The Elephant and the Mouse

John Lowndes

AuthorHouse™
1663 Liberty Drive
Bloomington, IN 47403
www.authorhouse.com
Phone: 1 (800) 839-8640

Published by AuthorHouse 03/02/2018

ISBN: 978-1-5462-2442-6 (sc)
978-1-5462-2443-3 (e)

Library of Congress Control Number: 2018900469

Print information available on the last page.

This book is printed on acid-free paper.

authorHOUSE®

Dedication:

I would like to dedicate this book to my family. Without them I would truly not be the man I am today! To Pam, who has never wavered in her love for me. To my boys who keep me thinking about new ideas for books, and to my parents who have always been there. Also to my many friends around the world from many diverse cultures and backgrounds who have taught me to love, learn, and live life fully! Finally I want to thank God who rescued me from certain destruction. I'm forever grateful.

Edward Elephant was having a great day. He, of course, was on top of the world, and he had just heard about a new water hole not far from where he was.

“I think I’ll go find that new water hole,” Edward Elephant said to himself. So Edward Elephant went ***Crashing***, ***Bashing,*** and ***Smashing*** through the jungle as he usually did. You see, Edward Elephant was on top of the world!

Crash, Bash, Smash went Edward Elephant through the jungle. You see, being on top of the world, you don't often see the little things under your big, ***Crashing, Bashing, Smashing*** *feet*.

"I can smell that nice new water hole," Edward Elephant said to himself. "I think it's right over there!" ***Crash, Bash, Smash*** went Edward Elephant through the jungle. "I'm on top of the world!" Edward Elephant said to himself.

As Edward Elephant ***Crashed, Bashed,*** and ***Smashed*** his way along, something was happening right under his big, ***Crashing, Bashing, Smashing*** feet, and it was not a pretty sight!

You see, those on top of the world like Edward Elephant are often unaware of those who are under their big, ***Crashing, Bashing,*** and ***Smashing*** feet.

As Edward Elephant ***Crashed, Bashed,*** and ***Smashed*** his way along, those who were under his big, ***Crashing, Bashing***, ***Smashing*** feet were being ***Flipped, Skipped,*** and ***Tripped*** right out of their beds!

Crash, Bash, Smash! Flip, Skip, Trip went Marty Mouse and his family. You see, Edward Elephant was on top of the world!

As the ***Crashing, Bashing,*** and ***Smashing*** faded into the distance, Marty Mouse and his family got up after being ***Flipped, Skipped,*** and ***Tripped*** right out of their beds.

"What was that?" asked Baby Mouse. "I was just ***Flipped, Skipped,*** and ***Tripped*** right out of my bed!"

"That ***Crashing, Bashing,*** and ***Smashing*** was one of those elephants who ***Flipped, Skipped,*** and ***Tripped*** us right out of our beds," said Marty Mouse. "They think they are on top of the world!"

As Marty Mouse and his family picked themselves up, Marty Mouse decided he could not have his family ***Crashed, Bashed***, and ***Smashed*** by Edward Elephant. "I will not have my family ***Flipped, Skipped***, and ***Tripped*** right out of their beds!" said Marty Mouse.

Marty Mouse followed the sound of those big, ***Crashing, Bashing***, and ***Smashing*** feet right up to the new water hole where Edward Elephant was drinking loudly. ***Slurp, Glurp, Burp*** guzzled Edward Elephant. You see, Edward Elephant was on top of the world!

Tippity-Tip-Tap went Marty Mouse, aware of everything under his feet. You see, Marty Mouse was not on top of the world. ***Slurp, Glurp, Burp*** guzzled Edward Elephant from the new water hole.

Marty Mouse ***Tippity-Tip-Tapped*** right up to Edward Elephant, who was still ***Slurping, Glurping***, and ***Burping*** from the new water hole.

Smack, Boot, Toot went little Marty Mouse when he walked up to Edward Elephant. "What was that?" said Edward Elephant to himself, stopping his ***Slurping, Glurping***, and ***Burping.***"

I felt a ***Smack,*** a ***Boot***, and I thought I heard a ***Toot***."

“Down here!” shouted Marty Mouse. “Your ***Crashing***, ***Bashing***, and ***Smashing*** caused my family to ***Flip***, ***Skip***, and ***Trip*** out of our beds!”

“I’m on top of the world,” said Edward Elephant, “and I’ll ***Crash***, ***Bash***, and ***Smash*** wherever I want, and I don’t care if I ***Flipped***, ***Skipped***, and ***Tripped*** you out of your beds.”

"This is our home," said Marty Mouse, "and your ***Crashing***, ***Bashing***, and ***Smashing*** around the water hole will mean we have to leave our home."

"Humph!" said Edward Elephant, ***Crashing***, ***Bashing***, and **Smashing** his big feet on the ground. "This is my new water hole, and I'll be telling all my elephant friends where to find it."

A small tear ran down Marty Mouse's cheek as he realized those on top of the world did not care about those who are not on top of the world.

As Mr. Mouse began to walk away, Edward Elephant realized they were not alone. All the little animals had come out of their homes and were looking at Edward Elephant.

“Let’s go,” said Marty Mouse to all the other families. “Edward Elephant is on top of the world and does not care about us little animals under his big, ***Crashing***, ***Bashing***, and ***Smashing*** feet.”

As all the little families began to leave their homes, something came over Edward Elephant that he had not felt for a long time. Did my big, ***Crashing*, *Bashing*, *Smashing*** feet cause all these little families to leave their homes? wondered Edward Elephant.

As Edward Elephant wondered if his big, ***Crashing, Bashing***, ***Smashing*** feet had done all this, he felt a ***Tap, Tap, Tap*** on his big, ***Crashing***, ***Bashing***, ***Smashing*** feet.

Edward Elephant looked down and saw Baby Mouse. "It's okay, Mr. Elephant," said Baby Mouse, handing him a flower. "You can keep your water hole. We'll just move somewhere else!"

As Baby Mouse began to walk away, something happened inside Edward Elephant—he remembered something he had not thought about for a long time.

When he was small, just a baby elephant, his life changed forever. It was the day, Edward Elephant's mom and dad had taken him to their water hole. ***Smash, Bash, Crash*** went little Edward Elephant and his family through the grass to their water hole.

As Edward Elephant and his family were ***Slurping***, ***Glurping***, and ***Burping***, there was a loud ***Bang, Bang, Bang*** and a shout from Edward elephant's parents. "Run, Edward Elephant, run!"

You see, there was a day when Edward Elephant was not on top of the world, and those who were on top of the world changed his life forever. Ever since, Edward Elephant had been ***Smashing***, ***Bashing***, and ***Crashing*** his way through the jungle.

As Edward Elephant watched all the little families walk away from their homes, a tear fell from his eye. That single tear soon became a river of tears.

"Wait!" shouted Edward Elephant "Wait! I'm sorry! I'm sorry my ***Crashing, Bashing***, ***Smashing*** feet caused all of this. Wait, don't leave!"

As all the little families turned around, Edward Elephant felt a ***Tap, Tap, Tap*** on his big, ***Smashing, Bashing***, ***Crashing*** feet. Edward Elephant looked down, and there was Baby Mouse, hugging Edward Elephant's big trunk.

"Thank you, Mr. Elephant," said Baby Mouse. "Does that mean I can stay in my house?" Baby Mouse looked into Edward Elephant's big, teary eyes.

As Elephant looked down at Baby Mouse, something happened in Edward Elephant's big heart—something wonderful.

"Wait!" Edward Elephant shouted to all the little families. With tears still falling from his eyes, he looked down at baby Mouse. "I'll take care of you," Edward Elephant said to Baby Mouse.

From that day forward, you could find Edward Elephant standing at the head of the trail, directing traffic to the water hole. “There’s another entrance over there,” Edward Elephant would tell the other animals heading for the water hole.

You see, Edward Elephant began to understand that those on top of the world have a responsibility to take care of those who have been hurt by their big, ***Crashing***, ***Bashing***, ***Smashing*** feet.

So Edward Elephant and Baby Mouse became the best of friends, and every day you could find them on the edge of their little town, directing all the bigger animals to the new water hole.

CPSIA information can be obtained
at www.ICGtesting.com
Printed in the USA
FSHW01n0502061018
52798FS

9 781546 224426

ECDL Expert

The Complete Coursebook for ECDL Advanced Modules AM3–AM6 for Office 2000

ECDL Expert

The Complete Coursebook for ECDL Advanced Modules AM3–AM6 for Office 2000

Covering ECDL Advanced Word Processing, Spreadsheets, Databases and Presentation

Paul Holden, Brendan Munnelly, Judith Cuppage and Sadhbh O'Dwyer

Harlow, England • London • New York • Boston • San Francisco • Toronto • Sydney • Singapore • Hong Kong
Tokyo • Seoul • Taipei • New Delhi • Cape Town • Madrid • Mexico City • Amsterdam • Munich • Paris • Milan

Pearson Education Limited
Edinburgh Gate
Harlow
Essex CM20 2JE
England

and Associated Companies throughout the world

Visit us on the World Wide Web at:
www.pearsoned.co.uk

First published in Great Britain 2006

Compiled from:

ECDL Advanced Word Processing
by Brendan Munnelly and Paul Holden
ISBN 0 130 98984 3
Copyright © Rédacteurs Limited 2002

ECDL Advanced Spreadsheets
by Sharon Murphy and Paul Holden
ISBN 0 130 98983 5
Copyright © Rédacteurs Limited 2002

ECDL Advanced Databases
by Judith Cuppage and Paul Holden
ISBN 0 13 120240 5
Copyright © Rédacteurs Limited 2004

ECDL Advanced Presentation
by Sadhbh O'Dwyer and Paul Holden
ISBN 0 13 120241 3
Copyright © Rédacteurs Limited 2004

ISBN-13: 978-0-13-197630-6
ISBN-10: 0-13-197630-3

British Library Cataloguing-in-Publication Data
A catalogue record for this book is available from the British Library

Library of Congress-in-Publication Data
A catalog record for this book is available from the Library of Congress

10 9 8 7 6 5 4 3 2 1
10 09 08 07 06

Typeset in 11pt Times New Roman PS by 30.
Printed and bound by Ashford Colour Press Ltd, Gosport, Hampshire

The Publisher's policy is to use paper manufactured from sustainable forests.

Complete Coursebook for ECDL Expert

This coursebook provides everything you need to prepare for and pass all four of the ECDL Advanced Syllabus modules on Word Processing; Spreadsheets; Databases; and Presentations, and consequently to gain the new ECDL Expert qualification to develop your office skills to a more advanced level.

ECDL Advanced Modules

The ECDL Advanced qualification is designed to progress your computer skills from the internationally successful European Computer Driving Licence® (ECDL) to the next level of competence.

ECDL Advanced will prove that your competence with computer use is well above the basic skill level, and will help determine suitability for jobs involving computer use at a higher level.

The extensive use of computers in many business functions today has brought into existence a variety of roles that rely on extensive knowledge of particular computing tools. An employee holding an ECDL Advanced certificate can prove they have the competence to effectively and efficiently use these tools.

What is ECDL Expert?

The ECDL Expert Certificate is a new qualification that is available for all candidates who have successfully completed all four ECDL Advanced modules, in any order. No additional testing is required to gain this certificate – the certificate is awarded upon successful completion of the fourth modules at an accredited test centre request and delivers an additional qualification for successful candidates which:

- Recognizes the achievement of all passing four modules
- Increases your chances of promotion and employment
- Provides a route to Associate Membership of the British Computer Society (AMBCS), including use of AMBCS post-nominal letters
- Requires no additional tuition or testing

Overall, ECDL Expert delivers an additional benchmark level of recognized, accredited achievement in IT skills.

Advanced Word Processing

Brendan Munnelly
and Paul Holden

ECDL Advanced Approved
Courseware Syllabus AM3 Version 1.0

Harlow, England • London • New York • Boston • San Francisco • Toronto • Sydney • Singapore • Hong Kong
Tokyo • Seoul • Taipei • New Delhi • Cape Town • Madrid • Mexico City • Amsterdam • Munich • Paris • Milan

Preface

What is ECDL?

ECDL, or the European Computer Driving Licence, is an internationally recognized qualification in Information Technology skills. It is accepted by businesses internationally as a verification of competence and proficiency in computer skills.

The ECDL syllabus is neither operating system nor software specific.

For more information about ECDL, and to see the syllabus for *ECDL Module 4, Word Processing, Advanced Level*, visit the official ECDL website at www.ecdl.com.

About this book

This book covers the ECDL Advanced Word Processing syllabus Version 1.0, using Microsoft Word 2000 to complete all the required tasks. It is assumed that you have already completed the word processing module of ECDL 3 using Microsoft Word, or have an equivalent knowledge of the product.

The chapters in this book are intended to be read sequentially. Each chapter assumes that you have read and understood the information in the preceding chapter.

Every chapter contains the following elements:

- **Learning objectives:** This sets out the skills and concepts that you will learn in the chapter.
- **New words:** A list of the key terms introduced and defined in the chapter.
- **Syllabus reference:** A list the items from the ECDL Advanced Word Processing Syllabus that are covered in the chapter:
- **Exercises:** Practical, step-by-step tasks to build your skills.
- **Tasks summary:** A list of the key procedures covered in the chapter.
- **Concepts summary:** A brief guide to the key ideas in the chapter.
- **Quick quiz:** A series of multiple-choice questions to test your knowledge of the material contained in the chapter.

Exercises files

Almost all chapters are accompanied by 'before' and 'after' exercises files. Use the 'before' files as directed. You can check the correctness of your work by comparing them against the 'after' files.

Hardware and software requirements

Your PC should meet the following specifications:

- Pentium 75MHz or higher processor
- Windows 98 ME, NT, 2000 or XP
- 64MB RAM
- Word 2000
- Excel 2000

Typographic conventions

The following typographic conventions are used in this book:

- **Bold face text** is used to denote the names of Microsoft Word menus and commands, buttons on toolbars, tabs and buttons in dialog boxes, and keyboard keys.
- *Italicized text* is used to denote the names of Microsoft Word dialog boxes, and lists, options and checkboxes within dialog boxes.

Good luck with your ECDL studies and test. And remember: 'What one fool can learn, so can another'.

Contents

Chapter 1: Finish faster by beginning differently: outlines

Chapter 2: Do once what you used to do every day: styles

Chapter 3: Recycle content and formatting: templates

Chapter 4: Separating content from format: templates and styles

Chapter 5: Here's one I prepared earlier: AutoText

Chapter 6: Word checks your documents: AutoCorrect

Chapter 7: Word typesets your documents: AutoFormat As You Type

Chapter 8: Word updates your documents: fields

Chapter 9: Word does everything: macros

Chapter 10: 'Are you sure about this?': comments and document protection

Chapter 11: Displaying, accepting and rejecting revisions: change tracking

Chapter 12: Many subdocuments, one document: master documents

Chapter 13: 'Please complete and return': Word forms

Chapter 14: Tables: merging, splitting, sorting and totalling

Chapter 15: Spreadsheets in Word

Chapter 16: Charts in Word

Chapter 17: Footnotes and endnotes

Chapter 18: Bookmarks and cross-references

Chapter 19: Tables of contents

Chapter 20: Captions

Chapter 21: Indexes

Chapter 22: Font and paragraph effects

Chapter 23: Text boxes and text orientation

Chapter 24: Graphics in Word

Chapter 25: Many columns, one document

Chapter 26: Many sections, one document

Chapter 27: Mail merge

1 Finishing faster by beginning differently: outlines

Objectives

In this chapter you will learn how to:

- Use Outline view to enter headings for a new document
- Display an existing document in Outline view
- Promote and demote headings in Outline view
- Move headings within a document in Outline view
- Control the display of headings and text in Outline view

New words

In this chapter you will meet the following terms:

- Heading level
- Outline
- Outline view
- Outline numbering

Exercise files

In this chapter you will work with the following Word files:

- `Chapter1_Exercise_1-1_Before.doc`
- `Chapter1_Exercise_1-2_Before.doc`
- `Chapter1_Exercise_1-3_Before.doc`
- `Chapter1_Exercise_1-4_Before.doc`

Syllabus reference

In this chapter you will cover the following item of the ECDL Advanced Word Processing Syllabus:

- **AM3.1.2.6**: Use outline options.

Getting past page 1

When writing a new document, which do you find more difficult: writing the first page or two, or getting beyond the first few pages?

Typically, it's the second step. Why? Because you fall into the trap of trying to perfect your first pages before moving on to the remainder of your document.

Here's the solution: *start differently*.

- Don't begin by focusing on your first sentence, paragraph or page.
- Do begin by considering your entire document.

This method is called *outlining*. It means asking yourself – and perhaps your colleagues – questions such as 'How many sections will be needed?' and 'What subsections will be in each section?'

Only when you have completed your outline, and agreed it with your colleagues, do you write the content of the document.

Outlines: what do they look like?

An outline is a list of a document's headings. Most documents are unlikely to need more than three heading types or *heading levels*: main headings, subheadings and sub-subheadings.

In Word, main headings are called level-1 headings, subheadings are level-2 headings, and so on.

In the following example, you can see five level-1 headings. Of these, only the second ('Codes of Conduct') and fifth ('Help Us To Help You') contain level-2 headings.

Mission Statement
Codes of Conduct
    Standards of Individual Behaviour
    Consultant-based Services
    Nursing Services
Standards of Service
Teaching and Research
Help Us To Help You
    Keeping Us Informed
    Submitting Feedback
    Making a Complaint

Heading Level

The relative importance of a heading in a document. Typically, two or three heading levels are sufficient: main headings (level-1 headings), subheadings (level-2 headings) and sub-subheadings (level-3 headings).

In outlines, lower-level headings are indented ('moved in') progressively from the left margin. Indents in an outline have one purpose only: to show the relative importance of the various headings. The indents do *not* affect how the document appears when printed.

Outline

A list of the headings in a document, with indentation used to represent the level of each heading.

Promoting and demoting

In an outline, the act of changing a heading from a lower to a higher level is called *promoting* the heading. Conversely, changing a heading from a higher to a lower level is called *demoting* the heading.

Outlining: the benefits to you

With outlines, you can:

- **Agree structure before writing content**. Will other people be reviewing your document? If so, it makes sense to write the main content only *after* you have secured agreement on the overall structure.

  Otherwise, the document you write, although excellent in many ways, may not be the one that your colleagues and superiors actually want – an example of climbing to the top of a ladder only to discover that it is leaning against the wrong wall.

- **Begin with what's easy**. You can begin by writing those parts you feel more confident about – the middle of section three, for example, or the first four subsections of section two.

  Sections that you find more difficult or awkward can be left until the end. You will feel more confident about tackling these when your document is 80–90% complete.

- **Identify problem areas quickly**. Some sections of your document may need information that you do not have to hand.

  You are more likely to meet your deadline if you identify these sections at the start of the project than in the middle or towards the end.

- **Delegate content tasks**. If you are managing a document-creation project, you can delegate different sections of the outline to other contributors.

Outlines in Word

In Word, an outline is one of four available views of a document. (The other views are Normal, Print Layout and Web Layout.) If you have a document currently open, you can see its outline by choosing **View | Outline**.

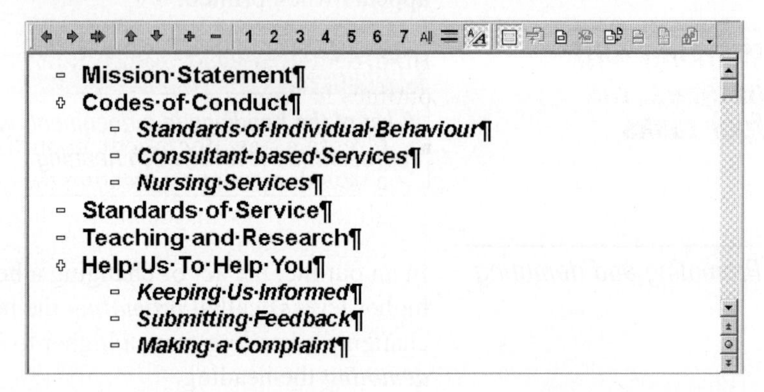

Outlines and styles

Outline heading levels are tied to Word's built-in heading styles, as shown below. (You will learn more about built-in heading styles in Chapter 2.)

Outline heading level	Paragraph style
Level-1 heading	Heading 1
Level-2 heading	Heading 2
Level-3 heading (etc.)	Heading 3 (etc.)
Body text	Normal

You can use styles other than heading styles in your outlines, but it's cumbersome and the methods are not covered in this book.

If a document contains only a single style such as Normal, it displays in Outline view without any organization or structure.

Outline view

A view in Word that displays a document outline. Outline view provides options to change headings levels, reorder headings, and control which heading levels and other paragraphs are displayed.

The Outlining toolbar

By default, Word's Outline view contains an Outlining toolbar with buttons for promoting and demoting headings, moving headings (and associated text) within the document, and controlling how many heading levels are displayed.

⇦ ⇨ ⇨	⇧ ⇩	+ −	1 2 3 4 5 6 7 All ☰

You will learn the purpose of each Outlining toolbar button as you use it in the exercises. A list of buttons and their functions is included at the end of this chapter for easy reference.

Working with outlines: the four tasks

Here are the four tasks that you need to be able to perform with outlines in Word:

- **Create a new document in outline view**. When you begin a new document by creating the document outline, you gain all the benefits associated with outlines and document creation. Exercise 1.1 provides an example.
- **Reorganize an already-written document in Outline view**. As Exercise 1.2 shows, you can quickly and easily restructure the content of an existing document by manipulating its outline.
- **Apply paragraph numbering in Outline view**. In Outline view, you can apply sequential numbering to paragraphs with a single mouse click. You may find this feature useful when working with legal and other highly-structured documents. See Exercise 1.3.
- **Exploit automatic paragraph renumbering**. If you rearrange numbered paragraphs in Outline view, Word automatically renumbers the paragraphs for you. Exercise 1.4 takes you through the steps.

Working with outlines of new documents

As you will see in Exercise 1.1, creating an outline can be the first step in writing a new document. After typing your headings and applying the correct heading levels to them, you then can switch from Outline to Normal or Print Layout view, and type the body text of your document.

Following this method provides you with two benefits:

- Your document is structured correctly from the start.
- Your headings are formatted automatically with the appropriate built-in heading styles.

Exercise 1.1: Creating a document in Outline view

In your first exercise, you will use Word's outline features to help you create a patients' charter for a fictitious organization, the Elmsworth Health Trust.

1) Open Word. If a new, blank document is not created by default, create one.

2) Choose **View | Outline**. Alternatively, click the **Outline View** button at the lower left of the Word window.

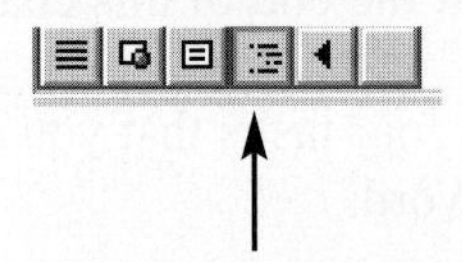

Outline View button

3) Type the following lines of text, pressing the **Enter** key after every line except the last one:

```
Codes of Conduct
Individual Standards of Behaviour
Courtesy
Privacy
Religious Beliefs
Consultant-based Services
Nursing Services
```

By default, Word positions your paragraphs as main (level-1) headings.

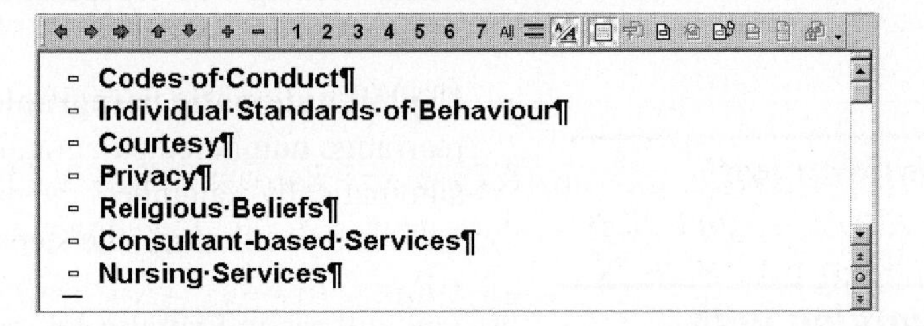

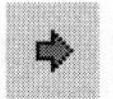

Demote button

4) Click anywhere in the second paragraph, and click the **Demote** button on the Outlining toolbar. The paragraph is now a level-2 heading and looks like this:

Codes·of·Conduct¶
Individual·Standards·of·Behaviour¶
Courtesy¶

(Another way to demote a heading is to click anywhere in the paragraph and press the **Tab** key.)

5) Drag the mouse over paragraphs three to seven to select them, and click the **Demote** button twice. Your selected paragraphs are now level-3 headings. Click anywhere outside the five paragraphs to deselect them.

Codes·of·Conduct¶
- *Individual·Standards·of·Behaviour¶*
  - Courtesy¶
  - Privacy¶
  - Religious·Beliefs¶
  - Consultant-based·Services¶
  - Nursing·Services¶

Promote button

6) Select the last two paragraphs, and click the **Promote** button to make them level-2 headings. Click anywhere outside the two paragraphs to deselect them.

Codes·of·Conduct¶
- *Individual·Standards·of·Behaviour¶*
  - Courtesy¶
  - Privacy¶
  - Religious·Beliefs¶
- *Consultant-based·Services¶*
- *Nursing·Services¶*

(Another way to promote a paragraph is to click anywhere in the paragraph and press the **Shift+Tab** keys.)

7) Choose **View | Print Layout**. You can see that your outline heading levels now appear as paragraph styles.

8) Save your sample document with the following name:

`Chapter1_Exercise_1-1_After_`*`Your_Name`*`.doc`

Then close the sample document.

Working with outlines of already-written documents

As you will discover in Exercise 1.2, you can open an existing document, display it in Outline view, and, as you need

- **Change heading levels**. For example, you can demote a level 1 heading to a level-2 heading, or promote a level-3 heading to a level-2 heading, and so on.
- **Reorder content**. You can move content within documents simply by moving the relevant headings in the outline.

  That's right – when you move a heading in Outline view, all subordinate content, both lower-level headings and body text, moves with it.

Reorganizing a lengthy document in Outline view with just a few mouse clicks is faster and less likely to lead to errors than the alternative: working in Normal or Print Layout view, and scrolling repeatedly through pages to perform multiple cut-and-paste operations.

Exercise 1.2: Reorganizing a document in Outline view

In this exercise, you will use Word's outline features to reorder the content of a document, the patients' charter of Elmsworth Health Trust.

1) Open the following file:

   `Chapter1_Exercise_1-2_Before.doc`

2) Choose **View | Outline**.

3) Click the **Show Heading 3** button on the Outlining toolbar.

   3

   Show Heading 3 button

   This displays only heading levels 1, 2 and 3. Any lower-level headings and text in Normal style are not shown.

4) Click anywhere in the level-3 heading, 'Waiting Times During Appointments'.

5) Click the **Move Down** button twice. Click anywhere outside the heading to deselect it.

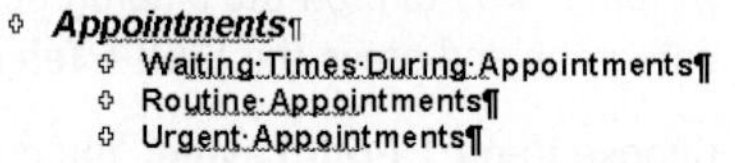

   Move down button

   Before:
   - *Appointments*
     - Waiting Times During Appointments
     - Routine Appointments
     - Urgent Appointments

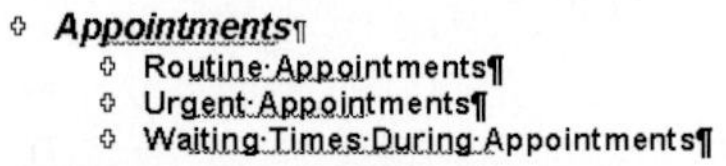

   After:
   - *Appointments*
     - Routine Appointments
     - Urgent Appointments
     - Waiting Times During Appointments

6) Select the level-2 heading 'Appointments' and the three level-3 headings beneath it.

   - *Appointments*
     - Waiting Times During Appointments
     - Routine Appointments
     - Urgent Appointments

7) Click the **Move Up** button four times. Click anywhere outside the headings to deselect them. Word reorders the selected headings like this:

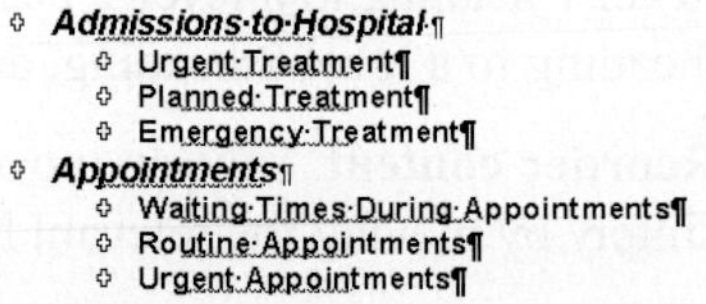

   Move up button

   Before:
   - *Admissions to Hospital*
     - Urgent Treatment
     - Planned Treatment
     - Emergency Treatment
   - *Appointments*
     - Waiting Times During Appointments
     - Routine Appointments
     - Urgent Appointments

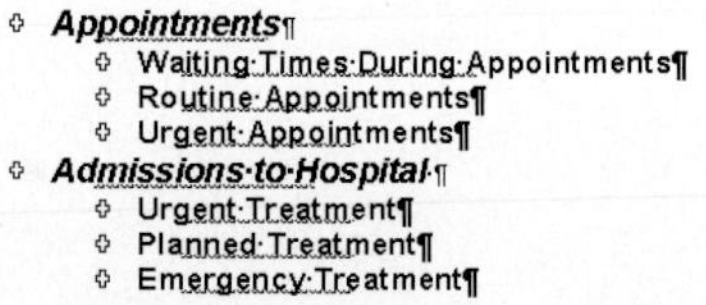

   After:
   - *Appointments*
     - Waiting Times During Appointments
     - Routine Appointments
     - Urgent Appointments
   - *Admissions to Hospital*
     - Urgent Treatment
     - Planned Treatment
     - Emergency Treatment

8) In the final part of this exercise, you will move the heading 'Help Us To Help You' and its subordinate headings so that they are at the end of the document.

   One way is to select the four relevant headings as shown, and then click the **Move Down** button repeatedly.

- Help·Us·To·Help·You
  - *Keeping·Us·Informed¶*
  - *Submitting·Feedback¶*
  - *Making·a·Complaint¶*

1

Show Heading 1 button

Let's try another approach. Click the **Show Heading 1** button on the Outlining toolbar, so that only level-1 headings are shown.

- Elmsworth·Health·Trust:·Patient's·Charter¶
- Mission·Statement¶
- Codes·of·Conduct¶
- Standards·of·Service¶
- Teaching·and·Research¶
- Help·Us·To·Help·You
- Information·and·Records

Click anywhere in the heading 'Help Us To Help You', and click the **Move Down** button. Click anywhere outside the heading to deselect it.

9) Let's check if moving the selected level-1 heading also moved the subordinate level-2 headings.

2

Show Heading 2 button

Click the **Show Heading 2** button on the Outlining toolbar, so that Word displays both level 1 and level 2 headings.

As you can see, Word automatically moved the subordinate level-2 headings.

Before:

- Help·Us·To·Help·You
  - *Keeping·Us·Informed¶*
  - *Submitting·Feedback¶*
  - *Making·a·Complaint¶*
- Information·and·Records
  - *Delays·and·Postponements¶*
  - *Identity·of·Staff¶*
  - *Medical·Information¶*

After:

- Information·and·Records
  - *Delays·and·Postponements¶*
  - *Identity·of·Staff¶*
  - *Medical·Information¶*
- Help·Us·To·Help·You
  - *Keeping·Us·Informed¶*
  - *Submitting·Feedback¶*
  - *Making·a·Complaint¶*

10) Save your sample document with the following name:

`Chapter1_Exercise_1-2_After_`*`Your_Name`*`.doc`

You can close the document.

Did you notice the grey lines under the headings in this exercise? In Outline view, a grey line under a heading indicates that the heading contains undisplayed lower-level headings and/or body text.

Working with outlines and outline numbering

Many engineering, legal and other highly-structured documents contain numbered headings, such as:

- 'According to section 4.5, that window should be on the other wall.'
- 'I refer the court's attention to subsection 4.29.'

When documents have multiple heading levels, lower-level headings *inherit* their leading numbers (or letters) from the relevant higher ones as shown below:

5. A level-1 heading	8.3. A level-2 heading
5.1. A level-2 heading	8.3. (a) A level-3 heading
5.2. Another level-2 heading	8.3. (b) Another level-3 heading

In Word, the sequential numbering (or alphabetizing) of headings is called *outline numbering*. You can apply outline numbering to a document's headings in Print Layout, Outline or Normal view. It is better to apply outline numbering through styles (using the **Format | Style** command) than by direct formatting (the **Format | Bullets and Numbering** command).

Outline Numbering

The application of sequential numbering to headings of a document. Lower-level headings inherit their leading numbers from higher-level headings.

When you reorder numbered headings in Outline view, Word renumbers the headings to take account of their new location in the document. This automatic renumbering is a huge time-saver: you can imagine the effort needed to renumber headings manually.

Exercise 1.3: Applying outline numbering to a document

In this exercise, you will apply outline numbering to the headings of a document.

1) Open the following file:

   `Chapter1_Exercise_1-3_Before.doc`

   If you are not viewing the document in Print Layout view, choose **View | Print Layout**.

2) Click in any heading in the Heading 1 style – for example, the document title 'Elmsworth Health Trust: Patients' Charter'.

3) Choose **Format | Style** and click the **Modify** button.

4) In the *Modify Style* dialog box, click the **Format** button and choose **Numbering** from the menu displayed.

5) Click the **Outline Numbered** tab of the dialog box displayed.

   You must select a sample numbering format that contains the word 'heading'. Click the format selected below, and then click **OK**, **OK** and **Apply** to close the box.

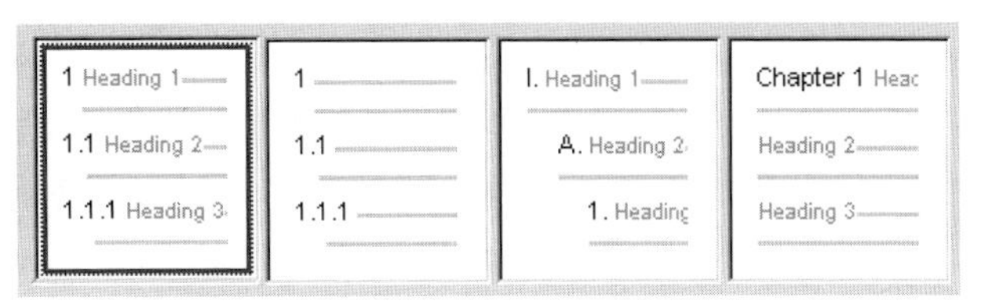

Word applies the outline numbering to your document.

3

Show Heading 3 button

6) Choose **View | Outline**, and click the **Show Heading 3** button on the Outlining toolbar to verify that Word has applied outline numbering to all three heading levels in your document, as in the following example:

1→Elmsworth·Health·Trust:·Patient's·Charter¶
2→Mission·Statement¶
3→Codes·of·Conduct¶
3.1 → Individual·Standards·of·Behaviour¶
3.1.1 → Courtesy¶
3.1.2 → Privacy¶
3.1.3 → Confidentiality¶
3.1.4 → Religious·Beliefs¶
3.2 → Consultant-based·Services¶
3.3 → Nursing·Services¶
4→Standards·of·Service¶
4.1 → Appointments¶
4.1.1 → Routine·Appointments¶

7) Close and save your sample document with the following name:

`Chapter1_Exercise_1-3_After_Your_Name.doc`

Exercise 1.4: Reordering numbered headings in Outline view

In this exercise, you will change the order of sequentially numbered headings.

1) Open the following file:

`Chapter1_Exercise_1-4_Before.doc`

2) Choose **View | Outline**.

3) Click anywhere in the level-1 heading called 'Teaching and Research'.

4) Click the **Move Down** button four times. Click anywhere outside the heading to deselect it.

5→Information·and·Records¶
5.1 → Delays·and·Postponements¶
5.2 → Identity·of·Staff¶
5.3 → Medical·Information¶
6→Help·Us·To·Help·You¶
6.1 → Keeping·Us·Informed¶
6.2 → Submitting·Feedback¶
6.3 → Making·a·Complaint¶
7→Teaching·and·Research¶

Notice that Word automatically renumbers the headings that you moved.

5) Close and save your sample document with the following name:

`Chapter1_Exercise_1-4_After_Your_Name.doc`

You have now completed the four exercises in this chapter.

Chapter 1: quick reference

Outlining toolbar: ***Promote*** *and* ***Demote*** *buttons*

Button	Description
⇦	Promotes a paragraph to a higher heading level.
⇨	Demotes a paragraph to a lower heading level.
⇨	Demotes a paragraph to body text (Normal style).

Outlining toolbar: ***Move Up*** *and* ***Move Down*** *buttons*

Button	Description
⇧	Moves a paragraph up above the preceding paragraph.
⇩	Move a paragraph down after the following paragraph..

Outlining toolbar: ***Show Heading*** *buttons*

Button	Description
1	Displays level-1 headings only.
2	Displays level-1 and level-2 headings only.
3	Displays level-1, level-2 and level-3 headings only.
═	Displays all heading levels and the first line only of body text paragraphs.
All	Displays the entire document, both headings and body text.

Shortcut keys

Keys	Description
Tab	Demotes the paragraph in which the insertion point is located.
Shift+Tab	Promotes the paragraph in which the insertion point is located.

Tasks summary

Task	Procedure
Display Outline view of the active document.	Choose **View | Outline**.
Promote or demote a heading.	Click anywhere in the heading and click the **Promote** or **Demote** button on the Outlining toolbar.
Move a heading (and subordinate content).	Select the heading and click the **Move Up** or **Move Down** button on the Outlining toolbar.
Control which headings are displayed.	Click the relevant **Show Heading** button on the Outlining toolbar.
Apply outline numbering to headings.	Click in any level-1 heading and choose **Format | Style**. Click **Modify**, **Format**, **Numbering**. Click the **Outline Numbered** tab, select a style that contains the word 'heading', and click **OK**, **OK** and **Apply**.

Concepts summary

In general, an *outline* is a list of the headings in a document. A *heading level* indicates the importance of a heading in relation to other headings. Outlines use indentation to represent the level of each heading, with lower-level headings indented further than higher-level ones.

In Word, an outline is a view of document. The outline heading levels shown are tied to the *built-in heading styles* applied in the document. Outline view includes the *Outlining toolbar*, which provides options for changing heading levels and reordering the headings.

For a new document, working in Outline view enables you to focus on the entire document and gain agreement from colleagues on its overall structure before you write the main content.

When working on an already-written document, Outline view allows you to restructure the document's content quickly and easily by manipulating the outline headings. This is because moving a heading in Outline view also moves all subordinate content, both lower-level headings and body text.

For legal and technical documents, you can apply sequential *outline numbering* to headings. If you move headings that are sequentially numbered, Word automatically renumbers them to take account of their new location in the document.

Chapter 1: quick quiz

Circle the correct answer to each of the following multiple-choice questions about outlines in Word.

Q1	A document outline is ...
A.	A list of the styles and fonts used in a document.
B.	A list of a document's headings, with lower-level headings indented progressively to reflect their relative importance.
C.	A list of the first lines of each paragraph in a document, arranged vertically in a single-column table.
D.	A first draft of a document that has not been checked for spelling or grammar, and that does not include a table of contents.

Q2	A Word outline cannot help you perform which of the following tasks?
A.	Gain agreement from colleagues about the overall structure of a document before the content is written.
B.	Begin writing the body of the document with the headings already formatted in the appropriate heading style.
C.	Identify sections of a document for delegation to colleagues.
D.	Display the readability statistics of a document.

Q3	You want to display the active document in Word's Outline view. Which action do you perform?
A.	Choose **File | Outline View**, select the *Outlining* checkbox, and click **OK**.
B.	Choose **Format | Views | Outlining**.
C.	Choose **View | Outline**.
D.	Choose **Tools | Document**, select the **Outline view only** option, and click **Apply**.

Q4	In Word, which of the following statements about outlines and styles is true?
A.	Heading levels in the outline are tied to heading styles in the document.
B.	A document can have heading styles or outline heading levels, but it cannot have both.
C.	Only the styles Outline 1, Outline 2 and Outline 3 can be used in a document outline.
D.	Text in Normal style cannot be displayed in a Word outline.

Q5	When creating a new Word document in Outline view, which of the following tasks are you most likely to perform?
A.	Create a single-column Word table for storing the names of people who will review your document.
B.	Specify the page margins for your new document
C.	Select the default folder for storing your document's template.
D.	Type your document's headings and arrange them in the appropriate order.

Q6	You are working on an already-written Word document in Outline view. Which of the following tasks are you most likely to perform?
A.	Move headings and subordinate content up and down in a document.
B.	Change the attributes of numbered bullets.
C.	Edit the body text, and check for errors in spelling and grammar.
D.	Check that the correct language setting is selected.

Q7	In a Word outline, what happens to numbered headings when you move them up or down in the document?
A.	Word displays an error message, telling you that numbered headings cannot be moved in Outline view.
B.	Word removes the numbers from the headings that you move.
C.	Word automatically renumbers the headings in the document to reflect their new location.
D.	The headings are preserved but not renumbered – you need to renumber them manually.

Q8	In Word Outline view, which toolbar button do you click to display level-1 and level-2 headings only?
A.	
B.	2
C.	
D.	1

Q9	In Word Outline view, which toolbar button do you click to promote a selected paragraph to a higher level?
A.	All
B.	1
C.	
D.	

Q10	In Word outline view, which toolbar button do you click to demote a selected heading to body text (Normal style)?
A.	➾
B.	⇩
C.	⇨
D.	≡

Q11	In Word outline view, which toolbar button do you click to move a heading up in the document?
A.	1
B.	⇩
C.	⇨
D.	⇧

Q12	In Word Outline view, what is the effect of pressing the key combination Shift+Tab?
A.	Word displays the entire document, and not just the document's headings.
B.	The paragraph that contains the insertion point is moved forward in the document.
C.	Only levels-1 and level-2 headings are displayed. Other headings and body text are hidden.
D.	The paragraph that contains the insertion point is promoted one level.

Answers

1: B, **2:** D, **3:** C, **4:** A, **5:** D, **6:** A, **7:** C, **8:** B, **9:** C, **10:** A, **11:** D, **12:** D.

2 Do once what you used to do every day: styles

Objectives

In this chapter you will learn how to:

- View the styles available to a document
- Identify the styles that are used in a document
- Create new paragraph and character styles
- Modify existing paragraph and character styles

New words

In this chapter you will meet the following terms:

- Heading styles
- Character styles
- Style Area
- Paragraph styles
- Style Box
- Direct formatting

Exercise files

In this chapter you will work with the following Word files:

- `Chapter2_Exercise_2-1_Before.doc`
- `Chapter2_Exercise_2-2_Before.doc`
- `Chapter2_Exercise_2-3_Before.doc`
- `Chapter2_Exercise_2-4_Before.doc`
- `Chapter2_Exercise_2-5_Before.doc`

Syllabus reference

In this chapter you will cover the following items from the ECDL Advanced Word Processing Syllabus:

- **AM3.1.2.4**: Create new character or paragraph styles.
- **AM3.1.2.5**: Modify existing character or paragraph styles.

Styles in Word: one click does it all

A style is a named set or ensemble of attributes that can be created, saved and then applied to items within documents.

Styles save you significant formatting effort and time, perhaps up to 80% with longer documents. Why? Because by applying a style, you can apply a wide range of attributes in a single operation. That's so much faster than applying each attribute individually.

An example of a style at work:

1. You select the text:

Word Styles: The Benefits

A style is a named set of multiple attributes that can be created, saved and applied to selected text, tables or other objects. I've known long-time Microsoft Word users who have

2. You select the style that you want from the Style Box:

3. Word applies the style's various attributes, such as font, indent and borders, in a single action.

Word Styles: The Benefits

A style is a named set of multiple attributes that can be created, saved and applied to selected text, tables or other objects. I've known long-time Microsoft Word users who have

Word's built-in styles

Word contains approximately 100 built-in, ready-to-use styles. The ones that you are likely to use most often are listed below, together with their default values.

Built-in style name	Font	Weight	Font size (points)	Additional spacing (points)
Heading 1	Arial	Bold	16	12 before, 3 after
Heading 2	Arial	Bold	14	12 before, 3 after
Heading 3	Arial	Bold	13	12 before, 3 after
Normal	Times New Roman	Normal	12	None

Although somewhat plain, Word's built-in styles are adequate for many documents.

Paragraph and character styles

Word's styles are of two types:

- **Paragraph styles**. These can control all aspects of a paragraph's appearance. You can apply a paragraph style only to entire paragraphs – not to selected text within a paragraph.
- **Character Styles**. These contain font, border and language attributes. You can apply character styles to an entire paragraph or to selected text within a paragraph.

Both paragraph and character styles are covered by the ECDL syllabus. Typically, you will use paragraph styles much more frequently than character styles. For this reason, the exercise for character style is located at the end of this chapter.

> **Paragraph style**
>
> *A named set of formatting, positioning and other attributes that can be applied to paragraphs.*

Heading styles

The styles Heading 1, Heading 2, etc., are called heading styles. By default, Word uses these styles for displaying outlines and generating tables of contents.

You don't have to use these styles for headings in your documents, but you will find it easier to exploit other Word features if you do.

> **Heading styles**
>
> *The styles named Heading 1, Heading 2, and so on. By default, Word uses these in outlines and tables of contents.*

Direct formatting

Direct formatting is an alternative to using styles. You select text and change its attributes with menu commands or toolbar buttons. Direct formatting overrides the attributes applied with styles.

> **Direct formatting**
>
> *Formatting applied by means other than by styles. Typically, formatting or alignment applied with buttons on the Formatting toolbar, or with the **Format | Font, Format | Paragraph** and **Format | Borders and Shading** commands.*

Styles: how you benefit

Styles, as you have learnt, enable you to apply a wide range of attributes in a single operation. Here are some other benefits provided by styles in Word:

- **Consistency**. Documents formatted with styles have a consistent, professional appearance.
- **Ease of updating**. You can change the appearance of all headings in a document simply by amending the relevant styles.
- **Automation and organization**. Styles enable you to take advantage of time-saving features in Word, such as outlines, AutoFormat, table-of-contents generation and master documents.
- **Faster operation**. Word has to work harder at displaying and managing files that contain a lot of direct formatting. Documents formatted with styles are smaller in file size and display on screen more quickly.
- **Document exporting**. If you need to export a Word document to a file format used by desktop publishing (DTP) software or to the web, you'll be glad that you used styles.

Most DTP software can recognize and work with Word styles, and Word styles can be incorporated within cascading style sheets (CSS) in Hypertext Mark-up Language (HTML) documents.

Styles and templates

Styles are related to another Word feature: templates. The relationship between styles and templates is less than straightforward, and is covered in Chapter 4.

Styles: the five tasks

Here are the five tasks that you need to be able to perform with styles:

- **View styles available to a document**. You can use the Style Box on the Formatting toolbar to display the styles available to your current document. Exercise 2.1 shows you how.
- **Identify styles used in a document**. Word offers two convenient features to help you identify the styles applied to text in any document. You will discover how to use them in Exercise 2.2.
- **Amend the attributes of an existing style**. You can amend the attributes of any style, whether it is a built-in Word style or a user-created style. See Exercise 2.3.

- **Create a new style**. In Exercise 2.4, you learn how to create a new style and define its attributes.
- **Work with character styles**. Exercise 2.5 takes you through the steps of creating, amending and deleting a character style.

Displaying style information

In the first two exercises of this chapter, you will work with paragraph styles that already exist: you will begin by displaying a list of the styles available to a document, and then view the styles that are already applied within the document.

Exercise 2.1: Viewing the styles available to a document

1) Start Word and open the following file:

```
Chapter2_Exercise_2-1_Before.doc
```

2) On the Formatting toolbar, click the **Style Box** drop-down arrow.

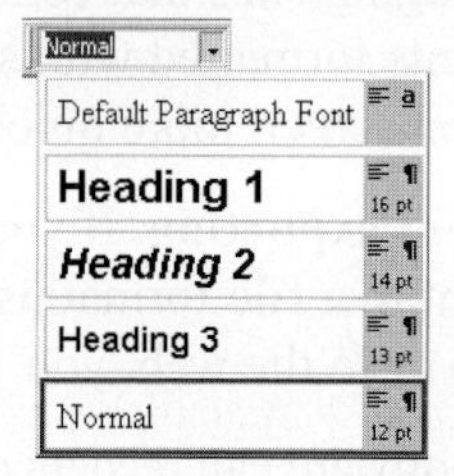

Word displays an abbreviated list of the styles that are available to your current document. Each style is formatted, so that you can see what it looks like before you apply it.

Click anywhere in the document to close the drop-down list.

3) Hold down the **Shift** key and click the **Style Box** drop-down arrow. Word now shows all available styles, not just the main ones.

Click anywhere in the document to close the drop-down list.

Then close the sample document.

> **Style Box**
>
> *A box on the Formatting toolbar that can display a drop-down list of the styles available to a document. The styles are formatted, so that you can see what they look like before you apply them.*

Exercise 2.2: Viewing styles used in a document

Ever wonder what styles are used in a particular Word document? In this exercise you discover how to find out, using two Word features – What's This? and the Style Area.

1) Open the following file:

```
Chapter2_Exercise_2-2_Before.doc
```

2) Choose **Help | What's This**. Notice how Word displays a question mark beside the cursor.

3) Click on any text for Word to display a pop-up window containing the relevant style details.

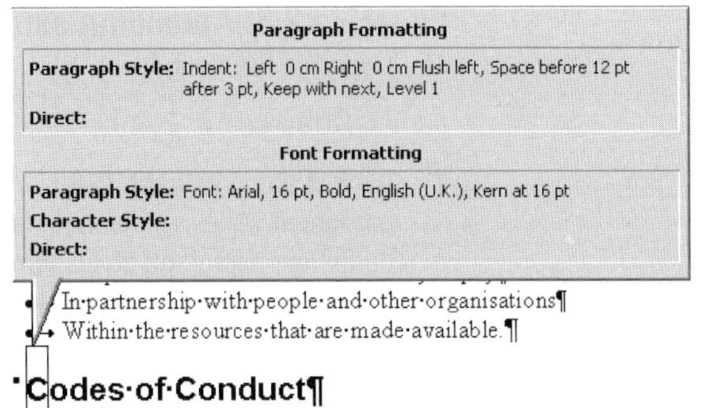

You can continue clicking on text throughout your document to view the relevant style details.

When finished, press **Esc** to close the pop-up window.

4) Switch to Normal view.

5) Choose **Tools | Options**, and click the **View** tab in the dialog box displayed.

6) Enter a Style Area width of 2.5 cm.

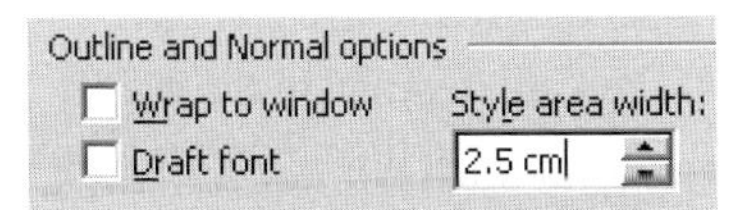

7) Click **OK**. Your current document now looks as shown in the next example. Notice the Style Area at the left of the Word window. You can use the mouse to resize the Style Area.

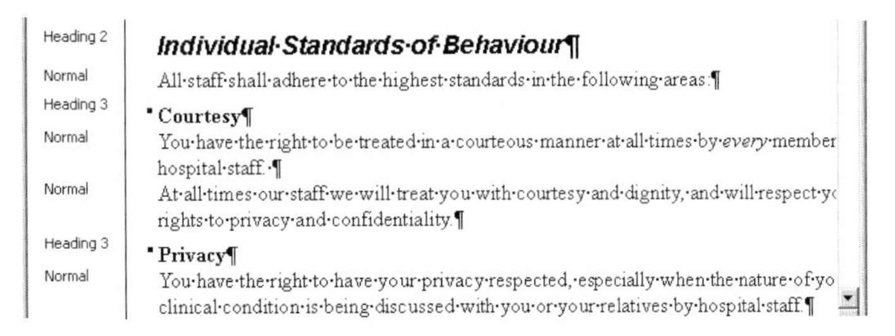

8) When you have finished, close your document.

Style Area

A resizable pane that can be displayed in Normal or Outline view to show the styles used throughout a document.

Working with existing styles

In Exercise 2.3, you will open a sample document, amend attributes of the Body Text and Heading 1 built-in styles, and then save the document.

Exercise 2.3: Amending existing styles

1) Open the following file:

   `Chapter2_Exercise_2-3_Before.doc`

2) Click in any paragraph that is in the Normal style. (When modifying paragraph styles, you don't need to select an entire paragraph. By definition, paragraph styles apply to paragraphs, so it's enough just to position the insertion point in a paragraph whose style you want to modify.)

3) Choose **Format | Style**, and click the **Modify** button.

4) In the *Modify Style* dialog box, click the **Format** button, and then click the **Font** option.

5) Select Garamond, Regular style, 12 point, and click **OK**.

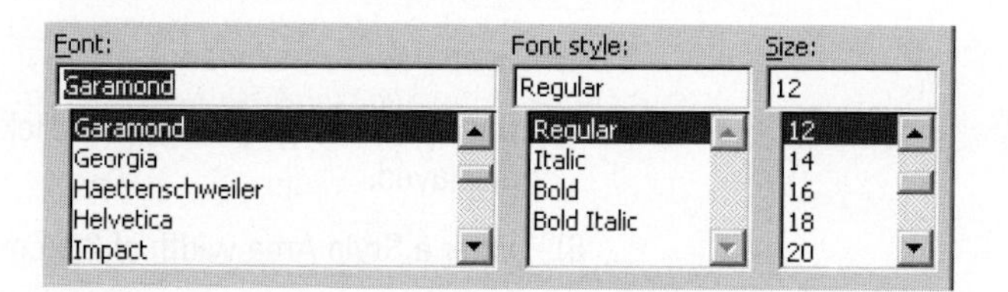

6) You are returned to the *Modify Style* dialog box. Click the **Format** button, and then the **Paragraph** option.

   In the *Spacing* area, enter 6 pt in the *After* box. Click OK.

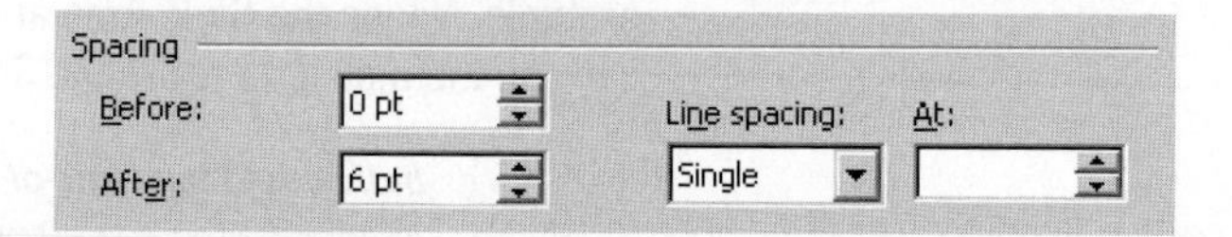

7) You are returned to the *Modify Style* dialog box. Ensure that the *Add to template* and *Automatically update* checkboxes are deselected.

   Click **OK.** You are returned to the *Style* dialog box. Click **Apply**.

   Notice that *all* paragraphs in the Normal style are amended.

8) Click in any paragraph that is in the Heading 1 style, choose **Format | Style**, and click the **Modify** button.

9) In the *Modify Style* dialog box, click the **Format** button, and then the **Border** option.

10) Select a 1-point top border. Click **OK**.

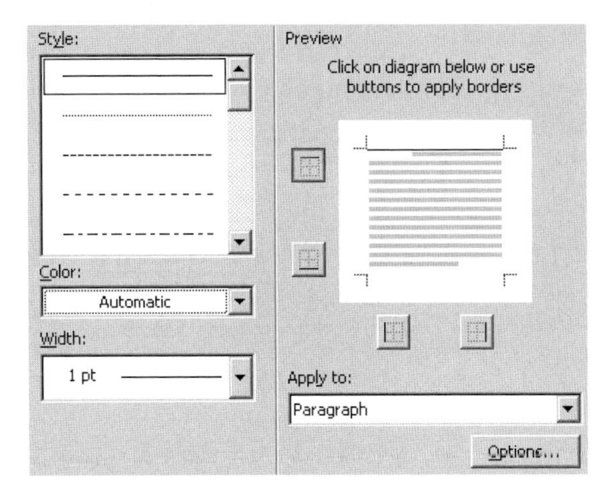

11) You are returned to the *Modify Style* dialog box. Click the **Format** button, and then the **Paragraph** option.

12) In the *Spacing* area, increase the value in the *Before* box to 24 pt. Click **OK**.

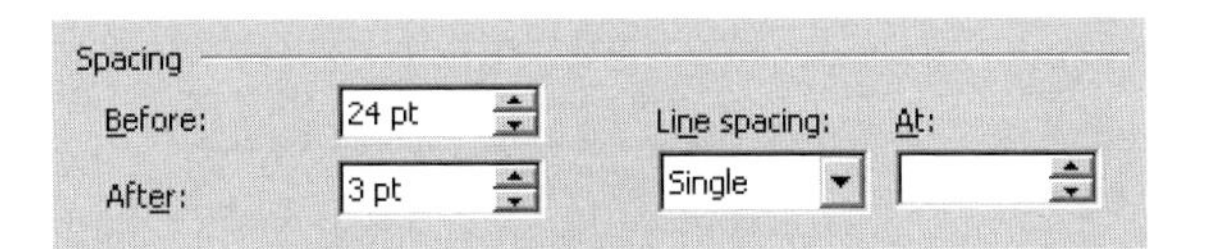

13) You are returned to the *Modify Style* dialog box. Ensure that the *Add to template* and *Automatically update* checkboxes are deselected.

    Click **OK**. You are returned to the *Style* dialog box. Click **Apply**.

    Notice that *all* paragraphs in the Heading 1 style are amended.

14) Close and save your sample document with the following name:

    `Chapter2_Exercise_2-3_After_`*`Your_Name`*`.doc`

Working with new styles

Through the **Format | Style** command, Word gives you complete control over every aspect of a new paragraph style that you create. Style attributes are available in the seven categories:

- Font
- Paragraph
- Tabs
- Border

- Language
- Frame
- Numbering

You can access each category of attributes by clicking the **Format** button in the *New Style* dialog box.

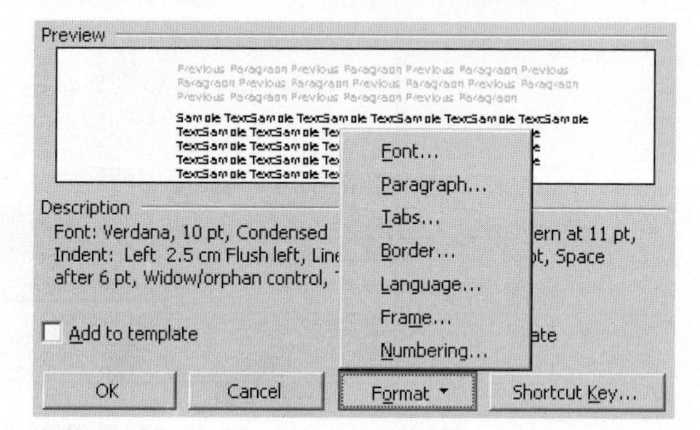

In addition to these various attributes, there are six other important fields available in the *New Style* dialog box:

Field name	Description
Name: My New Style1	You must give a unique name to each new style that you create. You can rename styles as often as you want.
Style type: Paragraph (Paragraph, Character)	You must choose either *Paragraph* or *Character*. You cannot change the style type at a later stage.
Based on: ¶ Normal	Optionally, you can select an existing style on which your new style will be based. Except where you specify otherwise, your new style takes on the attributes of the selected Based on style. If you do not select a Based on style, ensure that you set a language for your new style, otherwise the default will be No proofing. You can add, remove or change the Based on style at a later stage.

Field name	Description
Style for following paragraph: ¶ Normal	You must specify the style that Word will apply to a paragraph created by pressing **Enter** after a paragraph in your new style. For both headings and body text, your typical choice for this field will be the Normal style. You can change the style for the following paragraph at a later stage.
Add to template	If you select this checkbox, your new style is saved to the document template, not just to the document. It is then available to all other documents based on the same template.
Automatically update	If you select this checkbox, Word will redefine the style to reflect any changes you make with direct formatting.

Based on style

A style that supplies default attributes to one or more other styles. If the Based on style changes, so do all the attributes that the dependent styles share with the Based on style – that is, those that were specified explicitly by the user.

Style shortcut keys

Another option provided by the *New Style* dialog box is the ability to associate a shortcut key with a new style. If you plan to use a style frequently, it makes sense to give it a shortcut key. You can also assign keyboard shortcuts to existing styles.

You access this option by clicking the **Shortcut Key** button in the *New Style* (or *Modify Style*) dialog box.

Do not assign styles to keyboard shortcuts already used for common Word tasks, such as applying bold (**Ctrl+B**) or italics (**Ctrl+I**), or saving (**Ctrl+S**) and printing (**Ctrl+P**).

Exercise 2.4: Creating a new style

In this exercise, you will create a new style and explore how direct formatting can affect a style's attributes.

1) Open the following file:

```
Chapter2_Exercise_2-4_Before.doc
```

2) Click in any paragraph that is in the Heading 1 style.

3) Choose **Format | Style**, and in the dialog box displayed, click the **New** button.

4) In the *Name* box, enter 'Heading 1 *Your Name*', select a *Style type* of 'Paragraph', a *Based on* style of 'Heading 1', and a *Style for following paragraph* of 'Normal'. The following example shows how Ken Bloggs might fill in the details.

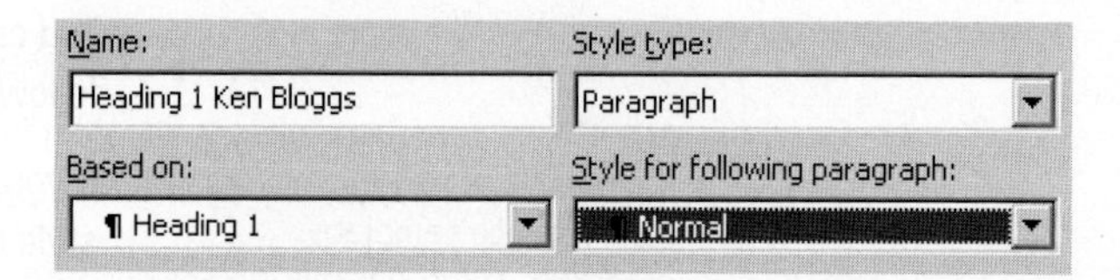

Click the **Format** button, click **Font**, change the *Color* to red, and click **OK**.

5) Click the **Shortcut Key** button. With the insertion point in the *Press new shortcut key* box, type the combination of keys that you want to assign to your new style. For example, **Ctrl+Shift+F1**.

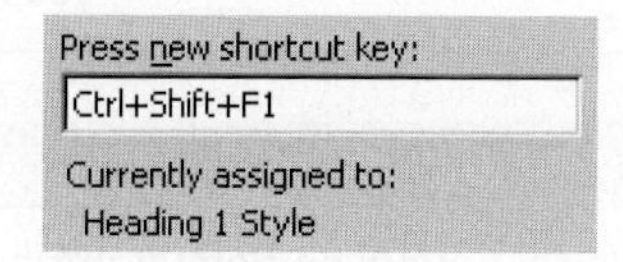

If the keyboard shortcut you entered is already assigned to another style or to another Word feature, Word displays a message beneath the box. You can override any previous keyboard shortcut.

6) Click the drop-down arrow to the right of the *Save changes in* box, and select the template Normal (Normal.dot) as the location in which you want to store your keyboard shortcut.

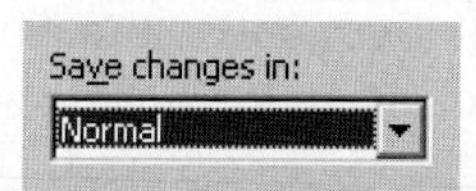

When finished, click **Assign**, and then click **Close**.

7) You are returned to the *New Style* dialog box. Leave the *Add to template* checkbox deselected. Select the *Automatically update* checkbox.

8) Click **OK** to close the *New Style* dialog box, then click **Apply** to close the *Style* dialog box. You are returned to your document.

Notice that Word applies the new style to the paragraph in which the insertion point is located.

9) Choose **Edit | Replace**, and replace all occurrences of the Heading 1 style with your new Heading 1 Your Name style.

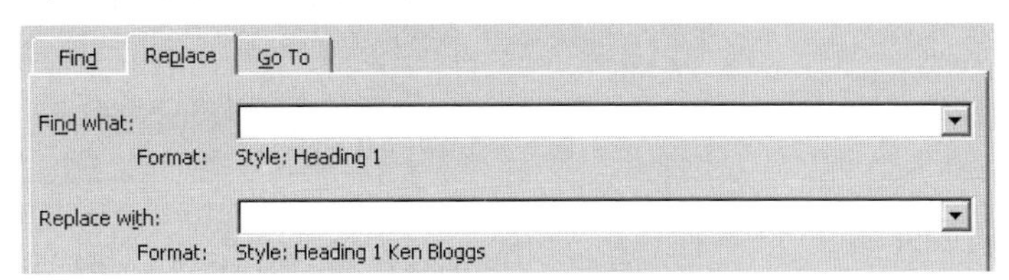

10) Select any paragraph in the Heading 1 *Your Name* style, choose **Format | Font**, and change the font to Arial Narrow.

    Notice that Word changes all other paragraphs in the Heading 1 *Your Name* style to Arial Narrow. This is because you selected the *Automatically update* checkbox when creating the new style.

11) Click in any paragraph in the Heading 1 Your Name style. Choose **Format | Style**, click **Modify**, deselect the *Automatically update* checkbox, click **OK** and click **Apply**. This prevents further direct formatting from affecting the attributes of your new style.

12) Close and save your sample document with the following name:

    `Chapter2_Exercise_2-4_After_`*`Your_Name`*`.doc`

Reapplying styles after direct formatting changes

Direct formatting, applied using the Formatting toolbar or with commands such as **Format | Font** and **Format | Paragraph**, overrides the style-based attributes that are applied to the relevant paragraphs.

Sometimes, after a paragraph has been formatted directly, you will want to change the paragraph's attributes back to those of its style. In other words, you want to reapply the style.

Reapplying a style means applying a style to a paragraph that meets the following conditions:

- The paragraph has direct formatting applied to it.
- The paragraph is already in the style you are about to apply, but it looks different from other paragraphs in the same style because of the direct formatting.

When using the Style Box you reapply a style to such a paragraph, Word displays a *Modify Style* dialog box similar to this:

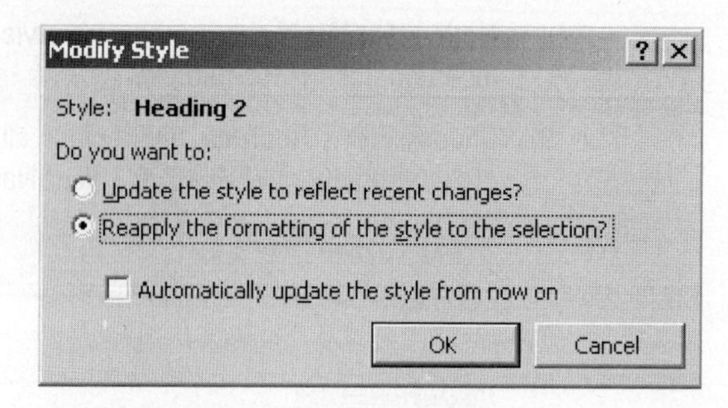

Typically, you will select the second option, *Reapply the formatting of the style to the selection*, because you will not want the relevant style definition to be amended.

If you select the first option, *Update the style to reflect recent changes*, Word redefines the style so that it has the attributes of the directly formatted paragraph. It has the same effect as selecting the *Automatically update* checkbox displayed when creating or modifying the style with the **Format | Style** command.

Working with character styles

Earlier in this chapter, you learnt about character styles that contain only font, border and language attributes. Unlike paragraph styles that apply to entire paragraphs, you can apply character styles to a paragraph or to selected text within a paragraph.

Take a look at the styles in the drop-down Style Box list. Notice that only paragraph styles have the paragraph mark symbol (¶) beside their style name.

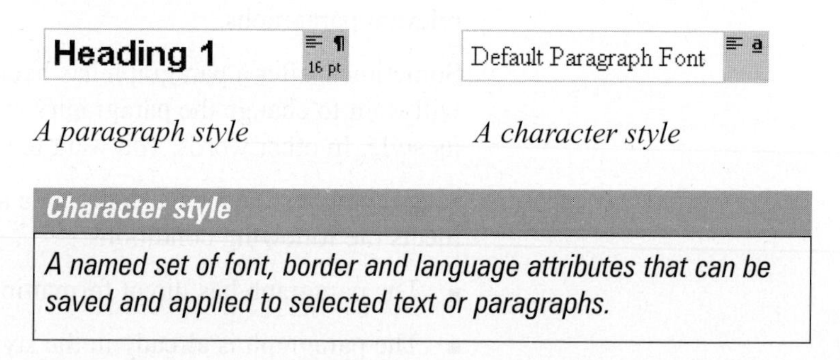

A paragraph style *A character style*

Character style

A named set of font, border and language attributes that can be saved and applied to selected text or paragraphs.

In Exercise 2.5, you will create and amend a character style.

Exercise 2.5: Creating and amending a character style

1) Open the following file:

   `Chapter2_Exercise_2-5_Before.doc`

2) Choose **Format | Style**, and in the dialog box displayed, click the **New** button.

3) In the *Name* box, enter 'Char Style *Your Name*', select a *Style type* of Character, and a *Based on* style of Default Paragraph Font.

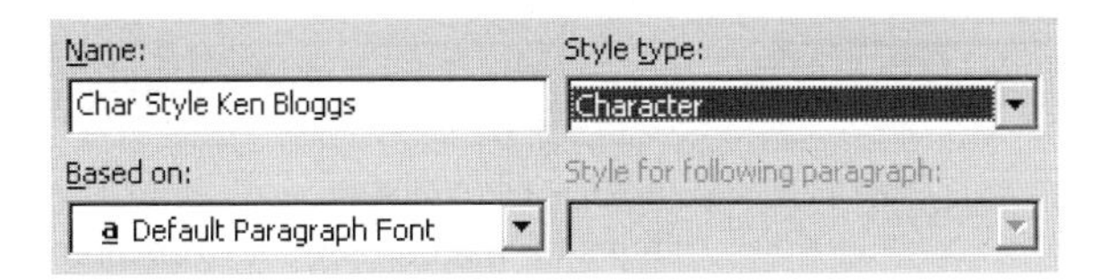

Character styles do not offer a *Style for following paragraph* option.

4) Click the **Format** button, click **Font**, select Arial, Regular, 10 pt, and click **OK**.

5) You are returned to the *New Style* dialog box. Leave the *Add to template* check box deselected. The *Update automatically* checkbox is not available for character styles.

   Click **OK** to close the *New Style* dialog box, and then click **Apply** to close the *Style* dialog box. You are returned to your document.

6) In the sample document, select the text 'Elmsworth Health Trust' in the first paragraph under the heading 'Elmsworth Health Trust: Patients' Charter', click the Style Box drop-down arrow, and select your new character style. Click anywhere else in the document to deselect the text.

Elmsworth Health Trust: Patients' Charter

At Elmsworth Health Trust, we are committed to delivering a world-class service. standards apply whether you are:

7) Your next step is to modify your character style.

   Click anywhere in the text that you selected in Step 6, and choose **Format | Style**. In the dialog box displayed, select the new style from the *Styles* list and click the **Modify** button.

8) Click the **Format** button, click **Font**, select Arial Narrow, Regular, 10 pt, and click **OK**.

9) You are returned to the *New Style* dialog box. Leave the *Add to template* checkbox deselected.

   Click **OK** to close the *New Style* dialog box, and then click **Apply** to close the *Style* dialog box. You are returned to your document.

   Notice that Word applies the style change to the selected text.

   Close and save your sample document with the following name:

   `Chapter2_Exercise_2-5_After_`*`Your_Name`*`.doc`

Chapter 2: quick reference

Tasks summary

Task	Procedure
To view all available styles for the current document.	Hold down the **Shift** key and click the Style Box drop-down arrow on the Formatting toolbar.
To view the style applied to text.	Choose **Help | What's This?** This and click in the text to display a pop-up information window.
To view styles applied in a document.	In Normal view, choose **Tools | Options**, click the **View** tab, enter a Style Area Width of 2.5 cm, and click **OK**. Word displays the Style Area to the left of the document.
To create a new style.	Choose **Format | Style**, click **New**, define the style attributes, select a *Style for following paragraph* (for paragraph styles only), click **OK** and **Apply**. Optionally, you can define a *Based on* style, and assign a shortcut key for the style.
To amend a style.	Click in an occurrence of the style, choose **Format | Style**, click **Modify**, amend the attributes, click **OK**, and click **Apply**.
To allow style redefinition through direct formatting.	When creating or amending the style, select the *Automatically update* checkbox. Word will redefine the style when you apply direct formatting to any paragraph in that style.

Concepts summary

A *style* is a named set of attributes that can be created, saved and then applied to items within documents. Styles enable you to apply a wide range of attributes in a single operation. And when you change the attributes of a style, all text in that style changes accordingly.

Word contains almost 100 built-in, ready-to-use styles. The ones that you are likely to use most often are *heading styles* (Heading 1, Heading 2, ...) and *Normal* (for body text). You can create new styles, and amend built-in styles and user-created styles.

Word's styles are of two types: *paragraph styles* that can control every aspect of a paragraph's appearance and position, and *character styles* that contain font, border and language attributes only. A *Based on* style is one that supplies default attributes to one or more other styles.

Chapter 2: quick quiz

Circle the correct answer to each of the following multiple-choice questions about styles in Word.

Q1	In Word, a style is ...
A.	A named set of attributes that can be saved and then applied to selected items in a document.
B.	A file containing preset formatting and standard content that provides a pattern for individual Word documents.
C.	A list of a document's headings, with lower-level headings indented progressively to reflect their relative importance.
D.	A list of installed Windows fonts that are available for use in Word documents.

Q2	Which of the following is not an advantage of using styles in a Word document?
A.	You will find it easier to export the document to HTML and other non-Word formats.
B.	You are provided with an automatically-created backup in the event of document corruption or loss.
C.	You can change the document's appearance by modifying the relevant style or styles.
D.	Your document has a smaller file size and displays more quickly than a document that has formatting applied manually.

Q3	Which of the following is not a built-in heading style in Word?
A.	Heading 3.
B.	Heading 1.
C.	Word File Heading.
D.	Heading 5.

Q4	Which of the following statements about Word's Style Box is untrue?
A.	The Style Box is located on the Formatting toolbar.
B.	The Style Box is located on the Standard Toolbar.
C.	Holding down the **Shift** key before clicking the **Style Box** drop-down arrow displays the full list of available styles.
D.	Styles listed in the Style Box are formatted, so that you can see what each one looks like before you apply it.

Q5	Which of the following statements about Word's paragraph and character styles is untrue?
A.	Paragraph styles can control every aspect of a paragraph's appearance and position.
B.	Character styles contain only font, border and language attributes.
C.	The *Update automatically* checkbox within the **Format | Style** command is not available for paragraph styles.
D.	Character styles can be applied to paragraphs or to selected text within paragraphs.

Q6	Which of the following methods do you use to display Word's Style Area?
A.	Click anywhere in the document and choose **Help | What's This?**
B.	Click the **Style Area** button beside the Styles Box on the Standard toolbar.
C.	In Print Layout view, choose **Tools | Customize**, select the *Style area* checkbox, and click **OK**.
D.	In Normal view, choose **Tools | Options**, click the **View** tab on the dialog box displayed, enter a non-zero style area width, and click **OK**.

Q7	**When using Word's Format | Style command, which of the following statements best describes the effect of selecting the *Automatically update* checkbox?**
A.	It updates the document's table of contents to reflect any changes to the heading styles.
B.	It updates other documents that are based on the same template with the most recent style modifications.
C.	It prevents direct formatting from affecting the style's attributes.
D.	It tells Word to update the style definition whenever direct formatting is applied to a paragraph in that style.

Q8	**Which of the following statements about the *Based on* feature of styles in Word is true?**
A.	For any particular style, you can change the *Based on* style chosen at the time that the style was created.
B.	Only Word's collection of approximately 100 built-in styles can be used as *Based on* styles.
C.	You cannot specify a *Based on* style for a character style.
D.	You cannot specify a *Based on* style for a heading style.

Q9	**Which of the following statements about the *Style for following paragraph* feature of styles in Word is true?**
A.	For any particular style, you cannot change the *Style for following paragraph* style chosen at the time that the style was created.
B.	Only Word's collection of approximately 100 built-in styles can be selected as *Style for following paragraph* styles.
C.	A typical choice for the *Style for following paragraph* is the Normal style.
D.	The *Style for following paragraph* feature is optional. You need not choose such a style for every new style that you create.

Q10	Which of the following statements about the shortcut key feature of styles in Word is true?
A.	Keyboard shortcuts can be applied only to paragraph styles.
B.	Keyboard shortcuts can be applied to paragraph and character styles.
C.	A keyboard shortcut, once assigned to a style, cannot be changed.
D.	Keyboard shortcuts can be assigned only to Word's collection of approximately 100 built-in styles.

Q11	Directly applied formatting is ...
A.	Formatting applied to selected text or paragraphs in a document through the use of styles.
B.	Formatting applied with the **Format | Font, Format | Paragraph, Format | Borders and Shading** commands, or with the buttons on the Formatting toolbar.
C.	Formatting applied to a template file.
D.	Formatting applied to a document before it is saved.

Q12	What happens when you reapply a style to a paragraph that is already in that style, but that contains directly applied formatting?
A.	Word modifies the style so that it takes on the attributes of the directly applied formatting.
B.	Word gives you the choice of removing the directly applied formatting or of redefining the style to match that formatting.
C.	Word modifies the style but saves the modifications only to the document and not to the associated template.
D.	Word removes the directly applied formatting and restores the attributes of the paragraph back to those of the reapplied style.

Answers **1:** A, **2:** C, **3:** C, **4:** B, **5:** C, **6:** D, **7:** D, **8**: A, **9:** C, **10:** A, **11:** C, **12**: B

Recycle content and formatting: templates

Objectives

In this chapter you will learn how to:

- Create a template based on a document
- Create a document based on a user-built template
- Make changes to a template
- Create a new template based on an existing template

New words

In this chapter you will meet the following term:

- Template

Exercise files

In this chapter you will work with the following Word files:

- `Chapter3_Exercise_3-1_Before.doc`
- `Chapter3_Exercise_3-2_Before.doc`
- `Chapter3_Exercise_3-3_Before.dot`
- `Chapter3_Exercise_3-4_Before.dot`

Syllabus reference

In this chapter you will cover the following items from the ECDL Advanced Word Processing Syllabus:

- **AM3.1.3.1**: Change basic formatting and layout options in a template.
- **AM3.1.3.2**: Create a new template based on an existing document or template.

Patterns in document content and structure

If a document begins with the discovery of an unidentified body and concludes with the unmasking of a murderer, the chances are that it's a crime novel.

If it starts with executive summary, contains a competitive analysis and a sales forecast, and ends with pro forma income statements, it's more probably a business-plan document.

When reading any individual document, generally you can tell the category or genre to which it belongs because of the features it shares with other documents in its category:

- **Familiar content**. The same elements tend to reappear in documents of a particular category.
- **Predictable sequence**. The elements tend to be present in the same order as in other documents of that category.

Document patterns and Word templates

Behind every Word document is a pattern or template that can control its appearance and content. Among the things that you can build into templates are page settings, paragraph styles, and standard text and images.

You minimize effort and maximize output by:

- **Categorizing your documents**. Consider the types of documents that you create most frequently. Identify the formatting and content that are common to documents in each category.
- **Building category templates**. Create Word templates for each document type to provide a basis for individual documents.

Examples of business document types that lend themselves to templating are:

- Fax cover sheets
- Letters
- Reports
- Memos
- Press releases
- Business plans

Word comes with almost 30 templates suitable for different document types – CVs, brochures, manuals, and so on. You can customize Word's built-in templates according to your needs. A document is not tied forever to a particular template, and you can change the template associated with a document at any stage. (You will learn more about this in Chapter 4.)

Templates: the benefits to you

The value of templates is simply this: the more standard content and formatting settings that you include in your templates, the less work you need to perform on individual documents.

Working with templates

Here are the four template-related tasks that you need to be able to perform:

- **Create a template based on a document.** Got a document that would be suitable as a template – a company memo, perhaps, or a monthly sales report?

  Exercise 3.1 takes you through the steps of removing all but general-purpose text from such a document, and then saving the document as a template.

  While you can save a document as a template, the reverse is not true: you cannot save a template as a document.

  Word templates end in the file name extension .dot in contrast to .doc for Word documents.

- **Create a document based on a user-built template.** In Exercise 3.2 you use the template that you created in Exercise 2.1 as the basis for a new Word document.
- **Make changes to a template**: You can open, amend and then resave Word templates just as you would Word documents. Exercise 3.3 provides an example.
- **Create a new template based on an existing template.** If you want to create a template that is similar to one you already have, you can open the first template, customize it, and then save the template with a new name. See Exercise 3.4.

Template

A file that provides a pattern for individual Word documents. Template files, which end in .dot, can contain formatting settings and standard text, images and fields.

Exercise 3.1: Creating a new template based on a document

In this exercise, you will use a Word document, an internal company memo, as the basis for a new template.

1) Open Word, and open the following file:

   `Chapter3_Exercise_3-1_Before.doc`

2) In the table beneath the title 'Memo', delete the details specific to this memo. The table should then look like this:

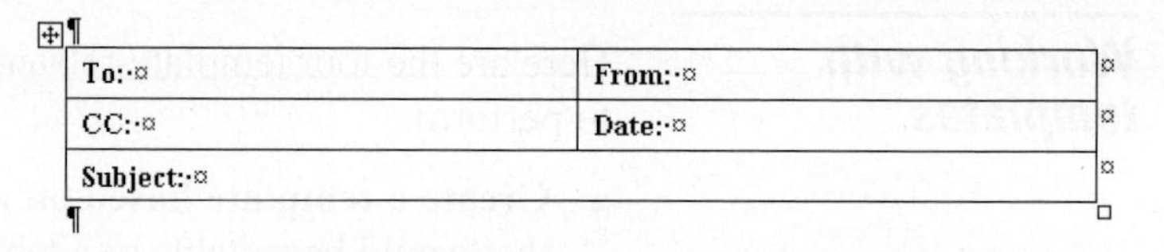

3) Delete the body text of the memo. Leave three paragraph marks beneath the table to facilitate the typing of text in individual memos.

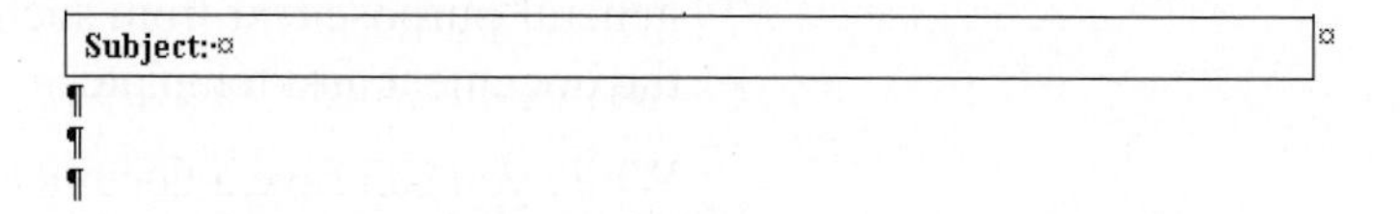

At the bottom of the page you can see a footer with a border along its top. You can leave this footer as it is.

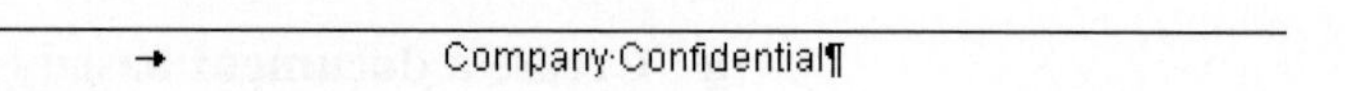

Your memo now contains only standard, general-purpose text, and it is ready to be saved as a template.

4) Choose **File | Save As**. In the dialog box displayed, click the *Save as type* drop-down arrow, and select the *Document Template* option.

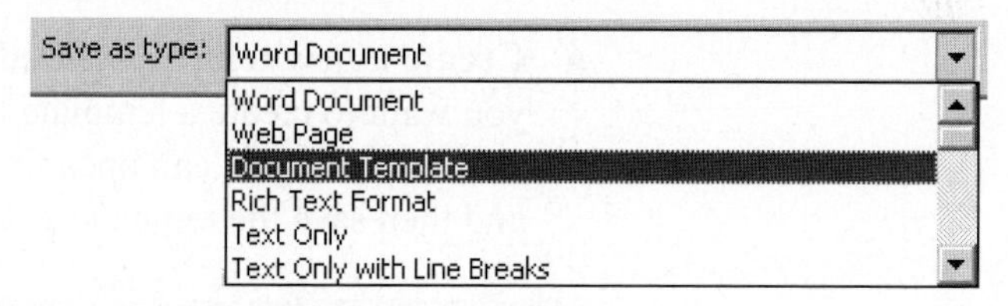

By default, Word prompts you to save templates in the folder named \Templates. Accept this location.

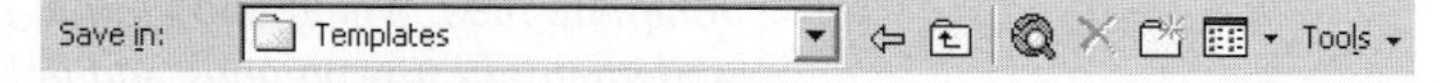

(You can learn more about the \Templates folder in '*Where are templates stored?*' below.)

5) In the *File name* box, type the following:

`Chapter3_Exercise_3-1_After_`*`Your_Name`*

Word automatically adds the file name extension .dot to your new template.

6) Click **Save**. You can close your new template.

Where are templates stored?

You can save a template in any location on your PC, but you can make life easier by storing your templates in the \Templates folder. Where is that? It depends on your version of Windows:

Windows 95, 98, ME

`C:\Windows\Application Data\Microsoft\Templates`
-or-
`C:\Windows\Profiles\`*`User_Name`*`\Application Data\Microsoft\Templates`
-or-
`C:\Windows\Profiles\`*`User_Name`*`\Templates`

Windows 2000
`C:\Documents and Settings\`*`User_Name`*`\Application Data\Microsoft\Templates`

Still can't find your \Templates folder? Use the **Search** command on the **Start** menu to locate it. Document template files that you store in the \Templates folder appear on the *General* tab of the **File | New** dialog box, where they are easy to find when you need them.

If you create a subfolder within \Templates and save your templates in it, your subfolder's name appears as a new tab on the **File | New** dialog box.

Exercise 3.2: Creating a document based on a user-built template

In this Exercise, you will use a memo template as the basis for a new memo document.

1) Choose **File | New** to create a new document.

   In the *New* dialog box, click the *General* tab if it is not displayed already.

2) Click the following template:

   `Chapter3_Exercise_3-2_Before.dot`

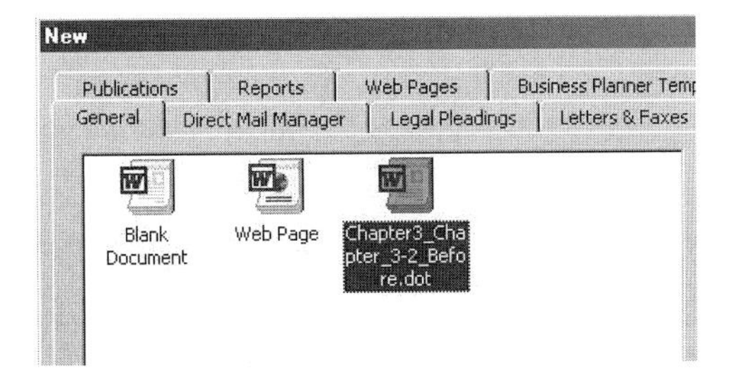

3) Select the *Create New Document* option, and click **OK**.

4) Type some text in the memo, and save the document with the following name:

   Chapter2_Exercise_3-2_After_*Your_Name*.doc

5) Save and close the sample memo document.

Exercise 3.3: Making changes to a template

In this exercise, you will amend some aspects of the template similar to the one you created in Exercise 3.1 and used as the basis for a document in Exercise 3.2.

1) Open the following file:

   Chapter3_Exercise_3-3_Before.dot

2) Click to the right of the heading 'Date:'. Press the Spacebar so that the insertion point is one empty space to the right of the colon.

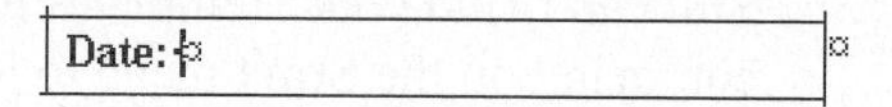

3) Choose **Insert | Field**. In the *Categories* list, select *Date and Time*. In the *Field names* list, select *Date*.

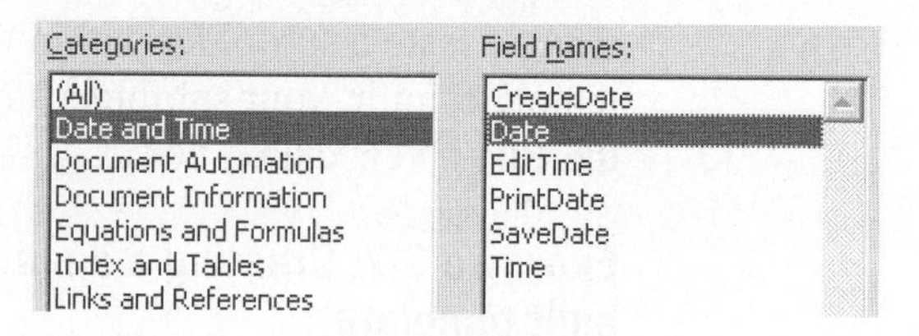

4) Click **OK**.

5) Choose **File | Save As**. By default, Word prompts you to save the amended template in the folder named \Templates. Accept this location.

   In the *File name* box, type the following:

   Chapter3_Exercise_3-3_After_Your_Name

6) Click **Save**. Word automatically adds the file name extension .dot to your new template. You can close the template file.

   In future, whenever the template is opened, the date field will be updated to show the current date. You will learn more about Word fields in Chapter 8.

Exercise 3.4: Creating a new template based on an existing template

In this exercise, you will open a memo template similar to the one that you worked on in Exercise 3.3 and use it to create a template for a fax cover sheet.

1) Open the following file:

    `Lesson3_Exercise_3-4_Before.dot`

2) Replace the title 'Memo' with the new title 'Fax Message'.

3) Click anywhere in the table cell containing the word 'From:', choose **Table | Select | Cell**, and then select **Edit | Cut**.

4) Drag across the two cells in the top row of the table, and choose **Table | Merge Cells**. The top row should now look like this:

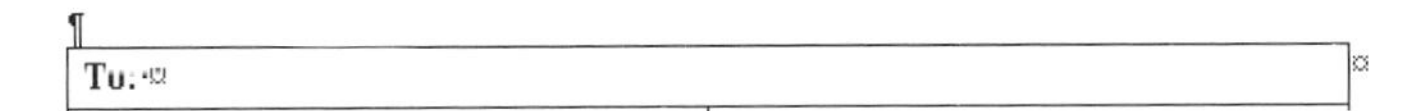

5) Click anywhere in the table cell containing 'CC:', choose **Table | Select | Cell**, and then **Select Edit | Cut.**

6) Drag across the two cells in the second row of the table and choose **Table | Merge Cells**.

7) Choose **View | Header and Footer**, delete the footer text 'Company Confidential', and click **Close** on the Header and Footer toolbar.

8) Choose **File | Save As**. In the dialog box displayed, click the *Save as type* drop-down arrow, and select the *Document Template* option.

    By default, Word prompts you to save templates in the folder named \Templates. Accept this location.

    In the *File name* box, type the following:

    Chapter3_Exercise_3-4_After_*Your_Name*

9) Click Save. Word automatically adds the file name extension .dot to your new template. You can close the template file.

Chapter 3: quick reference

Tasks summary

Task	Procedure
Create a new template based on a document.	Remove all but general-purpose text from the document. Choose **File | Save As**, select *Save as type* as *Document Template*, and click **Save**.
Create a document based on a particular template.	Choose **File | New**, select your required template from the dialog box, select the *Create New Document* option, and click **OK**.
Amend a template.	Open the template, make the required changes, and resave it.
Create a new template based on an existing template.	Open the template, make the required changes, and save it under a new name.

Concepts summary

A template is a pattern for documents that can hold preset formatting and standard content, including text, images and fields. The more content and formatting that you include in your templates, the less work you need to perform on individual documents.

Examples of business document types that lend themselves to templating include fax cover sheets, company memos, letters, press releases, reports and business plans.

To create a new template from an existing document, remove all but general-purpose text from the document and then save it as a template. You can open, amend and then resave Word templates just as you would Word documents. You cannot save a template as a document.

By default, Word prompts you to save templates in the folder named \Templates. Templates stored in the \Templates folder appear on the *General* tab of the **File | New** dialog box, where they are easy to find when you need them.

Word templates end in the file name extension .dot in contrast to .doc for Word documents.

Chapter 3: quick quiz

Circle the correct answer to each of the following multiple-choice questions about templates in Word.

Q1	A Word template is …
A.	A free upgrade program supplied by Microsoft to registered Word users.
B.	A file containing preset formatting and standard content that provides a pattern for individual Word documents.
C.	A list of a document's headings, with lower-level headings indented progressively to reflect the relative importance.
D.	An automatically created back-up version of a document.

Q2	Which of the following is a benefit provided by templates?
A.	Documents based on built-in Word templates load and display more quickly.
B.	Creating templates for commonly-used document types reduces effort because individual documents based on the templates will already contain standard formatting and content.
C.	Templates provide automatic back-ups in the event of file corruption or loss.
D.	Templates make it easier to convert documents to outlines.

Q3	Which of the following files is a Word template?
A.	Template.doc
B.	Update.dot.doc
C.	Template_fax.wrd
D.	Report.dot

Q4	Which of the following statements about Word templates is untrue?
A.	A template can be saved as a document.
B.	A document can be saved as a template.
C.	A built-in Word template (such as Fax.dot) can be modified and saved under a new template name (such as Fax2.dot).
D.	A template can be deleted.

Q5	Which of the following statements about Word's \Templates folder is untrue?
A.	The \Templates folder may store both built-in and user-created templates.
B.	The \Templates folder is the default location for storing files with a file type of document template (.dot).
C.	Templates saved in the \Templates folder appear on the **General** tab of the **File | Open** dialog box.
D.	Templates must be stored in the \Templates folder.

Q6	You want to base a new Word document on a template that you have created. Which of the following actions do you take?
A.	Click the **New** button on the Standard toolbar.
B.	Choose **File | New** and select the required template from the *Template options* drop-down list.
C.	Remove Normal.dot from the \Templates folder.
D.	Choose **File | New**, select the required template from the dialog box displayed, and click **OK**.

Answers

1: B, **2:** B, **3:** D, **4:** A, **5:** D, **6:** D.

Separating content from format: templates and styles

Objectives

In this chapter you will learn how to:

- Save a style and a style modification in a template
- Base a new document on a selected template
- Change the template on which a document is based
- Apply Word's AutoFormat feature to a plain, unformatted document

New words

In this chapter you will meet the following terms:

- Template-based formatting
- AutoFormat

Exercise files

In this chapter you will work with the following Word files:

- `Chapter4_Exercise_4-1_Before.doc`
- `Chapter4_Exercise_4-1_Template1.dot`
- `Chapter4_Exercise_4-1_Template2.dot`
- `Chapter4_Exercise_4-2_Doc1.doc`
- `Chapter4_Exercise_4-2_Doc2.doc`
- `Chapter4_Exercise_4-2_Template1.dot`
- `Chapter4_Exercise_4-2_Template2.dot`
- `Chapter4_Exercise_4-3_Before.doc`

Syllabus reference

In this chapter you cover the following items from the ECDL Advanced Word Processing Syllabus:

- **AM3.1.2.5**: Modify existing character or paragraph styles.
- **AM3.1.3.1**: Change basic formatting and layout options in a template.
- **AM3.1.1.4**: Apply automatic text formatting options.

Styles and templates: a review

You covered Word's styles in Chapter 2 and templates in Chapter 3. Let's begin this chapter by summarizing what you know:

- **Style**. A named *set of attributes* that can be created, saved and then applied to items within documents. When you change the attributes of a style, all text in that style changes accordingly.
- **Template**. A pattern for documents that can hold *preset formatting* and *standard content*, including text, images and fields.

In this chapter you will explore the *relationship* between templates and styles, and discover how that relationship affects the documents that you work with.

Style location: document or template?

Ask yourself the question, where is style stored? Unlike a document or a template, a style is not a separate file. Yet each style must be stored somewhere – but where?

You can store a new style that you create in either of two locations: in the current document, or in the current template (that is, the template on which the current document is based).

- **Current document**. A style stored in the current document is available in that document only.

  This is the sensible choice for one-off styles that you create for use only in a single document and are unlikely to ever need again.

- **Template**. A style stored in a template is available to all other documents that are also based on that template.

  When you want to reuse a style in multiple documents – for example, all fax cover sheets or all sales reports – but the best place to store the style is in the template.

The Add to template *checkbox*

What controls where a new style is stored? Answer: the settings of the *Add to template* checkbox, which appears in the *New Style* dialogue box within the **Format | Style** command.

When you select *Add to template*, you are telling Word: 'This is a style that I may want to use in other documents. So store my new style in the current template.'

When you leave the *Add to template* checkbox deselected (its default value), Word stores your new style in the current document only.

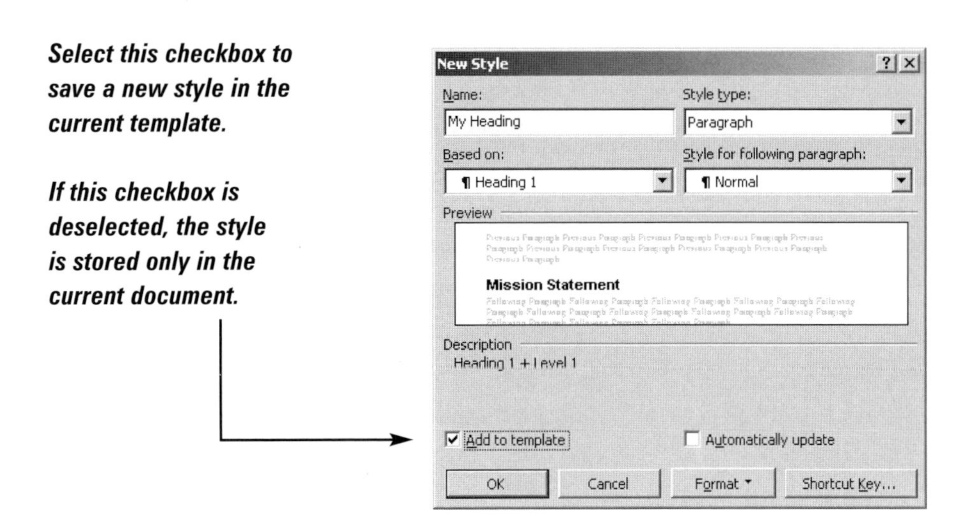

Separating content from format: the benefits

When you store styles in a template, you take away control of the document's format from the document itself and pass that control to another file: the template file.

This approach to formatting a document with styles saved in a template is called template-based formatting or style-sheet-based formatting. (The terms *template* and *style sheet* are often used interchangeably.) This approach offers the following advantages:

- **Consistency across multiple documents**. You can ensure that multiple documents share the same appearance simply by basing them on a common template.
- **Multiple document reformatting**. You can change the appearance of multiple documents simply by amending a *single* file, the template file. All documents based on that template, whether they number 10 or 10,000, change accordingly.

Template-based formatting

An approach in which documents are formatted by applying styles saved in a common template. It enables the formatting of multiple documents to be managed from a single template file.

Templates and documents: how they are first connected

New button

Every Word document is based on a template. The association between a document and its underlying template is made in one of two ways:

- **Word chooses the template**. If you create a document by clicking the **New** button on the Standard toolbar, Word associates your document with the so-called Normal template, also known as Normal.dot.

- **You choose the template**. If you create a document by choosing **File | New**, Word displays a dialog box and prompts you to select your required template.

When you click on a template icon, select the *Create New Document* option, and click **OK**, Word creates a new document based on the template that you have selected.

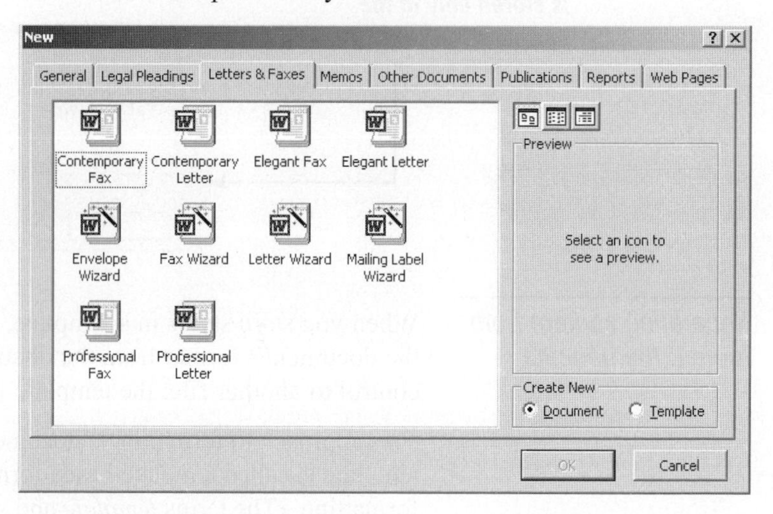

Changing the template on which a document is based

A document is not tied forever to the template chosen at the time it was created. You can change a document's template as often as you wish.

Exercise 4.1: Attach a new template to a document

In this exercise, you open a document containing text, attach a new template to it, and discover how the new template affects the document's appearance.

1) Open Word, and open the following file:

   `Chapter4_Exercise_4-1_Before.doc`

   A sample from the document is shown below.

The·New·Era·of·e-Business:·Part·1¶

Introduction¶

By·transforming·the·way·that·people·and·businesses·communicate·and·interact,·the·Internet·has·dramatically·changed·the·face·of·business.¶

Impressed·by·the·Internet's·rising·popularity,·many·businesses·have·established·an·online·presence.·A·rich·variety·of·business·information·—·from·product·and·service·catalogues·to·press·releases·to·company·contacts·—is·now·available·to·Internet·users.¶

Today,·many·businesses·realise·that,·in·order·to·compete·successfully,·they·need·to·sell·their·goods·and·services·directly·to·consumers·or·other·businesses·over·the·Internet.¶

Formatting is applied to the document using Word's built-in Heading 1, Heading 2, Normal and List Bullet styles.

2) Choose **Tools | Templates** and **Add-Ins**.

3) Click **Attach** to display the templates located in your \Templates folder, click the following template to select it, and then click **Open**:

    `Chapter4_Exercise_4-1_Template1.dot`

    You are returned to the *Templates and Add-ins* dialog box.

4) Select the *Automatically update document styles* checkbox. The dialog box should now look similar to this:

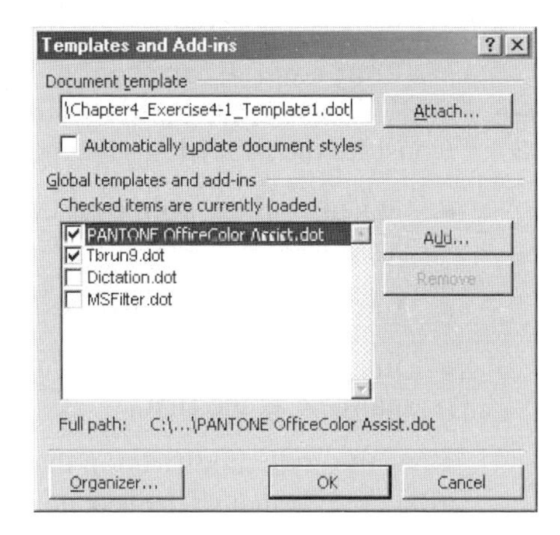

5) Click **OK** to close the dialog box and attach the selected template to your selected document.

    Notice how your sample document has changed appearance. This is because the style definitions for Heading 1, Heading 2, Normal and List Bullet in the new template are different to those of the document's original template, Normal.dot.

    The·New·Era·of·e-Business:·Part·1¶

    Introduction¶

    By·transforming·the·way·that·people·and·businesses·communicate·and·interact,·the·Internet·has·dramatically·changed·the·face·of·business.¶

    Impressed·by·the·Internet's·rising·popularity,·many·businesses·have·established·an·online·presence.·A·rich·variety·of·business·information·—from·product·and·service·catalogues·to·press·releases·to·company·contacts·—is·now·available·to·Internet·users.¶

    Today,·many·businesses·realise·that,·in·order·to·compete·successfully,·they·need·to·sell·their·goods·and·services·directly·to·consumers·or·other·businesses·over·the·Internet.¶

6) Repeat steps 2 to 4, but this time select the following template:

    `Chapter4_Exercise_4-1_Template2.dot`

Notice again how your sample document has changed appearance.

> **The·New·Era·of·e-Business:·Part·1¶**
>
> **Introduction¶**
>
> By·transforming·the·way·that·people·and·businesses·communicate·and·interact,·the·Internet·has·dramatically·changed·the·face·of·business.¶
>
> Impressed·by·the·Internet's·rising·popularity,·many·businesses·have·established·an·online·presence.·A·rich·variety·of·business·information·–·from·product·and·service·catalogues·to·press·releases·to·company·contacts·–·is·now·available·to·Internet·users.¶
>
> Today,·many·businesses·realise·that,·in·order·to·compete·successfully,·they·need·to·sell·their·goods·and·services·directly·to·consumers·or·other·businesses·over·the·Internet.¶

7) Close and save your sample document with the following name:

`Chapter4_Exercise_4-1_After_Your_Name.doc`

Style modifications and templates

Consider the following sequence of events:

- When working with a particular document, you modify the attributes of a style.
- You save and close the document.
- You then open another document that is based on the same template as the first.

Does the style modification that you made in the first document affect the format of the second document? The answer is that it depends.

Everything that you have learnt so far about styles and templates also applies to style modifications and templates. When you modify a style – that is, change its attributes in some way – you can store the modification in the current document or template.

- **Style in template, modification in document**. It is possible to store a style in a template, and to store a modification to the same style in a document.

  In this case, the original style is available to all documents based on the template, but the newer, modified style is available only to the current document.

- **Style in document, modification in template**. You can create a new style and store it in the current document only. Later, you can amend the style's attributes in some way and save the modified version of the style in the current template.

  In this case, the original style is available to the current document only, but the modified style is available to all documents based on the relevant template.

As with new styles, the storage location of a style modification depends on the setting of the *Add to template* checkbox. This checkbox, which appears in the *New Style* dialog box, also appears within the *Modify Style* dialog box. Both dialog boxes are available through the **Format | Style** command.

Exercise 4.2: Modifying a style stored in a template

In this exercise, you work with two documents that are based on the same template. You will redefine a style in one document, and discover the effects of the style modification on the other document.

1) Open the following file:

   `Chapter4_Exercise_4-2_Doc1.doc`

2) Choose **Tools | Templates and Add-Ins**. Click **Attach** to display the templates located in your \Templates folder, click the following template, and then click **Open**:

   `Chapter4_Exercise_4-2_Template2.dot`

   You are returned to the *Templates and Add-ins* dialogue box.

   Select the *Automatically update document styles* checkbox.

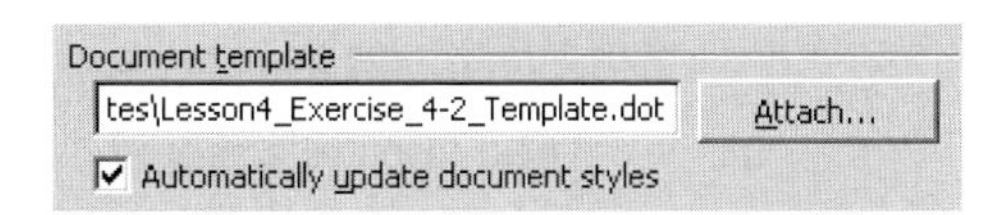

3) Click **OK** to close the dialog box and attach the selected template to your sample document. Notice how your sample document has changed appearance. Leave this document open.

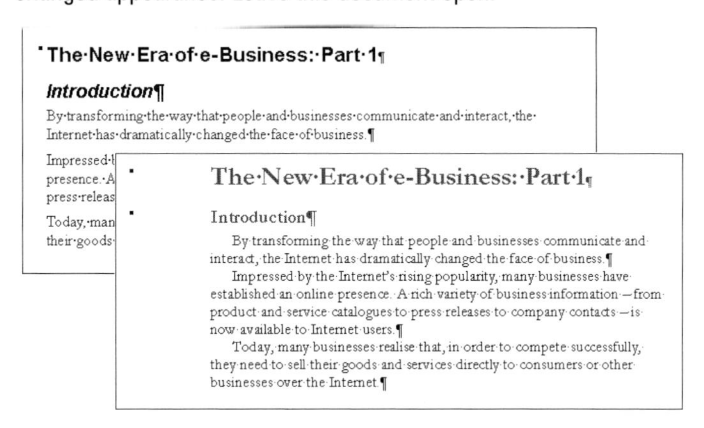

4) Open the second file:

   `Chapter4_Exercise_4-2_Doc2.doc`

5) Choose **Tools | Templates and Add-Ins**, click **Attach** to attach the following template, and then click **Open**:

   `Chapter4_Exercise_4-2_Template.dot`

Select the *Automatically update document styles* checkbox, and click **OK** to close the *Templates and Add-ins* dialog box.

Leave this second document open. You now have two documents based on the same template.

6) In your first sample document, click anywhere in the main heading, 'The New Era of e-Business: Part 1'. It is in the Heading 1 style.

7) Choose **Format | Style**, click **Modify**, **Format**, **Font**, change the *Color* to a different colour, and click **OK**.

   You are returned to the *Modify Style* dialog box. Select the *Add to template* checkbox, click **OK**, and then click **Apply** to close the dialog box. The document's main heading is now shown in your selected new colour.

8) Close your first sample document by clicking the **Close** box or by choosing **File | Close**. Word displays the following message box:

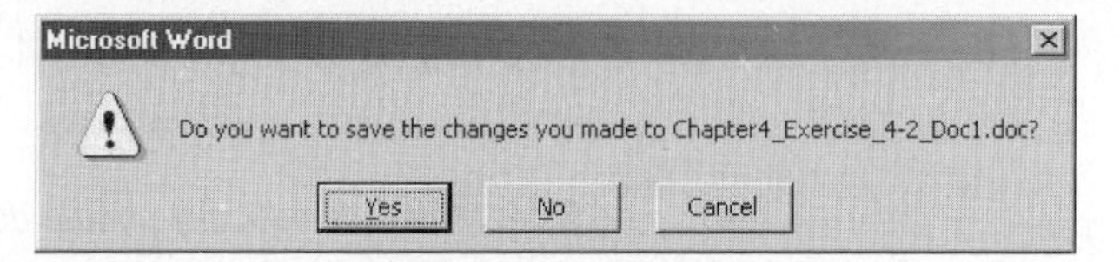

   Click **Yes** to save the change to your document.

9) Word next displays a second dialog box, asking you if you want to save the change to the template.

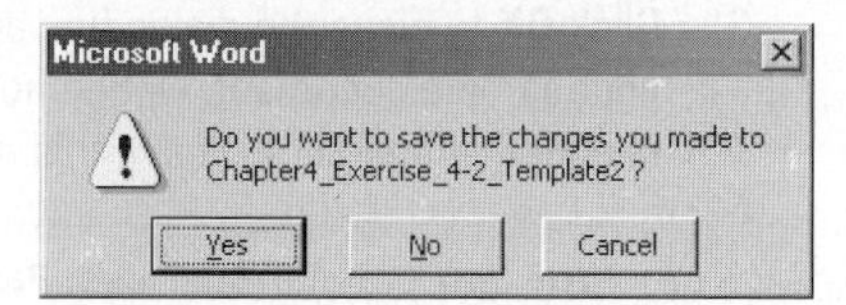

   Click **Yes** to save the change to your template.

   Only your second sample document is now open on your screen.

10) Look at the colour of the main heading in the second sample document. You can see that it has not been effected by the colour change that you made in step 8. For the style modification to take effect, you need to *reattach* the template containing the amended style to the document.

11) Choose **Tools | Templates and Add-Ins**, click **Attach** to attach the following template, and click **Open**:

```
Chapter4_Exercise_4-2_Template2.dot
```

   Do not select the *Automatically update document styles* checkbox. Click **OK** to close the *Templates and Add-ins* dialog box.

   You can see that the main heading is still in its original colour.

12) Choose **Tools | Templates and Add-Ins**, click **Attach** to attach the following template, and click **Open**:

    Chapter4_Exercise_4-2_Template2.dot

13) This time, select the *Automatically update document styles* checkbox. Click **OK** to close the *Templates and Add-ins* dialog box.

14) Now you can see that the main heading is in the new colour, reflecting the modification to the Heading 1 style saved in the document's template.

15) Choose **Format | Style**, click **Modify**, **Format**, **Font**, change the *Color* to its original colour, and click **OK**.

    You are returned to the *Modify Style* dialog box. Select the *Add to template* checkbox, click **OK**, and then click **Apply** to close the dialog box. The document's main heading is now in its original colour.

16) You can close and save your second sample document, saving the change to its template as you do.

17) Reopen Chapter4_Exercise_4-2_Doc1.doc and Chapter4_Exercise_4-2_Doc2.doc, reattach them to the Chapter4_Exercise_4-2_Template1.dot template, and close and save them.

The Automatically update document styles *checkbox*

Available within the **Tools | Templates and Add-Ins** command, the setting of this checkbox determines whether style modifications, saved in the document's template, affect the format of a document:

- **Checkbox selected**. The document is affected by the latest style modifications that are saved in the document's template.
- **Checkbox deselected**. The document is unaffected by style modifications saved in the template since the connection between the document and template was last made.

Select this checkbox to ensure that a document contains the latest template-based style modifications.

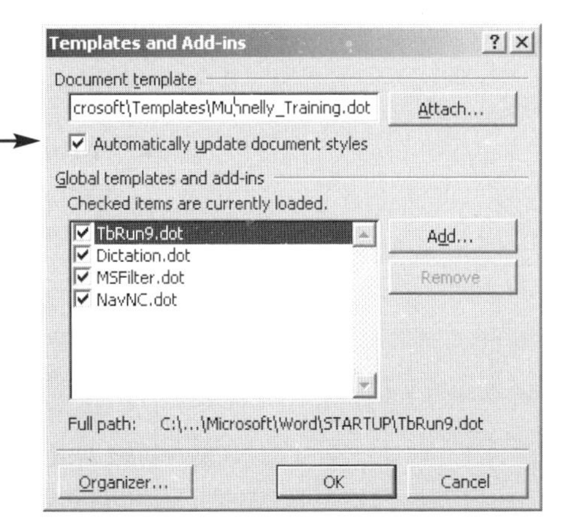

Template-based formatting: a review

In summary, if you create a new style or modify an existing one, and you want the new or modified style to be available to other documents based on the same template, you must:

- When using the **Format | Style** command to create or modify a style, select the *Add to template* checkbox.
- When closing the document that was open when you created or modified the style, save the changes to the template when prompted.
- Reattach the template to other documents, using the **Tools | Templates and Add-Ins** command, and ensure that you select the *Automatically update document styles* checkbox.

Applying styles with AutoFormat

If you need to apply styles to an unformatted document – for example, a plain-text, ASCII file imported from a non-Word source – you will find the AutoFormat feature a great time-saver.

AutoFormat works by examining factors such as line length (shorter lines are probably headings) and detecting the presence of special characters (a line beginning with an asterisk (*) and followed by a space or a tab is probably a bullet). It then applies appropriate heading and other styles to the document.

AutoFormat is, in effect, automated guesswork by Word. Its choices may not always be correct, but it is a valuable aid nonetheless.

AutoFormat also offers a number of other features that help tidy up a document, as does a related Word feature called AutoFormat As You Type. You will learn more about these features in Chapter 7.

You have two options when applying AutoFormat to all or selected parts of a document:

- **AutoFormat now**. This automatically formats the document or selected paragraphs based on your chosen settings.
- **AutoFormat and review each change**. This prompts you every time AutoFormat detects something in the document that it thinks it should reformat, and asks you whether you want to apply or ignore its suggested formatting.

AutoFormat

A Word feature that automatically applies appropriate heading, list and other styles to an unformatted or partly-formatted document based on an analysis of that document's structure.

AutoFormat style options

The main AutoFormat options relating to styles are shown in the following table. You access these options by choosing **Format | AutoFormat**, and clicking the **Options** button.

AutoFormat option	Effect on document
Headings	Paragraphs identified as headings are converted to the appropriate heading style – Heading 1, Heading 2, etc.
Lists	Paragraphs identified as items in a bulleted or numbered list are converted to the appropriate paragraph styles – List Bullet or List.
Automatic bulleted lists	Paragraphs identified as items in a bulleted or numbered list are converted to the Normal style, but bulleted or numbering formatting is applied to them within that style. If you select both the *Lists* and the *Automatic bulleted lists* options, the *Lists* option takes preference.
Other paragraphs	Paragraphs identified as body text are converted to the Normal style.
Preserve styles	Any paragraph styles already applied to text in the document are unchanged by AutoFormat. The exception is Plain Text style (Word default style for plain-text, unformatted documents).

Exercise 4.3: Applying styles with AutoFormat

In this exercise, you will apply AutoFormat to an unformatted document.

1) Open the following file:

   `Chapter4_Exercise_4-3_Before.doc`

   Notice that the entire document is in Plain Text style, Word's default style for plain-text, unformatted documents.

   There are no heading styles, and the asterisk character (*) is used to indicate items in a bulleted list.

2) Choose **Format | AutoFormat**, and click **Options**. Select the options shown below and click **OK**.

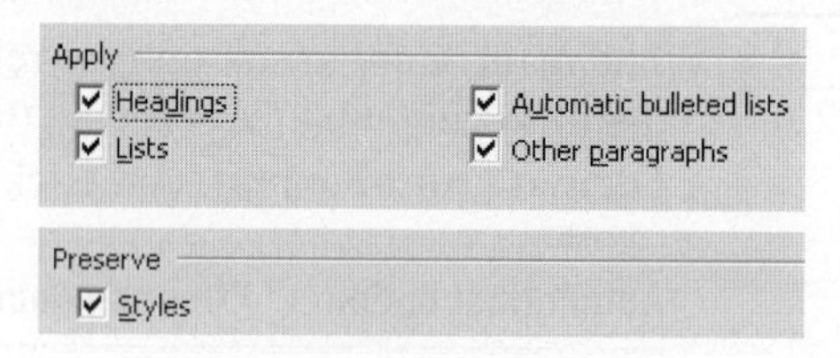

3) You now have two options: you can run AutoFormat in a single pass, or you can ask Word to prompt you for confirmation before it makes any changes. Click the *AutoFormat and review each change* option.

   Select a document type to guide Word's formatting operation: *General document* (your current template), *Letter* or *Email*. In this case, select the *General document* option.

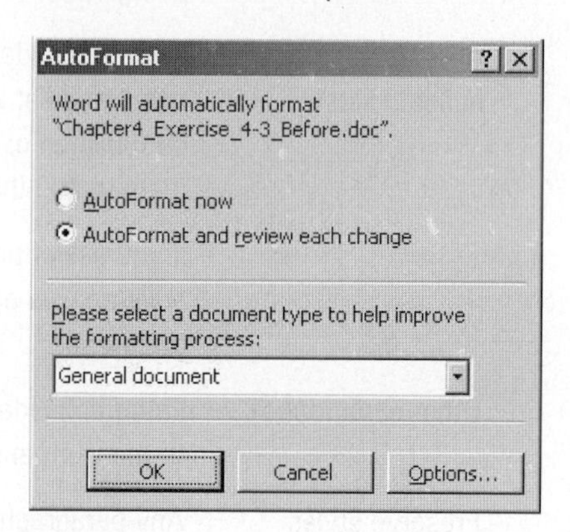

4) Click **OK**.

   (If you had selected the *AutoFormat now* option in step 3, Word would now apply the formatting changes. If you are unhappy with the changes made, you can choose **Edit | Undo** to reverse them.)

5) AutoFormat applies the changes to the sample document, which you can see on your screen. You can use the scrollbar or navigation keys to move through your document to inspect how well Word has formatted your document.

6) In the foreground, you can see the following dialog box:

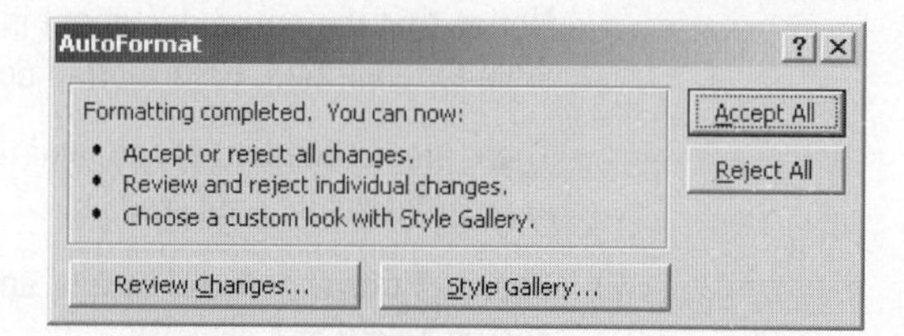

   If you approve of the changes, click **Accept All**.

   If the changes suggested are not at all what you want, click **Reject All**.

Selecting either option ends the AutoFormat procedure and returns you to the document.

7) If you want to accept some changes but not others, click **Review Changes**.

   Word now highlights each suggested formatting change on screen. Insertions are marked in blue and deletions in red. All changes are indicated by a vertical bar in the page margin.

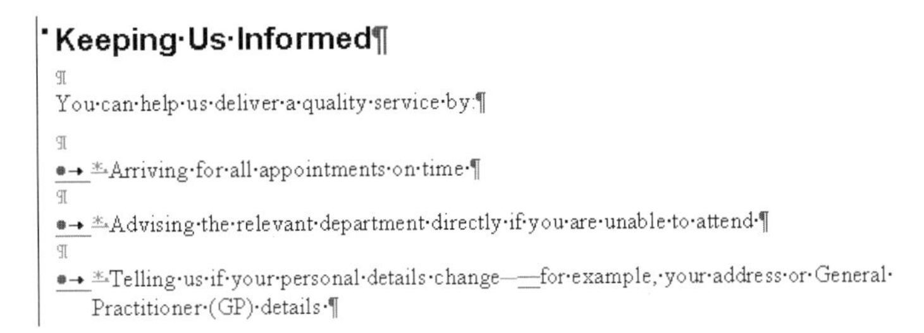

   A new dialog box, shown below, appears in the foreground. Click the **Hide Marks** button if you do not want Word to display the revision marks.

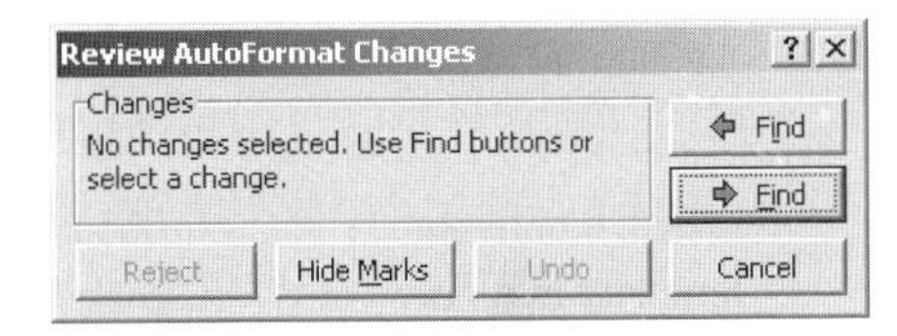

8) To inspect each formatting change, click **-> Find**. Word displays a dialog box indicating the first suggested formatting change.

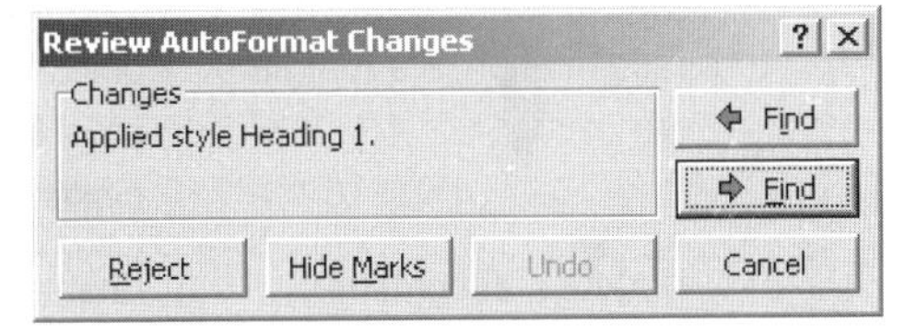

   Click **Reject** to reject the suggested change. Click **-> Find** to accept the suggested change and display the next one.

9) Repeat step 8 until you have moved through all the suggested changes. You now see the following dialog box:

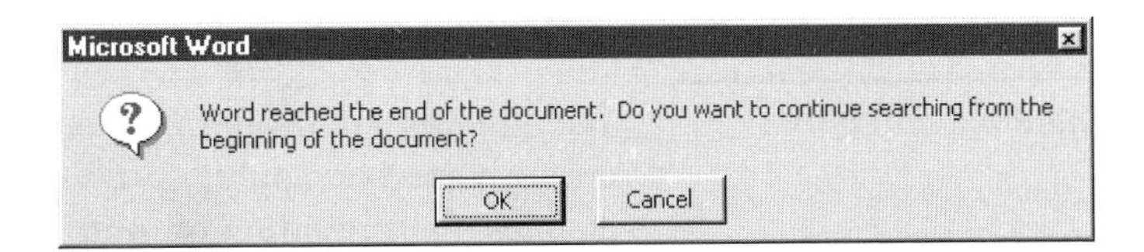

   Click **Cancel**.

10) Word again shows the *Review AutoFormat Changes* dialog box. Click **Cancel**.

11) You are now shown the AutoFormat dialog box. Click **Accept All**. This implements only those changes that you have accepted by clicking the **-> Find** button in Steps 8 and 9, and not any changes that you did not accept by clicking the **Reject** button.

    You have now completed the AutoFormat procedure.

12) Choose **File | Save As**, and save your document with the following name:

    `Chapter4_Exercise_4-3_After_`*`Your_Name`*`.doc`

    You can now close your document.

Chapter 4: quick reference

Tasks summary

Task	Procedure
Base a new document on a template other than the Normal template.	Choose **File | New**, click on a template icon from the dialog box, select the *Create New Document option*, and click **OK**.
Attach a different template to a new document.	Choose **Tools | Templates and Add-Ins**, click **Attach**, select the new template, select the *Automatically update document styles* checkbox, and click **OK**.
Save a style or a style modification in a template.	Within the **Format | Style** dialog box, select the *Add to template* checkbox, and save the template when prompted as you close the document.
Update a document's format to reflect the latest style modifications saved in the document's template.	Reattach the document template: choose **Tools | Templates and Add-Ins**, click **Attach**, select the current template, select the *Automatically update document styles* checkbox, and click **OK**.

Concepts summary

Template-based formatting is an approach in which documents are formatted by applying styles saved in a common template. It enables the formatting of multiple documents to be managed from a single template file.

An advantage of this approach is that is enables you to enforce a common format across multiple documents by basing the documents on the same template. In addition, you can change the appearance of multiple documents simply by amending their template file.

To apply the template-based formatting approach in Word, styles – and style modifications – must be saved in a template rather than in individual documents. When styles are added or modified, the template must be saved when the document is closed. Also, individual documents must be reattached to their template so that they reflect the latest updates to styles that are saved in the templates.

Chapter 4: quick quiz

Circle the correct answer to each of the following multiple-choice questions about templates, styles and AutoFormat in Word.

Q1	You want to base a new Word document on a template other than the Normal template. Do you...
A.	Click the **New** button on the Standard toolbar?
B.	Choose **File | New**, and select the required template from the *Template Options* drop-down list?
C.	Remove Normal.dot from the \Templates folder?
D.	Choose **File | New**, select the required template from the dialogue box displayed, and click **OK**?

Q2	Which of the following statements about styles and templates in Word is untrue?
A.	A style can be stored only in the Normal.dot template.
B.	A style can be stored in a template or a document.
C.	A style can be stored in a template, while a modification to the same style can be stored in a document.
D.	Two documents with the same styles can look very different.

Q3	When using Word's Format | Style command, what is the effect of selecting the *Add to template* checkbox?
A.	It ensures that the style is saved to the Normal.dot template.
B.	It merges the styles in your current template to the Normal.dot template.
C.	It makes the style or style modification available to the current template and not just to the current document.
D.	It converts all character styles to paragraph styles.

Q4	Two Word documents share the same template and styles but look different. Which of the following is a possible reason for this?
A.	The user modified a style when working on the second document but saved the style changes only to the second document, and not to the template.
B.	Both documents are based on the Normal template.
C.	Neither document is based on the Normal template.
D.	The template is not located in the \Templates folder.

Q5	What happens when you apply AutoFormat to an unformatted Word document?
A.	Word automatically applies the AutoFormat template (AutoFormat.dot) to the document.
B.	Word examines the document's structure and applies appropriate headings and other styles accordingly.
C.	Word runs a built-in macro on the document that corrects automatically any spelling and grammar errors.
D.	Word makes a back-up copy of the document and applies style-based formatting to the back-up copy. The original document is unaffected.

Answers

1: D, **2**: A, **3:** C, **4:** A, **5**: B.

5 Here's one I prepared earlier: AutoText

Objectives

In this chapter you will learn how to:

- Add a new text, table and image entries to AutoText
- Insert an AutoText entry in a document
- Amend an AutoText entry
- Delete an AutoText entry

New words

In this chapter you will meet the following term:

- AutoText

Exercise files

In this chapter you will work with the following Word files:

- `Chapter5_Exercise_5-1.doc`
- `Chapter5_Exercise_5-2_Before.dot`

Syllabus reference

In this chapter you will cover the following item from the ECDL Advanced Word Processing Syllabus:

- **AM3.1.1.5**: Use automatic text entry options.

About AutoText

AutoText is a Word feature for storing and inserting commonly-used text, graphics, tables and fields.

Two kinds of AutoText entries

Items stored in AutoText are called *AutoText entries*. There are two kinds: those supplied with Word, and those you add yourself.

- **Built-in entries**. Word offers a categorized range of supplied AutoText entries.

  Most are simple text entries relevant to letter-writing. Others are items suitable for insertion in document headers or footers.

- **User-created entries**. You can add your own AutoText entries. For example, your organization's name and contact details, formatted tables, and standard paragraphs such as disclaimers.

  You can also add images to AutoText, such as a scanned image of your signature.

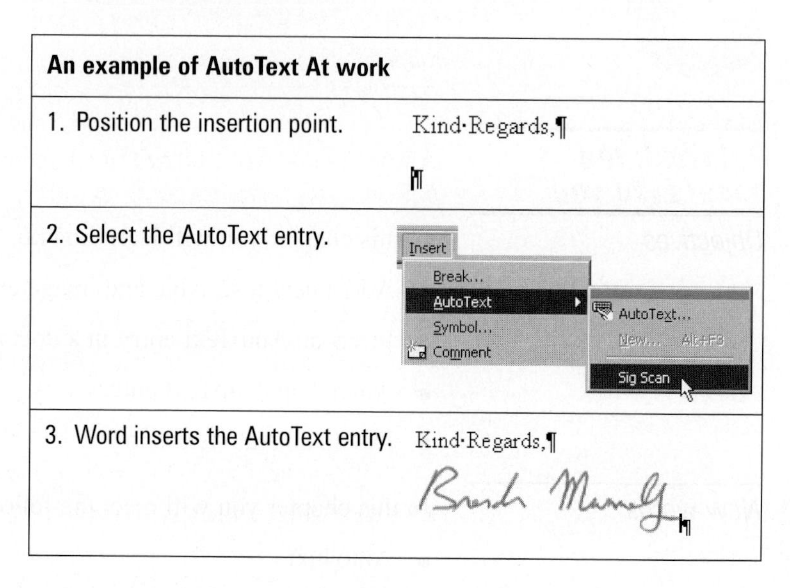

An example of AutoText At work	
1. Position the insertion point.	Kind·Regards,¶
2. Select the AutoText entry.	Insert / Break... / AutoText / Symbol... / Comment / AutoText... / New... Alt+F3 / Sig Scan
3. Word inserts the AutoText entry.	Kind·Regards,¶

*The **AutoText** tab*

To display your current AutoText entries, choose **Tools | AutoCorrect**. Click the **AutoText** tab, and scroll through the entries. When finished, click **OK**.

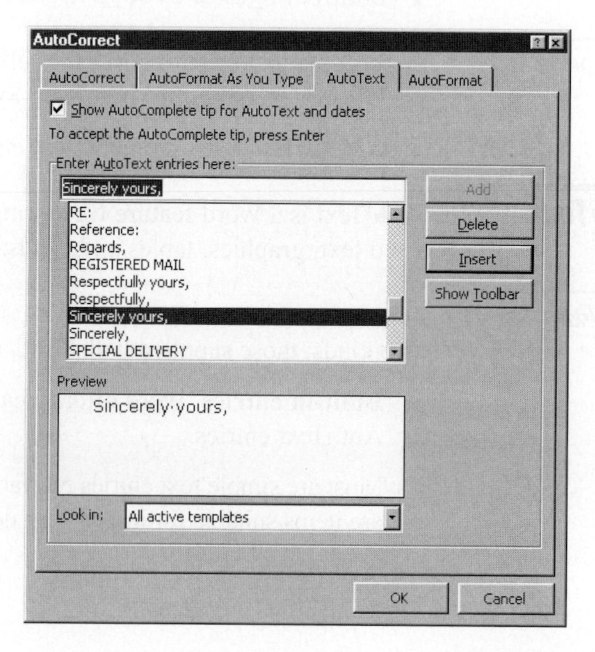

How much information can you store in an AutoText entry? Answer: it depends on the size of your PC's memory.

AutoText
A Word feature that stores frequently used text, tables and graphics, and enables users to insert these items as needed in individual documents.

AutoText: the benefits to you

A template, as you learned in Chapter 3, can store standard content – text, tables, graphics and fields – or automatic inclusion in any individual document based on that template. So what does AutoText offer that templates do not?

AutoText is valuable for:

- **Content that appears frequently but not always.** Like templates, AutoText can store ready-made content. But unlike templates, AutoText gives you the option of inserting or not inserting the content.
- **Content that appears across different document types**. Templates work best with narrowly categorized documents. AutoText entries can be applied more widely across many different document types – from one-page letters to lengthy reports.

Both templates and AutoText offer common benefits. They:

- **Save time**. AutoText can help eliminate a lot of repetitive typing.
- **Reduce errors**. Less typing results in documents with fewer misspellings and other errors.

Working with AutoText: the four tasks

Here are the four tasks you need to be able to perform with AutoText in Word:

- **Create new AutoText entries**. Exercise 5.1 takes you through the steps of creating new AutoText entries for a text paragraph, a table and an image.
- **Insert AutoText entries in a document**. In Exercise 5.2, you discover how to insert AutoText entries in a document.
- **Amend an AutoText entry**. Sometimes, you may want to modify an AutoText entry. Exercise 5.3 shows you how.
- **Delete an AutoText entry**. Finally, in Exercise 5.4, you learn how to delete an entry from AutoText.

Working with new AutoText entries

Two topics you need to understand before you create new AutoText entries are storage location and formatting.

AutoText and templates

Built-in AutoText entries are stored in the Normal template, from where they are available to every document that you work on.

User-created AutoText entries, however, are stored in the Word template associated with the document that was open when you created the entry. If this was Normal.dot, then your AutoText entry is available to all documents. If it was another template – say, Fax.dot – the entry is available only to documents based on that template.

AutoText and formatting

Typically, you create AutoText entries by selecting existing text, tables or graphics, and then storing them in AutoText. How does AutoText deal with formatting? The rules are straightforward:

- **Character formatting**. AutoText entries retain their character formatting (font, bold, italic, etc.).

  If you do not want a new AutoText entry to include paragraph formatting, select the paragraph without its paragraph mark.

- **Paragraph formatting**. If you want an AutoText entry to retain its paragraph formatting (alignment, indents, borders, tabs, etc.), include the paragraph mark when you select the entry.

Exercise 5.1: Creating AutoText entries

In this exercise, you will create three new AutoText entries: a text paragraph, a table, and a scanned image of a signature.

1) Open the following file:

   `Chapter5_Exercise_5-1.doc`

2) Select the following text paragraph, including the paragraph mark at the end.

3) Choose **Insert | AutoText | New**.

   (This option is available only if you have selected either text or a graphic within the document.)

4) In the *Create AutoText* dialog box, type a short, descriptive name for the entry. AutoText names can include spaces. In this example, type the name 'Slogan'.

Click **OK**.

5) Click anywhere in the Monthly Sales Report table, choose **Table | Select Table**.

6) Choose **Insert | AutoText | New**. In the *Create AutoText* dialog box, type the name 'Monthly Sales Report Table' and click **OK**.

7) Click on the image of the scanned signature to select it.

8) Choose **Insert | AutoText | New**. In the *Create AutoText* dialog box, type the name 'BM Sig Scan' and click **OK**.

9) You can close the sample document without saving it.

   Your work – the addition of three new AutoText entries – is contained in the template, not in the document.

Working with existing AutoText entries

The best way to gain an appreciation of AutoText is to use this feature in creating a document.

Exercise 5.2: Inserting AutoText entries in a document

In this exercise, you will insert the AutoText entries that you created in Exercise 5.1, together with two built-in Word AutoText entries.

1) Choose **File | New** and select the following template from the **General** tab:

   `Chapter5_Exercise_5-2_Before.dot`

   Click **OK**.

   Word now displays a new document based on the selected template.

2) Position the insertion point before the paragraph mark that is above the word 'Memo'.

3) Choose **Insert | AutoText | Normal | Slogan**.

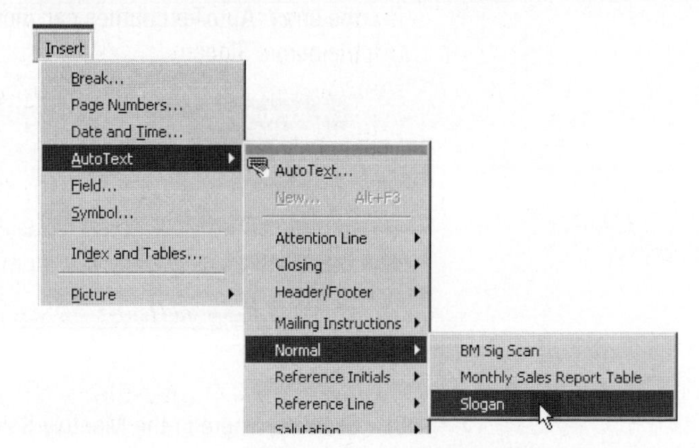

Word inserts the AutoText entry as shown.

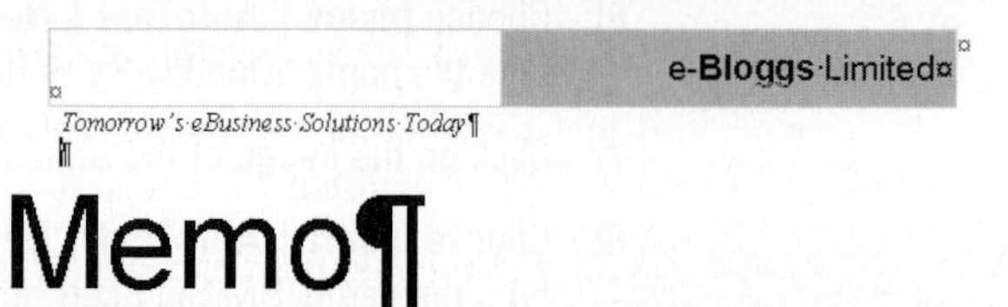

4) Position the insertion point at the third paragraph mark beneath the table.

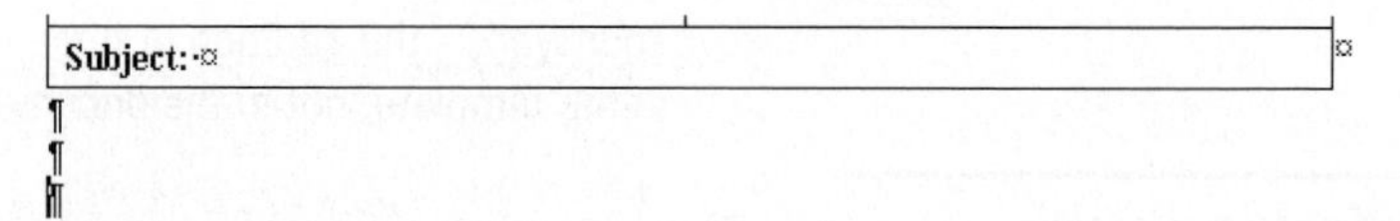

5) Choose **Insert | AutoText | Salutation | To Whom It May Concern**. Word inserts the AutoText entry.

6) Press **Enter** three times.

7) Choose **Insert | AutoText | Normal | Monthly Sales Report Table**. Word inserts the AutoText entry.

8) Press **Enter** three times.

9) Choose **Insert | AutoText | Closing | Best Regards**. Word inserts the AutoText entry.

10) Press **Enter** twice.

11) Choose **Insert | AutoText | Normal | BM Sig Scan**. Word inserts the AutoText entry.

12) Save your sample document with the following name, and close it:

`Chapter5_Exercise_5-2_After_`*`Your_Name`*`.doc`

Can you amend an AutoText entry? Not directly. But you can insert an entry in a document, modify the entry in the document, and then resave the entry in AutoText under the same name. The amended AutoText entry then overwrites the original entry.

Exercise 5.3: Amend an AutoText entry

In this exercise, you will modify an AutoText entry by amending it in a document and then resaving it to AutoText.

1) Click the **New** button on the Standard toolbar to create a new, blank document.
2) Choose **Insert | AutoText | Normal | Monthly Sales Report Table**. Word inserts the AutoText entry.
3) Select the text 'Monthly Sales Report'.
4) Choose **Format | Font**, change the font colour to light grey, and click **OK**.
5) Click anywhere in the Monthly Sales Report table, and choose **Table | Select Table**.
6) Choose **Insert | AutoText | New**. In the *Create AutoText* dialog box, type the name 'Monthly Sales Report Table' and click **OK**.
7) Word prompts you like this:

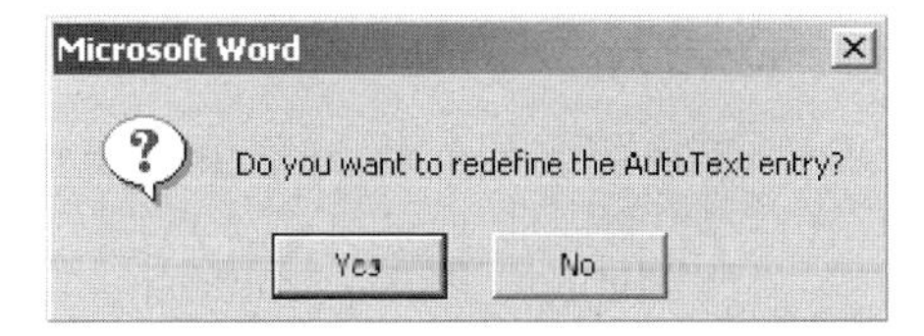

Click **Yes**. The named AutoText entry is now amended.

You can close the document without saving it. Your work – the modification of an AutoText entry – is contained in the template, not in the document.

Exercise 5.4: Deleting an AutoText entry

Removing an entry from AutoText is a simple task, as this exercise demonstrates.

1) Choose **Tools | AutoCorrect**, and click the **AutoText** tab.
2) Scroll through the list of AutoText entries to find an entry that you want to delete.
3) When you see the entry you want to delete, click to select it.
4) Click the **Delete** button.
5) Repeat steps 2 to 4 to remove any other AutoText entries you don't want.
6) When finished, click **OK** to close the dialog box.

Chapter 5: quick reference

Tasks summary

Task	Procedure
Save selected item as an AutoText entry.	Select the item, choose **Insert | AutoText | New**, type a short name for the entry, and click **OK**. To include the item's paragraph formatting, select the paragraph mark at the end of the item.
Insert an AutoText item in the current document.	Position the insertion point, choose **Insert | AutoText**, and click the required entry on the submenu.
Amend an AutoText entry.	In a document, type the amended entry, choose **Insert | AutoText | New**, and type the short name for the entry you want to amend. When prompted to redefine the entry, click **Yes**.
Delete an AutoText entry.	Choose **Tools | AutoCorrect**, click the **AutoText** tab, select the entry for deletion, click **Delete**, and click **OK**.

Concepts summary

AutoText is a Word feature that stores frequently-used content, and enables users to insert these items as needed in individual documents. Items stored in AutoText can include text, tables, graphics and fields.

Like templates, AutoText can store ready-made content. But unlike templates, AutoText gives you the option of inserting or not inserting the content.

Word includes a categorized range of *built-in AutoText entries*. Most are simple text entries relevant to letter-writing. Others are items suitable for insertion in document headers or footers.

You can add your own AutoText entries, such as your organization's name, contact details and logo. AutoText entries retain their character formatting (bold, italic, etc.) and, optionally, their paragraph formatting (alignment, indents, etc.).

User-created AutoText entries are stored in the Word template associated with the document that was open when the entry was created.

Items suitable for inclusion in AutoText are those that are relevant across many different document types – from one-page letters to lengthy reports.

Chapter 5: quick quiz

Circle the correct answer to each of the following multiple choice questions about AutoText in Word.

Q1	Which of the following statements best describes the AutoText feature in Word?
A.	AutoText checks a document's readability statistics and automatically makes such improvements as are necessary.
B.	AutoText generates document outlines automatically, based on the document's headings and subheadings.
C.	AutoText applies paragraph styles to a document based on factors such as line length and presence of bullet characters and numbers at the beginning of paragraphs.
D.	AutoText stores frequently-used text, tables, graphics and fields, and enables users to insert these items as needed in individual documents.

Q2	Which of the following is not an advantage of using AutoText in Word documents?
A.	Reduced likelihood of spelling errors as commonly-used text items can be retrieved from AutoText and inserted as needed in individual documents.
B.	Availability of automatically-created back-ups in the event of document corruption or loss.
C.	Documents look more professional, as logos and other standard graphics can be retrieved quickly from AutoText and inserted in individual documents.
D.	Faster production of documents containing sales figures and other numerical data, as highly-formatted tables can be retrieved from AutoText and inserted in individual documents.

Q3	Which of the following items can you not store as an AutoText entry in Word?
A.	Multiple paragraphs of text.
B.	A colour image.
C.	A template.
D.	A date field.

Q4	Which of the following factors determines the maximum size of the entries that you can store in AutoText?
A.	Your version of Word.
B.	The size of your PC's memory.
C.	The speed of your internal network connection.
D.	None of the above – entries may not exceed 256 characters.

Q5	Which of the following commands do you choose to create an AutoText entry from a selected item in a Word document?
A.	**Insert | AutoText | New.**
B.	**Tools | AutoText | Add.**
C.	**Insert | Add | AutoText.**
D.	**Format | AutoCorrect | AutoText | New.**

Q6	Which of the following commands do you choose to insert an AutoText entry in an open Word document?
A.	**Insert | AutoText | New.**
B.	**Insert | AutoText | <Submenu Name> | <AutoText Entry Name>.**
C.	**Format | Add | <AutoText Entry Name>.**
D.	**Format | AutoCorrect | AutoText | <Submenu Name> | <AutoText Entry Name>.**

Q7	You want to include an item's paragraph formatting attributes when adding it as an AutoText entry in Word. Do you...
A.	Exclude the item's paragraph mark when selecting it?
B.	Hold down the **Shift** key when selecting the item?
C.	Include the item's paragraph mark when selecting it?
D.	Hold down the **Ctrl** key when selecting the item?

Q8	Which of the following statements about amending AutoText entries is correct?
A.	Only user-created, not built-in, AutoCorrect entries can be amended.
B.	An entry can be amended directly in the *AutoText* dialog box.
C.	An entry can be amended only by saving a modified version of the entry with the same name as the entry you want to amend.
D.	Only text entries, not tables, can be amended.

Answers

1: D, **2:** B, **3:** D, **4:** B, **5:** A, **6:** D, **7:** C, **8:** C.

6 Word checks Your documents: AutoCorrect

Objectives

In this chapter you will learn how to:

- Turn AutoCorrect on and off
- Apply AutoCorrect options selectively
- Include and exclude the Office 2000 spellchecker in AutoCorrect
- Add a new AutoCorrect entry
- Amend an AutoCorrect entry
- Delete an AutoCorrect entry
- Use AutoCorrect exceptions.

New words

In this chapter you will meet the following term:

- AutoCorrect

Syllabus reference

In this chapter you will cover the following item of the ECDL Advanced Word Processing Syllabus:

- **AM3.1.1.3**: Use automatic text correction options.

About AutoCorrect

AutoCorrect is a Word feature that can improve your documents by automatically detecting and correcting:

- **Misspelled words**. For example, 'teh' instead of 'the', and 'calulated' instead of 'calculated'.
- **Grammatical errors**. For example, 'might of had' instead of 'might have had'.
- **Missing interword spaces**. For example, 'aboutit' instead of 'about it'.

- **Incorrect capitalization**. For example, 'tuesday' instead of 'Tuesday'.
- **Unformatted symbols**. For example, '(c)' instead of the copyright symbol '©'.

By default, AutoCorrect runs interactively in the background as you type and edit text. Whenever you type anything that it regards as an error, AutoCorrect fixes your entry as soon as you press the **Spacebar** or **Enter** key.

An example of AutoCorrect at work	
1. You mistype a word.	and·then·teh¶
2. You press the **Spacebar**.	
3. AutoCorrect fixes your error.	and·then·the¶

A lot of the time, you may not even notice AutoCorrect making its corrections.

Two kinds of AutoCorrect entries

Items stored in AutoCorrect are called *AutoCorrect entries*. There are two kinds:

- **Built-in entries**. AutoCorrect contains almost 1000 common errors and solutions.
- **User-created entries**. You can add your own AutoText entries. These may be spelling mistakes that you make most often, or the full form of abbreviations that you commonly use.

For example, you could create an AutoCorrect entry that replaces 'asap' with 'as soon as possible', or 'spec' with 'specifications'.

The AutoCorrect *dialog box*

To view the AutoCorrect entries available to your current document, choose **Tools | AutoCorrect**, click the **AutoCorrect** tab, and scroll through the entries in the lower half of the dialog box. When finished, click **Cancel**.

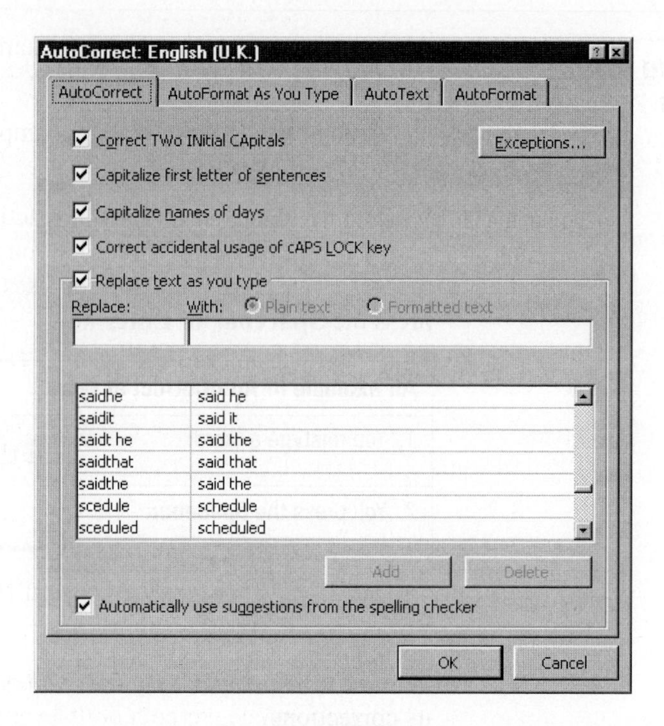

AutoCorrect and the Office 2000 spellchecker

By default, AutoCorrect also draws on the many thousands of errors and their replacements contained in the Microsoft Office 2000 spelling dictionary.

AutoCorrect, when working with the Office 2000 spellchecker, does not replace every suspect word you type. AutoCorrect replaces a typed word only if it decides that what you have typed is an error. You many find this feature either helpful or annoying, and therefore choose to either leave it on or switch it off.

In effect, AutoCorrect offers not one but two options for detecting and correcting misspellings: one based on AutoCorrect entries, and a second based on the Office 2000 spellchecker.

The two options are independent of each other. You can decide to activate one, both, or neither.

AutoCorrect

A Word feature that automatically detects and corrects various errors as you type. AutoCorrect can fix misspellings, incorrect capitalization, missing interword spaces, and unformatted symbols, and can draw on the errors and replacements contained in the Office 2000 spelling dictionary.

Working with AutoCorrect

Here are the tasks that you need to be able to perform with AutoCorrect:

- **Switch AutoCorrect on and off**. Exercise 6.1 shows you how.
- **Apply AutoCorrect options selectively**. Sometimes, you may want to use some AutoCorrect options but not others. Follow Exercise 6.2 to discover how to apply AutoCorrect selectively.
- **Using the Office 2000 spellchecker in AutoCorrect**. You can decide to include or exclude automatic spell checking and replacement within AutoCorrect. Exercise 6.3 takes you through the steps.
- **Add new AutoText entries**. You are not limited to using only Word's AutoCorrect built-in entries.

  Exercises 6.4 and 6.5 show you how to add unformatted and formatted entries of your own.
- **Amend and delete existing AutoCorrect entries**. You can modify and delete both built-in and user-created entries in AutoText. Exercise 6.6 takes you through the steps.
- **Work with AutoCorrect exceptions**. Imagine that your organization is named *Teh Limited* or *Taht Enterprises*, for example. You would not want Word 'correcting' your name every time you typed it. See Exercise 6.7.

Working with AutoCorrect settings

In the first three exercises, you will explore various settings within AutoCorrect.

Exercise 6.1: Switching AutoCorrect off and on

Before performing this exercise, start Word and open a new, blank document. The **Tools | AutoCorrect** menu command is available only when you have at least one document open.

1) Choose **Tools | AutoCorrect**, and click the **AutoCorrect** tab of the dialog box displayed.
2) Deselect or select the *Replace text as you type* checkbox, as appropriate.

   ☑ Replace text as you type

   Deselecting this checkbox disables the four AutoCorrect options above this check box, regardless of whether the checkboxes are selected.

   Selecting or deselecting this checkbox does not affect the *Automatically use suggestions from the spelling checker* checkbox.

It is possible to disable AutoCorrect entries yet still use AutoCorrect to implement spelling corrections automatically from the Office 2000 Spellchecker.

3) Click **OK**.

Word saves your AutoCorrect settings. You can close the sample document without saving it.

Exercise 6.2: Applying AutoCorrect options selectively

Before performing this exercise, first open a new, blank Word document. The **Tools | AutoCorrect** menu command is available only when you have at least one document open.

1) Choose **Tools | AutoCorrect**, and click the **AutoCorrect** tab of the dialog box displayed.

Ensure that the *Replace text as you type* checkbox is selected. This check box must remain selected through all the steps in this exercise.

☑ Replace text as you type

2) Select the first of the four AutoCorrect checkboxes, deselect the other three as shown, and click **OK**.

☑ Correct TWo INitial CApitals
☐ Capitalize first letter of sentences
☐ Capitalize names of days
☐ Correct accidental usage of cAPS LOCK key

3) Type the following text and press **Enter** twice:

```
THe lazy brown fox
```

Notice how AutoCorrect corrects your typing error.

4) Choose **Tools | AutoCorrect**, click the **AutoCorrect** tab, select the second of the four AutoCorrect checkboxes, deselect the other three, and click **OK**.

5) Type the following text and press **Enter** twice.

```
the lazy brown fox
```

Notice how AutoCorrect corrects your typing error.

6) Choose **Tools | AutoCorrect**, click the **AutoCorrect** tab, select the third of the four AutoCorrect checkboxes, deselect the other three, and click **OK.**

7) Type the following text and press Enter twice:

```
the lazy brown fox on friday
```

Notice how AutoCorrect corrects your typing error.

8) Choose **Tools | AutoCorrect**, click the **AutoCorrect** tab, select the fourth of the four AutoCorrect checkboxes, deselect the other three, and click **OK**.

9) Type the following text:

```
The lazy br
```

10) Press the **Caps Lock** key

11) Type the following text and press **Enter** twice:

```
OWN fox
```

Notice how AutoCorrect corrects your typing error. This correction option applies only to the use of the **Caps Lock** key, not the **Shift** key.

You can close the sample document without saving it.

Exercise 6.3: Using the Office 2000 spellchecker in AutoCorrect

Before performing this exercise, first open a new, blank Word document. The **Tools | AutoCorrect** menu command is available only when you have at least one document open.

1) Choose **Tools | Options**, click the **Spelling & Grammar** tab, and select the *Check spelling as you type* checkbox if it is not selected already.

Click **OK** to close the dialog box. You must select this option if you want to use the Office 2000 spellcheck feature within AutoCorrect.

2) Choose **Tools | AutoCorrect**, and click the **AutoCorrect** tab of the dialog box displayed.

Ensure that the *Replace text as you type* checkbox is selected.

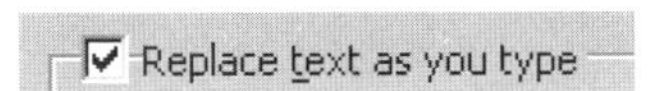

3) Select the *Automatically use suggestions from the spelling checker* checkbox.

Automatically use suggestions from the spelling checker

4) Click **OK** to close the dialog box.

5) Type the following text and press **Enter**:

```
The greene carrrot
```

6) Notice that Word replaces 'carrrot' with 'carrot', but not 'greene' with 'green'. This is because Word decided that only 'carrrot' was a definitely a misspelling.

You can close the sample document without saving it.

If you prefer not to use the Office 2000 spellchecker option within AutoCorrect, choose **Tools | AutoCorrect**, click the **AutoCorrect** tab, deselect the *Automatically use suggestions from the spelling checker* checkbox. and click **OK**.

Working with new AutoCorrect entries

When adding an AutoCorrect entry, you can choose whether to include paragraph formatting with the entry by selecting the paragraph mark immediately after it.

Exercise 6.4: Adding an unformatted AutoCorrect entry

In this Exercise you will add an unformatted entry to AutoText. Unformatted entries may be up to 256 characters in length.

1) Open a new, blank Word document, type the following text, and press **Enter** twice:

   `No pizza is complete without plenty of chese`

2) Select the item in the currently open document that you want AutoCorrect to replace. In this instance, select the word 'chese'.

   No·pizza·is·complete·without·plenty·of·chese¶

   (If the item is a complete paragraph, or if if is text at the end of a paragraph, do not include the paragraph mark in your selection. Including the paragraph mark in your selection has the effect of including the formatting of your selected item. See Exercise 6.5.)

3) Choose **Tools | AutoCorrect**, and click the **AutoCorrect** tab of the dialog box displayed.

4) In the *Replace* and *With* boxes, type your text items.

   (Because you began this procedure by selecting text, the *Replace* box already contains your selected text.)

5) Click **Add** to add your entry to AutoCorrect.

   You can repeat steps 3 and 4 to add further entries.

6) When finished, click **OK** to close the dialog box.

   You have now added an unformatted entry to AutoCorrect.

7) As a test, on a new line type the following word and press **Space**:

   `Chese`

   Notice how AutoCorrect corrects your misspelling.

   You can close the sample document without saving it.

Exercise 6.5: Adding a formatted AutoCorrect entry

In this exercise, you will add a formatted entry to AutoText. Word does not place a limit on the size of formatted AutoCorrect entries.

1) Open a new, blank Word document, type the following text, and press **Enter** twice:

    `ABC Training Services`

2) Select your typed text, choose **Format | Font**, select Arial for *Font*, 14 point for *Size*, change the colour to red, and click **OK**.

3) With your text still selected, click the **Center** button on the Formatting toolbar.

4) Select the item that you want AutoCorrect to insert in your document – not the item you want AutoCorrect to replace.

    In this instance, select 'ABC Training Services'.

    If the item is a complete paragraph, or if it is text at the end of a paragraph, include the paragraph mark in your selection. You do this because you want the AutoText entry to include both paragraph and character attributes.

5) Choose **Tools | AutoCorrect**, and click the **AutoCorrect** tab of the dialog box displayed.

6) The *With* box contains your selected text. By default, the *Formatted text* checkbox is selected.

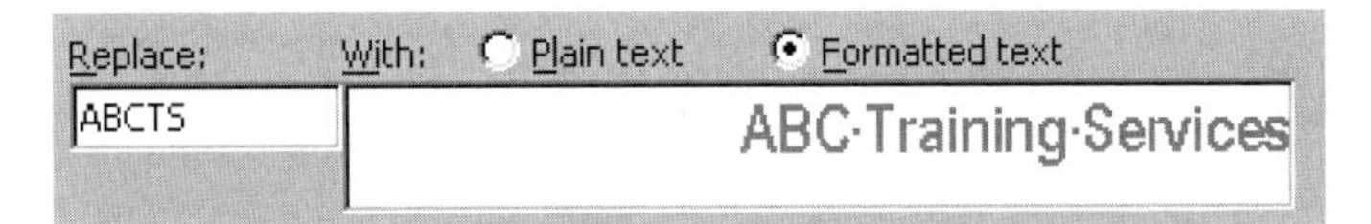

    In the *Replace* box, type the text you want AutoCorrect to replace.

    In this instance, type the following:

    ABCTS

7) Click **Add** to add your entry to AutoCorrect, and click **OK** to close the dialog box.

8) As a test, on a new line type the following text and press **Enter**:

    ABCTS

    Notice how AutoCorrect replaces your typed abbreviation with the formatted AutoCorrect entry.

    You can close the sample document without saving it.

AutoCorrect entries and templates

When you create an AutoCorrect entry, Word stores the entry in the current document's template. The AutoCorrect entry is then available to all new documents that are also based on that template.

Working with existing AutoCorrect entries

Word allows you to modify and delete AutoCorrect entries, whether they are Word's built-in entries or those added you have added yourself.

Exercise 6.6: Amending or deleting an AutoCorrect entry

This exercise takes you through the steps of modifying and deleting AutoCorrect entries.

1) Choose **Tools | AutoCorrect**, and click the **AutoCorrect** tab of the dialog box displayed.

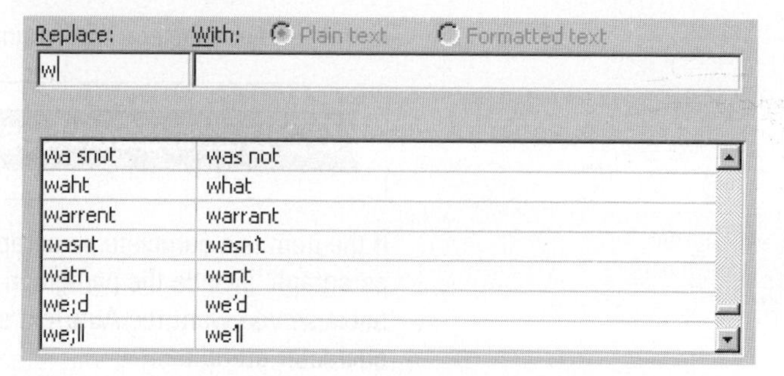

2) Scroll down through the list to locate the relevant entry.

   When you find the relevant entry, click it to select it.

3) Word displays the entry in the *Replace* and *With* boxes.

4) To amend the selected entry, edit the text in the *With* box and click **Amend**.

   If the AutoText entry contains formatted text (as indicated by an asterisk), you can amend only the *Replace* box and not the *With* box. To amend such an entry completely, recreate it, overwriting and original entry.

   To remove the selected entry, click **Delete**.

5) Repeat steps 2 to 4 to amend or delete further AutoCorrect entries.

6) When finished, click **OK** to close the dialog box.

Working with AutoCorrect exceptions

You may want to take advantage of AutoCorrect's helpful features when working on your documents – but there may be some words or abbreviations that you do not want AutoCorrect to replace automatically.

AutoCorrect allows you to enter *exceptions* in three categories:

- **First letter after full stop exceptions**. Use this option to override the *Capitalize first letter of sentences* option in specified instances.

  A number of built-in exceptions of this type are supplied with Word. For example, 'approx.' and 'dept.' and 'subj.'. You can remove or modify these, or add new ones of your own.

- **Initial capitals exceptions**. If your organization is named 'Global EBusiness Incorporated', you can prevent AutoCorrrect from changing this to 'Global Ebusiness Incorporated'.

- **Other exceptions**. This is a miscellaneous category. If your organization is named 'Teh Limited' or TAHT.COM', for example, you would enter the exception in this category.

Exercise 6.7: Working with AutoCorrect exceptions

How do you add or modify AutoCorrect exceptions? How do exceptions affect what you type? Follow this exercise to find out.

1) Open a new, blank Word document, type the following text, and press **Enter** twice:

   ```
   Please deliver a qty. of 10 pallets.
   ```

2) Choose **Tools | AutoCorrect**, click the **AutoCorrect** tab of the dialog box displayed, and click the **Exceptions** button.

3) Click the **First Letter** tab, and locate the 'qty.' entry.

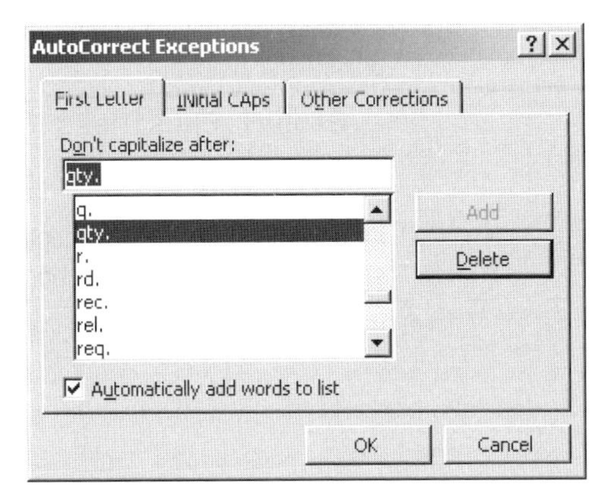

4) Click the **Delete** button to remove the exception. Click **OK** to close the *AutoCorrect Exceptions* dialog box, and click **OK** again to close the *AutoCorrect* dialog box.

5) On a new line of your sample document, type the following text and press *Enter* twice:

   ```
   Please deliver a qty. of 10 pallets.
   ```

Notice that this time, AutoCorrect changes the first letter after 'qty.' to an upper-case 'O'. This is because Word incorrectly identified the full stop after 'qty' as the end of a sentence.

6) Choose **Tools | AutoCorrect**, click the **AutoCorrect** tab, click the **Exceptions** button, and click the **First Letter** tab.

7) In the *Don't capitalize after* box, type 'qty.', click **Add**, click **OK**, and then click **OK** again. You have re-entered this exception to AutoCorrect.

8) Choose **Tools | AutoCorrect**, click the **AutoCorrect** tab, click the **Exceptions** button, and click the **INitial CAps** tab.

9) In the *Don't correct* box, type 'EBusiness' and click **Add**.

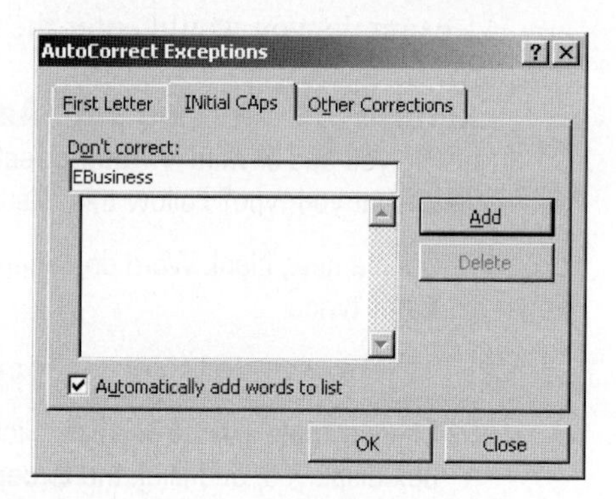

10) Click **OK**, and then click **OK** again.

11) On a new line of your sample document, type the following text and press *Enter* twice:

```
Global EBusiness Corporation.
```

Notice that AutoCorrect did not change 'EBusiness' to 'Ebusiness'.

12) Remove the 'EBusiness' exception, retype the line that you typed in step 11, and notice what happens.

13) When finished, click **OK** to close the dialog box.

Chapter 6: quick reference

Tasks summary

Task	Procedure
Access AutoCorrect options.	Choose **Tools | AutoCorrect** to display the *AutoCorrect* dialog box, select or deselect the relevant checkboxes, and click **OK**.
Switch AutoCorrect on or off.	Select or deselect the *Replace text as you type* checkbox within the *AutoCorrect* dialog box.
Include and exclude the Office 2000 spellchecker in AutoCorrect.	Choose **Tools | Options**, click the **Spelling & Grammar tab**, select the *Check spelling as you type* checkbox, and click **OK**.
	Choose **Tools | AutoCorrect**, select the *Automatically use suggestions from the spelling checker* checkboxes, and click **OK**.
Add an AutoCorrect entry.	Select the item in the current document that you want AutoCorrect to replace, choose **Tools | AutoCorrect**, type the replacement in the *With* box, click **Add** and click **OK**.
	To include paragraph formatting with an entry, include its paragraph mark when selecting it.
Amend an AutoCorrect entry.	Recreate it, overwriting the original entry.
Delete an AutoCorrect entry.	Choose **Tools | AutoCorrect**, select the entry, click **Delete** and click **OK**.

Concepts summary

AutoCorrect can improve your documents by detecting and correcting errors automatically. AutoCorrect contains thousands of common errors and solutions, such as misspelled words, grammatical errors, missing interword spaces, incorrect capitalization, and unformatted symbols.

You can apply AutoCorrect options selectively, amend or delete entries, and add entries of you own. User-created AutoCorrect entries are stored in the Word template associated with the document that was open when the entry was created. The AutoCorrect entry is then available within all new documents based on that template.

Chapter 6: quick quiz

Circle the correct answer to each of the following multiple-choice questions about AutoCorrect in Word.

Q1	Which of the following statements about Word's AutoCorrect is untrue?
A.	It can apply built-in heading styles to text typed in a certain way.
B.	It can detect and automatically correct certain grammatical errors.
C.	AutoCorrect entries are stored in the current document template.
D.	You can add your own entries to AutoCorrect.

Q2	Which of the following items can Word's AutoCorrect feature not correct automatically?
A.	Missing interword spaces.
B.	Misspelled words.
C.	Incorrect capitalization.
D.	Two successive hyphens (--) used instead of an en dash (–).

Q3	Which of the following options within the Word' *AutoCorrect* dialog box switches off AutoCorrect?
A.	Automatically use suggestions from spelling checker.
B.	Replace text as you type.
C.	Define styles based on your formatting.
D.	AutoCorrect in use.

Q4	Which of the following options within the *AutoCorrect* dialog box switches on the Office 2000 spellchecker within AutoCorrect?
A.	AutoCorrect in use.
B.	Always suggest corrections.
C.	Automatically use suggestions from spelling checker.
D.	Show spelling errors in this document.

Q5	To include paragraph formatting with a new entry in AutoCorrect, you must ...
A.	Include the item's paragraph mark when selecting the item for adding to AutoCorrect.
B.	Hold down the **Shift** key when selecting the item for adding to AutoCorrect.
C.	Hold down the **Ctrl** key when selecting the item for adding to AutoCorrect.
D.	None of the above – you can include only character formatting and not paragraph formatting with AutoCorrect entries.

Answers

1: A, 2: D, 3: B, 4: C, 5: A.

7 Word typesets your documents: AutoFormat As You Type

Objectives

In this chapter you will learn how to:

- Apply AutoFormat As You Type options selectively.

New words

In this chapter you will meet the following terms:

- AutoFormat As You Type
- Ordinal
- En dash
- Curly quote

Syllabus reference

In this chapter you will cover the following item from the ECDL Advanced Word Processing Syllabus:

- **AM3.1.1.4**: Apply automatic text formatting options.

About AutoFormat As You Type

AutoFormat As You Type is a Word feature that can perform three types of tasks automatically:

- **Character replacement**. Word can replace certain typed characters with their more typographically correct alternatives.

  For example, Word can replace '17th' with '17th' and '3/4' with '¾'.

  Word can also replace straight quotes (" ") with curly quotes (“ ”), two successive hyphens (--) with a single en dash (–) and three successive hyphens with a column-wide line.

An example of AutoFormat As You Type: character replacement	
1. Type a fraction.	3/4
2. Press the **Spacebar**.	
3. AutoFormat As You Type replaces your typed fraction with the alternative fraction character.	¾

- **Bulleted and numbered list conversion**. If you begin a paragraph by typing an asterisk (*) followed by a space, Word can apply the bulleted format when you press **Enter** at the end of the paragraph.

An example of AutoFormat As You Type: lists	
1. Type an asterisk, a space and some text.	*·Item·one¶
2. Press **Enter**.	
3. AutoFormat reformats the line, and the line following it, as bullet points.	• → Item·one¶ • → ¶

- **Heading style application**. If you type some text and then press **Enter** twice, Word can apply the Heading 1 style to the text.

As its name suggests, AutoFormat As You Type runs interactively as you enter and edit text. Whenever you type something that it decides to format or replace, AutoFormat As You Type performs the operation as soon as you press the **Spacebar** or the **Enter** key (as appropriate).

AutoFormat As You Type and AutoFormat

In Chapter 4, you met Word's AutoFormat feature, which can apply formatting automatically to already-created documents. You can think of AutoFormat as 'AutoFormat *After* You Type'.

In contrast, AutoFormat As You Type works at the same time as you: it is not a feature that you apply after you have written a document.

Consequently, any change that you make to options within AutoFormat As You Type does not affect text that you have typed previously.

*The **AutoFormat As You Type** tab*

To view the AutoFormat As You Type options, choose **Tools | AutoCorrect** and click the **AutoFormat As You Type** tab. When finished, click **Cancel**.

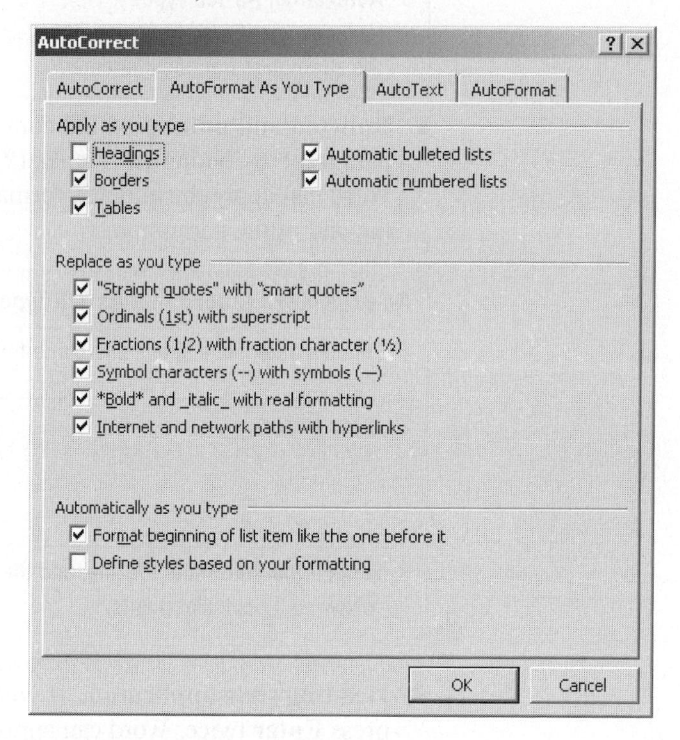

AutoFormat As You Type: the benefits to you

The options within AutoFormat As You Type offer the following benefits:

- **Professional-looking, typeset documents**. Items such as fraction symbols, curly quotes and en dashes give your Word documents the appearance of professionally typeset publications.

  In effect, AutoFormat As You Type provides the features of a typesetting machine within a word processing program.

- **Automatic performance**. AutoFormat As You Type does nothing that you cannot do manually using menu commands and toolbar buttons. For example, you can insert an en dash using the **Insert | Symbol** command.

  With AutoFormat As You Type, however, you can obtain professional typographic effects automatically.

Working with AutoFormat As You Type: the seven tasks

Here are the seven tasks that you need to be able to perform with AutoFormat As You Type:

- **Apply fraction character, ordinal-to-superscript and dash options**. Give your documents a professional appearance with these options. See Exercise 7.1.
- **Apply smart quote options**. Exercise 7.2 shows you how to produce typographically correct quotes and apostrophes automatically.
- **Apply hyperlink options**. Want Word to convert your typed e-mail and web addresses to hyperlinks? Follow Exercise 7.3 to discover how.
- **Apply fast bold and italic options**. Exercise 7.4 shows you how to format text in bold or italics without the usual mouse clicks or keystrokes – a real time-saver.
- **Apply line drawing options**. Exercise 7.5 shows you how to draw three types of line using only the keyboard.
- **Apply automatic list options**. Save effort by enabling Word to generate lists with bulleted and numbered formatting. See Exercises 7.6 and 7.7.
- **Using heading style options**. Exercise 7.8 shows you how Word can automatically apply heading styles to your typed text.

AutoFormat As You Type

AutoFormat As You Type can replace certain typed characters with their more typographically correct alternatives. It can also convert certain paragraphs to bulleted and numbered lists, and apply heading styles to text you enter.

Table options

AutoFormat As You Type can also convert text containing certain patterns of characters to tables. The table option may be useful when applying AutoFormat to ASCII documents (see Chapter 4). It is unlikely, however, that you will ever use the table option when working with AutoFormat As You Type.

Working with fractions, ordinals and dashes

The following three automatic replacement options with AutoFormat As You Type can make a real difference to the quality of your documents:

- **Fractions to fraction characters**. Word can replace three common fractions (1/4, 1/2 and 3/4) with their corresponding fraction characters (¼, ½ and ¾).

  Other fractions – for example, 1/3 or 3/8 – cannot be reformatted automatically. Be careful that this limitation does not lead to inconsistencies in your documents.

- **Ordinals to superscript**. Word can replace ordinals with their superscript alternatives. For example, '1st' and '17th' with '1st' and '17th'.

- **Hyphens to dashes**. Word can replace two successive hyphens (--) with a single en dash (–), and can also insert an en dash when you type a space, a hyphen and a space.

  The use of successive hyphens to create dashes is a throwback to the days of typewriters, which did not have dash keys. If you want to produce a document to publication standard, use dashes instead. See *Dashes: the three types* below for more information about when to use this feature.

Ordinal

A number indicating the place (such as 1st, 2nd, 3rd, etc.) occupied by an item in an ordered sequence.

Exercise 7.1: Automatic fractions, superscript and dashes

Before performing this exercise, start Word. Open a new, blank document. The **Tools | AutoCorrect** command is available only when you have at least one document open.

1) Choose **Tools | AutoCorrect**, and click the **AutoFormat As You Type** tab of the dialog box displayed.

2) Select the three checkboxes shown below, and click **OK**.

☑ Ordinals (1st) with superscript
☑ Fractions (1/2) with fraction character (½)
☑ Symbol characters (--) with symbols (—)

3) Type the following text and press **Enter**:

```
I will finish the first 1/2 of the 3rd
draft of the report on July 14th --
unless my PC crashes again.
```

As you type, notice that Word automatically replaces your fraction, ordinal and single hyphens with their typographic alternatives.

I will finish the first ½ of the 3rd draft of the report on July 14th – unless my PC crashes again.¶

4) Choose **Tools | AutoCorrect**, click the **AutoFormat As You Type** tab, deselect the three options selected in step 2, and click **OK**.

5) Retype the text you entered in step 3.

Notice that Word does not perform the automatic character replacements this time.

6) Choose **Tools | AutoCorrect**, click the **AutoFormat As You Type** tab, reselect the three options deselected in step 4, and click **OK**.

You can close your sample document without saving it.

Dashes: the three types

Now that you know how to use the automatic hyphen-to-dash replacement option, it's a good idea to learn when to use the different types of dashes.

Fonts contain three kinds of dashes: the hyphen, the en dash and the em dash.

- **Hyphen**. The shortest dash, obtained by pressing the hyphen key once.

Usage	Examples
To hyphenate words.	Pro-am, pre-packed
To separate telephone numbers.	353-1-9876543

- **En dash**. A longer dash. It is the width of a lower-case letter 'n' in the font.

Usage	Dash Examples
To combine words of equal weight.	East–West relations, the Manchester–London flight.
To denote a series of inclusive numbers.	January 4–6, aged 10–12, pages 223–6 of the book.
To set off a parenthetical clause in a sentence.	I think you would look fine wearing either the silk blouse – the one with the blue pattern – or the angora sweater.
To give a special emphasis to the end of the sentence.	Seeing the door slightly ajar, he gave it a push and it opened to reveal Jennifer – in the arms of Steven!

- **Em dash**: The longest dash. It is the width of a lower-case letter 'm' in the font. The em dash is little used now.

En dash

A dash that is the width of a lower-case 'n'. Used for separating words of equal weight, denoting series of inclusive numbers, setting off parenthetical clauses, and giving special emphasis to the end of a sentence.

Working with curly quotes and apostrophes

When typing the abbreviations for inches (") or feet ('), use straight quotes. For quotations or apostrophes, however, use *curly quotes* instead. Curly quotes (also called smart quotes or typographers' quotes) curve towards the text that they enclose.

The difference between curly and straight quotes is more apparent in serif fonts such as Times than sans serif ones such as Arial.

Exercise 7.2: Automatic quotes and apostrophes

Before performing this exercise, open a new, blank document.

1) Choose **Tools | AutoCorrect** and click the **AutoFormat As You Type** tab.

2) Select the "*Straight Quotes*" *with* "*Smart Quotes*" checkbox, and click **OK**.

☑ "Straight quotes" with "smart quotes"

3) Type the following text and press **Enter**:

```
The so-called "Book of Rules" is just a
collection of the author's prejudices.
```

Notice that Word converts your typed double and single quotes to curly quotes.

The so-called “Book of Rules” is just a collection of the author’s prejudices.¶

4) Choose **Tools | AutoCorrect**, click the **AutoFormat As You Type** tab, deselect the checkbox selected in step 2, and click **OK**.

5) Type the following text and press **Enter**:

```
The garden wall is 4' and 6" tall.
```

Notice that Word does not automatically replace your typed quotes with curly quotes.

6) Choose **Tools | AutoCorrect**, click the **AutoFormat As You Type** tab, reselect the option deselected in step 4, and click **OK**.

You can close your sample document without saving it.

Curly quotes

Also called smart or typographers' quotes, these curve towards the text that they enclose (“ ”). Used for quotations in typeset documents.

Working with hyperlinks

Word can automatically replace e-mail and web addresses that you type with clickable hyperlinks. You will find this feature useful when creating e-mails or documents for publication online. This feature within AutoFormat As You Type is selected by default.

When working with documents that are to be printed on paper, however, you may find this feature a nuisance and want to switch it off.

Exercise 7.3: Automatic hyperlinks

Before performing this exercise, open a new, blank document.

1) Choose **Tools | AutoCorrect** and click the **AutoFormat As You Type** tab.

2) Select the *Internet and network paths with hyperlinks* checkbox and click **OK**.

☑ Internet and network paths with hyperlinks

3) Type the following text and press **Enter**:

```
My e-mail address is joe@bloggs.com and my
website is at www.bloggs99.com.
```

Notice that Word converts the e-mail and web addresses to clickable hyperlinks.

My e-mail address is joe@bloggs.com and my website is at www.bloggs99.com.¶

4) Choose **Tools | AutoCorrect**, click the **AutoFormat As You Type** tab, deselect the checkbox selected in step 2, and click **OK**.

5) Retype the text you entered in step 3.

Notice that Word does not automatically convert your entered addresses to hyperlinks.

Leave this checkbox deselected. You can close your sample document without saving it.

Working with automatic bold and italic formatting

To apply bold or italics to text in a document, you usually select the text and then either click the relevant toolbar button or type the appropriate shortcut keys. AutoFormat As You Type offers alternative methods that do not interrupt your flow of typing:

- **Bold formatting**. Enclose the text in asterisks (*).
- **Italic formatting**. Enclose the text in underlines (_).

Exercise 7.4: Automatic bold and italic formatting

Before performing this exercise, open a new, blank document.

1) Choose **Tools | AutoCorrect** and click the **AutoFormat As You Type** tab.

2) Select the following checkbox and click **OK:**

☑ *Bold* and _italic_ with real formatting

3) Type the following text and press **Enter**:

```
I think it was *Abraham Lincoln* who
said: "I may walk slowly but I _never_
walk backwards."
```

Notice that Word converts the enclosed words to bold and italics.

I think it was **Abraham Lincoln** who said: "I may walk slowly but I *never* walk backwards."¶

4) Choose **Tools | AutoCorrect**, click the **AutoFormat As You Type** tab, deselect the checkbox selected in step 2, and click **OK**.

5) Retype the text you entered in step 3.

   Notice that Word does not perform the automatic replacement.

6) Choose **Tools | AutoCorrect**, click the **AutoFormat As You Type** *tab*, reselect the option deselected in step 4, and click **OK.**

   You can close your sample document without saving it.

Working with automatic line drawing

Word can automatically draw column-wide lines whenever you type three or more hyphens (-), underscore characters (_), or equals signs (=) and press **Enter**.

Word draws a thin, thick or double line, respectively. The line – in fact, it is a border – is applied to the paragraph *before* the one in which you type the hyphens, underscores or equals signs. To remove such a border, select the paragraph, choose **Format | Borders and Shading**, choose *None*, and click **OK.**

Exercise 7.5: Automatic line drawing

Before performing this exercise, open a new, blank document.

1) Choose **Tools | AutoCorrect** and click the **AutoFormat As You Type** tab.

2) Select the *Borders* checkbox and click **OK**.

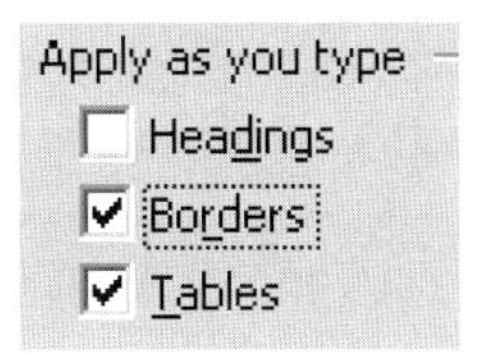

3) Press the hyphen key (-) three times and press **Enter**.

4) Type the following text and press **Enter**:

   Document Heading

5) Press the equals key (=) three times and press **Enter**.

6) Select your typed paragraphs and centre-align them. Your text should look like this:

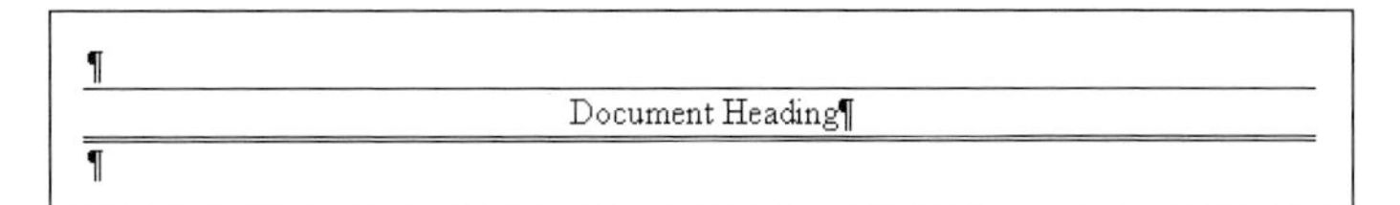

7) Choose **Tools | AutoCorrect**, click the **AutoFormat As You Type** tab, deselect the checkbox selected in step 2, and click **OK**.

8) Repeat steps 3 to 6.

   Notice that Word does not draw the column-wide lines.

9) Choose **Tools | AutoCorrect**, click the **AutoFormat As You Type** tab, reselect the option deselected in step 7, and click **OK**.

   You can close your sample document without saving it.

Working with automatic lists

Word can automatically format a bulleted list when you begin a paragraph with any of the these three characters, followed by a space or a tab:

- An asterisk (*)
- A closing angle bracket (>)
- A hyphen (-)

When you press **Enter** to add the next paragraph, Word inserts the next bullet automatically. To end the list of bullets, press **Enter** twice, or press **Backspace** to delete the last bullet in the list.

Also, Word can apply numbered list formatting if you type a number or letter, a full stop, and a space or tab at the beginning of a paragraph. When you press **Enter**, Word inserts the next number in the list automatically. To end the list of numbered bullets, press **Enter** twice, or press **Backspace** to delete the last number in the list.

Exercise 7.6: Automatic bulleted and numbered lists

Before performing this exercise, open a new, blank document.

1) Choose **Tools | AutoCorrect** and click the **AutoFormat As You Type** tab.

2) Select the following two checkboxes, and click **OK**:

   ☑ Automatic bulleted lists
   ☑ Automatic numbered lists

3) Type the four lines of text shown in the left-hand column below. Press **Enter** once after the first three lines, and **Enter** twice after the fourth:

What you type	*What Word displays*
*John	▪ John
Paul	▪ Paul
George	▪ George
Ringo	▪ Ringo

4) Type the four lines of text shown in the left-hand column below. Press **Enter** once after the first three lines, and **Enter** twice after the fourth:

1.John	1. John
Paul	2. Paul
George	3. George
Ringo	4. Ringo
What you type	***What Word displays***

5) Choose **Tools | AutoCorrect**, click the **AutoFormat As You Type** tab, deselect the two checkboxes selected in step 2, and click **OK**.

6) Retype the text you entered in steps 3 and 4.

   Notice that Word does not perform the automatic list formatting.

7) Choose **Tools | AutoCorrect**, click the **AutoFormat As You Type** tab, reselect the two options deselected in step 5, and click **OK**.

   You can close your sample document without saving it.

Automatic formatting at the beginnings of lists

Sometimes, you will want bold or italic formatting applied to a word or group of words at the beginning of each line in a list.

AutoFormat As You Type gives you the option of formatting only text at the beginning of the first list item, with Word repeating your character formatting for the other list items automatically.

Exercise 7.7: Automatic character formatting at the beginning of a list

Before performing this Exercise, open a new, blank document.

1) Choose **Tools | AutoCorrect** and click the **AutoFormat As You Type** tab.

2) Select the following three checkboxes and click **OK**.

   ☑ Automatic bulleted lists
   ☑ Automatic numbered lists

   ☑ Format beginning of list item like the one before it

3) Type the following line of text, but do not press **Enter** at the end of the line:

   `* Kennedy: A US president`

4) Select the word 'Kennedy', and apply bold formatting to it.

   *·**Kennedy**:·A·US·president¶

5) Click at the end of the line and press **Enter**. Your screen should look like this:

```
•→ Kennedy:·A·US·president¶
•→ ¶
```

6) Click after the bullet point on the second line, type the following text, and press **Enter**:

   `Wilson: A British prime minister`

   Word automatically applies your beginning-of-line formatting as shown:

```
•→ Kennedy:·A·US·president¶
•→ Wilson:·A·British·prime·minister¶
```

7) Choose **Tools | AutoCorrect**, click the **AutoFormat As You Type** tab, deselect the three checkboxes selected in step 2, and click **OK**.
8) Repeat steps 3 to 6.

   Notice that Word does not perform any of the list formatting actions.
9) Choose **Tools | AutoCorrect**, click the **AutoFormat As You Type** tab, reselect the three options deselected in step 7, and click **OK**.

   You can close your sample document without saving it.

Working with automatic heading styles

AutoFormat As You Type can apply Word's built-in heading styles to text that you enter in a certain way.

- **Heading 1 style**. If you type a line of text and press **Enter** twice, Word applies the Heading 1 style.
- **Heading 2 style**. If you press **Tab** on a new line, type some text and press **Enter** twice, Word applies the Heading 2 style.
- **Heading 3 style**. If you press **Tab** twice on a new line, type some text and press **Enter** twice, Word applies the Heading 3 style.

By default, this option is not selected with AutoFormat As You Type. It would be too distracting during normal word processing.

Exercise 7.8 Automatic heading styles

Before performing this exercise, open a new, blank document.

1) Choose **Tools | AutoCorrect** and click the **AutoFormat As You Type** tab.

2) Select the following checkbox and click **OK**:

Headings

3) Type the following text and press **Enter** twice:

```
Heading 1
```

Notice that Word applies the Heading 1 style to your text. Although you pressed **Enter** twice, the second paragraph mark is not displayed.

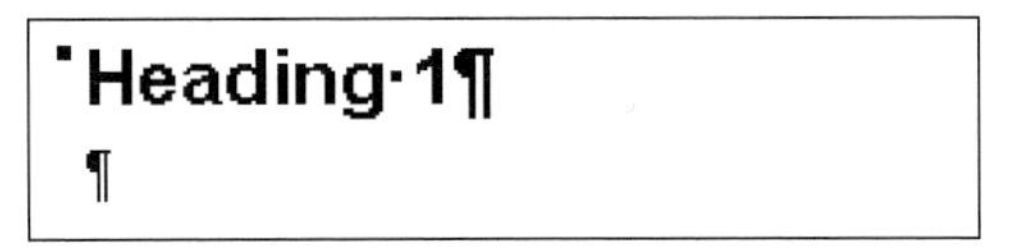

4) On a new line, press **Tab**, type the following text, and press **Enter** twice:

```
Heading 2
```

Notice that Word applies the Heading 2 style to your text. As in step 3, the second paragraph mark is not displayed.

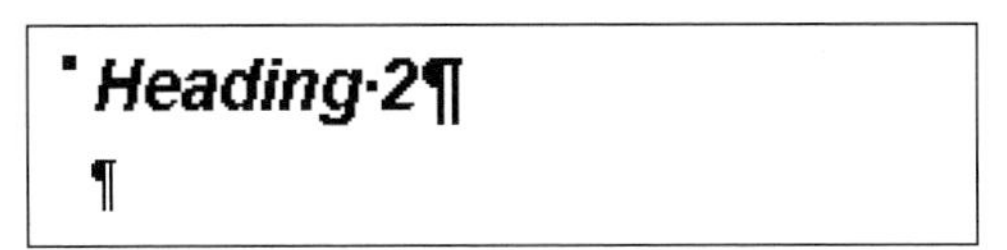

5) On a new line, press **Tab** twice, type the following text, and press **Enter** twice:

```
Heading 3
```

Notice that Word applies the Heading 3 style to your text. As in steps 3 and 4, the second paragraph mark is not displayed.

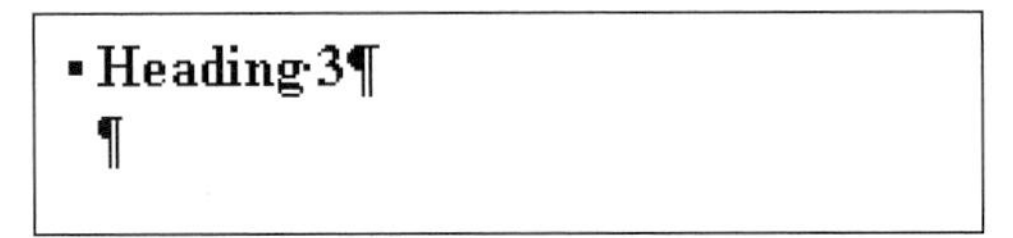

6) Choose **Tools | AutoCorrect**, click the **AutoFormat As You Type** tab, deselect the option selected in step 2, and click **OK**.

7) Repeat steps 3 to 5.

Notice that Word does not apply the heading styles.

Leave this checkbox deselected. You can close your sample document without saving it.

Defining styles based on formatting

At the bottom of the **AutoFormat As You Type** tab of the **Tools | AutoCorrect** dialog box, you can see the following option. By default, it is deselected.

Define styles based on your formatting

This option, when selected, enables Word to apply heading styles automatically to text that you type, based on how you format and position that text.

For example, if you type a few words on a single line, increase the font size, and centre the line, Word can automatically apply a heading style.

Unfortunately, this option can create more problems than it solves, because it can apply heading styles to lines you never intended as headings, with unwanted effects on outlines and tables of contents. Leave this option deselected – its default value.

Chapter 7: quick reference

Tasks summary

Task	Procedure
To activate or deactivate the various AutoFormat As You Type options.	Choose **Tools | AutoCorrect**, click the **AutoFormat As You Type** tab of the dialog box displayed, select or deselect the relevant checkboxes, and click **OK**.

Concepts summary

AutoFormat As You Type is a Word feature that can perform three types of tasks automatically:

- **Character replacement**. Word can replace certain typed characters with their more typographically correct alternatives. For example, '17th' with '17th' and '3/4' and '¾'. It can also replace straight quotes (" ") with curly quotes (“ ”), two successive hyphens (--) with a single en dash (–), and three successive hyphens with a column-wide line.
- **Bulleted and numbered list conversion**. If you begin a paragraph by typing an asterisk (*) followed by a space, Word can apply the bulleted format when you press **Enter** at the end of the paragraph.
- **Heading style application**. If you type some text and then press **Enter** twice, Word can apply the Heading 1 style to the text.

AutoFormat As You Type runs interactively as you enter and edit text. Whenever you type something that it decides to format or replace, AutoFormat As You Type performs the operation as soon as you press the relevant **Spacebar** or **Enter** key.

You can apply the various AutoFormat As You Type options selectively.

Chapter 7: quick quiz

Circle the correct answer to each of the following multiple-choice questions about Word's AutoFormat As You Type feature.

Q1	Which of the following statements about Word's AutoFormat As You Type feature is untrue?
A.	It provides the ability to produce typeset-standard documents without the need to insert special characters such as en dashes or fraction symbols manually.
B.	It can apply built-in heading styles to text typed in a certain way.
C.	It allows the user to insert commonly-used text items that are stored in the document template.
D.	It can apply bold and italic formatting to text enclosed in certain characters.

Q2	Which automatic character replacement can AutoFormat As You Type *not* perform?
A.	Tues with Tuesday.
B.	2nd with 2nd.
C.	29th with 29th.
D.	Two hyphens (--) with an en dash (–).

Q3	Which automatic character replacement can AutoFormat As You Type *not* perform?
A.	3/4 with $^{3}/_{4}$.
B.	1/8 with $^{1}/_{8}$.
C.	1/4 with $^{1}/_{4}$.
D.	1/2 with $^{1}/_{2}$.

Q4	To insert an en dash (–) with Word's AutoFormat As You Type feature, you…
A.	Use the **Insert | Symbol** menu command.
B.	Type two successive hyphens (--) and press **Enter**.
C.	Type a hyphen (-) while holding down the **Shift** key.
D.	Type a hyphen (-) while holding down the **Ctrl** key.

Q5	Which checkbox in Word's AutoFormat As You Type feature do you select to replace typed e-mail and web addresses with hyperlinks?
A.	*Internet and network paths with hyperlinks.*
B.	*Smart addresses active.*
C.	*Replace web addresses with smart hyperlinks.*
D.	*Automatic hyperlink replacement.*

Q6	Word's AutoFormat As You Type feature can apply bold formatting to text that you enclose in which characters?
A.	Underscores (_).
B.	Ampersands (&).
C.	Asterisks (*).
D.	Dollar signs ($).

Q7	Word's AutoFormat As You Type feature can apply italic formatting to text that you enclose in which characters?
A.	Dollar signs ($).
B.	Underscores (_).
C.	Ampersands (&).
D.	Asterisks (*).

Q8	In Word's AutoFormat As You Type feature, what is the effect of selecting the *Borders* checkbox?
A.	Word draws a column-wide line when you type three successive hyphens (---) and press **Enter**.
B.	Word applies the currently selected border style to any border that you create.
C.	Word applies a thin border to the header at the top of every page of the document.
D.	Word applies a thin border to the footer at the bottom of every page of the document.

Q9	In Word's AutoFormat As You Type feature, what is the effect of selecting the *Automatic list formatting* checkbox?
A.	Word applies the built-in list style to paragraphs that begin with an asterisk (*) followed by a space or a tab.
B.	Word applies a list style stored in AutoText to paragraphs that begin with an asterisk (*) followed by a space or a tab.
C.	Word applies list formatting when you type a paragraph that begins with an asterisk (*) followed by a space or a tab.
D.	Word applies a list style stored in the Normal template to paragraphs that begin with an asterisk (*) followed by a tab.

Answers

1: C, **2:** A, **3**: B, **4:** B, **5:** A, **6:** C, **7:** B, **8:** A, **9**: C.

Word updates your documents: fields

Objectives

In this chapter you will learn how to:

- Insert a field
- Switch between the display of field codes and field values
- Update a field directly
- Lock a field to prevent updating
- Delete a field

New words

In this chapter you will meet the following terms:

- Field
- Field locking

Exercise files

In this chapter you will work with the following Word files:

- Chapter8_Exercise_8-1_Before.doc
- Chapter8_Exercise_8-2_Before.doc
- Chapter8_Exercise_8-3_Before.doc
- Chapter8_Exercise_8-4_Doc1.doc
- Chapter8_Exercise_8-4_Doc2_Before.doc
- Chapter8_Exercise_8-5_Before.doc
- Chapter8_Exercise_8-6_Before.doc
- Chapter8_Exercise_8-7_Before.doc

Syllabus reference

In this chapter you will cover the following items from the ECDL Advanced Word Processing Syllabus:

- **AM3.3.2.1**. Insert a field code.
- **AM3.3.2.2**. Edit or update a field code entry.

- **AM3.3.2.3**. Lock or unlock a field.
- **AM3.3.2.4**. Delete a field code.

Fields: instructions and the results of instructions

In a Word document, fields are *containers* that hold two things: instructions and the results of instructions. Let's look at each more closely:

- **Instructions**. These tell Word to 'show today's date', for example, or to 'show the number of pages in the current document'. A field's instructions remain fixed unless you amend them.

  The set of instructions in a particular field is called a *field* code.

- **Result**. A field also holds the result generated by the field's instructions. This may change with time or as other conditions change.

  For example, a field that instructs Word to show your document's page count will contain changing results as you increase or decrease the number of pages.

  The current result in a particular field is called the *field value*.

In summary, field codes remain fixed while field values may change.

Fields: where do they get their information?

Fields that display text (in this context, 'text' includes numbers and dates) in a document can extract their information from a range of sources, including:

- **System clock**. Some fields can detect the current date and time from your computer's clock.
- **Current document**. Some fields extract information from the document that you are currently working on, including information stored in the tabs of the **File | Properties** dialog box.
- **User information**. Some fields can access the details that you entered when installing Word on your PC.

The Field *dialog box*

You insert fields in your documents with the *Field* dialog box, which you display by choosing the **Insert | Field** command.

The *Field* dialog box contains two lists:

- **Categories**. On the left of the dialog box, you can select a grouping of fields types – Date and Time fields, User Information fields, and so on.
- **Field names**. On the right of the dialog box, you can select an individual field from the field category selected on the left.

If you select the field category of *User Information*, for example, the fields available in this category include *UserName* and *UserInitials*.

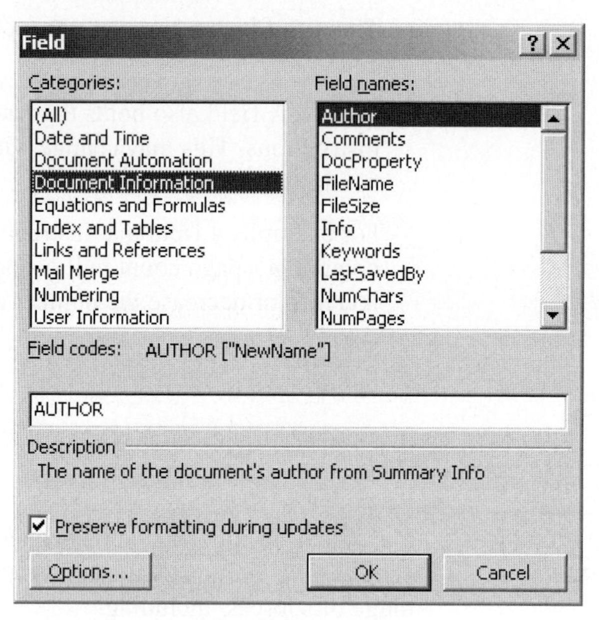

Fields: the benefits to you

Fields offer two main advantages. They:

- **Save time**. Where a suitable field is available, it is generally faster to insert the field than to type the information directly into a document.
- **Reduce errors**. As fields can update automatically over time or with changing conditions, you can be sure that your document contains the most up-to-date, accurate information.

> ***Field***
>
> *A container that holds an instruction (**field code**) and the result of the instructions (**field value**). By extracting data from sources such as the current document and the system clock, fields can display continuously updated information.*

Working with fields: the five tasks

Here are the five tasks you need to be able to perform with fields in Word:

- **Insert a field**. Exercise 8.1 takes you through the steps of inserting a field in a Word document. In Exercise 8.2, you will discover how to insert a field from AutoText in a Word document.
- **Change how fields display**. Sometimes, you will want to display the results of fields (the field values). On other occasions, you will prefer to see the instructions that generate the results (the field codes). Exercise 8.3 shows you how to switch between the two views.
- **Update a field directly**. Different types of fields can be updated in different ways or as the result of different conditions. Follow Exercise 8.4 to discover how to update one or all fields in a document directly.
- **Lock a field to prevent updating**. *Locking*, as you will learn in Exercise 8.5, is the act of preventing a particular field from being updated. In Exercise 8.6, you will learn how to unlock a locked field.
- **Delete a field**. Finally, in Exercise 8.7 you learn how to delete a field from a document.

Working with new fields

How are fields placed in a document? Some fields are inserted by Word as the result of running a particular Word feature:

- Word's *tables of contents* and *indexes* require fields for their operation.
- Automatic *page numbering* in headers or footers is based on the use of fields to display updated information.
- *Mail merge* letters contain fields such as *Surname* and *StreetAddress* to indicate the type of details to be extracted from a data source.

In your first field exercise, you will insert a field directly.

Exercise 8.1: Inserting fields in a document

In this exercise, you will insert two fields in a sample document.

1) Open the following file:

```
Chapter8_Exercise_8-1_Before.doc
```

2) Click in the second table cell – the one to the right of the words 'Current Date'.

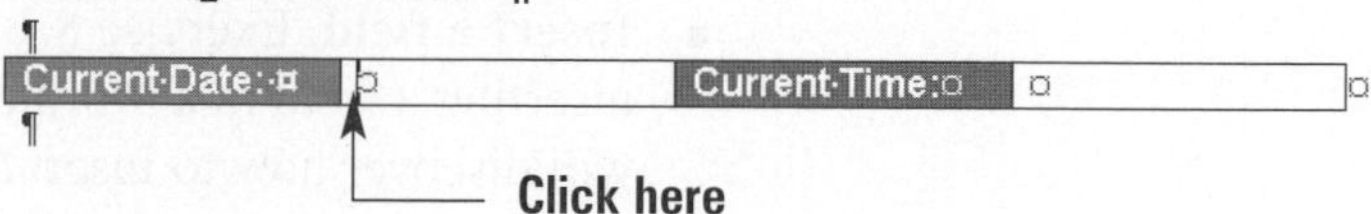

3) Choose **Insert | Field** to display the *Field* dialog box.
4) On the left of the dialog box, click to select the category of *Date and Time*.
5) On the right of the dialog box, click to select the field name of *Date*.

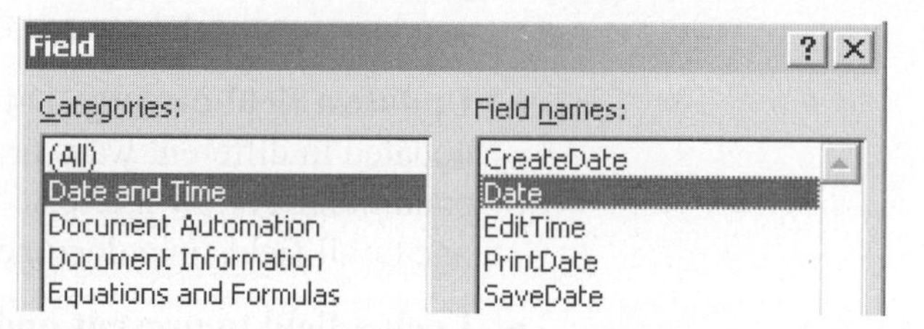

6) Typically, you will leave the *Preserve formatting during updates* checkbox at its selected default value.

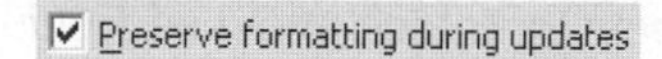

This means that if you later apply italics or other formatting to your field, Word will not change that formatting whenever it updates the field.

7) Click **OK**. Word inserts the field and closes the dialog box.
8) Click in the fourth table cell – the one to the right of the words 'Current Time'.
9) Choose **Insert | Field** to display the *Field* dialog box.
10) On the left of the dialog box, click to select the category of *Date and Time*.
11) On the right of the dialog box, click to select the field name of *Time*.
12) Again, leave the *Preserve formatting during updates* checkbox at its default value of selected.
13) Click **OK**. Word inserts the field and closes the dialog box.

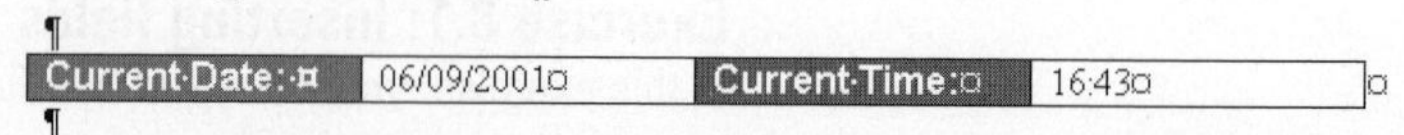

14) Save the document with the following name:

`Chapter8_Exercise_8-1_After_`*`Your_Name`*`.doc`

You can now close the document.

Exercise 8.2: Inserting AutoText fields in a document

In this exercise, you will insert two fields in a sample document.

1) Open the following file:

   `Chapter8_Exercise_8-2_Before.doc`

2) Choose **View | Header and Footer** to display the Header and Footer toolbar.

   By default, Word positions the insertion point in the *Odd Page Header* box.

3) Click the **Insert AutoText** button to display the AutoText fields available.

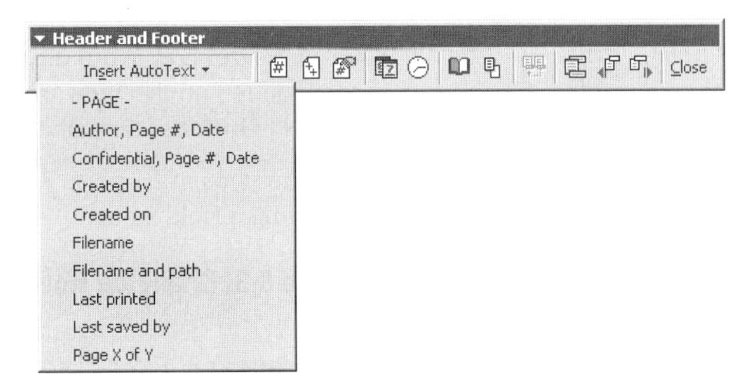

4) Choose the option *Filename and path*. Word inserts the AutoText field.

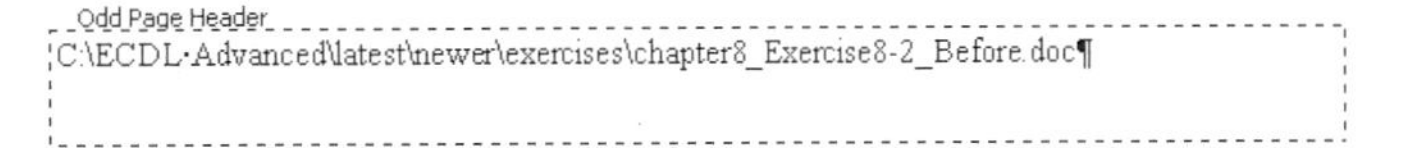

5) Click the **Show Next** button on the Header and Footer toolbar. Word displays the *Even Page Header* box.

6) Click the **Insert AutoText** button and choose the *Author, Page #, Date* option. Word inserts the AutoText field.

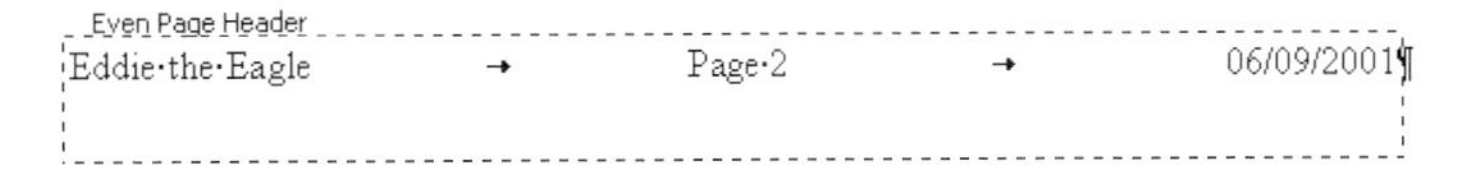

7) Save the document with the following name:

   `Chapter8_Exercise_8-2_After_`*`Your_Name`*`.doc`

   You can now close the document.

Working with existing fields

Typically, what you see in a document is the *result* of a field's instructions, and not the underlying field code. Field results, when clicked, are displayed against a grey background to indicate the presence of a field. The grey background is not shown on print-outs.

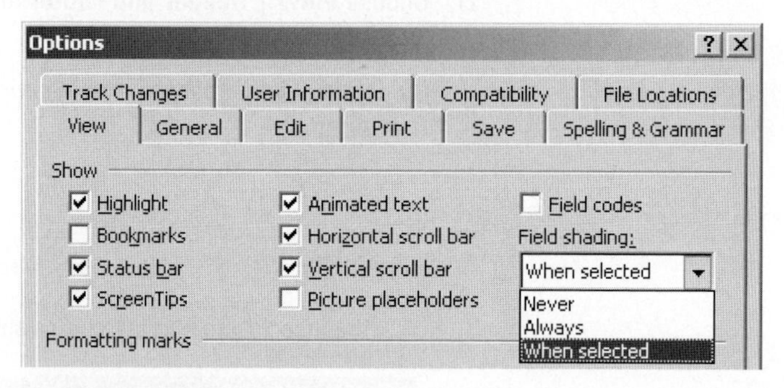

You can control how Word displays field results with the *Field shading* option on the **View** tab of the dialog box displayed with the **Tools | Options** command.

Follow the steps in Exercise 8.3 to view the underlying field code behind a field value.

Exercise 8.3: Changing How Fields Display

1) Open the following file:

   `Chapter8_Exercise_8-3_Before.doc`

2) Click anywhere in the table cell that contains the date field. Notice how a grey background appears behind the date. This indicates that the date is not regular typed text but a value generated by an underlying field code.

Before selecting the field *After selecting the field*

3) Right-click on the *Date* field and choose *Toggle field codes* from the pop-up menu displayed. Word replaces the field result with the field code.

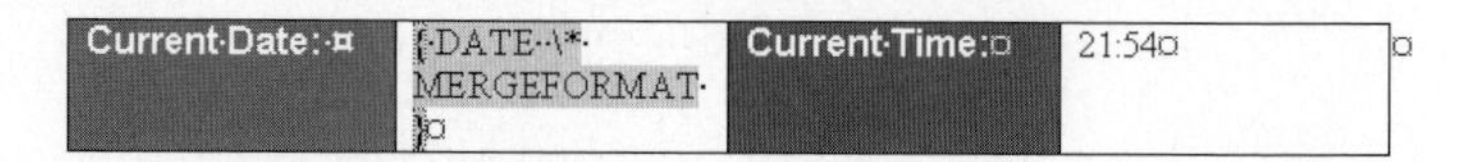

4) Repeat step 3 for the *Time* field in the fourth table cell. Both field codes are now displayed.

5) Save the document with the following name:

   Chapter8_Exercise_8-3_After_*Your_Name*.doc

You can now close the document.

As its name suggests, the *Toggle field codes* command also works in reverse. If you right-click on a field that currently shows the field code, Word replaces the code with the field value.

The shortcut key combination for toggling the display of a selected field is **Shift+F9**. You can toggle the display of *all* fields throughout a document by first selecting all the text in the document and then pressing **Shift+F9**.

To show field codes rather than field values by default, choose **Tools | Options**, click the **View** tab, select the *Field codes* checkbox, and click **OK.**

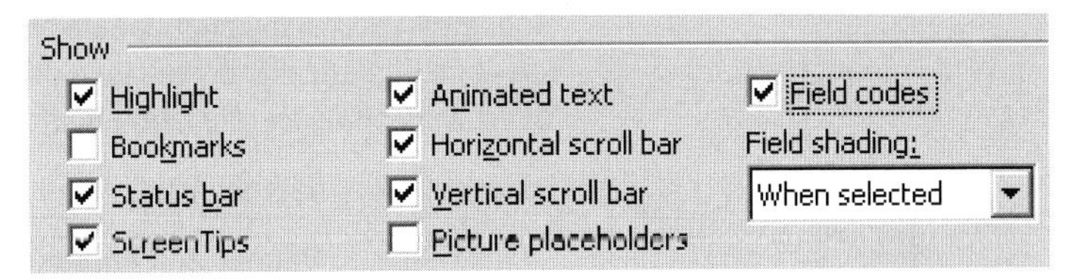

Working with field updates

Different types of fields are updated in different ways:

- **Automatic page numbering fields**. When you add, remove or reorder pages in a document, Word automatically adjusts the page numbering fields automatically.
- **Date and time fields**. When you open a document that contains date or time fields, Word updates the field results automatically.
- **Updates from printing**. The **Options** button within Word's **File | Print** dialog box offers an *Update fields* checkbox. If this is selected, Word will update all fields in the current document before printing.

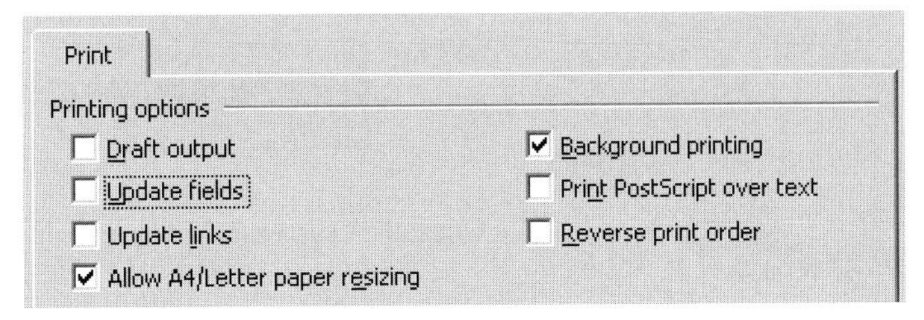

The next exercise takes you through the steps of updating fields directly.

Exercise 8.4: Updating a field directly

1) Open the following file:

```
Chapter8_Exercise_8-4_Doc1.doc
```

2) Do nothing for a couple of minutes. Then right-click anywhere in the table cell that contains the time field and choose *Update field* from the pop-up menu.

   Word updates the field to show the latest time. You can now close the sample document without saving it.

3) Open the following file:

   `Chapter8_Exercise_8-4_Doc2_Before.doc`

4) Choose **File | Save As** and save the file with the following name:

   `Chapter8_Exercise_8-4_Doc2_After_`*`Your_Name`*`.doc`

   Notice that Word does not update the file name displayed in the header automatically. If you close the document and then reopen it, Word will update the file name field for you.

   Instead, let's update the field directly.

5) Choose **View | Header and Footer** to display the Header and Footer toolbar.

6) By default, Word positions the insertion point in the *Odd Page Header* box. The file name field is selected.

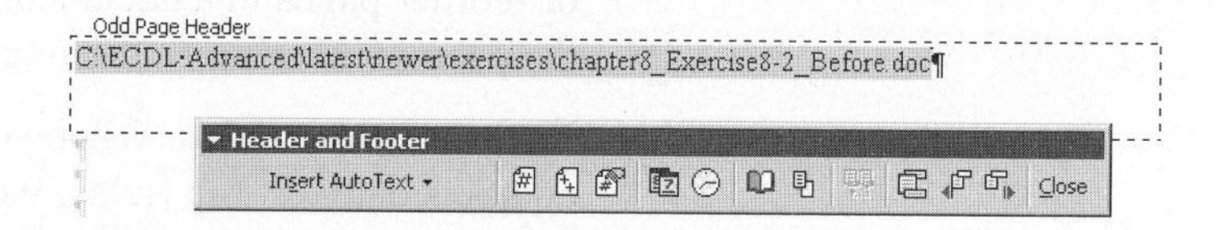

7) Right-click anywhere in the field and choose *Update field* from the pop-up menu.

   Word updates the field as shown below:

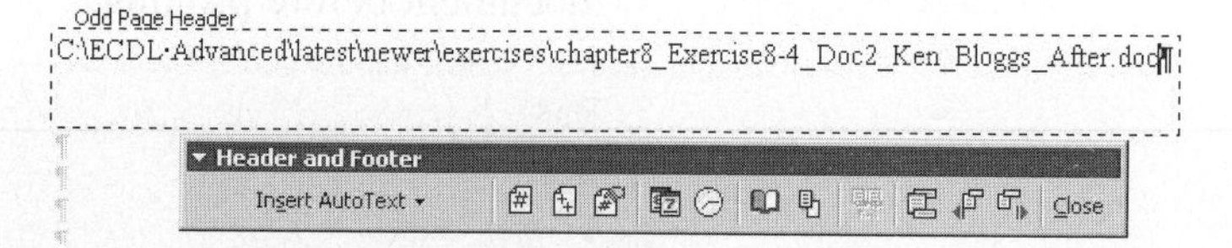

8) Close and save your sample document.

The shortcut key combination for updating a selected field is **F9**. You can update *all* fields throughout a document by first selecting all the text in the document and then pressing **F9**.

Working with locked fields

There may be times when you don't want a particular field to be updated, even when you are updating other fields in the same document.

Word allows you to *lock* a selected field or fields, so that the values remain fixed. You can later unlock the field or fields. Locking a field also prevents it from being amended.

Exercise 8.5: Locking a field to prevent updates

1) Open the following file:

   `Chapter8_Exercise_8-5_Before.doc`

2) Click anywhere in the table cell that contains the *Time* field and press **CTRL+F11**.

   (There is no menu command for this option: you need to know the keyboard shortcut.)

3) Right-click on the field. Notice that the *Update field* command is not available on the pop-up menu.

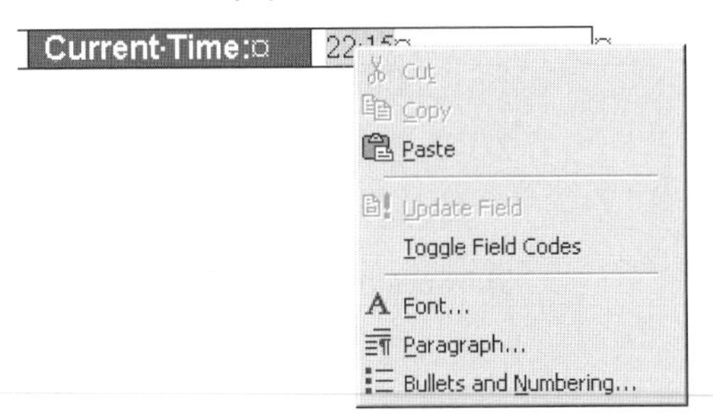

4) Save the document with the following name:

   `Chapter8_Exercise_8-5_After_Your_Name.doc`

   You can now close the document.

Exercise 8.6: Unlocking a field to allow updates

Field locking is a reversible operation. In Exercise 8.6, you will unlock a field similar to the one that you locked in Exercise 8.5.

1) Open the following file:

   `Chapter8_Exercise_8-6_Before.doc`

2) Click anywhere in the table cell that contains the *Time* field and press **Ctrl+Shift+F11**.

   (There is no menu command for this option: you need to know the keyboard shortcut.)

3) Right-click on the field. Notice that the *Update field* command is again available on the pop-up menu.

4) Save the document with the following name:

   `Chapter8_Exercise_8-6_After_`*`Your_Name`*`.doc`

   You can now close the document.

To lock (or unlock) *all fields* throughout a document, first select the entire document and then press **Ctrl+F11** (or **Ctrl+Shift+F11**).

Locking
Preventing a selected field or fields from being updated. The field values remain fixed after locking. Locked fields can be unlocked at a later stage if required.

Deleting fields

Don't want a particular field in a document any more? Deleting a field is fast and easy.

Exercise 8.7: Deleting a field

1) Open the following file:

   `Chapter8_Exercise_8-7_Before.doc`

2) Drag across the *Time* field to select it and then press the **Delete** key.

   Word removes the selected field from the document.

3) Save the document with the following name:

   `Chapter8_Exercise_8-7_After_`*`Your_Name`*`.doc`

   You can now close the document.

Chapter 8: quick reference

Shortcut keys

Keys	Description
Shift+F9	Toggles the display format of a selected field or fields between field code and field value.
F9	Updates the selected field or fields so that they show the latest value.
Ctrl+F11	Locks a selected field or fields to prevent updates.
Ctrl+Shift+F11	Unlocks a selected field or fields to allow updates.

Tasks summary

Task	Procedure
Change how a field is displayed.	Right-click in the field and choose *Toggle field codes*. Or click anywhere in the and press **Shift+F9**.
Update a field so that it shows the latest value.	Right-click in the field and choose *Update field*. Or click anywhere in the field and press **F9**.
Lock a field to prevent it from being updated.	Click anywhere in the field and press **Ctrl+F11**.
Unlock a field to permit updates.	Click anywhere in the field and press **Ctrl+Shift+F11**.

Concepts summary

In a Word document, *fields* are containers for holding instructions (*field codes*) and the results of instructions (*field values*). Field codes remain fixed unless you change them. Field values change over time or as conditions change. You can choose to display field codes or values, as required.

Fields can obtain their information from a range of sources, including the system clock, the current document properties, and the Word user's profile.

Opening a Word document typically updates all field in the document, and Word can also update fields when printing a document. You can *update fields directly*. You can *lock* fields to prevent updates, and *unlock* them later, as required

A number of common Word features, including tables of contents, indexes, automatic page numbering and mail merge rely on fields for their operation.

Chapter 8: quick quiz

Circle the correct answer to each of the following multiple-choice questions about fields in Word.

Q1	Which of the following statements best describes a field in Word?
A.	A named set of attributes that can be saved and then applied to selected items in a document.
B.	A file containing formatting settings and content that provides a pattern for individual Word documents.
C.	A container that holds instructions and the result of the instructions. Field values can change over time or as conditions change.
D.	A list of installed Windows fonts that are available for use in Word documents.

Q2	Which of the following is not a source from which a field may extract information for display in a Word document?
A.	The PC's system clock.
B.	The current Word document.
C.	The current document template.
D.	The details entered by the user when installing Word on the PC.

Q3	Which of the following Word features does not rely on the use of fields for its operation?
A.	Generation of a table of contents.
B.	Automatically updated page numbers in headers or footers.
C.	Mail merge.
D.	Character styles.

Q4	By default, how is a selected field value displayed in a Word document?
A.	In dark blue text.
B.	With a light grey background.
C.	In reverse type (white text against black background).
D.	As a hyperlink.

Q5	Which of the following commands would you choose to insert a new field in a Word document?
A.	Tools | Options | Fields | New.
B.	Insert | Field.
C.	Format | Field Insertion.
D.	Insert | Field | New Field.

Q6	Which of the following shortcut key combinations would you press to toggle between the display of field codes and field values?
A.	Alt+F11.
B.	Shift+F9.
C.	Shift+F11.
D.	F11.

Q7	Which of the following shortcut key combinations would you press to update a field directly?
A.	F9.
B.	F11.
C.	Alt+F9.
D.	Ctrl+Shift+F11.

Q8	Preventing a field in a Word document from being updated is called ...
A.	Unlocking.
B.	Linking.
C.	Unlinking.
D.	Locking.

Q9	Which of the following shortcut key combinations would you press to lock a particular field in a Word document?
A.	Alt+F9.
B.	F11.
C.	Shift+F9.
D.	Ctrl+F11.

Q10	Which of the following shortcut key combinations would you press to unlock a particular field in a Word document?
A.	Ctrl+Shift+F11.
B.	Shift+F9.
C.	Ctrl+Shift+F9.
D.	Alt+F9.

Answers

1: C, **2:** C, **3:** D, **4:** B, **5:** B, **6:** B, **7:** A, **8:** D, **9:** D, **10:** A.

9 Word does everything: macros

Objectives

In this chapter you will learn how to:

- Record a macro
- Run a macro
- Assign a macro to a keyboard shortcut
- Assign a macro to a toolbar custom button
- Copy a macro between templates

New words

In this chapter you will meet the following terms:

- Macro
- Macro project

Exercise files

In this chapter you will work with the following Word files:

- `Chapter9_Exercise_9-1_Before.doc`
- `Chapter9_Exercise_9-2_Before.doc`
- `Chapter9_Exercise_9-3_Before.doc`
- `Chapter9_Exercise_9-5_Before.doc`
- `Chapter9_Exercise_9-6_Before.doc`
- `Chapter9_Exercise_9-7_Before.doc`

Syllabus reference

In this chapter you will cover the following item of the ECDL Advanced Word Processing Syllabus:

- **AM3.5.2.1**. Record a simple macro (e.g. page set-up changes).
- **AM3.5.2.2**. Copy a macro.
- **AM3.5.2.3**. Run a macro.
- **AM3.5.2.4**. Assign a macro to a custom button on a toolbar.

About macros

Ever feel like you have a million tasks to perform? Or that you are doing the same task a million times over?

Word's macro feature can help you with the second problem. Think of a macro as a tape recorder that records not music or voices but sequences of Word actions and menu commands.

When you have recorded Word actions in a macro, you can then play back the macro as often as you need. In Word, playing back a macro is called *running* a macro.

The Macros dialog box

You perform most macro-related tasks from the *Macros* dialog box, which you access by choosing the **Tools | Macro | Macros** command.

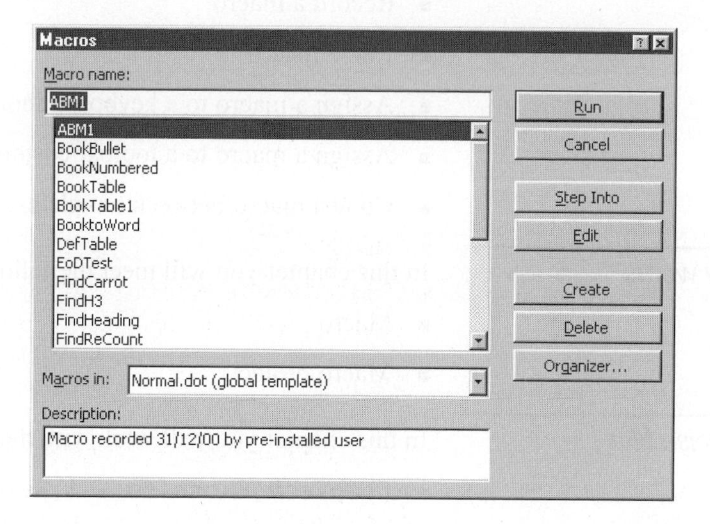

Other automation features in Word

Macros are not the only way of automating tasks in Word. Other automation features include:

- **Templates and styles**. These allow you to apply consistent formatting, standard text and page layout settings across a range of different documents. See Chapter 3.
- **AutoText entries**. These allow you to insert commonly-used text, with or without paragraph formatting, in different documents. See Chapter 5.

Macros are best suited for automating tasks that combine several different Word features. Examples might be combinations of text and paragraph formatting, mail merge operations, and the tidying-up of documents imported from the web or other non-Word sources.

Macros: the benefits to you

Macros offer two main advantages. They:

- **Save time**. By recording frequently-performed and repetitive tasks in macros, and running the macros as you need them, you can speed up your work greatly.
- **Reduce errors**. As the actions stored in a macro are performed in exactly the same way each time the macro is run, procedures are followed more reliably.

Working with macros: the five tasks

Here are the five macro-related tasks that you need to be able to perform in Word:

- **Record and run a macro**. Exercises 9.1, 9.3, 9.5 and 9.7 provide examples of the macro recording process in Word.
- **Run a macro**. Exercise 9.2 takes you through the steps of running a macro.
- **Assign a macro to a keyboard shortcut**: See Exercises 9.3 and 9.4.
- **Assign a macro to a toolbar button**. See Exercises 9.5 and 9.6.
- **Copy a macro between templates**. A macro, like a style, can be saved in a document or in a template. As Exercise 9.8 shows, you can copy macros between different documents and templates.

Macro

A series of Word actions and menu commands grouped together that when run, perform those actions and commands automatically. Macros are identified by a unique name, and can be stored in a template or document.

Working with simple macros

In the first exercise, you will create a simple macro that opens a new Word document and types some text in it.

Exercise 9.1: Record a simple macro

1) Start Word and open the following document:

    `Chapter9_Exercise_9-1_Before.doc`

2) Select the first paragraph of body text in the document.

Introduction¶

By·transforming·the·way·that·people·and·businesses·communicate·and·interact,·the·Internet·has·dramatically·changed·the·face·of·business.¶

Impressed·by·the·Internet's·rising·popularity,·many·businesses·have·established·an·online·

3) Choose **Tools | Macro | Record New Macro**.

   Alternatively, double-click the **REC** button on the Status Bar along the bottom of the Word window.

   Word displays the *Record Macro* dialog box.

4) In the *Macro name* box, type the following:

   ```
   AllCaps_Macro_Your_Name
   ```

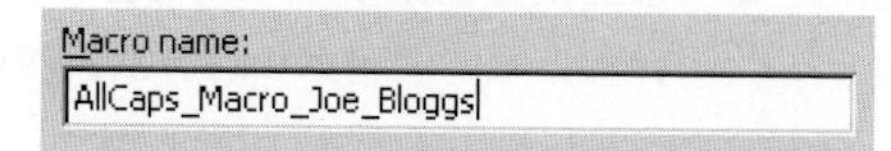

   Do not enter or change any other details in the dialog box. Click **OK**.

5) Word closes the dialog box and displays the Stop Recording toolbar on your screen.

   This has just two buttons: one to stop recording and another to pause/resume macro recording.

   You will now perform the sequence of actions for your macro to record:

   - Choose **Format | Font**.
   - Select the *All caps* checkbox.

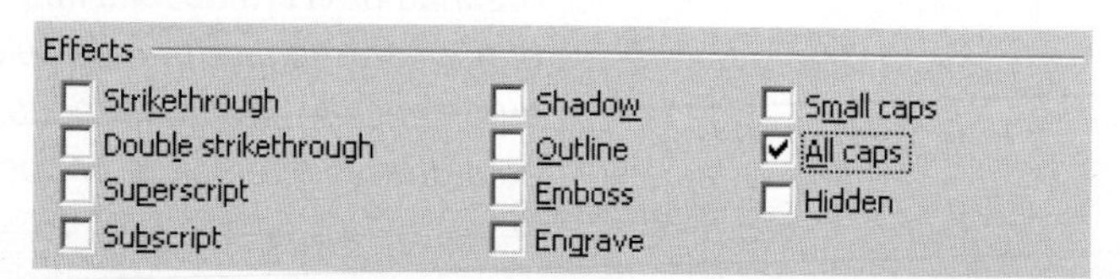

   - Click **OK**.

   This completes the actions.

7) Click the **Stop Recording** button on the Stop Recording toolbar. Word removes the toolbar from the screen.

   Your macro is now recorded. You can close the sample document without saving it. Your new macro is stored in the Normal template – not in the document.

Were you a little nervous as you recorded your first macro, knowing that Word was remembering your actions? Word does *not* record the speed at which you perform your actions. So you can take the time to think carefully about what steps you want to record.

- **I've made a slight mistake**. Don't panic. Just correct your error and keep going. Word records both your error and your correction as part of the macro, but Word plays back macros so fast that it's unlikely that anyone will notice.
- **I've really messed it up**. Click the **Stop Recording** button, and record the macro again. If you enter the same macro name, Word prompts you to overwrite the original macro. Click **Yes** and perform your actions again.

Running macros

Now that you've recorded your first macro, your next step is to play it back. The procedure in Exercise 9.2 will let you run any available macro. If the relevant macro has not been assigned to a menu, keyboard shortcut or toolbar, this is the *only* way that you can run the macro.

Exercise 9.2: Run a macro

1) Start Word and open the following document:

    `Lesson9_Exercise_9-2_Before.doc`

2) Select the first paragraph of body text in the document.

    ***Introduction*¶**

    By·transforming·the·way·that·people·and·businesses·communicate·and·interact,·the·Internet·has·dramatically·changed·the·face·of·business.¶

    Impressed·by·the·Internet's·rising·popularity,·many·businesses·have·established·an·online·

3) Choose **Tools | Macro | Macros...** to display the *Macros* dialog box.

4) In the *Macro name* box, select the macro that you recorded in Exercise 9.1.

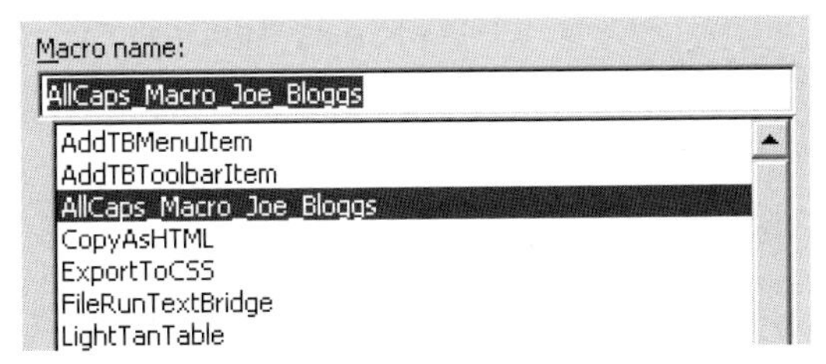

5) Click **Run**. Word runs the macro on the selected text.

    ***Introduction*¶**

    BY·TRANSFORMING·THE·WAY·THAT·PEOPLE·AND·BUSINESSES·COMMUNICATE·AND·INTERACT,·THE·INTERNET·HAS·DRAMATICALLY·CHANGED·THE·FACE·OF·BUSINESS.¶

    Impressed·by·the·Internet's·rising·popularity,·many·businesses·have·established·an·online·

6) Save your sample document with the following name:

`Chapter9_Exercise_9-2_After_Your_Name.doc`

You can close the sample document.

Working with macros and keyboard shortcuts

If you plan to run a macro frequently, you will find it convenient to assign it to a keyboard shortcut. You can then run the macro directly without displaying the *Macros* dialog box. You assign a macro to a keyboard shortcut:

- **When you record the macro**. This is the procedure that you will follow in Exercise 9.3.
- **After the macro has been recorded**. You can assign a keyboard shortcut to a macro that you or another user has already created, or amend a previously assigned shortcut. Exercise 9.4 takes you through the steps.

Do *not* assign macros to keyboard shortcuts already used for common Word tasks, such as applying bold (**Ctrl+B**) or italics (**Ctrl+I**), or saving (**Ctrl+S**) and printing (**Ctrl+P**).

Exercise 9.3: Record a macro and assign it to a keyboard shortcut

In this exercise, you will recreate the macro that you recorded in Exercise 9.1 and assign a keyboard shortcut to it.

1) Open the following document:

`Chapter_Exercise_9-3_Before.doc`

2) Select the first paragraph of text in the document.
3) Choose **Tools | Macro | Record New Macro** to display the *Record Macro* dialog box.
4) In the *Macro name* box, type the same name as you gave your first macro in Exercise 9.1:

`AllCaps_Macro_Your_Name`

5) Click the **Keyboard** button. Word prompts you as follows:

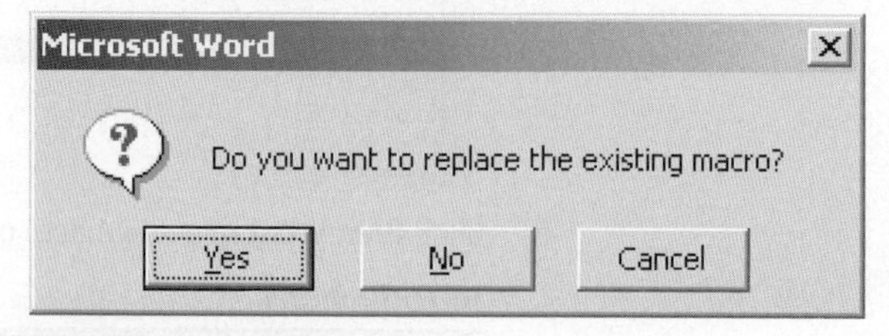

Click **Yes**.

6) Word now displays the *Customize Keyboard* dialog box. Click in the *Press new shortcut key* box, and press **Ctrl+B**.

Word responds by telling you that this keyboard shortcut is already assigned. You could override the current assignment, but that would not be a good idea as this shortcut is for bold formatting.

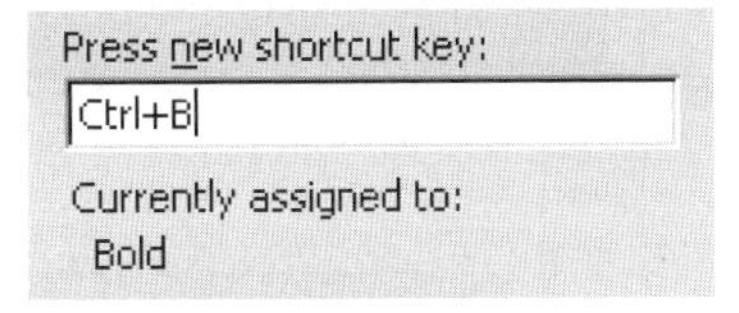

Delete **Ctrl+B** from the box.

7) With the insertion point still in the *Press new shortcut key* box, press the following key combination:

   Alt+Ctrl+X

   Word responds by telling you that this keyboard shortcut is not assigned to any other action.

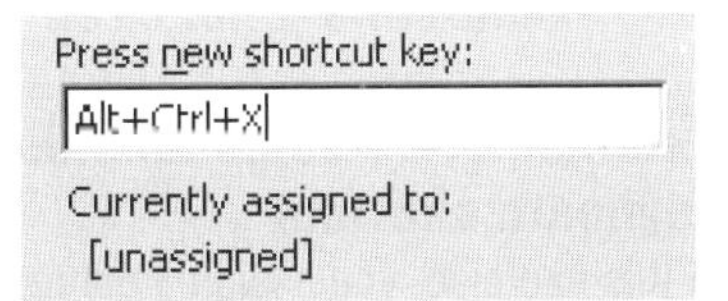

8) Click **Assign** to assign the shortcut key combination, and then click **Close** to close the dialog box.

9) You will now perform the sequence of actions for your macro to record:

   - Choose **Format | Font**.
   - Select the *All caps* checkbox.
   - Click **OK**.

   This completes the actions.

10) Click the **Stop Recording** button on the Stop Recording toolbar. Word removes the toolbar from the screen.

11) Your macro is now recorded. You can close the sample document without saving it. Your new macro is stored in the Normal template – not in the document.

12) Let's check that your macro is assigned correctly. Open the following document:

    `Chapter9_Exercise_9-3_Before.doc`

    Select the second paragraph of text and press **Alt+Ctrl+X**. Your macro should have the effect shown:

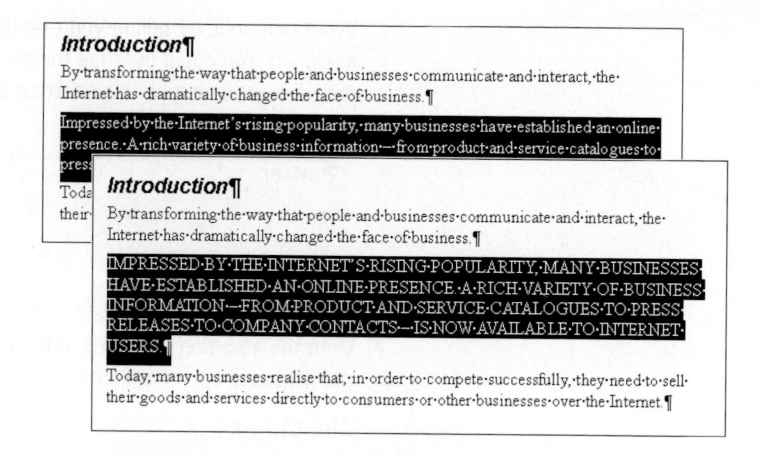

13) Close and save your sample document with the following name:

`Chapter9_Exercise_9-3_After_Your_Name.doc`

Exercise 9.4: Assign an existing macro to a keyboard shortcut

In this exercise, you assign a different keyboard shortcut to the macro that you created in Exercise 9.3. You do not need to have a document open to reassign a macro keyboard shortcut – unless the macro is stored in a particular document rather than a template.

1) Right-click any displayed Word toolbar, such as the Standard toolbar, and choose **Customize**.
2) In the *Customize* dialog box, click the **Commands** tab, and click the **Keyboard** button to display the *Customize Keyboard* dialog box.
3) In the *Categories* list, click *Macros*. In the *Macros* list, click the macro that you created in Exercise 9.3.

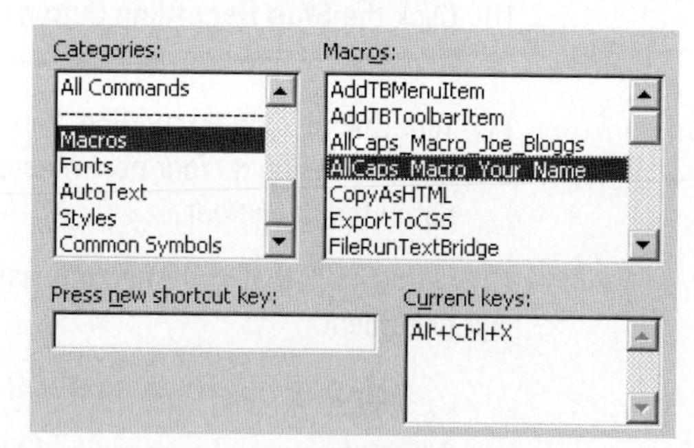

4) Word displays the currently assigned keyboard shortcut for the selected macro. In this case, the keyboard shortcut is **Alt+Ctrl+X**. If no shortcut was assigned to the macro, the *Current keys* box would be empty.

   Your next step is to assign a second shortcut key combination to the macro.

5) Click in the *Press new shortcut key* box, and press the following key combination:

Alt+Ctrl+;

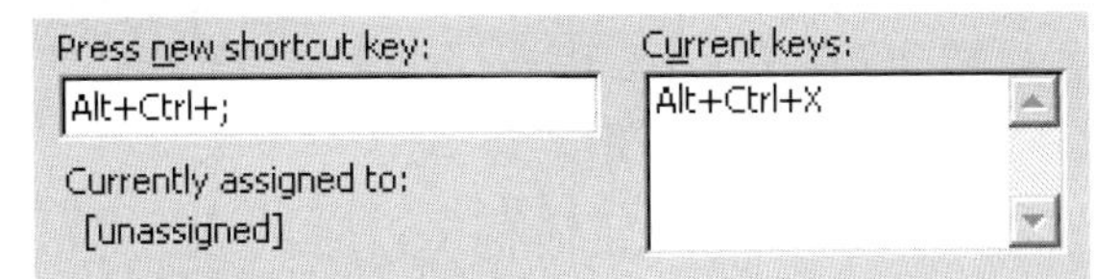

6) Click **Assign**. Word assigns the keyboard shortcut. The macro now has two keyboard shortcuts associated with it. In future, using either shortcut will run the macro.

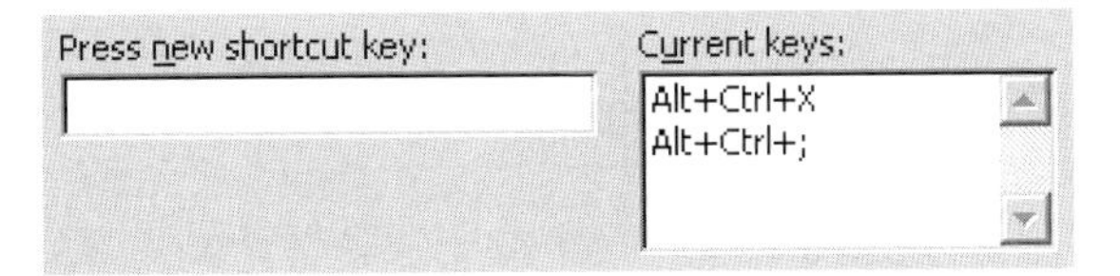

7) Click **Close** to close the *Customize Keyboard* dialog box, and click **Close** to close the *Customize* dialog box.

8) You have completed this exercise. You do not need to save any documents: the new keyboard assignment is already saved to your Normal template.

Working with macros and toolbar buttons

The procedure for assigning a macro to a toolbar button is very similar to that for assigning a macro to a keyboard shortcut. You can assign the macro when you record, as shown in Exercise 9.5, or at a later time, as in Exercise 9.6.

Exercise 9.5: Record a macro and assign it to a toolbar button

In this exercise, you will create a new macro and assign it to a button on a Word toolbar.

1) Is the Word toolbar to which you want to assign the macro displayed? If not, choose **View | Toolbars** to display it now.

2) Open the following document:

   `Chapter9_Exercise_9-5_Before.doc`

3) Select the first paragraph of text in the document.

4) Choose **Tools | Macro | Record New Macro** to display the *Record Macro* dialog box.

5) In the *Macro name* box, type the following:

   `BlueCaps_Macro_Your_Name`

6) Click the **Toolbars** button. Word now displays the *Customize* dialog box.

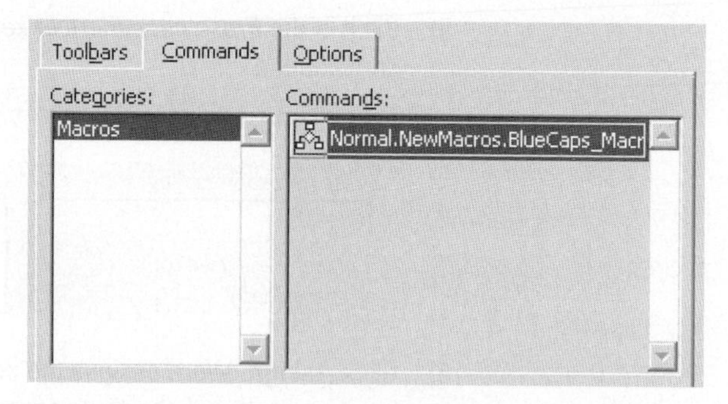

In the *Commands* list of the **Commands** tab, click on the macro that you have just named and drag it to the relevant toolbar.

In the example below, the button for the macro is positioned on the Standard toolbar.

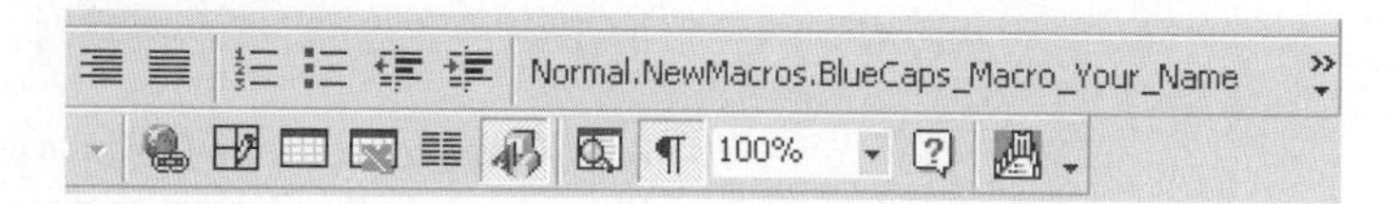

When you have dragged the macro name to the toolbar, click **Close** to close the *Customize* dialog box.

7) You will now perform the sequence of actions for your macro to record:

   - Choose **Format | Font**.
   - Change the font colour to blue, and select the *All caps* checkbox.
   - Click **OK**.

   This completes the actions.

8) Click the **Stop Recording** button on the Stop Recording toolbar. Word removes the toolbar from the screen.

9) Your macro is now recorded. You can close the sample document without saving it. Your new macro is stored in the Normal template – not in the document.

10) Let's check that your macro is assigned correctly. Open the following document:

    `Chapter9_Exercise_9-5_Before.doc`

    Select the second paragraph of text, and click the macro button on the toolbar. Your macro should have the effect shown.

Impressed·by·the·Internet's·rising·popularity,·many·businesses·have·established·an·online·presence.·A·rich·variety·of·business·information·—·from·product·and·service·catalogues·to·pres

IMPRESSED·BY·THE·INTERNET'S·RISING·POPULARITY,·MANY·BUSINESSES·HAVE·ESTABLISHED·AN·ONLINE·PRESENCE.·A·RICH·VARIETY·OF·BUSINESS·INFORMATION·—·FROM·PRODUCT·AND·SERVICE·CATALOGUES·TO·PRESS·RELEASES·TO·COMPANY·CONTACTS·—·IS·NOW·AVAILABLE·TO·INTERNET·USERS.¶

11) Close and save your sample document with the following name:

`Chapter9_Exercise_9-5_After_Your_Name.doc`

Exercise 9.6: Assign an existing macro to a toolbar button

In this exercise, you will assign a toolbar button to the macro that you previously created in Exercise 9.3.

1) Right-click any displayed Word toolbar, such as the Standard toolbar, choose **Customize** to display the *Customize* dialog box, and click the **Commands** tab.

2) In the *Categories* list, click *Macros*.

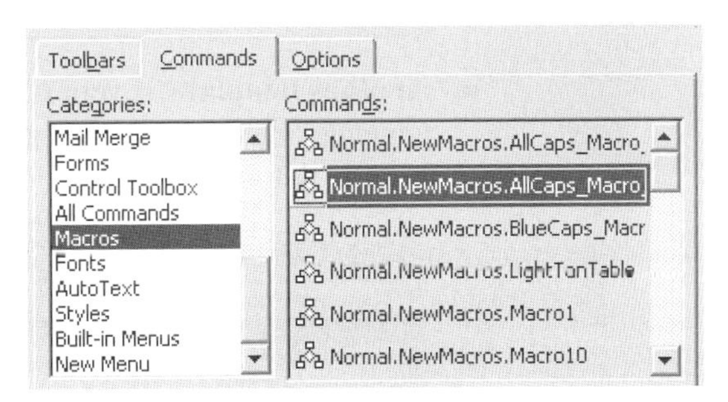

3) In the *Commands* list, click the macro that you created in Exercise 9.3 and drag it to the relevant toolbar.

   When finished, click **Close** to close the *Customize* dialog box.

4) Let's check that your macro is assigned correctly to the toolbar. Open the following document:

   `Chapter9_Exercise_9-6_Before.doc`

5) Select the third paragraph of body text, and click the macro button on the toolbar. Close and save your sample document with the following name:

   Chapter9_Exercise_9-6_After_*Your_Name*.doc

   Want to remove the macro button from your toolbar? Hold down the **Alt** key and drag the button down off the toolbar.

Working with macros and templates

A Word macro is not a separate file but is stored in a template or document.

- **Normal template**. If your current document is based on the Normal template (Normal.dot), Word gives you the choice of storing a new macro in the Normal template or in the current document.

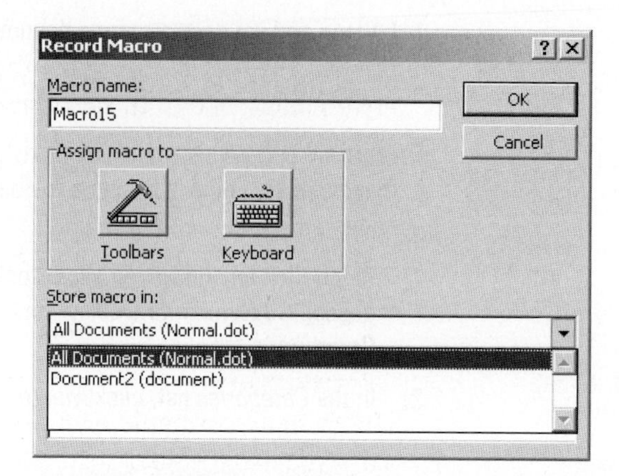

- **Another template**. If your current document is based on a template other than Normal.dot, you can store a new macro in Normal.dot, in the current template, or in the current document.

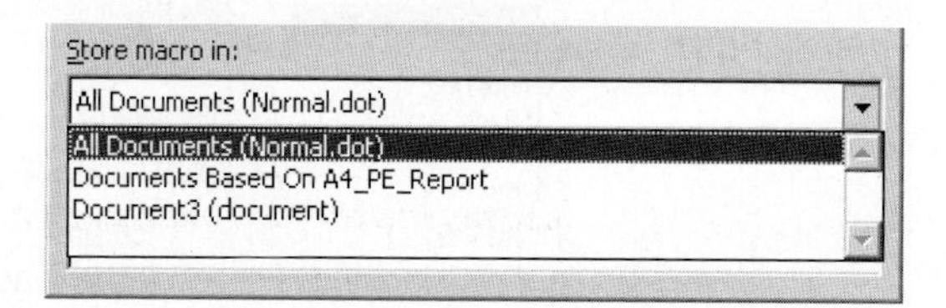

When you store a macro in the Normal template, it is available to all documents on *your* PC. When you store a macro in a document, it is available to any Word user who opens that document on *any* PC.

Macro projects and the Word 2000 Organizer

The area within a Word document or template in which macros are stored is called the *macro project*. A document or template may have more than one macro project. The first or default macro project in every Word document or template is called NewMacros.

Macro project

A group of one or more macros saved in an individual Word template or document. The first or default macro project in every document or template is called NewMacros.

Using the Word 2000 Organizer, you can copy a macro project (and all the macros it contains) between templates, between documents, and between documents and templates.

In the *Organizer* dialog box (available from the *Macros* dialog box), you can display two lists:

- **Macros in active document**. On the left, Word can display the macro projects stored in the active document, in Normal.dot and, if the current document is based on another template, in that other template.

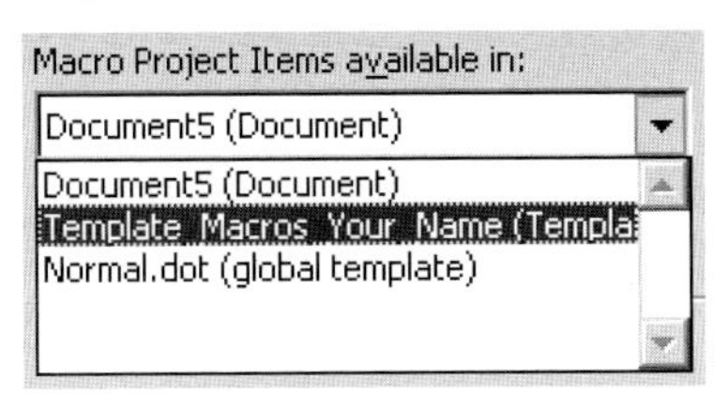

  In the above example, you can select the macro project from any one of three locations: the current document (Document5), the current template (Template_Macros_Your_Name) or Normal.dot.

- **Macros in Normal template**. On the right, Word shows the macro project in the Normal document template only.

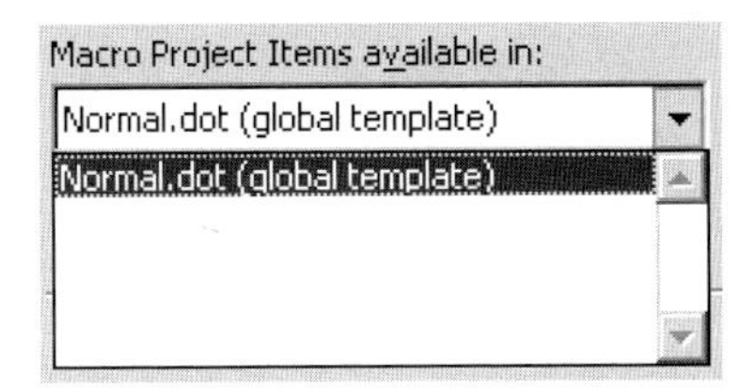

In Exercise 9.7, you will record a macro and store it in the current document rather than in a template. In Exercise 9.8, you use the Word 2000 Organizer to copy the macro project that contains your macro from the document to the Normal template.

Exercise 9.7: Record a macro and store it in a document

1) Open the following blank document:

   `Chapter9_Exercise_9-7_Before.doc`

2) Choose **Tools | Macro | Record New Macro** to display the *Record Macro* dialog box.

3) In the *Macro name* box, type the following name:

   `Landscape_Macro_`*`Your_Name`*

4) In the *Store macro in* list, select the current document option. Click **OK** to close the dialog box.

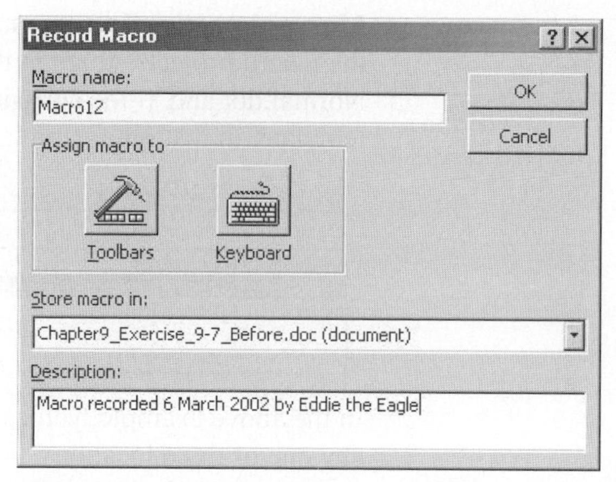

5) You will now perform the sequence of actions for your macro to record.
   - Choose **File | Page Setup**.
   - Click the **Paper Size** tab.
   - Change the orientation to *Landscape*.
   - Click **OK**.

   This completes the actions.
6) Click the **Stop Recording** button on the Stop Recording toolbar. Word removes the toolbar from the screen. Your macro is now recorded.
7) Close and save the document with the following name:

   `Chapter9_Exercise_9-7_After_`*`Your_Name`*`.doc`

In the next exercise, you will copy your macro, saved in the document, to the Normal template.

Exercise 9.8: Copy a macro using the Word 2000 Organizer

1) Open the document that you saved at the end of Exercise 9.7:

   `Chapter9_Exercise_9-7_After_`*`Your_Name`*`.doc`
2) Choose **Tools | Macro | Macros** to display the *Macros* dialog box and click the **Organizer** button.
3) Select the **Macro Project Items** tab.

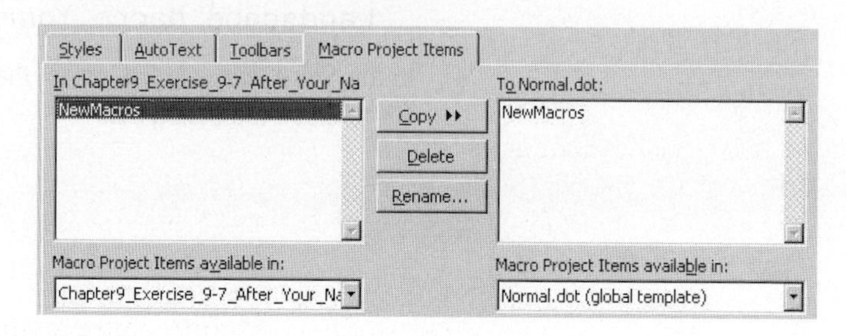

4) In the left-hand list, which shows the macro project for the current document, click *NewMacros* to select it, and then click **Copy**.

5) Word displays the following message box.

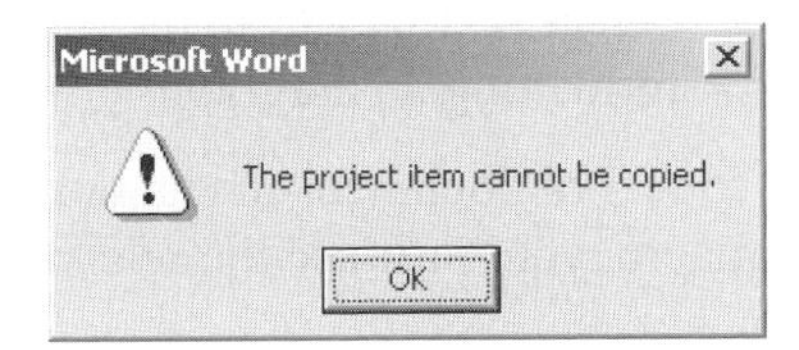

Why? Because you tried to copy a macro project named NewMacros to the Normal template, which already contains a macro project called NewMacros. You need to first rename the macro project before you can copy it.

6) With NewMacros still selected in the left list, click **Rename**, type the following new macro project name when prompted, and click **OK**:

```
MoreMacros
```

7) With MoreMacros still selected in the left list, click **Copy** to copy the macro project to the Normal template.

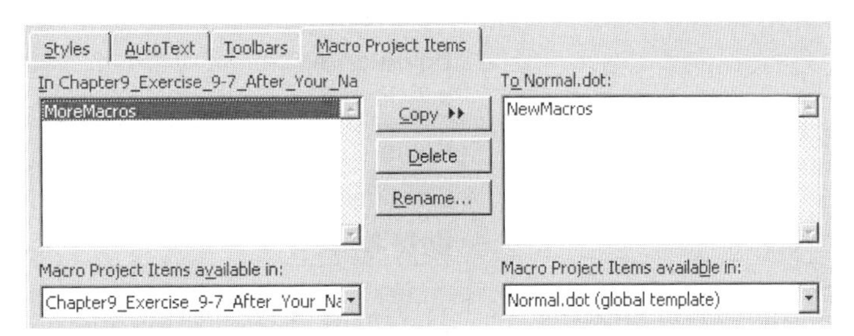

8) When finished, click **Close**.

9) Let's check that your landscape macro is actually stored in the Normal template, from where it is available to all documents based on that template.

Click the **New** button on the Standard toolbar to open a new document, choose **Tools | Macro | Macros**, and verify that your macro is present. When finished, you can close all open documents.

What a macro does and does not record

When you record a macro, which of your actions does the macro 'remember'? Macros record actions that affect the document, and ignore those that do not, such as switching display features on and off.

Macros and mouse actions

Macros do record mouse actions that choose menu commands (such as **File | Save**) and that click on toolbar buttons (such as the **Bold** button on the Formatting toolbar).

Macros do *not* record mouse actions that:

- **Change the location of the insertion point**. For example, to move a number of characters along a line, or to move forward or backward through a document
- **Select text**. For example, before copying a word or formatting a paragraph.

To record document-navigation and text-selection actions in a macro, you must use the relevant shortcut keys.

Navigation keys

The main shortcut keys for document navigation are:

Press	To move the insertion point
Left arrow	One character to the left.
Right arrow	One character to the right.
Ctrl+Left arrow	One word to the left.
Ctrl+ Right arrow	One word to the right.
Ctrl+Up arrow	One paragraph up.
Ctrl+Down arrow	One paragraph down.
Up arrow	Up one line.
Down arrow	Down one line.
End	To the end of a line.
Home	To the beginning of a line.
Ctrl+End	To the end of a document.
Ctrl+Home	To the beginning of a document.

Text-selection keys

The main text-selection shortcut keys are:

Press	To select text
Shift+ Right arrow	One character to the right.
Shift+Left arrow	One character to the left.
Ctrl+Shift+ Right arrow	To the end of a word.
Ctrl+Shift+Left arrow	To the beginning of a word.
Shift+End	To the end of a line.
Shift+Home	To the beginning of a line.
Shift+Down arrow	One line down.
Shift+Up arrow	One line up.
Ctrl+Shift+Down arrow	To the end of a paragraph.
Ctrl+Shift+Up arrow	To the beginning of a paragraph.
Ctrl+Shift+Home	To the beginning of a document.
Ctrl+Shift+End	To the end of a document.
Ctrl+A	The entire document.
F8+arrow keys	To a specific location in a document.

To display the document-navigation and text-selection keyboard shortcuts in Word's Online Help, choose **Help | Microsoft Word Help**, type 'shortcuts' in the search box, click **Search**, and then click *Keyboard Shortcuts* in the topics list. (Make sure you have hidden the Office Assistant before you do this.)

Before recording a macro

Here are some points to remember before recording any macro:

- **Templates**. Decide where you want to save the macro – in the current template or in the current document only.
- **Actions**. Plan the steps you want the macro to perform. It is possible to edit a macro, but you must be familiar with Visual Basic for Applications (VBA), the programming language in which macros are written. VBA is beyond the scope of this ECDL module and book.
- **Text selection**. If you are creating a macro that applies only to selected text in a document, consider whether you want the text-selection action recorded as part of the macro, or whether you want to select the text first before running the macro.

Chapter 9: quick reference

Macro properties

Property	Description
Name	This identifies the macro uniquely. Macro names can contain numbers, but they must begin with a letter and they cannot contain spaces. If you give a new macro the same name as an existing built-in Word macro, your new macro will replace the built-in Word macro – *without* warning!
Storage location	This can be the current template or document.
Description	Optionally, you can enter a description of your macro, up to 255 characters in length. This is your reference to help you remember what the macro does.
Keyboard shortcut	Optionally, you can assign a macro to a keyboard shortcut so that you can run it by pressing the appropriate keys.
Toolbar button	Optionally, you can assign a macro to a toolbar button so that you can run it by clicking the appropriate button.

Tasks summary

Task	Procedure
Record a new macro.	Click the **REC** button on the Status Bar or choose **Tools | Macro | Record New Macro**. Type a name and click **OK**. Perform the actions you want the macro to record. When finished, click the **Stop Recording** button.
Assign a macro to a keyboard shortcut.	When recording the macro, click the **Keyboard** button in the *Record Macro* dialog box, press the relevant key combination, click **Assign** and click **Close**.
Assign a macro to a toolbar button.	When recording the macro, click the **Toolbar** button in the *Record Macro* dialog box. In the *Commands* list, click the macro and drag it to the relevant toolbar.
Copy a macro.	Choose **Tools | Macro | Record New Macro**, click **Organizer**, select the macro project, click **Copy** and then click **Close**.

Concepts summary

Word's macro feature enables you to *record* and, as often as needed, play back or *run* sequences of Word actions and menu commands. By recording frequently-performed and repetitive tasks in macros, you can speed up your work greatly. As the actions stored in a macro are performed in exactly the same way each time the macro is run, you can ensure that procedures are followed more reliably.

Macros are identified by a unique name and, optionally, can be assigned to a keyboard shortcut or toolbar button for fast access. You can make the keyboard or toolbar assignment when recording the macro or at a later time.

Word does *not* record the speed at which perform your actions. If you make a slight mistake, you can correct your error and keep going. If you make a serious error, stop the recording and begin again.

Macros *do* record *mouse actions* that choose menu commands and click on toolbar buttons, but they do not record mouse actions that change the location of the insertion point or select text. To record navigation and selection actions in a macro, you must use the relevant *shortcut keys*.

A Word macro is not a separate file but is stored in the current template or document. The area within a Word document or template in which macros are stored is called the *macro project.*

A document or template may have more than one macro project. The first or default macro project in every Word document or template is called *NewMacros*.

Using the *Word 2000 Organizer*, you can copy a macro project (and all the macros it contains) between templates, between documents, and between documents and templates.

Chapter 9: quick quiz

Circle the correct answer to each of the following multiple-choice questions about macros in Word.

Q1	A Word macro is ...
A.	An AutoText entry that is inserted automatically when a new Word document opens.
B.	A built-in Word program that can copy text and graphics between templates.
C.	A series of recorded actions that, when run, performs those actions automatically.
D.	An AutoText entry that is inserted automatically when a Word document is saved and closed.

Q2	Which of the following statements about Word macros is untrue?
A.	Macros can be protected by passwords for security.
B.	Macros enable procedures to be followed consistently because the actions are performed in the same way each time the macro is run.
C.	Macros enable repetitive tasks to be recorded once and then run as often as needed.
D.	Macros can be stored in a document or a template.

Q3	Which button on Word's Status Bar can you click to begin recording a new macro?
A.	**MACRO.**
B.	**RECORD.**
C.	**MAC REC.**
D.	**REC.**

Q4	Which Word command can you choose to record a new macro?
A.	**File | New | Macro.**
B.	**Tools | Macro | Record New Macro.**
C.	**Format | Automation | New Macros.**
D.	**Tools | Macro | New.**

Q5	In Word, which of the following items must you specify for each new macro that you record?
A.	Macro description.
B.	Keyboard shortcut.
C.	Toolbar button.
D.	Macro name.

Q6	In Word, which of the following is the default storage location for a new macro that you record?
A.	The current document.
B.	The current template.
C.	The Normal template.
D.	AutoText Check.

Q7	In Word, which of the following keyboard shortcuts is a good choice for assigning a macro to?
A.	Ctrl+B.
B.	Ctrl+C.
C.	Ctrl+V.
D.	Alt+Ctrl+X.

Q8	In Word's *Record Macro* dialog box, which series of actions do you perform to assign a macro to a keyboard shortcut?
A.	Click the **Shortcut Key** button, press the relevant key combination, click the **Assign Now** button, and then click **OK**.
B.	Select an unassigned keyboard shortcut from the *Keyboard* list and click **Copy** to copy it to the *Assigned keys* list.
C.	Click the **Keyboard** button, press the relevant key combination, click the **Assign** button, and then click **Close**.
D.	Select an unassigned keyboard shortcut from the *Keyboard* list and click the **Assign** button.

Q9	In Word's *Record Macro* dialog box, which series of actions do you perform to assign a macro to a toolbar button?
A.	Click the **Toolbar** button. In the *Commands* list, click the macro to select it and drag it to the relevant toolbar.
B.	Click the **Toolbar** button. In the *Toolbars* list, click to select the relevant toolbar, click the **Assign** button and click **OK**.
C.	Click the **Assign Toolbar** button. In the *Macros* list, right-click the macro to select it and drag it to the relevant toolbar.
D.	Click the **Toolbar** button. In the *Available Toolbars* list, click to select the relevant toolbar, click the **Copy** button and click **OK**.

Q10	In Word, which series of actions do you perform to assign an already-recorded macro to a shortcut key?
A.	Right-click on the toolbar and choose **Customize**. On the *Commands* tab, click the **Keyboard** button, select *Macros* in the *Categories* list, select the macro in the *Macros* list, press the key combination, click **Assign**, click **Close,** and then click **Close** again.
B.	Choose **Tools | Macro | Macros**, click the **Shortcut Key** button, press the relevant key combination, click the **Assign Now** button, and then click **OK**.
C.	Right-click on the toolbar and choose **Customize**. On the **Commands** tab, click the **Keyboard** button, select the macro in the *Macros* list, press the key combination, click the **Assign** button, and click **OK**.
D.	Choose **Tools | Macro | Macros**, select an unassigned keyboard shortcut from the *Keyboard* list, click the **Assign** button, and click **OK**.

Q11	In Word, which series of actions do you perform to assign an already-recorded macro to a toolbar button?
A.	Choose **Tools | Macro | Macros**, click the **Shortcut Key** button, press the relevant key combination, click the **Assign Now** button, and then click **OK**.
B.	Right-click on the toolbar and choose **Customize**. On the **Commands** tab, select *Macros* in the *Categories* list, click the macro in the *Macros* list, drag it to the relevant toolbar, and click **Close**.
C.	Choose **Tools | Macro | Macros**, select a toolbar from the *Toolbars* list, select the macro from the *Macros* list, click the **Assign** button, and click **OK**.
D.	Right-click on the toolbar and choose **Customize.** On the **Commands** tab, right-click the macro in the *Available macros* list, drag it to the relevant toolbar, and click **OK**.

Q12	In Word, the area within a document or template in which macros are stored is called ...
A.	A macro field.
B.	A macro subfolder.
C.	A macro AutoText entry.
D.	A macro project.

Q13	The first or default macro project in every Word document or template is called ...
A.	DefaultMacros.
B.	NewMacros.
C.	Macros_Default.
D.	MacrosNew.

Q14	By default, the left-hand list in the *Word Organizer* dialog box shows ...
A.	The macro projects stored in the Normal template.
B.	The macro projects stored in the Normal template and, if the current document is based on another template, in that other template.
C.	The macro projects stored in the current document.
D.	The macro projects stored in the active document, in Normal.dot and, if the current document is based on another template, in that other template.

Answers

1: C, **2:** A, **3:** D, **4:** B, **5:** D, **6:** C, **7:** D, **8:** C, **9:** A, **10:** A, **11:** B, **12:** D, **13:** B, **14:** D.

10 'Are you sure about this?': comments and document protection

Objectives

In this chapter you will learn how to:

- Insert comments in a document
- Hide, display and edit comments
- Remove comments from a document
- Change the identifying details associated with inserted comments
- Add password protection to a document
- Remove password protection from a document

New words

In this chapter you will meet the following terms:

- Comment
- Comment mark
- Password-protected document

Exercise files

In this chapter you will work with the following Word files:

- Chapter10_Exercise_10-1_Before.doc
- Chapter10_Exercise_10-2_Before.doc
- Chapter10_Exercise_10-3_Before.doc
- Chapter10_Exercise_10-4_Before.doc
- Chapter10_Exercise_10-5_Before.doc

Syllabus reference

In this chapter you will cover the following items from the ECDL Advanced Word Processing Syllabus:

- **AM3.1.4.1**. Add or remove text comments.
- **AM3.1.4.2**. Edit text comments.

- **AM3.3.4.1**. Add password protection to a document.
- **AM3.3.4.2**. Remove password protection from a document.

About comments

Any document you write will usually benefit from review by one or more of your colleagues. Word offers a *comments* feature to help document authors gather feedback from reviewers. Sometimes, authors insert comments for their own benefit – such as a reminder to add further text or to check particular facts. A few important points about comments in Word:

- Comments do not change the body of a document. Think of a comment as a kind of electronic Post-it™ note.
- The presence of a comment in a document is indicated by a comment mark. Double-click a comment mark to display the comment text in a separate *comment pane* at the bottom of the document window.
- Word numbers comments automatically, and labels each comment to identify the person making the comment.
- Comments can be edited and removed.

The Reviewing toolbar

Word offers a special toolbar for working with comments. To display it, choose **View | Toolbars | Reviewing**. Only four buttons are relevant to comments.

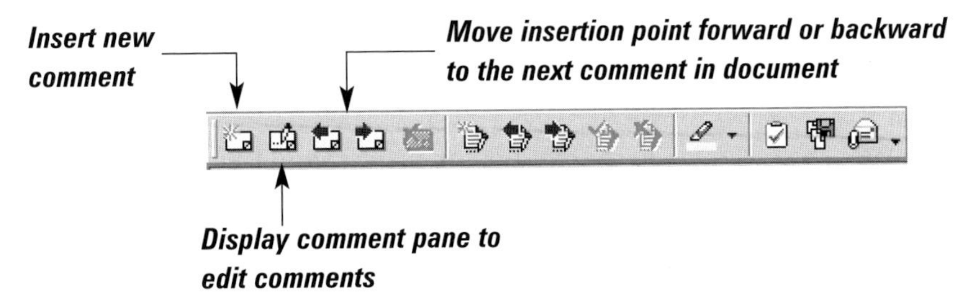

Comment

A short note or annotation applied to a particular location in a document. Comments do not affect a document's content.

Comments and printing

By default, Word does not print comments. To change this, choose **File | Print**, click **Options**, click the *Comments* checkbox and click **OK**, **OK**.

Include with document

- [ ] Document properties
- [ ] Field codes
- [x] Comments
- [ ] Hidden text
- [x] Drawing objects

Word then prints the comments at the end of the document, beginning on a new page.

Comments and document protection

To ensure that your reviewers insert only comments and do not otherwise change your document, you can *password-protect* your document against modification.

Comments: the benefits for authors and reviewers

In the past, authors typically gathered feedback on a document by printing multiple copies, circulating the copies to reviewers, collecting the reviewed copies, and reading and implementing the reviewers' comments. Reviewers generally wrote their comments or annotations by hand on the printed review copies.

Word's comment feature streamlines the review process in three ways:

- **Electronic document distribution**. Documents can be circulated for review in electronic rather than printed form, eliminating the need for printing, photocopying and physical distribution.
- **Electronic comment capture**. Annotations are entered directly on the document file, removing the legibility problems that arise from difficult-to-read handwriting.
- **Single document version**. Because Word automatically identifies the person who inserts each comment, the same Word file can be reviewed successively by different people. This eliminates the version-management issues associated with multiple review copies of the same document.

Working with comments: the four tasks

Here are the four comment-related tasks you need to be able to perform:

- **Insert a comment in a document**. Exercise 10.1 takes you through the steps.
- **Display and hide comments**. You will learn about the various comment displays options in the text following Exercise 10.1.

- **Edit an existing comment**. You can edit comment text in the same way that you edit text in a document. See Exercise 10.2.
- **Remove a comment**. Typically, you will want to remove comments when preparing a final draft of a document. Exercise 10.3 shows you how.

Exercise 10.1: Insert a comment in a document

1) Start Word and open the following file:

   `Chapter10_Exercise_10-1_Before.doc`

2) Is the Reviewing toolbar displayed? If not, display it now by choosing **View | Toolbars | Reviewing**.
3) In the first line of the text under the document title, click just before the word 'committed'.

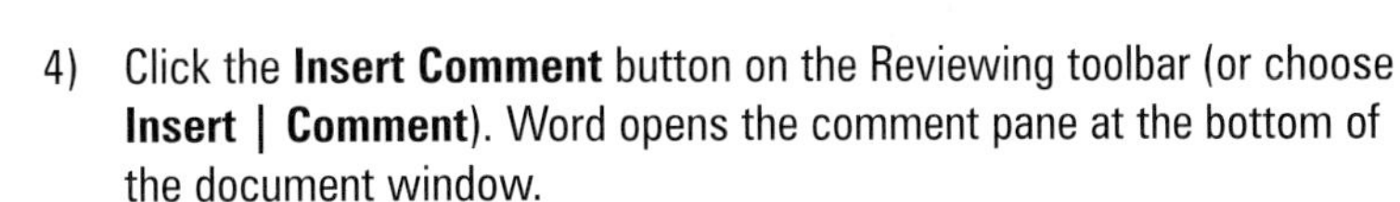

Elmsworth·Health·Trust:·Patients'·Charter¶
At·Elmsworth·Health·Trust,·we·are·committed·to·delivering·a·world-class·service.·Our·

Click here

Insert Comment button

4) Click the **Insert Comment** button on the Reviewing toolbar (or choose **Insert | Comment**). Word opens the comment pane at the bottom of the document window.
5) Type the comment 'totally' in the comment pane.

Comments From: All Reviewers
Close
[EE1]totally¶

   You can resize the comment pane by dragging the grey border between it and the document.

6) When finished, click **Close** on the comment pane.

Show/Hide button

7) Is the **Show/Hide** button on the Standard toolbar selected? If not, click it now.

   Notice that Word displays a comment mark in the document to indicate that a comment is present at that location.

Elmsworth·Health·Trust:·Patients'·Charter¶
At·Elmsworth·Health·Trust,·we·are·committed·[EE1]to·delivering·a·world-class·service.·

Comment mark

8) Close and save your sample document with the following name:

   Chapter10_Exercise_10-1_After_*Your_Name*.doc

Comments and hidden text

Comments are examples of Word's hidden text – text that can be hidden from display and shown only when you want to view it.

If you want to display hidden text at all times, and not just when the **Show/Hide** button on the Standard toolbar is selected:

- Choose **Tools | Options** and click the **View** tab.
- Select the *Hidden text* checkbox and click **OK**.

Another useful option on the **View** tab within the *Options* dialog box is the *ScreenTips* checkbox. When you select this, Word:

- Displays a yellow background behind comments, regardless of whether the **Show/Hide** button on the Standard toolbar is selected.
- Displays a yellow pop-up box when you position the cursor over a comment mark.

If your document contains comments from different reviewers, Word highlights each reviewer's comments with a different background colour.

Comment marks

If your document has been commented on by different reviewers, how can you tell which comments were made by individual reviewers?

Whenever a comment is inserted in a document, Word attaches the reviewer's details to that comment. Word takes the reviewer's details from the **User Information** tab of the dialog box accessed from **Tools | Options**. This information is entered during Word installation, but it may be amended at any stage.

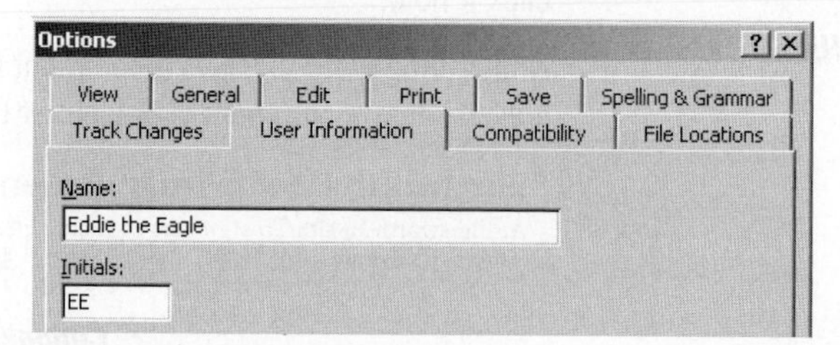

When using another person's PC to insert comments, you can use **Tools | Options** to change the user information details, and then change them back again when you have completed your comments.

In addition to user details, Word also attaches a sequentially increasing number to each comment, and displays the unique comment number in the comment mark. Word automatically updates the comment numbers as you add new comments and remove existing ones.

Comment mark
A mark that indicates the presence of a comment in a document. Comment marks identify the comment maker and show the comment's unique number.

Exercise 10.2: Edit a comment

1) Open the following file:

    `Chapter10_Exercise_10-2_Before.doc`

2) Is the Reviewing toolbar displayed? If not, display it now by choosing **View | Toolbars | Reviewing**.

3) Double-click the comment mark after the word 'committed'.

    Elmsworth Health Trust: Patients' Charter

    At Elmsworth Health Trust, we are committed [EE1]to delivering a world-class service.

    Double-click here

    Word opens the comment pane at the bottom of the document window.

4) In the comment pane, change the text 'totally' to 'totally and absolutely'.

5) When finished, click **Close** on the comment pane.

6) Close and save your sample document with the following name:

    Chapter10_Exercise_10-2_After_*Your_Name*.doc

Exercise 10.3: Remove a comment

1) Open the following file:

    `Chapter10_Exercise_10-3_Before.doc`

2) Is the Reviewing toolbar displayed? If not, display it now by choosing **View | Toolbars | Reviewing**.

3) Right-click the comment mark after the word 'committed' to display a pop-up menu.

Elmsworth Health Trust: Patients' Charter

At Elmsworth Health Trust, we are committed [E... ass service.

Our standards apply whether you are:

- A patient
- A relative or friend of a patient
- Someone simply seeking advice.

This Patient Charter sets out what we can do for ... led to.

Mission Statement

The purpose of the Elmsworth Health Trust is to:

- Promote good health

Cut
Copy
Paste
Edit Comment
Delete Comment
Font...
Paragraph...
Bullets and Numbering...

4) Choose **Delete Comment** to remove the comment and close the pop-up menu.

5) Close and save your sample document with the following name:

`Chapter10_Exercise_10-3_After_`*`Your_Name`*`.doc`

Document protection

To ensure that your reviewers insert only comments and do not alter the document itself, use Word's document-protection feature.

Word offers two kinds of password protection:

- **Document-open password protection**. You can protect a document so that it cannot be opened without the user entering the correct password.
- **Document-modify password protection**. You can protect a document so that it can be opened for reading by anyone, but only people who know the correct password can modify the document.

  This second option is suitable for documents that you want to circulate to reviewers, because reviewers can insert comments in a document-modify protected file without knowing the correct password.

  Note, however, that this option does not prevent someone saving your Word document under a new file name, and then making changes to it.

The procedures for applying the document-open and document-modify protections methods are very similar. You perform each from the same dialog box within the **File | Save As** command.

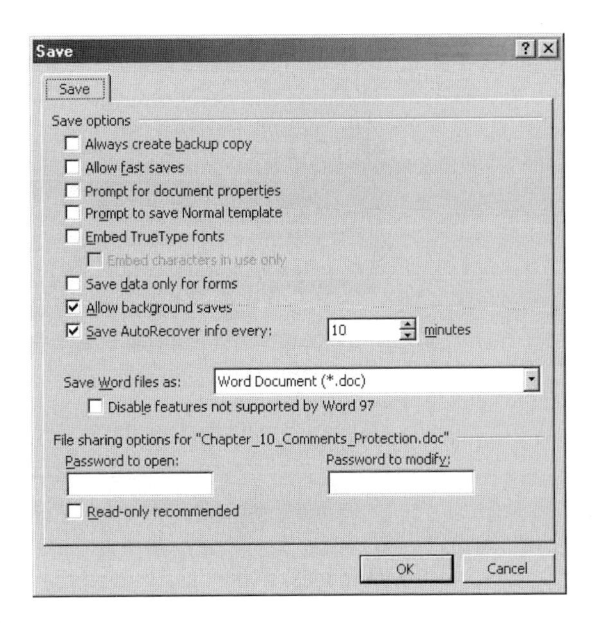

About passwords

In Word, passwords are case sensitive and can contain up to 15 characters, including letters, numerals and symbols. You might want to write down your passwords and keep them in a secure place.

If you lose the password to a document-open protected Word file, you will not be able to open it. If you lose the password to a document-modify protected Word file, you will be able to open it only in read-only mode.

Working with document protection: the two tasks

Here are the two document protection tasks you need to be able to perform:

- **Add password protection to a document**. See Exercise 10.4.
- **Remove password protection from a document**. See Exercise 10.5.

Exercise 10.4: Add password protection to a document

1) Open the following file:

   `Chapter10_Exercise_10-4_Before.doc`

2) Choose **File | Save As**.
3) Click the **Tools** button in the dialog box, and from the pop-up menu select **General Options**.

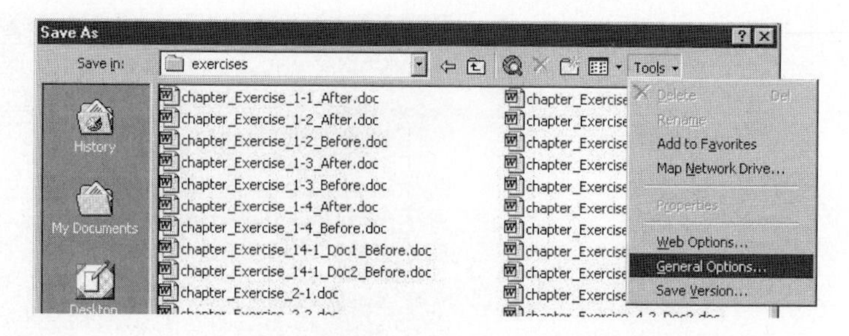

4) At the bottom of the dialog box, in the *Password to modify* box, type a password.

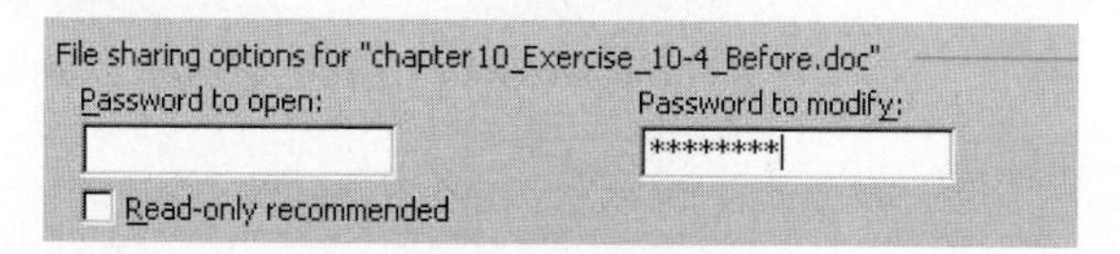

Word masks your password as you type it, displaying only asterisks.

5) Click **OK**. Word displays the *Confirm Password* dialog box.

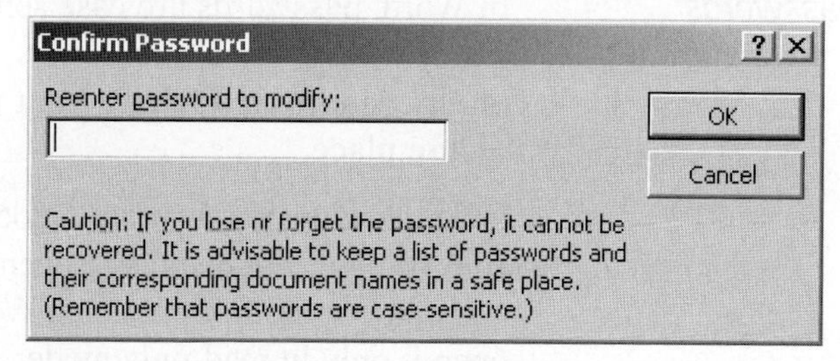

6) Retype your password and click **OK**.

7) You are returned to the *Save As* dialog box. In the *File name* box, type the following file name:

`Chapter10_Exercise_10-4_After_`*`Your_Name`*`.doc`

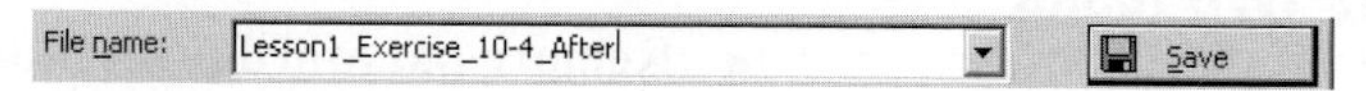

8) Click **Save**.

You can now close your sample document.

Exercise 10.5: Remove password protection from a document

1) Open the following file:

`Chapter10_Exercise_10-5_Before.doc`

2) Word prompts you to enter a password.

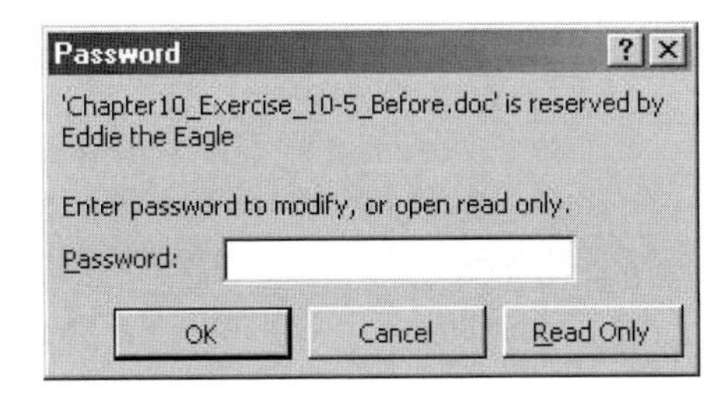

3) Type the following password and click **OK**.

   `blah`

4) Word now opens your sample document. You now need to resave the document – but without the password protection.

   Choose **File | Save As**, click the **Tools** button and choose **General Options**.

5) Delete the password from the *Password to modify* box and click **OK**.

6) You are returned to the **Save As** dialog box. In the *File name* box, type the following file name:

   `Chapter10_Exercise_10-5_After_`*`Your_Name`*`.doc`

7) Click **Save**.

   You can now close your sample document.

   You can also use the procedure described in this exercise to change the password that protects a document.

Lesson 10: quick reference

Reviewing toolbar: comment buttons

Keys	Description
	Inserts a new comment at the insertion point in the current document.
	Displays the comment pane at the foot of the document window, enabling you to edit comments.
	Moves the insertion point forward to the location of the next comment in the document.
	Moves the insertion point back to the location of the previous comment in the document.

Tasks summary: comments

Task	Procedure
Insert a comment at the insertion point in the document.	Click the **Insert Comment** button on the Reviewing toolbar or choose **Insert | Comment**. Type the comment text and click **Close**.
Show/hide comments.	Click the **Show/Hide** button on the Standard toolbar.
Always show comments.	Choose **Tools | Options**, click the **View** tab, click the *Hidden text* checkbox, and click **OK**.
Show/hide coloured background behind comments.	Choose **Tools | Options**, click the **View** tab, select the *ScreenTips* checkbox, and click **OK.**
Edit a comment.	Double-click the comment mark to display the comment pane. Edit the text and click **Close**.
Delete a comment.	Right-click the comment mark and choose **Delete Comment** from the pop-up menu.

Tasks summary: password protection

Task	Procedure
Apply password protection to a document.	Choose **File | Save As**, click the **Tools** button, choose **General Options**, enter open and/or modify password(s), click **OK**, retype password(s), click **OK** and click **Save**.
Remove password protection from a document.	Choose **File | Save As**, click the **Tools** button, choose **General Options**, delete and/or modify password(s), click **OK** and click **Save**.

Concepts summary: comments

Word's *comments* feature enables reviewers to insert annotations or short notes in a document.

The presence of a comment in a document is indicated by a *comment mark*, which shows a sequential comment number and the identity of the comment-maker. Double-clicking a comment mark displays the comment text in a separate *comment pane* at the bottom of the document window.

Once inserted, comments can be edited and removed as required.

By default, Word does not print comments. If comments are selected for printing, Word prints them on a separate page at the end of the document.

Comments do not change the content of a document. Think of a comment as a kind of electronic Post-it™ note.

Concepts summary: password protection

Word allows you to *protect* a document so that it may not be opened without the entry of the correct password; alternatively, it may be opened but not modified without the entry of the correct password.

In Word, *passwords* are case sensitive and can contain up to 15 characters, including letters, numerals and symbols.

When a document is password-protected against modification, users who do not enter the correct password may open the document in *read-only* mode only. Users may insert comments in a read-only document, however. This makes this type of password protection suitable for documents circulated to reviewers.

Password-protecting a Word document against modification does not prevent anyone saving the document under a new file name and then making changes to it.

Chapter 10: quick quiz – comments

Circle the correct answer to each of the following multiple-choice questions about comments in Word.

Q1	In Word, a comment is ...
A.	A text amendment in a Word document that is highlighted with a revision mark.
B.	A text item that is attached at a particular location in a Word document.
C.	One item in a list of amendments made to a document, and contained in a separate, automatically-created file
D.	An annotation stored in the **File | Document Properties** dialog box.

Q2	Which of the following is not an advantage of using the comments feature in Word?
A.	Documents can be circulated for commenting in electronic rather than printed form.
B.	You are provided with a separate file containing all comments.
C.	Comments can be typed directly to the document file, rather than handwritten on a print-out.
D.	Each comment is labelled with the identity of the reviewer.

Q3	Which action do you take to insert a new comment in a Word document?
A.	Click the **New Comment** button on the Standard toolbar.
B.	Choose **Tools | Comment | New**.
C.	Choose **Insert | Comment**.
D.	Click the **New Comment** button on the Formatting toolbar.

Q4	In a Word document, which action do you take to ensure that comments are always displayed?
A.	Choose **Tools | Options**, click the **View** tab, select the *Show comments* checkbox, and click **OK**.
B.	Click the **Show Comments** button on the Reviewing toolbar.
C.	Choose **Tools | Options**, click the **View** tab, select the *Hidden text* checkbox, and click **OK**.
D.	Choose **Tools | Options**, click the **Comments** tab, select the *Show comments in document* checkbox, and click **OK**.

Q5	You want to edit a comment in a Word document. Which action do you *not* take?
A.	Right-click the comment mark and choose **Remove Comment** from the pop-up menu.
B.	Click the **Edit Comment** button on the Reviewing toolbar to display the comment text in the comment pane.
C.	Click anywhere in the comment mark and choose **Insert | Comments | Edit**.
D.	Double-click the comment mark to display the comment text in the comment pane.

Q6	You want to delete a comment from a Word document. Which action do you take?
A.	Right-click the comment mark and choose **Delete Comment** from the pop-up menu.
B.	Double-click the comment mark and choose **Delete Comment** from the pop-up menu.
C.	Choose **Insert | Comments | Remove**.
D.	Double-click the comment mark to display the comment pane, delete the comment and its label, and click **Close**.

Q7	To ensure Word always displays a coloured background behind comments you ...
A.	Choose **Tools | Options**, click the **View** tab, select the *ScreenTips* checkbox, and click **OK**.
B.	Click the **Show Comments** button on the Reviewing toolbar.
C.	Choose **Tools | Options**, click the **Comments** tab, select the *Show colored background* checkbox, and click **OK**.
D.	Choose **Tools | Options**, click the **View** tab, select the *Comment background* checkbox, and click **OK**.

Answers

1: B, **2:** B, **3:** C, **4:** C, *5:* A, **6:** A, **7:** A.

Chapter 10: quick quiz – password protection

Circle the correct answer to each of the following multiple-choice questions about password protection in Word.

Q1	Which of the following is a valid type of password protection in Word?
A.	Document-delete password protection.
B.	Document-format password protection.
C.	Document-modify password protection.
D.	Document-template password protection.

Q2	Which statement correctly describes document-modify password protection in Word?
A.	Without knowing the correct password, a user may not modify the document content but may insert comments in the document.
B.	Without knowing the correct password, a user may open the document but the document text is masked behind asterisks.
C.	Without knowing the correct password, a user may not modify the document content and may not insert comments in the document.
D.	Without knowing the correct password, a user may not open the document.

Q3	Which statement correctly describes document-open password protection in Word?
A.	Without knowing the correct password, a user may open the document but may not modify it in any way.
B.	Without knowing the correct password, a user may open the document but the document text is masked behind asterisks.
C.	Without knowing the correct password, a user may not modify the document content but may insert comments in the document.
D.	Without knowing the correct password, a user may not open the document.

Q4	Which of these statements about password protection of documents in Word is true?
A.	A user must specify the same password to protect a document against opening and against modification.
B.	The document-modify password protection feature prevents a user from resaving a Word document under a new file name and then making changes to it.
C.	A user may specify one password to protect a document against opening, and a different password to protect it against modification.
D.	Word stores on your PC a list of your document passwords that you can view in the event of you forgetting or losing a password.

Q5	Which of these statements about passwords in Word is untrue?
A.	Passwords can contain up to 15 characters.
B.	Passwords are case-sensitive.
C.	Passwords may include letters, numerals and symbols.
D.	Passwords, once entered, may not be amended.

Q6	Which command in Word do you choose to work with the password-protection options?
A.	**Tools | Security.**
B.	**File | Properties.**
C.	**Format | Password Protection.**
D.	**File | Save As.**

Answers

1: C, **2:** A, **3:** D, **4:** C, **5**: D, **6:** D.

11 Displaying, accepting and rejecting revisions: change tracking

Objectives

In this chapter you will learn how to:

- Switch change tracking on and off
- Display and hide tracked changes
- Control how tracked changes are displayed
- Accept and reject tracked changes

New words

In this chapter you will meet the following terms:

- Change tracking
- Compare documents

Exercise files

In this chapter you will work with the following Word files:

- `Chapter11_Exercise_11_4_Original_Before.doc`
- `Chapter11_Exercise_11_4_Edited_Before.doc`

Syllabus reference

In this chapter you will cover the following items from the ECDL Advanced Word Processing Syllabus:

- **AM3.1.4.3**. Use highlighting options to track changes in a document.
- **AM3.1.4.4**. Accept or reject changes in a document.

About change tracking

Change tracking is a feature that records amendments made to a Word document by highlighting them with the following *revision marks*:

- **New text**. Word identifies text added to a document by formatting it in colour with underlining.
- **Deleted text**. Word identifies deleted text by formatting it in colour with strikethrough.

- **All amended text**. Word indicates all text additions and deletions by placing a vertical bar in the document's left margin.

> **Discharge from Hospital**
>
> ~~We~~ Staff will ensure that you and your family are involved in the planning of your discharge from hospital, where practical.
>
> A discharge plan will be provided for your continuing health and social care needs. This will be communicated to your General Practitioner. Your GP will be notified ~~promptly~~ in a reasonable period of time regarding ~~of~~ your discharge.

Change tracking helps authors locate the changes made by others to a Word document, identify who made the changes, and then accept or reject each change as required.

When different reviewers make changes to the same document, Word highlights each person's additions or deletions in a different colour.

The Reviewing toolbar

Word offers a special toolbar for working with tracked changes. To display it, choose **View | Toolbars | Reviewing**. Five buttons are relevant to change tracking.

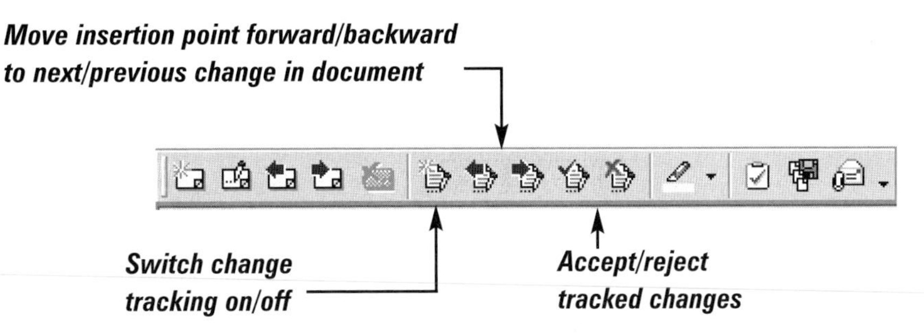

Change tracking: the benefits to you

Change tracking offers two main benefits. It:

- **Highlights relevant areas**. The vertical bar in the left margin helps you locate reviewers' edits quickly. For long documents, this is a significant time-saver.
- **Saves retyping of reviewer feedback**. When you meet a change that you want to accept, a single mouse click is all that is needed to insert the change.

Change tracking

A feature that tracks additions or deletions made by reviewers to a Word document, highlights the changes with revision marks, and enables the author or editor to accept or reject such revisions.

Working with tracked changes: the four tasks

Here are the four tasks that you need to be able to perform with Word's tracked changes feature:

- **Switch change tracking on and off**. Change tracking is not appropriate for every document that you and your colleagues work on. Exercise 11.1 shows you how to switch this feature on and off.
- **Hide and display change tracking as you work**. Word gives you the option of displaying or hiding revisions marks as you work. See Exercise 11.2.
- **Control how tracked changes are displayed**. As Exercise 11.3 shows, Word allows you customize the display of tracked changes.
- **Accept or reject tracked changes**. Some changes from reviewers you will want to accept; others you will want to reject. Exercise 11.4 takes you through the steps of performing both tasks.

Exercise 11.1: Switch change tracking on and off

By default, change tracking is not activated in Word. To use it, you first need to turn it on. When you no longer want to track your changes, you can turn it off again.

Before performing this exercise, start Word and open a new, blank document. Change tracking is available only when you have at least one document open.

Track Changes button

1) Double-click the **TRK** button on the Status Bar at the foot of the main Word window. Alternatively, click the **Track Changes** button on the Reviewing toolbar. Repeat this step to switch change tracking off again.

Exercise 11.2: Hide and display change tracking on screen

With change tracking switched on, you may not always want to view your revisions recorded on screen as you work. This exercise shows you how to hide or display change tracking as you type.

Before performing this Exercise, first open a new, blank Word document. The **Tools | Track Changes** menu command is available only when you have at least one document open.

1) Choose **Tools | Track Changes | Highlight Changes**.
2) As required, deselect or select the *Highlight changes on screen* checkbox.

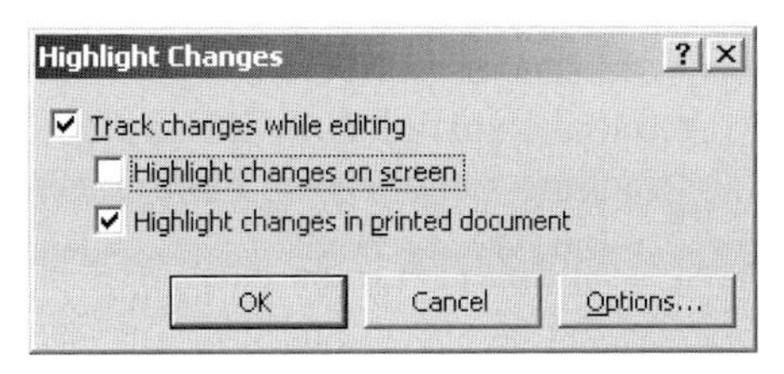

(Ensure that the *Track changes while editing* checkbox is selected.)

3) Click **OK**.

Exercise 11.3: Controlling how Word displays tracked changes

Revision marks indicate where a deletion, insertion or other editing change has been made in a document. This exercise shows how you can customize Word's display of revision marks.

Before performing this exercise, first open a new, blank Word document. The **Tools | Track Changes** menu command is available only when you have at least one document open.

1) Choose **Tools | Track Changes | Highlight Changes**, and click the **Options** button.
2) Word displays a dialog box that allows you to amend the mark and colour that you want applied to different kinds of revisions.

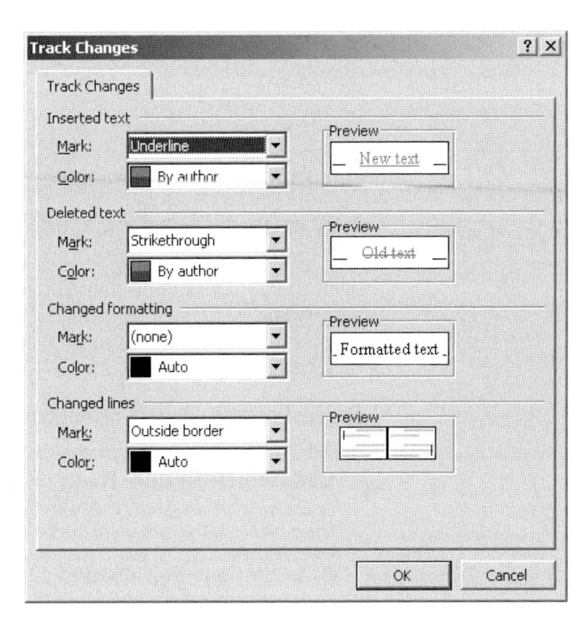

3) Make your amendments as required and click **OK**, **OK** to return to your document.

Accepting or rejecting tracked changes

You send a Word document to a reviewer. You ask the reviewer to make any edits directly in the document, with change tracking switched on. The reviewer then returns the document to you. What's next?

As the document author, you can use change tracking, in combination with another Word feature called compare documents, to:

- Identify the amendments made to a document.
- Accept or reject each amendment as appropriate, without having to retype amendments you accept.

Compare documents
A feature that identifies differences between two open Word documents, typically the original document and a second, edited copy of the original.

Exercise 11.4: Accept or reject tracked changes

In this exercise, you will open and work with two documents: an original document without tracked changes, and an edited document with tracked changes.

1) Open the following file, which represents the original, unedited document:

   `Chapter11_Exercise_11_4_Original_Before.doc`

2) Choose **Tools | Track Changes | Compare Documents**.

   Word opens the *Select File to Compare With Current Document* dialog box, prompting you to select the edited document against which you want to compare the original document. Select the following file and click **Open**:

   `Chapter11_Exercise_11_4_Edited_Before.doc`

   The first part of the original document should look like this:

   Elmsworth·Health·Trust:·Patients'·Charter¶

   At·Elmsworth·Health·Trust~~is~~,·we·are·committed·to·delivering·a·world-class·service.·Our·standards·apply·whether·you·are:¶

   - A·patient¶
   - A·relative·or·friend·of·a·patient¶
   - Someone·simply·seeking·advice.¶

   ~~Our~~This·Patient·Charter·sets·out·what·we·can·do·for·you·and·what·you·are·entitled·to.¶

   One way to accept or reject the reviewer's changes is to scroll through the document, locate each change, click anywhere in it, and then click the **Accept Change** or **Reject Change** button on the Reviewing toolbar.

Another method – one that gives you more information and options – is to choose **Tools | Track Changes | Accept or Reject Changes**. This displays the *Accept or Reject Changes* dialog box shown below.

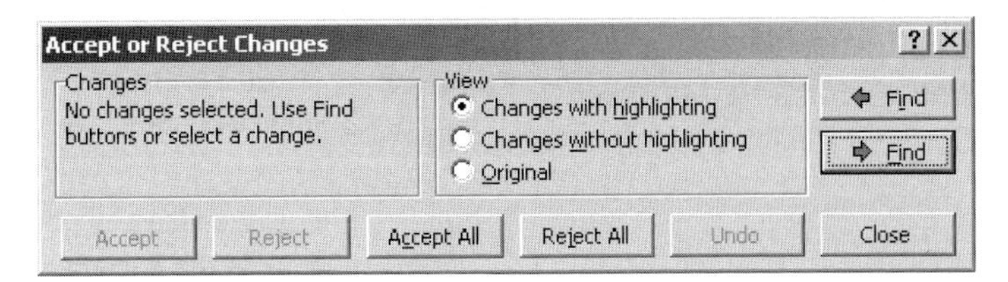

3) Click **-> Find** to tell Word to locate the first tracked change in the document.

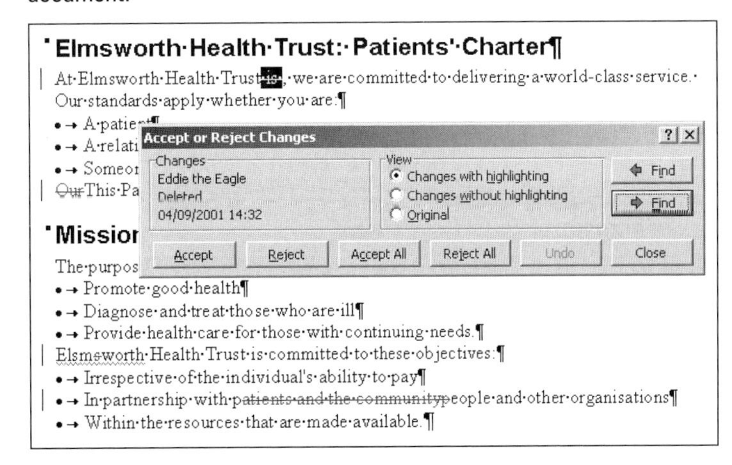

4) Click the **Accept** button to accept each change as Word leads you through the document.

5) When Word has presented you with all the tracked changes, it displays the following message box:

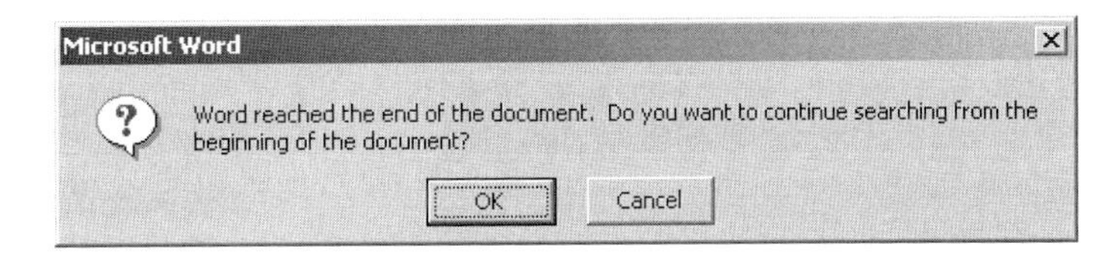

Click **Cancel**, and then click **Close** to close the *Accept or Reject Changes* dialog box.

6) Close and save your sample document under the following file name:

`Chapter11_Exercise_11_4_Final_Draft.doc`

Chapter 11: quick reference

Reviewing toolbar: change tracking buttons

Button	Description
	Switches change tracking on or off.
	Moves the insertion point forward to the location of the next change in the document.
	Moves the insertion point back to the location of the previous change in the document.
	Accepts the selected change.
	Rejects the selected change.

Tasks summary

Task	Procedure
Turn change tracking on/off.	Double-click the **TRK** button on the Status Bar or click the **Track Changes** button on the Reviewing toolbar.
Show/hide revision marks on screen.	Choose **Tools | Track Changes | Highlight Changes**, select/deselect the *Highlight changes on screen* checkbox, and click **OK**.
Customize display of revision marks.	Choose **Tools | Track Changes | Highlight Changes**, click **Options**, customize the revision mark options, and click **OK**, **OK**.
Accept/reject tracked changes by comparing the original with the edited document.	Open the original document, choose **Tools | Track Changes | Compare Documents**, select the edited document and click **Open**.
	Choose **Tools | Track Changes | Accept or Reject Changes** and click **->Find**.
	Click **Accept** or **Reject** as Word leads you through the tracked changes in the document.
	When finished, click **Cancel** and **Close** when prompted.

Concepts summary

Change tracking is a feature that highlights amendments made to a Word with *revision marks*. New text is formatted in colour with underlining, and deleted text is formatted in colour with strikethrough. When different reviewers make changes to the same document, Word highlights each person's additions or deletions in a different colour.

Word flags all changes, whether additions or deletions, by positioning a *vertical bar* in the document's left margin. Word allows you to customize how you format the on-screen revision marks.

When you type and edit text with change tracking switched on, you may find the display of revision marks distracting. You can opt to hide the revision marks. Later, when you want to inspect your work, you can then switch them back on again.

An advantage of change tracking is that when used with the *compare documents* feature, it allows you to work with two documents – an original and an edited document – and selectively accept or reject changes made in the edited document.

Chapter 11: quick quiz

Circle the correct answer to each of the following multiple-choice questions about change tracking in Word.

Q1	Change tracking in Word is ...
A.	A feature that automatically corrects errors of spelling and grammar in a document.
B.	A feature that automatically generates a second copy of a document, and stores any changes separately in the second document.
C.	A feature that highlights changes with revision marks, and facilitates the acceptance or rejection of such changes.
D.	A feature that formats changes as hyperlinks, and offers the option to insert such changes by clicking on the hyperlinks.

Q2	By default, which revision mark does Word's change tracking feature use to indicate new text added to document?
A.	Colour with single-line underlining.
B.	Colour with double-line underlining.
C.	Colour with italics.
D.	Colour with strikethrough.

Q3	By default, which revision mark does Word's change tracking feature use to indicate text deleted from a document?
A.	Colour with single-line underlining.
B.	Colour with italics.
C.	Colour with bold.
D.	Colour with strikethrough.

Q4	By default, how does Word's change tracking feature indicate a change of any kind made to a document?
A.	Word places a grey background behind the amended text.
B.	Word places a vertical bar in the document's left margin.
C.	Word places a solid border around the amended text.
D.	Word places a vertical bar in the document's right margin.

Q5	Which action do you take to turn on change tracking in Word?
A.	Right-click the **TRK** button on the Status Bar at the foot of the main Word window.
B.	Choose **Tools | Change Tracking I On**.
C.	Double-click the **TRK** button on the Status Bar at the foot of the main Word window.
D.	Choose **Format | Track Changes**.

Q6	With change tracking switched on in Word, which action do you take to hide revision marks on the screen?
A.	Click the **Hide Revision Marks** button on the Reviewing toolbar.
B.	Choose **Tools | Track Changes | Highlight Changes**, deselect the *Highlight changes on screen* checkbox, and click **OK**.
C.	Double-click the **TRK** button on the Status Bar at the foot of the main Word window.
D.	Choose **Tools | Track Changes | Revision Marks**, deselect the *Highlight changes on screen* checkbox, and click **OK**.

Q7	**In Word, which command do you choose to compare an original document with an edited copy of the same document?**
A.	Open both documents, switch to the original document, and choose **Tools | Documents | Compare**.
B.	Open the edited document, choose **Tools | Track Changes | Compare Documents**, select the original document, and click **Open**.
C.	Open both documents, switch to the original document, and choose **Tools | Track Changes | Compare Documents**.
D.	Open the original document, choose **Tools | Track Changes | Compare Documents**, select the edited document, and click **Open.**

Q8	**Which of the following is not an advantage of Word's change tracking feature?**
A.	All amendments are highlighted, making them easier to locate.
B.	Errors in spelling and grammar are corrected automatically.
C.	The process of accepting or rejecting reviewers' amendments is simplified.
D.	All amendments are labelled with the identity of the reviewer, making document management easier.

Answers

1: C, **2:** A, **3:** D, **4:** B, **5:** C, **6:** B, **7:** D, **8:** B.

12 Many subdocuments, one document: master documents

Objectives

In this chapter you will learn how to:

- Save a style and a style modification in a template
- Base a new document on a selected template
- Change the template on which a document is based
- Apply Word's AutoFormat feature to a plain, unformatted document

New words

In this chapter you will meet the following terms:

- Master document
- Subdocument

Exercise files

In this chapter you will work with the following Word files:

- `Chapter12_Exercise_12-1_Before.doc`
- `Chapter12_Exercise_12-2_Before.doc`
- `Chapter12_Exercise_12-2_SubDoc1.doc`
- `Chapter12_Exercise_12-2_SubDoc2.doc`
- `Chapter12_Exercise_12-2_SubDoc3.doc`
- `Chapter12_Exercise_12-2_SubDoc4.doc`
- `Chapter12_Exercise_12-3_Before.doc`
- `Chapter12_Exercise_12-4_Before.doc`

Syllabus reference

In this chapter you will cover the following items of the ECDL Advanced Word Processing Syllabus:

- **AM3.2.1.1**: Create a new master document.
- **AM3.2.1.2**: Create a subdocument based on heading styles within a master document.
- **AM3.2.1.3**: Add or remove a subdocument within a master document.

What are master documents?

In Word, a *master document* is a file that can contain links to a series of individual Word documents called *subdocuments*. Master documents are used most commonly in networked environments because they enable different people on different PCs to work separately on different parts of a single large publication, such as a business plan, technical manual or annual report.

Master documents: the benefits to you

Imagine that you are a manager responsible for a publication project that consists of several, individual Word documents, some or all of which are written by different people. What benefits can you expect from using Word's master document feature?

- **Consistent style formatting**. Because all subdocuments are based on the template of the master document, it is easier for the manager to enforce common formatting standards throughout all the subdocuments in the publication.
- **Multi-document editing**. The manager can open and display all subdocuments in the master document at once, rearrange their order, and move text and graphics within and between subdocuments.
- **Automatic updating**. When any material is moved within or between subdocuments in the master document, Word automatically updates all numbered headings, footnotes, cross-references and page numbers to reflect their new location.
- **Multi-document navigation**.A single table of contents and index can be created and kept up to date for all the subdocuments in the master document.
- **Multi-document printing**. The manager can print all subdocuments in the master document in a single operation.

Different writers who work on individual subdocuments also gain from the use of the master document feature:

- **File size efficiency**. It is easier and faster to work on a small Word document than on a large one: the file opens and saves more quickly, and there is less need to navigate through large amounts of text.
- **Parallel production**. Individual writers can work on different subdocuments at the same time and focus only on their own contribution.

Master documents and outlines

Master documents are very similar to outlines: the publication manager works with master documents in Outline view, and the options needed are available as buttons on the Outlining toolbar.

You will learn the purpose of the toolbar buttons as you use them in the exercises. A list of buttons and their functions is included at the end of this chapter for easy reference.

Master documents

A Word file that can act as a container for one or more individual Word documents, called subdocuments. Within a master document, subdocuments can be opened, formatted and edited as if they were single documents.

Working with master documents: the four tasks

Here are the four master document tasks that you need to be able to perform:

- **Create a new master document and new subdocuments**. Exercise 12.1 shows you how to create a new master document, and then create subdocuments within it.
- **Create a new master document with inserted subdocuments**. In Exercise 12.2, you create a new master document by inserting existing Word documents as subdocuments within the master document.
- **Add a subdocument to a master document**. The procedure for adding subdocuments to a master document is similar to that for creating a master document by the insertion of subdocuments. See Exercise 12.3.
- **Remove a subdocument from a master document**. No longer need a subdocument within a master document? Exercise 12.4 shows you how to remove a subdocument.

Working with new master documents

In effect, a master document is a Word document that contains one or more subdocuments. Word allows you to create subdocuments, and as a result, transform your currently open document into a master document, in either of two ways. You can convert outline headings to new subdocuments or insert existing documents as subdocuments. Let's examine each approach in more detail.

Converting outline headings to new subdocuments

Here are the main steps in this approach:

- You begin by creating a new document or opening an existing one. This document will become your master document.
- You switch to Outline view. If this is a new document, you create your outline headings. If it is an existing document, you ensure that your headings are formatted with heading styles.
- Finally, you designate some or all of your outline headings as subdocuments by selecting them and clicking the **Create Subdocument** button on the Outlining toolbar.

Create Subdocument button

Because your current document now contains subdocuments, it is a master document.

Exercise 12.1 provides an example of this approach.

Inserting existing documents as subdocuments

Here are the main steps in this approach:

- You create a new document or open an existing one.
- You switch to Outline view.
- You insert one or more existing Word documents as subdocuments in your open document. You do this using the **Insert Subdocument** button on the Outlining toolbar.

Insert Subdocument button

This is the approach that you follow in Exercise 12.2.

Which is the better way to create master documents?

Creating an outline and then converting the outline headings to subdocuments gives you more control over the document management process. In practice, however, a publication manager is often asked to build a master document from a number of already-written documents.

On many occasions, a hybrid approach may be necessary: you may begin with a new outline, convert some outline headings to subdocuments, and then insert some already-written documents into your master document.

Saving a master document

You save a master document as you would any Word document – by pressing **CTRL+S**, clicking the **Save** button on the Standard toolbar, or choosing **File | Save** – but the effect is very different.

When you save a master document containing outline headings that you have selected for conversion to subdocuments, Word:

- Creates a new, separate file for each subdocument.
- Assigns subdocument file names based on the text of the outline headings.
- Stores the subdocuments in the same folder as the master document.

If you are managing a multi-author document on a PC network, it's a good idea to create a special folder for holding the master document and the subdocuments, and inform your colleagues of its location.

Exercise 12.1: Convert outline headings to subdocuments

In this exercise you, will open a Word document, display it in Outline view, designate all the level-1 headings as subdocuments, and then save it as a master document with subdocuments.

1) Open Word and open the following Word file:

   `Chapter12_Exercise_12-1_Before.doc`

2) Choose **View | Outline**. As you can see, the document has been formatted using Word styles that display as outline headings in Outline view.

   You want to split your open document into a series of smaller subdocuments, with each level-1 heading indicating the start of a new subdocument.

3) Click the **Show Heading 1** button on the Outlining toolbar so that Word displays only level-1 headings.

Create Subdocument button

4) Select the four level-1 headings by dragging across them with the mouse.
5) Click the **Create Subdocument** button on the Outlining toolbar.

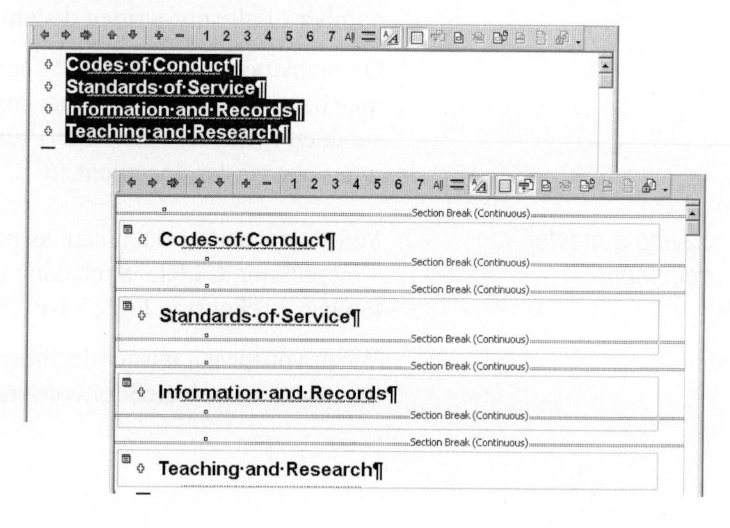

Word converts your selected outline headings to subdocuments.

Notice that it separates the subdocuments with continuous section breaks, surrounds each subdocument with a thin, grey border, and displays a subdocument icon at the top-left corner of each subdocument.

6) Click the **Show Heading 3** button on the Outlining toolbar to see how Word displays the subdocuments in this view.

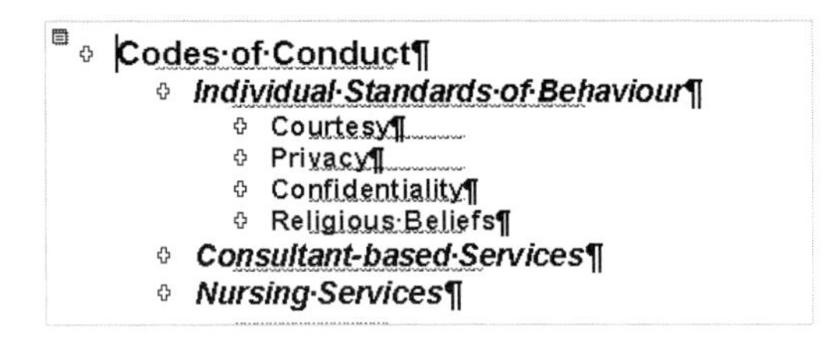

The section breaks are not shown, but a grey border still surrounds each subdocument.

7) Click the **Show All Headings** button on the Outlining toolbar to see how Word displays the subdocuments.

Both the sections breaks and the grey borders are shown in this view.

8) Save your new master document with the following file name, and close it:

`Chapter12_Exercise_12-1_After_`*`Your_Name`*`.doc`

In the final stage of this exercise, you will open your saved master document and verify that Word created the subdocuments as separate files.

9) Open the master document that you saved and named in step 8. It should look like this.

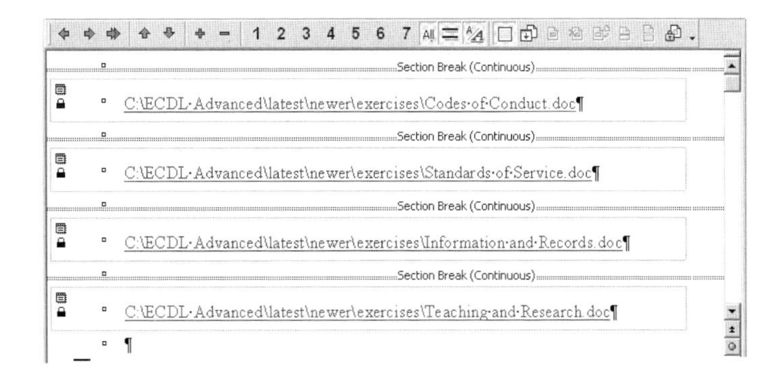

(The file path names may be different on your PC.)

10) Close your master document. Using Windows Explorer or My Computer, verify that the subdocument files, shown in your master document, actually exist on your PC.

In Exercise 12.1, you converted all level-1 headings in the outline to subdocuments. Word allows you to convert one or a selection of heading levels to a subdocument or subdocuments:

- **Single outline heading**. You can select and then convert any individual outline heading to a subdocument.
- **Selection of outline headings**. You can select and then convert a group of outline headings to subdocuments. Ensure that the *first* heading in your selection is in the heading level you want to use for splitting your document.

  For example, if you select a number of headings, the first one of which is at heading level 2, Word creates a new subdocument for every heading level 2 in your selection, even if the selection contains text formatted with heading level 1.

Exercise 12.2: Insert existing documents as subdocuments

In this exercise, you insert existing Word documents as subdocuments within a new, blank document, and then save the document as a master document.

1) Open a new, blank document and choose **View | Outline**.

Insert Subdocument button

2) On the Outlining toolbar, click the **Insert Subdocument** button to display the *Insert Subdocument* dialog box.
3) Select the following document and click the **Open** button:

   `Chapter12_Exercise_12-2_SubDoc1`

   Word inserts the selected file and moves the insertion point to the next line.
4) Repeat step 3 for the following documents:

   `Chapter12_Exercise_12-2_SubDoc2`

   `Chapter12_Exercise_12-2_SubDoc2`

   `Chapter12_Exercise_12-2_SubDoc4`

   Your master document should now look like this.

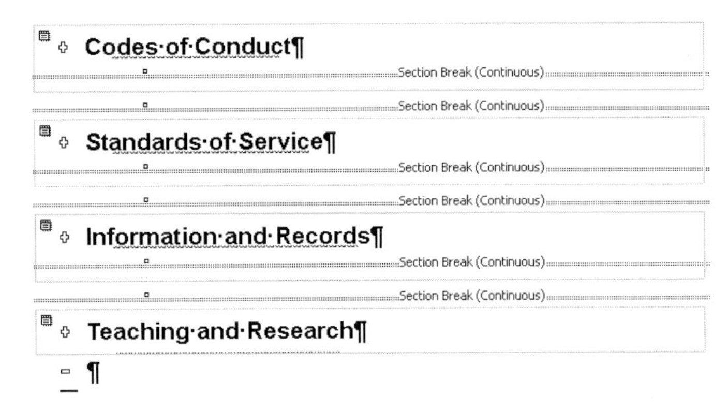

5) Save your document with the following name and close it:

   `Chapter12_Exercise_12-2_After_Your_Name.doc`

6) Open your saved master document. You should see the subdocuments as hyperlinked path and file names. As a test, click once on any subdocument to open it.

7) Close your master document and close the open subdocument.

Working with existing master documents

Here are some important points about working with master documents and subdocuments:

- **Displaying subdocuments within the master document.** When you open a master document in Outline view, the subdocuments are hidden – that is, they are collapsed into the master document and displayed only as hyperlinks.

  When the subdocuments are hidden, click the **Expand Subdocuments** button to view them. You can then switch to Normal or Print Layout view, as required.

Expand Subdocuments button

  To hide the subdocuments, click the **Collapse Subdocuments** button. The subdocuments appear as hyperlinked file names. Click on a hyperlink for Word to display a subdocument in a separate document window.

Collapse Subdocuments button

- **Working with a subdocument in the master document.** As a publication manager, you will typically work with subdocuments from within the master document.

  If the subdocuments are collapsed, just click on a subdocument name to display it. If they are expanded, switch to Normal or Print Layout view.

- **Working with subdocuments as separate files.** Individual writers open and work with subdocuments as separate Word files rather than from within the master document.

Locking subdocuments

Whenever you open a master document in Outline view, Word displays a small padlock icon to the left of each subdocument.

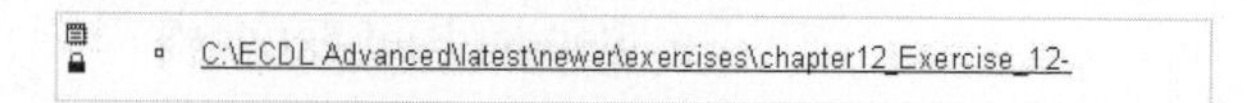

This indicates that Word has *locked* the subdocuments so that they can be displayed but not modified.

Click the **Expand Subdocuments** button on the Outlining toolbar to unlock the subdocuments. If any subdocument remains locked, it is because another person is working on it, or the author has password-protected it, or it is in a folder to which you have read-only access.

Unlock/Lock Document button

You can attempt to unlock a locked document by clicking the **Unlock/Lock Document** button on the Outlining toolbar.

Subdocument locations and filenames

It is important that individual authors do not save subdocuments to a different location or rename them. If they do, the links to the subdocuments within the master document are no longer valid, and the subdocuments disappear from the master document.

Exercise 12.3: Adding and removing subdocuments

You can add further subdocuments to a master document at any stage. The procedure is similar to the one you followed in Exercise 12.2 for building a master document by inserting subdocuments.

1) Open the master document that you created and saved in Exercise 12.2. Word opens the document in Outline view.

2) Click the **Expand Subdocuments** button on the Outlining toolbar.

Expand Subdocuments button

3) In this example, you want to add a Word document as the new third subdocument in the master document. It will be located after the 'Standards of Service' subdocument and before the 'Information and Records' subdocument.

   Click on the section break before the location where you want to insert the additional subdocument.

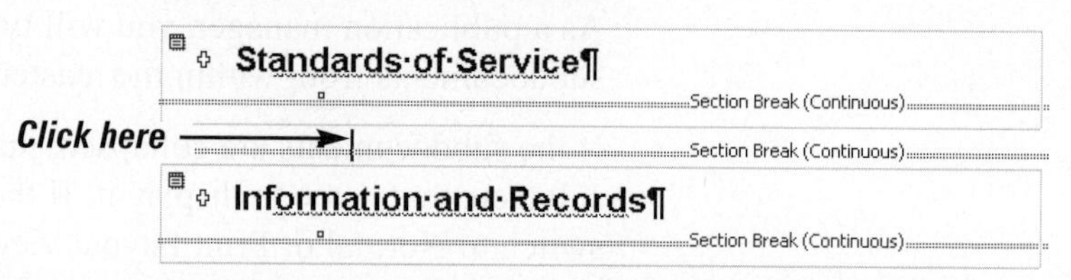

4) Press the **Enter** key to insert a new paragraph mark.

Insert Subdocument button

5) With the insertion point positioned at the new paragraph mark, click the **Insert Subdocument** button on the Outlining toolbar.

   In the *Insert Subdocument* dialog box, select the following document and click **Open**:

   `Chapter12_Exercise_12-3_SubDocNew.doc`

   Word inserts your selected document as a subdocument within the master document.

6) Close and save your document with the following name:

   `Chapter12_Exercise_12-3_After_`*`Your_Name`*`.doc`

Exercise 12.4: Removing a subdocument from a master document

1) Open the master document that you saved in Exercise 12.3. Word opens the document in Outline view.

2) Click the **Expand Subdocuments** button on the Outlining toolbar.

Expand Subdocuments button

3) Click the icon for the subdocument that you want to remove. In this example, click the icon to the left of the third subdocument, as shown.

Remove Subdocument button

4) Click the **Remove Subdocument** button on the Outlining toolbar.

5) Close and save your document with the following name.

   `Chapter12_Exercise_12-4_After_`*`Your_Name`*`.doc`

   Word breaks the connection between the removed subdocument and the master document, but the subdocument's content remains in the master document. You can delete some or all of this content from the master document, as required. If you no longer need a subdocument file, use My Computer or Windows Explorer to delete it.

Chapter 12: quick reference

Outlining toolbar: master document and subdocument buttons

Button	Description
	Creates subdocument(s) from the selected outline heading(s).
	Displays a dialog box that allows you to insert a Word document as a subdocument of the currently open document.
	Expands the subdocuments of the current master document so you can view and work with their content in Outline, Normal or Print Layout view.
	Collapses the subdocuments of the currently open master document. Word displays only the path and file names of the subdocuments as hyperlinks.

Tasks summary

Task	Procedure
Designate an outline heading as a subdocument.	Select the outline heading and click the **Create Subdocument** button on the Outlining toolbar.
Insert a subdocument in an outline.	Position the insertion point at the location where you want to insert the subdocument, click the **Insert Subdocument** button on the Outlining toolbar, select the Word document, and click **Open**.
Expand/collapse subdocuments.	In Outline view, click the **Expand Subdocuments** or **Collapse Subdocuments** button on the Outlining toolbar.
Add a subdocument to a master document.	In Outline view, click on the section break before the location where you want to insert the subdocument, press **Enter**, click the **Insert Subdocument** button on the Outlining toolbar, select the Word document, and click **Open**.
Remove a subdocument from a master document.	In Outline view, click the icon for the subdocument that you want to remove, and click the **Remove Subdocument** button on the Outlining toolbar.

Concepts summary

Word's *master document* feature enables a publication manager to open, display, format and create a table of contents and index for several individual Word documents as if they were a single document.

The individual Word documents are called *subdocuments*. The containing document that integrates the subdocuments is called the *master document*.

You work with a master document in *Outline view*, and use the relevant buttons on the *Outlining toolbar*. You can create a master document in two ways: by *converting outline headings* to subdocuments, or *inserting existing Word documents* as subdocuments.

When you save a master document containing outline headings that have been converted to subdocuments, Word creates a new, separate file for each subdocument, assigns subdocument file names based on the text of the outline headings, and stores the subdocuments in the same folder as the master document.

Different contributors to a publication can open and work on different subdocuments simultaneously. The publication manager, however, typically works on subdocuments from within the master document.

When a master document is opened, Word displays only a hyperlinked path and file name for each subdocument. Click a hyperlink to open the subdocument in its own window. To work on the master document as a whole, click the **Expand Subdocuments** button on the Outlining toolbar and switch to Normal or Print Layout view.

Chapter 12: quick quiz

Circle the correct answer to each of the following multiple-choice questions about master documents and subdocuments in Word.

Q1	In Word, a master document is ...
A.	A Word file that contains style definitions and standard text that can be used in multiple Word documents.
B.	A Word document that has been checked for errors in spelling and grammar and that is formatted with styles.
C.	A Word file that contains one or more individual Word documents, called subdocuments.
D.	A Word document that has been saved with the **File | Save As Master Document**.

Q2	In Word, which of the following is not an advantage of using the master document feature?
A.	Word automatically generates and displays version numbers in the headers of all subdocuments in the master document.
B.	A single table of contents and index can be generated for all subdocuments in the master document.
C.	Consistent style formatting because all subdocuments are based on the template of the master document.
D.	All the subdocuments can be edited as a single file.

Q3	In Word, which document view do you use when working with master documents and subdocuments?
A.	Print Layout view.
B.	Outline view.
C.	Master view.
D.	Master Document view.

Q4	In Word, which of the following statements about subdocuments is untrue?
A.	The document manager typically views and works with subdocuments from within the master document.
B.	Individual writers can open and work with subdocuments just as they would regular Word documents.
C.	Different writers can work on different subdocuments of the same master document simultaneously.
D.	Subdocuments can be opened as individual Word documents; but they can be edited and formatted only from within the master document.

Q5	In Word Outline view, which action do you take to designate a selected outline heading as a subdocument?
A.	Click the **Create Subdocument** button on the Outlining toolbar.
B.	Press **Shift+Tab**.
C.	Click the **Convert to Subdocument** button on the Master Document toolbar.
D.	Click the **New Subdocument** button on the Master Document toolbar.

Q6	In Word, what happens when you save a new master document containing outline headings that you have designated as new subdocuments?
A.	Word saves the master document and all the designated subdocuments within a new file.
B.	Word saves the master document and creates a new, separate file for each subdocument.
C.	Word saves the master document in one file and all the designated subdocuments in a second file.
D.	Word saves only the master document.

Q7	In Word Outline view, which action do you take to insert a Word document as a subdocument in a master document?
A.	Click the **New Subdocument** button on the Master Document toolbar, select the document, and click **Insert**.
B.	Click **Insert+Tab.**
C.	Choose **File | Insert | Subdocument**, select the Word document, and click **OK**.
D.	Click the **Create Subdocument** button on the Outlining toolbar, select the document, and click **Open**.

Q8	What type of break does Word insert between subdocuments in a master document?
A.	A continuous section break.
B.	An odd page break.
C.	An odd page section break.
D.	An even page break.

Q9	By default, how does Word display a master document when it is opened?
A.	Word displays the first heading level only for each subdocument.
B.	Subdocuments are show only as hyperlinked file names.
C.	Word displays the first three heading levels only for each subdocument.
D.	Subdocuments are shown only as hyperlinked file and path names.

Q10	On Word's Outlining toolbar, which button do you click to designate an outline heading as a new subdocument?
A.	
B.	
C.	
D.	

Q11	On Word's Outlining toolbar, which button do you click to insert a Word document as a subdocument in a master document?
A.	
B.	
C.	
D.	

Q12	On Word's Outlining toolbar, which button do you click to view the subdocuments within a master document?
A.	
B.	
C.	
D.	

Answers

1: C, **2:** A, **3:** B, **4:** D, **5:** A, **6:** B, **7:** D, **8:** A, **9:** D, **10:** A, **11:** B, **12:** C.

13 'Please complete and return': Word forms

Objectives

In this chapter you will learn how to:

- Identify the appropriate form field for a particular task
- Insert text, drop-down and checkbox fields in a form
- Amend a form field's properties
- Protect a form with and without a password
- Delete form fields

New words

In this chapter you will meet the following terms:

- Word form
- Form field
- Text form field
- Drop-down form field
- Checkbox form field

Exercise files

In this chapter you will work with the following Word files:

- `Chapter13_Exercise_13-1_Before.doc`
- `Chapter13_Exercise_13-2_Before.doc`
- `Chapter13_Exercise_13-2_Before.doc`
- `Chapter13_Exercise_13-3_Before.doc`
- `Chapter13_Exercise_13-4_Before.doc`
- `Chapter13_Exercise_13-5_Before.doc`
- `Chapter13_Exercise_13-6_Before.doc`
- `Chapter13_Exercise_13-7_Before.doc`
- `Chapter13_Exercise_13-8_Before.doc`

Syllabus reference

In this chapter you will cover the following items from the ECDL Advanced Word Processing Syllabus:

- **AM3.4.2.1**. Create and edit a form.
- **AM3.4.2.2**. Use available form field options: text field, checkbox, drop-down menu, and so on.
- **AM3.4.2.3**. Delete fields in a form.
- **AM3.4.2.4**. Protect a form.

So many forms, so little time

How many forms have you completed in your life? The answer is probably 'a lot' (or perhaps 'too many'). Typically, forms are of two main types:

- **Paper-based forms**. Examples include applications (for organization membership, for bank loans and mortgages), compliance documents (for employers and regulators), and satisfaction questionnaires (for customers).
- **Web-based forms**. Some websites ask you to complete an online form in which you reveal details of your personal or business interests. If you purchase a product over the web, you are typically requested to type your credit card details into an online form.

Now meet a third type of form: a Word form.

Word forms: how they are different

What makes a Word form different from a regular Word file? A Word form has identifying features:

- **Form fields**. It contains *interactive* areas called form fields in which users can type information.
- **Protection**. A Word form is a *protected* document. The result is that users can only input text and select options – they cannot amend the form content or layout.
- **Templates**. A Word form is made available as a template. When users open the template, Word opens a *copy of the form* on their screens, ready for them to complete.

In summary, if a Word file is a template, is protected, and contains form fields, it's a form.

Form fields

Word offers three types of form fields – text, drop-down list and checkboxes.

- **Text form fields**. These are blank boxes in which users type details such as their name, address, age, etc. In this context, the term 'text' also includes numbers and dates.

- **Drop-down form fields**. These display a list of preset choices from which a user may select only one.

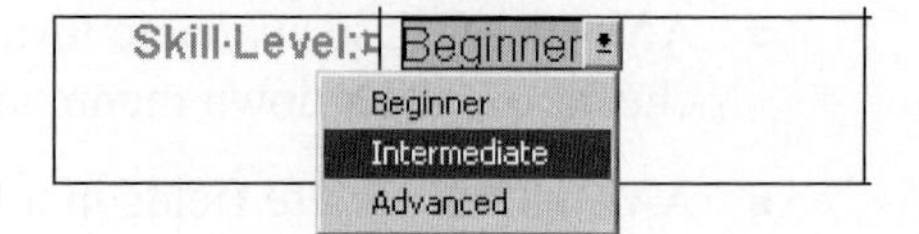

- **Checkbox form fields**. These enable you to offer users the ability to select more than one option from a given list.

Delicious·Toppings		
Choose·as·many·as·you·want!	Mozzarella	☒
	Ham	☐
	Pepperoni	☐
	Chicken	☐
	Tuna	☐
	Pineapple	☒
	Sweetcorn	☐
	Mushrooms	☒

Drop-down and checkbox form fields offer advantages for both the form creator and the form users:

- **For the form creator**. As you specify the options from which users may choose, you eliminate the risk of typos or other 'bad data' in your form.
- **For form users**. They help users to complete the form quickly and with a minimum of typing. Also, users need not remember the names of your products or services.

You will learn more about each type of form field later in this chapter.

> ***Form field***
>
> *An interactive area in a Word form where users type information in response to a question or indicate an appropriate response by choosing from drop-down lists or a series of checkboxes.*

The Forms toolbar

As a form creator, you work with form fields using Word's Forms toolbar. To display this Toolbar, choose **View | Toolbars | Forms**.

You will learn the purpose of each Forms toolbar button as you use it in the exercises.

You work with the parts of a form that are not form fields – the identifying text, instructions and questions – in the same way as you would work with text in a non-form Word document. You can also insert pictures and other graphics (such as a company logo) in a form.

Typically, tables are used when creating Word forms as they help the form creator to position questions and form fields left to right across the page.

Word form
A Word file that contains form fields, is protected, and is made available as a template. Form fields and descriptive text are typically arranged using one or more Word tables.

Word forms: the lifecycle

Consider the stages in the life of a Word form:

- **Form creation**. Someone creates a Word form using the Form toolbar for the form fields and Word's text editing, formatting, tables and graphics features for the remainder of the form.
- **Form distribution**. Two options here: *physical* (passing the form around on a diskette) or *network-based* (making the form available for downloading from a server or attaching it to an e-mail.)
- **Form completion**. Users open a copy of the form based on the form template, and 'fill in' and 'tick' the form fields, as appropriate.
- **Form collection**. Users return the completed form document, typically by the same means as they received it.
- **Data collation**. Someone extracts the users' responses from the returned Word forms. The collated responses are typically inserted into a database for reporting and analysis.

This chapter is essentially about learning two skills:

- The ability to choose the correct type of form field for a particular information-gathering task.
- The ability to use the options available on the Forms toolbar and the form field dialog boxes.

Working with forms: the six tasks

Here are the six tasks that you need to be able to perform with forms in Word:

- **Create a new form**. Exercise 13.1 takes you through the steps of inserting form fields in a Word document.
- **Protect a form**. In Exercises 13.2 and 13.3, you discover how to protect a form, without and with a password.
- **Work with text fields**. Learn how to manipulate form fields of this type in Exercises 13.4 and 13.5.
- **Work with drop-down list fields**. See Exercise 13.6.
- **Work with checkbox fields**. See Exercise 13.7.
- **Delete form fields**. See Exercise 13.8.

Working with new forms

In the first exercise, you will open a Word document and insert text, drop-down and checkbox form fields into it. The document already contains labels – text that identifies the purpose of each form field. A table is used to position both the field labels and the form fields.

Exercise 13.1: Creating a New Form

1) Start Word and open the following file:

   `Chapter13_Exercise_13-1_Before.doc`

2) Choose **View | Toolbars | Forms**.

3) Click in the second cell of the first row.

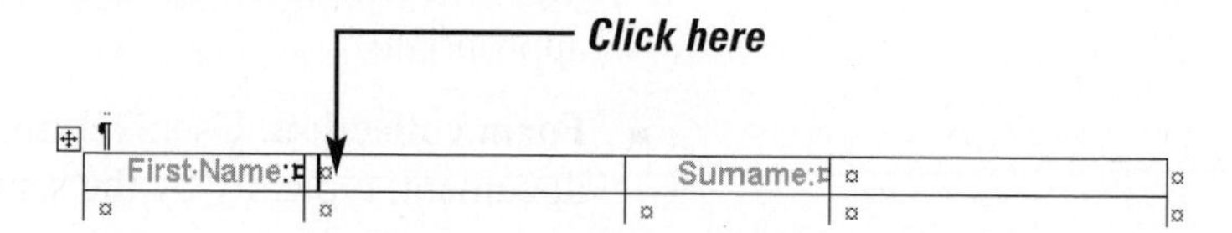

4) Click the **Text Form Field** button on the Forms toolbar.

   Word displays your inserted text form field as a grey rectangle containing a number of hollow dots.

ab|

Text Form Field button

5) Click in the fourth cell of the first row.

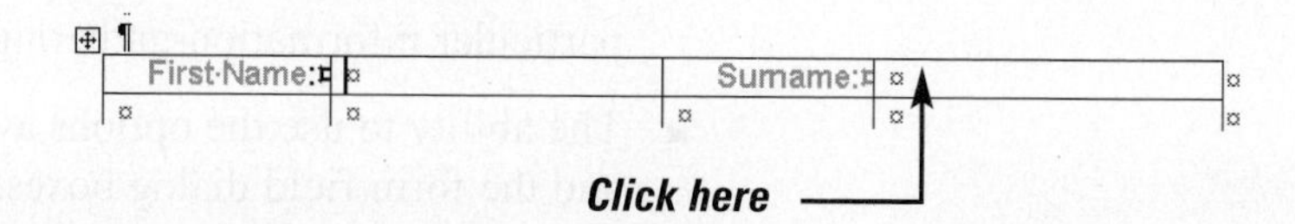

6) Click the **Text Form Field** button on the Forms toolbar. The first row of your table should now look like this:

First Name:		Surname:	

7) Click in the second cell of the third row.

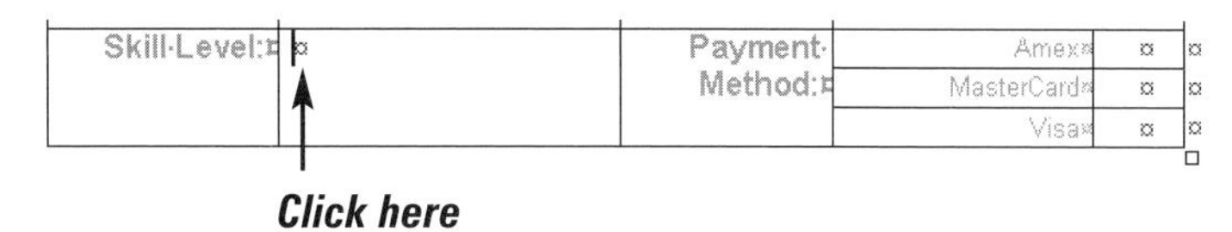

Drop Down Form Field button

8) Click the **Drop-Down Form Field** button on the Forms toolbar.

   Word displays your inserted drop-down form field as a solid grey rectangle.

Form Field Options button

9) Click anywhere in your drop-down list and click the **Form Field Options** button on the Forms toolbar. Alternatively, right-click on the field and choose **Properties** from the pop-up menu displayed.

   In the *Drop-down item* box, type the three options, 'Beginner', 'Intermediate' and 'Advanced', clicking the **Add** button after each one.

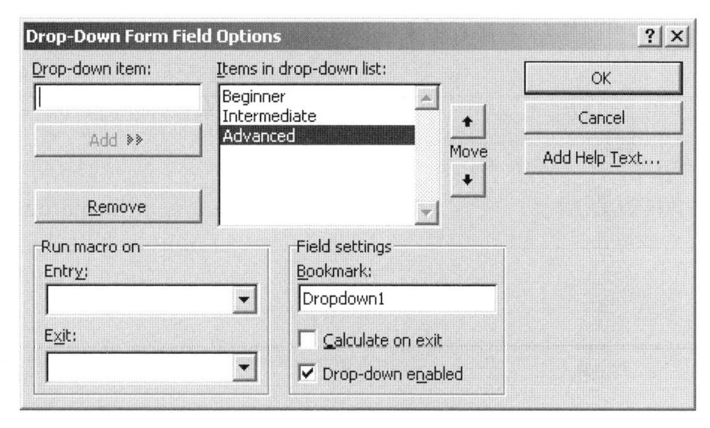

   When finished, click **OK** to close the dialog box.

10) On the third row, click in the cell to the right of the word 'Amex'.

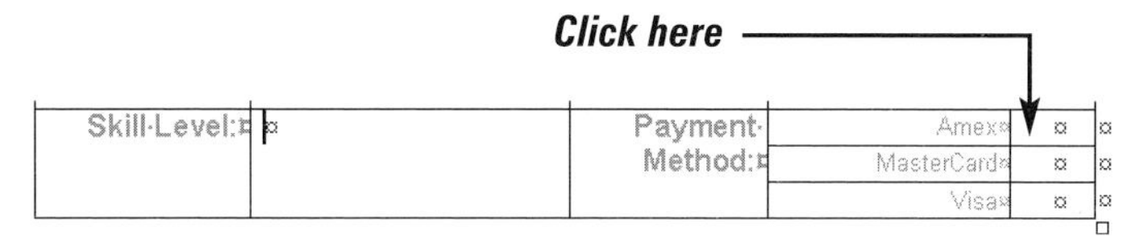

Check Box Form Field button

11) Click the **Check Box Form Field** button on the Forms toolbar.

   Word displays your inserted checkbox form field as a grey square block containing a smaller, hollow black square.

   ☐

12) Repeat step 11 in the cells to the right of the words 'MasterCard' and 'Visa'. Your document should look like this:

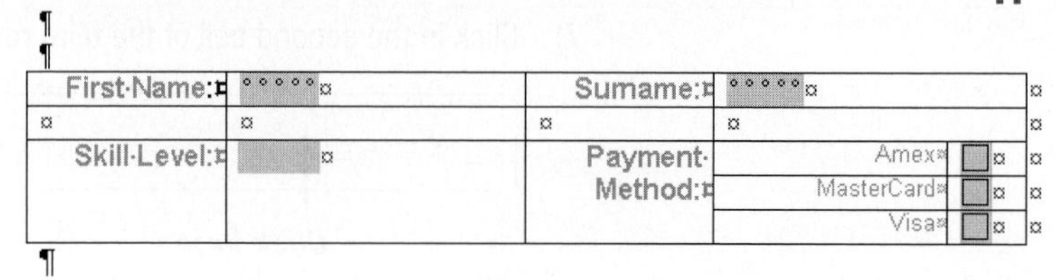
TRAINING BOOKING FORM

First Name:		Surname:	
Skill Level:		Payment Method:	Amex
			MasterCard
			Visa

13) Close and save your sample document with the following name:

`Chapter13_Exercise_13-1_After_`*`Your_Name`*`.doc`

Checkboxes and exclusive options

In Exercise 13.1, you used checkboxes for the credit card options. These are *exclusive* choices: you want your form users to select only *one* credit card. A drop-down list is a safer choice for such a purpose, as it prevents users from incorrectly selecting more than one option.

For form users, however, checkboxes are more convenient, because they need to click just once to indicate a choice. A drop-down list demands that users click twice – once to open the list, and a second time to select the required option.

Working with form protection

The form that you created and saved in Exercise 13.1 is not yet interactive. That is, information cannot be typed into its text fields, nor can options be selected from its drop-down or checkbox fields. A form becomes interactive only after it has been *protected.*

Word offers you two ways of protecting a form:

- **Without a password**. A form that is protected without a password can be unprotected by anyone.
- **With a password**. A form that is protected with a password can be unprotected only by someone who knows the correct password.

Users cannot alter the content or layout of a protected form. They can only interact with its form fields.

Which type of protection is better? Typically, the form creator first protects the form without a password and then tests the form's fields. When the creator is satisfied that the fields work correctly, he or she then applies password protection to the form, saves it as a template, and makes it available for use.

In the next two exercises, you apply protection to a form without and with a password.

Exercise 13.2: Protecting a form without a password

1) Open the following Word file:

   `Chapter13_Exercise_13-2_Before.doc`

   Is the Forms toolbar displayed? If not, choose **View | Toolbars | Forms**.

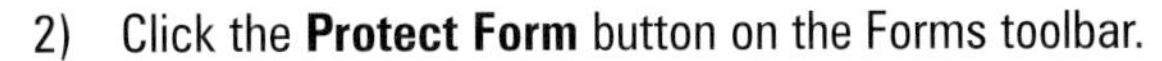

Protect Form button

2) Click the **Protect Form** button on the Forms toolbar.

   Alternatively, choose **Tools | Protect Document** to display the *Protect Document* dialog box. In the *Protect document for* area, select *Forms* and click **OK**.

   Your form is now protected. Let's check that its fields work correctly.

3) Click in the *First Name* field and type 'Charles'. Press **Tab** to move the insertion to the *Surname* field and type 'Kennedy'.

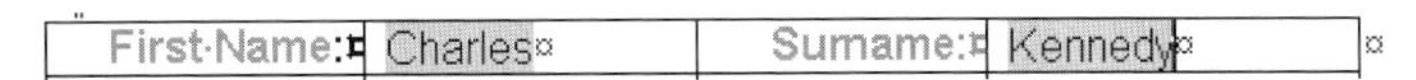

4) Click anywhere in the *Skill Level* field. Notice that Word displays a drop-down list. Select the *Advanced* option.

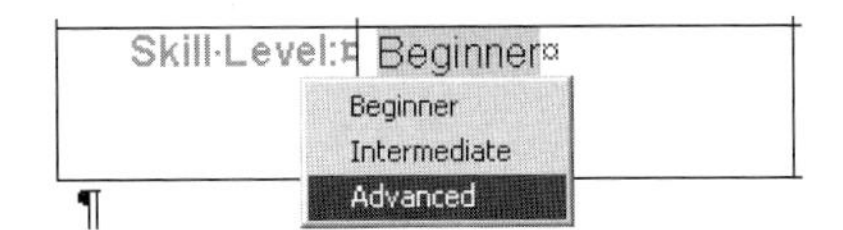

5) In the *Payment Method* area of your form, click in each of the three credit card fields. Notice that Word displays an 'X' in each field that you click on.

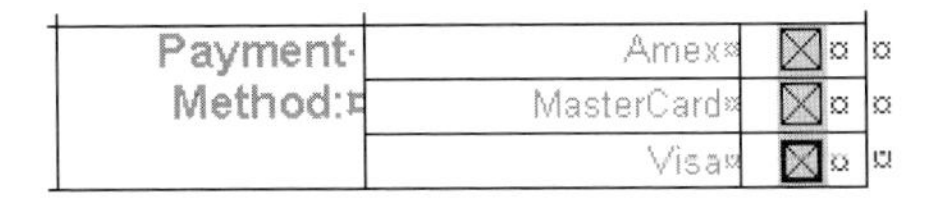

6) Your form appears to work correctly. Before continuing further, you need to remove the test information.

   Click again in each credit card field to deselect it. Click in the *Skill Level* drop-down list and select the *Beginner option*. Click in the *First Name* and *Surname* fields and use the **Backspace** or **Delete** keys to remove the text.

7) Close and save your sample protected form with the following name:

   Chapter13_Exercise_13-2_After_*Your_Name*.doc

Exercise 13.3: Protecting a form with a password

1) Open the following Word file:

   `Chapter13_Exercise_13-3_Before.doc`

   Is the Forms toolbar displayed? If not, choose **View | Toolbars | Forms**.

Protect Form button

2) The form is currently protected *without* a password. Your first task is to unprotect it.

   Click the **Protect Form** button on the Forms toolbar. Alternatively, choose **Tools | Unprotect Document**. You have removed the protection from the form.

3) Choose **Tools | Protect Document** to display the *Protect Document* dialog box.

4) In the *Protect document for* area, select *Forms*. Type the password 'hello', and click **OK**.

5) Word prompts you to re-enter your password.

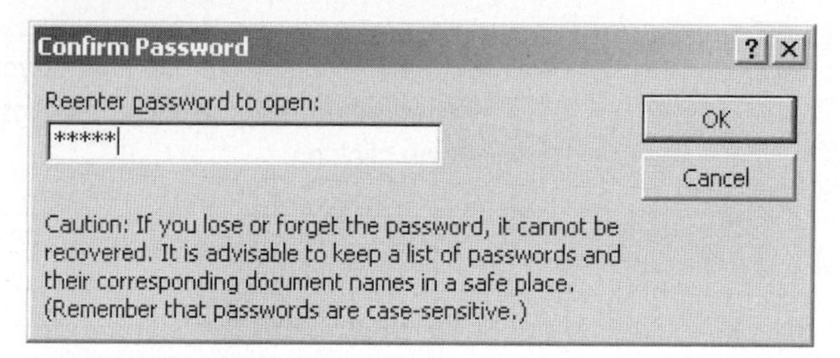

   Type 'hello' again and click **OK**.

6) Close and save your password-protected form with the following name:

   `Chapter13_Exercise_13-3_After_`*`Your_Name`*`.doc`

You can unprotect the form at any time by choosing **Tools | Unprotect Document** and entering the correct password when prompted.

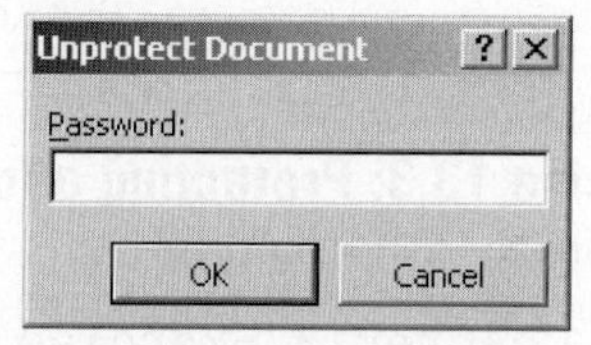

You cannot apply or remove password protection by using the **Protect Form** button on the Forms toolbar. You must use the **Tools | Protect Document** or **Tools | Unprotect Document** command on the Tools menu. The **Protect Form** button applies or removes only non-password protection.

Form fields and default values

To speed up users' completion of a form, you can provide preset responses – *default values* – in your form fields.

Text fields may contain default text, numbers or dates. In a drop-down list, the first item is selected by default; a checkbox may be defined as selected.

Default value

In a Word form, a choice made by the form creator when the user does not type information, or select an alternative answer or option.

Working with text form fields

Text form fields offer a range of attributes. For example, you can specify the type of text that users may enter (options include regular text, a date, a number or a calculation), the maximum number of characters, and the text case. The full list of options for text form fields is shown at the end of this chapter.

Text form field

In a Word form, an area in which users can type a text response to a question or instruction. Depending on the format specified, the field can contain alphanumeric characters, numbers only, dates, times or calculations.

Exercise 13.4: Working with text form fields

In this exercise, you will amend the properties of text form fields in a Word form.

1) Open the following Word file:

   `Chapter13_Exercise_13-4_Before.doc`

   Is the Forms toolbar displayed? If not, choose **View | Toolbars | Forms**.

2) A text form field is located to the right of the words 'Invoice Number:'. Right-click on it and choose the **Properties** command from the pop-up menu.

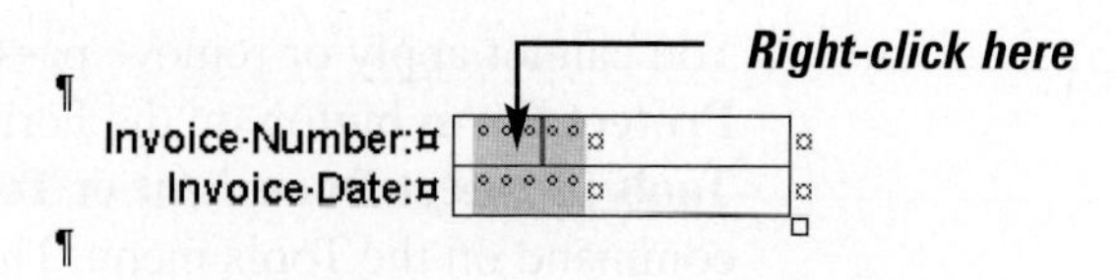

Word displays the *Text Form Field Options* dialog box.

In the *Type* box, select the *Number* option and click **OK**.

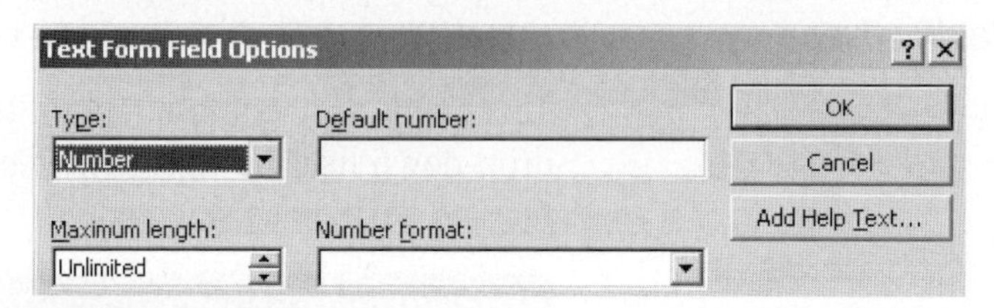

3) Right-click in the text form field to the right of 'Invoice Date:' and choose the **Properties** command.

   In the *Type* box, select the *Current date* option. In the *Date format* box, select *dd/MM/yyyy* and click **OK**.

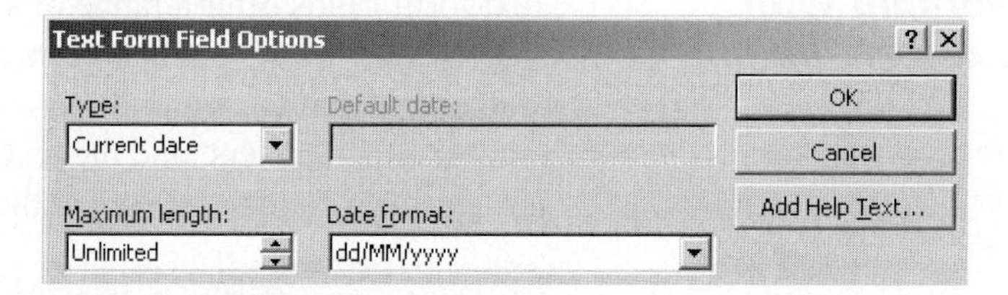

4) Right-click in the text form field beneath the 'Qty' heading and choose the **Properties** command.

   In the *Type* box, select the *Number* option. In the *Default number* box, type 0; in the *Number format* box, select 0. Click **OK**.

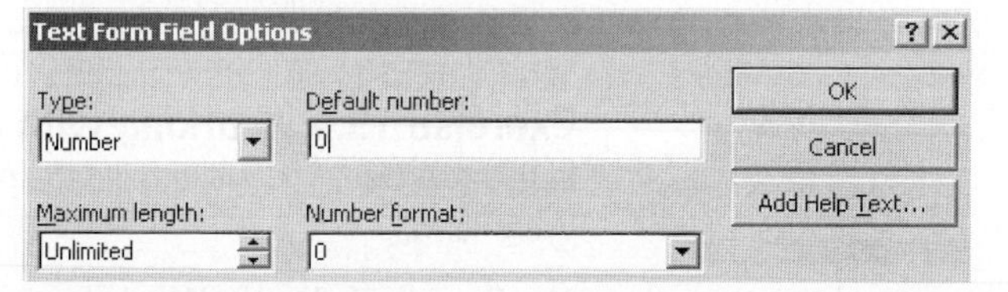

5) Select the text form field that you amended in step 4 by dragging across it.

   Press **Ctrl+C** and use **Ctrl+V** to paste it successively in each of the other five cells in the 'Qty' column. Your fields should look like this:

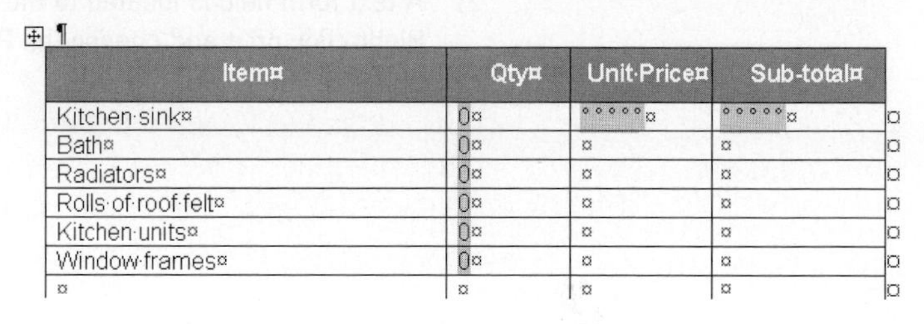

Item	Qty	Unit Price	Sub-total
Kitchen sink	0		
Bath	0		
Radiators	0		
Rolls of roof felt	0		
Kitchen units	0		
Window frames	0		

6) Right-click in the text form field beneath the 'Unit Price' heading and choose the **Properties** command.

   In the *Type* box, select the *Number* option. In the *Default number* box, type 0. In the *Number format* box, select the currency option – it's displayed as £#,##0.00;(£#,##0.00). Click **OK**.

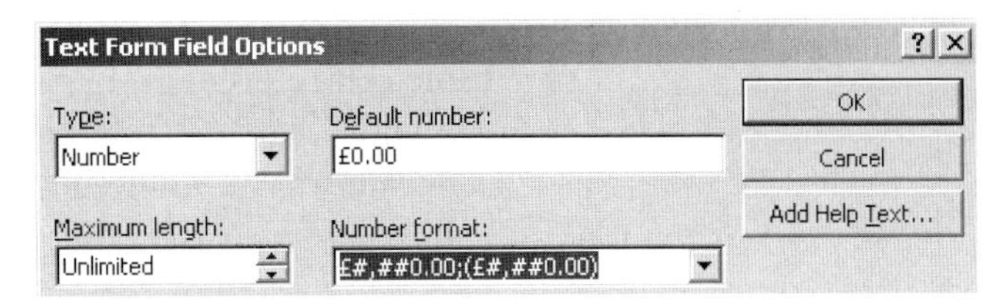

7) Select the text form field that you amended in step 6 by dragging across it.

   Press **Ctrl+C** and use **Ctrl+V** to paste it successively in each of the other five cells in the 'Unit Price' column.

8) Right-click in the text form field beneath the 'Sub-total' heading and choose the **Properties** command.

9) In the *Type* box, select the *Number* option. In the *Default number* box, type 0. In the *Number format* box, select the currency option. Click **OK**.

10) Select the text form field that you amended in step 9 by dragging across it.

    Press **Ctrl+C**, and use **Ctrl+V** to paste it successively in each of the other five cells in the 'Sub-total' column. Also, paste it in the *Total* field at the bottom right of the form. Your fields should look like this:

Item	Qty	Unit Price	Sub-total
Kitchen sink	0	£0.00	£0.00
Bath	0	£0.00	£0.00
Radiators	0	£0.00	£0.00
Rolls of roof felt	0	£0.00	£0.00
Kitchen units	0	£0.00	£0.00
Window frames	0	£0.00	£0.00
Total			£0.00

11) Click the **Protect Form** button on the Forms toolbar to protect your form.

12) Close and save your sample form with the following name:

    `Chapter13_Exercise_13-4_After_`*`Your_Name`*`.doc`

Calculations in text form fields

The form that you created in Exercise 13.4 does not take advantage of a very useful type of text form field – the *calculation* type. This field type can generate a result based on values entered by the form user in other fields of the form.

By inserting text form fields of the calculation type, your Word form can act like an Excel worksheet. As with formulas and functions in Excel, calculation fields in Word always being within an equals (=) sign. How do you identify which fields in your form contain the values needed to generate the result? Word gives you two options:

- **Table cell references**. If your form fields are located in a Word table, you can reference the cells in the table in the same way as you would the cells in an Excel worksheet.

  An example of a calculation using table cell references is:

  ```
  =SUM(C1:C4)
  ```

  In this instance, C1 is the cell in the third column of the first row, and C4 is the cell in the third column of the fourth row.

- **Form field bookmarks**. Word automatically assigns a bookmark name to each form field that you insert. You can view a form field's bookmark by selecting it and clicking the **Form Field Options** button on the Forms toolbar.

  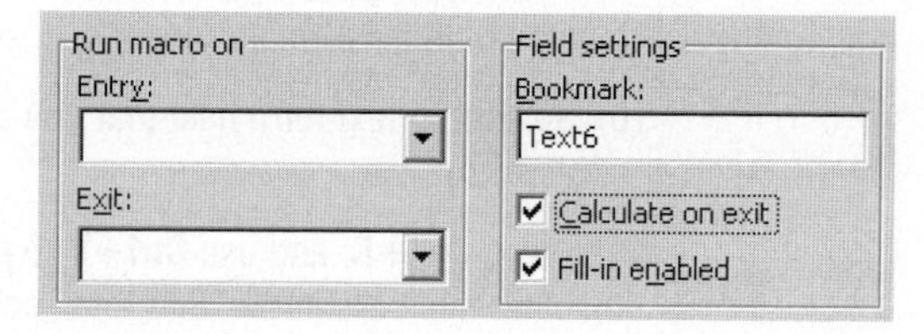

  An example of a calculation using bookmarks is:

  ```
  =SUM(Text5:Text8)
  ```

To use a form field as the basis for a calculation, you must select the *Calculate on exit* checkbox for that field. You do not select this checkbox for the field that performs the actual calculation. Exercise 13.5 provides an example of calculation-type text form fields in action.

Exercise 13.5: Working with calculations in text form fields

1) Open the following Word file:

   `Chapter13_Exercise_13-5_Before.doc`

   Is the Forms toolbar displayed? If not, choose **View | Toolbars | Forms**.

2) In turn, click on each of the six fields in the 'Qty' column of the form, click the **Form Field Options** button on the Forms toolbar, select the *Calculate on exit* checkbox, and click **OK**.

   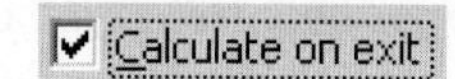

3) Repeat step 2 for each of the six fields in the 'Unit Price' column.

4) Click on the first field in the 'Sub-total' column beneath the column heading, click the **Form Field Options** button on the Forms toolbar, change the *Type* from *Number* to *Calculation*, and type the following in the *Expression* box:

```
=b2*c2
```

Cell references b2 and c2 represent the cells in the 'Qty' and 'Unit Price' columns of the same row of the table. Do not select the *Calculate on exit* option. Notice that the *Fill-in enabled* option is deselected.

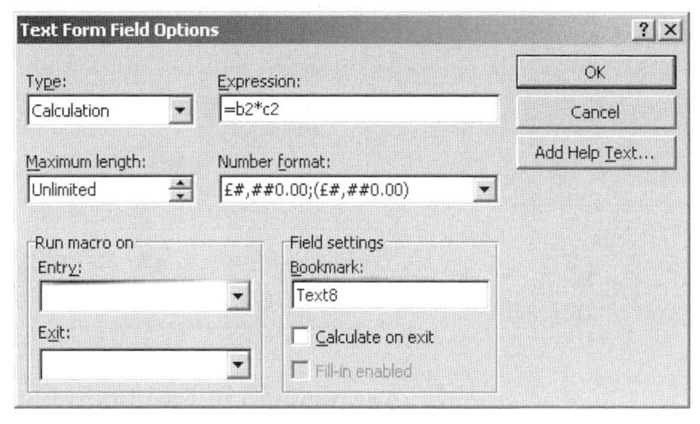

Click **OK** to close the dialog box.

5) Repeat step 4 for the other five cells in the 'Sub-total' column, but type different cell references in the *Expression* box for each cell, as follows:

```
=b3*c3
=b4*c4
=b5*c5
=b6*c6
=b7*c7
```

6) Click in the *Total* cell at the bottom right of your form, change the *Type* from *Number* to *Calculation*, and type the following in the *Expression* box:

```
=sum(d2:d7)
```

Click **OK** to close the dialog box.

7) Click the **Protect Form** button on the Forms toolbar to protect your document without a password.

8) Close and save your sample document with the following name:

Chapter13_Exercise_13-5_After_*Your_Name*.doc

9) Open your form and type some sample numbers and amounts in the 'Qty' and 'Unit Price' columns. Press the **Tab** key to move from one cell to the next.

Notice that Word generates new results in the 'Sub-total' column each time you enter or amend values in the 'Qty' or 'Unit Price' columns. You can close your form without saving it.

Working with drop-down form fields

A drop-down form field lets users select *one option* from a list of mutually exclusive alternatives. Drop-down form fields help to:

- Ensure accuracy, because users do not need to remember product or service names.
- Eliminate the risk of typos, because form users do not need to type their entries

Drop-down lists are not a good choice for printed forms because only the first item in each list will appear on the printed form.

Drop-down form field

In a Word form, a field that allows users to display a list of choices from which they can select a single response.

Exercise 13.6: Working with drop-down form fields

In this exercise, you will insert one drop-down form field, change the order of items in a second field, and remove and add items in a third field.

1) Open the following file:

   `Chapter13_Exercise_13-6_Before.doc`

   Is the Forms toolbar displayed? If not, display it now.

2) Click in the cell beneath the 'Flying To:' heading.

Flying From:	Flying To:	Departure Month:	Departure Year:
Dublin		January	2000
		All flights depart on 2nd of each month	

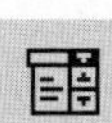

Drop-Down Form Field button

3) Click the **Drop-Down Form Field** button on the Forms toolbar. Word displays your inserted drop-down form field as a solid grey rectangle.

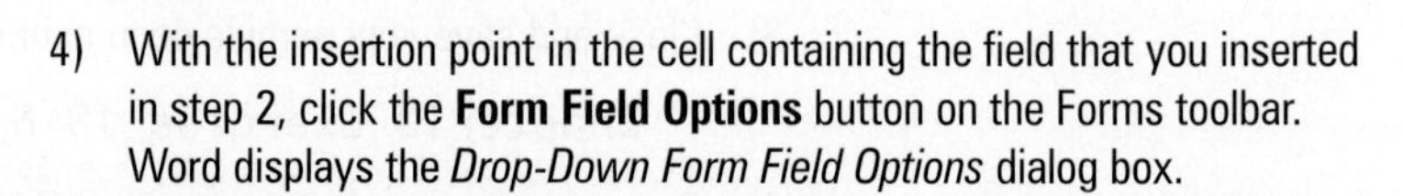

Form Field Options button

4) With the insertion point in the cell containing the field that you inserted in step 2, click the **Form Field Options** button on the Forms toolbar. Word displays the *Drop-Down Form Field Options* dialog box.

5) In the *Drop-down item* box, type the following locations, clicking the **Add** button after each one:

```
Berlin
Cork
Frankfurt
Glasgow
```

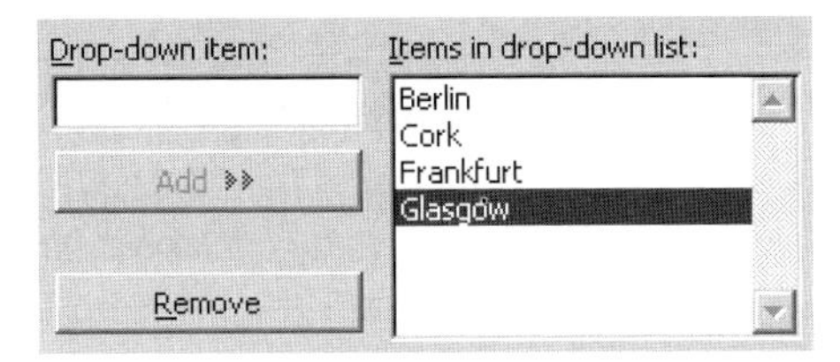

When finished, click **OK** to close the dialog box.

6) Right-click on the field in the field beneath the 'Departure Month' heading and choose **Properties** from the pop-up menu displayed. Word displays the *Drop-Down Form Field Options* dialog box.

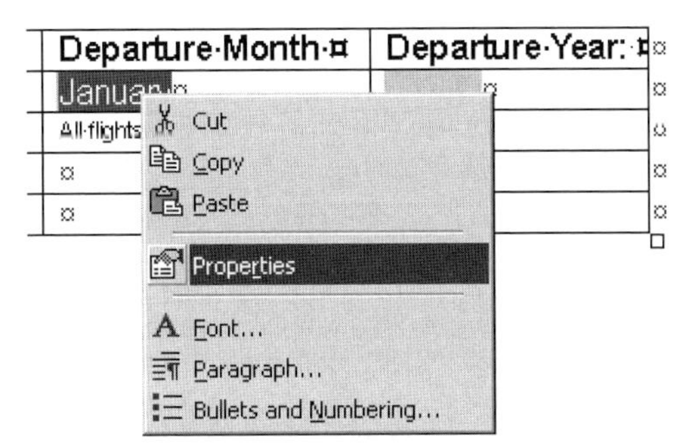

7) In the *Items in drop-down list* box, click March, and then click the **Move Up** button.

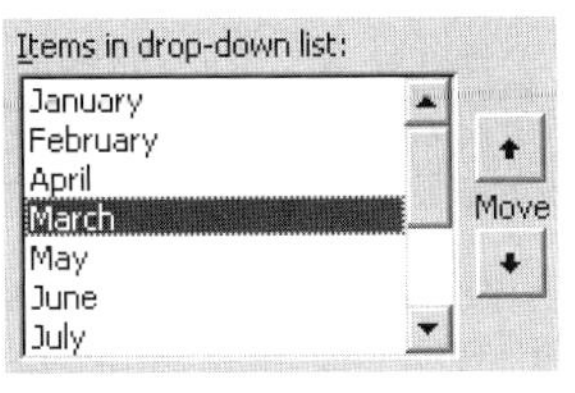

Before

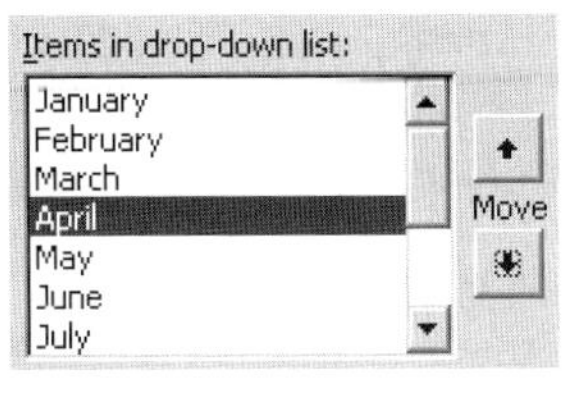

After

The months are now in the correct order. When finished, click **OK**.

8) Right-click in the field beneath the 'Departure Year' heading and choose **Properties**. Word displays the *Drop-Down Form Field Options* dialog box.

9) In the *Items in drop-down list* box, click 2000 and then click **Remove**.

10) In the *Drop-down item* box, type '2003'. Click **Add** and then **OK**.

11) Close and save your sample document with the following name:

Chapter13_Exercise_13-6_After_*Your_Name*.doc

Working with checkbox form fields

Checkbox fields help users complete a Word form quickly because they don't need to type their responses. Unlike the drop-down form fields, where users can select only one option, checkboxes allow form users to make multiple choices.

Checkbox form field
In a Word form, a field that allows users to select from among multiple options by clicking a checkbox.

Exercise 13.7: Working with checkbox form fields

1) Open the following file:

   Chapter13_Exercise_13-7_Before.doc

   Is the Forms toolbar displayed? If not, display it now.

2) Click in the cell to the right of the cell containing the word 'Mozzarella'.

Click here

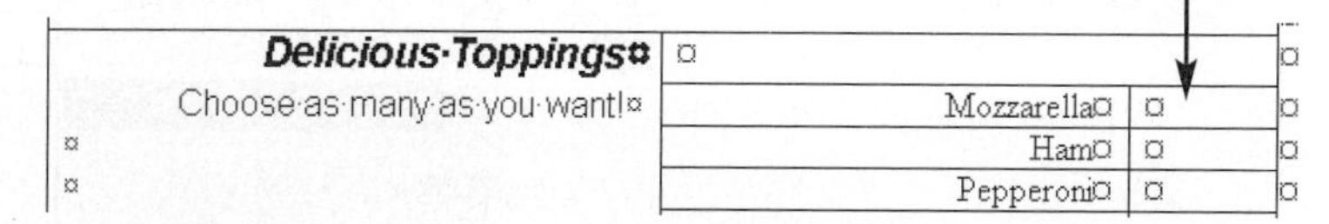

Delicious Toppings		
Choose as many as you want!	Mozzarella	
	Ham	
	Pepperoni	

Check Box Form Field button

3) Click the **Check Box Form Field** button on the Forms toolbar. Word displays your inserted checkbox form field as a grey square block containing a smaller, hollow, black square.

   ☐

4) Select the checkbox form field that you inserted in step 3 by dragging across it.

5) Press **Ctrl+C** and use **Ctrl+V** to paste it successively in each of the other seven cells that represent pizza toppings. Your fields should look like this:

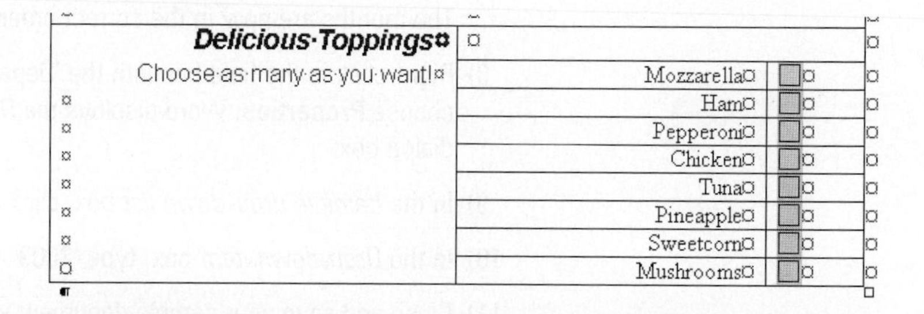

Delicious Toppings		
Choose as many as you want!	Mozzarella	☐
	Ham	☐
	Pepperoni	☐
	Chicken	☐
	Tuna	☐
	Pineapple	☐
	Sweetcorn	☐
	Mushrooms	☐

Form Field Options button

6) Click in the table cell containing the checkbox field for the mozzarella topping, and click the **Form Field Options** button. Word displays the *Check Box Form Field Options* dialog box.

7) In the *Default value* area, select the *Checked* option. Click **OK** to close the dialog box.

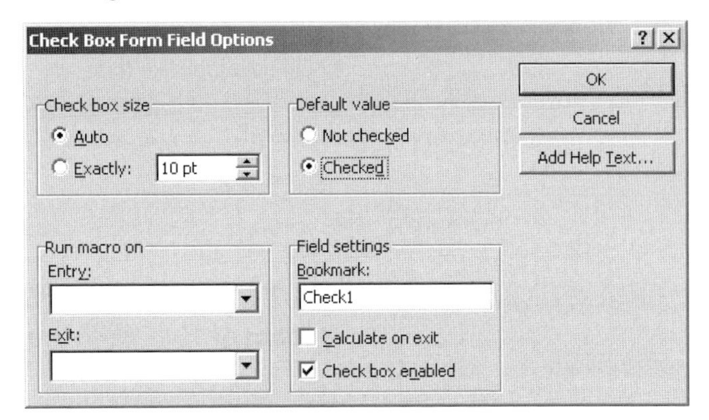

The mozzarella topping checkbox now looks like this:

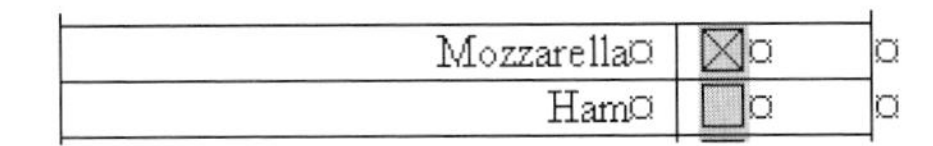

Protect Form button

8) Click the **Protect Form** button on the Form toolbar. Your form is now protected.

9) Close and save your sample document with the following name:

`Chapter13_Exercise_13-7_After_`*`Your_Name`*`.doc`

In the final exercise of this chapter, you will learn how to delete fields from a form.

Exercise 13.8: Deleting a form field

1) Open the following file:

`Chapter13_Exercise_13-8_Before.doc`

Is the Forms toolbar displayed? If not, display it now.

2) Click in the second cell of the first row to select the text form field. Word displays the selected field as a solid black rectangle.

Press the **Delete** key to remove the field from the form.

3) Click in the fourth cell of the first row to select the text form field, and press **Delete** to remove the field.

4) Click in the second cell of the third row to position the insertion point in the cell. Press **Delete** once to select the field and a second time to remove it.

5) In the third row, click in the cell to the right of the word 'Amex'.

Press **Delete**. Word selects the checkbox field. Press **Delete** a second time to remove the field.

6) Repeat step 5 to remove the other two credit card fields. Your table should now look like this:

First Name:		Surname:		
Skill Level:		Payment Method:	Amex	
			MasterCard	
			Visa	

7) Close and save your sample document with the following name:

Chapter13_Exercise_13-8_After_*Your_Name*.doc

Chapter 13: quick reference

Forms toolbar

Button	Description
ab|	Inserts a text box field in a document.
	Inserts a checkbox field in a document.
	Inserts a drop-down field in a document.
	Displays the *Form Field Options* dialog box for the selected field.
	Protects the form to enable users to interact with its fields.

Form fields

Field type	When used
Text	The user's response consists of text, a number or a date.
Checkbox	The user may select *multiple* choices from a series.
Drop-down list	The user must select one choice from a list.

Text form field types

Text field type	Permitted content
Regular text	Any characters, including letters, numbers and symbols.
Number	Numeric entries only. If you specify a number format, Word converts the user's entries accordingly.
Date	Calendar date entries only. If you specify a date format, Word converts the user's entries accordingly.
Current date	A display-only field that shows the date on which the user opened the form.
Current time	A display-only field that shows the time on which the user opened the form.
Calculation	Arithmetic expressions. For example, the total of a column of numbers, or the order quantity multiplied by the unit price.

Tasks summary

Task	Procedure
Insert a form field.	Click the appropriate form field button on the Forms toolbar.
Amend the properties of a form field.	Select the field and click the **Form Field Options** button on the Forms toolbar. Alternatively, right-click on the field and choose **Properties** from the drop-down menu.
Delete a form field.	Select the field and press **Delete**.
Protect a form without a password.	Click the **Protect Form** button on the Forms toolbar.
	Alternatively, select the field, choose **Tools | Protect Document**, select *Forms* in the *Protect document for* area, and click **OK**.
Protect a form with a password.	Choose **Tools | Protect Document**, select *Forms* in the *Protect document for* area, type your password, click **OK**, retype your password and click **OK**.
Unprotect a form.	If not password-protected, click the **Protect Form** button on the Forms toolbar.
	If password-protected, choose **Tools | Unprotect Document**, type the password, and click **OK**.

Concepts summary

A form is a Word *template* file that contains interactive areas called *form fields* in which users can type information and select options. When users open the template, Word opens a copy of the form on their screens, ready for them to complete. A Word form is a protected document. Users can input text and select options but cannot amend the form content or layout.

Word offers three kinds of form fields: *text* (blank boxes in which users can enter text, numbers, date and calculations), *drop-down* (which offer a list of preset choices from which a user may select only one), and *checkbox* (which allow users to select more than one option from a given range). You can specify default values for each field type to speed up form completion.

Chapter13: quick quiz

Circle the correct answer to each of the following multiple-choice questions about forms in Word.

Q1	Which of the following is not an essential feature of a Word form?
A.	A Word form is a protected document.
B.	A Word form is distributed as a template.
C.	A Word form is formatted using heading styles.
D.	A Word form must contain at least one form field.

Q2	Why are Word forms made available as templates?
A.	It enables users to create and complete a new Word document that is based on the selected form template, without affecting the template itself.
B.	Templates are easier to share among multiple users on a PC network.
C.	Form fields can be inserted in Word templates only and not in Word documents.
D.	Word templates can be password-protected against unwanted modification. Word documents cannot.

Q3	In Word, which of the following is not a type of form field?
A.	Drop-down list.
B.	Form ID.
C.	Text.
D.	Checkbox.

Q4	On the Forms toolbar in Word, which button do you click to insert a text form field?
A.	
B.	
C.	
D.	ab|

Q5	In a Word form, which form field type would you use to accept the entry of a person's date of birth?
A.	Text form field.
B.	Date form field.
C.	Calendar form field.
D.	Checkbox form field.

Q6	In a Word form, which form field type would you use to accept the entry of a financial amount?
A.	Floating-point form field.
B.	Currency form field.
C.	Text form field.
D.	Checkbox form field.

Q7	In a Word form, which type of user entry is permitted in a text form field?
A.	Text.
B.	Calculation.
C.	Number.
D.	All of the above.

Q8	In a Word form, which of the following would not be accepted as a valid calculation in a text form field?
A.	=B2*B4/52
B.	=SUM(E2:E6)
C.	=Text1+Text3
D.	SUM(D2:E6)

Q9	When defining a text form field in a Word form, what is the effect of selecting the *Calculate on exit* checkbox?
A.	The field's user-entered value can be the input to a calculation that is defined in another field on the form.
B.	Word automatically updates all the form's text fields whenever the user saves the form.
C.	The field can calculate a result that is based on values entered in other fields by the form user.
D.	Word automatically updates all the form's text fields whenever the user closes the form, regardless of whether the user saves the form.

Q10	On the Forms toolbar in Word, which button do you click to insert a drop-down form field?
A.	
B.	
C.	
D.	ab|

Q11	When creating a Word form, you would insert a drop-down list field when you want …
A.	The form user to enter a calendar date.
B.	To allow the form user to select more than one response from a series of options.
C.	The form user to enter a number.
D.	To prevent the form user from selecting more than one response from a series of options.

Q12	In Word, which of the following statements about drop-down list form fields is untrue?
A.	The first option in the list is the default choice.
B.	The form creator can edit the drop-down list to rearrange the order of the options in the list.
C.	The form user can select more than one option from the drop-down list.
D.	The form creator can remove an option from a drop-down list.

Q13	On the Forms toolbar in Word, which button do you click to insert a checkbox form field?
A.	
B.	
C.	
D.	ab|

Q14	When creating a Word form, you would insert a checkbox field when you want ...
A.	The form user to enter a calendar date.
B.	To allow the form user to select more than one response from a series of options.
C.	The form user to enter the input to a calculation.
D.	To prevent the form user from selecting more than one response from a series of options.

Q15	In Word, which of the following statements about checkbox form fields is untrue?
A.	The form creator can specify that a checkbox is selected by default.
B.	Form users can interact with a checkbox field in either of three ways: they leave it deselected, they can click to select it, or they can double-click to double-select it.
C.	Word automatically applies a bookmark name to each checkbox inserted by the form creator.
D.	The form creator can remove a checkbox from a form.

Q16	On the Forms toolbar in Word, which button do you click to apply or remove form protection?
A.	
B.	
C.	
D.	

Q17	In Word, which of the following statements about form protection is true?
A.	The form creator does not need to protect a form to enable the form users to interact with the fields on the form.
B.	Form protection without a password prevents form users from changing the form content or layout.
C.	Form protection without a password does not enable the form users to interact with the form fields.
D.	Form protection with a password enables the form users to interact with the form's fields but prevents them from changing the form content or layout.

Q18	In Word, which of the following statements about form protection is true?
A.	The form creator can apply or remove password-protection using the relevant buttons on the Forms toolbar.
B.	The form creator can apply or remove password-protection using the **Protect Document** or **Unprotect Document** commands on the **Tools** menu.
C.	The form creator cannot apply or remove non-password protection using the relevant buttons on the Forms toolbar.
D.	Password protection, once applied to a form, cannot be removed at a later stage.

Answers

1: C, **2:** A, **3:** B, **4:** D, **5:** A, **6:** C, **7:** D, **8:** D, **9:** A, **10:** A, **11:** D, **12:** C, **13:** B, **14:** B, **15:** B, **16:** D, **17:** D, **18:** B.

14 Tables: merging, splitting, sorting and totalling

Objectives

In this chapter you will learn how to:

- Convert tabbed text to a table
- Merge and split cells in a table
- Sort cells in a table
- Total columns of numbers in a table

New words

In this chapter you will meet the following terms:

- Table
- Sorting
- Separator character
- Sort order

Exercise files

In this chapter you will work with the following Word files:

- `Chapter14_Exercise_14-1_Before.doc`
- `Chapter14_Exercise_14-2_Before.doc`
- `Chapter14_Exercise_14-4_Before.doc`
- `Chapter14_Exercise_14-5_Before.doc`
- `Chapter14_Exercise_14-6_Before.doc`

Syllabus reference

In this chapter you will cover the following items from the ECDL Advanced Word Processing Syllabus:

- **AM3.4.1.1**. Use merge and split cell options in a table.
- **AM3.4.1.2**. Convert tabbed text into a table.
- **AM3.4.1.3**. Sort data (alphabetic or numeric) in a table (ascending or descending order).

- **AM3.4.1.4**. Perform addition calculations on a numeric list in a table.

About tables

Tables provide a way of arranging content – text, numbers, images or fields – in vertical *columns* and horizontal *rows*. The rectangular boxes in a table are called *cells*.

UK Premiership Top Scorers 2000-01

Player	Team	From Play	Penalties	Total Goals
Phillips	Sunderland	24	6	30
Shearer	Newcastle	18	5	23
Yorke	Manchester United	20	0	20
Bridges	Leeds United	19	0	19
Cole	Manchester United	19	0	19
Henry	Arsenal	15	2	17
Di Canio	West Ham	14	2	16
Iversen	Tottenham Hotspur	14	0	14
Quinn	Sunderland	14	0	14

Column
Row
Cell

Tables: when you need to use them

In Word, you will most commonly use tables to:

- **Present numerical information**. Material that includes numbers (such as a sales report) or conveys some kind of ranking (such as a list of best-selling products) is generally shown in tables.
- **Create multicolumn layout**. For brochures and other highly formatted documents, tables offer a quick, precise way of arranging content in multiple columns. (See Chapter 25 for more about Word's newspaper-style columns, which allow text to flow between columns.)
- **Design Word forms**. Tables offer the best way of positioning fields and labels in Word electronic forms (see Chapter 13).

When table cells contain numbers, you can perform arithmetical and statistical calculations on those numbers. In effect, you can use such a table as a spreadsheet.

Table

An arrangement of material (text, numbers, images or fields) in rows and columns. The individual elements of a table are called cells.

Working with tables: the four tasks

Here are the four tasks that you need to be able to perform with tables in Word:

- **Convert tabbed text to a table**. Exercise 14.1 takes you through the steps of creating a table from paragraphs of text that contain tabs.
- **Merge and split cells**. Sometimes, you may want to merge two or more cells into a single cell. At other times, you may want to split a single cell into a number of smaller cells. Exercises 14.2 and 14.3 show you how.
- **Sort cells in a table**. As Exercises 14.4 and 14.5 show, you can change the order of rows in a table.
- **Perform calculations in a table**. Tables are not just for layout. You can also perform calculations in tables. See Exercise 14.6.

Converting tabbed text to tables

Word provides an option for quickly converting text to a table when that material contains two *separator characters*:

- **A column separator character**. Word can use this character – typically a tab – to identify the beginning of a new column.
- **A row separator character**. Word can use this character – typically a paragraph mark or line break – to identify the beginning of a new row.

Generally, there are two situations when you want to converted tabbed text to tables:

- **The information was entered in tabbed format**. Tabs are an alternative to tables for creating multiple column layouts.
- **The information was imported in tab-delimited format**. You may find yourself working with text that has been imported, in tab-delimited format, from a non-Word file.

  As its name suggests, a tab-delimited file is one where text on the same row but in different columns is separated by tab characters.

Separator character

A character such as a tab or paragraph break that represents a logical division in the structure of a set of information.

When converting tabbed text to a table, ensure that each paragraph of text that you select for conversion contains the same number of tabs.

Extra tabs within any paragraph result in Word creating a row with empty, unwanted cells.

Exercise 14.1: Converting tabbed text to a table

In this exercise, you create a table by selecting and converting a number of paragraphs that contain tabs. The material is taken from *Designing Tomorrow's Education: Promoting Innovation with New Technologies*, EU Commission, March 2000.

1) Start Word and open the following file:

   `Chapter14_Exercise_14-1_Before.doc`

2) Select all the paragraphs of text that contain tabs.

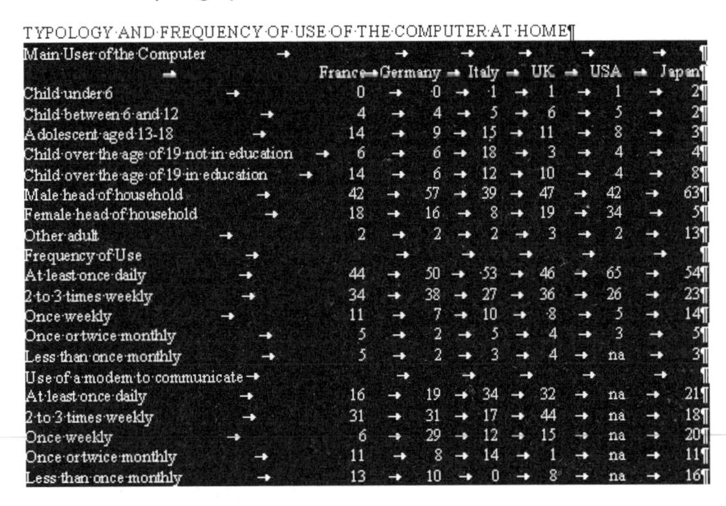

TYPOLOGY AND FREQUENCY OF USE OF THE COMPUTER AT HOME

Main User of the Computer						
	France	Germany	Italy	UK	USA	Japan
Child under 6	0	0	1	1	1	2
Child between 6 and 12	4	4	5	6	5	2
Adolescent aged 13-18	14	9	15	11	8	3
Child over the age of 19 not in education	6	6	18	3	4	4
Child over the age of 19 in education	14	6	12	10	4	8
Male head of household	42	57	39	47	42	63
Female head of household	18	16	8	19	34	5
Other adult	2	2	2	3	2	13
Frequency of Use						
At least once daily	44	50	53	46	65	54
2 to 3 times weekly	34	38	27	36	26	23
Once weekly	11	7	10	8	5	14
Once or twice monthly	5	2	5	4	3	5
Less than once monthly	5	2	3	4	na	3
Use of a modem to communicate						
At least once daily	16	19	34	32	na	21
2 to 3 times weekly	31	31	17	44	na	18
Once weekly	6	29	12	15	na	20
Once or twice monthly	11	8	14	1	na	11
Less than once monthly	13	10	0	8	na	16

3) Choose **Table | Convert Text to Table** to display the *Convert Text to Table* dialog box.

4) Word examines all your selected lines, finds the line containing the greatest number of tabs, and displays this number as the suggested value in the *Number of columns* box.

   In this example, accept the suggested value of seven columns.

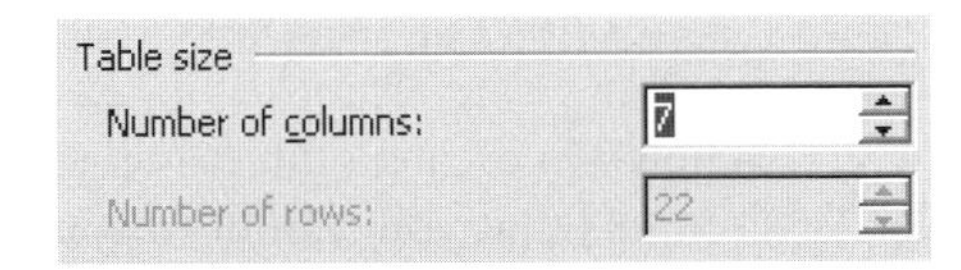

You cannot change the value in the *Number of rows* box. This is fixed by the number of paragraph marks or line breaks in the selected text.

Of the three available AutoFit options, select *AutoFit to contents*. This tells Word to adapt the width of each column to accommodate the text within it.

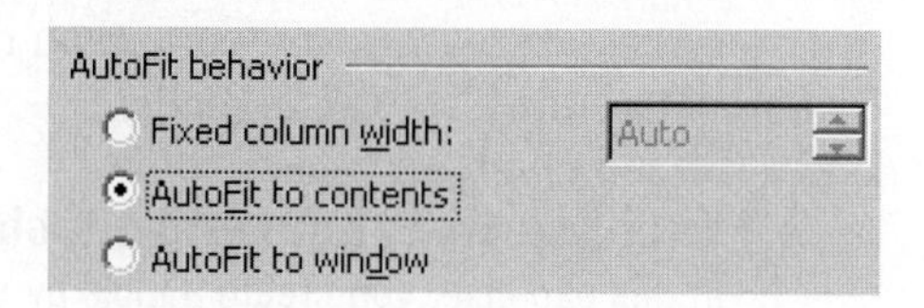

5) Word gives you the option of applying an AutoFormat layout to format your table by. Leave this field at its default value of *None*.

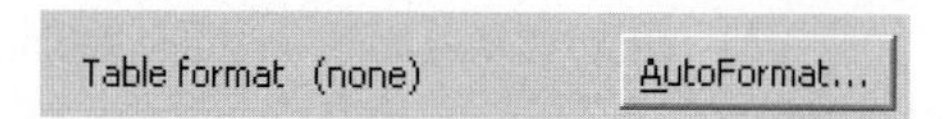

6) As your selected text contains tabs, Word correctly guesses that tabs are the separator character for the table conversion operation.

Separate text at
Paragraphs
Commas
Tabs
Other: -

Click **OK**, and then click anywhere outside your table to deselect it. Your converted table should look like this:

TYPOLOGY AND FREQUENCY OF USE OF THE COMPUTER AT HOME

Main User of the Computer						
	France	Germany	Italy	UK	USA	Japan
Child under 6	0	0	1	1	1	2
Child between 6 and 12	4	4	5	6	5	2
Adolescent aged 13-18	14	9	15	11	8	3
Child over the age of 19 not in education	6	6	18	3	4	4
Child over the age of 19 in education	14	6	12	10	4	8
Male head of household	42	57	39	47	42	63
Female head of household	18	16	8	19	34	5
Other adult	2	2	2	3	2	13
Frequency of Use						
At least once daily	44	50	53	46	65	54
2 to 3 times weekly	34	38	27	36	26	23
Once weekly	11	7	10	8	5	14
Once or twice monthly	5	2	5	4	3	5
Less than once monthly	5	2	3	4	na	3
Use of a modem to communicate						
At least once daily	16	19	34	32	na	21
2 to 3 times weekly	31	31	17	44	na	18
Once weekly	6	29	12	15	na	20
Once or twice monthly	11	8	14	1	na	11
Less than once monthly	13	10	0	8	na	16

7) Save your sample document with the following name, and close it:

`Chapter14_Exercise_14-1_After_Your_Name.doc`

Merging and splitting cells in tables

When you create a table, you must specify the number of columns that you want it to contain. As you work with a table, however, you may want to reduce or increase the number of cells in a particular row or rows. Word allows you to manipulate the number of cells in selected rows by merging or splitting their cells.

Exercise 14.2: Merging cells in a table

In this exercise, you will open an existing table and merge cells within some of its rows.

1) Open the following file:

   `Chapter14_Exercise_14-2_Before.doc`

2) Select the first row of the table by clicking just to the left of it.

TYPOLOGY AND FREQUENCY OF USE OF THE COMPUTER AT HOME

Main User of the Computer						
	France	Germany	Italy	UK	USA	Japan
Child under 6	0	0	1	1	1	2

3) Choose **Table | Merge Cells**.

   Word merges the seven cells so that the row now contains just a single cell. Click anywhere outside the row to deselect it. It should look like this:

TYPOLOGY AND FREQUENCY OF USE OF THE COMPUTER AT HOME

Main User of the Computer						
	France	Germany	Italy	UK	USA	Japan
Child under 6	0	0	1	1	1	2

4) Select the row that contains the words 'Frequency of Use' and repeat step 3.

Other adult	2	2	2	3	2	13
Frequency of Use						
At least once daily	44	50	53	46	65	54

5) Select the row that contains the words 'Use of a Modem to Communicate' and repeat step 3.

Less than once monthly	5	2	3	4	na	3
Use of a Modem to Communicate						
At least once daily	16	19	34	32	na	21

6) Save your sample document with the following name, and close it:

   Chapter13_Exercise_14-2_After_*Your_Name*.doc

What happens when the cells you select for merging contain text? The answer is that Word inserts paragraph marks to separate the text that was originally in different cells.

Joseph	Bloggs

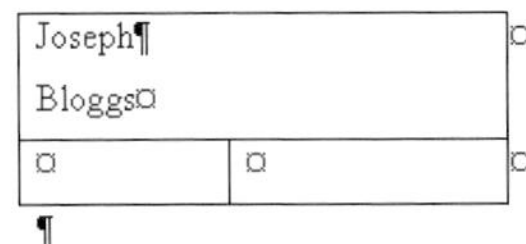

Joseph Bloggs	

Before ***After***

Exercise 14.3: Splitting cells in a table

In this exercise, you will create a table and then split a selected cell within it.

1) Click the **New** button on the Standard toolbar to create a new, blank document.
2) Choose **Table | Insert Table**, accept the dialog box default options as shown below, and click **OK**.

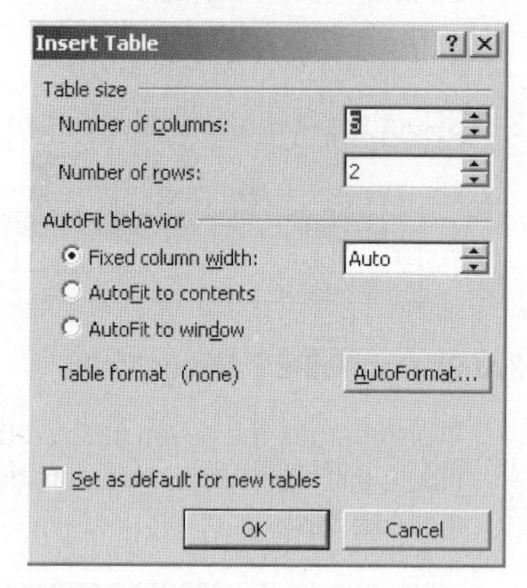

Word creates a new table as shown:

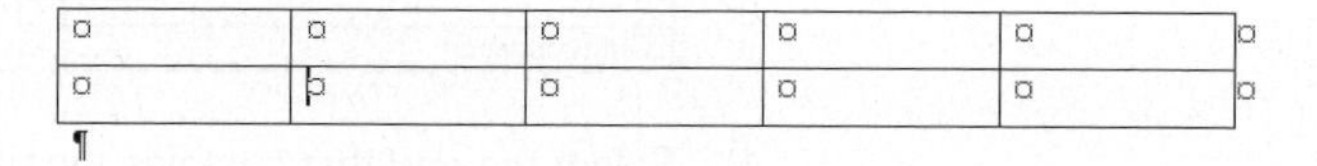

3) Click in the last cell of the second row and choose **Table | Split Cells**.
4) Accept the default dialog box options as shown, and click **OK**.

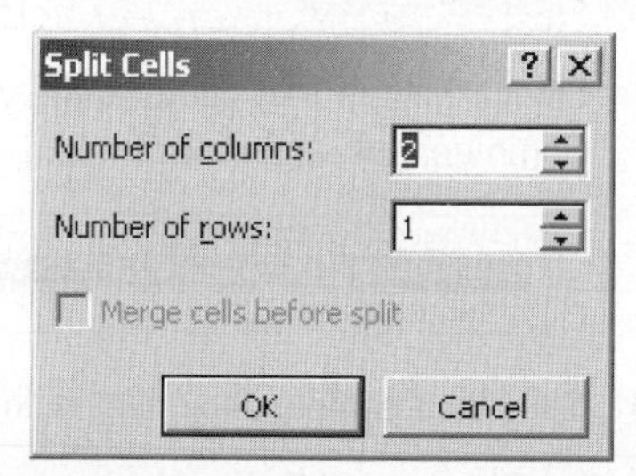

5) Click anywhere outside the table to deselect it. Your table should now look like this:

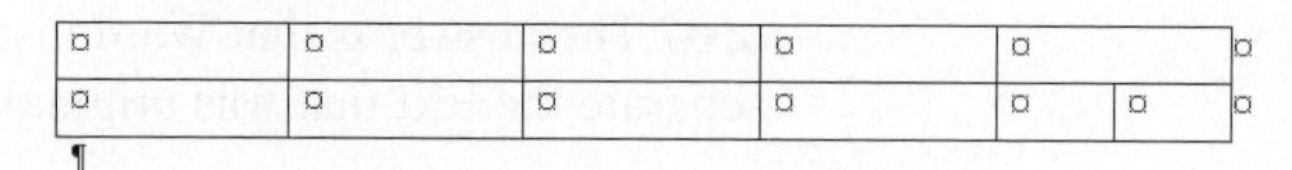

You can close the sample document without saving it.

What happens when the cell you select for splitting contains text? Word positions the text that was in the original cell in the *first* of the new cells.

If the text in the original, single cell contained paragraph marks, Word positions the text after the first paragraph mark in the second split cell, the text after the second paragraph mark in the third split cell, and so on.

Sorting rows in tables

Word allows you to rearrange the rows of a table, so that the rows are displayed in an order different to that in which they are currently displayed.

- **Alphabetically**. You may want to sort the rows alphabetically, in ascending (A–Z) or descending (Z–A) order.

  For example, when working with a table containing various customer details, it is generally easier to find a particular customer when the rows are sorted alphabetically by customer name.

Table sorted in ascending alphabetical order based on Name *column*

Name	Area	First Sale	Sales Value
Andrews	Region 4	21/05/99	234,987
Byrne	Region 2	12/09/00	340,344
Carlton	Region 6	03/07/01	125,000
Dunlop	Region 1	01/01/01	456,234
Engert	Region 2	12/09/01	520,988
Friars	Region 5	30/10/00	198,643
Greyfield	Region 4	17/10/99	231,040

- **Numerically**. You can also sort table rows according to the values of the numbers that they contain. Again, you can select an ascending (0–9) or descending (9–0) sort order.

  In the example of a table containing customer details, you might want to show customers in the order of their sales value.

Name	Area	First Sale	Sales Value
Engert	Region 2	12/09/01	520,988
Dunlop	Region 1	01/01/01	456,234
Byrne	Region 2	12/09/00	340,344
Andrews	Region 4	21/05/99	234,987
Greyfield	Region 4	17/10/99	231,040
Friars	Region 5	30/10/00	198,643
Carlton	Region 6	03/07/01	125,000

Table sorted in descending numeric order based on Sales Value *column*

Sorting does not change the content of a table, only the order in which the table rows are displayed.

Sorting
Rearranging rows in a table based on the values in one or more columns.

Exercise 14.4: Sorting rows in a table

In this exercise, you will sort a table that displays the top goal scorers in the English Football Premiership for the 2000–2001 season. This is an example of a one-level or 'simple' sort.

1) Open the following file:

   `Chapter14_Exercise_14-4_Before.doc`

   The rows are currently sorted in order of total goals scored, with the top scorers listed first.

   UK·Premiership·Top·Scorers·2000-01¶

Name	Team	From·Play	Penalties	Total·Goals
Phillips	Sunderland	24	6	30
Shearer	Newcastle	18	5	23
Yorke	Manchester·United	20	0	20
Bridges	Leeds·United	19	0	19
Cole	Manchester·United	19	0	19
Henry	Arsenal	15	2	17
Di·Canio	West·Ham	14	2	16
Iversen	Tottenham·Hotspur	14	0	14
Quinn	Sunderland	14	0	14

¶

2) Click in any cell of the *Name* column, and choose **Table | Sort** to display the *Sort* dialog box.

3) Notice that Word detects the column (in this case the *Name* column) in which you placed the insertion point.

   For text items, the sort order always defaults to ascending (A–Z). Also selected by default is the *Header row* option. Typically, your tables contain header rows that you do not want included in the sort operation.

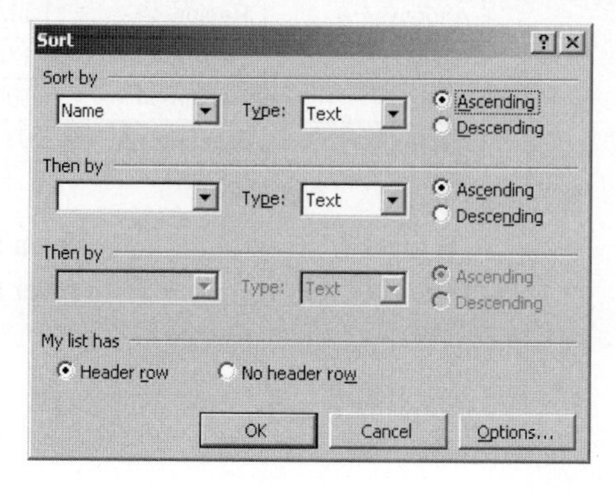

Accept the default dialog box values as shown above and click **OK**.

4) Word reorders the table rows in ascending order of player name, so that Bridges is listed first, Cole second and Yorke last.

UK·Premiership·Top·Scorers·2000-01¶

Name	Team	From·Play	Penalties	Total·Goals
Bridges	Leeds·United	19	0	19
Cole	Manchester·United	19	0	19
Di·Canio	West·Ham	14	2	16
Henry	Arsenal	15	2	17
Iversen	Tottenham·Hotspur	14	0	14
Phillips	Sunderland	24	6	30
Quinn	Sunderland	14	0	14
Shearer	Newcastle	18	5	23
Yorke	Manchester·United	20	0	20

Save your sample document with the following name, and close it:

`Chapter14_Exercise_14-4_After_Your_Name.doc`

Sorting by more than one column

Word enables you to specify up to three levels of sorting:

- **Single-level sort**. Rows are sorted according to the values in one column only (see Exercise 14.4).
- **Two-level sort**. Rows are sorted according to values in one column, *and*, where multiple rows contain the same value, the second sort order determines how these rows are ranked.

  Imagine that you have a customer table containing several customers who share the name Smith. If you sort the table by descending sales value within customer name, the Smiths with the higher sales values are listed first.
- **Three-level sort**. An example would be a customer table sorted by sales region within sales value within customer name. The third sort order takes effect only when multiple customers share the same name *and* the same sales value. In such rows, the values in the sales region column determine how the customers are listed.

Sort order

A way of sorting a table. Sort orders can be alphabetical or numeric, and can be in ascending (0–9, A–Z) or descending (Z–A, 9–0) sequence.

Exercise 14.5: Performing a two-level sort

In this exercise, you will perform a two-level sort: by player name within total goals scored. That is, you will list the table rows in order of goals scored. Where two players have scored the same number of goals, they will be sorted by name.

1) Open the following file:

   `Chapter14_Exercise_14-5_Before.doc`

2) Click anywhere in the table and choose **Table | Sort** to display the *Sort* dialog box.

3) In the *Sort by* area, select *Total Goals*, *Number* and *Descending*.

4) In the *Then by* area, select *Name*, *Text* and *Ascending*.

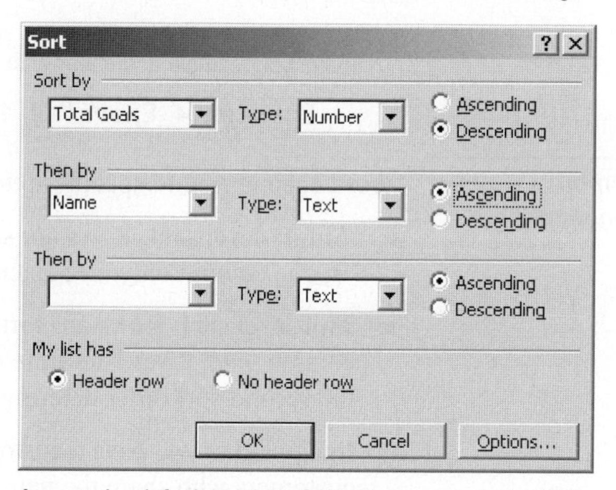

   Accept the default setting of *Header row* and click **OK**.

5) Word sorts the table rows as shown below:

UK·Premiership·Top·Scorers·2000-01¶

Name	Team	From·Play	Penalties	Total·Goals
Phillips	Sunderland	24	6	30
Shearer	Newcastle	18	5	23
Yorke	Manchester·United	20	0	20
Bridges	Leeds·United	19	0	19
Cole	Manchester·United	19	0	19
Henry	Arsenal	15	2	17
Di·Canio	West·Ham	14	2	16
Iversen	Tottenham·Hotspur	14	0	14
Quinn	Sunderland	14	0	14

¶

Notice that rows 4 and 5 under the header row contain the same value in the *Total Goals* column (19), but that Bridges is listed before Cole. And in rows 7 and 8 (*Total Goals*, 14) Iversen appears before Quinn.

6) Save your sample document with the following name, and close it:

`Chapter13_Exercise_14-5_After_`*`Your_Name`*`.doc`

Performing calculations in tables

A table in Word also offers the ability to arrange content in multiple columns, and, where the cells contain numbers, to perform spreadsheet-like calculations.

Exercise 14.6: Totalling numbers in a table

In this exercise, you add numbers that are arranged in vertical and horizontal lists within a table.

1) Open the following file:

`Chapter14_Exercise_14-6_Before.doc`

2) Click in the second cell on the bottom row of the table.

Customer	Jan	Feb	Mar	Total
Andrews	23	45	12	
Brittan	34	50	45	
Cranshaw	12	29	41	
Dunlop	45	63	71	
Edgars	12	18	31	

Click here

3) Choose **Table | Formula** to display the *Formula* dialog box.

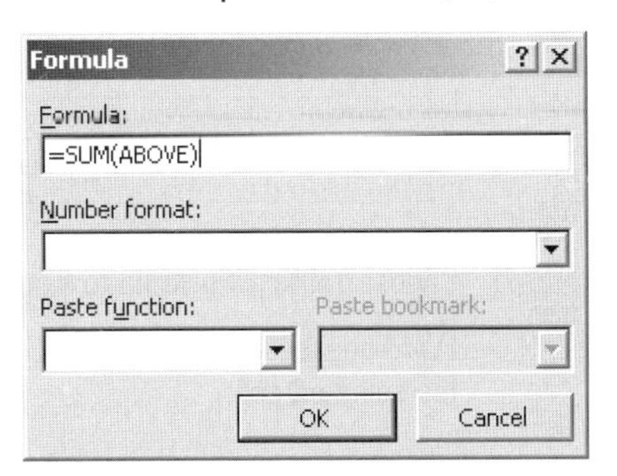

Word guesses correctly that you want to add numbers in the cells directly above the selected cell. Click **OK** to close the dialog box.

Word displays the sum of the cells in the second column (126) in the selected cell.

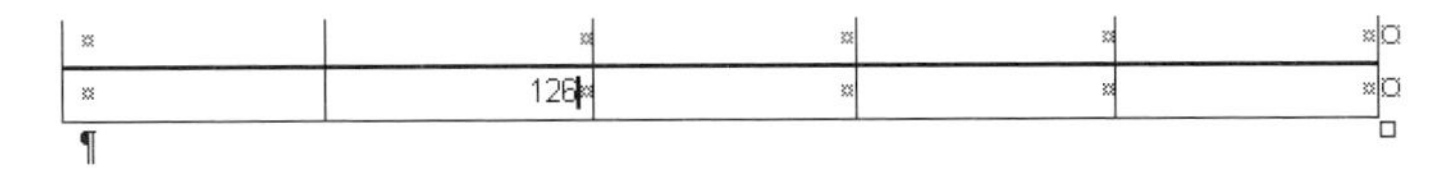

	126			

4) Click in the third cell on the bottom row of the table, and choose **Table | Formula** to display the *Formula* dialog box.

   In this case, Word guesses – incorrectly – that you want to add the cells to the left of the selected cell.

   Formula:
   =SUM(LEFT)

   Amend the value in the *Formula* box to the following:

   =SUM(ABOVE)

   Click **OK**.

5) Word displays the sum of the cells in the third column (205) in the selected cell.

   Click in the fourth cell of the bottom row and repeat step 4. Word should display the number 200 in this cell.

6) In the above steps, you have added numbers *vertically* in the table. In the remaining steps, you will add numbers *horizontally* across the table rows.

   Click in the last cell of the first row under the table header.

   Click here

Customer	Jan	Feb	Mar	Total
Andrews	23	45	12	
Brittan	34	50	45	
Cranshaw	12	29	41	
Dunlop	45	63	71	
Edgars	12	18	31	
	126	205	200	

7) Choose **Table | Formula** to display the *Formula* dialog box.

   Word guesses correctly that you want to add the cells to the left of the selected cell.

   Formula:
   =SUM(LEFT)

   Click **OK** to close the dialog box.

8) Click in the last cell of the second row under the header row and choose **Table | Formula** to display the *Formula* dialog box.

   In this case, Word guesses – incorrectly – that you want to add the cells above the selected cell.

Amend the value in the *Formula* box to the following:

=SUM(LEFT)

Click **OK**.

9) Click in the last cell of the third, fourth, fifth and seventh rows under the header row, and repeat step 9 in each case.

Your table should now look like this:

Customer	Jan	Feb	Mar	Total
Andrews	23	45	12	80
Brittan	34	50	45	129
Cranshaw	12	29	41	82
Dunlop	45	63	71	179
Edgars	12	18	31	61
	126	205	200	531

Save your sample document with the following name, and close it:

Chapter14_Exercise_14-6_After_*Your_Name*.doc

Chapter 14: quick reference

Tasks summary

Task	Procedure
Convert tabbed text to a table.	Select the text, choose **Table | Convert Text to Table**, select the number of columns, the column width, and the tab separator character, and click **OK**.
Merge multiple cells.	Select the cells and choose **Table | Merge Cells**.
Split a single cell.	Select the cell, choose **Table | Split Cells**, specify the number of columns and the rows that you want to split the selected cell into, and click **OK**.
Sort table rows.	Click in any cell, choose **Table | Sort**, select the column(s) to sort by and their sort order(s), specify whether the table contains a header row, and click **OK**.
Total numbers in a row or column.	Click in any cell, choose Table | Formula, accept or amend the suggested formula, and click **OK**. Typical formulas are as follows: =SUM(ABOVE) and =SUM(LEFT)

Concepts summary

Typically, you will use tables in Word to present *numerical information*, to create *multicolumn* layouts for brochures and newsletters, and to position fields and labels in Word *forms*.

You can *merge* multiple cells into a single cell, or *split* a single cell in multiple cells.

Tabbed text, including text imported in tab-delimited format, can be converted quickly to a table. The conversion process is based on Word identifying the tab character as the beginning of a new column and the paragraph mark or line break character as the beginning of a new row. Each tabbed paragraph should contain the same number of tabs. Extra tabs within any paragraph result in Word creating a row with empty, unwanted cells.

You can *sort* the rows of a table on the basis of the values in one, two or three columns. The *sort orders* available are alphabetical or numeric, and ascending (0–9, A–Z) or descending (Z–A, 9–0).

When table cells contain numbers, you can perform spreadsheet-like *calculations* on them.

Chapter 14: quick quiz

Circle the correct answer to each of the following multiple-choice questions about tables in Word.

Q1	Which of the following items cannot be stored in a Word table?
A.	A field.
B.	An image.
C.	A macro.
D.	Text.

Q2	In Word, which action do you take to begin converting selected tabbed text to a table?
A.	Click the **Convert Tabbed Text** button on the Tables and Borders toolbar.
B.	Right-click on the selected tabbed text and choose the **Convert Now** command from the pop-up menu.
C.	Choose the **Table | Convert Text to Table** command.
D.	Choose the **Tools | Conversion Options | Tabbed Text to Table** command.

Q3	Which of the statements about tabbed-text-to-table conversion in Word is not true?
A.	Word uses the tab character to identify where a new column should begin.
B.	Word uses the tab character to identify where a new row should begin.
C.	Word uses the line break character to identify where a new row should begin.
D.	For best results, all lines in the selected text should have the same number of tabs.

Q4	In a Word table, you merge four cells, each of which contains text, into a single new cell. Which statement describes the result?
A.	Word deletes the text that was in the original, pre-merged cells.
B.	Word displays the text that was in the first of the four cells in the new, merged cell. The text that was in the other cells is deleted.
C.	Word displays the text of the original cells in the single cell, with paragraph marks indicating the pre-merged cell boundaries.
D.	None of the above – you cannot merge a cell that contains text.

Q5	In a Word table, you split a cell that contains text into four new cells. Which statement describes the result?
A.	Word displays the text in the first of the four split cells.
B.	Word deletes the text that was in the original, unsplit cell.
C.	Word displays the text in all four of the new cells.
D.	None of the above – you cannot split a cell that contains text.

Q6	A single-column Word table lists numbers in the following order: 3, 8, 12, 45. How is the table sorted?
A.	Alphabetical, ascending.
B.	Numeric, ascending.
C.	Numeric, descending.
D.	Alphabetical, descending.

Q7	A single-column Word table lists names in the following order: Adams, Bergkamp, Dixon, Henry. How is the table sorted?
A.	Alphabetical, ascending.
B.	Numeric, descending.
C.	Numeric, ascending.
D.	Alphabetical, descending.

Q8	A Word table is sorted by customer name within sales value. What does this mean?
A.	Rows are listed in order of customer name. When two or more customers share the same name, the relevant rows are listed in order of sales value.
B.	The customer with the highest sales value is shown first, and the customer whose name begins with Z is shown last.
C.	Rows are listed in order of sales value. When two or more customers share the sales value, the relevant rows are listed in order of customer name.
D.	The customer with the highest sales value is shown last, and the customer whose name begins with Z is shown last.

Q9	Which of the following is a valid formula for adding numeric cells in a Word table?
A.	=ADD(LEFT)
B.	=TOTAL(ABOVE)
C.	=SUM(BENEATH)
D.	=SUM(LEFT)

Answers

1: C, **2:** C, **3:** B, **4:** C, **5:** A, **6:** B, **7:** A, **8:** A, **9:** D.

15 Spreadsheets in Word

Objectives

In this chapter you will learn how to:

- Embed worksheet cells in a Word document
- Modify embedded spreadsheet cells in Word

New words

In this chapter you will meet the following term:

- Embedded object

Exercise files

In this chapter you will work with the following files:

- `Chapter15_Exercise_15-1_Before.doc`
- `Chapter15_Exercise_15-1_Before.xls`
- `Chapter15_Exercise_15-2_Before.doc`

Syllabus reference

In this chapter you will cover the following item from the ECDL Advanced Word Processing Syllabus:

- **AM3.4.4.1:** Modify an embedded worksheet in a document.

About embedded objects

When working with files created in different MS Office 2000 applications, such as Word, Excel and PowerPoint, you can:

- Copy or cut an item from one type of file to the Clipboard.
- Use the **Edit | Paste Special** command to *embed* that item in the second type of file.

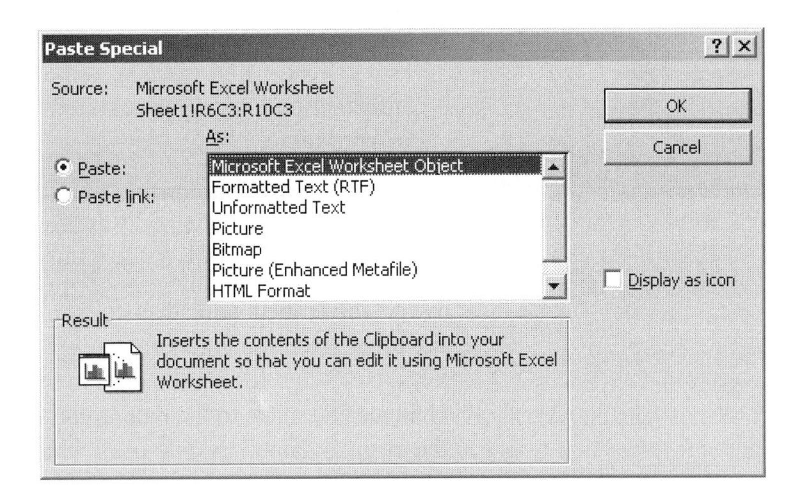

In this chapter, you will work with cells copied from Excel worksheets and embedded into Word documents. The cells are examples of *embedded objects*.

Pasting versus embedding

How does embedding differ from pasting?

- **Pasting.** When you paste Excel cells into a Word document, Word treats the worksheet cells as a Word table. You can edit and format the cells in the same way as you would the cells of a table.

  In effect, the pasted data become part of the Word document.

- **Embedding**. When you embed Excel cells into a Word document, the embedded cells bring with them the functionality of the worksheet from which they came. When you double-click the embedded cells, Word's menus and toolbars disappear from the screen and are replaced by Excel's.

  Although they are positioned within the Word document, the embedded data or 'objects' remain, in effect, part of Excel.

Embedded object

Data created in one MS Office application that are positioned in another application but that retain all the functionality of the original application.

Embedded objects: the benefits to you

Generally, there is a combination of two reasons why you will want to embed selected Excel cells, or an entire Excel worksheet, into a Word document:

- **The information is already entered in an Excel worksheet**. Consequently, it makes no sense to retype the information and any associated formulas and functions into a Word table.
- **The information contains complex calculations and/or large amounts of data**. It is easier to work with such information in an Excel worksheet than in a Word table.

When you embed worksheet cells in a Word document, you can use all of Excel's menu commands, toolbar buttons and shortcut keys to edit and format the cells in the embedded worksheet. Any changes you make to the data in the embedded object do not affect the original data in the file from which the object was copied.

Working with spreadsheets in Word: the two tasks

Here are the two tasks that you need to be able to perform with embedded spreadsheet cells in Word:

- **Embed worksheet cells in a Word document**. Exercise 15.1 takes you through the steps of embedding selected worksheet cells in a Word document.
- **Modify embedded spreadsheet cells in Word**. In Exercise 15.2 you discover how to manipulate worksheet cells that have been embedded in Word documents.

Embedding spreadsheet cells in Word

Exercise 15.1: Embed Excel worksheet cells in a Word document

In this exercise, you will select and copy a cell range from an Excel worksheet and then embed the cells in a Word document.

1) Start Word and open the following document:

   `Chapter15_Exercise_15-1_Before.doc`

2) Start Excel and open the following Excel workbook:

   `Chapter15_Exercise_15-1_Before.xls`

3) From Sheet1 in the Excel workbook, select the cell range B1:G39 and copy it to the Clipboard. You may now close the Excel workbook.
4) In the Word document, click at the second paragraph mark beneath the heading 'Balance Sheet for XYZ Enterprises'. This is the place at which you will embed the worksheet cells.
5) Choose **Edit | Paste Special** to display the *Paste Special* dialog box. In the *As* section of the dialog box, select *Paste* and select *Microsoft Excel Worksheet Object*.

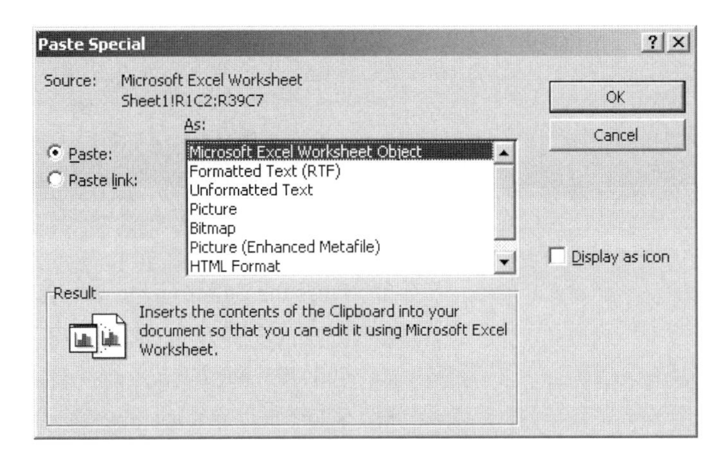

Click **OK**.

Word pastes the worksheets cells in your document as an embedded object.

6) Save your sample document with the following name, and close it:

`Chapter15_Exercise_15-1_After_`*`Your_Name`*`.doc`

Working with worksheet cells embedded in Word

When you create a table, you must specify the number of columns that you want it to contain. As you work with a table, however, you may want to reduce or increase the number of cells in a particular row or rows. Word allows you to manipulate the number of cells in selected rows by merging or splitting their cells.

Exercise 15.2: Amend embedded worksheet cells

In this exercise, you will amend a Word document that contains embedded worksheet cells and then edit and format those cells using Excel's functionality.

1) Open the following file:

`Chapter15_Exercise_15-2_Before.doc`

2) Double-click on the embedded worksheet cells, and click in the cell containing the words 'BALANCE SHEET'.

Notice that Word's menus and toolbars are replaced by the corresponding Excel ones.

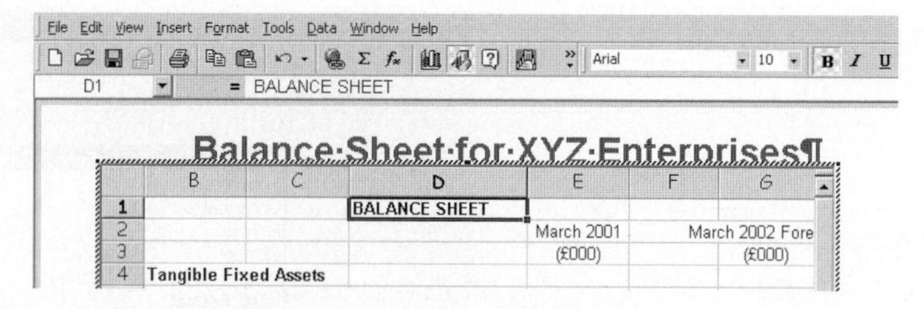

3) Press the **Delete** key to remove the words 'BALANCE SHEET'.
4) Click in cell E22 to select it, edit the cell content from '560' to '650', and press **Enter**.
5) Select the cell range B39:G39 and choose **Format | Cells**.
6) Click the **Borders** tab, select the *Outline* border, and click **OK**. Word places a border around the selected cells.
7) Scroll back up to the top of the embedded cells.
8) Double-click anywhere outside the embedded cells to deselect them. Notice that Excel's menus and toolbars disappear and are replaced by the corresponding Word ones.
9) Save your sample document with the following name, and close it:

`Chapter15_Exercise_15-2_After_`*`Your_Name`*`.doc`

Chapter 15: quick reference

Tasks summary

Keys	Description
Embed Excel worksheet cells in a Word document.	In Excel, select the cells and copy or cut them to the Clipboard.
	In Word, position the insertion point where you want to locate the cells and choose **Edit | Paste Special**.
	In the *As* section of the dialog box, select *Paste* and *Microsoft Excel Worksheet Object*, and click **OK**.
Modify worksheet cells that have been embedded in a Word document.	Double-click anywhere in the embedded cells to replace Word's menus and toolbars with the corresponding Excel ones.
	Perform the required actions. When finished, double-click anywhere outside the embedded cells to redisplay Word's menus and toolbars.

Concepts summary

When Excel cells are *embedded* into a Word document, they bring with them the functionality of the worksheet from which they came. When you double-click the embedded cells, Word's menus and toolbars disappear from the screen and are replaced by Excel's.

Chapter 15: quick quiz

Circle the correct answer to each of the following multiple-choice questions about embedded objects in Word.

Q1	Which one of the following commands do you choose to embed worksheet cells in a Word document?
A.	**Edit | Paste.**
B.	**Insert | Embedded Objects.**
C.	**Edit | Paste Special.**
D.	**Insert | New Objects.**

Q2	In Word, which of the following statements about embedded objects is untrue?
A.	Embedded objects bring with them the functionality of the application from which they came.
B.	You can embed data only from Excel in Word documents, and not data from PowerPoint or other MS Office applications.
C.	If you double-click on an embedded object, Word's menus and toolbars are replaced with those of the application in which the object was created.
D.	It is easier to work with complex calculations and/or large amounts of data in an embedded Excel worksheet than in a Word table.

Q3	In Word's *Paste Special* dialog box, which option do you select to embed cells from an Excel worksheet?
A.	Microsoft Excel Worksheet Object.
B.	Microsoft Workbook Object.
C.	Excel Worksheet Cells.
D.	Microsoft Excel Worksheet Cell Range.

Answers

1: C, **2:** B, **3:** A.

16 Charts in Word

Objectives

In this chapter you will learn how to:

- Create a chart with Microsoft Graph
- Modify chart formatting
- Reposition a chart in a Word document

New words

In this chapter you will meet the following terms:

- Microsoft Graph
- Data series
- Data label
- Plot area
- Datasheet
- Data point
- Chart area

Exercise files

In this chapter you will work with the following Word files:

- `Chapter16_Exercise_16-1_Before.doc`
- `Chapter16_Exercise_16-2_Before.doc`
- `Chapter16_Exercise_16-3_Before.doc`
- `Chapter16_Exercise_16-4_Before.doc`
- `Chapter16_Exercise_16-5_Before.doc`
- `Chapter16_Exercise_16-6_Before.doc`
- `Chapter16_Exercise_16-7_Before.doc`
- `Chapter16_Exercise_16-8_Before.doc`

- Chapter16_Exercise_16-9_Before.doc
- Chapter16_Exercise_16-10_Before.doc
- Chapter16_Exercise_16-11_Before.doc
- Chapter16_Exercise_16-12_Before.doc
- Chapter16_Exercise_16-13_Before.doc

Syllabus reference

In this chapter you will cover the following items from the ECDL Advanced Word Processing Syllabus:

- **AM3.4.4.2**: Create a chart from a table or pasted worksheet data in a document.
- **AM3.4.4.3**: Modify the formatting of a chart created from a table or pasted worksheet data.
- **AM3.4.4.4**: Position a chart in a document.

About Microsoft Graph

Word is supplied with a small application call *Microsoft Graph* that enables you to create and amend a variety of bar, column, pie and other charts based on information contained in tables. To present data in a Word table as a chart, you:

- Select the table, or cells within the table, in the Word document.

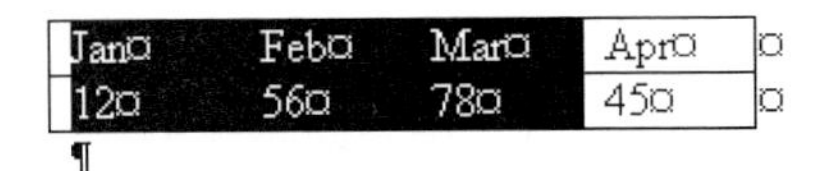

- Choose **Insert | Picture | Chart** to activate the Microsoft Graph application.

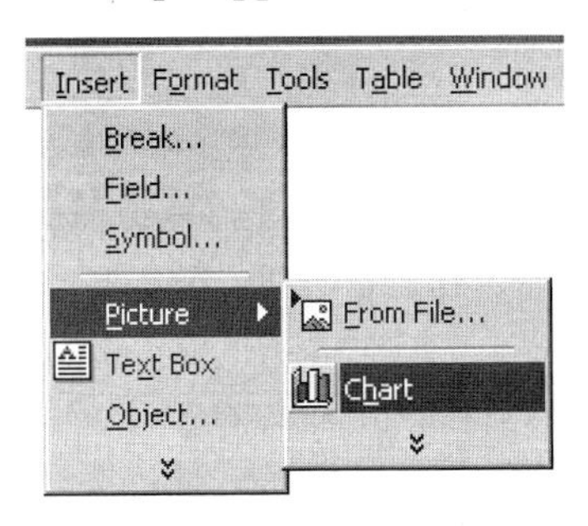

Microsoft Graph then creates a chart of the default type – a 3D bar chart – as an *embedded object* within your Word document.

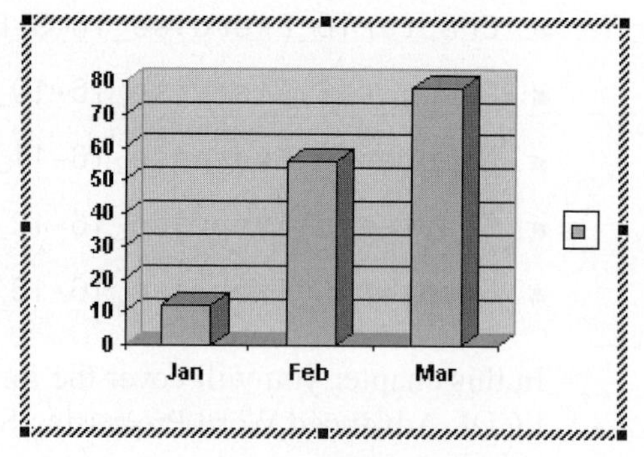

Want to change your chart format in any way? Just right-click on it to access a wide range of options that allow you to change the chart type and amend selected chart elements, such as font, background, axes and data labels. When finished, you can click outside the chart to return to Word.

Microsoft graph
A small application supplied with Word that enables you to create charts based on data in a table.

Charts and datasheets

Whenever you double-click a chart, you are shown another element called the *datasheet* – a small window that you use to modify the chart content. You do this by typing in your own numbers and text, over-writing those already present.

Document2 - Datasheet

		A	B	C	D	E
		Jan	Feb	Mar		
1	3-D Colum	12	56	78		
2						
3						
4						

To relocate the datasheet to a different part of your screen, click and drag its title bar. The datasheet is removed from the screen when you click anywhere outside the embedded chart. When you change an item in the datasheet, Microsoft Graph updates the chart immediately.

Datasheet
A table displayed by Microsoft Graph with every chart. You use the datasheet to modify the chart content.

Chart menu commands

When your embedded chart is active – that is, when you double-click on it – Word's menus disappear from the screen and are replaced by Microsoft Graph menus of charting commands.

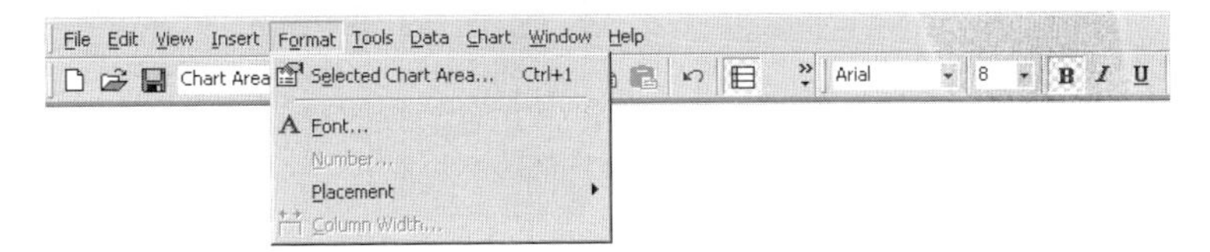

Working with charts in Word: the three tasks

Here are the three charting tasks that you need to be able to perform in Word:

- **Create a chart from a table**. Exercise 16.1 takes you through the steps of creating a chart from data in a Word table.
- **Modify chart formatting**. In Exercises 16.2 to 16.12, you discover the various options for amending the format of an embedded chart.
- **Reposition a chart in a document**. In Exercise 16.13, you learn how to relocate an embedded chart within a Word document.

Working with new charts

The starting point for the creation of a new chart is a table containing numbers and, usually, some text to identify the numbers. The table:

- may have been created directly in the Word document itself; or
- may have been created as a result of pasting Excel worksheet cells into the Word document.

Exercise 16.1: Create a chart from a word table

1) Start Word and open the following document:

   `Chapter16_Exercise_16-1_Before.doc`

2) Select all the columns except *Totals* on the right.

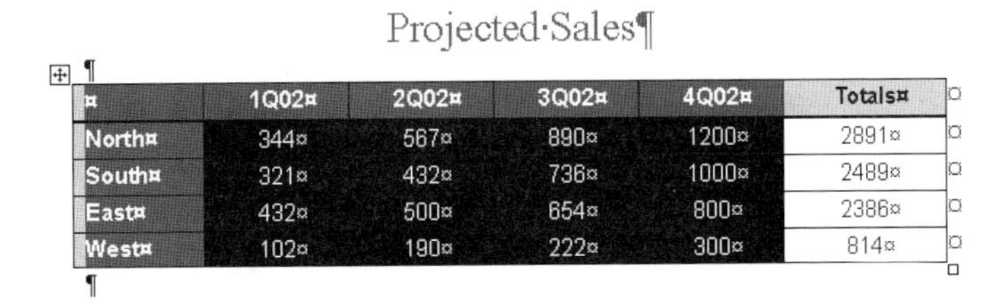

Projected Sales

	1Q02	2Q02	3Q02	4Q02	Totals
North	344	567	890	1200	2891
South	321	432	736	1000	2489
East	432	500	654	800	2386
West	102	190	222	300	814

3) Choose **Insert | Picture | Chart.**

4) Word activates Microsoft Graph, which inserts an embedded chart and an associated datasheet in your Word document.

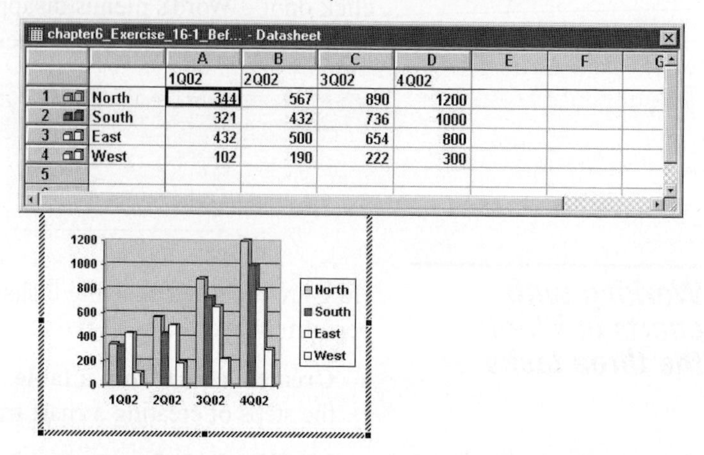

		A	B	C	D	E	F	G
		1Q02	2Q02	3Q02	4Q02			
1	North	344	567	890	1200			
2	South	321	432	736	1000			
3	East	432	500	654	800			
4	West	102	190	222	300			
5								

You can move the datasheet to a different part of your screen by dragging its title bar.

Click anywhere outside the embedded chart to close Microsoft Graph and return to Word.

5) Click once on your chart and drag its bottom right sizing handle until your chart is about the same width as the Word table above it. Click anywhere outside the chart to deselect it. Your document should look like this:

Projected·Sales¶

¶

¤	1Q02¤	2Q02¤	3Q02¤	4Q02¤	Totals¤
North¤	344¤	567¤	890¤	1200¤	2891¤
South¤	321¤	432¤	736¤	1000¤	2489¤
East¤	432¤	500¤	654¤	800¤	2386¤
West¤	102¤	190¤	222¤	300¤	814¤

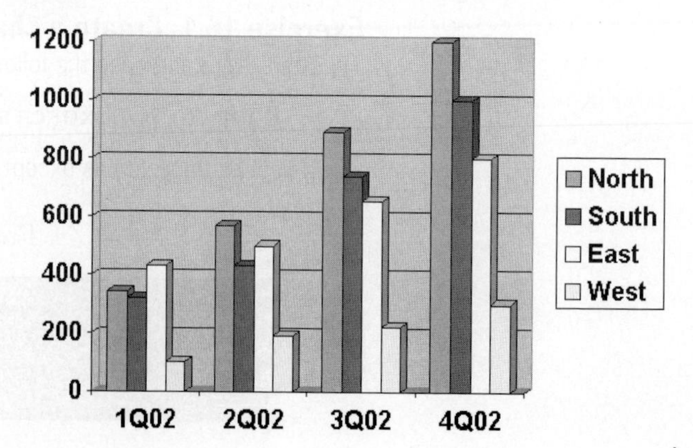

6) Save your sample document with the following name, and close it:

`Chapter16_Exercise_16-1_After_Your_Name.doc`

Working with chart elements

Data points, data series and data labels

Before working with chart formatting, it is important to understand a number of key terms relating to charting operations.

All charts are made up of *data points*. Each data point contains an item and its numerical value. Consider the four examples below:

Item	Value
Apples	4
Pears	3
Bananas	6

Item	Value
January	£ 1,965.34
February	£ 2,451.50
March	£ 8,301.49

Item	Value
Mary	15.00%
Catherine	50.00%
Margaret	35.00%

Item	Value
Sales	£4,954,032.00
Costs	£394,823.00
Overheads	£25,068.00

Each example consists of individual items (fruit, months, people and financial categories) and their associated numerical values. In the first example, the three data points are apples and 4, pears and 3, and bananas and 6. Other data points from the above examples are February and £2,451.50, Catherine and 50%, and overheads and £25,068.00

Data point

An item being measured and its measured value.

A collection of data points is called a *data series*. For instance, you may want to create a chart that shows the company's sales figures for different months, or a chart that compares one month's sales figures for different departments.

Data series

A group of related data points. A data series may compare different items measured at the same time, for example, or single items measured at different times.

By default, Microsoft Graph does not display labels. You can add two types of data labels to a chart:

- **Value labels**. These indicate the numerical values of the individual data points. See Exercise 16.2.
- **Text labels**. These display the names of the data points. By default, Microsoft Graph already displays these names on an axis. See Exercise 16.3.

Data label

The name or numerical value of a data point in a plotted data series.

Chart area and plot area

The region within an embedded chart consists of two distinct areas: the chart area and the plot area.

Chart area: the margin area surrounding the actual chart

Plot area: the area of the plotted chart

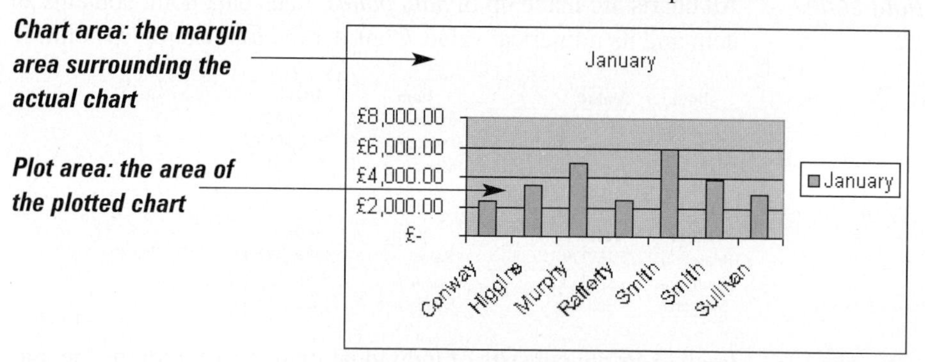

Chart area

The margin area inside the chart boundaries but outside the actual plotted chart. It typically holds labels identifying the chart axes.

Plot area

The area containing the actual plot. It is bounded by the two chart axes and is enclosed within the chart area.

Exercise 16.2: Add value labels to a chart

1) Open the following document:

   `Chapter16_Exercise_16-2_Before.doc`

2) Double-click anywhere on the chart to activate Microsoft Graph.
3) Right-click on the chart area (the margin area surrounding the actual chart), choose **Chart Options** from the pop-up menu, and select the **Data Labels** tab of the dialog box.
4) Select the *Show Value* option and click **OK**.

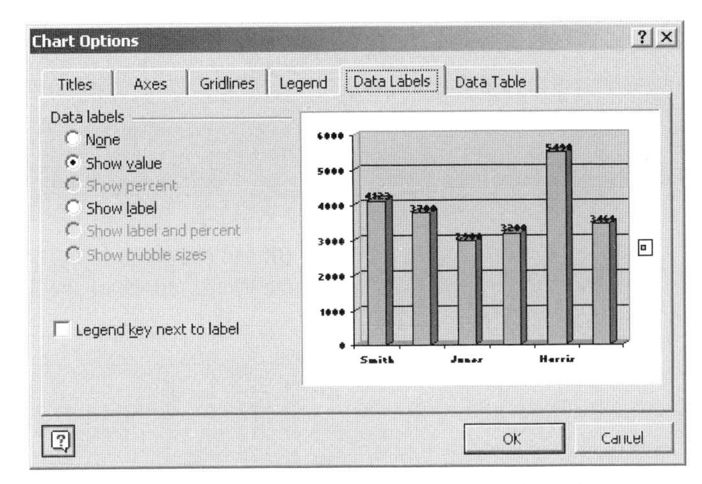

5) Right-click on the chart area, choose **Chart Type** from the pop-up menu, and select the 1D clustered column chart subtype.

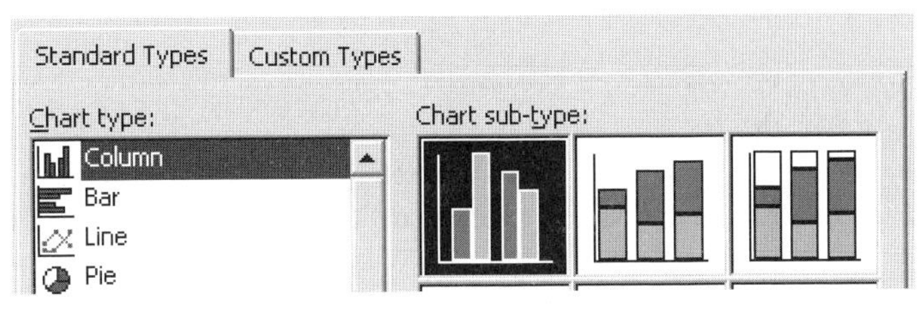

6) Click OK and click outside the chart to close Microsoft Graph and return to Word. Your chart should look like this.

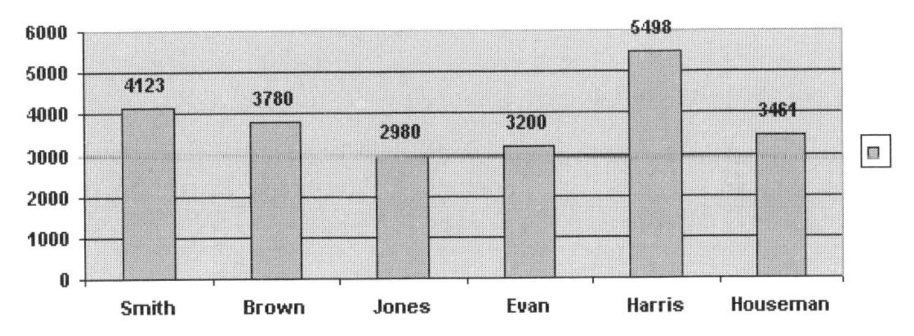

7) Save your sample document with the following name, and close it:

   `Chapter16_Exercise_16-2_After_`*`Your_Name`*`.doc`

Exercise 16.3: Add text labels to a chart

1) Open the following document:

   `Chapter16_Exercise_16-3_Before.doc`

2) Double-click anywhere on the chart to activate Microsoft Graph.

3) Right-click on the chart area (the margin area surrounding the actual chart), choose **Chart Options** from the pop-up menu, and select the **Data Labels** tab of the dialog box.

4) Select the *Show label* option.

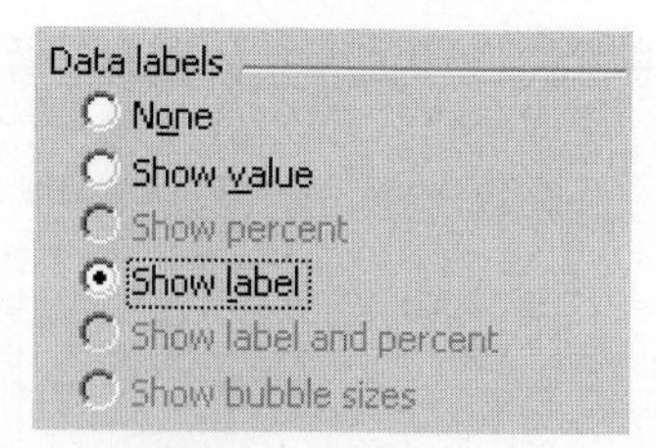

5) Click **OK** and click outside the chart to close Microsoft Graph and return to Word. Your chart should look like this:

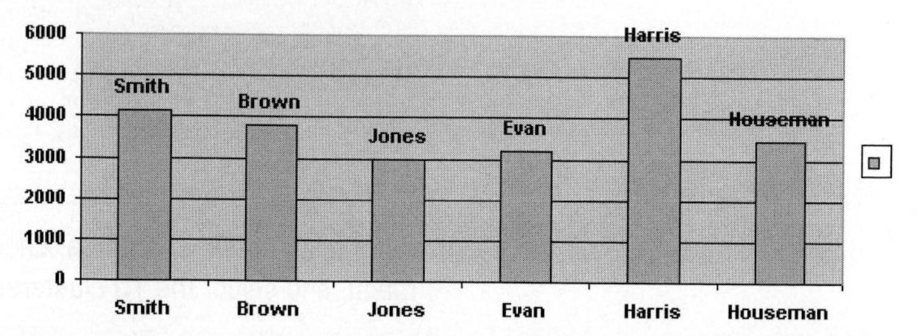

6) Save your sample document with the following name, and close it:

`Chapter16_Exercise_16-3_After_`*`Your_Name`*`.doc`

To format text and value labels, right-click on a label and choose **Format Data Labels** from the pop-up menu.

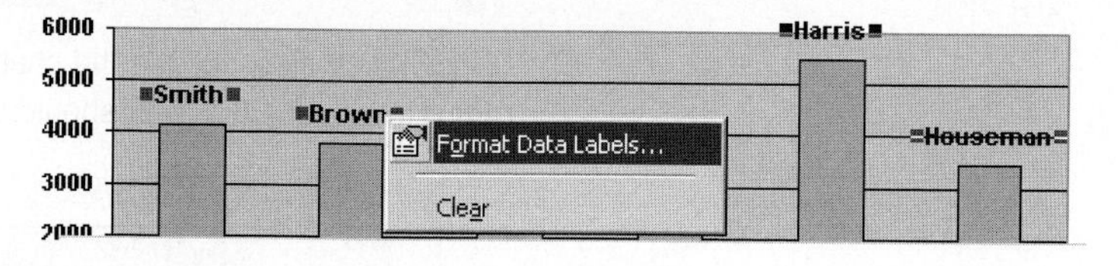

Select your required options from the following four dialog box tabs – **Patterns, Font**, **Number** and **Alignment** – and click **OK**.

Chart titles and legends

A chart title is text describing the chart. By default, Microsoft Graph centres the chart title in the chart area above the plot area.

A legend is a box that identifies the colours or patterns that are assigned to the data series or categories in a chart. Microsoft Graph offers the following placement options for a chart legend: bottom, corner, top, right and left. By default, the legend is located on the right. If you select a different placement, Microsoft Graph resizes the plot area automatically to accommodate it.

Exercise 16.4: Add a chart title

1) Open the following document:

`Chapter16_Exercise_16-4_Before.doc`

2) Double-click anywhere on the chart to activate Microsoft Graph.

3) Right-click on the chart area (the margin area surrounding the actual chart), choose **Chart Options** from the pop-up menu, and select the **Titles** tab of the dialog box.

4) In the *Chart title* box, type the following text and click **OK**:

    `Unit Sales in Third Quarter`

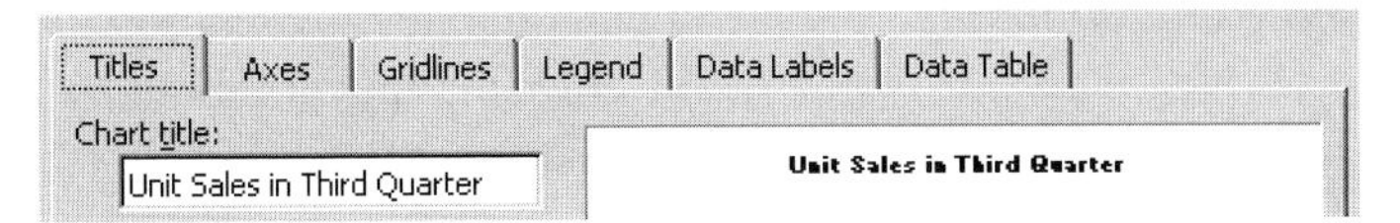

Click outside the chart to close Microsoft Graph and return to Word.

5) Save your sample document with the following name, and close it:

    `Chapter16_Exercise_16-4_After_`*`Your_Name`*`.doc`

To edit the chart title, double-click the chart to activate Microsoft Graph, and then click anywhere within the title text. You can now edit the text. To remove the chart title, click on it oncc and prcss **Dclctc**.

To reformat the chart title, right-click anywhere on it and choose **Format Chart Title** from the pop-up menu displayed.

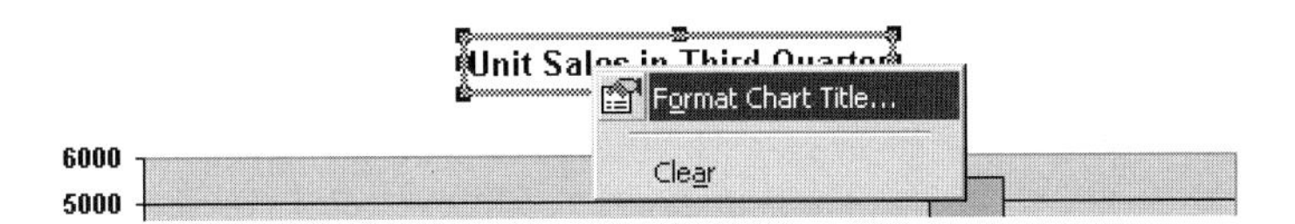

Select the options you require from the three tabs of the dialog box – **Patterns**, **Font** and **Alignment** – and click **OK** when finished.

Exercise 16.5: Move and delete a chart legend

1) Open the following document:

    `Chapter16_Exercise_16-5_Before.doc`

2) Double-click anywhere on the chart to activate Microsoft Graph.

3) Right-click on the chart area (the margin area surrounding the actual chart), choose **Chart Options** from the pop-up menu, and select the **Legend** tab of the dialog box.

4) Click on the various *Placement* options and notice the effect of relocating the legend in the preview area on the right of the dialog box.

5) Click the show *legend* option to deselect it and click **OK**.

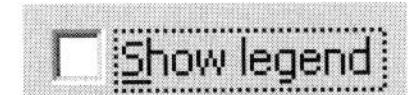

6) Click outside the chart to close Microsoft Graph and return to Word. You can see that the legend is no longer displayed.

7) Save your sample document with the following name, and close it:

`Chapter16_Exercise_16-5_After_`*`Your_Name`*`.doc`

Chart axes formatting

You can change how Microsoft Graph displays a chart axis by right-clicking anywhere on it and choosing **Format Axis** from the pop-up menu displayed.

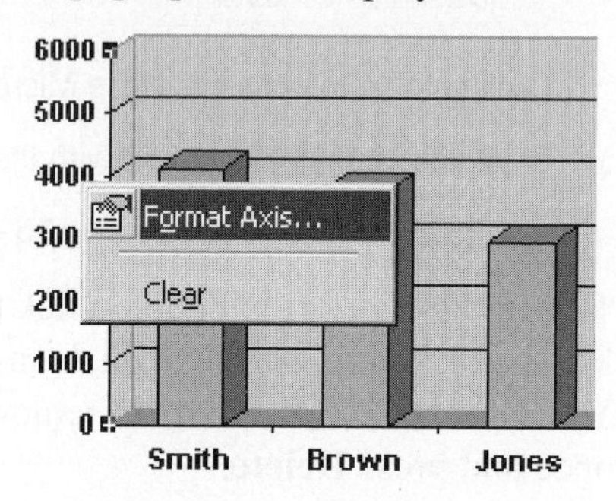

Select the options you require from the five tabs of the dialog box – **Patterns**, **Scale**, **Font**, **Number** and **Alignment** – and click **OK** when finished.

Exercise 16.6: Amend chart axis format

1) Open the following document:

`Chapter16_Exercise_16-6_Before.doc`

2) Double-click anywhere on the chart to activate Microsoft Graph.

3) Right-click on the horizontal category axis and choose the **Format Axis** command from the pop-up menu displayed.

4) In the dialog box displayed, click the **Font** tab and change the colour to red.

5) Click the **Patterns** tab and change the colour to red.

6) Click **OK** to close the dialog box.

7) Repeat steps 3 to 6 for the horizontal category value axis.

8) Click outside the chart to close Microsoft Graph and return to Word. You can see that the axis text is in the colour you chose.

9) Save your sample document with the following name, and close it:

`Chapter16_Exercise_16-6_After_`*`Your_Name`*`.doc`

Chart axes values

On the **Scale** tab of the *Format Axis* dialog box, Microsoft Graph allows you to change the minimum, maximum and increment values displayed for each axis, the units in which the chart values are shown, and the point at which the two axes cross. The three more commonly used options that can help you make a chart axis more readable are:

- **Minimum value**. Typically, you will want your chart to highlight the *relative differences* between the various data series rather than the absolute value of each series. See Exercise 16.7.
- **Units**. Does your chart consist of large numbers? If, for example, the chart values range from 1,000,000 to 50,000,000, you can display the numbers on the axis as 1 to 50 and show a label that indicates that the units express millions. See Exercise 16.8.
- **Increment value**. If the axis values are too crowded, you can increase the increment between each display value, say, from 1000 to 2000. See Exercise 16.9.

Exercise 16.7: Change the minimum axis value

1) Open the following Word document:

    `Chapter16_Exercise_16-7_Before.doc`

2) You can see that none of the data series have a value of less than 3000.

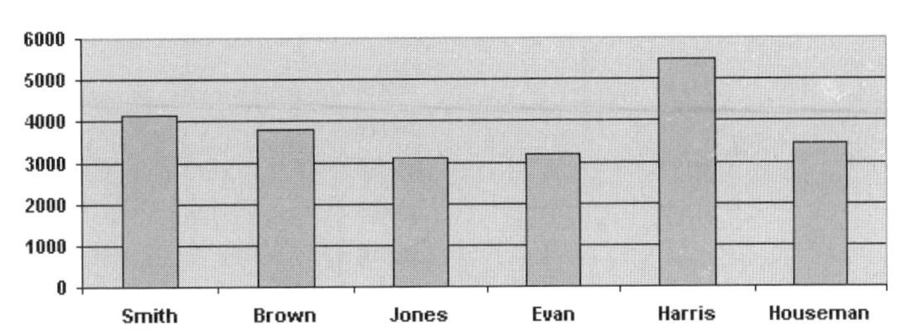

    By changing the minimum value to 3000, you will be able to see more clearly how the various data series differ from each other.

    Double-click anywhere on the chart to activate Microsoft Graph.

3) Right-click on the vertical value axis and choose the **Format Axis** command from the pop-up menu displayed.
4) In the dialog box displayed, click the **Scale** tab, and change the *Minimum* value to 3000. The *Category (X) Axis Crosses* at value automatically changes to 3000.

Value (Y) axis scale

Auto

- [ ] Minimum: 3000
- [x] Maximum: 6000
- [x] Major unit: 500
- [x] Minor unit: 100
- [x] Category (X) axis

Crosses at: 3000

5) Click **OK** to close the dialog box. Click outside the chart to close Microsoft Graph and return to Word. Your chart should now look like this:

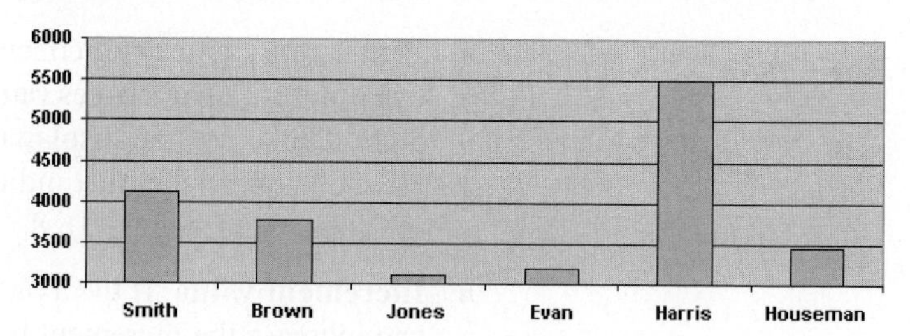

6) Save your sample document with the following name, and close it:

`Chapter16_Exercise_16-7_After_`*`Your_Name`*`.doc`

Exercise 16.8: Change the axis units

1) Open the following Word document:

`Chapter16_Exercise_16-8_Before.doc`

2) You can see that the data series values range from 300,000 to 600,000.

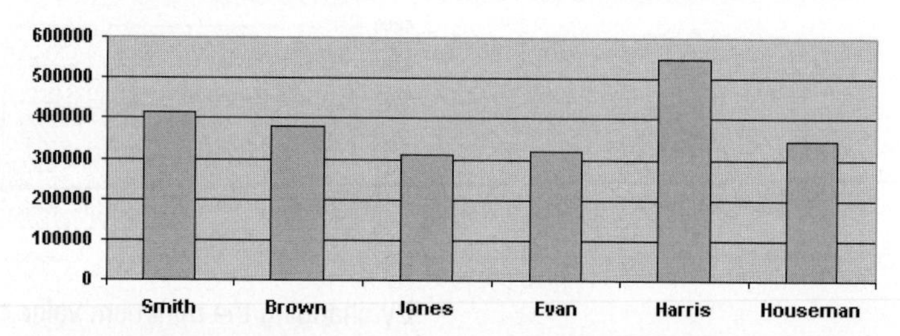

By changing the chart units to thousands, you can make your *y* axis easier to read.

Double-click anywhere on the chart to activate Microsoft Graph.

3) Right-click on the vertical value axis and choose the **Format Axis** command from the pop-up menu displayed.

4) In the dialog box displayed, click the **Scale** tab, and select the *Thousands* option from the *Display units* drop-down list.

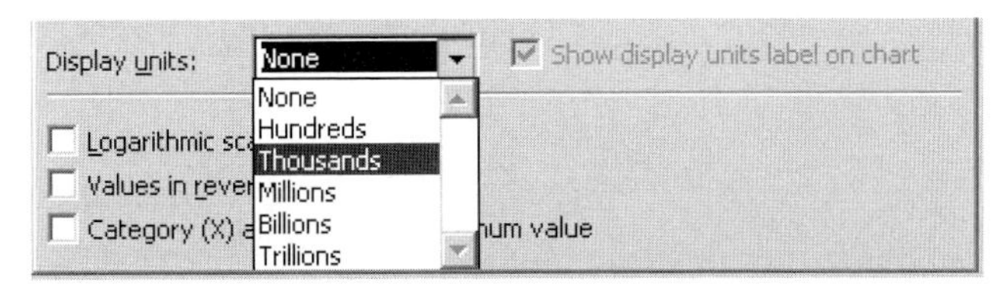

Ensure that the *Show display units label on chart* checkbox is selected.

5) Click **OK** to close the dialog box. Click outside the chart to close Microsoft Graph and return to Word. Your chart should now look like this:

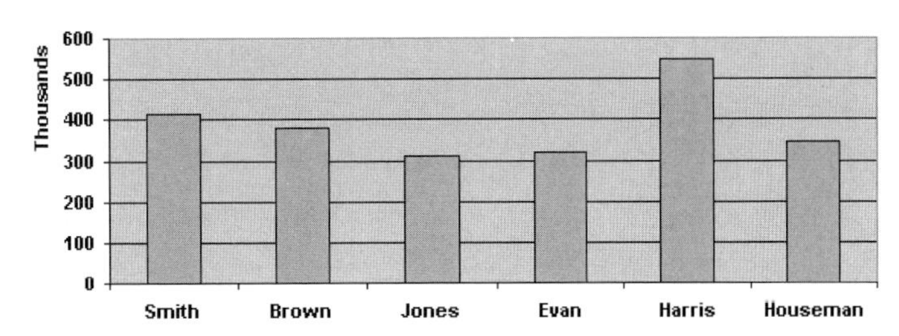

6) Save your sample document with the following name, and close it:

   Chapter16_Exercise_16-8_After_*Your_Name*.doc

Exercise 16.9: Change the axis unit increments

1) Open the following Word document:

   Chapter16_Exercise_16-9_Before.doc

   You can see that the *y* axis is divided into increments of 1000.

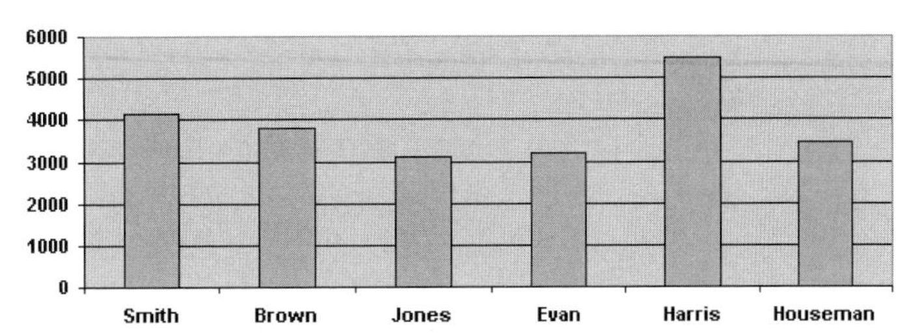

2) Double-click anywhere on the chart to activate Microsoft Graph.

3) Right-click on the vertical value axis and choose the **Format Axis** command from the pop-up menu displayed.

4) In the dialog box displayed, click the **Scale** tab, and change the value in the *Major unit* box from 1000 to 2000.

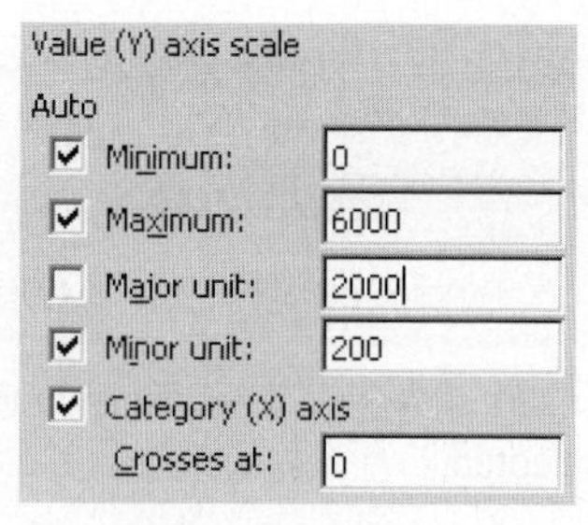

5) Click **OK** to close the dialog box. Click outside the chart to close Microsoft Graph and return to Word. Your chart should now look like this:

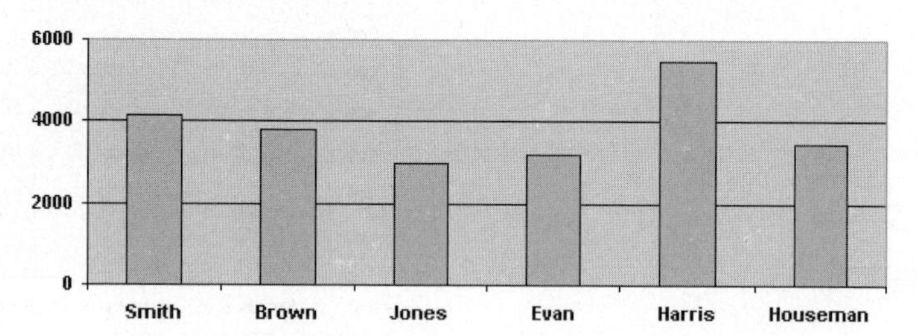

6) Save your sample document with the following name, and close it:

`Chapter16_Exercise_16-9_After_`*`Your_Name`*`.doc`

Chart gridlines

Gridlines are lines that extend across the plot area from the increment values on one or both axes. They make it easier for the reader to evaluate the chart's data values.

- On column charts, gridlines typically extend only from the *y* axis.
- On bar charts, gridlines typically extend only from the *x* axis.

Microsoft Graph offers two kinds of gridlines: *major gridlines*, which are displayed by default, and *minor gridlines* for more precise data evaluation. Pie charts have no gridlines.

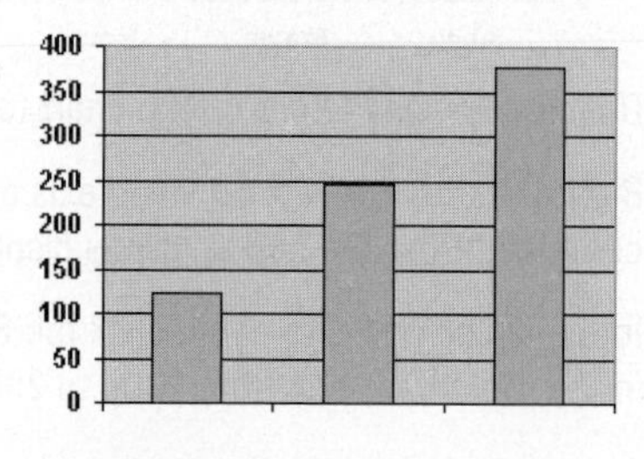

Column chart with gridlines from y axis

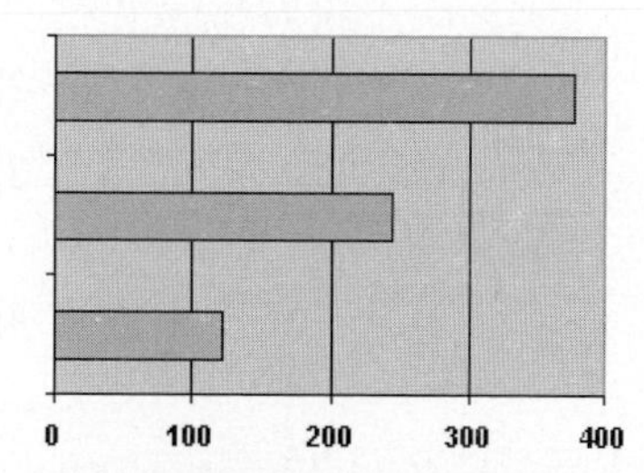

Bar chart with gridlines from x axis

Exercise 16.10: Amend chart gridlines

1) Open the following Word document:

   `Chapter16_Exercise_16-10_Before.doc`

   You can see major gridlines extending horizontally from the *y* axis.

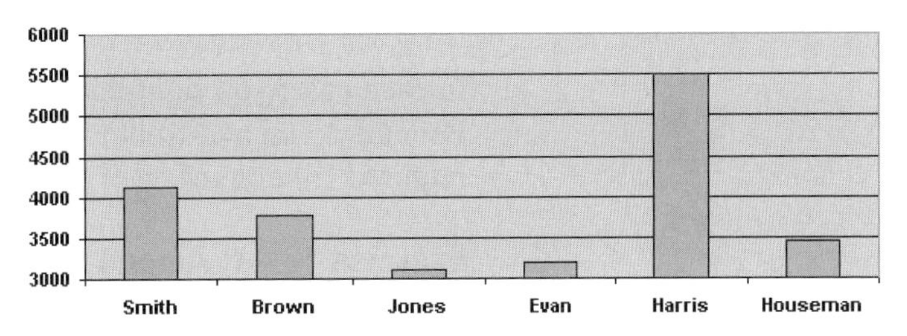

2) Double-click anywhere on the chart to activate Microsoft Graph.
3) Right-click on the chart area (the margin area surrounding the actual chart), choose **Chart Options** from the pop-up menu, and select the **Gridlines** tab.
4) In the dialog box displayed, click the *Minor gridlines* checkbox in the *Value (y) axis* section. The *Major gridlines* checkbox is selected by default.

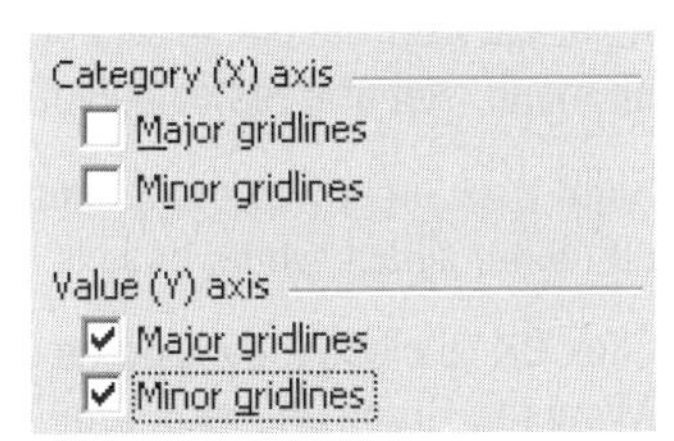

5) Click **OK** to close the dialog box. Click outside the chart to close Microsoft Graph and return to Word. You chart now looks as shown.

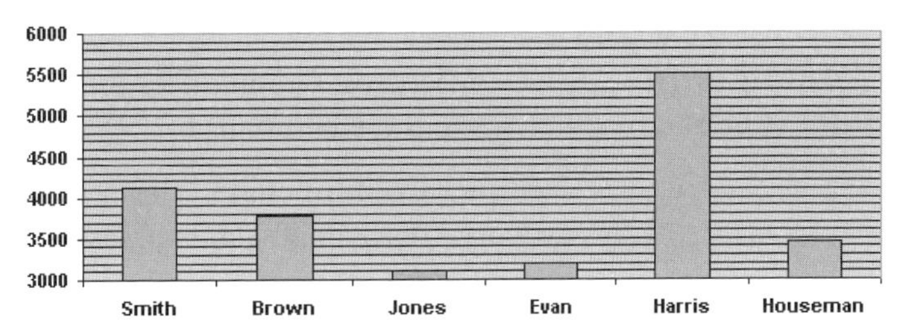

6) Save your sample document with the following name, and close it:

   Chapter16_Exercise_16-10_After_*Your_Name*.doc

Working with chart colours

Microsoft Graph enables you to change the colours of three parts of a chart:

- **Chart area**. This is the margin area surrounding the chart.
- **Plot area**. This is the area of the actual chart.
- **Data series**. This is the data plotted by the chart. Depending on the chart type, this can consist of columns, bars or 'slices' of a pie.

In each case, you right-click on the relevant element, choose the **Format** command from the pop-up menu, and select your required fill colour. See Exercise 16.11.

Exercise 16.11: Amend chart colours

1) Open the following Word document:

   `Chapter16_Exercise_16-11_Before.doc`

   As you can see, the chart area is currently coloured white, the plot area is grey, and the data series is blue.

2) Double-click anywhere on the chart to activate Microsoft Graph.
3) Right-click on the chart area, choose **Format Chart Area** from the pop-up menu, select a light yellow colour, and click **OK**.
4) Right-click on the plot area, choose **Format Plot Area** from the pop-up menu, select a red colour, and click **OK**.
5) Right-click on any column, choose **Format Data Series** from the pop-up menu, select white, and click **OK**.

   Click **OK** to close the dialog box. Click outside the chart to close Microsoft Graph and return to Word.

6) Save your sample document with the following name, and close it:

   Chapter16_Exercise_16-11_After_*Your_Name*.doc

Working with chart types

Microsoft Graph offers more than a dozen chart types. Here are the three main ones:

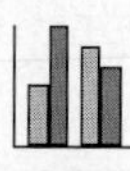

- **Column chart**. The default type, in which items are shown horizontally and values vertically.

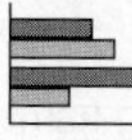

- **Bar chart**. A sideways column chart that shows items horizontally and values vertically.

- **Pie chart**. Shows the proportion of each item that makes up the total.

Changing the chart type

To change the current type of a chart, double-click the chart to activate Microsoft Graph, right-click anywhere within the chart, choose the **Chart Type** command from the pop-up menu, and select a different type (or subtype) from the *Chart Type* dialog box.

In Exercise 16.12 you will convert an existing column chart, the default type, to a bar chart.

Exercise 16.12: Changing a column chart to a bar chart

1) Open the following Word document:

   `Chapter16_Exercise_16-12_Before.doc`

2) Double-click anywhere on the column chart to activate Microsoft Graph.

3) Right-click on the chart area, and choose **Chart Type** from the pop-up menu.

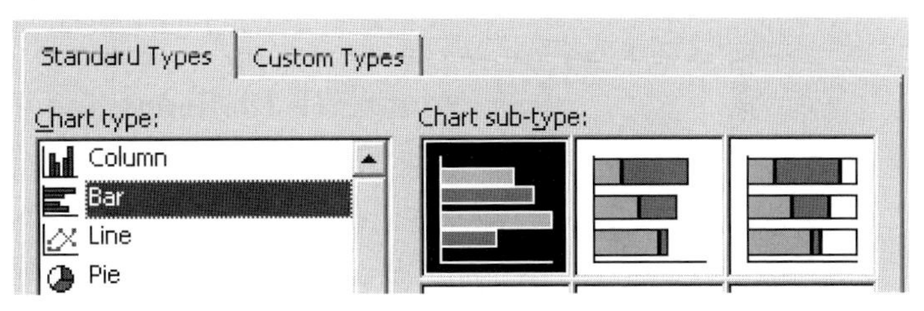

4) In the *Chart type* area, select *Bar* and click **OK** to close the dialog box.

5) Click outside the chart to close Microsoft Graph and return to Word. Your chart should now look like this:

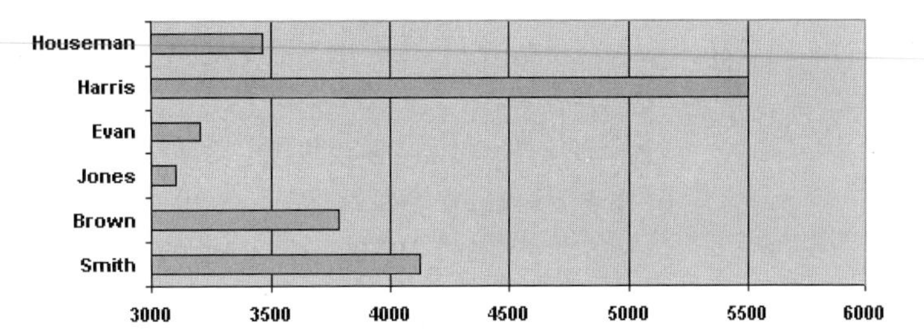

6) Save your sample document with the following name, and close it:

   Chapter16_Exercise_16-12_After_*Your_Name*.doc

Repositioning and resizing a chart

When you double-click on an embedded chart, you activate Microsoft Graph and can use all its charting functions. When you have finished working with the chart, you can then click anywhere outside the chart area to return to Word.

When you click *once* on an embedded chart, you remain within Word and you can work with the chart as if it were an inserted picture.

- **Repositioning a chart**. By default, Word treats an embedded chart as a paragraph, just as it does an inserted picture. You can reposition such a chart with the **Format | Paragraph** command.

  Alternatively, you can right-click the embedded chart, choose **Format Object**, click the **Layout** tab, select the *Behind text* or *In front of text* option, and click **OK**.

  Your embedded chart is no longer a paragraph but a free-floating object that you can click on and drag to a new position with the mouse.

- **Resizing a chart**. Click once anywhere in the chart to select it, click on a sizing handle, and then drag it to the required size.

Exercise 16.13: Reposition a chart

1) Open the following Word document:

   `Chapter16_Exercise_16-13_Before.doc`

2) Select the table at the bottom of the page.

Security¤	90%¤	¤
Can't·see·or·touch·product¤	69%¤	¤
Privacy·of·giving·personal·info¤	67%¤	¤
Customer·recourse¤	64%¤	¤
Prefer·other·ways·of·shopping¤	59%¤	¤
Too·new/people·aren't·ready¤	16%¤	¤
Hard·to·find·what·you're·looking·for¤	9%¤	¤

3) Choose **Insert | Picture | Chart**.

4) Word activates Microsoft Graph, which inserts an embedded chart and an associated datasheet in your Word document.

   Click anywhere outside the chart to return to Word.

5) Select the table that supplied the data for the chart, and choose **Edit | Cut** to remove it from the Word document.

6) Click the chart once, choose **Format | Paragraph**, change the left indentation from 5 to 0 cm, and click **OK**.

7) Click once on your chart, and drag its bottom-right sizing handle to the right margin of the page.

8) Double-click anywhere on the column chart to activate Microsoft Graph.

9) Right-click on the chart legend, choose **Format Legend** from the pop-up menu, click the **Font** tab, change the font to 10 point, and click **OK**.

10) Right-click on the *y* axis, choose **Format Axis** from the pop-up menu, click the **Font** tab, change the font to 10 point, and click **OK**. Your sample document should now look like this:

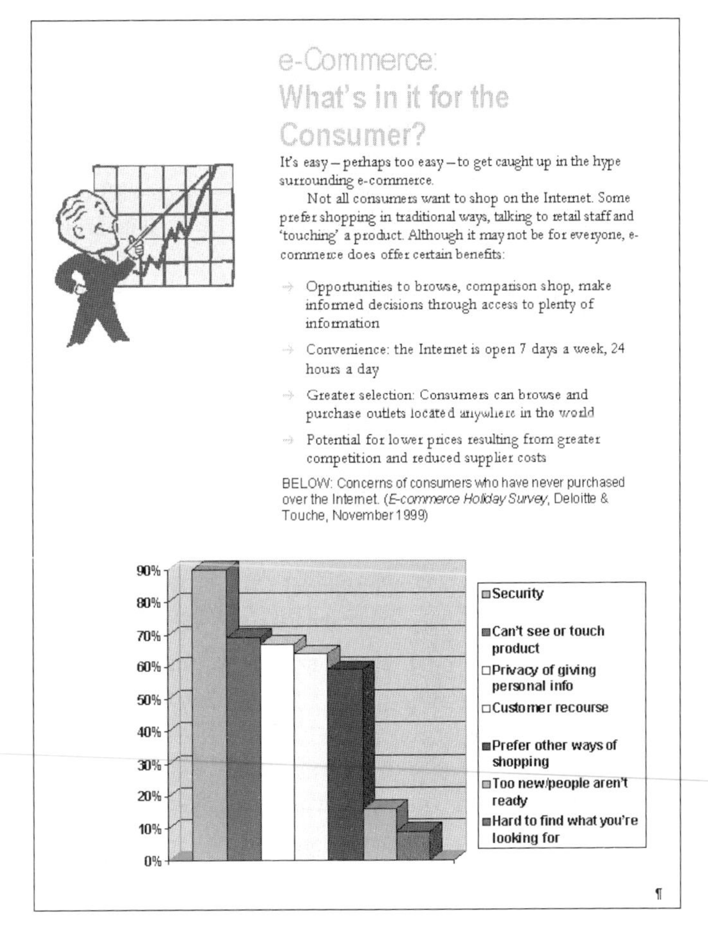

e-Commerce:
What's in it for the Consumer?

It's easy – perhaps too easy – to get caught up in the hype surrounding e-commerce.

Not all consumers want to shop on the Internet. Some prefer shopping in traditional ways, talking to retail staff and 'touching' a product. Although it may not be for everyone, e-commerce does offer certain benefits:

- Opportunities to browse, comparison shop, make informed decisions through access to plenty of information
- Convenience: the Internet is open 7 days a week, 24 hours a day
- Greater selection: Consumers can browse and purchase outlets located anywhere in the world
- Potential for lower prices resulting from greater competition and reduced supplier costs

BELOW: Concerns of consumers who have never purchased over the Internet. (*E-commerce Holiday Survey*, Deloitte & Touche, November 1999)

11) Save your sample document with the following name, and close it:

Chapter16_Exercise_16-13_After_*Your_Name*.doc

Chapter 16: quick reference

Tasks summary

Task	Procedure
Create a chart based on data in a table.	Select the table, or cells within the table, in the Word document, and choose **Insert | Picture | Chart**.
Add value labels to a chart.	Right-click on the chart area, choose **Chart Options**, click the **Data Labels** tab, select the Show Value option, and click **OK**.
Add text labels to a chart.	Right-click on the chart area, choose **Chart Options**, click the **Data Labels** tab, select the *Show label* option, and click **OK**.
Add a chart title.	Right-click on the chart area, choose **Chart Options**, click the **Titles** tab, enter the title in the *Chart title* box, and click **OK**.
Reposition or delete a legend.	Right-click on the chart area, choose **Chart Options**, click the **Legend** tab, select your required options, and click **OK**.
Amend axis format.	Right-click on an axis, choose **Format Axis**, select your required options on the **Font** and **Patterns** tabs, and click **OK**.
Change axis minimum value.	Right-click on an axis, choose **Format Axis**, click the **Scale** tab, change the minimum value, and click **OK**.
Change axis units.	Right-click on an axis, choose **Format Axis**, click the **Scale** tab, select from the *Display units* drop-down list, and click **OK**.
Change the chart axis unit increments.	Right-click on an axis, choose **Format Axis**, click the **Scale** tab, change the major unit, and click **OK**.
Amend gridlines display.	Right-click on the chart area, choose **Chart Options**, click the **Gridlines** tab, select your required options, and click **OK**.
Amend chart colours.	Right-click on the chart area, plot area or a data series, choose **Format**, select your required fill colour, and click **OK**.
Change chart type.	Right-click on the chart area, choose **Chart Type**, select a different type (or subtype), and click **OK**.
Reposition a chart.	In Word, click the chart, choose **Format | Paragraph**, enter your new value(s), and click **OK**. Alternatively, right-click the chart, choose **Format Object**, click the **Layout** tab, select the *Behind text* or *In front of text* option, and click **OK**. You can then drag the chart with the mouse.

Concepts summary

Word is supplied with a small application named *Microsoft Graph* that enables you to create and amend a variety of bar, column, pie and other charts based on information contained in tables.

To present data in a Word table as a chart, select all or part of the table and choose **Insert | Picture | Chart**. Microsoft Graph then creates a chart of the default type – a 3D bar chart – as an *embedded object* within your Word document. You can return to Word by clicking anywhere outside the chart.

Associated with every chart is a *datasheet* – a small window that you use to modify the chart content. You do this by typing in your own numbers and text, over-writing those already present.

A chart contains three main areas: the *chart area* (the margin area surrounding the chart), the *plot area* (the area of the actual chart), and the *data series* (the data plotted by the chart). Depending on the *chart type*, the data series can consist of columns, bars or slices of a pie.

In any chart, a *data point* is an item being measured and its measured value. You can add *value labels* to indicate the numerical values of the individual data points, and *text labels* to display the names of the data points. You can also add a *chart title* to describe the chart, and you can amend, move or delete the chart legend – the box that identifies the colours or patterns of the data series.

Options for working with the *chart axes* include the ability to change the *minimum value* to highlight the relative rather than absolute value of the data series, the units in which the values are expressed (for example, hundreds or thousands), and, if the axis values are too crowded, the increment value.

Gridlines are lines that extend across the plot area from the increment values on one or both axes. They make it easier for the reader to evaluate the chart's data values. Microsoft Graph offers major gridlines (displayed by default) and optional minor gridlines for more precise data evaluation. Pie charts have no gridlines.

You can change the colour of any element by right-clicking on it, choosing the **Format** command from the pop-up menu, and selecting your required fill colour.

By default, Word treats an embedded chart as a paragraph, just as it does an inserted picture. You can reposition such a chart with the **Format | Paragraph** command. Alternatively, you can right-click the embedded chart, choose **Format Object**, click the **Layout** tab, select the *Behind text* or *In front of text* option, and click **OK**. You can then drag the chart with the mouse.

Chapter 16: quick quiz

Circle the correct answer to each of the following multiple-choice questions about charts in Word.

Q1	What is the name of the application supplied with Word that enables users to create and work with charts?
A.	Microsoft Chart Maker.
B.	Microsoft Graph Builder.
C.	Microsoft Chart.
D.	Microsoft Graph.

Q2	In Word, which command do you choose to create a chart based on data contained in table cells?
A.	**Insert | Picture | Chart.**
B.	**Format | Chart | New.**
C.	**Tools | Insert | Chart.**
D.	**Format | Chart | Insert.**

Q3	By default, which item(s) does Microsoft Graph display within the area of an embedded chart?
A.	The chart only.
B.	The datasheet only.
C.	The chart and its associated datasheet.
D.	The chart and its associated worksheet.

Q4	In Word, which action do you take to return from Microsoft Graph to the Word document that contains the chart?
A.	Click anywhere outside the chart.
B.	Choose **Chart** | **Exit**.
C.	Choose **File** | **Close Chart and Return to Word**.
D.	Choose **File** | **Close**.

Q5	In a Word document, which action do you take to work with an embedded chart?
A.	Right-click anywhere on the chart.
B.	Double-click anywhere on the chart.
C.	Right-click on the plot area.
D.	Right-click on the plot area and choose **Format** | **Object**.

Q6	In Microsoft Graph, which action do you take to access the options for changing the format of a chart axis?
A.	Right-click on the axis, choose **Axis Pattern**, and select your required options from the **Font** and **Shading** tabs.
B.	Click to select the axis and select your required options on the **Format** tab.
C.	Right-click on the axis, choose **Format Axis**, and select your required options on the **Font** and **Pattern** tabs.
D.	Click to select the axis and select your required options on the **Format** and **Color** tabs.

Q7	In Microsoft Graph, which of the following chart axis actions can you not perform?
A.	Change the minimum value displayed by the chart axis.
B.	Set the chart axis width to zero.
C.	Amend the units in which the chart axis values are displayed.
D.	Change the increment between the displayed chart axis units.

Q8	In Microsoft Graph, which of the following statements about gridlines is untrue?
A.	On column charts, gridlines extend by default only from the *y* axis.
B.	Pie charts do not display gridlines by default.
C.	On bar charts, gridlines extend by default only from the *x* axis.
D.	Column charts do not display gridlines by default.

Q9	In Microsoft Graph, which of the following statements is untrue?
A.	The chart area is the plot area and the data series it contains.
B.	A data point indicates a particular value within a data series.
C.	The plot area is the area of the actual chart. It is bounded by the two chart axes and is enclosed within the chart area
D.	A data series is a collection of data points. Depending on the chart type, the data series can consist of columns, bars or slices of a pie.

Answers

1: D, **2:** A, **3:** C, **4:** A, **5:** B, **6:** C, **7:** B, **8:** D, **9:** A.

17 Footnotes and endnotes

Objectives

In this chapter you will learn how to:

- Create footnotes and endnotes
- Amend the content, format and placement of footnotes and endnotes
- Remove footnotes and endnotes

New words

In this chapter you will meet the following terms:

- Footnote
- Endnote

Exercise files

In this chapter you will work with the following Word files:

- `Chapter17_Exercise_17-1_Before.doc`
- `Chapter17_Exercise_17-2_Before.doc`
- `Chapter17_Exercise_17-3_Before.doc`
- `Chapter17_Exercise_17-4_Before.doc`
- `Chapter17_Exercise_17-5_Before.doc`
- `Chapter17_Exercise_17-6_Before.doc`
- `Chapter17_Exercise_17-7_Before.doc`

Syllabus reference

In this chapter you will cover the following items from the ECDL Advanced Word Processing Syllabus:

- **AM3.3.3.1:** Create or delete footnotes and endnotes.
- **AM3.3.3.2:** Modify existing footnotes or endnotes.
- **AM3.3.3.3:** Modify format and positioning of footnotes or endnotes.

About footnotes and endnotes

You can use footnotes and endnotes to supply additional information about text in a document, or to cite references or sources. The main difference between footnotes and endnotes is their location. Here are some important points about footnotes and endnotes:

- **Positioning**. Footnotes typically appear at the bottom of individual pages. Endnotes typically appear at the end of the document.
- **Footnotes and endnotes together**. You can include both footnotes and endnotes in the same document.
- **Reference marks**. Every footnote or endnote consists of text and an indicator called a reference mark – this is a superscripted symbol or number that appears in the body of the document to indicate that a footnote or endnote is present.

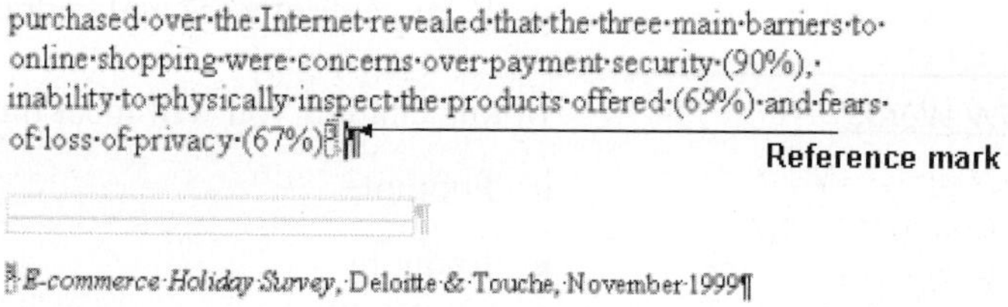

purchased·over·the·Internet·revealed·that·the·three·main·barriers·to·online·shopping·were·concerns·over·payment·security·(90%),·inability·to·physically·inspect·the·products·offered·(69%)·and·fears·of·loss·of·privacy·(67%)[1]¶

Reference mark

[1] *E-commerce·Holiday·Survey*,·Deloitte·&·Touche,·November·1999¶

- **Symbol reference marks**. Symbols are a good choice as reference marks when you have only one or two footnotes or endnotes in a document. For example, **Subject to status or availability* or *♦Certain conditions may apply.*
- **Sequential numbering**. By default, Word inserts sequential numbers as references marks. When you move, delete or relocate a numbered footnote or endnote, Word automatically updates all other footnotes or endnotes in the document.
- **Editing and formatting**. In Print Layout view, you edit and format footnote and endnote text in the same way that you edit and format text in the body of a document.

The Footnote and Endnote *dialog box*

You insert footnotes and endnotes with the **Insert | Footnote** command.

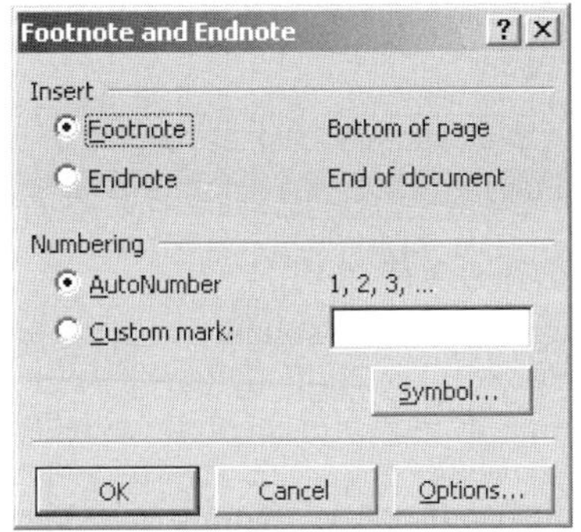

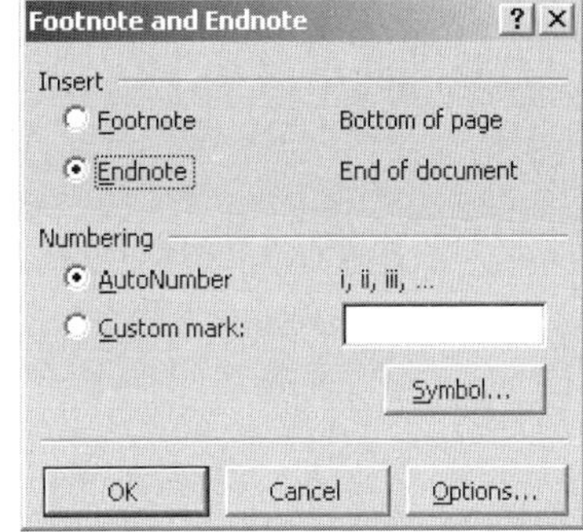

Footnotes, endnotes and document views

In Print Layout view, you edit and format individual footnotes and endnotes simply by positioning the insertion point over them and clicking and selecting the note text, as required.

In Normal view, Word does not display notes by default. To view them, choose **View | Footnotes**. Word opens a separate window at the bottom of your screen in which you can access and work with all footnotes and endnotes in your document.

Working with footnotes: the four tasks

Here are the four tasks that you need to be able to perform with footnotes and endnotes in Word:

- **Create footnotes and endnotes**. Exercises 17.1 and 17.2 take you through the steps of creating footnotes with sequential numbers and with custom symbols. In Exercise 17.6, you learn how to create numbered endnotes.
- **Edit note text**. Exercise 17.3 shows you how to amend footnote text. You edit endnote text in a similar way.
- **Amend note format**. In Exercise 17.4, you discover the various options for modifying footnote format. You reformat endnotes in a similar way.
- **Delete notes**. You delete a footnote in Exercise 17.5 and delete an endnote in Exercise 17.7.

Working with new footnotes

In the first two exercises, you will create new footnotes in two documents.

Exercise 17.1: Create numbered footnotes

1) Start Word and open the following document:

   `Chapter17_Exercise_17-1_Before.doc`

2) Are you in Print Layout view? If not, choose **View | Print Layout**.

3) Click in the location where you want the footnote reference mark to appear.

   In this example, click at the end of the first paragraph of body text, after the '2005' but before the full stop.

   INTRODUCTION¶

   Internet·usage·continues·to·grow·dramatically·throughout·the·world.· From·a·base·of·40·million·users·in·1996,·the·number·of·online·users· is·predicted·to·reach·1·billion·in·2005.¶

4) Choose **Insert | Footnote** to display the *Footnote and Endnote* dialog box.

5) In the *Insert* area, select *Footnote*. In the *Numbering* area, select *AutoNumber*. The default numbering system for footnotes is 1,2,3, …

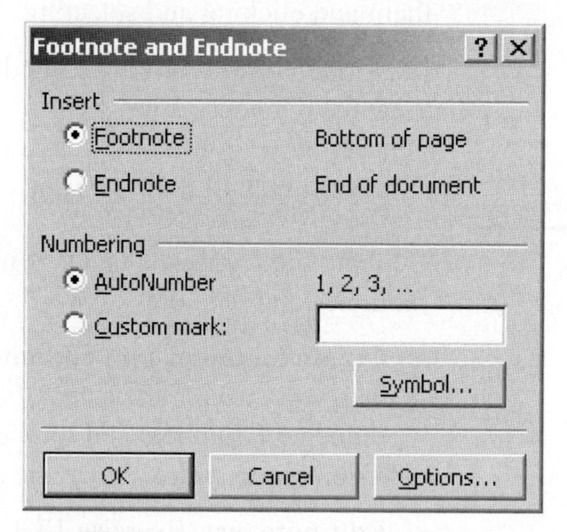

   Click **OK**.

6) Word moves the insertion point to the bottom of the page. You can see a line and the number 1. This is where the footnote will appear.

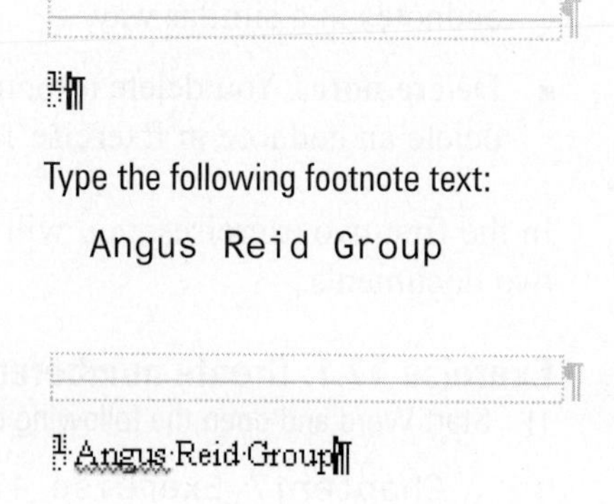

   Type the following footnote text:

   Angus Reid Group

   1·Angus·Reid·Group¶

7) Move to the second page of the sample document, and locate the paragraph of body text that begins with 'By 2003'.

8) Click in the end of the paragraph, after the word 'models' but before the full stop.

only·2.7%·of·new·car·sales·currently·take·place·over·the·Net,·but·as·many·as·40%·of·purchases·involve·the·Net·at·some·point,·with·consumers·using·it·to·compare·prices·or·look·at·the·latest·models.¶

9) Choose **Insert | Footnote**, select *Footnote*, select *AutoNumber*, and click **OK**.

   Word moves the insertion point to the bottom of the page. Type the following footnote text:

   The Economist, Feb. 2000

10) Drag over the words 'The Economist', and click the **Italics** button on the Formatting toolbar. Your footnote should now look like this:

¶

[1]·*The·Economist*,·Feb.·2000¶

11) Move to the next paragraph, which begins with the words 'Not all consumers'. Click at the end of the paragraph, after the '(67%)' but before the full stop.

online·shopping·were·concerns·over·payment·security·(90%),·inability·to·physically·inspect·the·products·offered·(69%)·and·fears·of·loss·of·privacy·(67%).¶

12) Choose **Insert | Footnote**, select *Footnote*, select *AutoNumber*, and click **OK**.

13) Word moves the insertion point to the bottom of the page. Type the following footnote text:

    E-commerce Holiday Survey, Deloitte & Touche, November 1999

14) Drag over the words 'E-commerce Holiday Survey', and click the **Italics** button on the Formatting toolbar. Your footnote should now look like this:

¶

[1]·*The·Economist*,·Feb.·2000¶

[2]·*E-commerce·Holiday·Survey*,·Deloitte·&·Touche,·November·1999¶

15) Click anywhere in the body text of your sample document. Save your document with the following name, and close:

    Chapter17_Exercise_17-1_After_*Your_Name*.doc

Exercise 17.2: Create footnotes with custom symbols

1) Open the following Word document:

    Chapter17_Exercise_17-2_Before.doc

    Are you in Print Layout view? If not, choose **View | Print Layout**.

    Click in the end of the first paragraph of body text, after the '2005' but before the full stop.

    INTRODUCTION¶
    Internet·usage·continues·to·grow·dramatically·throughout·the·world.·
    From·a·base·of·40·million·users·in·1996,·the·number·of·online·users·
    is·predicted·to·reach·1·billion·in·2005¶

2) Choose **Insert | Footnote** to display the *Footnote and Endnote* dialog box.

3) In the *Insert* area, select *Footnote*. In the *Numbering* area, click the **Symbol** button.

4) Word displays the *Symbol* dialog box. Click the asterisk symbol (*) to select it and click **OK**.

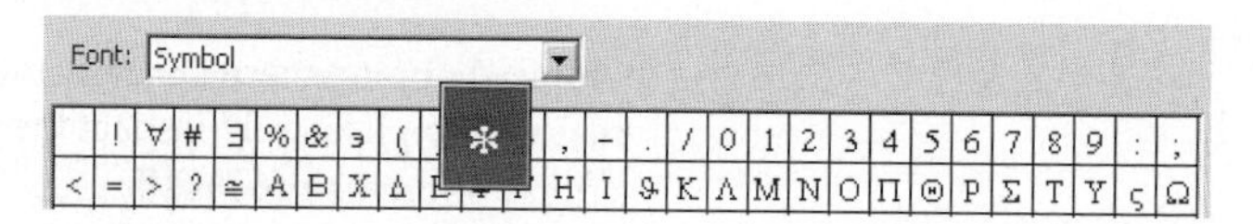

5) You are returned to the *Footnote and Endnote* dialog box. Notice that the *Custom mark* checkbox is selected and the asterisk is shown in the box to its right.

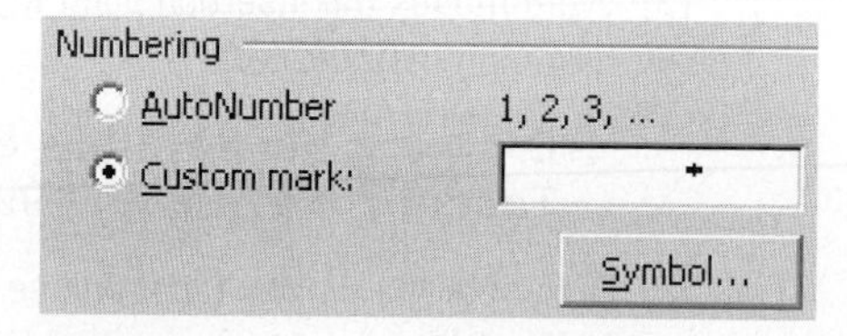

6) Click **OK**.

7) Word moves the insertion point to the bottom of the page. You can see a line and the asterisk symbol. This is where the footnote will appear.

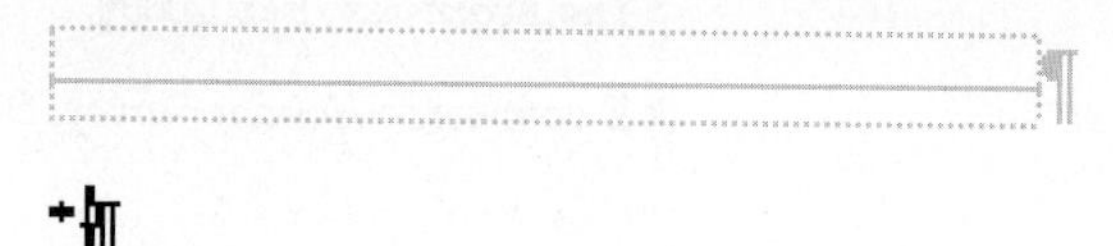

8) Type the following footnote text:

```
Angus Reid Group
```

9) Move to the second page of the sample document, and locate the paragraph of body text that begins with 'By 2003'.

   Click in the end of the paragraph, after the word 'models' but before the full stop.

   only·2.7%·of·new·car·sales·currently·take·place·over·the·Net,·but·as·many·as·40%·of·purchases·involve·the·Net·at·some·point,·with·consumers·using·it·to·compare·prices·or·look·at·the·latest·models¶

10) Choose **Insert | Footnote**. In the *Insert* area, select *Footnote*. In the *Numbering* area, click the **Symbol** button.

11) In the *Symbol* dialog box, click the diamond symbol (♦) to select it and click **OK**.

12) Word moves the insertion point to the bottom of the page. Type the following footnote text:

```
The Economist, Feb. 2000
```

13) Drag over the words 'The Economist', and click the **Italics** button on the Formatting toolbar. Your footnote should now look like this:

   ♦·*The·Economist,*·Feb.·2000¶

14) Move to the paragraph, that begins with the words 'Not all consumers'. Click in the end of the paragraph, after the '(67%)' but before the full stop.

   online·shopping·were·concerns·over·payment·security·(90%),·inability·to·physically·inspect·the·products·offered·(69%)·and·fears·of·loss·of·privacy·(67%)¶

15) Choose **Insert | Footnote**. In the *Insert* area, select *Footnote*. In the *Numbering* area, click the **Symbol** button.

16) In the *Symbol* dialog box, click the degree symbol (°) to select it and click **OK**.

17) Word moves the insertion point to the bottom of the page. Type the following footnote text:

```
E-commerce Holiday Survey, Deloitte &
Touche, November 1999
```

18) Drag over the words 'E-commerce Holiday Survey', and click the **Italics** button on the Formatting toolbar. Your footnote should now look like this:

* *The Economist*, Feb. 2000¶

* *E-commerce Holiday Survey*, Deloitte & Touche, November 1999¶

19) Click anywhere in the body text of your sample document. Save your document with the following name, and close:

    Chapter17_Exercise_17-2_After_*Your_Name*.doc

Working with footnote content

In Exercise 17.3, you will edit the content of an existing footnote.

Exercise 17.3: Amend the content of footnotes

1) Open the following Word document:

    Chapter17_Exercise_17-3_Before.doc

    Are you in Print Layout view? If not, choose **View | Print Layout**.

2) Move to the footnote at the bottom of the first page, and edit the text from 'Angus Reid Group' to 'XYZ Consultants'.

    Your footnote should now look like this:

XYZ Consultants¶

3) Click anywhere in the body text of your sample document. Save your document with the following name, and close:

    Chapter17_Exercise_17-3_After_*Your_Name*.doc

Working with footnote format

Word allows you to amend the format of a footnote in a number of ways:

- **Font**. You can select all or part of a footnote and amend aspects of its appearance – such as the font or font colour – with the **Format | Font** command.

  Alternatively, as in Exercises 17.1 and 17.2, you can amend the format of selected footnote text by clicking the relevant buttons on the Formatting toolbar.

- **Paragraph**. You can select a footnote and amend its left and right indents, and the spacing above and below it, with the **Format | Paragraph** command.

- **Style**. You can change the font and paragraph attributes of *all* footnotes in a document, or in all documents based on a particular template, by changing the built-in Footnote Text style with the **Format** | **Style** command.
- **Separator line**. You can delete the horizontal line that Word inserts above footnotes and, optionally, insert an alternative. To do so, switch to Normal view and use the options within the **View** | **Footnotes** command.
- **Numbering format**. When your footnotes follow an automatic sequence, you use the **Options** button within the **Insert** | **Footnote** command to change from the default pattern (1,2,3, …) to another of your choice (such as a,b,c, ...).
- **Placement**. You can change the placement of all footnotes in a document from the default location at the bottom of the page to beneath the last line of text on each page.

Exercise 17.4: Amend the format of a footnote

1) Open the following Word document:

    `Chapter17_Exercise_17-4_Before.doc`

    Are you in Print Layout view? If not, choose **View** | **Print Layout**.

2) Click anywhere in the footnote at the bottom of the first page, and choose **Format** | **Style**. Word displays the *Style* dialog box with Footnote Text style selected automatically. Click the **Modify** button.
3) In the *Modify Style* dialog box, click **Format** and then **Font**.
4) Change the font to Arial, 10 point, and change the font colour to blue. Click **OK**, **OK** and **Apply**.
5) Move to the second page of your sample document and verify that the other footnotes have also changed appearance.
6) Choose **View** | **Normal** to switch to Normal view, and then choose **View** | **Footnotes**. Word opens a separate footnote pane at the bottom of your screen.
7) Click *Footnote Separator* in the drop-down list that appears just above the footnotes.

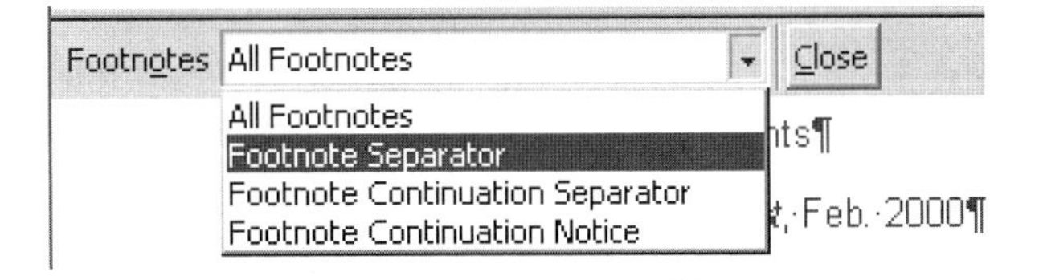

8) Click to the left of the separator line to select it.

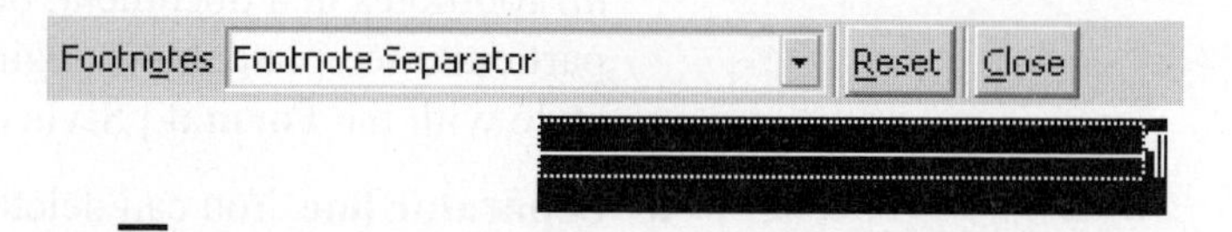

9) Press **Delete** to remove it.

10) Click at the paragraph mark where the separator line used to be.

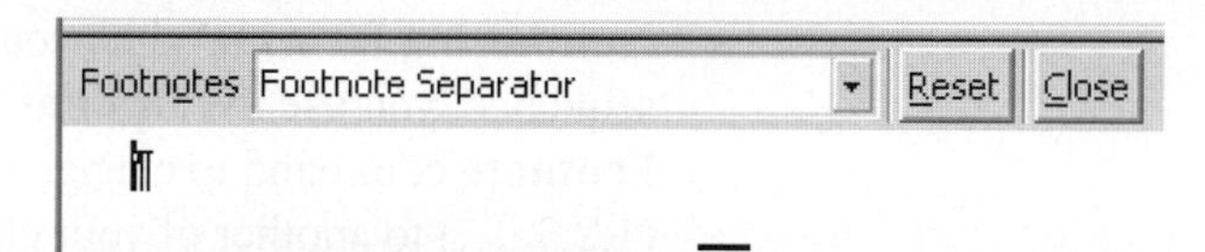

Choose **Format | Borders and Shading**. On the **Borders** tab, click *Box*, change the style to a double line, and deselect all borders except the bottom one.

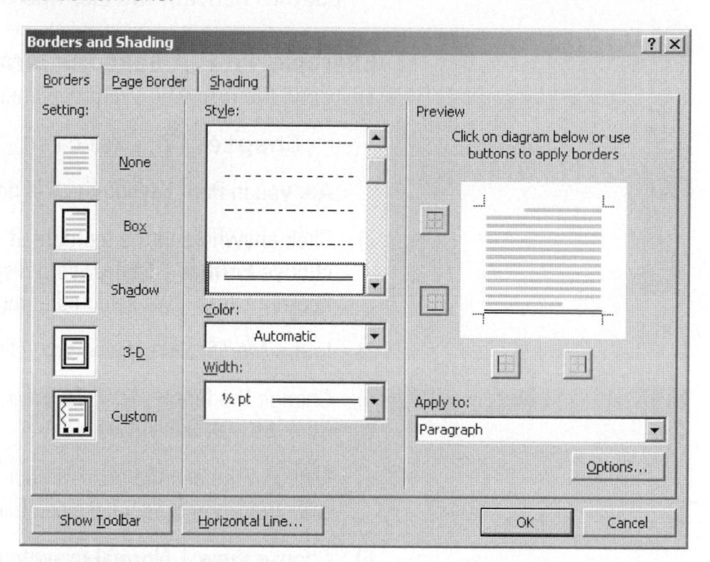

Click **OK**.

11) Choose **View | Print Layout** and verify that your footnote separator has changed.

12) Click anywhere in the footnote at the bottom of the sample document's first page and choose **Insert | Footnote**.

13) Click the **Options** button. In the *Place at* list, select *Beneath text*. In the *Number format* list, select *A, B, C, ...*

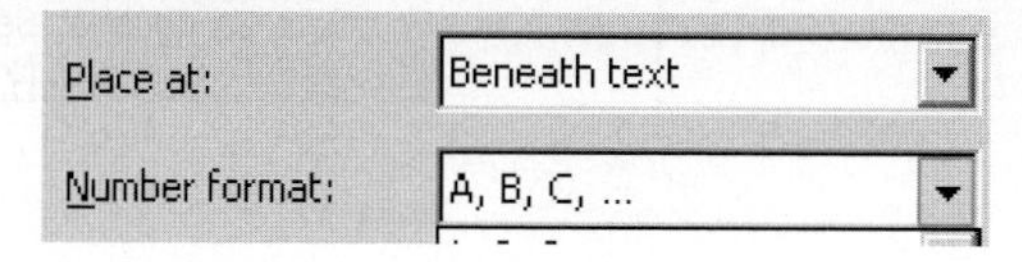

When finished, click **OK** and **OK**.

Notice that Word has inserted a new footnote symbol. This is as a result of using the **Insert | Footnote** command.

¶

XYZ·Consultants¶

Click to the left of this and press **Backspace**. Your footnote should now look like this:

¶

XYZ·Consultants¶

14) Move to the second page of your sample document to verify that the footnote numbering sequence and placement has changed.

15) Click anywhere in the body text of your sample document. Save your document with the following name, and close:

    Chapter17 Exercise_17-4_After_*Your_Name*.doc.

Want to remove a footnote? Just select the reference marker in the body text and press **Backspace** or **Delete**. Word removes the footnote and, if you are using the AutoNumber option, automatically renumbers all remaining footnotes. See Exercise 17.5.

Exercise 17.5: Deleting a footnote

1) Open the following Word document:

    Chapter17_Exercise_17-5_Before.doc

    Are you in Print Layout view? If not, choose **View | Print Layout**.

2) Select the first footnote marker in your document by dragging across it.

    Internet·usage·continues·to·grow·dramatically·throughout·the·world. From·a·base·of·40·million·users·in·1996,·the·number·of·online·users· is·predicted·to·reach·1·billion·in·2005.¶

3) Press **Delete** or **Backspace**. Word removes the footnote.

4) Move to the second page of your sample document to verify that the footnote numbering sequence has changed.

5) Click anywhere in the body text of your sample document. Save your document with the following name, and close:

    Chapter17_Exercise_17-5_After_*Your_Name*.doc

Working with new endnotes

In Exercise 17.6, you will create new endnotes in a sample document.

Exercise 17.6: Create numbered endnotes

1) Start Word and open the following document:

    `Chapter17_Exercise_17-6_Before.doc`

2) Are you in Print Layout view? If not, choose **View | Print Layout**.

3) Click in the location where you want the endnote reference mark to appear.

    In this example, click at the end of the first paragraph of body text, after the '2005' but before the full stop.

    INTRODUCTION¶

    Internet·usage·continues·to·grow·dramatically·throughout·the·world.· From·a·base·of·40·million·users·in·1996,·the·number·of·online·users· is·predicted·to·reach·1·billion·in·2005¶

4) Choose **Insert | Footnote** to display the *Footnote and Endnote* dialog box.

5) In the *Insert* area, select *Endnote*. In the *Numbering* area, select *AutoNumber*. The default numbering system for endnotes is 1,2,3, ...

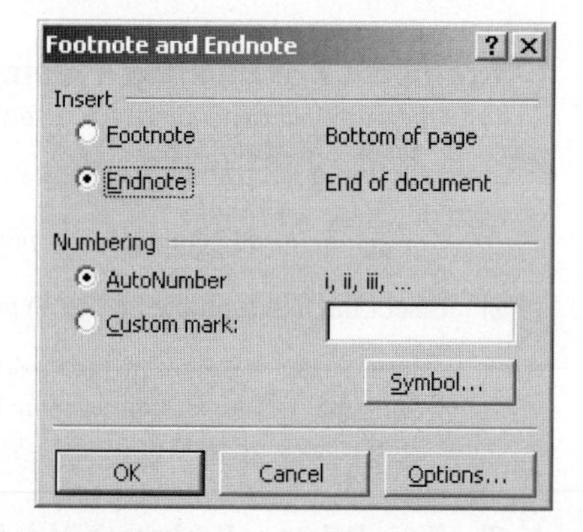

6) Click **OK**.

7) Word moves the insertion point to the end of your document. You can see a line and the number 1. This is where the endnote will appear.

Type the following endnote text:

```
Angus Reid Group
```

¶

[1] Angus·Reid·Group¶

8) Move to the second page of the sample document, and locate the paragraph of body text that begins with 'By 2003'.

   Click in the end of the paragraph, after the word 'models' but before the full stop.

   only·2.7%·of·new·car·sales·currently·take·place·over·the·Net,·but·as·many·as·40%·of·purchases·involve·the·Net·at·some·point,·with·consumers·using·it·to·compare·prices·or·look·at·the·latest·models¶

9) Choose **Insert | Footnote**, select *Endnote*, select *AutoNumber*, and click **OK**.

10) Word moves the insertion point to the end of your document. Type the following endnote text:

```
The Economist, Feb. 2000
```

11) Drag over the words 'The Economist', and click the **Italics** button on the Formatting toolbar. Your endnote should now look like this:

   ¶

   [2] *The·Economist*,·Feb.·2000¶

12) Move to the next paragraph, which begins with the words 'Not all consumers'. Click at the end of the paragraph, after the '(67%)' but before the full stop.

   online·shopping·were·concerns·over·payment·security·(90%),·inability·to·physically·inspect·the·products·offered·(69%)·and·fears·of·loss·of·privacy·(67%)¶

13) Choose **Insert | Endnote**, select *Endnote*, select *AutoNumber*, and click **OK**.

14) Word moves the insertion point to the end of the document. Type the following endnote text:

```
E-commerce Holiday Survey, Deloitte &
Touche, November 1999
```

15) Drag over the words 'E-commerce Holiday Survey', and click the **Italics** button on the Formatting toolbar. Your endnotes should now look like this:

i Angus Reid Group¶

ii *The Economist*, Feb. 2000¶

iii *E-commerce Holiday Survey*, Deloitte & Touche, November 1999¶

16) Click anywhere in the body text of your sample document. Save your document with the following name, and close:

`Chapter17_Exercise_17-6_After_Your_Name.doc`

Working with endnote content and format

The procedures for modifying existing endnotes are similar to those for working with footnotes:

- **Content**. To change the text of any endnote in Print Layout view, click in the endnote and make the text changes.
- **Font**. You can select all or part of an endnote and amend aspects of its appearance – such as the font or font colour – with the **Format | Font** command.

  Alternatively, as in Exercise 17.4, you can amend the format of selected endnote text by clicking the relevant buttons on the Formatting toolbar.
- **Paragraph**. You can select an endnote and amend its left and right indents, and the spacing above and below it, with the **Format | Paragraph** command.
- **Style**. You can change the font and paragraph attributes of *all* endnotes in a document, or in all documents based on a particular template, by changing the built-in Endnote Text style with the **Format | Style** command.
- **Separator line**. You can delete the horizontal line that Word inserts above endnotes and insert an alternative. To do so, switch to Normal view and use the options within the **View | Footnotes** command.
- **Numbering Format**. When your endnotes follow an automatic sequence, you use the **Options** button within the **Insert | Footnote** command to change from the default pattern (1,2,3, …) to another of your choice (such as a,b,c, ...).

Exercise 17.7: Deleting a endnote

1) Open the following Word document:

`Chapter17_Exercise_17-7_Before.doc`

Are you in Print Layout view? If not, choose **View | Print Layout**.

2) Select the first endnote marker in your document by dragging across it.

Internet·usage·continues·to·grow·dramatically·throughout·the·world.· From·a·base·of·40·million·users·in·1996,·the·number·of·online·users·is· predicted·to·reach·1·billion·in·2005i.¶

3) Press **Delete** or **Backspace**. Word removes the endnote.

4) Move to the end of your sample document to verify that the endnote numbering sequence has changed.

i·*The·Economist*,·Feb.·2000¶

ii·*E-commerce·Holiday·Survey*,·Deloitte·&·Touche,·November·1999¶

5) Click anywhere in the body text of your sample document. Save your document with the following name, and close:

Chapter17_Exercise_17-7_After_*Your_Name*.doc

Chapter 17: quick reference

Tasks summary

Task	Procedure
Insert a footnote or endnote.	Position the insertion point where you want to reference mark to appear, choose **Insert | Footnote**, select the required options, and click **OK**.
Edit a footnote or endnote.	In Print Layout view, you can edit notes in the same way that you edit and format text in the body of a document.
Reformat a footnote or endnote.	In Print Layout view, select the note text and click the buttons on the Formatting toolbar, or use the options within the **Font**, **Paragraph** and **Style** commands on the **Format** menu.
Modifying sequential numbering pattern in footnotes or endnotes.	Select your required option from the list available with the **Options** button in the **Insert | Footnote** command.
Change the placement of footnotes or endnotes.	Select your required options from the list available with the **Options** button in the **Insert | Footnote** command.

Concepts summary

Use *footnotes* and *endnotes* to supply additional information about text in a document, or to cite references or sources. Footnotes typically appear at the bottom of individual pages.

Endnotes typically appear at the end of the document. You insert both types of notes with the same command: **Insert | Footnote**.

Every footnote or endnote consists of text and an indicator called a *reference mark*. This is the superscripted symbol or number that appears in the body of the document to indicate that a footnote or endnote is present. By default, Word inserts sequential numbers as reference marks. When you move, delete or relocate a numbered footnote or endnote, Word automatically updates all other footnotes or endnotes in the document accordingly. You can also use symbols as reference marks.

In Print Layout view, you edit and format footnote and endnote text just as you would text in the body of a document. In Normal view, Word does not display notes by default. To view them, choose **View | Footnotes**. Word opens a separate window at the bottom of your screen in which you can access and work with all footnotes and endnotes in your document.

Chapter 17: quick quiz

Circle the correct answer to each of the following multiple-choice questions about footnotes and endnotes in Word.

Q1	A footnote is ...
A.	Additional information or references regarding the main text that appears at the end of document.
B.	A summary of information about a document that can be displayed with the **File | Properties** command.
C.	Additional information or references regarding the main text that appears at the bottom of a page within a document.
D.	A text box positioned in a page footer with the **Insert | Text Box** command.

Q2	An endnote is ...
A.	Additional information or references regarding main text that appears at the end of document.
B.	A summary of information about a document that can be displayed with the **File | Properties** command.
C.	Additional information or references regarding the main text that appears at the bottom of a page within a document.
D.	A text box positioned in the page footer with the **Insert | Text Box** command.

Q3	In Word, which command do you choose to insert a footnote or endnote in a document?
A.	Insert | Footnote.
B.	Tools | Options | Notes.
C.	Insert | Notes | Footnote.
D.	Format | AutoNotes.

Q4	In Word, a footnote or endnote reference mark is ...
A.	A superscripted number that appears in the body of a document to indicate that a footnote or endnote is present.
B.	A symbol or number positioned in a page header.
C.	A superscripted letter 'F' or 'N' that that appears in the body of a document to indicate that a footnote or endnote is present.
D.	A superscripted symbol or number that appears in the body of a document to indicate that a footnote or endnote is present.

Q5	In which type of documents are you mostly likely to use custom symbols as reference marks for footnotes?
A.	Financial or business documents of any length.
B.	Lengthy, multi-page documents of any type.
C.	Technical documents of any length.
D.	Short or single-page documents of any type.

Q6	In which type of documents are you mostly likely to use an automatically increasing number sequence as reference marks for footnotes or endnotes?
A.	Financial or business documents of any length.
B.	Lengthy, multi-page documents of any type.
C.	Technical documents of any length.
D.	Short or single-page documents of any type.

Q7	In which of the following Word document views can you edit footnotes or endnotes just as you would body text?
A.	Print Layout view.
B.	Outline view.
C.	Notes view.
D.	Normal view.

Q8	In which of the following Word document views can you edit all the footnotes or endnotes in a document within a separate window?
A.	Print Layout view.
B.	Outline view.
C.	Notes view.
D.	Normal view.

Q9	In Word, which of the following statements about footnote and endnote formatting is untrue?
A.	You can change the appearance of all footnotes or endnotes in a document with the **Format | Style** command.
B.	You can change the appearance of a selected footnote or endnote with the **Format | Footnote** command.
C.	You can change the appearance of a selected footnote or endnote with the **Format | Paragraph** command.
D.	You can change the appearance of a selected footnote or endnote by clicking the relevant buttons on the Formatting toolbar.

Answers

1: C, **2:** A, **3:** A, **4:** D, **5:** D, **6:** B, **7:** A, **8:** D, **9:** B.

18 Bookmarks and cross-references

Objectives

In this chapter you will learn how to:

- Insert a bookmark
- Display a bookmark
- Move to a bookmark
- Delete a bookmark
- Insert a cross-reference
- Navigate with cross-references
- View cross-references
- Delete a cross-reference

New words

In this chapter you will meet the following terms:

- Bookmark
- Cross-reference

Exercise files

In this chapter you will work with the following Word files:

- `Chapter18_Exercise_18-1_Before.doc`
- `Chapter18_Exercise_18-4_Before.doc`
- `Chapter18_Exercise_18-5_Before.doc`
- `Chapter18_Exercise_18-6_Before.doc`
- `Chapter18_Exercise_18-9_Before.doc`

Syllabus reference

In this chapter you will cover the following items from the ECDL Advanced Word Processing Syllabus:

- **AM3.3.1.1**. Add or delete a bookmark.
- **AM3.3.1.3**. Create or delete a cross-reference.

About bookmarks

Word's bookmark feature enables the reader to move quickly to a particular location in a document, without needing to remember page numbers or headings.

The Bookmark *dialog box*

You insert bookmarks with the *Bookmark* dialog box, displayed with the **Insert | Bookmark** command.

Bookmark names

Bookmark names must begin with a letter. They can contain numbers but not spaces. To separate words, you can use the underscore character, for example, 'Sales_Figures'. A bookmark can have up to 40 characters.

Bookmark

A named mark placed on a selected item in a document that enables readers to move to that location without needing to know the relevant page number.

About cross-references

A cross-reference is a way to direct readers to related or otherwise relevant material located elsewhere in the same document. For example, 'For more information about software solutions, see page 32.'

Word enables you to create cross-references to various document elements, including:

- Headings formatted with built-in styles
- Bookmarks
- Footnotes and endnotes

Cross-reference

An entry in a document that, if clicked, takes the reader to another location in the same document. Cross-references are useful for directing readers to related or otherwise relevant material.

The Cross-reference *dialog box*

You insert cross-references with the **Insert | Cross-reference** command. The associated dialog box provides all the options you need.

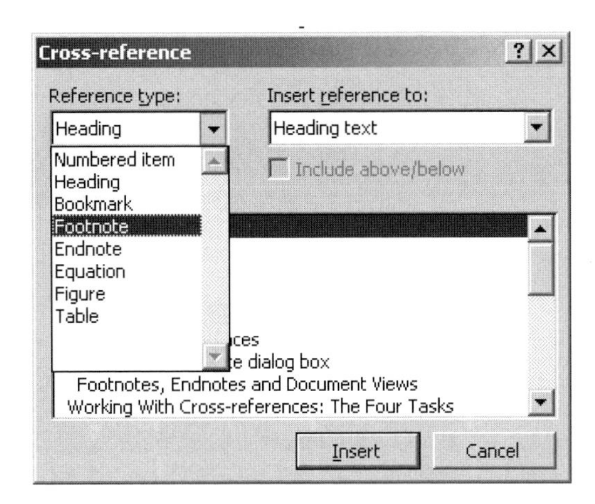

Updating cross-references

If you add or delete pages to a document that contains cross-references, you may need to update your cross-references. To do so, press **Ctrl+A** to select the entire document, and then press the **F9** key.

Working with bookmarks: the four tasks

Here are the four tasks that you need to be able to perform with bookmarks in Word:

- **Insert a bookmark**. Exercise 18.1 takes you through the steps of inserting bookmarks in a document.
- **Display all bookmarks**. Exercise 18.2 shows you how to display all bookmarks in a document.
- **Move to a bookmark**. Follow Exercise 18.3 to discover how to move to a specific bookmark in a document.
- **Delete a bookmark**. Exercise 18.4 shows you how to remove a bookmark from a document.

Working with cross-references: the four tasks

Here are the four tasks that you need to be able to perform with cross-references in Word:

- **Insert a cross-reference**. Exercises 18.5 and 18.6 take you through the steps of inserting cross-references in built-in headings and bookmarks, respectively.
- **Navigate with cross-references**. Follow Exercise 18.7 to discover how to move to material in a document by clicking cross-references.
- **Display cross-references**. Exercise 18.8 shows you how to display cross-reference field codes in a document.
- **Delete a cross-reference**. You delete a cross-reference in Exercise 18.9.

Working with bookmarks

Exercise 18.1: Inserting bookmarks

1) Start Word and open the following document:

   `Chapter18_Exercise_18-1_Before.doc`

2) Select the text, table, graphic or other item you want to bookmark.

   In this example, select the 'Codes of Conduct' heading on the first page.

   Codes·of·Conduct¶

   Our·staff·will·introduce·themselves·to·you·and·explain·how·they·can·help.·All·staff·will·wear·a·name·badge·to·enable·you·to·identify·them.¶

3) Choose **Insert | Bookmark** to display the *Bookmark* dialog box.

4) In the *Bookmark name* text box, type the following:

   `Codes_of_Conduct`

5) Click the **Add** button to insert the bookmark – the dialog box closes automatically.

6) Select the next heading, 'Individual Standards of Behaviour'.

7) Press **Ctrl+C** to copy the text to the Clipboard, and choose **Insert | Bookmark**.

8) Click in the *Bookmark name* box, press **Backspace** or **Delete** to remove the currently display bookmark name, and press **Ctrl+V** to paste the selected text.

9) Edit the bookmark name to read:

   `Individual_Standards_of_Behaviour`

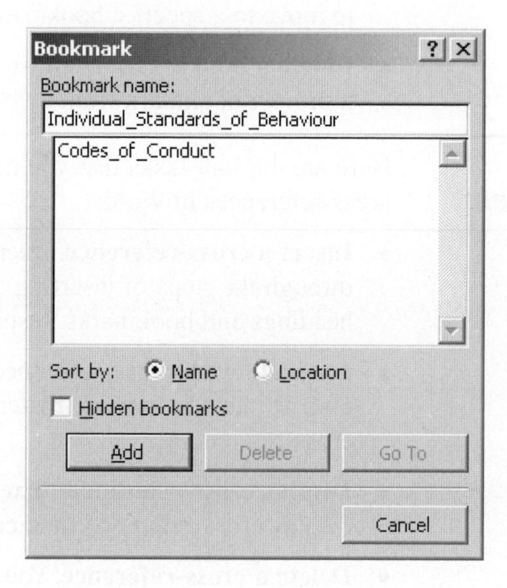

10) Click **Add**.

11) Move to the second page of the document, select the 'Consultant-based Services' heading, repeat steps 7 and 8, and modify the bookmark name to read:

    `Consultant_based_Services`

    When finished, click **Add**.

12) Save your document with the following name, and close:

    `Chapter18_Exercise_18-1_After_`*`Your_Name`*`.doc`

Exercise 18.2: Display all bookmarks

1) Open the Word document that you saved at the end of Exercise 18.1.

2) Choose **Tools | Options** and click the **View** tab. In the *Show* area, select the *Bookmarks* checkbox, and click **OK**.

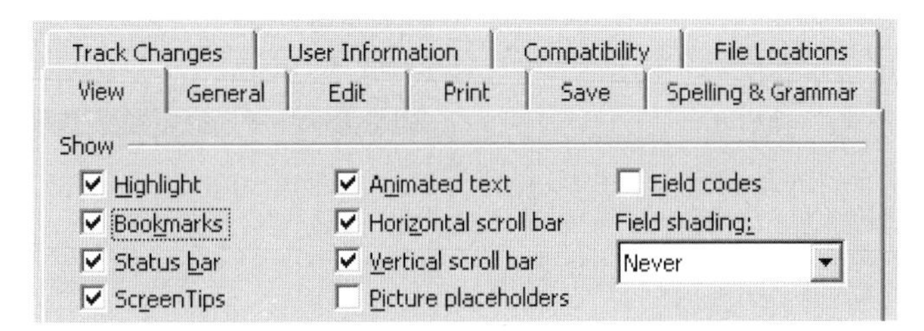

3) Scroll through your sample document. Notice that Word displays bookmarked text within dark grey or black brackets. These brackets do not appear on print-outs.

4) You can close your sample document without saving it.

Exercise 18.3: Move to a bookmark

1) Open the Word document you saved at the end of Exercise 18.1.

2) Choose **Edit | Go To** or press **F5**. Word displays the **Go To** tab of the *Find and Replace* dialog box.

3) In the *Go to what* list box, select *Bookmark*. In the *Enter bookmark name* list box, select the bookmark that you want to move to.

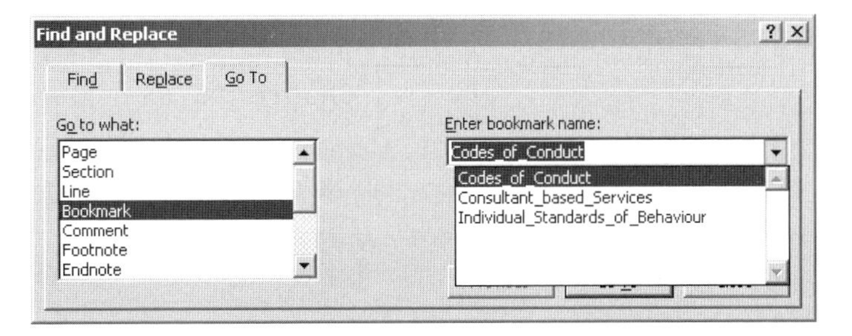

4) Click **Go To**. Word takes you to your selected location in the document. The bookmarked item is selected and the dialog box remains open.

5) You can select further bookmarks or click **Close** to close the dialog box.

6) When finished, you can close your document without saving it.

Exercise 18.4: Delete a bookmark

1) Open the following Word document:

   `Chapter18_Exercise_18-4_Before.doc`

2) Choose **Insert | Bookmark** and select the bookmark that you want to delete. In this example, select the 'Individual_Standards_of_Behaviour' bookmark.

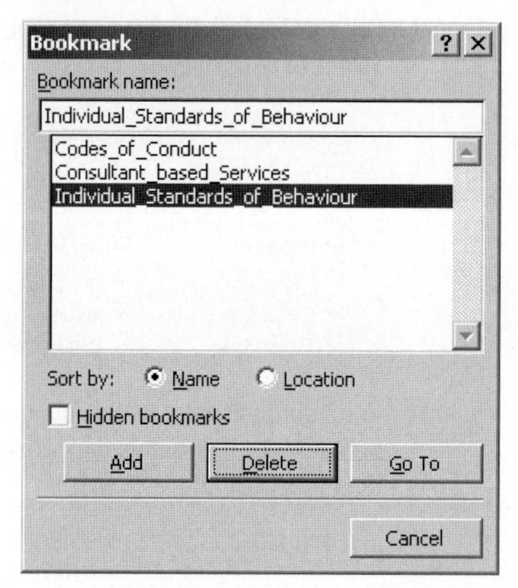

3) Press **Delete**. Word removes the selected bookmark from the document. The dialog box remains open. You can remove further bookmarks or press **Close** to close the dialog box.

4) Save your document with the following name, and close:

   Chapter18_Exercise_18-4_After_*Your_Name*.doc

Working with cross-references

Exercise 18.5: Insert cross-references to built-in headings

1) Open the following Word document:

   `Chapter18_Exercise_18-5_Before.doc`

2) Move to the second page, click at the end of the paragraph beneath the 'Nursing Services' heading, and press **Enter**.

Nursing·Services¶

We·will·ensure·that·a·named,·qualified·nurse,·midwife·or·other·health·care·professional·takes·a·personal·responsibility·for·your·treatment·and·care·during·your·time·with·us.¶

¶

3) Type the text that you want to appear before the cross-reference. In this example, type the following, followed by a single space:

   See:

4) Choose **Insert | Cross-reference**. In the *Reference type* list, select *Heading*. In the *For which heading* list, select *Individual Standards of Behaviour*.

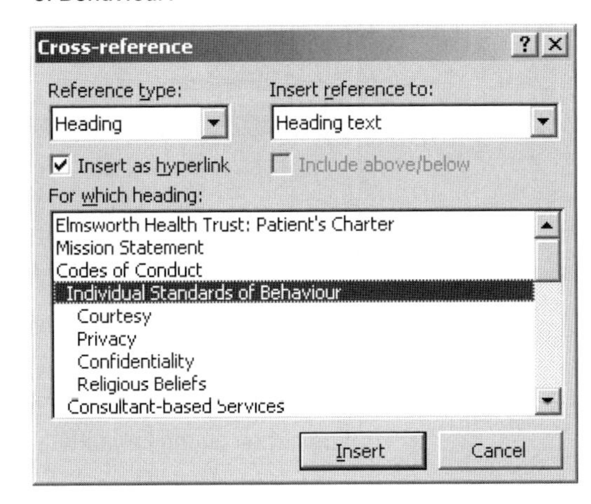

   To allow readers to jump to the cross-referenced item, tick the *Insert as hyperlink* checkbox.

   Click **Insert** to insert the cross-reference, and then click **Close** to close the dialog box.

5) Select the cross-reference text by dragging across it, and click the **Italics** button on the Formatting toolbar.

   See: *Individual Standards of Behaviour*¶

6) Move to the first page, click at the end of the paragraph beneath the 'Codes of Conduct' heading, and press **Enter**.

   Codes·of·Conduct¶

   Our·staff·will·introduce·themselves·to·you·and·explain·how·they·can·help.·All·staff·will·wear·a·name·badge·to·enable·you·to·identify·them.¶

   ¶

7) Type the following text, followed by a single space:

   See:

8) Choose **Insert | Cross-reference**. In the *Reference type* list, select *Heading*. In the *For which heading* list, select *Standards of Service*.

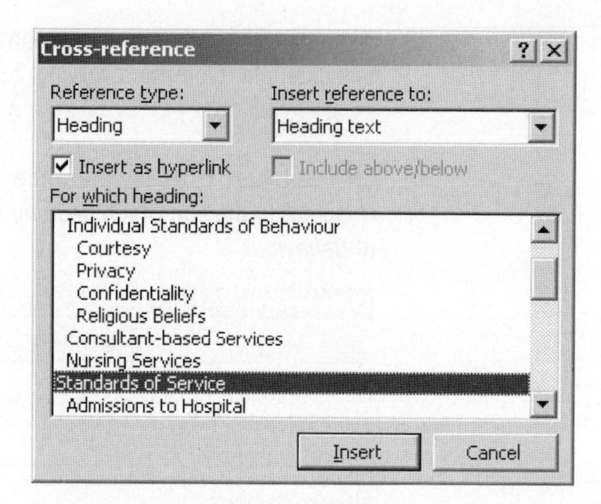

Ensure that the *Insert as hyperlink* checkbox is selected.

Click **Insert** to insert the cross-reference, and then click Close to close the dialog box.

9) Select the cross-reference text by dragging across it, and click the **Italics** button on the Formatting toolbar.

See:·*Standards·of·Service*¶

10) Save your document with the following name, and close:

    Chapter18_Exercise_18-5_After_*Your_Name*.doc.

Exercise 18.6: Insert cross-references to bookmarks

1) Open the following Word document:

    Chapter18_Exercise_18-6_Before.doc

2) On the first page, click at the end of the paragraph beneath the 'Codes of Conduct' heading and press **Enter**.

·Codes·of·Conduct¶

Our·staff·will·introduce·themselves·to·you·and·explain·how·they·can·help.·All·staff·will·wear·a·name·badge·to·enable·you·to·identify·them.¶

¶

3) Type the text that you want to appear before the cross-reference. In this example, type the following, followed by a single space:

    See also:

4) Choose **Insert | Cross-reference**. In the *Reference type* list, select *Bookmark*. In the *For which bookmark* list, select *Individual_Standards_of_Behaviour*.

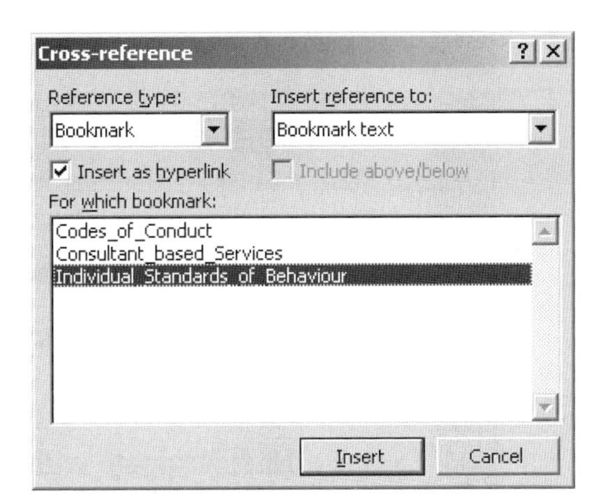

Ensure that the *Insert as hyperlink* checkbox is selected.

Click **Insert** to insert the cross-reference, and then click **Close** to close the dialog box.

5) Select the cross-reference text by dragging across it, and click the **Underline** button on the Formatting toolbar.

See·also:·Individual·Standards·of·Behaviour¶

6) Move to the second page, click at the end of the paragraph beneath the 'Nursing Services' heading, and press **Enter**.

Nursing·Services¶
We·will·ensure·that·a·named,·qualified·nurse,·midwife·or·other·health·care·professional·takes·a·personal·responsibility·for·your·treatment·and·care·during·your·time·with·us.¶
¶

7) Type the following text, followed by a single space:

```
See also:
```

8) Choose **Insert | Cross-reference**. In the *Reference type* list, select *Bookmark*. In the *For which bookmark* list, select *Codes_of_Conduct*.

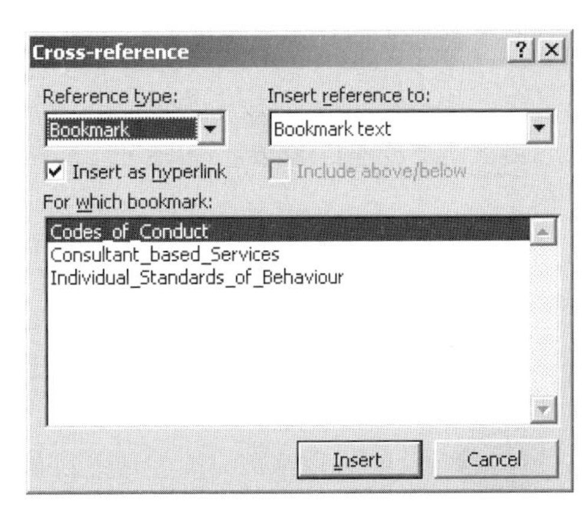

Ensure that the *Insert as hyperlink* checkbox is selected.

Click **Insert** to insert the cross-reference, and then click **Close** to close the dialog box.

9) Select the cross-reference text by dragging across it, and click the **Underline** button on the Formatting toolbar.

See·also:·Codes·of·Conduct¶

10) Save your document with the following name, and close:

    Chapter18_Exercise_18-6_After_*Your_Name*.doc.

Exercise 18.7: Navigate with cross-references

1) Open the Word document that you saved at the end of Exercise 18.5.

2) Hold the cursor over the cross-reference named 'See: Standards of Service' located under the 'Codes of Conduct' heading.

   Notice how the cursor changes shape to a pointing hand.

3) Click once on the cross-reference. Word moves you to the relevant location in the document. You can close the document without saving it.

4) Open the Word document that you saved at the end of Exercise 18.6.

5) Hold the cursor over the cross-reference named 'See also: Individual Standards of Behaviour' located under the 'Codes of Conduct' heading.

   Notice how the cursor changes shape to a pointing hand.

6) Click once on the cross-reference. Word moves you to the relevant location in the document. You can close the document without saving it.

Exercise 18.8: Viewing cross-references

1) Open the document that you saved at the end of Exercise 18.6.

2) Press **Ctrl+A** to select the entire document.

3) Press **Alt+F9** to display all the fields in the document.

4) Scroll through the document to display the cross-reference field codes. The first one is displayed below:

   ·Codes·of·Conduct¶

   Our·staff·will·introduce·themselves·to·you·and·explain·how·they·can·help.·All·staff·will·wear·a·name·badge·to·enable·you·to·identify·them.¶

   See·also:·{·REF·Individual_Standards_of_Behaviour·\h··*·MERGEFORMAT·}¶

5) You can close your sample document without saving it.

Exercise 18.9: Delete a cross-reference

1) Start Word and open the following document:

   `Chapter18_Exercise_18-9_Before.doc`

2) Drag across the first cross-reference to select it. It is located after the text beneath the 'Codes of Conduct' heading.

   ·Codes·of·Conduct¶

   Our·staff·will·introduce·themselves·to·you·and·explain·how·they·can·help.·All·staff·will·wear·a·name·badge·to·enable·you·to·identify·them.¶

   See·also:·Individual·Standards·of·Behaviour¶

3) Press the **Delete** or **Backspace** key. Word removes the cross-reference. Next, select and delete the 'See also: ' text that introduced the cross-reference. Finally, delete the paragraph mark to remove the now-empty line.

4) Save your document with the following name, and close:

   Chapter18_Exercise_18-9_After_*Your_Name*.doc

Chapter 18: quick reference

Tasks summary: bookmarks

Task	Procedure
Insert a bookmark.	Select the text, table, graphic or other item you want to bookmark, choose **Insert | Bookmark**, type a bookmark name, and click **OK**.
Display all bookmarks in a document.	Choose **Tools | Options** and click the **View** tab. In the *Show* area, select the *Bookmarks* checkbox and click **OK**.
Move to a specific bookmark in a document.	Choose **Edit | Go To** (or press **F5**) and click the **Go To** tab. In the *Go to what* list box, select *Bookmark*. In the *Enter bookmark name* box, select the bookmark that you want to move to, and click **Go To**.
Delete a bookmark from a document.	Choose **Insert | Bookmark**, select the bookmark that you want to delete, click **Delete,** and then click **OK**.

Tasks summary: cross-references

Task	Procedure
Insert a cross-reference.	Click where you want to insert the cross-reference, choose **Insert | Cross-reference**, select the relevant items from the *Reference type* list and in the *For which* list, ensure that the *Insert as hyperlink* checkbox is selected, and click **Insert**.
Display all cross-references in a document.	Press **Ctrl+A** to select the entire document, and then press **Alt+F9** to display all the fields in the document.
Delete a cross-reference from a document.	Drag across a cross-reference to select it, and press **Delete** or **Backspace**.

Concepts summary

Word's *bookmark* feature enables the reader to move quickly to a particular location in a document, without needing to remember page numbers or headings. You insert bookmarks with the *Bookmark* dialog box, displayed with the **Insert | Bookmark** command.

Bookmark names must begin with a letter. They can contain numbers but not spaces. To separate words, you can use the underscore character, for example, 'Sales_Figures'. A bookmark can have up to 40 characters.

A *cross-reference* is a way to direct readers to related or otherwise relevant material located elsewhere in the same document. For example, 'For more information about software solutions, see page 32.'

Word enables you to create cross-references to various document elements, including headings formatted with built-in styles and bookmarks.

You insert cross-references with the **Insert | Cross-references** command. The associated dialog box provides all the options you need.

Chapter 18: quick quiz

Circle the correct answer to each of the following multiple-choice questions about bookmarks and cross-references in Word.

Q1	A bookmark is ...
A.	Additional information or references regarding the main text that appears at the end of document.
B.	A summary of information about a document that can be displayed with the **File | Properties** command.
C.	A named mark placed in a document that enables readers to move to that location without needing to know the relevant page number.
D.	A text box positioned in a page footer with the **Insert | Text Box** command.

Q2	A cross-reference is ...
A.	A named mark placed in a document that enables readers to move to that location without needing to know the relevant page number.
B.	An entry in a document that, if clicked, takes the reader to another location in the same document.
C.	Additional information or references regarding the main text that appears at the bottom of a page within the document.
D.	A text box positioned in the page footer with the **Insert | Text Box** command.

Q3	In Word, which command do you choose to insert a bookmark in a document?
A.	**Format | Bookmarks.**
B.	**Insert | Bookmark.**
C.	**Tools | Options | Bookmarks | New.**
D.	**Insert | Marks| Bookmark.**

Q4	In Word, which command do you choose to insert a cross-reference in a document?
A.	**Insert | New| Reference.**
B.	**Tools | Cross-references.**
C.	**Insert | Cross-reference.**
D.	**Format | Auto | Reference.**

Q5	In Word, which actions do you take to display all bookmarks in a document?
A.	Choose **Tools | Options** and click the **View** tab. In the *Show* area, select the *Bookmarks* checkbox, and click **OK**.
B.	Choose **Insert | Bookmarks**, click the **Options** button, select the *View bookmarks* checkbox, and click **OK**.
C.	Click the **Book** button on the Status bar.
D.	Choose **View | Toolbars**, and select **Bookmarks**.

Q6	In Word, which actions do you take to move to a specific bookmark in a document?
A.	Click the **Find Bookmark** button on the Standard toolbar, select the bookmark that you want to move to, and click **Go To**.
B.	Choose **Edit | Find | Bookmark**, select the bookmark that you want to move to, and click **Find Now**.
C.	Press **Shift+F6**, select the bookmark that you want to move to, and click **Find Bookmark**.
D.	Choose **Edit | Go To** (or press **F5**) and click the **Go To** tab. In the *Go to what* list box, select *Bookmark*. In the *Enter bookmark name* list box, select the bookmark that you want to move to, and click **Go To**.

Q7	In Word, which actions do you take to delete a bookmark from a document?
A.	Choose **Tools | Bookmark | Delete**, select the bookmark that you want to delete, and click **OK**.
B.	Choose **Insert | Bookmark**, select the bookmark that you want to delete, click **Delete** and then click **OK**.
C.	Press **Ctrl+F8**, select the bookmark that you want delete, click **Delete** and then click **OK**.
D.	Choose **Insert | Bookmark**, select the bookmark that you want to delete, click **Remove Now** and then click **Apply**.

Q8	In Word, which actions do you take to insert a cross-reference in a document?
A.	Click where you want to insert the cross-reference, choose **Insert | Cross-reference**, type the cross-reference name, ensure that the *Insert as hyperlink* checkbox is selected, and click **Insert**.
B.	Click the **Insert Cross-reference** button on the Standard toolbar, select the relevant item from the *Reference type* list, type the cross-reference name, and click **Insert Now**.
C.	Choose **Insert | Cross-reference**, select the relevant items from the *Reference type* list and the *For which* drop-down list, ensure that the *Insert as hyperlink* checkbox is selected, and click **Insert**.
D.	Press **Ctrl+F8**, select the relevant items from the *Reference type* list and the *For which* drop-down list, and click **Insert**.

Q9	In Word, which actions do you take to displays all cross-references in a document?
A.	Press **Ctrl+A** to select the entire document, and then press **Alt+F9** to display all the fields in the document.
B.	Choose **Insert | Cross-reference**, select the *Display cross-references* checkbox, and click **OK**.
C.	Press **Ctrl+A** to select the entire document, and then display all the fields in the document by pressing **Shift+F8**.
D.	Click the **Show Cross-references** button on the Reviewing toolbar.

Q10	In Word, which actions do you take to remove a cross-reference from a document?
A.	Drag across a cross-reference to select it, and press **Delete** or **Backspace**.
B.	Choose **Tools | Cross-references | Delete**, select the cross-reference that you want to delete, and click **OK**.
C.	Choose **Insert | Cross-reference**, select the cross-reference that you want to delete, click **Remove Now** and then click **Apply**.
D.	Press **Ctrl+F8**, select the cross-reference that you want delete, click **Delete** and then click **OK**.

Q11	In Word, which of the following document elements can you not create a cross-reference to?
A.	Footnote.
B.	Footer.
C.	Built-in heading.
D.	Bookmark.

Q12	In Word, which of the following statements about bookmark names is untrue?
A.	Bookmark names can contain numbers.
B.	Bookmark names must begin with a letter.
C.	Bookmark names can have up to 40 characters.
D.	Bookmark names can contain spaces.

Answers

1: C, **2:** B, **3:** B, **4:** C, **5:** A, **6:** D, **7:** B, **8**: C, **9:** A, **10:** A, **11:** B, **12:** D.

19 Tables of contents

Objectives

In this chapter you will learn how to:

- Create a new table of contents using default settings
- Create a new table of contents using non-default settings
- Update an existing table of contents
- Format a table of contents

New words

In this chapter you will meet the following term:

- Table of contents

Exercise files

In this chapter you will work with the following Word files:

- `Chapter19_Exercise_19-1_Before.doc`
- `Chapter19_Exercise_19-2_Before.doc`
- `Chapter19_Exercise_19-3_Before.doc`
- `Chapter19_Exercise_19-4_Before.doc`

Syllabus reference

In this chapter you will cover the following items of the ECDL Advanced Word Processing Syllabus:

- **AM3.2.2.1**. Create a table of contents.
- **AM3.2.2.2**. Update and modify an existing table of contents.
- **AM3.2.2.3**. Apply formatting options to a table of contents.

About tables of contents

Let's begin with a precise definition of a table of contents.

Table of contents

A listing of a document's headings in the order in which they appear, along with the corresponding page numbers, shown at the beginning of a document. Typically, lower-level headings are indented further than higher-level ones.

Don't confuse a table of contents with an *index*. An index (see Chapter 21) appears at the end of a document, and is generally more thorough than a table of contents. It identifies the items – topics, terms, names and places – contained in the document, and shows their corresponding page numbers.

A table of contents lists items in the order in which they appear in the document; an index lists items alphabetically by name.

Word's 30-second table of contents

If you have applied heading styles in a document, Word can generate an acceptable table of contents for you in half a minute or less. Anyone who has ever created a table of contents manually will be impressed with this feature.

A sample from an automatically generated table of contents is shown below:

Standards of Service 2
  Admissions to Hospital 2
    Urgent Treatment 2
    Planned Treatment 3
    Emergency Treatment 3
  Appointments 3
    Waiting Times During Appointments 3
    Routine Appointments 3
    Urgent Appointments 3
  Accident and Emergency Services 3
  Discharge from Hospital 4
  Services For Children 4

Tables of contents: default settings

Word can generate a contents table very quickly because it makes a number of default choices for you. Lets look at these defaults in detail.

- **Three heading levels**. By default, Word includes paragraphs in the following styles only: Headings 1, 2 and 3. If there are more heading levels in your document, Word ignores them.
- **Progressive indentation**. As in outlines, lower heading levels are indented further from the left margin. This is a publishing convention; it results in a table of contents that is easier to read.
- **Right-aligned page numbers**. Again, Word follows the convention of aligning page numbers against the right page margin.

- **Tab leaders**. Another convention followed by Word: the insertion of dotted or continuous lines that draw the reader's eye from the left-aligned headings to the right-aligned page numbers.
- **Styles**. Word has a series of built-in styles, named TOC 1, TOC 2, and so on, that it applies to corresponding heading levels in a table of contents.

The Index and Tables *dialog box*

You insert a table of contents using the **Table of Contents** tab of the *Index and Tables* dialog box, displayed by choosing the **Insert | Index and Tables** command.

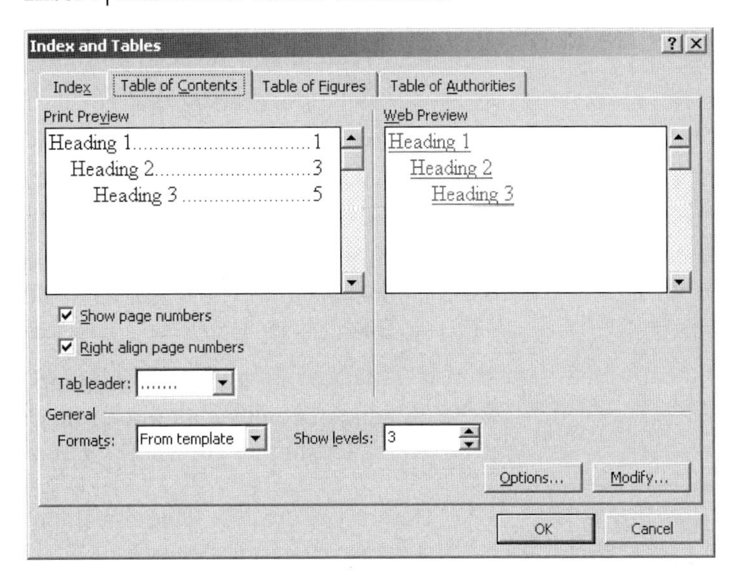

Modifying the table of contents defaults

Which default settings are you most likely to want to modify?

- **Heading levels**. The *Show levels* box enables you to override Word's default number of heading levels.
- **Styles**. It is not a good idea to apply styles other than the built-in styles to a table of contents. But, using the **Format | Style** command, you will probably want to change the attributes of these styles to something less plain.

  Another option is to select from Word's built-in gallery of formats for tables of contents. The choices include formats with names such as Classic, Distinctive and Formal.

Updating the table of contents

Typically, you will create a table of contents only once but will need to update it several times. This may be because you have added new content to your document, reordered existing content, or both.

The power of Word's automated table of contents feature is not just that it can create a new table of contents, but that it can recreate the table as often as necessary, with just a few mouse clicks.

Working with tables of contents: the four tasks

Here are the four tasks that you need to be able to perform with tables of contents in Word:

- **Create a new table of contents using default settings**. This is the fast and easy approach. See Exercise 19.1.
- **Create a new table of contents using non-default settings**. This takes a little longer, as you override Word's preset options. Exercise 19.2 takes you through the steps.
- **Update an existing table of contents**. There is more than one way to do this. You will discover your options in Exercise 19.3.
- **Formatting a table of contents**. Learn how to give your table of contents a more professional appearance by using the techniques shown in Exercise 19.4.

Creating a new table of contents

Before you start

Before you create a table of contents, ensure that the following steps have been performed:

- **Heading styles**. Check that built-in heading styles have been applied to your document's headings. You might find it easier to verify this in Outline view.

  Word's table of contents generate feature can find in a document only what you have placed in that document. Only by using paragraph styles consistently can you expect to achieve a logically organized table of contents.
- **Hidden text**. If your document uses hidden text, ensure that it is actually hidden.
- **Fields**. If your document contains fields, ensure that the fields display values rather than codes, and that the necessary fields have been updated.

Exercise 19.1: Create a table of contents with default values

In this exercise, you will generate a new table of contents for a document, based on Word's default settings.

1) Open the following file:

   Chapter19_Exercise_19-1_Before.doc

2) Position the insertion point in the blank line under the first heading.

   Elmsworth·Health·Trust:·Patients'·Charter¶

   ¶

   At·Elmsworth·Health·Trust,·we·are·committed·to·delivering·a·world-class·service.·Our·standards·apply·whether·you·are:¶

3) Choose **Insert | Index and Tables**, and click the **Table of Contents** tab.

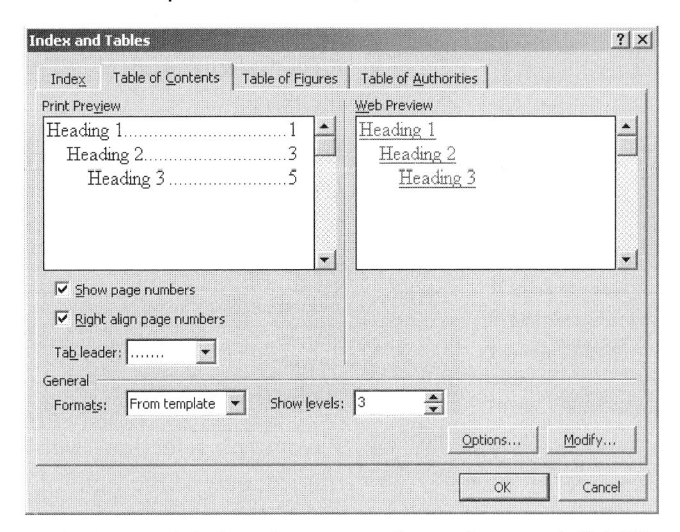

4) Verify that the default options are as shown above, and click **OK**.

   Word generates a table of contents, and positions it at the location of your insertion point. Part of the table of contents is shown below:

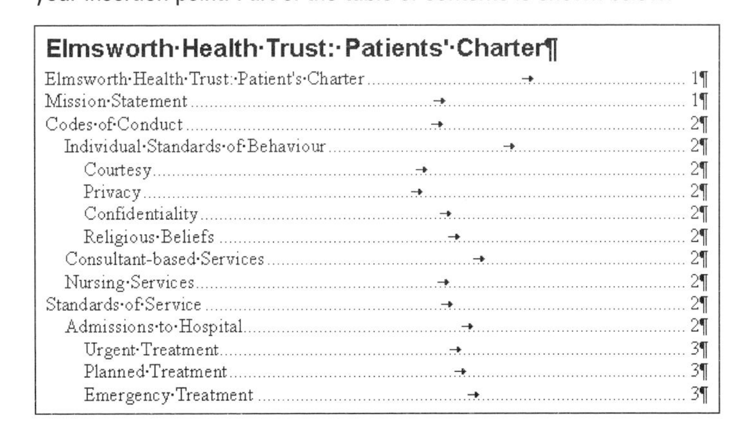

Elmsworth·Health·Trust:·Patients'·Charter¶

Elmsworth·Health·Trust:·Patient's·Charter → 1¶
Mission·Statement → 1¶
Codes·of·Conduct → 2¶
Individual·Standards·of·Behaviour → 2¶
Courtesy → 2¶
Privacy → 2¶
Confidentiality → 2¶
Religious·Beliefs → 2¶
Consultant-based·Services → 2¶
Nursing·Services → 2¶
Standards·of·Service → 2¶
Admissions·to·Hospital → 2¶
Urgent·Treatment → 3¶
Planned·Treatment → 3¶
Emergency·Treatment → 3¶

5) Save the document with the following name:

`Chapter19_Exercise_19-1_After_`*`Your_Name`*`.doc`

You can now close the document.

Tables of contents and hyperlinks

When you click on a line within a Word table of contents, the line behaves like a hyperlink on a web page: it takes you to the relevant heading within the document. This feature can be a nuisance when you want to perform an action on the contents table, such as deleting a particular line or applying direct formatting to it.

To work with a Word table of contents, click in the left margin *beside* the table. This has two effects:

- **Grey background**. Word places a grey background behind the table.

  If the grey background does not appear, choose **Tools | Options**, and click the **View** tab. In the *Field shading* box, select *When selected*, and click **OK**.

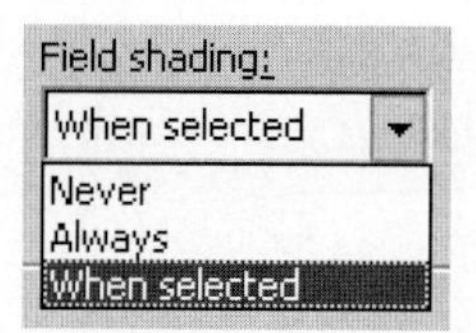

- **Paragraph selection**. Word selects the paragraph immediately to the right of the insertion point.

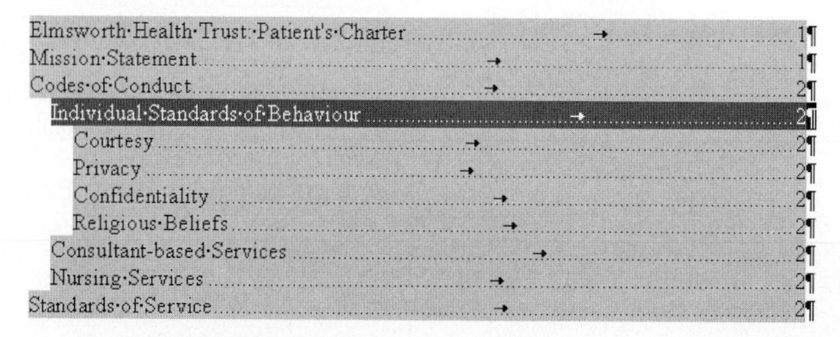

  You can now apply formatting to the paragraph, or press the **Delete** or **Backspace** key to remove it.

To select an entire table of contents, click in the left margin beside the first paragraph of the table of contents. Word then selects the entire table so that you can format it or delete it.

Exercise 19.2: Create a table of contents with non-default values

In this exercise, you will generate a new table of contents for a document based on some modifications that you make to Word's default settings.

1) Open the following file:

   `Chapter19_Exercise_19-2_Before.doc`

2) Position the insertion point in the blank line under the first heading.

3) Choose **Insert | Index and Tables**, and click the **Table of Contents** tab of the dialog box displayed.

4) In the *Tab leader* box, select the continuous line option. This replaces the default dotted line option.

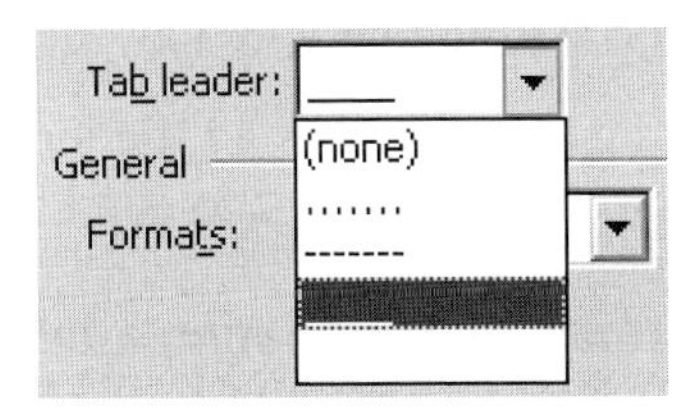

5) Change the setting of the *Show levels* box to 2. This replaces the default setting of three heading levels.

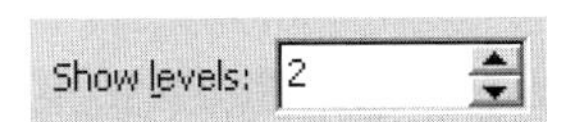

   Click **OK**. Word generates and inserts the table of contents, part of which is shown below:

   Elmsworth·Health·Trust:·Patients'·Charter¶

   Elmsworth·Health·Trust:·Patient's·Charter → 1¶
   Mission·Statement → 1¶
   Codes·of·Conduct → 1¶
   Individual·Standards·of·Behaviour → 1¶
   Consultant-based·Services → 2¶
   Nursing·Services → 2¶
   Standards·of·Service → 2¶
   Admissions·to·Hospital → 2¶
   Appointments → 3¶

6) Save the document with the following name:

   Chapter19_Exercise_19-2_After_*Your_Name*.doc

   You can now close the document.

Updating an existing table of contents

You have created a table of contents for your document, but the document has changed, with the result that the table of contents is no longer accurate. How can you update your table of contents?

Word offers two options:

- **Update page numbers only**. Select this option if you have amended, added or removed content in the document *other than* headings. If you run this option after changing your headings in any way, your heading changes will not be reflected in the updated table of contents.

  Updating only the page numbers does not affect any direct formatting that you may have applied to your table of contents.

- **Update the entire table**. Select this option if you have amended, added or removed headings in the document.

  Updating the entire table of contents removes any direct formatting that you may have applied to it.

Word generally takes a little longer to update an entire table than to update only page numbers.

Exercise 19.3: Updating a table of contents

In this exercise, you will make some changes to a table of contents, reorder text within a document, and then update the table of contents to reflect the changes.

1) Open the following file:

   `Chapter19_Exercise_19-3_Before.doc`

2) Position the insertion point in the blank line under the first heading.

   Elmsworth·Health·Trust:·Patients'·Charter¶

   ¶

   At·Elmsworth·Health·Trust,·we·are·committed·to·delivering·a·world-class·service.·Our·standards·apply·whether·you·are:¶

3) Choose **Insert | Index and Tables**, click the **Table of Contents** tab of the dialog box displayed, and click **OK**.

   Word generates the table of contents, and positions it at the location of your insertion point.

4) As you can see, Word includes your document's title ('Elmsworth Health Trust: Patients' Charter') as the first item in the table of contents. Let's remove this.

   If you click to the left of this first line, Word selects the entire table of contents and not just the first line. Instead, click at the paragraph mark at the end of the first line, hold down the **Shift** key, and press the left arrow key. (Before you do this, toggle the **Show/Hide** button to display paragraph marks.)

Elmsworth·Health·Trust:·Patients'·Charter¶

¶

Press **Delete** or **Backspace** to remove the selected first line from your table of contents.

5) Click at the beginning of the first paragraph of text beneath the table of contents.

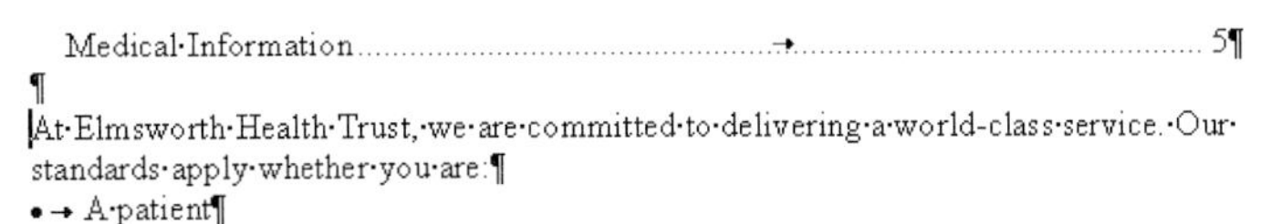

Choose **Insert | Break**, select the *Page break* option, and click **OK**.

Show Heading 1 button

Move Up button

6) Next, you will reorder a level-1 heading within the document.

Choose **View | Outline**, and click the **Show Heading 1** button on the Outlining toolbar.

7) Click anywhere in the last paragraph ('Information and Records'), and then click the **Move Up** button.

Before	***After***
Help·Us·To·Help·You¶ Information·and·Records¶	Information·and·Records¶ Help·Us·To·Help·You¶

Click anywhere else on the screen to deselect the heading. You have reordered two document headings.

8) Choose **View | Print Layout**, and navigate to the page that contains the table of contents.

Hold the mouse anywhere over the contents table. Notice that the cursor changes to a 'hand' shape. (Alternatively, click anywhere in the left margin of the contents table.)

9) Right-click with the mouse. From the pop-up menu, choose the **Update Field** command. (Alternatively, press **F9**.)

10) Word displays the *Update Table of Contents* dialog box.

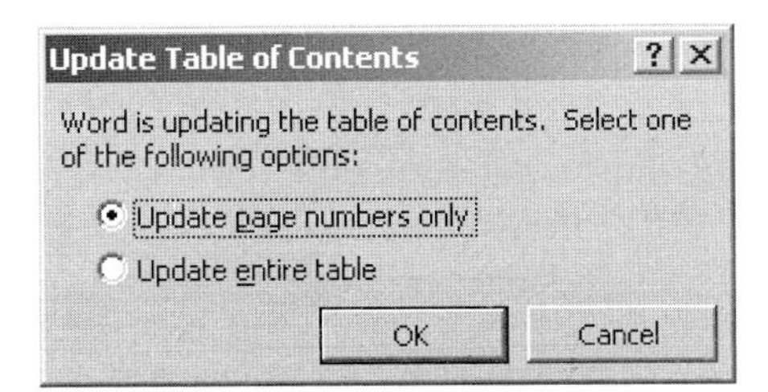

11) Select the *Update entire table* option and click **OK**.

Word updates the table of contents.

12) Save the document with the following name:

`Chapter19_Exercise_19-3_After_Your_Name.doc`

13) You can now close the document.

Formatting a table of contents

Word's default table of contents formatting may not be what you want for your documents. You have three reformatting options:

- **Apply direct formatting**. You can select one or more paragraphs in the table of contents, and use the **Format | Font, Format | Paragraph** and **Format | Borders and Shading** commands to format them.

  All such formatting is removed when you update the table with the *Update entire table* option table of contents.

- **Apply a built-in style from the table of contents gallery**. Another option is to select from Word's built-in gallery of table of contents formats. The choices include Classic, Distinctive and Formal.
- **Change the style attributes**. This is the preferred option.

Exercise 19.4: Amending the appearance of a table of contents

In this exercise, you will use various methods to modify the appearance of a document's table of contents.

1) Open the following file:

   `Chapter19_Exercise_19-4_Before.doc`

2) Click in the margin to the left of the first line of the table of contents. This selects the entire table.
3) Choose **Insert | Index and Tables**, and click the **Table of Contents** tab of the dialog box displayed.
4) In the *Formats* drop-down list, select *Formal* and click **OK**.

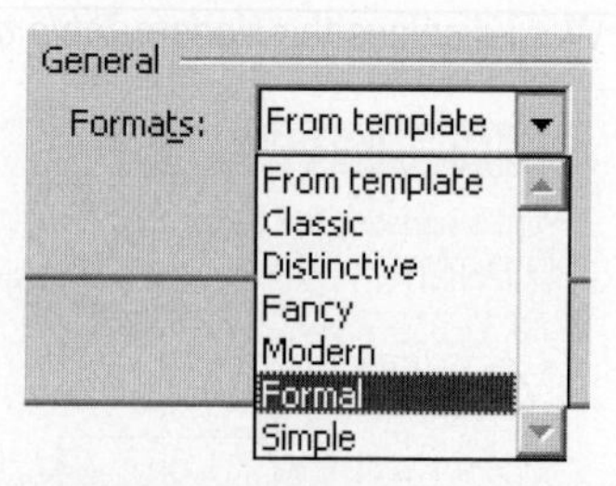

5) Word now displays the following dialog box:

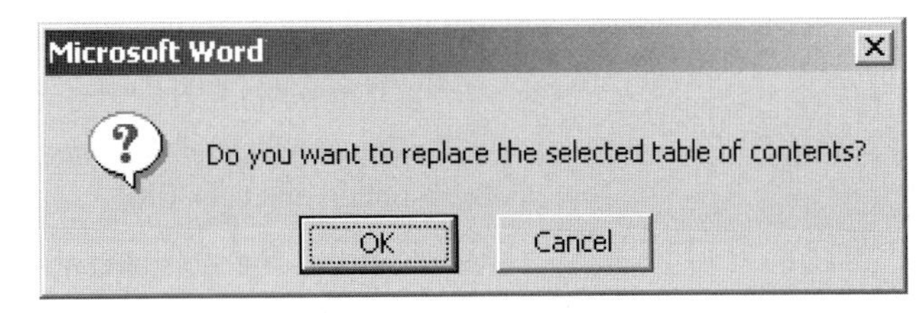

6) Click **OK**. Word now reformats the table, part of which is shown below:

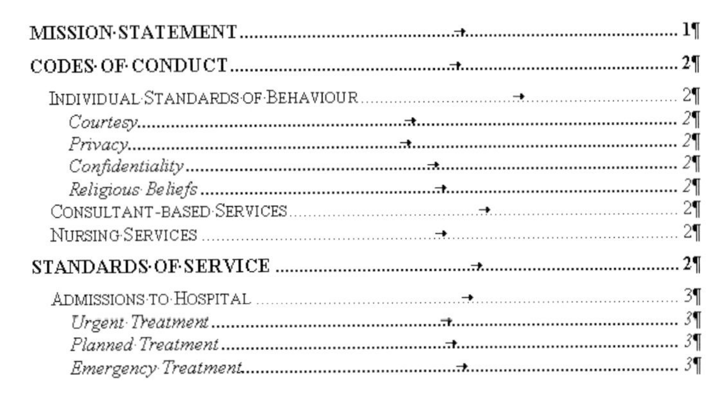

MISSION·STATEMENT → 1¶
CODES·OF·CONDUCT → 2¶
INDIVIDUAL·STANDARDS·OF·BEHAVIOUR → 2¶
Courtesy → 2¶
Privacy → 2¶
Confidentiality → 2¶
Religious·Beliefs → 2¶
CONSULTANT-BASED·SERVICES → 2¶
NURSING·SERVICES → 2¶
STANDARDS·OF·SERVICE → 2¶
ADMISSIONS·TO·HOSPITAL → 3¶
Urgent·Treatment → 3¶
Planned·Treatment → 3¶
Emergency·Treatment → 3¶

Notice that the Formal style uses upper-case letters for first- and second-level headings.

Next, you will apply some direct formatting to the table.

7) Click in the margin to the left of the first line of the table of contents. This selects the entire table.

8) On the Formatting toolbar, select the Garamond font in the *Font* box.

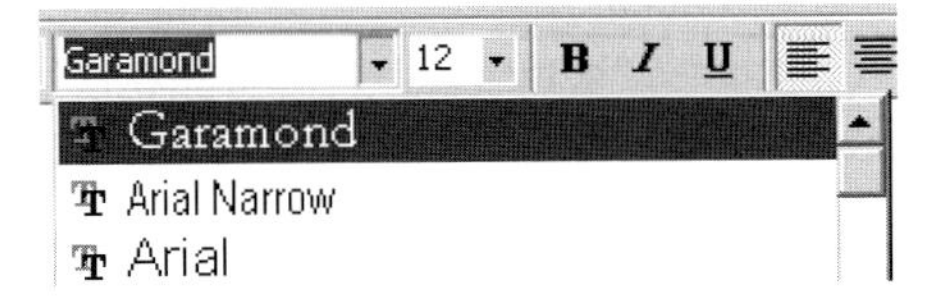

Word applies the font to the table. Click anywhere outside the table to deselect it. Your table should now look like this:

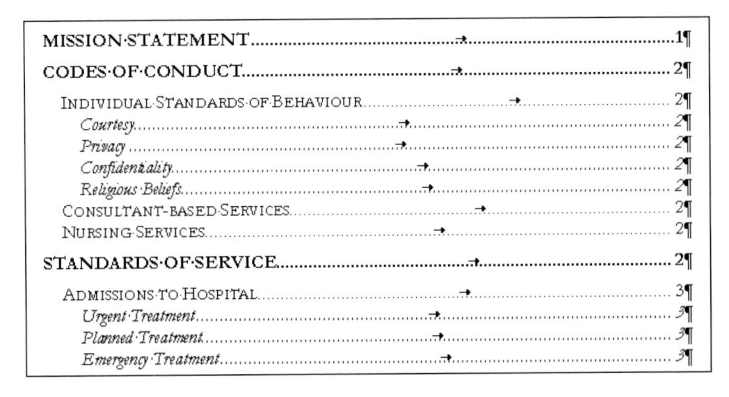

MISSION·STATEMENT → 1¶
CODES·OF·CONDUCT → 2¶
INDIVIDUAL·STANDARDS·OF·BEHAVIOUR → 2¶
Courtesy → 2¶
Privacy → 2¶
Confidentiality → 2¶
Religious·Beliefs → 2¶
CONSULTANT-BASED·SERVICES → 2¶
NURSING·SERVICES → 2¶
STANDARDS·OF·SERVICE → 2¶
ADMISSIONS·TO·HOSPITAL → 3¶
Urgent·Treatment → 3¶
Planned·Treatment → 3¶
Emergency·Treatment → 3¶

9) Hold the mouse anywhere over the table of contents and right-click. From the pop-up menu displayed, choose the **Update Field** command.

   In the *Update Table of Contents* dialog box, select the *Update entire table* option and click **OK**.

   Word updates the table of contents and removes the direct formatting that you applied in step 8.

10) Click in the left margin beside any heading (except the very first one) that is in the TOC 1 style.

11) Choose **Format | Style**, click **Modify**, click **Format**, and select the **Font** option. In the *Color* box, select *Dark Blue*, and click **OK**.

    In the *Modify Style* dialog box, do not select either the *Add to template* or *Automatically update* checkboxes, click **OK** and click **Apply**.

    Word applies the new modified style to the level-1 heading in the table. Click anywhere outside the table to deselect it.

12) Save the document with the following name:

    `Chapter19_Exercise_19-4_After_`*`Your_Name`*`.doc`

    You can now close the document.

Chapter 19: quick reference

Tasks summary

Task	Procedure
Insert a table of contents with default settings.	Choose **Insert | Index and Tables**, click the **Table of Contents** tab of the dialog box displayed, and click **OK**. Word generates tables of contents, and positions it at the location of your insertion point.
Update a table of contents to reflect changes in the document.	Click to the left of the table of contents and press **F9**.
Change the appearance of a table of contents.	Select a table of contents entry in the style you want to change, choose **Format | Style**, then specify the style characteristics you want to apply.
Delete a line from a table of contents.	Click to the left of the line and press **Delete** or **Backspace**.

Concepts summary

A *table of contents* is a listing of a document's headings in the order in which they appear, along with the corresponding page numbers. You can use Word to generate a table of contents based on a document's heading styles through the **Table of Contents** tab available with the **Insert | Index and Tables** command.

Word applies the following settings by default when generating a table of contents: *three heading levels*, with lesser headings indented further from the left-margin; *right-aligned page numbers*; and *dotted lines* joining the left-aligned headings with the right-aligned page numbers.

When you click on a line within a Word table of contents, the line acts as a hyperlink: it takes you to the relevant heading within the document.

To work with a Word table of contents, click in the *left margin* beside the table. To select the entire table of contents, click in the left margin beside the first line of table of contents. Word then selects the full table so that you can format it or delete it.

You have three *reformatting* options for a table of contents: apply direct formatting, select a built-in style from the table of contents gallery, or change the table of contents style attributes.

Word provides two ways for *updating* a table of contents: *page numbers only*, or the entire *table* of headings and page numbers. The second option removes any direct formatting that you have applied to the table.

Chapter 19: quick quiz

Circle the correct answer to each of the following multiple-choice questions about tables of contents in Word.

Q1	Which of the following statements about tables of contents is not true?
A.	A table of contents appears at the beginning of a document.
B.	A table of contents can include more than one heading level.
C.	A table of contents is a listing of a document's headings in the order in which they appear, along with the corresponding page numbers.
D.	A table of contents appears at the end of a document.

Q2	Which of the following is not a publishing convention in tables of contents?
A.	Lower heading levels are indented further from the left margin.
B.	Page numbers are aligned against the right page margin.
C.	Page numbers are shown in italics.
D.	The inclusion of dotted or continuous lines from the headings to the page numbers.

Q3	Which of the following items is not a default setting within Word's table of contents feature?
A.	Three levels of headings.
B.	Dotted lines joining headings with page numbers.
C.	Right-aligned page numbers.
D.	Four levels of headings.

Q4	Which of the following actions do you perform to create a table of contents in a Word document?
A.	Choose **Insert | Index and Tables**, select the *Generate Contents* option, and click **Apply**.
B.	Select all the text in the document and click the **New** button on the Table of Contents toolbar.
C.	Choose **Insert | Index and Tables**, click the **Table of Contents** tab, and click **OK**.
D.	Select all the text in the document, and choose the **Insert | Index and Tables** command.

Q5	What happens when you click on a line within a Word table of contents?
A.	Word displays Outline view, with the relevant line selected.
B.	You are taken to the relevant heading within the document.
C.	The line is selected.
D.	Nothing.

Q6	How do you select an entire table of contents in Word?
A.	Click in the left margin beside the first line of the table.
B.	Click anywhere in the left margin of the table.
C.	Right-click on the first line of the table.
D.	Click in the left margin beside any level-1 heading.

Q7	What choices does Word offer you for updating a table of contents?
A.	Two options: update the entire table or just the page numbers.
B.	Three options: update the entire table, the headings only, or the page numbers only.
C.	One option: update both the headings and the page numbers.
D.	Two options: update the headings and page numbers only, or update the styles only.

Q8	What happens to a Word table of contents that contains direct formatting when you update it with the *Update entire table* option selected?
A.	Word updates the table without affecting the direct formatting.
B.	Word does not update any headings or page numbers that contain direct formatting.
C.	Word updates the table but removes headings and numbers with direct formatting.
D.	Word updates the table and removes direct formatting from headings and page numbers.

Answers

1: D, **2:** C, **3:** D, **4:** C, **5:** B, **6:** A, **7:** A, **8:** D.

20 Captions

Objectives

In this chapter you will learn how to:

- Insert captions and modify the default options
- Apply chapter and caption numbers
- Update caption numbers
- Activate automatic captioning

New words

In this chapter you will meet the following term:

- Caption

Exercise files

In this chapter you will work with the following files:

- Chapter20_Exercise_20-1_Before.doc
- Chapter20_Exercise_20-2_Before.doc
- Chapter20_Exercise_20-3_Before.doc
- Chapter20_Exercise_20-4_Before.doc
- Chapter20_Exercise_20-4_Worksheet.xls
- Chapter20_Exercise_20-5_Before.doc

Syllabus reference

In this chapter you will cover the following items from the ECDL Advanced Word Processing Syllabus:

- **AM3.4.6.1**: Add or update a caption to an image or table.
- **AM3.4.6.2**: Apply a numbered caption to an image, figure, table or worksheet.
- **AM3.4.6.3**: Use automatic caption options.

About captions

A caption is a numbered label, such as 'Figure 12' or 'Table 3–8', that you add to items such as pictures, tables and Excel worksheet cells in a Word document.

The components of a caption

Let's examine the various components of a caption in Word:

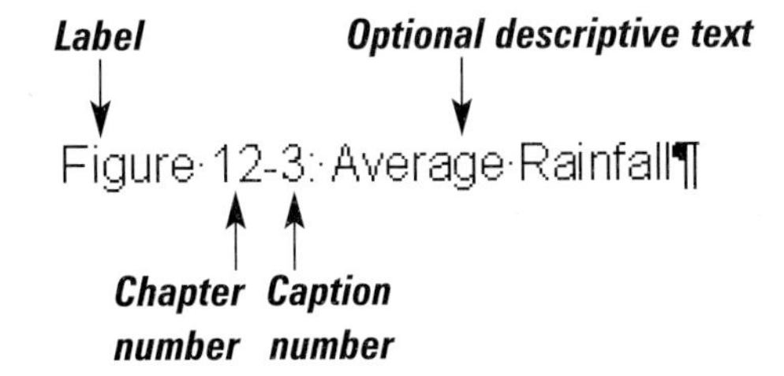

- **Label**. This is the standard text that appears in each caption. Word includes built-in labels such as 'Figure' and 'Table'.

  If required, you can create and use new labels, for example, 'Picture', 'Chart' or 'Screenshot'.
- **Caption number**. Word inserts an automatically incrementing number with each caption. For example, 'Table 1', 'Table 2', and so on.
- **Chapter number**. In multi-chapter documents, caption numbers are typically preceded by the relevant chapter number. For example, 'Table 3–5' or 'Figure 6–5'.
- **Optional text**. You can include additional text with a caption to identify or describe the item captioned. For example 'Annual Sales' or 'Average Rainfall'.

By default, captions are positioned *beneath* pictures but *above* tables or worksheet cells.

Caption

A numbered label added to pictures, tables, worksheet cells or equations in a Word document. Captions can optionally include the relevant chapter number and additional descriptive text.

The Caption dialog box

You add captions using the *Caption* dialog box, displayed by choosing the **Insert | Caption** command.

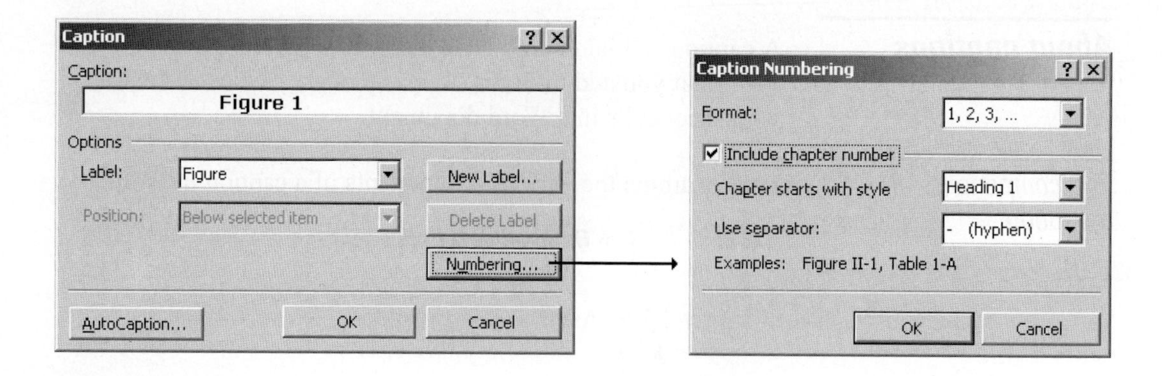

Working with captions: the five tasks

Here are the five tasks that you need to be able to perform with captions in Word:

- **Insert captions with default options**. This is the fast and easy approach. See Exercise 20.1.
- **Insert captions with non-default options**. Exercise 20.2 shows you how to take greater control over Word's captioning feature.
- **Insert captions that include chapter numbers**. Add a professional appearance to your Word documents by including the relevant chapter number with each inserted caption. See Exercise 20.3.
- **Insert captions automatically**. In Exercise 20.4, you learn how to set up automatic captioning so that Word adds a caption to every item of a particular type that you insert in your documents.
- **Update captions in a document**. Captions are fields. If you delete or move a caption, you need to update the caption numbers manually. See Exercise 20.5.

Inserting captions without chapter numbers

In the first two exercises, you will insert simple captions to accompany pictures in Word documents. The procedures for adding captions to tables and worksheet cells are similar.

Exercise 20.1: Insert captions with default options

1) Open the following file:

```
Chapter20_Exercise_20-1_Before.doc
```

2) On the first page of your sample document, click the first picture to select it.

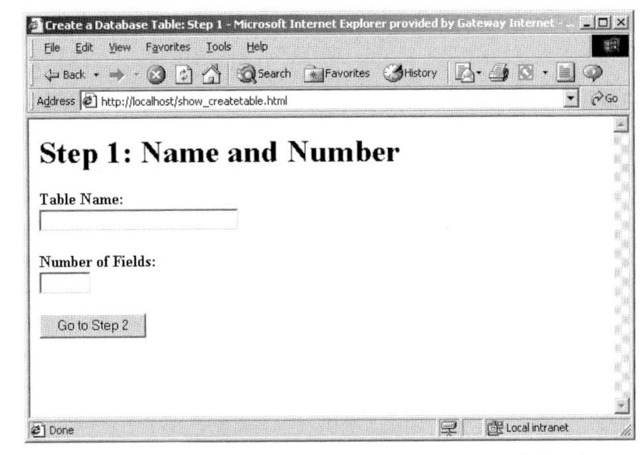

3) Choose **Insert | Caption** to display the *Caption* dialog box.

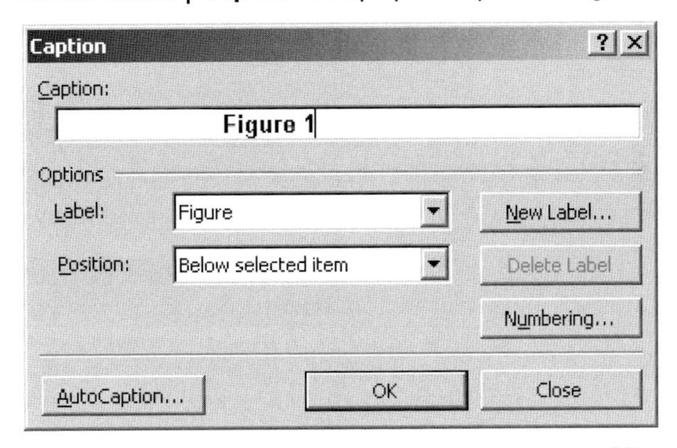

4) Accept the default options as shown above, and click **OK**.

   Word inserts the caption as shown here:

   Figure·1¶

5) Move to the second page of your sample document and insert captions for the three pictures on the page. Your captions should look like this:

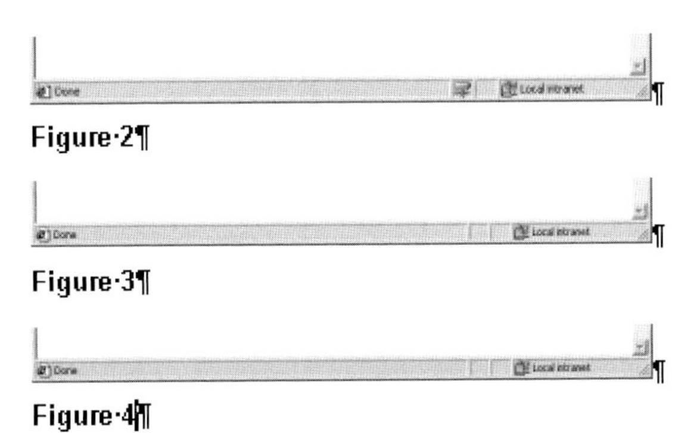

6) Save the document with the following name:

   `Chapter20_Exercise_20-1_After_Your_Name.doc`

   You can now close the document.

Exercise 20.2: Insert captions with non-default options

1) Open the following file:

   `Chapter20_Exercise_20-2_Before.doc`

2) On the first page of your sample document, click the first picture to select it and choose **Insert | Caption**.

3) Click the **New Label** button, type the label text 'Screen', and click **OK**.

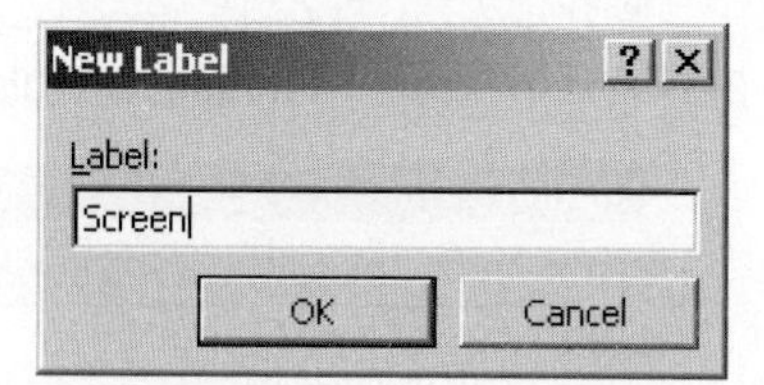

   The label 'Screen' is now available as an option in the drop-down *Label* list. It is also selected by default in the *Caption* box.

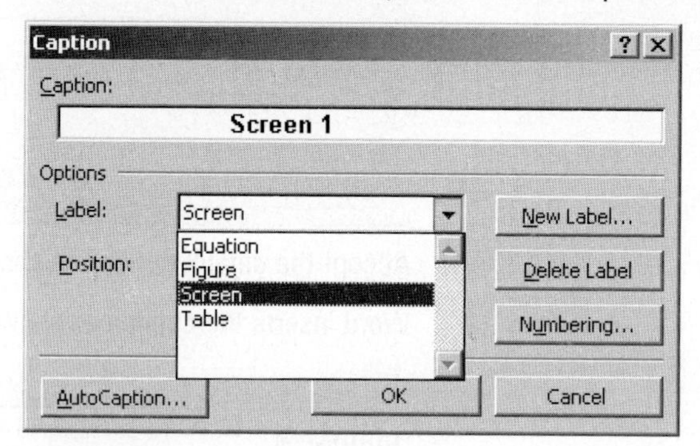

4) Click in the Caption box after the 'Screen 1' label, type the following additional text, and click **OK**:

   `: Creating the Table`

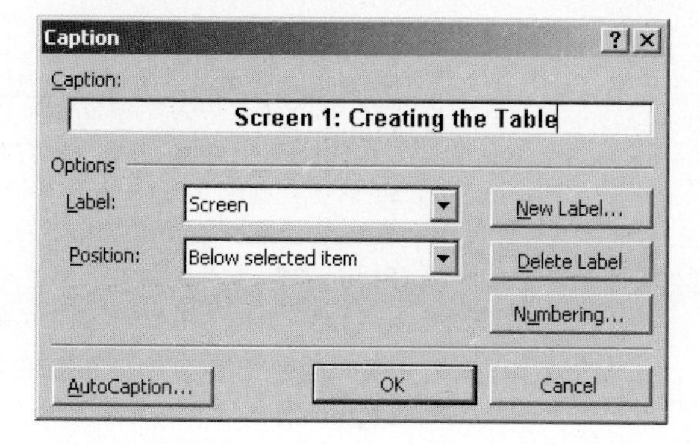

5) Move to the second page of your sample document and add the captions shown below for the three pictures on the page:

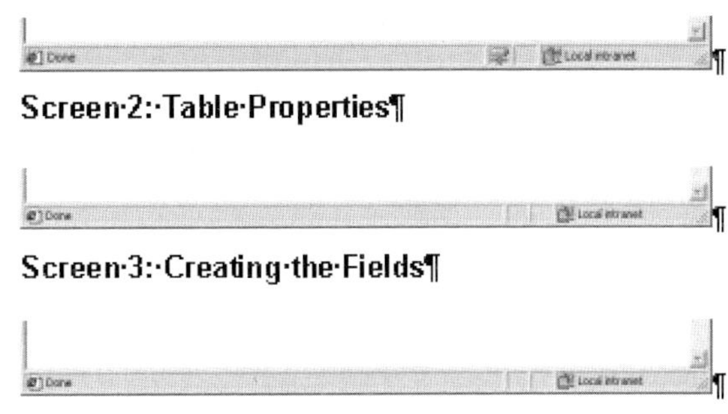

6) Save the document with the following name:

   `Chapter20_Exercise_20-2_After_`*`Your_Name`*`.doc`

   You can now close the document.

Inserting captions with chapter numbers

In multi-chapter documents, it is conventional to precede each caption number with the relevant chapter number – for example, 'Figure 1-A' or 'Table 4:6'.

Word can insert chapter numbers automatically, but only if the chapter title text is:

- Formatted in a built-in heading style. Typically, this is Heading 1 or Heading 2.
- Has outline numbering applied to it (see Chapter 1).

The word 'chapter' in this context simply means an individual document within a set of such documents. Chapters need not be named 'chapters'. You can name them 'Sections', 'Lessons', 'Units', or whatever you want.

Exercise 20.3: Insert captions with chapter numbers

1) Open the following file:

   `Chapter20_Exercise_20-3_Before.doc`

2) The headings in your sample document are formatted with the built-in heading styles Heading 1, Heading 2 and Heading 3. Your first step is to apply outline numbering to these headings. This is best done in Outline view.

   Choose **View | Outline**, and click the **Show Heading 3** button on the Outlining toolbar to display heading levels 1, 2 and 3 from your document.

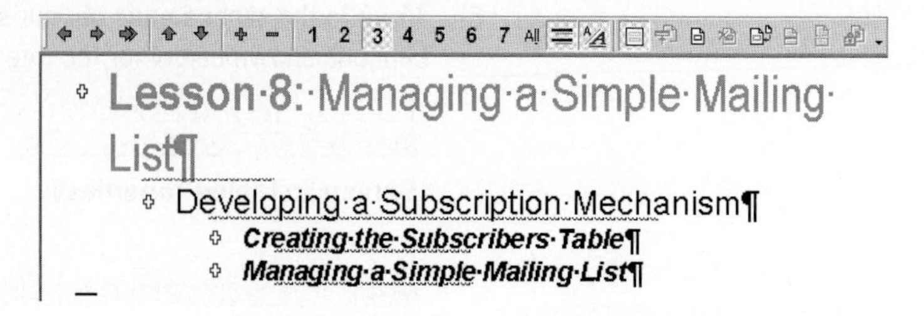

3) Position the insertion point anywhere in the level-1 heading, choose **Format | Bullets and Numbering**, click the **Outline Numbered** tab, and click to select the first of the four lower options in the dialog box.

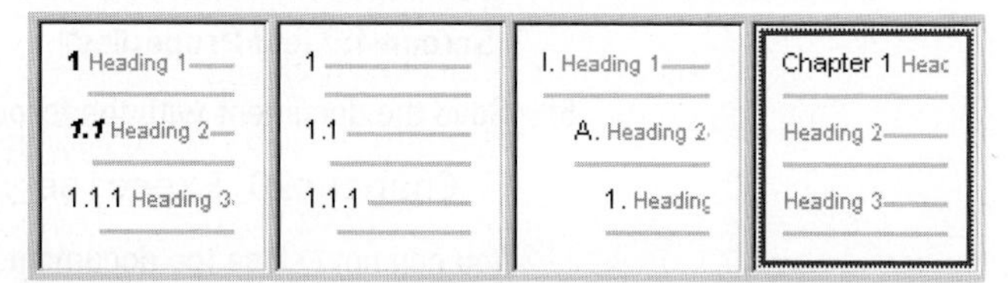

4) Click **Customize**. In the *Number format* box, change 'Chapter' to 'Lesson'. Change the *Start at* value from 1 to 8. Type a colon (:) after the number '8' in the *Number format* box.

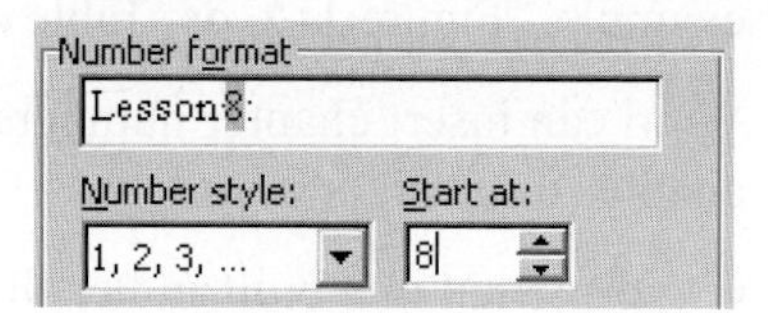

5) Click **Font**. Set the font attributes to Arial Narrow, bold, 28 point and dark grey.

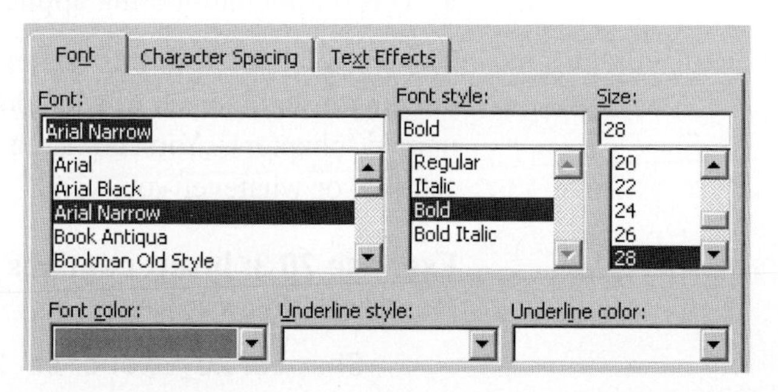

Click **OK** and **OK** to close the dialog boxes.

6) Choose **View | Print Layout**. You can see that the text 'Lesson 8:' now appears twice. The first is inserted automatically by Word's outline numbering feature.

Select the second 'Lesson 8:' and press **Delete** to remove it.

Lesson 8: Lesson·8:·Managing·a·Simple·Mailing·List¶

You are now ready to insert captions that include the chapter (or, in this example, the lesson) number.

7) On the first page of your sample document, click the first picture to select it, choose **Insert | Caption**, and click **Numbering** to display the *Caption Numbering* dialog box.

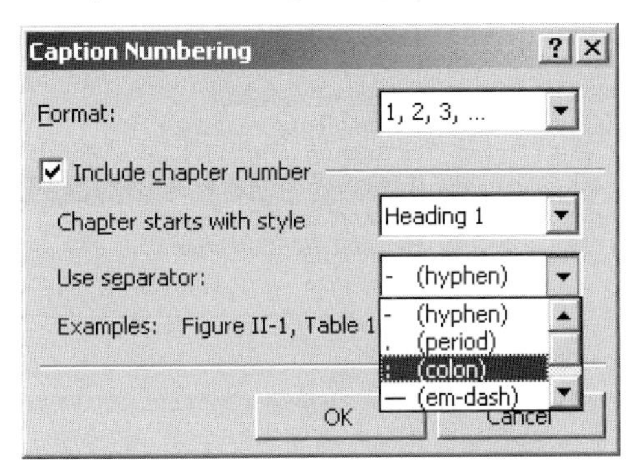

Select the *Include chapter number* checkbox. In the *Use separator* list, select the colon option. Click **OK** and **OK** to close the dialog boxes.

Word inserts the following caption beneath the selected picture:

Screen·8:1¶

8) Move to the second page of your sample document, and add the captions shown below for the three pictures on the page:

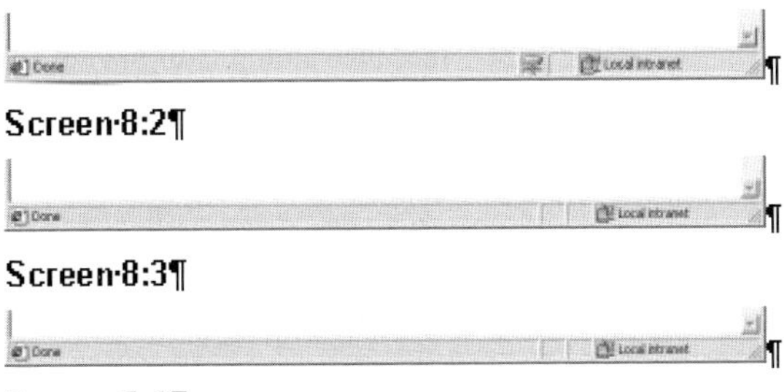

Screen·8:2¶

Screen·8:3¶

Screen·8:4¶

9) Close and save the document with the following name:

   `Chapter20_Exercise_20-3_After_`*`Your_Name`*`.doc`

Inserting captions automatically

If you are working with a document into which you plan to insert many pictures, tables, Excel worksheet cells or equations, you can take advantage of Word's automatic captioning feature.

You can include chapter numbering with automatic captioning if the chapter title text is formatted in a built-in heading style and has outline numbering applied to it.

Word's automatic captioning options are available within the *AutoCaption* dialog box, accessed by clicking the **AutoCaption** button on the *Caption* dialog box.

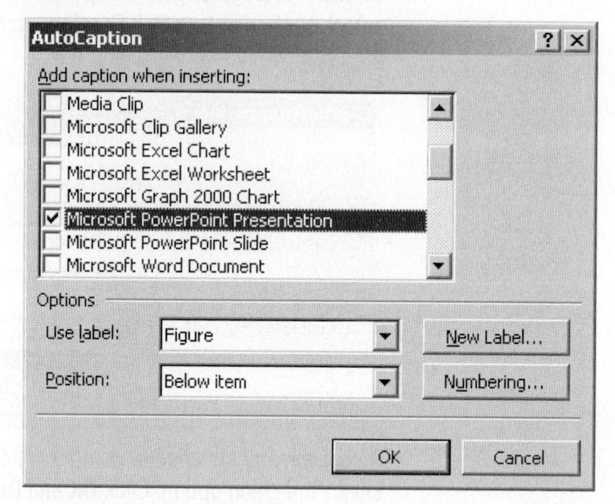

The *AutoCaption* dialog box lists a range of file types for which Word can automatically add appropriate captions. The content of the list depends on the software applications that you have installed on your PC.

Exercise 20.4: Insert captions automatically

1) Open the following file:

   `Chapter20_Exercise_20-4_Before.doc`

2) Your first action is to switch on automatic captions for Excel worksheet cells. Choose **Insert | Caption** and click **AutoCaption**.

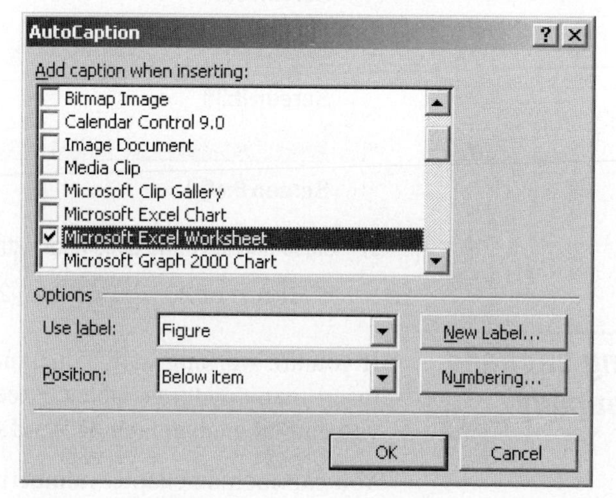

Select the checkbox for *Microsoft Excel Worksheet* and click **OK**.

3) You are now ready to insert Excel worksheet cells into your Word document.

Click at the second paragraph mark beneath the heading 'Balance Sheet for XYZ Enterprises'. This is the location at which you will insert the worksheet cells.

Choose **Insert | Object**, click the **Create from File** tab, and click the **Browse** button. Select the following sample file and click **Insert**:

`Chapter20_Exercise_20_4_Worksheet.xls`

Word redisplays the *Object* dialog box and shows the name of the file that you have selected for insertion.

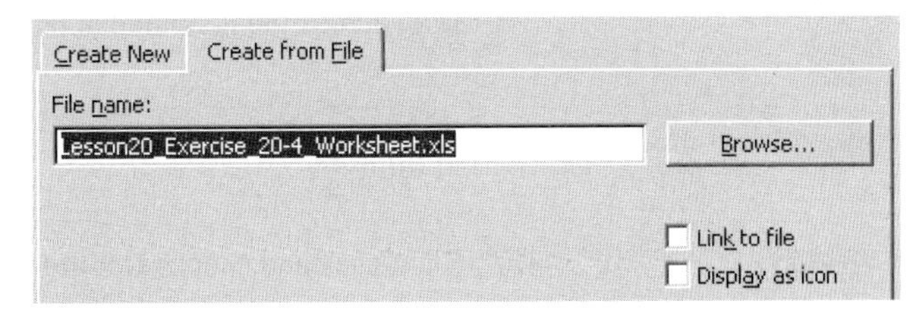

Click **OK**.

Beneath the inserted worksheet cells you can see that Word has automatically created the caption 'Figure 1'.

Donation reserve	873	882
	28,058	**30,413** ¶

Figure·1¶

4) Choose **Insert | Caption**, click **AutoCaption**, deselect the *Microsoft Excel Worksheet* checkbox, and click **OK**.

5) Close and save the document with the following name:

`Chapter20_Exercise_20-4_After_`*`Your_Name`*`.doc`

Updating caption fields

Word's captioning feature is based on fields (see Chapter 8). When you insert new captions, Word updates all other caption numbers in the document automatically. Word does this regardless of whether you insert new captions after all previous captions or *within* a series of already captioned items.

If you delete or move captions within a document, however, you need to update the caption numbers to reflect your changes. You can do this as follows:

- Select the entire document and update all fields.

  A selected caption or captions can be updated by pressing the **F9** key or by right-clicking on the selection and choosing the **Update Field** command.

- Alternatively, save and close the document, then open it again. Word will update the caption fields automatically.

Exercise 20.5: Update caption numbers

1) Open the following file:

   `Chapter20_Exercise_20-5_Before.doc`

2) Select the first picture and the caption beneath it, then press **Delete**.

3) Move to the second page. Notice that the caption numbers are now incorrect: the first caption in the document is named 'Figure 2', the second is 'Figure 3', and the third is 'Figure 4'.

4) Drag across the first caption number to select it.

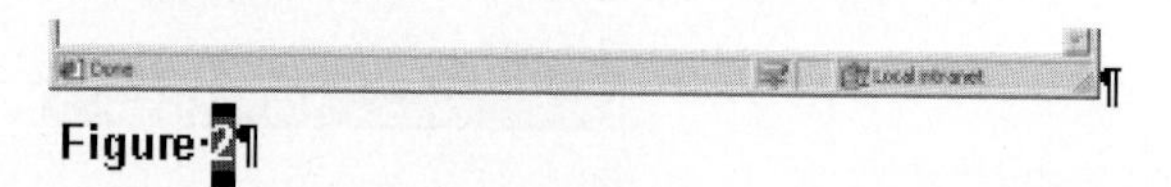

5) Right-click and choose **Update Field**. Word updates your first caption as shown:

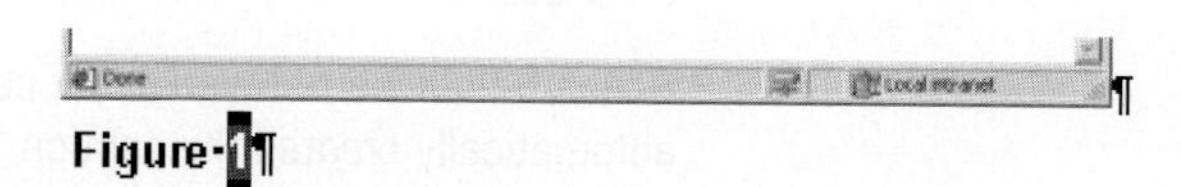

6) The two other caption numbers in your document are still incorrect. Let's update them by saving and closing the document and then opening it again.

   Save the document with the following name, then close it:

   Chapter20_Exercise_20-5_After_*Your_Name*.doc

7) Reopen your document. Notice that the second and third captions now contain the correct caption numbers. You can now close your sample document.

Chapter 20: quick reference

Tasks summary

Task	Procedure
Insert a caption.	Select the picture, table or other item for captioning, choose **Insert | Caption**, select or create a label, accept or amend the default caption position, and click **OK**.
Amend caption numbering format.	Choose **Insert | Caption**, click **Numbering**, select another numbering format, and click **OK** and **OK**.
Insert captions with chapter numbers.	Word can insert chapter numbers automatically, but only if the chapter title text is formatted in a built-in heading style and has outline numbering applied to it.
	Select the picture, table or other item for captioning, choose **Insert | Caption**, select or create a label, accept or amend the default caption position, click **Numbering**, select the *Include chapter number* checkbox, and click **OK** and **OK**.
Switch automatic captioning on or off.	Choose **Insert | Caption**, click **AutoCaption**, select or deselect the required file type(s), and click **OK** and **OK**.
Update captions.	Select a single caption or part or all of the document. Press **F9** or right-click on the selection and choose **Update Field**.
	Alternatively, close and save the document and then reopen it.

Concepts summary

A *caption* is a numbered label, such as 'Figure 12' or 'Table 3–8', that you can add to items such as pictures, tables, worksheet cells or equations in a Word document. By default, captions are positioned *beneath* pictures but *above* tables or worksheet cells.

The *caption label* is the standard text that appears in each caption. Word includes built-in labels, such as 'Figure' and 'Table'. If required, you can create and use new labels, for example, 'Picture' or 'Chart'. Optionally, you can include additional text with a caption label to identify or describe the item captioned.

Every caption includes a *caption number* field. When you insert new captions, Word updates all other caption numbers in the document automatically. Word does this regardless of whether you insert new captions after all previous captions or within a series of already captioned items. If you delete or move captions within a document, however, you need to update the caption number field to reflect your changes.

In multi-chapter documents, caption numbers are typically preceded by the relevant *chapter number*. For example, 'Table 3-5' or 'Picture 6-5'. Word can insert chapter numbers automatically, but only if the chapter title text is formatted in a built-in heading style and has outline numbering applied to it.

You add captions using the *Caption* dialog box, displayed by choosing the **Insert | Caption** command.

Chapter 20: quick quiz

Circle the correct answer to each of the following multiple-choice questions about captions in Word.

Q1	A caption is ...
A.	Additional information or references regarding the main text that appears at the end of document.
B.	A numbered label added to pictures, tables, worksheet cells or equations in a Word document.
C.	A summary of information about a document that can be displayed with the **File | Properties** command.
D.	Additional information or references regarding the main text that appears at the bottom of a page within document.

Q2	In Word, which command do you choose to insert a caption in a document?
A.	**Insert | Caption.**
B.	**Tools | Captions | Insert.**
C.	**Insert | New | Captions.**
D.	**Insert | Bookmarks or Captions.**

Q3	In Word, a caption label is ...
A.	An automatically incrementing number that Word inserts in each caption.
B.	Optional text such as 'Sales Figures' or 'Annual Rainfall' that you can add to further describe the item captioned.
C.	Standard text such as 'Figure' or 'Table' that appears in each caption.
D.	None of the above.

Q4	In Word, which of the following items can you not add a caption to?
A.	Picture.
B.	Footnote.
C.	Table.
D.	Equation.

Q5	By default, where does Word position captions for tables?
A.	Beneath the table.
B.	To the left of the table.
C.	Above the table.
D.	None of the above – you cannot add captions to tables.

Q6	By default, where does Word position captions for pictures?
A.	Beneath the picture.
B.	To the left of the picture.
C.	Above the picture.
D.	None of the above – you cannot add captions to pictures.

Q7	In Word, which action can you not perform after clicking the **Numbering** button on the *Caption* dialog box?
A.	Update the caption number fields throughout the document.
B.	Change the separator symbol between chapter and the caption number.
C.	Include the current chapter number with the caption numbers.
D.	Change the format that Word applies to the automatically incrementing caption numbers.

Q8	Which action do you take to activate automatic captioning in Word?
A.	Choose **Insert | Caption**, click **Numbering**, select the *Number all captions* checkbox, and click **Apply** and **OK**.
B.	Choose **Tools | Options**, click the **General** tab, select the *Automated captioning* checkbox, and click **OK**.
C.	Choose **Insert | Caption**, click **AutoCaption**, select the required file type(s), and click **OK** and **OK**.
D.	Choose **Format | Captions**, click the **Numbering** tab, select the *Automated captioning* checkbox, and click **OK**.

Q9	In Word, when can you automatically include chapter numbers with caption numbers?
A.	When the document is based on the Normal template (Normal.dot)
B.	When the chapter title text is formatted in a built-in heading style.
C.	When the document's headings are formatted with styles rather than with direct formatting.
D.	When the chapter title text is formatted in a built-in heading style and has outline numbering applied to it.

Answers

1: B, **2:** A, **3:** C, **4:** B, **5:** C, **6:** A, **7:** A, **8:** C, 9: D.

21 Indexes

Objectives

In this chapter you will learn how to:

- Mark text for indexing
- Compile an index
- Update an index

New words

In this chapter you will meet the following term:

- Index

Exercise files

In this chapter you will work with the following Word files:

- `Chapter21_Exercise_21-1_Before.doc`
- `Chapter21_Exercise_21-2_Before.doc`
- `Chapter21_Exercise_21-3_Before.doc`
- `Chapter21_Exercise_21-4_Before.doc`

Syllabus reference

In this chapter you will cover the following item from the ECDL Advanced Word Processing Syllabus:

- **AM3.3.1.2**: Create or edit an index.

About indexes

Let's begin with a more precise definition of an index.

Index
An alphabetical listing of the main items in a document, along with the corresponding page numbers, shown at the end of a document.

Don't confuse an index with a *table of contents*. A table of contents (see Chapter 19) is generally less thorough than an index and appears at the beginning of a document.

Indexing: the two steps

Word offers a number of features to help you build and update document indexes. In Word, indexing is a two-step process:

- **Marking the index entries**. The first step in building an index is to mark all the items in your document that are to be included in the index.

  Word positions an index entry field code (XE) at each item that you mark for indexing.

- **Creating the index**. When you have marked all your index entries, you then *compile* the actual index. Word generates the page number references in the index automatically.

  This is also the stage at which you specify the index format: the number of columns, the alignment of page numbers, and which (if any) tab leaders you want to use. As with tables of contents, Word's indexing feature offers a gallery of built-in formats, with names such as Classic and Modern.

A sample Word-created index is shown below:

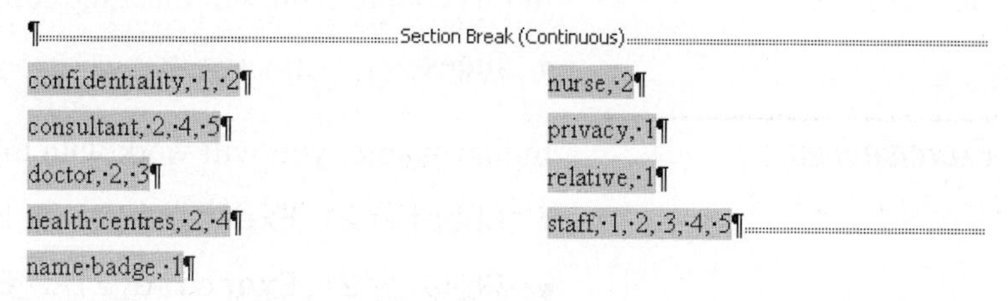

The Index and Tables *dialog box*

You insert an index using the **Index** tab of the *Index and Tables* dialog box, displayed by choosing the **Insert | Index and Tables** command.

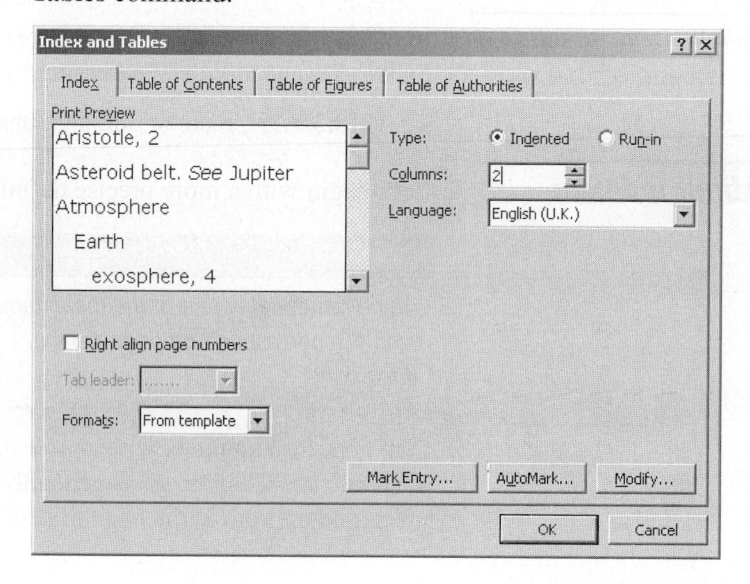

Updating the index

Typically, you compile an index only once but will need to update it several times. This may be because you have added new content to your document, reordered existing content, or both.

You can update an index by selecting it and pressing **F9**. Alternatively, right-click on the index and choose **Update Field** from the pop-up menu.

Working with indexes: the four tasks

Here are the four tasks that you need to be able to perform with indexes in Word:

- **Mark index entries**. Exercise 21.1 shows you how to mark text for inclusion in an index.
- **Compile an index**. In Exercise 21.2, you compile an index using the default options.
- **Formatting a table of contents**. Learn how to customize the appearance of your index using the techniques shown in Exercise 21.3.
- **Update an index**. Exercise 21.4 shows you how to update an index to reflect changes in the content of your document.

Working with index entries

In the first exercise, you mark items in a sample document for later inclusion in an index.

Exercise 21.1: Mark entries for indexing

1) Open the following file:

    `Chapter21_Exercise_21-1_Before.doc`

2) On the first page after the document's table of contents, under the heading 'Codes of Conduct', select the two words 'name badge'.

    ·Codes·of·Conduct¶

    Our·staff·will·introduce·themselves·to·you·and·explain·how·they·can·help.·All·staff·will·wear·a·name·badge·to·enable·you·to·identify·them.¶

3) Choose **Insert | Index and Tables**, click the **Index** tab of the dialog box, and select the **Mark Entry** button to display the *Mark Index Entry* dialog box.

    You can see the text you selected in the *Main entry* box.

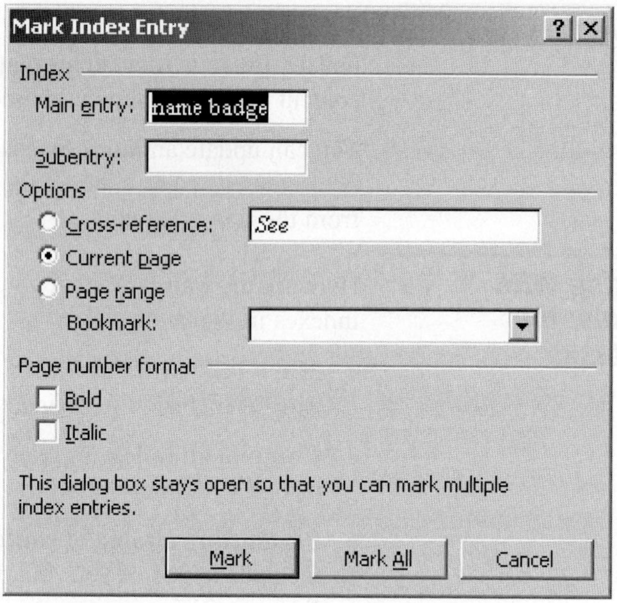

Mark Index Entry

Index

Main entry: name badge

Subentry:

Options

Cross-reference: *See*

Current page

Page range

Bookmark:

Page number format

Bold

Italic

This dialog box stays open so that you can mark multiple index entries.

Mark | Mark All | Cancel

4) Click the **Mark** button and then click **Close** to close the dialog box. You can see the index entry field in hidden text format. Can't see the XE field? Click the **Show/Hide** button on the Standard toolbar.

Codes·of·Conduct¶

Our·staff·will·introduce·themselves·to·you·and·explain·how·they·can·help.·All·staff·will·wear·a·name·badge{·XE·"name·badge"·}·to·enable·you·to·identify·them.¶

5) Move to the next page of the document. Under the heading 'Nursing Services', select the word 'nurse'.

***Nursing·Services*¶**

We·will·ensure·that·a·named,·qualified·nurse,·midwife·or·other·health·care·professional·takes·a·personal·responsibility·for·your·treatment·and·care·during·your·time·with·us.¶

6) Press the following shortcut key combination: **Alt+Shift+X**.

This displays the *Mark Index Entry* dialog box. Click the **Mark** button, and then click **Close** to close the dialog box. Your text should look like this:

***Nursing·Services*¶**

We·will·ensure·that·a·named,·qualified·nurse{·XE·"nurse"·},·midwife·or·other·health·care·professional·takes·a·personal·responsibility·for·your·treatment·and·care·during·your·time·with·us.¶

7) Further down the same page, under the heading 'Standards of Services', select the text 'health centres' and press **Alt+Shift+X**.

Standards·of·Service¶

Staff·at·our·hospitals·and·health·centres·are·committed·to·achieving·specified·standards·in·the·following·areas:¶

8) Click the **Mark All** button, and then click **Close** to close the dialog box. Your text should look like this:

Standards·of·Service¶

Staff·at·our·hospitals·and·health·centres{·XE·"health·centres"·}·are·committed·to·achieving·specified·standards·in·the·following·areas:¶

Move forward in your sample document to the heading called 'Keeping Us Informed'. You can see that other occurrences of the text 'health centres' also contain index entry marks.

- → Showing·consideration·for·other·people·in·the·hospital·and·health·centres{·XE·"health·centres"·},·and·keeping·noise·levels·to·a·minimum·¶
- → Complying·with·signs·around·the·hospital·and·health·centres{·XE·"health·centres"·},·including·those·asking·you·not·to·smoke,·not·to·use·mobile·phones,·and·our·advice·on·the·number·of·visitors·and·visiting·times.¶

9) Move back to the first page of text in your sample document. Select the word 'patient' in the first bullet point, press **Alt+Shift+X**, click **Mark All**, then click **Close**.

10) Locate occurrences of the following words in your sample document. In each case, select the word, press **Alt+Shift+X**, click **Mark All**, then click **Close**:

`relative, staff, privacy, confidentiality, consultant, doctor`

11) Save the document with the following name:

`Chapter21_Exercise_21-1_After_`*`Your_Name`*`.doc`

You can now close the document.

Options when marking index entries

In Exercise 21.1, you first selected each item of text that you wanted to mark as an index entry. Word displays the text that you select in the *Main entry* box of the *Mark Index Entry* dialog box.

Codes·of·Conduct¶

Our·staff·will·introduce·themselves·to·you·and·explain·how·they·can·help.·All·staff·will·wear·a·name·badge·to·enable·you·to·identify·them.¶

Word offers the following options when marking index entries:

- Want to change the word or phrase in the *Main entry* box? Simply edit the displayed text as required.

- Want to create an index entry for a word or phrase that does not appear in your document? Do not select any text before pressing **Alt+Shift**+X. Word displays the *Mark Index Entry* dialog box without any text present in the *Main entry* box. You can then type in the text that you require.

Compiling an index

In this exercise, you will compile an index based on the index entries that you marked in Exercise 21.2.

Exercise 21.2: Compile an index

1) Open the following file:

   `Chapter21_Exercise_21-2_Before.doc`

2) Click at the paragraph mark on the last page of the document. This is the location at which you will create the index.

3) Choose **Insert | Index and Tables**, click the **Index** tab, verify that the default options are as shown below, and click **OK**.

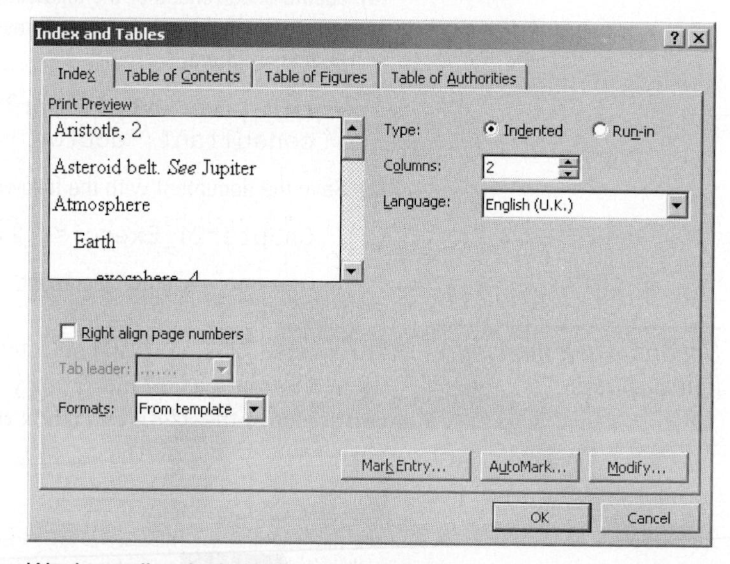

Word compiles the index as shown below:

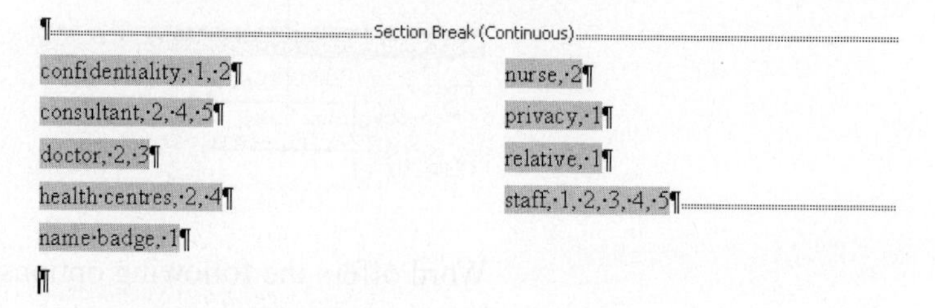

Can't see a grey background behind each indexed item? Choose **Tools | Options**, and click the **View** tab. In the *Field shading* box, select *When selected*, and click **OK**.

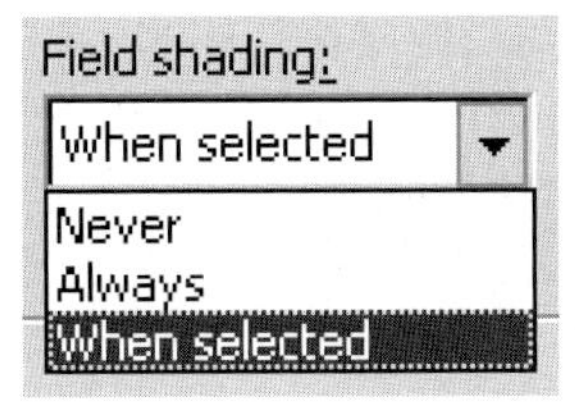

4) Save the document with the following name:

   `Chapter21_Exercise_21-2_After_`*`Your_Name`*`.doc`

   You can now close the document.

Index and section breaks

As you discovered in Exercise 21.2, Word places an index in a section of its own. Why? Because, by default, Word formats the index in a different number of columns to the remainder of the document. You will learn more about sections in Chapter 26.

Index formatting options

If Word's default index formatting is not to your taste, you have three reformatting options

- **Apply direct formatting**. You can select one or more paragraphs in the index, and use the **Format | Font**, **Format | Paragraph** and **Format | Borders and Shading** commands to format them.
- **Apply a built-in style from the index gallery**. Another option is to select from Word's built-in gallery of index formats. The choices include Classic, Distinctive and Formal.
- **Change the style attributes**. Word contains nine built-in styles for use in indexes, named Index Heading, Index 1, Index 2, etc. By changing the attributes of these styles with the **Format | Style** command, you can change the appearance of your index.

In Exercise 21.3, you will generate an index based on some modifications that you make to Word's default formatting settings.

Exercise 21.3: Compile an index with non-default formatting

1) Open the following file:

   `Chapter21_Exercise_21-3_Before.doc`

2) Click at the paragraph mark on the last page of the document, choose **Insert | Index and Tables**, and click the **Index** tab.
3) In the Formats drop-down list, select the *Classic* option, and click **OK**.

   Word generates and inserts the index like this:

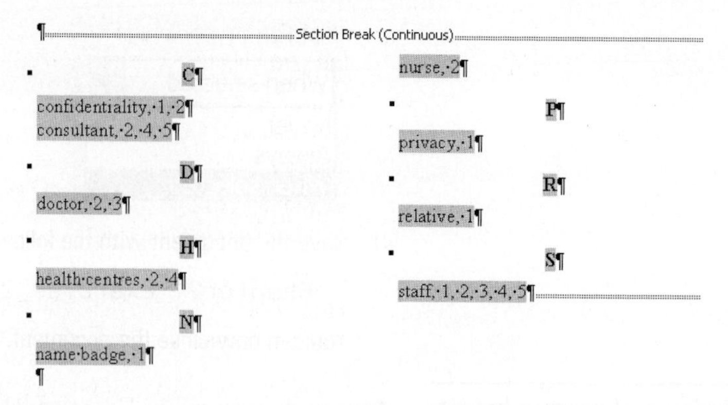

Section Break (Continuous)

C

confidentiality, 1, 2
consultant, 2, 4, 5

D

doctor, 2, 3

H

health centres, 2, 4

N

name badge, 1
nurse, 2

P

privacy, 1

R

relative, 1

S

staff, 1, 2, 3, 4, 5

4) Click at any of the index headings (the upper-case letters that precede each alphabetic group of index entries).

5) Choose **Format | Style**, click **Modify**, then click **Format** and **Paragraph**. In the *Alignment* box, select *Left,* and click **OK**, **OK**, and **Apply**. Your index should look like this:

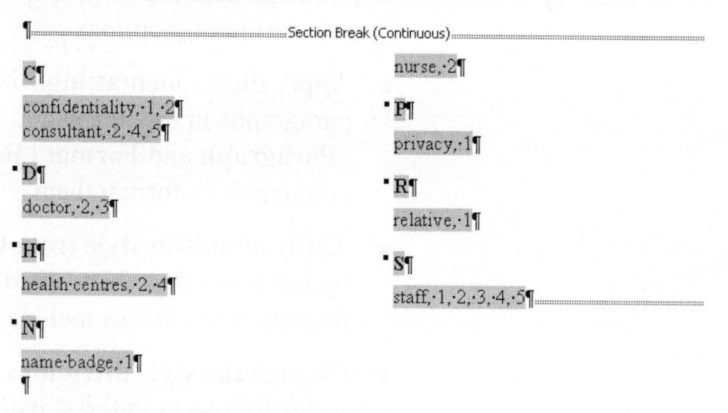

Section Break (Continuous)

C

confidentiality, 1, 2
consultant, 2, 4, 5

D

doctor, 2, 3

H

health centres, 2, 4

N

name badge, 1
nurse, 2

P

privacy, 1

R

relative, 1

S

staff, 1, 2, 3, 4, 5

6) Save the document with the following name:

`Chapter21_Exercise_21-3_After_Your_Name.doc`

You can now close the document.

Updating an index

You have created an index for your document – but the document has changed, with the result that the index is no longer accurate. How can you update your index?

In Exercise 21.4, you will make some changes to a document, and then update the index to reflect the changes.

Exercise 21.4: Update an index

1) Open the following file:

`Chapter21_Exercise_21-4_Before.doc`

2) Move to the last page of text in your sample document, and select the first bullet point beneath the heading 'Medical Information'.

▪ *Medical·Information¶*

You·have·the·right·to·be·informed·of·the·nature·of·your·illness·or·condition·in· language·that·you·can·fully·understand,·and·to·be·informed·concerning:·¶

- → The·results·of·your·tests·and·x-rays{·XE·"x-rays"·}¶
- → The·purpose,·method,·likely·duration·and·expected·benefit·of·the·proposed· treatment·¶

Press **Delete** to remove it. The paragraph contained a marked index entry. You need to update your index to reflect your editing change

3) Move to the final page of the document, i.e. the page that contains the index.

Hold the mouse over any index field and either press **F9** or right-click with the mouse and choose **Update Field** from the pop-up menu.

Word updates the index. You can see that the entry for 'X-rays, 6' is removed.

4) Save the document with the following name:

`Chapter21_Exercise_21-4_After_`*`Your_Name`*`.doc`

You can now close the document.

Chapter 21: quick reference

Tasks summary

Task	Procedure
Mark an index entry.	Select the text, press **Alt+Shift+X**, click **Mark** or **Mark All**, and then click **Close**.
Compile an index.	Position the insertion point where you want the index to appear, select your required format from the built-in gallery, choose **Insert | Index and Tables**, click the **Index** tab, and click **OK**.
Change the appearance of an index.	Select the index text and apply direct formatting. Or modify the attributes of the built-in indexing styles.
Update an index to reflect changes in the document.	Click on any field in the compiled index and press **F9**.

Concepts summary

An *index* is an alphabetical listing of the main items in a document, along with the corresponding page numbers, shown at the end of a document. You can use Word to *mark* text items for inclusion in an index, and to create or *compile* the index itself. The marking and compilation options are available within the **Index** tab when you choose the **Insert | Index and Tables** command.

Word places *section breaks* before and after an index because, by default, the index is formatted in a different number of columns to the remainder of the document.

You have three *formatting* options for an index: apply direct formatting, select a built-in style from the Index gallery, or change the index style attributes. You can *update* an index to reflect changes in the document content.

Chapter 21: quick quiz

Circle the correct answer to each of the following multiple-choice questions about indexes in Word.

Q1	Which of the following statements about indexes is untrue?
A.	An index lists the important items in a document.
B.	Items in an index are listed in alphabetical order.
C.	An index appears at the end of a document.
D.	Items in an index are listed in page number order.

Q2	In Word, which of the following keyboard shortcuts can you use when marking an index entry?
A.	**Alt+Ctrl+X.**
B.	**Alt+F9.**
C.	**Alt+Shift+X.**
D.	**F9.**

Q3	In Word, which of the following command actions can you perform to mark an index entry?
A.	Choose **Tools | Index**, click **Index Entry**, and then click **OK**.
B.	Choose **Insert | Index and Tables**, click the **Index** tab, click **Mark Entry**, and then click **OK.**
C.	Choose **Format | Index**, click **Mark Entry**, and then click **Apply**.
D.	Choose **Insert | Index and Tables**, click the **Index** tab, click **Mark**, and then click **Close**.

Q4	In Word, how can you create an index entry for a word or phrase that does not appear in your document?
A.	Do not select any text before pressing **Alt+Shift+X**, type the required text in the dialog box, and then click **Mark** and **Close**.
B.	Choose **Tools | Index**, click **Index New Entry**, type the required text in the dialog box, and then click **OK**.
C.	Click anywhere in the document left margin, press **Alt+Ctrl+X**, type the required text in the dialog box, and then click **Mark** and **Close**.
D.	None of the above – you cannot create index entries for words or phrases that do not appear in a document.

Q5	In Word, what is the effect of clicking the **Mark All** button in the *Mark Index Entry* dialog box?
A.	Word compiles an index of all commonly occurring words and phrases in the document.
B.	You are taken to the relevant index entry in the compiled index.
C.	All occurrences of the text in the *Mark entry* box within the dialogue box will be included in the compiled index.
D.	All occurrences of text formatting with built-in heading styles will be included in the compiled index.

Q6	In Word, which of the following command actions do you take to compile an index?
A.	Choose **Format | Index**, click **Compile Now**, and then click **Apply**.
B.	Choose **Insert | Index and Tables**, click the **Index** tab, and click **OK**.
C.	Right-click on any index entry field in the document, and choose **Compile Index** from the pop-up menu displayed.
D.	Choose **Insert | Index and Tables**, click the **Compile Index** tab, click **Compile**, and then click **Close**.

Q7	Which of the following breaks does Word automatically insert before and after a compiled index?
A.	Column breaks.
B.	Page breaks.
C.	Text-wrapping breaks.
D.	Section breaks.

Q8	In Word, which of the following actions do you take to update an index?
A.	Right-click on any field in the compiled index and press **Alt+Shift+X**.
B.	Select the compiled index, choose **Format | Index**, click **Update** and then click **Apply**.
C.	Click on any field in the compiled index and press **F9**.
D.	None of the above – you must recompile the index if the document content changes.

Answers

1: D, **2:** C, **3:** D, **4**: A, **5:** C, **6:** B, **7:** D, **8:** C.

22 Font and paragraph effects

Objectives

In this chapter you will learn how to:

- Apply static and animated effects to selected text
- Apply borders and shading to paragraphs
- Apply widow and orphan controls to paragraphs

New words

In this chapter you will meet the following terms:

- Widow
- Orphan

Exercise files

In this chapter you will work with the following Word files:

- `Chapter22_Exercise_22-1_Before.doc`
- `Chapter22_Exercise_22-2_Before.doc`
- `Chapter22_Exercise_22-3_Before.doc`
- `Chapter22_Exercise_22-4_Before.doc`
- `Chapter22_Exercise_22-5_Before.doc`

Syllabus reference

In this chapter you will cover the following items from the ECDL Advanced Word Processing Syllabus:

- **AM3.1.1.1**: Apply text effect options: strikethrough, superscript, subscript, shadow, etc.
- **AM3.1.1.2**: Apply animated text effect options.
- **AM3.1.2.1**: Use paragraph shading options.
- **AM3.1.2.2**: Use paragraph border options.
- **AM3.1.2.3**: Apply widow and orphan controls to paragraphs.

Font and paragraph effects

Word offers the following effects that you can apply to text and paragraphs through the **Format | Font** and **Format | Paragraph** commands.

- **Font options**. These include font features such as superscript, shadow and small capitals.
- **Animated text**. You can apply animation to text that appears on the screen but not on print-outs.
- **Paragraph borders and shading**. You can place a variety of border types around paragraph. You can also insert coloured backgrounds behind paragraphs for emphasis or decorative effect.
- **Widows and orphans**. You can prevent Word from printing the first line of a paragraph alone at the bottom of a page (*orphan*) or the last line of a paragraph alone at the top of a page (*widow*).

Working with text and paragraph effects: the five tasks

Here are the five tasks that you need to be able to perform with text and paragraph effects in Word:

- **Apply font effects**. Exercise 22.1 shows you how to apply font effects.
- **Apply animated text effects**. In Exercise 22.2, you apply Word's animated text effects.
- **Apply paragraph borders**. Exercise 22.3 takes you through the steps of applying borders around paragraphs.
- **Apply paragraph shading**. You learn how to place coloured backgrounds behind paragraphs in Exercise 22.4.
- **Apply widow and orphan controls**. In Exercise 22.5 you discover how to switch off the Word feature that prevents single lines appearing at the top and bottom of pages.

Working with font effects

Word offers a wide range of font options within the **Font** tab of the **Format | Font** command.

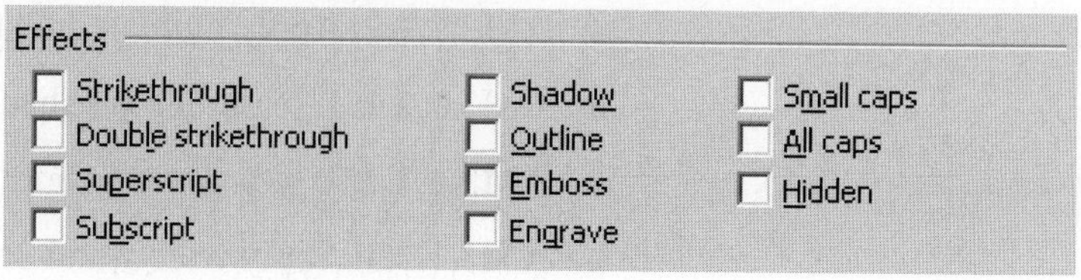

Effects

☐ Strikethrough	☐ Shadow	☐ Small caps
☐ Double strikethrough	☐ Outline	☐ All caps
☐ Superscript	☐ Emboss	☐ Hidden
☐ Subscript	☐ Engrave	

The table opposite lists and describes these font effects.

Name	Description	Example	Typical usage
Strikethrough	Applies a solid line through the middle of the text.	~~Coursebook~~	Revision tracking
Double strikethrough	Applies a double solid line through the middle of the text.	~~Coursebook~~	Revision tracking
Superscript	Raises the text and reduces its font size.	x^2+y^2	Exponents
Subscript	Lowers the text and reduces its font size.	H_2SO_4	Chemical formulas
Shadow	Applies a shadow behind the text.	Coursebook	Decorative headings
Outline	Displays character borders only.	Coursebook	Decorative headings
Emboss	Displays text as if it were raised off the page.	Coursebook	Decorative headings
Engrave	Displays text as if were pressed into the page.	Coursebook	Decorative headings
Small caps	Displays text in upper-case characters and reduces the font size.	COURSEBOOK	Decorative headings
All caps	Displays text in upper-case characters.	COURSEBOOK	Headings
Hidden	Makes text invisible. You can use the Show/Hide button to toggle the display of the text.		Revision tracking

In the first exercise, you will apply some font effects to a sample document.

Exercise 22.1: Apply font effects

1) Start Word and open the following document:

    Chapter22_Exercise_22-1_Before.doc

2) Select the word Danger, choose **Format | Font**, click the **Font** tab, select the *Outline* and *All caps* options, and click **OK**.

3) Select the words 'Hazardous Material' and 'Handle with Extreme Caution', choose **Format | Font**, click the **Font** tab, select the *Small caps* option, and click **OK**.

4) Select the words 'Sulphuric Acid', choose **Format | Font**, click the **Font** tab, select the *Shadow* option, and click **OK**.

5) In the line containing 'H2SO4', select the '2', choose **Format | Font**, click the **Font** tab, select the *Subscript* option, and click **OK**. Repeat this action for the '4' in 'H2SO4'.

    Your document should now look like this:

DANGER¶
HAZARDOUS·MATERIAL¶
HANDLE·WITH·EXTREME·CARE¶
Sulphuric·Acid¶
H_2SO_4¶

6) Save your sample document with the following name, and close it:

`Chapter22_Exercise_22-1_After_Your_Name.doc`

Working with animated text effects

Word offers a wide range of on-screen text animation effects within the **Animation** tab of the **Format | Font** command.

The following table lists and describes these text effects.

Name	Description
Blinking Background	Causes the text and background to alternate between black-on-white and white-on-black.
Las Vegas Lights	Surrounds the text with flashing, multi-coloured, neon-like dots.
Marching Black Ants	Surrounds the text with a dynamic, dashed, black border.
Marching Red Ants	Surrounds the text with a dynamic, dashed, red border.
Shimmer	Repeatedly blurs the text and then returns it to normal.
Sparkle Text	Displays a layer of flashing, multi-coloured sparkles over the text.

Exercise 22.2: Apply text animation effects

1) Open the following Word document:

   `Chapter22_Exercise_22-2_Before.doc`

2) Select the words 'Blinking Background', choose **Format | Font**, click the **Text Effects** tab, select the *Blinking Background* option, and click **OK**.

3) Select the words 'Las Vegas Lights', choose **Format | Font**, click the **Text Effects** tab, click the *Las Vegas Lights* option, and click **OK**.

4) Select the words 'Marching Black Ants', choose **Format | Font**, click the **Text Effects** tab, click the *Marching Black Ants* option, and click **OK**.

5) Select the words 'Marching Red Ants', choose **Format | Font**, click the **Text Effects** tab, click the *Marching Red Ants* option, and click **OK**.

6) Select the words 'Shimmer', choose **Format | Font**, click the **Text Effects** tab, click the *Shimmer* option, and click **OK**.

7) Select the words 'Sparkle Text', choose **Format | Font**, click the **Text Effects** tab, click the *Sparkle Text* option, and click **OK**.

8) Save your sample document with the following name, and close it:

   Chapter22_Exercise_22-2_After_*Your_Name*.doc

Working with paragraph borders and shading

You can call attention to paragraphs by adding borders (decorative boxes) and shading (coloured backgrounds) using the options available with the **Format | Borders and Shading** command.

Border options

To apply a border, select the paragraph (including its paragraph mark), choose **Format | Borders and Shading**, click the **Borders** tab, select your required options, and click **OK**.

Word offers a range of border settings. Use the *Preview* area on the right of the dialog box to select the edges that you want bordered. The default is all four edges. You can also control the border colour and width.

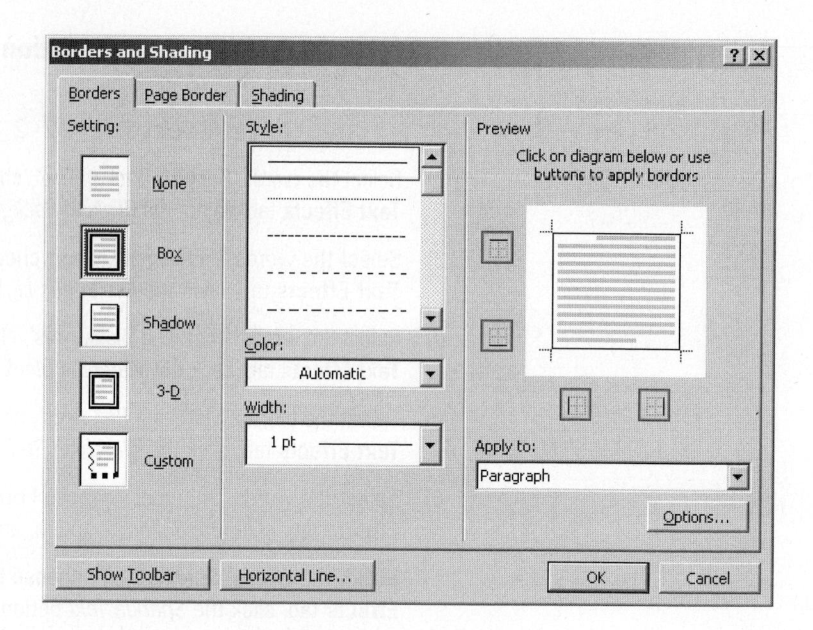

Exercise 22.3: Apply paragraph borders

1) Open the following Word document:

   `Chapter22_Exercise_22-3_Before.doc`

2) Select the 'Carpets Uncovered' paragraph, choose **Format | Borders and Shading**, and click the **Borders** tab.

   Click the *Shadow* setting and click **OK**.

3) Select the 'Everything Half Price' paragraph, choose **Format | Borders and Shading**, and click the **Borders** tab.

   In the *Width* box, select *3 pt*. In the *Preview* area, click the top box edge.

   In the *Width* box, select *1 pt*. In the *Preview* area, click the bottom box edge and click **OK**.

4) Select the 'Unit 42, Retail Park' paragraph, choose **Format | Borders and Shading**, and click the **Borders** tab.

   Click the *Box* setting. In the *Width* box, select *1½ pt* and click **OK**.

   Your document should look like this:

5) Save your sample document with the following name, and close it:

`Chapter22_Exercise_22-3_After_Your_Name.doc`

Shading options

To apply shading, select the paragraph (including its paragraph mark), choose **Format | Borders and Shading**, click the **Shading** tab, select your fill, style and colour options, and click **OK**.

- **Fill**. The text background colour. If you want to place a grey shade behind black text, use 25% or less of grey, otherwise the text will be difficult to read.
- **Style**. Allows you to apply tints (percentages of a colour) or patterns of a second colour (selected in the *Color* box) on top of the selected fill colour. Leave the *Style* box at its default value of *Clear* if you do not want to apply a second colour.
- **Colour**. If you have selected a pattern in the *Style* box, select the colour of the lines and dots in the pattern here.

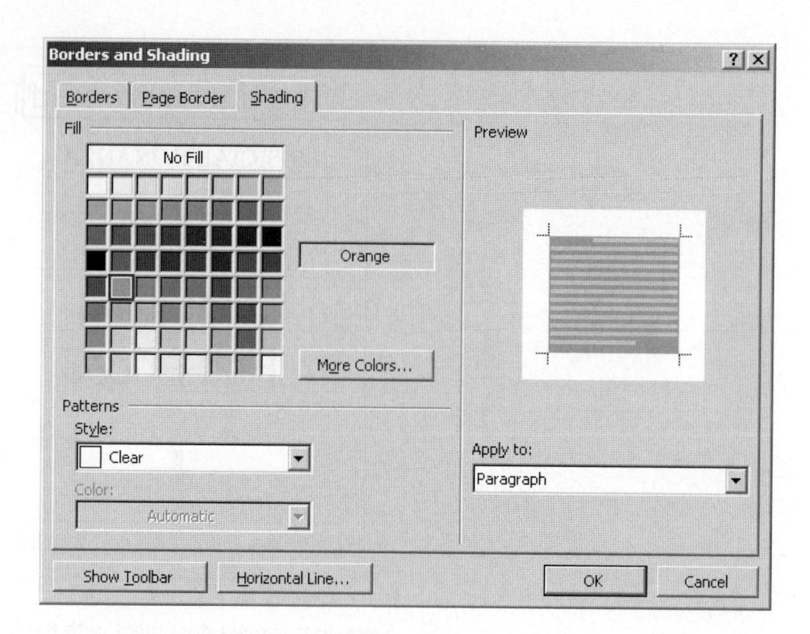

Paragraph bordering and shading options are commonly applied to the same paragraph to achieve visual effects.

Exercise 22.4: Apply paragraph shading

1) Open the following Word document:

    `Chapter22_Exercise_22-4_Before.doc`

2) Select the 'Carpets Uncovered' paragraph, choose **Format | Borders and Shading**, and click the **Shading** tab.

    In the *Fill* area, click *Gray-25%* and click **OK**.

3) Select the 'Everything Half Price' paragraph, choose **Format | Borders and Shading**, and click the **Shading** tab.

    In the *Fill* area, click *Black* and click **OK**.

    With the paragraph still selected, choose **Format | Font** and change the text colour to white.

4) Select the 'Unit 42, Retail Park' paragraph, choose **Format | Borders and Shading**, and click the **Borders** tab.

    Click the *Shadow* setting.

    Next, click the **Shading** tab. In the *Fill* area, click *Gray-25%* and click **OK**.

    Your document should now look like this:

5) Save your sample document with the following name, and close it:

`Chapter22_Exercise_22-4_After_Your_Name.doc`

Working with widows and orphans

Professional typesetters and designers follow two important rules when formatting multi-page documents:

- Never print the last line of a paragraph by itself at the top of a page. Such a line is called a *widow*.
- Never print the first line of a paragraph by itself at the bottom of a page. Such a line is called an *orphan*.

By default, Word prevents the occurrence of widows and orphans. You can switch off this setting by choosing **Format | Paragraph**, clicking the **Line and Page Breaks** tab, deselecting the *Widow/Orphan control* checkbox, and clicking **OK**.

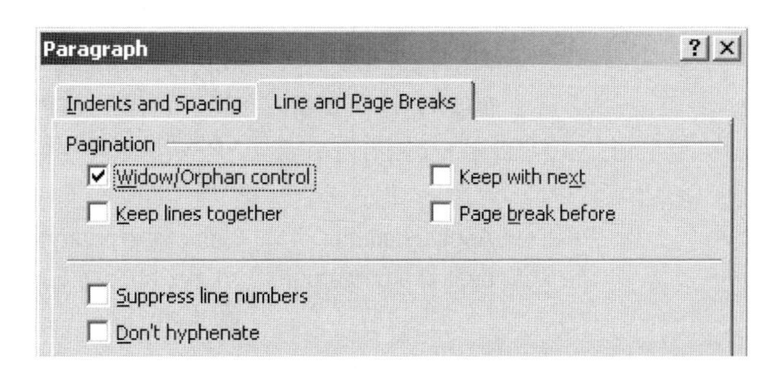

Widow

The last line of a paragraph displayed alone at the top of a page.

Orphan

The first line of a paragraph displayed alone at the bottom of a page.

Exercise 22.5: Switch off widow and orphan control

1) Open the following document:

   Chapter22_Exercise_22-5_Before.doc

2) Select the final paragraph of text, beginning with the words 'While it's easy ...'

   This paragraph runs from the bottom of the first page to the top of the second page.

3) Choose **Format | Paragraph**, click the **Line and Page Breaks** tab, deselect the *Widow/Orphan control* checkbox, and click **OK**.

   Notice that the last line of the paragraph now appears by itself at the top of the second page – a widow.

4) Save your sample document with the following name, and close it:

   Chapter22_Exercise_22-5_After_*Your_Name*.doc

Chapter 22: quick reference

Tasks summary

Task	Procedure
Apply font effects.	Select the text, choose **Format | Font**, click the **Font** tab, select a font effect checkbox or boxes, and click **OK**.
Apply animated text effects.	Select the text, choose **Format | Font**, click the **Text Effects** tab, select an animated effect from the list displayed, and click **OK**.
Apply borders around a paragraph.	Select the paragraph (including its paragraph mark), choose **Format | Borders and Shading**, click the **Borders** tab, select your required options, and click **OK**.
Apply shading behind a paragraph.	Select the paragraph (including its paragraph mark), choose **Format | Borders and Shading**, click the **Shading** tab, select your fill, style and colour options, and click **OK**.
Switch widow/ orphan control on/off.	Select the paragraph, choose **Format | Paragraph**, click the **Line and Page Breaks** tab, select or deselect the *Widow/Orphan control* check box, and click **OK**.

Concepts summary

Word offers a range of *font effects*, such as outline, shadow and subscript, which you can apply to selected text in documents. *Animated text effects* allow selected text to change dynamically on screen. These effects are available with the **Format | Font** command.

You can call attention to paragraphs by adding *borders* (decorative boxes) and *shading* (coloured backgrounds), using the options available with the **Format | Borders and Shading** command.

By default, Word prevents *widows* (the last line of a paragraph appearing alone at the top of a page) and *orphans* (the first line of a paragraph appearing alone at the bottom of a page). This setting is controlled within the **Line and Page Breaks** tab of the **Format | Paragraph** command.

Chapter 22: quick quiz

Circle the correct answer to each of the following multiple-choice questions about font and text effects, borders and shading, and widows and orphans in Word.

Q1	In Word, to which of the following types of text would you typically apply a subscript font effect?
A.	Chemical formulas.
B.	Exponents in mathematical text.
C.	Text that is marked for deletion.
D.	Decorative headings.

Q2	In Word, to which of the following types of text would you typically apply a small caps font effect?
A.	Body text.
B.	Decorative headings.
C.	Text that is marked for deletion.
D.	Exponents in mathematical text.

Q3	In Word, to which of the following types of text would you typically apply an outline font effect?
A.	Decorative headings.
B.	Body text.
C.	Field codes.
D.	Chemical formulas.

Q4	In Word, which of the following statements about animated text effects is untrue?
A.	Blinking Background and Shimmer are two animated text effects available with Word.
B.	Animated text effects appear both on screen and on print-outs.
C.	Animated text effects are controlled within the **Font** tab of the **Format | Font** command.
D.	Animated text effects appear on screen but not on print-outs.

Q5	In Word, which of the following statements about paragraph borders is untrue?
A.	A border can be applied selectively to one or more of the following edges of a paragraph: top, bottom, left and right.
B.	Paragraph borders are controlled within the **Borders** tab of the **Format | Borders and Shading** command.
C.	You can control the width but not the colour of paragraph borders.
D.	You can control both the width and the colour of paragraph borders.

Q6	In Word, which of the following statements about paragraph shading is untrue?
A.	Paragraph shading is controlled within the **Shading** tab of the **Format | Borders and Shading** command.
B.	Borders or shading, but not both at once, can be applied to a selected paragraph.
C.	The term 'fill' refers to the paragraph background colour.
D.	Borders and shading can be applied to the same paragraph.

Q7	In Word, which of the following statements about widows is untrue?
A.	Widow and orphan settings are controlled within the **Line and Page Breaks** tab of the **Format | Paragraph** command.
B.	A widow is the last line of a paragraph appearing alone at the top of a page.
C.	By default, Word prevents the occurrence of widows and orphans.
D.	A widow is the first line of a paragraph appearing alone at the bottom of a page.

Q8	In Word, which of the following statements about orphans is untrue?
A.	Widows and orphans settings are controlled within the **Line and Page Breaks** tab of the **Format | Paragraph** command.
B.	An orphan is the last line of a paragraph appearing alone at the top of a page.
C.	By default, Word prevents the occurrence of widows and orphans.
D.	An orphan is the first line of a paragraph appearing alone at the bottom of a page.

Answers

1: A, **2:** B, **3:** A, **4:** B, **5:** C, **6:** B, **7:** D, **8:** B

23 Text boxes and text orientation

Objectives

In this chapter you will learn how to:

- Create and delete text boxes
- Edit, resize and move text boxes
- Apply borders and shading to text boxes
- Link text boxes
- Orient text in text boxes and tables

New words

In this chapter you will meet the following terms:

- Text box
- Linked text boxes

Exercise files

In this chapter you will work with the following Word files:

- `Chapter23_Exercise_23-1_Before.doc`
- `Chapter23_Exercise_23-2_Before.doc`
- `Chapter23_Exercise_23-3_Before.doc`
- `Chapter23_Exercise_23-4_Before.doc`
- `Chapter23_Exercise_23-5_Before.doc`
- `Chapter23_Exercise_23-6_Before.doc`
- `Chapter23_Exercise_23-7_Before.doc`

Syllabus reference

In this chapter you will cover the following items from the ECDL Advanced Word Processing Syllabus:

- **AM3.4.3.1**. Insert or delete text boxes.
- **AM3.4.3.2**. Edit, move, or resize text boxes.

- **AM3.4.3.3**. Apply border and shading options in text boxes.
- **AM3.4.3.4**. Link text boxes.
- **AM3.1.1.7**. Use text orientation options.

About text boxes

In a Word document, text flows continuously from the beginning of the document to the end, from the top left of the first page to the bottom right of the last.

Sometimes, however, you might want to insert and position text in a block or container separate from the main text of the document. In publishing, such boxes are named call-outs or sidebars. In Word, the term used is *text boxes*.

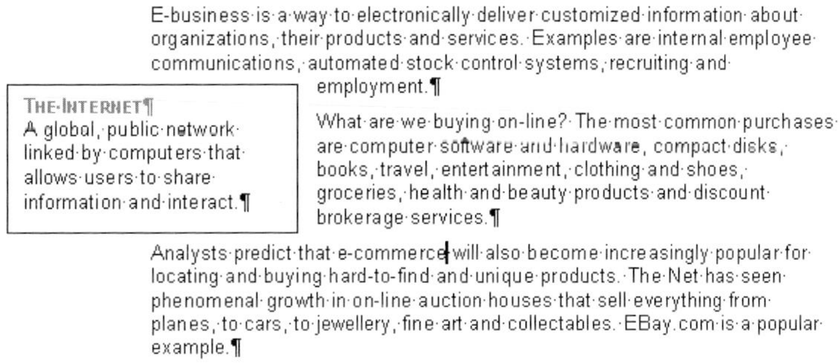

E-business is a way to electronically deliver customized information about organizations, their products and services. Examples are internal employee communications, automated stock control systems, recruiting and employment.¶

THE INTERNET¶
A global, public network linked by computers that allows users to share information and interact.¶

What are we buying on-line? The most common purchases are computer software and hardware, compact disks, books, travel, entertainment, clothing and shoes, groceries, health and beauty products and discount brokerage services.¶

Analysts predict that e-commerce will also become increasingly popular for locating and buying hard-to-find and unique products. The Net has seen phenomenal growth in on-line auction houses that sell everything from planes, to cars, to jewellery, fine art and collectables. EBay.com is a popular example.¶

An example of a text box in Word

You can insert several text boxes on the same page, format the text directly or with styles, add borders and shading (coloured backgrounds), and resize, move, copy, and cut and paste text boxes, as required.

Here are some of the items that you can include in a Word text box:

- Text
- Text in a table
- Pictures
- Fields

And here are some of the items that you cannot include:

- Columns
- Comments
- Footnotes and endnotes

Text box

A container for text or other items that is separate from the remainder of the text in the document. Text boxes can be formatted, sized, moved, copied, and cut and pasted, as required.

Text Box button

You can create a new text box by clicking the **Text Box** button on the Drawing toolbar, or by choosing **Insert | Text Box**. You then draw the text box by dragging with the mouse.

Formatting text boxes

Want to change any aspect of a text box? Just right-click on any of its edges, and choose **Format Text Box** from the pop-up menu displayed.

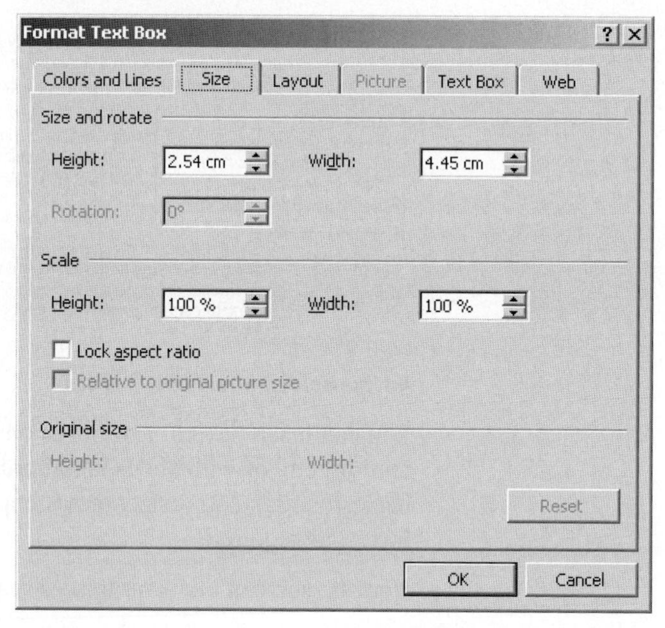

Linking text boxes

You can connect or *link* a series of text boxes so that text flows forward from one text box to the next. Linked text boxes are most commonly used in magazine or newsletter layouts, where, for example, a story that begins in a text box on one page can be continued in linked text boxes on later pages.

Text orientation

A feature that text boxes share with table cells is that the text that they contain can be oriented at 90 degrees. Text that is not inside a text box or table cell cannot be reoriented in this way.

Working with text boxes and text orientation: the five tasks

Here are the five tasks that you need to be able to perform with text boxes and text orientation in Word:

- **Add and remove text boxes**. Exercise 23.1 shows you how to insert and delete text boxes.

- **Edit, resize and move text boxes**. Follow Exercise 23.2 to learn how to edit the text in a text box, amend a box's size, and change a box's position.
- **Apply borders and shading to text boxes**. Exercises 23.3 and 23.4 take you through the steps of applying borders and coloured backgrounds to text boxes.
- **Link text boxes**. You discover how to connect a series of text boxes in Exercise 23.5.
- **Orient text in text boxes and tables**. See Exercises 23.6 and 23.7 to learn how to orient text in a text box and a table cell at 90 degrees.

Working with new text boxes

Exercise 23.1: Add and remove text boxes

1) Start Word and open the following document:

   `Chapter23 Exercise_23-1_Before.doc`

   Is the Drawing toolbar visible? If not, use **View | Toolbars** to display it.

Text Box button

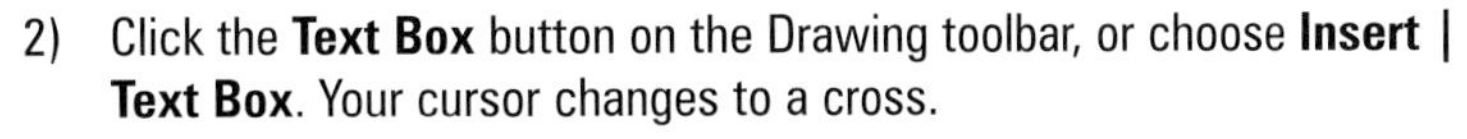

2) Click the **Text Box** button on the Drawing toolbar, or choose **Insert | Text Box**. Your cursor changes to a cross.
3) Drag the mouse to draw a text box to the left of the text beneath the heading 'Introduction'.

   Introduction¶
   By·transforming·the·way·that·people·and·businesses·communicate·and·
   ...et·has·dramatically·changed·the·face·of·business.¶
   ...Internet's·rising·popularity,·many·businesses·have·
   ...ine·presence.·A·rich·variety·of·business·information·–·from·
   ...e·catalogues·to·press·releases·to·company·contacts·–·is·
   ...nternet·users.¶
   ...nesses·realise·that,·in·order·to·compete·successfully,·they·
   need·to·sell·their·goods·and·services·directly·to·consumers·or·other·
   businesses·over·the·Internet.¶

4) Click at the paragraph mark in the text box, and type the following text:

   ```
   The Internet
   A global, public network linked by computers
   that allows users to share information and
   interact.
   ```

   Your sample document should look like this:

   Introduction¶
   The·Internet¶
   A·global,·public·network·linked·by·computers·that·allows·users·to·share·information·and·interact.¶
   By·transforming·the·way·that·people·and·businesses·communicate·and·
   ...et·has·dramatically·changed·the·face·of·business.¶
   ...Internet's·rising·popularity,·many·businesses·have·
   ...ine·presence.·A·rich·variety·of·business·information·–·from·
   ...e·catalogues·to·press·releases·to·company·contacts·–·is·
   ...nternet·users.¶
   ...nesses·realise·that,·in·order·to·compete·successfully,·they·
   need·to·sell·their·goods·and·services·directly·to·consumers·or·other·
   businesses·over·the·Internet.¶

5) Select the heading 'The Internet' in the text box. Using **Format | Font**, change it to Arial Narrow, small caps, and change the font colour to red.

6) Click on any edge of the text box. Notice that Word changes the pattern of the text box edges. This tells you that the text box is selected.

7) You can now copy, cut or delete the text box. Press **Delete** to remove the text box.

8) Click the **Text Box** button on the Drawing toolbar, or choose **Insert | Text Box**. Drag the mouse to draw a text box to the left of the text beneath the heading ' What is ebusiness?'.

·What·is·ebusiness?¶

E-business·is·a·way·to·electronically·deliver·customized·information·about·organizations,·their·products·and·services.·Examples·are·internal·employee·communications,·automated·stock·control·systems,·recruiting·and·

¶

ing·on-line?·The·most·common·purchases·are·computer·
dware,·compact·disks,·books,·travel,·entertainment,·clothing·
ies,·health·and·beauty·products·and·discount·brokerage·

hat·e-commerce·will·also·become·increasingly·popular·for·
g·hard-to-find·and·unique·products.·The·Net·has·seen·phenomenal·growth·in·on-line·auction·houses·that·sell·everything·from·planes,·to·cars,·to·jewellery,·fine·art·and·collectables.·EBay.com·is·a·popular·example.¶

9) Repeat steps 4 and 5 for your new text box.

10) Right-click on any edge of the text box, and choose **Format Text Box** from the pop-up menu. Click the **Layout** tab, select the *Square* option, and click **OK**.

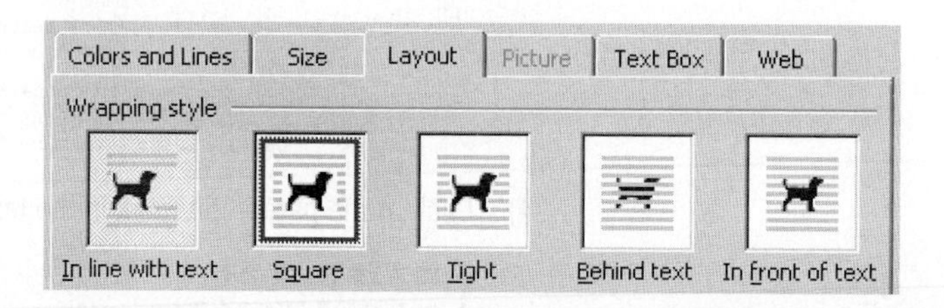

The main text of your document now flows around the text box. Click anywhere else in your document to deselect the text box. It should now look like this:

What is ebusiness?¶

E-business is a way to electronically deliver customized information about organizations, their products and services. Examples are internal employee communications, automated stock control systems, recruiting and employment.¶

THE INTERNET¶
A global, public network linked by computers that allows users to share information and interact.¶

What are we buying on-line? The most common purchases are computer software and hardware, books, travel, compact disks, entertainment, clothing and shoes, health and beauty products, groceries, and discount brokerage services.¶

Analysts predict that e-business will also become increasingly popular for locating and purchasing hard-to-find and unique products. The Net has seen huge growth in on-line auction websites that sell everything from cars to jewellery, fine art and collectables. Perhaps the most popular and successful example is www.ebay.com.¶

Don't worry if your text box is too large for the amount of text that it contains. You will learn how to resize text boxes in Exercise 23.2.

11) Save your sample document with the following name, and close it:

    Chapter23_Exercise_23-1_After_*Your_Name*.doc

Working with existing text boxes

Word allows you to perform a wide range of actions on a text box, as Exercise 23.2 shows.

Exercise 23.2: Edit, resize and move text boxes

1) Open the following Word document:

    Chapter23_Exercise_23-2_Before.doc

2) Click in the text box, and edit the text 'global, public network' to read 'public, global network'.
3) Select the heading 'THE INTERNET'. Change its font size to 12 point.
4) Select the text beneath the heading in the text box, and change its font size to 12 point, bold.

THE INTERNET¶
A public, global network linked by computers that allows users to share

5) You need to increase the size of your text box. Click on the middle sizing handle on the lower edge of the text box, and drag downwards with the mouse until all the text in the text box is visible.

   To size a text box more precisely, right-click on any of its edges, choose **Format Text Box**, click the **Size** tab, enter the dimensions you require, and click **OK**.

6) Click on any edge of the text box to select it, and drag with the mouse downwards until its lower edge is in line with the final paragraph above the heading 'What's in it for the consumer?'.

Analysts·predict·that·e-business·will·also·become·increasingly·popular·for·locating·and·purchasing·hard-to-find·and·unique·products.·The·Net·has·seen·huge·growth·in·on-line·auction·websites·that·sell·everything·from·cars·to·jewellery,·fine·art·and·collectables.·Perhaps·the·most·popular·and·successful·example·is·www.ebay.com.¶

Another·sector·that·has·mushroomed·is·on-line·investing.·Investors·can·buy·and·sell·stocks·and·shares,·keep·up-to-date·with·news·headlines·and·market·quotes·(delayed·or·real-time),·and·review·their·account·information.¶

THE·INTERNET¶
A·global,·public·network·linked·by·computers·that·allows·users·to·share·information·and·interact.¶

To make small, precise movements in a text box's position, select the text box, hold down the **Ctrl** key and press the arrow keys.

7) Save your sample document with the following name, and close it:

`Chapter23_Exercise_23-2_After_`*`Your_Name`*`.doc`

Working with borders and shading

You can call attention to text boxes by adding borders (decorative boxes). Word allows you to apply borders to a selected text box in two ways:

- Using the **Colors and Lines** tab of the *Format Text Box* dialog box, displayed by right-clicking on any edge of the text box and choosing the **Format Text Box** command from the pop-up menu.

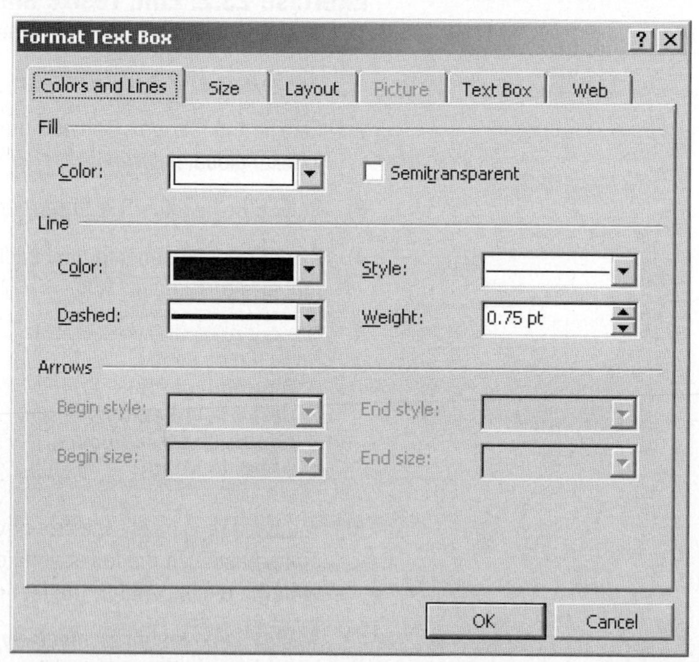

By default, Word applies a 0.75 pt continuous black border around all four sides of every new text box that you create. The default fill colour (background colour) is white.

- Using the options available with the **Format | Borders and Shading** command.

The second method is better because it offers more options and provides greater control. Before applying borders with **Format | Borders and Shading**, however, first *turn off the default border*. Exercise 23.3 takes you through the steps.

Exercise 23.3: Apply borders to a text box

1) Open the following Word document:

   `Chapter23_Exercise_23-3_Before.doc`

2) Right-click on any edge of the text box, choose the **Format Text Box** command, click the **Colors and Lines** tab, select *No Line* from the *Line Color* drop-down list, and click **OK**.

   You have removed the default text box border.

3) Select the text box, choose **Format | Borders and Shading**, and click the **Borders** tab.

   In the *Setting* area, click *None*. In the *Color* drop-down list, select *Red*.

   In the *Width* box, select *3 pt* in the *Preview* area, click the top box edge.

   In the *Width* box, select *1 pt*. In the *Preview* area, click the bottom box edge and click **OK**.

   If you cannot see the lower border of the text box, click the middle sizing handle on the lower edge of the text box, and drag downwards with the mouse until the lower border is visible. Click anywhere outside the text box to deselect it. Your text box should now look like this:

   THE·INTERNET¶
   A·global,·public·network·linked·by·computers·that·allows·users·to·share·information·and·interact.¶

   Analysts·predict·that·e-business·will·also·become·increasingly·popular·for·locating·and·purchasing·hard-to-find·and·unique·products.·The·Net·has·seen·huge·growth·in·on-line·auction·websites·that·sell·everything·from·cars·to·jewellery,·fine·art·and·collectables.·Perhaps·the·most·popular·and·successful·example·is·www.ebay.com.¶

   Another·sector·that·has·mushroomed·is·on-line·investing.·Investors·can·buy·and·sell·stocks·and·shares,·keep·up-to-date·with·news·headlines·and·market·quotes·(delayed·or·real-time),·and·review·their·account·information.¶

4) Save your sample document with the following name, and close it:

   Chapter23_Exercise_23-3_After_*Your_Name*.doc

Exercise 23.4: Apply shading to a text box

1) Open the following Word document:

   `Chapter23_Exercise_23-4_Before.doc`

2) Right-click on any edge of the text box, choose the **Format Text Box** command, click the **Colors and Lines** tab, and select *No Line* from the *Line Color* dropdown list.

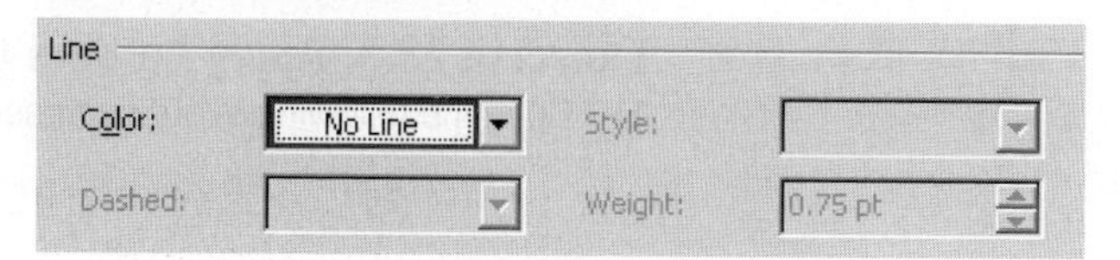
Line
Color:
No Line
Style:
Dashed:
Weight:
0.75 pt

   You have removed the default text box border.

3) In the *Fill Color* area, select a dark colour. Click **OK**.

4) Select the text in the text box and, using **Format | Font**, change the font colour to white. Your text box should now look like this:

THE·INTERNET¶
A·global,·public·
network·linked·by·
computers·that·allows·
users·to·share·
information·and·
interact.¶
Analysts·predict·that·e-business·will·also·become·increasingly·popular·for·locating·and·purchasing·hard-to-find·and·unique·products.·The·Net·has·seen·huge·growth·in·on-line·auction·websites·that·sell·everything·from·cars·to·jewellery,·fine·art·and·collectables.·Perhaps·the·most·popular·and·successful·example·is·www.ebay.com.¶
Another·sector·that·has·mushroomed·is·on-line·investing.·Investors·can·buy·and·sell·stocks·and·shares,·keep·up-to-date·with·news·headlines·and·market·quotes·(delayed·or·real-time),·and·review·their·account·information.¶

5) Save your sample document with the following name, and close it:

   Chapter23_Exercise_23-4_After_*Your_Name*.doc

Linking text boxes

Word enables you to link a series of text boxes so that text flows forward from one text box to the next. Here are the main points that you need to know about linked text boxes:

- Linked text boxes do not need to be on the same page. However, they must all be contained in a single document.
- You may have more than one series of linked text boxes in the same document.
- As you edit text in any box to make it shorter or longer, the text in the next linked text box moves backward or forward.
- If there is not enough text to fill all the linked boxes, the final box or boxes remain empty.
- If there is too much text to fit within the linked chain of boxes, the text runs below the lower edge of the final box.
- You can edit, resize, move and reformat linked text boxes in the same way that you would work with unlinked text boxes.

- In practice, you will want to add a line such as 'continued on page 2' for your linked text boxes. The best way to do so is to create a separate text box below the linked box, and type the 'continued ...' text in that separate box.

You link text boxes two at a time. Simply select the first box, click the **Create Text Box Link** button on the Text Box toolbar, and then select the second text box.

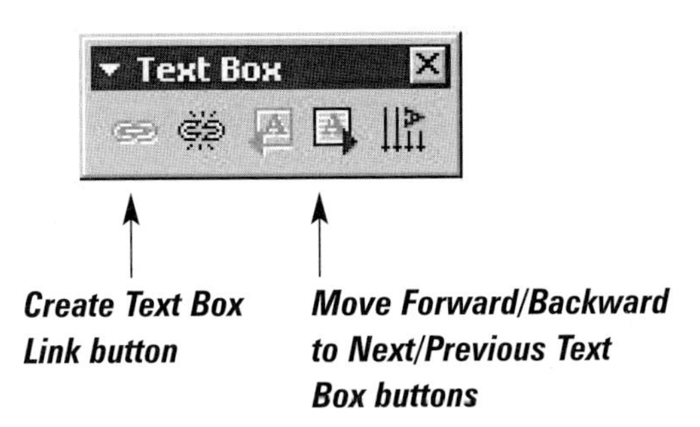

Create Text Box Link button

Move Forward/Backward to Next/Previous Text Box buttons

You can then link the second text box to a third box, and so on.

Linked text boxes

Two or more text boxes in a document that are connected such that text flows forward from the first to the second, and so on.

Exercise 23.5: Link text boxes

1) Open the following document:

    `Chapter23_Exercise_23-5_Before.doc`

2) Click any edge of the text box on the first page to select it. If the Text Box toolbar does not appear, use the **View | Toolbars** command to display it.

3) Click the **Create Text Box Link** button on the Text Box toolbar.

Create Text Box Link button

4) Move forward to the second page, and click any edge of the second text box to select it. The two text boxes in your sample document are now linked.

5) Select the final paragraph of text in the document, beginning with the words 'A rich variety of ...' and press **Ctrl+X** to cut it.

6) Click at the paragraph mark in the first of the two linked text boxes and press **Ctrl+V** to paste the text.

7) Move to the second page of your sample document. Notice that the text has flowed forward to this second text box.

As·with·any·other·
business·activity,·it's·
always·a·good·idea·
to·see·what·your·
competition·is·doing.·
If·they·have·a·web·

Continued·on·next·page

presence·and·seem·
to·be·benefiting·from·
it,·your·company·
might·want·to·follow·
their·example.¶

Continued·from·previous·page

8) Save your sample document with the following name, and close it:

   `Chapter23_Exercise_23-5_After_`*`Your_Name`*`.doc`

Working with text orientation

By default, Word displays text horizontally. You can use the **Format | Text Direction** command to display text vertically – but only if the text is in a text box or a table.

Exercise 23.6: Orient text in a text box

1) Open the following document:

   `Chapter23_Exercise_23-6_Before.doc`

Text Box button

2) Click the **Text Box** button on the Drawing toolbar, or choose **Insert | Text Box**. Your cursor changes to a cross.
3) Drag the mouse to draw a text box to the left of the heading 'Introduction'.

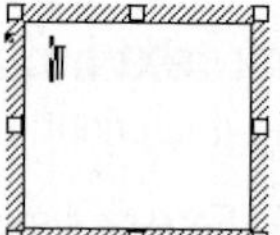

Introduction¶

By·transforming·the·way·that·people·and·businesses·communicate·and·interact,·the·Internet·has·dramatically·changed·the·face·of·business.¶

Impressed·by·the·Internet's·rising·popularity,·many·businesses·have·established·an·online·presence.·A·rich·variety·of·business·information·—·

4) Right-click on any edge of the text box to select it. Choose **Format | Text Box**, click the **Size** tab, change the height to 14 cm, and click **OK**.
5) Select the document heading, 'The New Era of e-Business', and press **Ctrl+X** to cut it.
6) Click at the paragraph mark in the text box and press **Ctrl+V** to paste the heading text in it.
7) With the cursor positioned anywhere in the text box, choose **Format | Text Direction**, click the bottom-to-top orientation option, and click **OK**.

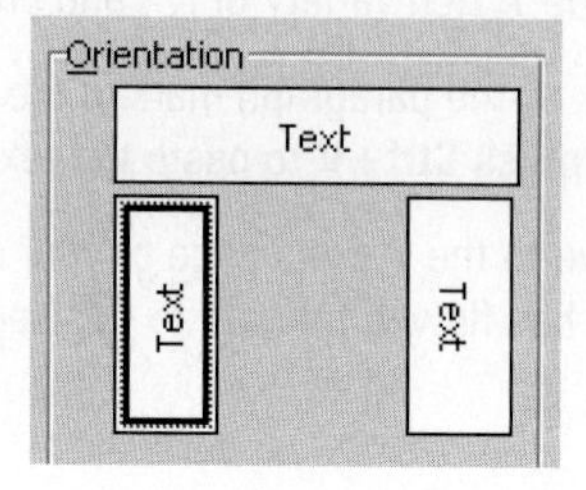

8) Click anywhere in the text box, and then click the **Align Top** button on the Formatting toolbar.

9) Click on the top edge of the text box to select it. Move to the second page of your sample document, click anywhere on the second page, and press **Ctrl+V** to paste the text box. Finally, drag the text box to reposition it at the top left of the page.

10) Both pages should now contain a vertical heading positioned just inside the left margin.

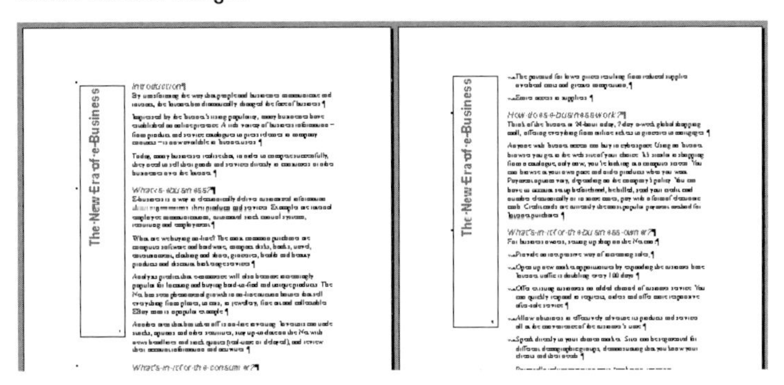

11) Save your sample document with the following name, and close it:

`Chapter23_Exercise_23-6_After_`*`Your_Name`*`.doc`

Exercise 23.7: Orient text in a table

1) Open the following document:

`Chapter23_Exercise_23-7_Before.doc`

2) Click just to the left of the first row of the table to select that row.

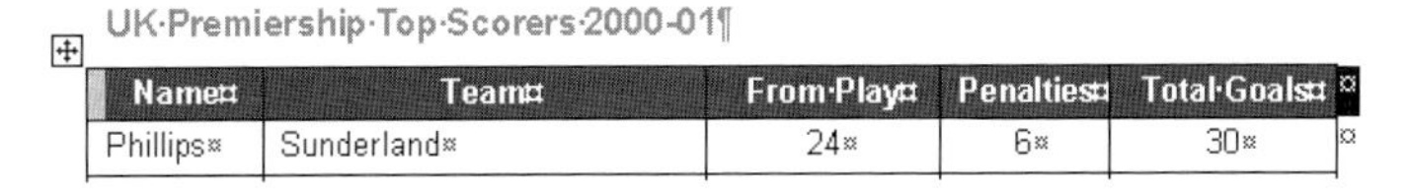

UK·Premiership·Top·Scorers·2000-01¶

Name¤	Team¤	From·Play¤	Penalties¤	Total·Goals¤
Phillips¤	Sunderland¤	24¤	6¤	30¤

3) Choose **Format | Text Direction**, click the top-to-bottom orientation option, and click **OK.**

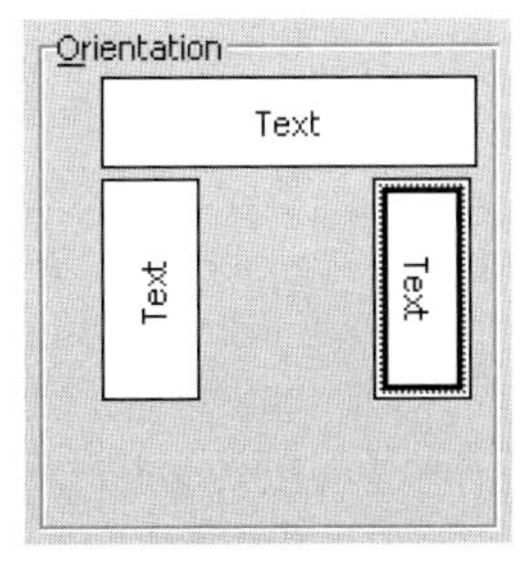

4) Click anywhere in the table, and then click the **Align Top** button on the Formatting toolbar.

5) With the top row still selected, choose **Table | Table Properties**, click the **Cell** tab, select the *Vertical alignment Center* option, and click **OK**.

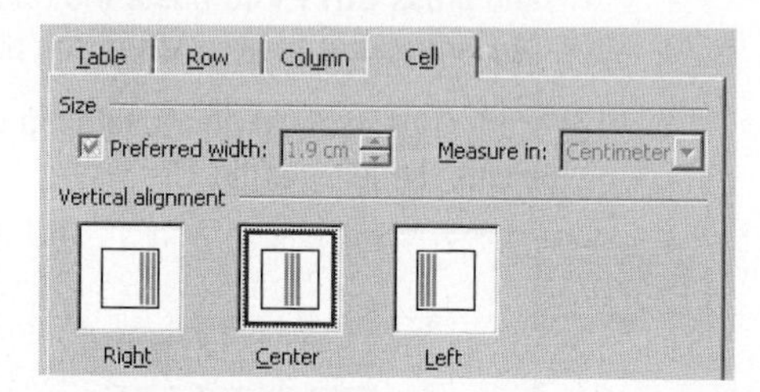

6) Click anywhere outside the top row to deselect it. The top row should now look like this:

Name	Team	From Play	Penalties	Total Goals
Phillips	Sunderland	24	6	30

7) Save your sample document with the following name, and close it:

`Chapter23_Exercise_23-7_After_Your_Name.doc`

Chapter 23: quick reference

Tasks summary

Task	Procedure
Create a text box.	Click the **Text Box** button on the Drawing toolbar, or choose **Insert | Text Box**. Then draw the text box by dragging with the mouse.
Resize a text box.	Click on any sizing handle and drag. Or right-click on any edge, choose **Format Text Box**, click the **Size** tab, enter the dimensions, and click **OK**.
Move a text box.	Click on any edge to select the text box and drag to a different part of the same page. Or cut the selected text box and paste it to another page.
Add borders to a text box.	Right-click on any edge, choose **Format Text Box** click the **Colors and Lines** tab, remove the default border, and click **OK**. Next, select the text box, choose **Format | Borders and Shading**, click the **Borders** tab, select your required border options, and click **OK**.

Add a background colour to a text box.	Right-click on any edge, choose **Format Text Box**, click the **Colors and Lines** tab, select the required fill options, and click **OK**.
Link two text boxes.	Select the first text box, click the **Create Text Box Link** button on the Text Box toolbar, and then select the second text box.
Orient text at 90° in a text box or table cell.	Click anywhere in the text box or cell, choose **Format | Text Direction**, select your required orientation option, and click **OK**.

Concepts summary

In Word, *text boxes* hold text and other items that are positioned separately from the main text of the document. You can insert several text boxes on the same page, format the text directly or with styles, add borders and shading (coloured backgrounds), and resize, move, copy, and cut and paste text boxes, as required.

You can connect or *link* a series of text boxes so that text flows forward from one text box to the next. Text located in text boxes or table cells can be *oriented* at 90 degrees to the remainder of the document.

Chapter 23: quick quiz

Circle the correct answer to each of the following multiple-choice questions about text boxes and text orientation in Word.

Q1	In Word, a text box is ...
A.	Text formatted with Word's built-in Text Box paragraph style.
B.	A container for holding text or other items that is separate from the main text in the document.
C.	Text surrounded by a solid border applied with the **Format | Borders and Shading** command.
D.	A storage area for holding commonly-used text for convenient insertion in multiple documents.

Q2	In Word, which of the following actions would you perform to create a text box?
A.	Choose **Insert | Picture | Text Box**, enter the box's dimensions, and click **Insert**.
B.	Click the **Text Box** button on the Drawing toolbar and drag with the mouse.
C.	Choose **File | New | Text Box**, select the required template, and click **Create**.
D.	Click the **New Text Box** button on the Formatting toolbar and drag with the mouse.

Q3	In Word, which of the following actions would you perform to resize a text box?
A.	Click anywhere in the box, choose **Resize**, and then drag with the mouse.
B.	Right-click on any sizing handle and drag with the mouse.
C.	Right-click on any edge, choose **Resize Text Box**, click the **Dimensions** tab, enter the dimensions, and click **OK**.
D.	Click on any sizing handle and drag with the mouse.

Q4	In Word, which of the following actions requires that you first select the text box by clicking on one of its edges?
A.	Deleting the text box.
B.	Editing the text contained in the text box.
C.	Applying direct formatting to the text in the text box.
D.	Pasting new text into the text box.

Q5	In Word, which of the following items cannot be included in a text box?
A.	Columns.
B.	Fields.
C.	Pictures.
D.	Tables.

Q6	In Word, which of the following statements about text boxes is untrue?
A.	By default, text boxes have a black, 0.75 pt border.
B.	You can insert several text boxes on the same page of a document.
C.	You can apply paragraph styles to text in a text boxes.
D.	A text box can have borders or shading, but not both.

Q7	In Word, which of the following statements about linked text boxes is untrue?
A.	Text flows forward from the first linked text box to the second, and so on.
B.	A document may contain several different and separate chains of linked text boxes.
C.	Text boxes in different documents may be linked together.
D.	If there is not enough text to fill all linked boxes, the final box or boxes remain empty.

Q8	In Word, which of the following actions do you perform to link two text boxes?
A.	Select all the text in the document, and choose **Format | Text Boxes | Link All**.
B.	Select the first text box, click the **Create Text Box Link** button on the Text Box toolbar, and then select the second text box.
C.	Select both text boxes, then click the **Create Text Box Link** button on the Text Box toolbar.
D.	Select both text boxes, choose **Insert | Text Box**, click the **Links** tab, select the *Create link* checkbox, and click **OK**.

Q9	In Word, which of these text types can you orient at 90 degrees with the Format | Text Direction command?
A.	Text in table cells only.
B.	Text in text boxes, table cells, and built-in heading styles only.
C.	Text formatted with built-in heading styles only.
D.	Text in table cells and text boxes only.

Answers

1: B, **2:** B, **3:** D, **4:** A, **5:** A, **6:** D, **7:** C, **8:** B, **9:** D.

24 Graphics in Word

Objectives

In this chapter you will learn how to:

- Create drawing objects with the drawing tools and AutoShapes
- Stack and group AutoShapes
- Create WordArt objects
- Change picture and ClipArt borders
- Wrap text around graphics
- Insert watermarks

New words

In this chapter you will meet the following terms:

- AutoShape
- WordArt
- ClipArt
- Watermark

Exercise files

In this chapter you will work with the following Word files:

- `Chapter24_Exercise_24-1_Before.doc`
- `Chapter24_Exercise_24-3_Before.doc`
- `Chapter24_Exercise_24-4_Before.doc`
- `Chapter24_Exercise_24-5_Before.doc`
- `Chapter24_Exercise_24-6_Before.doc`
- `Chapter24_Exercise_24-7_Before.doc`
- `Chapter24_Exercise_24-8_Before.doc`
- `Chapter24_Exercise_24-9_Before.doc`

Syllabus reference

In this chapter you will cover the following items from the ECDL Advanced Word Processing Syllabus:

- **AM3.4.5.1**: Modify image borders.
- **AM3.4.5.2:** Create a simple drawing using the drawing options.
- **AM3.4.5.3**: Use predefined shapes options.
- **AM3.4.5.4**: Send predefined shapes to the back or front.
- **AM3.4.5.5**: Send predefined shapes in front of or behind text.
- **AM3.4.5.6**: Group or ungroup predefined shapes.
- **AM3.4.5.7**: Add a watermark to a document.
- **AM3.1.1.6**: Use text-wrapping options.
- **AM3.1.1.8**: Use available text design gallery options.

About graphics in Word

In Word, the term *graphics* includes:

- **User-drawn shapes**. Examples include lines, rectangles and circles. You create these using the buttons available on Word's Drawing toolbar, which is positioned along the bottom of your screen.

Can't see the Drawing Toolbar? Use the **View | Toolbars** command to display it.

- **AutoShapes**. These are Word's built-in, ready-to-insert shapes that are divided into categories such as flowchart elements, stars and banners, and call-outs. You can modify AutoShapes to your own needs.

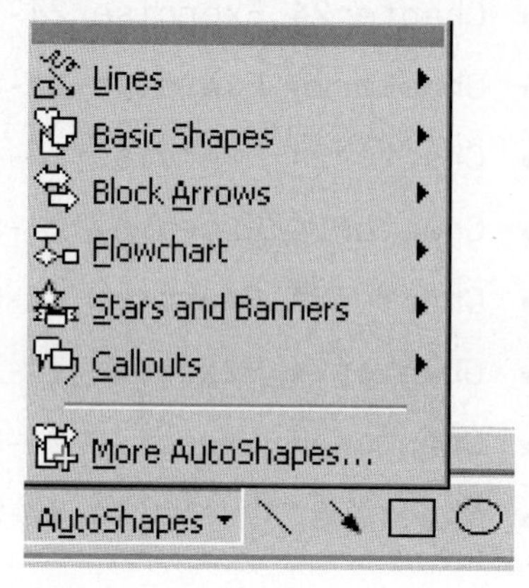

- **Pictures**. You can insert two types of picture into Word documents: ClipArt pictures from Word's built-in ClipArt library, and picture files created in other applications, such as Paintbrush, Photoshop and PaintShop Pro.

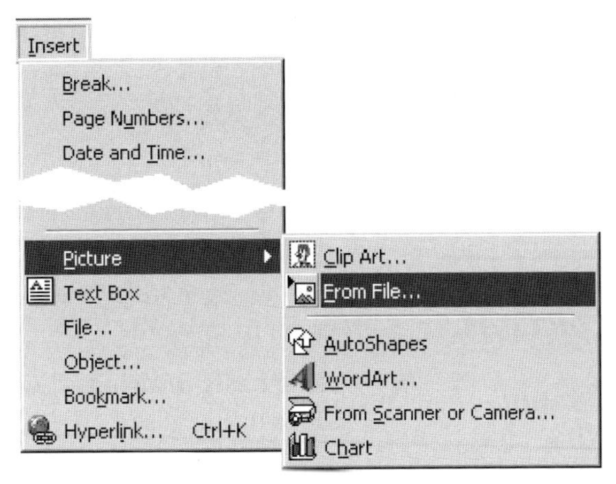

- **WordArt**. These are special effects that you can apply to selected text. You work with WordArt text in Word documents in the same way that you work with inserted pictures.

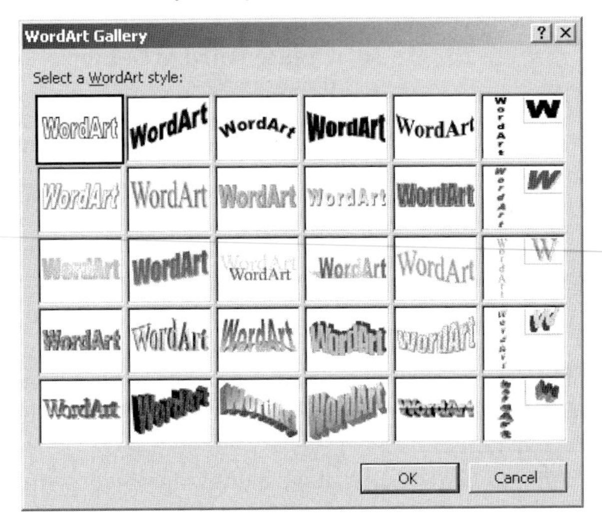

- **Watermarks**. These are graphics or text that appear either behind or on top of the document's main text. For example, you might want your company logo or the word 'Confidential' to appear in light print in the background of every page of a document.

Graphics and text flow

Typically, you will combine graphics with text on the same page. Word's **Format | AutoShape, Format | Picture** and **Format | WordArt** commands give you total control of how the text flows around graphics.

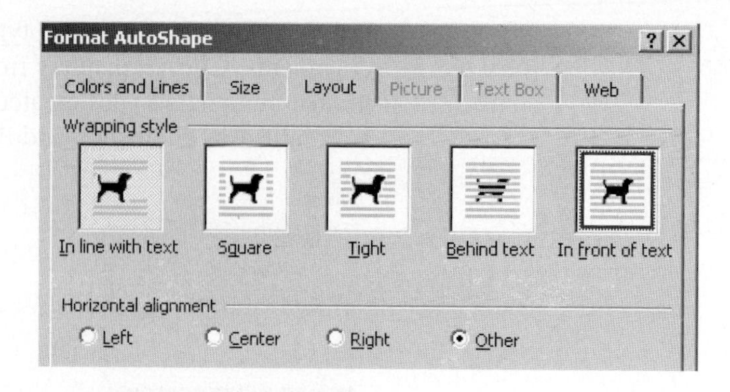

Working with drawings, pictures, WordArt, watermarks and text flow: the seven tasks

Here are the seven tasks that you need to be able to perform with graphics in Word:

- **Create basic drawings**. Learn how to draw some basic shapes in Exercise 24.1.
- **Create drawings with AutoShapes**. Exercise 24.2 shows you how to use Word's AutoShapes feature.
- **Stack and group AutoShapes**. Exercises 24.3 and 24.4 take you through the steps of stacking and grouping AutoShapes.
- **Create WordArt objects**. Apply decorative text effects in Exercise 24.5.
- **Change picture and ClipArt borders**. See Exercise 24.6.
- **Wrap text around graphics**. Explore Word text flow options in Exercise 24.7.
- **Insert watermarks**. Exercises 24.8 and 24.9 show you how to insert a watermark on one or all pages of a document.

Working with drawing objects

There are a number of common operations that you can perform on *drawing objects*, whether user-drawn shapes or AutoShapes.

Moving drawing objects

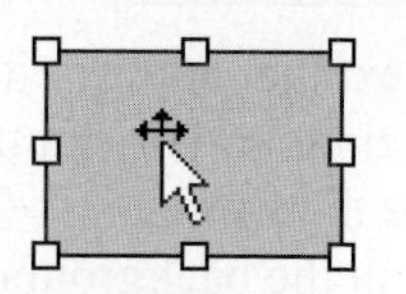

To move a drawing object within the same page, first select it by clicking anywhere on it. A cross appears at the tip of the cursor arrow. Then drag the object to its new position.

To move a drawing object between pages, select it and then cut and paste it.

Changing drawing object size and shape

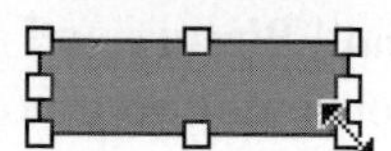

You can change the size and shape of a drawing object by selecting it and clicking on any of its sizing handles. The cursor appears as a double arrow. Next, drag a sizing handle until the drawing object forms the new shape that you require.

Deleting drawing objects

To delete a drawing object, click on it and press **Delete**. You can always reverse a deletion by clicking the **Undo** button on Word's Standard toolbar.

Working with Word's drawing tools

Line and arrow tools

Line button

Arrow button

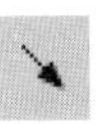

Arrow Style button

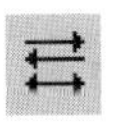

To draw a line, click the **Line** button on the Drawing toolbar, place the cursor where you want the line to begin, click and drag to where you want the line to end, and release the mouse button.

- To draw a perfectly horizontal or vertical line, hold down the **Shift** key while dragging.
- To draw a line ending in an arrow, click on the **Arrow** button and draw it in the same way.
- To change the style of the arrowhead, or the direction of the arrow, click the arrow to select it, click the **Arrow Style** button, and select a different style.

Rectangle and square tools

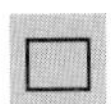

Rectangle button

To draw a rectangle, click the **Rectangle** button on the Drawing toolbar, place the cursor where you want one corner of the rectangle, click and drag diagonally to where you want the opposite corner of the rectangle, and release the mouse button.

To draw a perfect square, hold down the **Shift** key as you drag with the mouse.

Ellipse and circle tools

Oval button

To draw an ellipse (oval), click the **Oval** button, place the cursor where you want the shape to begin, click and drag until the shape is the size you want, and release the mouse button.

To draw a perfect circle, hold down the **Shift** key as you drag with the mouse.

Line colour and style

Line Color button

Line Style button

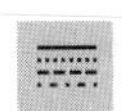

Dash Style button

In the case of lines, arrows and closed shapes (such as rectangles and circles), you can specify the colour and thickness of the line or shape border. Click the **Line Color** button and select a colour, either before you draw the line or closed shape, or, with the line or shape selected, after you have drawn it.

To delete a border around a closed shape, select *No Line* in the *Line Color* pop-up menu.

Change the thickness of a line or border by clicking the **Line Style** button.

Make a line or border a dashed line (in a choice of dash styles) by clicking the **Dash Style** button.

Fill colour

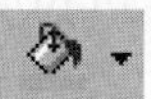

Fill Color button

Use the arrow to the right of the **Fill Color** button to select the colour with which the inside of the closed shape (such as a square or ellipse) should be filled.

You can choose the fill colour before you draw the shape, or you can select an existing shape and then choose a fill colour.

To make a closed object transparent, select *No Fill* in the *Fill Color* pop-up menu.

Shadow effects

Shadow button

To place a shadow behind a selected object, click the **Shadow** button and choose from the shadow styles available on the pop-up menu.

Exercise 24.1: Create basic drawings

1) Start Word and open the following document:

   `Chapter24_Exercise_24-1_Before.doc`

2) Click the **Rectangle** button on the Drawing toolbar, and draw a rectangle around the words 'First Aid Kit'.

   With the rectangle still selected, click the **Fill Color** button on the Drawing toolbar and choose *No Fill*. Click the **Line Color** button and select *Red*. Click the **Line Style** button and select *3 pt*. Your graphic should look like this

3) Click the **Oval** button on the Drawing toolbar and draw an oval around the word '£100'.

   With the oval still selected, click the **Fill Color** button on the Drawing toolbar and choose *No Fill*. Click the **Line Style** button and select *3 pt*. Your graphic should look like this:

4) Click the **Arrow** button on the Drawing Toolbar and draw an arrow to the left of the word '£100'.

   With the arrow still selected, click the **Line Style** button and select *6 pt*. Press **Ctrl+C** to copy the arrow, press **Ctrl+V** to paste it, and move the arrow to the right of the word '£100'. The pasted arrow is now selected. Click the **Arrow Style** button, and select the left-pointing arrow. Your graphic should now look like this:

5) Save your sample document with the following name, and close it:

   `Chapter24_Exercise_24-1_After_`*`Your_Name`*`.doc`

Working with AutoShapes

AutoShapes are ready-made shapes that you can insert in your documents. AutoShape categories include lines, basic shapes, flowchart elements, stars and banners, and call-outs.

To select an AutoShape, click the **AutoShapes** button on the Drawing toolbar and choose from the options offered by the pop-up menu.

AutoShapes

Ready-made shapes, including lines, geometric shapes and flowchart elements, that you can insert and modify in your Word documents.

Exercise 24.2: Create a drawing with AutoShapes

1) Open the following document:

   `Chapter24_Exercise_24-2_Before.doc`

2) Click at a paragraph mark after 'Carpets Unlimited' and before 'Everything Half Price'.

3) Click the **AutoShapes** button on the Drawing toolbar, click **Stars and Banners**, and click the first option, called 'Explosion 1'.

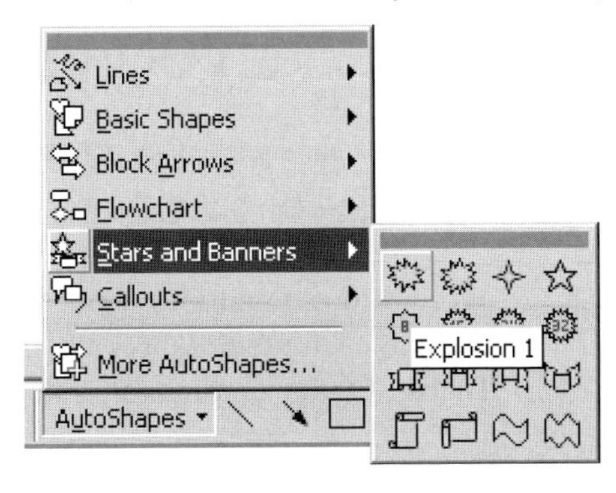

4) Draw the AutoShape under the 'Carpets Unlimited' heading as shown below:

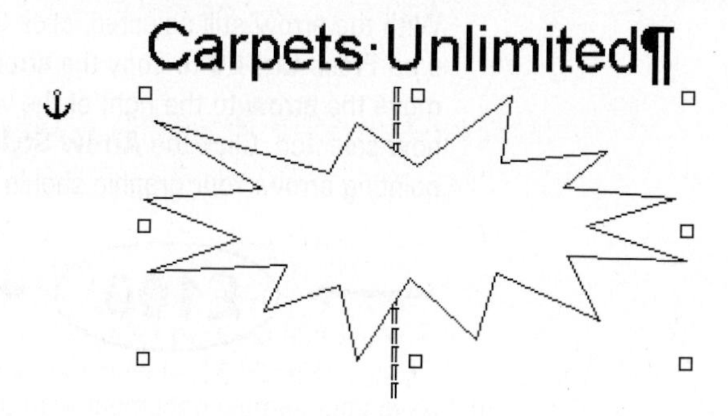

5) Right-click on the AutoShape, and choose the **Add Text** command from the pop-up menu.
6) At the paragraph mark that appears in the AutoShape, type the word 'SALE' in upper-case characters.
7) Select the word 'SALE'. Change it to Arial, 48 point, bold, and centre-aligned.
8) On the Drawing toolbar, click the arrow to the right of the **Fill Color** button.

Fill Color button

Select *Gray-50%*.

9) Select the word 'SALE' and change the font colour to white. The top of your sample document should look like this:

10) Save your sample document with the following name, and close it:

`Chapter24_Exercise_24-2_After_`*`Your_Name`*`.doc`

AutoShapes and stacks

Word allows you to layer or *stack* AutoShapes so that they overlap each other. You arrange AutoShapes in a stack using the **Draw | Order** command on the Drawing toolbar. You can bring an object to the front or send it to the back of a stack, or bring forward or send backward one level in a stack. You can also stack an AutoShape so that it appears behind the text in a document.

Exercise 24.3: Stacking AutoShapes

1) Open the following document:

   `Chapter24_Exercise_24-3_Before.doc`

2) Click anywhere in the first AutoShape, the one containing the words 'Lowest Prices'. Next, right-click on any of its borders. From the pop-up menu displayed, choose **Order | Send to Back**.

3) Click anywhere in the third AutoShape, the one containing the words 'Expert Service'. Next, right-click on any of its borders. From the pop-up menu displayed, choose **Order | Bring to Front**.

   Your AutoShapes should look like this:

4) Save your sample document with the following name, and close it:

   Chapter24_Exercise_24-3_After_*Your_Name*.doc

AutoShapes and text

Typically, an AutoShape drawn in a document that contains text is *stacked* in front of the text.

To display an AutoShape behind the text, right-click on the AutoShape and choose **Order | Send Behind Text** from the pop-up menu displayed.

If·you·require·accident·and·emergency·treatment,·and·arrive·at·your·Casualty·Department,·you·w[illegible]ll·[illegible]·assessed·immediately·by·a·professional·and·your·needs·identified.·Em[illegible]tment·will·always·take·priority·over·minor·injuries.·However,·we·[illegible]·the·patients·within·45·minutes·of·their·assessment.·If·this·is·not·possible,·[illegible]nation·will·be·given·to·you·by·a·member·of·staff.¶

If·you·need·to·be·a[illegible]mitted·to·hospital·from·the·Casualty·Department,·we·guarantee·to·admit·you·to·a·ward·as·soon·as·possible.·In·the·vast·majority·of·cases·this·should·be·within·one·hour·of·a·decision·being·taken·to·admit·you.¶

AutoShapes stacked in front of and behind text

AutoShapes and groups

You can group AutoShapes or other drawing objects so that you can move, format, stack or work with them as if they were a single object.

- **Grouping**. To group objects, hold down the **Shift** key and click on each of the objects in turn. Next, click the **Draw** button on the Drawing toolbar and choose **Group**. You can now work with them as if there were a single object.
- **Ungrouping**. To ungroup a selected group of objects, click the **Draw** button on the Drawing Toolbar and choose the **Ungroup** command.

Exercise 24.4: Grouping and ungrouping AutoShapes

1) Open the following document:

   `Chapter24_Exercise_24-4_Before.doc`

2) Hold down the **Shift** key, click anywhere in the first AutoShape, then in the second AutoShape, and finally in the third AutoShape.
3) Click the Draw button at the left of the Drawing toolbar. From the pop-up menu displayed, choose **Group**.

   Notice that one set of eight sizing handles now appears around the three AutoShapes. You can now work with the three AutoShapes as if they were a single drawing object.
4) Drag the grouped AutoShapes down to the bottom of the page.
5) Click on any of the grouped AutoShapes, click the **Draw** button at the left of the Drawing toolbar. From the pop-up menu displayed, choose **Ungroup**.

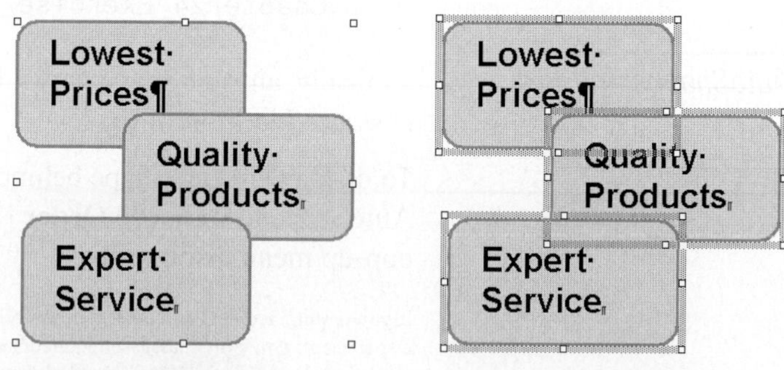

Grouped AutoShapes ***Ungrouped AutoShapes***

6) Save your sample document with the following name, and close it:

   `Chapter24_Exercise_24-4_After_`*`Your_Name`*`.doc`

Working with WordArt

WordArt enables you to apply special effects to selected text.

WordArt
A Word feature that enables you to apply decorative effects – such as colours, shadows, rotation and depth – to selected text. WordArt objects can be manipulated in a similar way to inserted pictures.

Exercise 24.5: Create text effects with WordArt

1) Open the following document:

   `Chapter24_Exercise_24-5_Before.doc`

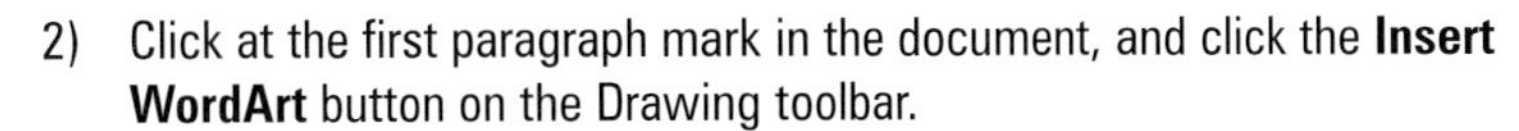

2) Click at the first paragraph mark in the document, and click the **Insert WordArt** button on the Drawing toolbar.

Insert WordArt button

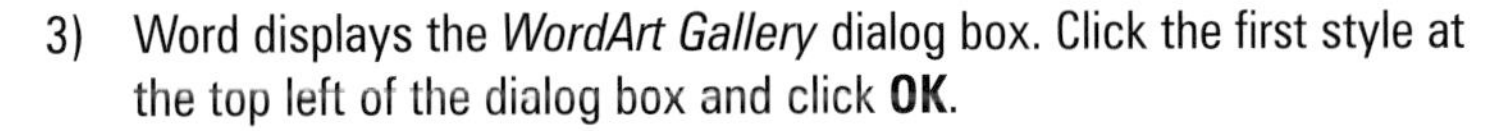

3) Word displays the *WordArt Gallery* dialog box. Click the first style at the top left of the dialog box and click **OK**.

4) Word displays the *Edit WordArt Text* dialog box. In the *Text* box is the sample text 'Your Text Here'.

   Delete this text, type the words 'Carpets Uncovered', and click **OK**.

   Word displays your WordArt text. Drag it up to the top of your document, and make it about 20% larger by dragging one of its corner handles.

5) Word displays the WordArt toolbar.

   Click the Format WordArt button. On the **Colors and Lines** tab, change the fill colour to red and click **OK**.

   The top of your sample document should look like this:

6) Save your sample document with the following name, and close it:

`Chapter24_Exercise_24-5_After_`*`Your_Name`*`.doc`

Working with pictures

ClipArt pictures

You can illustrate your documents by inserting pictures created in other software applications, scanned photographs or ClipArt.

Word includes a gallery of ClipArt pictures that you can use in different documents. They are grouped in categories, ranging from Academic to Food and Travel.

To insert a ClipArt picture in a Word document, choose **Insert | Picture | ClipArt**, click a picture category to select it, right-click your required picture, and choose **Insert** from the pop-up menu displayed. Finally, click the **Close** box at the top-right of the *Insert ClipArt* dialog box.

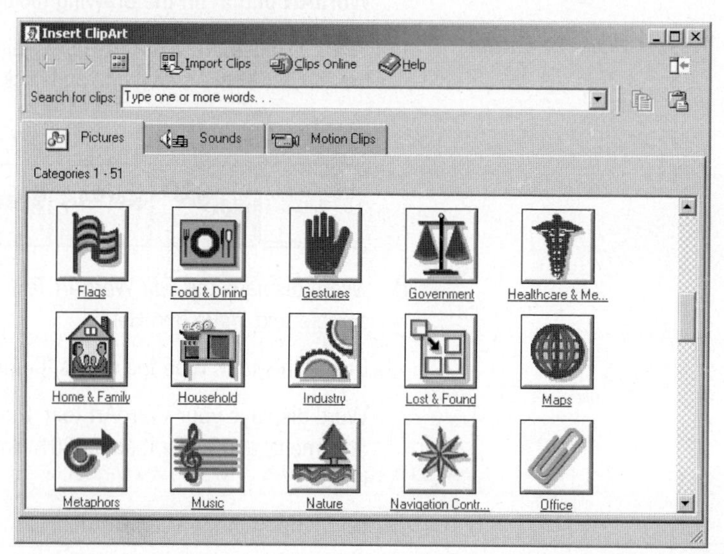

> **ClipArt**
>
> *Built-in standard or 'stock' pictures that can be used and reused in Word documents.*

Non-ClipArt pictures

To insert a picture of your own – your company logo, for example – in a document, choose **Insert | Picture | From File**, select the required picture file, and choose **Insert**. Word accepts pictures in most common picture file formats.

In ECDL Advanced Word Processing, you only need to know how to add a border to ClipArt and other pictures, and how to modify existing borders.

Exercise 24.6: Change borders around ClipArt and pictures

1) Open the following Word document

   `Chapter24_Exercise_24-6_Before.doc`

2) Right-click anywhere on the arrow, choose **Format AutoShape** from the pop-up menu displayed, and click the **Colors and Lines** tab.

3) In the *Line Color* drop-down list, select *Red*. In the *Weight* box, select *8 pt*.

   When finished, click **OK**.

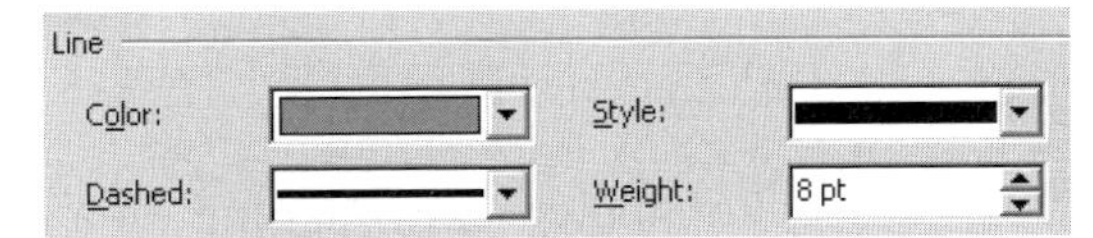

4) Right-click anywhere on the ClipArt picture at the bottom of the page, choose **Borders and Shading** from the pop-up menu displayed, and click the **Borders** tab.

5) In the *Settings* area, click *Shadow*. In the *Color* drop-down list, select *Green*. In the *Width* drop-down list, select *3 pt*.

   When finished, click **OK**.

6) Save your sample document with the following name, and close it:

   Chapter24_Exercise_24-6_After_*Your_Name*.doc

Working with text wrapping

Wrapping is the way in which text *flows* around a graphic, whether a drawing object, a picture or a WordArt object. Word offers the following options:

Text wrapping	Description	Example
In line with text	Positions the object in the document on the line that contains the insertion point. This is the default setting for pictures and WordArt. It is not available for AutoShapes.	
Square	Wraps text around an outer square or rectangular boundary of the object.	
Tight	Wraps text closely around the edges of the object.	

Text wrapping	Description	Example
Behind text	Places or *stacks* the object behind text in the document.	
In front of text	Places or *stacks* the object in front of text in the document. This is the default option for AutoShapes.	

To modify text wrapping for a selected object, right-click on it, select **Format AutoShape, Format WordArt** or **Format Picture** from the popup menu displayed, click the **Layout** tab, select your required wrapping option, and click **OK**.

Exercise 24.7: Wrap text around a picture

1) Open the following Word document:

   `Chapter24_Exercise_24-7_Before.doc`

2) Click at the beginning of the second paragraph of body text.

   By·transforming·the·way·that·people·and·businesses·communicate·and·interact,·the·Internet·has·dramatically·changed·the·face·of·business.¶

3) Choose **Insert | Picture | Clip Art**, click the **Business** category to select it, right-click the 'three desks' picture, and choose **Insert** from the pop-up menu.

4) Click **Close** to close the *Insert Clip Art* dialog box.

5) Reduce the inserted picture by 50% by dragging its lower right-hand corner handle. Your picture should look as shown. Notice that it is in line with Text, the default positioning option.

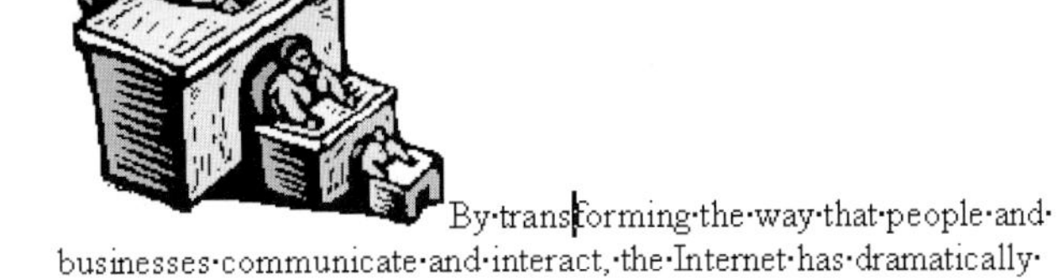

By·transforming·the·way·that·people·and·businesses·communicate·and·interact,·the·Internet·has·dramatically·changed·the·face·of·business.¶

6) Right-click the picture, choose **Format Picture**, click the **Layout** tab, click the **Square** option, and click **OK**. Your picture should now look like this:

From·a·base·of·40·million·users·in·1996,·the·number·of·online·users·is·predicted·to·reach·1·billion·in·2005.¶

By·transforming·the·way·that·people·and·businesses·communicate·and·interact,·the·Internet·has·dramatically·changed·the·face·of·business.¶

Impressed·by·the·Internet's·rising·popularity,·many·businesses·have·established·an·online·presence.·A·rich·variety·of·business·information·—·from·service·and·product·catalogues·to·press·releases·to·company·contacts·—·is·now·available·to·Internet·users.¶

7) Right-click the picture, choose **Format Picture**, click the **Layout** tab, click the **Tight** option, and click **OK**. Your picture should look like this:

By·transforming·the·way·that·people·and·businesses·communicate·and·interact,·the·Internet·has·dramatically·changed·the·face·of·business.¶

Impressed·by·the·Internet's·rising·popularity,·many·businesses·have·established·an·online·presence.·A·rich·variety·of·business·information·—·from·service·and·product·catalogues·to·press·releases·to·company·contacts·—·is·now·available·to·Internet·users.¶

8) Save your sample document with the following name, and close it:

`Chapter24_Exercise_24-7_After_`*`Your_Name`*`.doc`

Working with watermarks

A watermark is a picture, drawing object or text box that is:

- displayed *behind* the main text of page;
- of light or *feint* colour, so that it does not impair the legibility of the main text on the page.

Examples of text watermarks would be the words 'First draft' or 'Confidential'. Company logos are the most common examples of picture watermark. Usually, you will want to insert a watermark on either *one* or *all pages* of a document.

- **Single-page watermark**. If the watermark is a a picture, right-click on it, choose **Format Picture**, select the **Picture** tab, and select *Watermark* from the *Color* drop-down list. Click the **Layout** tab, select the *Behind text* option, and click **OK**.

  If the watermark is an AutoShape or WordArt object, right-click on it, choose **Format AutoShape** or **Format WordArt**, click the **Layout** tab, select the *Behind text* option, and click **OK**.

- **All-page watermark**. Choose **View | Header and Footer**. Insert the picture, or create the AutoShape or WordArt, in the header or footer. Right-click on the object, and use the **Format** command to stack the object behind the text. If using a picture, you can apply a watermark effect with the **Format** command.

  To apply a text watermark, insert a text box in the header or footer, type your watermark text in it, and format the text.

  If using odd and even page headers and footers, remember to insert your watermark into both the odd and even headers or footers.

Watermark

A picture, drawing or text box that appears behind the text on one or all pages of a document. Watermarks are typically of feint colour so that they do not impair the legibility of the main text on the page.

Exercise 24.8: Insert a picture watermark on a single page

1) Open the following Word document:

   `Chapter24_Exercise_24-8_Before.doc`

2) Click at the start of the paragraph containing the words 'Everything Half Price'.

   Everything↵
   Half·Price¶

3) Choose **Insert | Picture | Clip Art**, click the **Household** category to select it, right-click the 'furniture' picture, and choose **Insert** from the pop-up menu. Click **Close** to close the *Insert Clip Art* dialog box.

4) Click the picture to select it, then right-click it, choose **Format Picture**, click the **Picture** tab, select *Watermark* from the *Color* drop-down list, click the **Layout** tab, click the *Behind text* option, click the *Center horizontal alignment* option, and click **OK**. Your picture should look like this:

5) Save your sample document with the following name, and close it:

`Chapter24_Exercise_24-8_After_`*`Your_Name`*`.doc`

Exercise 24.9: Insert a text box watermark on every page

1) Open the following Word document:

`Chapter24_Exercise_24-9_After_`*`Your_Name`*`.doc`

2) Choose **View | Header and Footer**. Word displays the insertion point in the header of the first page.

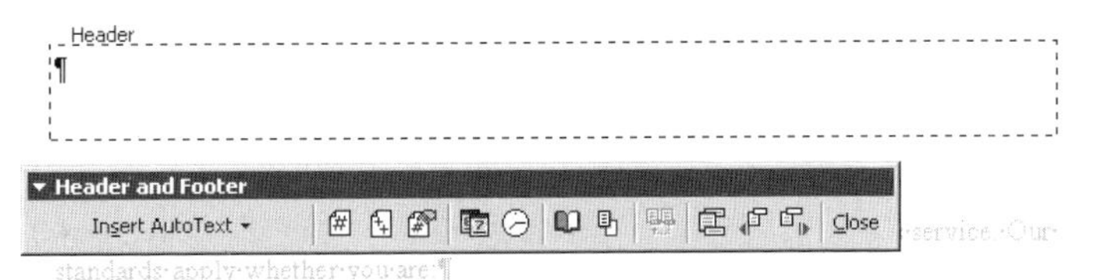

You may find it helpful to reduce the page display to 50%.

3) Choose **Insert | Text Box**, draw the text box, and type in the words 'Draft Copy Only'.

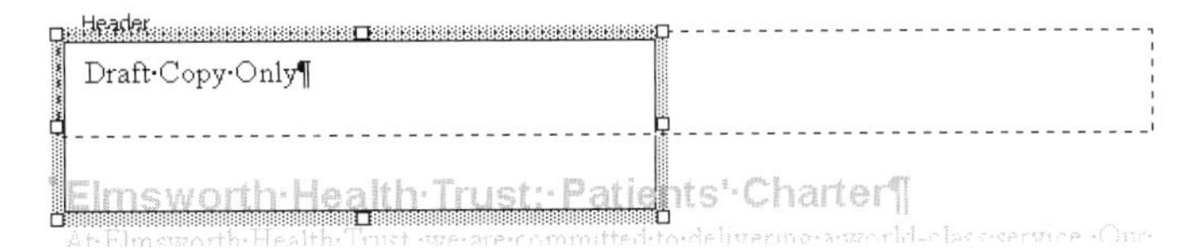

4) Select the text in the text box, format it in Arial, bold, 36 point, and change the font colour to light grey. If necessary, increase the size of the text box to accommodate the text.

5) Drag the text box to the centre of the page.

6) Right-click the border of the text box, choose **Format Text Box** and click the **Colors and Lines** tab. In the *Line Color* drop-down list, click *No Line*, and click **OK**.

7) Click the **Close** button on the Header and Footer toolbar. Scroll through your document to verify that the watermark appears on every page.

8) Save your sample document with the following name, and close it:

`Chapter24_Exercise_24-9_After_`*`Your_Name`*`.doc`

Chapter 24: quick reference

Drawing toolbar buttons

Button	Description
	Draws a straight line. To draw a perfectly horizontal or vertical line, hold down the **Shift** key as you drag with the mouse.
	Draws a line ending in an arrow.
	Draws a rectangle. To draw a perfect square, hold down the **Shift** key as you drag with the mouse.
	Draws an ellipse (oval). To draw a perfect circle, hold down the **Shift** key as you drag with the mouse.
	Applies WordArt – decorative effects such as colours, shadows, rotation and depth – to selected text.
	Specifies the colour with which the inside of a closed shape (such as a square or ellipse) should be filled.
	Specifies the colour and thickness of the line or shape border.
	Specifies the thickness of a line or a shape border.
	Specifies the style of a line or shape border.
	Specifies the arrow line style.

Tasks summary: drawing basic shapes

Task	Procedure
Draw a line.	Click the **Line** button on the Drawing toolbar, place the cursor where you want the line to begin, click and drag to where you want the line to end, and release the mouse button. To draw a perfectly horizontal or vertical line, hold down the **Shift** key as you drag with the mouse.
Draw a rectangle or square.	Click the **Rectangle** button on the Drawing toolbar, place the cursor where you want one corner of the rectangle, click and drag diagonally to where you want the opposite corner of the rectangle, and release the mouse button. To draw a perfect square, hold down the **Shift** key as you drag with the mouse.
Draw an oval or circle.	Click the **Oval** button on the Drawing toolbar, place the cursor where you want the shape to begin, click and drag until the shape is the size you want, and release the mouse button. To draw a perfect circle, hold down the **Shift** key as you drag with the mouse.

Tasks summary: lines, borders and fills

Task	Procedure
Change line or border colour.	Click the **Line Color** button on the Drawing toolbar, select a colour, either before you draw the line or closed shape, or, with the line or shape selected, after you have drawn it. To delete a border around a closed shape, select *No Line* in the **Line Color** pop-up menu.
Change fill colour.	Use the arrow to the right of the **Fill Color** button to select the colour with which the inside of the closed shape (such as a square or ellipse) should be filled. You can choose the fill colour before you draw the shape, or you can select an existing shape and then choose a fill colour. To make a closed object transparent, select *No Fill* in the **Fill Color** pop-up menu.

Tasks summary: AutoShapes

Task	Procedure
Insert an AutoShape.	Click the **AutoShapes** button on the Drawing toolbar, and select the AutoShape category and the individual AutoShape.
Stack AutoShapes.	Select an AutoShape, choose the **Draw | Order** command on the Drawing toolbar, and select your required option, such as **Bring to Front**, **Send to Back** or **Send Behind Text**.
Group/ungroup AutoShapes.	To group objects, hold down the **Shift** key and click on each of the objects in turn. Next, click the **Draw** button on the Drawing toolbar and choose **Group**. To ungroup a selected group of objects, click the **Draw** button on the Drawing Toolbar and choose **Ungroup**.

Tasks summary: WordArt, pictures and watermarks

Task	Procedure
Insert WordArt.	Place the cursor where you want the WordArt to appear, click the **WordArt** button on the Drawing toolbar, select your required style, click **OK**, type your text, select a font and font size, and click **OK**.
Change picture borders.	Right-click the picture, choose **Format Picture**, click the **Colors and Lines** tab, select your required options, and click **OK**.
Create a watermark on a single page.	If you want to use a picture object, right-click on it, choose **Format Picture**, select the **Picture** tab, select *Watermark* from the *Color* drop-down list, click the **Layout** tab, select the *Behind text* option, and click **OK**. If you are using an AutoShape or WordArt object, right-click on it, choose **Format AutoShape or Format WordArt**, click the **Layout** tab, select the *Behind text* option, and click **OK**.
Insert a watermark on all pages of a document.	Choose **View | Header and Footer**, and insert the picture, or create the AutoShape, WordArt or text box in the header or footer. Right-click on the object, and use the **Format** command to stack the object behind the text. If using a picture you can also apply a watermark effect with the **Format** command.

Tasks summary: text wrapping

Task	Procedure
Control text wrapping.	Right-click on the object, choose **Format**, click the **Layout** tab, select your required text flow option, and click **OK**.

Concepts summary

Word's Drawing toolbar, which is positioned along the bottom of your screen, enables you to draw a wide range of graphic objects.

Lines, rectangles and circles are examples of *user-drawn shapes*. *AutoShapes* are Word's built-in, ready-to-insert shapes that are divided into categories such as flowchart elements, stars and banners, and call-outs. You can modify AutoShapes to your needs.

You can layer or *stack* AutoShapes so that they overlap each other. You can bring an object to the front or send it to the back of a stack, or bring it forward or send it backward one level in a stack. You can also stack an AutoShape so that is appears behind the text in a document. A collection of AutoShapes can be *grouped* together and manipulated as if they were a single object.

You can insert two types of *pictures* into Word documents: ClipArt pictures from Word's built-in ClipArt library, and picture files created in other applications. You can add a *border* to ClipArt and other pictures, and modify existing borders.

WordArt is a feature that enables you to apply decorative effects – such as colours, shadows, rotation and depth – to selected text. WordArt objects can be manipulated in a similar way to inserted pictures.

Text wrapping is the way in which text *flows* around a drawing graphic, whether a user-drawn shape, an AutoShape, a picture or a WordArt object.

A *watermark* is a picture, drawing object or text box that is displayed behind the main text of a page. Watermarks are coloured lightly so that they do not impair the legibility of the main text on the page. You can insert a watermark on a single page or, using the header or footer area, on all pages of a document.

Chapter 24: quick quiz

Circle the correct answer to each of the following multiple-choice questions about user-created drawings, AutoShapes, WordArt, pictures, text flow and watermarks in Word.

Q1	To draw a perfectly horizontal or vertical line in Word, you ...
A.	Click the **Line** button on the Drawing toolbar and hold down the **Shift** key as you drag with the mouse.
B.	Click the **Straight Horizontal Line** button on the Drawing toolbar and drag with the mouse.
C.	Click the **Line** button on the Drawing toolbar and hold down the **Ctrl** key as you drag with the mouse.
D.	Click the **Straight Line** button on the Drawing toolbar and hold down the **Ctrl** key as you drag with the mouse.

Q2	On Word's Drawing toolbar, which of the following buttons do you click to draw a line with an arrow?
A.	
B.	
C.	
D.	

Q3	To draw a perfect square in Word, you ...
A.	Click the **Square Box** button on the Drawing toolbar and hold down the **Ctrl** key as you drag with the mouse.
B.	Click the **Perfect Square** button on the Drawing toolbar and drag with the mouse.
C.	Click the **Rectangle** button on the Drawing toolbar and hold down the **Shift** key as you drag with the mouse.
D.	Click the **Rectangle** button on the Drawing toolbar and hold down the **Ctrl** key as you drag with the mouse.

Q4	In which part of the Word window is the Drawing toolbar displayed by default?
A.	In the top left of the Word window.
B.	Along the bottom of the Word window.
C.	As part of the Formatting toolbar.
D.	Along the top of the Word window.

Q5	To draw a perfect circle in Word, you ...
A.	Click the **Perfect Circle** button on the Drawing toolbar and drag with the mouse.
B.	Click the **Oval** button on the Drawing toolbar and hold down the **Shift** key as you drag with the mouse.
C.	Click the **Oval** button on the Drawing toolbar and hold down the **Ctrl** key as you drag with the mouse.
D.	Click the **Circle** button on the Drawing toolbar and hold down the **Ctrl** key as you drag with the mouse.

Q6	On Word's Drawing toolbar, which of the following buttons do you click to change the colour of a line or border?
A.	
B.	
C.	
D.	

Q7	On Word's Drawing toolbar, which of the following buttons do you click to change the inside colour of a closed shape?
A.	
B.	
C.	
D.	

Q8	In Word, which of the following actions do you perform to insert an AutoShape?
A.	Choose **Insert | AutoShape**.
B.	Choose **Format | AutoShapes**.
C.	Choose **Insert | Pictures | AutoShapes**.
D.	Click the **AutoShapes** button on the Drawing toolbar.

Q9	In Word, which of the following is not an AutoShape category?
A.	Stars and Banners.
B.	Academic.
C.	Flowchart.
D.	Callouts.

Q10	In Word, which of the following statements about AutoShapes is untrue?
A.	AutoShapes can be stacked so that they overlap each other.
B.	AutoShapes are not displayed in Normal view.
C.	A collection of AutoShapes can be grouped so that they can be manipulated as a single object.
D.	AutoShapes cannot be stacked behind the main text in a document.

Q11	In Word, the term WordArt refers to …
A.	Built-in standard or stock pictures that can be used and reused in Word documents.
B.	Pictures stored in AutoText.
C.	A feature that enables decorative effects – such as colours, shadows, rotation and depth – to be applied to selected text.
D.	Word's built-in gallery of ready-to-insert drawing objects.

Q12	In Word, which of the following statements about WordArt is untrue?
A.	You apply WordArt effects by clicking the **WordArt** button on the Drawing toolbar.
B.	You can amend the default font and font size when applying WordArt effects to selected text.
C.	You apply WordArt effects by choosing the **Insert | Picture | WordArt** button on the Drawing toolbar.
D.	WordArt objects cannot be manipulated in a similar way to inserted pictures.

Q13	In Word, which of the following statements about text wrapping is untrue?
A.	You apply text wrapping to a graphic by selecting it, choosing **Format | Text Flow**, selecting the required text flow option, and clicking **OK**.
B.	In front of text is the default text wrapping option for AutoShapes.
C.	You apply text wrapping to an object by right-clicking on it, choosing **Format**, clicking the **Layout** tab, selecting the required text flow option, and clicking **OK**.
D.	In line with text is the default text wrapping option for pictures and WordArt. It is not available for AutoShapes.

Q14	In Word, which of the following statements about watermarks is untrue?
A.	Watermarks are typically of feint colour so that they do not impair the legibility of the main text on the page.
B.	Pictures, drawings, WordArt objects and text boxes can be used as watermarks.
C.	The **Picture** tab of the **Format Picture** command includes an option to prepare a picture for use as a watermark.
D.	Only pictures, drawings and WordArt objects can be used as watermarks.

Q15	In Word, which of these methods do you follow to insert a watermark on every page of a document?
A.	Insert the graphic in the header or footer of the document.
B.	Add the graphic to AutoText, and then insert from AutoText into the first page of the document.
C.	Insert the graphic in the document template.
D.	Choose the **Insert | All Pages** command when inserting the graphic.

Answers

1: A, **2:** D, **3:** C, **4:** B, **5:** B, **6:** A, **7:** C, **8:** D, **9:** B, **10:** D, **11:** C, **12:** D, **13:** A, **14:** D, **15:** A.

25

Many columns, one document

Objectives

In this chapter you will learn how to:

- Apply a multi-column layout to a Word document
- Modify column widths and interline spacing
- Change the number of columns
- Insert vertical lines between columns
- Prevent paragraphs from breaking across columns
- Insert and remove column breaks

New words

In this chapter you will meet the following term:

- Multi-column layout

Exercise files

In this chapter you will work with the following Word files:

- `Chapter25_Exercise_25-1_Before.doc`
- `Chapter25_Exercise_25-2_Before.doc`
- `Chapter25_Exercise_25-3_Before.doc`
- `Chapter25_Exercise_25-4_Before.doc`
- `Chapter25_Exercise_25-5_Before.doc`

Syllabus reference

In this chapter you will cover the following items from the ECDL Advanced Word Processing Syllabus:

- **AM3.2.4.1**. Create multiple-column layouts.
- **AM3.2.4.2**. Modify column layouts.
- **AM3.2.4.3**. Modify column width and spacing.
- **AM3.2.4.4**. Insert a column break.
- **AM3.2.4.5**. Delete a column break.

Multi-column layouts

Like tables, columns enable you to position text, tables and graphics side by side on a page. Unlike tables, however, columns allow text to flow from the bottom of one column to the top of the next column.

Columns: the benefits to you

What are the advantages of using multi-column layouts?

- **Professional-looking newsletters**. Word's column features enable you to produce stylish newsletters quickly and easily.
- **Easier-to-read text**. Text line length within columns is shortened, with the result that the text is easier to read.
- **More content in less space**. You can generally fit more text and graphics into a multi-column layout than in a page-wide, single-column layout.

Columns: toolbar button or menu command?

You can create columns in either of two ways:

- **Toolbar button**. Click the **Columns** button on the Standard toolbar, drag with the mouse to select a layout of up to four columns, and then click.

- **Menu command**. Choose **Format | Columns** to display the *Columns* dialog box, select your required options, and click **OK**.

  Using the toolbar button is the fast and easy approach. The menu command, however, offers more options and gives you greater control over the layout.

In this chapter, you will apply columns to entire documents only. Applying columns to selected parts of a document is covered in Chapter 26 because this requires the use of section breaks.

Columns and document views

Word displays multi-column layouts on screen only in Print Layout view.

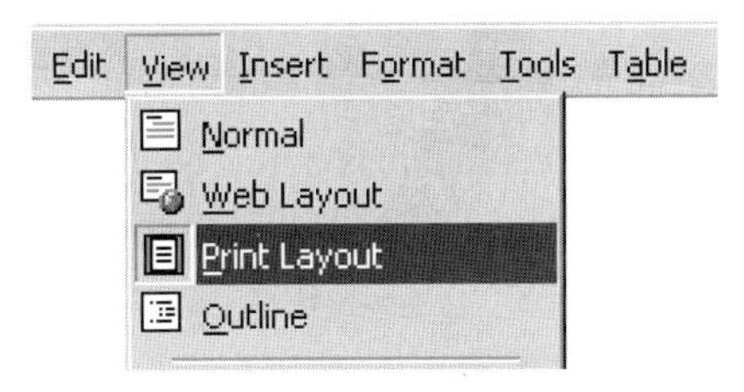

In Normal view, multiple columns are not displayed side by side but appear as a single column. Before performing the exercises in this chapter, check that Print Layout view is selected.

Multi-column layout

A layout in which text, tables and graphics are positioned side by side in such a way that text flows from the bottom of one column to the top of the next column. Multi-column layouts are commonly used in newsletters.

Working with columns: the four tasks

Here are the four tasks that you need to be able to perform with columns in Word:

- **Create multiple-column layouts**. Learn how to apply a simple, multi-column layout in Exercise 25.1 using both the Standard toolbar button and the **Format | Columns** command.
- **Change column width and spacing**. Exercise 25.2 shows you how to make your columns wider or narrower, and intercolumn spacing narrower or wider.
- **Modify multiple-column layouts**. In Exercise 25.3, you discover how to change the number of columns, add a vertical line between columns, and prevent a paragraph of text from breaking across two columns.
- **Insert and remove column breaks**. Column breaks are added and removed automatically by Word as you apply and modify column layouts. However, you can also insert and remove column breaks directly, as Exercises 25.4 and 25.5 demonstrate.

Working with new columns

In Exercise 25.1, you will apply a basic, two-column layout using Word's default options. You apply the columns first with the toolbar button and then with the menu command.

Exercise 25.1: Create a simple multi-column layout

1) Open the following document:

    `Chapter25_Exercise_25-1_Before.doc`

2) Click anywhere in the document.

3) Click the **Columns** button on the Standard Toolbar, and then choose the two-column layout.

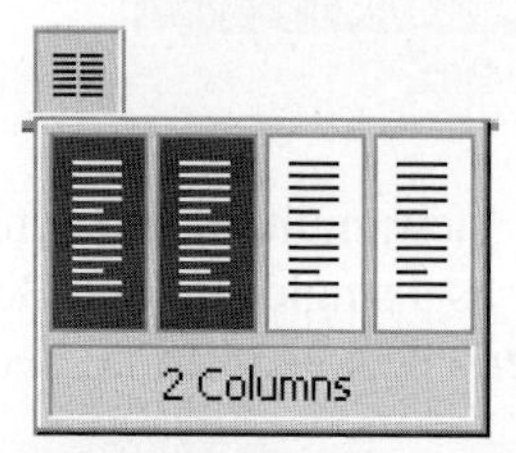

Word applies the two-column layout to your entire document.

Choose **Edit | Undo Columns**. You will now reapply the columns with the **Format | Columns** command.

4) With the insertion point positioned anywhere in the document, choose **Format | Columns** to display the *Columns* dialog box.

5) In the *Presets* area, click *Two*. Accept the default values of the other options, and click **OK**.

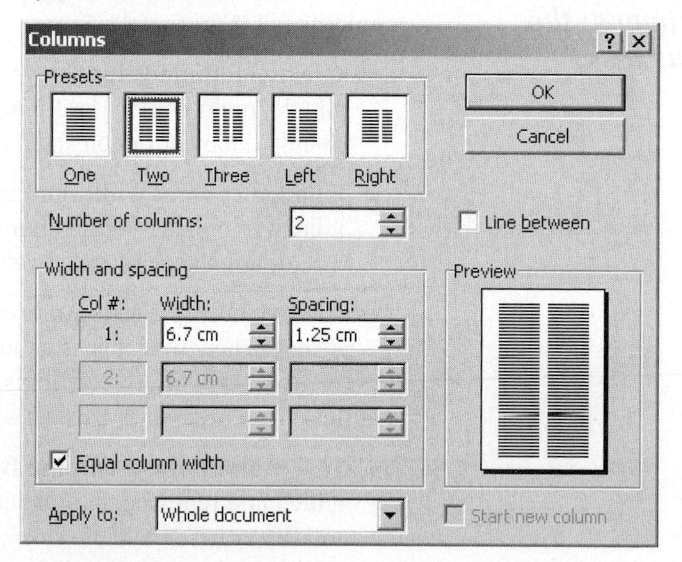

6) Word applies the two-column layout. The upper part of your document should look like this:

·The·New·Era·of·eBusiness¶

Introduction¶

By·transforming·the·way·that·people·and·businesses·communicate·and·interact,·the·Internet·has·dramatically·changed·the·face·of·business.¶

Impressed·by·the·Internet's·rising·popularity,·many·businesses·have·established·an·online·presence.·A·rich·variety·of·business·information·–·from·service·and·product·catalogues·to·press·releases·to·company·contacts·–·is·now·available·to·Internet·users.¶

that·not·all·consumers·want·to·shop·on-line.·Some·people·prefer·shopping·in·the·traditional·manner:·talking·to·sales·staff,·lingering·in·the·aisles,·'touching'·products,·and·interacting·with·other·customers.·Although·it·may·not·be·for·everyone·at·all·times,·e-business·does·offer·certain·benefits:¶

- → Opportunities·to·browse,·comparison·shop·and·make·purchases·from·the·comfort·of·their·desktop;¶
- → Convenience·–·shops·are·always·open·for·business·on·the·Net;¶
- → An·expanded·marketplace.·The·Net·is·a·global·shopping·mall.·Purchase·from·a·company·in·Paris,·Tokyo·or·San·Francisco;¶

7) Save your sample document with the following name, and close it:

`Chapter25_Exercise_25-1_After_`*`Your_Name`*`.doc`

Modifying column layouts

Word provides a range of features that you can use to modify your columns to make them appear precisely as you want.

Column width and spacing

In Exercise 25.2, you will learn how to adjust column width and intercolumn spacing. The two settings are inversely related:

- If you make your columns *wider*, Word automatically makes your intercolumn spacing *narrower*.
- If you make your columns *narrower*, Word automatically makes your intercolumn spacing *wider*.

Exercise 25.2: Change column width and spacing

1) Open the following three-column document:

`Chapter25_Exercise_25-2_Before.doc`

2) Choose **Format | Columns** to display the *Columns* dialog box. Notice that all three columns are 4.5 cm wide, and that the intercolumn spacing is 1.25 cm. Click **Cancel** to close the dialog box.

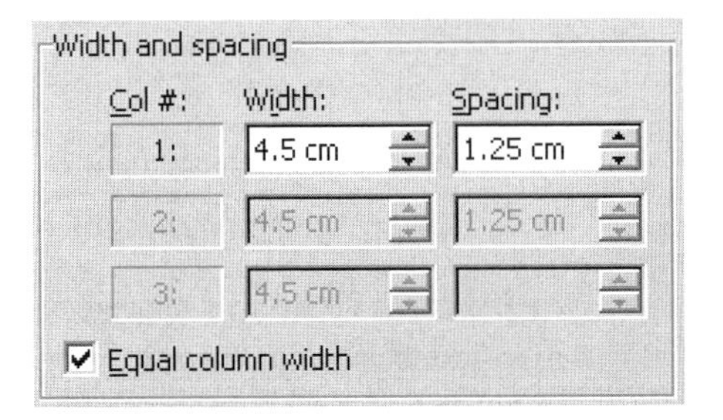

3) Choose **File | Page Setup**. On the *Margins* tab, you can see that the left and right page margins are both 2.5 cm.

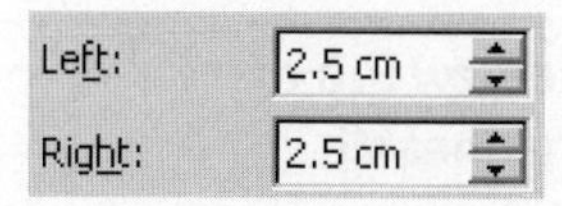

Change the two margins to 3 cm, and click **OK**. You have now reduced the distance between the two margins – the area available to the text – by 1 cm.

4) Choose **Format | Columns** to display the *Columns* dialog box. Notice that Word has automatically adjusted the column width as a result of the change in page margins. The intercolumn spacing remains unaffected.

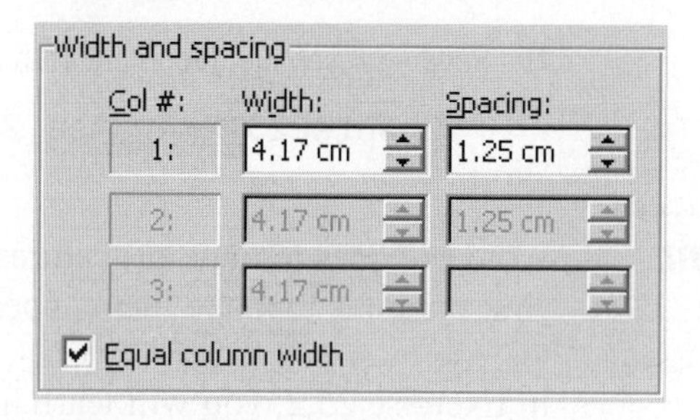

5) Click in the *Width* box for the first column, and change the value from 4.17 to 4 cm. Click **OK**.

   Because the *Equal column width* checkbox is selected, the other two columns will be affected by your change to the first column Click **OK**.

6) Choose **Format | Columns** to display the *Columns* dialog box. Because you reduced the column widths from 4.17 cm to 4 cm, Word increased the column spacing from 1.25 cm to 1.5 cm.

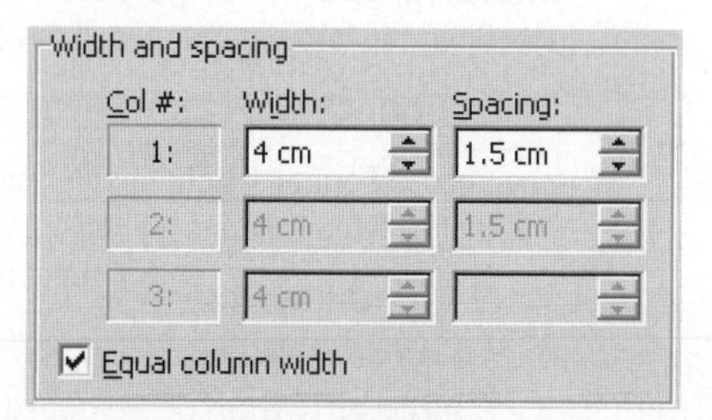

7) Save your sample document with the following name, and close it:

   `Chapter25_Exercise_25-2_After_`*`Your_Name`*`.doc`

In Exercise 25.2, you changed the column width and Word responded by adjusting the intercolumn spacing. The opposite is also true: if you change the intercolumn spacing, Word adjusts the column width accordingly.

Column layout options

Other layout options available with columns in Word include the ability to:

- change the number of columns, say from two to three, or three to four;
- insert a vertical line between columns;
- prevent a paragraph of text from breaking across two columns.

Exercise 25.3 provides examples of each feature.

Exercise 25.3: Change column layout

1) Open the following document:

   `Chapter25_Exercise_25-3_Before.doc`

2) Choose **Format | Columns** to display the *Columns* dialog box.

   In the *Number of columns* box, replace 3 with 2, and click **OK**. You have now converted a three-column layout to a two-column layout.

3) Choose **Format | Columns** to display the *Columns* dialog box.

4) Select the *Line between* checkbox and click **OK**.

   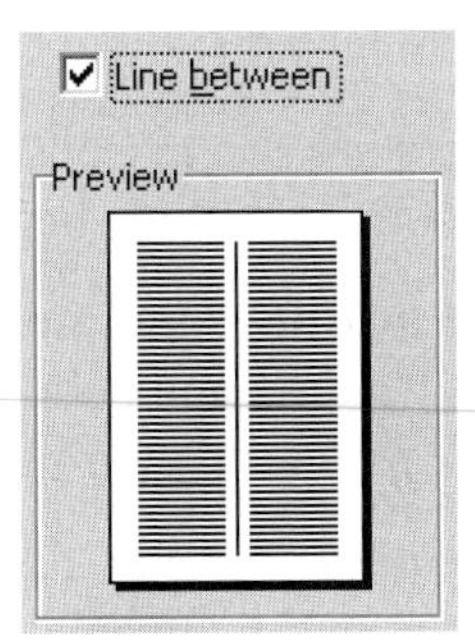

   Word inserts a vertical line between your two columns.

5) Notice that the paragraph of body text beginning with the word 'Another area that has taken off' begins at the bottom of the first column and ends at the top of the second column.

6) Click anywhere in this paragraph, choose **Format | Paragraph**, click the **Line and Page Breaks** tab, select the *Keep lines together* checkbox, and click **OK**.

   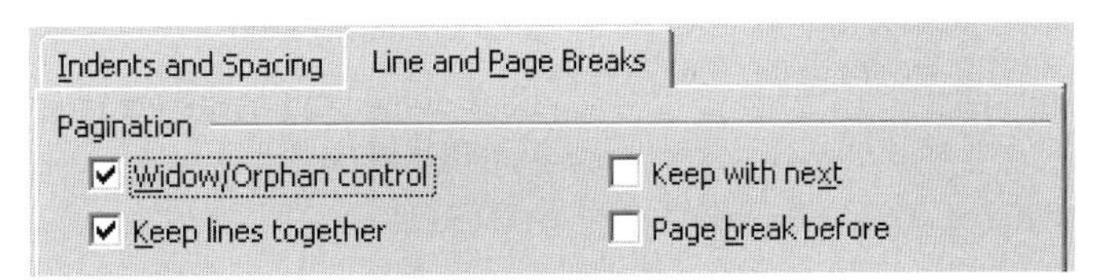

Word now positions this paragraph in its entirety at the top of the second column. The upper part of your document should now look like this:

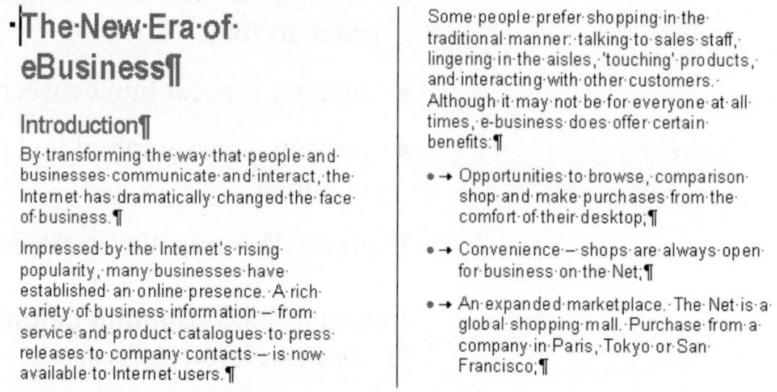

·The·New·Era·of·eBusiness¶

Introduction¶

By·transforming·the·way·that·people·and·businesses·communicate·and·interact,·the·Internet·has·dramatically·changed·the·face·of·business.¶

Impressed·by·the·Internet's·rising·popularity,·many·businesses·have·established·an·online·presence.·A·rich·variety·of·business·information·–·from·service·and·product·catalogues·to·press·releases·to·company·contacts·–·is·now·available·to·Internet·users.¶

Some·people·prefer·shopping·in·the·traditional·manner:·talking·to·sales·staff,·lingering·in·the·aisles,·'touching'·products,·and·interacting·with·other·customers.·Although·it·may·not·be·for·everyone·at·all·times,·e-business·does·offer·certain·benefits:¶

- Opportunities·to·browse,·comparison·shop·and·make·purchases·from·the·comfort·of·their·desktop;¶
- Convenience·–·shops·are·always·open·for·business·on·the·Net;¶
- An·expanded·marketplace.·The·Net·is·a·global·shopping·mall.·Purchase·from·a·company·in·Paris,·Tokyo·or·San·Francisco;¶

7) Save your sample document with the following name, and close it:

Chapter25_Exercise_25-3_After_*Your_Name*.doc

Working with column breaks

As you apply and modify multi-column layouts in a document, Word automatically inserts column breaks at the appropriate locations. Sometimes, however, you will want to insert or remove such breaks directly.

Typically, there are two reasons why you might want to force the end of a column and the beginning of another:

- **Highlight headings and introductions**. You might want a document heading and perhaps some introductory text or graphic to appear on their own in the first column on a page.
- **Balance column length**. Text in the final column is often shorter than that in preceding columns. By inserting a column break, you can give your multi-column page a more even appearance.

Exercise 25.4: Insert a column break

1) Open the following document:

Chapter25_Exercise_25-4_Before.doc

2) Move to the bottom of the page. You can see that the right column is shorter than the left.

Click at the start of the paragraph beginning with the words 'Deciding whether to have'.

3) Choose **Insert | Break** to display the *Break* dialog box.

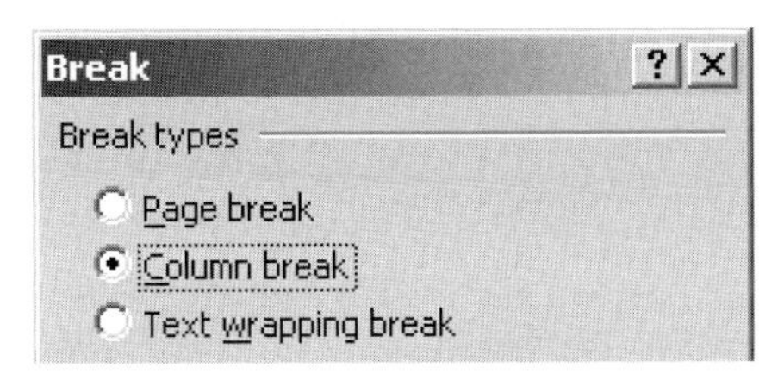

Select *Column break* and click **OK**.

Word inserts the column break at your selected location.

• → Depending·on·the·type·of·business,·your·website·can·be·used·to·link·with·suppliers,·order·raw·materials,·check·stock·levels·and·conduct·sales.¶

..................Column Break..................

4) Save your sample document with the following name, and close it:

`Chapter25_Exercise_25-4_After_`*`Your_Name`*`.doc`

Exercise 25.5: Remove a column break

1) Open the following document:

`Chapter25_Exercise_25-5_Before.doc`

2) Move to the bottom of the page. Click just to the left of the column break at the bottom of the left column.

• → Depending·on·the·type·of·business,·your·website·can·be·used·to·link·with·suppliers,·order·raw·materials,·check·stock·levels·and·conduct·sales.¶

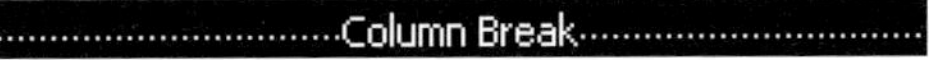

3) Press the **Delete** key. Word removes the column break.

4) Save your sample document with the following name, and close it:

`Chapter25_Exercise_25-5_After_`*`Your_Name`*`.doc`

Removing multi-column layouts

Want to remove a multi-column layout from a document? Click anywhere in the document, click the **Column** button on the Standard toolbar, and choose the single column layout. Word removes the multi-column layout.

Alternatively, with the cursor anywhere in the document, choose **Format | Columns**. In the *Number of columns* box, type 1. Finally, click **OK**.

Chapter 25: quick reference

Tasks summary

Task	Procedure
Apply a multi-column layout to a document.	Click the **Columns** button on the Standard toolbar and choose a layout of up to four columns.
	Alternatively, choose **Format | Columns**, select the required number of columns, specify any other layout options, and click **OK.**
Change column width.	Choose **Format | Columns**, type a new width for the column(s) or intercolumn spacing(s), and click **OK**.
Change the number of columns.	Choose **Format | Columns**. In the *Presets* area, type the number of columns you require, and click **OK**.
Insert or remove vertical lines between columns.	Choose **Format | Columns**. Select or deselect the *Line between* checkbox, and click **OK**.
Control paragraph breaks across columns.	Click anywhere in the text paragraph, choose **Format | Paragraph**, select or deselect the *Keep lines together* checkbox, and click **OK**.
Insert a column break.	Click in the text where you want the break to appear, choose **Insert | Break**, select the *Column break* option, and click **OK**.
Remove a column break.	Select the column break and press **Delete**.

Concepts summary

Word's *columns* feature enables you to position text, tables and graphics side by side on a page so that text flows from the bottom of one column to the top of the next column. Multi-column layouts are commonly used for *newsletters*.

You can generally fit *more content* into a multi-column layout than in a page-wide, single-column layout. Also, because text line length within columns is shorter, the resulting text can be *easier to read*.

You can create columns before or after you type text. Word gives you complete control of multi-column layouts, including the ability to change column width and intercolumn spacing, change the number of columns, add or remove vertical lines between columns, and insert or delete column breaks directly. You can also prevent particular paragraphs from breaking across columns.

Chapter 25: quick quiz

Circle the correct answer to each of the following multiple-choice questions about columns in Word.

Q1	In Word, which of the following statements about multi-column layouts is untrue?
A.	You cannot change the number of columns in an existing multi-column layout.
B.	Columns allow text to flow from the bottom of one column to the top of the next column.
C.	You can insert vertical lines between columns.
D.	You can insert and remove column breaks directly.

Q2	In Word, which of the following buttons on the Standard toolbar can you click to begin inserting columns?
A.	
B.	
C.	
D.	

Q3	In Word, which of the following menu commands can you click to begin inserting columns?
A.	**Tools | Options | Columns.**
B.	**Format | Columns.**
C.	**Table | New Columns.**
D.	**Insert | Columns.**

Q4	In Word, which of the following statements about column width and intercolumn spacing is untrue?
A.	The wider the columns, the narrower the intercolumn spacing.
B.	When you change column width, Word adjusts the intercolumn spacing automatically.
C.	The narrower the columns, the wider the intercolumn spacing.
D.	When you decrease intercolumn spacing, Word reduces the column widths automatically.

Q5	To insert vertical lines between columns in a Word document, you ...
A.	Right-click in the intercolumn gap, and choose **Insert Vertical Line** command from the pop-up menu displayed.
B.	Choose **Format | Columns**, select the *Line between* checkbox, and click **OK**.
C.	Right-click in the intercolumn gap, and choose the **Lines | Vertical** command from the pop-up menu displayed.
D.	Choose **Insert | Columns**, select the *Vertical line* checkbox, and click **OK**.

Q6	To change the number of columns in a Word document, you ...
A.	Choose **Format | Columns**, select a different preset value, and click **OK**.
B.	Right-click on any column, choose **Change Columns**, type the number of columns, and click **OK**.
C.	Choose **Insert | Columns**, select a different number of columns from the drop-down list, and click **OK**.
D.	Right-click on any column, choose **Column Number**, type the number of columns, and click **OK**.

Q7	In Word, how do you prevent a particular paragraph from breaking across two columns?
A.	Click anywhere in the text paragraph, choose **Format | Paragraph**, select the *Keep with next* checkbox, and click **OK**.
B.	Click anywhere in the text paragraph, choose **Format | Columns**, deselect the *Break paragraph* checkbox, and click **OK**.
C.	Right-click on the paragraph, choose **Breaks**, deselect the *Paragraph break* checkbox, and click **OK**.
D.	Click anywhere in the text paragraph, choose **Format | Paragraph**, select the *Keep lines together* checkbox, and click **OK**.

Q8	In a Word document, which of the following actions do you take to insert a column break?
A.	Choose **Format | Columns | Break**, select the *New column break* checkbox, and click **OK**.
B.	Right-click where you want to break to appear, and choose **Breaks | Column**.
C.	Choose **Insert | Break**, select the *Column break* option, and click **OK**.
D.	None of the above – you cannot insert a column break directly

Q9	In Word, which of the following actions do you take to remove a column break?
A.	Click at the column break to select it and press **Delete**.
B.	Right-click on the column break, and choose **Cut** from the pop-up menu displayed.
C.	Click at the column break to select it and press **Ctrl+V**.
D.	None of the above – you cannot remove a column break directly

Answers

1: A, **2:** D, **3:** B, **4:** D, **5:** B, **6:** A, **7:** A, **8:** C, **9:** A.

26 Many sections, one document

Objectives

In this chapter you will learn how to:

- Insert section breaks
- Delete section breaks
- Print the following parts of a document: odd-numbered pages, even-numbered pages, and selected text
- Print multiple copies of a document of part or a document

New words

In this chapter you will meet the following term:

- Section

Exercise files

In this chapter you will work with the following Word files:

- `Chapter26_Exercise_26-1_Before.doc`
- `Chapter26_Exercise_26-3_Before.doc`
- `Chapter26_Exercise_26-4_Before.doc`
- `Chapter26_Exercise_26-5_Before.doc`
- `Chapter26_Exercise_26-6_Before.doc`

Syllabus reference

In this chapter you will cover the following items from the ECDL Advanced Word Processing Syllabus:

- **AM3.2.3.1**. Create sections in a document.
- **AM3.2.3.2**. Delete section breaks in a document.
- **AM3.6.1.1**. Print odd-numbered pages only.
- **AM3.6.1.2**. Print even-numbered pages only.
- **AM3.6.1.3**. Print a defined selection.
- **AM3.6.1.4**. Print a defined number of pages per sheet.

About sections

The section break feature in Word enables you to split a document into two or more parts or *sections*, and to apply different layout settings to each section. A section may consist of a single paragraph or can be several pages long. Inserting a single section break in a document creates *two* sections: the section before the section break and the section after it.

Varying the layout between sections in a document

Here are some of the layout elements that can differ between sections of the same document:

- Options within the **File | Page Setup** command – for example, page margins, paper size or orientation, and paper source for a printer.

  This command also controls header and footer settings, such as whether headers or footers are displayed on the first page, or are different on left and right pages.

- Text and numbering in headers and footers, and any other options available with the **View | Headers and Footers** command.
- Page border and shading features applied with the **Format | Borders and Shading** command.
- Footnotes and endnotes inserted and formatted with the **Insert | Footnote** command.
- Multi-column layouts.

To change the layout of a section, move the insertion point to somewhere within it, and apply your layout changes to that section.

Section

A part of a Word document that can have layout settings – such as page margins, headers and footers, and columns – that are different from the rest of the document. Sections are bounded by sections breaks, and can range in length from a single paragraph to several pages.

Multiple sections: the benefits to you

You are most likely to use section breaks to perform the following two layout actions in Word documents:

- **Column layouts**. Vary the number of columns on a single page or in a single document.

- **Tables of contents**. Interrupt page numbering between a table of contents and the text that follows. As a result, the pages on which the table of contents appears are not counted by the table of contents.

About section breaks

By default, Word documents consist of only one section. To divide the document into sections you need to:

- **Insert section breaks directly**. You do this by positioning the insertion point where you want your new section to start, choosing the **Insert | Break** command, selecting your required section break type, and clicking **OK**.

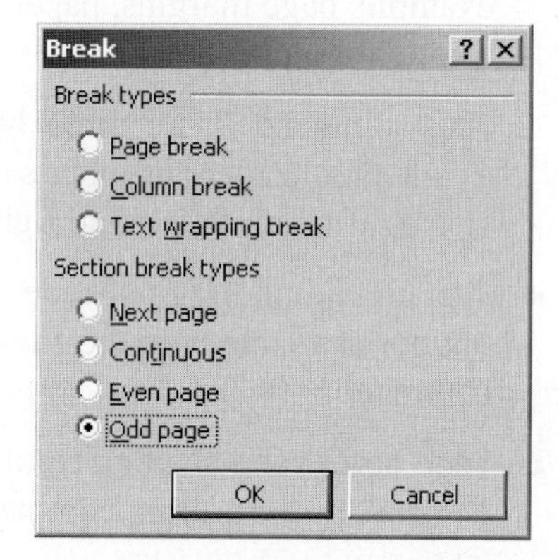

- **Use a Word feature that inserts section breaks for you**. An example is multi-column layout. If you select part of a document and apply columns, Word inserts section breaks automatically *before* and *after* the text that you selected.

Working with sections in Word: the two tasks

Here are the two tasks that you need to be able to perform with section breaks in Word:

- **Create sections in a document**. Exercises 26.1 and 26.3 take you through the steps of inserting sections breaks in Word documents. In Exercise 26.2, you discover how Word inserts section breaks automatically whenever you apply a multi-column layout to part of a document.
- **Delete sections from a document**. In Exercise 26.4, you remove section breaks from a Word document and learn how this affects a document's formatting.

Working with section breaks and multi-column layouts

In Exercise 26.1, you will create a page layout that consists of a heading that runs left to right across the top of the page with two columns of text beneath it.

Exercise 26.1: Multiple columns and directly inserted section breaks

1) Start Word and open the following document:

   `Chapter26_Exercise_26-1_Before.doc`

2) Click at the start of the heading 'Introduction'. This is where you want the new section to begin.

   .The·New·Era·of·ebusiness¶

   Introduction¶

   By·transforming·the·way·that·people·and·businesses·communicate·and·interact,·the·Internet·has·dramatically·changed·the·face·of·business.¶

3) Choose **Insert | Break** to display the *Break* dialog box. Select the *Continuous* option and click **OK**.

   .The·New·Era·of·ebusiness¶ Section Break (Continuous)

   Introduction¶

   By·transforming·the·way·that·people·and·businesses·communicate·and·interact,·the·Internet·has·dramatically·changed·the·face·of·business.¶

4) Click anywhere in the text beneath the section break and choose **Format | Columns**.

5) In the *Presets* area, select *Two*. Select the *Line between* option.

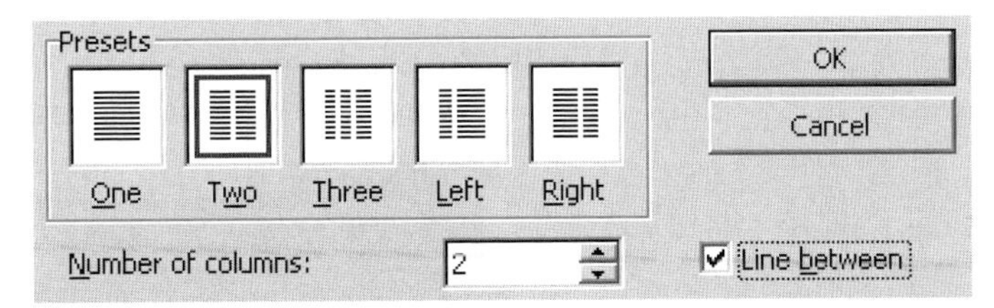

   Click **OK**.

6) Click just to the left of the page heading 'The New Era of eBusiness' to select it, and click the **Center** button on the Formatting toolbar.

   The upper part of your page should look like this:

   The·New·Era·of·ebusiness Section Break (Continuous)

   Introduction¶

   By·transforming·the·way·that·people·and·businesses·communicate·and·interact,·the·Internet·has·dramatically·changed·the·face·of·business.¶

   Impressed·by·the·Internet's·rising·popularity,·many·businesses·have·established·an·online·presence.·A·rich·variety·of·business·

   What's·In·It·for·the·consumer?¶

   While·it's·easy·to·get·caught·up·in·the·hype·surrounding·e-commerce,·not·all·consumers·want·to·shop·on-line.·Some·people·prefer·shopping·in·traditional·ways,·talking·to·sales·staff·and·"touching"·a·product.·Although·e-commerce·may·not·be·for·everyone,·it·does·offer·certain·benefits:¶

7) Save your sample document with the following name, and close it:

   Chapter26_Exercise_26-1_After_*Your_Name*.doc

Section breaks: more than one type

In Exercise 26.1, you inserted a section break of the continuous (same page) type. Word provides four section break types:

Section break type	Description
Continuous	Starts the new section on the same page.
Next page	Starts the new section on the next page.
Even page	Starts the new section on the next even-numbered page. Typically, this is a left-hand page.
Odd page	Starts the new section on the next odd-numbered page. Typically, this is a right-hand page.

In Exercise 26.2, you will select part of a document, apply a two-column layout, and observe that Word inserts section breaks automatically before and after your selected text.

Exercise 26.2: Multiple columns and automatically inserted section breaks

1) Open the following document:

   `Chapter26_Exercise_26-2_Before.doc`

2) Go to the heading 'Introduction' and select it and the three paragraphs beneath it, as far as, but not including, the 'What is ebusiness?' heading.

   Introduction¶
   By·transforming·the·way·that·people·and·businesses·communicate·and·interact,·the·Internet·has·dramatically·changed·the·face·of·business.¶
   Impressed·by·the·Internet's·rising·popularity,·many·businesses·have·established·an·online·presence.·A·rich·variety·of·business·information—from·product·and·service·catalogues·to·press·releases·to·company·contacts—is·now·available·to·Internet·users.¶
   Today,·many·businesses·realise·that,·in·order·to·compete·successfully,·they·need·to·sell·their·goods·and·services·directly·to·consumers·or·other·businesses·over·the·Internet.¶

3) Choose **Format | Columns.**
4) In the *Presets* area, select *Two*. Click **OK**.

   The upper part of your page should look like this:

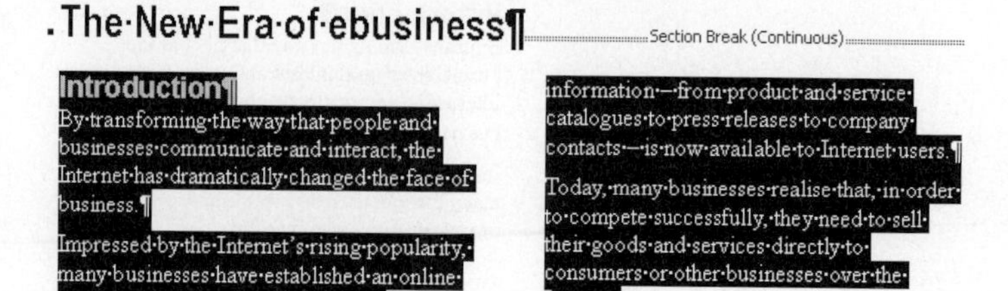
.The·New·Era·of·ebusiness¶ Section Break (Continuous)
Introduction¶
By·transforming·the·way·that·people·and·businesses·communicate·and·interact,·the·Internet·has·dramatically·changed·the·face·of·business.¶
Impressed·by·the·Internet's·rising·popularity,·many·businesses·have·established·an·online·presence.·A·rich·variety·of·business·information—from·product·and·service·catalogues·to·press·releases·to·company·contacts—is·now·available·to·Internet·users.¶
Today,·many·businesses·realise·that,·in·order·to·compete·successfully,·they·need·to·sell·their·goods·and·services·directly·to·consumers·or·other·businesses·over·the·Internet. Section Break (Continuous)
¶

Notice the continuous (same-page) section breaks inserted automatically before and after the text that you selected for conversion to columns. Click anywhere outside the text to deselect it.

5) Save your sample document with the following name, and close it:

   `Chapter26_Exercise_26-2_After_`*`Your_Name`*`.doc`

Working with section breaks and tables of contents

There is a Zen saying that an ideal list is one that includes itself. A table of contents, however, should *not* include itself.

In Exercise 26.3, you will insert an odd-page section break in a document after a table of contents and before the main text. You will then update the page numbering in the footers, and regenerate the table of contents to reflect the new page numbering.

Exercise 26.3: Section breaks and tables of contents

1) Open the following Word document:

   `Chapter26_Exercise_26-3_Before.doc`

2) Move through the seven pages of the document, noting the page numbers at the bottom of each page. You can see that the cover page and the table of contents page are numbered '1' and '2', respectively.

   You want to change this so that:

   - the cover and contents pages do not display page numbers;
   - the first page of text (currently 3) remains a right-hand page, and is numbered 1.

3) Click the page break at the bottom of the table of contents page to select it, and press **Delete** to remove the page breaks.

4) Click at the beginning of the first paragraph of text, which starts with the words 'At Elmsworth Health Trust'.

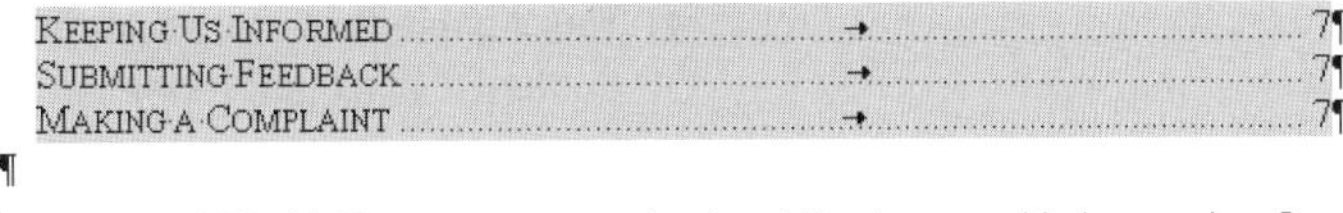
KEEPING US INFORMED → 7¶
SUBMITTING FEEDBACK → 7¶
MAKING A COMPLAINT → 7¶
¶
At·Elmsworth·Health·Trust,·we·are·committed·to·delivering·a·world-class·service.·Our·standards·apply·whether·you·are:¶

5) Choose **Insert | Break** to display the *Break* dialog box. Select the *Odd page* option and click **OK**.

Switch Between Header and Footer button

6) Click anywhere in the text after the section break, choose **View | Header and Footer**, and click the **Switch Between Header and Footer** button on the Header and Footer toolbar.

7) Notice that the **Same as Previous** button on the Header and Footer toolbar is selected by default. Click it to deselect it.

Same as Previous button

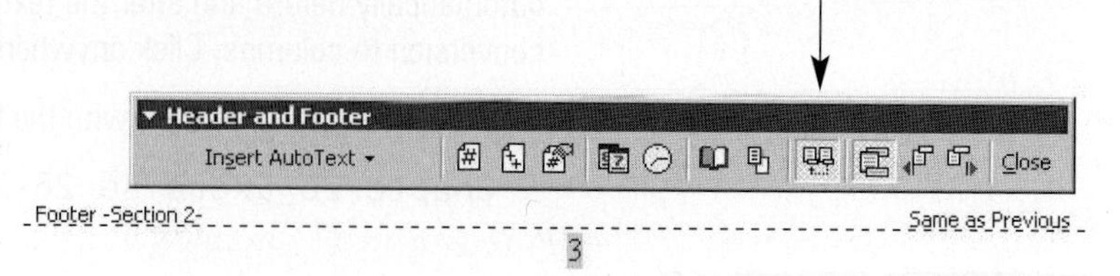

8) Click on the '3' in the footer, and click the **Format Page Number** button on the Header and Footer toolbar.

9) In the *Page numbering* area of the *Page Number Format* dialog box, click the *Start at* option. Word inserts a '1' in the associated text box. Click **OK**.

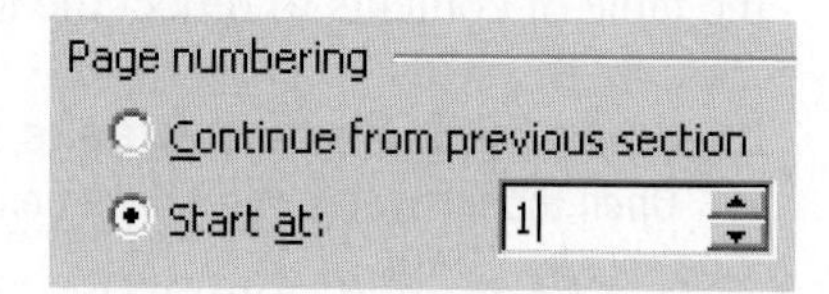

10) Click the **Show Next** button on the Header and Footer toolbar. Notice that the **Same as Previous** button on the Header and Footer toolbar is again selected by default. Click it to deselect it. Click the **Close Header and Footer** button.

11) Click anywhere on the first page of your sample document, choose **View | Header and Footer**, and click the **Switch Between Header and Footer** button on the Header and Footer toolbar.

12) Delete the page number '1' from the footer, click the **Show Next** button on the Header and Footer toolbar, and delete the page number '2' from the footer. Click the **Close Header and Footer** button.

13) Inspect the page numbers in your document. You can see that you have achieved your desired result: the cover and contents pages have no page numbers, and the pages of text are numbered from 1 to 5.

14) Your final task is to update the page numbering in the table of contents. Click just to the left of any line of the table of contents.

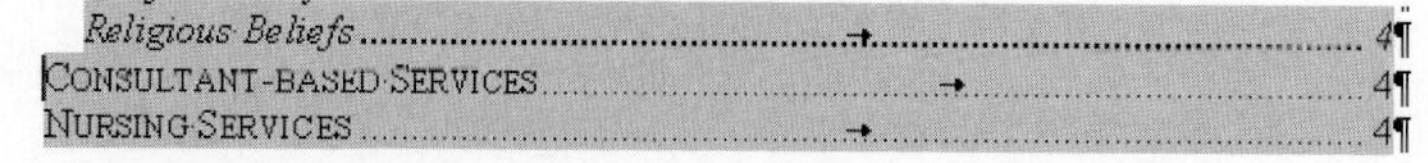

15) Press **F9**. Word displays the *Update Table of Contents* dialog box. Accept the default *Update page numbers only* option and click **OK**.

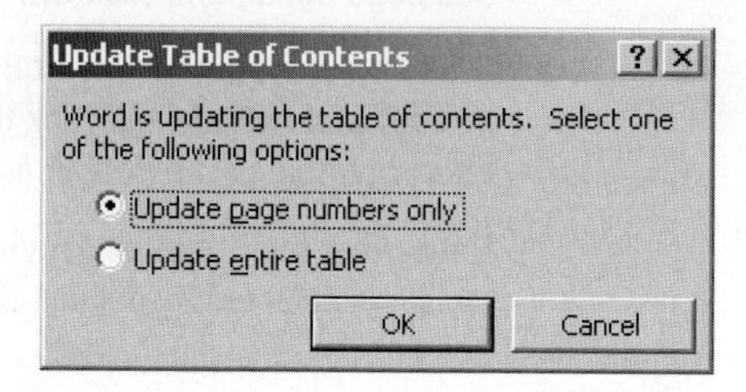

16) Word updates your table of contents to reflect the new page numbering. Save your sample document with the following name, and close it:

Chapter26_Exercise_26-3_After_*Your_Name*.doc

Removing section breaks

Want to remove a section break? Click at the start of the section break and press the **Delete** key.

Section breaks and formatting

A section break controls text formatting in the section that precedes it. When you delete a section break, Word:

- removes section-specific formatting from the text that was before the section break; and
- applies to that text the formatting of the text *after* the deleted section break.

Exercise 26.4 demonstrates the effects on document formatting of deleting section breaks.

Exercise 26.4: Remove section breaks

1) Open the following Word document:

Chapter26_Exercise_26-4_Before.doc

2) Click at the beginning of the second section break, which marks the end of the two-column layout.

Today,·many·businesses·realise·that,·in·order·to·compete·successfully,·they·need·to·sell·their·goods·and·services·directly·to·consumers·or·other·businesses·over·the·Internet.::::::::Section Break (Continuous)::::::::

3) Press the **Delete** key to remove the section break. Notice that Word removes the two-column formatting with the deleted section break.

4) Click at the beginning of the first section break and press **Delete**. No formatting change is applied, because the text before and after the deleted section break had single-column formatting.

The upper part of your page should look ike this:

.The·New·Era·of·eBusiness¶

Introduction¶

By·transforming·the·way·that·people·and·businesses·communicate·and·interact,·the·Internet·has·dramatically·changed·the·face·of·business.¶

Impressed·by·the·Internet's·rising·popularity,·many·businesses·have·established·an·online·presence.·A·rich·variety·of·business·information·—·from·product·and·service·catalogues·to·press·releases·to·company·contacts·—·is·now·available·to·Internet·users.¶

Today,·many·businesses·realise·that,·in·order·to·compete·successfully,·they·need·to·sell·their·goods·and·services·directly·to·consumers·or·other·businesses·over·the·Internet.¶

5) Save your sample document with the following name, and close it:

   `Chapter26_Exercise_26-4_After_Your_Name.doc`

Working with Word's print options

In Word, you are not limited to printing a document in its entirety. Nor are you confined to printing just a single copy in one print operation. Follow Exercise 25.6 to discover the range of print options available to you.

Exercise 26.5: Print document parts and multiple copies

1) Open the following Word document:

   `Chapter26_Exercise_26-5_Before.doc`

2) Choose **File | Print**. From the *Print* drop-down list, select *Odd pages*, and click **OK**.

   Word should print only the following pages: the cover, page 1, page 3 and page 5.

3) Choose **File | Print**. From the *Print* drop-down list, select *Even pages*, and click **OK**.

   Word should print only the following pages: the table of contents, page 2, and page 4.

4) Go to the first page of text in your sample document – the page that follows the table of contents page. Select the 'Mission Statement' heading and the eight lines of text beneath that heading.

   Mission·Statement¶

   The·purpose·of·the·Elmsworth·Health·Trust·is·to:¶

   •→ Promote·good·health¶

   •→ Diagnose·and·treat·those·who·are·ill¶

   •→ Provide·health·care·for·those·with·continuing·needs.¶

   Elmsworth·Health·Trust·is·committed·to·these·objectives:¶

   •→ Irrespective·of·the·individual's·ability·to·pay¶

   •→ In·partnership·with·people·and·other·organisations¶

   •→ Within·the·resources·that·are·made·available.¶

5) Choose **File | Print**. In the *Page range* area, select the *Selection* option, and click **OK**.

   Word should print only the selected text from the document. Click anywhere outside the selected text to deselect it.

6) Choose **File | Print**. In the *Pages per sheet* box, select *4 pages*, and click **OK**.

Word should print two pages of paper. The first should contain the cover, the contents page, page 1 and page 2. The second should contain pages 3, 4 and 5.

7) You can close your sample document without saving it.

Chapter 26: quick reference

Tasks summary: sections

Task	Procedure
Insert a section break directly.	Position the insertion point where you want the new section to begin, choose **Insert | Break**, select your required section break type,and click **OK**.
Remove a section break.	Click at the start of the section break and press the **Delete** key.

Tasks summary: printing

Task	Procedure
Print odd- or even-numbered pages only.	Choose **File | Print**. From the *Print* drop-down list, select *Odd pages* or *Even pages*, and click **OK**.
Print the currently selected part of a document.	Choose **File | Print**. In the *Page range* area, select the *Selection* option, and click **OK**.
Print multiple pages of a document on a single sheet of paper.	Choose **File | Print**. In the *Pages per sheet* box, select 1 to 16 pages, and click **OK**.

Concepts summary

A *section* is a part of a Word document that can have layout settings – such as page margins, headers and footers, and columns – that are different from the rest of the document. Sections are bounded by *section breaks*.

You are most likely to use section breaks to vary the number of columns on a single page or in a single document, and to interrupt page numbering between a table of contents and the text that follows.

Word provides four section break types: *continuous* (starts the new section on the same page), *next page* (starts the new section on the next page), *even page* (starts the new section on the next even-numbered page), and *odd page* (starts the new section on the next odd-numbered page).

Word's *print options* include the ability to print odd- or even-numbered pages or selections only, and to output multiple copies.

Chapter 26: quick quiz

Circle the correct answer to each of the following multiple-choice questions about sections and print options in Word.

Q1	A section in a Word document is …
A.	The part of a document that contains the cover page and the table of contents.
B.	The part of the document that contains preset formatting and standard content supplied by the document's template.
C.	Any part of the document that can have layout settings that are different from the rest of the document.
D.	Any part of the document that uses text, graphics or other content inserted by the AutoText feature.

Q2	Which of the following actions do you take to insert a section break in a Word document?
A.	Choose **Insert | Break**, select your required section break type, and click **OK**.
B.	Right-click where you want the break to appear, and choose the **New Break** command from the pop-up menu.
C.	Choose **Insert | Section Break**, and click **OK**.
D.	Click the **Insert Section Break** button on the Formatting toolbar, select your required section break type, and click **OK**.

Q3	Which of the following Word features inserts one or more section breaks in a document automatically?
A.	A table of contents.
B.	A multiple column layout applied only to a selected part of a document.
C.	Any table.
D.	None of the above – you must insert section breaks directly.

Q4	In Word, which of the following is not a section break type?
A.	First page.
B.	Odd page.
C.	Next page.
D.	Continuous.

Q5	Which of the following formatting features requires the division of a Word document into sections?
A.	The Chapter heading built-in paragraph style applied to the first paragraph of a document.
B.	Multiple column layouts applied only to a selected part of a document.
C.	A table of contents.
D.	An index.

Q6	Which of the following formatting features, applied to only part of a document, does not require the division of a Word document into sections?
A.	Page border and shading features.
B.	Text and numbering in headers and footers.
C.	Footnotes and endnotes.
D.	An index.

Q7	Which of the following actions do you take to remove a section break from a Word document?
A.	Click anywhere on the section break and choose **Breaks | Delete**.
B.	Switch to Outline view, click the **View Breaks** button, select the section break, and press the **Backspace** or **Delete** key.
C.	Click at the start of the section break and press the **Delete** key.
D.	Right-click on the section break and choose **Breaks | Delete** from the pop-up menu.

Q8	In Word, how does the removal of a section break affect the formatting of the text before the deleted section break?
A.	The formatting after the deleted section break is applied to the text that was before the deleted section break.
B.	The formatting before the deleted section break is applied to the text that was after the deleted section break.
C.	The text reverts to the paragraph styles in the associated document template. Any directly applied formatting is removed.
D.	None of the above – the removal of a section break does not affect document formatting.

Q9	In Word, which of the following is not a print option?
A.	Print odd-numbered pages only.
B.	Print the document template only.
C.	Print even-numbered pages only.
D.	Print the selected part of the document only.

Answers

1: C, **2:** A, **3:** B, **4:** A, **5:** B, **6:** D, **7:** C, **8:** A, **9:** B.

27 Mail merge

Objectives

In this chapter you will learn how to:

- Edit a mail merge data source
- Perform a mail merge with a sorted data source
- Perform a mail merge with a queried data source

New words

In this chapter you will meet the following terms:

- Form letter
- Data source
- Sorting
- Query

Exercise files

In this chapter you will work with the following Word files:

- `Chapter27_Exercise_27-1_Before.doc`
- `Chapter27_Exercise_27-2_Form_Letter_Before.doc`
- `Chapter27_Exercise_27-2_Data_Source.doc`
- `Chapter27_Exercise_27-3_Form_Letter_Before.doc`
- `Chapter27_Exercise_27-3_Data_Source.doc`
- `Chapter27_Exercise_27-4_Form_Letter_Before.doc`
- `Chapter27_Exercise_27-4_Data_Source.doc`

Syllabus reference

In this chapter you will cover the following items from the ECDL Advanced Word Processing Syllabus:

- AM3.5.1.1: Edit a mail merge data source or data file.
- AM3.5.1.2: Sort data source or data file records.
- AM3.5.1.3: Merge a document with a data source or data file using given merge criteria.

About mail merge elements

Word's mail merge feature enables you to generate letters containing personalized details, such as names and addresses, for sending to large numbers of people. Three elements are required for the production of mail merge letters: the form letter, the data source and the merge fields. Let's review each element in turn.

Form letters

A form letter holds the text that remains the same in every letter, plus punctuation, spaces and perhaps graphics. You don't type the personalized details in the form letter, because these will be different on each copy of the final, merged letter.

Form letter

A Word document containing information (text, spaces, punctuation and graphics) that remains the same in each copy of the merged letter.

Data sources

A data source holds the information that changes for each copy of the final, merged letter – the names and addresses of the people that you want to send the merged letters to.

Data sources can be created in Word, or in a spreadsheet (such as Excel) or database (such as Access).

Data source

A file containing information (such as names and addresses) that will be different in each merged copy of the final letter.

Merge fields

Merge fields are special instructions that you insert in your form letter. They tell Word which details you want to merge from your data source, and where Word is to position them in your merged letter.

«FirstName»¶

«Title»·«LastName»,¶

«Company».¶

Merge fields have names such as Job Title, First Name and Town, and are enclosed within double angle brackets. When you merge the form letter and the data source, Word replaces the merge fields in the form letter with the associated details from the data source. For example, Word might replace the merge field called Town with Bristol, Carlisle or Derby on different copies of the merged letter.

Merge field

An instruction to Word to insert a particular type of information, such as job title or a line of an address, in a specified location on the form letter.

About mail merge procedures

You perform mail merge actions with Word's *Mail Merge Helper* dialog box, which is displayed by choosing the **Tools | Mail Merge** command, and with the various buttons on the Mail Merge toolbar.

The Mail Merge Helper *dialog box*

You use this dialog box chiefly for creating new form letters and data sources, or for selecting already-created ones.

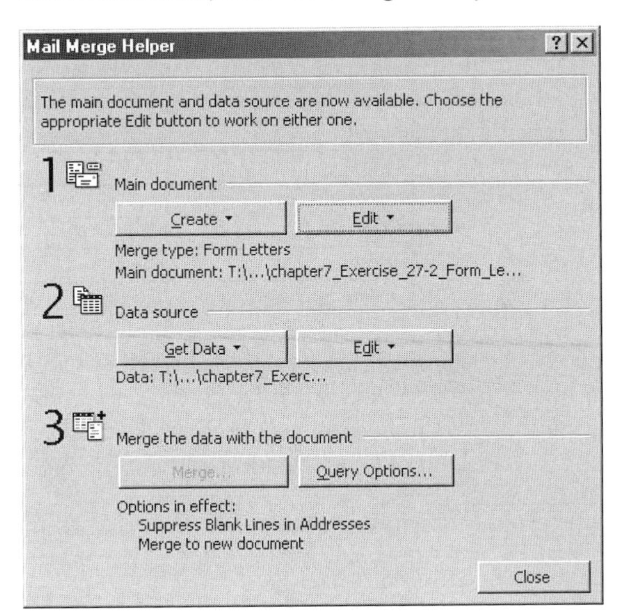

The Mail Merge toolbar

Word displays this toolbar after you create or open a form letter and select a data source. You can use its buttons to insert the merge fields, perform sort and query operations on the data source, and preview merge letters before printing them.

What's advanced about advanced mail merge?

ECDL Advanced Word Processing introduces two new mail merge features, both of which relate to the data source. These are *sorting* and *querying*.

Whichever file type you use as a data source for a mail merge, two conditions apply:

- The data source contents must be arranged in a table, with horizontal rows and vertical coloumns.
- The top row must contain titles identifying the information categories in the columns underneath, such as LastName or PostCode.

Spreadsheets and databases, by nature, can display information in this way. When using a Word document as a data source, you must enter the information in a table, similar to that shown below.

FirstName	LastName	StreetAddress	District	PostCode
Pamela	Connors	59 High Road	Santry	Dublin 9
Margaret	Conroy	12 Crescent Gardens	Tenenure	Dublin 6
Ismail	Corboy	17 Laurel Avenue	Sanymount	Dublin 4
Denis	Collins	29 Sandhills Road	Tallaght	Dublin 24
Derek	Corcoran	33 Beechwood Heights	Drumcondra	Dublin 9
Maurice	Shelbourne	Health Centre	Drumcondra	Dublin 9
Deborah	Cosgrave	The Park Clinic	Santry	Dublin 9
Mary	Costello	63 The Vaults	Thomas Street	Dublin 8
James	Pearce	12 Road	Raheny	Dublin 5
Edward	Lawson	87 Booterstown Avenue	Booterstown	Dublin 4

Each horizontal row, whether in a Word table, a spreadsheet or a database, is referred to as a *record*, and holds details of an individual person. Each vertical column is called a *field*, and holds information of the same type about each person.

Sorting the data source

The order in which records were originally typed into a data source may not be the order in which, later on, you would prefer to generate mail merge letters. The act of rearranging one or more records into a different sequence is called *sorting*.

For example, you could sort records by the LastName field, so that Adams is displayed first, followed by Brown, then Callaghan, Dickens, and so on.

It is particularly useful in mail merges to be able to sort records by postal district, because you can then collate the printed letters in a manner most helpful to your distribution system.

Sorting

Rearranging records in a data source based on the values in one or more fields, with the result that the mail merge letters are printed according to postal district or some other user-chosen sequence.

You learn how to sort a data source in Exercise 27.3.

Querying the data source

Sometimes, you may want to generate mail merge letters for only *some* people in your data source: only those in a certain postal district, for example. Or, if your data source also holds financial information, only for those people with unpaid bills. This is called *querying* the data source.

Querying

Selecting from a data source only those records that meet your chosen criteria, with the result that mail merge letters are generated only for the relevant people.

You learn how to query a data source in Exercise 27.4.

Working with advanced mail merge: the three tasks

Here are the three tasks that you need to be able to perform with mail merge in Word:

- **Edit a mail merge data source**. Exercise 27.1 takes you through the steps of amending a mail merge data source file. The file is a Word document containing a table.
- **Sort records in a data source**. In Exercise 27.3, you sort a data file before generating a mail merge.
- **Merge a form letter with a queried data source**. Exercise 27.4 shows you how to query a data source for printing mail merge letters for selected people only.

Editing a mail merge source

In Exercise 27.1, you will open a mail merge data source file and amend it in the following ways: edit a record, add a new record, and finally delete a record.

Exercise 27.1: Amend a mail merge data source file

1) Start Word and open the following document:

   `Chapter27_Exercise_27-1_Before.doc`

   Your document consists of names and addresses arranged in a table. Each table row corresponds to a record of an individual person's details.

   Your first task is to edit a record.

2) Locate the record containing the details for 'Dennis Collins', and click in the cell containing the first name 'Dennis'. Edit the text to 'Derek'.

Your next task is to add a new record, i.e. a new row, to the Word table.

3) Click anywhere in the bottom row of the table, and choose **Table | Insert I Rows** Below.

In the new row, type the following details:

FirstName	Anne
SecondName	Byrne
StreetAddress	54 Baggot Street
District	Grand Canal
PostCode	Dublin 2

Finally, you will delete a record from the table.

4) Click just to the left of the row containing the name 'EM Gallagher' to select the row. Choose **Table | Delete | Rows**.

5) Save your sample document with the following name, and close it:

`Chapter27_Exercise_27-1_After_`*`Your_Name`*`.doc`

Mail merge: an overview

In Word, mail merging is a five-step process. Let's review each step before continuing further. All steps are available within the **Tools | Mail Merge** command:

1. **Prepare your form letter**. You can open an already-typed letter to use as your form letter, or you can create a new letter as part of the mail merge operation.

2. **Select your data source**. You can select a Word file containing a table or a file created in another software application, such as Microsoft Access or Excel.

3. **Insert merge fields in your form letter**. Using the **Insert Merge Field** button on the Mail Merge toolbar, you can select and then position the merge fields in your form letter.

4. **Preview your merged letters**. Before you produce your merged letters, click on the **View Merged Data** toolbar button to preview the first one or two merged letters.

5. **Print your merged letters**. Happy with the preview? Click the **Mail Merge** toolbar button to perform the complete merge operation. Select the *Merge to printer* option to output copies of your merged letters.

In Exercise 27.2, you will perform a basic mail merge operation. You will use the form letter created and its associated data source as the basis for performing the sorting and querying tasks in Exercises 27.3 and 27.4

Exercise 27.2: Perform a simple mail merge

1) Open the following Word document:

   `Chapter27_Exercise_27-2_Form_Letter_Before`

   This will be the form letter for your mail merge operation.

2) Choose **Tools | Mail Merge**. In the *Main document* area of the *Mail Merge Helper* dialog box, click **Create** and then choose **Form Letters**.

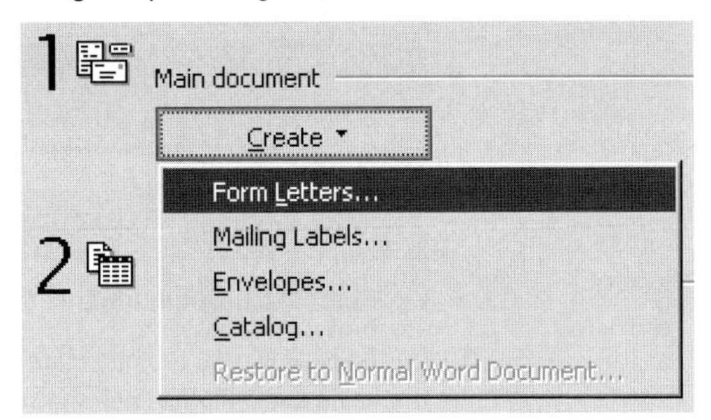

3) In the next dialog box displayed, click **Active Window**.

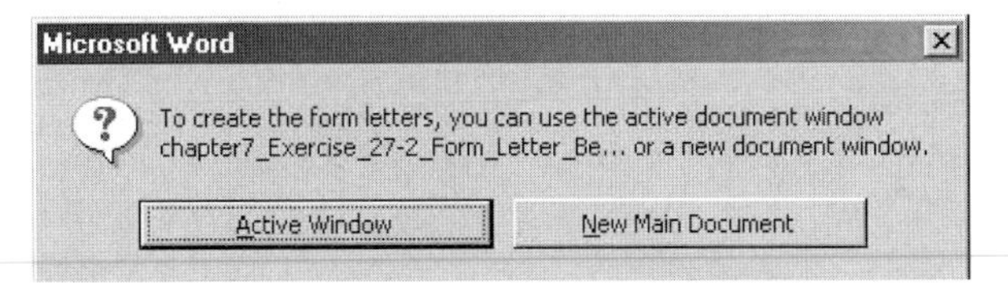

   Word redisplays the *Mail Merge Helper* dialog box.

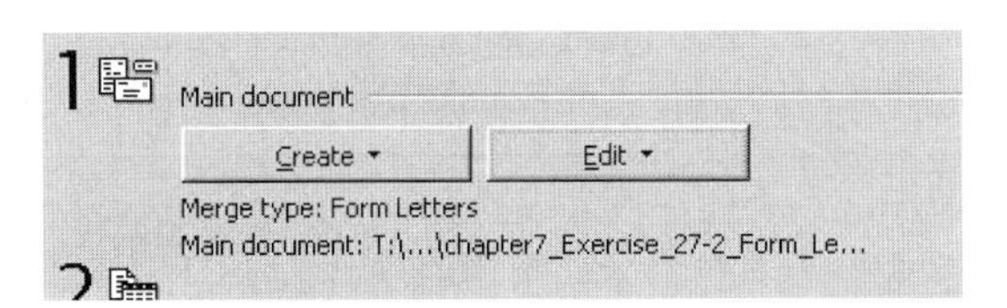

4) In the *Data source* area of the dialog box, click **Get Data**, and then choose **Open Data Source**.

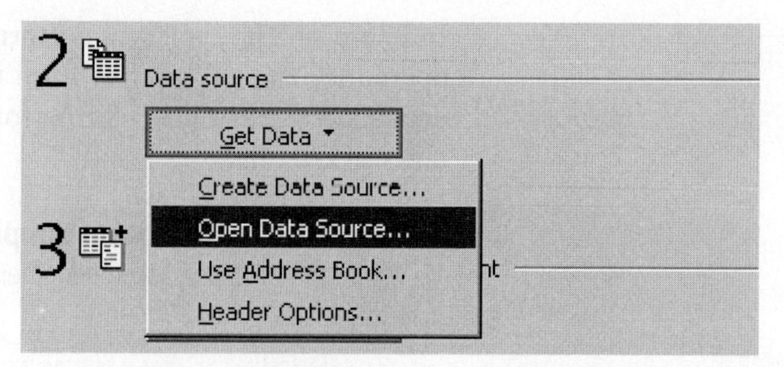

5) Select the following Word document as your data source, and click **Open**:

`Chapter27_Exercise_27-2_Data_Source`

6) Word now displays the following dialog box.

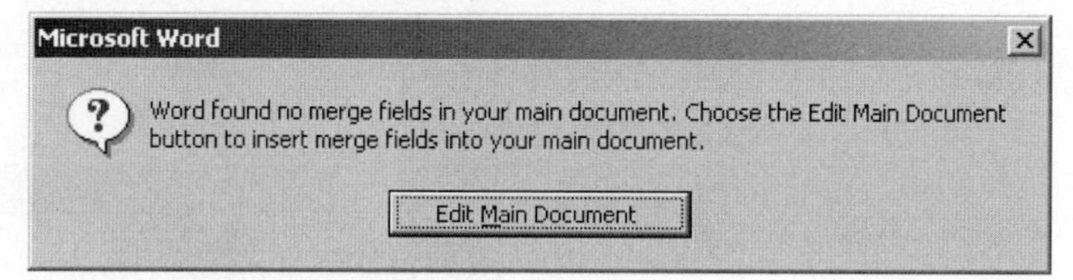

Click **Edit Main Document**, as directed.

7) On the Mail Merge toolbar, click the Insert Merge Field button to view the fields available for merging to your form letter.

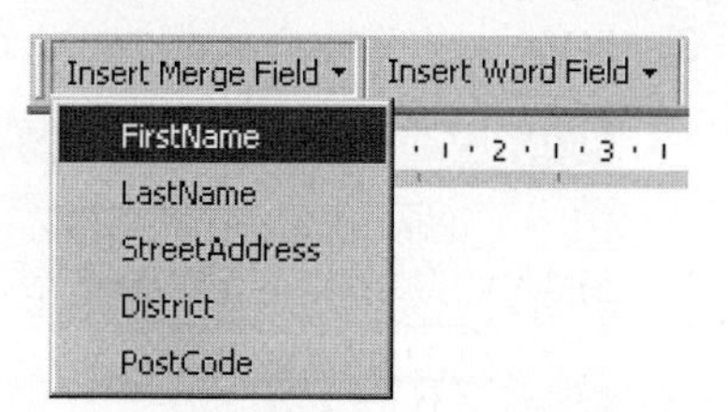

8) For each merge field, place the cursor in the appropriate position in your form letter, click the **Insert Merge Field** button, and click the relevant field title from the drop-down list. Continue until your form letter looks like this:

¶
To: → «FirstName»·«LastName»,¶
→ → «StreetAddress»,¶
→ → «District»,¶
→ → «PostCode».¶
¶
¶
¶
¶
¶
→ → → → → → → → → → 20/11/2001¶
¶
¶
Dear·«FirstName»,¶
¶

Do not forget to type spaces between merge fields just as you would between ordinary text.

Now everything is in place for the mail merge operation.

View Merged Data button

9) Click the **View Merged Data** button on the Mail Merge toolbar. Word displays the first merged letter. It should look like this:

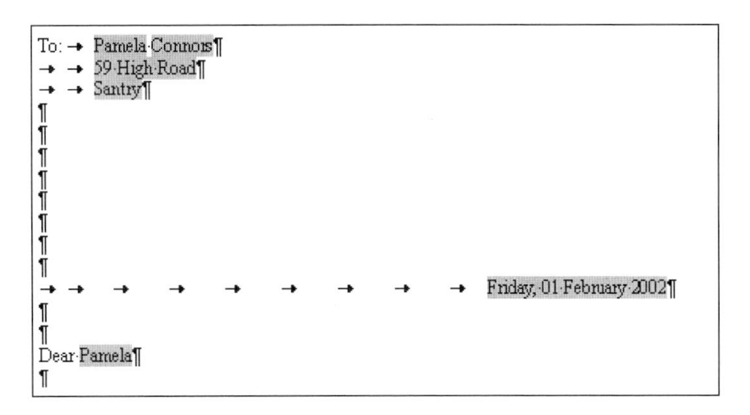

10) You can move forwards and backwards through the merged letters by clicking the **Next Record** and **Previous Record** buttons on the Mail Merge toolbar.

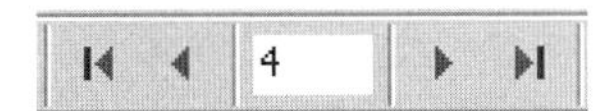

You are now ready to perform the mail merge.

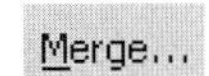

Start Mail Merge button

11) Click the **Start Mail Merge** button on the Mail Merge toolbar to display the *Merge* dialog box.

Select the options as shown below and click **Merge**.

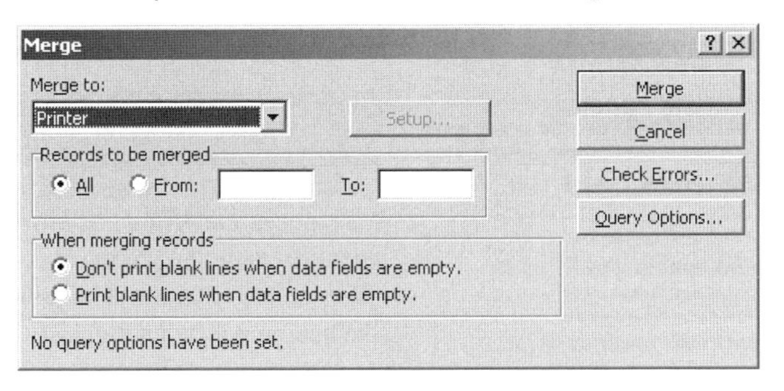

12) Word now displays the *Printer* dialog box. Click **OK** to print your merged letters – or click **Close** to exit from the merge operation without printing.

13) Save your form letter with the following name, and close it:

`Chapter27_Exercise_27-2_Form_Letter_`
`After_`*`Your_Name`*`.doc`

Working with a sorted data source

In Exercise 27.3, you will open a form letter similar to the one that you saved in Exercise 27.2. Like the form letter in the previous exercise, the form letter in Exercise 27.3 is linked to a data source. As a result, Word displays the Mail Merge toolbar when you open the form letter. You will then sort the records in the data source and view how this affects the sequence in which the mail merge letters are printed.

Exercise 27.3: Perform a mail merge from sorted data source

1) Open the following document:

   `Chapter27_Exercise_27-3_Form_Letter_Before.doc`

Start Mail Merge button

2) Click the **Start Mail Merge** button on the Mail Merge toolbar.
3) Click the **Query Options** button on the *Merge* dialog box to display the *Query Options* dialog box, and then click the **Sort Records** tab.
4) Select the *LastName* field in the *Sort by* drop-down list. Accept the default sort order of *Ascending*. Click **OK**.

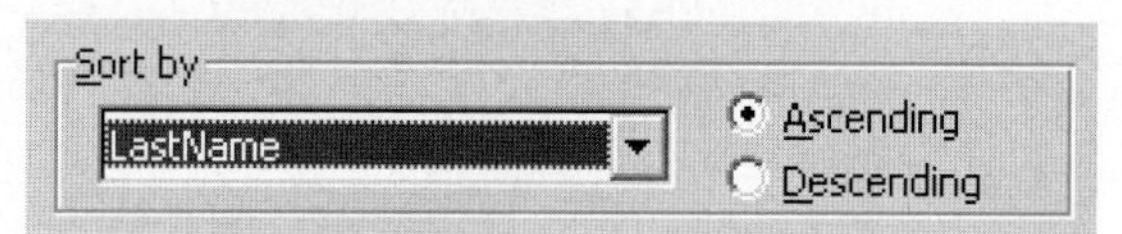

5) Word redisplays the *Merge* dialog box. Click **Close** to close it and return to your form letter.

View Merged Data button

6) Let's inspect the effect of your sort on your mail merge letters. Click the **View Merged Data** button on the Mail Merge toolbar, and then click the **Next Record** and **Previous Record** buttons on the Mail Merge toolbar.

   You can see that Word has arranged the letters in a new, alphabetic sequence according to the recipient's last name. For example, the letter to Anne Byrne will be printed first, and that to Maurice Shelbourne will be printed last.

7) You can now produce the merged letters by clicking the **Start Mail Merge** button on the Mail Merge toolbar to display the *Merge* dialog box, selecting your required options, and, when Word displays the *Printer* dialog box, clicking **OK**.

8) Save your form letter with the following name, and close it:

    Chapter27_Exercise_27-3_Form_Letter_
    After_*Your_Name*.doc

Working with a queried data source

In Exercise 27.4, you will open a form letter that is linked to a data source. As a result, Word displays the Mail Merge toolbar when you open the form letter. You will then query the records in the data source and view how your query limits the number of mail merge letters that will be printed.

Exercise 27.4: Perform a mail merge from a queried data source

1) Open the following Word document:

    Chapter27_Exercise_27-4_Form_Letter_
    Before.doc

Start Mail Merge button

2) Click the **Start Mail Merge** button on the Mail Merge toolbar.
3) Click the **Query Options** button on the *Merge* dialog box to display the **Filter Records** tab.
4) In the *Field* drop-down list, select *LastName*. In the *Comparison* drop-down list, select *Equal to*. In the *Compare to* box, type the name Byrne.

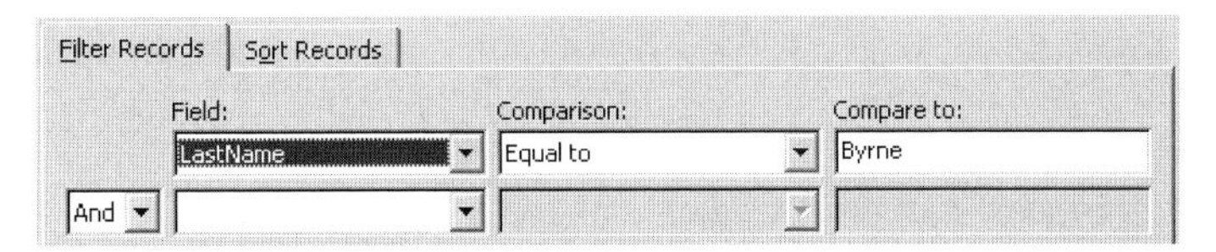

Click **OK** and then **Close** to return to your form letter.

View Merged Data button

5) Let's inspect the effect of your sort on your mail merge letters. Click the **View Merged Data** button on the Mail Merge toolbar, and then click the **Next Record** and **Previous Record** buttons on the Mail Merge toolbar.

6) You can see that Word has created just a single mail merge letter – the letter to Anne Byrne.
7) You can now produce the merged letter by clicking the **Start Mail Merge** button on the Mail Merge toolbar to display the *Merge* dialog box, selecting your required options, and, when Word displays the *Printer* dialog box, clicking **OK**.
8) Save your form letter with the following name, and close it:

    Chapter27_Exercise_27-4_Form_Letter_
    After_*Your_Name*.doc

Chapter 27: quick reference

Tasks summary

Task	Procedure
Perform a mail merge from a sorted data source.	Open a form letter that has a data source associated with it. Click the **Start Mail Merge** button on the Mail Merge toolbar and click the **Sort Records** tab. Select your required field in the *Sort by* drop-down list, accept or amend the sort order, and click **OK** and then **Close**.
Perform a mail merge from a queried source.	Open a form letter that has a data source associated with it. Click the **Start Mail Merge** button on the Mail Merge toolbar. On the **Filter Records** tab, select your required field in the *Field* drop-down list and your required operator in the *Comparison* drop-down list. Type the query text in the *Compare to* box, and click **OK** and then **Close**.

Concepts summary

Mail merge is the process of combining a *form letter* (which holds the unchanging letter text) and a *data source* (which holds the names, addresses and other details that are different in every merged letter).

The data source can be created in Word, in a spreadsheet or in a database. Whichever file type is used, its contents must be arranged in a table, with the top row containing the field titles. *Merge fields* in the form letter indicate which details are taken from the data source, and where they are positioned on the final, merged letter.

You can *sort* the records in a data source to print the mail merge letters in a particular sequence, such as according to postcode. You can also *query* the data source so that Word prints mail merge letters only for selected people.

Chapter 27: quick quiz

Circle the correct answer to each of the following multiple-choice questions about mail merge in Word.

Q1	In Word, which of the following elements is not required to generate mail merge letters?
A.	Merge fields.
B.	Form letter.
C.	Mail merge template.
D.	Data source.

Q2	In Word, which of the following statements about form letters is true?
A.	They may contain text but not graphics.
B.	They can be created in a spreadsheet or database.
C.	They are limited to a single page of text.
D.	They hold the content that remains the same in every letter

Q3	In Word, which of the following statements about mail merge fields is untrue?
A.	They are stored in the mail merge template.
B.	They are enclosed within double angle brackets.
C.	They have names such as JobTitle, FirstName and Town.
D.	They tell Word which details to merge from the data source.

Q4	In Word, which of the following statements about data sources is untrue?
A.	Their contents must be arranged in a table.
B.	A spreadsheet or database file can be used as a data source.
C.	They contain records regarding the people who are to receive the merged letters.
D.	They are enclosed within double angle brackets.

Q5	In a mail merge operation in Word, which of the following tasks would you perform first?
A.	Select the data source.
B.	Open an already-typed letter to use as your form letter.
C.	Sort and/or query the data source.
D.	Insert the merge fields.

Q6	Which of the following toolbar buttons would you click to preview mail merge letters before printing them?
A.	Merge...
B.	«» ABC
C.	
D.	

Q7	In Word, what effect does sorting records in the data source have on the mail merge letters?
A.	It enables more than one data source to be used in printing the letters.
B.	It restricts the number of letters printed according to the user-selected sort criteria.
C.	It changes the sequence in which the letters are produced by the printer.
D.	None of the above.

Q8	In Word, what effect does querying the records in the data source have on the mail merge letters?
A.	It restricts the number of letters printed according to the user-specified query criteria.
B.	It changes the sequence in which the letters are produced by the printer.
C.	It enables multiple data sources to be used in printing the letters.
D.	None of the above.

Answers

1: C, **2:** D, **3:** A, **4:** D, **5:** B, **6:** B, **7:** C, **8:** A.

Index

ECDL Advanced Spreadsheets

Sharon Murphy
and Paul Holden

ECDL Advanced Approved
Courseware Syllabus AM3 Version 1.0

Harlow, England • London • New York • Boston • San Francisco • Toronto • Sydney • Singapore • Hong Kong
Tokyo • Seoul • Taipei • New Delhi • Cape Town • Madrid • Mexico City • Amsterdam • Munich • Paris • Milan

Preface

What is ECDL?

ECDL, or the European Computer Driving Licence, is an internationally recognized qualification in information technology skills. It is accepted by businesses internationally as a verification of competence and proficiency in computer skills.

The ECDL syllabus is neither operating system nor software specific.

For more information about ECDL, and to see the syllabus for *ECDL Module 4, Spreadsheets, Advanced Level*, visit the official ECDL website at www.ecdl.com.

About this book

This book covers the ECDL Advanced Spreadsheets syllabus Version 1.0, using Excel 2000 to complete all the required tasks. It is assumed that you have already completed the spreadsheets module of ECDL 3 using Excel, or you have an equivalent knowledge of the product.

The chapters in this book are intended to be read sequentially. Each chapter assumes that you have read and understood the information in the preceding chapters.

Each exercise in the book builds on the results of previous exercises. The exercises should be completed in order.

Additional exercises, labelled *Over to you*, have been posed for you to complete. These exercises provide limited guidance as to how to go about performing the tasks, since you should have learned what you need in the preceding exercises. Some of these exercises are marked as mandatory and others as optional. The changes you make in the mandatory exercises are used in later exercises in the book.

Hardware and software requirements

Your PC should meet the following specifications:

- Pentium 75 MHz or higher processor.
- Windows 95 or later.
- 22 MB RAM if you are running Excel on Windows 95 or 98, or 36 MB RAM on later versions of Windows.
- CD-ROM drive.
- 500 KB of free space on your hard disk.
- Excel 2000.
- Microsoft Query.
- Word 2000.

Typographic conventions

The following typographic conventions are used in this book:

Bold text is used to denote command names, button names, menu names, the names of tabs in dialog boxes, and keyboard keys.

Italicized text is used to denote cross-references within the book, as well as field names, options in drop-down lists and list boxes, dialog box names, areas in dialog boxes, toolbars, cells in spreadsheets, and text entered in cells and fields.

ARIAL NARROW TEXT is used to denote the names of folders and files, and, when italicized, the names of worksheets in Excel workbooks.

Contents

Chapter 12: Customizing charts *103*

Chapter 13: Using statistical and database functions *117*

Chapter 14: Using financial functions *125*

1 Introduction

The case study

The exercises in this book relate to the spreadsheets used by a fictitious company, Murphy's Flatpack Furniture, or MFPF.

MFPF is a family-run business, producing a range of flatpack furniture. The current range includes five indoor pieces (bed, wardrobe, chest of drawers, coffee table and kitchen organizer), and two outdoor pieces (garden chair and garden table).

MFPF sells furniture to six retailers: three in Cullenstown, where MFPF is based, and three in neighbouring villages.

Mr and Mrs Murphy are not salaried, but they retain any profits made by the business. Their daughter works in the warehouse and receives a monthly salary.

Regular business expenses are materials, warehouse rental, petrol, electricity and telephone.

You have just been hired as a bookkeeper for the business. Your duties include looking after invoices, maintaining records on the financial transactions of the business, and producing reports, summaries and forecasts when requested.

The CD

The CD supplied with this book contains the following files:

- DELIVERY_COSTS.TXT – a delimited text file that lists the road distance to each customer and the delivery charge applied to their orders.
- INVOICE_MFPF.XLT – an Excel template for sales invoices.
- LETTER.DOC – the start of a letter to the local bank manager, in relation to a business loan.
- LOGO.GIF – MFPF's company logo.
- MFPF_FINANCE.XLS – the start of a spreadsheet used to track the business's annual incomings, outgoings and profits.

- MFPF_ORD.MDB – an Access database containing details of MFPF's customers and all the orders they placed in 2000.
- OUTGOING.TXT – a delimited text file that lists the monthly costs of regular business expenses.
- PASTE_SPECIAL.XLS – a spreadsheet containing an assortment of miscellaneous information.
- PRICES.TXT – a delimited text file listing the costs of materials for each furniture type produced, and the price at which the finished products are sold.

You will use these files when completing the exercises in the book.

Before you start

Before you begin working through the exercises in this book, you will need to copy the files from the CD to your computer.

Copying files from the CD

In the following exercise, you will copy the INVOICE_MFPF.XLT template to Excel's templates folder, then create a working folder to which you will copy the remainder of the files from the CD.

Exercise 1.1: Copying files from the CD to your computer

1) Copy the Excel template INVOICE_MFPF.XLT from the CD to the following folder:
   Application Data\Microsoft\Templates
   Where this folder is located will depend on how your computer has been set up.
2) Create a folder called ECDL_EXCEL anywhere on your computer. This will be your working folder for the exercises in this book.
3) Copy all the other files from the disk to the ECDL_EXCEL folder.

Turning off adaptive menus

Excel's adaptive menus show the commands you have used most recently first. Since the exercises in this book require less commonly used commands, you should turn off adaptive menus before you start.

Exercise 1.2: Turning off adaptive menus

1) Start Excel.
2) Select **View | Toolbars | Customize ...** .
   The *Customize* dialog box opens.
3) Click the **Options** tab.
4) Uncheck the box beside *Menus show recently used commands first* and click **Close**.

2 Using Templates in Excel

In this chapter

Every time you create a new spreadsheet in Excel, you base it on a template.

In this chapter you will learn about templates in Excel: what they are, what information they contain, and how to use them. You will also learn how to edit templates, and how to create templates of your own.

New skills

At the end of this chapter you should be able to:

- Explain what a template is
- Explain why you would want to use a template
- Give examples of the type of information that can be stored in a template
- Find Excel templates on your PC
- Create spreadsheets from templates
- Create and edit templates

New words

At the end of this chapter you should be able to explain the following terms:

- Template
- Boilerplate text

Creating spreadsheets from templates

Every time you create a new spreadsheet in Excel, you use a template that defines the default settings and content for the spreadsheet.

Template
In Excel, a template is a type of spreadsheet that contains default information and settings, and is used to create new spreadsheets with the same look and feel. Excel templates have the file extension .xlt.

Even the 'empty' workbook that opens by default when you start Excel is based on a template. The template contains no text or numeric data, but it does have default layout and style content.

Start Excel and have a closer look at the default workbook that opens.

Normally, the default workbook contains three worksheets. (The default may have been changed on your computer.) Each worksheet has 256 columns and 65,536 rows. Every column has a standard width; every row has a standard height. The font in every cell is Arial 10 point. All of this is defined by the default template.

Most templates you use in Excel contain default text, such as row and column labels, which is included in every new spreadsheet generated from the template. This text is known as boilerplate text.

Boilerplate text
Default text included in a template is called boilerplate text. It is added to every spreadsheet created from that template.

Templates can also contain layout and style formatting, numbers, formulae, macros, charts and any other type of information or setting that can be added to a spreadsheet in Excel.

Using a template to generate a particular type of spreadsheet that you use regularly can save you a lot of time and effort. Only the case-specific data will need to be added each time.

Creating an invoice from a template

Mr Murphy has given you your first task for Murphy's Flatpack Furniture. He wants you to issue an invoice to a customer, using Excel. The invoice should indicate who has issued it and when, who it was issued to, and what goods were ordered and how much they cost. MFPF will keep an electronic copy of the invoice for its own records and print out a copy to send to the customer.

To create the invoice, you could start with the default workbook and add labels and numbers for the required details, and then apply formatting before printing it and sending it to the customer. Fortunately, though, there's an invoice template available with all the default information already there.

> **Note:** If you didn't complete *Exercise 1.1* on page 2 you should go back and do it now. The exercises use files supplied on the disk that comes with the book. These files must be in specific locations before you start.

Exercise 2.1: Creating a spreadsheet from a template

1) Start Excel, if it is not already open.
2) Select **File | New ...**
   The *New* dialog box opens.
3) Click the **General** tab.
   A list of available templates is shown.

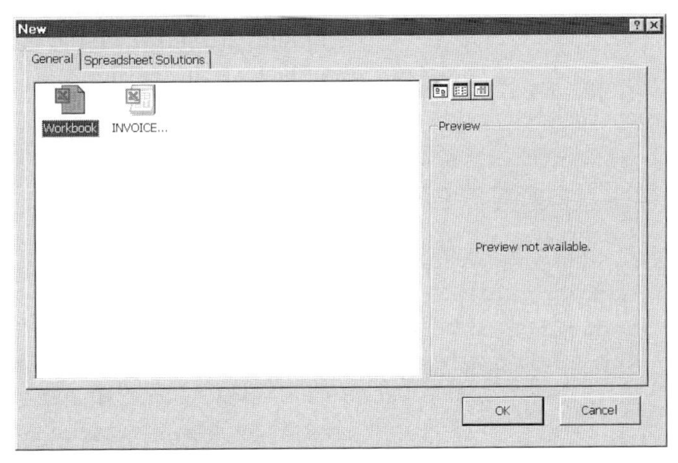

4) Select INVOICE_MFPF.XLT and click **OK**.
   A new spreadsheet opens.
   This spreadsheet contains all the default information and settings defined by the template.
   To write an invoice, you just need to fill in the blanks.

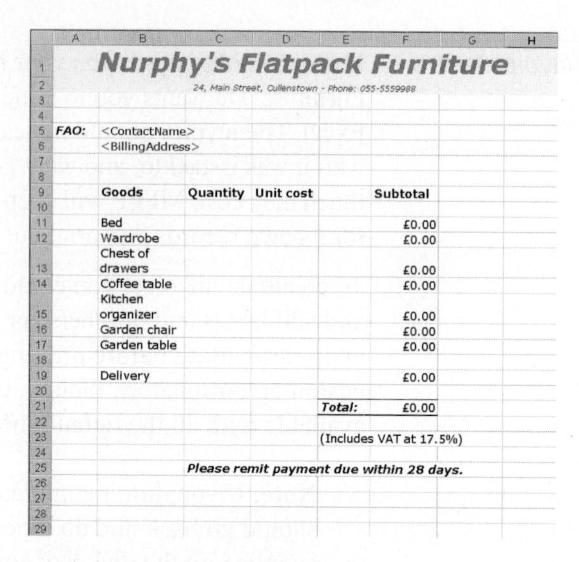

A B C D E F G H
Nurphy's Flatpack Furniture
24, Main Street, Cullenstown - Phone: 055-5559988
FAO: <ContactName>
<BillingAddress>
Goods Quantity Unit cost Subtotal
Bed £0.00
Wardrobe £0.00
Chest of drawers £0.00
Coffee table £0.00
Kitchen organizer £0.00
Garden chair £0.00
Garden table £0.00
Delivery £0.00
Total: £0.00
(Includes VAT at 17.5%)
Please remit payment due within 28 days.

Save button 

5) Select **File | Save**, or click the **Save** button on the *Standard* toolbar. The *Save As* dialog box opens.

6) Name the spreadsheet INVOICE1.XLS, and save it in your working folder, ECDL_EXCEL.

Over to you: optional

Next, you will look at some more templates.

The *New* dialog box lists all the templates available on your computer. The **Spreadsheet Solutions** tab contains four templates that have been provided by Microsoft. All other templates are shown on the **General** tab. *Workbook* is the default template we saw earlier.

- Open the other templates on your computer and see what information and settings they contain. Try to think of other spreadsheet templates you might find useful.

Creating templates

You can create a new template by adding the default information and settings you want in the template to a spreadsheet, and then saving the spreadsheet as a template using **File | Save as ...** .

When you save a spreadsheet as a template, Excel automatically changes the file extension to .XLT and opens the correct folder for saving Excel templates.

You can add templates to the **General** tab of the *New* dialog box by putting Excel template files in any of these folders:

- C:\<OS>\PROFILES\<USERNAME>\APPLICATIONDATA\MICROSOFT\TEMPLATES
- C:\<OS>\PROFILES\<USERNAME>\APPLICATIONDATA\MICROSOFT\EXCEL\XLSTART
- The folder specified in the *Default file location* field on the **General** tab of the dialog box opened by selecting **Tools | Options ...** .

In the first two of these, <OS> should be replaced by the name of the operating system you are running, for example WINNT, and <USERNAME> should be replaced by your username on the computer.

Editing templates

There are two ways to edit an existing template:

- Select **File | Open ...** , locate the template, edit it directly, and save your results.
  – or –
- Select **File | New ...** , create a new spreadsheet based on the template, make changes to the spreadsheet, then save it as a template, using the name of the existing template.

The second option is preferable, because if you decide at any point that you are not happy with your changes, you still have the original template and have not lost any work.

Editing a template

There are some problems with the invoice template you used earlier. There is a typo in the company name on the first page, and despite a request that the invoice be paid within 28 days there is nowhere to indicate what date it was issued!

In the following exercise, you will create a spreadsheet from the invoice template, edit the spreadsheet to fix these problems and make some other formatting changes, and then save it as a template, replacing the original INVOICE_MFPF.XLT.

Exercise 2.2: Editing a template

1) Create a new spreadsheet based on the invoice template.
2) Select **File | Save**, or click the **Save** button on the *Standard* toolbar.
3) Name your file INVOICE_MFPF.XLS and save it in the ECDL_EXCEL folder.
4) Make the following changes to the spreadsheet:
   - On the **Customer Invoice** worksheet, fix the typo in the spelling of *Murphy*.
   - Increase the font size for the invoice total in cell *F21* to 12 point.
   - Decrease the font size for the list of goods in cell range *B11:B19* to 10 point.
   - The invoice should be paid within 28 days, but the issue date is not indicated anywhere. Enter the label *Date*: in cell *E5*, and format it as bold italic.
5) Save your workbook when you are done.
6) Select **File | Save as ...** , and select *Template (*.xlt)* from the *Save* as *type* drop-down list.
   Excel changes the file extension and automatically opens the TEMPLATES folder.
7) Select the existing INVOICE_MFPF.XLT to replace it, and click **Save**.
   A dialog box appears, asking you to confirm that you want to replace the existing INVOICE_MFPF.XLT.
8) Click **Yes**.

Congratulations! You just saved your first template. Just think about how much time and energy you will save in the future when you have created templates for all of the spreadsheets you use regularly.

Over to you: optional

To see that your changes are now part of the invoice template, you will create a new spreadsheet based on the template.

- Create a new spreadsheet based on INVOICE_MFPF.XLT. Check that the changes you made in *Exercise 2.2* on page 10 are now part of the default information in the template. Close Excel when you are finished.

Chapter summary

In Excel, a template is a type of spreadsheet that contains default information and settings, and is used to create new spreadsheets with the same look and feel. Excel templates have the file extension .xlt.

Templates can contain any type of information or setting that can be added to a spreadsheet in Excel, including text, layout and style formatting, numbers, formulae, macros and charts.

Default text included in a template is called boilerplate text. It is added to every spreadsheet created from that template.

3 Importing Data into a Spreadsheet

In this chapter

From time to time, you may find that you want to reuse all or same of the data from another source in an Excel spreadsheet.

For example, you might want to reuse a list of staff members from a telephone list as row labels in a worksheet where you will calculate your annual salary budget. Or you might want to include petty cash records from a database in your expenses calculations.

Excel's data import facility allows you to import all or part of the data in a delimited text file or a database into a spreadsheet. In this chapter you will learn how to import data from delimited text files and from an Access database into Excel.

New skills

At the end of this chapter you should be able to:

- Import data from delimited text files
- Import data from a database using a query
- Run a saved database query
- Edit a database query
- Add filter and sort requirements to a database query

New words

At the end of this chapter you should be able to explain the following terms:

- Delimited text file
- Text qualifier
- Query
- Criteria
- Filter

Importing data from an external source

In ECDL 3 you imported objects created in other programs into Excel spreadsheets. These objects included images and text files.

You can also choose to import text from an external source and include it in the cells of an Excel spreadsheet. These data can then be formatted, manipulated and used in formulae, just like any other data in Excel.

When you import data from an external source, Excel remembers which file or database you imported your data from, and the setting you used to import it. If the data in the source file change, you can update the imported data in Excel by selecting the imported data, and then selecting **Data | Refresh Data** or clicking the **Refresh Data** button on the *External Data* toolbar.

Refresh Data button

If you cannot see the *External Data* toolbar, you can turn it on by selecting **View | Toolbars | External Data**.

Importing data from text files

When you import data from a text file, the text file will usually be formatted in rows and columns. You can use Excel's *Text Import Wizard* to specify how the data have been formatted, so that you can preserve the row and column structure when you import the data into Excel.

Structured text files

When importing structured text files, Excel treats each new line as a row. Excel recognizes two different ways that columns can be represented:

- The columns can be *delimited*, which means that a particular character or set of characters is used to indicate where one column stops and the next begins.
- The columns can be structured with a *fixed width*, which means that a number of tabs and spaces, or a combination of the two, is used to make all the entries in a column line up.

Delimited text file

A text file in which columns of information are separated from each other by a particular character or set of characters is known as a delimited text file.

Text qualifiers

If any of the data elements in your delimited text file contain the character that has been used as a delimiter, you can use a text qualifier to mark the beginning and end of the data element. The *Text Import Wizard* ignores any delimiter characters that appear between a pair of text qualifiers.

Text qualifier

A character used to mark the beginning and end of a data element in a delimited text file. Usually, single or double quotation marks are used as text qualifiers.

Importing delimited text files

Mrs Murphy has asked you to import data about MFPF's business expenses from three delimited text files into spreadsheets, where the data can be used in calculations of monthly running costs.

The three files are:

- OUTGOING.TXT, which is space-delimited and shows the regular expenses incurred by the business every month.
- PRICES.TXT, which is tab-delimited and shows the cost of the materials for each type of furniture produced by the business, and the wholesale price for which they are sold.
- DELIVERY_COSTS.TXT, which is comma-delimited and shows the distance to each customer's premises, and the delivery charge for each order.

Each file uses double quotation marks as text qualifiers.

In the next exercise, you will import the first of these files into the MFPF_FINANCE.XLS spreadsheet.

Exercise 3.1: Importing a space-delimited text file

1) Open the spreadsheet MFPF_FINANCE.XLS.

2) Select **Data | Get External Data | Import Text File ...** .
   The *Import Text File* dialog box opens.

3) Select outgoing.txt in your working folder and click **Import**.
   The *Text Import Wizard* opens.

4) Indicate that your data are *Delimited*, and that you want to *Start import at row 1*.
   Click **Next**.

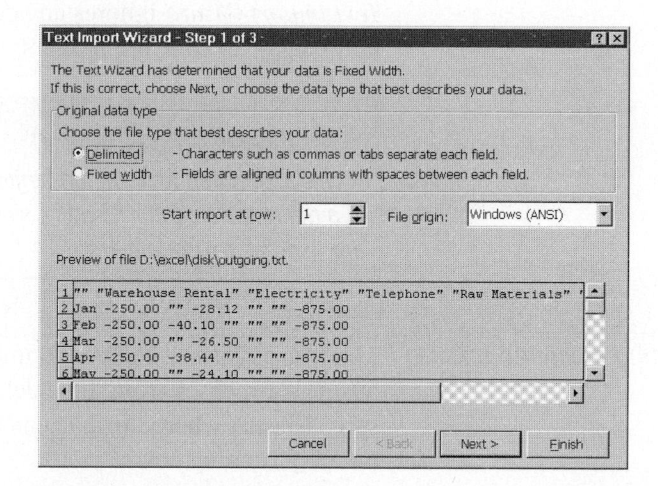

5) The file you are importing is space-delimited, so in the *Delimiters* area on the dialog box that now appears, check the box beside *Space.*

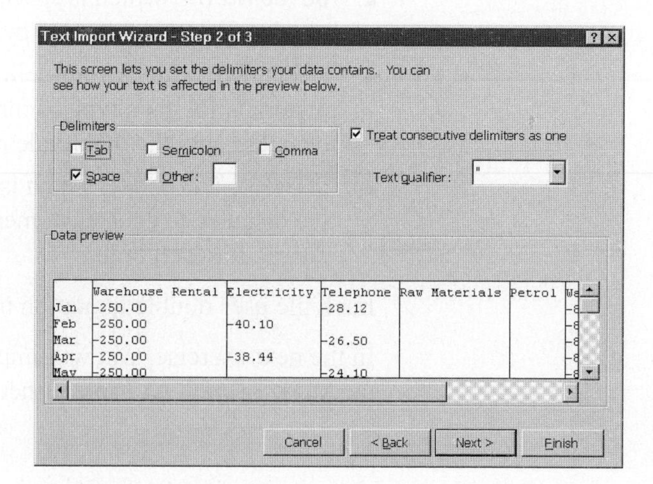

In the *Text qualifier* field, select the double quotation mark.
Click **Next**.

6) In the *Column data format* area, you can specify a format for the column selected in the *Data preview* area, or select *Do not import column* to skip the column when importing.

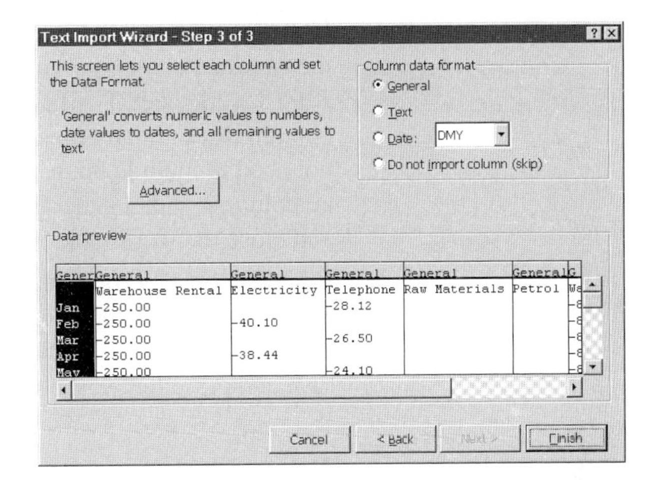

To select a column, click anywhere in it in the *Data preview* area of the dialog box.
In this case, you will import all the columns with a *General* format.
Click **Finish**.
The *Import Data* dialog box opens.

7) Specify that you want to add the data to the *OUTGOING* worksheet, in the cell range starting in cell *A1*.
Either enter the details below manually, or open the *OUTGOING* worksheet and click in cell *A1* to automatically add the correct cell reference to the *Existing worksheet* field of the *Import Data* dialog box.

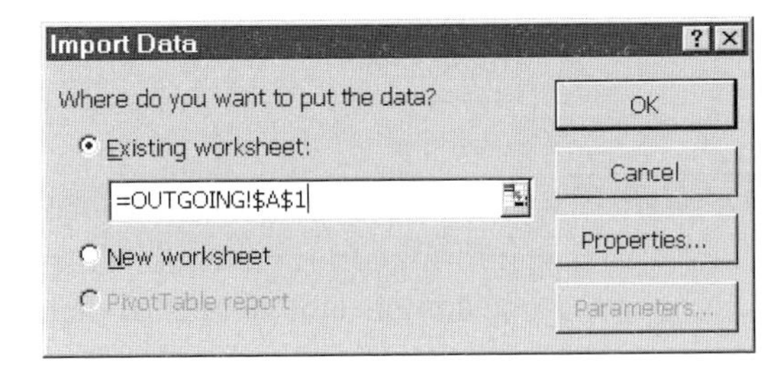

Click **OK**.
The data from the text file are added to the *OUTGOING* worksheet.

8) Save your workbook.

Well done! You have just imported a year's worth of expenses information from a space-delimited text file into a spreadsheet in a matter of minutes.

Over to you: mandatory

Next, you will import the other two delimited text files into other worksheets.

- Import the data from PRICES.TXT into MFPF_FINANCE.XLS. Add the data in a cell range starting at cell *A15* on the *SALES TOTALS* worksheet. The first row in PRICES.TXT contains the column titles already present on this worksheet, so you do not need to include them: start your import at row *2*. Import all columns with a general format. When you are done, save and close the workbook.
- Create a new workbook called DELIVERIES.XLS based on the default template. Rename one of the worksheets *CHARGES* and import DELIVERY_COSTS.TXT into it. When you are done, save and close the workbook.

Querying a database from Excel

You have successfully imported data from a variety of delimited text files. Next, you will learn how to import data from a database.

To import data from a database, you create a query that specifies the information you want. Then you run the query, and put the results in your Excel spreadsheet.

Query

A query is a set of rules that specifies what records, or parts of records, to retrieve from a database, and how to display those data.

Creating a simple query

The Access database MFPF_ORD.MDB contains contact information for each of Murphy's Flatpack Furniture's customers, and details of their orders for the year 2000.

You have been asked to import from the database only those columns that indicate the date of an order, the company that made the order, the town it is based in, and how many units of each type of furniture it ordered.

In the next exercise, you will create a simple query to import the specified columns from MFPF_ORD.MDB. You will also save the query you create so that you can run it again later.

Exercise 3.2: Creating a simple database query in Excel

1) Create a new workbook called MFPF_ORD.XLS, based on the default template, and rename the first worksheet *COMPLETE*.

2) Select **Data | Get External Data | New Database Query ...** .
The *Choose Data Source* dialog box opens.

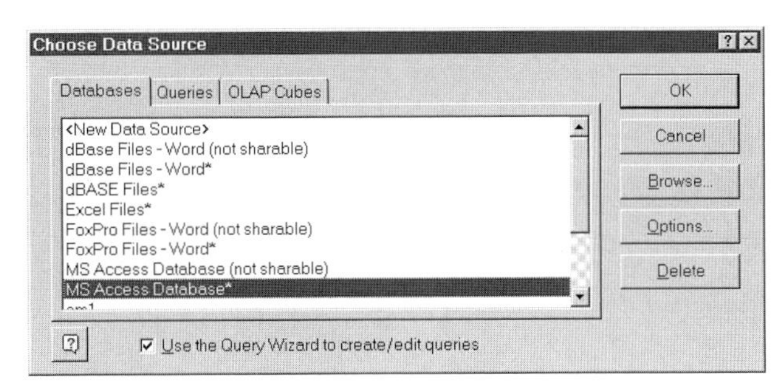

3) Select *MS Access Database** from the list of databases.
Make sure the box beside *Use the Query Wizard to create/edit queries* is checked, then click **OK**.
The *Select Database* dialog box opens.

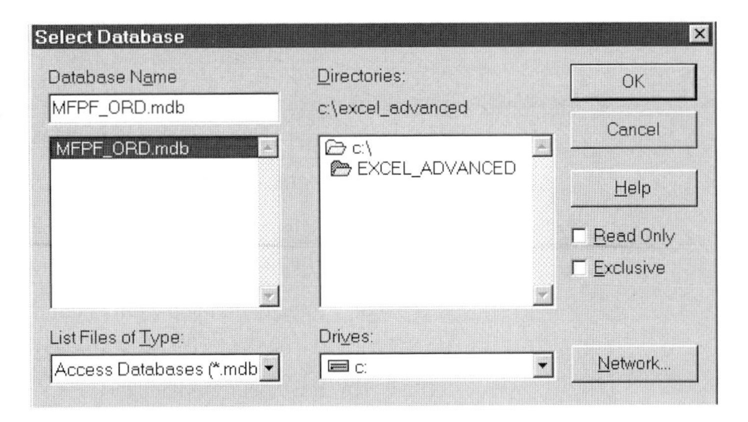

4) Select the MFPF_ORD.MDB database in your working folder.
If your working folder is not on the C drive, you will need to select the correct drive in the *Drives* field first.
Click **OK**.

The *Query Wizard – Choose Columns* dialog box opens.

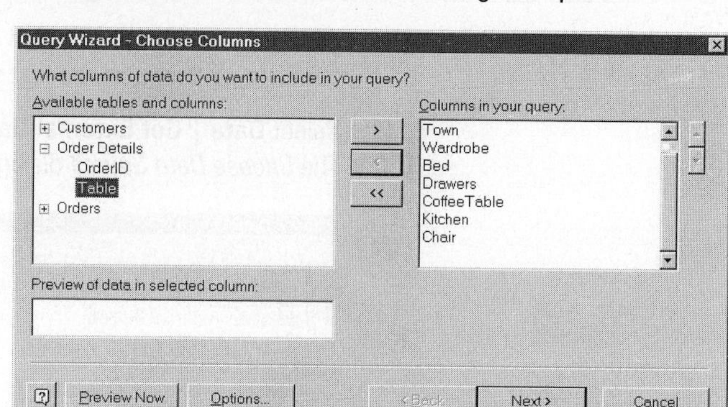

5) Select the following columns in this order:
   - *OrderDate* from the *Orders* table.
   - *CompanyName* and *Town* from the *Customers* table.
   - *Wardrobe, Bed, Drawers, CoffeeTable, Kitchen, Chair* and *Table* from the *Order Details* table.

   Keep clicking **Next** until you get to the *Query Wizard – Finish* dialog box.
6) Select **Save Query ...** .
   The *Save As* dialog box opens.
7) Name the query *MFPF_Q1.DQY* and click **Save**.
8) Select *Return Data to Microsoft Excel* and click **Finish**.
   The *Returning External Data to Microsoft Excel* dialog box opens.
9) Specify that you want to put the data in the cell range beginning in cell *A1* on the *COMPLETE* worksheet, and click **OK**.
10) Save your workbook.

Over to you: mandatory

Next, you will create a query to retrieve the columns that indicate the order date and company name for each order placed. These details will be used later to calculate delivery charges and petrol costs for each order.

- Open DELIVERIES.XLS and create a query that retrieves from MFPF_ORD.MDB the following columns (in order): *DeliveryDate* and *CompanyName* from the *Orders* table. Add the results to a new worksheet. Name the new worksheet *DELIVERIES*.

When you are done, save and close the workbook.

Using filter and sort in a database query

When you import data from delimited text files, you choose which columns to include, and at which row to start the import.

When you import data from a database, you have much more control over which rows (or records) to include. You can specify a set of criteria that the records you import should satisfy.

Criteria
Criteria are rules that specify what records are imported, based on the value in a particular field.

For example, you could use criteria to indicate that the value in a particular field must match exactly a specified value.

Criteria are combined together to create a filter.

Filter
A filter limits the records imported from a database to those that satisfy a set of criteria.

You can even sort the records before importing them into your spreadsheet.

Running a saved query

Mrs Murphy has asked you to add two more worksheets to the MFPF_ORD.XLS workbook. The first should show order details for outdoor furniture (garden chairs and garden tables). The second should show details for indoor furniture (bed, wardrobe, chest of drawers, coffee table and kitchen organizer).

Additionally, she only wants to see the records for sales to customers in Cullenstown on each of these sheets.

In the next exercise, you will run the query you saved earlier to import order records into a new worksheet.

Exercise 3.3: Running a saved query

1) Open MFPF_ORD.XLS, and name one of the empty worksheets *INDOOR*.
2) Select **Data | Get External Data | Run Saved Query ...** . The *Run Query* dialog box opens.
3) Select *MFPF_Q1.DQY* (the query you saved earlier) and click **Get Data.**
   The *Returning External Data to Microsoft Excel* dialog box opens.
4) Specify that you want to put the data in the cell range beginning in cell *A1* on the *INDOOR* worksheet and click **OK**.
5) Save your workbook.

The *INDOOR* worksheet now contains the same information you imported into the *COMPLETE* worksheet when you first created and ran the MFPF_Q1.DQY query.

Editing queries

In the next exercise, you will edit the query to import information about sales of indoor furniture only. You will also add a filter so that only records relating to customers in Cullenstown are imported. Finally, just to make the results easier to read, you will sort the records in reverse chronological order, so that the most recent orders appear first.

> **Note:** You will not save the changes you make to the query, so the next time you run it, the results will be unfiltered and unsorted, as before.

Exercise 3.4: Editing a query

Edit Query ... button

1) Select any cell in the range that contains the imported data, and select **Data | Get External Data | Edit Query ...** , or click the **Edit Query ...** button on the *External Data* toolbar.
   If you cannot see the *External Data* toolbar, open it by selecting **View | Toolbars | External Data**.
2) Remove the columns for the sales of *Chairs* and *Tables*.
   Click **Next**.

The *Query Wizard – Filter Data* dialog box opens.

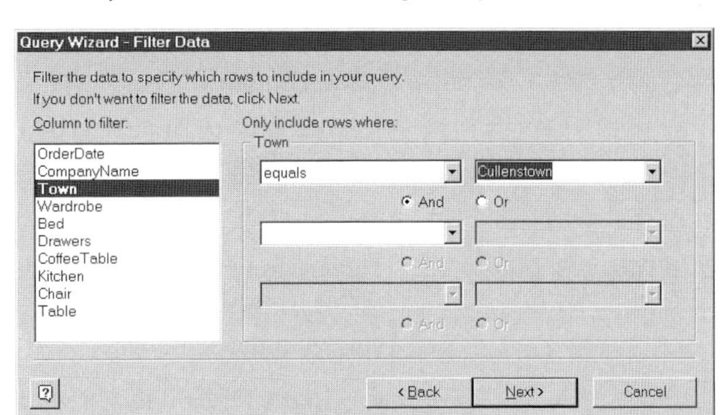

3) In this dialog box, you will create a filter to limit the records returned by the query to those related to orders from customers in Cullenstown.
Select *Town* in the *Column to filter* list box, then select *equals* and *Cullenstown* in the *Only include rows where* area.
This is a criterion in your filter.
You could add any number of other criteria to *Town* and other columns in this dialog box, if you wanted to.
You can combine the criteria for a single column using either logical AND or logical OR.
The filter requirements for different columns are combined using logical AND. This means that for a record to get through the filter, it should satisfy the filter requirements you set for each column.

4) Click **Next**.
The *Query Wizard – Sort Order* dialog box opens.

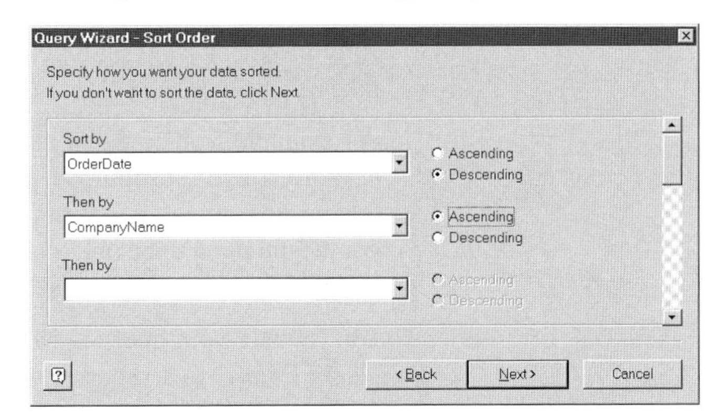

5) Sort by *OrderDate Descending* to see the most recent sales first.
Then select *CompanyName Ascending*, so that if more than one sale was made on the same date, the sales for that date will be listed alphabetically by customer.
Click **Next**.

6) Select *Return Data to Microsoft Excel* and click **Finish**.

7) Save your workbook.

Well done! You've accomplished a lot this time. You have learned how to run a saved query, how to edit that query, and how to use filter and sort when querying.

Over to you: mandatory

Next, you will filter the results from the saved query MFPF_Q1.DQY to show results for outdoor furniture, filtered and sorted in the same way.

- In the MFPF_ORD.XLS workbook, create a worksheet called *OUTDOOR*.
- Run the saved query MFPF_Q1.DQY and put the results on the *OUTDOOR* worksheet, starting in cell *A1*.
- Edit the query to show records for outdoor furniture sold in Cullenstown only, sorted in reverse chronological order.
- Save your workbook.

Advanced querying

Looking at the query results on the *INDOOR* and *OUTDOOR* worksheets, you can see that there are rows where none of the specified types of furniture were sold. These records are not really of any interest, but there is no way to filter them out using the *Query Wizard*.

Although you can combine the criteria for a given column using logical AND or logical OR, the sets of criteria for different columns are always combined using logical AND in the *Query Wizard*.

For example, you could create a filter to find orders where one or more of every furniture type was ordered, but not one where one or more of any one furniture type was ordered. To do that, you would need to be able to combine column filters using logical OR.

You can edit your query in Microsoft Query, instead of in the *Query Wizard*, to set more complex filters, using both logical AND and logical OR to combine all of your criteria, regardless of which columns they refer to.

Filters in Microsoft Query

In Microsoft Query, criteria are combined using logical AND and logical OR to create a set of distinct filter requirements.

Here is an example of how a set of filter requirements is represented in Microsoft Query:

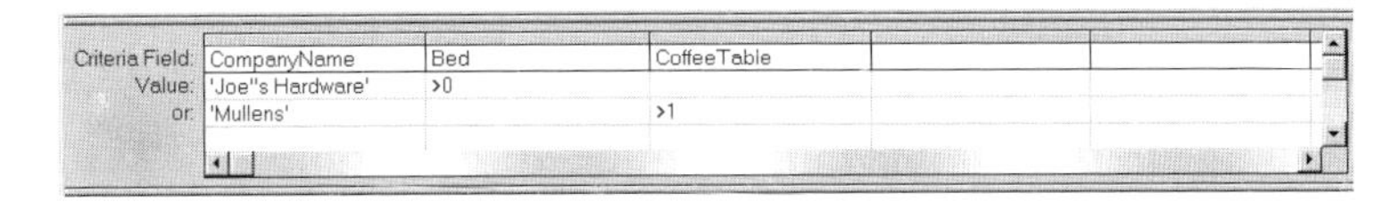

Criteria consist of *Criteria Fields* and *Values*. If a *Value* cell is left blank, then any value for the corresponding *Criteria Field* is acceptable.

Each row represents a single filter requirement, where the criteria are combined using logical AND.

The individual rows are combined using logical OR.

So, for a record to get through the filter, it must satisfy all of the criteria in any one row.

In the example shown, a record will get through the filter if it is an order from *Joe's Hardware* AND at least one *Bed* was ordered, OR if it is an order from *Mullens* AND at least two *Coffee Tables* were ordered. No other records will get through.

Before you start to define a filter in Microsoft Query, you should be clear *exactly* what your filter requirements are, and how they relate to each other.

Creating an advanced filter

You want to filter out the records on the *INDOOR* and *OUTDOOR* worksheets of MFPF_ORD.XLS where no furniture was ordered. Remember that Mrs Murphy asked only to see records for customers in Cullenstown.

The individual filter requirements you will need to create are:

- The customer is from Cullenstown AND at least one bed was ordered
  OR
- The customer is from Cullenstown AND at least one wardrobe was ordered
  OR
- etc.

In the next exercise, you will use Microsoft Query to create an advanced query filter that finds records where at least one piece of indoor furniture was ordered by a shop in Cullenstown.

Exercise 3.5: Using advanced filtering in Microsoft Query

1) Open MFPF_ORD.XLS and go to the *INDOOR* worksheet.
2) Select any cell in the query results, and select **Data | Get External Data | Edit Query ...** , or click the **Edit Query ...** button on the *External Data* toolbar.
   The *Query Wizard* opens.
3) Click **Cancel**.
   A dialog box opens asking you if you would like to continue editing the query in Microsoft Query.
4) Click **Yes**.
   Microsoft Query opens.

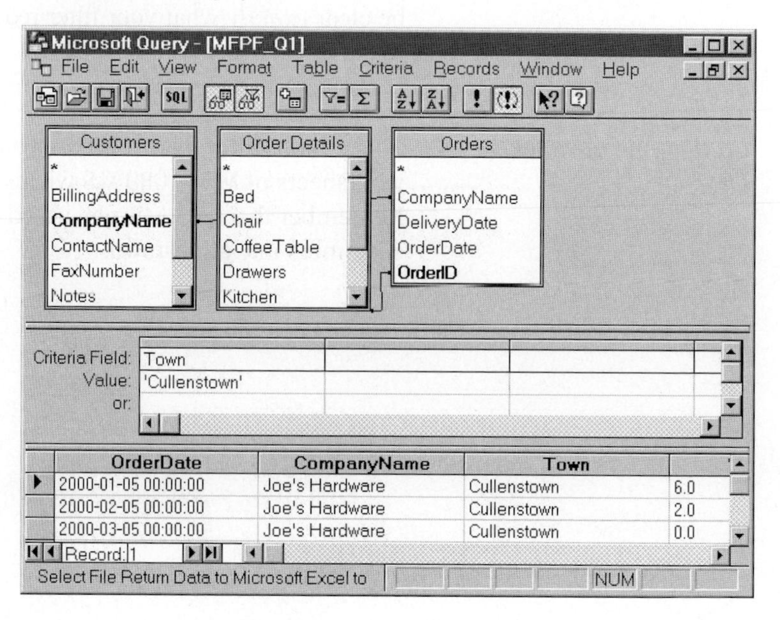

5) Select **Criteria | Remove All Criteria** to delete the filter you set earlier for the *Town* column area, before you add new filter rules.

6) You could add your criteria by typing directly in the *Criteria Field* and *Value* cells, but instead you will use the *Add Criteria* dialog box. Select **Criteria | Add Criteria ...** .
The *Add Criteria* dialog box appears.

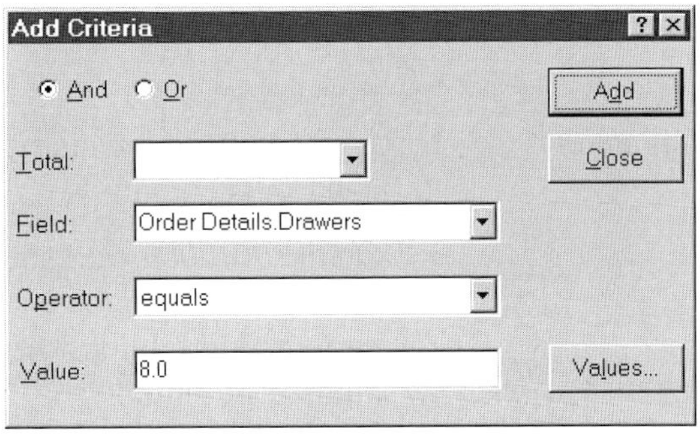

Add Criteria
And Or
Total:
Field: Order Details.Drawers
Operator: equals
Value: 8.0
Add
Close
Values...

7) Add the following criteria to your filter in order, clicking **Add** after specifying each one:

And/Or	Field	Operator	Value
	Order Details.Bed	Is greater than	*0*
Or	Order Details.Wardrobe	Is greater than	*0*
Or	Order Details.Drawers	Is greater than	*0*
Or	Order Details.CoffeeTable	Is greater than	*0*
Or	Order Details.Kitchen	Is greater than	*0*
And	Customers.Town	Equals	Cullenstown

Each criterion you add through the *Add Criteria* dialog box is combined with all the other criteria you have already entered using the selected logical operator.
By adding the *AND Customers.Town Equals Cullenstown* criterion last, you combine this requirement with all of the *Order Details* criteria. You could not have done this if you had added the *Town* criterion first.
When you have finished adding criteria, click **Close**.

Return Data button

8) Select **File | Return Data to Microsoft Excel**, or click the **Return Data** toolbar button.

9) Save your workbook.

Well done! You just created an advanced filter in MS Query, combining a range of criteria using both logical AND and logical OR.

Microsoft Query allows you to select any column in the database when you create a criterion, not only those that you are importing. This makes Microsoft Query a more powerful filtering tool than the *Query Wizard*.

Over to you: mandatory

Next, you will edit the query results on the *OUTDOOR* worksheet to show similar results.

- On the *OUTDOOR* worksheet of MFPF_ORD.XLS, add an advanced filter to the query results to show records for customers in Cullenstown who ordered at least one item of outdoor furniture.
- Save your workbook.

Chapter summary

A delimited text file is a text file in which columns of information are separated from each other by a particular character or set of characters, known as delimiters. Excel allows you to import data from delimited text files using the *Text Import Wizard*. You can choose to import all of the columns in a delimited text file, or only a subset of them. You can also specify at which row of the text file you should start the import.

Excel also allows you to import database records using a *query*. A query is a set of rules that specifies what records, or parts of records, to retrieve from the database, and how to display those data.

When you create a query, you can define a *sort order* for the results. You can sort by the values in any number of columns.

You can also include a filter in your query to import only those records that satisfy specific criteria. Excel's *Query Wizard* allows you to set simple filter requirements based on the values in the database columns you are importing. You can edit your query in Microsoft Query to set much more complex filter requirements based on the values in any of the database columns.

4

Sorting Data in a Spreadsheet

In this chapter

In ECDL 3, you learned how to sort the information in a column numerically and alphabetically, in ascending and descending order.

When you defined a query in Chapter 3, you edited that query to sort the returned data by the values in multiple columns. Now you will find out how to sort by multiple columns in an Excel spreadsheet.

You will learn how to use Excel's custom sort orders to sort data in a non-alphabetic and non-numeric order – for example, by days of the week.

Finally, you will learn how to define a custom sort order of your own.

New skills

At the end of this chapter you should be able to:

- Sort by the values in multiple columns
- Sort columns using a custom sort order
- Create a custom list

New words

At the end of this chapter you should be able to explain the following term:

- Custom list

Sorting data in Excel

Typically, you will sort data in an Excel spreadsheet so that they are presented in a way that is easier to read and understand. For example, you might sort a list of birthdays in chronological order, or a list of mountain ranges by height.

In ECDL 3, you used Excel's **Sort** command to sort the data in a single column into ascending or descending order. In fact, you can sort data by the values in up to three columns in Excel.

> **Note:** When you sorted records in a database query, there was no limit to the number of columns you could sort by.

Sorting multiple columns at the same time

Mrs Murphy liked the way you sorted the results from the query you created earlier. She would like to see the data on the *COMPLETE* worksheet of MFPF_ORD.XLS sorted by customer, with the orders from each customer sorted in reverse chronological order.

In the following exercise, you will rearrange the rows on the *COMPLETE* worksheet of MFPF_ORD.XLS as Mrs Murphy asked.

Exercise 4.1: Sorting by multiple columns

1) Open MFPF_ORD.XLS and go to the COMPLETE worksheet.
2) Select columns *A* to *J*, then select **Data | Sort ...** .
   The *Sort* dialog box opens.
3) In the *Sort by* field, select *CompanyName* and *Ascending*.
   In the *Then by* field, select *OrderDate* and *Descending*.

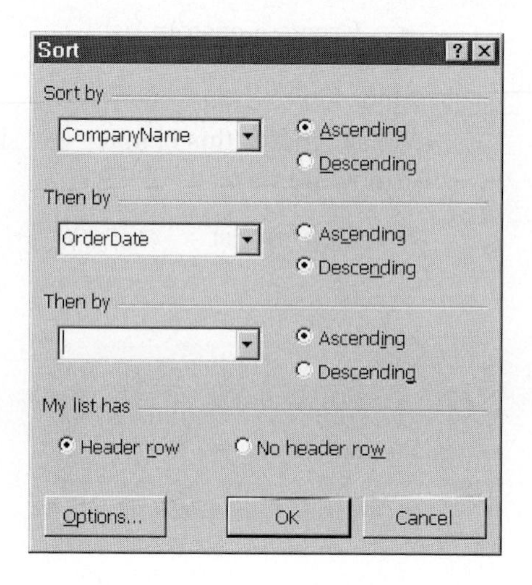

4) Click **OK**.
   Your data are now sorted alphabetically by the values in the *CompanyName* column, with the orders for each company listed in reverse chronological order.

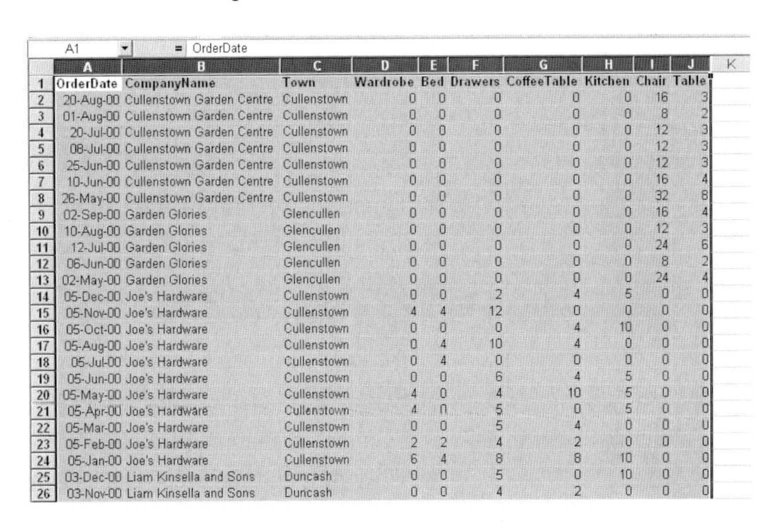

A1 = OrderDate

	A	B	C	D	E	F	G	H	I	J
1	OrderDate	CompanyName	Town	Wardrobe	Bed	Drawers	CoffeeTable	Kitchen	Chair	Table
2	20-Aug-00	Cullenstown Garden Centre	Cullenstown	0	0	0	0	0	16	3
3	01-Aug-00	Cullenstown Garden Centre	Cullenstown	0	0	0	0	0	8	2
4	20-Jul-00	Cullenstown Garden Centre	Cullenstown	0	0	0	0	0	12	3
5	08-Jul-00	Cullenstown Garden Centre	Cullenstown	0	0	0	0	0	12	3
6	25-Jun-00	Cullenstown Garden Centre	Cullenstown	0	0	0	0	0	12	3
7	10-Jun-00	Cullenstown Garden Centre	Cullenstown	0	0	0	0	0	16	4
8	26-May-00	Cullenstown Garden Centre	Cullenstown	0	0	0	0	0	32	8
9	02-Sep-00	Garden Glories	Glencullen	0	0	0	0	0	16	4
10	10-Aug-00	Garden Glories	Glencullen	0	0	0	0	0	12	3
11	12-Jul-00	Garden Glories	Glencullen	0	0	0	0	0	24	6
12	06-Jun-00	Garden Glories	Glencullen	0	0	0	0	0	8	2
13	02-May-00	Garden Glories	Glencullen	0	0	0	0	0	24	4
14	05-Dec-00	Joe's Hardware	Cullenstown	0	0	2	4	5	0	0
15	05-Nov-00	Joe's Hardware	Cullenstown	4	4	12	0	0	0	0
16	05-Oct-00	Joe's Hardware	Cullenstown	0	0	0	4	10	0	0
17	05-Aug-00	Joe's Hardware	Cullenstown	0	4	10	4	0	0	0
18	05-Jul-00	Joe's Hardware	Cullenstown	0	4	0	0	0	0	0
19	05-Jun-00	Joe's Hardware	Cullenstown	0	0	6	4	5	0	0
20	05-May-00	Joe's Hardware	Cullenstown	4	0	4	10	5	0	0
21	05-Apr-00	Joe's Hardware	Cullenstown	4	0	5	0	5	0	0
22	05-Mar-00	Joe's Hardware	Cullenstown	0	0	5	4	0	0	0
23	05-Feb-00	Joe's Hardware	Cullenstown	2	2	4	2	0	0	0
24	05-Jan-00	Joe's Hardware	Cullenstown	6	4	8	8	10	0	0
25	03-Dec-00	Liam Kinsella and Sons	Duncash	0	0	5	0	10	0	0
26	03-Nov-00	Liam Kinsella and Sons	Duncash	0	0	4	2	0	0	0

5) Save your workbook when you are done.

Over to you: optional

To impress Mrs Murphy even more, you decide to rearrange the data on the *COMPLETE* worksheet again, this time sorting by three columns.

- First, you will sort by *Town* in ascending order, then by *CompanyName* in ascending order, and finally by *OrderDate* in descending order.
  All of the orders for each customer will still be grouped together, as Mrs Murphy requested, but now the customers themselves will be grouped according to which town they are from.

Custom sort orders

Look at the following column of data, which lists the first three months of the year in an arbitrary order:

	A	B	C
1	January		
2	March		
3	February		
4			

What order do you think it should be sorted in? If you tried simply to sort the months in ascending order, Excel would sort them alphabetically, resulting in:

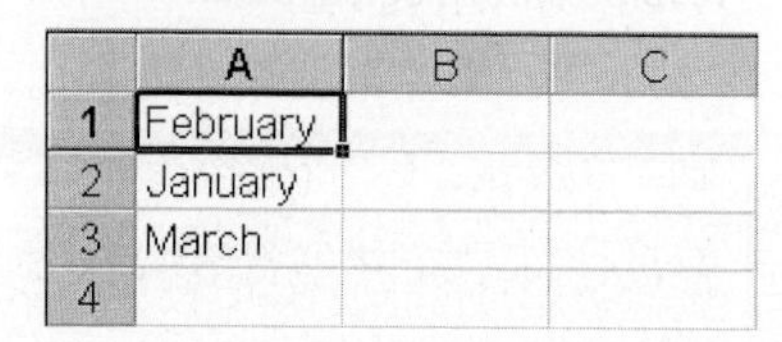

	A	B	C
1	February		
2	January		
3	March		
4			

Chances are, you would rather sort the data so that they appeared in this order:

	A	B	C
1	January		
2	February		
3	March		
4			

How do you tell Excel that you want to use a special order for sorting columns containing the months of the year? You use a custom sort order.

Using a custom sort order

A custom sort order is defined using a custom list that lists the values in the required order. Excel comes with custom lists for days of the week and months of the year by default.

Custom list

A custom list is a list that specifies a non-alphabetic and non-numeric order for a series of data elements – for example, the days of the week in chronological order.

Custom lists are used when performing custom sorts and can also be used to autofill cell ranges. You learned about AutoFill functionality in ECDL 3.

In the next exercise, you will use a custom sort order to sort cells containing entries for the months January, February and March into their usual chronological order.

Exercise 4.2: Sorting using a custom sort order

1) Open a new workbook based on the default template.
2) In the cell range *A1:A3*, enter the values *January, March, February.*
3) Select the cell range, and select **Data | Sort ...** .
   The *Sort* dialog box opens.

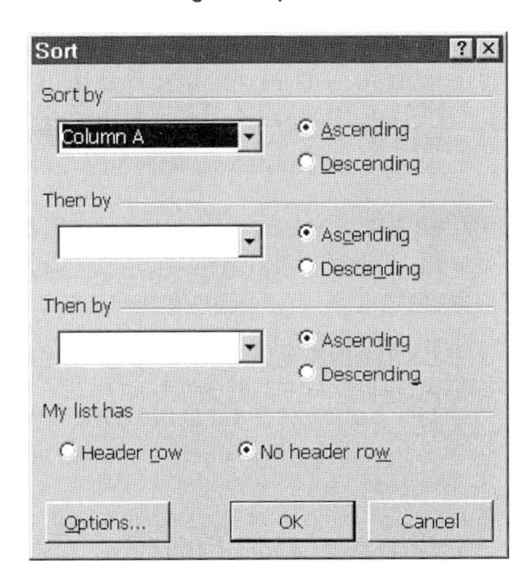

4) In the *Sort by* field, select *Column A*.
5) Click **Options ...** .
   The *Sort Options* dialog box opens.

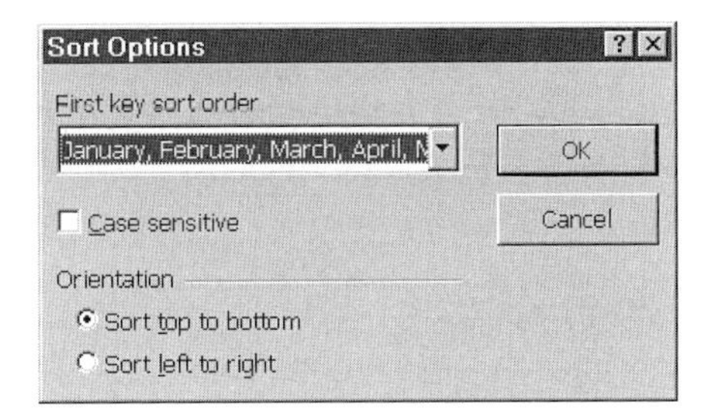

6) In the *First key sort order* field, select the entry beginning *January, February, March*, then click **OK**.
7) Click **OK**.
   The data in the cell range are now sorted in the order you would usually expect.

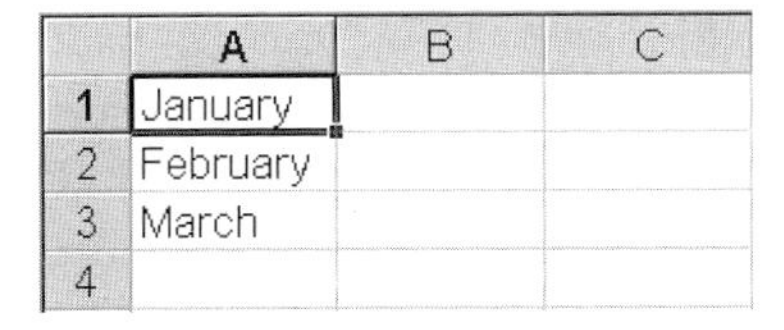

	A	B	C
1	January		
2	February		
3	March		
4			

8) Close your workbook without saving when you are done.

Defining a custom list

You can add any number of additional custom lists to Excel; for example, you can list employee names by seniority, or groceries according to which aisle they are in in the supermarket. Custom lists are stored as part of Excel and will be available to you in any workbook.

Mr Murphy has heard about your superior sorting skills. He asks you to sort order information by how far away each customer is. This will let him stock the delivery van so that the goods for the cutomer furthest away are loaded first and unloaded last.

In the next exercise you will create a custom list that lists the customers in order of how far away they are.

Exercise 4.3: Adding a custom list to Excel

1) Start Excel if it is not already started. It does not matter which workbook is open, because your custom list will be stored as part of Excel.
2) Select **Tools | Options ...** .
   The *Options* dialog box opens.
3) Select the **Custom lists** tab.
   The custom lists already known to Excel are shown in the *Custom lists* area.

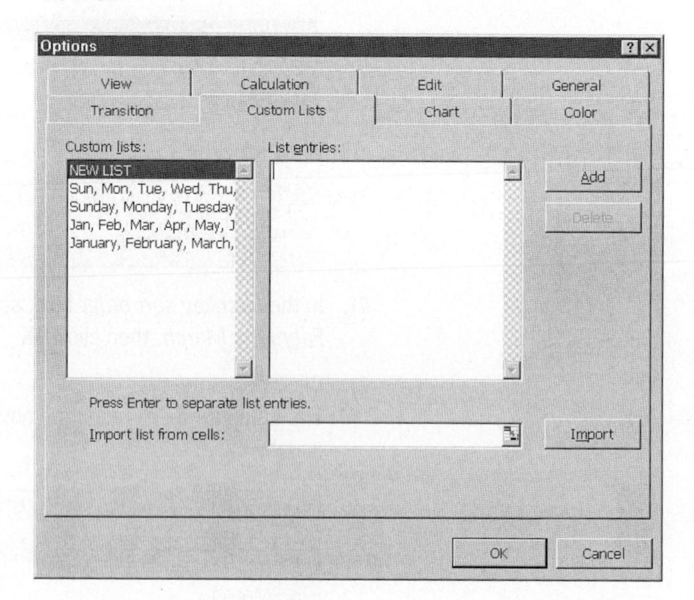

4) In the *Custom lists* area, select *NEW LIST*, then add the following data in the *List entries* area:
Joe's Hardware
Cullenstown Garden Centre
The DIY Centre
Mullens
Garden Glories
Liam Kinsella and Sons

Pay close attention to the spelling and punctuation used. Later, Excel will use this list to sort entries in your spreadsheet, and it will not recognize values that do not exactly match those in this list.

5) Click **Add**.
Your new entry is now shown in the *Custom lists* area.

6) Click **OK**.

Well done! You just added a custom list to Excel. You will be able to use this list in future to specify a custom sort order when you sort data or autofill cell ranges in any spreadsheet.

Over to you: optional

Next, you will sort the data on the *COMPLETE* worksheet by customer name, using the custom list you just defined to specify the correct sort order.

- Use the custom list of customer names you defined in *Exercise 4.3* on page 34 to sort the entries on the *COMPLETE* worksheet in MFPF_ORD.XLS.

Chapter summary

Excel's sort facility allows you to reorder the rows in a spreadsheet according to the values in multiple columns. You can choose to sort data in ascending or descending alphabetic or numeric order, or in a custom order.

Custom sort orders allow you to sort data in a specific non-alphabetic and non-numeric order. Custom sorts use custom lists to define the correct order to use when sorting data.

A custom list is a list that specifies a non-alphabetic and non-numeric order for a series of data elements – for example, the days of the week in chronological order.

You can create your own custom lists in Excel.

5 Naming Cells and Adding Comments

In this chapter

When dealing with large spreadsheets, it is easy to lose track of what particular cell ranges are for, and why you have decided to perform your calculations in a particular way.

Usually, you use labels to indicate what the contents of a particular cell, row or column represent. Sometimes, because of the layout or complexity of your data, it might not be possible to label them in this way. For example, you may want to assign a single overall label to a group of labelled cells or cell ranges.

In this chapter you will learn about two other ways you can assign additional information to a cell or cell range: custom names and comments.

New skills

At the end of this chapter you should be able to:

- Give a cell or cell range a custom name
- Navigate a worksheet or workbook using custom names
- Use a named cell or cell range in a formula
- Add comments to your spreadsheet
- Read comments in a spreadsheet
- Edit spreadsheet comments
- Delete spreadsheet comments

New words

At the end of this chapter you should be able to explain the following terms:

- Custom name
- Comment

Cell names

Every cell in a worksheet has a unique name.

By default, a cell's name is determined by the column and row it occupies. For example, *A1* is the default name of the cell that appears in column *A* of row *1* in every Excel worksheet.

When you select a cell, its name appears in the *Name Box* to the left of the formula bar.

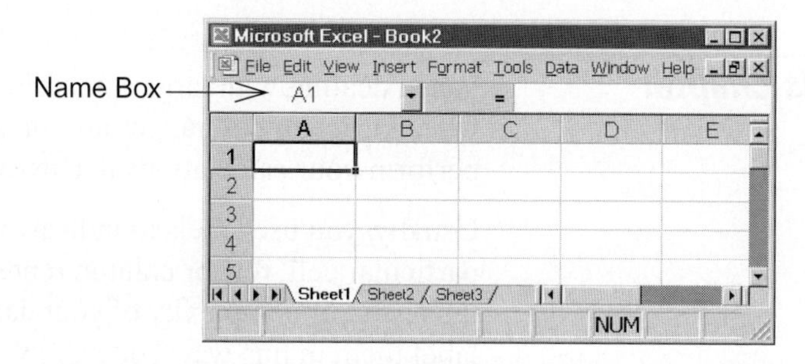

You can also enter a cell's name in the *Name Box* and press **Enter** to select that cell.

Custom cell names

You can associate a custom name with any cell or cell range. Because cell names must be unique, you can only use a particular name once in any workbook. But you can associate as many different custom names as you like with any cell or cell range.

Custom name
A custom name is a unique name in a workbook that can be used to identify a cell or cell range.

You can see a list of all of the custom names associated with cells and cell ranges in your workbook by clicking the down arrow to the right of the *Name Box*. If you select a name from this list, Excel will instantly select the cell or cell range that uses that name.

Custom cell names and formulae

You can use custom cell names instead of the default ones when you refer to cells and cell ranges in formulae. This can often make formulae easier to read and to edit.

Have a look at cell *C15*, which has been named *INC_TOT*, on the *INCOMING* worksheet of MFPF_FINANCE.XLS. It contains the formula:

=SUM(Products)+SUM(Delivery)

Compare this with:

=SUM(B2:B13)+SUM(C2:C13)

Although each formula calculates exactly the same thing, the first is much easier to understand.

Assigning a custom name to a cell range

There are a lot of data in the MFPF_FINANCE.XLS workbook. Naming particular cells and cell ranges will make the workbook easier to use.

In the next exercise, you are going to assign a custom name to a cell range.

Exercise 5.1: Naming a cell range

1) Open MFPF_FINANCE.XLS and go to the *SALES TOTALS* worksheet.
2) Select the cell range *A1:H13*.
   This cell range will be used to hold the monthly sales figures for each product.
3) In the *Name Box*, enter the word *SALES* and press **Enter**.

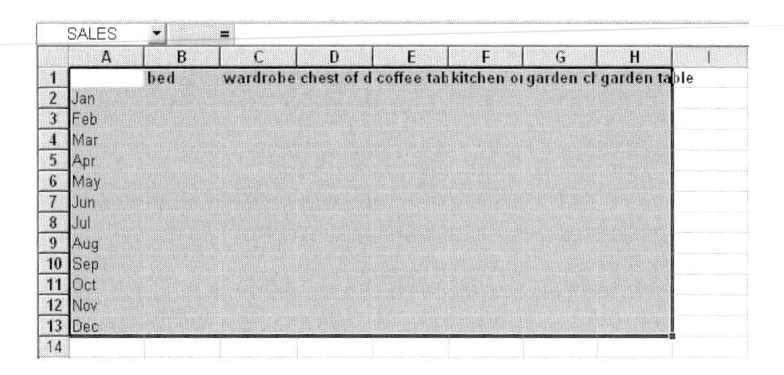

4) Save the workbook.

If you look at the *Name Box* list, *SALES* is now included.

The procedure for naming a single cell is exactly the same.

Over to you: mandatory

Next, you will name some cell ranges yourself, and then use the custom names in a formula.

- On the *OUTGOING* worksheet of MFPF_FINANCE.XLS, name the cell ranges referring to particular payment types (for example, assign the name *RENT* to the cell range *B2:B13*).
- Enter a formula in cell *C15* that adds up the totals for each payment type for the year, using the cell range names you just defined.
- Assign the name *TOTAL_OUTGOING* to cell *C15*; then save your workbook.

Comments

Comments are a useful way to add notes to cells in your worksheets. You might add a comment to remind yourself of why you calculated a value using one method rather than another. Or you might use a comment to let a colleague who will work with the spreadsheet later know what needs to be done next.

Comment
A comment is a type of note that can be associated with a spreadsheet cell.

Comment text is normally hidden from view, so that you can continue working with an uncluttered spreadsheet. A cell with an associated comment has a small red triangle in its top right corner:

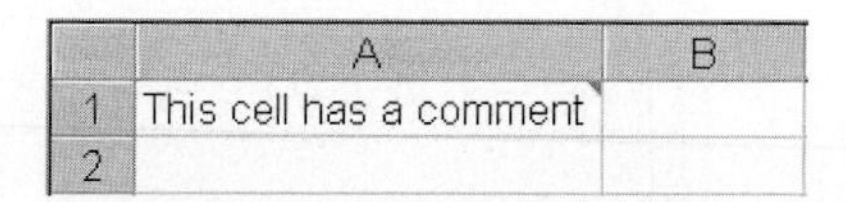

The *Reviewing* toolbar contains buttons for most of the commands you will use when creating, reading, editing and deleting comments. If you cannot see the *Reviewing* toolbar, you can open it by selecting **View | Toolbars | Reviewing**.

Adding comments

Earlier, you assigned the name *SALES* to a cell range in MFPF_FINANCE.XLS. At the moment, there are no numeric data in this cell range. What is the cell range there for? How will someone else editing the worksheet know if it will be required later, or if you have already used it and it can be deleted?

In the next exercise, you will add a comment to the *SALES* cell range explaining what it represents and what it will be used for.

Exercise 5.2: Adding a comment to a cell

1) Go to the cell range named *SALES* in MFPF_FINANCE.XLS.
2) Right-click cell *A1*, and select **Insert Comment** from the shortcut menu that appears.
   – or –
   Select cell *A1* and click the **New Comment** button on the *Reviewing* toolbar.
   A comment box opens.

   New Comment button

3) Enter the following text in the comment box:
   This table shows the total sales of each product type each month. The data will be used later to calculate our incoming sales revenue on the INCOMING worksheet.
4) If you cannot see all of the comment text, resize the comment box by clicking and dragging one of the white resize handles that appear around the edge of the box.
5) Save your workbook when you are done.

Reading comments

There are several different ways to display the comment associated with a cell in order to read it:

- If you place your cursor over the cell with the comment, a pop-up box displays the contents of the comment. The pop-up box closes when you move your cursor away.

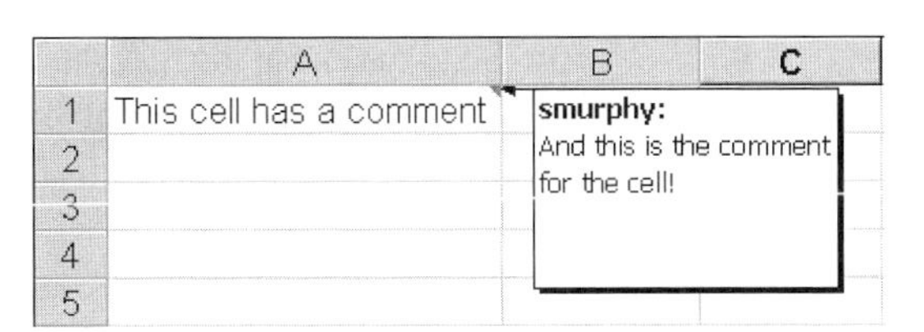

Show/Hide Comment button

- If you select the cell with the comment, you can click the **Show/Hide Comment** button on the *Reviewing* toolbar to display the comment associated with that cell. The comment will remain open until you click the **Show/Hide Comment** button a second time.
- If you right-click a cell with an associated comment, you can select **Show Comment** from the shortcut menu that opens. The comment will remain open until you right-click the cell again and select **Hide Comment** from the shortcut menu.

You can also choose to display all spreadsheet comments. There are two ways to do this:

- If you select **View | Comments**, all comments will be displayed. You can deselect **View | Comments** to hide all comments again.

Show/Hide All Comments button

- If you click the **Show/Hide All Comments** button on the *Reviewing* toolbar, all comments will be displayed. Click the **Show/Hide All Comments** button again to hide the comments.

Editing comments

You can reopen a comment to edit its text at any time.

In the next exercise, you will edit the comment you added to the *SALES* cell range in *Exercise 5.2* on page 41.

Exercise 5.3: Editing a comment

1) Go to the cell range named *SALES* in MFPF_FINANCE.XLS.
2) Right-click cell *A1*, and select **Edit Comment** from the shortcut menu that appears.
   – or –
   Edit Comment button
   Select cell *A1* and click the **Edit Comment** button on the *Reviewing* toolbar.
   The comment box opens for editing.
3) Go to the end of the text you entered earlier and add the following text: *and also our materials expenses on the OUTGOING worksheet.*
4) Save your workbook when you are done.

Deleting comments

If you select a cell with an associated comment and press **Delete**, you delete the cell contents but not the comment. This means that you can add a comment saying what the value in the cell represents and not worry about losing your comment if you delete or change the value in the cell.

In the next exercise, you will find out how to delete the comment you added to the *SALES* cell range in *Exercise 5.2* on page 41.

Exercise 5.4: Removing a comment

1) Go to the cell range named *SALES* in MFPF_FINANCE.XLS.
2) Right-click cell *A1*, and select **Delete Comment** from the shortcut menu that appears.
   – or –
   Select cell *A1* and click the **Delete Comment** button on the *Reviewing* toolbar.
   The comment is deleted from the cell.
3) Save and close your workbook when you are done.

Delete Comment button 

Chapter summary

Every cell in every Excel worksheet has a default name that is defined by the column and row it is in – for example, *A1*. You can assign a unique custom name to a cell or cell range. These custom names can be used in formulae.

A comment is a type of note that can be associated with a spreadsheet cell. A small red triangle in a cell indicates that it has an associated comment. Usually comments are hidden so that you can work with an uncluttered worksheet.

6 Using Paste Special

In this chapter

Every cell in an Excel spreadsheet has many different types of information associated with it. It will have some kind of formatting. It may contain a value or formula, or an associated comment.

Usually, when you copy a cell's contents and paste them somewhere else, you paste all of the information associated with that cell.

Excel's **Paste Special** command allows you to select specific elements of a copied cell's information to paste. You can also manipulate copied data in a variety of ways before pasting them to their destination cell.

New skills

At the end of this chapter you should be able to:

- Paste specific elements of copied data to a destination cell
- Perform simple mathematical operations using **Paste Special**
- Create links between cells using **Paste Special**

New words

There are no new words in this chapter.

Why Paste Special?

When you copy data from a cell in an Excel spreadsheet, and paste them to another cell, Excel pastes *all* of the data associated with the cell you copied to the new cell.

If you copied the value 12, formatted in 14-point Arial with a bright yellow background, then when you paste the value to a new cell, it will be formatted in 14-point Arial with a bright yellow background. If the value in the cell you copied was the result of a formula, you probably will not even get the same value when you paste it, unless the formula used absolute cell references.

When you use the **Paste Special** command instead of **Paste**, the *Paste Special* dialog box opens, and you can choose which part or parts of the data you really want to paste.

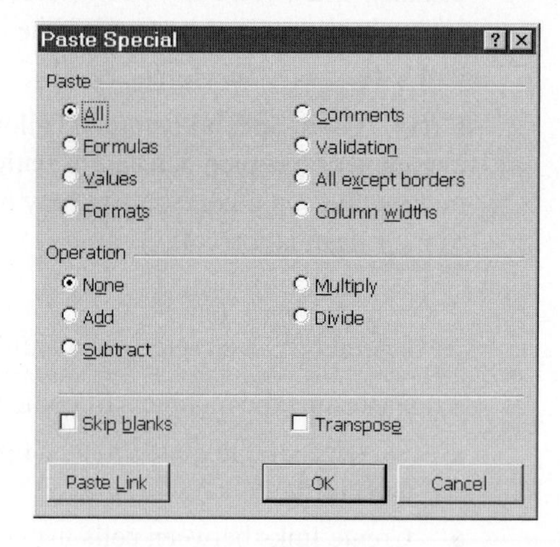

Note: If you are pasting data other than Excel spreadsheet cells, **Edit | Paste Special** opens the standard *Paste Special* dialog box common to all Microsoft Office software.

Pasting different types of information

In the *Paste* area of the *Paste Special* dialog box, you can choose which part, or parts, of the copied data you want to paste to the destination cells.

You can only choose one option at a time from the *Paste* area. If you want to paste a combination of the data elements – for example, a formula and its associated comment – you must use **Paste Special** more than once to paste each piece of data.

The following table lists the different options in the *Paste* area of the *Paste Special* dialog box and explains what each one does.

Option	Action
All	Paste all data from the copied cell.
Formulas	Paste the formula from the copied cell, if there is one. Paste the value from the copied cell if there is no formula.
Values	Paste the value from the copied cell. If the copied cell contains a formula, paste the result of that formula as a value.
Formats	Paste the formatting data from the copied cell.
Comments	Paste the comment from the copied cell.
Validation	Paste the validation, or data entry, rules from the copied cell.
All except borders	Paste the formula (or value if there is no formula) and the formatting data from the copied cell, but do not include border formatting.
Column widths	Paste the column width from the copied cell.

In the following exercises, you will copy cells from the workbook PASTE_SPECIAL.XLS, and use the options in the *Paste Special* dialog box to paste particular parts of the copied data to destination cells.

Note: To deselect a cell range after you have copied it, press **Esc**.

Exercise 6.1: Pasting formulae

1) Open the PASTE_SPECIAL.XLS workbook.

	A	B	C	D	E	F	G	H
1								
2		2	3	4	5	6	10	
3		4	6	8	10	0	10	
4		6	9	12	15	18	10	
5		8	12	16	20	0	10	
6		10	15	20	25	30	10	
7		12	18	24	30		10	
8		14	21	28	35	42	10	
9		16	24	32	40		10	
10		18	27	36	45	54	10	
11		20	30	40	50		10	
12	yOuR vAlUe HeRe:							
13	TOTALS	110						
14								

2) Copy the contents of cell *B13*.

3) Select the cell range *C13:E13*.

4) Select **Edit | Paste Special**.

5) In the *Paste* area, select *Formulas* and click **OK**.
The relative SUM formula from cell *B13* is the only piece of data pasted to the cells in the cell range *C13:E13*.

Exercise 6.2: Pasting values

1) Copy the contents of cell *B13*.

2) Select cell *J2*.

3) Select **Edit | Paste Special**.

4) In the *Paste* area, select *Values* and click **OK**.
The result of the formula in cell *B13* is pasted to cell *J2*.

Exercise 6.3: Pasting formats

1) Copy the contents of cell *A13*.

2) Select the cell range *C13:E13*.

3) Select **Edit | Paste Special**.

4) In the *Paste* area, select *Formats* and click **OK**.
The cell and font formatting from cell *A13* is pasted to cells *C13:E13*.

Exercise 6.4: Pasting all cell information except borders

1) Copy the cell range named *Table1*.
2) Select cell *B15*.
3) Select **Edit | Paste Special**.
4) In the *Paste* area, select *All except borders* and click **OK**.
   All of the copied cell information except borders is pasted to a cell range starting in cell *B15*.

Exercise 6.5: Pasting column widths

1) Copy the cell range named *Table1*.
2) Select cell *H15*.
3) Select **Edit | Paste Special**.
4) In the *Paste* area, select *Column widths* and click **OK**.
   The column widths used in *Table1* are pasted to a cell range starting in cell *H15*.

Exercise 6.6: Pasting comments

1) Copy the contents of cell *A13*.
2) Select the cell range *C13:E13*.
3) Select **Edit | Paste Special**.
4) In the *Paste* area, select *Comments* and click **OK**.
   The comment in cell *B13* is pasted to cells *C13:E13*.

Exercise 6.7: Pasting validation

1) Copy the contents of cell *B12*.
   Cell *B12* has associated validation rules that allow you to enter only whole numbers in the cell.
2) Select the cell range *C12:E12*.
3) Select **Edit | Paste Special**.
4) In the *Paste* area, select *Validation* and click **OK**.
   The validation rules from cell *B12* are pasted to cells *C12:E12*.

The Operation area

You can combine numeric data from a copied cell with numeric data in a destination cell when you use **Paste Special**. The value in the destination cell is replaced by the result of the operation. Available operations are listed in the *Operation* area of the *Paste Special* dialog box.

The selection you make in the *Operation* area is combined with your selection from the *Paste* area.

The following table lists the different options in the *Operation* area of the *Paste Special* dialog box and explains what each one does:

Option	**Action**
None	Do not perform any operation.
Add	Add the data in the copied cell to the data in the destination cell, and place the result in the destination cell.
Subtract	Subtract the data in the copied cell from the data in the destination cell, and place the result in the destination cell.
Multiply	Multiply the data in the copied cell by the data in the destination cell, and place the result in the destination cell.
Divide	Divide the data in the destination cell by the data in the copied cell, and place the result in the destination cell.

In the next exercise, you will use the *Add* operation in the *Paste Special* dialog box to combine numeric data in two cell ranges.

Exercise 6.8: Pasting with operations

1) Copy the contents of cells *B2:B11*.
2) Select the cell range *G2:G11*.
3) Select **Edit | Paste Special**.
4) In the *Paste* area, select *All*.
   In the *Operations* area, select *Add*.
5) Click **OK**.
   The values in the cells in the copied range are added to the values in the corresponding cells in the destination cell range, and the totals replace the original values in the cell range *G2:G11*.

Special options

There are three additional special options in the *Paste Special* dialog box: *Skip blanks*, *Transpose* and **Paste Link**.

Skip blanks

A 'blank' cell is one that contains no values or formulae, though it may have any of the other information types associated with it, such as formatting, comments or validation rules.

The *Skip blanks* option can be used in conjunction with options from the *Paste* and *Operation* areas of the *Paste Special* dialog box. If *Skip blanks* is selected, then no data are pasted for any copied cell that does not contain either a value or a formula.

If you try to divide a number by zero in Excel, an error message, *#DIV/0!*, appears in the cell where the calculation was attempted. When you use operations, blank cells are treated as though they contain zeros. The *Skip blanks* option is especially useful when used in combination with the *Divide* operation.

In the next exercise, you will use the *Skip blanks* option on the *Paste Special* dialog box to tell Excel to ignore blank cells in a copied cell range when performing a *Divide* operation.

Exercise 6.9: Skip blanks

1) Copy the contents of cells *F2:F11*.
2) Select the cell range *G2:G11*.
3) Select **Edit | Paste Special**.
4) In the *Paste* area, select *Values*.
   In the *Operations* area, select *Divide*.
   Check the box beside *Skip blanks*.
   Click **OK**.

	A	B	C	D	E	F	G	H
1								
2		2	3	4	5	6	2	
3		4	6	8	10	0	#DIV/0!	
4		6	9	12	15	18	0.888889	
5		8	12	16	20	0	#DIV/0!	
6		10	15	20	25	30	0.666667	
7		12	18	24	30		22	
8		14	21	28	35	42	0.571429	
9		16	24	32	40		26	
10		18	27	36	45	54	0.518519	
11		20	30	40	50		30	
12	yOuR vAlUe HeRe:							
13	TOTALS	110						
14								

In the cell range *G2:G11*, *#DIV/0!* errors are shown in the cells where you actually divided by zero.
Where the cell in the copied cell range was blank, the value in the pasted range does not change.

Transpose

You can combine the *Transpose* option with selections from the *Paste* and *Operation* areas of the *Paste Special* dialog box. If you copy a range of cells that are in a column orientation, you can use the *Transpose* option to paste them in a row orientation, and vice versa.

In the next exercise, you will copy a cell range in a column orientation, and use the *Transpose* option to paste it to another cell range in a row orientation.

Exercise 6.10: Transpose

1) Copy the contents of cells *G2:G11*.
2) Select the cell *A1*.
3) Select **Edit | Paste Special**.
4) In the *Paste* area, select *Values*.
   Check the box beside *Transpose*.
   Click **OK**.
5) The data from the column of cells *G2:G11* are pasted to the row of cells *A1:A10*.

Paste Link

If it is important that a cell in your spreadsheet should always contain the value from another cell, you can create a link from the second cell to the first. If the value in the first cell changes, the value in the second cell automatically updates to reflect the change.

You can use the **Paste Link** option in the *Paste Special* dialog box to link the destination cell to the copied cell.

In the next exercise, you will create links from cells in a destination range to cells in a source range using the **Paste Link** option.

Exercise 6.11: Paste link

1) Copy the contents of cells *A13:E13*.
2) Select the cell *H13*.
3) Select **Edit | Paste Special**.
4) Click **Paste Link**.
   A link is created from each of the cells in the range *H13:L13* to their corresponding cells in the source range, *A13:E13*.
   The values in cells *H13:L13* will update automatically to reflect changes to the values in cells *A13:E13*.

Over to you: optional

Continue to experiment with different combinations of options in the *Paste Special* dialog box, until you are comfortable with it. Save and close PASTE_SPECIAL.XLS when you are done.

Chapter summary

A cell in an Excel spreadsheet has many different types of information associated with it: values, formatting, comments, etc. When you use **Copy** and **Paste** to copy the contents of one cell to another in a worksheet, all of the different information types are pasted. You can use **Paste Special** to select a subset of the information types to paste.

Paste Special allows you to combine numeric data from copied cells with numeric data in destination cells using simple mathematical operations. The results of the operation replacc the original values in the destination cells.

The *Skip blanks* option allows you to choose not to paste any information from blank copied cells. A blank cell is one that contains no value or formula, though it may contain other information, such as formatting or a comment.

The *Transpose* option allows you to change the orientation of the copied cells when you paste them, from row to column or from column to row.

The **Paste Link** option allows you to create a link from a destination cell to a source cell. The value in the destination cell will update automatically if the value or formula in the source cell changes.

7 Summarizing Data Using PivotTables

In this chapter

Occasionally, you will want to create a report summarizing the data in a spreadsheet. Your report will probably perform a particular type of calculation using the data. You might even want to filter the data you include in a particular calculation.

Where the spreadsheets you are working with are large and detailed, creating a summary report can be a complicated and demanding task.

Excel's PivotTable functionality allows you to create dynamic, interactive summaries of a set of data.

In this chapter, you will learn how to create and use PivotTables.

New skills

At the end of this chapter you should be able to:

- Create a PivotTable
- Filter data in a PivotTable
- Group data in a PivotTable
- Refresh a PivotTable

New words

At the end of this chapter you should be able to explain the following terms:

- PivotTable
- Field
- Group

What are PivotTables?

A PivotTable is a useful Excel tool for summarizing large amounts of information in a dynamic report.

PivotTable
A PivotTable is an interactive table that allows you to dynamically create reports summarizing large amounts of data.

PivotTables can be used to generate reports on data from external databases or from Excel spreadsheets. You do not need to include all of the columns from your data source in a PivotTable, only the ones that are of interest to you.

The columns in your original data are referred to as fields when you include them in a PivotTable. This is to avoid confusion with the columns of the PivotTable itself.

Field
A field in a PivotTable corresponds to a column in the data source that the PivotTable is being used to summarize.

You can select the field or fields on which summary calculations should be performed. Summary functions include sum, average, minimum and maximum.

PivotTable layout

When you define the layout for a PivotTable, you add fields to four areas: *Page*, *Row*, *Column* and *Data*.

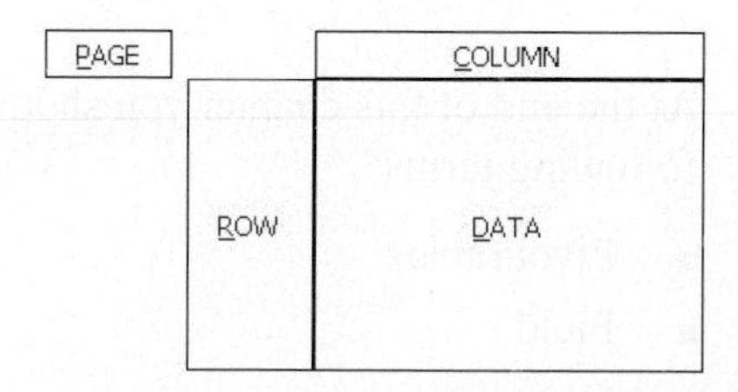

The *Page*, *Column* and *Row* areas show the fields you add and their different values. These values act as labels for the summary results, which are calculated in the *Data* area.

You can use the fields in the *Row*, *Column* and *Page* areas to filter the records from the data source that are included in the PivotTable.

Each field in the *Data* area must have a data function associated with it. This function determines what type of summary result is shown for that field. You can calculate more than one type of summary value from the data in any field.

You do not have to add fields to the *Page*, *Row* and *Column* areas, but the *Data* area must contain at least one field and an associated data function.

Filtering using fields

If you click the arrow to the right of any field name in a PivotTable, you open a drop-down list that contains a list of all the possible values that field might have. The list of values is determined by the values in the records in your data source.

You can check or uncheck the box beside each value to include or exclude records in which the field has that value.

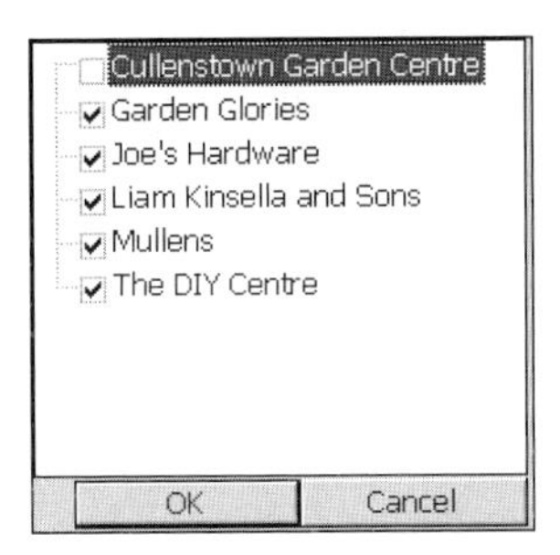

When you have finished making your selections, click **OK** to return to the PivotTable, which will now only display records matching those values.

The drop-down list for a *Page* field is slightly different: it does not have checkboxes beside each value. You can only select one value at a time. But it does have an extra value, *All*, which allows you to include all possible values for the field.

Example of a PivotTable

Here is an example of a PivotTable that is based on the data in the *COMPLETE* worksheet of MFPF_ORD.XLS:

	A	B	C	D
1	Town	Cullenstown		
2				
3	CompanyName	Data	Total	
4	Cullenstown Garden Centre	Sum of Chair	108	
5		Average of Chair2	15.42857143	
6	Joe's Hardware	Sum of Chair	0	
7		Average of Chair2	0	
8	The DIY Centre	Sum of Chair	36	
9		Average of Chair2	3	
10	Total Sum of Chair		144	
11	Total Average of Chair2		4.8	
12				

This PivotTable calculates:

- The total number of chairs ordered by each company over the year.
- The average number of chairs ordered by each company per order.

The *Town* field is used in the *Page* area, and the *CompanyName* field in the *Row* area. The *Town* field has been used to filter results in the table to show those from customers in *Cullenstown* only.

The *Data* area includes two different calculations on the data in the *Chair* field: one to calculate the sum, and one to calculate the average. When a field is used more than once in a single PivotTable, it is relabelled to include a number, for example, *Chair* and *Chair2* in the example shown.

At the bottom of the PivotTable, grand totals show the total number of chairs ordered, and the average number of chairs per order.

Creating PivotTables

You need to produce figures that show MFPF's total sales for each product by month to add to the *SALES TOTALS* worksheet of MFPF_FINANCE.XLS.

In the next exercise, you will begin to calculate these totals by creating a PivotTable to summarize the sales data in the cell range *A1:J55* on the *COMPLETE* worksheet of MFPF_ORD.XLS.

Exercise 7.1: Creating a PivotTable

1) Open MFPF_ORD.XLS.

2) Select **Data | PivotTable and PivotChart Report ...** .
   – or –
   Click the **PivotTable Wizard** button on the *PivotTable* toolbar.
   If you cannot see the *PivotTable* toolbar, you can open it by selecting **View | Toolbars | PivotTable.**
   The *PivotTable and PivotChart Wizard* opens.

PivotTable Wizard button

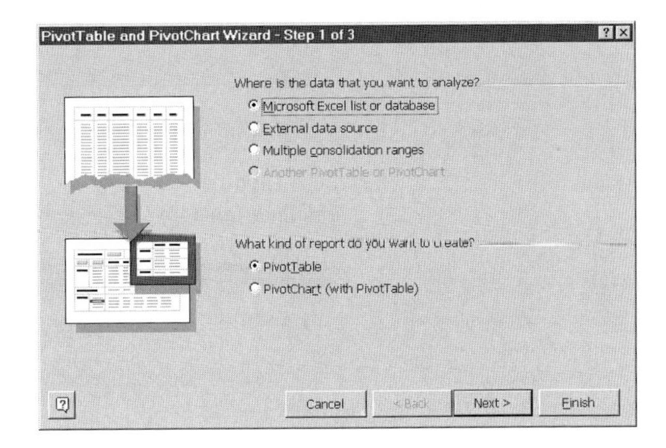

3) In the *Where is the data that you want to analyze?* area, select *Microsoft Excel list or database*.
   In the *What kind of report do you want to create?* area, select *PivotTable*.
   Click **Next**.
   A dialog box opens where you can specify the cell range that contains the source data for the PivotTable.

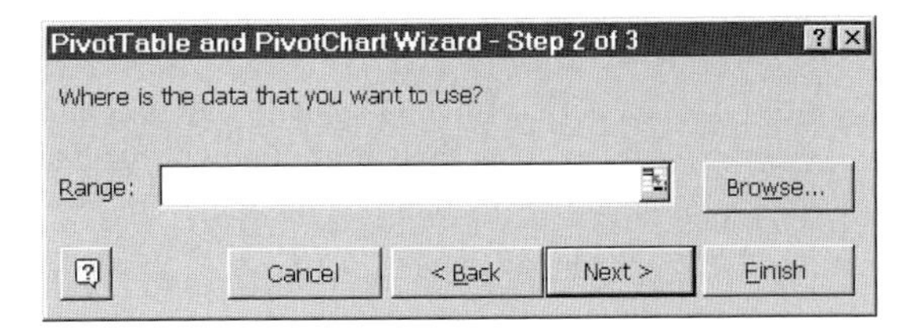

4) Open the *COMPLETE* worksheet and select the cell range *A1:J55*. The reference for the cell range is automatically filled in to the *Range* field.
   Click **Next**.

A dialog box opens where you can select where to put your PivotTable.

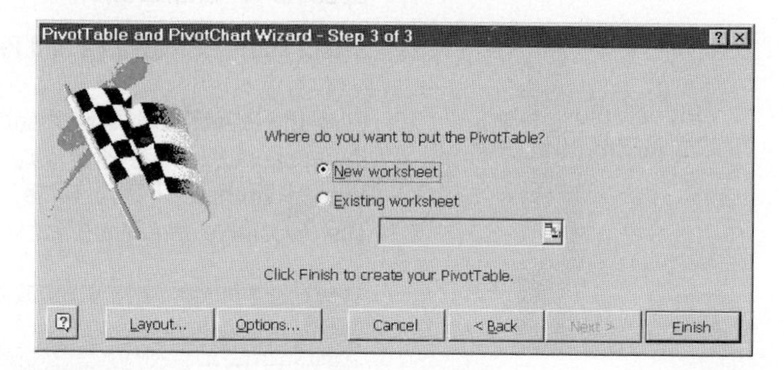

5) Specify that you want to put the PivotTable on a *New worksheet*.

6) Click **Layout**.
The *PivotTable and PivotChart Wizard – Layout* dialog box opens.

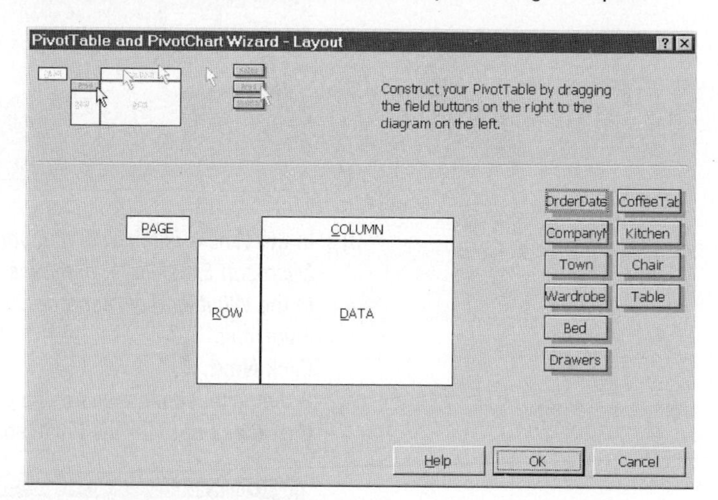

7) You add fields to different areas of the PivotTable by dragging the buttons from the right-hand side of the dialog box to the PivotTable diagram on the left.

- Drag **OrderDate** to the *Row* area.
- Drag the following (in order) to the *Data* area: **Bed, Wardrobe, Drawers, CoffeeTable, Kitchen, Chair, Table.**

The fields in the *Data* area are labelled to indicate the data function associated with them.

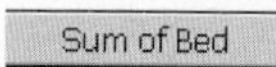

For this exercise, they should all use the data function *Sum of*. You can change the data function for a field by double-clicking the field and selecting a function from the list that appears.
Click **OK**.

8) Click **Finish**.
The PivotTable is added to your workbook on a new worksheet. It is laid out according to the settings you made.

	A	B	C	D
1	Drop Page Fields Here			
2				
3	OrderDa	Data	Total	
4	03-Jan-00	Sum of Bed	6	
5		Sum of Wardrobe	0	
6		Sum of Drawers	12	
7		Sum of CoffeeTable	2	
8		Sum of Kitchen	0	
9		Sum of Chair	0	
10		Sum of Table	0	
11	05-Jan-00	Sum of Bed	4	
12		Sum of Wardrobe	6	
13		Sum of Drawers	8	
14		Sum of CoffeeTable	8	
15		Sum of Kitchen	10	
16		Sum of Chair	0	
17		Sum of Table	0	
18	24-Jan-00	Sum of Bed	0	
19		Sum of Wardrobe	0	
20		Sum of Drawers	8	
21		Sum of CoffeeTable	6	
22		Sum of Kitchen	10	
23		Sum of Chair	0	
24		Sum of Table	0	
25	03-Feb-00	Sum of Bed	0	
26		Sum of Wardrobe	2	
27		Sum of Drawers	2	

9) Name the new worksheet *PIVOT* and save your workbook.

Grouping data in PivotTables

You now have 360 rows of data showing sales totals for each furniture type on particular dates. You also have a grand total for sales of each furniture type for the year. You want to know the total for each month.

You could select a subset of *OrderDates* for each month and take the grand totals calculated for those, but that would take a lot of time and clicking.

Not to worry! Another feature of PivotTables is that you can group fields to make it easier to view or select subsets of information in one go.

Group
A group is a set of objects that is treated as a single object.

In the next exercise, you will create a group for all of the order dates in January.

Exercise 7.2: Grouping data in a PivotTable

1) In the *OrderDate* field, select the cells that contain a January date.

2) Right-click and select **Group and Outline | Group** from the shortcut menu that appears.
An extra field (*OrderDate2*) is added to the *Column* area of the PivotTable.
An entry in this column called *Group1* covers all the cells in *OrderDate* related to January.

	A	B	C	D	E
1					
2					
3	OrderDate2	OrderDate	Data	Total	
4	Group1	03-Jan-00	Sum of Bed	6	
5			Sum of Wardrobe	0	
6			Sum of Drawers	12	
7			Sum of CoffeeTable	2	
8			Sum of Kitchen	0	
9			Sum of Chair	0	
10			Sum of Table	0	
11		05-Jan-00	Sum of Bed	4	
12			Sum of Wardrobe	6	
13			Sum of Drawers	8	
14			Sum of CoffeeTable	8	
15			Sum of Kitchen	10	
16			Sum of Chair	0	
17			Sum of Table	0	
18		24-Jan-00	Sum of Bed	0	
19			Sum of Wardrobe	0	
20			Sum of Drawers	8	
21			Sum of CoffeeTable	6	
22			Sum of Kitchen	10	
23			Sum of Chair	0	
24			Sum of Table	0	
25	03/02/2000	03-Feb-00	Sum of Bed	0	
26			Sum of Wardrobe	2	

You can ungroup the dates in any group again by selecting the group, right-clicking, and selecting **Group and Outline | Ungroup** from the shortcut menu that appears.

3) Double-click the group name to hide the details of the group members in the *OrderDate* field.

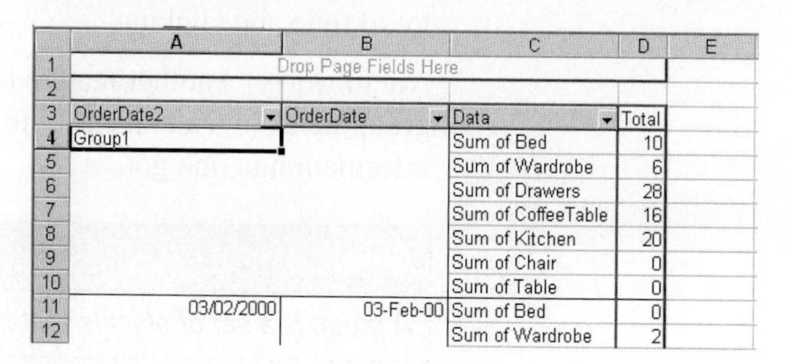

	A	B	C	D	E
1	Drop Page Fields Here				
2					
3	OrderDate2	OrderDate	Data	Total	
4	Group1		Sum of Bed	10	
5			Sum of Wardrobe	6	
6			Sum of Drawers	28	
7			Sum of CoffeeTable	16	
8			Sum of Kitchen	20	
9			Sum of Chair	0	
10			Sum of Table	0	
11	03/02/2000	03-Feb-00	Sum of Bed	0	
12			Sum of Wardrobe	2	

Now the numbers shown in the *Data* area refer to the month as a whole.

4) Select the text *Group1*, and in the formula bar enter the text *January* and press **ENTER**.
The group is renamed.

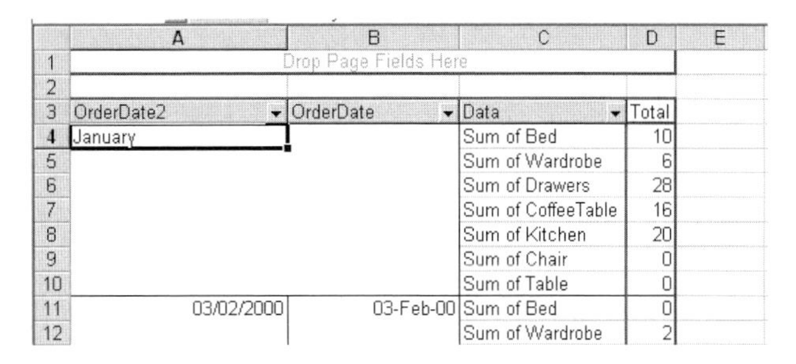

	A	B	C	D	E
1	Drop Page Fields Here				
2					
3	OrderDate2	OrderDate	Data	Total	
4	January		Sum of Bed	10	
5			Sum of Wardrobe	6	
6			Sum of Drawers	28	
7			Sum of CoffeeTable	16	
8			Sum of Kitchen	20	
9			Sum of Chair	0	
10			Sum of Table	0	
11	03/02/2000	03-Feb-00	Sum of Bed	0	
12			Sum of Wardrobe	2	

5) Save your workbook.

Over to you: mandatory

The PivotTable now displays sales totals for each furniture type for January and for all other dates in the year.

Next, you will finish grouping the PivotTable data and add the results you calculate to MFPF_FINANCE.XLS.

- Group the dates for each of the other months together, hide the details in the *OrderDate* field, and rename the groups.
- Finally, copy the monthly totals into the space left for them on the *SALES TOTALS* worksheet in the MFPF_FINANCE.XLS workbook. You will need to use **Edit | Paste Special** to paste the values and transpose them.

Save both workbooks when you are done.

Refresh PivotTables

In Chapter 3, you learned that you could update data imported from a delimited text file or from a database to match the source data at any time.

You can also refresh PivotTables so that they reflect the most current data in the data source defined.

In the next exercise, you will make a change to the sales data on the *COMPLETE* worksheet of MFPF_ORD.XLS and refresh your PivotTable to see this.

Don't worry – if you manually change the information in the PivotTable, you won't affect the database the results came from. In fact, you can refresh your PivotTable, and the values will change back to their original values again.

Exercise 7.3: Updating the data in a PivotTable

1) Go to the *COMPLETE* worksheet of MFPF_ORD.XLS.
   Change any one of the orders to include a request for 2000 wardrobes.
2) Go to the *PIVOT* worksheet.
3) Select **Data | Refresh Data**.
4) Look for the total that has been affected by the change you made.
   A month with in excess of 2000 wardrobe orders is easy to find!

Over to you: optional

Experiment with creating PivotTables to summarize the data on the *COMPLETE* worksheet of MFPF_ORD.XLS.

Here are some ideas for reports you could generate:

- A report showing the average order by a given customer for each furniture type in a year.
- A report showing the largest orders for specific furniture types by each company.
- A report showing the total sales of each furniture type in specific towns.

Chapter summary

A PivotTable is an interactive table that allows you to dynamically create reports summarizing large amounts of data.

PivotTables can be based on data from databases or from Excel spreadsheets.

A field in a PivotTable corresponds to a column in the data source that the PivotTable is based on.

You can group fields in a PivotTable to make it easier to view or select subsets of records. A group is a set of objects that is treated as a single object.

PivotTables can be refreshed at any time to reflect changes in their data source.

Linking Data in Spreadsheets

In this chapter

In Chapter 6, you created a link from one cell to the value in another using **Paste Special**. In this chapter you will find out how to create links between cells using link formulae.

You will also see how Excel charts remain linked to their source data, and how changes in the source values are reflected automatically in the charts.

Finally, you will learn how to add a link from a Word document to a cell range in an Excel spreadsheet.

New skills

At the end of this chapter you should be able to:

- Create links to cells on the same worksheet
- Create links to cells on other worksheets
- Create links to cells in other workbooks
- Add a chart linked to a cell range in one worksheet to any worksheet or workbook
- Create links from Word to cells in an Excel spreadsheet

New words

There are no new words in this chapter.

Linking to a cell on the same worksheet

You have used formulae in Excel before to perform calculations.

For example, the formula *=SUM(A1:A12)* uses the SUM function to add together the values in each cell in the range *A1:A12*, and displays the result.

When you create a link from one cell to another in an Excel spreadsheet, you use a link formula to refer to a cell's contents.

To create a link from one cell on a worksheet to another, you use a link formula in the form *=cellname*, for example, *=A1*.

If you had named the cell, you could refer to it by this custom name instead. The result would be the same; the data shown in the cell containing the link is the value in the linked cell.

In the next exercise, you will link a cell on the *OUTGOING* worksheet of MFPF_FINANCE.XLS to another cell on the same worksheet.

Exercise 8.1: Linking cells on a worksheet

1) Open MFPF_FINANCE.XLS and go to the *OUTGOING* worksheet.
2) In cell *A17*, enter the label *Outgoing total*.
3) In cell *C17*, enter the link formula *=C15*.
   Cell *C17* is now linked to the value in cell *C15*.
4) Enter number values in blank cells in the *Petrol* column and observe that the numbers in cells *C15* and *C17* both change.

Linking to cells in other worksheets

To create a link from a cell in one worksheet to a cell in another worksheet, you use the same principle, but you add an extra piece of information to your link formula that tells Excel which worksheet in the current workbook to look at.

A link from a cell in one worksheet to a cell in another worksheet in the same workbook is in the form *=sheetname!cellname* – for example, *=Sheet1!A1*.

A cell can have a default name and any number of custom names at the same time. A worksheet can only have one name, and this must be the name used in the link formula.

In the next exercise, you will create a link on the *PROFIT* worksheet of MFPF_FINANCE.XLS to the cell containing the value for total annual outgoings on the *OUTGOING* worksheet.

Exercise 8.2: Linking cells across worksheets

1) Go to the *PROFIT* worksheet of MFPF_FINANCE.XLS.
2) In cell *A17*, enter the label *Outgoing Total*.
3) In cell *C17*, enter the link formula *=OUTGOING!C17*.
   Cell *C17* is now linked to cell *C17* of the *OUTGOING* worksheet in the same workbook.
4) Delete the entries you added in the *Petrol* column on the *OUTGOING* worksheet in *Exercise 8.1* on page 66.
   The contents of cells *C15* and *C17* on the *OUTGOING* worksheet, and those of cell *C17* on the *PROFIT* sheet, update automatically to reflect your changes.

Linking to cells in other workbooks

You can even create a link from a cell in one workbook to a cell in another workbook. The link formula is in the form *=[bookname]sheetname!cellname* – for example, *=[book1.xls]sheet1!A1*.

> **Note:** If both workbooks are in the same folder, you only need to give the filename in the square brackets. If the files are in different folders, you will need to enter the full path, including filename, between the square brackets in the link formula.

Exercise 8.3: Linking cells across workbooks

1) Add a new worksheet to MFPF_FINANCE.XLS.
2) In cell *A1* on the new worksheet, enter the link *=[MFPF_ORD.XLS]OUTDOOR!$A$1*
   The value in cell *A1* on the *OUTDOOR* worksheet of MFPF_ORD.XLS now appears in cell *A1* of the new worksheet.
3) Delete the added worksheet, and save your workbook.

Cell references in formulae

The format used in link formulae to refer to cells in other worksheets and workbooks can be used in other formulae too.

For example, the following formula adds the contents of cell *A1* on *sheet1* of the current workbook to the contents of cell *A1* on *sheet1* of a workbook called *book1.xls*:
=sheet1!A1+[book1.xls]sheet1!A1.

Linking to cells in Excel workbooks from Word

Using Word's **Paste Special** command, you can create a link from a Word document to a cell range in an Excel workbook.

When you change the Excel spreadsheet, the linked data in the Word document are updated automatically to reflect your changes.

Mr Murphy is applying for a business loan to buy new machinery for the warehouse. He has already been to see the local bank manager, who has asked to see a summary of the business's incomings and outgoings for the previous year before agreeing to the loan. You have been asked to add these details to a letter Mr Murphy has written.

Although you have not finished working out the figures in MFPF_FINANCE.XLS, you do know which cell range they will go in.

You can add a link to the relevant cell range now, and then when you're finished making your calculations, all you will need to do is open the letter and print it. The data from the cell range in the workbook will be filled into the letter automatically.

In the next exercise, you will add a link from a letter written in a Word document to a cell range in the *PROFIT* worksheet of MFPF_FINANCE.XLS.

Exercise 8.4: Linking from Word to cells in a spreadsheet

1) Go to the *PROFIT* worksheet of MFPF_FINANCE.XLS.
2) Copy the cell range *A1:D15*.
3) Open the Word document LETTER.DOC, and go to the empty paragraph after the line 'I trust they will be to your satisfaction.'
4) Select **Edit | Paste Special** in Word.
   The *Paste Special* dialog box opens.

5) Select *Paste link*, then select *Microscoft Excel Worksheet Object* from the *As* area.

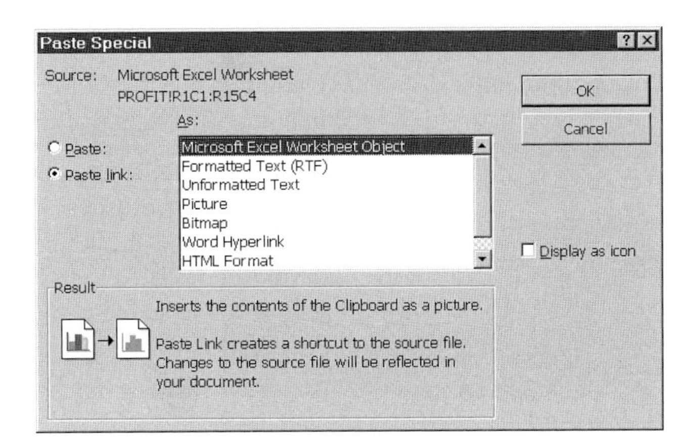

Click **OK**.

A link is added from the Word document to the copied cells in the Excel spreadsheet.

Your letter should now look like this:

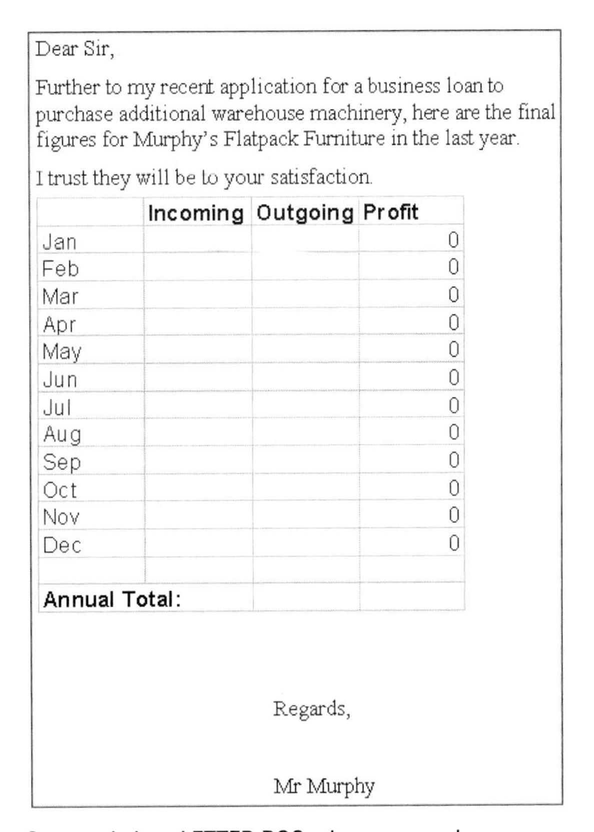

Dear Sir,

Further to my recent application for a business loan to purchase additional warehouse machinery, here are the final figures for Murphy's Flatpack Furniture in the last year.

I trust they will be to your satisfaction.

	Incoming	Outgoing	Profit
Jan			0
Feb			0
Mar			0
Apr			0
May			0
Jun			0
Jul			0
Aug			0
Sep			0
Oct			0
Nov			0
Dec			0
Annual Total:			

Regards,

Mr Murphy

6) Save and close LETTER.DOC when you are done.

Note: You can create a link from a Word document to an Excel chart in exactly the same way.

Over to you: optional

Next, you will check that the link you created from the Word document to the Excel worksheet cell range really works.

- Add some numbers to the *INCOMING* and *OUTGOING* columns in the *PROFIT* worksheet in MFPF_FINANCE.XLS. Open LETTER.DOC and check that the cells in the Word document have been updated to reflect your changes. Delete the numbers you added to the *PROFIT* worksheet when you are done.

Linking charts

When you create a chart in Excel, it is linked automatically to the source data from which it was generated. When you edit the source data, the chart updates automatically to reflect your changes.

When you create a chart, you are given the option of adding it to the current worksheet or to a new worksheet in the same workbook. To add the chart to another existing worksheet of the current workbook, or to a worksheet in a different workbook, you must use **Copy** and **Paste**. Copies of the chart remain linked to the source data.

In the following exercise, you will create a chart that shows MFPF's monthly telephone bill expenditure.

Exercise 8.5: Creating a linked chart

1) Go to the *OUTGOING* worksheet of MFPF_FINANCE.XLS.
2) Select the non-adjacent cell ranges *A2:A13* and *D2:D13*.
(To select non-adjacent cell ranges, select the first range, then holding down the **CTRL** key, select the second range.)
3) Select **Insert | Chart ...** .
– or –
Click the **Chart Wizard** button on the *Standard* toolbar.
The *Chart Wizard* opens.

Chart Wizard button 

4) In the *Chart Wizard*, select *Column* in the *Chart type* field and click **Finish**.
5) A column chart indicating how much was spent on the telephone bill each month is inserted into the current worksheet.

In the next exercise, you will add copies of the chart you just created to a new worksheet in MFPF_FINANCE.XLS and to a worksheet in a new workbook. You will then edit the value of the phone bill for one month and see all three charts update to reflect that change.

Exercise 8.6: Creating copies of a linked chart

1) Select the chart you created in the last exercise.
2) Select **Edit | Copy**.
3) Select **Insert | Worksheet** to add a new worksheet to MFPF_FINANCE.XLS.
4) Open the new worksheet and select **Edit | Paste**.
5) Select **File | New ...** and create a new workbook based on the default template.
6) In the new workbook, paste the copied chart to the *Sheet1* worksheet in the new workbook.
7) Change the entry in cell *D3* on the *OUTGOING* worksheet in MFPF_FINANCE.XLS to – 10 and press **Enter**.
   All three copies of the chart you created update to reflect the change.

When you are done, delete the entry in cell *D3* on the *OUTGOING* worksheet in MFPF_FINANCE.XLS.

Close all your workbooks without saving again when you are done.

Chapter summary

You can create a link from a cell in an Excel spreadsheet to any other cell in any worksheet in any workbook. The complete format for such links is *=[bookname]sheetname!cellname* – for example, *=[Book1.xls]Sheet1!A1*.

Charts created in Excel are linked automatically to the source data they were generated from. Even if a chart is copied to another worksheet or workbook, it remains linked to its source data and updates automatically to reflect changes in those data.

You can use Word's **Paste Special** command to create a link from a Word document to a cell range or chart in an Excel workbook. If the values in the cell range change, the values in the Word document update to reflect the changes.

Formatting your Spreadsheets

In this chapter

When you have added data to your spreadsheet, you will usually add some formatting to make the information clearer and more appealing to the eye.

In ECDL 3 you learned how to apply text and number formats to cells in an Excel spreadsheet.

In this chapter you will learn about other more advanced formatting options in Excel.

New skills

At the end of this chapter you should be able to:

- Freeze row and column titles
- Use Excel's AutoFormat option
- Create and apply a custom number format
- Use conditional formatting

New words

There are no new words in this chapter.

Freezing row and column titles

Where a spreadsheet contains many rows and columns, you may find that when you scroll down or across the worksheet, you are looking at a part of the spreadsheet where no row or column titles are visible. Unless the information in each column is very distinctive, for example, Name, Address and Telephone Number, the data may be difficult to read.

As an example, open MFPF_ORD.XLS, go to the *COMPLETE* worksheet, and look at cell *H50*. What does this number refer to? All the cells around it contain similar data. Unless you have a very large, high-resolution monitor, you probably cannot see the column title for the cell.

To determine what the number in the cell you are looking at refers to, you could scroll to the top of the sheet to see the column label and then scroll back again. But it would be good to be able to see the column labels all the time, no matter how far down the spreadsheet you scrolled.

Well, you can. Excel allows you to select a row, or set of rows, at the top of a spreadsheet and 'freeze' them so that you can see them no matter how far down the rest of the sheet you scroll. You can also freeze a column or group of columns at the left of the spreadsheet to have permanently visible row labels.

In the next exercise, you will create frozen column and row titles on the *COMPLETE* worksheet of MFPF_ORD.XLS.

Exercise 9.1: Freezing row and column titles

1) Open MFPF_ORD.XLS and go to the *COMPLETE* worksheet.

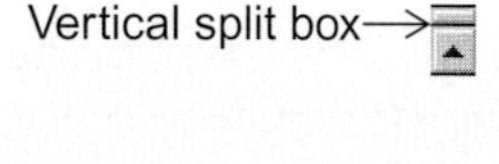

2) Click and drag the vertical split box, located at the top of the vertical scroll bar, to just below row 1.
   The column titles are separated from the rest of the spreadsheet.

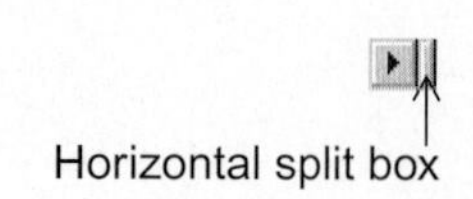

3) Click and drag the horizontal split box, located at the right of the horizontal scroll bar, to the right of column *B*.
   The cells containing the *OrderDate* and *CompanyName* for each row are separated from the rest of the spreadsheet.

Your worksheet should now look like this:

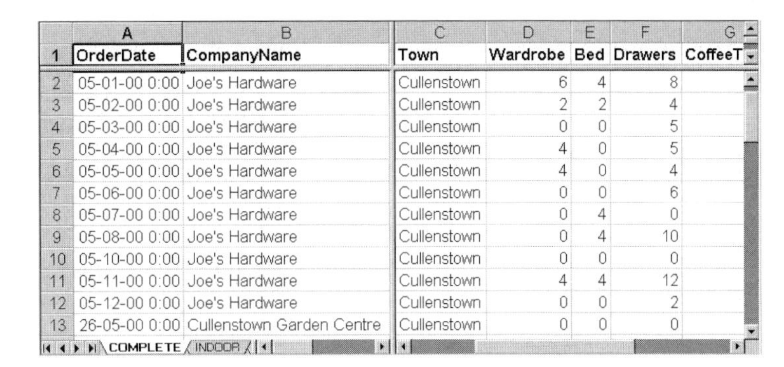

	A	B	C	D	E	F	G
1	OrderDate	CompanyName	Town	Wardrobe	Bed	Drawers	CoffeeT
2	05-01-00 0:00	Joe's Hardware	Cullenstown	6	4	8	
3	05-02-00 0:00	Joe's Hardware	Cullenstown	2	2	4	
4	05-03-00 0:00	Joe's Hardware	Cullenstown	0	0	5	
5	05-04-00 0:00	Joe's Hardware	Cullenstown	4	0	5	
6	05-05-00 0:00	Joe's Hardware	Cullenstown	4	0	4	
7	05-06-00 0:00	Joe's Hardware	Cullenstown	0	0	6	
8	05-07-00 0:00	Joe's Hardware	Cullenstown	0	4	0	
9	05-08-00 0:00	Joe's Hardware	Cullenstown	0	4	10	
10	05-10-00 0:00	Joe's Hardware	Cullenstown	0	0	0	
11	05-11-00 0:00	Joe's Hardware	Cullenstown	4	4	12	
12	05-12-00 0:00	Joe's Hardware	Cullenstown	0	0	2	
13	26-05-00 0:00	Cullenstown Garden Centre	Cullenstown	0	0	0	

COMPLETE / INDOOR

With the worksheet divided in this way, you can scroll independently in each quadrant.

4) Select **Window | Freeze panes**.
   The split dividers disappear and are replaced by lines.
   You can now only scroll in the lower right quadrant.

5) Scroll down the worksheet. The frozen column titles remain visible no matter which rows you are looking at.
   Next, scroll across the worksheet. The frozen cells indicating the *OrderDate* and *CompanyName* for each order remain visible no matter which columns you are looking at.

6) Save and close your workbook when you are done.

You can unfreeze areas by selecting **Window | Unfreeze Panes**. Then, to get rid of the split entirely, select **Window | Remove Split**.

> **Note:** If you want to freeze horizontal and vertical portions of the screen, you must add both splits before freezing. Once a window has been frozen, you cannot split it again. You can only make one split in each direction.

Using AutoFormat

When you apply formatting to a spreadsheet, you can spend a lot of time deciding how you want your data to look, and then applying different fill colours, fonts, etc.

Excel's **AutoFormat** facility allows you to select one of 17 pre-defined design schemes and apply it to a cell range. Each scheme defines formats for numbers, borders, fonts, patterns, alignment, and cell width and height.

In the next exercise, you will format the accounting information on the *OUTGOING* worksheet of MFPF_FINANCE.XLS using an Excel **AutoFormat** option.

Exercise 9.2: Applying AutoFormat

1) Open MFPF_FINANCE.XLS and go to the *OUTGOING* worksheet.
2) Select the cell range *A1:G15*.
3) Select **Format | AutoFormat ...** .
   The *AutoFormat* dialog box opens.
   A sample of each format you can apply is shown in the left-hand panel of the dialog box, with its name below it.
4) Select the style *Classic 3* by clicking it once.
   A black border appears around the format to indicate that it has been selected.
5) Click **Options ...** .
   The *Formats to apply* area opens at the bottom of the dialog box, where you can specify a subset of the format elements of the format you want to use.

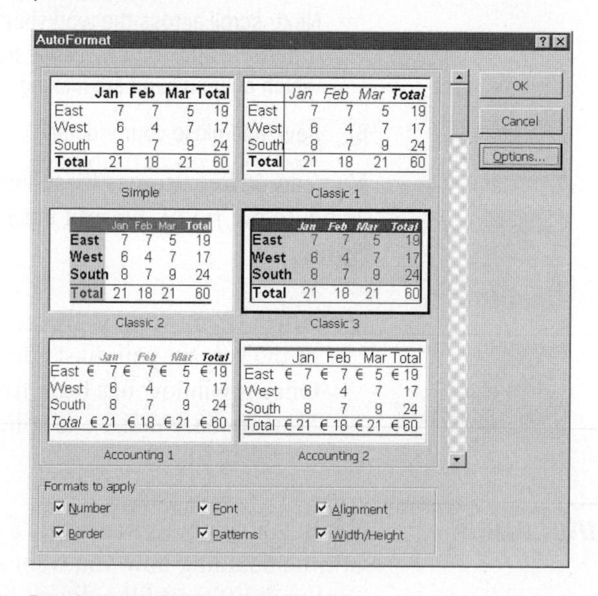

   Deselect the *Border* option.
   Each format preview changes to show how the format looks without borders.
6) Click **OK**.
   The *Classic 3* format is applied to the cell range *A1:G15* on the *OUTGOING* worksheet.
7) Save your workbook when you are done.

Over to you: optional

Try applying other **AutoFormat** styles to the cell range you just formatted. When you find one you like, apply the same format to the accounting information on the *INCOMING* and *PROFIT* worksheets.

Custom number formats

In ECDL 3 you learned how to apply number formats to cells in a worksheet to define how numeric data should appear – for example, with a certain number of decimal places, with a particular thousands indicator, or with a particular currency symbol.

If you want to use a number format that doesn't already exist in Excel, you can define a custom number format.

Mr Murphy has asked you to format numbers in a cell range in DELIVERIES.XLS as distances in kilometres. There is no default number style in Excel that will let you do this. If you just added the letters *km* to the numbers in each cell, the cell contents would be treated as text, and you would not be able to use the data in calculations later.

In the next exercise, you will create a custom number format to indicate kilometre distances, and then apply it to a cell range.

Exercise 9.3: Creating a custom number format

1) Open DELIVERIES.XLS and go to the *CHARGES* worksheet.
2) Select column *B*, which lists the distances to each customer's premises.
3) Select **Format | Cells ...** .
   – or –
   Click the **Format Cells** button on the *Formatting* toolbar.
   The *Format Cells* dialog box opens.

   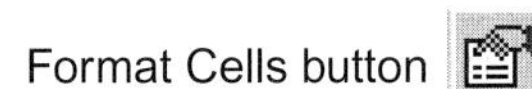
   Format Cells button
4) Click the **Number** tab.
5) Select *Custom* in the *Category* list.
6) In the *Type* field, enter the text *0.0 "km"* (including the quotation marks) and press **Enter**.
   All the cells in column *B* that contain numeric data are now formatted to have one decimal place, and the letters *km* appear after the numbers.
7) Save and close your workbook when you are done.

Conditional formatting

Sometimes you will want to apply a certain type of formatting to data only if they satisfy certain criteria. For example, you might want to format every negative number in a cell range in bold, red text.

You could look at the values in each cell, identify the negative ones, and manually apply the required formatting to each one. Alternatively, you could use conditional formatting to automatically check the values in each cell of a cell range and format the negative ones in bold, red text.

You can also format the contents of one cell in a particular way if the value in another cell satisfies certain criteria.

For example, in cell *D9* on the *PERSONAL NOTES* worksheet of INVOICE_MFPF.XLT, the text *Late* has been entered and formatted in white so that it cannot be seen. The cell has conditional formatting associated with it: if the payment date in cell *C9* is more than 28 days after the invoice date in cell *C8*, then the text in this cell is formatted in red.

MFPF have estimated maximum payments for each utility. The estimated maximum for any electricity bill is £40. You have been asked to automatically flag any bill that exceeds that amount.

In the next exercise, you will apply conditional formatting to data in the *Electricity* column on the *OUTGOING* worksheet of MFPF_FINANCE.XLS, so that any payment exceeding £40 is shown in bold, red text.

Exercise 9.4: Applying conditional formatting

1) Go to the *OUTGOING* worksheet of MFPF_FINANCE.XLS.
2) Select the cell range *C2:C13*, which contains the values for electricity payments made by the business.
3) Select **Format | Conditional Formatting ...** .
   The *Conditional Formatting* dialog box opens.

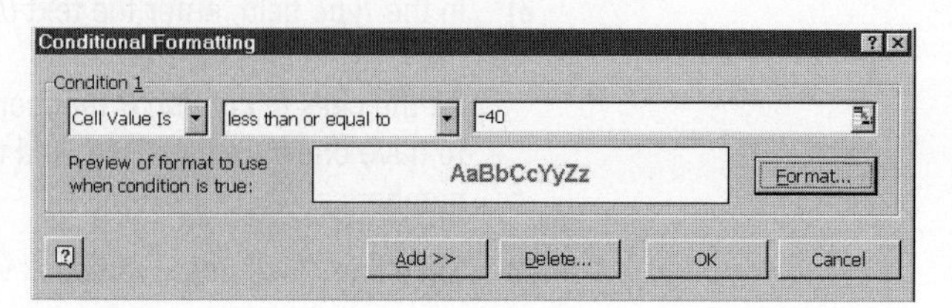

4) In the *Condition 1* area of the *Conditional Formatting* dialog box, set the following condition:
Cell Value Is less than or equal to –40.
Remember, because the numbers on this worksheet indicate money that is being paid out by the business, they have been entered as negative values.

5) Click **Format ...** to open the *Format Cells* dialog box, where you will specify the format to apply if the condition is met.

6) In the *Format Cells* dialog box, select *Bold* in the *Font Style* area, and *Red* in the *Color* drop-down list.
Click **OK**.
You could add more conditional formatting rules to the cell by clicking **Add**. For now, you will only apply one conditional format.

7) Click **OK**.

8) Save your workbook.

The value in cell *C3* is now formatted in bold, red text as it exceeds the estimated maximum, as defined in *Condition 1.*

Over to you: optional

To impress the Murphys, you decide also to flag entries where the payment amount is close to the estimated maximum.

- Apply conditional formatting rules to format payments of £39 and over in bold, orange text, and those of £38 and over in bold, yellow text.

  Note: Excel applies formatting to the contents of a cell according to which of the defined conditions is satisfied first. Thus, the order in which you define your conditional formatting rules is important. £41 is obviously greater than £38, £39 and £40. If you specify the rules in the order given, £41 will be formatted in red; however, if you were to specify them in the reverse order, it would be formatted in yellow.

Chapter summary

Excel allows you to select a row, or set of rows, at the top of a spreadsheet and 'freeze' them so that you can see them no matter how far down the rest of the sheet you scroll. You can also freeze a column or group of columns at the left of the spreadsheet to have permanently visible row labels.

Excel's **AutoFormat** facility allows you to select one of 17 pre-defined design schemes and apply it to a cell range. Each scheme defines formats for numbers, borders, fonts, patterns, alignment, and cell width and height.

You can define custom number formats to use when formatting cells in Excel.

You can also use conditional formatting rules to format data in a certain way if they satisfy specified criteria.

10 Using Excel Macros

In this chapter

Excel allows you to save time on repetitive tasks in several ways.

Earlier, you learned how to use a template to save default content and settings for a type of spreadsheet you would use many times.

In this chapter, you will learn the equally useful skill of defining your own commands in Excel to perform any series of actions that you repeat regularly.

New skills

At the end of this chapter you should be able to:

- Record a macro
- Run a recorded macro
- Assign a recorded macro to a toolbar button

New words

At the end of this chapter you should be able to explain the following term:

- Macro

What are macros?

From time to time, you will want to perform the same series of actions on a cell or cell range in several worksheets.

For example, say you use Excel to keep track of all the phone calls you make in a month. Each month you create a new worksheet and add the numbers you dial in column *A* and the call durations in column *B*. At the end of the month, you sort the entries on the sheet by the number dialled, then apply different formatting to columns *A* and *B*. You also apply conditional formatting to column *B* to highlight any calls that went on for over an hour.

Because you perform these exact actions in exactly the same way every month, it would save you time in the long run to have a single Excel command that could perform this task.

Well, you can create a command that performs all of these actions and save it in Excel.

Excel allows you to record a series of actions that are always performed in the same way, and in the same order, and save the series as a new command, called a macro.

Macro
A macro is a custom command defined to perform a series of specific actions in the same way and in the same order every time the macro is run.

Macros are associated with Excel workbooks. You can save a macro in one of three places:

- Personal Macro Workbook – The Personal Macro Workbook is stored in the Excel start-up folder. Any macros you save in this workbook will be available to you whenever you run Excel, no matter what workbook you are editing.
- New Workbook – You can choose to create a new workbook and save the macro there. The macro will be available to you when you edit the new workbook.
- This Workbook – If you save the macro in the workbook you create it in, it will be available to you whenever you edit that workbook.

Note: If a workbook you open contains macros, a dialog box will appear alerting you to this fact, and asking if you want to enable or disable the macros. If you disable the macros, they cannot run. This allows you to protect yourself from macro viruses.

Recording macros

To record a macro in Excel, you first tell Excel to start recording what you are doing, then you perform the actions you want the macro to perform whenever you run it. When you have finished, you tell Excel to stop recording your actions. Everything you do from the time you tell Excel to start recording to when you tell it to stop is included in the macro.

If you apply formatting to a cell, then change your mind and change it to something else, both of the formatting actions are remembered and performed, in order, by the macro when it is run. Every action included in the macro increases its size, so you must be clear before you start recording exactly what it is that you want to record.

Another important aspect of macros is that they can be absolute or relative.

Absolute macros

An absolute macro is one that performs exactly the same set of actions on the exact same cell or cell range whenever it is run. An absolute macro might always change the format for columns *A* and *D*, or always delete the contents of the cell range *A3:D5*, for example.

Relative macros

A relative macro performs the set of recorded actions relative to the cell or cell range selected when you run the macro.
A relative macro might assign a particular background colour, text colour, font and number format to the contents of the selected cell or cell range when it is run, for example.

Mr Murphy urgently needs the *COMPLETE*, *INDOOR* and *OUTDOOR* worksheets of MFPF_ORD.XLS reformatted. He has asked you to apply a certain type of formatting to all three sheets in the next five minutes.

You know that you can apply the required formatting to one of the sheets in five minutes, but you doubt you'll have time to format the other two sheets as well. But, if you record the changes you make to the first sheet in a macro, then you can reapply all of the changes to each of the other sheets in seconds.

In the next exercise, you will record an absolute macro to apply formatting to data imported using the MFPF_Q1.DQY query you created and saved earlier.

Exercise 10.1: Recording a macro

1) Open MFPF_ORD.XLS and go to the *COMPLETE* worksheet.
2) You will include commands to split and freeze the first row and first two columns of the selected worksheet in your formatting macro.
   To remove the freezes already applied to the data in the *COMPLETE* worksheet, select **Window | Unfreeze panes**, then select **Window | Remove Split**.
   Now you are ready to start recording your macro.
3) Select **Tools | Macros | Record New Macro ...** .
   The *Record Macro* dialog box opens.

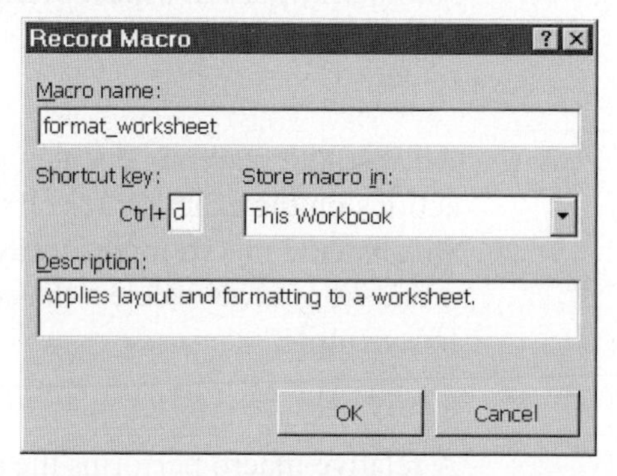

4) In the *Macro name* field, enter *format_worksheet*.
   In the *Shortcut key* field enter *d*.
   In the *Store macro in* field, select *This Workbook*.
   In the *Description* field, enter the text *Applies layout and formatting to a worksheet*.
   Click **OK**.
   The *Record Macro* dialog box closes, and the *Stop Recording* toolbar appears.

Everything you do from now until you stop recording will be saved in the new macro.

Relative Reference button 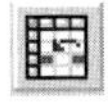

5) You want to record an absolute macro, so make sure that the **Relative Reference** button on the *Stop Recording* toolbar is not pressed.
   If you wanted to record a relative macro, you would press this button first, before making any other changes you wanted to include in the macro.

6) Apply the following formatting changes:
   - Add a horizontal split below row *1*.
   - Add a vertical split to the right of column *B*.
   - Select **Window | Freeze**.
   - Format the text in row *1* as dark blue italics.
   - Add a background fill of pale yellow to the cells in row *1*.
   - Format the cells in column *A* as dates, selecting 14-Mar-98 from the *Type* area on the **Number** tab of the *Format Cells* dialog box.

Stop Recording button

7) Select **Tools | Macro | Stop recording.**
   – or –
   Click the **Stop recording** button on the *Stop Recording* toolbar.

8) Save your workbook when you are done.

Running macros

Next, you will learn how to run your saved macro on the *INDOOR* and *OUTDOOR* worksheets, and in a matter of seconds you will have a perfectly consistent set of formatted query results.

In the next exercise, you will run your macro from the *Macro* dialog box and by using the shortcut you defined when recording the macro.

Exercise 10.2: Running a macro

1) Go to the *INDOOR* worksheet of MFPF_ORD.XLS.

2) Select **Tools | Macro | Macros ...** .
   The *Macro* dialog box opens.
   This dialog box lists all of the macros saved in the current workbook.

3) Select the macro called *format_worksheet* and click **Run**.

4) Go to the *OUTDOOR* worksheet.
   Press **Ctrl** and **d** to run the macro using the shortcut you defined when you created it.
5) Save your workbook when you are done.

All three worksheets are now formatted identically thanks to your macro.

Adding macros to a toolbar

You can add a custom toolbar button to any of Excel's toolbars and assign any command, including a recorded macro, to the new toolbar button.

The toolbar button will always appear on the toolbar, no matter what workbook you are editing. If you click the button when you are editing a different workbook, Excel will open the workbook where the macro is saved in order to run it.

Mrs Murphy wants you to create several more worksheets containing the results of the MFPF_Q1.DQY query, with different sort and filter requirements on each. She wants to have all of the query results formatted in the same way. You decide to add a button to the *Formatting* toolbar so that you can run your macro in one click in future.

In the next exercise, you will add a new button to the *Formatting* toolbar, and assign your macro to that button.

Exercise 10.3: Assigning a macro to a toolbar button

1) Go to any worksheet in MFPF_ORD.XLS.
2) Select **View | Toolbars | Customize ...** .
   The *Customize* dialog box opens.
3) Go to the **Commands** tab of the *Customize* dialog box.

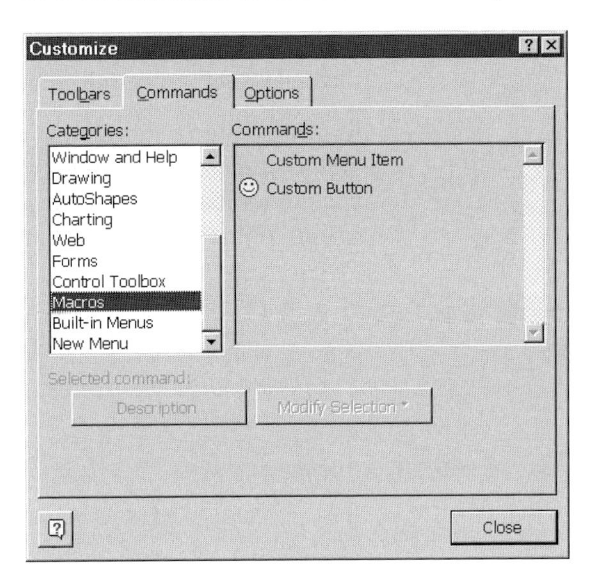

4) In the *Categories* area, select *Macros*.
5) Click the *Custom Button* option in the *Commands* area, and drag it to the *Formatting* toolbar.
6) Right-click the new toolbar button and select *Assign Macro* from the shortcut menu that opens.
   The *Assign Macro* dialog box opens.
7) In the *Macro name* area, select *format_worksheet*, and click **OK**.
8) Click **Close**.
   Your toolbar button now appears on the *Formatting* toolbar. Whenever you click it, it will run your recorded macro.
9) Save and close your workbook when you are done.

Over to you: optional

Next, you will use your new toolbar button to apply formatting to query results in a new workbook.

- Create a new workbook, run the saved query MFPF_Q1.DQY, and click the toolbar button to run your formatting macro. Close the new workbook without saving when you are done.

Chapter summary

A macro is a custom command defined to perform a series of specific actions in the same way and in the same order every time the macro is run.

An absolute macro is one that performs the exact same set of actions on the exact same cell or cell range whenever it is run.

A relative macro performs the set of recorded actions relative to the cell or cell range selected when you run the macro.

You can define a shortcut when you are recording your macro and use that shortcut to run your macro. You can also add a custom toolbar button to any Excel toolbar and assign your macro to that new toolbar button.

11 Using Reference and Mathematical Functions

In this chapter

Up to now, you have done a lot of work setting up your Excel spreadsheets and adding raw data to them. Now you can start to generate some figures for MFPF's incoming revenue and outgoing expenses in the MFPF_FINANCE.XLS workbook.

In this chapter, you will use some of Excel's mathematical functions and commands to generate these numbers.

You will also use reference functions and learn how to nest functions.

New skills

At the end of this chapter you should be able to:

- Use HLOOKUP and VLOOKUP reference functions
- Use the **Subtotals** command
- Create a 3D sum function
- Use the SUMIF mathematical function
- Use the ROUND mathematical function

New words

There are no new words in this chapter.

Maths with Paste Special

In Chapter 6 you learned that you can use Excel's **Paste Special** command to combine copied numerical data with numerical data in a destination cell or cell range using simple mathematical functions. Now you will use this functionality to calculate sales revenue and materials costs for the products sold by MFPF over the year.

The *INCOMING* worksheet of MFPF_FINANCE.XLS has an empty column, *Products*, where you will put figures for incoming revenue from product sales.

To work out these figures, you will combine the sales figures you calculated in Chapter 7 with the data you imported from PRICES.TXT in Chapter 3. Both of these sets of numbers are on the *SALES TOTALS* worksheet of MFPF_FINANCE.XLS.

In the next exercise, you will create a copy of the named cell range *SALES*, and combine the data in the cell range with the prices in the *Sell for* row to work out the revenue generated by sales of each product each month.

Exercise 11.1: Multiplying numbers using Paste Special

1) Open MFPF_FINANCE.XLS and go to the cell range named *SALES*.
2) Copy the *SALES* cell range, and paste the data to a new cell range starting in cell *A18* on the *SALES TOTALS* worksheet.
3) Name the new cell range *REVENUE*.
4) Copy the product price data in cells *B16:H16*.
5) Select the cell range *B19:H30*.
6) Select **Edit | Paste Special**.
   The *Paste Special* dialog box opens.
7) In the *Paste* area, select *Values*.
   In the *Operation* area, select *Multiply*.
   Click **OK**.
8) Save your workbook.

The *REVENUE* cell range now indicates the total money earned by MFPF by selling each product type each month.

Over to you: mandatory

Now that you know how much was earned by selling each product type each month, you will calculate the total revenue for the month by adding all of these figures up.

- Using the SUM function, which you learned about in ECDL 3, add up the revenue figures for all product types each month.
- Copy and paste the final revenue figures for each month into the *Products* column on the *INCOMING* worksheet.

Next, you will work out how much was spent on the materials needed to make the ordered furniture each month, and add those figures to the *Materials* column on the *OUTGOING* worksheet.

- Create another copy of the *SALES* range on the *SALES TOTALS* worksheet.
- Combine the data in the new cell range with the figures in the *Materials* row to calculate materials costs for each furniture type each month.
- Calculate the monthly total for materials purchases, and copy and paste the final figures to the *Materials* column on the *OUTGOING* worksheet.

Save your workbook when you are done.

Reference functions

There are only two more sets of figures left to calculate to complete the records on the *INCOMING* and *OUTGOING* worksheets: revenue from delivery charges, and expenditure on petrol while making the deliveries.

To calculate these figures, you will use the data in DELIVERIES.XLS. The *CHARGES* worksheet indicates how far away each customer is, and what delivery charge they pay for each order. The *DELIVERIES* worksheet lists the date of each delivery, and the customer to which the delivery was made.

You will add a third column to the *DELIVERIES* worksheet, which shows the delivery charge paid for each order.

To calculate this value, you will need to check which customer each row in the *DELIVERIES* worksheet refers to, and then look up the delivery charge for that customer on the *CHARGES* worksheet.

To do this, you will use a reference function, VLOOKUP.

VLOOKUP

VLOOKUP is an Excel function that checks a cell range for a row starting with a specified value, and returns the value in a specified column of that row.

The reference function VLOOKUP has the following format:

=VLOOKUP(Lookup_value, Table_array, Col_index_num, Range_lookup)	
Lookup_value	The value to look for in the first column of the *Table_array*.
Table_array	The cell range to look at. Entries in the *Table_array* must be sorted by the first column in ascending order if you specify a value of *1* for *Range_lookup*.
Col_index_num	The number (not letter) for the column in the table array that contains the value you want returned.
Range_lookup	*1 (TRUE)* or *0 (FALSE)*. If you leave this value blank, 0 is used by default. If *Range_lookup* is *1*, then if the *Lookup_value* is not found, the row starting with the closest value less than the *Lookup_value* is used instead. This is why the entries in the *Table_array* must be sorted by the first column in ascending order. If *Range_lookup* is *0*, then an error will be given if an exact match to your *Lookup_value* is not found in the first column of the *Table_array*.

Note: The parts of the function in the brackets are called parameters. They should always be separated by commas.

Some parameters are optional, and you do not have to specify a value for them. If you do not specify a value for a parameter, you should include a blank space instead of that parameter, and separate it from the other parameter values using commas – this tells Excel that the next value given is for the next parameter and not for the one you are skipping. If an optional parameter comes at the end of the parameter list, you can simply leave it out.

In the next exercise, you will use the VLOOKUP function to find the corresponding *Delivery charge* in column *C* on the *CHARGES* worksheet for the *CompanyName* in column *B* of every record on the *DELIVERIES* worksheet.

Exercise 11.2: Using VLOOKUP

1) Open DELIVERIES.XLS and go to the *DELIVERIES* worksheet.
2) Label column *C Delivery charge*.
3) In cell *C2* on the *DELIVERIES* worksheet, enter the following formula:
   =VLOOKUP(B2,CHARGES!$A$1:$C$7,3)
   to find the value in the third column of the table array on the *CHARGES* worksheet for the company listed in cell *B2* of the *DELIVERIES* worksheet.
4) Copy the formula to the other cells in column *C*.

   Column *C* now contains the charge for each delivery listed.

   Note: The relative *B2* cell reference is updated to reflect the appropriate row in the copied formulae, but the absolute references used to define the table array mean that the same cell range on the *CHARGES* worksheet is used in each formula.

Over to you: mandatory

Next, you will work out how much was spent on petrol for each delivery.

- Label column *D* on the *DELIVERIES* worksheet *Petrol*.
- In cell *D2*, enter a formula that multiplies the distance to the customer listed in cell *B2* for each delivery by 2 to get the round-trip distance, and then by £0.06 (the average cost Mr Murphy pays for petrol per km). Use a VLOOKUP function to find the distance to the customer in the same table array used in the previous exercise.

HLOOKUP

A similar function to VLOOKUP, called HLOOKUP, checks a cell range for a column starting with a specified value, and returns the value in a specified row of that column.

The reference function HLOOKUP has the following format:

=HLOOKUP(Lookup_value, Table_array, Col_index_num, Range_lookup)	
Lookup_value	The value to look for in the first row of the *Table_array*.
Table_array	The cell range to look at. Entries in the *Table_array* must be sorted by the first row in ascending order if you specify a value of *1* for *Range_lookup*.
Row_index_num	The number for the row in the table array that contains the value you want returned.
Range_lookup	*1 (TRUE)* or *0 (FALSE)*. If you leave this value blank, 0 is used by default. If *Range_lookup* is *1*, then if the *Lookup_value* is not found, the column starting with the closest value less than the *Lookup_value* is used instead. This is why the entries in the *Table_array* must be sorted by the first row in ascending order. If *Range_lookup* is *0*, then an error will be given if an exact match to your *Lookup_value* is not found in the first row of the *Table_array*.

Next, you will work out the delivery charge for each order using a transposed table array and HLOOKUP.

Exercise 11.3: Using HLOOKUP

1) Go to the *CHARGES* worksheet of DELIVERIES.XLS.
2) Copy the cell range *A1:C7.*
3) Insert a new worksheet into the workbook and name it *CHARGES2*.
4) Use **Paste Special**'s *Transpose* option to paste the values from the copied data to cell rage *A1:G3*.
5) In cell *E2* on the *DELIVERIES* worksheet, enter the following formula:
   =HLOOKUP(B2,CHARGES2!$A$1:$G$3,3)
   to find the value in the third fow of the table array on the *CHARGES2* worksheet for the company listed in cell *B2* of the *DELIVERIES* worksheet.
6) Copy the formula to the other cells in column *E*.

The numbers in column *E* should be the same as those in column *C*.

Subtotalling

Now you know the charge and the cost of petrol for each delivery. Next, you will work out what the monthly total for each one is, using Excel's **Subtotals** command.

The **Subtotals** command allows you to create subtotals of the values in specified columns in a sorted list. Excel looks for changes in the values in specified sorted columns to identify the end of a group, and adds a subtotal at that point.

In the next exercise, you will sort the data on the *DELIVERIES* worksheet of DELIVERIES.XLS by month, and calculate monthly subtotals for delivery charges and petrol.

Before calculating monthly subtotals, you will change the format of the entries in the *DeliveryDate* column to show the month and year only, otherwise each change in the day of the month will be identified as the end of a group, and you will calculate subtotals for each day instead of for each month.

Exercise 11.4: Calculating subtotals

1) Go to the *DELIVERIES* worksheet of DELIVERIES.XLS and select column *A*.

2) Select **Format | Cells ...** .
   – or –
   Click the **Format Cells** button on the *Formatting* toolbar.
   The *Format Cells* dialog box opens.

3) Click the **Number** tab.

4) In the *Category* area, select *Date*, and in the *Type* area, select *Mar-98*.
   This will format the dates to show only their month and year components.
   Click **OK**.

5) Select columns *A* to *D*, and then select **Data | Subtotals ...** .
   The *Subtotal* dialog box opens.

6) In the *At each change in* field, select *DeliveryDate*.
   In the *Use function* field, select *Sum*.
   In the *Add subtotal to* area, check the boxes beside *Delivery Charge* and *Petrol*
   Your dialog box should now look like this:

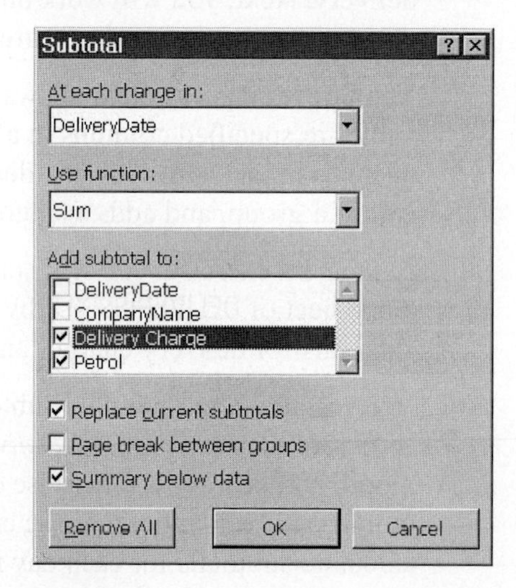

   Click **OK**.

Excel calculates subtotals for the specified columns, and adds them to your worksheet.

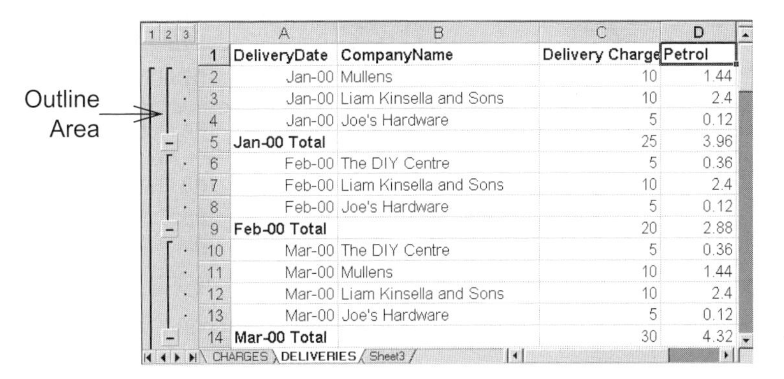

	A	B	C	D
1	DeliveryDate	CompanyName	Delivery Charge	Petrol
2	Jan-00	Mullens	10	1.44
3	Jan-00	Liam Kinsella and Sons	10	2.4
4	Jan-00	Joe's Hardware	5	0.12
5	Jan-00 Total		25	3.96
6	Feb-00	The DIY Centre	5	0.36
7	Feb-00	Liam Kinsella and Sons	10	2.4
8	Feb-00	Joe's Hardware	5	0.12
9	Feb-00 Total		20	2.88
10	Mar-00	The DIY Centre	5	0.36
11	Mar-00	Mullens	10	1.44
12	Mar-00	Liam Kinsella and Sons	10	2.4
13	Mar-00	Joe's Hardware	5	0.12
14	Mar-00 Total		30	4.32

CHARGES / DELIVERIES / Sheet3

7) Click the '-' symbols in the *Outline* area to hide the record rows and show only the subtotal results.

8) Save your workbook when you are done.

Over to you: mandatory

Next, you will add the subtotals for each month to MFPF_FINANCE.XLS.

- Using **Copy** and **Paste Special**, copy the monthly revenue from deliveries and the monthly petrol expenses to the spaces left for them on the *INCOMING* and *OUTGOING* worksheets of MFPF_FINANCE.XLS. Save both workbooks when you are done, and close DELIVERIES.XLS.

  Note: You will have to copy each figure individually instead of copying the cell range. If you try to copy the cell range containing the results, you will also copy the cells in the hidden rows.

3D sum

In ECDL 3, you learned how to use the SUM function to add up the values in a 2D cell range on a worksheet. You can also use the SUM function to sum in three dimensions, across a series of worksheets, where the numbers you want to add up appear in the same cell or cell range on each worksheet.

A 3D sum function has the following format:

=SUM(First_sheet:Last_sheet!Cell)	
First_sheet	The first worksheet in the 3D range.
Last_sheet	The last worksheet in the 3D range.
Cell	The cell or cell range on all of the worksheets in the specified range that contains the values you want to sum.

On the *INCOMING* and *OUTGOING* worksheets of MFPF_FINANCE.XLS, the total amounts of money each year that are earned by the business and paid out by the business are calculated in cell *C15*.

In the next exercise, you will add a 3D sum to the *PROFIT* worksheet, which adds up the values that appear in cell *C15* on each sheet.

Exercise 11.5: Creating a 3D sum

1) Go to the *PROFIT* worksheet of MFPF_FINANCE.XLS.
2) Select cell *C15*.
3) Click the **Autosum** button on the *Standard* toolbar.

Autosum button Σ

4) Go to the *INCOMING* worksheet and select cell *C15*.
5) Hold down the **Shift** key and click the tab for the *OUTGOING* worksheet.
6) Press **Enter**.
7) Save your workbook when you are done.

The total calculated by adding together the values in cell *C15* on each of the worksheets is now displayed in cell *C15* on the *PROFIT* worksheet.

SUMIF

You can specify that you want to sum data only if they satisfy certain criteria using Excel's SUMIF function.

The mathematical function SUMIF has the following format:

=SUMIF(Range_to_eval, Criteria, Sum_range)	
Range_to_eval	The range of cells to check against your criteria.
Criteria	The tests to perform to see whether to include the data in the sum.
Sum_range	The range of cells containing the data you want to sum. If you do not specify a *Sum_range*, the values in the *Range_to_eval* will be summed instead. There should be a one-to-one correspondence between cells in the *Range_to_eval* and *Sum_range*.

Note: Criteria are enclosed in quotation marks, can be any comparisons using the expressions <, >, =, <= (which means less than or equal to) or >= (which means greater than or equal to), and can include cell references as well as numeric and text values.

MFPF currently requires a minimum order of eight for garden chairs. Mr Murphy is thinking about increasing this number to 12. He has asked you to look at last year's figures and work out how many chairs would have been sold if MFPF had refused to fill orders for less than 12 chairs at a time.

In the next exercise, you will calculate how many chairs were sold last year in total, and how many of them were sold in orders for 12 or more chairs.

Exercise 11.6: Using the SUMIF function

1) Open MFPF_ORD.XLS and go to the *COMPLETE* worksheet.
2) In cell *I56*, below the column giving order numbers for garden chairs, enter the formula *=SUM(I2:I55)*.
3) In cell *I57* enter the formula *=SUMIF(I2:I55, ">=12")*.

The number in cell *I57* is smaller than the number in *I56*, because only those orders for 12 or more chairs were included in the sum.

Over to you: optional

Next, check how many garden tables would have been sold if no order for less than three tables at a time was filled. Save and close the workbook when you are done.

SUMPOSITIVE

As you know, ECDL is a vendor-independent certification. One of the Advanced Spreadsheets syllabus requirements is to know about SUMPOSITIVE. SUMPOSITIVE is a Lotus 1-2-3 function that sums only the positive values in a cell range. You can use Excel's SUMIF function to do the same job using the formula *=SUMIF(Range_to_eval, ">0", Sum_range)*.

ROUND

Occasionally, you will want to round numbers on a spreadsheet to a particular number of decimal places. Excel's ROUND function allows you to specify any number of digits before or after the decimal point to which you can round the number.

The mathematical function ROUND has the following format:

=ROUND(Number, Num_digits)	
Number	The number you want to round.
Num_digits	The number of digits before or after the decimal point to round to. A negative number indicates a position to the left of the decimal point, and a positive number indicates a position to the right.

Mrs Murphy has asked you to provide her with a list of the monthly profits on the *PROFIT* worksheet of MFPF_FINANCE.XLS, with each value rounded to the nearest £100.

In the next exercise, you will add a column to the *PROFIT* worksheet, which shows rounded profit figures for each month.

Exercise 11.7: Using the ROUND function

1) Open MFPF_FINANCE.XLS and go to the *PROFIT* worksheet.
2) Label column *E* Rounded Profit.
3) In cell *E2*, enter the formula *=ROUND(D2, –2)*.
4) Copy the formula to the cells *E3:E13*.

Column *E* now shows the profits for each month of the year rounded to the nearest £100.

D	E
Profit	Rounded Profit
£3,482.84	£3,500.00
£1,057.78	£1,100.00
£605.32	£600.00
£465.94	£500.00
£3,060.26	£3,100.00
£2,590.76	£2,600.00
£3,695.02	£3,700.00
£2,997.06	£3,000.00
£508.74	£500.00
£185.98	£200.00
£1,648.84	£1,600.00
£598.00	£600.00

Nesting

In the previous exercise, you used the ROUND function to manipulate a number generated by a SUM function. You could have combined both functions in a single formula by nesting them.

If you use one function as an argument in another function, then the first function is nested in the second.

You can nest up to seven functions inside a function.

In the next exercise, you will create a nested function to calculate the profit figure for a month and round it to the nearest £100.

Exercise 11.8: Nesting functions

1) Open MFPF_FINANCE.XLS and go to the *PROFIT* worksheet.
2) Label column *F Rounded Profit (using nesting)*.
3) In cell *F2*, enter *=ROUND(SUM(B2:C2),_2)*.
   This formula first calculates the sum of the values in the cells in the cell range *B2:C2*, and then applies the ROUND function to show the result rounded to the nearest hundreds value.
4) Copy the formula to cells *F3:F13*.

The results in column *F* are identical to those in column *E* and were achieved using just one formula.

When you are done, save and close your workbook.

Chapter summary

VLOOKUP is an Excel function that checks a cell range for a row starting with a specified value, and returns the value in a specified column of that row.

HLOOKUP is an Excel function that checks a cell range for a column starting with a specified value, and returns the value in a specified row of that column.

The **Subtotals** command allows you to create subtotals of values in a sorted list. Excel looks for changes in the values in one specified column to identify the end of a group, and creates a subtotal at that point.

You can use the SUM function to sum in three dimensions, across a series of worksheets, where the numbers you want to add up appear in the same cell or cell range on each worksheet.

You can specify that you want to include data in a calculation only if they satisfy certain criteria, using the SUMIF function.

The ROUND function allows you to specify any number of digits before or after the decimal point to which the number is to be rounded.

You can combine a number of functions in a single formula by nesting them inside one another, using parentheses.

12 Customizing Charts

In this chapter

In ECDL 3 you learned how to create charts in Excel, and how to make simple changes to them.

In this chapter you will learn how to make more advanced changes to charts after you have added them.

New skills

At the end of this chapter you should be able to:

- Delete a data series from a chart
- Change the angle of pie-chart slices
- Explode all the segments in a pie chart
- Format the text or numbers on a chart axis
- Reposition chart titles, legends and data labels
- Widen the gap between columns or bars in a chart
- Insert an image into a chart

New words

There are no new words in this chapter.

Deleting a data series from a chart

Sometimes, you may find that after you have created a chart you need to remove a particular data series. Maybe one data series dominates the chart, making it difficult to see the others. Maybe you accidentally included values for a salesperson who deals with a different geographical area from the one covered by the chart.

You could delete your chart, reselect the source data, and generate a new chart that shows only the relevant data series.

But Excel allows you to edit the chart directly and remove the data series there, preserving any other changes you have made in the meantime.

Mrs Murphy has asked you to generate a chart that shows the sales of each product each month over the year.

In the next exercise, you will create the chart, and add it to a new worksheet in MFPF_FINANCE.XLS.

Exercise 12.1: Creating a column chart

1) Open MFPF_FINANCE.XLS and select the cell range named *SALES*.
2) Select **Insert | Chart ...** .
   – or –
   Click the **Chart Wizard** button on the *Standard* toolbar.
   The *Chart Wizard* dialog box appears.
3) In the *Chart type* area, select *Column*.
   In the *Chart sub-type* area, select *Clustered column with a 3-D visual effect*.

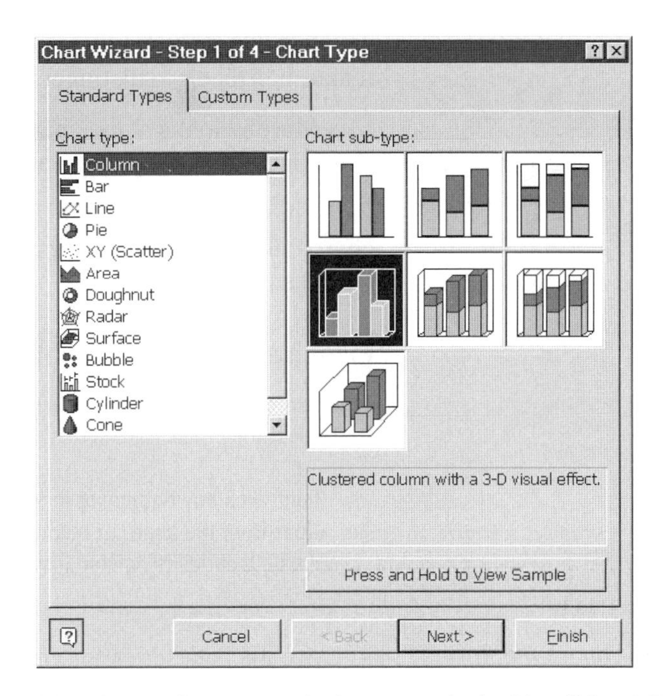

4) Click **Next** until you get to the last screen in the *Chart Wizard: Chart Location*.

5) Select *Add as new sheet*, and click **Finish**.
Your chart is created and added to a new worksheet named *Chart1*.
Your chart should look like this:

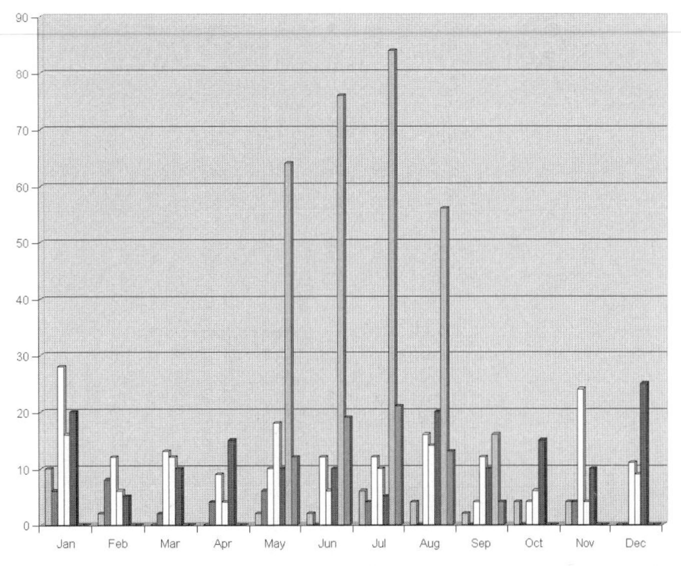

There is a trend for a lot of garden furniture to be bought in the summer months. Because of these high summer sales, the data series for garden chairs swamps the rest of the data in the chart.

The fact that there are up to seven columns in each cluster also makes it difficult to distinguish one column from another.

Mrs Murphy looks at the chart, and asks you to change it to show data for sales of bedroom furniture only.

In the next exercise, you will begin to delete data series from the chart you already generated, instead of regenerating the chart with the required data only.

Exercise 12.2: Deleting a data series from a chart

1) Click any data point (i.e., column) in the *Garden Chair* data series to select the whole data series, and press the **Delete** key.
   – or –
   Right-click any data point in the *Garden Chair* data series and select **Clear** from the shortcut menu that appears.
   The data series is deleted from the chart.

Over to you: mandatory

Remove the data series for *Garden Table*, *Kitchen Organizer* and *Coffee Table* in the same way.

Your chart now contains three columns in each cluster of data points. It is much easier to read than the original graph.

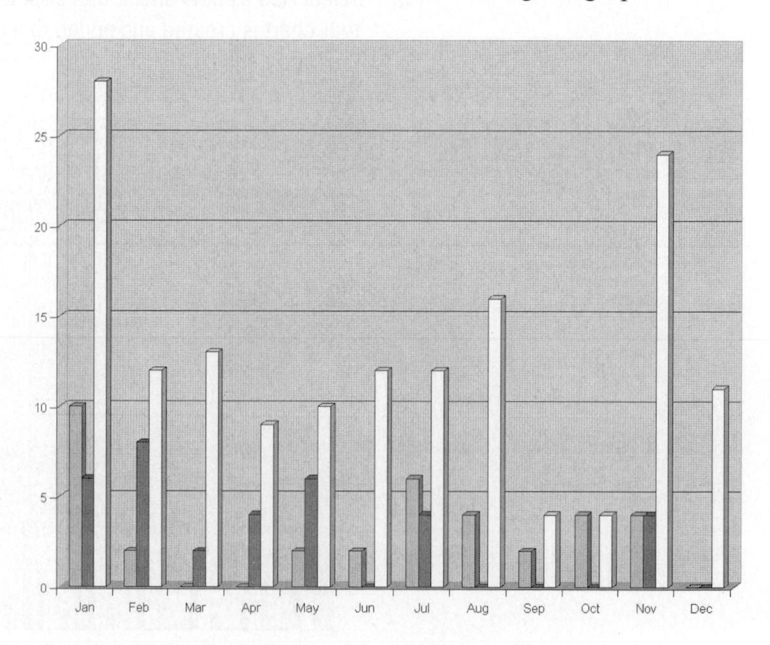

Save the workbook when you are done.

Modifying the chart type for a data series

MFPF have a black-and-white printer. It will still be difficult to distinguish which column represents which product when the chart is printed. Excel allows you to represent each data series in a chart in a different chart type. You decide to apply a different chart type to each data series in your chart to make the distinction clearer.

In the next exercise, you will change the chart type for the *Wardrobe* data series to *Cylinder*.

Exercise 12.3: Changing the chart type for a data series

1) Right-click the *Wardrobe* data series, and select **Chart Type** from the shortcut menu that opens.
   The *Chart Type* dialog box appears.

2) In the *Chart type* area, select *Cylinder*.

3) In the *Options* area, select *Apply to selection* to change the chart type for the selected data series only.

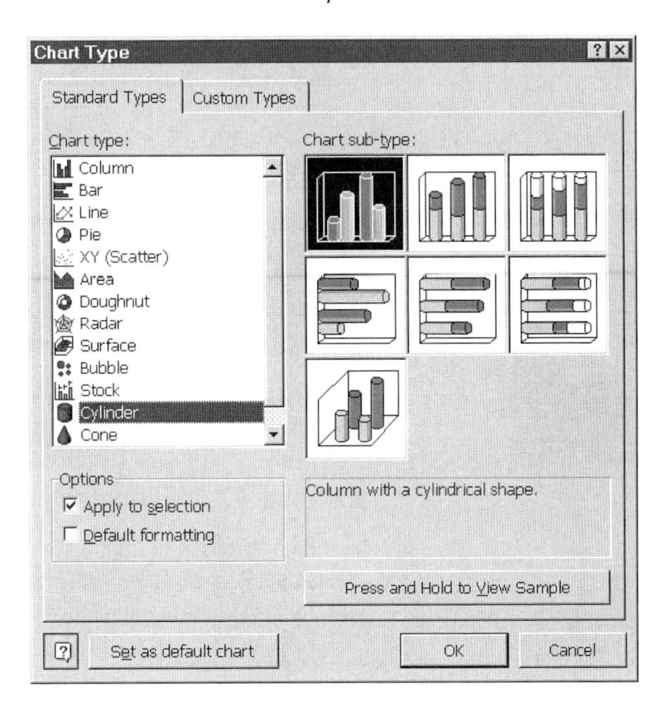

4) Click **OK**.

Over to you: mandatory

Next, change the chart type for the *Chest of Drawers* data series to *Cone* and save the workbook when you are done.

Your chart should now look like this:

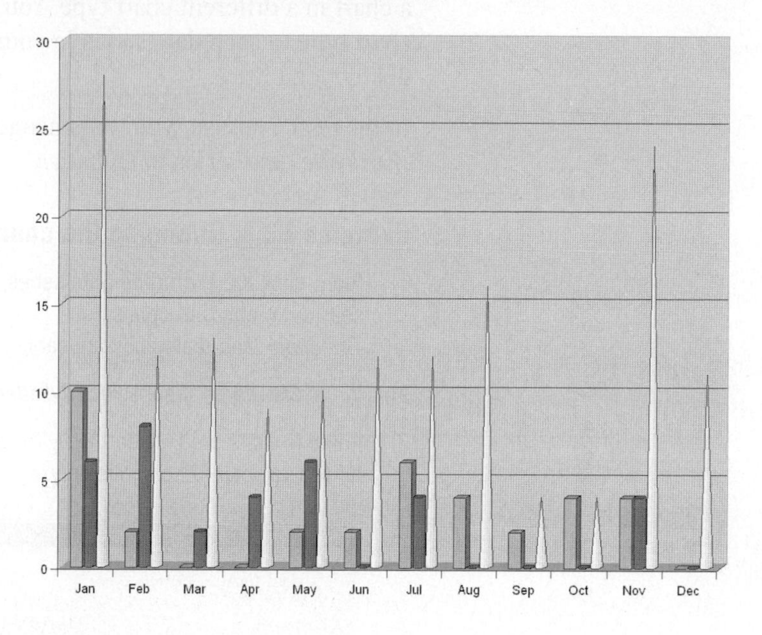

Formatting chart axes

You can change the font attributes for any text that appears in your chart.

You decide to make some more changes to the chart to improve the legibility of the data shown.

In the next exercise, you will change the font attributes of the text on the axes of the chart.

Exercise 12.4: Formatting chart axes

1) Right-click the horizontal axis showing the months of the year to select it.
   A small white square appears at each end of the axis line when it is selected.
2) Select **Format Axis** from the shortcut menu that appears.
   The *Format Axis* dialog box opens.
3) Click the **Font** tab.

4) Assign the following font settings:

- *Font: Verdana*
- *Size: 11*
- *Color: Dark blue*

5) Click **OK**.
Your font format changes are applied to the text on the axis.

Over to you: mandatory

Format the numbers on the vertical axis to appear with the same font settings.

Widening the gaps between columns in a chart

Excel adds a certain amount of space between the columns in a chart by default. You can change how much space appears between columns if you want.

Mrs Murphy asks you to change your chart to a 2D column representation, and to add extra space between the column clusters and between the columns in each cluster to make it easier to read the chart.

In the next exercise, you will change the chart type for all the data series, and add extra space between the columns in each cluster and between the individual clusters.

Exercise 12.5: Widening the gaps between columns in a 2D chart

1) Right-click any data series in your chart, and select **Chart Type** from the shortcut menu that opens.
The *Chart Type* dialog box appears.

2) In the *Chart type* area, select *Column*.

3) Make sure that the check box beside *Apply to selection* is unchecked.

4) Click **OK**.
The chart is reformatted so that all data series are 2D columns.

5) Right-click any data series, and select **Format Data Series** from the shortcut menu that opens.
The *Format Data Series* dialog box opens.

6) Click the **Options** tab.

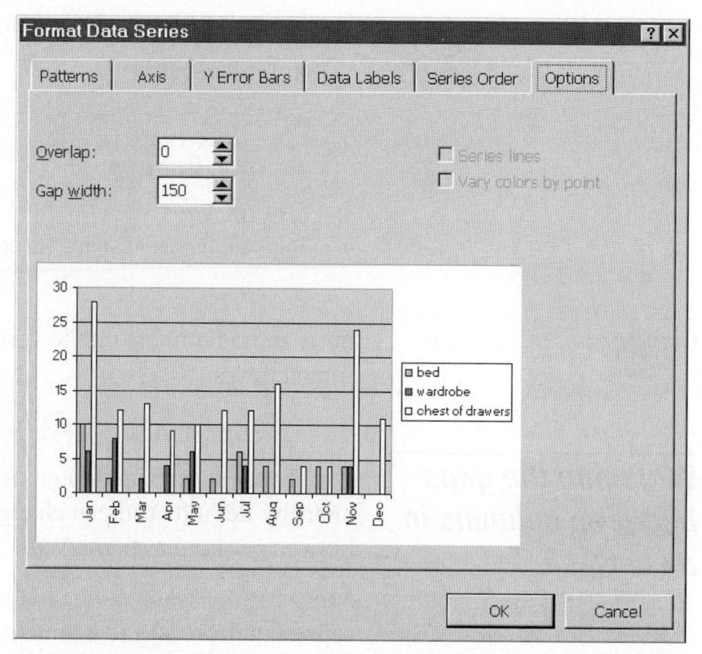

7) In the *Overlap* field, enter *–50*, either by entering the number in the box, or by using the up/down arrows to the right of the box to change the value.
   Overlap refers to the size of the gap between the columns in each cluster.
   In the *Gap width* field, enter *400*.
   Gap width refers to the gap between adjacent clusters.
   The graph on the lower half of the tab changes to show the effect of your changes.

8) Click **OK**.
   Extra space is added between the columns.

Inserting a picture in a chart

Excel allows you to add a graphic to the plot area, the chart area, a data series, or a data point in your chart.

You decide to change the default background of the plot area to the MFPF logo.

In the next exercise, you will add the company logo as a background to the chart area.

Exercise 12.6: Adding a graphic to a chart

1) Right-click the plot area and select **Format Plot Area** from the shortcut menu that opens.
   The *Format Plot Area* dialog box opens.

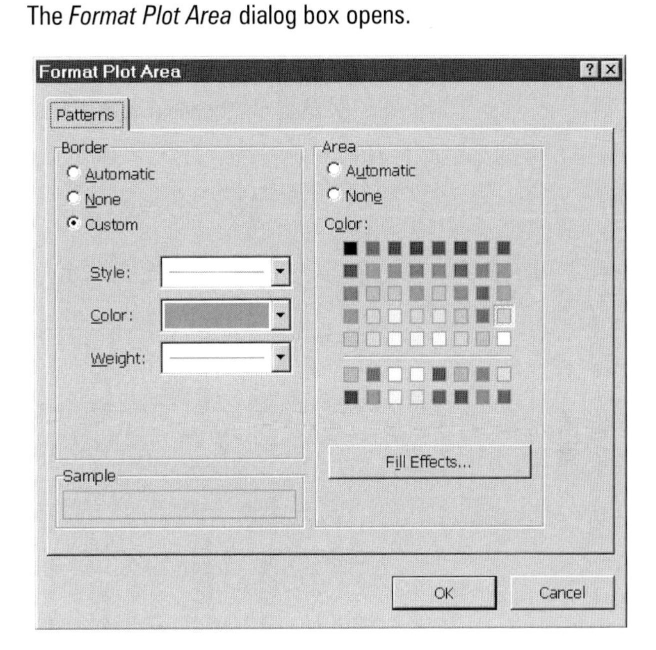

2) Click **Fill Effects ...** .
   The *Fill Effects* dialog box opens.

3) Click the **Picture** tab.

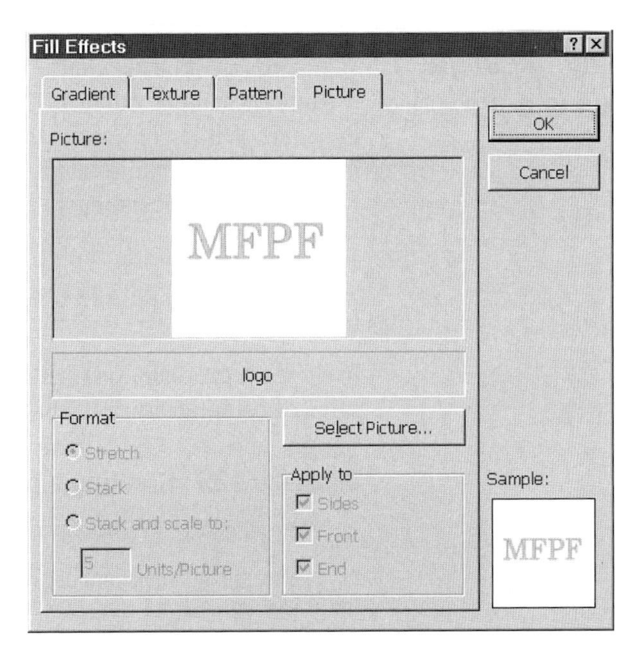

4) Click **Select Picture ...** .
   The *Select Picture* dialog box opens.

5) Select the file LOGO.GIF from your working folder, and click **Insert**.

6) Click **OK**.

7) Click **OK**.
   Your chart should now look like this:

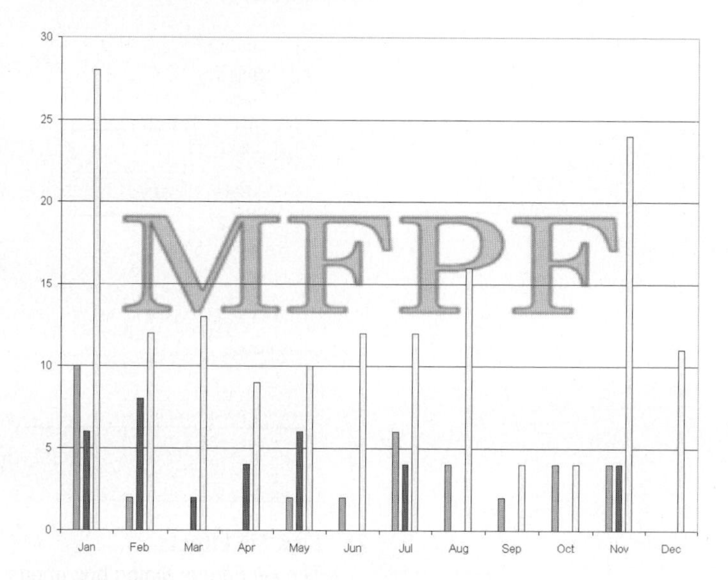

8) Save your workbook when you are done.

Changing the angle of slices in a pie chart

When you insert a pie chart, the order of the slices is determined by the order of the values in the worksheet cells used to generate the chart. While you cannot change the order the slices appear in in the chart, you can rotate a pie chart to change the angle at which the first slice appears relative to the 12 o'clock position.

July was the busiest month for MFPF. Mrs Murphy has asked you to generate a pie chart showing the breakdown of sales in that month.

In the next exercise, you will generate a pie chart showing the sales of each furniture type for the month of July.

Exercise 12.7: Creating a pie chart

1) Go to the *SALES TOTALS* worksheet of MFPF_FINANCE.XLS.

2) Select the non-adjacent cell ranges *A1:H1* and *A8:H8*.

3) Select **Insert | Chart ...** .
   – or –
   Click the **Chart Wizard** button on the *Standard* toolbar.
   The *Chart Wizard* opens.
4) In the *Chart type* area, select *Pie*.
5) Click **Next** until you get to the last screen in the *Chart Wizard: Chart Location*.
6) Select *Add as new sheet*, and click **Finish**.
   Your chart is created and added on to a new worksheet named *Chart2*.

Garden chairs make up most of the sales. Mrs Murphy would like the pie slice representing garden chairs to be the last one in the pie, ending at the 12 o'clock position.

In the next exercise, you will change the angle of the pie chart, so that the pie slice for garden chairs appears last. You will also add data labels to each slice to show how many units of furniture each one represents.

Exercise 12.8: Changing the angle of slices in a pie chart

1) Right-click the pie chart and select **Format Data Series** from the shortcut menu that opens.
   The *Format Data Series* dialog box opens.
2) Click the **Options** tab.

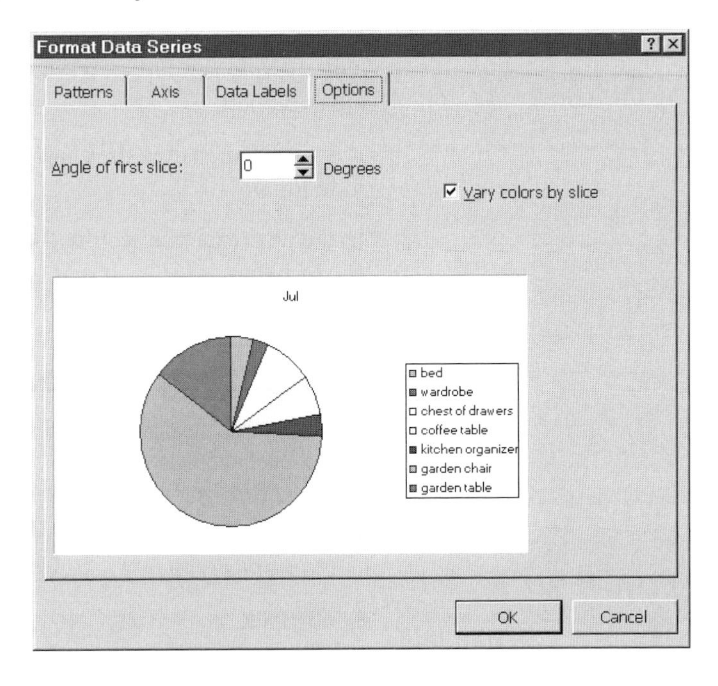

3) Change the value in the *Angle of first slice* box to *54*, either by entering the number in the box, or by using the up/down arrows to the right of the box to change the value.
   If you use the up/down arrows to change the angle, you can see the pie chart rotate in the preview area on this screen.
4) Click the **Data Labels** tab.
5) In the *Data labels* area, select *Show values*.
6) Click **OK**.
   Your pie chart is rotated as specified on the **Options** tab, and data labels have been added to each slice, showing the number of units of each furniture type sold.

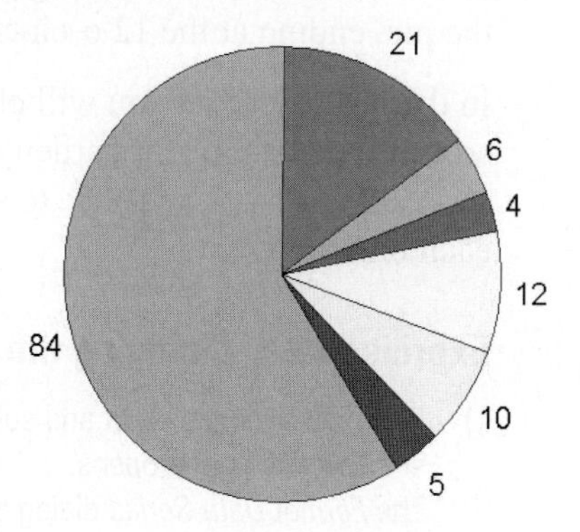

Exploding all the slices in a pie chart

In ECDL 3, you learned how to explode individual slices in a pie to make them easier to see. There is also a pie-chart subtype called *Exploded Pie*, in which all of the slices of the pie chart are exploded.

It is easier to change the chart subtype than to explode each slice individually.

In the next exercise, you will change the chart subtype from *Pie* to *Exploded Pie*, so that you can see the smaller slices more clearly.

Exercise 12.9: Changing the chart type

1) Right-click the pie chart, and select **Chart Type** from the shortcut menu that opens.
   The *Chart Type* dialog box appears.
2) *Pie* is already selected in the *Chart type* area.
   In the *Chart sub-type* area, select *Exploded pie*.
3) Click **OK**.
   Your chart is now an exploded pie chart

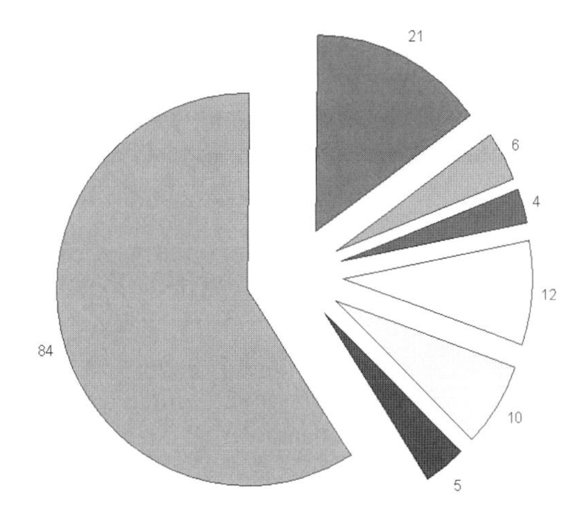

Repositioning chart elements

The chart title, legend and data labels are added to default positions in a chart in Excel. If you would prefer to see them in different positions, you can select any one of them and drag it to any other position on the chart that you like.

In the next exercise, you will reposition the title of the pie chart, so that instead of appearing above the chart, it appears just to the left of it.

Exercise 12.10: Repositioning a chart title

1) Select the chart title, *Jul*, by clicking it once.
   A rectangle of small black boxes appears around the text box when it is selected.
2) Click the border of the text box, and drag it to its new position, just left of the chart.

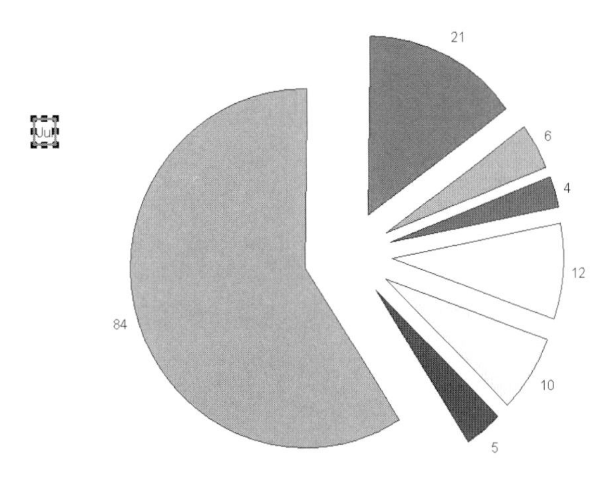

Over to you: mandatory

Next, you will move some other chart elements.

- Move the legend, by default located in a box to the right of the chart, to just below the chart title on the left of the chart.
- Drag the data labels for each pie slice on to the relevant slice.

When you are done, save and close MFPF_FINANCE.XLS.

Chapter summary

You can make changes to a chart after it has been created. You can remove individual data series, or represent each data series in a chart by a different chart type.

You can change the font attributes for any text in your chart.

You can change how much space appears between columns in a column chart, or rotate a pie chart to change the angle at which the first slice appears relative to the 12 o'clock position.

You can add graphics to the plot area, the chart area, data series, and data points in your chart.

You can move chart elements to new positions if you are not happy with the default layout.

13 Using Statistical and Database Functions

In this chapter

Sometimes, you will want to count the number of cells in a range that contain a particular type of data, although you don't want to do anything with the values in the cells.

In this chapter you will learn how to count the number of cells in a range that contains a certain type of value or that satisfy specified criteria.

You will also learn about Excel 'databases', and find out how to count fields and sum the values they contain using criteria to specify which fields to include. You will also learn how to find minimum and maximum values in Excel database fields.

New skills

At the end of this chapter you should be able to:

- Use the COUNT function
- Use the COUNTA function
- Use the COUNTIF function
- Use the DSUM function
- Use the DMIN and DMAX functions
- Use the DCOUNT function

New words

At the end of this chapter you should be able to explain the following term:

- Excel database

Statistical functions

The statistical functions you will learn about in this chapter are used to count the number of cells in a cell range that contain a particular type of data, or data that satisfy specified criteria.

COUNT

COUNT is an Excel function that looks at a list of values and calculates how many of them are numeric. Blanks and text values are disregarded.

The statistical function COUNT has the following format:

COUNT(Value1, Value2, ...)	
Value1, Value2, ...	A list of values or a cell range containing the data elements to count. Only the numeric values are counted.

Mr Murphy asks you to calculate exactly how many orders were made in the year.

You could calculate the total number of orders by looking at the row number of the first entry and the row number of the last, and subtracting one from the other. But using COUNT, you can simply tell Excel to look at any of the columns that contain order numbers and count how many entries in that range are numbers.

In the next exercise, you will use COUNT to calculate how many of the cells in column *J* contain numeric values and thereby determine how many orders were made.

> **Note:** If you completed the optional SUMIF exercise on page 100, you should delete the SUM and SUMIF formulae you added in column *J* of the *COMPLETE* worksheet in MFPF_ORD.XLS. The results of these formulae are numeric values and would be counted by the functions in the following exercises.

Exercise 13.1: Using COUNT

1) Open MFPF_ORD.XLS and go to the *COMPLETE* worksheet.
2) In cell *N2*, enter the formula *=COUNT(J:J)* to count all the rows in column *J* that contain a number.
   The answer is 54.
   Cell *J1*, which contains label text, and the blank cells in the column were not counted.
3) Save your workbook when you are done.

COUNTA

COUNTA is an Excel function that looks at a list of values and counts how many of them are non-blank. Any numeric or textual value will add to the count total.

COUNTA is the Excel function equivalent to Lotus 1-2-3's PURECOUNT.

The statistical function COUNTA has the following format:

COUNTA(Value1, Value2, ...)	
Value1, Value2, ...	A list of values or a cell range containing the data elements to count. All non-blank values are counted.

In the next exercise, you will count how many cells in column *J* of the *COMPLETE* worksheet of MFPF_ORD.XLS contain values.

Exercise 13.2: Using COUNTA

1) Go to the *COMPLETE* worksheet of MFPF_ORD.XLS.
2) In cell *N3*, enter the formula *=COUNTA(J:J)*.
   The answer is 55.
   Cell *J1* contains text, so it was included in the count, but the blank cells in the column were ignored again.
3) Save your workbook when you are done.

COUNTIF

COUNTIF is an Excel function that looks at a list of values, and calculates how many of them satisfy specified criteria.

The statistical function COUNTIF has the following format:

COUNTIF(Range, Criteria)	
Range	The cell range containing the values to be counted.
Criteria	The criteria the value in a cell must satisfy for that cell to be included in the count.

Earlier, you used SUMIF to see how many chairs MFPF would have sold if no orders for fewer than 12 at a time had been filled. How many actual orders would not have been filled?

In the next exercise, you will use COUNTIF to find the number of values in the *Chairs* column on the *COMPLETE* worksheet of MFPF_ORD.XLS that are lower than 12.

Exercise 13.3: Using COUNTIF

1) Open MFPF_ORD.XLS and go to the *COMPLETE* worksheet.
2) In cell *I58*, enter the formula *=COUNTIF(I2:I55,"<12")*.
   There were 38 occasions on which fewer than 12 chairs were ordered.
3) Save your workbook when you are done.

Database functions

The 'database' referred to in the term 'database function' is not an external one, such as Microsoft Access. It is a table or list of related data in an Excel spreadsheet.

Excel database
An Excel database is a table or list of related data in an Excel spreadsheet that can be treated as a database of records.

Excel database functions are used to make calculations based on the data in specific fields of a table or list row, where the row satisfies specified criteria.

DSUM

DSUM is an Excel function that looks at a list or table of values, finds the rows that satisfy specified criteria, and adds up the values in a specified column of those rows.

The database function DSUM has the following format:

=DSUM(Database, Field, Criteria)	
Database	The cell range you will use as your database for the purposes of this calculation.
Field	The number (not letter) for the column that contains the values you want to sum.
Criteria	The criteria that must be satisfied for the row values to be included in the sum. Criteria for database functions are specified as a range of cell pairs, where one cell contains a column name and the cell below it contains the value that should appear in that column. Each of the criteria specified must be satisfied for the row values to be included in the sum.

In the next exercise, you will use the DSUM function to calculate the total number of garden chairs ordered by the Cullenstown Garden Centre, using the data on the *COMPLETE* worksheet of MFPF_ORD.XLS as your database.

The cell range containing the query results you will use as your database was automatically given the custom name of *MFPF_Q1* when you imported the data. You will use that name to identify the cell range in the function.

Exercise 13.4: Using DSUM

1) Go to the *COMPLETE* worksheet of MFPF_ORD.XLS.
2) Enter the label *CompanyName* (with no spaces) in cell *N6*.
   Enter the value *Cullenstown Garden Centre* in cell *N7*.
   This is the criterion you will use to find the rows in the database to include in the sum.
3) In cell *N9*, enter the label *Chairs ordered*.
4) In cell *O9*, enter the formula *=DSUM(MFPF_Q1,9,N6:N7)*.
   108 chairs were ordered in the year by Cullenstown Garden Centre.

DMIN

DMIN is an Excel function that looks at a list or table of values, finds the rows that satisfy specified criteria, and determines the minimum value in a specified column of those rows.

The database function DMIN has the following format:

=DMIN(Database, Field, Criteria)	
Database	The cell range you will use as your database for the purposes of this calculation.
Field	The number of the column in which you want to find the minimum value.
Criteria	The cell range containing the criteria for the rows to include.

In the next exercise, you will use the DMIN function to find the smallest order for garden chairs placed by the Cullenstown Garden Centre.

Exercise 13.5: Using DMIN

1) Open MFPF_ORD.XLS, and go to the *COMPLETE* worksheet.
2) In cell *N10*, enter the label *Smallest chair order.*
3) In cell *O10*, enter the formula *=DMIN(MFPF_Q1,9,N6:N7)*.
   The smallest order was for eight chairs.

DMAX

DMAX is an Excel function that looks at a list or table of values, finds the rows that satisfy specified criteria, and determines the maximum value in a specified column of those rows.

The database function DMAX has the following format:

=DMAX(Database, Field, Criteria)	
Database	The cell range you will use as your database for the purposes of this calculation.
Field	The number of the column in which you want to find the maximum value.
Criteria	The cell range containing the criteria for the rows to include.

In the next exercise, you will use the DMAX function to find the largest order for garden chairs placed by the Cullenstown Garden Centre.

Exercise 13.6: Using DMAX

1) Open MFPF_ORD.XLS, and go to the *COMPLETE* worksheet.
2) In cell *N11*, enter the label *Largest chair order.*
3) In cell *O11*, enter the formula *=DMAX(MFPF_Q1,9,N6:N7)*.
   The largest order was for 32 chairs.

DCOUNT

DCOUNT is an Excel function that looks at a list or table of values, finds the rows that satisfy specified criteria, and counts them.

The database function DCOUNT has the following format:

=DCOUNT(Database, Field, Criteria)	
Database	The cell range you will use as your database for the purposes of this calculation.
Field	The number of the column that contains the values you want to count.
Criteria	The cell range containing the criteria for the rows to include.

In the next exercise, you will use the DCOUNT function to find how many orders for 12 or more garden chairs were placed by the Cullenstown Garden Centre.

Exercise 13.7: Using DCOUNT

1) Open MFPF_ORD.XLS, and go to the *COMPLETE* worksheet.
2) In cell *O6*, enter the criterion label *Chair*.
   In cell *O7*, enter *>=12*.
3) In cell *N13*, enter the label *12+ chairs*.
4) In cell *O13*, enter the formula *=DCOUNT(MFPF_Q1,9,N6:O7)*.
   This formula tells Excel to count the entries in the ninth column of the *MFPF_Q1* database (named cell range) that match the criteria defined in the cell range *N6:O7*.
   (*N6:N7* specifies the Cullenstown Garden Centre; *O6:O7* specifies 12 or more chairs; N6:O7 combines the two.)
   The result shows that Cullenstown Garden Centre made six orders for 12 or more chairs.

Chapter summary

Excel's COUNT function looks at a list of values, and calculates how many are numeric. Blanks and text values are disregarded.

The COUNTA function calculates how many of the values are non-blank. Any numeric or textual value will add to the count total. COUNTA is the Excel function equivalent of Lotus 1-2-3's PURECOUNT.

The COUNTIF function looks at a list of values, and calculates how many of them satisfy specified criteria.

An Excel database is a table or list of related data in an Excel spreadsheet that can be treated as a database of records.

The database function DSUM looks at a list or table of values, finds the rows that satisfy specified criteria, and adds up the values in a specified column of those rows.

DMIN finds the rows that satisfy specified criteria, and determines the minimum value in a specified column of those rows. Similarly, DMAX determines the maximum value in a specified column.

The DCOUNT function looks at a list or table of values, finds the rows that satisfy specified criteria, and counts them.

14 Using Financial Functions

In this chapter

So far in this book, you have learned about reference, mathematical, statistical and database functions in Excel.

Most of the time, Excel is used to keep track of financial information. Because of this, Excel also includes a set of functions specifically designed to handle financial data. These functions calculate typical accounting figures, such as the future value of a series of investments at a fixed interest rate.

In this chapter, you will learn how to use some of Excel's financial functions.

New skills

At the end of this chapter you should be able to:

- Use the NPV function
- Use the PV function
- Use the FV function
- Use the PMT function
- Use the RATE function

New words

There are no new words in this chapter.

NPV

NPV is an Excel function that calculates the net present value of an investment or debt. This gives the value in today's money of your investment or debt at the end of the investment period.

Because of factors such as inflation and depreciation, an investment you own today may not be worth as much in relative terms in the future.

The financial function NPV has the following format:

=NPV(Rate, Value1, Value2, ...)	
Rate	The discount rate per period of investment (for example, the inflation rate per period).
Value1, Value2, ...	A list of the payments made into the investment (negative numbers), and the income earned on the investment (positive numbers) over the total investment period. The values can be of variable size, but they must occur at regular intervals. The interval should be the same as the period of the discount rate.

MFPF puts 10% of profits each month for the year 2000 in a bank account with a negligible interest rate. Inflation for the year was 5.5%, or approximately 0.46% per month.

The total amount of money saved over the year was £2089.65. Taking inflation into account, what would the NPV of MFPF's £2089.65 savings have been at the start of the 12-month period?

In the next exercise, you will calculate the NPV of MFPF's savings at the start of the investment period.

Exercise 14.1: Using NPV

1) Open MFPF_FINANCE.XLS and go to the *PROFIT* worksheet.
2) In cell *H1*, enter the label *Savings*.
3) In cell *H2*, enter the formula *=_D2*0.1*, to calculate 10% of the profit value in column *D*.
   The '_' is because the amounts are then paid into a savings account. Copy the formula to the other cells in the range *H2:H13*.
4) In cell *A18*, enter the label *Discount Rate*.
5) In cell *B18*, enter the formula *=0.055/12* to calculate the monthly rate of inflation.

6) In cell *A19*, enter the label *NPV*.

7) In cell *B19*, enter the formula *=NPV(B18,H2:H13)*.
   The result tells you that the NPV of the investment at the start of the year was £2034.93.

MFPF can buy £2089.65 worth of goods at the end of the year, using the money saved. Twelve months earlier, the same goods would have cost £2034.93. Prices will have increased due to the 5.5% annual inflation rate.

PV

PV is an Excel function, similar to NPV, that calculates the present value of an investment where all the payments made are the same size and made at regular intervals.

The financial function PV has the following format:

=PV(Rate, Nper, Pmt, Fv, Type)	
Rate	The discount rate per period.
Nper	The number of payment periods in the investment.
Pmt	The value of the payment made each period. This value cannot change over the lifetime of the investment. **Note:** You must supply a value for either *Pmt* or *Fv*, but not both.
Fv	The future value the investment or debt should reach at maturity. If you are paying back a loan, the value of *Fv* is *0*. If you do not fill in a value, *0* is assumed. **Note:** You must supply a value for either *Pmt* or *Fv*, but not both.
Type	*1* or *0*. *1* indicates that payment is made at the start of each period, and *0* that it is made at the end of the period. If you do not specify a value, *0* is assumed.

If MFPF had invested £150 each month instead of 10% of profits, £1800 would have been saved over the year. What would the PV of the £1800 have been at the start of the 12-month period?

In the next exercise, you will calculate the PV at the start of the investment period of £150 savings per month over the 12-month period.

Exercise 14.2: Using PV

1) Open MFPF_FINANCE.XLS and go to the *PROFIT* worksheet.
2) In cell *A20*, enter the label *Fixed sum*.
3) In cell *B20*, enter the value *–150*.
4) In cell *A21*, enter the label *PV*.
5) In cell *B21*, enter the formula *=PV(B18,12,B20)*.
   Cell *B18* contains the *Rate value*, 12 is the number of payment periods (*Nper*), and cell *B20* contains the value for *Pmt*. No values are specified for the *Fv* or *Type* parameters.
   The result tells you that the PV of the investment at the start of the year was £1747.50.

FV

FV is an Excel function used to calculate the future value of an investment or debt, where fixed payments are made at regular intervals. FV only considers the interest rate being applied to the investment or debt, and ignores inflation and devaluation.

The financial function FV has the following format:

=FV(Rate, Nper, Pmt, Pv, Type)	
Rate	The interest rate per period.
Nper	The number of payment periods in the investment.
Pmt	The value of the payment made each period. This value cannot change over the lifetime of the investment. **Note:** You must supply a value for either *Pmt* or *Pv*, but not both.
Pv	The present value of all of the future payments. If you do not fill in a value, *0* is assumed. **Note:** You must supply a value for either *Pmt* or *Pv*, but not both.
Type	*1* or *0*. *1* indicates that payment is made at the start of each period, and *0* that it is made at the end of the period. If you do not specify a value, *0* is assumed.

The Murphys are considering opening a savings account that will pay 7.5% interest per annum if at least £200 is deposited each month. If MFPF invests £200 each month for 12 months, how much money will there be in the account, including interest?

In the next exercise, you will calculate how much money will be in the savings account at the end of a year if £200 is invested monthly.

Exercise 14.3: Using FV

1) Open MFPF_FINANCE.XLS and go to the *PROFIT* worksheet.
2) In cell *A23*, enter the label *Fixed sum*.
3) In cell *B23*, enter the value *–200*.
4) In cell *A24*, enter the label *Interest rate*.
5) In cell *D24*, enter thc formula *–0.075/12*.
6) In cell *A25*, enter the label *FV*.
7) In cell *B25*, enter the formula *=FV(B24, 12, B23)*.
   Cell *B24* contains the *Rate value*, 12 is the number of payment periods, and cell *B23* contains the value for *Pmt*.
   The result tells you that the future value of an account where £200 is invested each month for 12 months at an annual interest rate of 7.5% is £2484.24.

PMT

You can use Excel's PMT function to calculate the size of fixed payments needed on an investment or debt in order to reach a target value in a certain number of payments, where you already know the interest rate per period.

The financial function PMT has the following format:

=PMT(Rate, Nper, Pv, Fv, Type)	
Rate	The interest rate per period.
Nper	The number of payment periods in the investment.
Pv	The present value of all of the future payments combined. If you are calculating the size of payments to pay back a loan, this is the value of the loan. If you do not fill in a value, *0* is assumed.
Fv	The future value the investment or debt should reach at maturity. If you are paying back a loan, the value of *Fv* is *0*. If you do not fill in a value, *0* is assumed.
Type	*1* or *0*. *1* indicates that payment is made at the start of each period, and *0* that it is made at the end of the period. If you do not specify a value, *0* is assumed.

Mr Murphy would like to buy a new delivery van. A local showroom has promised to sell him one used for display and test drives for £5500 at the end of next year. MFPF already has £2089.65 in savings from last year, so the company needs to save a further £3410.35 in the next 12 months to be able to buy the van.

Mr Murphy asks you to work out how much he would need to save each month in the account offering 7.5% interest per annum if he wanted to save exactly £3410.35 after 12 months, including interest.

In the next exercise, you will calculate the payment Mr Murphy must make into the savings account to achieve his target in 12 months.

Exercise 14.4: Using PMT

1) Open MFPF_FINANCE.XLS and go to the *PROFIT* worksheet.
2) In cell *A26*, enter the label *PMT.*
3) In cell *B26*, enter the formula *=PMT(B24, 12, 0, 3410.35)*.
   Cell *B24* contains the interest rate, 12 is the number of payment periods, 0 is the present value of the account, and £3410.35 is the target final value.

The result tells you that MFPF needs to put £274.56 in the savings account each month to save £3410.35, including interest, by the end of the 12-month period.

RATE

RATE is an Excel financial function used to determine the interest rate on an investment where the number of payments and constant payment size are known, as well as either the PV or FV of the investment.

The financial function RATE has the following format:

=RATE(Nper, Pmt, Pv, Fv, Type, Guess)	
Nper	The number of payment periods in the investment.
Pmt	The value of the payment made each period. This value cannot change over the lifetime of the investment. **Note:** If you do not supply a value for *Pmt*, you must supply one for *Fv*.
Pv	The present value of all of the future payments combined. If you are calculating the size of payments to pay back a loan, this is the value of the loan. If you do not fill in a value, *0* is assumed.
Fv	The future value the investment or debt should reach at maturity. If you are paying back a loan, the value of *Fv* is *0*. If you do not fill in a value, *0* is assumed. **Note:** If you do not supply a value for *Fv*, you must supply one for *Pmt*.
Type	*1* or *0*. *1* indicates that payment is made at the start of each period, and *0* that it is made at the end of the period. If you do not specify a value, *0* is assumed.
Guess	Your guess for what you think the rate will be. This field can be left blank. If you do not supply a guess, 10% is assumed.

Mr Murphy has asked you to find out what interest rate an account should have for him to be able to save enough to pay for the new van by investing only £265 per month.

In the next exercise, you will work out the optimum interest rate for a savings account, so that the final amount in the account after 12 months will be £3410.35, including interest, when £265 is invested each month.

Exercise 14.5: Using RATE

1) Open MFPF_FINANCE.XLS and go to the *PROFIT* worksheet.
2) In cell *A28*, enter the label *Rate*.
3) In cell *B28*, enter the formula *=RATE(12, –265, 0, 3410.35)*.
   The result tells you that Mr Murphy will need to find a savings account offering 1.26% interest per month (equivalent to 15.15% per annum) to achieve his target in 12 months.
   (You may need to apply cell formatting to see this result to two decimal places.)

Chapter summary

Excel's NPV function calculates the net present value of an investment or debt, where payments are at regular intervals but of variable size. PV is similar to NPV, but calculates the present value of an investment where all the payments are the same size and made at regular intervals.

FV calculates the future value of an investment or debt, where fixed payments are made at regular intervals.

PMT calculates the size of fixed payments needed on an investment or debt in order to reach a target value in a certain number of payments, where you already know the interest rate per period.

RATE determines the interest rate on an investment where the number of payments and constant payment size are known as well as either the PV or FV of the investment.

15 Using Text and Date Functions

In this chapter

In general, you will use Excel spreadsheets to keep track of numeric information and to perform numeric calculations. But there are other types of data you can include in your spreadsheets – for example, text and dates.

Excel includes a number of functions that you can use to manipulate text and date information in your spreadsheets.

In this chapter you will learn how to manipulate text data, change the case, and create concatenated strings.

You will also learn about the date functions in Excel, which allow you to generate and manipulate date information.

New skills

At the end of this chapter you should be able to:

- Use the PROPER, UPPER and LOWER text functions
- Use the CONCATENATE text function
- Use the TODAY date function
- Use the DAY, MONTH and YEAR date functions

New words

At the end of this chapter you should be able to explain the following term:

- String

Text functions

Earlier, you looked at functions, such as ROUND, that took numeric values as arguments, made some change to the value, and displayed the result. There are also Excel functions that take text values as arguments, make a change to the text, and display the result.

In this chapter, you will learn about text functions that allow you to change the case (upper or lower) of text, and that allow you to combine text values into longer strings, and to combine text and numeric values into a single value.

String
A string is a value that contains text, or text and numbers.

Note: When using a string as an argument to a function in Excel, you must enclose it in double quotation marks (").

PROPER

PROPER is an Excel function that takes a string as an argument and capitalizes the first letter of each word.

In the next exercise, you will add a formula to a cell in PASTE_SPECIAL.XLS that retrieves the string in another cell, reformats it with the first letter of each word capitalized, and displays the result.

Exercise 15.1: Using PROPER

1) Open PASTE_SPECIAL.XLS. Note that cell *A12* contains the string "yOuR vAlUe HeRe".
2) In cell *A28*, enter the formula *=PROPER(A12)*.
   The text from cell *A12* is now shown in cell *A28*, reformatted so that the first letter of each word is capitalized.

UPPER

UPPER is an Excel function that takes a string as an argument and capitalizes every letter.

In the next exercise, you will add a formula to another cell in PASTE_SPECIAL.XLS that will retrieve the PROPER case string you generated in *Exercise 15.1* and reformat it with every letter capitalized.

Exercise 15.2: Using UPPER

1) Open PASTE_SPECIAL.XLS.
2) In cell *A29*, enter the formula *=UPPER(A28)*.
   The text from cell *A28* is shown in cell *A29*, reformatted so that every letter is capitalized.

LOWER

LOWER is an Excel function that takes a string as an argument and changes every letter to lower case.

In the next exercise, you will add a formula to another cell in PASTE_SPECIAL.XLS, retrieve the upper-case string you generated in *Exercise 15.2*, and reformat it with every letter in lower case.

Exercise 15.3: Using LOWER

1) Open PASTE_SPECIAL.XLS.
2) In cell *A30*, enter the formula *=LOWER(A29)*.
   The text from cell *A29* is shown in cell *A30*, reformatted so that every letter is in lower case.

Reusing text values in longer strings

Sometimes, you may want to join values together in a spreadsheet to create new strings. For example, say a spreadsheet listing staff members has first names in column *A* and surnames in column *B*. You could join the values from the cells in columns *A* and *B* in each row together to generate full names.

Joining a series of text strings together is known as concatenation, and Excel has a text function, CONCATENATE, that can do just that.

CONCATENATE

CONCATENATE is an Excel function that takes a series of arguments separated by commas and joins them together to create a single string. Arguments can be cell references, numbers or text.

Note: When using CONCATENATE, you must include any spaces you want to appear between concatenated terms. The spaces should appear inside quotation marks or they will be ignored. Space is not added automatically between arguments.

In the next exercise, you will use the CONCATENATE function to join two strings and the value from a cell together to create a new string.

Exercise 15.4: Using CONCATENATE

1) Open PASTE_SPECIAL.XLS.
2) In cell *A32*, enter the formula *=CONCATENATE("The text in cell A12 says: ",A12,"!!")* and press **ENTER**.
   The value in cell A32 is now: *The text in cell A12 says: yOuR vAlUe HeRe:!!*
3) Save and close your workbook when you are done.

Date

Excel's date functions allow you to generate and manipulate date information. In this section, you will look at formulae that allow you to automatically retrieve the current day's date, and to display individual elements of a date, such as the month.

TODAY

TODAY is an Excel date function that returns the current date. This function can be a useful timesaver, as you neither have to find the current date nor type it in.

In the next exercise, you will edit the invoice template, INVOICE_MFPF.XLT, and add the TODAY function to automatically fill in the date when an invoice is edited.

Note: When you have finished writing an invoice, you should use **Copy** and **Paste Special** to replace the date formula with the value it generates. Otherwise, the next time you open the document to read or edit it, the date will be updated again.

Exercise 15.5: Using TODAY

1) Create a new spreadsheet based on the INVOICE_MFPF.XLT template.
2) In cell *F5*, enter the formula *=TODAY()*.
3) Save the spreadsheet as a template, replacing the original INVOICE_MFPF.XLT.

DAY, MONTH and YEAR

DAY, MONTH, and YEAR are Excel functions that take a date as an argument, and return the number value of the day, month and year portions of that date, respectively.

In the next exercise, you will use CONCATENATE in conjunction with DAY, MONTH and YEAR to create a sentence that lists the number values for the day, month and year of the date generated by TODAY.

Exercise 15.6: Using DAY, MONTH and YEAR

1) Open a new, blank spreadsheet.
2) In cell *A1*, enter the label *Today's date*.
3) In cell *A2*, enter the formula *=TODAY()*.
   In cell *C1*, enter the formula *=CONCATENATE("Today is day ",DAY(A2)," of month ",MONTH(A2),", ",YEAR(A2),".")*
4) Close the workbook without saving when finished.

Chapter summary

A string is a value that contains text, or text and numbers.

The PROPER text function takes a string as an argument and capitalizes the first letter of each word. UPPER capitalizes every letter, and LOWER reformats the text so that every letter is in lower case.

CONCATENATE takes a series of strings and joins them all together to create a single string. Arguments can be cell references, numbers or text.

The TODAY date function returns the current date. The DAY, MONTH and YEAR functions take a date as an argument and return the number value of the day, month and year portions of that date, respectively.

16 Using Logical Functions

In this chapter

Earlier, you learned how to apply formatting to a cell if the value it contained satisfied certain criteria (conditional formatting). Sometimes, you may want to check whether a value satisfies certain criteria but not do anything to the data itself.

For example, you might want to check if your profits for any month are below a certain value, but not apply any special formatting to the value. Otherwise it will be the first thing a bank manager or prospective investor notices when looking at your accounts!

Excel's logical functions allow you to check the value of data in a cell against certain criteria. The functions return a value of TRUE if the criteria are satisfied, and FALSE if they are not.

New skills

At the end of this chapter you should be able to:

- Use the IF function
- Use the AND and OR functions
- Use the ISERROR function

New words

There are no new words in this chapter.

IF

Excel's logical functions are used to check if the value in a cell satisfies certain criteria. They return a value of *TRUE* if it does, and *FALSE* if it does not.

You can use Excel's IF function to perform a logical test and return custom messages for *TRUE* and *FALSE* results. The logical test can be any comparison using the operators <, >, =, <= (which means less than or equal to) or >= (which means greater than or equal to), and can include cell references as well as numeric and text values. The logical test can even be another logical function – for example, an AND test.

The logical function IF has the following format:

=IF(Logical_test, Value_if_true, Value_if_false)	
Logical_test	The logical test or comparison to perform, for example, *A1>B1*.
Value_if_true	The value to return if the result of the logical test is *TRUE*. If the value is a string, it should be enclosed in quotation marks – for example, *"Passed Test"*.
Value_if_false	The value to return if the result of the logical test is *FALSE*. If the value is a string, it should be enclosed in quotation marks – for example, *"Failed Test"*.

Mrs Murphy has asked you to indicate, beside the profit figure for each month, whether the profits have gone up or down from the previous month.

In the next exercise, you will use the IF function to compare the profit figure for each month with the one for the previous month. You will return a message of *UP* if a month's profit is greater than the profit for the previous month, and *DOWN* if it is less than the profit for the previous month.

Exercise 16.1: Using IF

1) Open MFPF_FINANCE.XLS and go to the *PROFIT* worksheet.
2) Select column *F*, where you calculated rounded profit using a single formula, and delete its contents.
3) In cell *F1*, enter the label *TREND.*

4) In cell *F3*, enter the formula *=IF(D3>D2,"UP","DOWN")*.

5) Copy the formula to the other cells in the range *F3:F13*.
As you do not have a profit value for December 1999 to compare with the January 2000 value, you should not enter a formula in cell *F2*.

6) Save your workbook when you are done.

Over to you: mandatory

In the invoice template, INVOICE_MFPF.XLT, the white text *Late* in cell *D9* is conditionally formatted in red if the customer pays more than 28 days after the invoice was issued. If you changed the fill colour of cell *D9* to any other colour, the white text would be visible. Use the IF function to generate the *Late* text instead.

- Create a new spreadsheet based on the template INVOICE_MFPF.XLT.
- Delete the text in cell *D9* on the *PERSONAL NOTES* worksheet, and change the text colour for the cell to black.
- Add an IF function to the cell, which checks whether the difference between *Date Paid* and *Date Invoiced* is greater than 28, and returns the text *Late* if it is, and no message otherwise.
- Save the spreadsheet as a template, replacing the original INVOICE_MFPF.XLT.

AND

AND is an Excel function that examines a list of logical tests or comparisons, and returns a value of *TRUE* if *all* of the logical tests are true. Otherwise, the function returns a value of *FALSE*.

The logical function AND has the following format:

=AND(Logical1, Logical2, ...)	
Logical1, Logical2, ...	The list of logical tests or comparisons to perform.

To return a custom message instead of TRUE or FALSE, you could nest this function in an IF function, as the *Logical_test* argument.

For example, the formula

=IF(AND(B1<2,B2<2),"Both < 2","Not both < 2")

returns the string *Both < 2* if the values in both cells *B1* and *B2* are less than 2, making the AND function return *TRUE*, and returns the string *Not both < 2* if the AND function returns *FALSE*.

Mr Murphy is wondering whether he should sell garden tables and garden chairs packaged together as sets. He asks you to look at the orders for the last year to see if customers usually buy both garden chairs and garden tables at the same time.

In the next exercise, you will use the logical AND function to find the orders where both garden chairs and garden tables were ordered at the same time.

Exercise 16.2: Using AND

1) Open MFPF_ORD.XLS and go to the *COMPLETE* worksheet.
2) In cell *K1*, enter the label *Chairs and Tables*.
3) In cell *K2*, enter the formula *=AND(I2>0,J2>0)*.
4) Copy the formula to the other cells in column *K*.
   The message *TRUE* appears in the rows where both garden chairs and garden tables were ordered.
   The message *FALSE* appears where either no garden chairs or garden tables were ordered, or where only one or the other was ordered.

OR

OR is an Excel function that examines a list of logical tests or comparisons, and returns a value of *TRUE* if one or more of the logical tests is true. Otherwise, the function returns a value of *FALSE*.

The logical function OR has the following format:

=OR(Logical1, Logical2, ...)	
Logical1, Logical2, ...	The list of logical tests or comparisons to perform.

The results in column *K* show which customers bought both garden tables and garden chairs. Next, you will see who bought garden tables or garden chairs or both, using the OR function. By comparing the values, you will be able to see who bought one but not the other.

In the next exercise, you will use the OR function to check which customers ordered either garden chairs or garden tables or both.

Exercise 16.3: Using OR

1) Open MFPF_ORD.XLS and go to the *COMPLETE* worksheet.
2) In cell *L1*, enter the label *Chair and/or Tables*.
3) In cell *L2*, enter the formula *=OR(I2>0,J2>0)*.
4) Copy the formula to the other cells in column *L*.
   Orders where either garden chairs or garden tables were ordered, and orders where both garden chairs and garden tables were ordered, are now flagged as *TRUE* in column *L*.

Over to you: mandatory

By looking at columns *K* and *L* together, you can see which customers bought either garden chairs or garden tables but not both of them. You could see this information more clearly if you used another logical function to compare the results of both tests.

- In column *M*, use an AND function to flag orders that have a *FALSE* value in column *K* and a *TRUE* value in column *L*.
  A *TRUE* result in column *M* indicates an order where either chairs or tables but not both were bought.

Over to you: optional

You could also construct a nested function to perform this check in a single step.

- Create an AND function that uses AND and OR functions as arguments to determine which customers bought either garden chairs or garden tables, but not both.

ISERROR

ISERROR is an Excel function that examines the value in a cell, and returns a value of *TRUE* if the value is an Excel error message. Otherwise, the function returns a value of *FALSE*.

The information function ISERROR has the following format:

=ISERROR(Value)	
Value	The cell to check for an error message.

You have decided to add a worksheet to MFPF_FINANCE.XLS that will contain ISERROR checks for all of the formulae used in the workbook. This means that when you make changes to the data in your workbook, you can see quickly and easily if your changes contravene any of the formulae you use just by looking at this one sheet.

In the next exercise, you will add a new worksheet to MFPF_FINANCE.XLS and start adding ISERROR checks for cells containing formulae.

Exercise 16.4: Using ISERROR

1) Open MFPF_FINANCE.XLS and add a new worksheet.
   Name the new worksheet *ERRORS*.
2) In cell *A1*, enter the label *NPV*.
3) In cell *B1*, enter the formula *=ISERROR(PROFIT!B19)*.
   The value is *FALSE* because there is no error in cell *B19* on the *PROFIT* worksheet.

Over to you: optional

If you would like to reassure yourself that the ISERROR function really works, go to the *PROFIT* worksheet and edit the NPV formula to say *=NPV(I2,E2:E13)/0*. This generates a *#DIV/0!* error, and changes the value in cell *B1* on the *ERRORS* worksheet to *TRUE*.

Chapter summary

Excel's logical functions are used to check if the value in a cell satisfies certain criteria. They return a value of *TRUE* if it does, and *FALSE* if it does not.

IF performs a logical test and can return custom messages for *TRUE* and *FALSE* results.

AND examines a list of logical tests or comparisons, and returns a value of *TRUE* if *all* of the logical tests are true. OR returns a value of *TRUE* if one or more of the logical tests is true.

ISERROR examines the value in a cell, and returns a value of *TRUE* if the value is an Excel error message.

17 Using Data Tables and Scenarios

In this chapter

What if you invested in a savings account with a 4% interest rate instead of one with a 3% interest rate? What if you invested £170 per month instead of £150? What effect would one or more of these changes have on the value of your savings in a year's time?

To answer questions like these, where you have several alternative values you could use for an argument and you want to know what the result would be if you used each of them, you could create a formula for each possibility and enter it in your spreadsheet.

Aside from this method, Excel offers you two ways to deal with such 'What if?' calculations: data tables and scenarios.

In this chapter you will learn how to use each of these tools.

New skills

At the end of this chapter you should be able to:

- Use a 1-input data table
- Use a 2-input data table
- Create a named scenario
- View a named scenario
- Generate a scenario summary report

New words

At the end of this chapter you should be able to explain the following terms:

- Data table
- Scenario

Data tables

In Chapter 14, you calculated how much money Mr Murphy needed to save each month in an account with a particular interest rate to have saved a target amount at the end of 12 months. Then you calculated what interest rate an account would need to attract for him to be able to save a smaller amount each month and reach the same goal.

You could have created a data table to find the ideal combination of RATE and PMT values to achieve a target FV result.

> **Data table**
>
> *A data table is a range of cells that shows the results of substituting different values in one or more formulae.*

There are two types of data table:

- *1-input data table*: In a 1-input data table, you can substitute different values for one variable, and see the effect each value has on the results of one or more formulae.
- *2-input data table*: In a 2-input data table, you can substitute different values for two variables, and see the effect each variable value combination has on a single formula.

1-input data tables

With a 1-input data table, you can see the effect that changing a single variable value has on the results of any number of formulae that use that value. You could have used a 1-input data table to work out the future value your savings would have for a range of different interest rates.

A 1-input data table lists the possible values for a single variable on one axis and a series of formulae that use that value on the other axis. Excel completes the data table by filling in the results for each of the formulae using the different variable values.

In the following example, a 1-input data table has been set up with a list of possible interest rates in a column orientation and an FV formula in a row orientation. Results have not yet been calculated.

The FV formula will be used to calculate the possible future values of an investment of a fixed sum of £200 over 12 payment periods. Initially, the FV formula takes the interest rate value from cell *B1*. To fill in the data table with the value of FV for each interest rate, you must tell Excel to replace the value in cell *B1* with the values in the column axis of the table.

	A	B	C	D
1	**Interest rate per period**	0.0025		
2				
3			=FV(B1,12,-200)	
4	**Interest rates**	0.0025		
5		0.005		
6		0.0075		
7		0.01		
8		0.0125		
9		0.015		
10				

The formulae refer to a specific cell on the worksheet, but the value in that cell is replaced by each variable value to calculate the final results.

Note: If you enter your variables in a *column* orientation, you should add your first formula in the cell one column to the right of, and one row above, the cell containing the first variable value. Any other formulae should be entered in the cells to the right of the first formula.

If you enter your variable in a *row* orientation, you should add your first formula in the cell one column to the left of, and one row below, the cell containing the first variable value. Any other formulae should be entered in the cells below the first formula.

In the next exercise, you will create the 1-input data table shown in the example, and fill in the final results.

Exercise 17.1: Using a 1-input data table

1) Create a new worksheet, based on the default template, and save it as INVEST.XLS.

2) In cell *A1* of the first worksheet, enter the label *Interest rate per period*.

3) In cell *B1*, enter the value *0.0025* – a quarter of one per cent.

4) In cell *A4*, enter the label *Interest Rates*.

5) Change the formatting of cell *A4* so that the text in it is bold and rotated through 90 degrees.

6) In the cell range *B4:B9*, enter the variable values *0.0025*, *0.005*, *0.0075*, *0.01*, *0.0125* and *0.015*.
These are the variable values you will substitute in place of the interest rate in cell *B1*.

7) In cell *C3*, enter the formula *=FV(B1,12,_200)*.

8) Select the range *B3:C9*, and select **Data | Table ...** .
The *Table* dialog box opens.

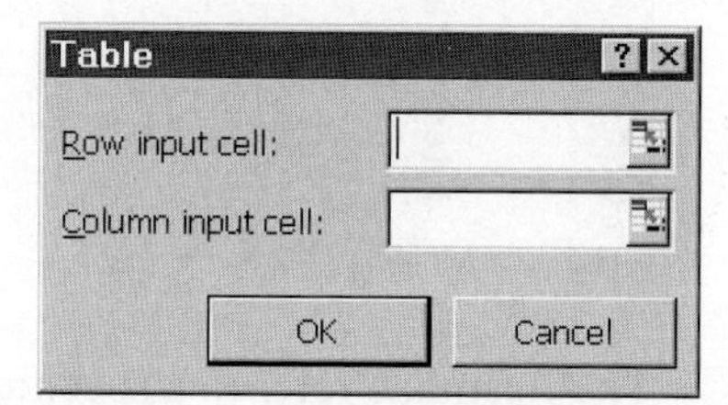

9) In this dialog box, you will tell Excel which cell referred to in your formulae should be replaced by the variable values in either the column or row orientation in your data table.
Enter the cell *B1* in the *Column input cell* field.
Click **OK**.
The data table is filled in with the values calculated for FV with each possible interest rate.

	A	B	C	D
1	**Interest rate per period**	0.0025		
2				
3			2433.276553	
4	**Interest rates**	0.0025	2433.276553	
5		0.005	2467.112475	
6		0.0075	2501.517271	
7		0.01	2536.500603	
8		0.0125	2572.072284	
9		0.015	2608.242286	
10				

(You may need to apply additional cell formatting to see your results to the same number of decimal places shown in the illustration.)

10) Save your workbook when you are done.

2-input data tables

You can also create a 2-input data table to calculate the possible results of a single formula where the values of two of the inputs can change. For example, to calculate FV, if there are a variety of interest rates to choose from, and several possible values for PMT, you could create a 2-input data table.

In this case, one set of variables is entered in the row orientation of the data table and the other in the column orientation.

The formula should be entered in the cell immediately above the first entry in the column of variable values, and the row of variable values should be entered in the cell range starting with the first cell to the right of the formula.

In the next exercise, you will create a 2-input data table that calculates the value of FV where both the interest rate per period and the payment amount are variables.

Exercise 17.2: Using a 2-input data table

1) In cell *C1* of the first worksheet in INVEST.XLS, enter the label *Payment*.
2) In cell *D1*, enter the value *–150*.
3) In cell *A11*, enter the formula *=FV(B1,12,D1)*.
   Cell *B1* contains the value for *Rate*, 12 is the number of payment periods, and cell *D1* contains the value for *Pmt* (the payment amount).
4) In the cell range *A12:A17*, enter the variable values *0.0025*, *0.005*, *0.0075*, *0.01*, *0.0125* and *0.015*.
   These are the variable values you will substitute for the interest rate in cell *B1*.
5) In the cell range *B11:G11*, enter the variable values –150, –160, *–170*, *–180*, *–190* and *–200*.
   These are the variable values you will substitute for the payment amount in cell *D1*.
6) Select the cell range *A11:G17* and select **Data | Table ...** .
   The *Table* dialog box opens.
7) In the *Column Input Cell* field, enter *B1*.
   In the *Row Input Cell* field, enter *D1*.
   Click **OK**.

The data table is filled in with the values calculated for FV with each interest rate and payment amount combination.

	A	B	C	D	E	F	G
1	**Interest rate per period**	0.0025	Payment	-150			
2							
3			$2,433.28				
4	**Interest Rates**	0.0025	2433.277				
5		0.005	2467.112				
6		0.0075	2501.517				
7		0.01	2536.501				
8		0.0125	2572.072				
9		0.015	2608.242				
10							
11	1824.9574	-150	-160	-170	-180	-190	-200
12	0.0025	1824.957	1946.621	2068.285	2189.949	2311.613	2433.277
13	0.005	1850.334	1973.69	2097.046	2220.401	2343.757	2467.112
14	0.0075	1876.138	2001.214	2126.29	2251.366	2376.441	2501.517
15	0.01	1902.375	2029.2	2156.026	2282.851	2409.676	2536.501
16	0.0125	1929.054	2057.658	2186.261	2314.865	2443.469	2572.072
17	0.015	1956.182	2086.594	2217.006	2347.418	2477.83	2608.242
18							

8) Save your workbook when you are done.

Named scenarios

What if you wanted to substitute a variable number of payment periods in the formula, too? You cannot do this in a data table, but you can use Excel's Scenarios functionality to substitute values for any number of variables.

Scenario

A scenario is a named set of values that can be substituted into a set of selected cells in a spreadsheet.

When you create a scenario, you define a set of values that should be entered in particular cells on a worksheet, and assign a name to that scenario. You can select any one scenario to view at one time, and all the defined values in that scenario are substituted into your worksheet.

Creating a scenario

In the next exercise, you will create a scenario that specifies a particular combination of values for the number of payment periods in an investment, the payment amount per period, and the interest rate per period.

Exercise 17.3: Creating a named scenario

1) In cell *E1* of the first worksheet in INVEST.XLS, enter the label *Payment Periods*.
2) In cell *F1*, enter the value *12*.
3) In cell *A2*, enter the label *FV*.
4) In cell *B2*, enter the formula *=FV(B1,F1,D1)*.
   Cell *B1* contains the value for *Rate*, cell *F1* contains the value for *Nper* (the number of payment periods), and cell *D1* contains the value for *Pmt*.
5) Select **Tools | Scenarios ...** .
   The *Scenario Manager* dialog box opens.
6) Click **Add ...** .
   The *Add Scenario* dialog box opens.

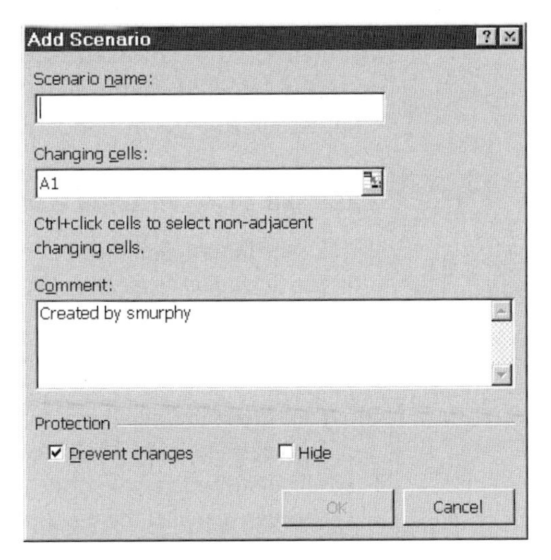

7) In the *Scenario name* field, enter *Savings1*.
   In the *Changing cells* field, enter *B1,D1,F1*.
   Click **OK**.
   The *Scenario Values* dialog box opens.

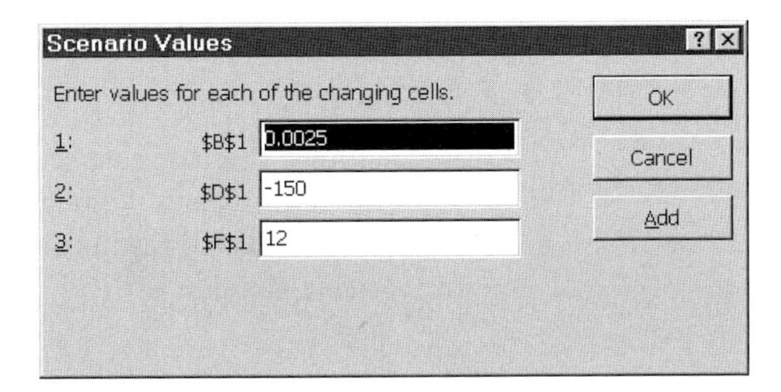

8) In the *Scenario Values* dialog box, the current values in the selected cells are shown.
You can edit one or more of these values, and save all three in the current scenario by clicking **OK**.
For now, you will save the default values in the *Savings1* scenario.

9) Click **OK**.

10) Click **Close** to close the *Scenario Manager* dialog box.

Over to you: mandatory

Continue to add scenarios using different combinations of values for interest rate per period in cell *B1*, number of periods in the investment in cell *F1*, and payment amount per period in cell *D1*. Add at least two more scenarios.

Viewing a scenario

When you have defined your scenarios, you can select any one of them to view. All of the scenario values you defined are filled in to the selected changing cells, and the results of any formulae that use these cells are updated.

Exercise 17.4: Viewing a scenario

1) Select **Tools | Scenarios ...** .
The *Scenario Manager* dialog box opens.

2) In the *Scenarios* area, select one of the two additional scenarios you defined and click **Show**.

3) Click **Close** to close the *Scenario Manager* dialog box.
The values for cells *B1*, *D1* and *F1* specified in the scenario are substituted into the worksheet and the result of the formula in cell *B2* changes to reflect the new values in cells *B1*, *D1* and *F1*.

4) Save your workbook when you are done.

Scenario summaries

Unlike data tables, which show all possible results at once, you can only see the data for one scenario at a time. This makes it difficult to compare the effect each set of values has just by looking at the results.

Excel allows you to create scenario summary reports, which show the set of values defined in each scenario and also the final numbers in selected results cells on the worksheet that rely on the variable values.

In the next exercise, you will create a summary report that shows the settings for, and results of, each scenario you have defined on the first worksheet of INVEST.XLS.

Exercise 17.5: Creating a scenario summary

1) Select **Tools | Scenarios ...** .

2) Click **Summary ...** .
   The *Scenario Summary* dialog box opens.

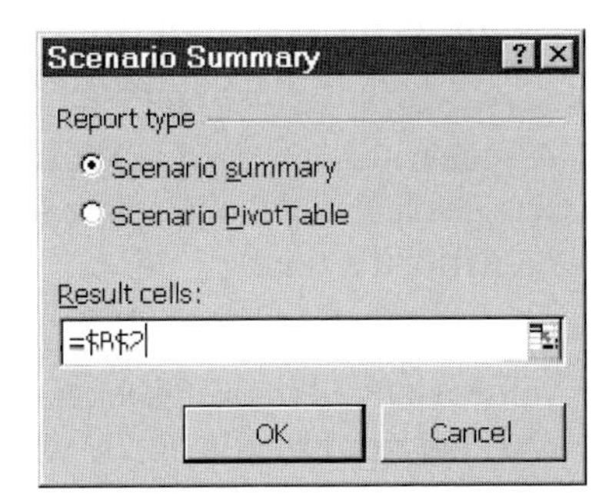

3) In the *Report type* area, select *Scenario summary.*

4) In the *Result cells* area, enter *$B$2*.
   This is the cell that contains the FV formula that uses the data from the changing cells.

5) Click **OK**.

6) A new worksheet is added to your workbook.
   The worksheet contains a summary report of the scenarios you defined. It shows the changing cells and their values for each scenario, as well as the results cells and their values.

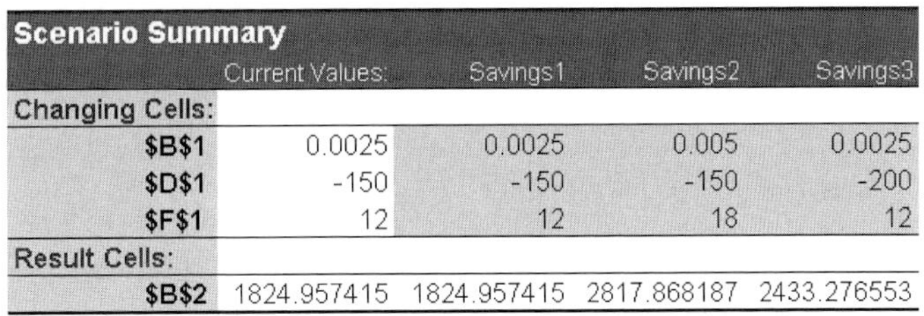

Scenario Summary

	Current Values:	Savings1	Savings2	Savings3
Changing Cells:				
$B$1	0.0025	0.0025	0.005	0.0025
$D$1	-150	-150	-150	-200
$F$1	12	12	18	12
Result Cells:				
$B$2	1824.957415	1824.957415	2817.868187	2433.276553

Notes: Current Values column represents values of changing cells at time Scenario Summary Report was created. Changing cells for each scenario are highlighted in gray.

7) Save and close your workbook when you are done.

Chapter summary

A data table is a range of cells that shows the results of substituting different values in one or more formulae.

There are two types of data table:

- *1-input data table*: In a 1-input data table, you can substitute different values for one variable, and see the effect each value has on the results of one or more formulae.
- *2-input data table*: In a 2-input data table, you can substitute different values for two variables, and see the effect each variable value combination has on a single formula.

A scenario is a named set of values that can be substituted into a set of selected cells in a spreadsheet. You can only view one scenario at a time.

You can create scenario summary reports that show the set of values defined in each scenario and also the final numbers in selected results cells on the worksheet that rely on the variable values.

18 Auditing your Spreadsheets

In this chapter

Congratulations! Your workbooks are now completed. You have entered or imported all of the required data, and you have made all of your calculations.

But how can you tell which cells contain pure values, and which contain formulae? How can you track which formulae use data from which cells?

In this chapter, you will learn how to audit your worksheets to locate the cells containing formulae, and to track which cells contain values used in formulae, and which cells contain the formulae that use them.

New skills

At the end of this chapter you should be able to:

- Locate and display formulae on a worksheet
- Trace precedent and dependent cells

New words

There are no new words in this chapter.

Formulae and locations

In *Exercise 16.4* on page 144, you started to add ISERROR functions to a worksheet, which would check the formulae in your workbook for errors. But, how can you tell which cells in your worksheets contain formulae, without checking each cell individually?

Excel allows you to identify the cells in a worksheet that contain formulae in two ways:

- Using the **Go To** command to select all the cells that contain formulae.
- Choosing to display the formulae in cells, instead of the values they generate.

Go To

In the next exercise, you will use Excel's **Go To** command to select all of the cells on the *PROFIT* worksheet of MFPF_FINANCE.XLS that contain formulae.

Exercise 18.1: Highlighting cells that contain formulae

1) Open MFPF_FINANCE.XLS and go to the *PROFIT* worksheet.
2) Select **Edit | Go To ...** .
   The *Go To* dialog box opens.
   This dialog box lists named cell ranges on the current worksheet.
   If you select a range and click **OK**, that range is selected in the worksheet.

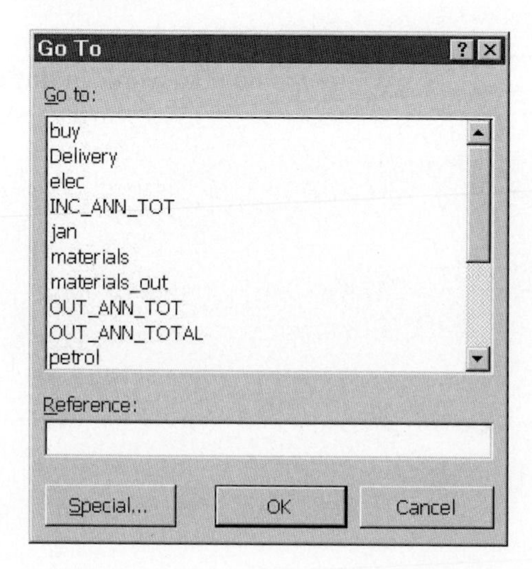

3) Click **Special ...** .
   The *Go To Special* dialog box opens.

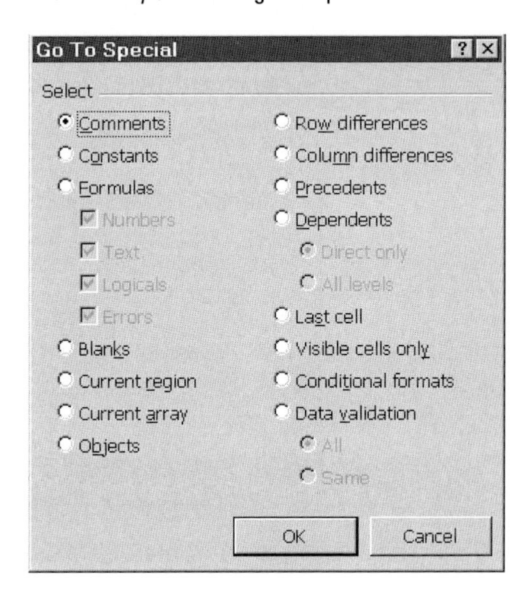

   This dialog box lets you select a particular cell property that the cells you want to select have.
   When you click **OK**, any cell with the selected property is selected.
   If multiple cells have the property, they are all selected.

4) Select *Formulas*, and check all of the formula types.

5) Click **OK**.
   All of the cells on the *PROFIT* worksheet that contain formulae are now selected.

You can select all cells containing formulae using **Go To**, but to see the actual formula in a given cell, you need to select that cell and read the formula from the formula bar. When you do this, you deselect all of the other cells again.

Displaying formulae

You can specify that you want to show all formulae in a worksheet instead of the values they generate.

In the next exercise, you will display all of the formulae in the *INCOMING* worksheet of MFPF_FINANCE.XLS.

Exercise 18.2: Showing formulae instead of values

1) Go to the *INCOMING* worksheet of MFPF_FINANCE.XLS.

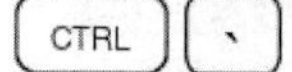

2) Press **Ctrl** and ' (the open single inverted comma key).
   The formulae used to calculate values on this sheet are shown instead of the values.

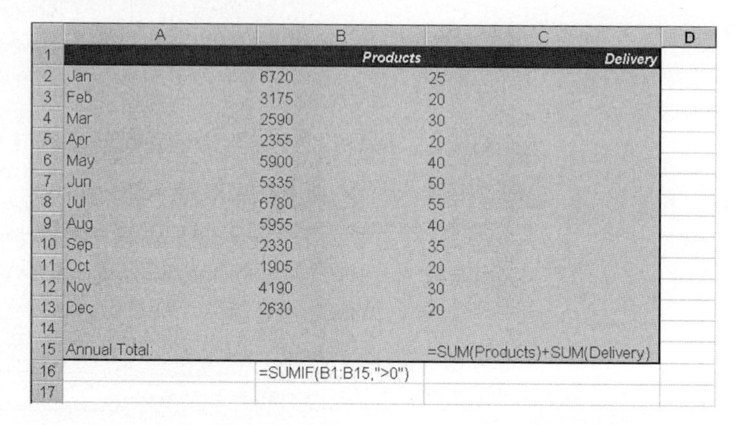

	A	B	C	D
1		Products	Delivery	
2	Jan	6720	25	
3	Feb	3175	20	
4	Mar	2590	30	
5	Apr	2355	20	
6	May	5900	40	
7	Jun	5335	50	
8	Jul	6780	55	
9	Aug	5955	40	
10	Sep	2330	35	
11	Oct	1905	20	
12	Nov	4190	30	
13	Dec	2630	20	
14				
15	Annual Total:		=SUM(Products)+SUM(Delivery)	
16		=SUMIF(B1:B15,">0")		
17				

You can toggle between formulae and values by pressing **Ctrl** and ' repeatedly.

Tracing precedent cells

Without reading the list of arguments for a formula, how can you tell which cells it gets data from?

Excel's **Trace Precedents** command locates all of the cells referred to by the formula in a selected cell, and connects them to the cell containing the formula using arrows.

If any of the precedent cells are not on the same worksheet as the selected cell, a spreadsheet icon is shown at the other end of the precedent's arrow.

If you double-click the spreadsheet icon, the *Go To* dialog box opens with a list of all the precedent cells not on the current worksheet. You can select one of these cell references and click **OK** to go to that cell.

In the next exercise, you will use the **Trace Precedents** command to indicate the cells that contain input data for the NPV formula on the *PROFIT* worksheet of MFPF_FINANCE.XLS.

Exercise 18.3: Tracing precedent cells

1) Open MFPF_FINANCE.XLS and go to the *PROFIT* worksheet.
2) Select cell *B19*, which contains the NPV formula.
3) Select **Tools | Auditing | Trace Precedents.**
   Arrows appear on the worksheet to indicate the cells used as input to the NPV formula.
   The cell range *H2:H13* is surrounded by a border, and a single arrow indicates that the values in all of these cells are used.

	A	B	C	D	E	F	G	H	I
1		**Incoming**	**Outgoing**	**Profit**	**Rounded Profit**	**Trend**		**Savings**	
2	Jan	£6,745.00	-£3,262.16	£3,482.84	£3,500.00			-£348.28	
3	Feb	£3,195.00	-£2,137.22	£1,057.78	£1,100.00	DOWN		-£105.78	
4	Mar	£2,620.00	-£2,014.68	£605.32	£600.00	DOWN		-£60.53	
5	Apr	£2,375.00	-£1,909.06	£465.94	£500.00	DOWN		-£46.59	
6	May	£5,940.00	-£2,879.74	£3,060.26	£3,100.00	UP		-£306.03	
7	Jun	£5,385.00	-£2,794.24	£2,590.76	£2,600.00	DOWN		-£259.08	
8	Jul	£6,835.00	-£3,139.98	£3,695.02	£3,700.00	UP		-£369.50	
9	Aug	£5,995.00	-£2,997.94	£2,997.06	£3,000.00	DOWN		-£299.71	
10	Sep	£2,365.00	-£1,856.26	£508.74	£500.00	DOWN		-£50.87	
11	Oct	£1,925.00	-£1,739.02	£185.98	£200.00	DOWN		-£18.60	
12	Nov	£4,220.00	-£2,571.16	£1,648.84	£1,000.00	UP		-£164.88	
13	Dec	£2,650.00	-£2,052.00	£598.00	£600.00	DOWN		-£59.80	
14									
15	**Annual Total:**		**20896.54**						
16									
17	Outgoing total		-29353.46						
18	**Discount Rate**	0.004583333							
19	**NPV**	-£2,089.65							
20	**Fixed sum**	-£150.00							
21	**PV**	£1,747.50							
22									

Note: To remove the trace arrows you have added to your worksheet, select **Tools | Auditing | Remove All Arrows**.

Over to you: optional

In this exercise, you will locate precedent cells on other worksheets.

- Select cell *C15* on the *PROFIT* worksheet of MFPF_FINANCE.XLS and trace its precedent cells.
  There are two cells: one on the *INCOMING* worksheet and one on the *OUTGOING* worksheet.
- Double-click the spreadsheet icon at the end of the Precedents arrow and follow the link to one of the precedent cells.

Tracing dependent cells

You could have worked out the precedent cells for any formula by reading the formula. How would you find out whether a particular cell is used by any formula in your spreadsheet, without checking each formula individually?

Excel's **Trace Dependents** command indicates the cells containing formulae that refer to a selected cell.

Note: Trace Dependents will only find dependent cells in worksheets in the same workbook as the selected cell.

In the next exercise, you will trace the dependent cells for one of the monthly profit totals on the *PROFIT* worksheet of MFPF_FINANCE.XLS.

Exercise 18.4: Tracing dependent cells

1) Open MFPF_FINANCE.XLS and go to the *OUTGOING* worksheet.
2) Select cell *B5*.
3) Select **Tools | Auditing | Trace Dependents.**
   Arrows appear on the worksheet to indicate the cells that use cell *B5* as an input.

	A	B	C	D	E	F	G	H	I
1		Warehouse Rental	Electricity	Telephone	Raw Materials	Petrol	Wages	Outgoing total	
2	Jan	-£250.00		-£28.12	-£2,113.00	£3.96	-£875.00	-£3,262.16	
3	Feb	-£250.00	-£40.10		-£975.00	£2.88	-£875.00	-£2,137.22	
4	Mar	-£250.00		-£26.50	-£867.50	£4.32	-£875.00	-£2,014.68	
5	Apr	-£250.00	[illegible]		-£740.50	£2.00	-£875.00	£1,909.06	
6	May	-£250.00		-£24.10	-£1,737.00	£6.36	-£875.00	-£2,879.74	
7	Jun	-£250.00	-£39.08		-£1,637.00	£6.84	-£875.00	-£2,794.24	
8	Jul	-£250.00		-£28.06	-£1,994.00	£7.08	-£875.00	-£3,139.98	
9	Aug	-£250.00	-£36.34		-£1,842.00	£5.40	-£875.00	-£2,997.94	
10	Sep	-£270.00		-£26.50	-£691.00	£6.24	-£875.00	-£1,856.26	
11	Oct	-£270.00	-£38.90		-£558.00	£2.88	-£875.00	-£1,739.02	
12	Nov	-£270.00		-£24.48	-£1,406.00	£4.32	-£875.00	-£2,571.16	
13	Dec	-£270.00	-£37.88		-£872.00	£2.88	-£875.00	-£2,052.00	
14									
15	Annual Total:		-£29,353.46						
16									
17	Outgoing total		-£29,353.46						
18									

Note: Cell *C15* is a dependent of cell *B5*. Cell *C15* is itself a precedent of cell *C15* on the *PROFIT* worksheet. If a dependent cell is itself a precedent cell for the formula in another cell, no arrow appears to indicate this. You will need to check each dependent cell for further dependents.

Chapter summary

Excel allows you to identify the cells in a worksheet that contain formulae by using the **Go To** command, or by switching between displaying formulae and the values they generate.

The **Trace Precedents** command locates all of the cells referred to by the formula in a selected cell, and connects them to the cell containing the formula using arrows.

The **Trace Dependents** command indicates the cells in a workbook containing formulae that refer to a selected cell in the same workbook.

19 Sharing and Protecting your Spreadsheets

In this chapter

There are many reasons you might want to share your spreadsheet with other people: for information purposes only, or so that they can add specific data that you need, for example.

When you give copies of your spreadsheets to other people for information purposes, you may want them to see final values in all of the cells, but not the formulae used to generate them.

If you want someone to add specific data, you might want them to fill in certain values and see a result calculated. You don't want them to change the formulae used, or edit any existing data, you just want them to be able to edit specific cells.

In this chapter, you will look at different ways you can protect all or part of a workbook before sharing it with someone else.

New skills

At the end of this chapter you should be able to:

- Hide and unhide columns and rows in a worksheet
- Hide and unhide worksheets in a workbook
- Protect individual cells in a worksheet
- Apply password protection to worksheets and workbooks

New words

There are no new words in this chapter.

Hiding columns and rows

You can hide individual columns and rows in any Excel worksheet.

After hiding a column or row, you will need to password-protect either the worksheet or the workbook containing the hidden column or row, otherwise anyone can unhide the column or row at any time.

Hiding a column

Joe Molloy from Joe's Hardware lost the books he kept his order records in, so he needs to recreate them. He has asked Mr Murphy for a copy of the delivery records he kept. Mr Murphy has agreed, and asks you to give Joe a copy of the *DELIVERIES* worksheet of DELIVERIES.XLS. Before handing it over, though, you should hide the column that shows the petrol cost for each delivery.

In the next exercise, you will hide column *D* on the *DELIVERIES* worksheet of DELIVERIES.XLS, which shows the cost of petrol for each delivery.

Exercise 19.1: Hiding a column

1) Open DELIVERIES.XLS, and go to the *DELIVERIES* worksheet.

2) Select column *D*.

3) Select **Format | Column | Hide**.
The column disappears.
You can see the location of the hidden column, because the columns in the worksheet now go: *A*, *B*, *C*, *E*, *F*, ...

	A	B	C	E
1	DeliveryDate	CompanyName	Delivery charge	
2	Jan-00	Mullens	10	
3	Jan-00	Liam Kinsella and Sons	10	
4	Jan-00	Joe's Hardware	5	

Unhiding a column

In the next exercise, you will unhide the column you hid in *Exercise 19.1*.

Exercise 19.2: Unhiding a column

1) Open DELIVERIES.XLS, and go to the *DELIVERIES* worksheet.
2) Select the columns either side of the hidden column, in this case columns *C* and *E*.
3) Select **Format | Column | Unhide**.
   Column *D* reappears.
4) Save and close your workbook when you are done.

Note: If column *A* is hidden, you cannot use the above method to unhide it. Instead, select **Edit | Go To ...** to open the *Go To* dialog box, type *A1* in the *Reference* field, and click **OK**. Then you can select **Format | Column | Unhide** to show the hidden column.

Hiding and unhiding rows

The procedures for hiding and unhiding rows are the same, except that you select the **Row** option on the **Format** menu instead of the **Column** option.

Hiding worksheets

As well as hiding individual rows and columns in a worksheet, you can select a whole worksheet and hide it from view in your workbook.

Joe Molloy has asked the Murphys to send him his invoices by e-mail in future. They have agreed to send him a copy of the Excel spreadsheet for each invoice.

The invoice template you use, INVOICE_MFPF.XLT, contains two worksheets: *CUSTOMER INVOICE* and *PERSONAL NOTES*. When you pass an invoice on to Joe, you will need to hide the *PERSONAL NOTES* worksheet first.

In the next exercise, you will hide the *PERSONAL NOTES* worksheet of INVOICE1.XLS.

Exercise 19.3: Hiding a worksheet

1) Open INVOICE1.XLS and go to the *PERSONAL NOTES* worksheet.
2) Select **Format | Sheet | Hide**.
   The *PERSONAL NOTES* worksheet disappears.
3) Save the workbook.

You have hidden a whole worksheet in your workbook.

Unhiding worksheets

To unhide worksheets in a workbook, you open a dialog box that lists all of the hidden worksheets in the book, and select the one to unhide.

In the next exercise, you will unhide the worksheet you hid in *Exercise 19.3*.

Exercise 19.4: Unhiding a worksheet

1) Open INVOICE1.XLS.
2) Select **Format | Sheet | Unhide ...** .
   The *Unhide* dialog box appears.

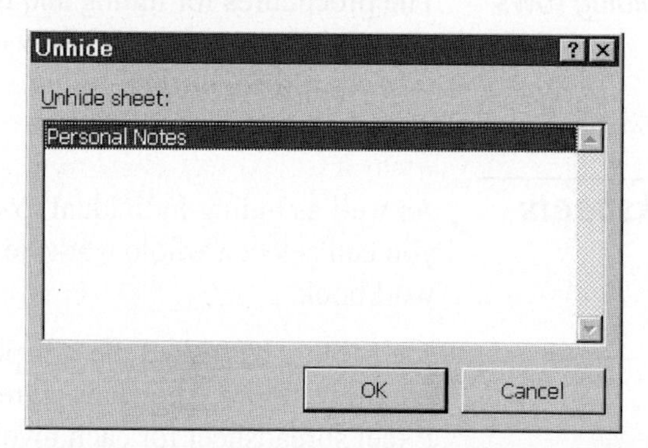

3) The *Unhide* dialog box lists all of the hidden worksheets in the current workbook.
   Select *PERSONAL NOTES* and click **OK**.
   The *PERSONAL NOTES* worksheet reappears.
4) Finally, select **Edit | Repeat Hide** to hide the worksheet again.

Note: Unless you password-protect your workbook, Joe will be able to unhide the worksheet again just like you did in this exercise. You will learn about password-protecting workbooks in *Protecting workbooks* on page 171.

Protecting cells

When you share a spreadsheet with other people, you can prevent them from making any changes to it, or you can restrict them to changing only certain cells.

If you are issuing an invoice, you will not want the customer to be able to change any of the details in the invoice. If you are using a spreadsheet as an order form, on the other hand, you will want the customer to be able to enter a quantity for each product, but not change the product list or prices.

You can assign two types of protection to a cell:

- *Locked:* If a cell is locked, you cannot edit the cell's contents.
- *Hidden:* If a cell is hidden, you can see the value in the cell, but if a formula was used to calculate the value, you cannot see the formula.

By default, when you protect a worksheet or workbook, Excel assumes that you want all cells to be locked but not hidden.

> **Note:** The protection setting for a cell is not enforced until you protect the worksheet or workbook containing the cell.

Specifying protection settings for a cell

Joe Molloy has asked you to leave an editable area in the electronic copies of the invoices you send him, where he can enter the date he paid the invoice. Remember, by default all cells will be locked when you password-protect your workbook.

In the next exercise, you will set the protection for a cell on the *CUSTOMER INVOICE* worksheet of INVOICE1.XLS so that Joe can enter into it the date the invoice was paid.

Exercise 19.5: Setting protection for a cell

1) Open INVOICE1.XLS and go to the *CUSTOMER INVOICE* worksheet.
2) In cell *E30*, enter the label *Date paid:*.
3) Select cell *F30*.
4) Select **Format | Cells ...** .
   The *Format Cells* dialog box opens.
5) Click the **Protection** tab.

6) Uncheck the checkboxes beside *Locked* and *Hidden*, then click **OK**.
Cell *F30* is now unprotected so that even after password protection has been added to the worksheet or workbook, the value in this cell can be edited.

Protecting worksheets

To protect the contents of a worksheet, and to enforce the protection settings applied to cells within it, you will need to protect the sheet itself. You can choose to protect a worksheet with or without a password, but if you do not use a password, then anyone can unprotect the worksheet again.

You can choose to protect one or more of the following:

- *Contents:* If you protect contents in the worksheet, then you cannot edit locked cells and you cannot see the formulae in hidden cells.
- *Objects:* If you protect objects in the worksheet, then embedded objects, for example, graphics, cannot be edited.
- *Scenarios:* If you protect scenarios, then scenario definitions cannot be edited.

In the next exercise, you will protect the contents of the *CUSTOMER INVOICE* worksheet of INVOICE1.XLS.

Exercise 19.6: Protecting a worksheet

1) Open INVOICE1.XLS and go to the *CUSTOMER INVOICE* worksheet.
2) Select **Tools | Protection | Protect Sheet ...** .
The *Protect Sheet* dialog box opens.

3) Check the boxes beside *Contents*.
As there are no objects or scenarios in this workbook, it does not matter whether you check the boxes beside *Objects* and *Scenarios* or leave them unchecked.

4) Enter a password in the *Password* field, and click **OK**.
   The *Confirm Password* dialog box opens.

5) Re-enter your password and click **OK**.

You can unprotect the worksheet again at any time by selecting **Tools | Protection | Unprotect sheet** and entering the password you used to protect it.

Protecting workbooks

You can hide or protect individual worksheets in a workbook, but you can still unhide, add and delete worksheets (even protected ones) as long as the workbook itself is unprotected.

You can choose to protect two different aspects of a workbook:

- *Structure:* If you protect the structure of a workbook, you cannot add, remove, hide or unhide worksheets. Also, you cannot unhide rows or columns, or change the protection on cells or worksheets.
- *Windows:* If you protect the windows, then the size and location on the screen of the workbook will be the same every time it is opened. You might want to use this setting to resize the Excel window to exactly frame a specific cell range when a workbook is opened.

To make sure that Joe does not unhide the *PERSONAL NOTES* worksheet, you will protect the workbook containing his invoice.

In the next exercise, you will assign password protection to INVOICE1.XLS, so that no further changes can be made to the workbook.

Exercise 19.7: Protecting a workbook

1) Open INVOICE1.XLS.
2) Select **Tools | Protection | Protect Workbook ...** .
The *Protect Workbook* dialog box opens.

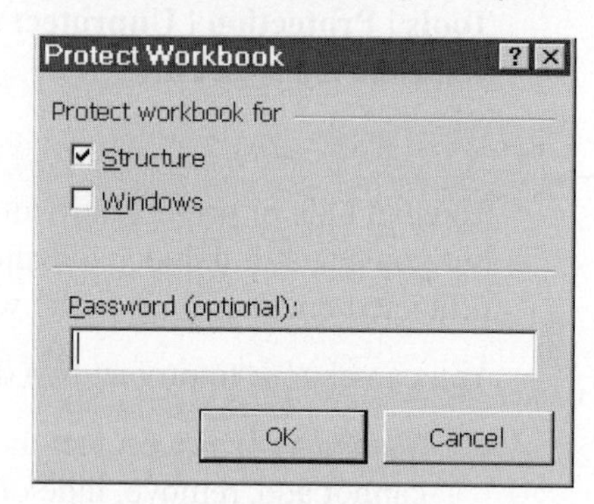

3) Check the checkbox beside *Structure*.
4) Enter a password in the *Password* field and click **OK**.
The *Confirm Password* dialog box opens.
5) Re-enter your password and click **OK**.
6) Save and close your workbook when you are done.

You can remove the protection again by selecting **Tools | Protection | Unprotect Workbook** and entering the password you used to protect the workbook.

Chapter summary

You can hide individual columns and rows in any Excel worksheet. You can also select a whole worksheet and hide it from view in your workbook.

You can protect any cell against editing, or hide formulae in cells, so that only the final calculated value can be seen.

You can choose to protect data in a worksheet, embedded objects, scenario definitions, or any combination of these three.

You can choose to protect a workbook's structure so that you cannot add, remove, hide or unhide worksheets, unhide rows or columns, or change the protection on cells or worksheets. You can also protect a workbook so that its size and location on the screen of the workbook will be the same every time it is opened.

In conclusion

Now that you have completed all the tasks in this book, you have completed the required syllabus for ECDL Advanced Spreadsheets, and are able to:

- Save time on repetitive tasks by using templates and macros.
- Keep track of the data in your spreadsheets by using named cells and cell ranges, comments and auditing.
- Reuse data by importing them from text files and databases, using different Paste Special options, and creating links between spreadsheets or from Word documents.
- Make your data easier to read by performing multi-column sorts, applying cell and worksheet formatting, customizing charts, and summarizing large amounts of information in PivotTables.
- Use key reference, maths, statistics, database, finance, text, date, time and logical functions.
- Consider how changing the value of a variable will affect your calculations by using data tables and scenarios.
- Protect your work against unauthorized changes by protecting cells, workbooks and worksheets.

Also, thanks to your hard work, the Murphys now have a comprehensive set of spreadsheets that show their sales data for the year, and can track their financial incomings and outgoings. Hopefully, the bank manager will now approve their loan, and, based on the comparative information you have provided, the Murphys will invest wisely for the future.

Congratulations, you have done a great job!

Index

Advanced Databases

Judith Cuppage
and
Paul Holden

Harlow, England • London • New York • Boston • San Francisco • Toronto • Sydney • Singapore • Hong Kong
Tokyo • Seoul • Taipei • New Delhi • Cape Town • Madrid • Mexico City • Amsterdam • Munich • Paris • Milan

Contents

Chapter 5: Table design: relationships 61

Chapter 6: Table design: joins 77

Chapter 7: Query design: action queries 89

Chapter 8: Query design: total queries 99

Chapter 14: Report design 203

Chapter 15: Macros 227

Chapter 16: Importing, linking and exporting data 240

Chapter 17: In conclusion 262

Preface

What is ECDL?

ECDL, or the European Computer Driving Licence, is an internationally recognized qualification in information technology skills. It is accepted by businesses internationally as a verification of competence and proficiency in computer skills.

The ECDL syllabus is neither operating system nor application specific.

ECDL Advanced Database module

ECDL Module AM5, Database, Advanced Level, requires you to operate a database application effectively, at more than a basic level of competence, and to be able to realize much of the potential of the application.

It requires you to be able to use the database application to organize, extract, view and report on data using advanced data management skills, and also to create simple macros, and to import, export and link data.

For more information about ECDL, and to see the syllabus for ECDL Module AM5, Database, Advanced Level, visit the official ECDL website at www.ecdl.com.

About this book

This book covers the ECDL Advanced Database syllabus Version 1.0, using Microsoft Access 2000 to complete all the required tasks. It is assumed that you have already completed the database module of ECDL 3 or ECDL 4 using Microsoft Access, or have an equivalent knowledge of the product.

The chapters in this book are intended to be read sequentially. Each chapter assumes that you have read and understood the information in the preceding chapters.

Most chapters contain the following elements:

- **New skills:** This sets out the skills and concepts that you will learn in the chapter.
- **New words:** A list of the key terms introduced and defined in the chapter.
- **Exercise files:** A list of the exercise files that you will work with in the chapter (see 'Exercise files' below).
- **Syllabus reference:** A list of the items from the ECDL Advanced Database syllabus that are covered in the chapter.

- **Exercises:** Practical, step-by-step tasks to build your skills.
- **Chapter summary:** A brief summary of the concepts and skills covered in the chapter.
- **Quick quiz:** A series of multiple-choice questions to test your knowledge of the material contained in the chapter.

Case study

The exercises in this book guide you step-by-step through the tasks you need to be able to perform, using a library database as a case study.

The database in the case study is used by a village library that serves a small but growing local community. Library staff use the database to maintain information about the books available in the library and about loans of books to library members.

At present, all information is maintained manually, using a variety of paper forms, card indexes and ledgers. This system was adequate while the membership and library holdings were small. Now the membership is growing steadily and the library is expanding. It has been decided that a relational database system is necessary.

In the exercises in this book you will design and build the village library database, and the various queries, forms and reports needed to support the library services.

Note that the case study has been designed to illustrate the features necessary to cover the syllabus. It is not intended as a complete functioning database for a real library.

Exercise files

The CD accompanying this book contains a database file for most chapters. In each case, the database file provides the starting point for exercises in the chapter. For example, you work with the following database file when doing the exercises in Chapter 3:

- `Chp3_VillageLibrary_Database`

For some chapters, additional files (such as spreadsheets or text files) are provided for use with the exercises.

Before you begin working through the exercises, you need to copy all of the files from the CD to your computer. To do this, create a working folder anywhere on your computer and name it something like `ECDL_Database_Advanced`. Then copy all files from the CD to that folder.

Text conventions

The following conventions are used in this book:

- **Bold text** is used to denote the names of Access menus and commands, buttons on toolbars, tabs and command buttons in dialog boxes and keyboard keys.
- *Italicized text* is used to denote the names of Access dialog boxes, and lists, options and checkboxes within dialog boxes.
- The | symbol is used to denote a command sequence. For example, choose **Tools | Macro | Run Macro** means choose the **Tools** menu, then the **Macro** option on that menu, and finally the **Run Macro** option on the **Macro** sub-menu.
- Field names are often prefixed by the name of the table to which they belong. For example, Books.ISBN refers to the ISBN field in the Books table.

Hardware and software requirements

Your PC should meet the following specifications:

- Microsoft Access 2000 (including the Northwind sample database) (see next section)
- Microsoft Word 2000
- Microsoft Excel 2000
- 10 MB hard disk space for exercise files

Access 2000 service packs

Your Access 2000 installation must include the following service packs:

- Microsoft Office 2000 Service Release 1a (SR-1a)
- Microsoft Office 2000 Service Pack 3 (SP-3)

A service pack contains a collection of product updates that enhance, extend, and fix known errors in the original product. If you do not install the Microsoft Office 2000 service packs, you may encounter problems when creating and using the sample forms, reports, and macros in this book.

To check your version of Microsoft Access, start the application, and choose **Help | About Microsoft Access**.

- If both service packs have been installed, **SP-3** will appear as part of the version number at the top of the *About Microsoft Access* dialog box, and you do not need to take further action.

- If Service Release 1 or 1a has been installed, but not Service Pack 3, SR-1 will appear as part of the version number at the top of the *About Microsoft Access* dialog box. In this case you need to install Service Pack 3 and possibly Service Release 1a.
- If neither SR-1 nor SP-3 appears as part of the version number, you need to install both service packs.

Note that the installation procedure requires access to your original Office 2000 CD.

Installing the service packs

To update a single, stand-alone computer, you can download both service packs from the following Microsoft website:

```
http://office.microsoft.com/officeupdate/
default.aspx
```

The website provides a utility that scans your computer to detect which Office updates you need. The results list available updates for all your Microsoft products.

- If a Windows Installer update is included in the list, download and install this first, following the instructions on screen.
- If Office 2000 Service Release 1a (SR-1a) is included in the list, download and install it following the instructions on screen. You must download this update separately from other updates.
- If Office 2000 Service Pack 3 is included in the list, download and install it following the instructions on screen.

To update Office 2000 on a network, go to the following website:

```
http://www.microsoft.com/office/ork/2003/
admin/97_2000/default.htm
```

This lists administrative updates for Office 97–2000. The following items provide information on deploying Service Release 1a and Service Pack 3:

- Office 2000 Release 1a Now Available
- Office 2000 Service Pack 3 (SP3)

Access environment defaults

Access's *Options* dialog box presents a wide range of options that enable you to customize your Access working environment. You can, for example, specify the default formatting for datasheets, define the default field type and size for new fields in a table, and change the default behaviour of the **Enter**, **Tab** and **Arrow** keys in forms and datasheets.

The exercises and illustrations in this book assume that all the options have their original default values. To use the same settings, open the *Options* dialog, by choosing **Tools | Options**, and then apply the following settings:

Option	Settings
View tab	
Show in macro design Names column Conditions column	 Not selected Not selected
Double-click open	Selected
General tab	
New database sort order	General
Use four-digit year formatting This database All databases	 Not selected Not selected
Edit/Find tab	
Confirm Record changes Record deletions Action queries	 Selected Selected Selected
Keyboard tab	
Move after enter	Next field
Behaviour entering field	Select entire field
Arrow key behaviour	Next field
Forms/Reports tab	
Form template	Normal
Report template	Normal
Always use event procedures	Not selected

Option	Settings
Tables/Queries tab	
Default field sizes Text Number	 50 Long Integer
Default field type	Text
Query design Show table names Enable AutoJoin Output all fields	 Selected Selected Not selected

Windows Regional Settings

By default, Access displays numbers, currencies, and dates in the format specified in your Windows Regional Settings. The examples used in this book assume that your Regional Settings are set to *English (United Kingdom)*, that the default currency symbol is £, that the default date sequence and display format is dd-mm-yy, and that commas are used as the thousands separator.

It is recommended that you use the Regional Settings listed here. Otherwise, dates and numbers may display differently on your screen than in the examples and illustrations in this book. You can access your Regional Settings from the Windows Control Panel.

Note that, depending on which operating system you are using, the order and names of Regional Settings options may differ slightly from those listed here.

Setting	Value
Regional Settings	
Regional Settings	English (United Kingdom)
Number	
Decimal symbol	.
No. of digits after decimal	2
Digit grouping symbol	,
No. of digits in group	3
Negative sign symbol	–
Negative number format	–1.1
Display leading zeros	0.7
Measurement system	Metric

Currency	
Currency symbol	£
Position of currency symbol	£ 1.1
Negative number format	–£ 1.1
Decimal symbol etc.	Same as for numbers.
Date	
Short date style	dd-MM-yy
Date separator	–
Long date style	dd MMMM yyyy

1 Database development: overview

In this chapter

Creating a relational database requires careful planning and preparation. You need to understand not only how to create the database in Access, but also how to design the database so that you can quickly and easily retrieve any information you want.

This chapter provides an overview of the steps involved in creating a database and explains the benefits of good database design.

New skills

At the end of this chapter you should be able to:

- Explain what a relational database is
- Explain the advantages of good database design
- List the typical steps involved in designing and creating a relational database

New words

In this chapter you will meet the following terms:

- Relational database
- Relationship

What is a relational database?

A relational database consists of a collection of data organized into tables. Tables are linked together by defining relationships between them. These relationships are based on the tables having a common field, and they allow you to bring together data from different tables.

As an example, take the Books and Publishers tables shown below. Each record in the Books table has a related record in the Publishers table that provides details about the book's publisher. The relationship is established by including a PublisherID field in the Books table as well as in the Publishers table.

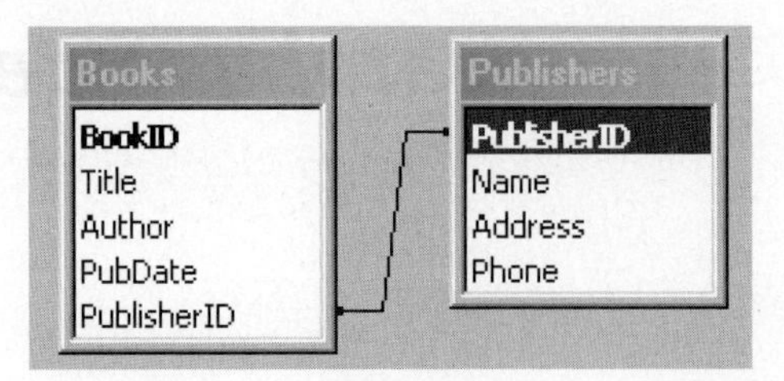

Knowing the PublisherID value for a particular book, Access can find the publisher with that PublisherID and so bring together the records from the two tables. In the example here, Access has retrieved the title and author of a book from the Books table and the name and address of the book's publisher from the Publishers table.

Title	Author	Name	Address
Mansfield Park	Jane Austen	Penguin	London, England

Relational database

A collection of data organized into tables.

Relationship

A connection between two tables that allows them to share data. It is based on the tables having at least one field in common.

Overview of database development

Developing a database involves a design phase and an implementation phase. In the design phase, you decide on the structure of the database. In the implementation phase, you build the database by using a Database Management System (DBMS) such as Microsoft Access.

Design phase

The object of the design phase is to determine a suitable structure for your database by answering the following questions:

- What tables do I need to create?
- What fields do I need to include in each table and what are their data types?
- What is the primary key of each table?
- What are the relationships between the tables?

It is important to spend time on this phase. A poorly designed database makes it difficult for users to retrieve certain information and may return inconsistent and inaccurate results. A well-designed database, on the other hand, provides the following benefits:

- The database will be compact, efficient and easy to modify.
- Data will be consistent, accurate and easy to maintain.
- Users will able to retrieve whatever information they want now and in the future.

Pen and paper or a word processing application are the best tools for roughing out and refining your database design. Only when you are satisfied with your design should you start to create the tables and enter data.

Implementation phase

In the implementation phase you use Access to create the tables you identified in the design phase, and to create the queries, forms and reports that you need to input data and retrieve and present information.

> ***Data and information***
>
> *Data is the values that you store in the database. Information is data that you retrieve from the database in some meaningful way.*

Steps for building a database

Here is an overview of the typical steps involved in designing and building a database.

1) **Determine the overall purpose and specific objectives of the database.** Establishing the purpose of your database provides a focus for your design. Establishing the specific tasks you want to accomplish with the database helps you to identify the main subjects of the database and the facts that you need to store about each subject.

   The subjects you identify are all candidates for tables in your database. The facts about a subject are all candidates for fields in that subject's table.

2) **Determine the tables and fields you need.** In this step you establish a preliminary set of tables and fields based on the subjects and facts you identified in step one. You then apply a set of design principles to these tables and fields in order to determine the final set of tables and the primary key for each.

3) **Determine the data type and properties for each field.** A field's data type determines the kind of data that the field will accept. A field's properties control such attributes as field size, default value and display format.

4) **Determine the table relationships.** In this step you determine how one table is related to another and the type of relationship in each case. You may need to add new fields or create new tables at this stage in order to define the relationships correctly.

5) **Implement the database design.** In this step you create the tables and relationships you identified during the design phase.

6) **Enter the database records.** Because it is much easier to change the database design before you have filled the tables with data, it is a good idea to first test the design. You can do this by entering sample data and checking that you can get the results you want. When you are satisfied that the database design suits your requirements, you can begin entering data in the tables.

7) **Create queries, forms and reports.** This final step involves designing and creating the queries, forms and reports you need for inputting data to the database and retrieving information from it.

Chapter 1: summary

A relational database consists of a collection of data organized into tables. You can retrieve a combination of information from different tables by defining relationships between the tables.

There are two main phases in creating a database: design and implementation. In the design phase you decide on the tables, fields and relationships you need. In the implementation phase you create the tables and relationships, and also the queries, forms and reports you need for inputting data and retrieving information.

2 Table design: what tables, what fields?

In this chapter

Designing an appropriate set of tables for your database is an essential first step in building an effective and efficient database.

In this chapter you will learn the principles of good database design and how to apply them to determine an appropriate set of tables for the Village Library database.

New skills

At the end of this chapter you should be able to explain:

- Why relational databases are preferable to flat databases
- The problems you might encounter in poorly designed databases
- The steps involved in designing a database
- The principles of good database design

New words

In this chapter you will meet the following terms:

- Flat database
- Redundancy
- Modification anomaly
- Multivalue field
- Multipart field

Why not a flat database?

A simple database can consist of a single table. However, most databases consist of a number of related tables. To see why, let's take a look at the problems you might encounter with a flat database and with poorly designed tables.

Flat database

A database consisting of a single table.

The following table contains data about members of a library and the books they have borrowed. You do not need to create this database in order to recognize its pitfalls.

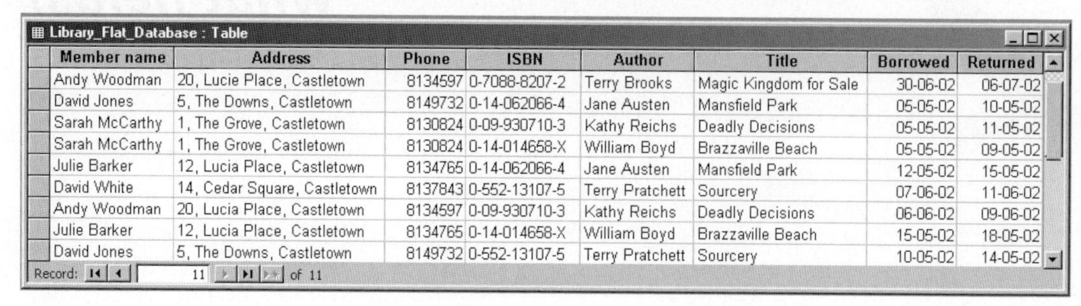

Library_Flat_Database : Table

Member name	Address	Phone	ISBN	Author	Title	Borrowed	Returned
Andy Woodman	20, Lucie Place, Castletown	8134597	0-7088-8207-2	Terry Brooks	Magic Kingdom for Sale	30-06-02	06-07-02
David Jones	5, The Downs, Castletown	8149732	0-14-062066-4	Jane Austen	Mansfield Park	05-05-02	10-05-02
Sarah McCarthy	1, The Grove, Castletown	8130824	0-09-930710-3	Kathy Reichs	Deadly Decisions	05-05-02	11-05-02
Sarah McCarthy	1, The Grove, Castletown	8130824	0-14-014658-X	William Boyd	Brazzaville Beach	05-05-02	09-05-02
Julie Barker	12, Lucia Place, Castletown	8134765	0-14-062066-4	Jane Austen	Mansfield Park	12-05-02	15-05-02
David White	14, Cedar Square, Castletown	8137843	0-552-13107-5	Terry Pratchett	Sourcery	07-06-02	11-06-02
Andy Woodman	20, Lucia Place, Castletown	8134597	0-09-930710-3	Kathy Reichs	Deadly Decisions	06-06-02	09-06-02
Julie Barker	12, Lucia Place, Castletown	8134765	0-14-014658-X	William Boyd	Brazzaville Beach	15-05-02	18-05-02
David Jones	5, The Downs, Castletown	8149732	0-552-13107-5	Terry Pratchett	Sourcery	10-05-02	14-05-02

Record: 11 of 11

The problems with this table, as with most poorly designed tables, can be summarized as follows:

- Redundancy
- Modification anomalies
- Multivalue fields
- Multipart fields

Redundancy

Have a look at the records in the table. Every time a member borrows a book, you must enter their name, address and phone number. The table contains each member's details many times.

This is a waste of space and a waste of time. It also increases the likelihood of data entry errors, creating inconsistencies between member details in different records. The unnecessary duplication of data in a database is referred to as *redundancy*.

The table also contains each book's details many times: more wasted space, more inconsistencies, more redundancy.

Redundancy

The unnecessary duplication of data in a database.

Modification anomalies

Member details may change over time. When they do, you must update *every* record containing those details. Otherwise there will be inconsistencies in the database. This is an example of an *update anomaly*.

What happens when you want to add a new book to the database but it hasn't yet been borrowed by a member? The member-related fields will be empty and the primary key will probably be missing or partly missing. So there will be no way to uniquely identify the new record. This is an example of an *insertion anomaly*.

What happens when a member cancels their library subscription and you want to remove them from the database? If you delete all their loan records, you also delete information about the books they have borrowed. And if they are the only member that has borrowed a particular book, you will lose all information about that book. This is an example of a *deletion anomaly*.

Multivalue fields

The table contains a single field for the author of a book. But what about books with multiple authors?

In a single table, you can approach this problem in one of three ways, each with its own problems:

- Include all the authors in the same field, referred to as multivalue field. However, this makes it difficult to work with the data in the field – for example, to search for a single author or to list authors alphabetically.
- Duplicate the entire record for each author, but this considerably increases redundancy and the possibility of inconsistencies.
- Include a separate field for each author. But how many fields should you create? However many you decide, all but one will be empty in most records. In addition, when searching for a particular author you will have to include all the fields in your query.

Multivalue field

A field that contains multiple values for the same data item.

Multipart fields

A multipart field is a field that contains more than one data item. The Library_Flat_Database table contains two typical examples:

- The Member name field contains both the member's first and last names. This makes it difficult to search for or sort members by their last name.
- There is only one address field. If the address contains a street address, a town or city name, and a postal code, it is difficult to manipulate these items separately.

Multipart field

A field that includes more than one data item.

Solution

The solution to multipart fields is to create a separate field for each data item. The solution to redundancy, modification anomalies, and multivalue fields is to separate your data into a number of tables and to define relationships between those tables.

But how do you know what is the correct set of tables? In formal database design theory, you use a process known as *normalization*. This chapter takes a more informal approach that achieves similar results.

Overview of table design

Here are the steps you should follow in order to determine the tables and fields required for a particular database:

1) Determine the purpose of the database.
2) Determine the tasks that you want to accomplish with the database.
3) Determine the subjects of the database and the facts (characteristics) you need to store about each subject.
4) Map the subjects and characteristics to tables and fields.
5) Apply the principles of good database design to the tables and fields.

Database purpose

Formally specifying the purpose of your database provides a focus for your database design and helps you draw up the list of tasks that the database must support.

In the case of the Village Library database, the purpose can be stated as:

> "The purpose of the Village Library database is to maintain the data that is used to support the library service. The database is intended to facilitate staff in cataloguing books, maintaining membership records, and tracking book loans."

Database tasks

Drawing up a list of the major tasks that the database must automate helps you to identify the subjects of the database and the characteristics of those subjects. You can subsequently map these to tables and fields.

In the case of the Village Library database, the tasks include the following:

- Maintain a catalogue of the library's holdings. The specific tasks to be supported include adding new books, removing missing and discarded books, and updating book details.
- Provide facilities for searching the catalogue by author, book, publisher, category, and so on.
- Provide links to author websites.
- Maintain membership records. The specific tasks to be supported include adding new members, removing members, and updating member details.
- Provide facilities for searching the membership records by name, address, and so on.
- Record all loans and returns, including any fines paid for late returns.
- Provide reports on overdue books, books currently on loan, fines paid, borrower activity, the most popular books and book categories, and so on.
- Enforce library lending rules. A member can have a maximum of five books on loan at any one time. The maximum lending period is ten days. Fines for overdue books are imposed at a rate of £0.50 per book per day, but library staff can apply a discount at their own discretion.

Database subjects

The subjects of a database are the people, things, or events about which the database must store data. The characteristics of a subject are the details that describe that subject.

To draw up a list of subjects, take a look at the database purpose and tasks that you have identified and list the subjects mentioned there, as shown below.

Catalogue
Books
Members
Loans
Publishers
Categories
Authors
Returns
Fines
Overdue books
Borrowers

You may intuitively realize that some items in the list are not subjects in their own right. But it is best to review the list methodically.

Are there any duplicates? Catalogue represents the same subject as Books, so one of these can be removed. The same is true of Members and Borrowers.

Does any subject represent a characteristic of another subject rather than a subject in its own right? What about Overdue books, Fines, and Returns? Being overdue is really a characteristic of a loan. The same is true for the return of a book, and for fines relating to late returns. So you can remove these subjects. You can also remove Categories, as a category is a characteristic of a book.

What about Authors and Publishers? Both are characteristics of books. However, if they have characteristics of their own, such as address, phone, and web address, then they are subjects in their own right. Let's leave them in the list for the moment.

Books Members Loans Authors Publishers

The subject list now includes only Books, Members, Loans, Authors, and Publishers.

Subject characteristics

To identify the characteristics of each subject, look at the list of tasks again and identify the characteristics mentioned there. In a real-world scenario you would find other characteristics by interviewing the library staff and examining the ledgers, reports, and index cards that they currently use.

Assume that the preliminary list of characteristics is as shown below.

Books	Members	Loans	Authors	Publishers
ISBN	Name	ISBN	Name	Name
Title	Address	Title	Web Address	
Author Name	Phone	Author		
Publication Year	Email	Member Name		
Publisher Name		Date Borrowed		
Category		Date Returned		
Date Purchased		Fine Paid		
Cost				

Again review the list methodically:

- Does each characteristic describe the subject under which it is listed and not another subject? Title and Author appear under Loans but they describe a book. So you can remove them from the Loans subject.
- Are there any duplicates?
  - Title and Author Name were duplicated but they have already been removed from the Loans subject.
  - Publisher Name appears under both Books and Publishers. As no other publisher details are required, a separate Publishers subject is unnecessary. So you can remove that subject. A publisher's name now appears only under the Books subject.

– What about ISBN? This is a characteristic of a book. However, it establishes the relationship between a particular loan and a particular book and so must appear under both subjects. Similarly, Member Name establishes the relationship between loans and members, and Author Name establishes the relationship between books and authors.

- Finally, make sure that no characteristics are missing. For example, does the library require statistics on the gender and age of members? If so you would add these characteristics under Members.

  For the moment you can assume that there are no further characteristics to be recorded. So the list of subjects and characteristics now looks as shown below.

Books	Members	Loans	Authors
ISBN	Name	ISBN	Name
Title	Address	Member Name	Web Address
Author Name	Phone	Date Borrowed	
Publication Year	Email	Date Returned	
Publisher Name		Fine Paid	
Category			
Date Purchased			
Cost			

Tables and fields

Each subject of a database is represented by a table in the database. Each characteristic of a subject represents a field in the corresponding table. So the list of subjects and characteristics maps directly to the list of tables and fields for the database.

When naming your tables and fields, follow these simple guidelines:

- Table and field names should be unique and meaningful.
- Keep table and field names as short as possible while maintaining their meaningfulness.
- For tables, use the plural form of the name. For fields, use the singular form of the name.
- If the same field appears in two tables, give it the same name in each.

With these guidelines in mind, the tables so far determined for the Village Library database might look like those below.

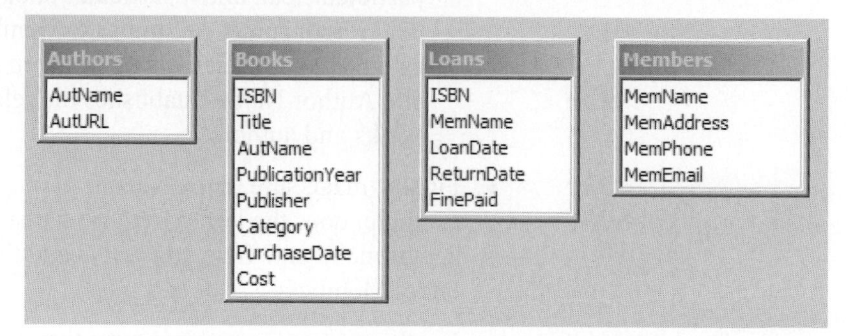

The tables and fields identified here are a good foundation for the Village Library database but they need further refinement, as described in the next section.

Design principles

The principles of good database design can be summarized as follows:

- One table, one subject
- One field, one value
- One table, one primary key
- The key, the whole key, and nothing but the key

One table, one subject

Each table in your database should represent a single subject only. Otherwise, you will have multiple repetitions of the same data in different records. The result: redundancy, inconsistencies, and modification anomalies. The tables identified in the previous section meet this criterion.

You could arrive at the same set of tables by analysing the Library_Flat_Database and eliminating redundancy.

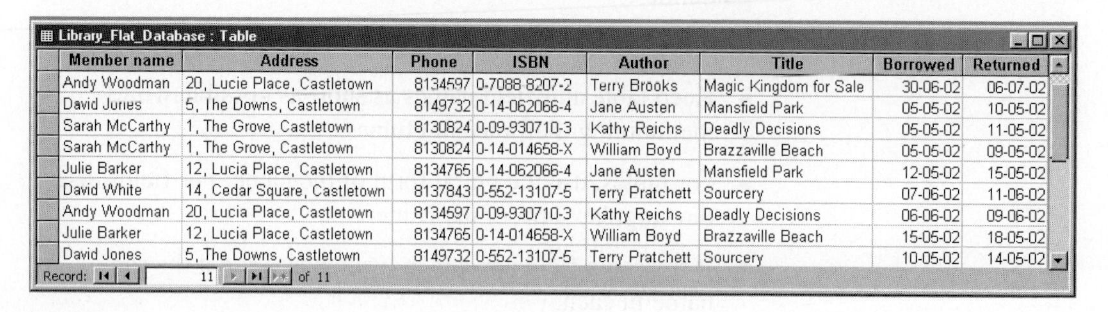

Library_Flat_Database : Table

Member name	Address	Phone	ISBN	Author	Title	Borrowed	Returned
Andy Woodman	20, Lucie Place, Castletown	8134597	0-7088 8207-2	Terry Brooks	Magic Kingdom for Sale	30-06-02	06-07-02
David Jones	5, The Downs, Castletown	8149732	0-14-062066-4	Jane Austen	Mansfield Park	05-05-02	10-05-02
Sarah McCarthy	1, The Grove, Castletown	8130824	0-09-930710-3	Kathy Reichs	Deadly Decisions	05-05-02	11-05-02
Sarah McCarthy	1, The Grove, Castletown	8130824	0-14-014658-X	William Boyd	Brazzaville Beach	05-05-02	09-05-02
Julie Barker	12, Lucia Place, Castletown	8134765	0-14-062066-4	Jane Austen	Mansfield Park	12-05-02	15-05-02
David White	14, Cedar Square, Castletown	8137843	0-552-13107-5	Terry Pratchett	Sourcery	07-06-02	11-06-02
Andy Woodman	20, Lucia Place, Castletown	8134597	0-09-930710-3	Kathy Reichs	Deadly Decisions	06-06-02	09-06-02
Julie Barker	12, Lucia Place, Castletown	8134765	0-14-014658-X	William Boyd	Brazzaville Beach	15-05-02	18-05-02
David Jones	5, The Downs, Castletown	8149732	0-552-13107-5	Terry Pratchett	Sourcery	10-05-02	14-05-02

Record: 11 of 11

- Whenever Andy Woodman borrows a book, his personal details are duplicated in a new record. To ensure that member details are stored only once, you would create a separate Members table.
- Whenever someone borrows *Sourcery* by Terry Pratchett, the book's ISBN, author and title must be repeated. To ensure that book details are stored only once, you would create a separate Books table.
- If you include an author's website address, then every time someone borrows a book, both the author name and web address must be repeated. To ensure that author details are stored only once, you would create a separate Authors table.
- The Borrowed and Returned dates are the only fields now remaining in the original table. These relate to loans and should be included in a Loans table. This table would also include ISBN and Member name fields so that you can relate the Loans and Books tables and the Loans and Members tables.

From this exercise, you have arrived at the same set of tables as you did by identifying the database subjects and characteristics.

One field, one value

Each field in a table should represent only one data item and should contain only one value for that data item. Otherwise it is difficult to search and sort on values in the field.

There are two examples of *multipart* fields in the Members table: MemName and MemAddress.

- MemName contains both the member's first and last names. This makes it difficult to search and sort on last names. So split the field in two: MemFirstname and MemLastname. And do the same for the AutName field in the Authors table.
- MemAddress contains house numbers, street names and towns. Whether you split this into different fields depends on whether you want to manipulate the different parts of the address separately.

  Let's assume that the library wants to produce statistics on how many members live in each town. In this case, MemTown should be a separate field.

There is one example of a *multivalue* field in the Books table: AutName.

- Books can have more than one author, but including them all in the one field makes it difficult to sort and search on the field.

  Resolving this problem involves creating a many-to-many relationship between the Books and Authors tables. You will learn how to do this in Chapter 5. For the moment, leave AutName in the Books table.

The database structure now looks as shown below.

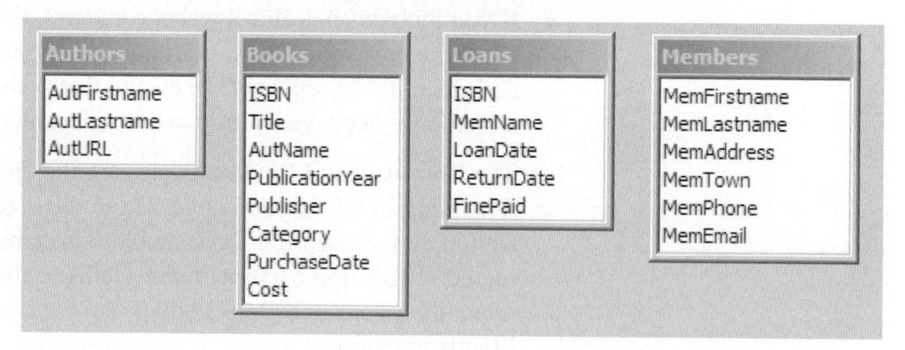

One table, one primary key

Every table must have a primary key that uniquely identifies each record in the table. The key can consist of a single field or a combination of fields (a composite key). If a table has more than one candidate for the primary key, choose the one with the least number of fields.

Let's look at each table in turn. Do any of the fields uniquely identify each record in the table?

- In the Members table, MemLastname is unlikely to be unique, as is the combination of MemFirstname and MemLastname. A combination of MemFirstname, MemLastname and MemAddress may also not be unique, as a parent and child living at the same address could have the same name.

  The solution is to add a MemID field and to make it the primary key. In the Loans table, you must then replace the MemName field with the MemID field.

- For the purposes of the case study, we assume that there is never more than one copy of a given book in the library, so that ISBN uniquely identifies a book. Therefore, you can use ISBN as the primary key for the Books table.

- In the Authors table, only the combination of AutFirstname, AutLastname name and AutURL is likely to be unique. But no primary key should include a field that is optional or may be empty, as is the case with AutURL.

  Again, the solution is to add an AutID field and make it the primary key. In the Books table, you must then replace the AutName field with the AutID field.

- In the Loans table, the combination of ISBN and LoanDate is unique for each record. So you can make this the primary key.

The database structure now looks as shown below (the primary key fields are in bold type).

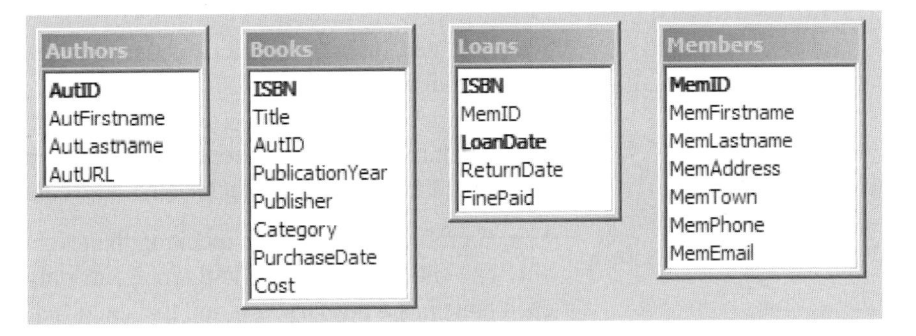

The key, the whole key, and nothing but the key

This phrase summarizes three important attributes of good database design.

- **The key ...** Each field in a table must directly describe the subject of that table, as represented by the primary key.

  For example, a PublisherAddress field should not be included in the Books table, as it describes a publisher and not a book. If you need to record that information, you would create a separate Publishers table.

- **... the whole key ...** When a table has a composite key, each non-key field must depend on the whole key and not just on part of it.

  If the Loans table included a Title field, that field would depend on the value in the ISBN field, but not on the value in the LoanDate field. So it doesn't belong in that table.

- **... and nothing but the key.** Each field in a table must depend on the primary key and on no other field in the table. That is, making a change to data in one non-key field must not require making a change to data in any other non-key field.

For example, if you include a PublisherAddress field in the Books table, then the value of the primary key (ISBN) determines the value of the PublisherAddress field only indirectly. If the value in the Publisher field changes, the value in the PublisherAddress field will also change. So PublisherAddress does not belong in the Books table.

Chapter 2: summary

The aim of good database design is to minimize redundancy and to ensure that each field is directly related to the subject of the table.

When designing a database, you should avoid unnecessary redundancy, multipart and multivalue fields, and modification anomalies.

The first step in designing a database is to establish the purpose of the database and the tasks you want to accomplish with it. From these you can draw up a list of subjects for the database and the characteristics of those subjects. You can then map subjects to tables, and characteristics to fields.

You can refine the tables by checking that each table represents only one subject, that each field represents only one value, that each table has a primary key, and that each field in a table depends on the primary key, the whole key, and nothing but the key.

Chapter 2: quick quiz

Q1	Which of these are problems associated with flat databases?
A.	Redundancy.
B.	Data entry errors.
C.	Modification anomalies.

Q2	True or false – a multivalue field includes more than one value for the same data item.
A.	True.
B.	False.

Q3	True or false – a multipart field includes more than one data item.
A.	True.
B.	False.

Q4	True or false – subjects map to tables and characteristics map to fields.
A.	True.
B.	False.

Q5	Which of these is *not* a principle of good database design?
A.	One table, one subject.
B.	One field, one value.
C.	One value, one key.

Answers

1: All, **2:** A, **3:** A, **4:** A, **5:** C.

3 Table design: data types, field sizes, field formats

In this chapter

The data type of a field determines the kind of data that can be stored in the field and the operations that can be carried out on that data. The properties of a field determine how data in the field is stored, handled and displayed.

In this chapter you will learn the purpose of each data type and related *Field Size* and *Format* properties.

New skills

At the end of this chapter you should be able to:

- Explain the purpose of each data type
- Apply each data type
- Specify field sizes and formats
- Explain the consequences of changing a field's data type

New words

There are no new terms in this chapter.

Exercise file

In this chapter you will work with the following Access file:

- `Chp3_VillageLibrary_Database`

You will also use the following Word file:

- `MansfieldPark-JaneAusten`

Syllabus reference

In this chapter you will cover the following items of the ECDL Advanced Database syllabus:

- **AM5.1.1.1:** Apply and modify data types such as text, memo, hyperlink, currency, date and time in a field, column.
- **AM5.1.1.2:** Understand the consequences of modifying data types.

About data types

Access supports the following data types:

- Text
- Currency
- Yes/No
- Memo
- Date/Time
- Hyperlink
- Number
- AutoNumber

It is important to choose the appropriate data type for each field when you create it.

Before you enter data in a table, you can change the data type of a field as and when you like. After you have entered data, changing a field's data type has consequences that you must take into account if you do not want to lose data.

Field sizes

Some data types have a *Field Size* property that you can use to set the maximum size for data in a field. Use the smallest possible setting as smaller data sizes can be processed faster and require less memory than larger ones. Users will not be able to enter values larger than the specified field size.

Be careful when reducing the size of a field that already contains data. You will lose data if existing values are larger than those supported by the new field size.

Field formats

Many data types have a *Format* property that you can use to specify how data is displayed and printed. This does not affect how data is stored in a field. For example, you can choose to display dates in any of the following formats:

```
23/05/03
23-May-03
Friday, May 23, 2003
```

For each data type, you can select from a list of predefined formats or you can create your own custom format.

For some predefined Number, Currency and Date/Time formats, Access uses the Regional Settings specified in the Windows Control Panel. The examples used in this book assume that your Regional Settings are set to *English (United Kingdom)*. (See 'Windows Regional Settings' in the Preface for further information.)

Applying data types and field properties

You apply data types to fields in Table Design View. In the Design View window, you use the *Field Name* column to specify the name of a field and you use the *Data Type* column to specify the field's data type.

When you click on a field in the upper part of the Design View window, that field's properties are displayed in the lower part of the window, and you can choose the options you want there.

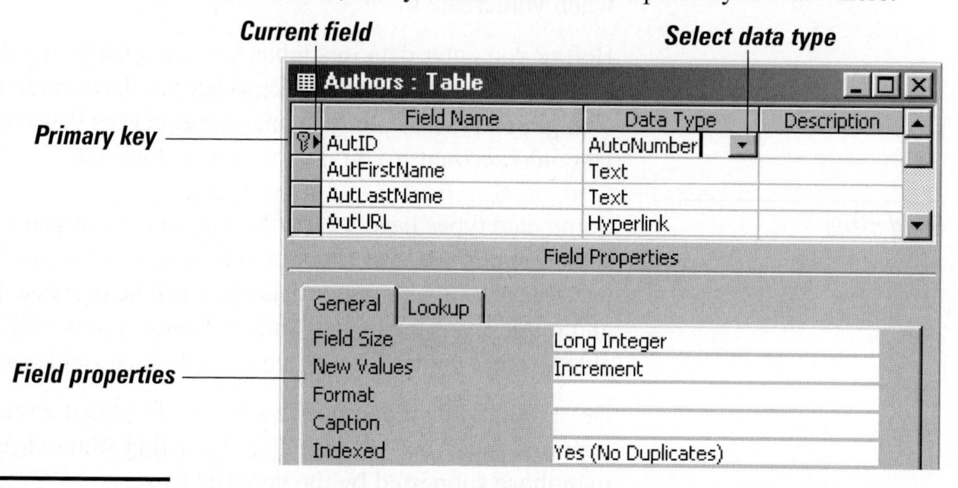

Text fields

Use a Text data type to store alphanumeric data that does not exceed 255 characters in length. For example, in the Village Library database, a Text data type is appropriate for name, address, ISBN and book title fields.

Use a Text data type also for numbers that are not required in calculations – for example, telephone numbers and postal codes.

The following are all Text fields.

MemFirstname	MemLastname	MemPhon
Andy	White	8134597
David	Jones	8149732

Be aware that in a Text field, numbers are sorted as text strings. If you want to sort them in numeric order, either change the data type to Number or add leading zeros to the number strings to make them all the same length.

Text	Text	Number
1	001	1
10	002	2
100	010	10
13	013	13
2	020	20
20	100	100

Text data type *Text data type* *Number data type*

Memo fields

Use a Memo data type to store alphanumeric data that is more than 255 characters long. Data in Memo fields can contain tabs and paragraph breaks.

In Datasheet View, you see only a single line of a Memo field at any one time. To view the full contents of the field, click in the field and press **Shift+F2**. This displays the *Zoom* dialog box where you can view and edit the contents of the field. You can use this feature for other field types as well.

Exercise 3.1: Creating a Memo field

In this exercise you will add a Review field to the Books table and set its data type to Memo.

1) Open the starting database for this chapter:

   `Chp3_VillageLibrary_Database`

2) Open the Books table in Design View. To do this, click on the table in the Database window and click the **Design** button.

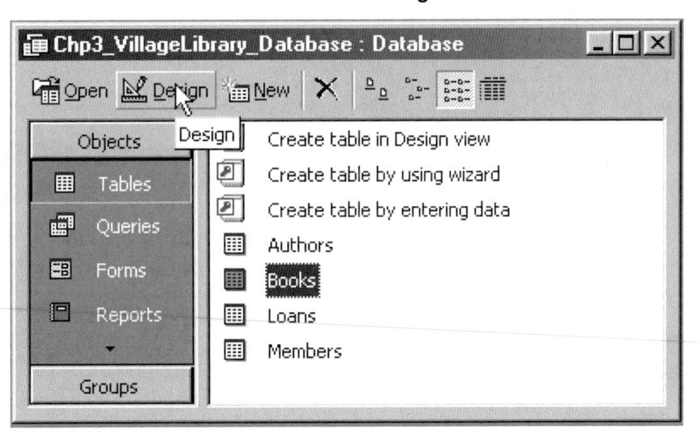

3) Add a new field at the end of the table. Name it Review and select Memo as its data type.

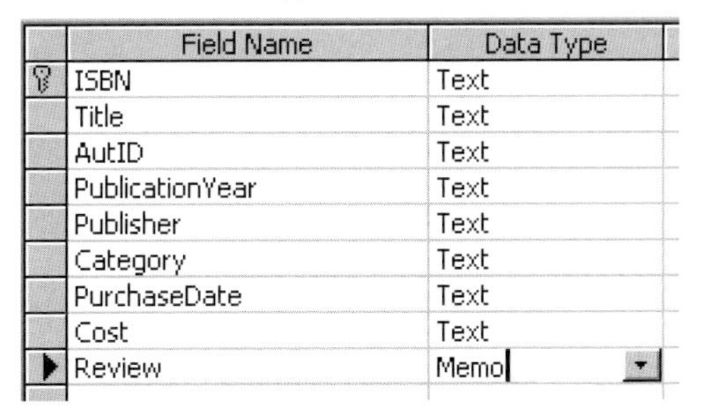

Field Name	Data Type
ISBN	Text
Title	Text
AutID	Text
PublicationYear	Text
Publisher	Text
Category	Text
PurchaseDate	Text
Cost	Text
Review	Memo

4) Switch to Datasheet View, saving the table as you do.

5) To see how a Memo field works, you need some sample text. To save time, open the Microsoft Access Help Window and copy a few paragraphs of text from there.

6) Click a Review field in the Books table and press **Shift+F2**.

7) When the *Zoom* dialog box appears, paste the copied text into it. Notice that Access preserves the text and paragraph breaks but not the formatting or any graphics.

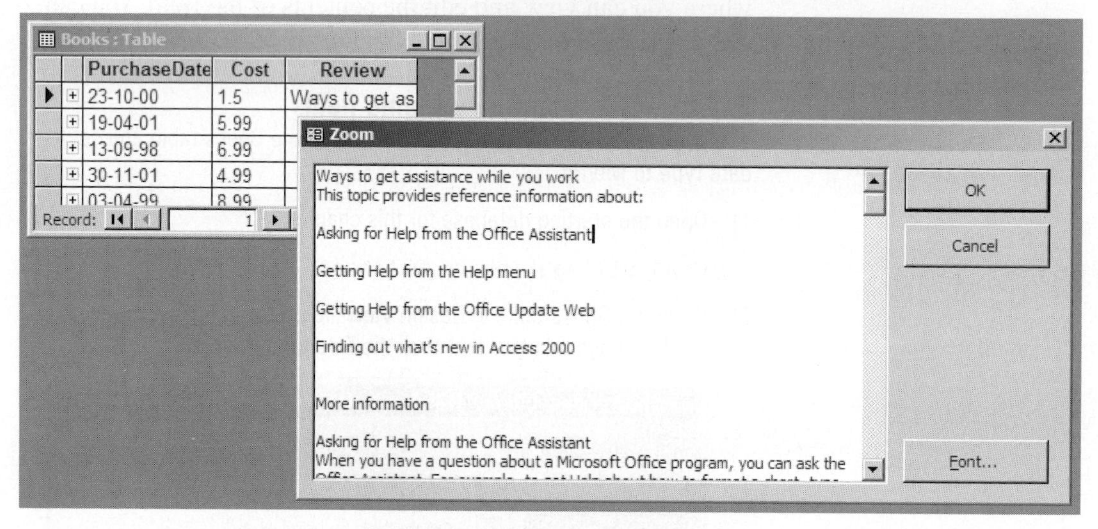

8) Click **OK** to close the *Zoom* dialog box.

9) Now try using the **Arrow** keys to scroll through the field contents. You can see that with any lengthy entry it is much easier to view the data in the *Zoom* dialog box and to edit it there.

10) Press **Shift+F2** again and make some changes to the data.

    You can use standard editing keys such as **Del** and **Backspace**, but to insert a paragraph break you must press **Ctrl+Enter** (pressing **Enter** is the same as clicking **OK**).

11) Click **OK** to save your changes. Then close the Books table.

Number fields

Use a Number data type to store numeric data that is to be used in calculations, except calculations involving currency values.

The following are all examples of Number fields.

Order ID	Quantity	Discount
10248	12	15%
10248	10	20%

Field Size

Use the *Field Size* property to set a specific number type. The options are shown in the following table.

Field Size	Description
Byte	Stores whole numbers from 0 to 255.
Integer	Stores whole numbers from –32,768 to 32,767.
Long Integer	Stores whole numbers from –2,147,483,648 to 2,147,483,647. This is the default size.
Single	Stores numbers from –3.402823E38 to –1.401298E–45 for negative values and from 1.401298E–45 to 3.402823E38 for positive values.
Double	Stores numbers from –1.79769313486231E308 to –4.94065645841247E–324 for negative values and from 1.79769313486231E308 to 4.94065645841247E–324 for positive values.
Replication ID	A special number type relevant only to database replication.
Decimal	Stores numbers from $-10^{28} - 1$ through $10^{28} - 1$.

When to use a Number data type

You can enter numeric data in Text, Number and Currency fields. How do you decide when to use a Number field and which field size to apply?

Data types for numbers

- If numbers are not going to be used in calculations, you can use the Text data type. Remember, however, that numbers in Text fields sort as text strings (see 'Text fields' above).
- If numbers represent a currency value, use the Currency data type.
- If numbers are going to be used in calculations or need to be sorted in numeric order, use the Number data type.

Number field sizes

- For numbers without fractions, use *Byte*, *Integer* or *Long Integer*, depending on the range of numbers required.
- For values with fractions, use *Single*, *Double* or *Decimal*, depending on the degree of precision required.

Single and *Double* number types can store extremely small and extremely large numbers. However, they use floating-point mathematics and you may encounter small rounding errors when you include them in calculations. If you require a high level of accuracy, and cannot afford even very small rounding errors, use *Decimal* instead, or use a Currency data type (this can store up to 15 digits to the left of the decimal point and up to four digits to the right).

Format

Access provides a number of predefined formats for Number fields. For example, you can choose to include a currency symbol, to include or exclude thousands separators, or to display a number as a percentage.

Exercise 3.2: Applying Number data types

In this exercise you will apply a Number data type to the Books.PublicationYear field so that you can perform calculations on its values. You will also change the field's *Field Size* and *Format* properties.

1) Open the Books table in Design View.
2) Change the *Data Type* setting for the PublicationYear field from *Text* to *Number*.
3) In the *Field Properties* box, you can see that Access sets the field size to *Long Integer* by default. However, no year entered in the Library database will be greater than 32,767 so an *Integer* field size is adequate.

   Click on the *Field Size* property and click the arrow to view the available field sizes. Then select the *Integer* option.

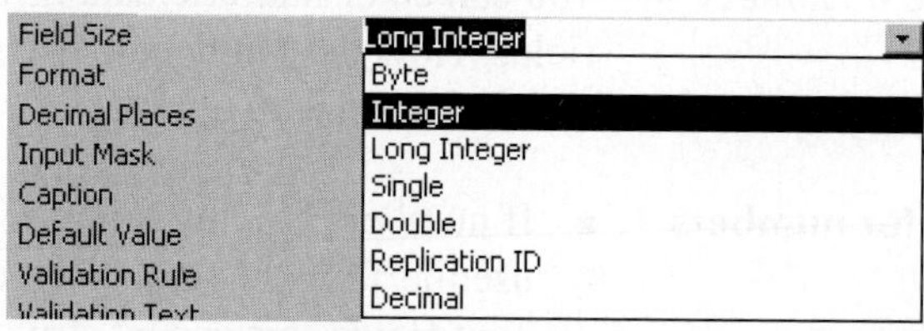

4) Click on the *Format* property and click the arrow to view the available formats.

   You do not want thousands separators, currency symbols or decimal places, so select the *General Number* option. This option does not display decimal places for integers.

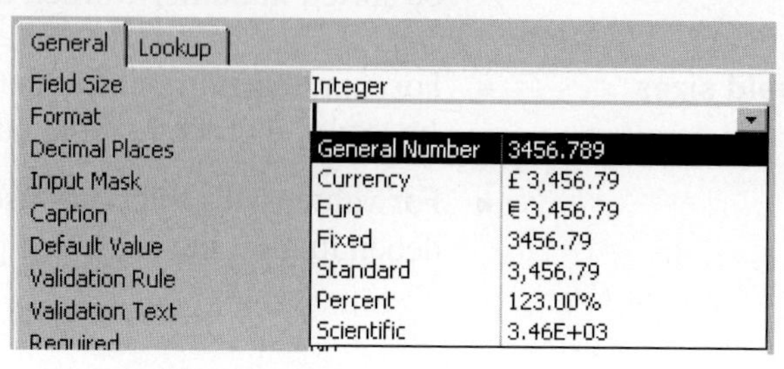

5) For an explanation of all Number formats, press **F1** with the *Format* property still selected. This displays a help topic that explains formats in general. Click the *Number and Currency Data Types* link for information on Number formats specifically. When you have finished, close the Help window.

6) Save the Books table.

Currency fields

Use a Currency data type for monetary values. The default currency symbol displayed depends on your Windows Regional Settings. You can also use a Currency data type for number fields that require a high level of accuracy, with no rounding off during calculations.

Cost
£3.87
£5.99

Exercise 3.3: Applying Currency data types

In this exercise you will apply a Currency data type to the Books.Cost field and select an appropriate *Format* option.

1) Open the Books table in Design View.

2) For the Cost field, change the *Data Type* setting to *Currency*.

3) Notice that the field's *Format* property is automatically set to *Currency*. Click in the property box and click the down arrow to see the display layout of this format.

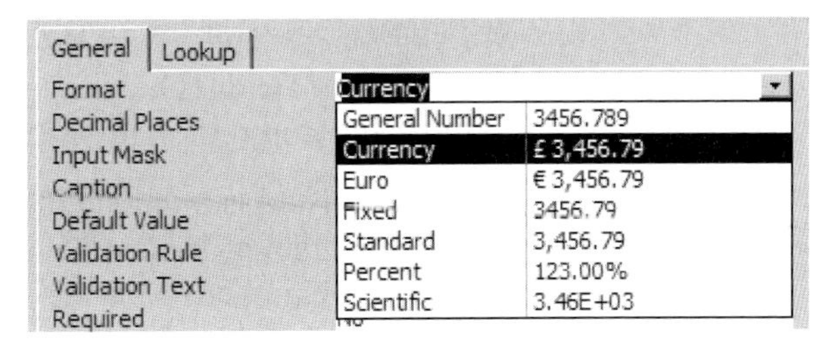

4) Save the Books table.

Date/Time fields

Use a Date/Time data type for dates and times.

By default, Access displays dates and times using the Short Date and Long Time settings in your Windows Regional Settings. If a value includes a date only, no time is displayed. If a value includes a time only, no date is displayed.

LoanDate	ReturnDate
24-May-02	27-05-02

Exercise 3.4: Applying Date/Time data types

In this exercise you will apply a Date/Time data type to the Books.PurchaseDate field and select an appropriate field format.

1) Open the Books table in Design View.
2) For the PurchaseDate field, change the *Data Type* setting to *Date/Time*.
3) Click on the *Format* property and click the arrow to view the available formats.
4) Select the *Medium Date* format.

Property	Format	Example
Format		
Input Mask	General Date	19-06-94 17:34:23
Caption	Long Date	19 June 1994
Default Value	Medium Date	19-Jun-94
Validation Rule	Short Date	19-06-94
Validation Text	Long Time	17:34:23
Required	Medium Time	05:34
Indexed	Short Time	17:34

5) Close the Books table, saving it as you do.

AutoNumber fields

Use an AutoNumber data type for fields that require unique, consecutive or random numbers. Access generates the numbers automatically. Typically this data type is used for primary key fields such as order numbers, IDs, invoice numbers, and so on.

MemID
000001
000002
000003

By default, Access assigns a *Field Size* property of *Long Integer* and a *New Values* property of *Increment* to AutoNumber fields. These are the most commonly used settings and don't normally need to be changed.

If the same field is included in more than one table, in order to link the two tables, it must have the same data type in both tables. AutoNumber fields are an exception. If a field in one table has an AutoNumber data type, then it must have a Number data type in the linked table and a field size of *Long Integer*.

Note that you cannot include more than one AutoNumber field in a table.

Exercise 3.5: Applying an AutoNumber data type

In this exercise, you will apply an AutoNumber data type to the Authors.AutID field and change the Books.AutID field's data type accordingly.

1) Open the Authors table in Design View.
2) Change the data type of the AutID field to *AutoNumber*. You can see that Access assigns a *Field Size* property of *Long Integer* and a *New Values* property of *Increment* by default. Leave these as they are.

3) Close and save the Authors table.

4) Open the Books table in Design View.

5) AutID is included here as a link to the Authors table. So set the data type to *Number* and the *Field Size* property to *Long Integer*.

6) Close and save the Books table.

Yes/No fields

Use a Yes/No data type for fields that can contain only one of two values.

By default, Access uses a checkbox control for Yes/No fields. However, you can change this to a text box or a combo box if you wish. You can then use the field's *Format* property to specify whether the values display as Yes/No, True/False or On/Off.

FineIssued	Fine
☑	€2.50
☐	€0.00

FineIssued	Fine
Yes	€2.50
No	€0.00

Exercise 3.6: Applying a Yes/No data type

In this exercise you will add a FineIssued field to the Loans table and set its data type to Yes/No.

1) Open the Loans table in Design View.

2) Insert a new field before the FinePaid field (click in the row for the FinePaid field and choose **Insert | Rows**). Name the new field FineIssued and set its data type to *Yes/No*.

3) The field's *Format* property is set by default to *Yes/No*. Have a look at the other options available but do not change the current setting.

4) Click on the **Lookup** tab in the *Field Properties* box. Then click the *Display Control* property and open its drop-down list. This lists the types of control that you can use for the field. *Check Box* is the default and most commonly used option, so leave this as it is.

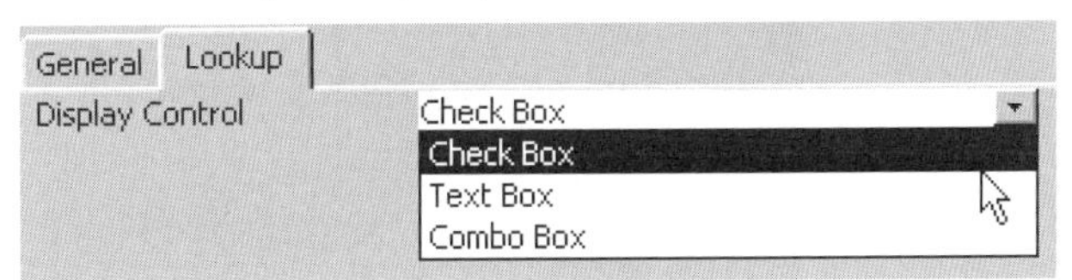

5) Switch to Datasheet View, saving the table as you do. Notice that Access has set the values in your new field to unselected checkboxes by default; this indicates a No value. To change a value, simply click in the checkbox.

6) Close the Loans table.

Hyperlink fields

Use a Hyperlink data type to store hyperlinks to websites, folders and files. Users can then click on the hyperlink to start the relevant application and display the destination of the link.

Exercise 3.7: Applying a Hyperlink data type

In this exercise you will change the data type of the Books.Review field from Memo to Hyperlink.

1) Open the Books table in Design View.
2) Change the Review field's data type to *Hyperlink*.
3) Switch back to Datasheet View, saving the table as you do.

Note that any values already in the Review field are converted to hyperlinks, but the links are invalid and will not work.

Exercise 3.8: Creating a hyperlink to a file

In this exercise you will create a hyperlink to a Word document that contains a review of *Mansfield Park* by Jane Austen.

1) With the Books table in Datasheet View, click in an empty Review field and choose **Insert | Hyperlink**.

   This displays a dialog box where you can browse to the file, folder or web page to which you want to create the link.

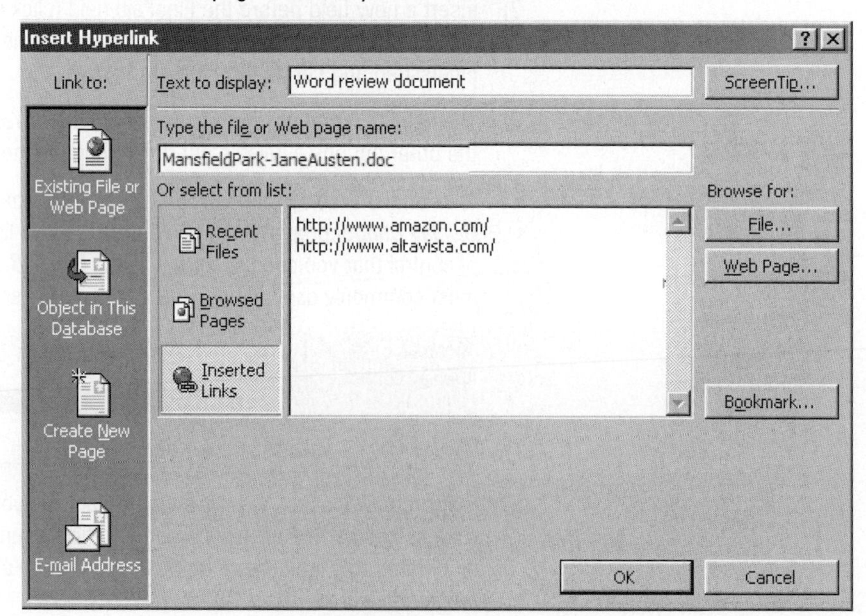

2) In the *Text to display* box, type the text you want to appear in the Hyperlink field in Access. For example:

   `Word review document`

3) Use the *Browse for: File* option to navigate to the folder to which you copied the contents of the CD that accompanies this book. Then select the following file by double-clicking on it:

   `MansfieldPark-JaneAusten`

4) Click **OK**. A hyperlink to the file is now inserted in the Review field.

5) Click on the link. This starts Microsoft Word and opens the review document.

6) Close the document, exit Word, and return to Access.

Exercise 3.9: Creating a hyperlink to a web page

In this exercise you will create a hyperlink to a review on a web page.

1) In the Books table, right-click on the link you created in the previous exercise and choose **Hyperlink | Edit Hyperlink** from the pop-up menu. This displays the *Edit Hyperlink* dialog box. Make sure that the *Link to: Existing File or Web Page* option is selected.

2) In the *Text to display* box, replace the existing text with the following:

   `Web review`

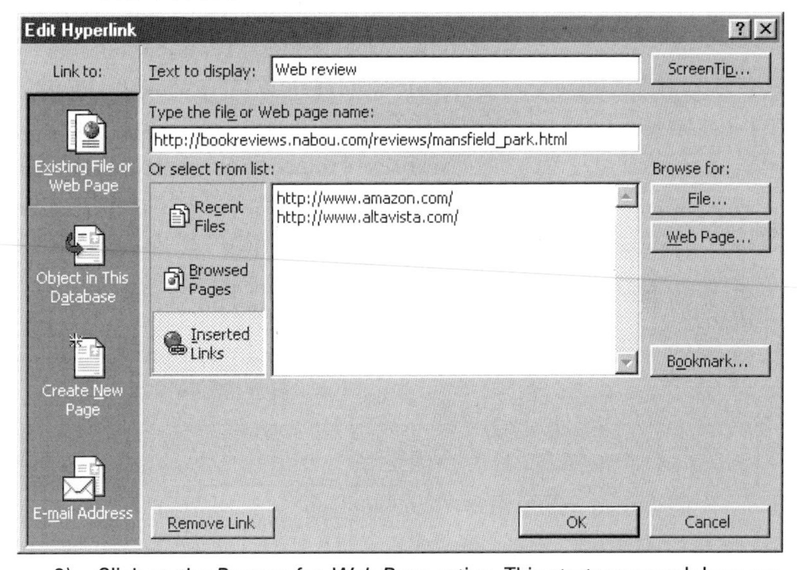

3) Click on the *Browse for: Web Page* option. This starts your web browser.

4) Connect to the Internet and go to the following address:

   `http://bookreviews.nabou.com/reviews/mansfield_park.html`

5) Close your Browser and disconnect. In the *Type the file or Web page name* box, Access automatically enters the address for the last web page you accessed. If it doesn't, you can select the web page from

the list displayed when you click the *Browsed Pages* option in the dialog box.

If you do not have an Internet connection, type the address directly in the *Type the file...* box.

6) Click **OK**. A hyperlink to the web page is now inserted in the Review field.

Review
Web review

7) Click on the link. This starts your web browser. When a connection to the Internet has been established, the web page to which you created the hyperlink is opened.

8) Exit your web browser and disconnect.

9) Return to Access and close the Books table.

Modifying data types

Before you enter data in a table, you can change the data type of a field as and when you like. After you have entered data, however, changing a field's data type may not always be possible or may have consequences that you need to be aware of if you don't want to lose data.

In general, Access can convert any data type to any other data type, provided that data already in the field is valid for the new data type. For example, in exercises in this chapter you changed the data type of fields in the Books and Authors tables without a problem.

However, there are conversions that are not possible or that may cause problems. When a data type modification will result in errors or deletions, Access always displays a warning message and gives you the option of either continuing with or abandoning the conversion.

The following table lists the most common data type conversions and any limitations you need to be aware of if a field already contains data.

From	To	Limitations
Any data type	AutoNumber	Not possible if the field contains values or is part of a relationship.
AutoNumber	Text, Currency, Number	Values may be truncated depending on the new *Field Size* setting.
Text	Memo	None.
Memo	Text	Text longer than 255 characters is truncated. Values may also be truncated depending on the new *Field Size* setting.

Text, Memo	Number, Currency	Text must contain only numbers and valid separators, otherwise it is deleted.
	Date/Time	Text must contain a recognizable date and/or time, otherwise it is deleted.
	Yes/No	Text must contain one the following values only: Yes, No, True, False, On or Off, otherwise it is deleted.
	Hyperlink	Text must contain a valid hyperlink, otherwise the link will not work.
Number	Text, Memo, Currency	Where relevant, make sure that values fit in the new field size.
	Yes/No	Zero and Null convert to No, any other value converts to Yes.
Currency	Text, Memo, Number	Where relevant, make sure that values fit in the new field size.
Date/Time	Text, Memo	None.
Yes/No	Text, Memo	None.
	Number, Currency	Yes converts to –1; No converts to 0.
Hyperlink	Text	Text longer than 255 characters is truncated.
	Memo	None.
	Any other type	Not possible.

Chapter 3: summary

The data type of a field determines the kind of data that can be stored in that field and the operations that can be carried out on the data.

You use a Text data type for alphanumeric data no more than 255 characters long and for numbers that do not require calculations and do not need to be sorted in numeric order. You use a Memo data type for long passages of unformatted text.

You use a Number or Currency data type for numeric data that is to be used in calculations. And you use an AutoNumber data type when you want Access to generate unique, sequential numbers for a field.

You use a Date/Time data type for date fields, a Hyperlink data type to store hyperlinks to websites and files, and a Yes/No data type for fields that have only two possible values.

The properties of a field determine how data in the field is stored, handled, and displayed. You use the *Field Size* property to set the maximum size for data in a field. You use the *Format* property to specify how data is displayed and printed.

Before you enter data in a table, you can change the data type of a field as and when you like. If you change a field's data type after you have entered data, make sure that data already in the field is valid for the new data type; otherwise the data may be lost.

Chapter 3: quick quiz

Q1	**True or false – you can apply data types to fields in both Datasheet and Design View.**
A.	True.
B.	False.

Q2	**To view a field's contents in the *Zoom* dialog you ...**
A.	Click in the field and press **Ctrl+F2**.
B.	Click in the field and press **Shift+F2**.
C.	Double-click on the field.
D.	Click in the field and choose **View | Zoom**.

Q3	**True or false – you use the *Format* property to set the number type (Integer, Decimal, and so on) for a Number field.**
A.	True.
B.	False.

Q4	**A Yes/No data type is useful for ...**
A.	Fields that require unique, sequential numbers.
B.	Fields that have only two possible values.
C.	Fields that you want to be able to hide and unhide.
D.	Field that you want to be able to freeze and unfreeze.

Q5	Which data type allows you to store links to Microsoft Word documents in a field?
A.	Memo.
B.	Hyperlink.
C.	Text.

Q6	Which data type allows you to store links to web pages in a field?
A.	Memo.
B.	Hyperlink.
C.	Text.

Answers

1: B, **2:** B, **3:** B, **4:** B, **5:** B, **6:** B.

4 Table design: advanced field properties

In this chapter

Setting an appropriate data type and field size provides a degree of control over the data that users can enter in a field. For more precise control, and to make data entry easier for users, you can also use lookup fields, input masks, validation rules, default values and required values.

In this chapter you will learn how to create and use these features, which are all field properties.

New skills

At the end of this chapter you should be able to:

- Understand and create lookup fields
- Understand and create input masks
- Understand and create validation rules
- Define default values
- Define required fields

New words

In this chapter you will meet the following terms:

- Lookup field
- Input mask
- Validation rule
- Default value
- Required value

Exercise file

In this chapter you will work with the following Access file:

- `Chp4_VillageLibrary_Database`

Syllabus reference

In this chapter you will cover the following items of the ECDL Advanced Database syllabus:

- **AM5.1.1.3:** Create and edit a lookup field, column.
- **AM5.1.1.4:** Create and edit a validation rule in a field, column.

- **AM5.1.1.5:** Create and edit an input mask in a field, column.
- **AM5.1.1.6:** Apply and modify default values in a field, column.
- **AM5.1.1.7:** Set a mandatory data field, column.

Lookup fields

A lookup field displays a list of values from which the user selects one to enter in the field. The field can look up its values in a table/query or in a value list that you define when you create the field.

- Use a lookup to another table when the lookup field duplicates values from that table.

  For example, the MemID field in the Loans table refers to MemID values in the Members table. So you could create Loans.MemID as a lookup field that lists members from the Members table and allows users to select a member from the list.

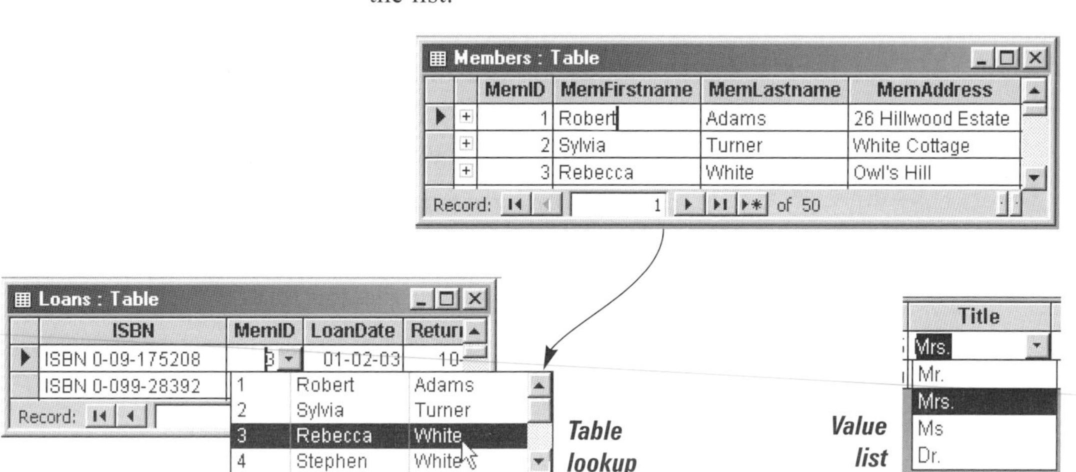

- Use a value list for fields with a limited set of values that do not change often. For example, a Title field with the options Mr, Mrs, and Ms.

> **Lookup field**
>
> *A field that displays a list from which you select the value to store in the field. The list can look up values either from a table or query or from a fixed value list.*

Using the Lookup Wizard

Access provides a *Lookup Wizard* for creating lookup fields. With the wizard you can either create a fixed value list for the field or specify fields in another table as the list source.

Exercise 4.1: Creating a lookup field with a fixed value list

In this exercise, you will change the Books.Category field to a lookup field and specify a set of values for the lookup list.

1) Open the starting database for this chapter:

   `Chp4_VillageLibrary_Database`

2) Open the Books table in Design View.

3) Change the data type of the Category field to *Lookup Wizard*. This starts the *Lookup Wizard*.

4) First the wizard prompts you to select the type of lookup field you want to create. Select the second option and click **Next**.

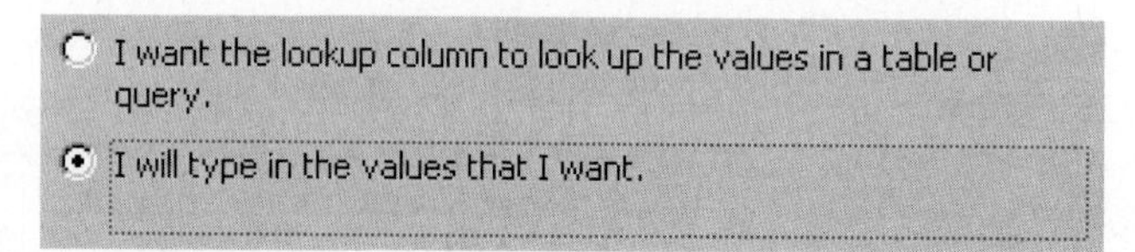

5) The wizard now prompts you for the layout and content of your list.

   You use the *Number of columns* option to specify the number of columns in the list. The default is 1 and is suitable for the category list, so leave this as it is. A single column is displayed in the area below and this is where you enter your list.

   Type the following categories in successive rows of the column, in alphabetical order:

   - Biography
   - Children
   - Computers
   - Cookery
   - Crime
   - Fantasy
   - Fiction
   - Reference
   - Science

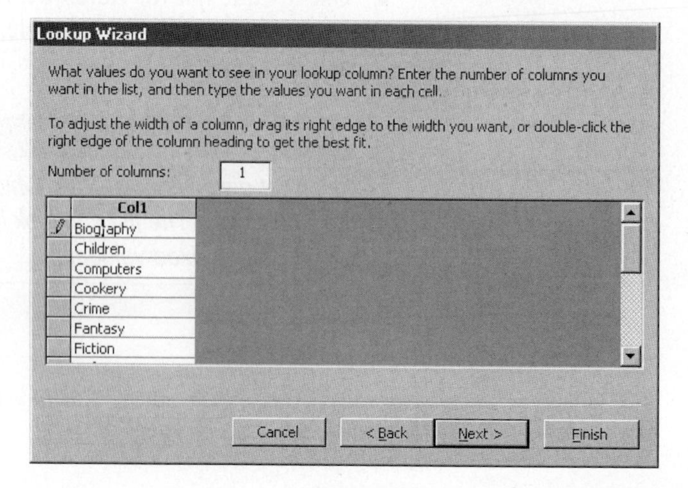

To adjust the column width to fit the longest entry, double-click on the right edge of the column heading. Then click **Next**.

6) When prompted for a name for your lookup field, accept the default (the field name) and click **Finish**.

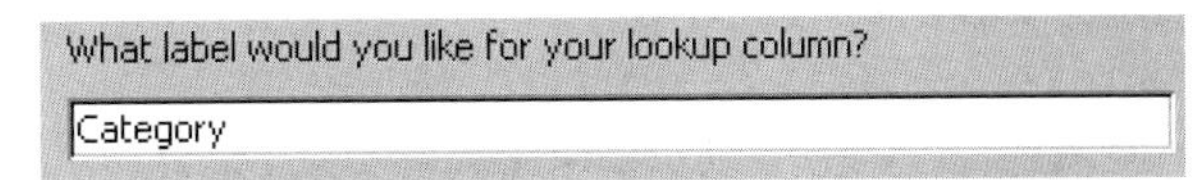

7) Switch to Datasheet View, saving the table as you do.

8) Click in a Category field and click the arrow that appears. This displays the list you have just created.

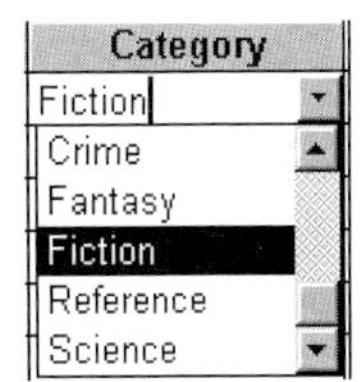

9) Select a category in the list. This is then entered in the Category field for you.

If you type an entry in the field instead, Access automatically displays the first list item that matches the characters entered.

If you type a value that is not in the list, Access allows the entry and stores the value in the field. However, it doesn't add the value to the list for future lookups.

10) Close the Books table.

If you want to change the list at a later stage, you can use the field's *Row Source* property to add, edit and remove values (see 'Creating and modifying lookup fields manually' below).

Exercise 4.2: Creating a field that looks up values in another table

In this exercise, you will change the Loans.MemID field to a lookup field that looks up values in the Members table.

1) Open the Loans table in Design View.

2) Change the data type of the MemID field to *Lookup Wizard*. This starts the *Lookup Wizard*.

3) In the first page of the wizard, select the first option and click **Next**.

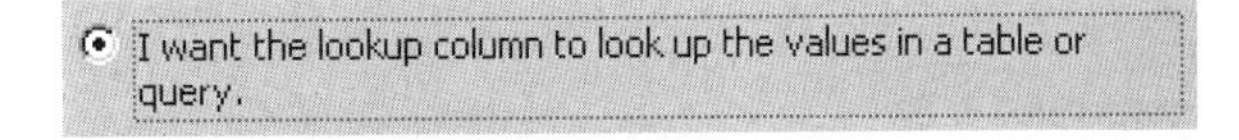

4) The wizard now displays a dialog where you specify the table to which you want to link the lookup field. Select the Members table and click **Next**.

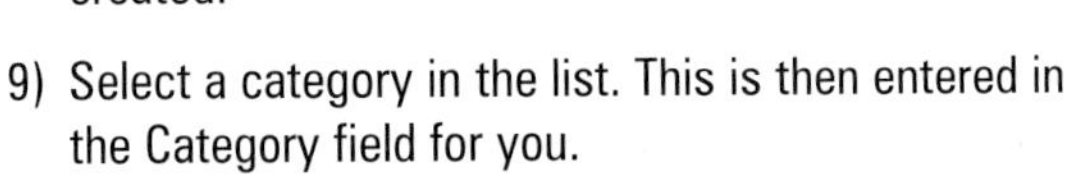

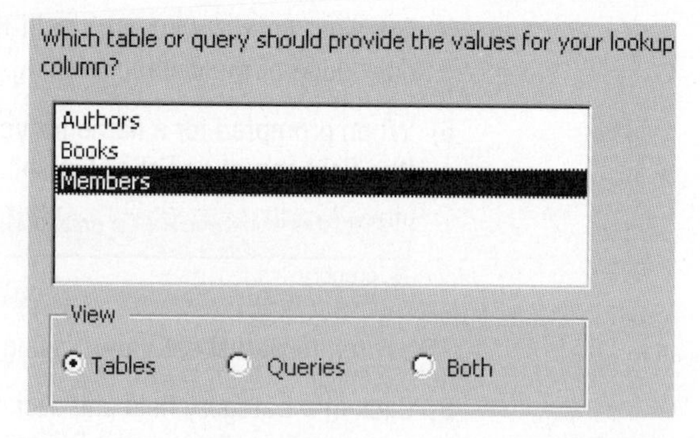

5) The wizard displays a list of the fields in the Members table and prompts you to select the ones you want to include in the lookup list. Select MemID, MemLastname and MemFirstname.

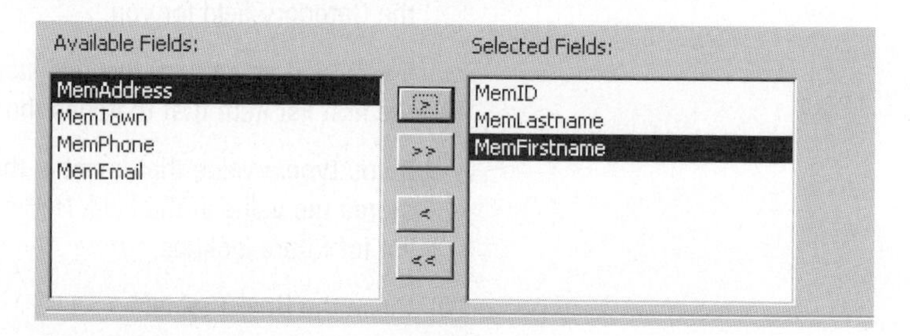

You need MemID because this is the value you want to enter in records in the Loans table. The other two fields make the list more meaningful. When you have selected the fields, click **Next**.

6) You can now adjust the layout of the columns. Access suggests that you hide the MemID column. However, users will need to be able to differentiate between members with the same first and last names, so deselect the *Hide key column* option.

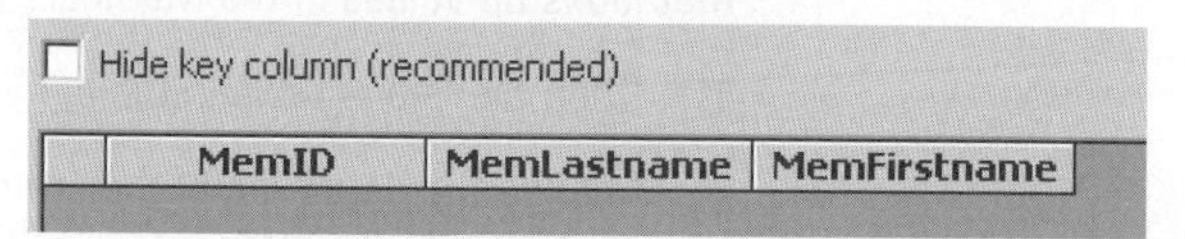

You can adjust the width of the columns the same way as you do in a datasheet. Make them just wide enough to fit the ID and name values.

Click **Next** when you have finished.

7) The wizard prompts you to select the field whose value you want to store in the Loans table. Select MemID and click **Next**.

8) The wizard prompts you for a label for the lookup field. This becomes the default name for the field in datasheets and forms. The default is the name of the field you selected in step 7. Leave this as it is and click **Finish**.

9) Save the table when prompted to do so and switch to Datasheet View.

10) Click in a MemID field and click the down arrow to view the lookup list you have just created. Then select a member from the list. Access enters the MemID value in the field for you.

11) Close the Loans table.

If some of the columns in the list are too narrow or too wide for the data they display, you can use the *Column Width* and *List Width* lookup properties to adjust the widths (see 'Creating and modifying lookup fields manually' below).

Basing a lookup field on a query

In the Loans table, it would useful if the ISBN field looked up its values in the Books table. It would be even more useful if the lookup list displayed not only each book's ISBN and title (from the Books table) but also its author's name (from the Authors table), as shown below.

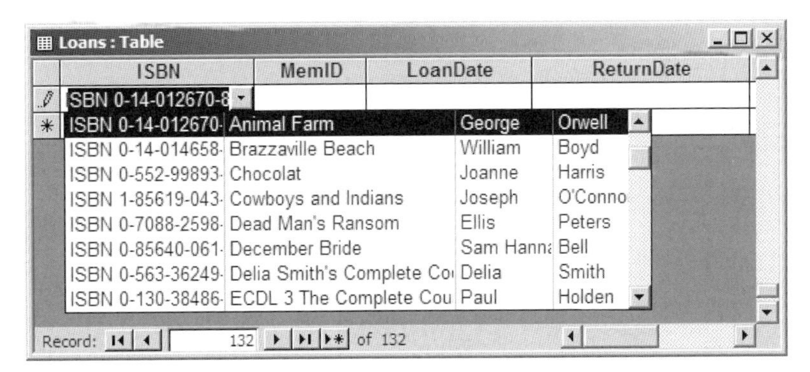

If you want to use the *Lookup Wizard* to create this lookup field, you must first create a query that includes all the fields you want to display, and then base the lookup field on that query. This is because the wizard doesn't allow you to select fields from different tables.

The `Chp4_VillageLibrary_Database` database includes a suitable query: ISBNLookupField. Open that query now in Design View and take a look at how it is defined. It includes the Books.ISBN, Books.Title, Authors.AutFirstname, and Authors.AutLastname fields, and is sorted by title (in ascending order).

Exercise 4.3: Creating a lookup field based on a query

In this exercise, you will create the ISBN lookup field based on the ISBNLookupField query.

1) Open the Loans table in Design View.

2) Change the data type of the ISBN field to *Lookup Wizard*. This starts the *Lookup Wizard*.

3) In the first page of the wizard, select the first option and click **Next**.

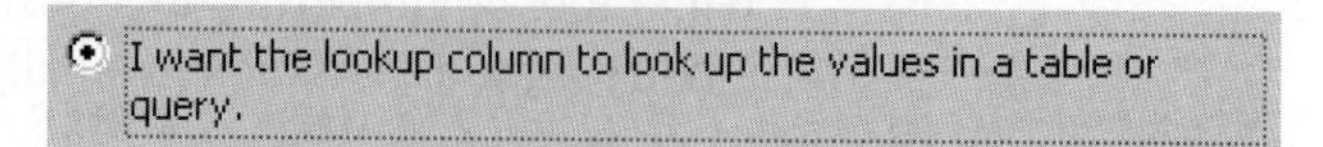

4) In the next page, select the *Queries* option, select the ISBNLookupField query, and then click **Next**.

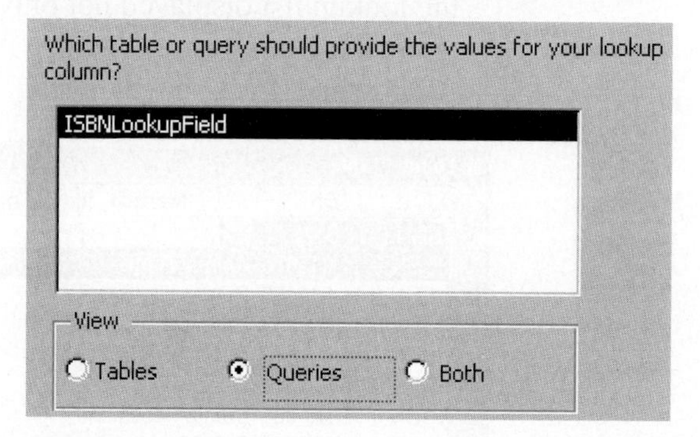

5) When prompted for the fields you want to include in the lookup list, select all the fields and click **Next**.

6) Now adjust the column widths to fit the field contents, as shown below, and click **Next** when you have finished.

ISBN	Title	AutFirstnar	AutLastnan
ISBN 1-85613-666-3	A Children's Treasury of Milligan	Spike	Milligan
ISBN 0-14-023171-4	A Good Man In Africa	William	Boyd
ISBN 0-7171-1738-3	A Simply Delicious Christmas	Darina	Allen
ISBN 0-552-99702-1	A Walk in the Woods	Bill	Bryson
ISBN 0-09-175208-6	An Evil Cradling	Brian	Keenan
ISBN 0-14-012670-8	Animal Farm	George	Orwell
ISBN 0-14-014658-X	Brazzaville Beach	William	Boyd

7) When prompted for the field whose value you want to store in the Loans table, select ISBN and click **Next**.

8) When prompted for a label for the lookup field, accept the default (which is the field name) and click **Finish**. This returns you to Design View.

9) Save the table and switch to Datasheet View.

10) Click in an ISBN field and click the down arrow to view the lookup list you have just created. Then select a book from the list. Access enters the ISBN value in the field for you.

11) Close the Loans table.

If some of the columns in the list are too narrow or too wide for the data they display, you can use the *Column Width* and *List Width* lookup properties to adjust the widths (see 'Creating and modifying lookup fields manually' below).

Creating and modifying lookup fields manually

In Design View, the **Lookup** tab in the *Field Properties* area displays the properties of a lookup field. The *Lookup Wizard* sets these properties automatically. To change them you can either rerun the wizard or make your changes directly to the properties on the **Lookup** tab.

The lookup properties shown here are those for the MemID lookup field that you created in Exercise 4.2.

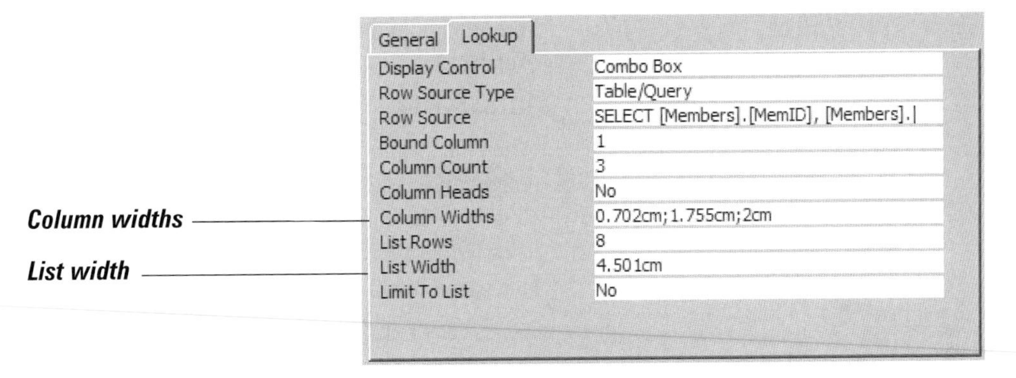

Once you are sufficiently familiar with creating lookup fields you may find it quicker and easier to create them by setting their properties on the **Lookup** tab instead of by using the wizard.

The following table explains each lookup property and the most commonly used options for those properties.

Property	Description
Display Control	Specifies the control to be used for displaying the lookup list. *Listbox:* On forms, the list is always displayed and the values are limited to those in the list. *Combo box:* On forms, the list doesn't display until you open it; so it uses less room than a list box. Also you can allow users to enter values that are not on the list.
Row Source Type	Specifies the type of source for the list values. For example, *Table/Query* or *Value List*.

Row Source	Specifies the source for the values in the lookup field.
	For a *value list*, this specifies the entries in the list. Each entry is enclosed in double quotes and separated from the next entry by a semicolon. For example:
	`"Biography";"Children";"Computers";`
	When the source is one or more *tables/queries*, this property typically takes the form of an SQL SELECT statement that specifies the source tables and fields. For example, if you look at this property for the Loans.MemID field, you will see the following:
	`SELECT [Members].[MemID],`
	`[Members].[MemLastname],`
	`[Members].[MemFirstname] FROM Members;`
	But you don't need to enter this manually. If the source is a single table and you want to include all its fields in the lookup list, select the table from the property's drop-down list. If the source is multiple tables, or you want to include only selected fields in the lookup list, click the ... button at the right of the property. This starts the *Query Builder* where you can create a query that includes the tables and fields you want to display in the lookup list.

Bound Column	When you include more than one column in a lookup list, Access needs to know which column is bound to the lookup field – that is, which column's data will be stored in the field when you select an item in the list. Columns are numbered 1 to *n*, in the order in which they appear in the list. For example, this property is set to 1 for the MemID lookup field, indicating that the value of Members.MemID will be stored in the field.
Column Count	Specifies the number of columns in the lookup list, including hidden columns.
Column Heads	Specifies whether column headings are included in the lookup list. The headings are taken from the field names in the underlying table or query.
Column Widths	Specifies the width of each column in the lookup list, separated by semicolons. For example: `0;4cm;2cm;2cm` You must include a width for each column. Enter 0 to hide a column.
List Rows	Specifies the maximum number of rows to be displayed in the lookup list at any one time.
List Width	Specifies the overall width of the lookup list.
Limit To List	Specifies whether users can enter any value in the field or only those that are included in the list.

What is SQL?

SQL (Structured Query Language) is the standard language used to create and query relational databases. For your convenience, Access provides graphical building tools for tables, queries, forms, and so on. Internally, however, it generates SQL statements to define these database objects.

For ECDL, you do not need to know how to use SQL. However, you will come across it in properties like the Row Source *property for lookup fields and combo box controls, and you can always view the SQL statement that a query uses by displaying the query in SQL View.*

Exercise 4.4: Modifying a fixed value list

In Exercise 4.1 you created a fixed-value lookup list for the Books. Category field. In this exercise, you will change the content and layout of this list.

1) Open the Books table in Design View and display the properties for the Category field.

2) Click the **Lookup** tab and take a look at the lookup properties for the field:

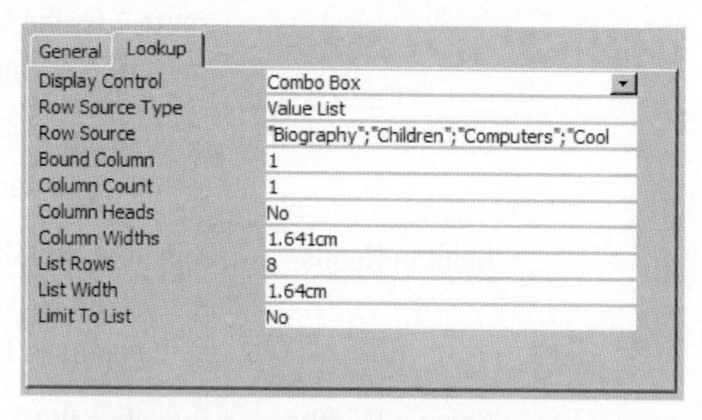

   – *Row Source Type*. This specifies that the source for the lookup field is a fixed value list.

   – *Row Source*. This specifies the values in the list. Each entry is enclosed in double quotes and separated from the next entry by a semicolon.

   – *Column Count*. This specifies that the list has one column.

   – *Column Widths*. This specifies the width of the column.

   – *List Rows*. This specifies that the list should display eight values at a time.

   – *List Width*. This specifies the overall width of the lookup list (in this case, the overall width is the same as the column width).

3) To add an Art category to the list, type the following at the start of the entries in the *Row Source* property:

```
"Art";
```

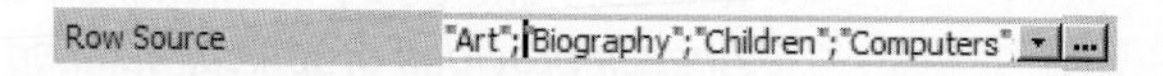

4) Now change the Children category to Children's Literature, as shown here:

5) The width of the lookup list is now too narrow to show the Children's Literature entry in full, so change the *Column Widths* and *List Width* properties as follows:

Column Widths	3.6cm
List Rows	8
List Width	3.6cm

6) Save the table and switch to Datasheet View to see the effect of your changes.

Exercise 4.5: Modifying a lookup field that looks up values in another table

In Exercise 4.2 you changed the Loans.MemID field to a lookup field that looks up values in the Members table. The lookup list displays the MemID, MemLastname, and MemFirstname field values for each member. In this exercise you will add the MemTown field to the list.

1) Open the Loans table in Design View and display the properties for the MemID field.

2) Click the **Lookup** tab and take a look at the lookup properties for the field:

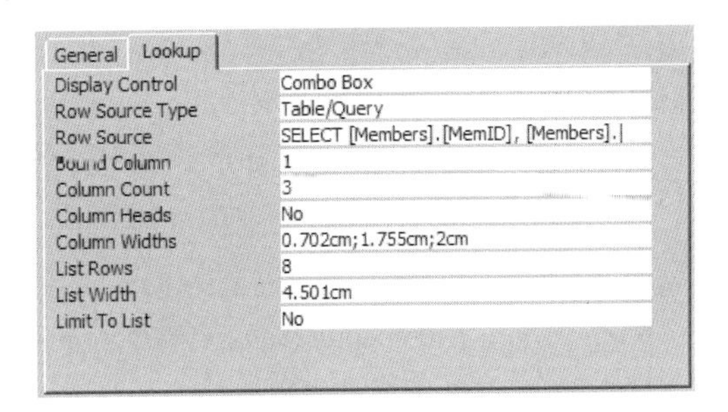

   - *Row Source Type*. This specifies that the source for the lookup field is a table.
   - *Row Source*. This consists of an SQL statement that specifies the source table and fields for the lookup list.
   - *Bound Column*. This specifies which value should be stored in the Loans.MemID field when users select an entry in the lookup list. In this case it is the value in the first column (that is, the MemID).
   - *Column Count*. This specifies that the list comprises three columns.
   - *Column Widths*. This specifies the width of each column.

3) Click the *Row Source* property and then click the ... button at the right of the property. This starts the *Query Builder*, which displays the SQL statement as a query.

4) In the *Query Builder* window, add the MemTown field to the query design grid. To do this, double-click the MemTown field in the field list in the upper part of the window.

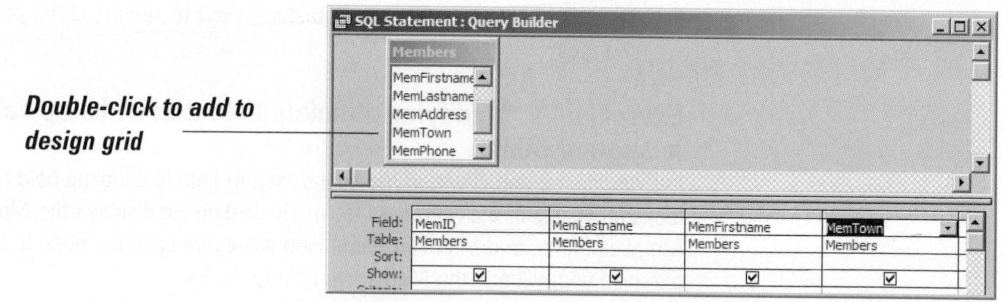

Double-click to add to design grid

5) Close the *Query Builder* window. When prompted to confirm your changes, click **Yes**. This updates the SQL statement in the *Row Source* property.

6) The lookup list now comprises four columns, so update the *Column Count* property as follows:

7) Enter a width for the new column in the *Column Widths* property, as follows:

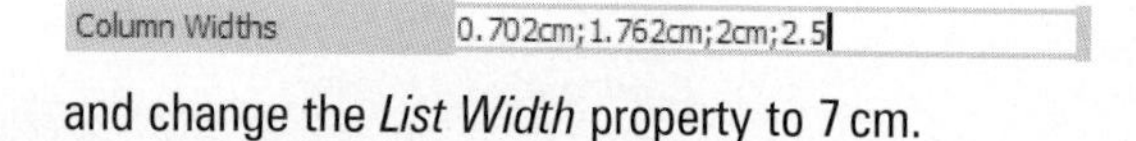

and change the *List Width* property to 7 cm.

8) Save the table and switch to Datasheet View to see the effect of your changes.

Input masks

An input mask is a template that specifies an exact pattern for data entered in a field and controls the type of data that can be entered at each position in the pattern. It makes data entry easier for users and helps to ensure entry of valid data.

Typically, an input mask consists of a combination of fixed characters (such as parentheses around telephone codes) and blank spaces where users fill in the field data.

For example, the telephone number input mask below enters the parentheses for you and requires entry of exactly three digits between the parentheses and seven digits after the parentheses.

Input masks are most commonly used for Text and Date/Time fields but are also available for Number and Currency fields. Here are just some of the ways in which they can aid and control data entry:

- Automatically enter and display characters common to all entries in a field. For example, parentheses around telephone codes, date separators, and fixed text such as ISBN or SSN.
- Restrict the type of data that can be entered in a field. For example, input could be restricted to digits only or to a fixed pattern of digits and letters, as might be required for user IDs or social security numbers.
- Control the number of characters that can be entered in a field. For example, input of a credit card number could be restricted to exactly sixteen digits.
- Convert between uppercase and lowercase characters. For example, the input mask for a first name field could convert the first letter to uppercase and all others to lowercase, regardless of how they are entered.

Text, Date/Time, Number and Currency fields all have an *Input Mask* property, which you use to create input masks. A wizard is available for creating Text and Date/Time input masks.

Input mask

A template that assists data entry and controls the type, number, and pattern of characters that can be entered in a field.

Input mask examples

The Books table includes two examples of input masks. These illustrate how input masks work. Open the Books table in Datasheet View and take a look at the following fields:

- **PublicationYear:** This has an input mask that restricts entries to exactly four digits. When you click in an empty field, four underline characters (_) are displayed to indicate where you enter the digits.

  You cannot enter letters, you cannot enter more than four digits, and if you exit the field with fewer than four digits entered, Access displays a warning message that forces you to input the correct number. Try it and see!

  (Note that if you enter a value in a *new* record without entering an ISBN value, which is the primary key, Access displays an error message when you try to move to a different record or to close the table. If this happens, click the **Undo** button to undo your entry and then continue normally.)

- **PurchaseDate:** This has an input mask that forces input of dates in Short Date format (for example, 28-01-02) and automatically enters the separators for you. The template appears when you click in an empty PurchaseDate field.

  Access rejects any input other than numbers and forces input of exactly two numbers each for day, month and year. Again, try it and see!

Creating an input mask with the wizard

The *Input Mask Wizard* offers predefined input masks for dates, phone numbers and postal codes, and allows you to modify these to your own requirements. It is available only for Text and Date/Time fields.

Exercise 4.6: Creating an input mask with the *Input Mask Wizard*

In this exercise you will use the *Input Mask Wizard* to create an input mask for the Members.MemPhone field.

1) Open the Members table in Design View and display the field properties for the MemPhone field.
2) Click the *Input Mask* property and click the ... button that appears. This starts the *Input Mask Wizard*.
3) The first page of the wizard displays a list of predefined input masks. Select the *Phone Number* option and click **Next**.

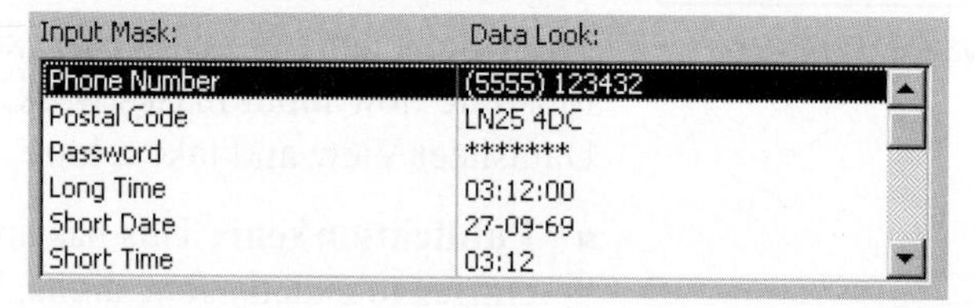

4) The second page of the wizard allows you to modify the selected mask and to select a placeholder character – that is, the character that indicates where data can or must be entered. The default is an underscore (_). Leave this as it is and click **Next**.
5) The third page of the wizard offers the option of storing the field data with or without any fixed characters. Again accept the default and click **Finish**.
6) Access now automatically inserts the input mask definition in the *Input Mask* property box. Ignore this for the moment and switch to Datasheet View, saving the table as you do.

7) Try entering some data in the MemPhone field. You will find that Access accepts any of the values shown here (spaces were entered where blanks are shown).

MemPhone
(   ) 3456677
(   ) 12345612
(1234) 233 1234

Input mask definitions

Now that you've seen how input masks work and how you can create them with a wizard, let's take a look at how input masks are defined.

Open the Members table in Design View and take a look at the *Input Mask* property for the MemPhone field. The property contains a string of characters as shown here. This is the *input mask definition*.

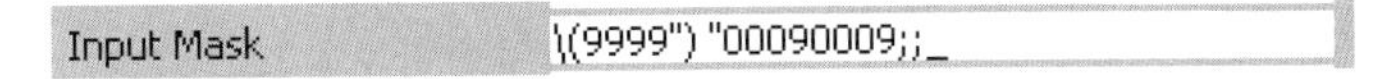

The definition has three sections, separated by semicolons. The last two sections specify whether fixed display characters are stored with the field data and which character is displayed for blanks in the input mask. These sections are optional and can usually be omitted. By default, Access doesn't store display characters with a field's data and it uses an underscore (_) as the placeholder character.

The first section of the input mask definition is the input mask string. This uses special characters to specify the type of data that can be entered at each position in the mask and whether entry is optional or mandatory.

For example, in the input mask for the MemPhone field, '9' indicates that you can enter a digit or a space, but that entry is optional. A '0' indicates that you can enter a digit (0–9) only and that entry is mandatory. So users can enter up to four digits between the parentheses in the input mask and from 6 to 8 digits after the parentheses.

Input mask characters

Here is a list of the special characters that you can use to create an input mask.

Note that leaving a position blank is not the same as entering a space character in it. The two may look the same when you are entering data but they are handled differently by input masks. Blank positions are omitted when the data is saved, while space characters are saved with the data.

Character	Meaning
0	A digit (0–9) must be entered at this position.
9	An entry is optional, but if entered it must be a digit (0–9) or a space character.
#	An entry is optional, but if entered it must be a digit (0–9), a space character, or a plus or minus sign.
L	A letter (A–Z, a–z) must be entered at this position.
?	An entry is optional, but if entered it must be a letter (A–Z, a–z).
A	A letter (A–Z, a–z) or digit (0–9) must be entered at this position.
a	An entry is optional, but if entered it must be a letter (A–Z, a–z) or digit (0–9).
&	Any character or a space character. Entry is mandatory.
C	Any character or a space character. Entry is optional.
.	Decimal placeholder. The actual character used depends on your Windows Regional Settings.
,	Thousands separator. The actual character used depends on your Windows Regional Settings.
:;-/	Date and time separators. The actual character used depends on your Windows Regional Settings.
<	Converts all following characters to lowercase.
>	Converts all following characters to uppercase.

!	Characters typed into the mask fill it from left to right, but when you exit the field, the characters are shifted to the right side of the mask.
	For example, if you type 1234567 into the following input masks, the results are displayed as follows:
	`!(999) 9999999` `( ) 1234567`
	`(999) 9999999` `(123) 4567`

Character	Meaning
\	Displays the next character as a literal character. This is used to display as a literal character any of the special characters listed in this table. For example, to display A you would enter \A. Characters that are not special input mask characters are automatically recognized as literals by Access and do not need to be specifically identified as such. However, when Access saves an input mask it automatically inserts the '\' character before a single literal character.
"literal"	Displays the enclosed characters as literal characters. This is used to display strings of special characters as literals. For example, to display CALL as a literal string, you could enter \C\A\L\L, but it is easier to enter "CALL". Strings that do not include special characters do not need to be enclosed by double quotes. However, when Access saves an input mask it automatically inserts double quotes around literal strings.

Input mask definition examples

Here is a list of input mask strings with examples of valid values for those masks.

Definition	Value examples
0000	1234 4562
(000) 0000000	(021) 2347654
(999) 9999999!	(021) 2347654 ( ) 1234567
>LOL OLO	Z2Y 1C3
AAA-AAA	123-xyz XyZ-354
000-999	123-456 123-45 123-
>L<?????????	Judith Robbie Jennifer

Modifying an input mask

To modify an input mask, you make the required changes to the input mask string in the *Input Mask* property.

Exercise 4.7: Modifying an input mask

In this exercise you will modify the MemPhone input mask so that users must enter a three-digit area code followed by a seven-digit phone number.

1) Open the Members table in Design View and display the field properties for the MemPhone field.
2) Change the input mask string to:

```
\(000") "0000000;;_
```

3) Switch to Datasheet View, saving the table as you do.

   You will now find that you *must* enter three digits between the parentheses, and seven digits after them. Spaces will not be accepted.

Creating an input mask manually

To create an input mask manually, you enter the input mask definition string directly in the *Input Mask* property.

Exercise 4.8: Creating an input mask manually

In this exercise you will create an input mask for the ISBN field in the Books table.

1) Open the Books table in Design View, and display the properties for the ISBN field.
2) Enter the following input mask definition string in the *Input Mask* property:

```
ISBN &&&&&&&&&&&&A
```

   An ISBN always consists of ten digits preceded by the letters ISBN. The ten digits are divided into four parts, separated by hyphens or spaces. The number of digits in the first three parts varies but the total number is always nine. The final part contains a single digit or X. For example:

   ISBN 0-14-014658-X   ISBN 0-099-28392-1   ISBN 1-85702-712-4

   The input mask you have just specified requires entry of 13 characters in total. The first 12 can be any combination of numbers and hyphens; the last character can be either a digit or a letter. Access enters the letters ISBN automatically.

3) Switch to Datasheet View, saving the table as you do.

4) Enter the following values in the ISBN field by typing the characters shown:

To get this ISBN value ...	Type ...
ISBN 0-14-014658-X	0-14-014658-X
ISBN 0-099-28392-1	0-099-28392-1

5) Save and close the Books table.

Field validation rules

While input masks provide control over the type and number of characters entered in a field, field validation rules set limits or conditions on the values that you can enter. For example, an input mask could specify that input must be three digits, and a validation rule could then specify that the values entered must be between 100 and 200.

Field validation rules are enforced when you add or edit data in a field. Access checks the new value against the rule when you attempt to leave the field. If the value breaks the rule, Access displays a warning message and you must then either change the value to one that is acceptable or use the **Undo** command to undo your entry.

Field validation rule

A rule that sets limits or conditions on the values that you can enter in a field.

Creating field validation rules

A validation rule is specified as an expression that consists of a combination of operators (for example, +, >, =), literal values (for example, 123.5, 23/1/03, "Hello"), field names, and functions.

Validation rule expressions follow the same rules, and use the same operators and functions, as expressions used in queries, forms, and reports. For full details, see Appendix A.

You enter a validation rule expression in the *Validation Rule* property of a field. And in the *Validation Text* property, you enter the error message to be displayed when the rule is broken.

Open the Books table in Design View and take a look at the *Validation Rule* and *Validation Text* properties for the PublicationYear field.

Validation Rule	>1900
Validation Text	Publication year must be later than 1900

The validation rule states that any value entered into the field must be greater than 1900. Try entering years like 1812 or 1899 in the field and see what happens!

To create a validation rule you can use the Expression Builder tool or you can enter the validation rule expression directly in the *Validation Rule* property. The Expression Builder is not explained here. If you want to try it out for yourself, you can open it by clicking on the *Validation Rule* property box and clicking the ... button.

Exercise 4.9: Creating a field validation rule

In this exercise you will add a validation rule to the Books.PurchaseDate field. The rule will ensure that dates entered in the field cannot be later than the current date.

1) Open the Books table in Design View and display the field properties for the PurchaseDate field.
2) Type the following expression in the *Validation Rule* property:

```
<=Date()
```

   Date() is a function that returns the current date.
3) Type the following message in the *Validation Text* property: A book's purchase date must be the current date or earlier.
4) Switch to Datasheet View, saving the table as you do.
5) The following message is displayed, warning you that existing data in the PurchaseDate field may break the validation rule and asking whether you want to test the data. Click **No**.

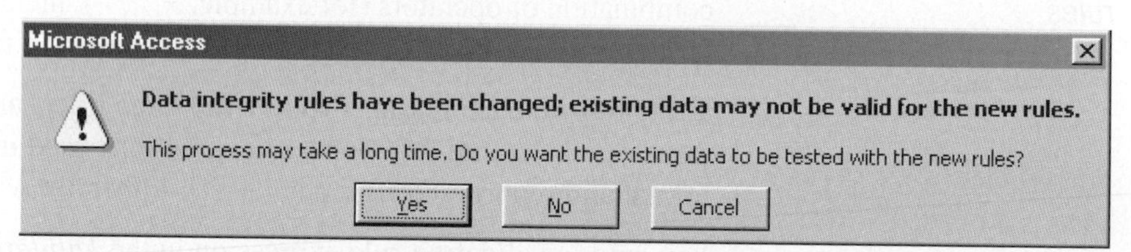
Microsoft Access
Data integrity rules have been changed; existing data may not be valid for the new rules.
This process may take a long time. Do you want the existing data to be tested with the new rules?
Yes
No
Cancel

6) Now try entering various dates in the PurchaseDate field and see what happens.

Modifying field validation rules

You modify a field validation rule by making the required changes to the expression in the *Validation Rule* property.

Exercise 4.10: Modifying a field validation rule

In this exercise you will modify the validation rule for the Books.PublicationYear field so that the field accepts only year values greater than 1900 and less than 2050.

1) Open the Books table in Design View and display the properties for the PublicationYear field.

2) Change the expression in the *Validation Rule* property to the following:

   >1900 And <2050

3) Change the message in the *Validation Text* property to read as follows:

   Publication year must be later than 1900 and earlier than 2050.

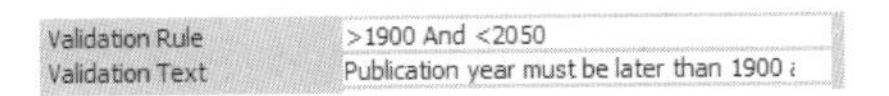

4) Switch to Datasheet View, saving the table as you do.

   A message is displayed, warning you that existing data in the table may break the new validation rule and asking whether you want to test the data. Click **No**.

5) Now try entering years like 2051 or 2075 in the PublicationYear field and see what happens.

Validation rule examples

The following table shows various field validation rule expressions and their meaning.

Note that text strings in expressions must be enclosed by double quotes (for example "Hello") and dates must be enclosed by hash (#) symbols (for example, #21-01-03#).

Rule	Explanation
>0	Value must be greater than zero.
>=0 And <=100	Value must be in range 0 to 100.
=0 Or >100	Value must be either 0 or greater than 100.
>=#01/01/02#	Value must be a date equal to or later than 1 January, 2002.
Between 1 And 100	Value must be in the range 1 to 100.
In ("Mr", "Mrs", "Ms")	Value must be one of those listed.
=Date()	Only today's date is valid in the field. For example, this would be a useful validation rule for the Loans.LoanDate field.
>=Date()+30	Value must be a date 30 days or more in the future.

Default values

A default value is a value that Access automatically enters in a field when you create a new record. Where the same value is frequently entered in a field, having a default value speeds up data entry considerably. If the default value is not appropriate, you can simply overwrite it.

For example, if most books in the library are in the Fiction category, you could make Fiction the default value for the Books.Category field. Or if most members live in Castletown, you could make that the default value for the Members.MemTown field.

Default value

A value that is automatically entered in a field when you create a new record.

Creating default values

The default value for a field can be any valid value for that field. You enter the expression for the default value in the field's *Default Value* property.

When including a text string in a default value expression, enclose it in double quotes (for example "Fiction"). When specifying a date, enclose it with hash (#) symbols (for example, #21-01-03#).

Note that when you create a Number field, Access automatically assigns a default value of 0. If this is not appropriate, simply delete it from the *Default Value* property.

When you create a Yes/No field, Access automatically defaults the value to *No* when you add a new record. This is usually the appropriate default value and so there is no need to change it.

Exercise 4.11: Creating a default value

In this exercise, you will set a default value for the Loans.LoanDate field.

1) Open the Loans table in Design View and display the field properties for the LoanDate field.
2) Type the following in the *Default Value* property:

3) Switch to Datasheet View, saving the table as you do.
4) Add a new record to the table and you will see that the current date is automatically entered in the LoanDate field.
5) Close the table.

Note that defining a default value for a field has no effect on existing records. It you want to enter the default value in an existing record, click on the relevant field and press **Ctrl+Alt+Spacebar**.

Default value examples

Here are some further examples of default values.

Expression	Default field value
"Castletown"	Castletown
Date()	Today's date
Now()	The current date and time
Date()+10	Today's date plus 10
"Fiction"	Fiction
10	10

Required values

All fields, other than AutoNumber fields, have a *Required* property that specifies whether or not the field is mandatory and must contain a value.

In most tables, there are fields where it doesn't matter if a value is entered or not – for example, Members.MemEmail and Authors.AutURL. And there are other fields that must contain a value if a record is to be meaningful – for example, Books.Title.

To force entry of a value in a field, you set the field's *Required* property to *Yes*. When you then create a new record, Access will not allow you to save the record until you have entered a value in the field.

Required field
A field in which it is mandatory to enter a value.

Exercise 4.12: Creating a required value

In this exercise, you will define the Books.Title field as a required field.

1) Open the Books table in Design View and display the field properties for the Title field.

2) Click on the *Required* property and select *Yes*.

Required
Allow Zero Length
Indexed
Yes
Yes
No

3) Save the table. The following message is displayed.

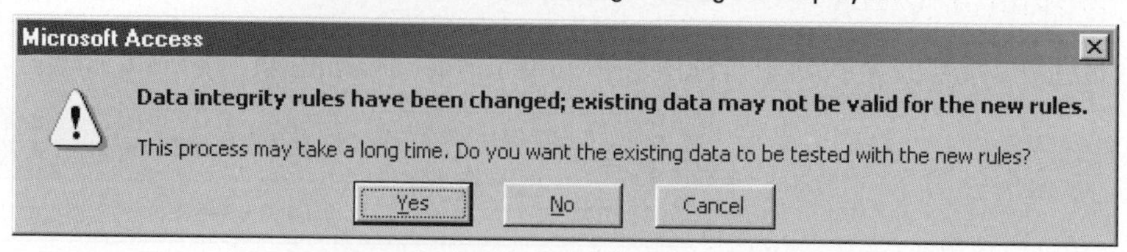
Microsoft Access
Data integrity rules have been changed; existing data may not be valid for the new rules.
This process may take a long time. Do you want the existing data to be tested with the new rules?
Yes
No
Cancel

This warns you that there may be existing records where there is no value in the Title field. It also gives you the option of checking whether this is so.

4) Click **No** to save the table without checking existing records and then switch to Datasheet View.

5) Add a new record to the table, leaving the Title field blank. When you move the focus from the new record, Access displays a message warning you that you must enter a value in the Title field. You can then either enter a value or use the **Undo** command to remove the new record.

6) Close `Chp4_VillageLibrary_Database`.

Chapter 4: summary

A *lookup field* displays a list of values from which the user selects one to enter in the field. The field can look up its values in a table or query or in a fixed value list. You can use the *Lookup Wizard* to create either type of lookup field.

An *input mask* is a template that specifies an exact pattern for data entered in a field and controls the type of data that can be entered at each position in the pattern. It makes data entry easier for users and helps to ensure entry of valid data. You enter the input mask definition for a field in the *Input Mask* property for that field.

A *field validation rule* set limits or conditions on the values that you can enter in a field. The rule is enforced when you add or edit data in the field. You enter the validation rule for a field in the *Validation Rule* property for that field.

A *default value* is a value that Access automatically enters in a field when you add a new record. Where the same value is frequently entered in a particular field, having a default value makes data entry much easier and quicker. You enter the default value for a field in the *Default Value* property for that field.

A *required field* is one in which it is mandatory to enter a value. You use a field's *Required* property to make it a required field.

Chapter 4: quick quiz

Q1	True or false – a lookup field can look up values in more than one table.
A.	True.
B.	False.

Q2	True or false – with the *Lookup Wizard* you can base a lookup field on either a table or a query.
A.	True.
B.	False.

Q3	Which of the following input masks specifies mandatory entry of exactly four digits?
A.	9999
B.	0000
C.	&&&&
D.	####

Q4	Which of these validation rules requires dates entered to be in the year 2000?
A.	In "2000"
B.	Year = 2000
C.	Between #01/01/2000# And #31/12/2000#
D.	>= #01/01/2000# And <= #31/12/2000#

Q5	Which of the following validation rules restricts a field's values to Mr, Mrs or Ms?
A.	In ("Mr", "Mrs", "Ms")
B.	"Mr" Or "Mrs" Or "Ms"
C.	="Mr" Or ="Mrs" Or ="Ms"

Q6	Which of these default value expressions enters today's date automatically in a date field?
A.	Date = (Today)
B.	Date(Today)
C.	Date()
D.	#99/99/99#

Answers

1: A, **2:** A, **3:** B, **4:** C and D, **5:** All, **6:** C.

5 Table design: relationships

In this chapter

When working with multiple tables, you need to tell Access how to bring together data from different tables so that you can retrieve meaningful information. You do this by defining relationships between the tables.

In this chapter you will learn how to define relationships and how to apply referential integrity to those relationships.

New skills

At the end of this chapter you should be able to:

- Understand and create a one-to-one and a one-to-many relationship
- Understand and resolve a many-to-many relationship
- Understand and apply referential integrity

New words

In this chapter you will meet the following terms:

- One-to-one relationship
- One-to-many relationship
- Many-to-many relationship
- Referential integrity

Exercise file

In this chapter you will work with the following Access database file:

- `Chp5_VillageLibrary_Database`

Syllabus reference

In this chapter you will cover the following items of the ECDL Advanced Database syllabus:

- **AM5.1.2.1:** Understand the basis for creating a valid relationship.
- **AM5.1.2.2:** Create, modify one-to-one and one-to-many relationships between tables.

- **AM5.1.2.3:** Understand and modify a many-to-many relationship between tables.
- **AM5.1.2.5:** Apply and use referential integrity.
- **AM5.1.2.6:** Apply automatic deletion of related records.

What is a valid relationship?

The purpose of creating a relationship between two tables is to enable Access to combine related records from the tables. For a valid relationship:

- The two tables must have a common field, so that Access can match values in those fields when joining the tables.
- The common fields must have the same data type; in the case of Number fields, they must also have the same field size.

  AutoNumber fields are an exception to this rule. If a field has an AutoNumber data type in one table, it must have a Number data type and a field size of *Long Integer* in the other table.
- Both fields usually have the same name.
- One of the fields is typically a primary key field and the related field is then referred to as a foreign key field.

In the example here, a relationship has been created between the Books and Authors tables based on their common AutID fields. AutID is the primary key field of the Authors table and is a foreign key field in the Books table.

The relationship enables Access to retrieve, for example, a list of book titles and their authors. To do this, it looks for a matching AutID value in the Authors table for each book in the Books table.

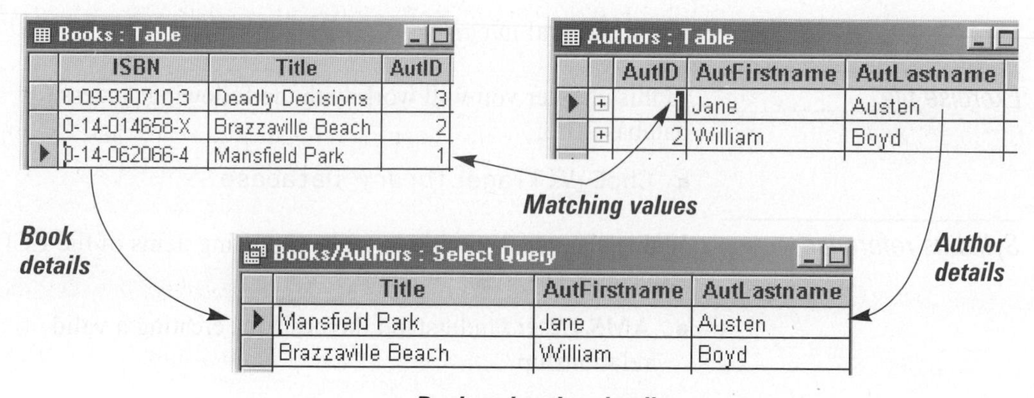

Book and author details

Relationship types

Relational databases support three types of relationship:

- One-to-one
- One-to-many
- Many-to-many

One-to-one

This is an unusual relationship type. Each record in one table can have no more than one matching record in the other table, and, typically, the two tables have the same primary key, as in the example here.

Books : Table

ISBN	Title	AutID	Publica	PublisherName	Category
0-09-930710-3	Deadly Decisions	3	2001	Arrow Books Ltd	Crime
0-14-014658-X	Brazzaville Beach	2	1991	Penguin Group	Crime
0-14-062066-4	Mansfield Park	1	1994	Penguin Group	Fiction
0-552-13107-5	Sourcery	4	1989	Transworld Ltd.	Fantasy
0-7000-0207-2	Magic Kingdom for	5	1986	Futura Publications	Fantasy

BooksConfidential : Table

ISBN	PurchaseDate	Cost
0-09-930710-3	24-08-01	€9.65
0-14-014658-X	23-06-00	€6.99
0-14-062066-4	23-06-00	€3.87
0-552-13107-5	23-06-00	€5.99
0-7088-8207-2	23-06-00	€6.42

The Books and BooksConfidential tables have a one-to-one relationship based on common ISBN fields. Each record in one table has no more than one matching record in the other table.

So why not merge the two tables? In this case, the library does not want members to have access to purchasing information. So the PurchaseDate and Cost fields have been moved to a separate table that members can't access.

The requirement to keep some information confidential is the most common reason for creating a one-to-one relationship. Another is to separate out data that is accessed infrequently. This speeds up access to the main table.

One-to-one relationship

A relationship in which each record in one table can have no more than one matching record in the other table.

One-to-many

This is by far the most common relationship type. Each record in one table can have many matching records in the second table, while records in the second table can have only one matching record in the first table.

In the Village Library database, the relationships between the Books and Loans tables and between the Members and Loans tables are examples of one-to-many relationships.

Let's take a look at the Loans and Members tables.

Loans : Table

	ISBN	MemID	LoanDate	ReturnDate
▶	ISBN 0-130-98983-5	1	04-06-01	13-06-01
	ISBN 0-130-98984-3	1	04-06-01	13-06-01
	ISBN 0-571-20408-2	1	[illegible]	[illegible]
	ISBN 1-862-30063-1	1		
	ISBN 0-130-38486-0	1		
	ISBN 0-563-36249-9	2		
	ISBN 0-552-99893-1	3		
	ISBN 0-14-062066-4	3		

Members : Table

	MemID	MemFirstname	MemLastname	MemAddress	MemTown
	1	Robert	Adams	26 Hillwood Estate	Burnford
	2	Sylvia	Turner	White Cottage	Belmount
	3	Rebecca	White	Owl's Hill	Belmount
	4	Stephen	White	Owl's Hill	Belmount
▶	5	Linda	White	Owl's Hill	Belmount

Each member can have many books out on loan, but each loan involves only one member. So the relationship between the two tables is one-to-many, based on a common MemID field. MemID is a primary key field in the Members table and a foreign key field in the Loans table.

If you want to view a list of the books currently out on loan, with details of their borrowers, Access can retrieve the borrower details for each loan by finding the record in the Members table that has the same MemID value as the MemID field in the loan record.

One-to-many relationship

A relationship in which each record in the first table can have many matching records in the second table. But each record in the second table can have only one matching record in the first table.

Many-to-many

A many-to-many relationship is one in which each record in the first table can have one or more related records in the second table and each record in the second table can have one or more related records in the first table.

So far in this book we've treated the Authors and Books tables as if they had a one-to-many relationship. In reality, however, they have a many-to-many relationship – each author can have many books, and each book can have many authors.

One book, many authors ***One author, many books***

Access does not support this type of relationship directly. A direct relationship between Books and Authors would involve, for example, including multiple records for some books in the Books table, one for each author of those books. The result? Redundancy, inconsistencies and wasted space.

Instead, you create a linking (or junction) table that matches books to authors using both their primary key fields, as shown below:

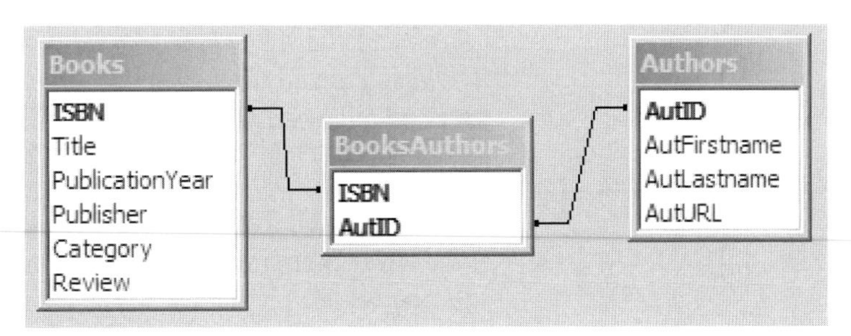

Instead of an unwieldy many-to-many relationship, you now have two standard one-to-many relationships, one between Books and the linking table, and one between Authors and the linking table. And Access can bring together information from Books and Authors indirectly, by using the linking table as an intermediary.

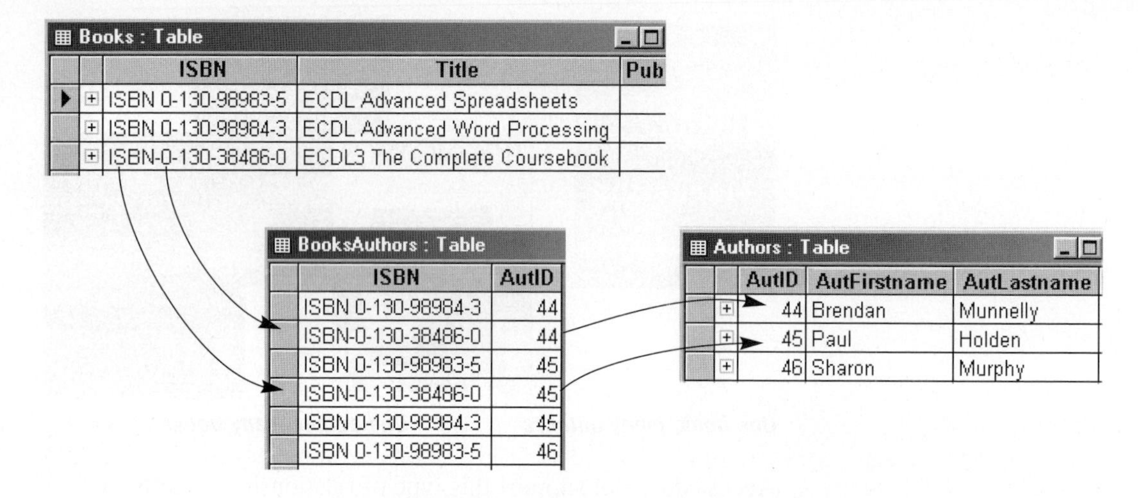

Books : Table

ISBN	Title	Pub
ISBN 0-130-98983-5	ECDL Advanced Spreadsheets	
ISBN 0-130-98984-3	ECDL Advanced Word Processing	
ISBN-0-130-38486-0	ECDL3 The Complete Coursebook	

BooksAuthors : Table

ISBN	AutID
ISBN 0-130-98984-3	44
ISBN-0-130-38486-0	44
ISBN 0-130-98983-5	45
ISBN-0-130-38486-0	45
ISBN 0-130-98984-3	45
ISBN 0-130-98983-5	46

Authors : Table

AutID	AutFirstname	AutLastname
44	Brendan	Munnelly
45	Paul	Holden
46	Sharon	Murphy

ISBN and AutID are foreign key fields in the BooksAuthors table. Neither field is limited to unique values in the table and so neither can act as its primary key. Instead, you can use a combination of ISBN and AutID, as each combination of these fields will be unique.

Many-to-many relationship

A relationship in which each record in the first table can have many matching records in the second table. And each record in the second table can have many matching records in the first table.

Primary tables

When two tables are related, one is referred to as the *primary table*, the other simply as the related table. The primary table is the one whose primary key is used as the linking field.

So, in a one-to-many relationship, the table on the 'one' side of the relationship is always the primary table. In a one-to-one relationship, either table can be the primary table. You make the choice when you create the relationship.

Which table is the primary table of a relationship is important when you enforce referential integrity for the relationship and allow cascading deletes and updates (see 'Referential integrity' below).

The Relationships window

You use Access's Relationships window to create, edit and view relationships.

Access's sample Northwind database includes a variety of tables with relationships already defined, so we'll use it to explore the Relationships window. Open that database now and then open its Relationships window.

Opening the Relationships window

To open the Relationships window, close any open tables, and then:

- Choose **Tools | Relationships**, or
- Click the **Relationships** button in the Access toolbar. 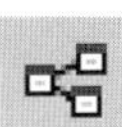

Provided that you haven't previously made any changes to the layout in Northwind's Relationships window, it should look as shown below.

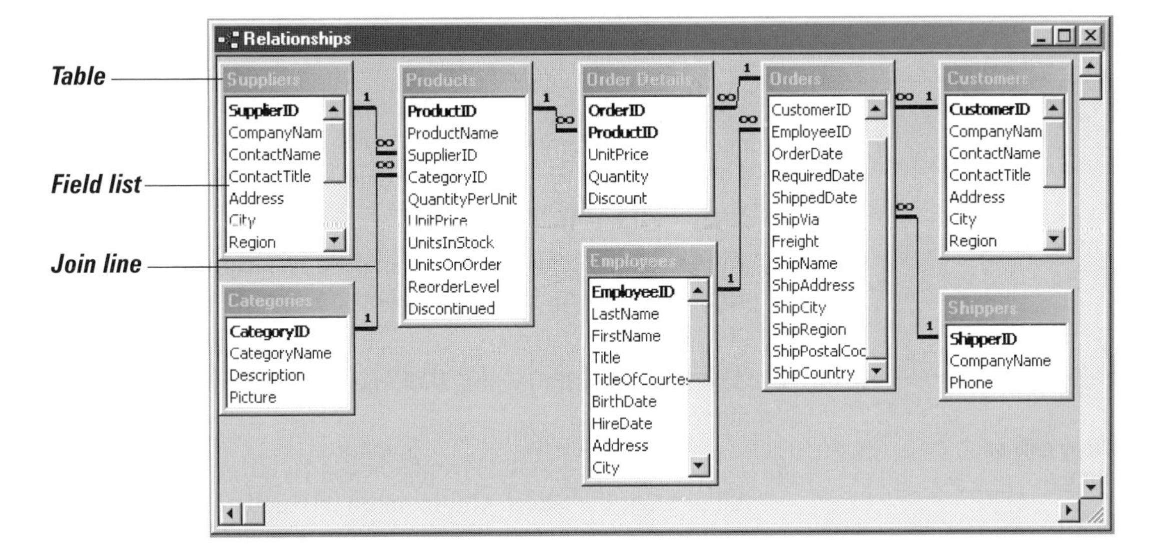

Understanding the Relationships window

In the Relationships window, you can display some or all of the tables in your database and the relationships between them:

- **Tables.** Each table is displayed with its field list. Primary key fields are displayed in bold type.
- **Relationships.** A relationship between two tables is represented by a join line between the two related fields.
- **Relationship types.** One-to-many relationships are indicated by a '1' at the 'one' end of the join line, and an infinity (∞) symbol at the 'many' end of the line. One-to-one relationships are indicated by a '1' at both ends.

When you open the Relationships window, a **Relationships** menu is added to the Access menu bar, and a number of buttons are added to the Access toolbar. Options are provided for:

- Organizing the layout of tables in the window. See 'Organizing the layout' below.
- Creating, editing and deleting relationships. See 'Creating and editing relationships' below.

A well-designed layout, like the Northwind example, clearly illustrates the structure of a database and makes it easy to understand the relationships between tables. Which tables you choose to display or not display in the layout affects only the layout here in the Relationships window; it does not affect the database in any way.

Organizing the layout

Initially, the Relationships window for a new database is empty. You can add and remove tables in various ways, as outlined here. Try out each option in Northwind's Relationships window, but do *not* save your new layout.

- To hide a table, click on it and choose **Relationships | Hide Table** or right-click on it and choose **Hide Table** from the pop-up menu.

Clear Layout button

- To clear the entire layout, click the **Clear Layout** button on the toolbar.

Show All button

- To add all tables to the layout, choose **Relationships | Show All** or click the **Show All** button on the toolbar. This works only for tables for which relationships have been defined.

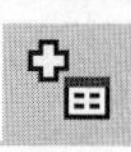

Show Table button

- To add selected tables to the layout, choose **Relationships | Show Table** or click the **Show Table** button on the toolbar. This displays the *Show Table* dialog box, which lists all your database tables. Double-click on each table you want to add to the layout and click **Close** when finished.

Access automatically arranges tables in rows across the layout, positioning each table that you add in the next available space. This can result in a confusing network of join lines. If you want to move a table you can do so by clicking on its title bar and dragging it to its new location.

You can save the current layout at any time by choosing **File | Save** or clicking the **Save** button on the toolbar. Whenever you open the Relationships window, the last saved layout is always displayed.

Creating and editing relationships

Provided that you have designed your tables appropriately, creating and editing relationships in the Relationships window is very straightforward:

- To create a relationship between two tables, drag the primary key field from the primary table to the related field in the other table.
- To edit a relationship, double-click on the relevant join line and make your selections in the *Edit Relationships* dialog box.
- To delete a relationship, right-click on the relevant join line and choose **Delete** from the pop-up menu.

Exercise 5.1: Creating and editing relationships

In this exercise you will create all the relationships required by the Village Library database.

1) Open the starting database for this chapter:

   `Chp5_VillageLibrary_Database`

2) Open the Relationships window and add all the database tables to the layout. Arrange them as shown here.

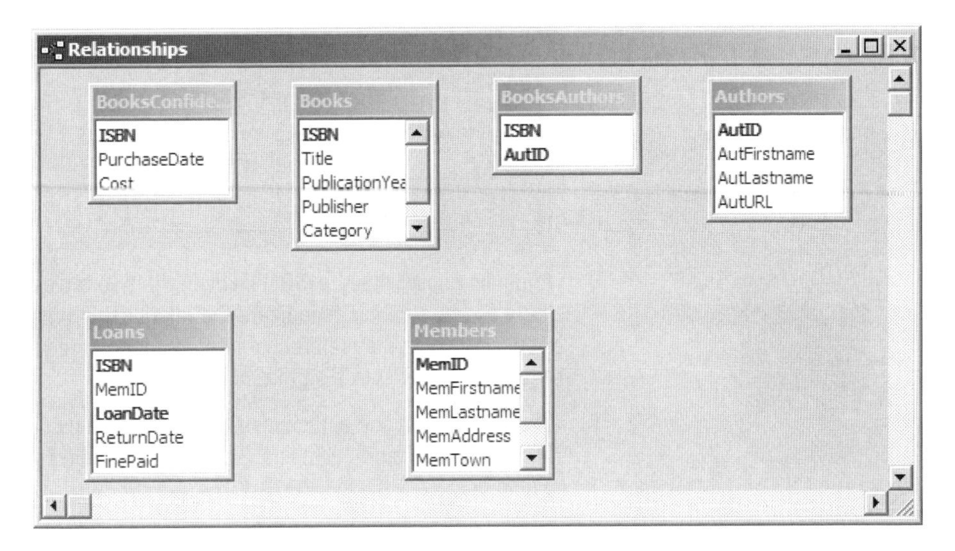

3) To create the one-to-one relationship between Books and BooksConfidential, drag the ISBN field from the Books table to the ISBN field in the BooksConfidential table.

   The *Edit Relationships* dialog box is now displayed. This lists the fields on which the relationship is based and indicates the type of relationship that will be created.

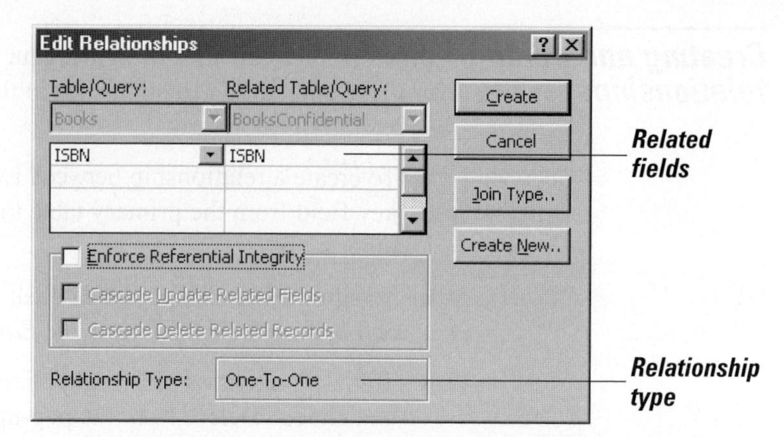

Access determines the relationship type automatically. It creates a one-to-one relationship if both fields are primary keys; it creates a one-to-many relationship if only one is a primary key. In the Books/BooksConfidential relationship, the Books table becomes the primary table because it is the table whose primary key you dragged to the other table.

4) For the moment, ignore the other options in the dialog box and click **Create** to create the relationship.

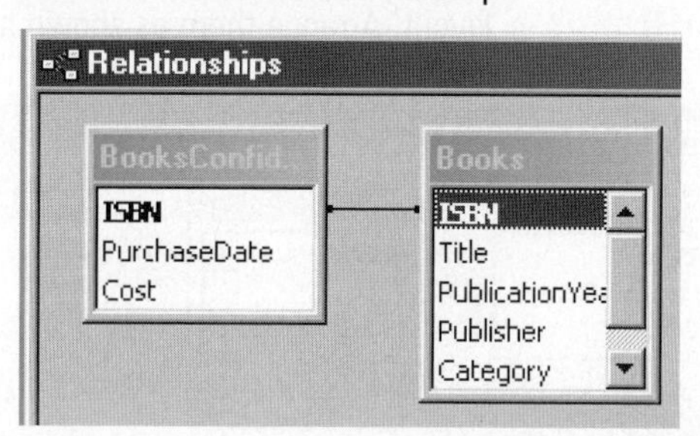

A join line now links the ISBN fields in the two tables. Notice that there are no symbols to indicate the relationship type – these are displayed only when referential integrity is enforced (see 'Referential integrity' below). Let's do that now.

5) Click on the join line and choose **Relationships | Edit Relationship**, or double-click on the join line. This redisplays the *Edit Relationships* dialog box.

6) Select the *Enforce Referential Integrity* option and click **OK**. The join line now indicates the relationship type.

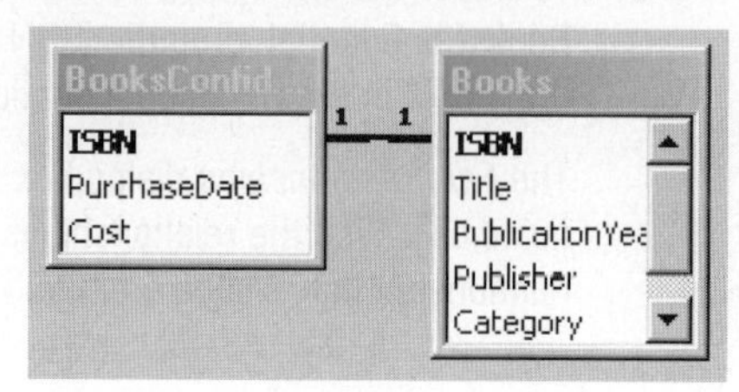

7) Now create the relationship between Books and BooksAuthors by dragging the ISBN field from the Books table to the ISBN field in BooksAuthors.

8) In the **Edit Relationships** dialog box, Access correctly identifies the relationship type as one-to-many. Select the *Enforce Referential Integrity* option and click **Create**.

9) Now create the following relationships, selecting the *Enforce Referential Integrity* option in each case:

Tables	Type	Related fields
Authors and BooksAuthors	one-to-many	AutID
Books and Loans	one-to-many	ISBN
Members and Loans	one-to-many	MemID

The Relationships window should now look similar to that shown here:

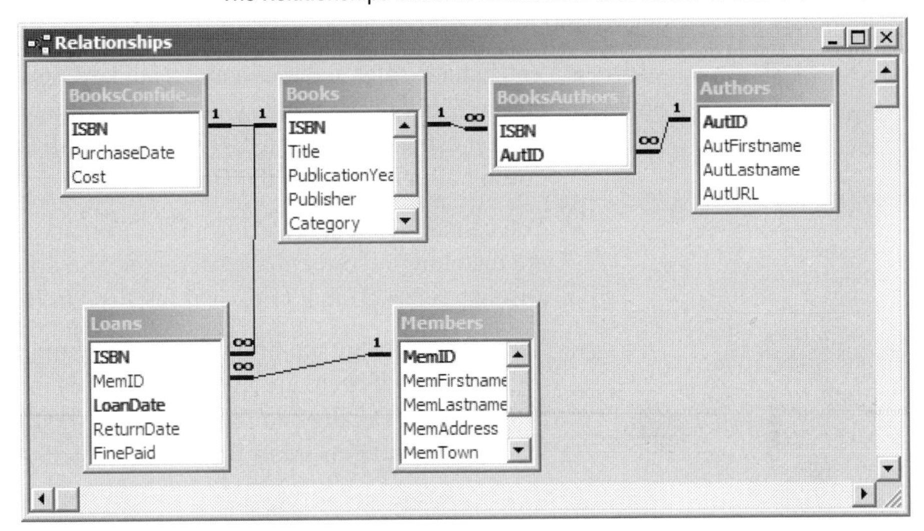

10) Close the Relationships window, saving the current layout as you do.

Referential integrity

You've seen how the relationship between the Books and BooksAuthors tables is based on including the primary key of the Books table (ISBN) as a foreign key in the BooksAuthors table.

To ensure consistency between the two tables, each ISBN value in BooksAuthors must have a matching value in the Books table – that is, it must point to a Books record that exists. If this is true, then the relationship has *referential integrity*.

Without referential integrity, the BooksAuthors table could have 'dangling' references that point nowhere, as shown below.

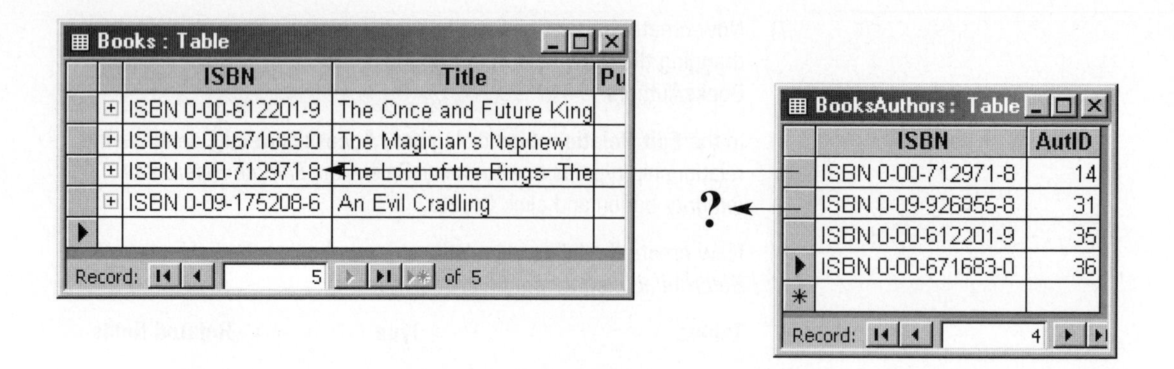

Books : Table

	ISBN	Title	Pu
+	ISBN 0-00-612201-9	The Once and Future King	
+	ISBN 0-00-671683-0	The Magician's Nephew	
+	ISBN 0-00-712971-8	The Lord of the Rings- The	
+	ISBN 0-09-175208-6	An Evil Cradling	

Record: 5 of 5

BooksAuthors : Table

ISBN	AutID
ISBN 0-00-712971-8	14
ISBN 0-09-926855-8	31
ISBN 0-00-612201-9	35
ISBN 0-00-671683-0	36

Record: 4

This would happen, for example, if you delete a Books record that is referenced by a record in the BooksAuthors table.

Referential integrity restrictions

When referential integrity is enforced, Access applies the following restrictions to relationships:

- You cannot enter a value in a foreign key field if that value doesn't exist in the primary key field of the primary table. So you cannot enter an ISBN value in BooksAuthors if it doesn't already exist in the Books table.
- You cannot delete a record from the primary table if there are matching records in a related table. So you cannot delete a Books record if that book is referenced in BooksAuthors.
- You cannot change the primary key value of a record in the primary table if there are matching records in a related table. So you cannot change an ISBN value in the Books table if that value is referenced in BooksAuthors.

Referential integrity

A set of rules that ensures that the relationships between records in related tables are valid, and that you do not accidentally delete or change related data.

Enforcing referential integrity

To enforce referential integrity in Access, you select the *Enforce Referential Integrity* option when creating or editing relationships between tables. You did this when you created the relationships in Exercise 5.1.

Overriding referential integrity restrictions

When you select the *Enforce Referential Integrity* option, two further options became available: *Cascade Update Related Fields* and *Cascade Delete Related Records*.

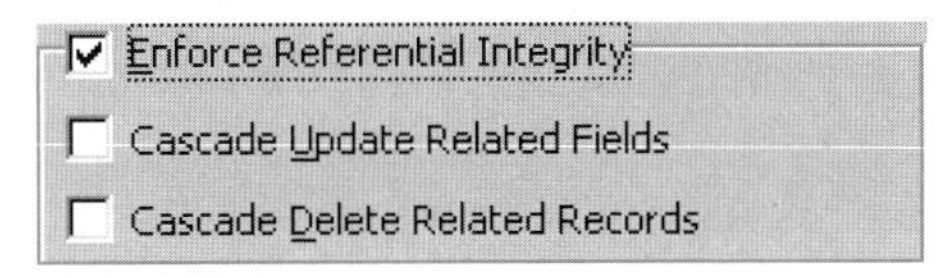

These allow you to perform the actions restricted by referential integrity but ensure that Access takes automatic action to prevent inconsistencies.

- **Cascade Update Related Fields.** When this is selected, if you change a primary key value in the primary table, Access automatically changes any matching values in related records.
- **Cascade Delete Related Records.** When this is selected, if you delete a record in the primary table, Access automatically deletes all matching records in the related table.

Note that cascades work in one direction only – changes to the primary table are automatically applied to the related table but not vice versa.

It is a good idea to enforce referential integrity for all relationships. However, enabling the *Cascade* options may result in Access automatically deleting or changing many records, so you should do so only after careful thought.

For example, let's suppose that both *Cascade* options have been enabled for all relationships in the Village Library database. These are some of the consequences:

- When you delete a record in the Books table, Access also deletes all records in the BooksConfidential, BooksAuthors, and Loans tables that have the same ISBN.
- When you update an ISBN value in the Books table, Access automatically updates any instances of that ISBN in the BooksConfidential, BooksAuthors, and Loans tables.
- When you delete a record in the Members table, Access also deletes all records in the Loans table that have the same MemID.

Applying automatic deletion of related records

Exercise 5.2: Using the *Cascade Delete Related Records* option

In this exercise you will enable the *Cascade Delete Related Records* option for some relationships and see what happens when you delete a record.

1) Open the Relationships window for the `Chp5_VillageLibrary_Database` database.
2) Double-click on the join line between the Books and BooksConfidential tables to display the *Edit Relationships* dialog box.
3) Select the *Cascade Delete Related Records* option and click **OK**.
4) When a table is the primary table in multiple relationships, you normally set the same referential integrity options for all the relationships. So repeat steps 2 and 3 for the other relationships involving the Books table – that is, Books and BooksAuthors, and Books and Loans.
5) Close the Relationships window.
6) Open the Books table and delete a record. Access displays a message similar to the following.

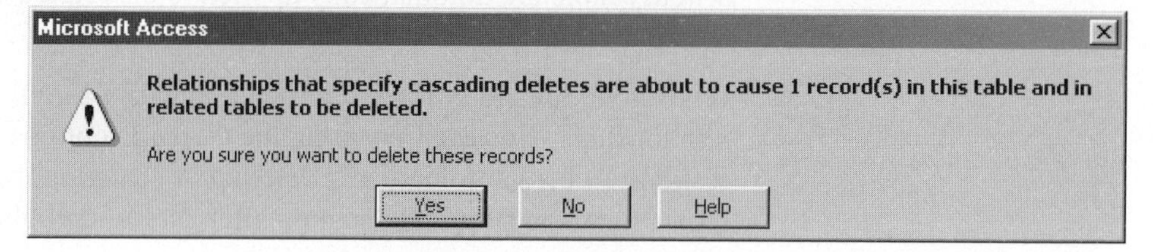

   This informs you that deleting the record will cause records in related tables to be automatically deleted.

7) Click **Yes**. Access now deletes the Books record and all related records in the BooksConfidential, BooksAuthors, and Loans tables.

Remember that changes to a primary table cascade down to related tables but not vice versa. To demonstrate this, open the Loans table and delete a record. This time Access prompts you to confirm the deletion and deletes only the selected record.

Chapter 5: summary

Defining a *relationship* between two tables enables Access to combine records from the two tables. The two tables must have a common field with the same data type (AutoNumber fields are an exception).

In a *one-to-one relationship*, each record in one table has no more than one matching record in the other table. In a *one-to-many relationship*, each record in the primary table can have many matching records in the related table, but records in the related table can have only one matching record in the primary table.

In a *many-to-many relationship*, each record in one table can have many matching records in the second table and vice versa. For this type of relationship, you create a linking table that contains the primary key fields from the two tables. You then create a one-to-many relationship between each of the two tables and the linking table.

You use the *Relationships window* to create and edit relationships. To create a relationship, simply drag the primary key field from the primary table to the related field in the other table.

Referential integrity ensures that foreign key values in a related table always have matching values in the primary key field of the primary table. This prevents records in the related table from including foreign keys that point to nonexistent records.

Chapter 5: quick quiz

Q1	For a valid relationship between two tables, which of the following statements must be true?
A.	The two tables must have a common field with shared values.
B.	The two tables must have the same number and types of fields.
C.	The fields that the two tables have in common must have the same Format properties.
D.	The fields that the two tables have in common must have the same data type, unless one is an AutoNumber field.

Q2	To create a relationship in the Relationships window, you ...
A.	Choose **Relationships | Create Relationship** and then drag the primary key field from one table to the related field in the other table.
B.	Select the two fields on which the relationship is to be based and choose **Relationships | Create Relationship**.
C.	Choose **Relationships | New**, select the two tables to be related, select the related fields in the two tables, and click **OK**.
D.	Drag the primary key field from the primary table to the related foreign key field in the other table.

Q3	How does Access know which type of relationship you want to create between two tables?
A.	You select the relationship type from the **Relationships** menu.
B.	You select the relationship type in the *Edit Relationships* dialog box.
C.	You select the relationship type by using the **Relationship Type** button on the toolbar.
D.	Access automatically creates a one-to-one relationship if both fields on which the relationship is based are primary key fields. And it automatically creates a one-to-many relationship if only one is a primary key.

Q4	True or false – when you enforce referential integrity for a relationship, you cannot delete a record in the primary table if there is a matching record in the related table.
A.	True.
B.	False.

Q5	True or false – when you select the *Cascade Delete Related Records* option for a relationship, you cannot delete a record from the primary table if there is a matching record in the related table.
A.	True.
B.	False.

Q6	Which of these options do you select if you want Access to automatically update the primary key value on the 'one' side of a relationship when you change it on the 'many' side?
A.	Cascade Update Related Fields.
B.	Cascade Update Related Records.
C.	Cascade Update Related Tables.
D.	Cascade Delete Related Records.

Answers

1: A and D, **2:** D, **3:** D, **4:** A, **5:** B, **6:** None.

Table design: joins

In this chapter

When a relationship has been defined between two tables, you can use a query to combine records from the tables based on values in their common fields. This operation is referred to as a *join*.

In this chapter you will learn about the different types of joins that you can use and how you apply them to relationships.

New skills

At the end of this chapter you should be able to:

- Understand and apply the different join types
- Create a query based on a self join
- Set the default join type for a relationship
- Override the default join type in a query
- Define relationships in a query

New words

In this chapter you will meet the following terms:

- Inner join
- Left outer join
- Right outer join
- Self join

Exercise file

In this chapter you will work with the following Access database file:

- `Chp6_VillageLibrary_Database`

Syllabus reference

In this chapter you will cover the following items of the ECDL Advanced Database syllabus:

- **AM5.1.2.4**: Apply inner, outer, and self joins.
- **AM5.1.2.7**: Relate/join data when designing queries.

Join types

The operation of combining records from two tables is referred to as a join. By default, when you run a query involving two tables, Access checks the values in the related fields, combines the records with matching values, and then returns only those records. This is one type of join – an inner join – but it is not the only type you can use.

In this section we will look at the following join types:

- Inner join
- Left outer join
- Right outer join
- Self join

To help you understand the different join types, the `Chp6_VillageLibrary_Database` database includes queries that use each type. Open the database now and take a look at the contents of the Members and Loans tables.

- The Members table contains records for 24 members, not all of whom have borrowed books.
- The Loans table contains records for 22 loans, some representing different books borrowed by the same member. It also contains two records where the MemID value does not have a matching record in the Members table (remember that this is possible only when referential integrity is not enforced).

In the following sections we will look at how different join types affect the results of queries run on these tables.

Join
The process of combining records from two tables.

Inner joins

An *inner join* is Access's default join type and the one with which you are probably most familiar. In this case, a query returns only records that have matching values in their related fields. It omits unmatched values in both tables.

The InnerJoin query in the `Chp6_VillageLibrary_Database` database performs an inner join on the Members and Loans tables. Open the database and run that query now.

The query combines all records with matching MemID values in the Loans and Members tables. There are 20 records in the Loans table with matching records in the Members table, so the query returns 20 records. It ignores the two records in the

Loans table that have no matching record in the Members table, and ignores all records in the Members table that have no matching record in the Loans table.

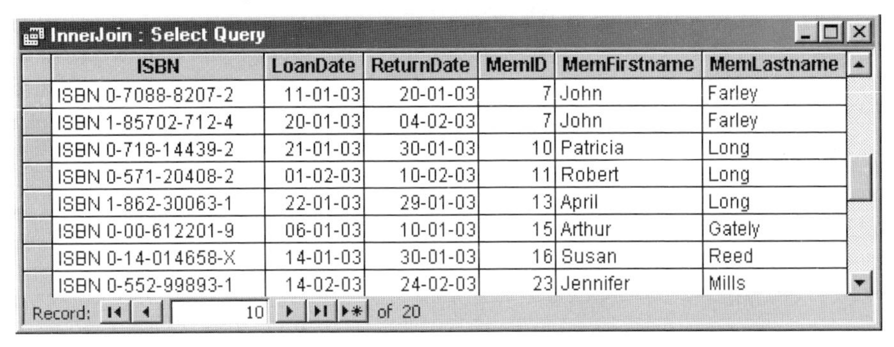

InnerJoin : Select Query

ISBN	LoanDate	ReturnDate	MemID	MemFirstname	MemLastname
ISBN 0-7088-8207-2	11-01-03	20-01-03	7	John	Farley
ISBN 1-85702-712-4	20-01-03	04-02-03	7	John	Farley
ISBN 0-718-14439-2	21-01-03	30-01-03	10	Patricia	Long
ISBN 0-571-20408-2	01-02-03	10-02-03	11	Robert	Long
ISBN 1-862-30063-1	22-01-03	29-01-03	13	April	Long
ISBN 0-00-612201-9	06-01-03	10-01-03	15	Arthur	Gately
ISBN 0-14-014658-X	14-01-03	30-01-03	16	Susan	Reed
ISBN 0-552-99893-1	14-02-03	24-02-03	23	Jennifer	Mills

Record: 10 of 20

Left outer joins

A *left outer join* is one in which a query returns *all* records from the primary table but only matching records from the related table.

The LeftOuterJoin query performs a left outer join on the Members and Loans tables. Run that query now and take a look at the records it returns.

The query combines all records with matching MemID values in the Loans and Members tables. It also returns all records from the Members table (the primary table) that do not have matching records in the Loans table. In these records the fields from the Loans table are blank. The query ignores the two records in the Loans table that have no matching record in the Members table.

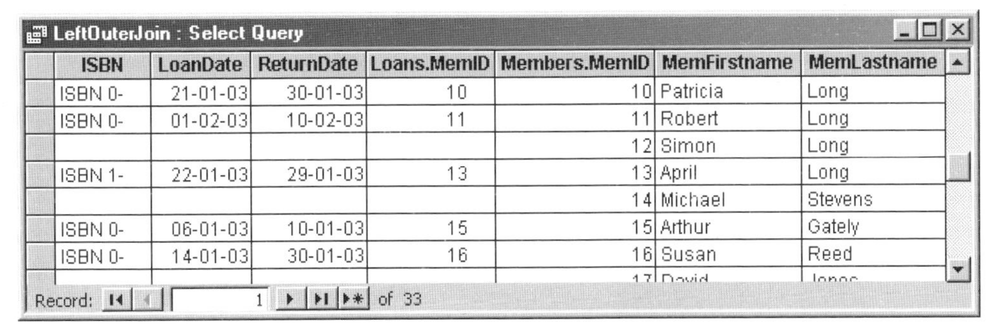

LeftOuterJoin : Select Query

ISBN	LoanDate	ReturnDate	Loans.MemID	Members.MemID	MemFirstname	MemLastname
ISBN 0-	21-01-03	30-01-03	10	10	Patricia	Long
ISBN 0-	01-02-03	10-02-03	11	11	Robert	Long
				12	Simon	Long
ISBN 1-	22-01-03	29-01-03	13	13	April	Long
				14	Michael	Stevens
ISBN 0-	06-01-03	10-01-03	15	15	Arthur	Gately
ISBN 0-	14-01-03	30-01-03	16	16	Susan	Reed

Record: 1 of 33

Right outer joins

A *right outer join* is one in which a query returns *all* records from the related table but only matching records from the primary table.

The RightOuterJoin query performs a right outer join on the Members and Loans tables. Run that query now and take a look at the records it returns.

The query combines all records with matching MemID values in the Loans and Members tables. It also returns the two records from the Loans table that do not have matching records in the Members table. In these records the fields from the Members table are blank. The query ignores records in the Members table that do not have matching records in the Loans table.

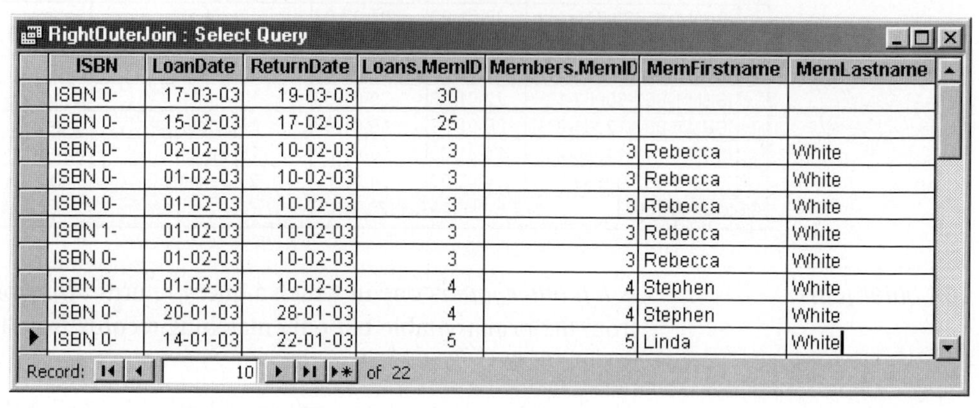

RightOuterJoin : Select Query

ISBN	LoanDate	ReturnDate	Loans.MemID	Members.MemID	MemFirstname	MemLastname
ISBN 0-	17-03-03	19-03-03	30			
ISBN 0-	15-02-03	17-02-03	25			
ISBN 0-	02-02-03	10-02-03	3	3	Rebecca	White
ISBN 0-	01-02-03	10-02-03	3	3	Rebecca	White
ISBN 0-	01-02-03	10-02-03	3	3	Rebecca	White
ISBN 1-	01-02-03	10-02-03	3	3	Rebecca	White
ISBN 0-	01-02-03	10-02-03	3	3	Rebecca	White
ISBN 0-	01-02-03	10-02-03	4	4	Stephen	White
ISBN 0-	20-01-03	28-01-03	4	4	Stephen	White
ISBN 0-	14-01-03	22-01-03	5	5	Linda	White

Record: 10 of 22

Self joins

A *self join* is one in which a table is joined to itself. This is useful, for example, when you want to find records that have the same values in one or more fields in the same table.

The SelfJoin query performs a self join on the Members table. Run that query now and take a look at the records it returns.

The query returns a list of all members who reside at the same address as another member. You will learn how to create this query later in the chapter.

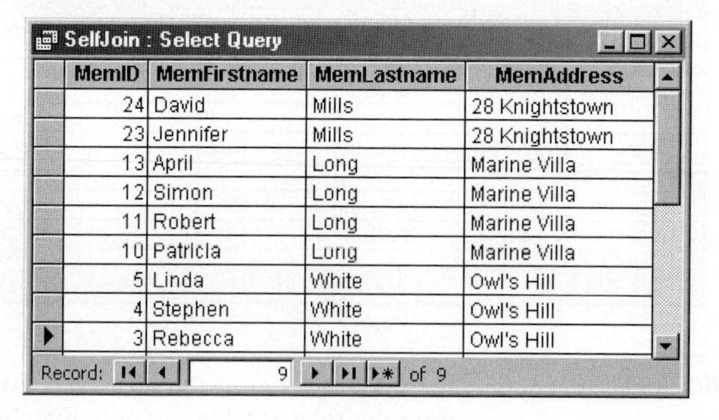

SelfJoin : Select Query

MemID	MemFirstname	MemLastname	MemAddress
24	David	Mills	28 Knightstown
23	Jennifer	Mills	28 Knightstown
13	April	Long	Marine Villa
12	Simon	Long	Marine Villa
11	Robert	Long	Marine Villa
10	Patricia	Long	Marine Villa
5	Linda	White	Owl's Hill
4	Stephen	White	Owl's Hill
3	Rebecca	White	Owl's Hill

Record: 9 of 9

Setting a default join type

When you create a relationship between two tables, Access applies an inner join as the default join type for the relationship. When you create a query on the two tables, this is the join type that is used by default.

You can change the default join type for any relationship in the Relationships window. You can also override the default join type in a query.

Exercise 6.1: Setting the default join type for a relationship

In this exercise you will change the default join type for the Books and Loans relationship.

1) Open the Relationships window for the `Chp6_VillageLibrary_Database` database.

2) Double-click on the join line linking the Books and Loans tables. This displays the *Edit Relationships* dialog box.

3) Click the **Join Type** button. This displays the *Join Properties* dialog box, which describes each of the available join types.

4) Select option *2*, which applies a left outer join, and click **OK**.

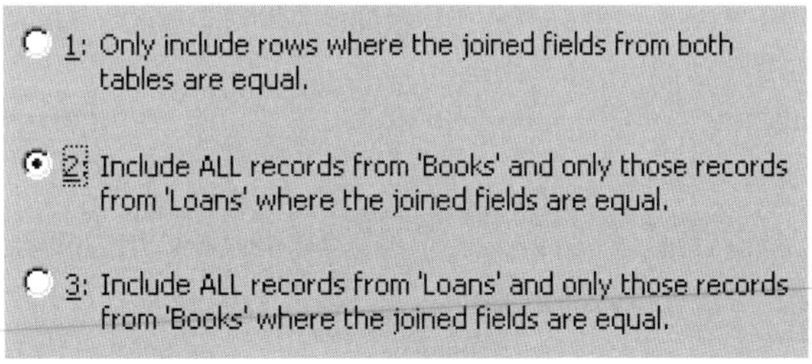

1: Only include rows where the joined fields from both tables are equal.

2: Include ALL records from 'Books' and only those records from 'Loans' where the joined fields are equal.

3: Include ALL records from 'Loans' and only those records from 'Books' where the joined fields are equal.

5) When returned to the *Edit Relationships* dialog box, click **OK** again.

6) Close the Relationships window.

The default join type for the Books and Loans tables is now a left outer join. Any queries you subsequently create on those tables will, by default, return all records from the Books table but only matching records from the Loans table.

Setting a join type in a query

Whatever the default join type defined for a relationship, you can override it when you create a query in Design View.

Exercise 6.2: Setting a join type in a query

The default join type for the Books and Loans relationship is now a left outer join. In this exercise you will create a query that overrides this default and joins the tables with an inner join instead.

1) Open a new query in Design View. To do this, click *Queries* in the *Objects* list in the Database window and then double-click the *Create query in Design view* option.

2) When prompted for the tables you want to include in the query, select Books and Loans. To do this, double-click on each of these tables in the list displayed and then click **Close**.

   Both tables are now displayed in the *Field List* area of the Query Design window, with a join line representing the relationship between them.

3) Add the following fields to the query design grid, in the order shown:

   – Books.ISBN

   – Books.Title

   – Loans.MemID

   – Loans.LoanDate

   – Loans.ReturnDate

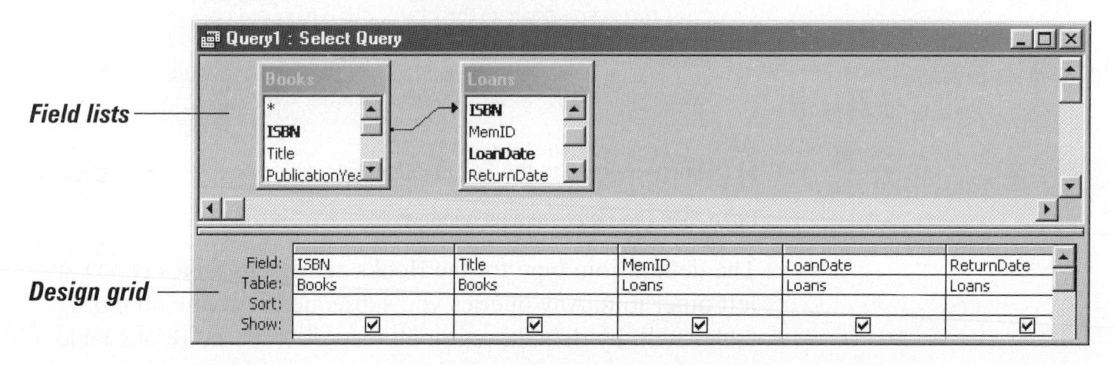

You can do this by using any of the following methods:

– Drag the field from the field list to an empty column in the design grid.

– Double-click the field in the field list. This adds the field to the next empty column in the design grid.

– Click in a *Field* cell in the design grid, click the arrow at the right of the cell, and then select a field from the list displayed.

Run button

4) Run the query by choosing **Query | Run** or by clicking the **Run** button on the toolbar. Then take a look at the results.

   There are many books in the Books table that have never been borrowed and so have no matching record in the Loans table. Because the default join for the two tables is a left outer join, all records in the Books table are listed anyway, with the fields from Loans left blank where there is no matching record.

5) Switch back to Design View.

6) Right-click on the join line between the tables and choose **Join Properties** from the pop-up menu, or double-click on the join line.

7) In the *Join Properties* dialog box, change the join type from option *2* to option *1* (an inner join) and click **OK**.

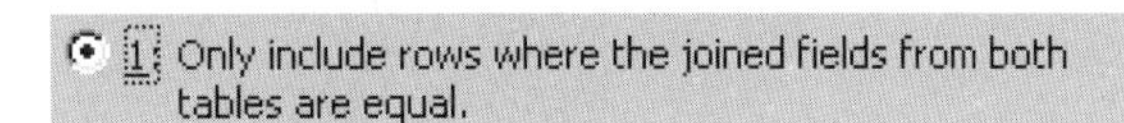

1: Only include rows where the joined fields from both tables are equal.

8) Now run the query again. This time only the records with matching ISBN values in both tables are displayed.

9) Save the query with the name BooksLoans and then close it.

Note that the default join type for the Books and Loans relationship remains a left outer join. When you set a join type in a query, it applies only to that query.

Creating self joins

A self join is not one of the join types offered in the *Join Properties* dialog box. A self join is actually a one-to-one relationship between two instances of the same table and must be set up manually.

Exercise 6.3: Creating a self join

In this exercise you will create the HouseMates query, which is a version of the SelfJoin query described in 'Self joins' above. The query returns a list of all members who reside at the same address as another member, as shown here.

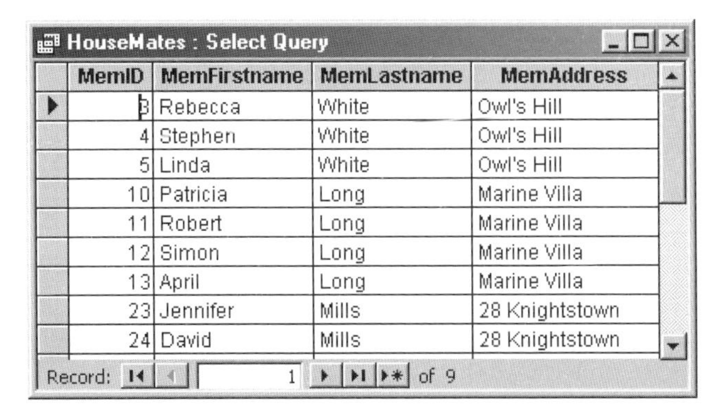

HouseMates : Select Query

MemID	MemFirstname	MemLastname	MemAddress
3	Rebecca	White	Owl's Hill
4	Stephen	White	Owl's Hill
5	Linda	White	Owl's Hill
10	Patricia	Long	Marine Villa
11	Robert	Long	Marine Villa
12	Simon	Long	Marine Villa
13	April	Long	Marine Villa
23	Jennifer	Mills	28 Knightstown
24	David	Mills	28 Knightstown

Record: 1 of 9

1) Open a new query in Design View. When prompted for the tables you want to include in the query, select Members twice. Two instances of the table are displayed – the second is named Members_1.

2) No relationship has been defined between these tables. However, Access allows you to relate tables in a query in the same way as you create a relationship in the Relationships window.

   In the case of the HouseMates query, you want to compare the Address fields in the two tables, so drag the Members.MemAddress field to the Members_1.MemAddress field. A join line now links the tables. By default, the join type is an inner join.

3) Add the following fields to the design grid and set a sort order of *Ascending* for the Members.MemID field.

   – Members.MemID

   – Members_1.MemID

   – Members.MemFirstname

   – Members.MemLastname

   – Members.MemAddress

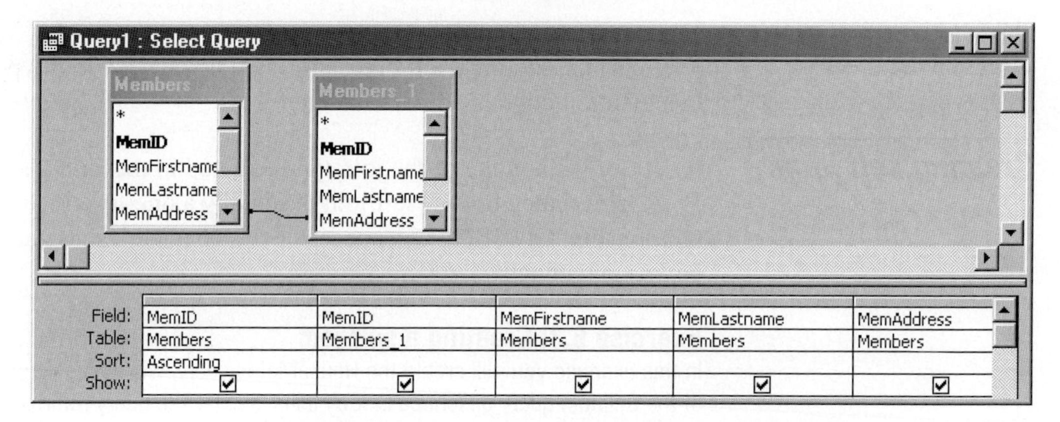

4) Run the query and take a look at the records it returns.

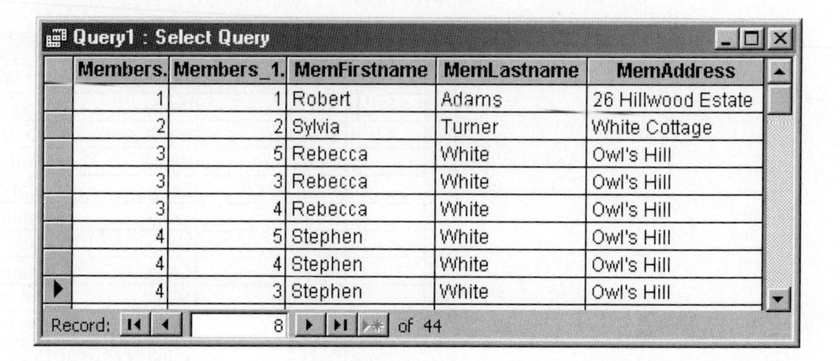
Query1 : Select Query

Members.	Members_1.	MemFirstname	MemLastname	MemAddress
1	1	Robert	Adams	26 Hillwood Estate
2	2	Sylvia	Turner	White Cottage
3	5	Rebecca	White	Owl's Hill
3	3	Rebecca	White	Owl's Hill
3	4	Rebecca	White	Owl's Hill
4	5	Stephen	White	Owl's Hill
4	4	Stephen	White	Owl's Hill
4	3	Stephen	White	Owl's Hill

Record: 8 of 44

As the two tables are joined on their Address fields, Access joins *every* record in Members to *every* record in Members_1 with a matching address value.

- Every record in Members has a duplicate record in Members_1, so Access displays a record for each of these combinations, showing that each member lives at the same address as himself or herself! The record for Robert Adams is an example.
- Some members share the same address, so Access also displays a record for each of these combinations. For example, the fifth record displayed joins the record for Rebecca White in the Members table to the record for Stephen White in the Members_1 table, and the eighth record joins the record for Stephen White in the Members table to the record for Rebecca White in the Members_1 table.

5) Switch back to Design View. You are now going to refine the query so that it excludes all members that don't share an address with another member and displays a single record for each member that does.

6) To exclude records that join members to themselves, enter the following expression in the *Criteria* row for the Members.MemID field:

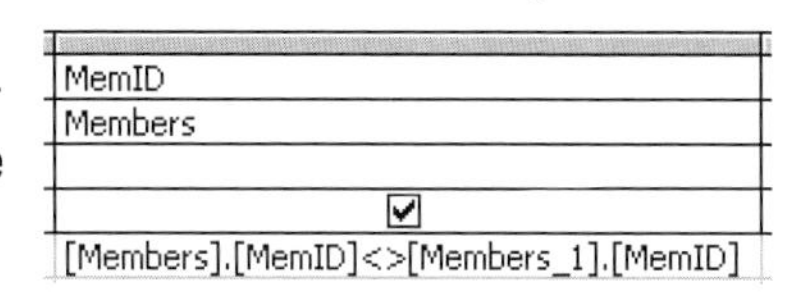


```
Members.MemID <> Members_1.MemID
```

This tells Access to return only records where the MemID value in the Members table is *not* equal to the MemID value in the Members_1 table – that is, to omit records that have the same MemID value in both tables.

7) Run the query and you will see that the results are now limited to members that share an address with other members. Then switch back to Design View.

8) Now you want limit the results to a single record for each member that shares an address with another member.

The properties of a query include a *Unique Values* property. This omits duplicates from the query results – a duplicate being a record that displays the same values as another record in all its fields. While the MemID fields from both tables are included in the results, there are no duplicates. However, if you remove Members_1.MemID, all records for the same member will display the same values in all fields. You can then use *Unique Values* to remove the duplicates.

So delete the Members_1.MemID field from the design grid by clicking its column selector and then pressing the **Delete** key. This affects only which fields the query displays, and not which records it displays. You can verify this by running the query.

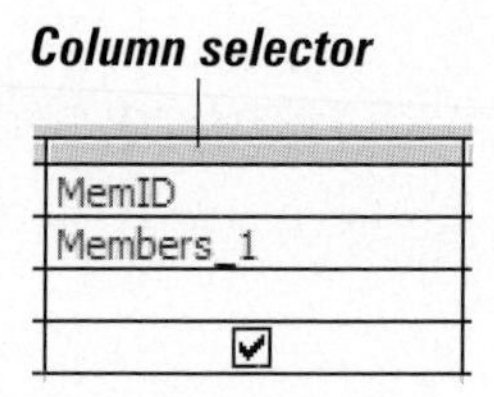

9) Now set the *Unique Values* property to *Yes*.

   To do this, right-click on a blank part of the field list area in the Query Design window and choose **Properties** from the pop-up menu. This displays the *Query Properties* dialog box. Select *Yes* in the drop-down list for the *Unique Values* property and then close the dialog box.

10) Run the query again. The results should be the same as those shown at the start of the exercise. At a glance you can see how many and which members live together at Owl's Hill or Marine Villa.

11) Save the query with the name HouseMates and then close it.

Defining relationships in a query

In the previous exercise, you were able to join the Members and Members_1 tables even though you had not previously defined a relationship between the tables.

This is possible for any two tables that share a field with the same or a compatible data type. To create the join simply drag the join field from one table to the related field in the other table.

It is important to know that you cannot apply Referential Integrity to tables related in this way, and that the relationship applies only to the query in which it was created. To define a permanent relationship between two tables you must use the Relationships window.

Chapter 6: summary

You can use a query to combine records from two related tables based on values in their common fields. This operation is referred to as a *join*. With an *inner join*, a query returns only records that have matching values in their related fields. With a *left outer join*, a query returns all records from the primary table, but only matching records from the related table. With a *right outer join*, a query returns all records from the related table, but only matching records from the primary table. With a *self join*, you combine records from two instances of the same table.

You set the *default join type* for a relationship when you create or edit that relationship in the Relationships window. You can then override this default join type for individual queries. You can also join tables in a query even if no relationship has been defined between them.

Chapter 6: quick quiz

Q1	In a query, which join type returns all records from the primary table but only matching records from the related table?
A.	Inner join.
B.	Left outer join.
C.	Right outer join.

Q2	In a query, which join type returns all records from the related table but only matching records from the primary table?
A.	Inner join.
B.	Left outer join.
C.	Right outer join.

Q3	Where do you set the default join type for a relationship?
A.	In the *Join Properties* dialog box when creating a query.
B.	In the *Edit Relationships* dialog box when creating a relationship in the Relationships window.
C.	In the *Join Properties* dialog box when creating a relationship in the Relationships window.

Q4	True or false – you can join two tables in a query even when no relationship has been created between the tables.
A.	True.
B.	False.

Q5	True or false – you can create a permanent relationship between two tables by joining them in a query.
A.	True.
B.	False.

Q6	Which of the following must be true in order to join two tables in a query?
A.	The related fields must have the same name.
B.	The related fields must have the same data type.
C.	The related fields must have the same or a compatible data type.

Answers

1: B, **2**: C, **3**: C, **4**: A, **5**: B, **6**: C.

7 Query design: action queries

In this chapter

Any queries you have used so far in this book relate to retrieving records for viewing or updating. This type of query is known as a *select query*.

In this chapter, you will learn about another query type – the action query – which you can use to copy, delete and modify multiple records at a time.

New skills

At the end of this chapter you should be able to:

- Create and use an update query
- Create and use a make-table query
- Create and use an append query
- Create and use a delete query

New words

In this chapter you will meet the following terms:

- Action query
- Update query
- Make-table query
- Append query
- Delete query

Exercise file

In this chapter you will work with the following Access file:

- `Chp7_VillageLibrary_Database`

Syllabus reference

In this chapter you will cover the following items of the ECDL Advanced Database Syllabus:

- **AM5.2.1.1**: Create and use a query to update data in a table.
- **AM5.2.1.2**: Create and use a query to delete records in a table.

- **AM5.2.1.3**: Create and use a query to save selected information as a table.
- **AM5.2.1.4**: Append records to a table using a query.

What is an action query?

If you need to copy, change, or delete a small number of records in a table it is easy enough to find those records in Datasheet View and make the changes manually. However, if you want to modify a large group of records, it is usually quicker and easier to use an action query.

There are four types of action query:

- **Update query**. Makes changes to values in a group of records from one or more tables.
- **Make-table query**. Creates a new table from data in one or more existing tables.
- **Append query**. Copies a group of records from one or more tables and appends them to the end of another table.
- **Delete query**. Deletes a group of records from one or more tables.

Access uses a different icon for each query type, as shown below. This means that you always know what type of action a query will perform before you run it.

Append query

Delete query

Make-table query

Select query

Update query 

Action query

A query that copies or changes groups of records from one or more tables.

Safeguarding your data

When you use an action query to modify records, in most cases you cannot then undo the changes. There are two methods you can use to ensure that you do not make unwanted and irreversible changes to your data.

- You can preview the records that will be modified by the action query and then decide whether or not you want to proceed with the action.
- You can make a copy of the table you want to modify before running the action query. If you need to undo the changes, you can then simply delete the modified table and rename the copy with the name of the original table.

In a real-life scenario, it is always advisable to make backup copies of your tables before running any action query other than a make-table query.

Update queries

You use an update query when you want to make global changes to data in one or more tables. Typical uses include:

- Updating all instances of a particular value in a field – for example, changing all instances of Yes to No, or changing all instances of a publisher's name.
- Updating all values in a field based on a mathematical expression – for example, updating all prices by 10%, or updating all prices less than £10 by 5% and all prices over £10 by 7%.
- Updating the values in one field based on the values in another field – for example, updating the Category value for all books by a particular author, or reducing the unit price of a product where the quantity ordered is greater than ten.

Creating an update query

In the following exercises, you will create update queries to update all instances of a particular value in a field and to update the values in one field based on values in another field.

Exercise 7.1: Creating a query to globally update a particular value

In this exercise you will create an update query to change all instances of the publisher name 'Penguin Books' to 'Penguin'.

1) Open the starting database for this chapter:

   `Chp7_VillageLibrary_Database`

2) Open a new query in Design View. When prompted for the tables you want to include in the query, select Books.

3) As the Publisher field is the one you want to update, add that field to the design grid.

Query Type button

4) By default, Access assumes that you want to create a select query. To specify an update query instead, choose **Update Query** in the **Query** menu or in the list displayed when you click the arrow next to the **Query Type** button on the Access toolbar. An *Update To* row is now added to the design grid. This is where you specify the new value for a field.

5) To specify that you want to update all instances of 'Penguin Books' in the Publisher field, type the following in the *Criteria* row for the field:

   `Penguin Books`

6) To specify 'Penguin' as the new value, type that value in the *Update To* row.

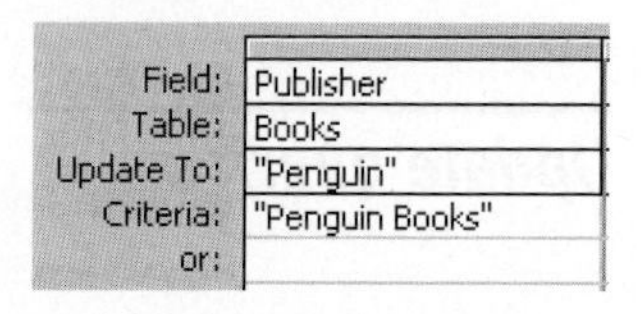

7) Now run the query. Access warns you that you are about to update a number of records and that you cannot undo the changes. Click **Yes**.

8) Save the query under the name PublisherUpdate and then close it.

You can now open the Books table and review the changes.

Exercise 7.2: Creating a query to update values in one field based on values in another field

In this exercise you will create an update query to change the Category value for all books written by J.K. Rowling.

1) Open a new query in Design View. When prompted for the tables you want to include in the query, add Books, BooksAuthors and Authors.

   You add the Books table because you want to update records in that table. You add Authors because you want to use a value in that table to select the records to be updated. Finally, you add BooksAuthors because this is the linking table between Books and Authors.

2) Add the Books.Category and Authors.AutLastname fields to the design grid.

3) Change the query type to an update query.

4) Type 'Rowling' in the *Criteria* row for the AutLastname field. This specifies that you want to update all records where the author's last name is 'Rowling'.

5) Type 'Fantasy' in the *Update To* row for the Category field. This specifies that you want to change the Category value to 'Fantasy' for all records that match the query criteria.

6) Run the query. Access warns you that you are about to update three records. Click **Yes**.

7) Close the query without saving it.

You can now open the Books table and review the changes. The category value for the 'Harry Potter' books has been updated to 'Fantasy'.

Make-table queries

You use a make-table query to create a new table from existing records in one or more tables. Typical uses include:

- Making backup copies of tables.
- Creating an archive table to store records no longer needed in the active table.
- Creating a table that contains selected fields from one or more tables.
- Creating a table containing summary data from one or more tables.

Creating a make-table qucry

The Village Library periodically removes old records from the Loans table and moves them to an archive table.

In the following exercise, you will use a make-table query to create the archive table and add the first batch of records to it. In later exercises, you will use a delete query to delete the archived records from the Loans table, and you will use an append query to add another batch of records to the new table.

Exercise 7.3: Using a make-table query to create an archive table

1) Open a new query in Design View. When prompted for the tables you want to include in the query, select Loans.
2) Add to the design grid the fields you want to include in the new table. In the case of the LoansArchive table, you want to include all fields from the Loans table, so add each in turn to the design grid.
3) Change the query type to a make-table query. When prompted for the name of the new table, enter LoansArchive, and click **OK**.

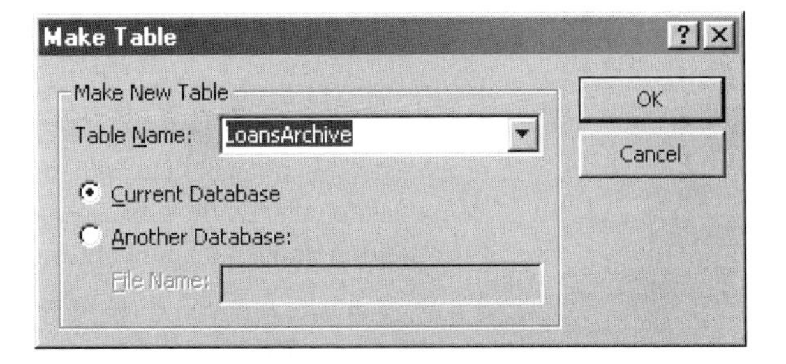

By default the new table is created in the current database.

4) Now you need to specify the criteria for selecting the records you want to add to the archive table. To do this, you enter an expression in the *Criteria* row for the ReturnDate field. For example:

Expression	Result
`<Date()-90`	Selects all records where the return date is more than 90 days ago.
`<=#31-12-01#`	Selects all records where the return date is 31 Dec 2001 or earlier.
`>=#01-01-02# And <=#31-03-02#`	Selects all records where the return date is between 1 Jan 2002 and 31 March 2002 (inclusive).

In a real-world scenario, you would probably choose the first example. You could then save the query and run it at the end of every quarter. For the purposes of this exercise, however, use the second example.

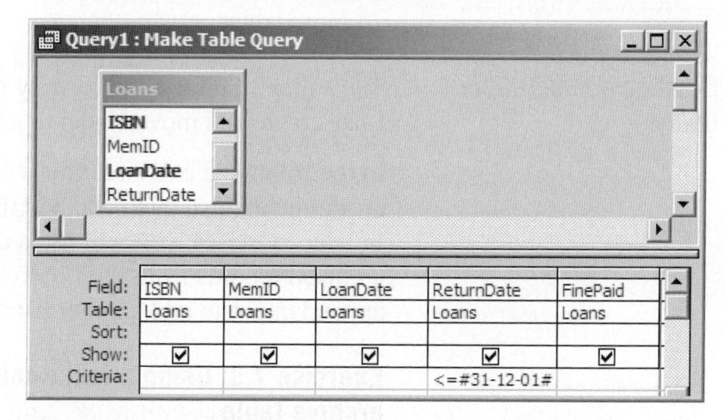

5) Run the query. Access warns you that you are about to paste three records into a new table. Click **Yes**.

6) Close the query without saving it.

The LoansArchive table is now listed in Tables view in the Database window. If you open the table, you will see that it has the same structure as the Loans table and currently contains three records.

Exercise 7.4: Creating a new table with selected fields from an existing table

In the `Chp7_VillageLibrary_Database` database, book costs and purchase dates are included in the Books table and not in a separate BooksConfidential table. In this exercise, you will use a make-table query to create the BooksConfidential table.

1) Open a new query in Design View. When prompted for the tables you want to include in the query, select Books.

2) Add to the design grid the fields you want to include in the new table – that is, ISBN, PurchaseDate and Cost.

3) Change the query type to a make-table query.

4) When prompted for the name of the new table, enter BooksConfidential, and click **OK**.

5) Run the query. Access warns you that you are about to paste a particular number of records into a new table. Click **Yes**.

6) Close the query without saving it.

The BooksConfidential table is now listed in Tables view in the Database window. If you open it, you will see that it contains complete copies of the ISBN, PurchaseDate and Cost fields from the Books tables.

Note that when you create a table with a make-table query, the new table is not assigned a primary key. You must do this manually.

Append queries

You use an append query to copy selected records from one or more tables and insert them into another table. Typical uses include:

- Copying records from an active table to an archive table.
- Importing data from an external source.
- Exporting data to an external destination.
- Copying records from one or more tables to a table that contains selected fields from those tables.

Creating an append query

Exercise 7.5: Creating an append query

In a previous exercise, you created an archive table for storing old records from the Loans table. In this exercise, you will copy more records from the Loans table to the LoansArchive table.

1) Open a new query in Design View. When prompted for the tables you want to include in the query, select Loans.

2) Add each field in the Loans table to the design grid.

3) Change the query type to an append query.

4) When prompted for the name of the destination table for the records, select LoansArchive from the *Table Name* drop-down list and click **OK**.

   An *Append To* row is now added to the design grid. You use this to specify the name of the destination field for each source field in the design grid. For fields with the same names in the source and destination tables, Access automatically fills in the *Append To* value. For those that don't, you must enter the *Append To* value manually.

Field:	ISBN	MemID	LoanDate	ReturnDate	FinePaid
Table:	Loans	Loans	Loans	Loans	Loans
Sort:					
Append To:	ISBN	MemID	LoanDate	ReturnDate	FinePaid

5) Enter the following expression in the *Criteria* row for the ReturnDate field:

   >=#01-01-02# And <=#31-12-02#

   This selects all records where the return date is in the year 2002.

6) Run the query. When prompted to confirm the append operation, click **Yes**.

7) Save the query with the name AppendArchiveLoans and then close it.

If you open the LoansArchive table now you will see that a number of new records have been added from the Loans table.

Appending records with AutoNumber fields

When an AutoNumber field is involved in an append operation, you can choose to copy its values from the original table to the destination table, or to have Access automatically create new AutoNumber values in the destination table.

- To copy the AutoNumber values from the original table, include the AutoNumber field in the design grid for the append query.
- If you want Access to automatically create AutoNumber values in the destination table, omit the AutoNumber field from the design grid.

Delete queries

You use a delete query to delete a group of records from one or more tables. With this type of query you always delete entire records, not just selected fields.

Remember that if you have enabled referential integrity for a relationship, but not cascade deletes, you will not be able to delete records from the primary table if there are matching records in the related table. In such a case, you must delete the records from the related table first, and only then delete the records from the primary table.

If you have enabled relational integrity and also the *Cascade Delete Related Records* option, Access allows you to delete records from the primary table, even if there are matching records in the related table, as it automatically deletes those matching records as well.

Creating a delete query

Exercise 7.6: Creating a delete query

In previous exercises, you copied records from the Loans table to an archive table. In this exercise, you will use a delete query to remove the archived records from the Loans table.

1) Open a new query in Design View. When prompted for the tables you want to include in the query, select Loans.
2) For a delete query, the only fields you *must* include in the design grid are those for which you want to set selection criteria. So add the ReturnDate field to the design grid. You need this to specify the criteria for selecting the records to be deleted.
3) Change the query type to a delete query. A *Delete* row is added to the design grid. Access automatically fills the appropriate values for this row.
4) In previous exercises, you archived all records with a return date of 31-12-02 or older. To select these records for deletion, enter the following expression in the *Criteria* row for the ReturnDate field:

   <=#31-12-02#

   This selects all records where the return date is 31 December 2002 or earlier.
5) Run the query. When prompted to confirm the delete operation, click **Yes**.
6) Save the query with the name DeleteArchivedLoans and then close it.

If you now open the Loans table you will see that all records with a return date of 31 December 2002 or earlier have been removed.

Chapter 7: summary

Action queries enable you to copy, delete, or update groups of records from one or more tables. It is always advisable to make backup copies of your tables before running action queries on them.

An *update query* makes global changes to data in one or more tables. A *make-table* query creates a new table from selected data in one or more tables. An *append query* copies a group of records from one or more tables and appends them to the end of another table. A *delete query* deletes a group of records from one or more tables.

You specify the type of query you are creating by choosing an option on the **Query** menu or by selecting an option from the list displayed when you click the arrow next to the **Query Type** button on the Access toolbar.

Chapter 7: quick quiz

Q1	Which type of query would you use to increase all prices in the Books table by 10%?
A.	An append query.
B.	An update query.
C.	A change values query.
D.	A make-table query.

Q2	True or false – with an update query, you can change the name of the publisher for all books written by a particular author.
A.	True.
B.	False.

Q3	True or false – with a make-table query you can create a table that combines records from the Books and Authors table.
A.	True.
B.	False.

Q4	Which type of query would you use to copy records from one table to another existing table?
A.	An append query.
B.	An update query.
C.	A make-table query.

Q5	How do you tell Access which records to delete with a delete query?
A.	Use the **Select Records** option on the **Query** menu.
B.	Use the *Show* checkbox in the design grid.
C.	Enter selection criteria in the *Criteria* row in the design grid.
D.	Enter selection criteria in the *Delete* row in the design grid.

Answers

1: B, **2**: A, **3**: A, **4**: A, **5**: C.

Query design: total queries

In this chapter

There are many types of calculations that you can perform in a query. In this chapter you will be introduced to the various types, and you will learn how to use Access's aggregate functions to summarize field values.

New skills

At the end of this chapter you should be able to:

- Calculate totals (sums, averages, and so on) for all records in a table
- Calculate totals for groups of records
- Use wildcards in queries
- Create and use a crosstab query
- Use logical operators in query criteria

New words

In this chapter you will meet the following terms:

- Aggregate function
- Wildcard
- Crosstab query

Exercise file

In this chapter you will work with the following Access file:

- `Chp8_VillageLibrary_Database`

Syllabus reference

In this chapter you will cover the following items of the ECDL Advanced Database Syllabus:

- **AM5.2.2.1**: Group information in a query.
- **AM5.2.2.2**: Use functions in a query: sum, count, average, max, min.
- **AM5.2.2.3:** Use a crosstab query.

- **AM5.2.2.4:** Use wildcards in a query.
- **AM5.2.2.5:** Use arithmetic, logical expressions in a query.

About query calculations

There are three types of calculations that you can perform in a query:

- You can use Access's aggregate functions to summarize field values. For example, you could calculate the total cost of books in the village library, or the total cost of books in each category.
- You can create a field that displays the result of calculations on other fields. For example, a FineDue field in the Loans table could calculate the default fine for overdue books – multiply the number of days each book is overdue by the daily fine amount.
- You can use calculations as criteria for selecting which records a query displays or performs an action on. For example, you could tell a query to return only records for late returns – subtract the LoanDate from the ReturnDate and return only records where the result is greater than 10.

You will learn about the latter two calculation types in Chapter 9.

About aggregate functions

Access provides a number of aggregate or 'totals' functions that you can use to summarize field values. The following table shows the ones you need to know for ECDL.

Function	Description
Sum	Returns the sum of the values in a field. This works with Number, Date/Time, Currency and AutoNumber data types.
Avg	Returns the average of the values in a field. This works with Number, Date/Time, Currency and AutoNumber data types.
Min	Returns the minimum value in a field. This works with Text, Number, Date/Time, Currency and AutoNumber data types.
Max	Returns the maximum value in a field. This works with Text, Number, Date/Time, Currency and AutoNumber data types.
Count	Returns a count of the number of values in a field. This works with Text, Memo, Number, Date/Time, Currency, AutoNumber, Yes/No and OLE Object data types.

About total queries

A total query uses aggregate functions to calculate summary field values for all records or for groups of records returned by the query.

This following query counts the number of books in the Books table and calculates their total cost, and their average, maximum and minimum prices.

CountOfISBN	SumOfCost	AvgOfCost	MinOfCost	MaxOfCost
56	£ 439.77	£ 7.85	£ 1.50	£ 24.80

And the following query groups the books by publisher. It then counts the number of books by each publisher, together with the total cost of those books, and their average, maximum and minimum prices.

Publisher	SumOfCost	AvgOfCost	MinOfCost	MaxOfCost	CountOfISBN
Pearson Education Ltd	£ 48.97	£ 16.32	£ 12.99	£ 18.99	3
Penguin Books	£ 91.12	£ 7.59	£ 4.15	£ 24.80	12
Picador	£ 17.45	£ 5.82	£ 5.55	£ 5.95	3
Puffin Books	£ 6.98	£ 3.49	£ 2.99	£ 3.99	2

If you open the BooksCostPerPublisher query in Design View, you will see how this query was created.

In a total query, a *Total* row is added to the query design grid, and it is here that you specify the fields by which you want to group the records and the type of calculation you want to perform on each field. A drop-down list provides all the available options.

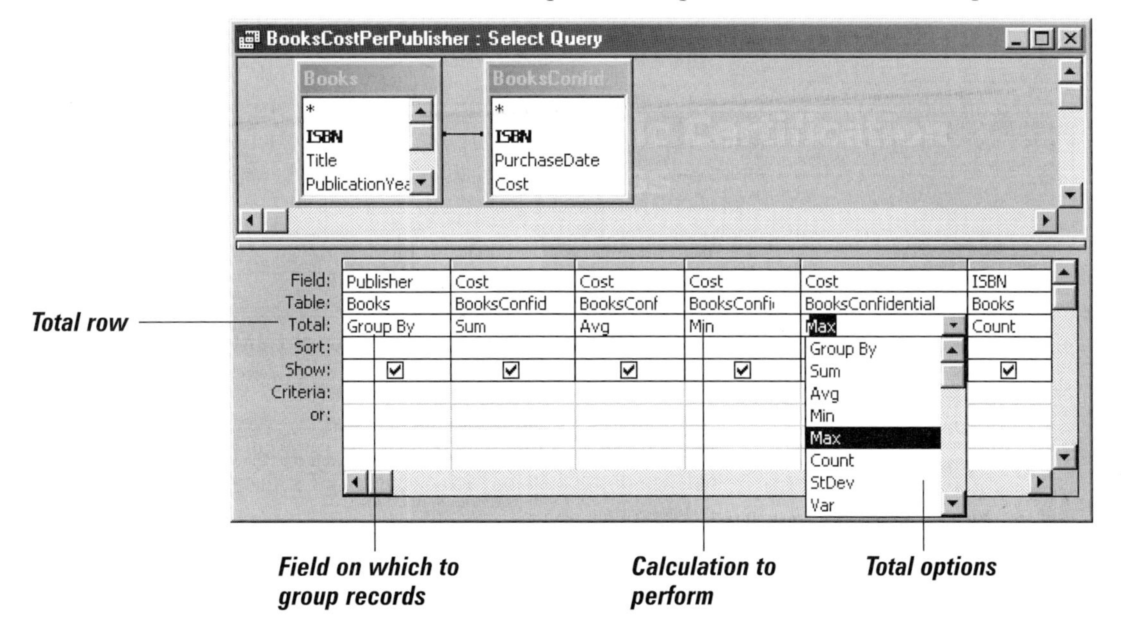

The only fields you need to include in the query are:

- The field(s) by which you want to group the results – BooksCostPerPublisher uses the Publisher field.
- The fields on which you want to perform calculations – BooksCostPerPublisher includes the Books.ISBN field, for counting the number of records per publisher, and four instances of the BooksConfidential.Cost field, so that several calculations can be performed on that field.
- The fields you want to use for setting selection criteria – see 'Using criteria in total queries' below.

If you switch to Datasheet View, you will see that, for the fields that perform calculations, Access automatically combines the function and field name to identify the column. But you can specify your own column names if you wish.

Total query

A query that calculates summary values for all records or for groups of records in tables/queries.

Creating total queries

You can create total queries with the *Simple Query Wizard* or in Query Design View. Using the wizard, however, has limitations:

- You can calculate totals only for Number fields.
- You cannot specify selection criteria for the query.

Totalling all records

Exercise 8.1: Calculating totals for all records in a query

In this exercise, you will create a query that displays the total number of books in the library and calculates totals for various fields in the BooksConfidential table.

1) Open the starting database for this chapter:

   `Chp8_VillageLibrary_Database`

2) Open a new query in Design View. When prompted for the tables you want to include in the query, select Books and BooksConfidential.

3) Add to the design grid all the fields on which you wish to perform calculations. To perform more than one calculation on a field, add an instance of the field for each calculation. For this exercise add the following fields:

   – Books.ISBN (to calculate the total number of books).

   – Two instances of BooksConfidential.Cost (to calculate the total and average cost of books).

   – Two instances of BooksConfidential.PurchaseDate (to calculate the earliest and latest dates on which books were purchased).

Totals button

4) Click the **Totals** button on the Query Design toolbar. This adds the *Total* row to the design grid.

5) By default, Access sets the *Total* row to *Group By* for all fields. Instead, select a calculation for each field, as shown here:

Field:	ISBN	Cost	Cost	PurchaseDate	PurchaseDate
Table:	Books	BooksConfidential	BooksConfidential	BooksConfidential	BooksConfidential
Total:	Count	Sum	Avg	Min	Max
Sort:					

6) Save the query with the name BookTotals and then close it.

You can now open the query in Datasheet View and see the results, which should be similar to those shown here.

CountOfISBN	SumOfCost	AvgOfCost	MinOfPurchaseDate	MaxOfPurchaseDate
56	£ 439.77	£ 7.85	24-02-98	16-03-03

- **CountOfISBN.** The number of records in the Books table.
- **SumOfCost.** The sum total of the values in the Cost field.
- **AvgOfCost.** The average of the values in the Cost field.
- **MinOfPurchaseDate.** The earliest date in the PurchaseDate field.
- **MaxOfPurchaseDate.** The latest date in the PurchaseDate field.

Why include the Books table in the query when you could use BooksConfidential.ISBN to count the books? Well, it is possible that some books would not have a record in BooksConfidential – for example, if they were donated and so had no PurchaseDate or Cost values. Using Books.ISBN to count the books covers this possibility.

Renaming fields in a query

In the previous exercise, Access automatically generated names for the calculated fields – a combination of the function name and field name. You can change these to more meaningful names in Design View.

In the *Field* row in the design grid, type the new name to the left of the field name, followed by a colon (:).

Field:	Number of Books: ISBN	Total Cost: Cost	Average Price: Cost	First Purchase: PurchaseDate	Last Purchase: PurchaseDate
Table:	Books	BooksConfidential	BooksConfidential	BooksConfidential	BooksConfidential
Total:	Count	Sum	Avg	Min	Max
Sort:					
Show:	☑	☑	☑	☑	☑

Design View

Datasheet View

Number of Books	Total Cost	Average Price	First Purchase	Last Purchase
56	£ 439.77	£ 7.85	24-02-98	16-03-03

Note that this changes only the name used as the column heading in Datasheet View. It does not change the actual field name.

Totalling groups of records

When totalling values, you will often want to see the totals for particular groups of records instead of for the entire table. For example, you might want the total cost of books for each publisher or for each book category.

To calculate totals for groups of records, you select the *Group By* option in the *Total* row for the field(s) on which you wish to group the records. When you group records by more than one field, Access groups records by values in the leftmost field(s) first.

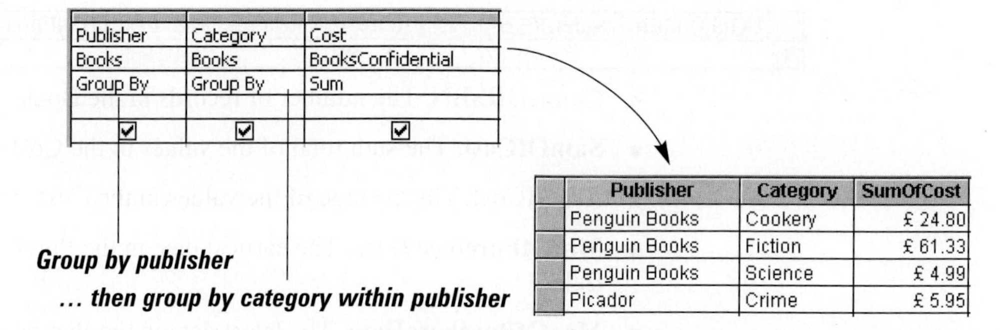

Publisher	Category	Cost
Books	Books	BooksConfidential
Group By	Group By	Sum
☑	☑	☑

Publisher	Category	SumOfCost
Penguin Books	Cookery	£ 24.80
Penguin Books	Fiction	£ 61.33
Penguin Books	Science	£ 4.99
Picador	Crime	£ 5.95

Exercise 8.2: Calculating totals for groups of records

In this exercise, you will create a query that displays the total number of books in each book category and the total, average, minimum and maximum cost of books in each category.

1) Open a new query in Design View. When prompted for the tables you want to include in the query, select Books and BooksConfidential.
2) Add the following fields to the design grid, in the order listed:
   - Books.Category (to group the records).
   - Books.ISBN (to count the records).
   - Four instances of BooksConfidential.Cost (to calculate the cost totals).
3) Click the **Totals** button to add the *Total* row to the design grid.
4) Rename the fields, and select a *Total* option for each field, as shown here:

Field:	Category	Quantity: ISBN	Total Cost: Cost	Avg Cost: Cost	Min Cost: Cost	Max Cost: Cost
Table:	Books	Books	BooksConfidential	BooksConfidential	BooksConfidential	BooksConfidential
Total:	Group By	Count	Sum	Avg	Min	Max
Sort:						
Show:	☑	☑	☑	☑	☑	☑

5) Save the query with the name BookCategoryTotals.

You can now run the query to see the results, which should be similar to those shown here.

Category	Quantity	Total Cost	Avg Cost	Min Cost	Max Cost
Biography	1	£ 12.75	£ 12.75	£ 12.75	£ 12.75
Children	6	£ 40.90	£ 6.82	£ 2.99	£ 18.99
Computers	3	£ 48.97	£ 16.32	£ 12.99	£ 18.99
Cookery	3	£ 48.78	£ 16.26	£ 5.99	£ 24.80
Crime	7	£ 33.93	£ 4.85	£ 2.09	£ 8.99
Fantasy	6	£ 36.74	£ 6.12	£ 4.99	£ 7.50
Fiction	25	£ 163.87	£ 6.55	£ 1.50	£ 13.60
Reference	1	£ 14.95	£ 14.95	£ 14.95	£ 14.95
Science	4	£ 38.88	£ 9.72	£ 4.99	£ 12.50

The Category column lists each book category. The Quantity field displays the number of books in each category. The remaining fields calculate totals for the cost of books in each category.

Using criteria in total queries

You can use criteria in total queries for three different purposes:

- To limit the records on which calculations are performed – for example, to calculate totals only for books that cost less than £20.
- To limit the groups on which calculations are performed – for example, to calculate totals only for Fiction, Fantasy and Crime books.
- To limit the records displayed based on the calculation results – for example, to display only groups where the total book cost is greater than £30.

Using multiple criteria

You enter selection criteria for a query in the *Criteria* and *Or* rows in the design grid. Criteria entered on different rows are combined using logical Or – that is, a record is selected if it satisfies *any* of the criteria. Criteria entered on the same row, but for different fields, are combined using logical And – that is, a record is selected only if it satisfies *all* the criteria.

You can, if you wish, combine different criteria in a single *Criteria* cell by including the logical operators in the criteria expression.

- Both the following examples select books published in 2000 by Penguin Books.

Field:	PublicationYear	Publisher
Table:	Books	Books
Sort:		
Show:	☑	☑
Criteria:	2000	"Penguin Books"
or:		

Field:	PublicationYear
Table:	Books
Sort:	
Show:	☑
Criteria:	2000 And [Publisher]="Penguin Books"

- This example selects books that are published either in 2000 or by Penguin Books or both.

Field:	PublicationYear	Publisher
Table:	Books	Books
Sort:		
Show:	☑	☑
Criteria:	2000	
or:		"Penguin Books"

- Both the following examples select books that are published in 2000 by either Puffin Books or Penguin Books.

Field:	PublicationYear	Publisher
Table:	Books	Books
Sort:		
Show:	☑	☑
Criteria:	2000	"Puffin Books"
or:	2000	"Penguin Books"

Field:	PublicationYear	Publisher
Table:	Books	Books
Sort:		
Show:	☑	☑
Criteria:	2000	"Penguin Books" Or "Puffin Books"

Limiting the records included in calculations

To limit the records on which a total calculation is performed:

1) Add to the design grid the field for which you wish to specify criteria. If you are also calculating a total for this field, you must add a second instance of the field for the calculation.

2) Select *Where* in the *Total* row for the field.

3) Enter your criteria for the field.

For example, when calculating totals for BooksConfidential.Cost, the criterion shown here specifies that only records where the cost is less than £20 are to be included in the calculation. To see this query in action, run the LimitRecords query.

Field:	Category	Cost	Cost
Table:	Books	BooksConfidential	BooksConfidential
Total:	Group By	Sum	Where
Sort:			
Show:	☑	☑	☐
Criteria:			<20

Before grouping or totalling, Access retrieves only books that cost less than £20

Note that Access always hides fields that have their *Total* row set to *Where*.

Limiting the groups on which calculations are performed

To limit the groups on which calculations are performed, you enter your selection criteria in the *Criteria* row(s) for the field(s) that define the groups.

For example, when grouping books by category and calculating total costs for each category, the criteria shown here specify that the calculations are to be performed only on the Fiction, Crime and Fantasy groups. To see this query in action, run the LimitGroups query.

Field:	Category	Cost	Cost
Table:	Books	BooksCo	BooksCo
Total:	Group By	Sum	Where
Sort:			
Show:	☑	☑	☐
Criteria:	"Fiction" Or "Crime" Or "Fantasy"		<20

Before totalling the cost, Access limits the groups to be totalled

Limiting the results to be displayed

To limit the records displayed by the query to those where a calculation result matches certain criteria, specify the criteria in the field that contains the calculation.

For example, when grouping books by category and calculating total costs for each category, the criteria shown here specify that the query is to return only those categories where the total cost is more than £50. To see this query in action, run the LimitResults query.

Field:	Category	Cost	Cost
Table:	Books	BooksConfi	BooksConfi
Total:	Group By	Sum	Where
Sort:			
Show:	☑	☑	☐
Criteria:	"Fiction" Or "Crime" Or "Fantasy"	>50	<20

After totalling the cost, Access returns only groups for which the total cost is over £50

Exercise 8.3: Specifying criteria for a total query

In this exercise, you will create a query that groups books by publisher, and for each publisher calculates the total cost of books in the 1990s. The query limits the results to publishers for which the total cost is more than £15.

1) Open a new query in Design View. When prompted for the tables you want to include in the query, select Books and BooksConfidential.
2) Add the following fields to the design grid in the order listed:
   - Books.Publisher (to group the selected records).
   - BooksConfidential.PurchaseDate (to select books bought in the 1990s).
   - BooksConfidential.Cost (to calculate the totals and specify the criteria those totals must satisfy).
3) Click the **Totals** button to add the *Total* row to the design grid.
4) Select *Where* in the *Total* row for the PurchaseDate field and enter the following criteria expression for that field:

   `Between #01-01-90# And #31-12-99#`
5) Select *Group By* in the *Total* row for the Publisher field.
6) Select *Sum* in the *Total* row for the Cost field and enter the following criteria expression for that field:

   >15

Field:	Publisher	PurchaseDate	Cost
Table:	Books	BooksConfidential	BooksConfidential
Total:	Group By	Where	Sum
Sort:			
Show:	☑	☐	☑
Criteria:		Between #01-01-90# And #31-12-99#	>15

7) Save the query with the name BookPublisherTotals.

You can now run the query to see the results, which should be similar to those shown here.

Publisher	SumOfCost
BBC Books	£ 17.99
Fourth Estate	£ 16.60
Penguin Books	£ 45.20
Virgin Publishing	£ 18.99

The Publisher column lists the Publishers for which the total cost of books bought in the 1990s was more than £15, and the SumOfCost column lists the total cost of those books for each publisher.

Using wildcards in queries

A wildcard character is a special character that takes the place of one or more other characters in a literal value.

You can use wildcards in query criteria to select values that match particular patterns of characters instead of specifying the values individually. For example, to select Publishers whose name begins with 'P', you could specify "P*" instead of "Penguin Books" Or "Puffin Books" Or "Picador". . ., and so on.

Wildcard

A special character that represents one or more other characters in a literal value.

Appendix A lists and explains the available wildcard characters. The following table presents some examples of using wildcard characters in query criteria.

Note that query criteria that include wildcard characters must be enclosed by double quotes, even when the values are numbers or dates. In addition, Access automatically adds the Like operator to criteria with wildcard characters (see Appendix A for details).

Field	Criteria	Result
Publisher	Like "P*"	Selects publishers whose name begins with the letter 'P'.
Publisher	Like "*Books"	Selects publishers whose name ends with the word 'Books'.
Publisher	Like "P[eu]*"	Selects publishers whose name begins with 'Pe' or 'Pu'. For example, Penguin Books and Puffin Books.
Publisher	Like "P[!eu]*"	Selects publishers whose name begins with 'P' and whose second letter is neither 'e' nor 'u'. For example, Picador.
Title	Like "*Potter*"	Selects titles that include the word 'Potter'. This would include the Harry Potter books and also 'From Potter's Field'.
PublicationYear	Like "200?"	Selects publication years from 2000 to 2009.
Cost	Like "*.99"	Selects cost values with 99 after the decimal point.
Cost	Like "*.9?"	Selects cost values with 90, 91, 92, and so on after the decimal point.
PurchaseDate	Like "??-??-0?"	Selects purchase dates in the years 2000 to 2009.

Note that you can use wildcard characters in any query, not just total queries.

About crosstab queries

A crosstab query is a special type of query that calculates totals for records that are grouped on more than one field and displays the results in a compact, spreadsheet-like format. For example, you could use a crosstab query to display the total number of books by category for each publisher.

Category groups

Publisher groups

Publisher	Children	Computers	Cookery	Crime	Fiction
Minerva					1
Pearson Education Ltd		3			
Penguin Books			1		10
Picador				1	2

Total for a particular publisher and category

The Publisher groups are displayed as row headings, the Category groups as column headings, and the totals are displayed in the intersection cells for each publisher and category.

You can use a standard total query to display the same data, as illustrated by the BooksByPublisherAndCategory query. If you run this query, you will get results similar to those shown here.

Publisher	Category	Count
Pearson Education Ltd	Compute	3
Penguin Books	Cookery	1
Penguin Books	Fiction	10
Penguin Books	Science	1
Picador	Crime	1
Picador	Fiction	2
Puffin Books	Children	2

In this case, both the Publisher and Category groups are displayed as row headings, with a separate record for each Publisher/Category combination. In this format, it is more difficult to compare the totals than it is in the corresponding crosstab query (CrosstabBooksByPublisherAndCategory).

The disadvantages of a crosstab query are that you can calculate only one total in the query and you cannot sort the results on the total values.

Crosstab query

A query that calculates totals for records that are grouped on more than one field and displays the results in a spreadsheet-like format.

Creating a crosstab query

You can create a crosstab query in Query Design View or by using the *Crosstab Query Wizard*. To include fields from more than one table when using the wizard, you must first create a query containing those fields and then use that query as the basis for the crosstab query.

Using the Crosstab Query Wizard

Exercise 8.4: Using the *Crosstab Query Wizard*

In this exercise you will create a crosstab query that groups books by publisher and category and calculates the total cost of books for each combination.

1) Click *Queries* in the *Objects* list in the Database window, click the **New** button on the window's toolbar, select the *Crosstab Query Wizard* option, and click **OK**.

2) When prompted for the table or query on which to base the new query, choose the PublisherCategoryCost query and then click **Next**.

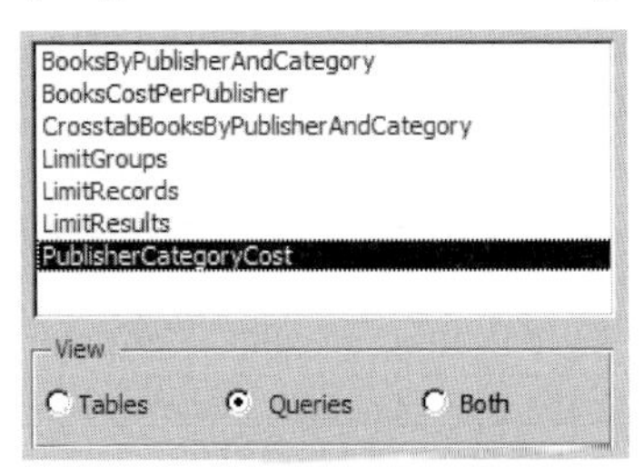

The PublisherCategoryCost query contains the Books.Publisher, Books.Category and BooksConfidential.Cost fields.

3) When prompted for the field whose values you want to use as row headings, select Publisher and click **Next**.

Note that the Sample in the lower part of each wizard window illustrates the result of your selection in that window.

4) When prompted for the field whose values you want to use as column headings, select Category and click **Next**.

5) When prompted for the calculation you want to perform, select *Sum*.

On the same page of the wizard, you are asked whether you want to summarize each row. The default is 'Yes', so leave this as it is. The results will include an overall total for each publisher, as well as category totals. Click **Next**.

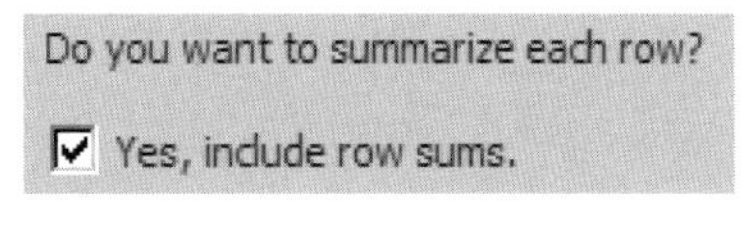

6) Finally, accept the default name for the query and click **Finish**.

The records displayed by the query should be similar to those shown here:

Publisher	Total Of Cost	Biography	Children	Computers	Cookery	Crime	Fantasy	Fiction	F
Anchor	£ 9.45							£ 9.45	
Arrow	£ 8.99					£ 8.99			
BBC Books	£ 17.99				£ 17.99				
Black Swan	£ 14.98							£ 14.98	
Blackstaff Press	£ 5.50							£ 5.50	
Bloomsbury	£ 24.43					£ 5.99	£ 18.44		
Collins	£ 14.48		£ 5.99				£ 6.99	£ 1.50	
Corgi Books	£ 5.99						£ 5.99		

The individual publishers are displayed as row headings on the left side of the datasheet. The categories are displayed as column headings. The intersection cell for each Publisher and Category displays the total cost of books for that Publisher/Category combination. In addition, there is a Total Of Cost column that displays a grand total for each publisher.

Using Query Design View

Now let's take a look at your crosstab query in Design View.

Field:	Publisher	Category	Cost	Total Of Cost: Cost
Table:	PublisherCategoryC	PublisherCategoryC	PublisherCategoryC	PublisherCategoryC
Total:	Group By	Group By	Sum	Sum
Crosstab:	Row Heading	Column Heading	Value	Row Heading
Sort:				
Criteria:				

The design grid includes a *Crosstab* row where you specify which fields contain the row headings, the column headings, and the calculated totals.

Note that you can include more than one row heading. In this example, the second row heading calculates the total cost of books from each publisher.

Exercise 8.5: Creating a crosstab query in Design View

In this exercise you will create a crosstab query that displays the number of books in each category that were purchased on a particular date.

1) Open a new query in Design View. When prompted for the tables to include in the query, select Books and BooksConfidential.
2) Add the following fields to the design grid, in the order listed:
   - BooksConfidential.PurchaseDate (to form the row headings).
   - Books.Category (to form the column headings).
   - BooksConfidential.ISBN (to count the records).
3) Choose **Query | Crosstab Query** to specify the query type. Both a *Total* row and a *Crosstab* row are added to the design grid.
4) For the field whose values you want displayed as row headings – PurchaseDate – select the *Row Heading* option in the *Crosstab* row. You must also select *Group By* in the *Total* row for this field.

5) For the field whose values you want displayed as column headings – Category – select the *Column Heading* option in the *Crosstab* row. You must also select *Group By* in the *Total* row for this field.

6) For the field whose values you want to total – ISBN – select the *Value* option in the *Crosstab* row and select the type of total you want to calculate in the *Total* row. Select *Count*.

Field:	PurchaseDate	Category	ISBN
Table:	BooksConfidential	Books	BooksConfidential
Total:	Group By	Group By	Count
Crosstab:	Row Heading	Column Heading	Value
Sort:			

7) Save the query with the name PurchaseDateCategoryCrosstab.

You can now run the query to see the results, which should be similar to those shown here.

PurchaseDate	Biography	Children	Computers	Cookery	Crime	Fantasy	Fiction	Reference	Science
24-02-98						1	4		
13-09-98		1		2	1	1	2		
03-04-99					1		4		1
07-07-99		3			1		3		1
01-05-00		1			2		3		
23-10-00				1	1		3		
19-04-01		1				1	3		

The individual purchase dates are displayed as row headings down the left side of the datasheet. The book categories are displayed as column headings. The intersection cell for each PurchaseDate/Category combination displays the number of books in that category that were purchased on that date.

Using criteria in crosstab queries

You can specify selection criteria for a crosstab query in the same way you do for other total queries. See 'Using criteria in total queries' above.

- To limit the records on which the total calculation is performed:
  1) Add to the design grid the field for which you wish to specify criteria.
  2) Select *Where* in the field's *Total* row.
  3) Enter your criteria for the field.
- To limit the row headings for which the calculation is performed, enter your criteria in the *Criteria* row for the field with *Row Heading* in its *Crosstab* row. For example, to include only purchase dates in the twenty-first century, enter the following expression in the PurchaseDate field's *Criteria* row:

  >=#01-01-00#

- To limit the column headings for which the calculation is performed, enter your criteria in the *Criteria* row for the field with *Column Heading* in its *Crosstab* row. For example, to include only the Fantasy and Fiction categories in the query, enter the following expression in the Category field's *Criteria* row:

```
Like "F*"
```

Chapter 8: summary

A *total query* uses functions such as Sum, Avg, Count, Max and Min to calculate and display summary field values. You can calculate totals for all records or for groups of records.

You can create total queries with the *Simple Query Wizard* or in Query Design View. In Design View you use the *Total* row options to specify the fields by which you want to group your records and the type of total calculation you want to perform for each field.

You use selection criteria in a total query to limit the records on which a total calculation is performed, to limit the groups on which it is performed, and to limit the results to be displayed.

A *crosstab query* calculates totals for records that are grouped on more than one field and displays the results in a compact, spreadsheet-like format. One group forms the row headings, another the column headings, and the total value for each row/column combination is displayed in the intersection cell for that row/column. You can specify criteria for crosstab queries in the same way you do for standard queries.

A *wildcard character* is a special character that represents one or more other characters in a literal value. You can use wildcards in query criteria to select values that match particular patterns of characters instead of specifying the values individually.

Chapter 8: quick quiz

Q1	Which of these total functions counts the number of values in a field?
A.	Sum.
B.	Max.
C.	Count.

Q2	True or false – with the *Simple Query Wizard* you can calculate totals for all records or for groups of records in a table/query.
A.	True.
B.	False.

Q3	You can specify criteria in a total query to ...
A.	Display only records where the calculation result satisfies certain criteria.
B.	Exclude certain records from the calculations.
C.	Calculate totals for certain groups only.

Q4	Which of these expressions selects all books that contain 'The' in the title?
A.	Like "*The".
B.	Like "The*".
C.	Like "*The*.
D.	Like "?The?".

Q5	True or false – you can use a single crosstab query to calculate the average and maximum cost of books for each publisher/category combination.
A.	True.
B.	False.

Q6 Which of the following query definitions calculates the total cost of books for each publisher by purchase date?

A.

Field:	PurchaseDate	Publisher	Cost
Table:	BooksConfidential	Books	BooksConfidential
Total:	Group By	Group By	Sum
Crosstab:	Row Heading	Column Heading	Value

B.

Field:	PurchaseDate	Publisher	Cost
Table:	BooksConfidential	Books	BooksConfidential
Total:	Group By	Group By	Sum
Crosstab:	Column Heading	Row Heading	Value

C.

Field:	PurchaseDate	Publisher	Cost
Table:	BooksConfidential	Books	BooksConfidential
Total:	Group By	Group By	Sum
Crosstab:	Row Heading	Row Heading	Value

Answers

1: C, **2**: A, **3**: All, **4**: C, **5**: B, **6**: A and B.

9 Query design: custom calculations

In this chapter

In the previous chapter you learned how to use Access's predefined aggregate functions to summarize field values in queries. In this chapter you will learn how to use your own custom calculations to define query criteria and to create calculated fields.

New skills

At the end of this chapter you should be able to:

- Use calculations in query criteria
- Create calculated fields
- Use aggregate functions in calculated fields

New words

In this chapter you will meet the following term:

- Calculated field

Exercise file

In this chapter you will work with the following Access file:

- Chp9_VillageLibrary_Database

Syllabus reference

In this chapter you will cover the following items of the ECDL Advanced Database Syllabus:

- **AM5.2.2.2**: Use functions in a query: sum, count, average, max, min.
- **AM5.2.2.5**: Use arithmetic, logical expressions in a query.

About custom calculations

A custom calculation uses arithmetic and/or logical expressions to perform calculations on values in one or more fields. You can use them to create new, calculated fields in a query – for example, DueDate (LoanDate plus 10) or FineDue (DaysOverdue multiplied by daily fine amount). You can also use custom calculations to specify query selection criteria.

The expressions can include one or more of the following operators (see Appendix A for more details):

- Arithmetic operators – that is, +, -, *, /.
- Aggregate functions – for example, Sum(), Avg() and Max().
- Logical functions – for example, IIf().

The values on which calculations are performed can be any of the following (see Appendix A for more details):

- Literal values – for example, 100, 2.5, 0.75.
- Field identifiers – for example, [Cost] and [ReturnDate].

The following table shows some examples of custom calculations.

Expression	Result
[Quantity] * [UnitPrice]	Calculates the total cost of an order by multiplying the unit price by the quantity ordered.
[DeliveryCharge]+ ([Quantity] * [UnitPrice])	Calculates the invoice amount by adding the delivery charge to the order value.
[Quantity]*[UnitPrice]*.95	Discounts the order amount by 5%.
Sum([Quantity]*[UnitPrice])	In a query grouped by customer, calculates the total value of each customer's orders.
([Bonus]/([Wages]+[Bonus]))* 100	Where total pay is the sum of wages and bonus, this calculates what percentage the bonus is of the total pay.
<Date()-30	As a query criterion, selects records where the date is more than 30 days earlier than the current date.
<#01/04/03# -30	As a query criterion, selects records where the date is more than 30 days earlier than 1 April 2003.

Note that field names must be enclosed within square brackets and expressions being evaluated by a function must be enclosed within parentheses. You also use parentheses to indicate the evaluation order of expressions.

Calculations as query criteria

You can use calculations as criteria for determining which records a query displays or performs an action on. The following exercise provides two examples.

Exercise 9.1: Using calculations in query criteria

In this exercise you will create a query that retrieves records for books that were returned late.

1) Open the starting database for this chapter:

   `Chp9_VillageLibrary_Database`

2) Open a new query in Design View. When prompted for the tables to include in the query, select Loans and Members.

3) Add the following fields to the design grid, in the order listed:

   – Loans.ISBN
   – Loans.LoanDate
   – Loans.ReturnDate
   – Members.MemLastname
   – Members.MemFirstname

4) In the *Criteria* row for the ReturnDate field, type the following:

   `>[LoanDate]+10`

Field:	ISBN	LoanDate	ReturnDate	MemLastname	MemFirstname
Table:	Loans	Loans	Loans	Members	Members
Sort:					
Show:	☑	☑	☑	☑	☑
Criteria:			>[LoanDate]+10		

   This limits the records retrieved to those where the return date is more than 10 days later than the loan date.

5) Switch to Datasheet View to confirm that the correct records have been retrieved.

Only books returned late are listed

ISBN	LoanDate	ReturnDate	MemLastname	MemFirstname
ISBN 0-00-671683-0	02-11-02	16-11-02	Long	April
ISBN 0-14-023171-4	19-11-02	01-12-02	Chase	Paul
ISBN 0-14-012670-8	19-11-02	01-12-02	Chase	Paul
ISBN 0-7088-8207-2	19-03-03	04-04-03	Mills	David
ISBN 0-14-023171-4	24-05-03	12-06-03	Woods	Richard
ISBN 0-14-012670-8	07-02-03	25-02-03	Worth	Richard
ISBN 0-14-014658-X	14-01-03	30-01-03	Reed	Susan

6) Switch back to Design View and replace the criteria expression with:

   `[ReturnDate]-[LoanDate]>10`

7) Switch to Datasheet View again and you will see that the results are the same.

8) Close the query without saving it.

Calculated fields

A calculated field is a query field that displays the result of a calculation on other fields in the query. For example, a calculated field named DueDate could calculate the due return date for a book by using the following expression:

```
[LoanDate]+10
```

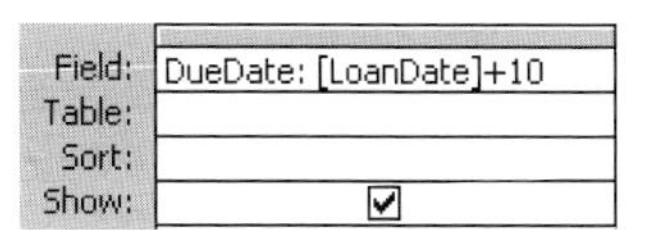

You create a calculated field by entering the field name and the required expression in the *Field* row of a blank column in the design grid. The example shown here creates the DueDate field.

Calculated fields are not stored in a database table. Instead Access reruns the calculation each time you run the query. To include calculated fields in a form or report, you can base the form or report on a query that contains those fields.

Calculated fields in the Village Library database

When library staff are processing book returns, they need to check if the books are overdue and to issue an appropriate fine if this is the case. This involves calculating the number of days that a book is overdue and then multiplying the result by the daily fine amount (£0.50).

Creating a query that includes the following fields would greatly facilitate this process.

Field	Description
DueDate	Members can borrow books for up to ten days. This calculated field displays the due date for borrowed books.
DaysOut	This calculated field displays the number of days that a book has been out on loan.
DaysOverdue	This calculated field displays the number of days by which a book is overdue (if any).
FineDue	The fine for overdue books is £0.50. This calculated field displays the amount due by multiplying the number of days overdue by 0.50.
FinePaid	Library staff have discretion to reduce fines in certain cases, so they must enter the actual amount paid manually in a table field where it can be stored for later analysis. FinePaid is that field.
Discount	This calculated field displays the percentage (if any) by which a fine was discounted.

The DueDate, DaysOut, FineDue and Discount fields involve straightforward calculations, as shown below.

Field	Expression
DueDate	[LoanDate]+10
DaysOut	[ReturnDate]-[LoanDate]
FineDue	[DaysOverdue]*0.5
Discount	(([FineDue]-[FinePaid])/[FineDue])*100

Calculating DaysOverdue, however, is more complicated, and requires use of the IIf() function.

Note that these calculations ignore books that have not yet been returned. You will learn how to deal with these in Chapter 10.

The IIf() function

For an overdue book, you can calculate DaysOverdue by subtracting 10 from DaysOut. For a book returned early or on time, however, this calculation returns a negative value, when what we want displayed is either zero or a blank field.

Basically we want Access to evaluate the result of the calculation before displaying it. Then if the result is greater than zero we want to display it, and if the result is zero or a negative value, we want to leave the field blank.

DaysOut	DaysOverdue
12	2
6	

Access provides the IIf() (or Immediate If) function to handle this type of situation – that is, to display one of two possible results depending on the evaluation of an expression. The IIf() function takes three arguments (that is, elements to which the function applies). Its syntax is:

```
IIf(expression, value_if_true, value_if_false)
```

where *expression* is the expression to be evaluated, *value_if_true* is the value to be displayed if the expression evaluates to true, and *value_if_false* is the value to be displayed if the expression evaluates to false.

In the case of the DaysOverdue field, we can use any of the following expressions to achieve the desired result:

```
IIf([DaysOut]>10,[DaysOut]-10,Null)
```

```
IIf([DaysOut]-10>0,[DaysOut]-10,Null)
```

```
IIf([ReturnDate]-[LoanDate]>10,[ReturnDate]-
[LoanDate]-10,Null)
```

The first example is the shortest and quickest. Access checks whether or not DaysOut is greater than ten (that is, whether the book is overdue). If it is, it calculates and displays the number of days overdue by subtracting ten from DaysOut. If it is not, it leaves the field blank.

Note that Null is a special value that indicates a blank field (see 'Null values' in Chapter 10). If you want DaysOverdue to display zero instead of Null, you would replace Null with 0 in the above expressions.

Creating calculated fields

You create a calculated field in a query by entering the field name and the required expression in the *Field* row of a blank column in the design grid.

Exercise 9.2: Creating calculated fields

In this exercise, you will create all the calculated fields described in 'Calculated fields in the Village Library database' above.

1) Open a new query in Design View. When prompted for the tables to include in the query, select Loans.
2) Add all fields from the table to the design grid.
3) Specify a sort order of *Descending* for the FinePaid field.
4) To create the DueDate field, insert a new column between the LoanDate and ReturnDate fields (click in the ReturnDate column and choose **Insert | Columns**). Then enter the following in the *Field* row of the new column:

   ```
   DueDate:[LoanDate]+10
   ```

   You can enter the expression directly in the *Field* cell, or you can display the *Zoom* dialog box and enter it there. The *Zoom* dialog box is the more flexible option, especially when entering or editing long expressions. To display the dialog box, click in the *Field* cell and press **Shift+F2**. When finished, close the dialog by clicking **OK.**
5) To create the DaysOut field, insert a new column after the ReturnDate field and enter the following in its *Field* row:

   ```
   DaysOut:[ReturnDate]-[LoanDate]
   ```
6) To create the DaysOverdue field, insert a new column after the DaysOut field and enter the following in its *Field* row:

   ```
   DaysOverdue:IIf([DaysOut]>10,[DaysOut]-10,Null)
   ```

7) To create the FineDue field, insert a new column after the DaysOverdue field and enter the following in its *Field* row:

```
FineDue:[DaysOverdue]*0.5
```

8) To create the Discount field, insert a new column after the FinePaid field and enter the following in its *Field* row:

```
Discount:(([FineDue]-[FinePaid])/[FineDue])*100
```

Field:	DueDate: [LoanDate]+10	ReturnDate	DaysOut: [ReturnDate]-[LoanDate]	DaysOverdue: IIf([DaysOut]>10,[DaysOut]-10,Null)
Table:		Loans		

9) Save the query with the name LoansExtended.

You can now run the query and see the results, which should be similar to those shown here. If you are prompted to enter a parameter instead, you have probably misspelled the name of a field in one of your calculations and should return to Design View and correct the mistake.

ISBN	MemID	LoanDate	DueDate	ReturnDate	DaysOut	DaysOverdue	FineDue	FinePaid	Discount
ISBN 0-1	39	07-02-03	17-02-03	25-02-03	18	8	4	£ 4.00	0
ISBN 0-1	28	24-05-03	03-06-03	12-06-03	19	9	4.5	£ 4.00	11.11111111
ISBN 0-1	16	14-01-03	24-01-03	30-01-03	16	6	3	£ 3.00	0
ISBN 0-7	24	19-03-03	29-03-03	04-04-03	16	6	3	£ 3.00	0
ISBN 0-1	23	14-04-03	24-04-03	30-04-03	16	6	3	£ 2.50	16.66666667
ISBN 0-3	43	21-01-03	31-01-03	05-02-03	15	5	2.5	£ 2.50	0
ISBN 0-1	26	30-01-03	09-02-03	13-02-03	14	4	2	£ 2.00	0

The calculated fields should be displaying the correct calculated values. However, you need to adjust the formatting of the FineDue and Discount fields. You will do this in the next exercise.

Changing calculated field properties

When you include a table field in a query, it inherits the properties defined for it in the table – for example, Format, Decimal Places and Input Mask. With a calculated field, however, there is no table field from which to inherit properties. Instead you can set the field's properties by using the **Properties** button on the *Query Design* toolbar. You can also use this option to change a table field's properties – the changes apply only to the query in which they are made.

Exercise 9.3: Changing calculated field properties

In this exercise, you will change the format of the FineDue field to Currency, and you will change the format of the Discount field to Percent.

Properties button

1) Open the LoansExtended query in Design View.
2) Click in the FineDue column and click the **Properties** button on the toolbar. This displays the *Field Properties* dialog box.

3) Select the *Currency* option in the *Format* property.

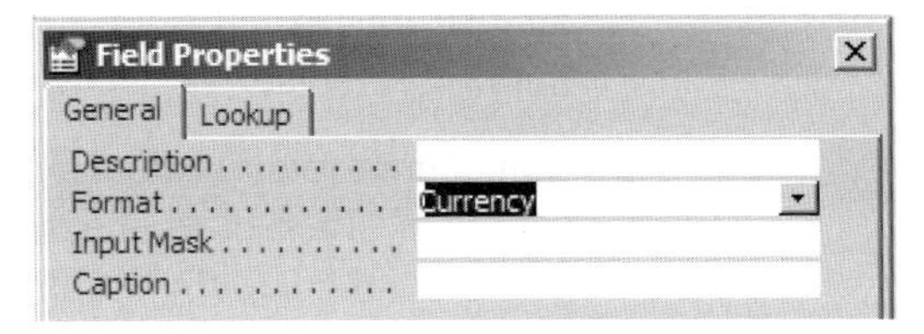

4) Click in the Discount column. That field's properties are now displayed in the *Field Properties* dialog box. Select *Percent* in the *Format* property.

5) When you apply a *Percent* format to a field, Access multiplies values in the field by 100 and appends a percent sign (%). The expression you used to create the Discount field also multiplies the values by 100. To avoid multiplying by 100 twice, change the expression to:

```
Discount:([FineDue]-[FinePaid])/[FineDue]
```

6) Save the query and then switch to Datasheet View to see the result of your changes. Both FineDue and Discount values are now more appropriately formatted.

FineDue	FinePaid	Discount
£ 4.00	£ 4.00	0.00%
£ 4.50	£ 4.00	11.11%
£ 3.00	£ 3.00	0.00%
£ 3.00	£ 3.00	0.00%

You could refine the Discount field still further by hiding all zero discount values. To do this you would change the field expression to:

```
Discount:IIf(([FineDue]-[FinePaid])=0,Null,
(([FineDue]-[FinePaid])/[FineDue]))
```

Sorting, totalling and defining criteria for calculated fields

Once you have set up the fields you want to include in a query, there are several design grid options that you can use to control the query output:

- **Sort**. You can use the *Sort* options to sort the records on one or more fields.
- **Show**. You can use the *Show* row to specify which fields to show or hide in the results.
- **Total**. You use the *Total* options to summarize the records.
- **Criteria**. You can enter selection criteria to limit the records that the query displays.

All these options are available for calculated fields, but with limitations:

- You cannot sort or specify criteria for calculated fields that reference another calculated field. For example, you can sort and specify criteria for DueDate but not DaysOverdue.

- You cannot hide a calculated field if it is referenced by another calculated field. For example, you can hide Discount but not FineDue.
- You cannot total a calculated field if it references another calculated field or includes the IIf() function. For example, you can calculate the minimum and maximum dates in DueDate but you cannot calculate the average value in DaysOverdue.

These appear to be serious limitations but there is a simple solution. Instead of specifying your sort orders, criteria, and so on in the original query, create a new query based on the original query and specify your sort orders, criteria and totalling requirements in this new query.

The SummaryOverdueBooks query provides an example of this type of query. If you open this query in Design View, you will see how it is defined.

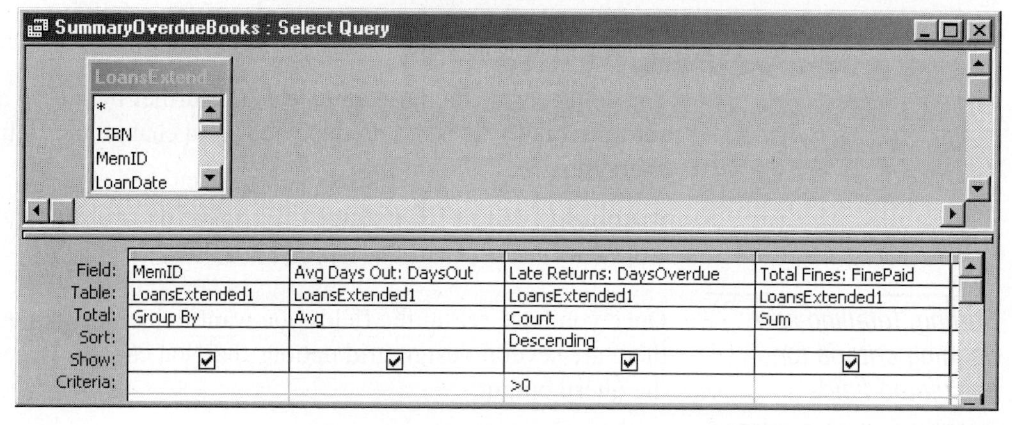

- The query is based on the LoansExtended1 query, which is a predefined version of your LoansExtended query.
- For each member, it calculates the average number of days they have had any books out on loan, the number of times that they have returned books late, and the total fines they have paid.
- It then groups records by MemID and limits the results to members who have returned books late on one or more occasions.
- The results are sorted by DaysOverdue in descending order.

If you run the query, the results should resemble those shown below.

MemID	Avg Days Out	Late Returns	Total Fines
9	8.75	2	£ 2.00
32	9.83	2	£ 2.00
23	9.00	1	£ 2.50
7	9.50	1	£ 2.00

Note that when you base a new query on an existing query, calculated fields in the new query do not inherit the properties set for those fields in the original query. You must reset them in the new query.

Using aggregate functions in calculated fields

The expression for a calculated field can include aggregate functions such as Sum() and Avg(). For example, the following calculated field returns the average daily fine paid for overdue books.

```
Daily Fine:Avg([FinePaid]/[DaysOverdue])
```

When calculated fields contain aggregate functions, you must display the *Total* row in the design grid and select *Expression* as the *Total* option for those fields. If there are other calculated fields in the query you must then select *Expression* in their *Total* rows also; you can leave the *Total* setting for non-calculated fields as *Group By*. This is not necessary if the calculated field(s) are the only fields in the query.

Field:	ISBN	MemID	LoanDate	ReturnDate	DaysOut: [ReturnDate]-[LoanDate]	FinePaid	Daily Fine: Avg([FinePaid]/[DaysOverdue])
Table:	Loans	Loans	Loans	Loans		Loans	
Total:	Group By	Group By	Group By	Group By	Expression	Group By	Expression
Sort:						Descending	
Show:	☑	☑	☑	☑	☑	☑	☑

Chapter 9: summary

Custom calculations in a query use arithmetic and logical expressions to perform calculations on values in one or more fields. You can use them to create new, calculated fields and to specify record selection criteria.

A *calculated field* is a query field that displays the result of a calculation on other fields in the query. You create a calculated field by entering the field name and the required expression in the *Field* row of a blank column in the query design grid. The field name must be immediately followed by a colon (:). You can change the properties of a calculated field in the same way you change the properties of other fields in a query – use the **Properties** button on the *Query Design* toolbar.

Calculated fields are not stored in a database table. Instead Access reruns the calculation each time you run the query.

You can use the IIf() function in a calculated field when you want Access to display different results depending on whether a particular condition is true or false. You can also use aggregate functions in a calculated field.

You can sort, total, and specify criteria for calculated fields, but there are limitations. When you want to perform these operations on calculated fields, it is often preferable to create the calculated fields in one query and then specify the sort orders, criteria, and total calculations in another query that is based on the original query.

Chapter 9: quick quiz

Q1	True or false – a calculated field can include more than one calculation.
A.	True.
B.	False.

Q2	Which of the following are valid calculated fields?
A.	DaysOverdue:[ReturnDate]-[LoanDate]>10
B.	DaysOverdue:[DaysOut]>10
C.	DaysOverdue:[DaysOut]-10

Q3	Which of these calculated fields displays Yes if a book was returned late and No if it was not?
A.	Overdue:IIf([DaysOut]>10,"No","Yes")
B.	Overdue:IIf([ReturnDate]-[LoanDate]>10,"Yes","No")
C.	Overdue:IIf([DaysOut]>10,"Yes","No")

Q4	For which of these calculated fields can you specify selection criteria?
A.	`DaysOut:[ReturnDate]-[LoanDate]`
B.	`DaysOverdue:[ReturnDate]-[DueDate]`
C.	`Overdue:IIf([ReturnDate]-[LoanDate]>10, "Yes","No")`
D.	`Overdue:IIf([DaysOut]>10,"Yes","No")`

Q5	True or false – the following is a valid calculated field: `AvgDaysOut:Avg([ReturnDate]-[LoanDate])`
A.	True.
B.	False.

Q6	True or false – you can sort and specify criteria for any calculated field in a query.
A.	True.
B.	False.

Answers

1: A, **2**: C, **3**: B and C, **4**: A and C, **5**: A, **6**: B.

10 Query design: refining queries

In this chapter

In this chapter you will learn various ways in which you can refine your queries and control their output.

New skills

At the end of this chapter you should be able to:

- Understand and use Null values
- Show and hide duplicate records and values
- Find unmatched records and values
- Display the highest or lowest range of values in a field
- Create and use parameter queries

New words

In this chapter you will meet the following terms:

- Null
- Duplicate record
- Unique record
- Unmatched record
- Top values
- Parameter query

Exercise file

In this chapter you will work with the following Access file:

- `Chp10_VillageLibrary_Database`

Syllabus reference

In this chapter you will cover the following items of the ECDL Advanced Database syllabus:

- **AM5.2.3.1**: Show duplicates.
- **AM5.2.3.2**: Show unmatched values.
- **AM5.2.3.3**: Show highest, lowest range of values in a query.
- **AM5.2.3.4**: Allow query input from a data prompt (parameter query).
- **AM5.2.3.5**: Refining queries using Null and NOT values.

Null values

Null is a special value that indicates missing or unknown data, or a field to which data is not applicable. Access automatically enters a Null value when you leave a field blank.

DueDate	ReturnDate	DaysOut	DaysOverdue	FineDue
05-12-02	01-12-02	6		
13-07-03				
29-11-02	01-12-02	12	2	£ 1.00
24-04-03	19-04-03	5		

All blank fields here contain Null values

Missing ***Unknown*** ***Not applicable***

Primary key fields cannot contain Null values and you can prevent other fields from accepting Null values by setting their *Required* property to Yes (see 'Required values' in Chapter 4).

You can use Null values in query criteria and calculated field expressions by entering the keyword **Null**. But Nulls have some special properties that can affect your query results.

- You cannot use the equal to (=) and not equal to (<>) operators with the Null keyword. For example, [ReturnDate]=Null is not a valid expression. Instead you must use the Is Null and Is Not Null operators or the IsNull() function (see below).
- Aggregate functions ignore Null values. For example, the result of an Avg() calculation is based only on fields with non-Null values. To include Null values in this type of calculation, you must first convert the Null values to zeros (see 'Nz() function' below).

  To include Null values when counting records, you can use Count(*) instead of Count().
- Expressions that include arithmetic operators (+, -, *, /) always return a Null value if any of the fields in the expression contain a Null value.

  For example, [OrderAmount]+[Freight] returns Null if there is no freight charge. To prevent this happening you can convert all Null values in the Freight field to zeros before performing the calculation (see 'Nz() function' below).
- When you use the criteria expression Like "*" for a field, the query does *not* return records that contain Nulls in that field.

Null

A special value (displayed as a blank field) that indicates missing or unknown data, or a field to which data is not applicable.

Is Null and Is Not Null operators

Is Null and Is Not Null are comparison operators that mean 'is equal to Null' and 'is not equal to Null' respectively.

Specifying Is Null as the selection criteria for a field returns all records where that field contains a Null value; specifying Is Not Null returns all records where the field does not contain a Null value.

For example, the BooksOnLoan query in `Chp10_VillageLibrary_Database` lists the books that are currently out on loan. If you open the query in Design View, you will see that the Is Null operator has been entered as the criteria for the ReturnDate field. This tells Access to display only records where the ReturnDate field is empty – that is, books that have been borrowed but not yet returned.

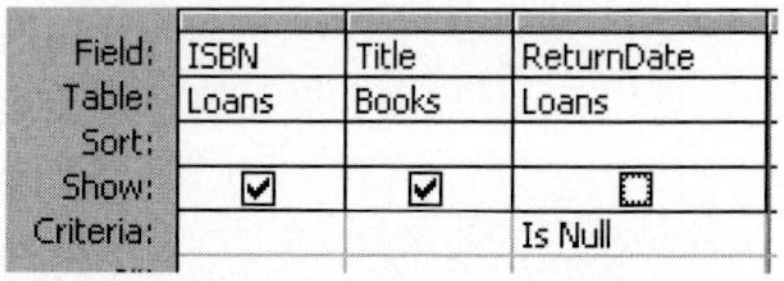

Field:	ISBN	Title	ReturnDate
Table:	Loans	Books	Loans
Sort:			
Show:	☑	☑	☐
Criteria:			Is Null

IsNull() function

IsNull() is a function that tests whether a value is Null. It is typically used in calculated fields in combination with the IIf() function.

Remember that the IIf() function returns one of two possible results depending on the evaluation of an expression. You can use the IsNull() function as the expression and so display one result if a field is Null and a different result if the field contains a non-Null value.

For example, take an InvoiceAmount field that is calculated as the sum of OrderAmount and Freight:

```
InvoiceAmount:[OrderAmount]+[Freight]
```

If no freight is being charged on an order, this calculation evaluates to Null because the freight value is Null. One way to overcome this problem is to use this expression instead:

```
InvoiceAmount:IIf(IsNull([Freight]),[OrderAmount],
[OrderAmount]+[Freight])
```

The IsNull([Freight]) expression tests whether the Freight value is Null. If it is, then the IIf() function returns the OrderAmount value. If it is not, then the IIf() function returns the sum of OrderAmount and Freight.

Exercise 10.1: Using the IsNull() function in calculated fields

In this exercise you will modify the LoansExtended query to include a new field: Overdue. This is a Yes/No field that indicates whether or not a book is overdue. Then you will change the expression in the DaysOverdue field so that it can handle books that have not yet been returned.

1) Open the LoansExtended query in Design View.

2) Take a look at the expression for the DaysOverdue field:

   ```
   DaysOverdue:IIf([DaysOut]>10,[DaysOut]-10,Null)
   ```

   If a book is overdue, the field displays the number of days that it is overdue. If a book is not overdue, the field displays Null. So to create an Overdue field that indicates whether or not a book is overdue, you can use the following expression:

   ```
   Overdue:IIf(IsNull([DaysOverdue]),"No","Yes")
   ```

3) Add a new column to the left of the DaysOverdue column, and create the Overdue field by using the above expression.

4) Save the query and then run it.

DueDate	ReturnDate	DaysOut	Overdue	DaysOverdue
29-11-02	01-12-02	12	Yes	2
29-11-02	01-12-02	12	Yes	2
13-03-03	14-03-03	11	Yes	1
23-07-03			No	

   Notice that 'No' has been entered for all books that have not yet been returned, even if they are overdue.

   Why? Because DaysOut is calculated by subtracting LoanDate from ReturnDate. For fields with no return date, this calculation returns Null, and this Null carries through to the DaysOut, DaysOverdue and Overdue fields, resulting in a 'No' value in the latter.

5) You need to modify the query to address this problem. Switch back to Design View and take a look at the expression in the DaysOut field.

   ```
   DaysOut:[ReturnDate]-[LoanDate]
   ```

   This calculates the number of days out, but only for books that have a ReturnDate value. For books that have not yet been returned, the calculation should be:

   ```
   Date()-[LoanDate]
   ```

   To enable the DaysOut field to handle both calculations, you need an IsNull() function to test whether ReturnDate is Null and an IIf() function so that one calculation is performed when ReturnDate is Null and the other is performed when ReturnDate is not Null. The appropriate expression is:

```
DaysOut:IIf(IsNull([ReturnDate]),Date()-
[LoanDate],[ReturnDate]-[LoanDate])
```

6) Replace the current definition of the DaysOut field with the new one shown above.
7) Save the query and then run it to see the result of your changes.

DueDate	ReturnDate	DaysOut	Overdue	DaysOverdue	FineDue
11-07-03		20	Yes	10	£ 5.00
11-07-03		20	Yes	10	£ 5.00
01-07-03	27-06-03	6	No		
11-07-03		20	Yes	10	£ 5.00

This time books that have not yet been returned are included in all the calculations. When a book is returned and a return date entered, the query will recalculate the calculated fields for that record.

Note that when you run the query, the results differ from those shown above. This is because, for books not yet returned, the value of DaysOut depends on the value returned by Date(), which is always the current date.

Nz() function

Expressions that include arithmetic operators always return Null if one of the fields in the expression contains a Null value. In a previous example, the following expression was used in an InvoiceAmount field to overcome the problem of Null freight values:

```
InvoiceAmount:IIf(IsNull([Freight]),[OrderAmount],
[OrderAmount]+[Freight])
```

But there is a shorter way to achieve the same result. This involves using the Nz() function.

The Nz() (or Null to Zero) function converts Null values to zeros before performing a calculation, so the results will never be Null. The syntax for the function is as follows:

```
Nz(expression,value_if_null)
```

where *expression* is the field or expression you want converted when it evaluates to Null and *value_if_null* is the value (typically 0) to which you want to convert Null values.

In the case of the InvoiceAmount field, you can use the following expression to overcome the problem of Null Freight values:

```
InvoiceAmount:[OrderAmount]+Nz([Freight],0)
```

Now when Freight contains a Null value, the Null is converted to zero before Freight is added to OrderAmount. This produces the desired result without having to use the IIf() function.

Duplicate records and values

Duplicate records are records that contain identical values in all their fields. Unique records are records that contain different values in at least one field.

By definition, values in the primary key field of a table must be unique, so a table with a primary key will contain only unique records. However, a query may return duplicate records if it doesn't include the primary keys of the tables on which it is based.

For example, this query here displays the MemLastname and MemTown fields from the Members table. Because some members share the same last name and address, the results include several duplicate records.

Turner	Belmount
White	Belmount
White	Belmount
White	Belmount
Woods	Newtown
Worth	Castletown
Worth	Castletown

Access provides the following features for working with duplicate records:

- *Find Duplicates Query Wizard*
- *Unique Values* property
- *Unique Records* property

Find Duplicates Query Wizard

The *Find Duplicates Query Wizard* enables you to find duplicate records in a table or query. You can use it to find entire duplicate records in a table. However, you are more likely to use it to find records that share the same value(s) in one or more fields. For example:

- Find all library members who live at the same address. In Chapter 6, you used a self join in a query to find this information. Using the *Find Duplicates Query Wizard* is a much simpler option.
- Find all books that have been borrowed more than once.
- Find all books that have been borrowed more than once by the same member.
- Find all books in a particular category that have been borrowed more than once.

To include fields from more than one table in the query, you must first create a query that includes those fields and then base the *Find Duplicates Query* on that query.

Exercise 10.2: Finding duplicate values in table fields

In this exercise you will create a query that lists all books that have been borrowed more than once.

1) Click the *Queries* option in the *Objects* list in the Database window, click the **New** button on the window's toolbar, select the *Find Duplicates Query Wizard* option, and click **OK**.

2) When prompted for the table or query in which you wish to search for duplicate field values, choose the Loans table and click **Next**.

3) When prompted for the field(s) that you want to check for duplicate values, choose ISBN and click **Next**.

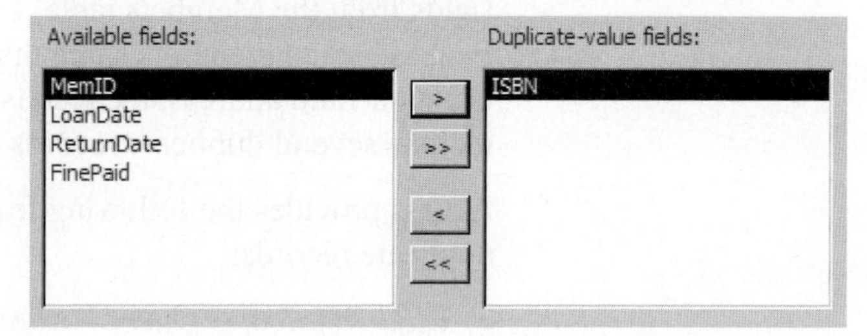

4) The wizard than asks you whether you want to include additional fields in the query, other than the ones with duplicate values:

   – If you don't select a field here, the query results will group records that have duplicate values in the field(s) specified in step 3 and display the number of duplicates in each group.

   – If you do select additional fields, the query results will display the records individually.

   For this exercise, you don't need additional fields, so just click **Next**.

5) When prompted to name the query, enter DuplicateLoanISBNs and click **Finish**.

ISBN Field	NumberOfDups
ISBN 0-00-6122	5
ISBN 0-00-7129	2
ISBN 0-099-283	4
ISBN 0-130-384	2

The query results display the ISBN value for each book that has been borrowed more than once and the number of times each of those books has been borrowed.

To see how the query works, switch to Design View. Notice that the design grid includes three instances of Loans. ISBN:

Field:	ISBN Field: ISBN	NumberOfDups: ISBN	ISBN
Table:	Loans	Loans	Loans
Total:	First	Count	Group By
Sort:			
Show:	☑	☑	☐
Criteria:		>1	

- **ISBN.** This instance is used to group records in the Loans table by ISBN value.
- **NumberOfDups.** This instance is used to count the number of records in each ISBN group and to limit the query results to those groups where the count is greater than one.
- **ISBN Field.** This instance is used to retrieve and display the ISBN value from the first record in each group.

To find all books that have been borrowed more than once by the same member, you would follow exactly the same procedure but select the MemID field as well as the ISBN field in step 3 of Exercise 10.2. The results would be similar to those shown here.

ISBN Field	MemID Field	NumberOfDups
ISBN 0-14-0390	41	2
ISBN 0-85640-0	32	2

Exercise 10.3: Including additional fields in a Find Duplicates Query

In this exercise you will create a query that lists all addresses where more than one member lives and the names of those members.

1) Start the *Find Duplicates Query Wizard*.
2) When prompted for the table or query in which you wish to search for duplicate field values, choose the Members table and click **Next**.
3) When prompted for the field(s) that you want to check for duplicate values, choose MemAddress and then click **Next**.
4) When prompted to select additional fields, choose MemFirstname and MemLastname and then click **Next**.
5) When prompted for a name for the query, enter DuplicateMemAddresses, and click **Finish**.

The query results display all addresses that are shared by more than one member and the names of those members. The following is an extract from those results.

MemAddress	MemFirstname	MemLastname
21 West Drive	Annabel	Worth
21 West Drive	Richard	Worth
28 Knightstown	David	Mills
28 Knightstown	Jennifer	Mills
Halfway House	Rodney	Black
Halfway House	Judith	Gibbs

To see how the query works, switch to Design View. In this case, a *subquery* is used to achieve the desired results. A subquery is a select query that is contained within another select query. You do not need to know about subqueries for ECDL.

Unique Values and Unique Records properties

By default, Access queries display all records retrieved by a query, including duplicates. If you want to omit duplicates, use one of the following query properties:

- **Unique Values**. Omits records with duplicate values in all fields displayed by the query, even if those records refer to different records in the underlying data source.

  For example, this query here is designed to show the range of book categories published by each publisher. The initial results include many duplicate records, representing individual books that share the same publisher and category. But if you set the *Unique Values* property, the query omits all but one of the records with duplicate values in the displayed fields.

Publisher	Category
Pearson Education Ltd	Computers
Pearson Education Ltd	Computers
Pearson Education Ltd	Computers
Penguin Books	Fiction
Penguin Books	Fiction
Penguin Books	Cookery
Penguin Books	Fiction
Penguin Books	Fiction

Unique Values not used

Publisher	Category
Pearson Education Ltd	Computers
~~Pearson Education Ltd~~	~~Computers~~
~~Pearson Education Ltd~~	~~Computers~~
Penguin Books	Fiction
~~Penguin Books~~	~~Fiction~~
Penguin Books	Cookery
~~Penguin Books~~	~~Fiction~~
~~Penguin Books~~	~~Fiction~~

Unique Values used

- **Unique Records**. Omits duplicates that represent the same record in the underlying data sources of a query. This property has an effect only when a query is based on more than one table and only if it displays fields from some, *but not all*, of those tables.

  For example, the following query is designed to list books that have been borrowed at least once. The initial results include many duplicates, representing books that have been borrowed many times. But if you set the *Unique Records* property, the query omits all but one of the duplicates that represent the same book.

ISBN	Title
ISBN 0-14-062010-9	Emma
ISBN 0-14-062010-9	Emma
ISBN 0-297-81410-9	The Man in the Ice
ISBN 0-297-81410-9	The Man in the Ice
ISBN 0-09-175208-6	An Evil Cradling
ISBN 0-552-13107-5	Sourcery
ISBN 0-552-13107-5	Sourcery

Unique Records not used

ISBN	Title
ISBN 0-14-062010-9	Emma
~~ISBN 0-14-062010-9~~	~~Emma~~
ISBN 0-297-81410-9	The Man in the Ice
~~ISBN 0-297-81410-9~~	~~The Man in the Ice~~
ISBN 0-09-175208-6	An Evil Cradling
ISBN 0-552-13107-5	Sourcery
~~ISBN 0-552-13107-5~~	~~Sourcery~~

Unique Records used

Unique Values and *Unique Records* are mutually exclusive options. For most queries to which *Unique Records* is applicable, using *Unique Values* produces the same results, but with one difference – queries that use *Unique Records* are updateable, while queries that use *Unique Values* are not.

What is an updateable query?

An updateable query is one that allows you to edit the records it returns. The changes are applied to the underlying table(s).

In general, single-table queries are updateable, as are multi-table queries based on tables with one-to-one relationships. Multi-table queries based on tables with one-to-many relationships are usually updateable but there are restrictions.

No query is updateable if it groups records, contains an aggregate function, or uses the Unique Values *property.*

Exercise 10.4: Using *Unique Records* and *Unique Values*

The UniqueValuesRecords query displays the publisher and category for all books that have been borrowed at least once. In this exercise, you will apply the *Unique Records* and *Unique Values* properties to see the different results that are returned by the query in each case.

1) Open the UniqueValuesRecords query in Design View.

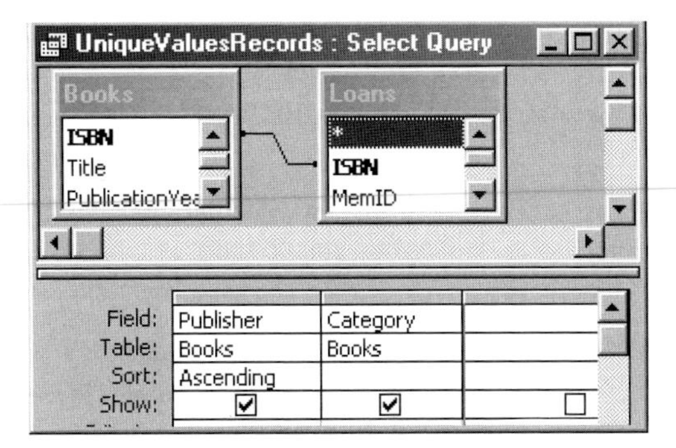

As you can see, the query includes the Books and Loans tables, related by an inner join on their ISBN fields. So the query compares values in the two ISBN fields and returns a record for each match found. For each record returned it then displays the Publisher and Category values.

2) Run the query and you will see that 131 records are displayed, including many duplicates. Basically, the query returns publisher and category details for each book loan. Some duplicates represent different books that have the same publisher and category. Others represent separate loans of the same book.

For example, a computer book from Pearson Education has been borrowed on five occasions. But we don't know whether these records represent the same or different books.

Publisher	Category
Pearson Education Ltd	Computers
Pearson Education Ltd	Computers
Pearson Education Ltd	Computers
Pearson Education Ltd	Computers
Pearson Education Ltd	Computers

3) Now let's see what effect the *Unique Values* and *Unique Records* properties have on the query. Switch back to Design View and open the *Query Properties* dialog box (click a blank part of the field list area and click the **Properties** button in the toolbar).

4) Select the *Yes* option in the *Unique Records* property.

5) Run the query. Only 46 records are now displayed, but there are still some duplicates. So which duplicates have been omitted?

   Remember that *Unique Records* omits duplicates that represent the same record in the underlying data source. So, in this query all duplicates that represent the same book are omitted. For example, the results now include three records for computer books published by Pearson Education. This indicates that three *different* computer books from that publisher have been borrowed at some time.

Publisher	Category
Pearson Education Ltd	Computers
Pearson Education Ltd	Computers
Pearson Education Ltd	Computers

6) Now switch back to Design View and set the *Unique Values* property to *Yes* (Access automatically sets the *Unique Records* property to *No* when you do this).

7) Run the query again. This time only 30 records are displayed and there are no duplicates.

Publisher	Category
Minerva	Fiction
Pearson Education Ltd	Computers
Penguin Books	Cookery

   Remember that *Unique Values* omits all but one of the records that have duplicate values in the displayed fields – that is, all records with the same publisher and category values. So the results include only one record for computer books by Pearson Education. This indicates that at least one computer book by that publisher has been borrowed at some time.

8) Close the query, saving it as you do.

Unmatched records

Most multi-table queries display results based on matching values in related tables. If, instead, you want to find the records in one table that have *no* matching records in another table, you can use the *Find Unmatched Query Wizard*. For example:

- Find all books that have never been borrowed.
- Find all members that have never borrowed a book.
- Find all books that were not borrowed in a particular time period.

Using the Find Unmatched Query Wizard

Exercise 10.5: Finding unmatched records

In this exercise you will use the *Find Unmatched Query Wizard* to create a query that lists the books that have never been borrowed.

1) Click the *Queries* option in the *Objects* list in the Database window, click the **New** button on the window's toolbar, select the *Find Unmatched Records Query Wizard* option, and click **OK**.
2) The first page of the wizard prompts you for the table that contains the unmatched records you want to view. You are looking for records in the Books table that have no matching records in the Loans table, so select the Books table and click **Next**.

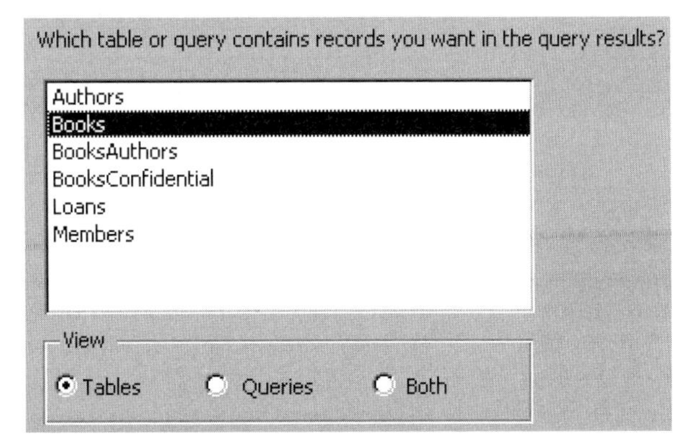

3) The second page prompts you for the related table. You are looking for books that have no entries in the Loans table, so select the Loans table and click **Next**.
4) The third page prompts you to select the field on which the two tables are joined. Select the ISBN field in both lists and click the <=> button. Then click **Next**.

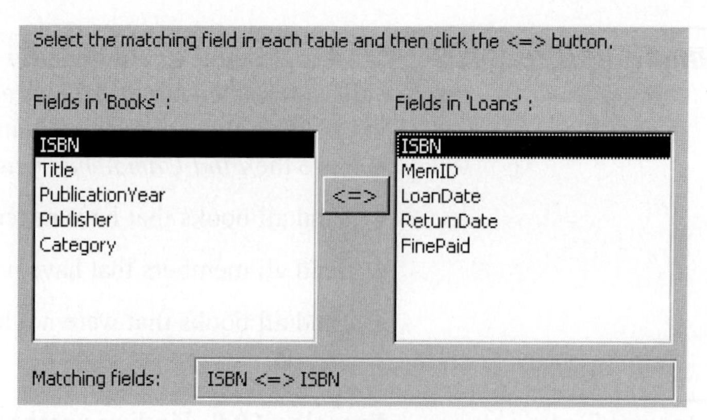

5) The fourth page prompts you for the fields that you want to display in the query results. Select ISBN, Title and Category and then click **Next**.

6) When prompted to name the query, enter BooksWithoutLoans and click **Finish**.

ISBN	Title	Category
ISBN 0-7171-1738-3	A Simply Delicious Christmas	Cookery
ISBN 0-283-06145-6	New Guide to the Planets	Science
ISBN 0-600-30451-5	The Adventurous Four	Children
ISBN 0-7548-0731-2	The New Guide to Cat Care	Referenc
ISBN 0-09-926855-8	Music & Silence	Fiction
ISBN 0-7088-2639-3	The Devil's Novice	Crime
ISBN 0-552-99702-1	A Walk in the Woods	Fiction
ISBN 0-451-16776-7	Feeling Good: The New Mood Ther	Science
ISBN 0-099-93072-0	Fatal Voyage	Crime
ISBN 0-14-012389-X	Love in the Time of Cholera	Fiction

The query results list all records in the Books table for which there are no matching records in the Loans table – that is, all books that have never been borrowed.

Unmatched Records queries in Design View

To see how the BooksWithoutLoans query works, open it in Design View and take a look at it there.

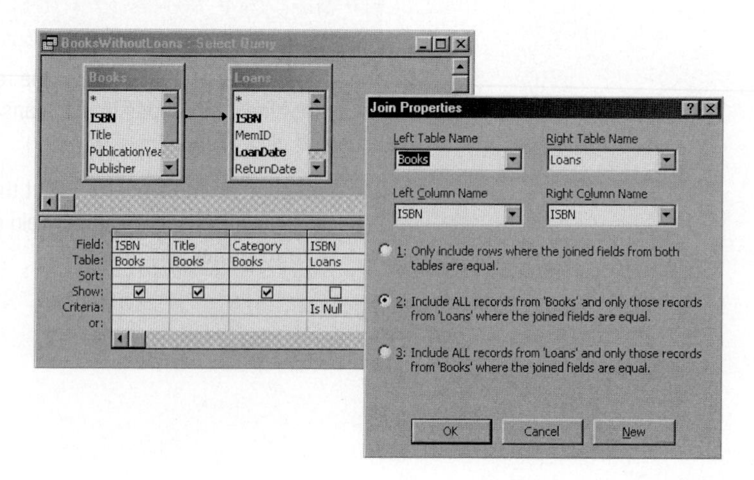

- Notice that the Books and Loans tables have been joined with a left outer join (option 2) so that the query returns all records from the Books table but only matching records from the Loans table. For books with no matching records in the Loans table, the fields from the Loans table will be blank – that is, they will contain a Null value. (See 'Left outer joins' in Chapter 6.)
- The records that have Null values in their Loan fields are the ones you are interested in, as they represent books that have never been borrowed. So, to limit the results to just those records, the query includes the Loans.ISBN field in the design grid and specifies Is Null as its selection criterion.

With the *Find Unmatched Records Wizard* you can't display fields from more than one table. For example, in the previous exercise, you couldn't include the author name in the query results. If you want to do this, you can use either of the following methods:

- Create a query that contains all the fields you want to display and base the BooksWithoutLoans query on that query, as shown here.

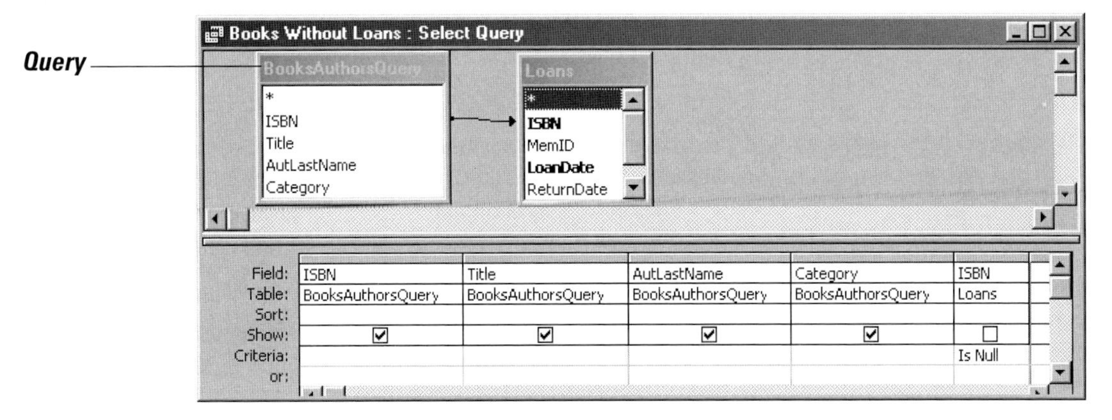

- Create the BooksWithoutLoans query as you did in Exercise 10.5 and then modify it in Design View, as shown here.

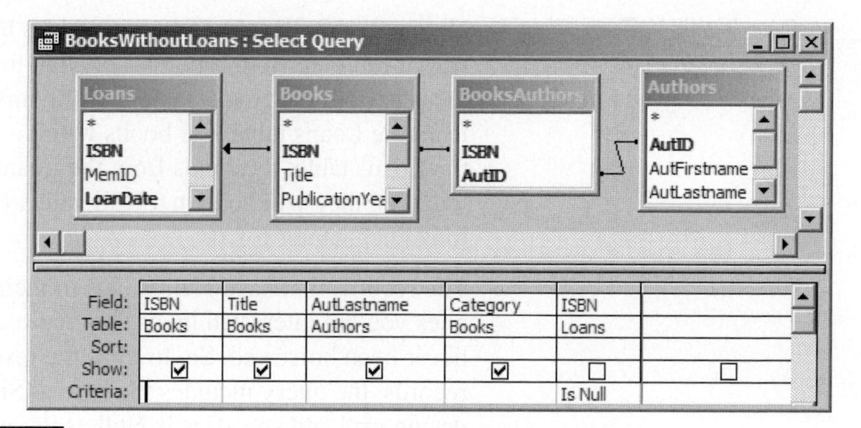

Unmatched values

Earlier in this chapter you learnt that you can use the Is Not Null operator in query criteria to exclude all records that contain a Null value in a particular field. To exclude records based on specific non-Null values you use the Not operator instead.

For example, to retrieve all books *not* published by Penguin Books, you would specify the following criterion for the Publisher field:

```
Not "Penguin Books"
```

The following table shows some examples of the Not operator in query criteria.

Field	Criteria	Result
Publisher	Not "P*"	Selects records where the publisher name does not begin with 'P'.
PublicationYear	Not 20??	Selects publication years that are not in the range 2000 to 2099.
ReturnDate	Not ([LoanDate]+10))	Selects return dates that are not the same as the due date.
Category	Not("Fiction" Or "Fantasy")	Selects all categories except Fiction and Fantasy.

Highest and lowest values

You can use a query's *Top Values* property to display a particular number or percentage of the records retrieved by the query – for example, to display only the first ten records retrieved. This property is particularly useful when used with sorted fields.

For example, if you set a descending sort order for the BooksConfidential.Cost field in a query, the most expensive books are displayed first in the results. If you also set the *Top Values* property to three, the query displays only the three most expensive books. If you specify an ascending sort order instead, the query displays the three cheapest books.

Books in descending order of cost

ISBN	Title	Cost
ISBN 0-718-14439-2	The Return of the Naked Chef	£ 24.80
ISBN 0-130-38486-0	ECDL 3 The Complete Courseboo	£ 18.99
ISBN 1-85613-666-3	A Children's Treasury of Milligan	£ 18.99
ISBN 0-563-36249-9	Delia Smith's Complete Cookery C	£ 17.99
ISBN 0-130-98984-3	ECDL Advanced Word Processing	£ 16.99
ISBN 0-7548-0731-2	The New Guide to Cat Care	£ 14.95
ISBN 0-571-20408-2	The History of the Kelly Gang	£ 13.60
ISBN 0-130-98983-5	ECDL Advanced Spreadsheets	£ 12.99
ISBN 0-09-175208-6	An Evil Cradling	£ 12.75
ISBN 0-297-81410-9	The Man in the Ice	£ 12.50

ISBN	Title	Cost
ISBN 0-718-14439-2	The Return of the Naked Chef	£ 24.80
ISBN 0-130-38486-0	ECDL 3 The Complete Courseboo	£ 18.99
ISBN 1-85613-666-3	A Children's Treasury of Milligan	£ 18.99

Top three records only

You can set the *Top Values* property in a query's property sheet or by using the *Top Values* box on the *Query Design* toolbar.

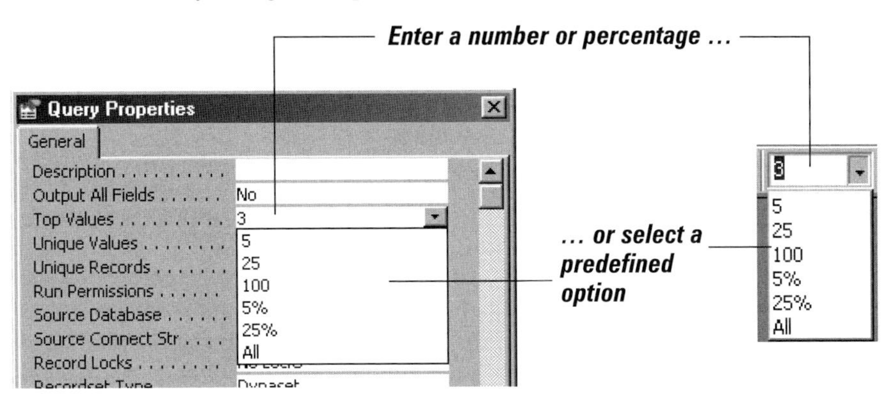

Exercise 10.6: Using the *Top Values* property

In this exercise you will create a query that displays the five most popular books in the library. You will do this by counting the number of times each book has been borrowed, sorting on this value in descending order, and limiting the results to five records.

1) Open a new query in Design View. When prompted for the tables to include in the query, select Loans and Books.
2) Add the following fields to the design grid, in the order listed here:
   - Loans.ISBN (to group all loans of the same book)
   - Books.Title
   - Loans.ISBN (to count the number of records in each group)
3) Change the name of the second instance of the ISBN field to Total Loans.
4) Click the **Totals** button in the *Query Design* toolbar to display the *Total* row in the design grid.
5) Select *Count* as the *Total* option for the Total Loans field and select *Descending* as its *Sort* option. Your query should now look like this:

Field:	ISBN	Title	Total Loans: ISBN
Table:	Loans	Books	Loans
Total:	Group By	Group By	Count
Sort:			Descending
Show:	☑	☑	☑

6) Set the query's *Top Values* property by typing 5 in the *Top Values* box on the *Query Design* toolbar and pressing **Enter**.

7) Save the query with the name TopFiveBooks and then run it.

ISBN	Title	Total Loans
ISBN 0-552-99893-1	Chocolat	8
ISBN 0-330-28414-2	The Name of the Rose	7
ISBN 0-7475-3007-6	Snow Falling On Cedars	7
ISBN 1-85702-242-4	The Shipping News	6
ISBN 0-571-20408-2	The History of the Kelly Gang	6

The five records displayed are those that have been borrowed the most number of times.

How does Access know that it is the Total Loans field whose top values you want to view? Because that is the field on which the results are sorted. If you are sorting on more than one field, the field whose top values you want to view must be the leftmost of those fields.

Note that when you specify a number (instead of a percentage) in the *Top Values* property, the query does not always display exactly that number of records. If the value of the top values field in the last record is shared by other records, those records are also displayed. For example, if more than two records have been borrowed six times, the TopFiveBooks query will display all those records and not just the first two.

Parameter queries

Up until now you have always entered your selection criteria for a query in the design grid. With a parameter query, however, Access instead prompts you for the criteria when you run the query. This means that you can use the same query to retrieve different information.

For example, the BooksInCategory query is designed to list the books in any specified category. When you run the query, Access prompts you for the category you want to view.

Try it and see what happens! Access prompts you to enter a category and then displays all books in that category.

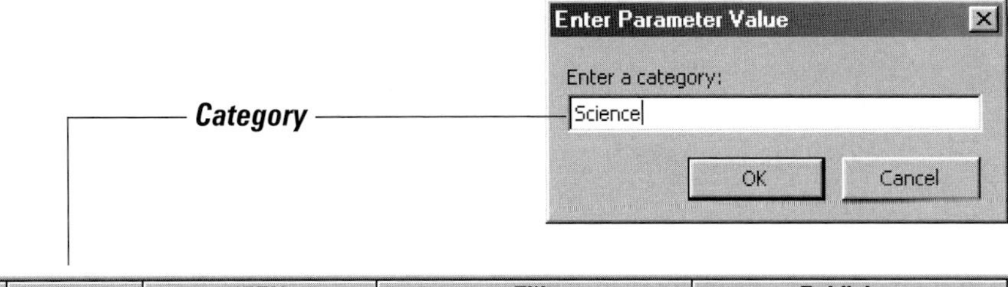

Category	ISBN	Title	Publisher
Science	ISBN 1-85702-712-4	Galileo's Daughter	Fourth Estate
Science	ISBN 0-283-06145-6	New Guide to the Planets	Sidgwick & Jackson
Science	ISBN 0-297-81410-9	The Man in the Ice	Weidenfeld and Nicholson
Science	ISBN 0-451-16776-7	Feeling Good: The New Mood	Penguin Books

You could also use a parameter query in the Village Library database to:

- Display the books by any specified author.
- Display the total cost of books in any specified category.
- Display the total cost of books in any specified category *and* from any specified publisher.
- Display the books still out on loan to any specified member.
- Display the books borrowed in any specified date range.

Parameter query

A query that prompts for record selection criteria when the query is run.

Creating a parameter query

To create a parameter query, you enter a parameter in the *Criteria* cell of a field instead of entering specific criteria. The parameter acts as placeholder for the actual criteria entered when the query is run. It consists of the text of the prompt to be displayed enclosed within square brackets.

For example, in the BooksInCategory query, '[Enter a category:]' has been entered as a parameter for the Books.Category field.

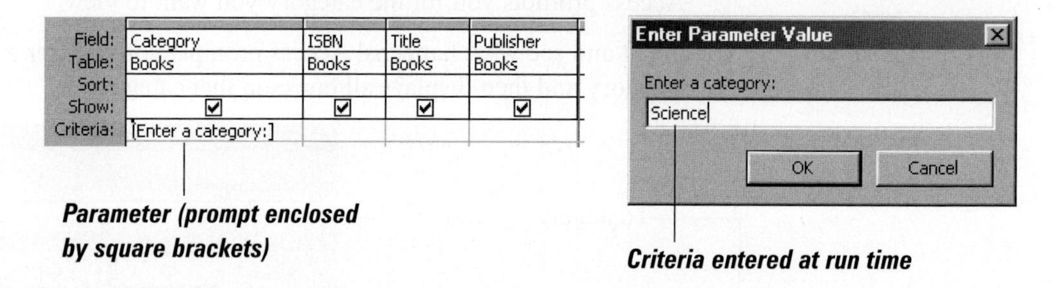

When you run the query, Access prompts you for a category and then uses the value you enter as the query criteria. Basically, Access substitutes the parameter in the query with the value that you enter at the prompt.

You can enter a parameter almost anywhere in criteria where you would normally enter a text string, a number, or a date. And you can include more than one parameter in a query. Access displays multiple prompts in the order that they appear in the design grid.

Exercise 10.7: Creating a parameter query

In this exercise you will convert the LoansExtended query to a parameter query. The modified query will prompt for a member's first name and last name and then display the loan records for that member.

1) Open the LoansExtended query in Design View and add the Members table to the query (choose **Query | Show Table** and then select the table in the normal way).

2) Add the Members.MemFirstname and Members.MemLastname fields to the right of the MemID field in the design grid.

3) Enter the following parameters in the *Criteria* rows for the MemFirstname and MemLastname fields respectively:

```
[Enter first name:]
[Enter last name:]
```

MemFirstname	MemLastname
Members	Members
☑	☑
[Enter first name:]	[Enter last name:]

4) Use the **File | Save As** command to save the query with the name LoansByMember and then run the query.

   Access prompts you for a first name and then for a last name. If you enter 'April' and 'Long', for example, the query returns all the loan records for April Long, as shown here.

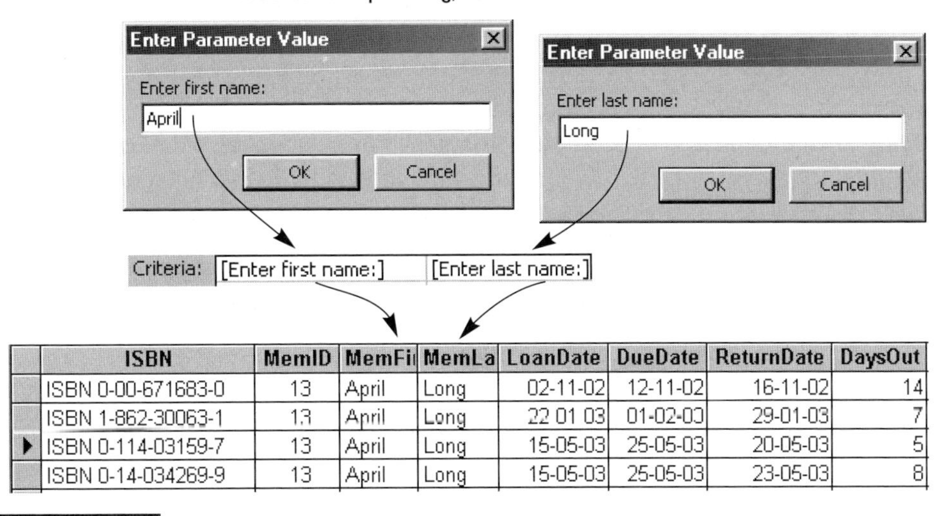

ISBN	MemID	MemFi	MemLa	LoanDate	DueDate	ReturnDate	DaysOut
ISBN 0-00-671683-0	13	April	Long	02-11-02	12-11-02	16-11-02	14
ISBN 1-862-30063-1	13	April	Long	22-01-03	01-02-03	29-01-03	7
ISBN 0-114-03159-7	13	April	Long	15-05-03	25-05-03	20-05-03	5
ISBN 0-14-034269-9	13	April	Long	15-05-03	25-05-03	23-05-03	8

Prompting for a date range

When you want to use a date range as the selection criteria for a query, you typically use the Between … And … operator. For example:

```
Between #01-01-02# And #31-12-02#
```

With a parameter query you can prompt for the start and end dates in the range instead of specifying them in the query.

For example, the LoansInPeriod query displays the loan records for books borrowed in any specified date range. Open that query in Design View and you will see that the *Criteria* row for the Loans.LoanDate field contains the following expression:

```
Between [Enter start date:] And [Enter end date:]
```

The expression includes two parameters instead of the start and end dates of a date range. When you run the query, Access prompts you for the dates that you want to use and then returns all records where the LoanDate value is in that range.

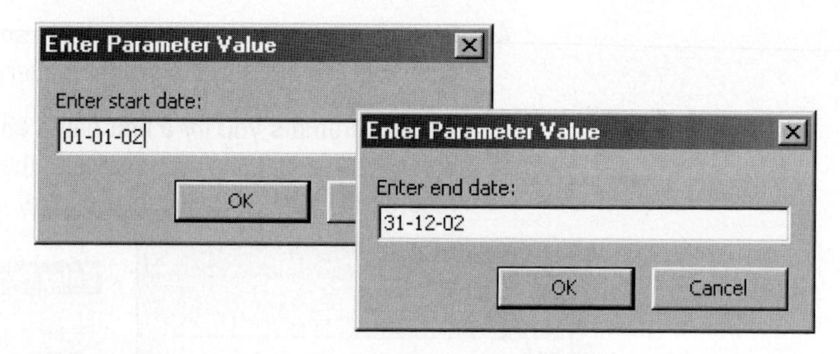

Using wildcards in parameters

Adding parameters to a query creates a more flexible query. Combining wildcards with the parameters creates a yet more flexible query again.

With a standard query you can retrieve all books in a category that begins with 'F' by entering the following criteria expression for the Books.Category field.

```
Like "F*"
```

With a parameter query you can retrieve all books where the category value begins with any character(s) entered by the user. To create this query you would enter the following criteria expression for the Books.Category field:

```
Like [Enter a category:] & "*"
```

Then if the user enters 'C' at the prompt, the query retrieves all books in the Children, Computer, and Cookery categories. And if the user enters 'Co', the query retrieves all books in the Computer and Cookery categories, and so on.

To retrieve records that include the entered characters *anywhere* in their Category value, use the following criteria expression:

```
Like "*" & [Enter a category:] & "*"
```

To retrieve records where the category value *ends with* the characters entered at the prompt, use the following criteria expression:

```
Like "*" & [Enter a category:]
```

Returning all records with a parameter query

When you combine the asterisk (*) wildcard with a parameter, entering nothing at the prompt retrieves all records where the parameter field does not contain Null. This is the same as entering "*" as the field criteria.

If you want to retrieve records that contain Null in the parameter field as well, you must add the following Or expression:

`[parameter] Is Null`

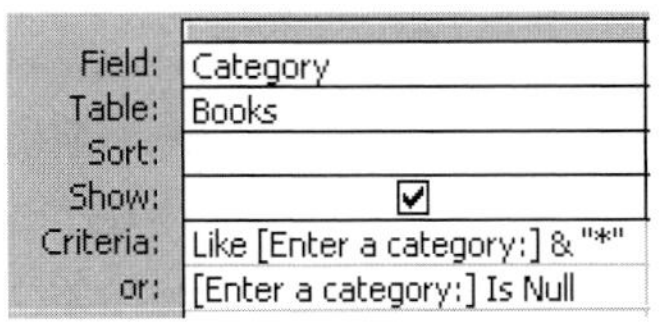

In the case of the BooksInCategory query, for example, entering nothing at the prompt will return all records, including those with Null values, if you enter the criteria shown here.

Chapter 10: summary

Null is a special value that indicates a missing, unknown, or inapplicable value. Access automatically enters a Null value when you leave a field blank. You can use Null values in query criteria and calculated fields but remember that aggregate functions ignore Null values, and expressions that use arithmetic operators always return Null if one of the fields in the expression contains Null.

You can use the Is Null operator in criteria expressions to select only records that contain Null in a particular field, and you can use the Is Not Null operator to select only records that contain non-Null values.

You can use the IsNull() function in calculated fields to test for Null values. Typically you use this function in combination with the IIf() function. You can use the Nz() function to convert Null values to zeros before performing a calculation.

A *duplicate record* is one that contains identical values to another record in all its fields. You can use the *Find Duplicates Query Wizard* to find duplicate records in a table or query and to find records that have the same values in selected fields. You use a query's *Unique Values* property to omit records that have duplicate values in the fields displayed by the query. You use the *Unique Records* property to omit duplicates that represent the same record in the underlying data source.

An *unmatched record* is one that has no matching record in a related table. You can use the *Find Unmatched Query Wizard* to find unmatched records.

In a query that specifies a sort order on a field, you can use the *Top Values* property to return a specified number or percentage of the highest or lowest values in that field.

A *parameter query* is a query that prompts for record selection criteria when you run the query. This allows you to use the same query to retrieve different information.

Chapter 10: quick quiz

Q1	True or false – an arithmetic expression always returns Null if one of the fields in the expression contains a Null value.
A.	True.
B.	False.

Q2	Which of these criteria expressions returns only records that contain Null in the criteria field?
A.	`IsNull()`
B.	`IsNull([ReturnDate])`
C.	`Is Null`

Q3	True or false – you use the *Unique Records* property to omit records that have duplicate values in the fields displayed by a query.
A.	True.
B.	False.

Q4	To display fields from two tables in a query you create with the *Find Unmatched Records Wizard*, you ...
A.	Create a query that contains all the fields you want to display and base the *Find Unmatched Records* query on that query.
B.	Select the two tables and the required fields in the wizard.
C.	Create the query and then modify the query in Design View to include the records from the second table.

Q5	To display the ten earliest publication years for books in the library, you ...
A.	Set the PublicationYear field's *Top Values* property to 10.
B.	Select a descending sort order for the PublicationYear field and set the query's *Top Values* property to 10.
C.	Select an ascending sort order for the PublicationYear field and set the query's *Top Values* property to 10.

Q6	Which of these criteria in the LoanDate field creates a query that allows users to enter a number (*n*) and then lists all books that were borrowed in the previous *n* days?
A.	`Date() - [Enter a number of days:]`
B.	`<=Date() - [Enter a number of days:]`
C.	`>=Date() - [Enter a number of days:]`

Answers

1: A, **2**: C, **3**: B, **4**: A and C, **5**: C, **6**: C.

11 Form design: controls

In this chapter

Forms are the main means of adding and editing data in a database. All information in a form is contained in controls such as labels, text boxes, list boxes and checkboxes. In this chapter you will learn about the most common form controls, when to use them, and how to create them.

New skills

At the end of this chapter you should be able to:

- Create text box, combo box, list box, checkbox and option group controls
- Create bound and unbound controls
- Create a record selector control
- Set the tab order for a form
- Add controls to form headers and footers

New words

In this chapter you will meet the following terms:

- Control
- Bound control
- Unbound control
- Tab order

Exercise file

In this chapter you will work with the following Access file:

- `Chp11_VillageLibrary_Database`

Syllabus reference

In this chapter you will cover the following items of the ECDL Advanced Database Syllabus:

- **AM5.3.1.1**: Create bound and unbound controls.
- **AM5.3.1.2**: Create, edit a combo box, list box, checkbox, option group.
- **AM5.3.1.4**: Set sequential order of controls on a form.
- **AM5.3.1.5**: Insert data field to appear within form header, footers on the first page or all pages.

About controls

A control is a graphical object that you place on a form to display data, to accept data input, to perform an action, or simply for decorative purposes.

Control types

The following list describes the controls that you need to know about for ECDL. You can see examples of these controls in the BookLoans form in the `Chp11_VillageLibrary_Database` database. If you open that form now you can try out each control as you read through the descriptions.

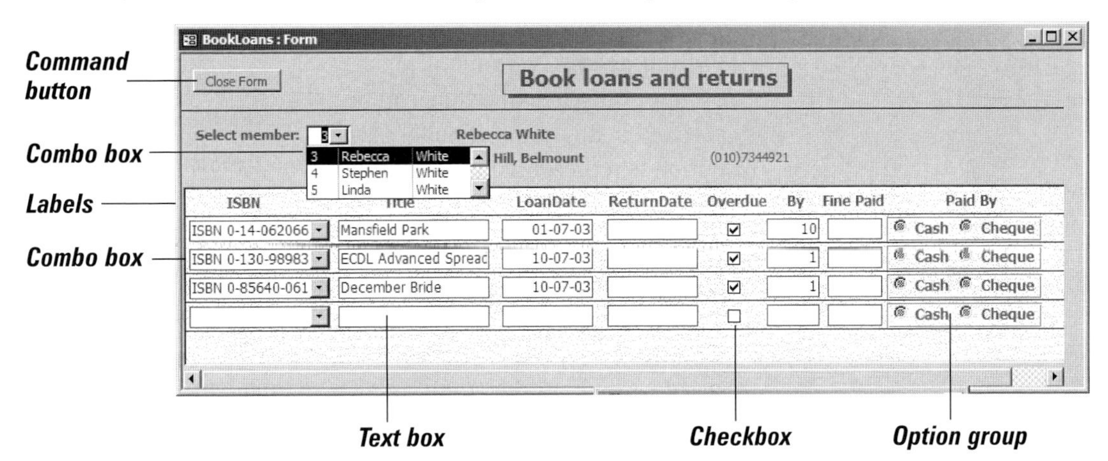

- **Label**. Displays descriptive text such as titles, headings, and instructions. By default, all controls that you add to a form have an attached label control.

  Loan Date: 05-05-03
  Label *Text box*

- **Text box**. Displays data from a table or query field and accepts input to that field. Text boxes can also display the results of calculations. In the BookLoans form, the member name, book title and loan date fields all use text box controls.

- **List box**. Displays a list from which users select a value. The list is always open, so this type of control is normally used only for short lists. Combo boxes are a more compact and flexible alternative.

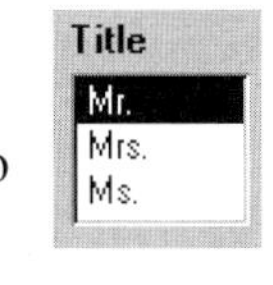

- **Combo box**. Combines a text box, where users can type a value, and a drop-down list box, where users can select a value instead. The list opens only when you click the down arrow in the control. In the BookLoans form, Select Member and ISBN are examples of combo box controls.

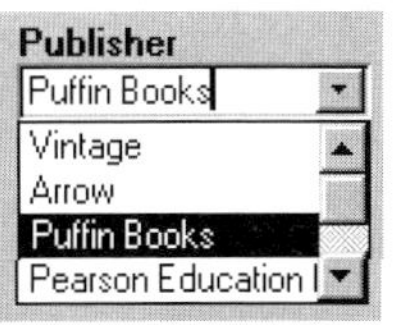

- **Checkbox**. A box that represents a Yes/No choice. Typically, checkboxes are used as stand-alone controls, with each checkbox representing a Yes/No choice that is independent of any other Yes/No choices. In the BookLoans form, Overdue is an example of a checkbox control.

☑ Overdue

- **Option button**. A small circle that represents a Yes/No choice. A blank circle represents a 'No' value; a small dot in the circle represents a 'Yes' value. Option buttons typically form part of an option group.
- **Option group**. A group of related options, only one of which can be selected at any time. Typically each option is represented by an option button control. Use option groups to present a few options only. If there are a large number of options, use a list box or combo box instead. In the BookLoans form, Paid By is an example of an option group.

Option group — Title: Mr. / Mrs. / Ms.
Option button

- **Command button**. A button control that starts an action or set of actions. In the BookLoans form, the Close Form button is an example of a command button. Clicking it closes the form. See Chapter 15 for further details.

Form control

A graphical object that you place on a form to display data, to accept data input, to perform an action, or simply for decorative purposes.

Bound and unbound controls

The tables and/or queries that provide the data for a form are referred to as the form's *record source*. The form is said to be *bound* to that record source. The form's controls can be either *bound* or *unbound*:

- A *bound control* is linked to a field in the form's record source. You use bound controls to display, enter, and update values in table or query fields.

  For example, in the BookLoans form, the ISBN, Title and Return Date controls are bound to fields in the LoansExtended query and can be used to add and edit values in those fields.

- An *unbound control* is not linked to a field in the form's record source. You use unbound controls, for example, to display descriptive text and to perform calculations and display their results. You cannot use an unbound control to update field values.

  In the BookLoans form, the form title and field labels are unbound. Overdue and By are also unbound, their data sources being calculated expressions.

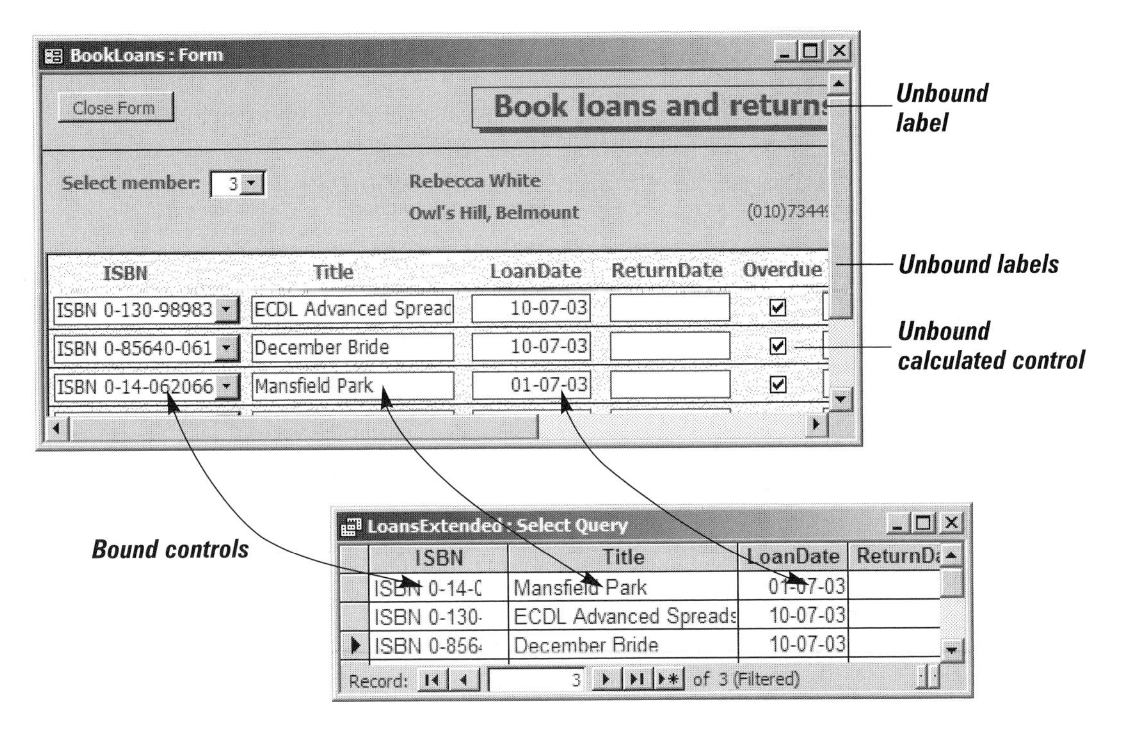

While most control types can be bound or unbound, only labels, text boxes and combo boxes are really useful for unbound data.

Record source

The table or query from which a form gets its data and whose fields it updates.

Bound control

A control that gets its values from a field in the form's record source and that you can use to update values in that field.

Unbound control

A control that is not linked to a table/query field. You can use unbound controls to display informational text, graphics and the results of calculations.

Form design tools

When you use a wizard to create a form, Access automatically creates controls for all the form fields. When you create a form in Design View you must create the controls manually, but you can choose the types of control to use and their content, layout and formatting.

Form Design View provides several design tools to help you create your forms, as shown here:

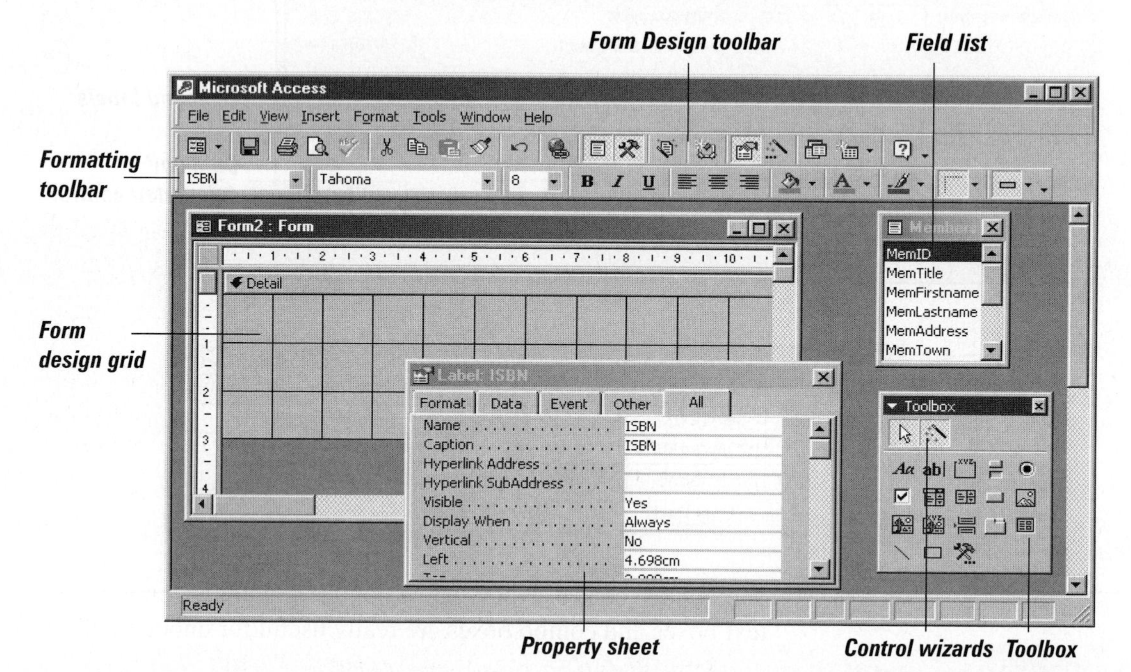

Before you create a form, let's take a look at how you use each of these tools. If you open the DesignToolsPractise form, you can experiment with each design tool as you read the descriptions.

Design grid

This is where you place a form's controls and arrange their layout. The grid lines provide a useful guide for aligning controls. The content and layout of the design grid correspond to the content and layout of the form you are creating.

- To change the height or width of a form, drag the bottom or right border of the design grid until it is the size you want.

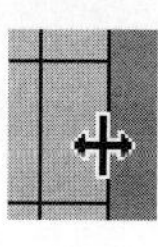

Field list

This lists all fields in the form's record source and you use it to add bound fields to a form. You can show or hide the list by clicking the **Field List** button on the *Form Design* toolbar.

- To add a bound field to a form, simply drag the field from the field list to the required position in the design grid.

  Access creates an appropriate control for the field, based on the field's data type. In most cases it creates a text box control. However, for a Yes/No or Lookup field it creates the control type specified by the field's *Display Control* property (see 'Lookup fields' in Chapter 4).

  By default, a label control is created for each field you add to the design grid.

- To add a block of fields to the design grid, click the first field in the block, hold down the **Shift** key, click the last field in the block, and then drag the fields to the design grid.

- To add several nonadjacent fields, hold down the **Ctrl** key, click each field to be added, and then drag to the design grid.

Toolbox

This provides tools for creating all types of form controls. You can show or hide the toolbox by clicking the **Toolbox** button on the *Form Design* toolbar. The following are the tools that you need to know about for ECDL.

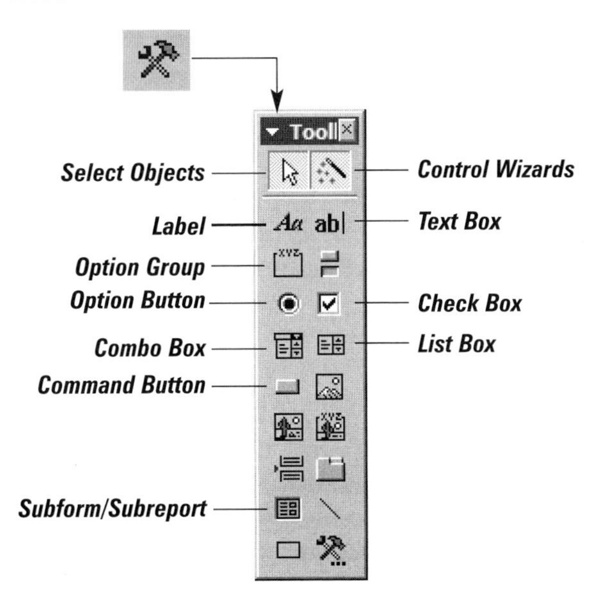

- To create a bound control of a particular type, select the required tool in the toolbox and then drag the field from the field list to the design grid.
- To create an unbound control, click the required tool in the toolbox. Then either click in the design grid or click in the design grid and drag until the control is the size you want. To specify the content for the control, you can use a Control Wizard or the control's property sheet (see below).

Control wizards

Access provides wizards for creating some control types. These guide you through the process of creating the control and defining its data source.

Control Wizards tool

If the **Control Wizards** tool in the toolbox is currently selected (pressed in), the appropriate wizard starts automatically when you add a combo box, list box or option group to the design grid. This is the simplest means of creating these control types.

Property sheets

Forms, form sections and form controls all have properties that define their appearance, behaviour, content and data sources. Access sets these properties automatically when you create a form, section or control.

You can view and edit properties in the *Property Sheet* window. For help with any property, click that property in the property sheet and press **F1**.

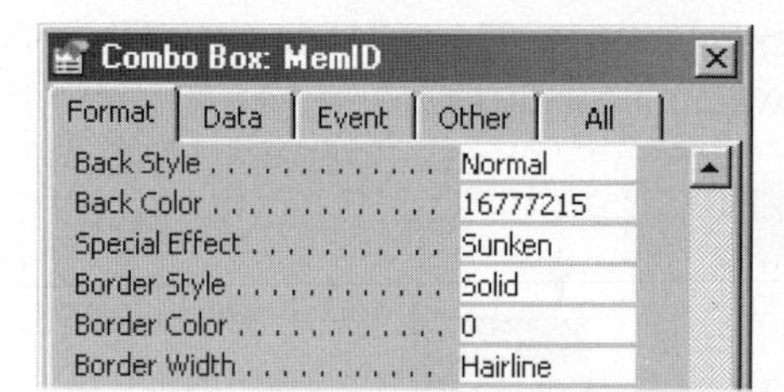

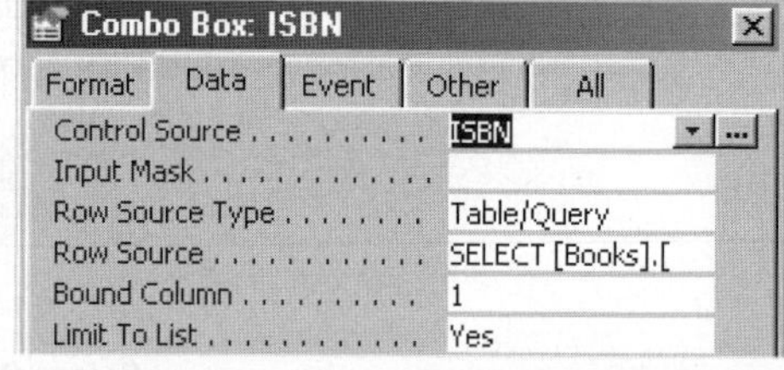

Properties button

To open the *Property Sheet* window, click the **Properties** button on the *Form Design* toolbar. Once the window is open, you can view the property sheet for any form element as follows:

- **Form**. Click the form selector.
- **Section**. Click the section selector.
- **Control**. Click the control.

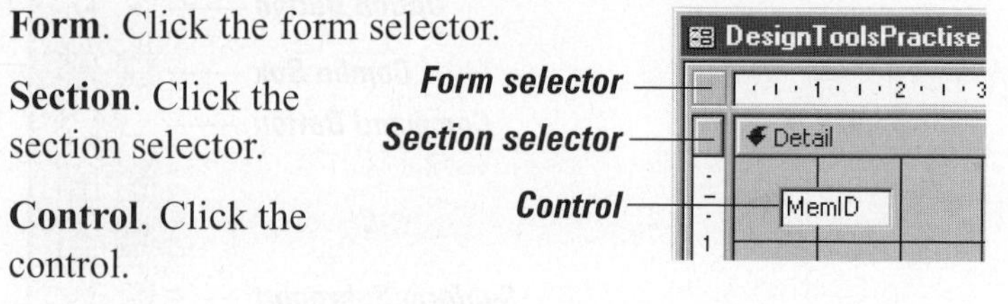

- **Any element**. Select the element in the *Object* list on the *Formatting* toolbar.

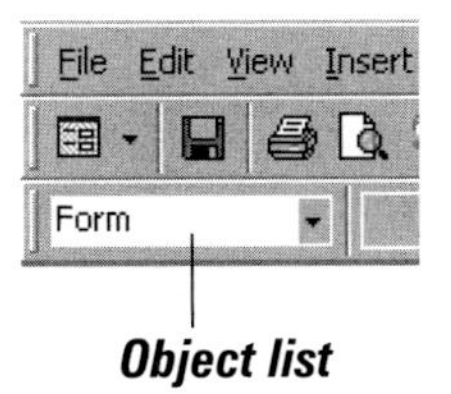

Object list

Here is a list of the most frequently used *form* properties.

- **Default View** (Format tab). Specifies the opening view for a form (see 'Default View' in Chapter 12).
- **Record Source** (Data tab). Specifies the source for data in the form. If you select a record source when creating the form, it is automatically entered in this property. To change the record source for a form:
  - Click the arrow at the right of the property box and select a table or query from the list displayed.
  - Click the **Build** button at the right of the property box. This opens the *Query Builder*. You can then modify the current query or create a new query for the form.

Build button

Here is a list of the most frequently used *control* properties.

- **Name** (Other tab). Every control has a name that identifies it uniquely, and which you can use to refer to the control's value in expressions.
  - The default name for a bound control is the name of the underlying field.
  - The default name for an unbound control is the control type followed by a unique number (for example, Label1, Combo6 or Text11). If you intend to refer to the control in expressions in other controls, it is a good idea to change the name to something more meaningful.
- **Caption** (Format tab). Specifies the text that appears in label controls.
  - When you create a control, the caption of the attached label is automatically set to the name of the control.
  - When you create a stand-alone label, its caption is whatever you type in the label.

  To change a label's caption, type the new caption in the label itself or in its *Caption* property.
- **Control Source** (Data tab). A form's *Record Source* property specifies the table or query to which the form is bound and from which it gets its data. The *Control Source* property for a control specifies the source of the data displayed by that control.

– For a bound control, the source is a field in the form's record source. When you drag a field from the field list to the design grid, this property is set automatically. To change the source field for a control, click the arrow at the right of the property box and select a field from the list displayed.

– For an unbound control, the source is typically an expression that you enter in the *Control Source* property.

- **Format and Decimal Places** (Format tab). These have the same function as the *Format* and *Decimal Places* properties for a query or table field. You use them to change the display format of date, number, and currency values.

Formatting toolbar

The *Format* properties for most controls include colour, font, border and other standard formatting options. The *Formatting* toolbar presents the same options and is easier and quicker to use than a property sheet.

Form Design toolbar

The *Form Design* toolbar includes buttons for showing/hiding the field list and toolbox and the *Property Sheet* window.

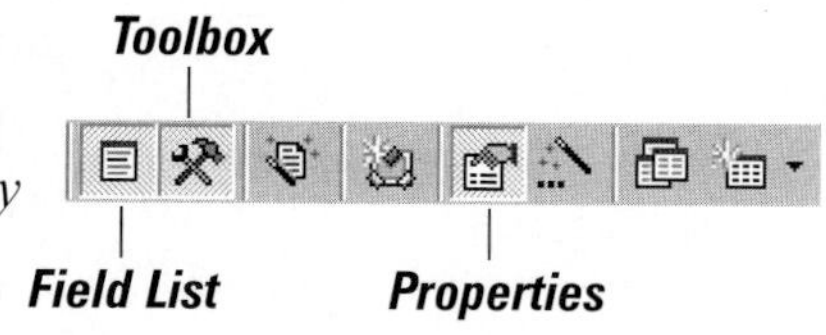

Creating forms in Design View

In the exercises in this chapter you will create a form for maintaining library membership records, as shown here.

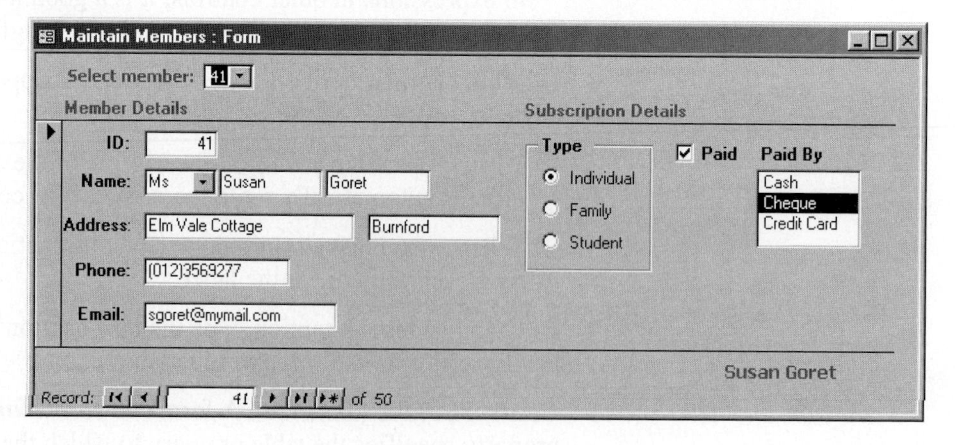

The form's record source is the Members table – that is, the form displays records from that table, and when you add, edit or delete records in the form, the table is updated accordingly.

In order to illustrate the use of combo box, list box, option group and checkbox controls, the following fields have been added to the table:

- **MemTitle**. The member's title.
- **MemType**. The member's membership type.
- **SubPaid**. A Yes/No field that indicates whether or not a member has paid their membership subscription.
- **PaidBy**. This indicates the payment method.

Exercise 11.1: Creating the Maintain Members form

In this exercise you will create a blank form that is bound to the Members table. In subsequent exercises you will add controls to the form.

1) Click *Forms* in the *Objects* list in the Database window and click the **New** button on the window's toolbar.

2) In the *New Form* dialog box, select the *Design View* option, select the Members table as the record source, and then click **OK.**

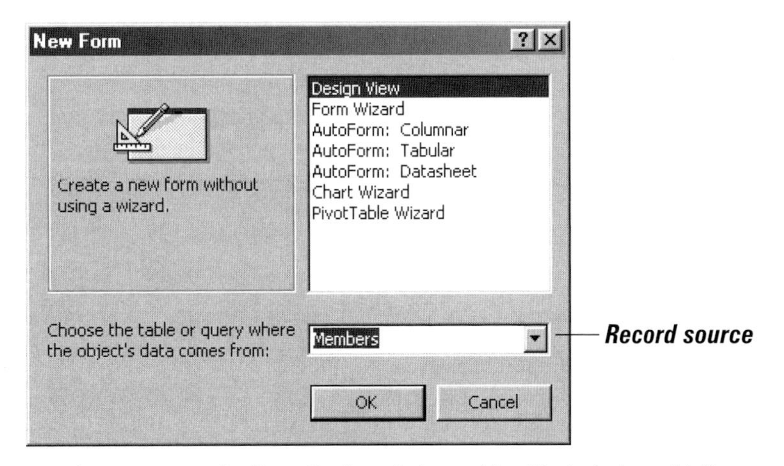

Access opens the *Form Design* window with a blank design grid. If you display the property sheet for the form, you will see that the *Record Source* property (Data tab) has been set to the Members table.

3) By default, any new form you create has only a Detail section. The Maintain Members form uses both Form Header and Form Footer sections, so add these by choosing **View | Form Header/Footer**.

4) To fit all the form controls, you need to increase the width of the design grid to about 15.5 cm, and change the height of the Form Header, Detail and Form Footer sections to about 1 cm, 4 cm and

0.75 cm respectively. You can do this by dragging the section borders. Use the horizontal and vertical rulers as guides.

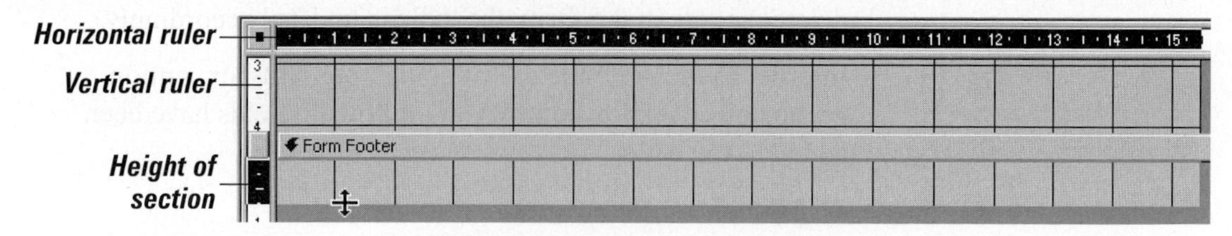

5) Choose **File | Save** to save the form. Name it Maintain Members.

Creating bound controls

In Exercises 11.2 to 11.6 you will add label, text box, combo box, list box, option group and checkbox controls to the Maintain Members form. All the controls, except the labels, will be bound to fields in the Members table.

Creating bound text boxes

A bound text box displays values from a field in the form's record source and you can use it to update the field.

Exercise 11.2: Creating bound text boxes

In this exercise you will create text box controls for the MemID, MemFirstname, MemLastname, MemAddress, MemTown, MemPhone and MemEmail fields.

Text Box tool

1) Select the **Text Box** tool in the toolbox.
2) Select the required fields in the field list. Remember that to select multiple, non-contiguous fields, you press and hold down the **Ctrl** key while selecting the fields.
3) Drag the fields to the centre of the Detail section in the design grid. A text box control, with attached label, is created for each field.
4) Now you need to position, size and format the controls as shown below (see steps 5 to 7). Use the rulers and grid lines to help you with the sizing and positioning.

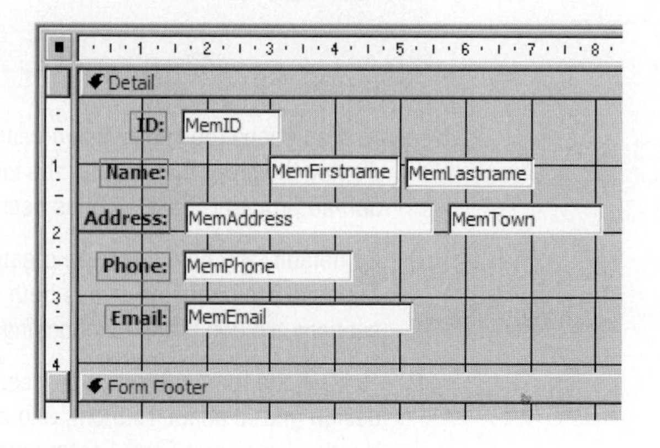

5) First delete the labels for the MemLastname and MemTown fields (click each label and press the **Delete** key), and then change the captions of the other labels as shown.

6) Now select all the label controls so that you can format them together. If the labels are in a single vertical column, you can do this by clicking on the horizontal ruler directly above them.

   - To change the label text to bold type, click the **Bold** button in the *Formatting* toolbar.
   - To right-align the label controls, choose **Format | Align | Right**.
   - To right-align the label text within the controls, click the **Align Right** button on the *Formatting* toolbar.
   - To resize the label controls to the size of the label text, choose **Format | Size | To Fit**.

7) Finally, reposition and resize the controls as shown above. Leave sufficient space between the Name label and the MemFirstname text box to insert a combo box control for the MemTitle field.

8) Save the form and switch to Form View to see how it looks.

If you need help with moving, sizing and aligning controls, the following Microsoft Help topic provides all the information you need: 'Move, size, align, and format text boxes or controls in a form or report'.

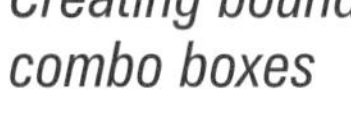

Creating bound combo boxes

A bound combo box control displays a list of values from which the user selects one to store in the field to which the control is bound. The control can look up its values either in a table or query, or in a fixed value list that you create manually.

Note that if you create a lookup field in a table and select a combo box as its default display control (see 'Lookup fields' in Chapter 4), Access automatically creates a combo box control for the field when you drag it from the field list to the design grid.

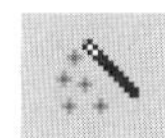

Control Wizards tool

Combo Box tool

Exercise 11.3: Creating a bound combo box control

In this exercise you will create a combo box control for the MemTitle field. This control will allow users to select a title from a predefined list. You will use a wizard to create the control.

1) Make sure that the **Control Wizards** tool is selected (presssed in) and then select the **Combo Box** tool.

2) Drag the MemTitle field from the field list to a blank area of the design grid. This starts the *Combo Box Wizard*.

3) First the wizard prompts you to select the type of combo box you want to create. Only the first two options are relevant for bound combo boxes.

   The first option creates a combo box that looks up its values in a table or query. The second option creates a combo box that looks up its values in a fixed value list. You met similar options when you created a lookup field in Chapter 4. Select the second option and click **Next**.

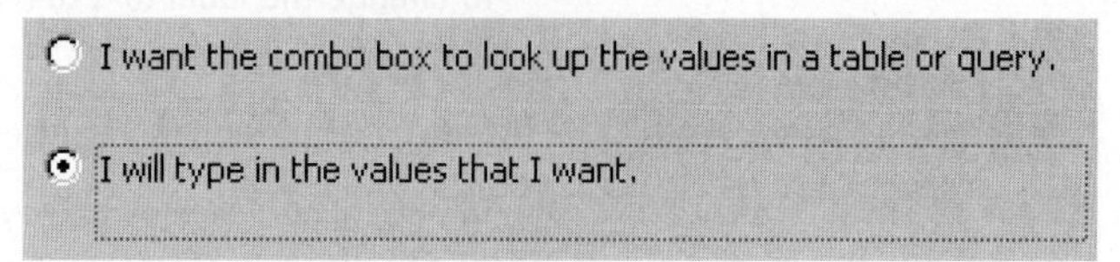

4) The wizard now prompts you for the list of values. Enter the values shown here and then click **Next**.

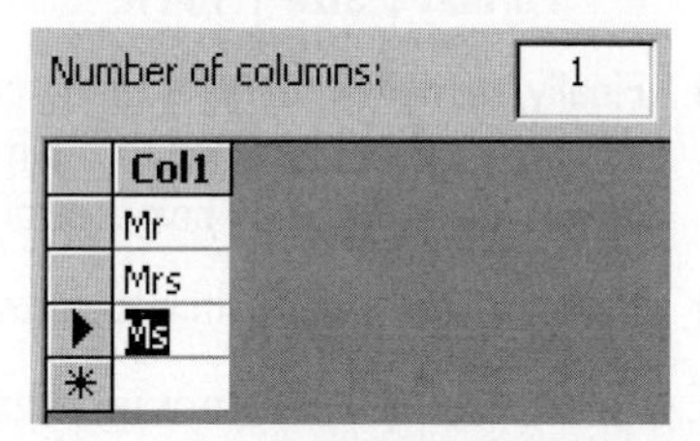

5) The wizard asks you what you want to do with a value selected in the list. Access can either save the value for later use (in a calculation, for example), or it can store the value in a table field. Because you based the combo box on the MemTitle field, the second option and the MemTitle field are selected by default. This is the option you want, so click **Next** to continue.

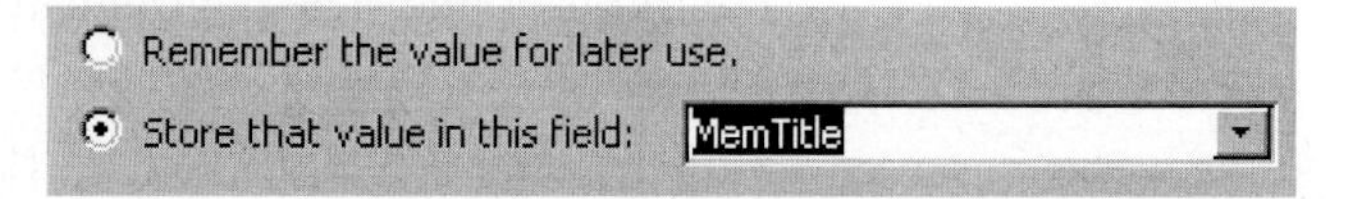

6) The last page of the wizard prompts you for a label for the combo box. The default is the field name. Leave this as it is and click **Finish**.

7) You are now returned to the design grid where the new combo box and attached label have been created for you. Delete the label, resize the combo box to the width of its longest entry, and move the control to the start of the Name row.

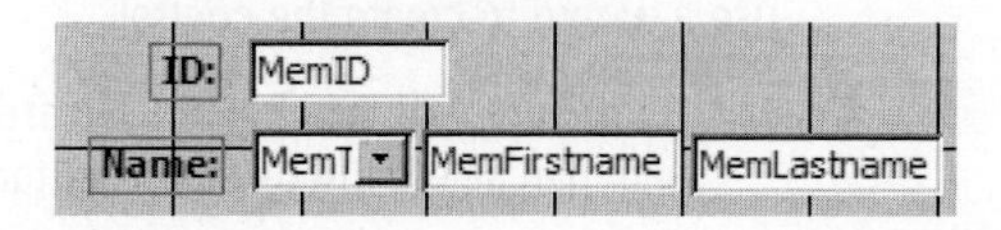

8) Save the form and switch to Form View to try out the new control.

What if you want to change the list displayed in the combo box? You could rerun the wizard and create the control again from scratch.

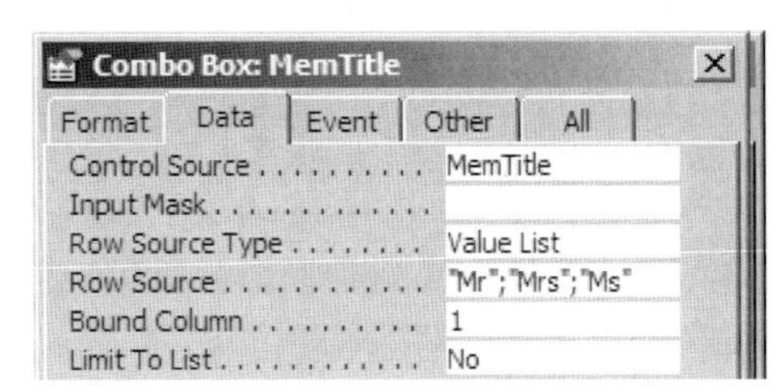

However, the list values are stored in the control's *Row Source* property and can be edited there.

Each entry in the list is enclosed in double quotes and separated from the next entry by a semicolon. To add 'Dr' to the list, for example, you would edit the list as follows:

```
"Mr";"Mrs";"Ms";"Dr"
```

Creating bound option groups

A bound option group presents a set of options from which the user selects one to store in the field to which the group is bound. Each option in the group has a label and a value. The label describes the option; the value is stored in the bound field when you select the option.

Exercise 11.4: Creating a bound option group

In this exercise you will create an option group control for the MemType field. You will use a wizard to create the control.

Option Group tool

1) Make sure that the **Control Wizards** tool is selected and then select the **Option Group** tool.
2) Drag the MemType field from the field list to a blank area of the design grid. This starts the *Option Group Wizard*.
3) First the wizard prompts you for the label for each option in the option group. Enter the values shown here and click **Next**.

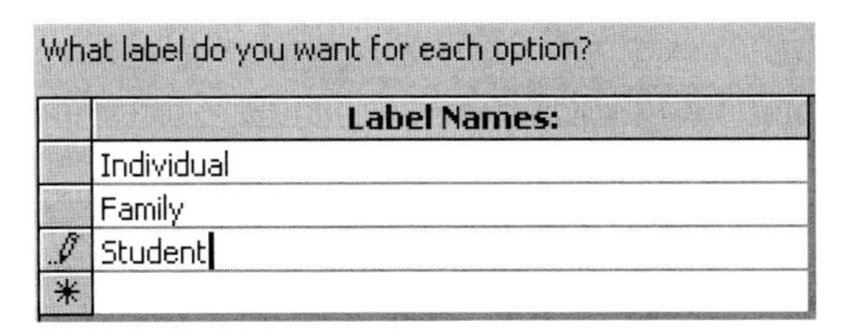

4) Next the wizard asks whether you want to specify a default option. It suggests that you use the first option: 'Individual'. As most library members are individual members, leave this as it is and click **Next**.
5) The wizard now asks you what value you want to assign to each option in the group. Only number values are valid.

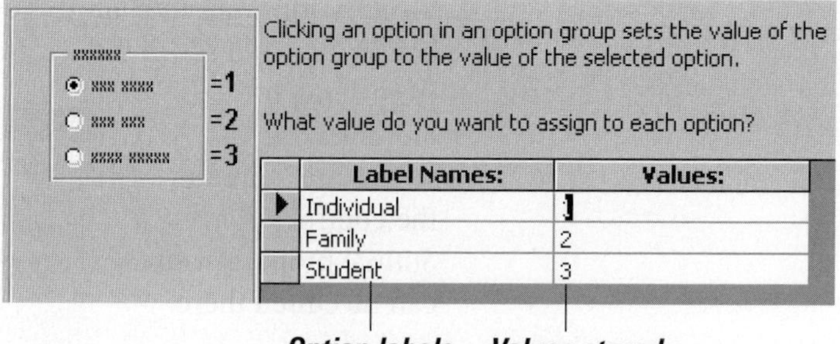

By default, the wizard assigns sequential numbers to the options. This makes sense, so accept these defaults by clicking **Next**. Now when a user selects the *Individual* option, Access stores 1 in the MemType field, when a user selects the *Family* option, Access stores 2 in the field, and so on.

6) The wizard now asks you what you want Access to do with the value of a selected option. Because you based the option group on the MemType field, the second option and the MemType field are selected by default. This is the option you want, so click **Next** to continue.

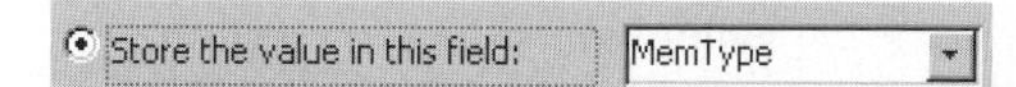

7) The wizard prompts you for the type of controls you want to use in the option group and the style to apply to the group and its controls. In the left part of the dialog box, your option group is displayed using the currently selected control type and style.

   For this exercise, accept the default options (*Option Buttons* and *Etched*) and click **Next**.

8) The last page of the wizard prompts you for a label for the option group. Enter 'Type' and click **Finish**.

9) You are now returned to the design grid where the new option group has been created for you. Make the option group label bold and resize it accordingly. Then select the option group by clicking its border, and move it to the position shown here.

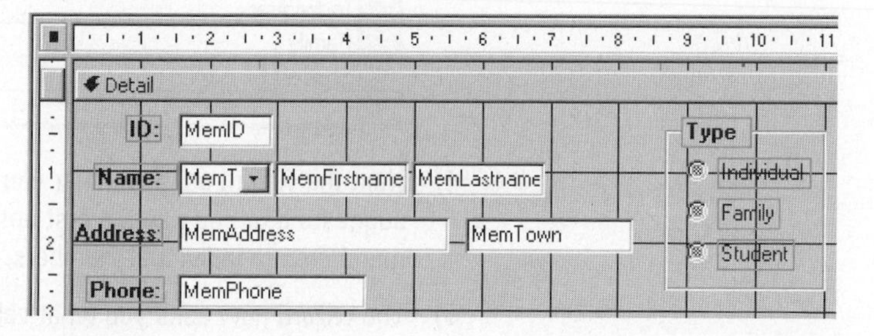

10) Save the form and switch to Form View to try out the new control.

What if you want to update the option group after you've created it?

- To change the label of an option button control within the group, type directly in the label control.
- To delete an option button control from the group, select it and press the **Delete** key.
- To add a new option button to the group, select the **Option Button** tool in the toolbox and click within the option group's borders. Then type the new option button's description in its label control.

A value is assigned to the new option automatically. For example, if you add a fourth option to an option group, it is given the value 4, if you add a fifth option, it is given the value 5, and so on.

Creating bound checkboxes

A bound checkbox displays values from a Yes/No field and you can use it to update the field. By default, Access automatically creates a checkbox control when you drag a Yes/No field from the field list to the design grid. If it does not, you can use the **Check Box** tool to create the control.

Exercise 11.5: Creating a bound checkbox

In this exercise you will create a checkbox control for the SubPaid field. There is no control wizard for creating checkboxes, but the procedure is simple.

Check Box tool

1) Select the **Check Box** tool in the toolbox.
2) Drag the SubPaid field from the field list to a blank area of the design grid. This creates a checkbox control that is bound to the SubPaid field. The attached label displays the field name.
3) Change the label to 'Paid', make it bold, and size it to the width of the text. Then position the check box and its label as shown here.

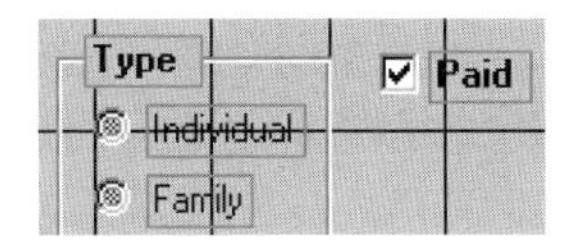

4) Save the form and switch to Form View to try out the control.

Creating bound list boxes

A bound list box control displays a list of values from which the user selects one to store in the field to which the control is bound. You create the control in the same way that you create a bound combo box control. The *List Box Wizard* presents the same options as the *Combo Box Wizard*; the only difference is the type of control created.

Exercise 11.6: Creating a bound list box

In this exercise you will create a list box control for the PaidBy field. This control will allow users to select a payment type from a predefined list. You will use a wizard to create the control.

List Box tool

1) Make sure that the **Control Wizards** tool is selected, and then select the **List Box** tool.
2) Drag the PaidBy field from the field list to a blank area of the design grid. This starts the *List Box Wizard*.
3) First the wizard prompts you to select the type of list box you want to create. Select the second option and click **Next**.
4) The wizard prompts you for the list of values to be displayed by the control. Enter the values shown here and click **Next**.

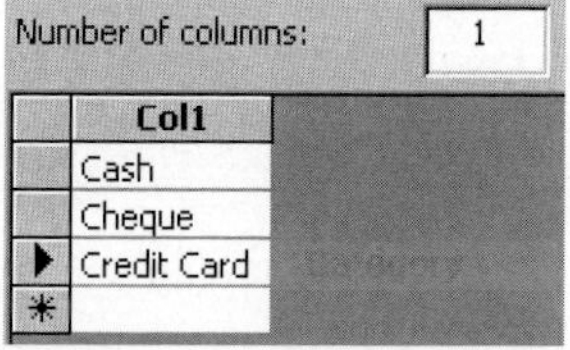

5) The wizard asks you what you want Access to do with a value selected in the list. Because you based the list box on the PaidBy field, the second option and the PaidBy field are selected by default. This is the option you want, so simply click **Next** to continue.
6) The last page of the wizard prompts you for a label for the list box. Enter 'Paid By' and click **Finish**.
7) You are now returned to the design grid where the new list box and attached label have been created for you. Note that the label may be positioned some distance from the list box, possibly overlying some other control in the design grid.

   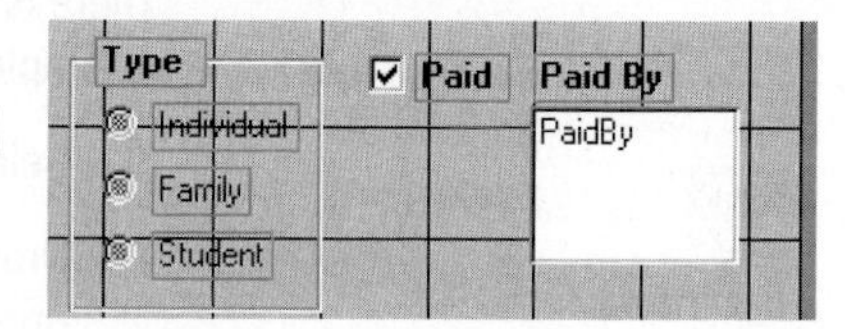

   Position and resize the list box and label as shown here and make the label bold.
8) Save the form and switch to Form View to try out the list box.

If you want to change the values in the list you can edit the control's *Row Source* property, as described under 'Creating bound combo boxes' above.

In Form View and in Design View, your form should now resemble that shown here.

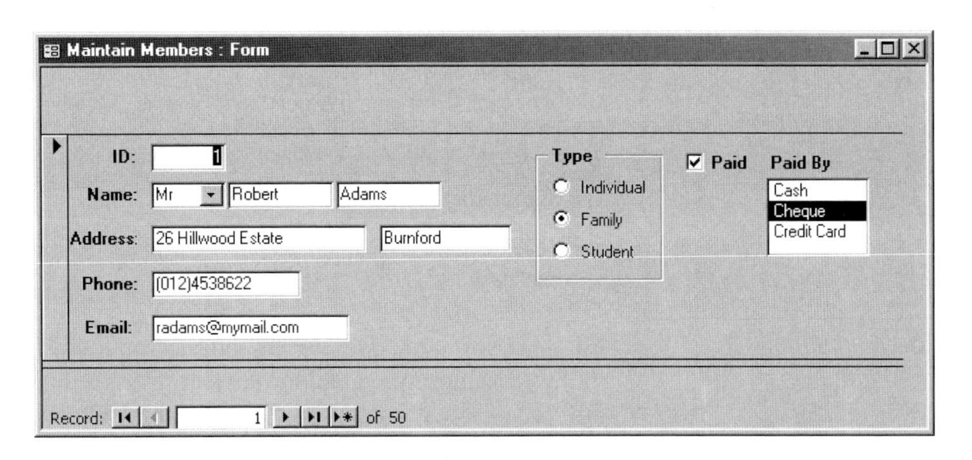

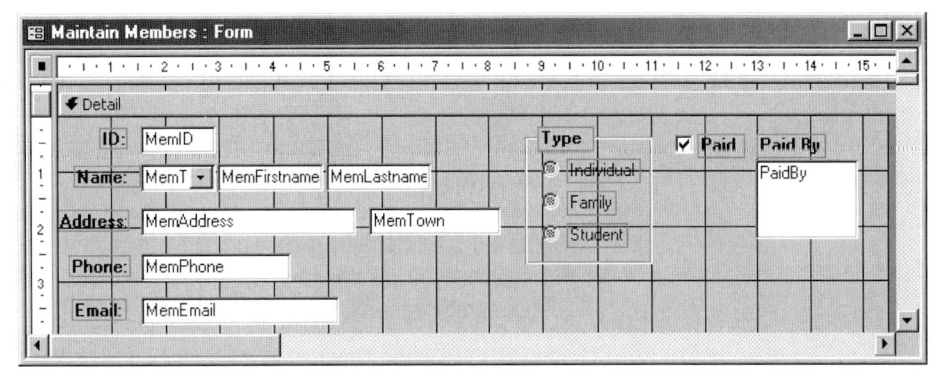

Creating unbound controls

In Exercises 11.7 to 11.9 you will add unbound label, combo box and text box controls to the Maintain Members form.

Creating unattached labels

Access automatically creates a label for each control you add to the design grid. These are attached labels that move with the control and describe its content. You use unattached (or stand-alone) labels for form titles, headings, instructions, and so on.

Exercise 11.7: Creating unattached label controls

In this exercise you will create label controls for the form headings, as shown here.

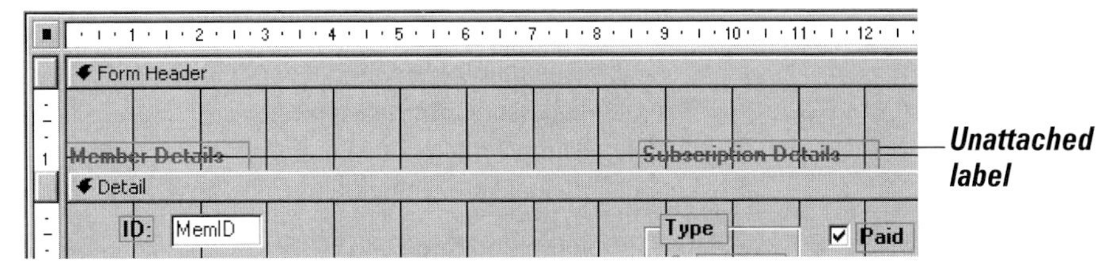

Label tool

1) Display the Maintain Members form in Design View and select the **Label** tool in the toolbox.

2) Click in the Form Header section where you want the upper left corner of the first heading to be and drag until the control is the size you want. Then type the label text – that is, 'Member Details'.
3) Make the text bold and apply a font colour of blue.
4) Repeat steps 1 to 3 for the second heading: Subscription Details.
5) Save the form and switch to Form View to see the result of your changes.

Creating unbound combo boxes

Like a bound combo box or list box, an unbound combo box looks up values in a table or query or in a fixed value list. The difference is that you do not bind the control to a table field and so a selected value is not stored in a table field. Instead Access stores the value internally for use by another control.

An unbound combo box can be very useful as a record selector, enabling users to select the record they want to view from the control's lookup list. When a user selects a value in the list, Access displays the corresponding record in the form.

Exercise 11.8: Creating a record selector combo box

In this exercise you will create a record selector combo box for the Maintain Members form.

1) Select the **Combo Box** tool in the toolbox and click in the Form Header section. This starts the *Combo Box Wizard*.
2) First the wizard prompts you to select the type of combo box you want to create. Select the *Find a record on my form . . .* option and click **Next**.

(•) Find a record on my form based on the value I selected in my combo box.

3) The wizard prompts you for the fields you want to display in the combo box list. Select MemID, MemFirstname and MemLastname and click **Next**.
4) You can now adjust the layout of the columns. Access suggests that you hide the MemID column. However, users need to be able to differentiate between members with the same first and last names, so deselect the *Hide key column* option. Then size the columns as shown here and click **Next**.

☐ Hide key column (recommended)

Mem	MemFirst	MemLast
1	Robert	Adams
2	Sylvia	Turner
3	Rebecca	White

5) The wizard prompts you to select the field whose value Access will use to find a record. Select MemID and click **Next**.

6) The wizard asks you what you want Access to do with a value selected in the list. Make sure the *Remember the value for later use* option is selected and click **Next**.

7) The last page of the wizard prompts you for a label for the combo box. Enter 'Select member:' and click **Finish**.

8) You are now returned to the design grid where the new combo box and attached label have been created for you. Make the label text bold and apply a font colour of blue. Then position and size the controls as shown here.

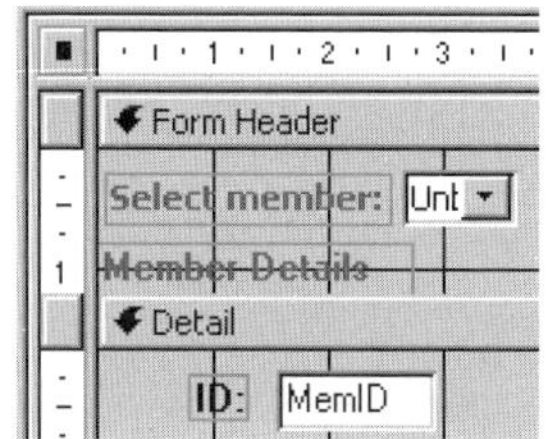

9) Save the form and switch to Form View to try out the new control. Select a member in the combo box and you will see that Access immediately displays the record for that member.

What if you want to add or remove columns from the combo box list or adjust the column widths? These attributes are all properties of the control and you can edit them in the control's property sheet.

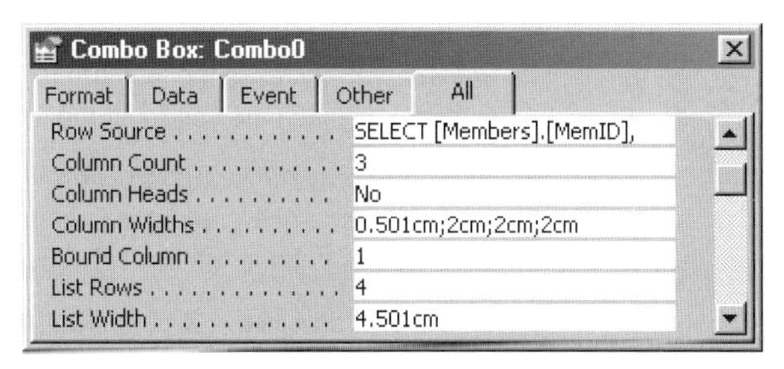

Many of the properties are the same as those for a lookup field in a table. For an explanation of these properties, see 'Creating and modifying lookup fields manually' in Chapter 4.

Creating unbound text boxes

You use unbound text box controls to display the results of expressions. An expression can consist of a calculation or a reference to a value in another control.

In the following exercise, you will create a text box control that references a value in another control. You will learn about calculated controls in Chapter 12.

Exercise 11.9: Creating an unbound text box

In this exercise you will create an unbound text box in the Footer section of the Maintain Members form. The text box will display the name of the member whose record is currently displayed in the form.

1) Select the **Text Box** tool in the toolbox and click in the Form Footer section. This creates an unbound text box and attached label. Delete the label.

2) Type the following expression in the text box:

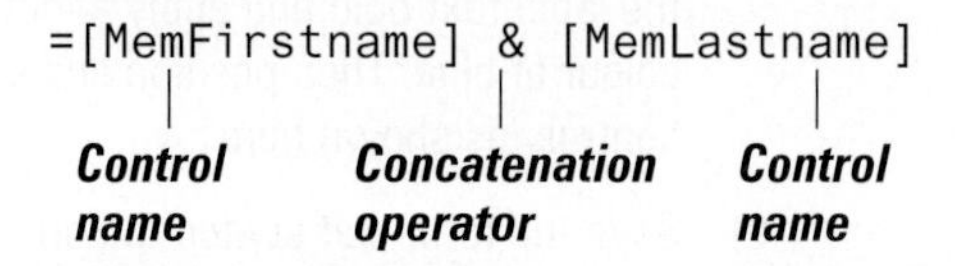

The & (concatenation) operator is a very useful operator that merges the values from two fields or controls and displays them as a single string. So the above expression combines the values in the MemFirstname and MemLastname controls.

3) As the control cannot be used to update a member's name, it is a good idea to use different formatting than you use for interactive text boxes.

Use the **Fill/Back Colour** and **Line/Border** buttons on the *Formatting* toolbar to change the control's background colour and border colour to *Transparent*. Increase the font size to 10 point, change its colour to blue, and then position the control at the far right side of the Footer section.

4) Save the form and switch to Form View. Notice that the first and last names are merged without any space in between. To insert a space, you need to change the control's expression as follows:

```
=[MemFirstname] & " " & [MemLastname]
```

This combines a member's first name, a space character, and the member's last name. Update the expression now and then save the form again.

In Form View and in Design View, your form should now resemble that shown here.

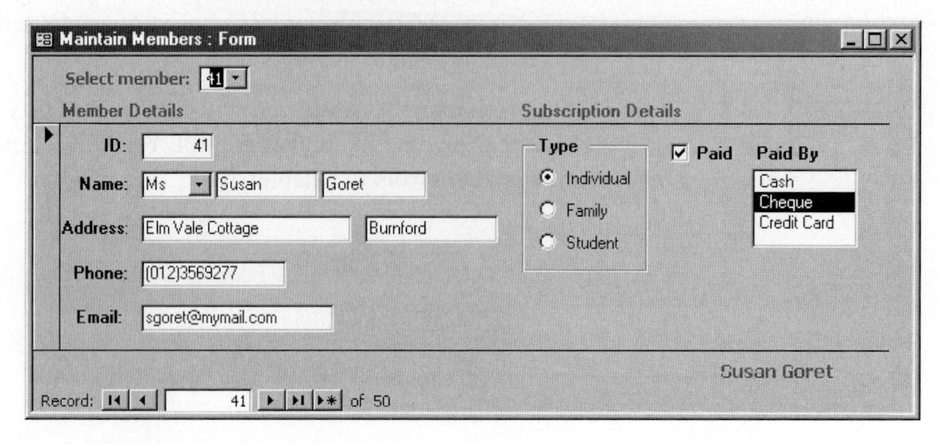

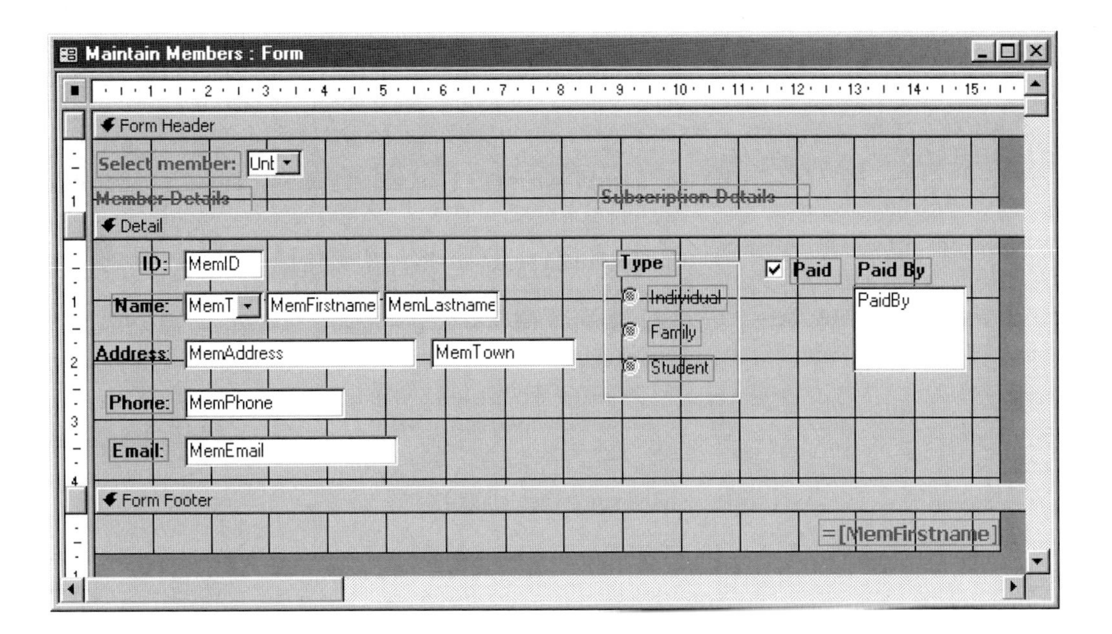

Setting the tab order for a form

In Form View users can press the **Tab** key to move from control to control. The order in which the focus moves through the controls is referred to as the *tab order*.

By default, the tab order corresponds to the order in which the controls were created. However, this may not be the most logical order for the form. In the Maintain Members form, for example, the MemTitle control comes after the MemEmail control in the tab order.

Exercise 11.10: Setting the tab order for a form

In this exercise you will set the tab order for the Maintain Members form.

1) Open the Maintain Members form in Design View and choose **View | Tab Order**. This displays the *Tab Order* dialog box.

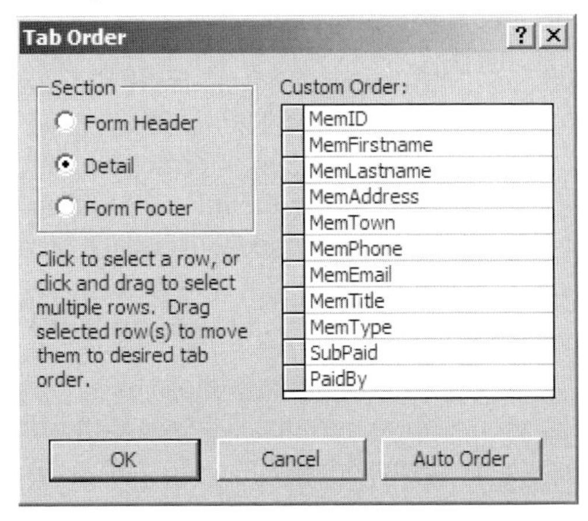

2) Each section in a form has a separate tab order. You select the section with which you want to work by selecting a *Section* option in the dialog box. Select the *Detail* option. The *Custom Order* box now lists the controls in the Detail section in their current tab order.

3) To change the position of a control in the tab order, drag it to its new position.

   First click the control selector. Then click it again and drag the control to its new position in the list. As you drag the control, a black line moves with the mouse pointer to indicate where the control will be inserted.

   Change the tab order to that shown here on the right. Then click **OK**.

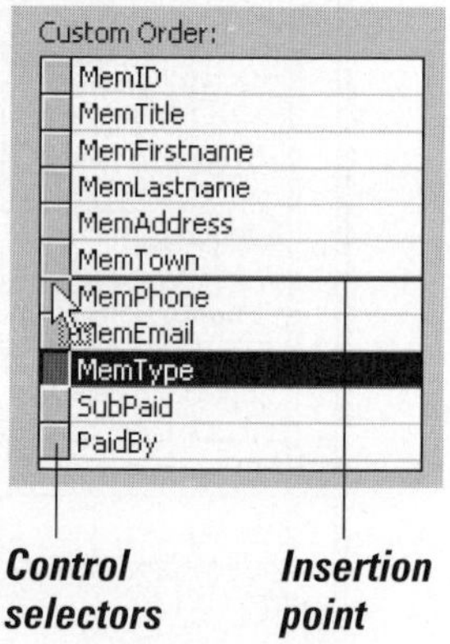

Custom Order:

MemID
MemTitle
MemFirstname
MemLastname
MemAddress
MemTown
MemPhone
MemEmail
MemType
SubPaid
PaidBy

Control selectors ***Insertion point***

4) Save the form.

Note that you can use the **Auto Order** button in the *Tab Order* dialog box to apply a left-to-right, top-to-bottom tab order automatically.

Tab order
The order in which the focus moves from control to control when a user tabs through a form.

Chapter 11: summary

All information in a form is contained in *controls* such as text boxes, list boxes, combo boxes and checkboxes. These controls can be either bound or unbound. A *bound control* is linked to a field in the form's record source and can be used to update that field. An *unbound control* (other than a label) is typically used as a record selector or to display the result of a calculation.

Access provides several tools for creating a form in Design View. The *field list* lists all fields in the form's record source. To create a bound field, drag the field from the field list to the design grid. The *toolbox* provides tools for all the controls you can include in a form. To create a bound control of a particular type, select the relevant tool in the toolbox before dragging the field from the field list. To create an unbound control, select the relevant tool in the toolbox and then click in the design grid where you want to position the control.

Wizards are available for creating combo boxes, list boxes and option groups. These are the simplest means of creating these control types.

Forms, form sections and form controls all have properties that define their appearance, behaviour, content and data sources. You can view and edit these properties in the *Property Sheet* window.

The *tab order* of a form is the order in which the focus moves from control to control when a user tabs through the form. The default tab order is the order in which the controls were created.

Chapter 11: quick quiz

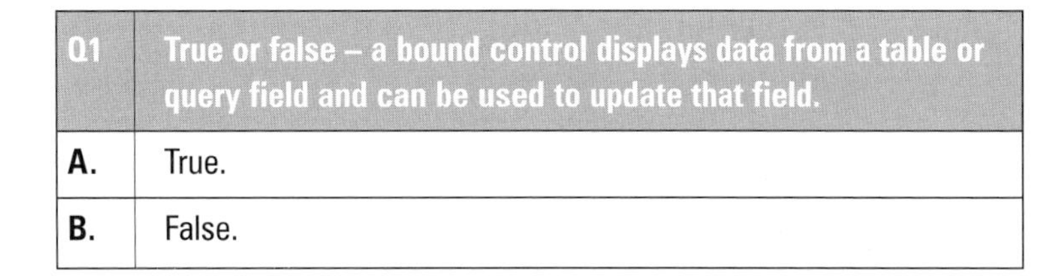

Q1	True or false – a bound control displays data from a table or query field and can be used to update that field.
A.	True.
B.	False.

Q2	True or false – an unbound control can display data from a table or query field but cannot be used to update that field.
A.	True.
B.	False.

Q3	Which of these tools do you use to create a text box?
A.	Aa
B.	ab|
C.	xyz

Q4	Which of these can you use as the source for a bound combo box or list box control?
A.	A field in the form's record source.
B.	A fixed value list.
C.	A field in any table or query in the database.

Q5	Which of these can you use as the source for a record selector combo box?
A.	A field in the form's record source.
B.	A fixed value list.
C.	A field in any table or query in the database.

Q6	Which of these expressions concatenates a member's title, firstname and lastname?
A.	`=[MemTitle] & [MemFirstname] & [MemLastname]`
B.	`=[MemTitle] # [MemFirstname] # [MemLastname]`
C.	`=[MemTitle] & " " & [MemFirstname] & " " & [MemLastname]`

Q7	Which of these properties defines the field that a bound control updates?
A.	Record Source.
B.	Control Source.
C.	Row Source.

Q8	Which of these properties defines the table/query from which a form gets its data?
A.	Record Source.
B.	Control Source.
C.	Row Source.

Answers

1: A, **2**: A, **3**: B, **4**: All, **5**: A, **6**: A and C (this latter expression inserts spaces between the concatenated fields), **7**: B, **8**: A.

12 Form design: calculated controls

In this chapter

You use calculated controls to display the results of calculations. The controls are unbound, so the calculation results are not stored in a database table. Instead Access reruns the calculation each time you open the form and whenever a value in the calculation expression changes.

In this chapter you will learn how to create calculated controls for single records and for summarizing and totalling values across records.

New skills

At the end of this chapter you should be able to:

- Create calculated controls
- Use aggregate functions in calculated controls
- Use the IIf(), Nz() and IsNull() functions in calculated controls.

New words

There are no new words in this chapter.

Exercise file

In this chapter you will work with the following Access file:

- `Chp12_VillageLibrary_Database`

Syllabus reference

In this chapter you will cover the following items of the ECDL Advanced Database Syllabus:

- **AM5.3.1.3**: Create arithmetic, logical expression controls on a form.

Calculated controls versus calculated fields

Calculated fields are query fields that display the results of calculations on other query fields (see Chapter 9). *Calculated controls* are controls that display the results of calculations on other controls in a form or report. You can use the same operators and functions in both cases.

When to use calculated fields

When you base a form on a query that includes calculated fields, those fields are available to the form in the same way as any other field. If you intend using the same calculations in multiple forms or reports, then put them in a query and base the forms/reports on that query. Otherwise you will find yourself creating the same calculated controls again and again.

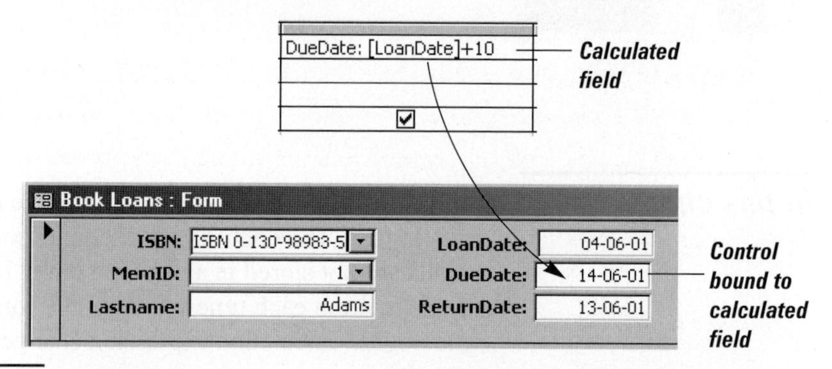

When to use calculated controls

Tables cannot include calculated fields. So when you base a form/report on a table, you must use calculated controls for any calculations you want to perform.

You also use calculated controls for summarizing values across multiple records. For example, this form here is based on a parameter query that allows users to retrieve the records for books in any specified category. The calculated control in the form's footer calculates the total cost of books in the category specified at the parameter prompt.

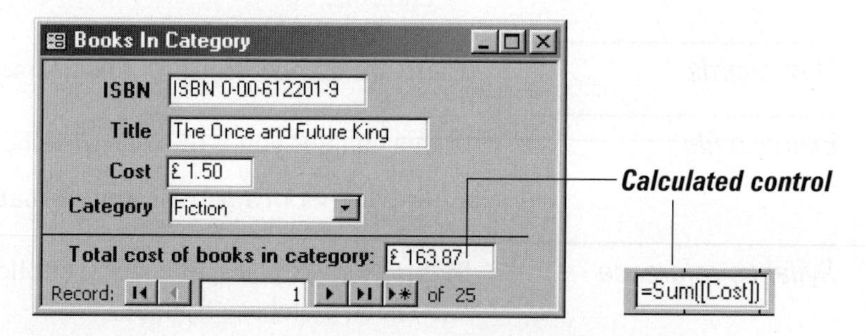

If you want to take a look at this form, it is included in `Chp12_VillageLibrary_Database` under the name BooksInCategory.

Exploring the Loans and Returns form

In the exercises in this chapter you will create the Loans and Returns form, which library staff use for processing book loans and returns.

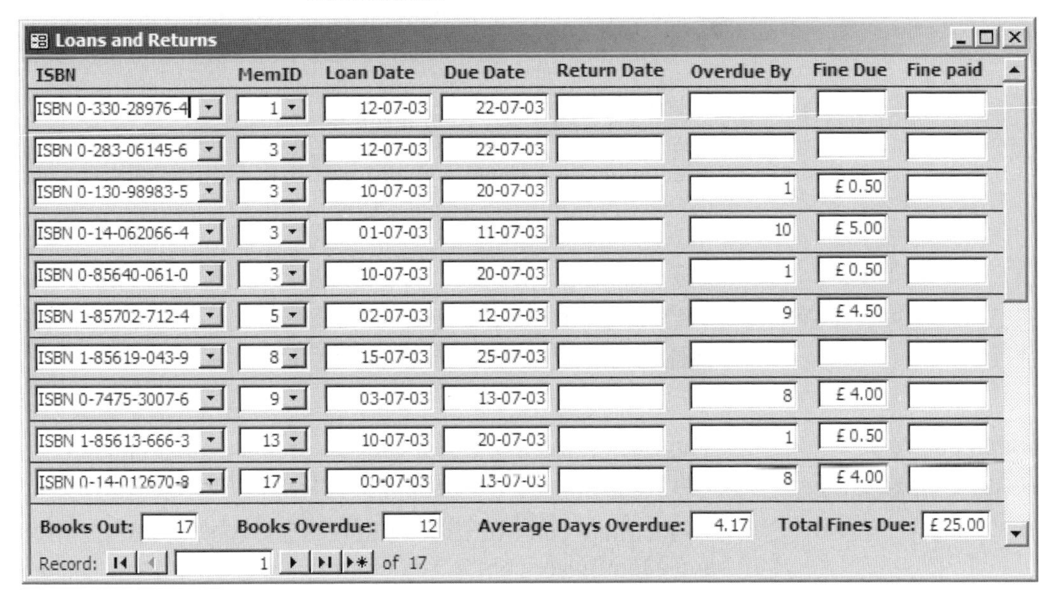
Loans and Returns

ISBN	MemID	Loan Date	Due Date	Return Date	Overdue By	Fine Due	Fine paid
ISBN 0-330-28976-4	1	12-07-03	22-07-03				
ISBN 0-283-06145-6	3	12-07-03	22-07-03				
ISBN 0-130-98983-5	3	10-07-03	20-07-03		1	£ 0.50	
ISBN 0-14-062066-4	3	01-07-03	11-07-03		10	£ 5.00	
ISBN 0-85640-061-0	3	10-07-03	20-07-03		1	£ 0.50	
ISBN 1-85702-712-4	5	02-07-03	12-07-03		9	£ 4.50	
ISBN 1-85619-043-9	8	15-07-03	25-07-03				
ISBN 0-7475-3007-6	9	03-07-03	13-07-03		8	£ 4.00	
ISBN 1-85613-666-3	13	10-07-03	20-07-03		1	£ 0.50	
ISBN 0-14-012670-8	17	03-07-03	13-07-03		8	£ 4.00	

Books Out: 17 Books Overdue: 12 Average Days Overdue: 4.17 Total Fines Due: £ 25.00

Record: 1 of 17

A finished copy of this form is available in `Chp12_VillageLibrary_Database` under the name LoansAndReturnsFinishedVersion. Open the latter form now and let's take a look at its contents, data sources, properties and behaviour.

Record source

When checking books out and in, library staff are not interested in records for books that have already been returned. To filter out these records, the form is bound to a query instead of to the Loans table.

Record Source .... BookReturns

The query (BookReturns) returns all fields in the Loans table but only for records that have no return date. You can view this query by opening it in Query Design View.

Default view

Forms can be presented to users in one of three different views. You set the view in which a form opens by using the form's *Default View property*. The available views are:

- **Single Form**. One record is displayed at a time. This is the view used for the Maintain Members form in Chapter 11.
- **Continuous Forms**. Multiple records are displayed at a time, each in its own copy of the form's Detail section.

Typically you use this view for records that have no more than two or three rows of controls.

- **Datasheet**. Multiple records are displayed at a time in rows and columns, in the same way as records are displayed in table and query datasheets. This view cannot display option groups, list boxes, graphics, headers and footers, or more than a single row of controls.

When checking books out and in, library staff want to be able to view multiple records at a time, so the *Default View* property for the LoansAndReturnsFinishedVersion form has been set to *Continuous Forms*. If set to *Datasheet* instead, the headers and footers would not display.

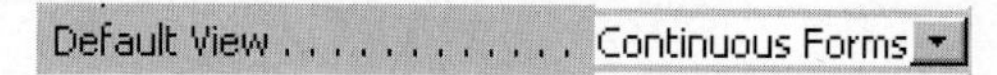

Bound controls

The ISBN, MemID, LoanDate, ReturnDate and FinePaid controls are all bound to fields in the BookReturns query.

To facilitate entry of ISBN numbers and member IDs, ISBN and MemID are combo box controls that look up their values in the Books and Members tables respectively. The other bound fields all use text box controls.

Calculated controls

Two types of calculated controls are included in the form:

- **Single-record calculated controls**. These perform calculations on values in a single record, in order to provide additional information about that record – that is, information that can be calculated from existing values in the record and does not need to be stored in a database table. You create this type of calculated control in the Detail section of a form.

Overdue By	Fine Due
8	£ 4.00
8	£ 4.00

  DueDate, OverdueBy and FineDue are all single-record calculated controls. They perform calculations on values in a single Loans record in order to provide information on the overdue status of a book loan. Any or all of these calculations could be performed by calculated fields in the BookReturns query instead of by calculated controls in the form.

  Note that DueDate, OverdueBy and FineDue are the control names (as defined in their *Name* properties) and not their labels. When the controls were first created, they were automatically given names like Text8, Text9, and so on. It is difficult to keep track of controls with names like these, particularly when you want to refer to them in calculations. So the names of the controls have been changed to something more meaningful.

- **Multi-record calculated controls.** These perform calculations that summarize values in a group of records by using Access's aggregate functions. You create this type of control in the Header or Footer sections of a form. The calculations are always performed on all records retrieved by the form.

  BooksOut, BooksOverdue, AverageDaysOverdue and TotalFinesDue are calculated controls that summarize information about all books that are currently out on loan. Again the control names have been changed from their default values to make them more meaningful.

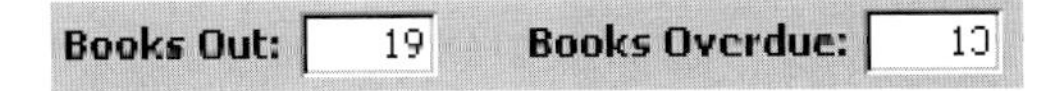

The calculations in a calculated control are rerun each time the form is opened and whenever a value in the calculation expression changes.

Exercise 12.1: Using the LoansAndReturnsFinishedVersion form

In this exercise you will update and add records in the form in order to see the calculated controls in action.

1) Open the LoansAndReturnsFinishedVersion form in Form View.
2) Go to any record with a loan date of 10-07-03 and take a look at the values in the DueDate, OverdueBy and FineDue controls.

   (Note that the calculations in the form use 21-07-03 as today's date, so a book with a loan date of 10-07-03 is overdue by one day.)
3) Change the loan date to 08-07-03. When you now move to another control, all the calculated controls for the record are automatically updated. When you move to another record, all the calculated controls in the form footer are also updated.
4) Now add a new record. Select a book in the ISBN control, a member in the MemID control, and enter 21-07-03 as the loan date. As soon as you leave the LoanDate control, the DueDate control will calculate and display the due date.
5) Enter a return date for any of the records. Then press **Shift+F9**. This command reruns the query on which the form is based and redisplays the records in the form. Notice that the record for which you entered

the return date is no longer displayed. This is because it no longer meets the criteria for the BookReturns query, which returns only records for which there is no return date.

6) Close the form.

Creating calculated controls

Typically you use text box controls for calculations. You can enter the calculation expression directly in the text box or in its *Control Source* property.

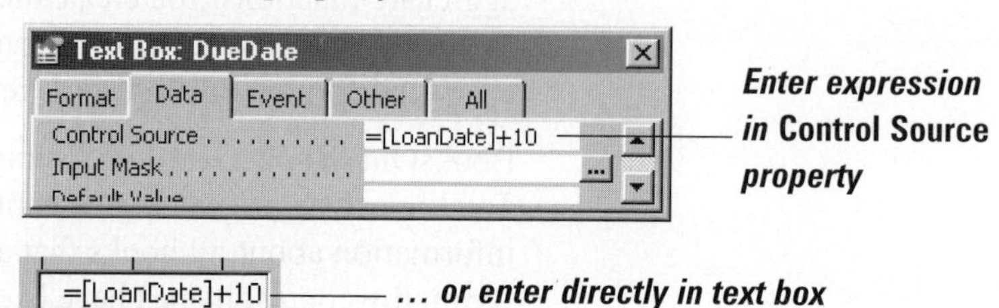

An expression in a calculated control must be preceded by the equal to (=) symbol. Otherwise the rules for control expressions are similar to those for calculated field expressions. And most expressions that you can enter in a calculated field you can also enter in a calculated control.

For example, all the calculation examples in 'About custom calculations' in Chapter 9 could also be used in calculated controls. Similarly, information in that chapter about the IIf() function applies equally to calculated controls, as does information in Chapter 10 about Null values, and the IsNull() and Nz() functions.

Appendix A summarizes all that you need to know about the operators, values, functions and field and control references that you can include in an expression.

Creating single-record calculated controls

In the exercises in this section you will create the DueDate, OverdueBy, and FineDue controls for the Loans and Returns form.

The form has already been started for you. All the bound controls have been created, and unbound text boxes have been created for the calculated controls. The controls are laid out in a single row in the Detail section. The labels have been moved to the Header section so that they are not repeated for each record in the form.

Exercise 12.2: Creating single-record calculated controls

1) Open the Loans and Returns form in Design View.

2) Click the DueDate text box control and type the following expression:

   ```
   =[LoanDate]+10
   ```

   In Form View this control will now display the due date for a book – that is, the loan date plus ten.

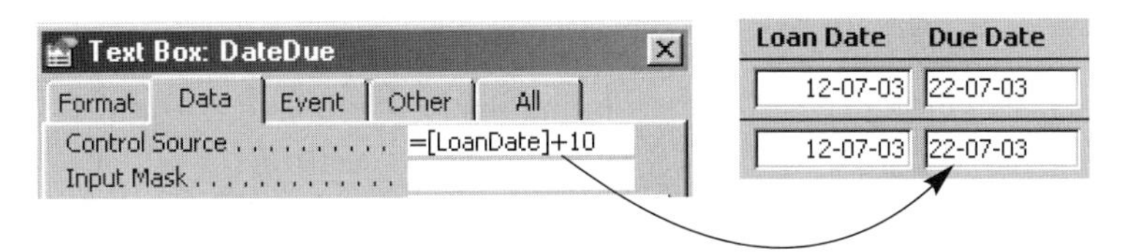

3) Display the property sheet for the OverdueBy text box control and click the **Data** tab to display its *Control Source* property. At the moment this is blank, but you will now enter an expression that calculates the number of days (if any) that a book is overdue, as follows:

   ```
   =IIf(Date()-[DueDate]>0,Date()-[DueDate],Null)
   ```

   As the expression is quite long, you will find it easier to enter and edit it in the *Zoom* dialog box. To open this, click in the *Control Source* property box and press **Shift+F2**. When you have finished, click **OK** and the expression is automatically entered in the *Control Source* property.

4) Switch to Form View to see the calculation results. The OverdueBy control now displays the number of days by which each book is overdue.

5) Note that the most recent loan dates in the database are in July 2003, so the number of days that books are overdue may be quite high by now. The data in the illustrations in this and subsequent chapters are based on a current date of 21-07-03. You can simulate this in your form by changing the OverdueBy expression as follows:

Overdue By
123
123

   ```
   =IIf(#21-07-03#-[DueDate]>0,#21-07-03#-
   [DueDate],Null)
   ```

   Switch back to Design View and do this now. Then take a look at the new calculation results.

6) In Design View, display the property sheet for the FineDue control and click the **Data** tab to display the control's *Control Source* property. Then enter this expression:

   ```
   =[OverdueBy]*0.5
   ```

7) Click the **Format** tab, and change the control's *Format* property to *Currency*.

8) Switch to Form View to see the results of this calculation. Then save the form.

Creating multi-record calculated controls

In the exercises in this section you will create the BooksOut, BooksOverdue, AverageDaysOverdue and TotalFinesDue controls for the Loans and Returns form. The calculations for these controls use the Count(), Avg() and Sum() functions. The controls are all located in the Form Footer section, as you want them to calculate totals for all records retrieved by the form and not just for a single record.

There is one important limitation when using aggregate functions in forms and reports. The functions *cannot* refer to the name of a *control*.

This isn't a problem when performing calculations on bound values. The calculation can refer to the bound *field* instead of to the *control*. So Count([ISBN]) will work.

Query field

ISBN
Loans

=Count([ISBN])

However, calculated controls do not store their values in table or query fields. So an aggregate function that summarizes the values in a calculated control can take its values from neither the calculated control nor an underlying field. In the case of the BooksOverdue control, for example, you can't use the expression Count([OverdueBy]).

=Count([OverdueBy])

The best solution is usually to create your single-record calculations as calculated query fields, as shown here on the right. Aggregate functions can then take their values from those fields.

Query field

OverdueBy: IIf(#21-07-03#-

=Count([OverdueBy])

Another solution is to repeat the expression from the single-record calculated control in the aggregate function, as shown here.

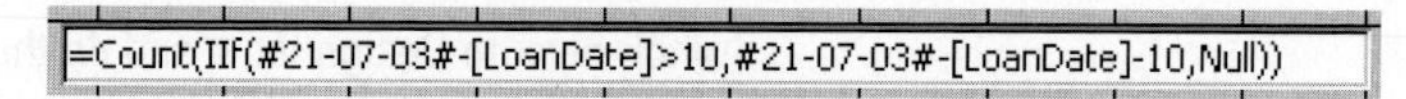
=Count(IIf(#21-07-03#-[LoanDate]>10,#21-07-03#-[LoanDate]-10,Null))

This is the method you will use in the following exercise.

Exercise 12.3: Creating multi-record calculated controls

1) Open the Loans and Returns form in Design View.
2) Enter the following expression in the BooksOut text box control:

```
=Count([ISBN])
```

This calculates the number of books that are currently out on loan. Remember that the Count() function ignores Null values. So, to count all the records in the form, you must specify a field that always contains a value. As a primary key field, ISBN is never Null and so is suitable for the calculation.

3) Enter the following expression in the BooksOverdue text box control:

```
=Count(IIf(#21-07-03#-[LoanDate]>10,#21-07-03#-
[LoanDate]-10,Null))
```

This calculates the number of books that are overdue, by counting only records for books that have been out on loan for longer than ten days.

Note that in a real-life scenario you would enter Date() instead of #21-07-03#. However, use #21-07-03# to maintain consistency between your calculation results and those shown in illustrations in this chapter.

4) Enter the following expression in the AverageDaysOverdue text box control:

```
=Avg(IIf(#21-07-03#-[LoanDate]>10,#21-07-03#-
[LoanDate]-10,Null))
```

This calculates the average number of days that books are overdue. Average() ignores Null values and so averages only books that have been out on loan for more than ten days.

5) Change the control's *Format* property to *Standard* and its *Decimal Places* property to *2*.

6) Enter the following expression in the TotalFinesDue text box control:

```
=Sum(IIf(#21-07-03#-[LoanDate]>10,#21-07-03#-
[LoanDate]-10,Null))*0.5
```

This calculates the total fines due on overdue books. The IIf() function returns the number of days that each overdue book is overdue and the Sum() function then adds these values.

7) Change the control's *Format* property to *Currency*.

8) Save the form and then switch to Form View to see the results of your changes.

In Form View and Design View, your form should now resemble that shown here.

Loans and Returns : Form

ISBN	MemID	Loan Date	Due Date	Return Date	Overdue By	Fine Due	Fine paid
ISBN 0-330-28976-4	1	12-07-03	22-07-03				
ISBN 0-130-98983-5	3	10-07-03	20-07-03		1	£ 0.50	
ISBN 0-14-062066-4	3	01-07-03	11-07-03		10	£ 5.00	
ISBN 0-85640-061-0	3	08-07-03	18-07-03		3	£ 1.50	
ISBN 0-283-06145-6	3	12-07-03	22-07-03				
ISBN 1-85702-712-4	5	02-07-03	12-07-03		9	£ 4.50	
ISBN 1-85619-043-9	8	15-07-03	25-07-03				
ISBN 0-7475-3007-6	9	03-07-03	13-07-03		8	£ 4.00	
ISBN 1-85613-666-3	13	10-07-03	20-07-03		1	£ 0.50	
ISBN 1-85613-666-3	17	21-07-03	31-07-03				

Books Out: 17 Books Overdue: 12 Average Days Overdue: 4.33 Total Fines Due: £ 26.00

Record: 1 of 17

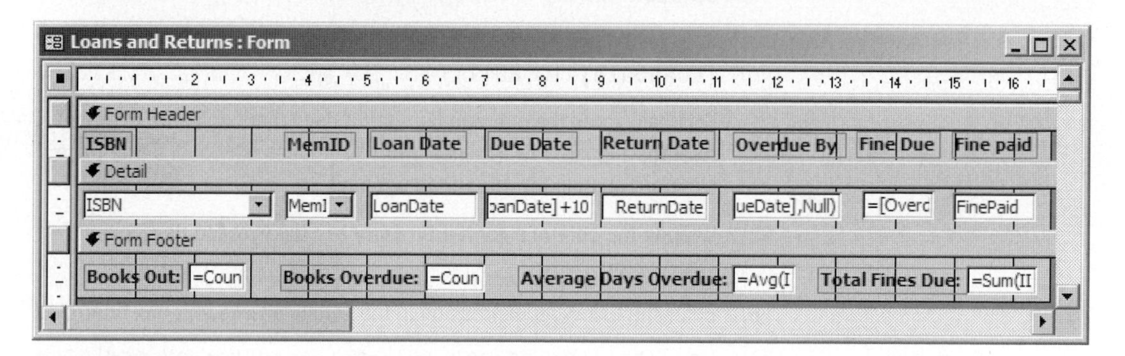

Chapter 12: summary

Calculated controls display the results of calculations. The controls are unbound, so the calculation results are not stored in the database. Instead Access reruns the calculation each time you open the form and whenever a value in the calculation expression changes.

If you intend to use the same calculations in multiple forms/reports, create them as calculated fields in a query and then base your forms/reports on that query.

Single-record calculated controls perform calculations on values in a single record, in order to provide additional information about that record. You create these controls in the Detail section of a form.

Multi-record calculated controls perform calculations that summarize values across multiple records by using Access's aggregate functions. You create these controls in the Header or Footer sections of a form.

When using aggregate functions in a calculated control, you cannot refer to the name of another control. For bound controls, you refer to the underlying field instead. For unbound controls, you can either add a calculated field to the record source and refer to that field in the aggregate function, or you can repeat the expression from the unbound control in the aggregate function.

Typically you use text boxes for calculated controls. You can enter the calculation expression directly in the text box or in its *Control Source* property. The expression must always be preceded by an equal to (=) symbol.

Chapter 12: quick quiz

Q1	True or false – form headers and footers do not display in Continuous Forms view.
A.	True.
B.	False.

Q2	True or false – a single-record calculated control performs calculations on the values in individual records.
A.	True.
B.	False.

Q3	True or false – a multi-record calculated control performs calculations across records retrieved by a form.
A.	True.
B.	False.

Q4	True or false – an equal to (=) symbol is optional at the start of a calculated control's expression.
A.	True.
B.	False.

Q5	Which of these control expressions calculates the average fine due for overdue books?
A.	`=Avg[OverdueBy]*0.5`
B.	`=Avg([OverdueBy])*0.5`
C.	`=Avg((IIf(Date()-[LoanDate]>10,Date()-[LoanDate]-10,Null))*0.5`

Q6	Which of these control expressions calculates the maximum number of overdue days for books in the library?
A.	`=Max([OverdueBy])`
B.	`=Max(Date()-[LoanDate]-10)`
C.	`=Max(IIf(Date()-[LoanDate]>10,Date()-[LoanDate]-10,Null))`
D.	`=TopValue([OverdueBy])`

Answers

1: B, **2**: A, **3**: A, **4**: B, **5**: C, **6**: B and C.

13 Form design: subforms

In this chapter

In previous chapters you created forms that display records from a single table or query. A form can also display a record from one table and all related records from another table. The records in the related table are displayed in a subform.

In this chapter you will learn about subforms and the various methods you can use to create them.

New skills

At the end of this chapter you should be able to:

- Understand subforms and their uses
- Create a subform with the *Form Wizard*
- Create a subform with the *Subform Wizard*
- Use an existing form as a subform
- Modify a subform to display different records

New words

In this chapter you will meet the following terms:

- Main form
- Subform

Exercise file

In this chapter you will work with the following Access file:

- `Chp13_VillageLibrary_Database`

Syllabus reference

In this chapter you will cover the following items of the ECDL Advanced Database Syllabus:

- **AM5.3.2.1**: Create a subform and link to parent.
- **AM5.3.2.2**: Modify the subform to change records displayed.

About subforms

A subform is a form that is contained within another form. The container or parent form is referred to as the main form.

In itself, a subform is not a special type of form. You can create and use it independently of the main form. It is a subform only when included in another form.

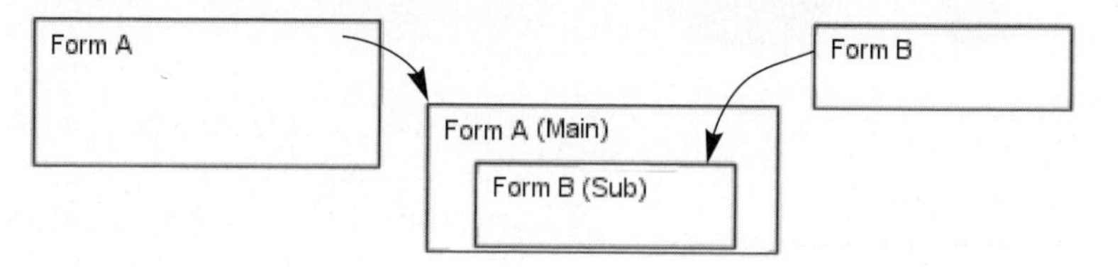

Subforms are especially useful for displaying records from tables with a one-to-many relationship, such as Books and Loans. For example, it would be very useful to be able to browse through the Books table and, as you move to each book, to see all the loans for that book. The BookLoans form shown here enables you to do just that.

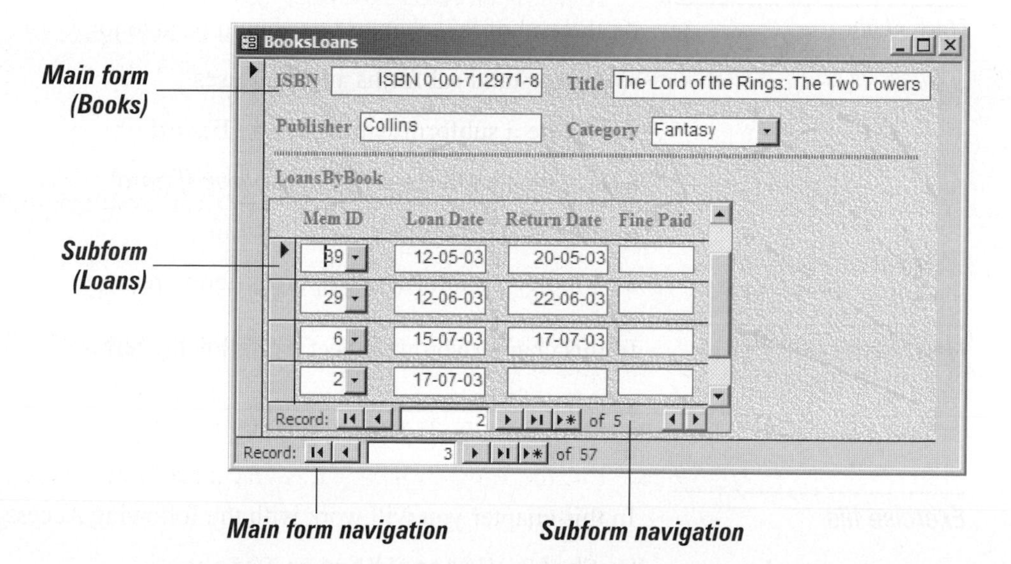

The main form displays a single record from the Books table – that is, from the 'one' side of the relationship. The subform displays multiple records from the Loans table – that is, from the 'many' side of the relationship. The two forms are linked in such a way that the subform displays only records related to the current record in the main form.

Exercise 13.1: Using forms with subforms

In this exercise you will explore the BookLoans form and its subform.

1) Open the BookLoans form in Form View.
2) Use the main form's navigation buttons to browse through the book records.
3) Use the subform's navigation buttons or its scroll bar to browse through the loan records for the current book.

New Record button

4) Use the subform's **New Record** button to enter a new loan record for the current book. The MemID field in the Loans table is a lookup field, so you can select a member from its lookup list. The ISBN number from the record in the main form is automatically saved as the ISBN number for the loan record.
5) Close the BookLoans form.
6) The subform exists as a form in its own right. It is named LoansByBook. Open that form now in Form View.

   Notice that when not acting as a subform, the form displays all records in the Loans table. Close the form.

Subform
A form that is contained within another form.

Main form
A form that contains a subform.

Creating subforms

You can use any of the following methods to create a form that contains a subform:

- Use the *Form Wizard* to create both forms.
- Use the *Subform Wizard* to create a subform in an existing form.
- Use an existing form as a subform.

Which method you use depends, for example, on whether you have existing forms that would be suitable as a main form or subform, whether you want to include headers and footers in the forms, and whether you want to include multiple subforms in the main form.

Note that you must use *Single Form* view for a main form. You can use any view for the subform, but *Continuous Form* view is generally the most useful.

In the following exercises you will create forms and subforms for processing book loans and returns. In each case, the main form will display details of an individual library member and the subform will list that member's loan records.

The main form will be based on the Members table (the 'one' side of the Members/Loans relationship). The subform will be based on the Loans table (the 'many' side of the relationship).

Using the Form Wizard

You use the *Form Wizard* to create a main form and subform at the same time.

Exercise 13.2: Using the *Form Wizard* to create a form and subform

1) Start the *Form Wizard*. To do this, click *Forms* in the *Objects* list in the Database window and then double-click the *Create form by using wizard* option in the forms list.

2) In the first page of the wizard, select the Members table in the *Tables/Queries* list and add all its fields to the *Selected fields* list. These are the fields that will be included in the main form.

   Then select the Loans table and add its ISBN, LoanDate, ReturnDate, and FinePaid fields to the list. These are the fields that will be included in the subform. You can omit Loans.MemID from the subform as it displays the same value as the MemID field in the main form.

   Select the Books table and add its Title field immediately below the ISBN field in the list. To do this, select the ISBN field in the right list before adding the Title field. Click **Next**.

   Note that you can select the tables and fields in any order. You don't have to select the table and fields for the main form first.

3) The wizard now asks you how you want to view your data. This is where you indicate the table/query to which you want to bind the main form. You must select a table on the 'one' side of a relationship. If you select a table on the 'many' side (in this case, Loans), the wizard creates a single form in which each record displays all the selected fields.

   Make sure that the *by Members* option is selected. This will create a main form that displays member records and a subform that displays loan records.

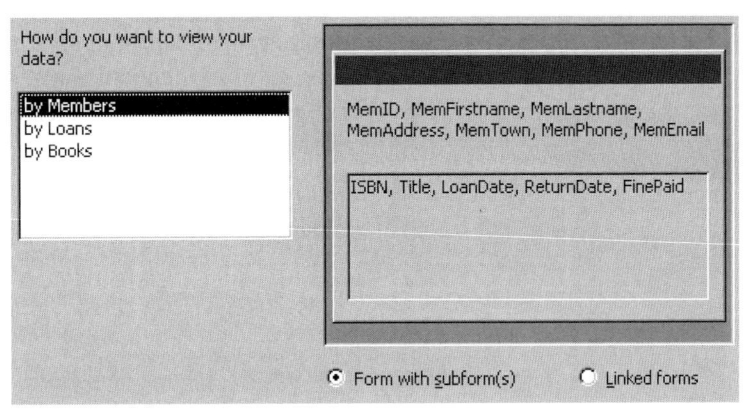

4) You now have the option of creating either a form with a subform or two linked forms. Make sure that the *Form with subform(s)* option is selected and click **Next**.

5) When prompted for a layout for the subform, select *Tabular* and click **Next**. This sets *Continuous Forms* as the default view for the subform.

6) When prompted for a form style, select *Expedition* and click **Next**.

7) When prompted for names for the two forms, enter FormWizard for the main form and FormWizardSubform for the subform. Click **Finish**.

Access now creates the main form and subform and displays the main form in Form View, as shown below.

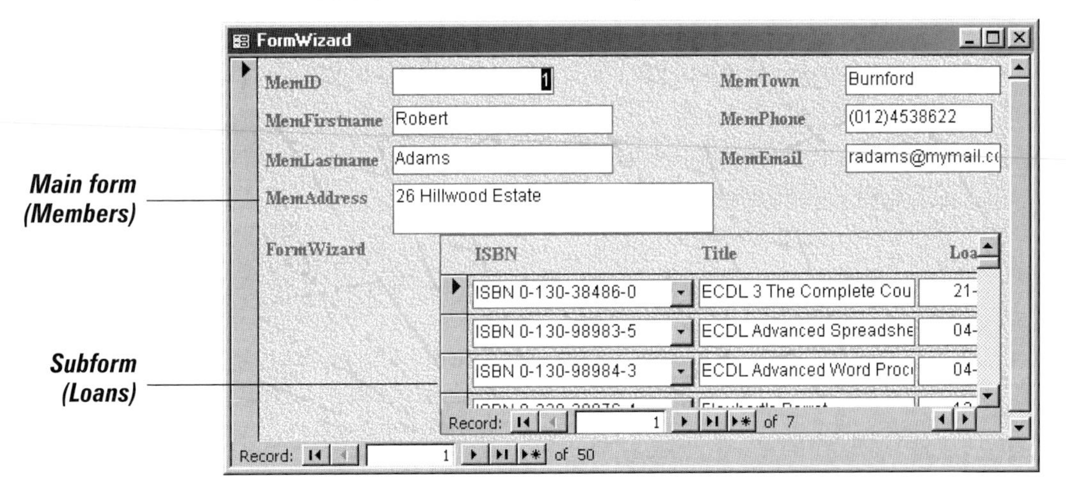

Using the *Form Wizard* is a quick and easy way to create a form and subform. However, the layout and formatting need some editing.

For example, the subform records don't display in full, the size of most fields needs to be adjusted, and the labels in the main form would be better without the 'Mem' prefix. You can make all these changes in Form Design View.

The Subform control

Like all other information in a form, a subform is displayed within a control in the main form. The control used is a Subform/Subreport control (referred to as the Subform control in the rest of this chapter).

Open the *FormWizard* form in Design View and take a look at its subform control:

- The subform control is displayed as a rectangular box. The subform is displayed in Design View within the box.

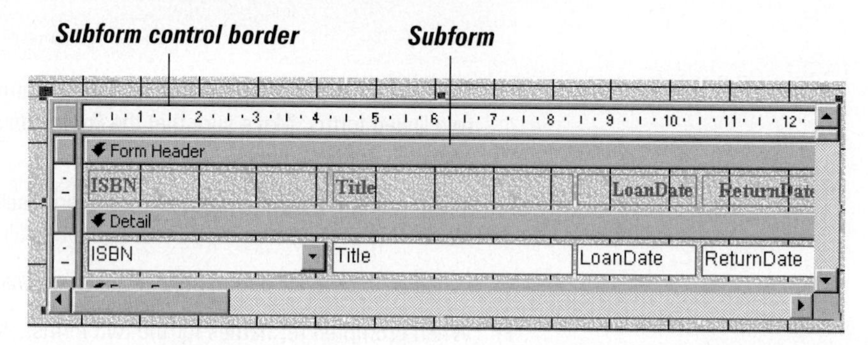

If the control is blank, it means that the subform is already open in a separate window; if this happens, close the main form and subform, and then reopen the main form.

- To select the subform control, click on its border. Alternatively, select the subform control in the *Object* list on the *Formatting* toolbar (it has the same name as the subform it contains).
- Once the control is selected, you can view its properties in its property sheet. The *Name* property specifies the name of the control; the *Source Object* property specifies the form that the control contains; and the *Link Child Fields* and *Link Master Fields* properties specify the fields that link the main form and the subform.

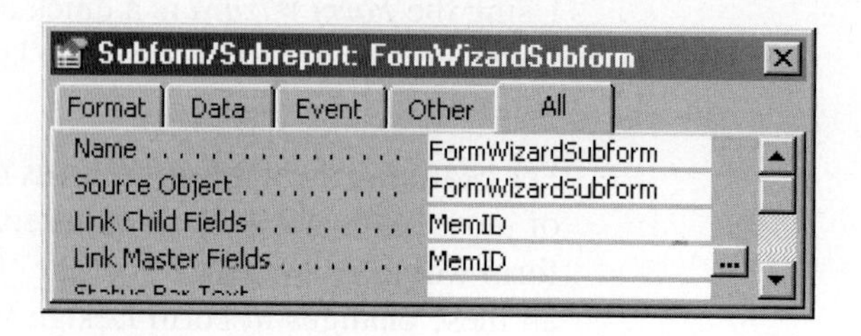

- Once the control is selected, you can also select any element of the subform in the normal way. For example, click the form selector to select the form, click a section selector to select a section, and click a control to select a control.
- When you select an element of the subform, you can edit it in the normal way.

While you can edit a subform from within a main form, it is usually easier to work with a subform in its own Design View window. To do this, close the main form, and then open the subform in Design View from the Database window.

Using the Subform Wizard

You use the *Subform Wizard* to create a subform within an existing form.

Exercise 13.3: Using the *Subform Wizard* to create a form and subform

For this exercise, a form based on the Members table has been prepared for you. You will create the subform that displays the loan records.

1) Open the Process Loans form in Form View.

   Notice that the form displays member records in *Single Form* view. A record selector combo box allows you to select the record you want to view from a lookup list. The MemFirstname and MemLastname values have been merged into a single string, as have the MemAddress and MemTown fields.

2) Switch to Form Design View and make sure that the **Control Wizards** tool is selected (pressed in) in the toolbox.

Subform tool

3) Click the **Subform** tool in the toolbox and click near the left edge of the Detail section, a little below the existing controls. This starts the *Subform Wizard*.

4) The wizard first asks you whether you want to use an existing form as the subform or whether you want to create a new subform. Make sure the *Use existing Tables and Queries* options is selected and click **Next**.

   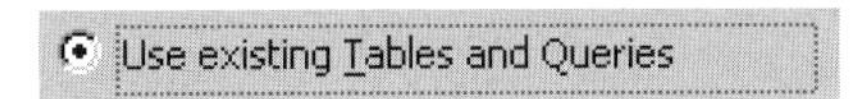

5) When prompted for the fields to include in the subform, select the following fields, in the order listed, and click **Next**:

   - Loans.ISBN
   - Books.Title
   - Loans.LoanDate
   - Loans.ReturnDate
   - Loans.FinePaid

6) The wizard next prompts you to specify the fields that link the subform and main form. The default options are *Choose from a list* and *Show Loans for each record in Members using MemID*. Leave these as they are and click **Next**.

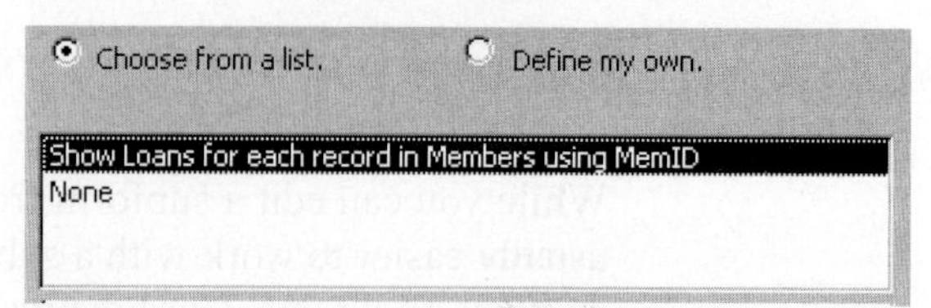

7) When prompted for a name for the subform, enter LoansSubform and click **Finish**. Access now creates the LoansSubform form and adds it to the subform control in the Process Loans form.

8) Switch to Form View to see what the subform looks like and how it works. When you select a member in the main form, the loan records for that member are displayed in the subform. This is what you want. However, the layout and formatting of the subform still need some work.

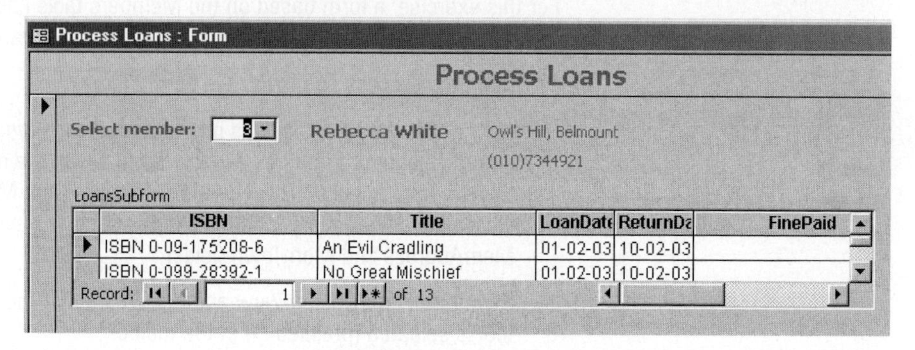

The height of the subform needs to be increased in order to display more records at a time; the field sizes need to be adjusted, and some of the labels could be more user friendly.

9) In the next exercise you will use the same main form and insert an existing form as the subform. So, switch back to Design View now and delete the subform control you have just created.

   To do this, select the control and press **Delete**. Then save and close the main form.

Using an existing form

Why go to the effort of creating a new subform when you already have a suitable form that you can use instead? The Loans and Returns form you created in Chapter 12 is well laid out and formatted, it displays only the records for current loans, and its calculated controls provide useful additional information.

Loans and Returns is an ideal candidate for the subform required by the Process Loans form. Just a few modifications are necessary, and these have already been made in the version of the form included in the `Chp13_VillageLibrary_Database` database.

Open the Loans and Returns form in Form View to see the changes:

- The Loans.MemID field has been removed from the form as it would have the same value as the ID in the main form. And the Books.Title field has been added to make the loan records more meaningful. The Books.Title field was first added to the BookReturns query on which the form is based.
- A new text box control has been added to the footer. This calculates the total amount of fines paid.
- The form's navigation buttons have been removed to avoid confusion with those on the main form. To do this the form's *Navigation Buttons* property was set to 'No'. You can still browse through the loan records by using the scroll bar.

Exercise 13.4: Using an existing form as a subform

In this exercise you will add the Loans and Returns form as a subform in the Process Loans form.

1) Make sure that the Loans and Returns form is closed. Then open the Process Loans form in Design View.
2) Rearrange the Database window and the form window so that you can see them both on your screen.
3) Click on the Loans and Returns form in the Database window and drag it into the form window, dropping it at the position shown here.

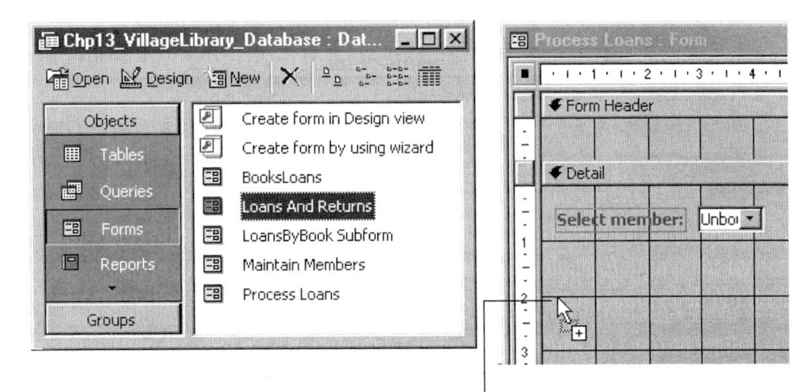

Access creates a subform control and displays the Loans And Returns form in Design View within it, as shown here.

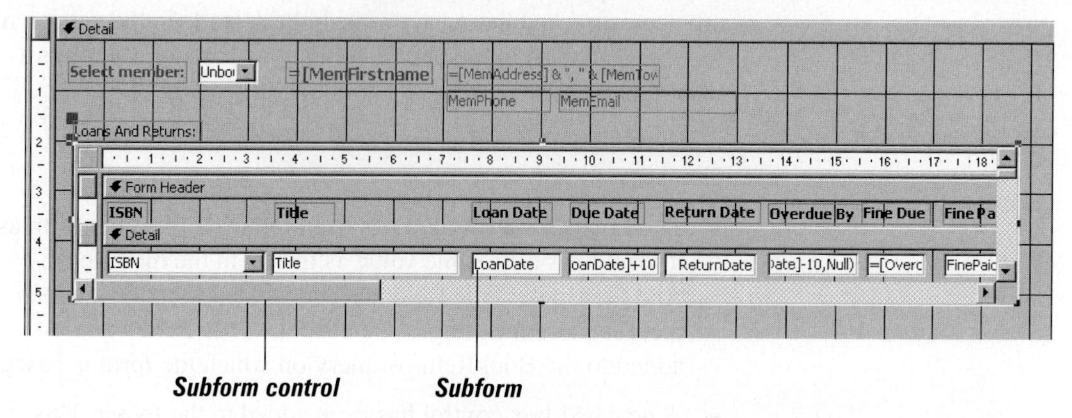

4) Save the Process Loans form and switch to Form View. Access has automatically linked the main form and subform so that the subform always displays the loans for the current member.

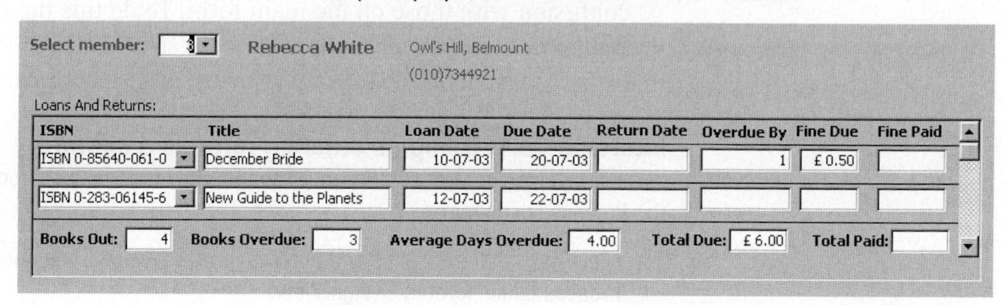

The form is now almost ready for use. Just two small changes: the subform's label should be the same colour as the other labels in the form; and the size of the subform control needs to be adjusted to display more than two records. Switch back to Design View to make these changes.

5) Change the subform control's label to 'Loans'. Make the text bold and the same colour as the other labels in the main form.

6) Members of the Village Library can have up to five books out on loan at the same time. To accommodate five records, the height of the subform control needs to be increased. Select the subform control to display its sizing handles. Then drag the lower edge of the control down to the end of the main form's Detail section and the beginning of the main form's Form Footer section. The control should have a height of about 5.5 cm.

7) Save the form and switch to Form View to see the result of your changes. Your form should now resemble that shown here.

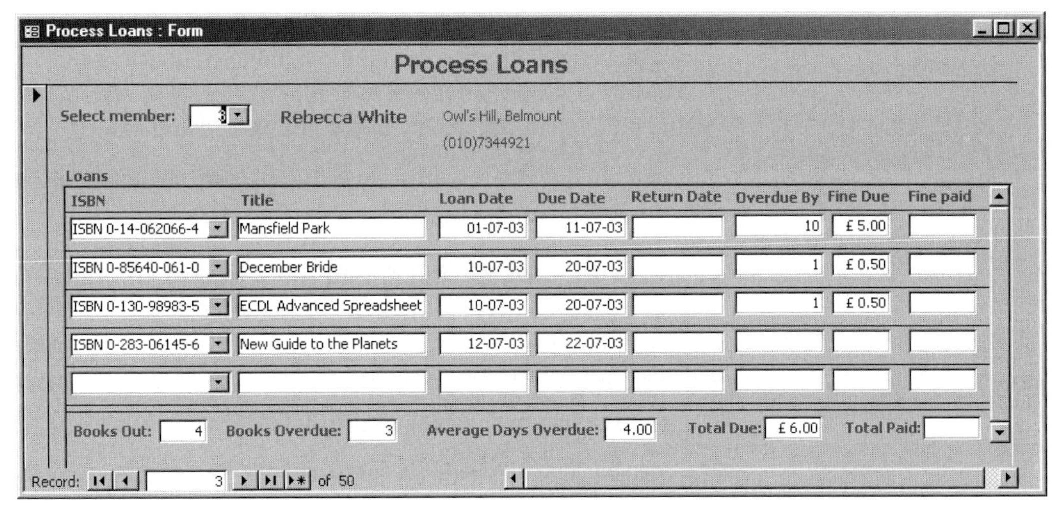

In this exercise, you added the Loans and Returns form to the Process Loans form by dragging it from the Database window. Here are two other methods you can use:

- Use the *Subform Wizard* and, in the first page of the wizard, select the Loans and Returns form as the subform.
- Create a blank subform control and then set its *Source Object* property to the Loans and Returns form.

Modifying the record source for a subform

Which records a subform displays is determined both by the current selection in the main form and by the subform's record source. The record source can be a table, a query or an SQL statement.

- Take a look at the *Record Source* property for the LoansByBook subform and you will see that its record source is the Loans table. The subform displays all records in the Loans table that relate to the book selected in the main form.
- Take a look at the *Record Source* property for the Loans and Returns subform and you will see that its record source is the BookReturns query, which retrieves only current loans – that is, loans where the ReturnDate value is Null.
- Take a look at the *Record Source* property for the FormWizardSubform and you will see that its record source is an SQL statement that retrieves all records from the Loans table and also the Title field from the Books table.

The record source is always an SQL statement when you include fields from more than one table or query in the subform and use a wizard to create it. The SQL statement is the equivalent of a query but is not named and saved.

You can change the record source for any form by changing its *Record Source* property.

Exercise 13.5: Modifying a subform's record source

In this exercise you will modify the record source for the FormWizardSubform subform so that it displays only current loans instead of a member's full borrowing history.

1) Open the subform in Design View from the Database window.
2) Open the form's property sheet and click the **Data** tab to display the *Record Source* property.

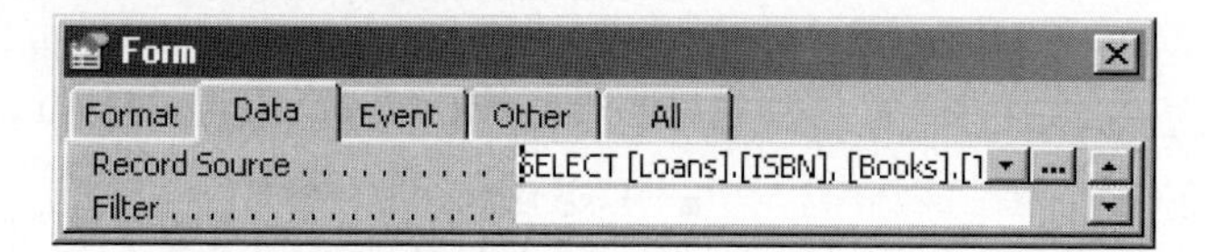

The property box displays both an arrow button and a **Build** button.

3) Click the arrow button. This displays a list of the tables and queries in the database and allows you to select one as the record source for your form instead of the SQL statement. Close the list without selecting an option. To do this, press the **Esc** button.
4) Click the **Build** button. This opens the *Query Builder*, which displays the SQL statement in Query Design View. You can now add and remove fields and specify criteria in the normal way.
5) Enter the following criteria for the ReturnDate field:

```
Is Null
```

6) Close the *Query Builder* window. When prompted to confirm your changes, click **Yes**. This updates the SQL statement in the *Record Source* property.
7) Close the form, saving it as you do.
8) Open the FormWizard form in Form View. When you select a member in the main form, the subform now displays only current loans.

You can modify the record source for the Loans and Returns subform in exactly the same way. Because the record source is a query, any changes you make are saved to that query. Alternatively, you can open the query in Design View from the Database window and make your changes there. The result is the same.

Chapter 13: summary

A *subform* is a form that is contained within another form. The container form is referred to as the *main form*.

Typically you use a main form and subform to display data from tables or queries with a one-to-many relationship. The main table displays records from the 'one' side of the relationship; the subform displays records from the 'many' side. The two forms are linked in such as a way that the subform displays only records that are related to the current record in the main form.

You use the *Form Wizard* to create a main form and subform at the same time. You use the *Subform Wizard* to create a subform in an existing main form. To use an existing form as a subform, open the main form in Design View and then drag the subform from the Database window to the Detail section of the main form.

You can change which records a subform displays by changing its *Record Source* property.

Chapter 13: quick quiz

Q1	True or false – you use a main form to display records from the 'many' side of a relationship.
A.	True.
B.	False.

Q2	To use an existing form as a subform ...
A.	Open the main form in Design View and drag the subform from the Database window into the main form.
B.	Create a blank subform control in the main form and set its *Source Object* property to the name of the subform.
C.	Open the main form in Design View and use the *Subform Wizard* to select the subform.

Q3	Which of these views can you use for a main form?
A.	Single Form.
B.	Datasheet.
C.	Continuous Forms.

Q4	True or false – you can modify a subform from within a main form.
A.	True.
B.	False.

Q5	True or false – you cannot view and use a subform independently of a main form.
A.	True.
B.	False.

Q6	True or false – a subform displays only records related to the current record in the main form.
A.	True.
B.	False.

Answers

1: B, **2**: All, **3**: A, **4**: A, **5**: B, **6**: A.

14 Report design

In this chapter

Reports are the main means of organizing, grouping and summarizing database information in a format suitable for printing and for online review. You can group records on significant fields, summarize and subtotal data within and across groups, create running sums, and perform complex calculations.

In this chapter, you will learn how to use these and other report features.

New skills

At the end of this chapter you should be able to:

- Create calculated controls in a report
- Use aggregate functions in a report
- Calculate percentages in a report
- Create running sums in a report
- Number items in a report
- Display data in headers and footers
- Display report sections on separate pages

New words

In this chapter you will meet the following term:

- Running sum

Exercise file

In this chapter you will work with the following Access file:

- `Chp14_VillageLibrary_Database`

Syllabus reference

In this chapter you will cover the following items of the ECDL Advanced Database Syllabus:

- **AM5.4.1.1**: Create arithmetic, logical calculation controls in a report.
- **AM5.4.1.2**: Calculate percentage calculation control in a report.

- **AM5.4.1.3**: Use formulas, expressions in a report such as sum, count, average, max, min, concatenate.
- **AM5.4.1.4**: Create running summaries in a report.
- **AM5.4.2.1**: Insert a data field to appear within report header, footers on the first page or all pages.
- **AM5.4.2.2**: Force page breaks for groups on reports.

Report controls

As with forms, all information in a report is contained in controls. The same controls are available for reports as for forms, and you create and modify them in the same way and with the same tools.

Most information in reports is presented in text box controls and labels. Reports are not interactive, so controls such as combo boxes, list boxes, option groups and command buttons are not appropriate.

Calculated controls

Calculated report controls are controls that display the results of calculations on other controls or fields in a report. You create them in the same way that you create calculated controls in a form and the same rules and guidelines generally apply.

- You can use calculated controls to perform calculations on values in single records, in order to provide additional information about those records. If you intend using the same calculations in multiple forms or reports, it is often easier to put the calculations in a query and base your report on that query.
- As with forms, you can use calculated controls to summarize values across all records. But, with reports, you can also group records and summarize values within each group.
- Remember that aggregate functions *cannot* refer to the name of a *control*. So an aggregate function cannot summarize values in a calculated control by referring to the control name.

  Instead you can either put the calculation in a query field and refer to that field in the aggregate function, or you can repeat the calculation expression in the aggregate function. For an example, see 'Creating multi-record calculated controls' in Chapter 12.

Exploring the Books By Category report

In the exercises in this chapter you will create the Books By Category report, which lists the full library catalogue, grouped by category, and summarizes the number and cost of books in each category and in the full catalogue.

A finished copy of this report is available in the `Chp14_VillageLibrary_Database` database under the name BooksByCategoryFinishedVersion. Open the report now in Print Preview View and take a look at its content and design.

Report header

The first page you see is the report header. A *report header* is displayed once at the start of a report. You use it to display items such as the report title and date.

In this report, the report header displays thc rcport title, the report date, and a picture. It is displayed on a page by itself.

Category groups

Use the report's navigation buttons to browse through the next few pages of the report. You can see that the main body of the report consists of a list of books and their cost. The books are grouped by category, with each category displayed on a separate page.

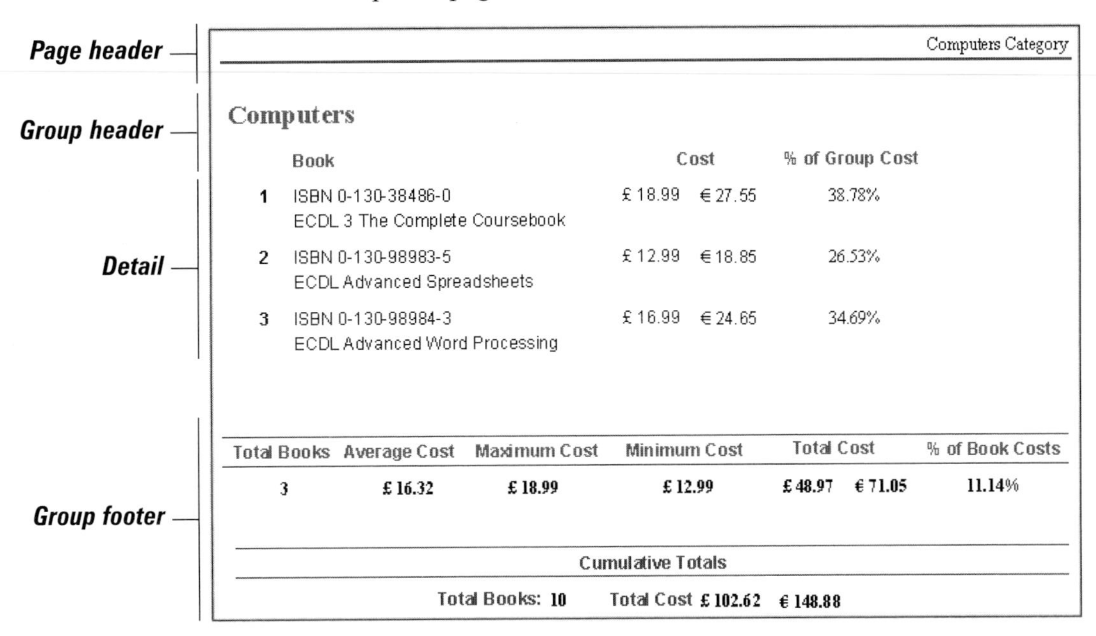

Computers Category

Computers

	Book	Cost		% of Group Cost
1	ISBN 0-130-38486-0 ECDL 3 The Complete Coursebook	£ 18.99	€ 27.55	38.78%
2	ISBN 0-130-98983-5 ECDL Advanced Spreadsheets	£ 12.99	€ 18.85	26.53%
3	ISBN 0-130-98984-3 ECDL Advanced Word Processing	£ 16.99	€ 24.65	34.69%

Total Books	Average Cost	Maximum Cost	Minimum Cost	Total Cost		% of Book Costs
3	£ 16.32	£ 18.99	£ 12.99	£ 48.97	€ 71.05	11.14%

Cumulative Totals

Total Books: 10 Total Cost £ 102.62 € 148.88

For each group there is a group header section, a detail section and a group footer section.

- The *group header* is displayed at the start of each group and you use it to display information that applies to the entire group. In this report, the group header displays the Category value and the column headings. Putting the column headings here means that they are displayed only once at the top of each group. If you include them in the detail section, they are repeated for each record in the group.
- The *detail* section displays the main report data. In this report, it lists the books in the current category and numbers the books sequentially within the group. For each book, the value of the BooksConfidential.Cost field is displayed and the euro equivalent is calculated. The percentage value displays the book cost as a percentage of the total cost of books in the category.

  Some books were donated to the library. In these cases, the word 'Donated' is displayed instead of costs. For examples of this, go to the Science and Reference categories.
- The *group footer* is displayed at the end of each group. You typically use it to display group totals. In this report, the group footer displays summary information about the number and cost of books in the current category. The percentage value displays the total cost of books in the category, as a percentage of the total cost of books in the library.

  The group footer in this report also displays running sums – that is, totals for all categories up to and including the current category.

Report footer

The *report footer* is displayed once at the end of a report. You use it to display items such as report totals. In this report, the report footer displays summary information about the number and cost of books in the library. It is displayed on a page by itself.

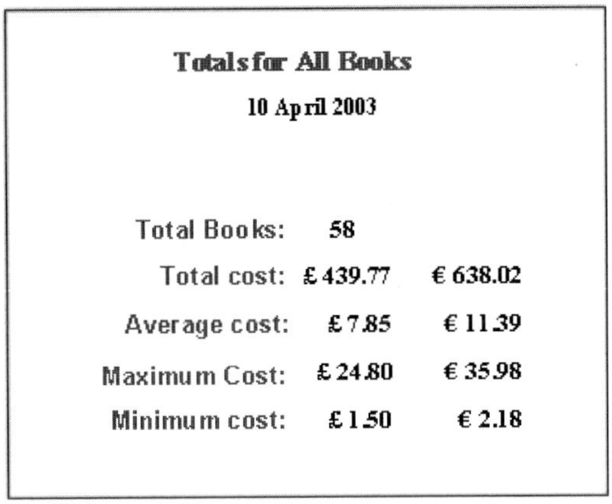

Totals for All Books

10 April 2003

Total Books:	**58**	
Total cost:	**£439.77**	**€638.02**
Average cost:	**£7.85**	**€11.39**
Maximum Cost:	**£24.80**	**€35.98**
Minimum cost:	**£1.50**	**€2.18**

Page headers and footers

Page headers and *page footers* are displayed at the top and bottom of each page. Typically you use the page header to display column headings, and the page footer to display page numbers.

In this report, the page header displays the name of the current category. The page footer displays the date and page number.

Page header — Science Category

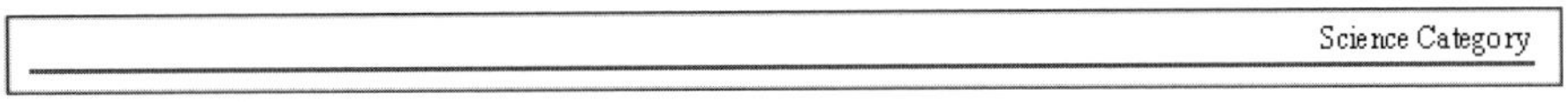

Page footer — **10-Apr-03** **Page 11 of 12**

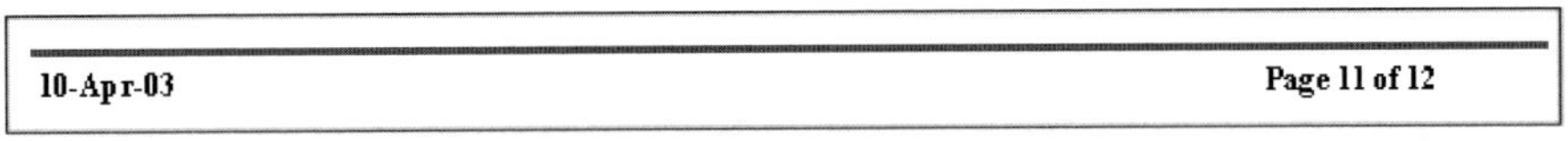

Design View

Now let's take a look at the report in Design View and see how it is defined.

- First display the property sheet for the report and take a look at its *Record Source* property. The report is based on a query named BooksByCategoryReportSource. You can open and view the query by clicking the **Build** button in the *Record Source* property box.

  This query joins the Books and BooksConfidential tables, and retrieves the ISBN, Title, Category and Cost fields from those tables. The tables are joined with a left outer join so that the query returns *all* records from the Books table, including those that have no matching record in the BooksConfidential table.

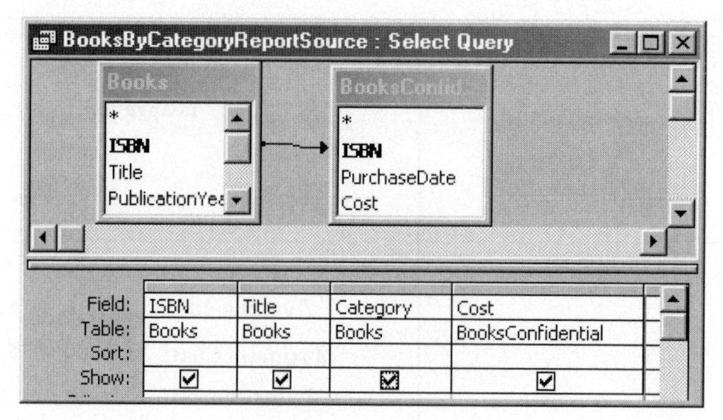

If you have opened the *Query Builder*, close it before continuing.

- If you open the **View** menu, you can see that both the **Page Header/Footer** and **Report Header/Footer** options are selected, so the report includes these sections.

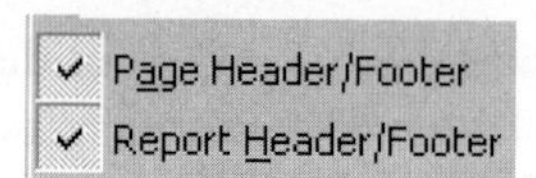

- If you open the *Sorting and Grouping* dialog box (choose **View | Sorting and Grouping**), you can see that a Category group has been created by selecting the Category field in the *Field/Expression* column and setting its *Group Header* and *Group Footer* properties to *Yes*. An ascending sort order has also been selected for the group.

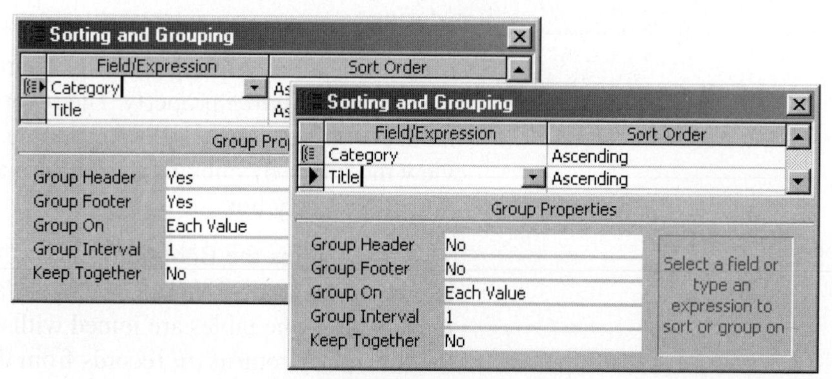

- To sort the books in ascending order of title, the Title field has been selected in the *Field/Expression* column and *Ascending* has been selected in the *Sort Order* column.

You can now close the BooksByCategoryFinishedVersion report. Do not save any changes you may have made.

Creating calculated controls

The BooksByCategoryFinishedVersion report includes calculated controls for a variety of calculation types and for different report sections. In the exercises in this section you will add these calculations to the Books By Category report.

This report has already been started for you. Open it now in Print Preview mode. You can see that it includes all the relevant sections and labcls, but no calculations, no page breaks between sections, and no information in the page header and footer.

Switch to Design View and you can see that most of the text box controls for the calculations have been created for you. Your task is to add the calculations themselves.

Note that in the exercises, controls are referred to by the names specified in their *Name* properties. For unbound controls, the names have been changed from the default names (Text1 and Text2, for example) to make them more meaningful.

Report width wider than page width warning

The Books By Category report is designed to be printed on A4 size paper. The report itself is a little less than 16 cm wide; the margins take up the rest of the page width. If the following message appears at any stage when you switch from Design View to Print Preview, it means that the report width has been increased beyond what will fit on one page.

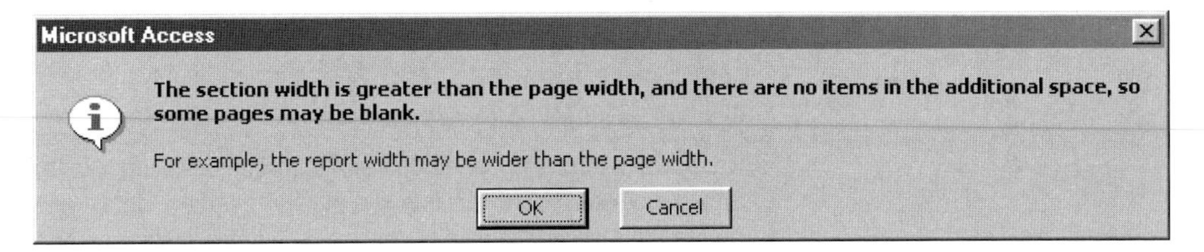

This can happen when you create a new control near the right edge of the report. If the control extends beyond the edge of the report, Access automatically increases the report width to accommodate it. If this happens, first move the control back from the edge of the report; then drag the report edge back to its original position (16 cm or less).

Creating calculated controls in the detail section

In the detail section of a report you create calculated controls that perform calculations on values in individual records.

Exercise 14.1: Creating calculated controls in the detail section

In this exercise you will add a calculation to display the euro cost of each book, and you will create a calculated field that displays the word 'Donated' for books that have no Cost value.

1) Open the Books By Category report in Design View and scroll to the detail section.

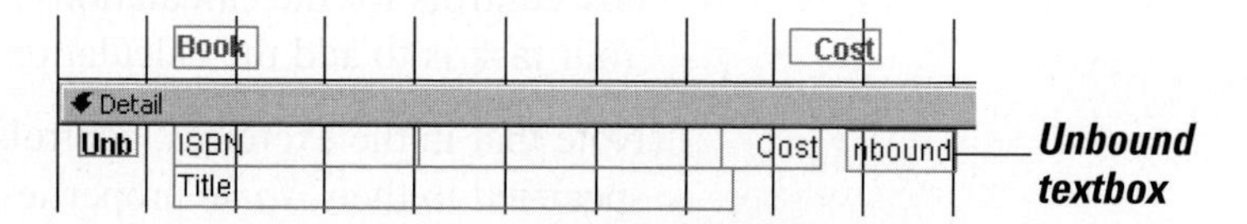

Notice that there are two controls below the Cost heading. The first is a text box control that is bound to the Cost field. The second is an unbound text box control (named EuroCost) that currently has no source.

2) Enter the following expression in the EuroCost text box control (you can type the expression directly in the control or in its *Control Source* property):

```
=[Cost]*1.4508
```

This calculates the euro equivalent of the values in the Cost field.

3) Display the property sheet for the EuroCost control and select the *Euro* option in its *Format* property. This format displays the € symbol and two decimal places only.

4) Now create a new unbound text box control by clicking the **Text Box** tool in the toolbox and clicking in a blank area of the detail section. Delete the attached label and change the control's *Name* property to 'DonatedBook'.

5) Enter the following expression in the control:

```
=IIf(IsNull([Cost]),"Donated",Null)
```

This checks if the Cost field is empty. If it is, the control displays the word 'Donated'. If it isn't, the control displays nothing.

6) You want the word 'Donated' to be displayed below the Cost heading, in place of the cost values. So change the width of the control to just fit the word 'Donated'; then position it on top of, and centred on, the Cost and EuroCost controls.

This may look confusing in Design View, but in Print Preview the DonatedBook control will always be empty if the other two controls contain values and vice versa.

Print Preview button

7) Save the report and switch to Print Preview to see the result of your changes. To see the DonatedBook control in action, go to the Science or Reference category.

ISBN 0-283-06145-6 £ 10.99 € 15.94
New Guide to the Planets

ISBN 0-00-219169-5 Donated
The Living Planet

Creating calculated controls in a group footer

In a group footer section of a report you typically create calculated controls that display group totals.

Exercise 14.2: Creating calculated controls in the group footer

In this exercise you will add calculations that display summary information about the number and cost of books in each category.

1) Open the Books By Category report in Design View and scroll to the group footer section (named Category Footer in this report).

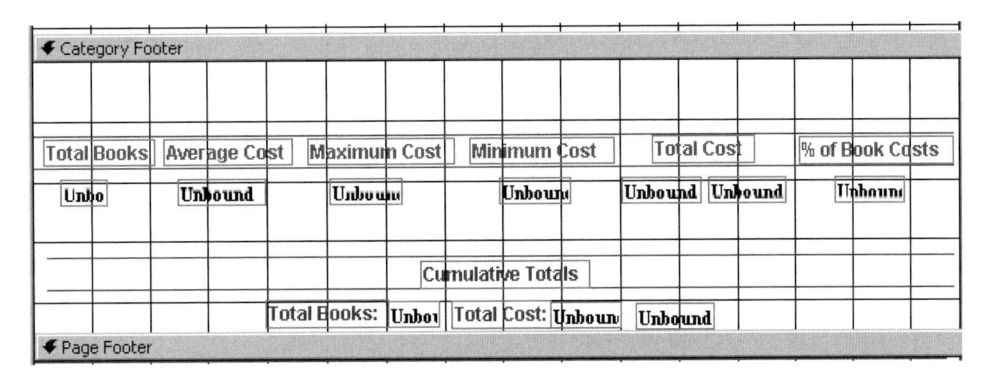

An unbound text box control has been created under each of the headings in the upper part of the section. These are where you will enter the group calculations.

2) In the TotalBooks text box control, enter the following expression:

```
=Count(*)
```

This counts all books in a group.

3) In the AverageCost text box control, enter the following expression:

```
=Avg([Cost])
```

This calculates the average cost of books in a group.

4) In the MaximumCost text box control, enter the following expression:

```
=Max([Cost])
```

This returns the maximum book cost in a group.

5) In the MinimumCost text box control, enter the following expression:

```
=Min([Cost])
```

This returns the minimum book cost in a group.

6) In the GroupTotalCostGBP text box control, enter the following expression:

```
=Sum([Cost])
```

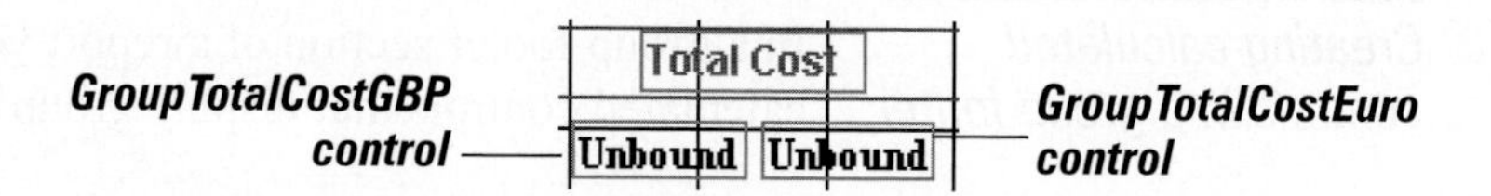

This totals the cost of books in a group.

7) In the GroupTotalCostEuro text box control, enter the following expression:

```
=Sum([Cost]*1.4508)
```

This totals the costs of books in a group, in euros. To include the euro symbol, select the *Euro* option in the control's *Format* property.

8) Save the report and switch to Print Preview to see the result of your changes. For example, the group footer for the Children category should now look as shown here.

Total Books	Average Cost	Maximum Cost	Minimum Cost	Total Cost	
6	£6.82	£18.99	£2.99	£40.90	€59.34

Creating calculated controls in the report footer

In the report footer section of a report you typically create calculated controls that display report totals.

Exercise 14.3: Creating calculated controls in the report footer

In this exercise you will add calculations that display summary information about the number and cost of books in the library as a whole.

1) Open the Books By Category report in Design View and scroll to the report footer section.

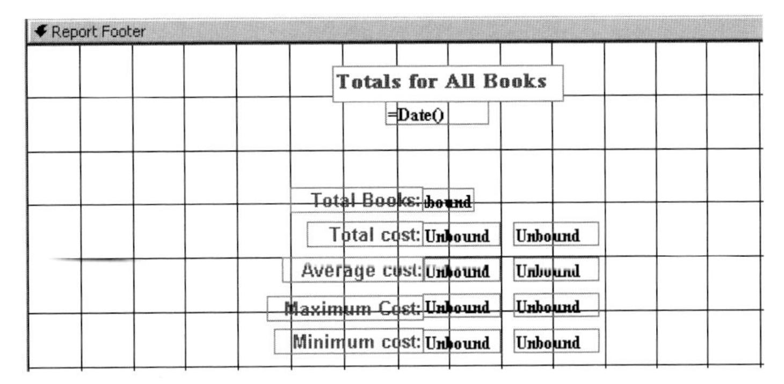

There are unbound text box controls beside each label in the section. These are where you will enter the overall report calculations.

2) In the ReportTotalBooks text box control, enter the following expression:

```
=Count(*)
```

This counts all books in the report.

3) In the RcportTotalCostGBP text box control, enter the following expression:

```
=Sum([Cost])
```

This calculates the total cost of books in the report.

4) In the ReportTotalCostEuro text box control, enter the following expression:

```
=Sum([Cost]*1.4508)
```

This calculates the total cost of books in euros.

5) In the ReportAverageCostGBP text box control, enter the following expression:

```
=Avg([Cost])
```

This calculates the average cost of books in the report.

6) In the ReportAverageCostEuro text box control, enter the following expression:

```
=Avg([Cost]*1.4508)
```

This calculates the average cost of books in euros.

7) In the ReportMaxCostGBP text box control, enter the following expression:

```
=Max([Cost])
```

This returns the maximum book cost in the report.

8) In the ReportMaxCostEuro text box control, enter the following expression:

```
=Max([Cost]*1.4508)
```

This returns the maximum book cost in euros.

9) In the ReportMinCostGBP text box control, enter the following expression:

```
=Min([Cost])
```

This returns the minimum book cost in the report.

10) In the ReportMinCostEuro text box control, enter the following expression:

```
=Min([Cost]*1.4508)
```

This returns the minimum book cost in euros.

11) Save the report and switch to Print Preview to see the result of your changes. The report footer should now look as shown here.

Totals for All Books

10 April 2003

Total Books:	58	
Total cost:	£439.77	€638.02
Average cost:	£7.85	€11.39
Maximum Cost:	£24.80	€35.98
Minimum cost:	£1.50	€2.18

Creating calculated controls in the report header

In the report header section of a report you typically create calculated controls for the date and perhaps for some summary data.

Exercise 14.4: Creating a calculated control in the report header

In this exercise you will add the current date to the report header.

1) Open the Books By Category report in Design View. There is an unbound text box control immediately below the report title. This is where you will enter the date expression.

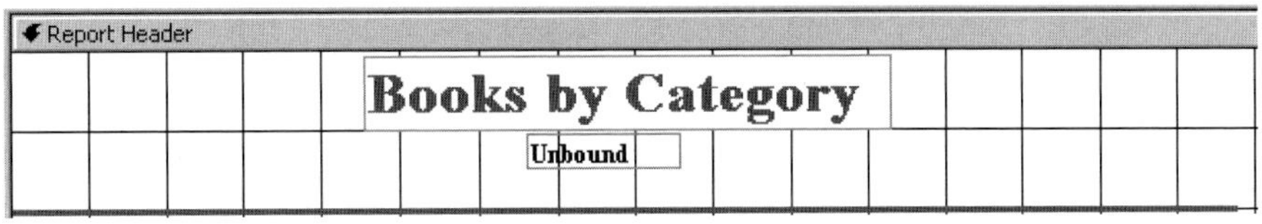

Report Header

Books by Category

Unbound

Note that the report header includes a decorative line and an image. For your information, these were created with the **Line** and **Unbound Object Frame** tools respectively. In the latter case, the image was selected from Microsoft's Clip Gallery.

2) In the HeaderDate text box control, enter the following expression:

```
=Date()
```

This returns the current date.

3) Save the report and switch to Print Preview to see the result of your change.

Creating calculated controls in the page header

You typically use the page header section to display column headings, but you can also use it to repeat the report date, the report title or a group heading, for example.

Exercise 14.5: Creating a calculated control in the page header

In this exercise you will add a calculated control to the page header to display the category heading for the first group on each page.

1) Open the Books By Category report in Design View.

2) Create a new text box control at the right side of the page header section. Delete the attached label, and make the text box about 3 cm wide.

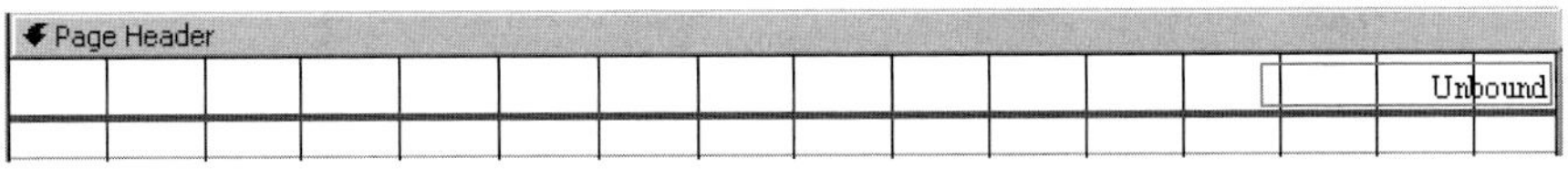

Page Header

Unbound

3) Enter the following expression In the control:

```
=[Category] & " Category"
```

This expression references the Category control in the group header. On each page, it will display the value of that control for the first group on the page. The concatenation expression appends the word 'Category' after the category value.

4) Save the report and switch to Print Preview to see the result of your change.

Computers Category

Computers

Book	Cost		% of Group Cost
ISBN 0-130-38486-0 ECDL 3 The Complete Coursebook	£ 18.99	€ 27.55	38.78%

Creating calculated controls in the page footer

You typically use the page footer section of a report to display the date and page numbers.

Exercise 14.6: Creating calculated controls in the page footer

In this exercise you will add the date and page number to the page footer. You could create the controls and expressions for these items manually, but it is quicker and easier to use the **Insert** menu options.

1) Open the Books By Category report in Design View.

2) Choose **Insert | Page Numbers**. This displays the *Page Numbers* dialog box, which presents various options for displaying page numbers. Select the following options:

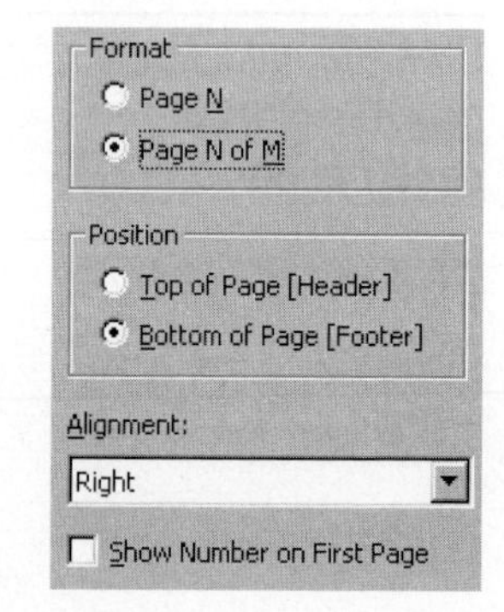

- *Format – Page N of M*
- *Position – Bottom of page (Footer)*
- *Alignment – Right*

Deselect the *Show Number on First Page* option. Then click **OK**.

3) Scroll to the page footer section and you can see that a text box control and appropriate expression have automatically been created for the page numbering.

4) Choose **Insert | Date and Time**. This displays the *Date and Time* dialog box.
5) Make sure the *Include Date* option is selected and then select the Medium Date format (for example, 10-Apr-03).
6) Deselect the *Include Time* option and click **OK**.

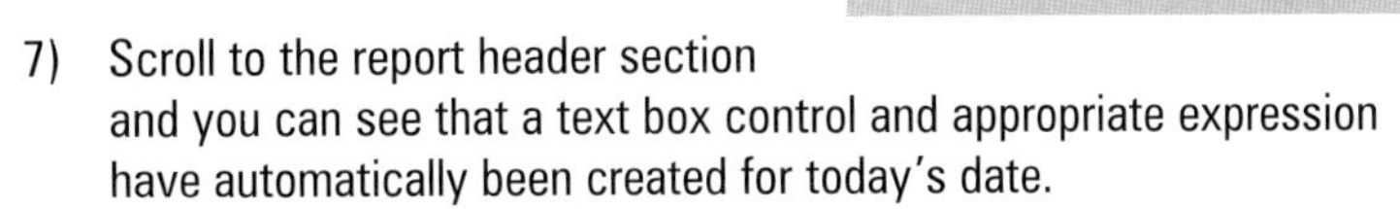

7) Scroll to the report header section and you can see that a text box control and appropriate expression have automatically been created for today's date.

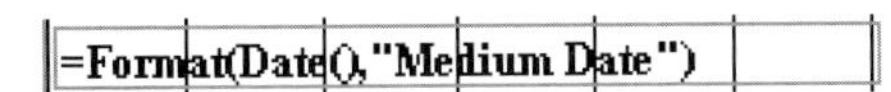

Select the control and drag it to the left side of the page footer section, as shown here.

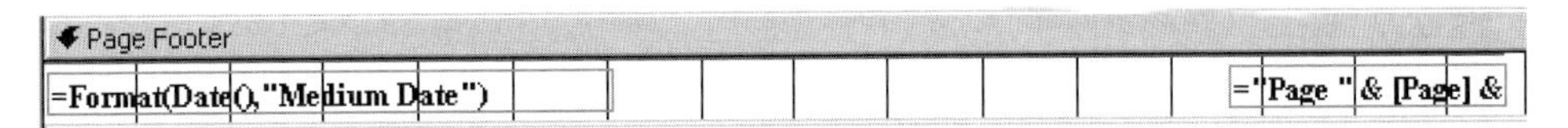

8) Save the report and switch to Print Preview to see the result of your changes.

Calculating percentages in a report

In a report you often need to calculate what percentage one value is of another. For example, what percentage a field value is of a group total and what percentage a group total is of a report total.

To do this you simply create an unbound text box control and enter an expression that divides the smaller value by the larger value. You then set the control's *Format* property to *Percent*.

Exercise 14.7: Calculating percentages

In this exercise you will add percentage calculations to the detail and group footer sections of the report.

1) Open the Books By Category report in Design View and scroll to the detail section.
2) There is an empty text box control (named PercentOfGroup) below the % of Group Costs heading. Enter the following expression in this control:

```
=[Cost]/[GroupTotalCostGBP]
```

This divides the cost of each book by the total cost of books in the group (as calculated in the GroupTotalCostGBP control), indicating what percentage the book cost is of the total group cost.

Select *Percent* in the *Format* property for the PercentOfGroup control.

3) There is another empty text box control (named PercentOfReport) in the Category Footer section, below the % of Book Costs heading. Enter the following expression in this control:

```
=[GroupTotalCostGBP]/[ReportTotalCostGBP]
```

This divides the total cost of books in a category by the total cost of books in the report (as calculated by the ReportTotalCostGBP control in the report footer), indicating what proportion the total category cost is of the total report cost.

Select *Percent* in the *Format* property for the PercentOfReport control.

4) Save the report and switch to Print Preview to see the result of your changes. For example, the information for the Reference category should now look as shown.

Reference

Book	Cost		% of Group Cost
ISBN 0-00-447823-1 Atlas of the World	Donated		
ISBN 0-7548-0731-2 The New Guide to Cat Care	£ 14.95	€ 21.69	100.00%

Total Books	Average Cost	Maximum Cost	Minimum Cost	Total Cost		% of Book Costs
2	**£ 14.95**	**£ 14.95**	**£ 14.95**	**£ 14.95**	**€ 21.69**	**3.40%**

Creating running sums

A running sum is a cumulative total of values in a report. You use a running sum to calculate record-by-record or group-by-group subtotals.

On the right is an example of a running sum that you could include in the Books By Category report. It displays a cumulative total for the Cost values in the detail section.

Cost	Running Sum
£ 18.99	£ 18.99
£ 2.99	£ 21.98
£ 3.99	£ 25.97
£ 3.99	£ 29.96
£ 5.99	£ 35.95
£ 4.95	£ 40.90

For each record, the running sum calculation adds the value of the Cost field to the previous value of the running sum, so accumulating the total Cost values record-by-record.

To create this running sum, you would create a text box control that is bound to the BooksConfidential.Cost field and then set the control's *Running Sum* property to either *Over Group* or *Over All*.

To create a running sum that increases for each record, you put it in the detail section. To create a running sum that increases for each group, you put it in the group header or group footer section.

You can choose to reset the running sum at the start of each group or to accumulate the totals through the entire report.

Running sum
A cumulative total of values in a report.

Exercise 14.8: Creating running sums

In this exercise you will add three running sums to the group footer.

1) Open the Books By Category report in Design View and scroll to the Category Footer section.

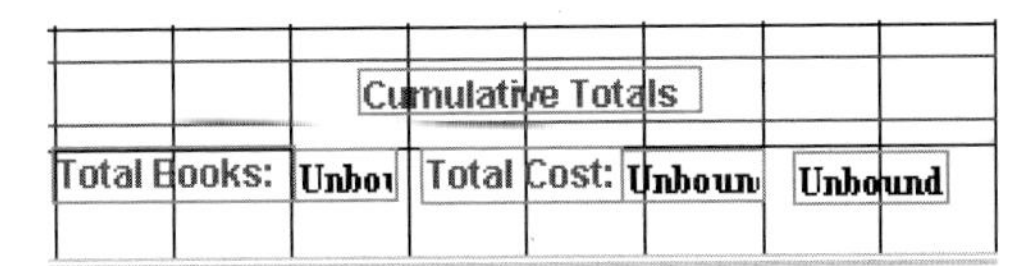

   There are three unbound text box controls below the Cumulative Totals heading. These are where you will create the running sums.

2) You are going to use the TotalCostCumulativeGBP control (the second in the row) to calculate a running sum for the total cost of books in each group.

   – To calculate the total cost of books in a group, enter the following expression in the TotalCostCumulativeGBP control:

     ```
     =Sum([Cost])
     ```

   – To create a running sum that accumulates until the end of the report, select the *Over All* option in the control's *Running Sum* property (**Data** tab).

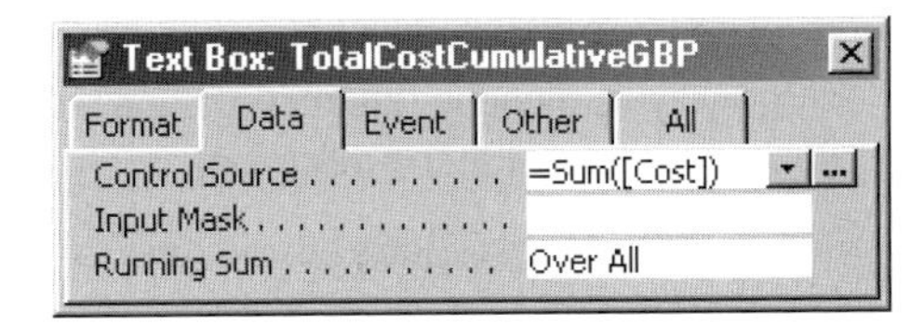

3) You are going to use the TotalCostCumulativeEuro control (the last in the row) to create an equivalent running sum in euros.

   – To calculate the total cost of books in a group in euros, enter the following expression in the TotalCostCumulativeEuro control:

     ```
     =Sum([Cost]*1.4508)
     ```

- To create a running sum that accumulates until the end of the report, select the *Over All* option in the control's *Running Sum* property.

4) You are going to use the TotalBooksCumulative control to calculate a running sum for the total number of books in each group.
   - To calculate the total number of books in a group, enter the following expression in the TotalBooksCumulative control:

     ```
     =Count(*)
     ```

   - To create a running sum that accumulates until the end of the report, select the *Over All* option in the control's *Running Sum* property.

5) Save the report and switch to Print Preview to see your running sums in action. Browse through the report from group to group and you will see that the running sum values accumulate through the report.

   Note that the running sum values for the last group represent the grand totals for the entire report, as shown here.

Cumulative Totals		
Total Books: 58	Total Cost £439.77	€ 638.02

Exercise 14.9: Repeating the grand total in the report footer

When a running sum is set to accumulate through the entire report, its final value represents the grand total for the report. In this exercise you will use this value to repeat the grand total in the report footer.

1) Open the Books By Category report in Design View and scroll to the report footer section.

2) The ReportTotalBooks text box control currently uses the Count() function to calculate the total number of books in the report. However, by the end of the report, the running sum in the TotalBooksCumulative control contains the same value.

3) To demonstrate this, change the expression in the ReportTotalBooks control to the following:

   ```
   =[TotalBooksCumulative]
   ```

   This simply references the value in the TotalBooksCumulative control.

4) Save the report and switch to Print Preview. Go to the report footer and you will see that the Total Books value is the same as before.

Numbering report items

In a report, it is often useful to number records and groups for easy reference. The running sum feature provides a very handy way to do this.

In the example here, a running sum is used to sequentially number book records in the detail section of a report.

1	ISBN 0-14-023171-4	A Good Man In Africa
2	ISBN 0-552-99702-1	A Walk in the Woods
3	ISBN 0-14-012670-8	Animal Farm
4	ISBN 0-14-014658-X	Brazzaville Beach
5	ISBN 0-552-99893-1	Chocolat

How do you create the running sum? Simply create an unbound text box control, set its *Control Source* property to '=1' and set its *Running Sum* property to either *Over Group* or *Over All*.

How does this work? The source value for the running sum is 1 and this is the running sum value for the first record. For each subsequent record, the running sum calculation adds its source value (that is, 1) to the current running sum value. This effectively increments the value of the control by 1 for each record.

Exercise 14.10: Number records in a report

In this exercise you will use a running sum to number the records in the Books By Category report.

1) Open the report in Design View and scroll to the detail section. There is a small, unbound text box control (named BookNumbers) at the start of this section. You will use this for the record numbers.

BookNumbers control

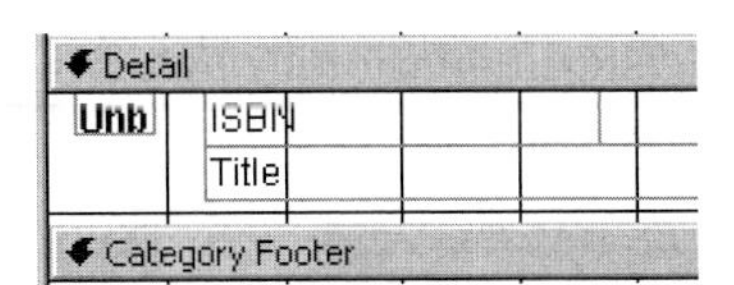

2) Enter the following expression in the BookNumbers control:

   =1

3) To create a running sum that is reset to its source value at the start of each group, select the *Over Group* option in the control's *Running Sum* property.

4) Save the report and switch to Print Preview to see the record numbering. For example, the Science category in the report should now look as shown below.

	Science			
	Book	Cost		% of Group Cost
1	ISBN 0-451-16776-7 Feeling Good: The New Mood Therapy	£ 4.99	€7.24	12.83%
2	ISBN 1-85702-712-4 Galileo's Daughter	£ 10.40	€15.09	26.75%
3	ISBN 0-283-06145-6 New Guide to the Planets	£ 10.99	€15.94	28.27%
4	ISBN 0-00-219169-5 The Living Planet	Donated		
5	ISBN 0-297-81410-9 The Man in the Ice	£ 12.50	€18.14	32.15%

Working with page breaks

By default, report sections have no page breaks between them. Each section and group is displayed on the same page as the previous section or group, provided there is sufficient space.

The report header and footer, group header and footer, and detail sections all have a *Force New Page* property that you can use to create page breaks before and/or after the sections. The options available are:

- **None**. The section is displayed on the same page as the previous section.
- **Before Section**. The section is displayed at the top of a new page.
- **After Section**. The next section is displayed at the top of a new page.
- **Before & After**. The section is displayed at the top of a new page, and the next section is also displayed at the top of a new page.

Exercise 14.11: Creating page breaks between sections

In this exercise you will modify the Books By Category report so that individual groups and the report header and footer are all displayed on separate pages.

1) Open the Books By Category report in Design View.
2) Display the property sheet for the Report Header section and select the *AfterSection* option in the *Force New Page* property. This inserts a page break after the report header, so that it appears on a page by itself.
3) Display the property sheet for the Category Header section and select the *BeforeSection* option in its *Force New Page* property. This inserts a page break before each group header, so that each group is displayed on a separate page.

4) Select *Yes* in the section's *Repeat Section* property. If a group spans more than one page, this causes the group header to be repeated on those pages.

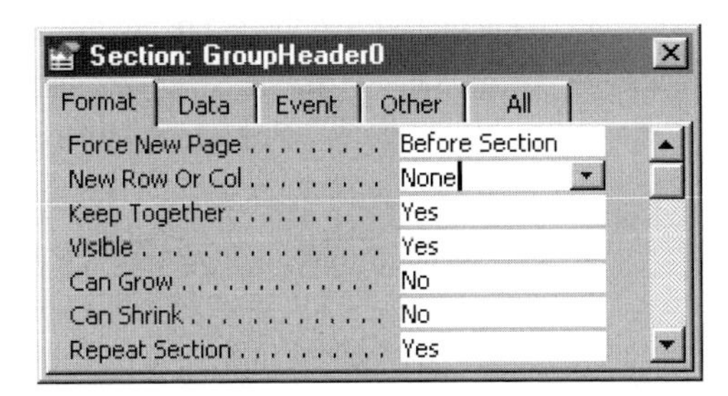

5) Display the property sheet for the report footer section and select the *BeforeSection* option in its *Force New Page* property.

   This inserts a page break before the report footer, so that it is displayed on a page of its own.

6) Save the report and switch to Print Preview to see the result of your changes.

Omitting page headers and footers

If you include page header and footer sections in a report, they are displayed on all pages by default. However, when you are using the report header as a title page, for example, you may want to omit the page header and footer from that page. Similarly, you may want to omit the page header and footer from the page that displays the report footer.

You use the report's *Page Header* and *Page Footer* properties to do this. The options are:

- **All Pages**. Displays the page header or footer on all pages.
- **Not with Rpt Hdr**. Omits the page header or footer from the report header page.
- **Not with Rpt Ftr**. Omits the page header or footer from the report footer page.
- **Not with Rpt Hdr/Ftr**. Omits the page header or footer from both the report header and report footer pages.

Exercise 14.12: Omitting page headers/footers from the report header/footer pages

In this exercise you will modify the Books By Category report so that the page header and footer are omitted from the report header page and the page header is omitted from the report footer page.

1) Open the Books By Category report in Design View and display the report's property sheet.
2) Select the *Not with Rpt Hdr/Ftr* option in the *Page Header* property. This omits the page header from both the report header and report footer pages.
3) Select the *Not with Rpt Hdr* option in the *Page Footer* property. This omits the page footer from the report header page but not from the report footer page.

4) Save the report and switch to Print Preview to see the result of your changes.

Chapter 14: summary

Reports are the main means of organizing, grouping and summarizing database information in a format suitable for printing and for online review. As with forms, all information in a report is contained in *controls*. The same controls are available for reports as for forms, and you create and modify them in the same way and with the same tools.

Calculated report controls are controls that display the results of calculations on other controls or fields in a report. You create them in the same way that you create calculated controls in a form, and the same rules and guidelines generally apply.

To perform calculations on single records in a report, put the calculated controls in the detail section. To summarize values in a group with Access's aggregate functions, put the calculated controls in the group header or footer. To summarize values across the entire report, put the calculated controls in the report footer. To include a data value on all pages, put the calculated control in the page header or footer.

A *running sum* is a cumulative total of values in a report. To create a running sum that increases for each record, put it in the detail section. To create a running sum that increases for each group, put it in the group header or footer section. In both cases you use the calculated control's *Running Sum* property to create the running sum.

You can also use a running sum to number records in a group and to number groups in a report.

The report header and footer, group header and footer, and detail sections all have a *Force New Page* property that you can use to create page breaks before and/or after the sections. The report itself has *Page Header* and *Page Footer* properties that you can use to omit the page header and footer from the pages that display the report header and/or report footer.

Chapter 14: quick quiz

Q1	True or false – aggregate functions cannot reference calculated controls.
A.	True.
B.	False.

Q2	Where do you create calculations that summarize group values?
A.	Detail section.
B.	Group header section.
C.	Group footer section.
D.	Report footer section.

Q3	Where do you create calculations that summarize values for an entire report?
A.	Detail section.
B.	Group header section.
C.	Report header section.
D.	Report footer section.

Q4	You can use a running sum to ...
A.	Number records sequentially within a group.
B.	Display a cumulative, record-by-record total for a value in a report.
C.	Number groups sequentially through an entire report.
D.	Display a cumulative, group-by-group total for a value in a report.

Q5	To display each group on a separate page, you ...
A.	Set the group header's *Force New Page* property to *Before Section*.
B.	Set the group footer's *Force New Page* property to *After Section*.
C.	Set the page header's *Force New Page* property to *Before & After*.
D.	Set the report header's *Force New Page* property to *Before & After*.

Q6	True or false – expressions in calculated report controls must start with an equal to (=) symbol.
A.	True.
B.	False.

Answers

1: A, **2**: B and C, **3**: C and D, **4**: All, **5**: A and B, **6**: A.

15 Macros

In this chapter

Macros provide a simple means of automating common database tasks. You can use them to automatically perform tasks that you repeat frequently and to make your database objects work together.

In this chapter, you will learn how to create macros and how to attach them to forms, reports and controls.

New skills

At the end of this chapter you should be able to:

- Create a macro
- Run a macro
- Attach macros to controls, forms and reports

New words

In this chapter you will meet the following terms:

- Macro
- Event

Exercise file

In this chapter you will work with the following Access file:

- `Chp15_VillageLibrary_Database`

Syllabus reference

In this chapter you will cover the following items of the ECDL Advanced Database Syllabus:

- **AM5.5.1.1**: Record a simple macro (e.g. close a form).
- **AM5.5.1.2**: Run a macro.
- **AM5.5.1.3**: Assign/attach a macro to a form, report, control.

About macros

A macro consists of a sequence of one or more database actions that can be triggered automatically or executed with a single command. A typical macro is one that opens a form or prints a report. But why create a macro to perform such a simple action?

The power of macros lies is their ability to run automatically in response to events that occur on forms, reports and controls. For example, a macro that simply opens the Maintain Members form is not very useful by itself. But, if it runs automatically when you click a command button in the Process Loans form, it becomes a useful tool for integrating the two forms.

In the exercises in this chapter you will add macros to the Process Loans form that you created in Chapter 13. A finished copy of this form is available in the `Chp15_VillageLibrary_Database` database under the name ProcessLoansFinishedVersion. Open that form now in Form View.

You can see that the main form has four command buttons, each of which triggers a macro. Click each command button in turn to see what happens.

- The **View Member** button displays the Maintain Members form for the currently selected member. If you change and save the member's details in the Maintain Members form, the changes are automatically reflected in the Process Loans form.

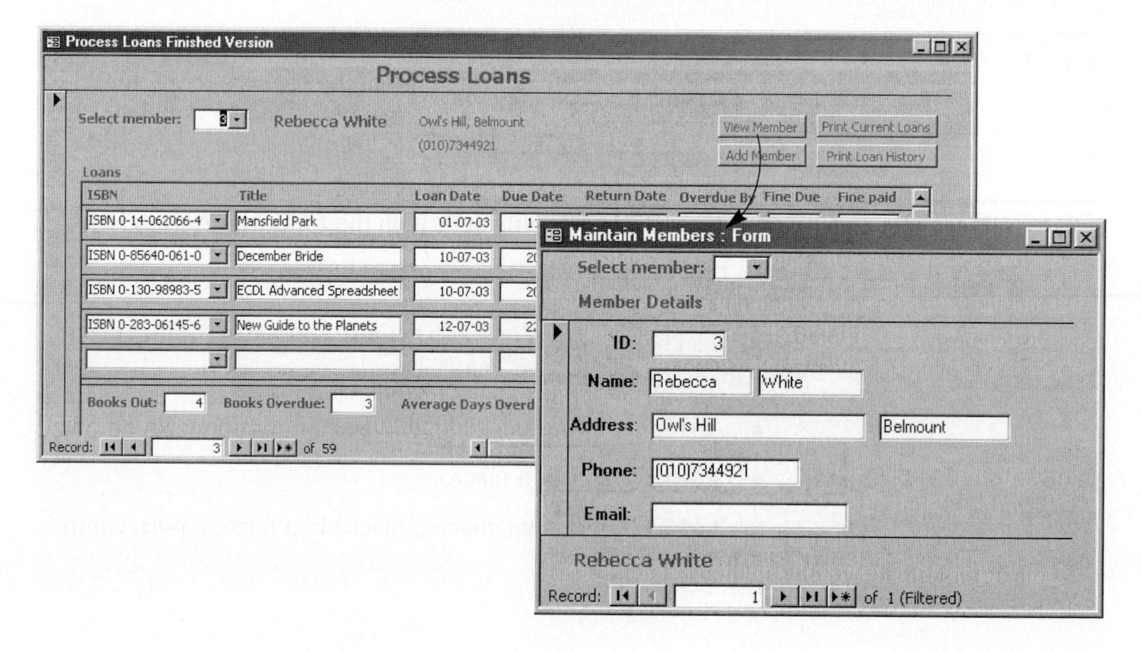

- The **Add Member** button opens the Maintain Members form at a new record, ready for you to enter details of a new member.
- The **Print Current Loans** button runs a report that lists the selected member's current loans. You can then print the report.
- The **Print Loan History** button runs a report that lists the selected member's past loans. You can then print the report.

With each of these examples, clicking a command button is the event that triggers execution of the macro. But there are many other events that can trigger macros, including opening and closing a form or report, moving from one record to another in a form, updating data in a form, deleting data in a form, and moving the focus to a particular form control.

Macro

A sequence of one or more database actions that can be triggered automatically or executed with a single command.

Event

An action that occurs on a form, report or control and that can trigger execution of a macro.

Creating a macro

Unlike Microsoft Office applications such as Word and Excel, Access does not have a facility for recording macros. Instead, you create macros manually in the Macro window, as shown here.

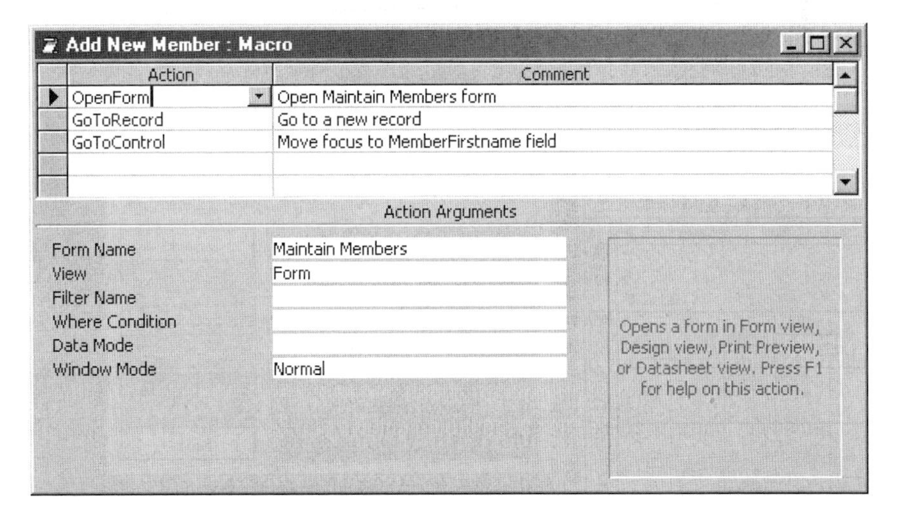

- In the *Action* column, you specify the actions you want the macro to perform, in the order you want them performed. The down arrow in an *Action* cell displays a list of actions and you select the action you want from this list.
- In the *Action Arguments* section of the window you specify the arguments for each action – that is, any additional information required to carry out the action. For example, an *OpenForm* action needs to know the name of the form to open and a *GoToRecord* action needs to know which record to go to.
- In the *Comment* column, you enter a description of each action. This is optional, but helps you to understand exactly what a macro does without having to browse through all its actions and arguments.
- A help message to the right of the action arguments provides help for the currently selected action or argument. For further help on the action or argument, press **F1**.

Exercise 15.1: Creating a macro that opens a form

In this exercise you will create a simple macro that opens the Maintain Members form.

1) Open the `Chp15_VillageLibrary_Database` database.

2) Click *Macros* in the *Objects* list in the Database window and click the **New** button on the window's toolbar. This opens the Macro window.

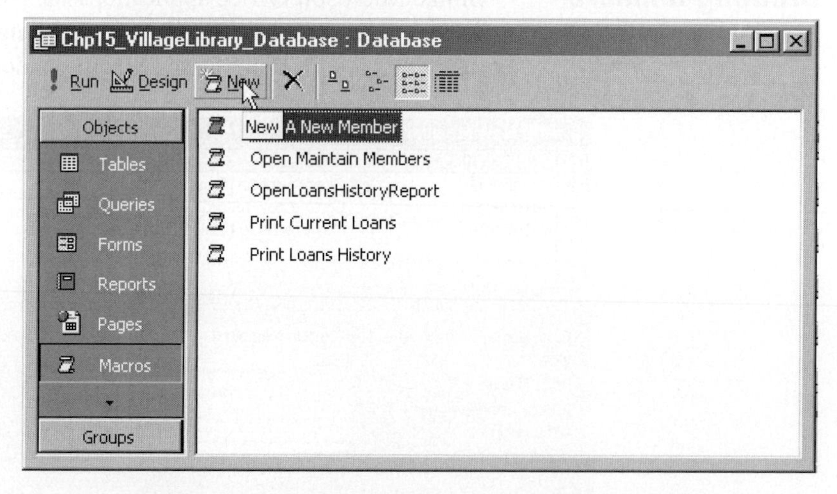

3) Click the down arrow in the first row of the *Action* column. This displays a list of all actions that a macro can perform. Select the *OpenForm* action. The arguments for the *OpenForm* action are now displayed in the *Action Arguments* section of the window.

4) Click the down arrow in the *Form Name* argument. This displays a list of all forms in the current database. Select *Maintain Members*, as this is the form that you want the macro to open.

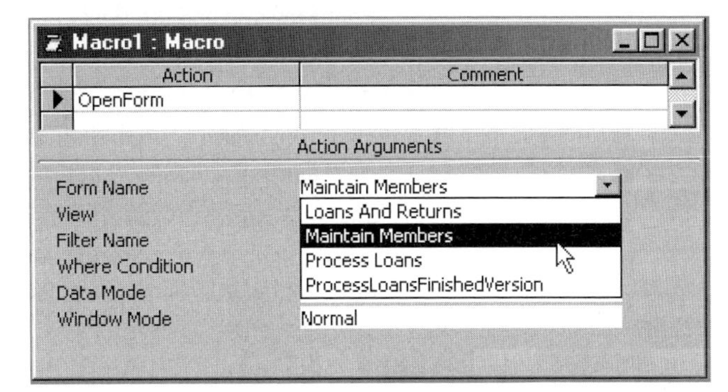

5) You can leave the other arguments as they are. The *View* argument specifies the View in which to open the form; the default is Form View. The *Where* argument allows you to specify which records the form displays. You will learn how to use this argument in a later exercise.

6) Close the Macro window, and when prompted to save the macro, click **Yes**. When prompted for a name for the macro, enter OpenMaintainMembersForm and click **OK**.

7) The new macro is now listed in the Database window. To run the macro, simply double-click it. The Maintain Members form automatically opens.

Exercise 15.2: Creating a macro that runs a report

The Current Loans By Member report lists all current loans, grouped by member. In this exercise you will create a simple macro that runs this report.

1) Click *Macros* in the *Objects* list in the Database window and click the **New** button on the window's toolbar. This opens the Macro window.

2) Click the down arrow in the first row of the *Action* column and select the *OpenReport* action. The arguments for this action are now displayed in the *Action Arguments* section of the window.

3) Click the down arrow in the *Report Name* argument. This displays a list of all reports in the current database. Select *Current Loans By Member*.

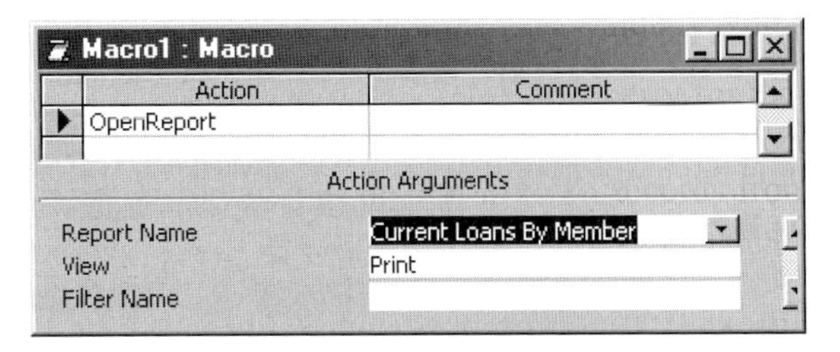

4) Click the down arrow in the *View* argument. This lists the views in which you can open the report. The *Print* option sends the report directly to the printer; the *Print Preview* option opens the report in Print Preview; and the *Design* option opens the report in Design View. Select the *Print Preview* option.

5) Close the Macro window, and when prompted to save the macro, click **Yes**. When prompted for a name for the macro, enter OpenCurrentLoansReport and click **OK**.

6) The new macro is now listed in the Database window. To run the macro, simply double-click it. The Open Current Loans By Member report automatically opens in Print Preview.

Exercise 15.3: Creating a macro that opens a blank record in a form

In this exercise you will create a macro that displays a blank record in the Maintain Members form, ready for you to enter a new record. The macro consists of several actions.

1) Open the Macro window for a new macro.

2) In the first row of the *Action* column, select the *OpenForm* action.

3) In the *Form Name* argument for this action, select *Maintain Members*.

4) In the second row of the *Action* column, select the *GoToRecord* action. With this action you can specify which record you want the macro to display in the form.

5) The arguments for the *GoToRecord* action include the type of object that contains the record you want to go to and the name of the object. In this case, there is no need to fill these two arguments; the previous action opens the Maintain Members form and this is taken as the default object.

6) The *Record* argument provides a list of options for specifying the record you want to go to in the form. Select the *New* option. This displays a blank record, the same as when you select the **New Record** button in the form itself.

7) In the third row of the *Action* column, select the *GoToControl* action. With this action you can specify which control you want the macro to put the focus on in the form.

8) There is only one argument for the *GoToControl* action – the control name. In the Maintain Members form, the first field that must be filled manually is the MemFirstname field (the MemID is generated automatically by Access). So enter MemFirstname in the *Control Name* argument.

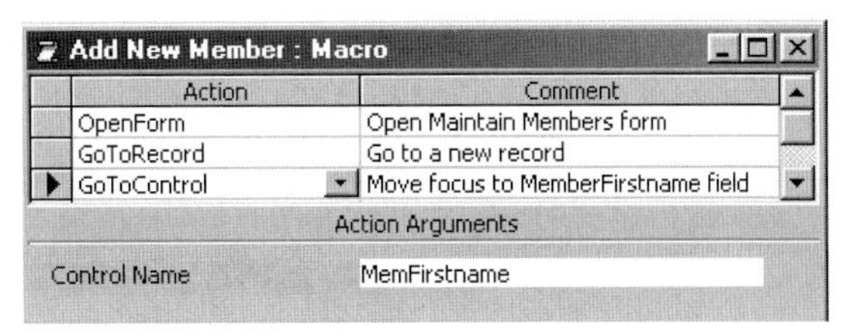

9) Close the Macro window and save the macro with the name AddNewMember.

10) Run the macro. The Maintain Members form opens automatically at a new record, with the focus on the MemFirstname field ready for you to enter details of a new member.

Attaching macros to control events

The power of macros lies in their ability to run in response to form, report, and control events. Every form control has a variety of associated events. These events are listed on the **Event** tab of the control's property sheet. Report controls do not have associated events.

Open the Process Loans form now in Design View and display the property sheet for the Print Loan History command button control. Then click the **Event** tab to see the list of control events. These include mouse events, keyboard key events and focus events.

For example, the *On Click* event occurs when you click the control, the *On Dbl Click* event occurs when you double-click the control, and the *On Got Focus* event occurs when the focus moves to the control.

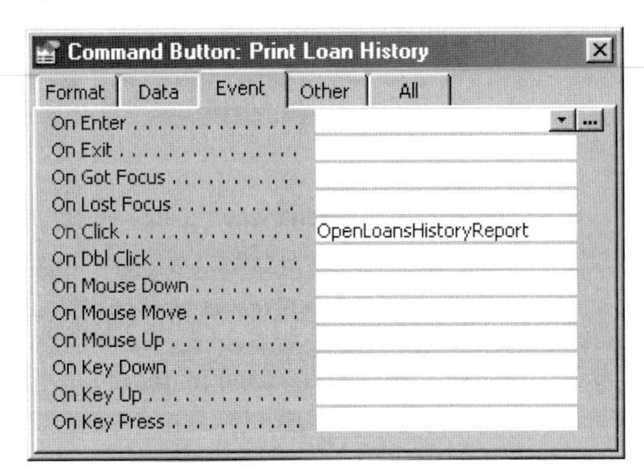

To attach a macro to a control, you simply click the event that you want to trigger the macro and then select the macro from the event's drop-down list.

In the case of the Print Loan History command button, the OpenLoansHistoryReport macro has been attached to the *On Click* event. This means that the macro runs automatically when you click the command button.

Exercise 15.4: Attaching macros to command buttons

In this exercise you will attach macros to the View Member and Add Member command buttons in the Process Loans form.

1) Open the Process Loans form in Design View.
2) Display the property sheet for the View Member command button control and click the **Event** tab to display the control's event properties.
3) In Exercise 15.1 you created the OpenMaintainMembersForm macro. To run this macro when a user clicks the View Member command button control, you attach the macro to the control's *On Click* event. To do this, click the *On Click* event and select *OpenMaintainMembersForm* from its drop-down list.

4) Now display the property sheet for the Add Member command button control and click the **Event** tab to display the control's event properties.
5) In Exercise 15.3 you created the AddNewMember macro. To run this macro when a user clicks the Add Member command button control, you attach the macro to the control's *On Click* event. To do this, click the *On Click* event and select *AddNewMember* from its drop-down list.

6) Save the form and switch to Form View to try out the command buttons. Note that clicking the **View Member** button opens the Maintain Members form. It does not, however, automatically display the record for the member currently selected in the Process Loans form. You will learn how to do this in a later exercise.

Exercise 15.5: Creating a command button that runs a macro

In this exercise you will create a new command button that runs the OpenCurrentLoansReport macro you created in Exercise 15.2.

1) Open the Process Loans form in Design View.
2) Make sure that the **Control Wizards** button in the toolbox is *not* selected.

Command Button tool

3) Click the **Command Button** tool in the toolbox and then click in the form where you want the top left corner of the control to be positioned. This creates a new command button control, as shown here. By default, the name of the control is used as the button's caption.

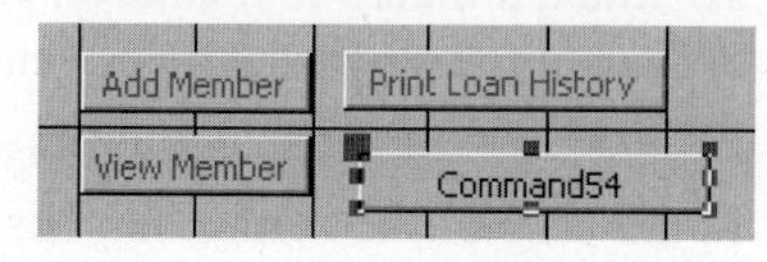

4) Display the property sheet for the new command button and enter Print Current Loans in the *Caption* property. This specifies the text to display on the button.

5) Click the **Event** tab to display the control's event properties.

6) To attach the OpenCurrentLoansReport macro to the control's *On Click* event, click that event and select OpenCurrentLoansReport from its drop-down list.

7) Save the form and switch to Form View to try out the new command button. When you click the button, the Current Loans By Member report is automatically run. It does not, however, automatically display the records for the member currently selected in the Process Loans form. You will learn how to do this in Exercise 15.6.

Synchronizing two forms or a form and a report

The **Print Loan History** button in the Process Loans form runs the Loans History By Member report and displays just the records for the member currently selected in the Process Loans form. To see how this is done, open the form in Design View and display the property sheet for the Print Loan History button.

The OpenLoansHistoryReport macro is attached to the control's *On Click* event. Take a look at that macro now by clicking the **Build** button at the right of the *On Click* property box.

The macro consists of a single *OpenReport* action that opens the Loans History By Member report. The following expression is entered in the *Where Condition* argument for that action (click the argument and press **Shift+F2** to open the expression in the *Zoom* window):

```
[MemID]=[Forms]![Process Loans]![SelectMember]
```

This tells the macro to select only records where the MemID value equals the value in the SelectMember control in the Process Loans form.

You can use a similar expression whenever you want to open a form or report and restrict its records to those that match the value of a control on another form. The syntax for the expression is:

```
[field]=Forms![form]![control]
```

where *field* is the name of a field in the record source of the form/report you want to open, *form* is the name of another form, and *control* is the name of a control on the other form.

You can close the Macro window now. Do not save any changes you may have made.

Exercise 15.6: Synchronizing forms and reports

In this exercise you will modify the OpenMaintainMembersForm and OpenCurrentLoansReport macros so that they display only records related to the member currently selected in the Process Loans form.

1) Open the Process Loans form in Design View.
2) Display the *On Click* event property for the View Member command button. Click in the property box and then click its **Build** button. This displays the OpenMaintainMembersForm macro in the Macro window.
3) Click the *Where Condition* argument for the *OpenForm* action and press **Shift+F2**. This opens the *Zoom* dialog box. Enter the following expression and then click **OK** to close the *Zoom* dialog box:

   ```
   [MemID]=[Forms]![Process Loans]![SelectMember]
   ```
4) Close the Macro window, saving the macro as you do.
5) Now repeat steps 2 to 4 for the Print Current Loans command button.
6) Save the form and switch to Form View to see the result of your changes.

   For example, display the record for Rebecca White in the Process Loans form and then click the **Print Current Loans** button. This runs the Current Loans By Member report and displays the current loans for Rebecca White only.

Attaching macros to form and report events

Clicking a command button in a form is one of the most common ways of running a macro. However, you can also attach a macro to form/report events such as the opening or closing of a form/report and the insertion or deletion of data in a form.

Exercise 15.7: Attaching a macro to a form event

In this exercise you will create a macro that runs automatically when the Process Loans form opens. The macro will display a message that tells users how to use the form.

1) Open the Macro window for a new macro.
2) In the first row of the *Action* column, select the *MsgBox* action.
3) Click the *Message* argument for this action and type the following text:

   ```
   This form displays the current loans for the
   member you select in the Select Member combo box.
   You can then add, delete, and edit loan records.
   ```
4) Close the Macro window and save the macro with the name ProcessLoansMessage.

5) Open the Process Loans form in Design View and display the property sheet for the form itself (double-click the form selector).

6) Click the **Event** tab to display the form events. Click the *On Open* event and select ProcessLoansMessage from its drop-down list.

7) Close the form, saving it as you do.

8) Now open the form in Form View from the Database window. Access displays your message and then opens the form when you click **OK**.

Exercise 15.8: Attaching a macro to a report event

In this exercise you will create a macro that runs automatically when you open the Current Loans By Member report. The macro will display a message that tells users about the report.

1) Open the Macro window for a new macro.

2) In the first row of the *Action* column, select the *MsgBox* action.

3) Click the *Message* argument for this action and type the following text:

```
This report lists current loans only. To view
non-current loans, run the Loans History By
Member report, or click the Print Loan History
button in the Process Loans form.
```

4) Close the Macro window and save the macro with the name CurrentLoansMessage.

5) Open the Current Loans By Member report in Design View and display the property sheet for the report itself (double-click the report selector).

6) Click the **Event** tab to display the report events. Click the *On Open* event and select CurrentLoansMessage from its drop-down list.

7) Close the report, saving it as you do.

8) Now open the report in Print Preview from the Database window. Access displays your message and then runs the report when you click **OK**.

Chapter 15: summary

A *macro* consists of a sequence of one or more database actions that can be triggered automatically or executed with a single command. The power of macros lies in their ability to run automatically in response to *events* that occur on forms, reports and controls.

In a form, *command button* controls are often used to trigger macros. You can also run a macro when the form opens or closes and when data in the form changes. You cannot attach macros to report controls, but you can run a macro when the report opens or closes, for example.

The **Event** tab on the property sheet for a form, report or control lists all the events to which you can attach a macro. You attach a macro to an event by clicking the event in the property sheet and then selecting the macro from the event's drop-down list.

You create macros in the *Macro* window. In the *Action* column you select the actions you want the macro to perform. In the *Action Arguments* section, you specify any additional information that the macro needs to perform these actions. For actions that open forms and reports, you can use the *Where Condition* argument to restrict the records displayed to those that match the value of a control on another form.

Chapter 15: quick quiz

Q1	Which of these events can trigger a macro?
A.	Opening a form.
B.	Double-clicking a form control.
C.	Opening a query.
D.	Closing a report.

Q2	Which of these macro actions would you use to open a report in Print Preview?
A.	SelectObject.
B.	PrintOut.
C.	OpenReport.
D.	OutputTo.

Q3	To run a macro when a form opens, to which form event would you attach the macro?
A.	On Activate.
B.	On Got Focus.
C.	On Open.
D.	On Current.

Q4	To view the definition of a macro that is attached to a command button . . .
A.	Run the macro from the Database window.
B.	Select the macro in the Database window and click the **Design** button on the window's toolbar.
C.	Open the form that contains the command button, display the button's event properties, click the event with which the macro is associated, and then select the macro from the event's drop-down list.
D.	Open the form that contains the command button, display the button's event properties, click the event with which the macro is associated, and then click the **Build** button for that event.

Q5	To run a macro when a report closes, to which event would you attach the macro?
A.	On Deactivate.
B.	On Unload.
C.	On Lost Focus.
D.	On Close.

Q6	Which of these *Where Condition* expressions restricts the records displayed by a report to those related to the record displayed in the Process Loans form?
A.	`[MemID]=[Process Loans]![SelectMember]`
B.	`[MemID]=[Forms]![Process Loans]![SelectMember]`
C.	`[MemID]=[Forms]![Process Loans.SelectMember]`
D.	`[Reports]![MemID]=[Forms]![Process Loans]![SelectMember]`

Answers

1: A, B, and D, **2**: C, **3**: C, **4**: B and D, **5**: D, **6**: B.

16 Importing, linking and exporting data

In this chapter

With Access you aren't limited to working with data in a single Access database. You can import data from other Access databases and from other file formats, you can link to data in external sources, and you can export data in various formats for use in other applications.

In this chapter, you will learn how to import, link to and export data in a variety of file formats.

New skills

At the end of this chapter you should be able to:

- Import dBASE, Paradox, spreadsheet and text files into an Access database
- Import database objects from another Access database
- Link to external data
- Export data to dBASE, Paradox, spreadsheet and text files

New words

In this chapter you will meet the following terms:

- Import
- Link
- Export
- Delimited text file
- Fixed-width text file

Exercise files

In this chapter you will work with the following Access file:

- `Chp16_VillageLibrary_Database`

You will also work with the following non-Access files:

- `MemPx` (a Paradox table)
- `MemDB` (a dBASE table)
- `LibraryExcel` (an Excel workbook)

- `LoansTxt` (a delimited text file)
- `MemTxt` (a fixed-width text file)

All these files are located in the folder to which you copied the contents of the CD that accompanies this book.

Syllabus reference

In this chapter you will cover the following items of the ECDL Advanced Database Syllabus:

- **AM5.6.1.1**: Import text, spreadsheet, csv, dBASE, Paradox files into a database.
- **AM5.6.1.2**: Export data in spreadsheet, txt, dBASE and Paradox formats.
- **AM5.6.1.3**: Link external data to a database.

About importing and linking data

Access provides two methods for working with data from external sources: *importing* and *linking*.

- **Importing**. When you import data, it is copied from the source file and converted from its original format to a set of Access records. There is no ongoing connection between the source data and the data in Access – changes to one do not affect the other.

  You use this method of working with external data when you no longer need to work with the data in its original format.

- **Linking**. When you link to external data, the data is not copied to your Access database. Instead, a connection is created between the external data and a table in Access, allowing you to view and work with the data in the source file from within Access. Changes you make to the data in Access are saved to the source file, and changes to the source file are reflected in your view of the data in Access.

  You use this method of working with external data when you need to share the data with users of a different database or application.

You can import and link to data from many different sources, including other Access databases, Paradox and dBASE database tables, spreadsheet files and text files.

Importing

Converts data from its original format and saves it to a new or existing Access table. There is no ongoing connection between the original data and the data in Access.

Linking

Creates a link to external data, allowing you to view and work with that data from within Access.

About exporting data

When you want to use data from an Access table or query in another application, you can export the data to a file format appropriate for that application. There is no ongoing connection between the data in Access and the exported data. Changes in one are not reflected in the other.

You can export data to a wide variety of file formats, including dBASE, Paradox, spreadsheet and text files.

Importing dBASE and Paradox tables

Both dBASE and Paradox are relational database applications. Paradox is part of the WordPerfect Office Suite from Corel. dBASE is a product of dBASE Inc.

All dBASE and Paradox tables are stored in separate table files, with the extensions .db (Paradox) and .dbf (dBASE). This means that you can import a single table to Access by importing the table file.

Exercise 16.1: Importing a Paradox table

In this exercise you will import a Paradox table to an Access database.

1) Open the `Chp16_VillageLibrary_Database` database.
2) Choose **File | Get External Data | Import**. This displays the *Import* dialog box.
3) In the *File of type* box, select the *Paradox* option. Then locate the `MemPx` file, select it, and click **Import**.

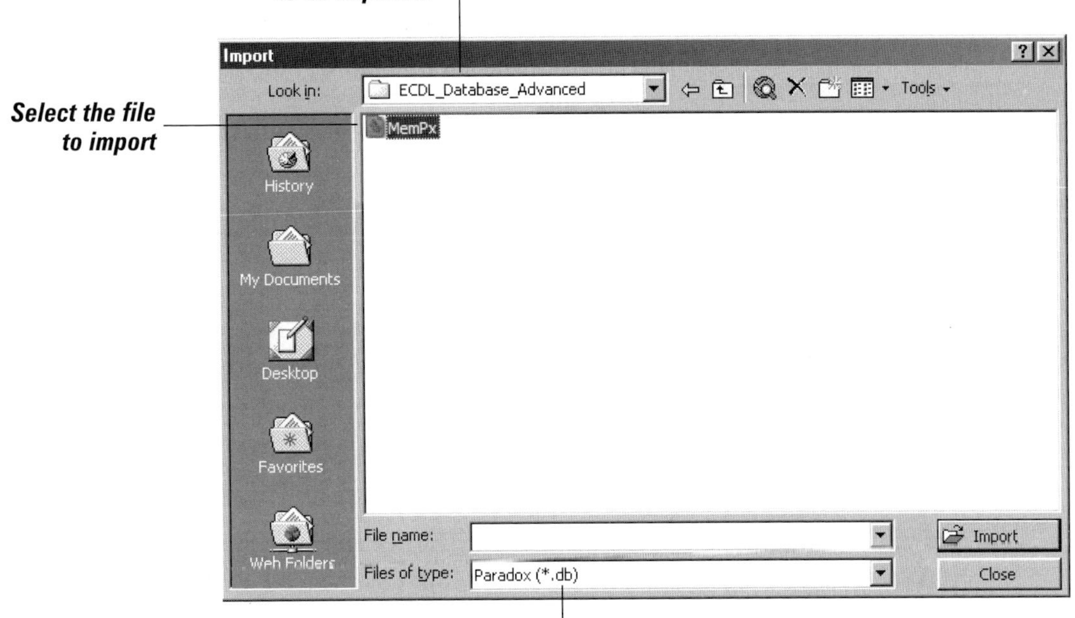

4) When the file has been successfully imported, a message to this effect is displayed. Click **OK** to close this message. Then click **Close** to close the *Import* dialog box.

5) In the Database window you can see that Access has created a new table named MemPx. If your database already contains a MemPx table, Access appends a number to the name to make it unique.

6) Open the MemPx table now in Datasheet View. You can see that it contains five records with similar fields to your own Members table.

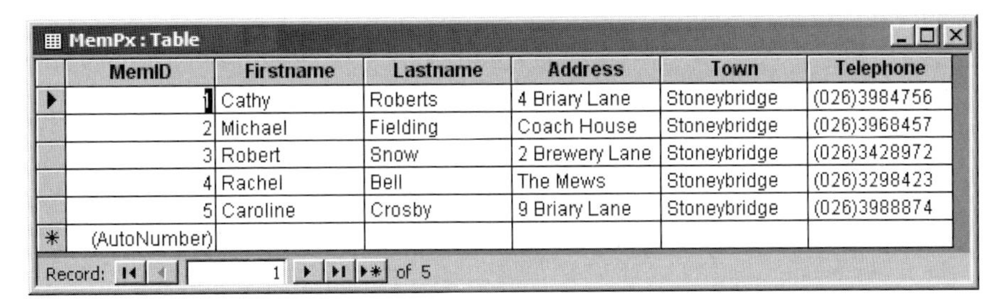

MemPx : Table

MemID	Firstname	Lastname	Address	Town	Telephone
1	Cathy	Roberts	4 Briary Lane	Stoneybridge	(026)3984756
2	Michael	Fielding	Coach House	Stoneybridge	(026)3968457
3	Robert	Snow	2 Brewery Lane	Stoneybridge	(026)3428972
4	Rachel	Bell	The Mews	Stoneybridge	(026)3298423
5	Caroline	Crosby	9 Briary Lane	Stoneybridge	(026)3988874
(AutoNumber)					

Record: 1 of 5

7) When you import data from any source, Access attempts to assign an appropriate data type and field size to the imported fields. However, you should always check these attributes to make sure that they meet your requirements.

Switch to Design View now to see the data types and field sizes that Access has assigned to the fields in the MemPx table. Then close the table.

You use almost exactly the same procedure to import a dBASE table. The only difference is that you select one of the dBASE file types in the *Import* dialog box instead of the Paradox file type. If you wish, you can try this with the `MemDB` file, which is in dBASE IV format.

Once you have imported a table, you can use an append query to add the new records to an existing table if you want (see Chapter 7). For example, to append the records in the MemPx table to the Members table, you would use the append query shown here.

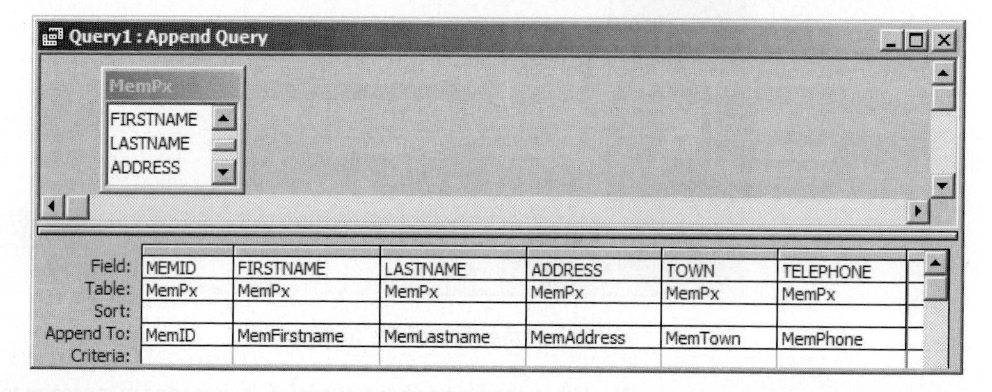

Importing spreadsheet data

You can import spreadsheet data from both Microsoft Excel and Lotus 1-2-3. The procedure is the same in both cases.

You can create a new table with the imported data or you can append the data to an existing table. However, in the latter case, the column headings must exactly match the field names in the Access table.

Preparing spreadsheet data

Before importing spreadsheet data, make sure that it is in a format suitable for conversion to an Access table:

- The data must be in tabular format, with each record on a separate row, and each field in a separate column. All data in a column must have the same data type. You can include column headings – Access converts these to field names.
- If a spreadsheet includes additional information such as totals and titles, you must either delete these from the spreadsheet or create a named range that includes only the data to be imported. A *named range* is a set of worksheet cells to which a name has been assigned.

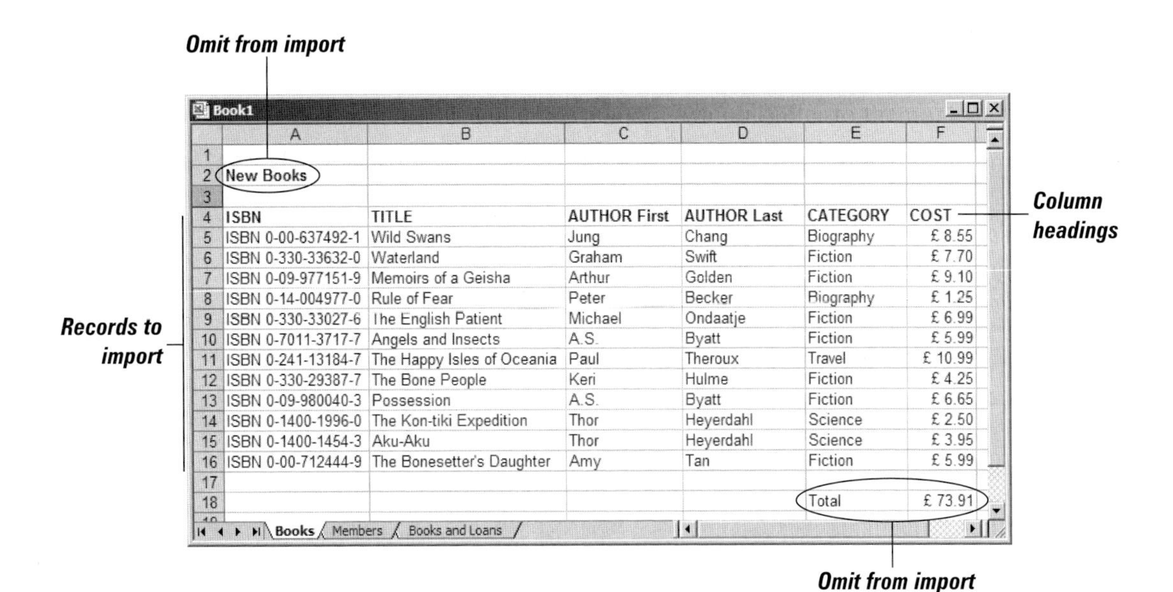

	A	B	C	D	E	F
1						
2	New Books					
3						
4	ISBN	TITLE	AUTHOR First	AUTHOR Last	CATEGORY	COST
5	ISBN 0-00-637492-1	Wild Swans	Jung	Chang	Biography	£ 8.55
6	ISBN 0-330-33632-0	Waterland	Graham	Swift	Fiction	£ 7.70
7	ISBN 0-09-977151-9	Memoirs of a Geisha	Arthur	Golden	Fiction	£ 9.10
8	ISBN 0-14-004977-0	Rule of Fear	Peter	Becker	Biography	£ 1.25
9	ISBN 0-330-33027-6	The English Patient	Michael	Ondaatje	Fiction	£ 6.99
10	ISBN 0-7011-3717-7	Angels and Insects	A.S.	Byatt	Fiction	£ 5.99
11	ISBN 0-241-13184-7	The Happy Isles of Oceania	Paul	Theroux	Travel	£ 10.99
12	ISBN 0-330-29387-7	The Bone People	Keri	Hulme	Fiction	£ 4.25
13	ISBN 0-09-980040-3	Possession	A.S.	Byatt	Fiction	£ 6.65
14	ISBN 0-1400-1996-0	The Kon-tiki Expedition	Thor	Heyerdahl	Science	£ 2.50
15	ISBN 0-1400-1454-3	Aku-Aku	Thor	Heyerdahl	Science	£ 3.95
16	ISBN 0-00-712444-9	The Bonesetter's Daughter	Amy	Tan	Fiction	£ 5.99
17						
18					Total	£ 73.91

- When importing from Excel (version 5.0 or later), you can import data from any worksheet within a workbook. When importing data from other multiple-spreadsheet sources, you must save each spreadsheet as a separate file before importing data from them.

Importing an Excel worksheet

The `LibraryExcel` file is an Excel workbook that contains book, member and loan records suitable for importing into the Village Library database. Open that workbook now and take a look at the contents of the Books worksheet.

Library Records for Import

	A	B	C	D	E	F
1	ISBN	TITLE	AUTHOR First	AUTHOR Last	CATEGORY	COST
2	ISBN 0-00-637492-1	Wild Swans	Jung	Chang	Biography	£ 8.55
3	ISBN 0-330-33632-0	Waterland	Graham	Swift	Fiction	£ 7.70
4	ISBN 0-09-977151-9	Memoirs of a Geisha	Arthur	Golden	Fiction	£ 9.10
5	ISBN 0-14-004977-0	Rule of Fear	Peter	Becker	Biography	£ 1.25
6	ISBN 0-330-33027-6	The English Patient	Michael	Ondaatje	Fiction	£ 6.99
7	ISBN 0-7011-3717-7	Angels and Insects	A.S.	Byatt	Fiction	£ 5.99
8	ISBN 0-241-13184-7	The Happy Isles of Oceania	Paul	Theroux	Travel	£ 10.99
9	ISBN 0-330-29387-7	The Bone People	Keri	Hulme	Fiction	£ 4.25
10	ISBN 0-09-980040-3	Possession	A.S.	Byatt	Fiction	£ 6.65
11	ISBN 0-1400-1996-0	The Kon-tiki Expedition	Thor	Heyerdahl	Science	£ 2.50
12	ISBN 0-1400-1454-3	Aku-Aku	Thor	Heyerdahl	Science	£ 3.95
13	ISBN 0-00-712444-9	The Bonesetter's Daughter	Amy	Tan	Fiction	£ 5.99
14						

Books | Members | Books and Loans

The records include information relevant to three different tables in the Village Library database: Books, BooksConfidential and Authors. This means that you cannot import the records directly into an existing table. Instead, you must import the records to a new table and then use one or more append queries to add selected fields to the other tables.

Exercise 16.2: Importing an Excel worksheet

In this exercise you will import the Books worksheet from the LibraryExcel workbook to the `Chp16_VillageLibrary_Database` database.

1) Switch to the Database window and choose **File | Get External Data | Import**.
2) In the *Import* dialog box, select *Microsoft Excel* as the file type, locate and select the `LibraryExcel` file, and click **Import**. This starts the *Import Spreadsheet Wizard*.
3) In the first page of the wizard you choose the worksheet or named range that you want to import. For this exercise, make sure that the *Show Worksheets* option and the *Books* worksheet are selected. Then click **Next**.

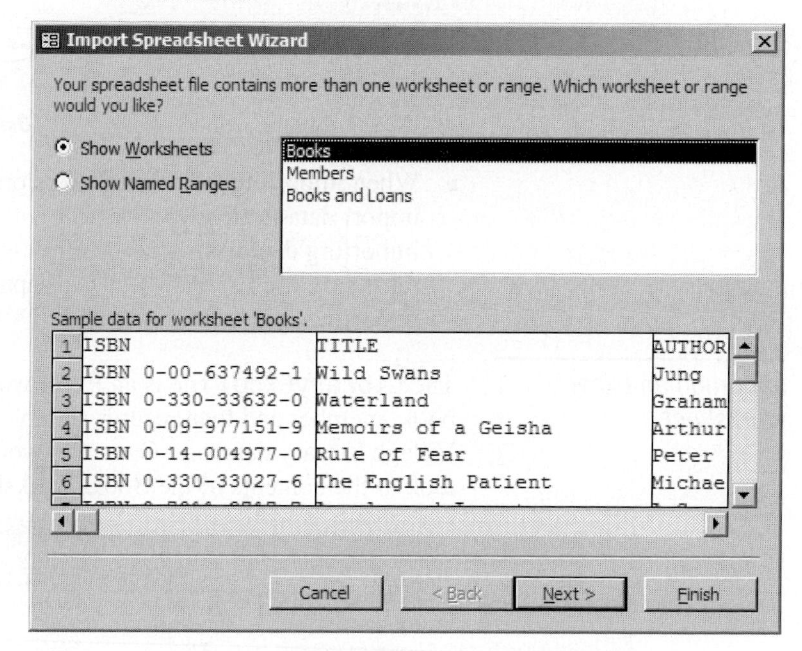

4) In the next page of the wizard, you specify whether or not the first row in the spreadsheet contains column headings. Select the *First Row Contains Column Headings* option and click **Next**.
5) When asked where you want to store the imported records, select the *In a New Table* option and click **Next**.

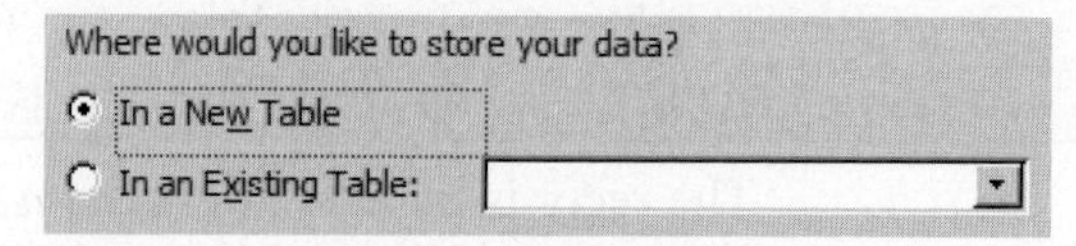

6) In the next page of the wizard you can specify various settings for the fields you are importing. The *Field Options* section of the dialog box displays the settings for the currently selected column.

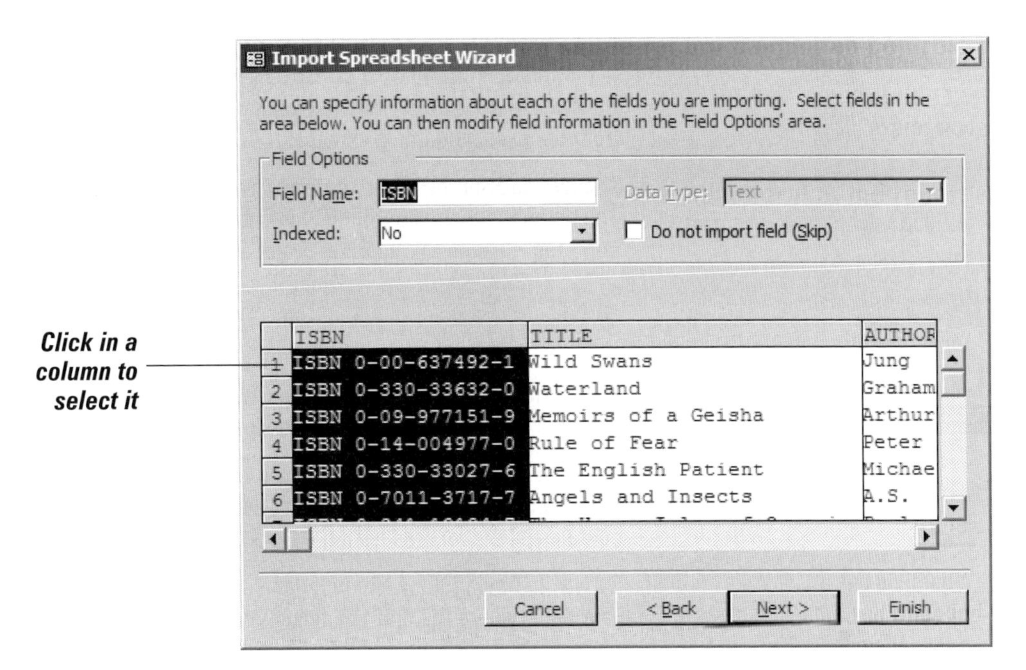

For this exercise, you do not need to make any changes to these options. Just click **Next**.

If you want to change the field settings, you can use the *Field Options* as follows:

- Use the *Field Name* option to change the name of the field to which the selected column will be imported.
- Use the *Data Type* option (when available) to change the data type for the field.
- Use the *Indexed* option to specify index settings for the field.
- Use the *Do not import field (Skip)* option to prevent a particular column being imported. This is particularly useful for omitting blank columns that may be included in a spreadsheet to separate other columns.

7) In the next page of the wizard you can specify a primary key for the new table. The records you are importing relate to three tables in your database and need to be appended to those tables at a later stage. So the table created to store the data is for temporary use only and does not need a primary key. Select the *No primary key* option and click **Next**.

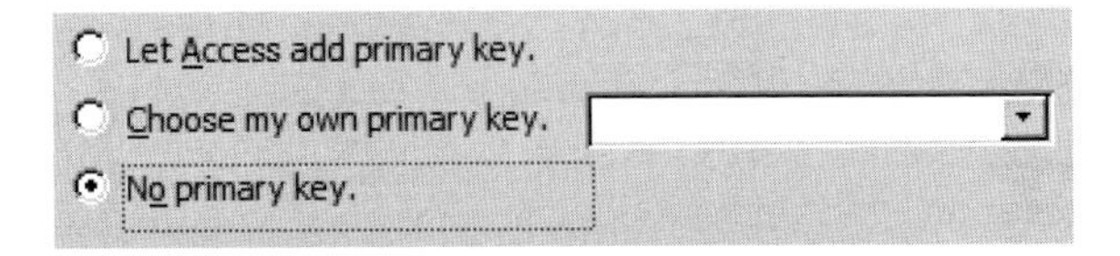

If you select the *Let Access add primary key* option instead, Access generates an AutoNumber primary key field for the table. If you select the *Choose my own primary key* option, you can select a primary key from the associated drop-down list.

8) The last page of the wizard prompts you for a name for the new table. The default is the name of the worksheet or named range being imported. Change this to BooksExcel and click **Finish**.

9) When the worksheet has been successfully imported, a message to this effect is displayed. Click **OK** to close this message.

10) In the Database window you can see that Access has created a new table named BooksExcel. Open that table now in Datasheet View. It contains all the records from the Books worksheet.

11) Switch to Design View and you can see that Access has assigned a Text data type to the first five fields, and has set their field size to 255 characters. It has also correctly assigned a Currency data type to the Cost field. When you have finished, close the table.

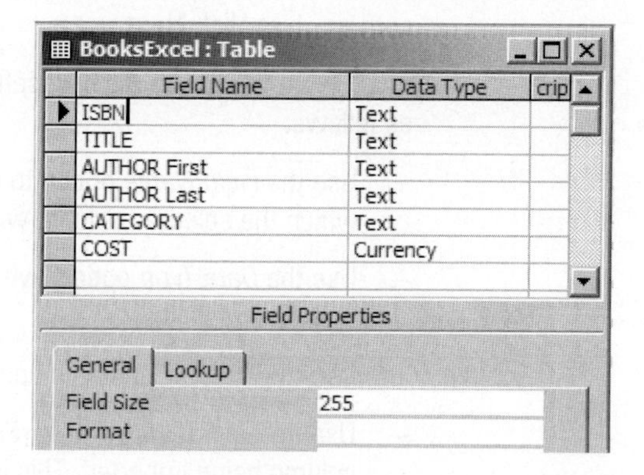

Importing text files

You can import data from text files provided that the data is organized and formatted appropriately:

- Each record must be on a separate line and the line must end with a paragraph break.
- All records must include the same fields and each field must contain the same type of data in all records.
- The file must be saved as a text file. The text file types to which you can save a file depend on the application you are using. The following are all appropriate for files you want to import to Access: Plain Text, Text Only, Text Document.

In order to convert data in a text file to a database table, Access needs to know where each field begins and ends. So the text file must be in one of the following formats:

- **Delimited text file**. Fields are separated by a special delimiter character such as a comma, tab or semicolon. Delimited files are often referred to as comma-delimited files or CSV (comma-separated values) files.

```
"ISBN 0-09-980040-3",2,01-07-03,
"ISBN 0-00-712444-9",6,03-06-31,
"ISBN 0-1400-1996-0",1,07-07-03,
```

- **Fixed-width text file**. Fields are aligned in columns. Spaces are inserted to fill out the fields so that they are the same width in all rows.

```
1··Cathy·····Roberts···4·Briary·Lane··Stoney·Bridge··(026)36792889¶
2··Michael···Fielding··Coach·House····Stoney·Bridge··(026)33886769¶
3··Robert····Snow······2·Brewery·Lane·Stoney·Bridge··(026)38471009¶
```

Preparing delimited text files

Before importing data from a delimited text file, make sure that the data is organized and formatted appropriately:

- Use the same delimiter character throughout the file – typically a comma.
- Enclose text values within double quotes.
- If you are including field names, enter them on the first row.

The `LoansTxt` file is a delimited text file that contains loan records suitable for appending to the Loans table in your database. Open the file now and take a look at its contents. You can open it in Notepad, WordPad, Microsoft Word, or some other word processing application.

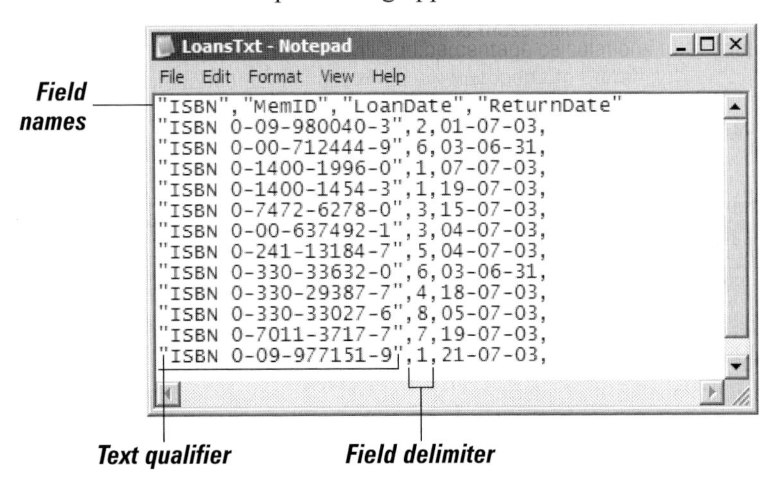

Note that each record is on a line of its own, with a paragraph break at the end of the line. The delimiter character is a comma (,). Text values, including the field headings, are enclosed within double quotes. Note also that the ReturnDate field is blank in all records.

Importing delimited text files

Exercise 16.3: Importing a delimited text file

In this exercise you will import the LoansTxt file and append its records to the Loans table.

1) Switch to the Database window and choose **File | Get External Data | Import**.

2) In the *Import* dialog box, select *Text Files* as the file type, locate and select the LoansTxt file, and click **Import**. This starts the *Import Text Wizard*.

3) The wizard first prompts you for the file type – that is, *Delimited* or *Fixed Width*. Make sure that the *Delimited* option is selected and click **Next**.

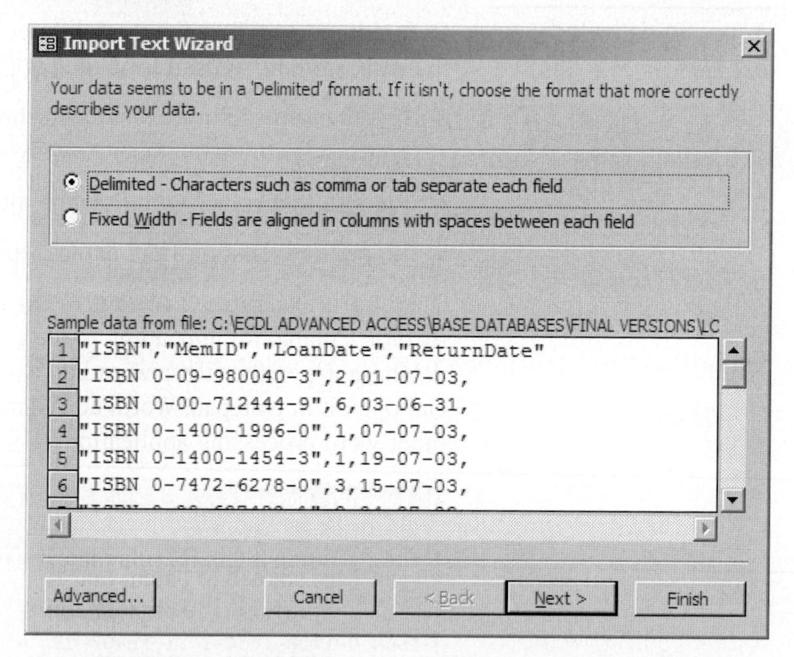

4) Next the wizard prompts you for information about the file format. Typically the wizard automatically selects the appropriate options, based on the contents of the text file. Make sure that *Comma* is selected as the field delimiter and that double quotes (") are selected as the text qualifier. Then select the *First Row Contains Field Names* option and click **Next**.

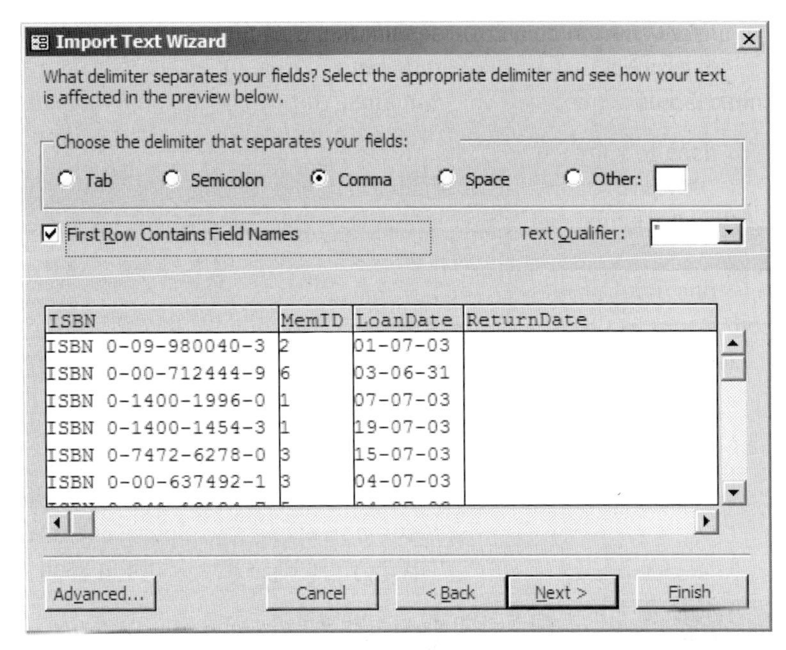

5) Next the wizard asks where you want to store the imported data. Select the *In an Existing Table* option and select the Loans table from the drop-down list. Then click **Next**.

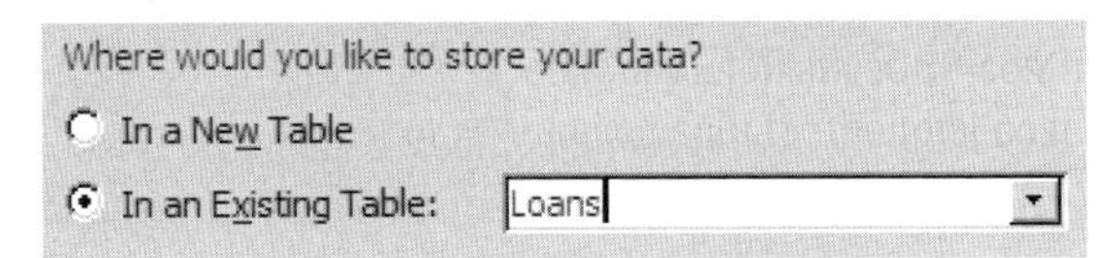

6) The last page of the wizard displays the name of the table to which the data will be imported. Make sure that this is the Loans table and then click **Finish**.

7) When the records have been successfully imported, a message to this effect is displayed. Click **OK** to close this message.

8) Now open the Loans table in Datasheet View and check that the records have been imported correctly. When you have finished, close the table.

Preparing fixed-width text files

Before importing data from a fixed-width text file, make sure that the data is organized and formatted appropriately:

- Access cannot import field names from a fixed-width text file. So, if the first row contains field names, delete that row.
- Make sure that each field is the same width in all rows. You need to apply a monospaced font (such as Courier New) to see this. If necessary, add or delete spaces in order to make fields the same width.

The MemTxt file is a fixed-width text file that contains several member records. Open the file now and take a look at its contents. You can open it in Notepad, WordPad, Microsoft Word, or some other word processing application.

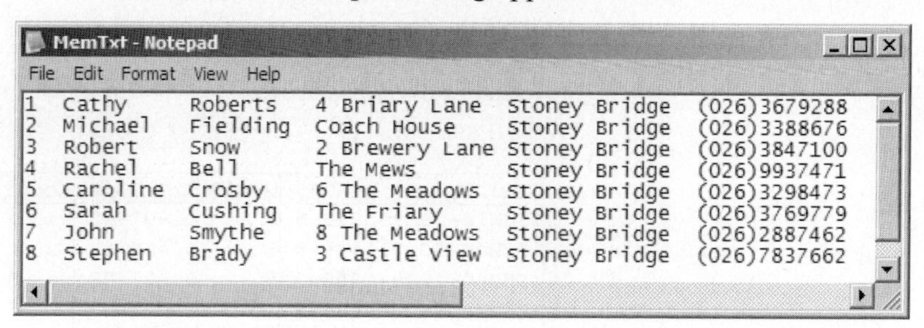

Note that each record is on a line of its own, with a paragraph break at the end of the line, and each field starts at the same position in every row. Spaces are used to fill out the fields so that they are the same width in each row.

Importing fixed-width text files

Exercise 16.4: Importing a fixed-width text file

In this exercise you will import the MemTxt file to a new table in your Access database.

1) Switch to the Database window and choose **File | Get External Data | Import**.

2) In the *Import* dialog box, select *Text Files* as the file type, locate and select the MemTxt file, and click **Import**. This starts the *Import Text Wizard*.

3) The wizard first prompts you for the file type. Make sure that the *Fixed-Width* option is selected and then click **Next**.

4) On the next page of the wizard, the records being imported are displayed with arrowed lines indicating the field breaks. The wizard makes a best guess at where field breaks occur, based on the contents of the source file.

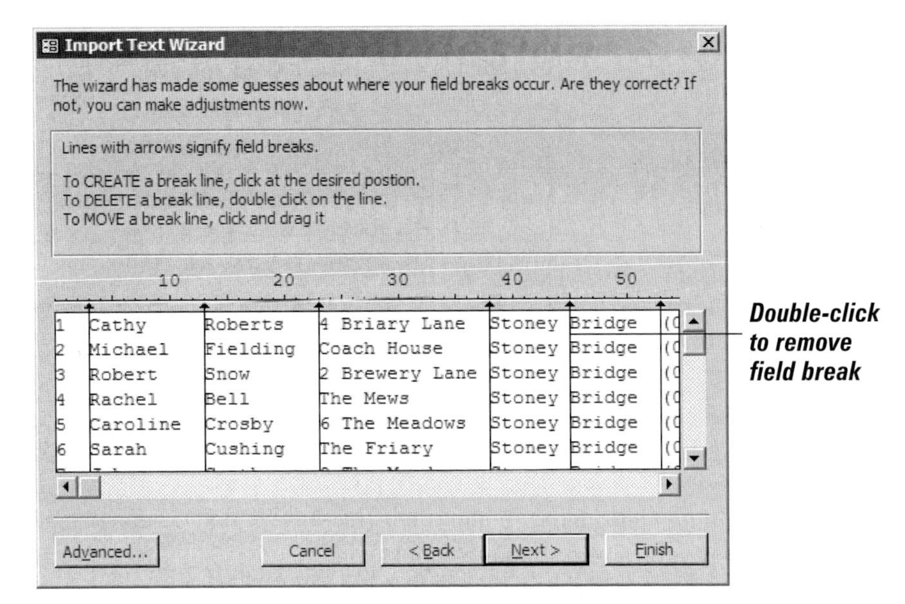

As you can see, the town name has been split into two fields. To remove the field break between the two parts of the name, double-click on the arrowed line. Then click **Next**.

5) Next the wizard asks you where you want to store the imported data. Select the *In a New Table* option and click **Next**.

6) In the next page of the wizard you can specify various settings for the fields you are importing. For this exercise, change the field names as follows:

Default name	New name
Field1	MemID
Field2	MemFirstname
Field3	MemLastname
Field4	MemAddress
Field5	MemTown
Field6	MemPhone

To change a field name, click the field in the lower part of the page and then type the new name in the *Field Name* box. When finished entering the new names, click **Next**.

7) In the next page of the wizard you can specify a primary key for the new table. Select the *No primary key* option and then click **Next**.

8) The last page of the wizard displays the name of the table to which the data will be imported. The default name is the name of the text file. Click **Finish** to create a new table with this name.

9) When the data has been successfully imported, a message to this effect is displayed. Click **OK** to close this message.

10) Now open the MemTxt table in Datasheet View and check that the records have been imported correctly. When you have finished, close the table.

Importing Access database objects

If there are database objects in one Access database that you want to include in another Access database, you can import them with the **Import** command. Here are some tips for importing objects from an Access database:

- When importing a table that contains lookup fields, also import the tables to which those fields refer (unless the tables already exist in your current database).
- When importing a form or report that is based on a query, import the query also.
- When importing a form that contains a subform, import the subform also.
- When importing a form that references other queries, forms, reports or macros, import those objects also.

Exercise 16.5: Importing a form from another Access database

In this exercise you will import the ProcessLoansFinishedVersion form from the Chp15_VillageLibrary_Database file.

1) With the Chp16_VillageLibrary_Database open in Access, switch to the Database window and choose **File | Get External Data | Import**.
2) In the *Import* dialog box, select *Microsoft Access* as the file type, locate and select the Chp15_VillageLibrary_Database file, and click **Import**. This displays the *Import Objects* dialog box.
3) Switch to the **Forms** tab and click the ProcessLoansFinishedVersion form to select it.

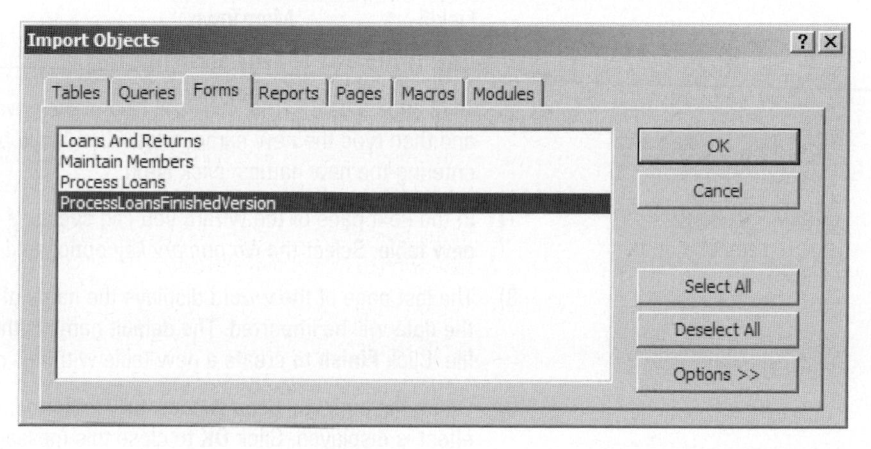

This form has a number of associated forms, queries, reports and macros, as follows:

- *Forms*: Loans and Returns; Maintain Members.
- *Query*: BookReturns.
- *Reports*: Current Loans by Member; Loans History by Member.
- *Macros*: Add a New Member; Open Maintain Members; Print Current Loans; Print Loans History; CurrentLoansMessage.

You need to import these objects also if you want to be able to use the ProcessLoansFinishedVersion form properly. So, switch to the relevant tabs and click each object to select it. When you have finished, click **OK**. Access now imports all the selected objects.

4) Open the ProcessLoansFinishedVersion form and check that it is working correctly. If any of its associated objects are missing, you can simply repeat the import operation for those objects. When you have finished, close the form.

Linking to an Excel worksheet

You can link to data in other Access databases, in Paradox and dBASE tables, in spreadsheet files, and in text files. The procedures are similar to those for importing data from those file types.

However, when you link to external data, you cannot change the table structure from within your database. And, depending on the source application, there may be some limitations to the operations you can perform on the data.

Exercise 16.6: Linking to an Excel worksheet

In this exercise you will create a link to the Books worksheet in the LibraryExcel workbook.

1) Switch to the Database window and choose **File | Get External Data | Link Files**.
2) In the *Link* dialog box, select *Microsoft Excel* as the file type, locate and select the `LibraryExcel` file, and click **Link**. This starts the *Link Spreadsheet Wizard*.
3) In the first page of the wizard, make sure that the *Show Worksheets* option and the *Books* worksheet are selected. Then click **Next**.
4) In the next page of the wizard select the *First Row Contains Column Headings* option and click **Next**.
5) The last page of the wizard displays the name that will be given to the linked table in Access. The default is the name of the worksheet. Change this to BooksExcelLinked and then click **Finish**.

6) When Access has successfully created the linked table, a message to this effect is displayed. Click **OK** to close this message.

7) BooksExcelLinked is now listed as a table in the Database window. As you can see, the table has a special icon consisting of the Excel logo preceded by an arrow. All linked tables in Access have this type of icon – an image that represents the source application preceded by an arrow, as shown below:

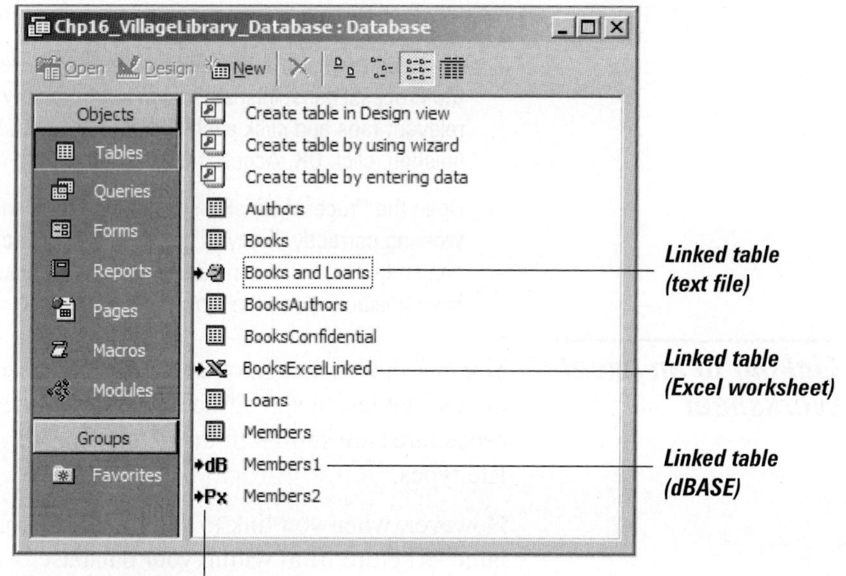

Open the BooksExcelLinked table in Datasheet View. As you can see, it looks the same as any other table in Access and you can base queries, forms, and reports on it in the normal way. However, the records are stored in the source file and not in your Access database. Also, you cannot make any changes to the table in Design View.

8) To see how linked tables work, open the BooksExcelLinked table in Datasheet View and make some changes to the data – for example, add a new record and change some values in existing records. Notice that you cannot delete a record here. When you have finished, close the table.

9) Now open the LibraryExcel workbook in Excel. Notice that the changes you made in Access have been saved to the workbook file and are included in the Books worksheet.

In the same way, any changes (including record deletions) that you make in Excel are included in the BooksExcelLinked table in Access the next time you open it. When you have finished viewing or updating the records in Excel, close the application.

Exporting data

You can export Access tables and queries to Paradox, dBASE, spreadsheet and text files. You use the same procedure for exporting to Paradox, dBASE and spreadsheet files. For text files, you use the *Export Text Wizard*, which enables you to choose a delimited or fixed-length format, and to specify various settings for the selected format.

Exercise 16.7: Exporting to an Excel spreadsheet

In this exercise you will export data from an Access query to an Excel worksheet.

1) Click *Queries* in the *Objects* list in the Database window and select the ExportQuery query. This query is a version of the LoansExtended query that you have worked with in previous chapters.
2) Choose **File | Export**. This displays the *Export Query* dialog box.
3) Select one of the *Excel* options in the *File of type* box, enter BookLoans as the destination file name, navigate to the folder where you want to save the file, and then click **Save**. The query data is now saved to an Excel workbook named BookLoans.
4) Open the BookLoans workbook in Excel. You can see that the query data has been copied to a worksheet with the same name as the query.

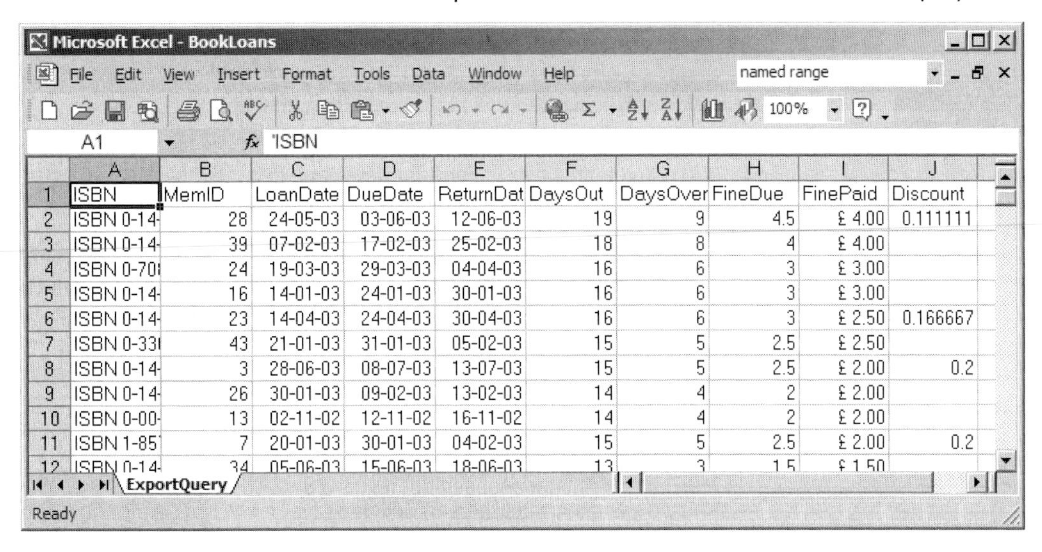

	A	B	C	D	E	F	G	H	I	J
1	ISBN	MemID	LoanDate	DueDate	ReturnDat	DaysOut	DaysOver	FineDue	FinePaid	Discount
2	ISBN 0-14-	28	24-05-03	03-06-03	12-06-03	19	9	4.5	£ 4.00	0.111111
3	ISBN 0-14-	39	07-02-03	17-02-03	25-02-03	18	8	4	£ 4.00	
4	ISBN 0-70	24	19-03-03	29-03-03	04-04-03	16	6	3	£ 3.00	
5	ISBN 0-14-	16	14-01-03	24-01-03	30-01-03	16	6	3	£ 3.00	
6	ISBN 0-14-	23	14-04-03	24-04-03	30-04-03	16	6	3	£ 2.50	0.166667
7	ISBN 0-33	43	21-01-03	31-01-03	05-02-03	15	5	2.5	£ 2.50	
8	ISBN 0-14-	3	28-06-03	08-07-03	13-07-03	15	5	2.5	£ 2.00	0.2
9	ISBN 0-14-	26	30-01-03	09-02-03	13-02-03	14	4	2	£ 2.00	
10	ISBN 0-00-	13	02-11-02	12-11-02	16-11-02	14	4	2	£ 2.00	
11	ISBN 1-85	7	20-01-03	30-01-03	04-02-03	15	5	2.5	£ 2.00	0.2
12	ISBN 0-14-	34	05-06-03	15-06-03	18-06-03	13	3	1.5	£ 1.50	

You can now work with the data in Excel. There is no connection between the data in Excel and the data in Access, so any changes you make affect only the Excel worksheet.

You use almost exactly the same procedure to export data to a dBASE or Paradox table. The only difference is that you select a dBASE or Paradox file type in the *Export* dialog box.

Exercise 16.8: Exporting to a text file

In this exercise you will export data from the Members table to a delimited text file.

1) In the Database window, click the Members table and then choose **File | Export**. This displays the *Export Table* dialog box.
2) Select *Text Files* in the *File of Type* box, enter MembersDelimited as the name of the destination file, navigate to the folder where you want to save the file, and then click **Save**. This starts the *Export Text Wizard*.
3) In the first page of the wizard you specify whether you want to export to a delimited text tile or to a fixed-width text file. Select each option in turn and see how this affects the format of the records displayed in the lower part of the window.

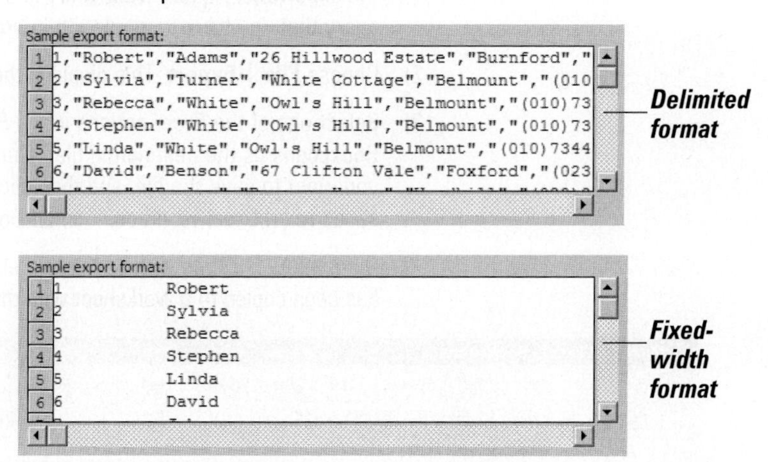

4) You are going to export the table to a delimited text file, so select this option and click **Next**.
5) In the next page of the wizard, you can change the field delimiter and text qualifier. You can also choose whether or not to export the field names with the records. Select the *Include Field Names on First Row* option and click **Finish**.
6) The wizard now creates a delimited text file named MembersDelimited and displays a confirmation message. Click **OK** to close this message.
7) Now open the MembersDelimited file to see the result of the export operation. You can open the file in Notepad, WordPad or Microsoft Word, for example.

Chapter 16: summary

Access provides two methods for working with data from external sources: *importing* and *linking*.

When you *import* data, it is copied from the source file and converted from its original format to a set of Access records. There is no ongoing connection between the source data and the data in Access – changes to one do not affect the other. You use this method of working with external data when you no longer need to work with the data in its original format.

When you *link* to external data, a connection is created between the external data and a table in Access, allowing you to view and work with the data in the source file from within Access. Changes you make to the data in Access are saved to the source file, and changes to the source file are reflected in your view of the data in Access. You use this method of working with external data when you need to share the data with users of a different database or application.

You can import and link to data from many different sources, including other Access databases, Paradox and dBASE database tables, spreadsheet files and text files. You use the **File | Get External Data | Import** option to import data and the **File | Get External Data | Link Files** option to link to data. Where necessary a wizard guides you through the procedure. Before importing a spreadsheet or text file, you usually need to prepare the file so that it is in a format suitable for conversion to an Access table.

When you want to use data from an Access database in another application, you can export the data to a file type appropriate for that application. There is no ongoing connection between the data in Access and the exported data. Changes in one are not reflected in the other. You can export Access tables and queries to a wide variety of file formats, including dBASE, Paradox, spreadsheet and text files.

Chapter 16: quick quiz

Q1	True or false – a linked table allows you to view and work with the same data in Access and in another application.
A.	True.
B.	False.

Q2	True or false – imported data is copied from the source file without retaining a link to that file.
A.	True.
B.	False.

Q3	When importing from a spreadsheet, the source data must not include . . .
A.	Column headings.
B.	Column totals and subtotals.
C.	Blank columns.

Q4	When importing from a text file, which of these requirements must the source data meet?
A.	Each field must contain the same type of data on all rows.
B.	Each record must be on a separate row.
C.	Each row must end with a paragraph break.
D.	All records must include the same fields.

Q5	True or false – when you import an object from another Access database, all associated objects are automatically imported as well.
A.	True.
B.	False.

Q6	True or false – when you export data from Access, a link is created between the source table or query and the exported data.
A.	True.
B.	False.

Answers

1: A, **2**: A, **3**: B, **4**: All, **5**: B, **6**: B.

17 In conclusion

In this chapter

Now that you have completed the topics and tasks in the previous chapters, you have covered the syllabus requirements for ECDL Advanced Databases.

This chapter summarizes what you have learnt. It also presents a final version of the Village Library database, with a more complete set of queries, forms, and reports than previous versions. An integrated Help file explains how and why the various elements of this database were created.

Exercise file

In this chapter you will work with the following Access file:

`Village Library Database`

Table design: summary

At the core of any database are the tables and fields that store the database data and the relationships that link the tables. These are determined by the purpose of the database, its subjects, and the tasks it is required to handle.

In Chapters 2 to 6 of this book you learnt how to:

- Design a set of tables that support the purpose of a database and the tasks it is intended to perform.
- Create relationships between the database tables.
- Enforce referential integrity to ensure consistency between related tables.
- Use the *Cascade Update* and *Cascade Delete* options to override referential integrity restrictions in a controlled manner.
- Specify a default join type for each relationship.
- Assign an appropriate data type and field size to each field.

- Create lookup fields, input masks, and default values to facilitate data entry.
- Create validation rules and specify required fields to ensure valid data entry.
- Select appropriate field formats to control how data is displayed.

You can view the resulting structure of the Village Library database by opening the `Village Library Database` and then opening the Relationships window (**Tools | Relationships**).

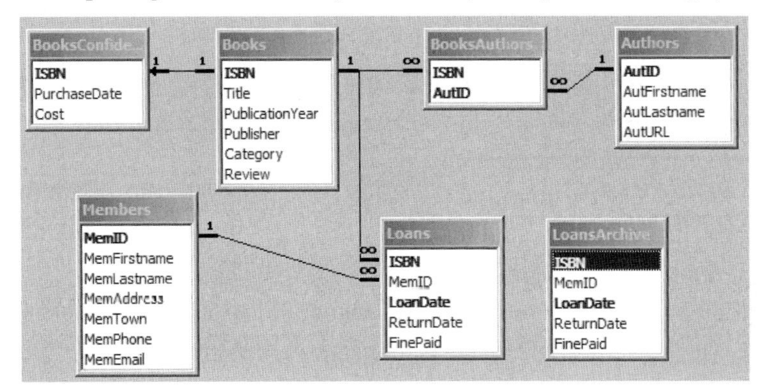

This provides an overview of the database structure, including the relationships between tables, the default join types, and the referential integrity options applied.

Query design: summary

You use select queries to retrieve data from your database, specifying the source tables and fields for the data and the criteria you want the retrieved data to meet. You can then use these queries as the record sources for forms and reports.

You use action queries to retrieve data from your database and then copy, delete, or modify the records retrieved.

In Chapters 7 to 10 of this book, you learnt how to:

- Create update, make-table, append and delete queries that enable you to act on multiple records at a time.
- Group records in a query.
- Create total queries that summarize (for example, count, sum, or average) field values in all records or in groups of records returned by the query.
- Create crosstab queries that calculate totals for records that are grouped on more than one field and display the results in a compact, spreadsheet-like format.

- Create calculated fields that return the result of calculations on other fields.
- Use calculations as criteria for determining which records are returned by a query.
- Include or exclude duplicate records and records that share the same value(s) in one or more fields.
- Find records that have no matching values in related tables.
- Display the records with the highest or lowest values in a particular field.
- Create parameter queries that prompt users for record selection criteria when they run the queries.

Form design: summary

Forms are the main means of adding and editing data in a database. All information in a form is contained in controls such as labels, text boxes, list boxes, and so on.

In Chapters 11 to 13 of this book, you learnt how to:

- Specify the record source for a form.
- Create controls that are linked to fields in the form's record source (bound controls).
- Create record selector controls.
- Create calculated controls that perform calculations on values in individual records.
- Create calculated controls that summarize values in a group of records.
- Specify the tab order for a form.
- Create a main form and subform that display records from one table/query and all related records from another table/query.

Report design: summary

Reports are the main means of organizing, grouping, and summarizing database information for printing or online review. All information in a report is contained in controls such as text boxes and labels.

In Chapter 14 you learnt how to:

- Create calculated controls that perform calculations on values in individual records in a report.
- Create calculated controls that display group totals.

- Create calculated controls that display report totals.
- Create calculated controls that display concatenated values, dates, and other expressions.
- Calculate percentages in a report.
- Create running sums and use running sums to number report items.
- Insert page breaks.
- Display/hide page headers and footers.

Macros: summary

Macros provide a simple means of automating common database tasks. You can use them to automatically perform tasks that you repeat frequently and to make your database objects work together.

In Chapter 15 you learnt how to:

- Create a macro.
- Create command buttons that trigger macros.
- Attach macros to form control events.
- Attach macros to form and report events.
- Use a macro to synchronize two forms or a form and a report.

Importing, exporting, and linking: summary

With Access you aren't limited to working with data in a single Access database. You can import data from other Access databases and from other file formats, you can link to data in external sources, and you can export data in various formats for use in other applications.

In Chapter 16 you learnt how to:

- Import dBASE and Paradox tables.
- Import spreadsheet data and text files.
- Import Access database objects.
- Link to data in an Excel worksheet.
- Export tables and queries to dBASE, Paradox, spreadsheet, and text files.

Village Library Database: final version

The case study in this book has been designed to illustrate the features required to cover the ECDL Advanced Database syllabus. Each chapter has its own version of the Village Library database, designed to support the skill sets dealt with in that chapter. This chapter presents a final version of the database (`Village Library Database.mdb`), which incorporates a more complete set of features than previous versions.

Remember that the database does not represent a complete functioning database for a real library. Such a database would require a more complex structure – one that is capable of storing and manipulating information about, for example, multiple copies and editions of books, media other than books, subscription rates, cancelled memberships, interlibrary loans, and so on. It might also exploit some of Access's more advanced features, such as SQL and the Visual Basic for Applications programming language.

Village Library Database: application

A database application consists of a set of database objects that are organized and linked together so that users can easily perform their tasks without having to work their way through long lists of queries, forms, reports, and so on.

Visual Basic for Applications (VBA) code is the most powerful tool that Access provides for developing database applications. However, you can create simple applications without any programming, using just the Access features you learnt about in this book or variations thereon.

The Village Library Database application accompanying this chapter uses only two features that you have not already met: the **Startup** feature and the **Help** feature. It consists of a set of tables, queries, forms, reports, and macros similar to those you created in earlier chapters. The features that turn it into a user-friendly application include:

- Startup settings
- Unbound forms
- Macros

Let's look at each of these now in turn.

Startup settings

Open the Village Library Database. You are immediately presented with a Welcome screen from which you can access all the application functionality.

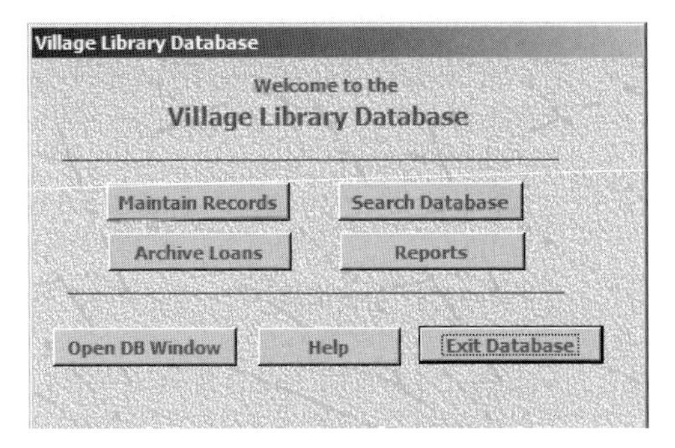

Notice that Access's Database Window is not displayed. Typically when you create an application, you automate access to all user functionality and you hide the underlying database objects so that users cannot interfere with them. So when you open the Village Library Database, Access's Database Window is hidden.

How do you get Access to display the Welcome screen and hide the Database Window? By using Access's **Startup** feature. Let's see how this works.

Having opened the database, choose the **Tools | Startup** command. This displays the *Startup* dialog box, as shown here.

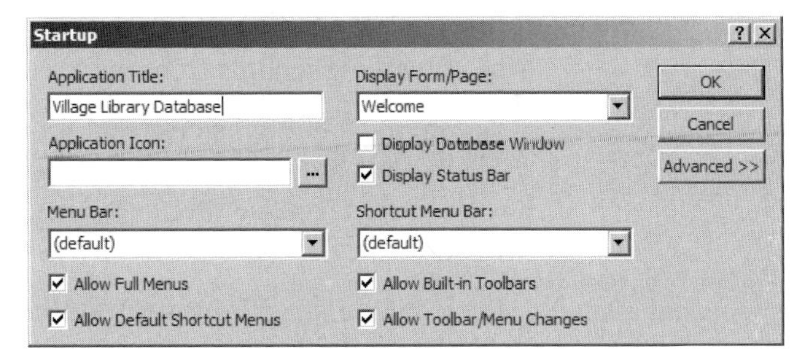

This controls how your application looks and behaves when it starts. The options relevant to the Village Library Database application are as follows:

- *Application Title*: This specifies the text displayed in Access's title bar, allowing you to use the name of your application in the title bar instead of 'Microsoft Access'.
- *Display Form/Page*: This enables you to specify a form to be displayed automatically when the database opens. In this case it is the Welcome form.

- *Display Database Window*: When this option is not selected, the Database Window is automatically hidden when the database is opened.

The other options relate to the use of built-in and custom menus and toolbars, which are not covered in this book. However, it is useful to know that you can customize Access's built-in menus and toolbars and that you can also create you own custom menus and toolbars. This gives you full control over the functionality available to users of your database, preventing access to all functionality except the user interface you have created.

Unbound forms

In this book you learnt how to create forms that display data from one or more tables and/or queries – that is, forms that are bound to some record source. It is also possible to create unbound forms – that is, forms with no record source. These are very useful for creating a user interface to your database objects.

The Welcome form is one such unbound form. Instead of displaying database records, it contains a set of command buttons that provide access to the main tasks that users will want to perform – that is:

- Maintaining records in the various database tables.
- Searching the database for particular records.
- Viewing reports.
- Archiving records from the Loans table.

A command button is provided for each of these tasks. The *On Click* event associated with each command button triggers a macro that takes the user to the next step in the task they want to perform.

For example, the **Maintain Database** button triggers a macro that opens the *Maintain Records* form. This is another unbound form, used only for navigating to the forms used for maintaining different tables.

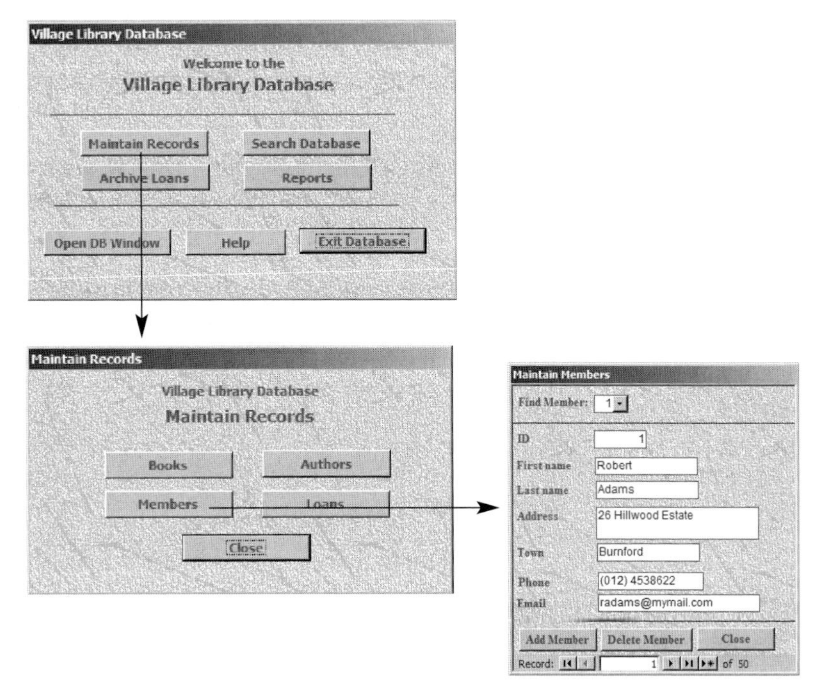

Additional command buttons on the Welcome form are shortcuts for displaying the Database Window, closing the Village Library Database, and accessing the Village Library Database's Help file.

Take some time now to browse through the user interface. You will see that it consists of a hierarchy of forms that allows users to quickly and easily access the functionality they want to use – all created with features you have already met in earlier chapters.

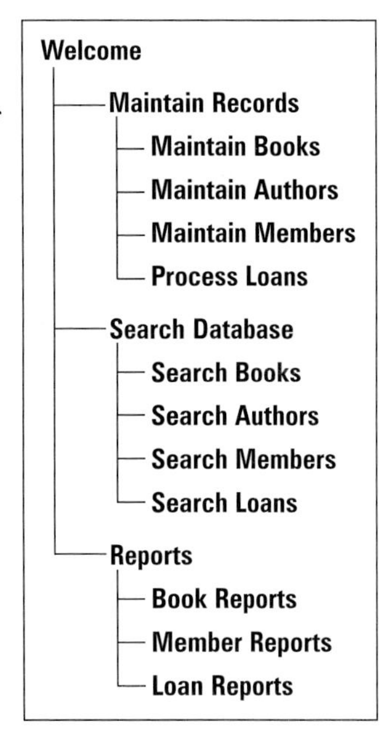

Macros

Macros form an important part of the user interface. They tie together the various forms and reports, and automate access to them.

- On all the unbound forms, macros are attached to each of the command buttons. These macros specify the action to be taken when a command button is clicked.
- On bound forms, such as the Maintain Members form, command buttons with attached macros are used to perform the various tasks associated with the form and to access related functionality.
- Macros have also been attached to some form and report events in order to refine the form/report functionality.

The following diagram illustrates the functionality of the Maintain Members form and the macros used to complete the table maintenance tasks.

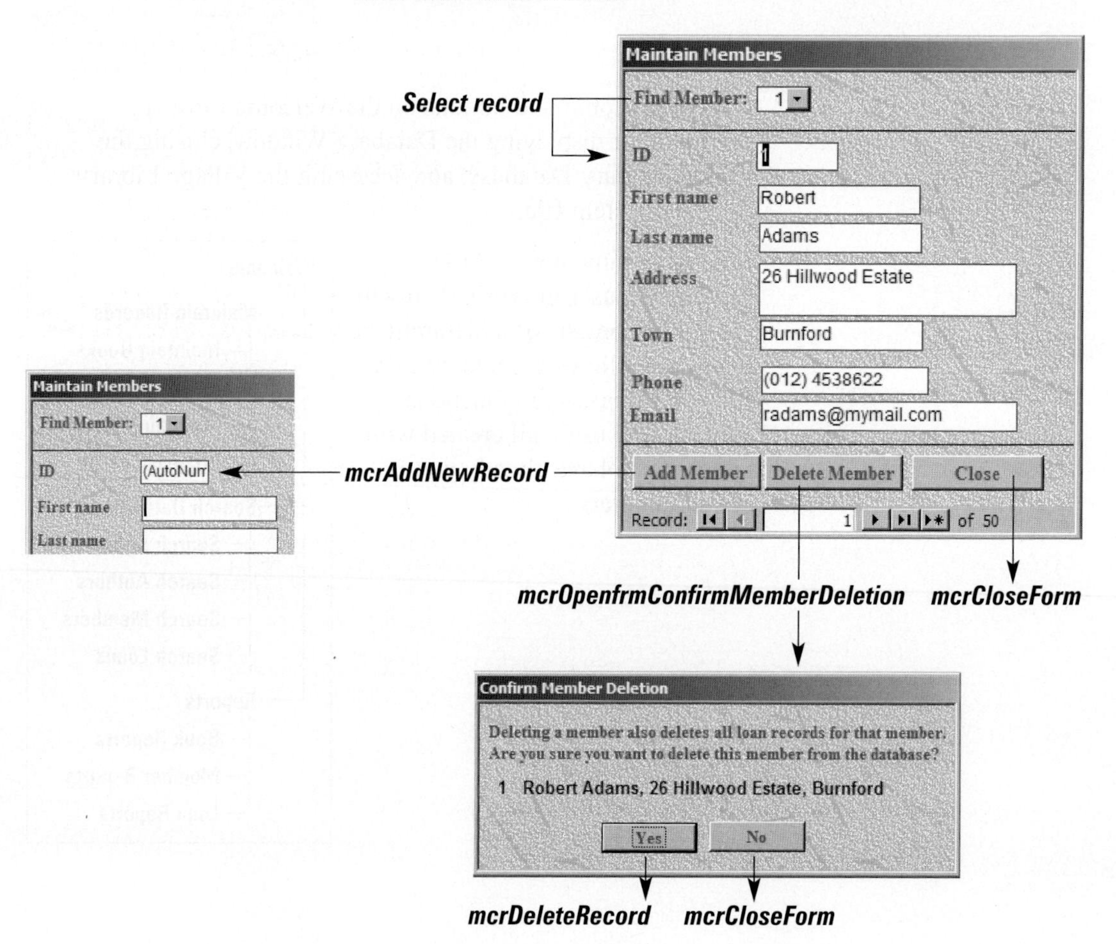

Village Library Database Help

A Help file is provided for the Village Library Database application and is integrated with it. This provides information on why and how the various elements of the database were created.

To display the Village Library Database Help, you can either:

- Click the **Help** button on the Welcome form. This opens a Help window with **Contents**, **Index**, and **Search** tabs.

  The **Contents** tab provides a table of contents for the entire Help file. The **Index** and **Search** tabs allow you to enter keywords to find particular help topics you want to view.

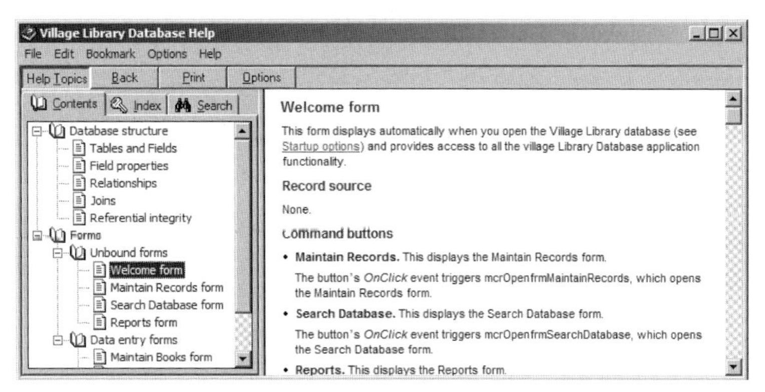

- Press **F1** (forms only). This displays help information specific to the active form.

As well as using the Village Library Help to get information about how the database was built, it will also be useful to open the database objects in Design View and take a look at their record sources, components, and properties.

Naming conventions

To make it easier to identify database objects when selecting them from lists and when referring to them in expressions, it is a good idea to use a consistent naming convention throughout the database.

Prefixes

One useful convention prefixes object names with a three/four letter tag that identifies the object type, as follows:

Object	Prefix	Example
Table	tbl	tblBooks
Query	qry	qryAllBooks
Form	frm	frmMaintainRecords
Subform	fsub	fsubLoansAndReturns
Report	rpt	rptLoansHistory
Macro	mcr	mcrCloseForm

This convention is used in the Village Library Database accompanying this chapter.

There is also a clear benefit to prefixing control names with the control type. This makes it easy to differentiate between controls and their underlying fields in expressions. The Village Library Database uses the following standard naming convention for controls:

Control	Prefix
Check box	chk
Combo box	cbo
Command button	cmd
Label	lbl
Line	lin
Listbox	lst
Option button	opt
Option group	grp
Subform/report	sub
Text box	txt

Spaces

Access supports spaces in object, field, and control names. However, there are disadvantages to including spaces in names.

In particular, Access does not recognize such names in expressions, unless you enclose them in square brackets – for example, [Purchase Date]. If you omit the spaces, Access will recognize the string as a name and automatically insert the square brackets for you.

In the Village Library Database accompanying this chapter, all object, field, and control names consist of a single string, with the first letter of each word (except the prefix) capitalized. This is a standard naming convention.

The default text displayed in the title bar of forms and reports, and in column headings in tables and queries, is the object or field name. To make these more user friendly, you can specify different text by using the object or field's *Caption* property.

And that's it!

The Village Library Database gives you a good idea of what you can achieve with the Access skills you have acquired while following this book. Good luck in your ECDL Advanced Databases examination!

A

Expressions

In this appendix

Expressions are a fundamental part of many Access operations. You use them, for example, when defining validation rules, default values, query criteria, and calculated fields.

This appendix presents all you need to know about the operators, values, functions, and field and control references that you can include in an expression.

What is an expression?

An expression consists of any combination of operators, identifiers, literal values, and functions that returns a result when applied to data in your database.

- **Literal value**. A value, such as a number, text string, or date, that Access uses exactly as written. You can use wildcard characters in literal values. See 'Literal values' and 'Wildcard characters' below.
- **Identifier**. Specifies the name of a field or control whose value you want to include in the expression. See 'Identifiers' below.
- **Operator**. Specifies the type of operation to be performed. In general, if you do not include an operator in an expression, Access assumes an equal to (=) operator. See 'Operators' below.
- **Function**. Returns a value based on a calculation or other operation. See 'Functions' below.

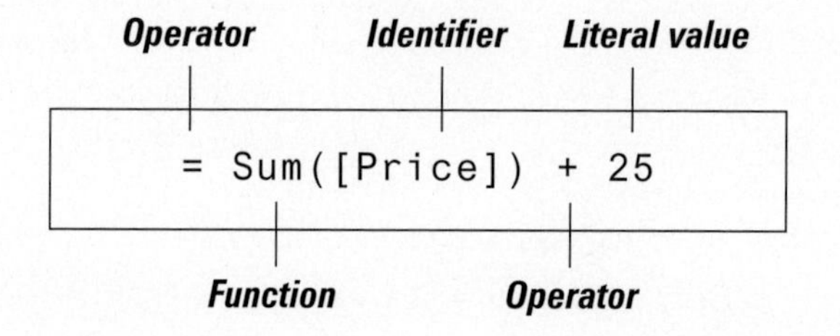

In form and report controls, all expressions must be preceded by the equal to (=) symbol.

Literal values

When including literal values in an expression:

- Enclose dates within hash (#) symbols – for example, #01-02-03#.
- Enclose strings within double quotes (") – for example, "Excellent".

Identifiers

When including field and control identifiers in an expression:

- Enclose the field or control name within square brackets ([ ]) – for example, [Cost].
- When a macro in one form refers to a control in another form, the reference must be in the following format:

  `Forms![Formname]![Controlname]`

Operators

Access provides several types of operators, including comparison, arithmetic, logical, and concatenation operators.

Operator	Meaning
Comparison	
=	Equal to.
<>	Not equal to.
<	Less than.
<=	Less than or equal to.
>	Greater than.
>=	Greater than or equal to.
In	Specifies a list of values. For example, the following validation rule specifies that only values from the list are valid in the field: `In ("Ireland", "England", "Scotland", "Wales")`
Between ... And ...	Specifies a range of values. For example, the following validation rule specifies that values entered must be between 1 and 100: `Between 1 And 100`

Operator	Meaning
Comparison	
Like	Searches for strings that match a specified pattern. (Typically used with wildcard characters.) For example, when used as selection criteria in a query field, the following expression specifies all values that begin with the word 'The': `Like "The*"`
Is Null	Is equal to Null.
Is Not Null	Is not equal to Null.
Arithmetic	
+	Add.
-	Subtract.
*	Multiply.
/	Divide.
Logical	
And	Use to combine expressions. All the expressions must evaluate to True. For example, the following validation rule specifies that values entered in the field must be *both* greater than 1 *and* less than 100: `>1 And <100`
Or	Use to combine expressions. Only one of the expressions need evaluate to True. For example, the following validation rule specifies that values entered in the field must begin *either* with 'A' *or* with 'B': `Like("A*") Or Like("B*")`
Not	Negates the result of an expression. For example, the following validation rule specifies that values in the field cannot begin with 'A': `Not Like ("A*")`
Concatenation	
&	Combines text strings from different fields or controls. If using to combine number values, Access automatically converts the numbers to text strings.

Functions

Access provides many different functions for use in expressions. Here is a list of the functions you are most likely to use.

Function	Meaning
Aggregate functions	
Sum()	Calculates the sum of a set of values.
Avg()	Calculates the average of a set of values (excluding Null values).
Min()	Returns the lowest value of a set of values (excluding Null values.)
Max()	Returns the highest value of a set of values (excluding Null values).
Count()	Returns a count of the values in a set of values (excluding Null values).
Count(*)	Returns a count of the values in a set of values (including Null values).
Date and time functions	
Date()	Returns the current date.
Time()	Returns the current time.
Now()	Returns the current date and time.
Year()	Returns the year of a specified date. For example, Year(01-01-03) returns 2003 and Year(Date()) returns the year part of the current date.
Logical functions	
IIf()	Returns one of two values, depending on the evaluation of an expression. The syntax is as follows: `IIf(expression, value_if_true, value_if_false)`
IsNull()	Tests whether or not a value is Null. Returns True if the value is Null. Otherwise returns False.
Conversion function	
Nz()	Converts Null values to zeros. The syntax is: `Nz(expression,0)`

Wildcard characters

A wildcard character is a special character that represents one or more other characters in a literal value.

Character	Meaning
?	Represents any single character in the same position. For example, the following represents 1002, 1112, 1562, 1762, 1222, 1AB2, 1FG2, and so on: `1??2`
*	Represents zero or more characters in the same position. For example, the following represents 'Bn', 'Brian', 'Brendan', 'Bern', 'Bergen', and so on: `B*n`
#	Represents any single number in the same position. For example, the following represents any three-digit number beginning with 1: `1##`

[ ]	Represents any single character within the brackets. You can specify either a list of characters or a range of characters.
	For example, the following represents 'fan', 'fin' and 'fun', but not 'fen' or 'faun':
	`f[aiu]n`
	And the following represents 'ban', 'can', and 'dan', but not 'fan':
	`[b-d]an`
	You can also specify multiple ranges. For example, the following represents 'ban', 'Ban' 'can', 'Can', and so on:
	`[B-D,b-d]an`

!	Represents any character except those listed within the brackets. For example, the following represents 'fen' but not 'fan', 'fin' or 'fun': `f[!aiu]n`

Glossary

In this appendix

This appendix presents a glossary of terms that you can use to quickly find definitions for most database terms used in this book.

Glossary terms and definitions

Action query
A query that copies or changes groups of records from one or more *tables*.

Aggregate function
An Access *function* that summarizes *field* values. Examples are Sum(), Avg() and Count().

Append query
A type of *query* that copies *records* from one or more *tables* and appends them to the end of another table.

Argument
A value or expression that provides information required by a *function* or *macro* action to perform its task.

AutoNumber data type
Access automatically generates unique sequential numbers in the *field*. This *data type* is typically used for *primary key* fields.

Bound control
A *control* that gets its values from a *field* in the *record source* of a *form* or *report*, and that you can use to update values in that field (forms only).

Calculated control
In a *form* or *report*, a *control* that displays the result of calculations.

Calculated field
A *query field* that contains a calculation *expression* and displays the result of that expression. Calculated fields are not stored in a database *table*. Instead Access reruns the calculations each time you run the query.

Checkbox control
A *control* that represents a Yes/No choice. Typically, checkboxes are used as stand-alone controls, with each checkbox representing a Yes/No choice that is independent of any other Yes/No choices.

Combo box control
A *control* that combines a *text box*, where users can type a value, and a drop-down *list box*, where users can select a value instead. A down-arrow appears when you click in the control; the drop-down list opens when you click this arrow.

Command button control
A *control* that starts an action.

Concatenation
The creation of a single string from a combination of *field* values and literal values.

Control
A graphical object that you place on a *form* or *report* to display data, to accept data input, to perform an action, or simply for decorative purposes.

Control name
The name that uniquely identifies a *control* within a *form* or *report*. The default name for a *bound control* is the name of the underlying *field*. The default name for an *unbound control* is the name of the control type followed by a unique number.

Control source
The source of the data displayed by a *control*. For a *bound control*, the control source is a *field* in the *form/report record source*. For an *unbound control*, the source is typically a calculation *expression*.

Criteria
See *Query criteria*.

Crosstab query
A *query* that calculates totals for *records* that are grouped on more than one *field* and displays the results in a spreadsheet-like format.

Currency data type
Stores numeric data with one to four decimal places. The data can be used in calculations and sorted in numeric order. By default, values are displayed with the currency symbol specified in your Windows Regional Settings.

Data and information
Data is the values that you store in the database. Information is data that you retrieve from the database in some meaningful way.

Datasheet View
Displays database information arranged in columns (one for each *field*) and rows (one for each *record*). Datasheet View is available for *tables*, *queries* and *forms*.

Data type
This determines the kind of data that can be stored in a *field* and the operations that can be carried out on that data.

Date/Time data type
Stores dates and times. The *Format* property allows you to specify the format in which dates and times are displayed.

Default value
A value that is automatically entered in a *field* when you create a new *record*.

Delete query
A type of *query* that deletes *records* from one or more *tables*.

Delimited text file
A text file in which fields are separated by a special delimiter character such as a comma, tab or semicolon. Delimited files are often referred to as comma-delimited files or CSV (comma-separated values) files.

Design View
The view in which you design *tables*, *queries*, *forms* and *reports*.

Duplicate records
Records that contain identical values in all their *fields*.

Event
An action that occurs on a *form*, *report* or *control* and that can trigger execution of a *macro* or an *event procedure*.

Event procedure
A procedure, written in Microsoft Visual Basic, that is executed in response to an *event*. *Macros* provide similar, though less powerful, functionality. For ECDL, you do not need to know how to create or use event procedures.

Expression
A combination of *operators*, *identifiers*, *literal values* and *functions* that returns a result when applied to data in your database.

Field
A single piece of information about the subject of a *table*.

Field size property
Determines the maximum size for data in a *field*.

Field validation rule
A rule that sets limits or conditions on the values that you can enter in a *field*.

Fixed-width text file
A text file in which fields are aligned in columns. Spaces are inserted to fill out the fields so that they are the same width in all rows.

Fixed value list
See *Value list*.

Flat database
A flat database consists of a single *table*.

Foreign key
One or more *fields* in a *table* that refer to the *primary key* field(s) of a related table.

Form
A database object used mainly for data input or onscreen display. Typically a form displays a single *record*, laid out and formatted in a user-friendly manner. A variety of *control* types are used to facilitate quick data entry and easy access to related data.

Form View
This is the view in which *forms* are presented to users. Single Form View displays a single *record* at a time. Continuous Form View displays multiple records at a time.

Format property
Determines how values in a *table field*, *query field*, *form control* or *report* control are displayed and printed. The format does not affect how the data is stored.

Function
A predefined formula that performs an operation (for example, a calculation or logical evaluation) and returns a value. The values on which the operation is performed are referred to as the function's *arguments*.

Grouped report
A *report* in which information is grouped by the values in one or more *fields*. Calculations may be performed on the data within each group.

Hyperlink data type
Stores hyperlinks to websites, folders and files. Users can click a hyperlink to start the source application and display the destination website, folder or file.

Identifier
The name of a *field* or *control* whose value you want to include in an *expression*.

Importing
Converts data from its original format and saves it to a new or existing Access *table*. There is no ongoing connection between the original data and the data in Access.

Index
A database feature that speeds up searching and sorting operations and that can force a *field* to have unique values. The *primary key* of a *table* is automatically indexed. You do not need to know about indexes for ECDL.

Inner join
When two *tables* are joined by an inner *join*, a *query* returns only records that have matching values in their related *fields*. Unmatched values in both tables are omitted.

Input mask
A template that assists data entry and controls the type, number and pattern of characters that can be entered in a *field*.

Join
The process of combining *records* from two *tables*.

Label control
A *form* or *report control* that displays descriptive text such as field captions, titles, headings and instructions.

Left outer join
When *two tables* are joined by a left outer *join*, a *query* returns all *records* from the *primary table* but only matching records from the related table.

Linked table
A *table* that is linked to external data, allowing you to view and work with that data from within Access. Changes you make to data in the linked table are saved to the external data source and not to your database.

Linking
Creates a link to external data, allowing you to view and work with that data from within Access.

List box control
A *form control* that displays a list from which users select a value. The list is always open and so is typically used to display a small number of options only.

Literal value
A value, such as a number, text string or date, that Access uses exactly as entered.

Lookup field
A *field* that displays a list from which you select the value to store in the field. The list can look up values either from a *table* or *query* or from a *fixed value list*.

Macro
A sequence of one or more database actions that can be executed with a single command or triggered automatically in response to a *form*, *report* or *control event*.

Main form
A *form* that contains a *subform*.

Make-table query
A type of *query* that creates a new *table* from data in one or more existing tables.

Many-to-many relationship
A *relationship* in which each *record* in the first *table* can have many matching records in the second table, and each record in the second table can have many matching records in the first table.

Memo data type
Stores alphanumeric data that is more than 255 characters long. The data can contain tabs and paragraphs but no formatting.

Multipart field
A *field* that includes more than one data item.

Multivalue field
A *field* that contains multiple values for the same data item.

Null
A special value (displayed as a blank *field)* that indicates missing or unknown data, or a field to which data is not applicable.

Number data type
Stores numeric data that can be used in calculations and sorted in numeric order.

One-to-one relationship
A *relationship* in which each *record* in *one* table can have no more than one matching record in the other table.

One-to-many relationship
A *relationship* in which each *record* in the first *table* can have many matching records in the second table. But each record in the second table can have only one matching record in the first table.

Operator
Specifies the type of calculation to be performed on data in an *expression*. Access supports the following types of operators: arithmetic, comparison, logical and concatenation.

Option button control
A *control* consisting of a small circle that represents a Yes/No choice. A blank circle represents a 'No' value; a small dot in the circle represents a 'Yes' value. Option buttons typically form part of an option group.

Option group control
A *control* consisting of a group of related options, only one of which can be selected at any time. Typically each option is represented by an *option button control*.

Parameter query
A *query* that prompts for *record* selection *criteria* when the query is run.

Primary key
A *field* (or combination of fields) in a database *record* that identifies that record uniquely.

Primary table
When two *tables* are related, the primary table is the one whose *primary key* is used as the linking *field*. So, in a *one-to-many relationship*, the table on the 'one' side of the relationship is always the primary table. In a *one-to-one relationship*, either table can be the primary table. You make the choice when you create the *relationship*.

Print Preview View
A view of database data as it will look when printed. This view is available for *forms*, *reports* and *datasheets*.

Query
A request to the database for *records* that match specified *criteria*. Queries are named and saved in the database and allow you to repeatedly retrieve up-to-date records that meet the query definition.

Query criteria
Expressions that restrict the *records* returned by a *query* to those that match specified conditions.

Record
One complete set of *fields* relating to the same item in a table.

Record source
The *table* or *query* from which a *form* or *report* gets its data and whose *fields* it updates (forms only).

Redundancy
Redundancy refers to the unnecessary duplication of data in a database.

Referential integrity
A set of rules that ensures that the *relationships* between *records* in related *tables* are valid, and that you do not accidentally delete or change related data.

Relational database
A collection of data organized into *tables*.

Relationship
A relationship is a connection between two *tables* that allows them to share data. It is based on the tables having at least one *field* in common.

Report
A database object used to organize, group and summarize database information in a format suitable for printing and for online review.

Required field
A *field* in which it is mandatory to enter a value.

Right outer join
When two *tables* are joined by a right outer *join*, a *query* returns all *records* from the related table but only matching records from the *primary table*.

Running sum
An accumulating total of values in a *report*.

Select query
A type of *query* that retrieves *records* for viewing and updating.

Self join
Joins a *table* to itself. A self *join* is based on a *one-to-one relationship* between two instances of the same table.

SQL
SQL (Structured Query Language) is the standard language used to create and query *relational databases*. For your convenience, Access provides graphical building tools for *tables*, *queries*, *forms*, and so on. Internally, however, it generates SQL statements to define these database objects. You do not need to know how to use SQL for ECDL.

Subform
A *form* that is contained within another form.

Subform control
A *form control*, represented by a rectangular box, that contains a *subform*.

Table
A collection of *records* with the same *fields* and relating to the subject.

Table subject
The people, things or events about which a *table* stores data.

Tab order
The order in which the focus moves from *control* to control when a user tabs through a *form*.

Text box control
Bound text boxes display data from a *table* or *query field* and accept input to that field. Unbound text boxes display the results of calculations.

Text data type
Stores alphanumeric data that does not exceed 255 characters in size.

Total query
A *query* that calculates summary values for all *records* or for groups of records in *tables/queries*.

Unbound control
A *control* that is not linked to a *table/query field*. You can use unbound controls to display informational text, graphics, and the results of calculations. You cannot use an unbound control to update field values.

Unique record
A *record* that contains a unique value in at least one of its *fields*.

Updateable query
A *query* that allows you to edit the *records* it returns. The changes are applied to the underlying *table(s)*.

Update query
A type of *query* that makes changes to values in multiple *records* in one or more *tables*.

Validation rule
A rule that sets limits or conditions on the values that you can enter in a *field* or *record*.

Value list
A fixed list of values that a *lookup field* or *combo box* can display for selection.

Wildcard
A special character that represents one or more other characters in a literal value.

Workbook
A Microsoft Excel file that contains one or more *worksheets*.

Worksheet
The primary document you use to store and work with data in Excel. Also referred to as a spreadsheet.

Yes/No data type
Stores Yes/No, True/False or On/Off values.

Index

Advanced Presentation

Sadhbh O'Dwyer
and Paul Holden

Approved
Courseware
Advanced
Syllabus AM 6
Version 1.0

Harlow, England • London • New York • Boston • San Francisco • Toronto • Sydney • Singapore • Hong Kong
Tokyo • Seoul • Taipei • New Delhi • Cape Town • Madrid • Mexico City • Amsterdam • Munich • Paris • Milan

Contents

Preface xi

Chapter 1: Getting started 1

Chapter 2: Information structure 3

Chapter 3: Design structure 14

Chapter 6: Action buttons and hyperlinks 72

Chapter 7: Custom shows and slide shows 87

Chapter 8: Transitions 98

Chapter 11: Linking *146*

Chapter 12: Macros and set-ups *160*

Preface

What is ECDL?

ECDL, or the European Computer Driving Licence, is an internationally recognised qualification in Information Technology skills. It is accepted by businesses internationally as a verification of competence and proficiency in computer skills.

The ECDL syllabus is neither operating system nor software specific.

For more information about ECDL, and to see the syllabus for *ECDL Module 6, Presentation, Advanced Level*, visit the official ECDL website at http://www.ecdl.com.

About this book

This book covers the ECDL Advanced Presentation Syllabus Version 1.0, using PowerPoint 2000 to complete all the required tasks. It is assumed that you have already completed the presentation module of ECDL 4.0 or earlier, using PowerPoint, or have an equivalent knowledge of the product.

Each chapter in this book contains a number of exercises. You can work through these exercises either sequentially or in any order you choose. Each exercise incorporates the results of preceding exercises. The starting points for the exercises are available on the CD that accompanies this book. If you are working though the book sequentially, you may wish to save your finished exercises in a different folder to the exercises supplied on CD.

Additional exercises, labelled Quick Quiz, have been posed for you to complete. These exercises provide limited guidance as to how to go about performing the tasks, since you should have learned what you need in the preceding exercises.

Hardware and software requirements

- CD-ROM drive
- 500 KB of free space on your hard disk
- PowerPoint 2000, PowerPoint 97 or PowerPoint XP
- Word 2000, Word 97 or Word XP

Note: The examples and exercises in this book are based on Microsoft Office 2000. If you are using a different version of Office, some of the screens and operations may be slightly different, but the general principles still apply.

Typographic conventions

The following typographic conventions are used in this book:

Bold face text is used to denote command names, button names, menu names, the names of tabs in dialog boxes, and keyboard keys.

Italicized text is used to denote options in drop-down lists and list boxes, dialog box names, areas in dialog boxes and toolbars.

CAPITALIZED TEXT is used to denote file types and exercise files.

1 Getting started

The case study

The exercises in this book relate to the presentations used by the fictitious company, Green Grocer Group, or GGG.

The Green Grocer Group is an organic food supplier. They supply major retailers with high quality organic fruit and vegetables. GGG source their produce from organic farmers in several locations. All produce of the Green Grocer Group is certified organic and is traceable. Due to the high demand for organic produce, GGG is expanding and is looking for new stockists and suppliers.

Your brief is to create an overview presentation that is of relevance to both the farmers who supply GGG with organic produce and the investors in the company.

The CD

The CD supplied with this book contains exercise files and the following supplementary files:

- GGG.DOC – Word outline of the presentation
- PREVIOUS.PPT – Previous PowerPoint presentation from the Green Grocer Group
- GGG.JPG – Green Grocer Group logo
- ORGANICS.JPG – Organic Farming in Europe logo
- FIELD.WMV – Organic farm video
- BOWL1.JPG – Fruit bowl graphic
- GREEN GROCER GROUP.MDB – Database of best-selling goods
- SUPPLIERS.XLS – Spreadsheet of suppliers
- WHAT OUR CUSTOMERS SAY.DOC – Word document
- END OF YEAR RESULTS.XLS – Spreadsheet of financial results

You will use these files when completing the exercises in the book.

Copying files from the CD

Before you begin working through the exercises in this book, you will need to copy the files from the CD to your computer. Create a folder on your computer and copy the files from the CD to it. Ideally, you should also create a subfolder within this folder into which you can save your completed exercises.

Exercise 1.1: Copying files from the CD to your computer

1) Create a folder called ECDL_PRESENTATIONS anywhere on your computer. This will be your working folder for the exercises in this book.

2) Copy all the files from the CD to the ECDL_PRESENTATIONS folder.

3) Create a sub-folder within the ECDL_PRESENTATIONS folder for completed exercises. Name this folder EXERCISE_COMPLETE. You can save your completed exercises into here.

2 Information structure

In this chapter

To communicate your message successfully you need to structure your information and present it clearly.

PowerPoint enables you to do both these things. In this chapter you will focus on structuring information in your PowerPoint presentation so that it is clear and easy to follow. You will gain an appreciation for the role of the audience in your presentation, and learn how to build your presentation around their needs.

New skills

At the end of this chapter you should be able to:

- Plan a presentation
- Build your presentation around the needs of the audience
- Organize your information into accessible units
- Import a Word document into a presentation

New words

At the end of this chapter you should be able to explain the following term:

- 7±2 rule

Syllabus reference

This chapter covers the following syllabus points:

- AM 6.1.1.1
- AM 6.1.1.2
- AM 6.1.3.1
- AM 6.2.1.2
- AM 6.2.1.3

Planning

A good presentation starts with a clear plan. A plan takes into account the following:

- Who am I talking to?
- What am I trying to say?
- How long will my presentation take?
- What hardware will I be using?
- Where will my presentation take place?

Don't open your presentation software yet; first you've got to think about your audience.

The audience

Think about it: you are giving this presentation so that your audience will be informed, convinced, entertained, influenced or educated. A good presentation, therefore, is planned around your audience, their needs and your message.

The more you know about the demographic profile of your audience, the better you can tailor your presentation to their needs. Ask questions such as – What are these people like? How old are they? Where do they live? What do they do? What is their level of education? What do they like? What do they dislike?

The answers to these questions help you to choose appropriate language and level of detail, tone, suitable examples, imagery and so on.

As the audience for the case study in this book consists of two distinct groups – suppliers of organic food, and shareholders in the organic food company, Green Grocer Group – your message should satisfy the needs of both. The suppliers will want to know about the growth of their produce and the shareholders will want to know about the growth of their shares!

Use of language

This audience is a mixture of the business community and the agricultural community. Some of the shareholders might need explanations of the agricultural terms; some of the suppliers might need explanations of the business terms. Accordingly, you may need to explain some terms that are specific to each group.

Keep your language consistent. Use the same terms to describe the same things, otherwise your audience might get confused. If you use jargon or technical terms, be sure that your audience understands them.

Cultural differences

An audience may misinterpret the message of a presentation due to cultural differences between them and the presenter. If you are presenting to a group from a different country, for example, you should be sensitive to possible misinterpretations. Some cultures, for example, read from right to left; if your slides depend on a left-right flow, such an audience might not be able to follow your presentation easily. Also, images and graphics in your presentation can symbolize different things in different cultures. For example, the owl is a symbol of foolishness in China, whereas it is a symbol of wisdom in the West. The audience in your case study scenario is fairly homogenous so you don't really need to worry about cultural differences here.

Presentation environment

Before you give your presentation you need to consider the physical environment in which you will be presenting. Ask yourself the following:

- Where will you be giving your presentation in a lecture theatre or a small room?
- How many people will be in your audience? (If you are talking to a large audience you might need a microphone.)
- Will you need to bring a laptop?
- Will there be a projector in the room?
- What type of lighting will be in the room?

It's always a good idea to familiarize yourself with the room and the hardware you will be using. You might simply need to know where to plug in your projector, but it's always good to know where the power points are before you begin your presentation, rather than looking for them half-way through!

Timing

How long will your presentation be? This might seem obvious, but you need to know how much time you can spend on each slide. A good guideline is to spend approximately one minute per slide and to allow time at the end for discussion. For example, if you expect to have your audience for half an hour, you might allow 20 slides for 20 minutes of presentation and keep 10 minutes for questions and answers at the end.

Writing your plan

Writing your plan can appear daunting at first. What information will you include? What information will you leave out? How long will your presentation be?

You may find it helpful to start by putting your main points in a Word document: use the Outline feature in Word to organize the points into a logical sequence. This will give you a structure for your presentation, which you can then import into PowerPoint.

Word outlines

Writing your outline in a word processor such as Microsoft Word can help you to order and prioritize the ideas that you want to communicate. It will help you to arrange your information into a logical sequence, so that the audience can follow the presentation.

Exercise 2.1: Exporting a Word document to a presentation

1) Open the Word document GGG.DOC that was supplied with this book.

Presenter

- Denis O'Dwyer, Green Grocer Group

Our Mission Statement

- Green Grocer Group works with 75 farmers in 23 locations to provide the finest organic fruit and vegetables

Company History

- The Green Grocer Group was founded in Devon by Johanna O'Brien and Jim Forster
- Our company philosophy

About Johanna O'Brien

- Johanna O'Brien worked for a major supermarket chain where she noticed a demand for organic fruit and vegetables
- This gave her the idea of setting up a company that supplies organic fruit and vegetables

About Jim Forster

- Jim Forster is an active member of the organic farming community in Devon
- With a background in both business and farming, he made the ideal business partner

2) In GGG.DOC, choose **File | Send To | Microsoft PowerPoint**.

3) PowerPoint opens a new presentation, with the Word document GGG.doc as its outline.

1 **Presenter**
- Denis O'Dwyer, Green Grocer Group

2 **Our Mission Statement**
- Green Grocer Group works with 75 farmers in 23 locations to provide the finest organic fruit and vegetables

3 **Company History**
- The Green Grocer Group was founded in Devon by Johanna O'Brien and Jim Forster
- Our company philosophy

4 **About Johanna O'Brien**
- Johanna O'Brien worked for a major supermarket chain where she noticed a demand for organic fruit and vegetables

4) Choose **File | Save** and save this presentation as EX2.1.PPT.

Congratulations! You now have the outline of your presentation.

Merging information from other presentations

You can sometimes save time by recycling parts of presentations that either you or your colleagues have previously made. You can easily merge slides from one presentation into another. How? Take a look at the following exercise.

Exercise 2.2: Merging slides from other presentations

1) Open EX2.1.PPT.

2) In the Outline pane, place your cursor at the end of the last bullet point in slide 1, titled 'Presenter'.

   1 **Presenter**
   - Denis O'Dwyer, Green Grocer Group

3) Choose **Insert | Slides from Files.**

4) Under the **Find Presentation** tab, click the **Browse** button to find PREVIOUS.PPT. (This is the presentation with the slides you want to recycle.)

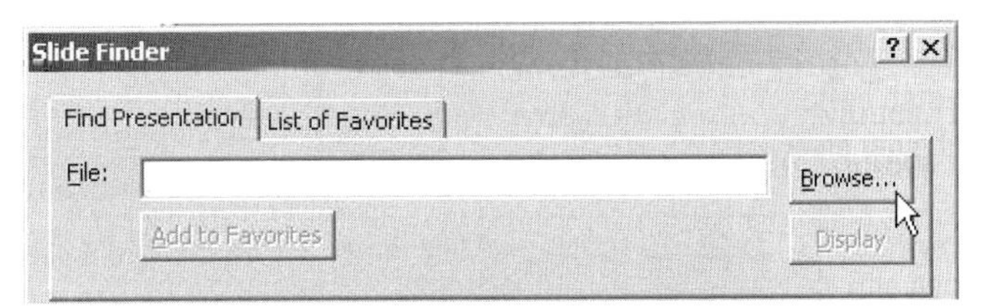

   Select the presentation and click **Open**.

5) In the *Select Slides* section, select the second slide, titled 'Green Grocer Group'.

   Click the **Insert** button and then click **Close**. (If you want to insert all the slides in a presentation, click the **Insert All** button – but that's not needed here!)

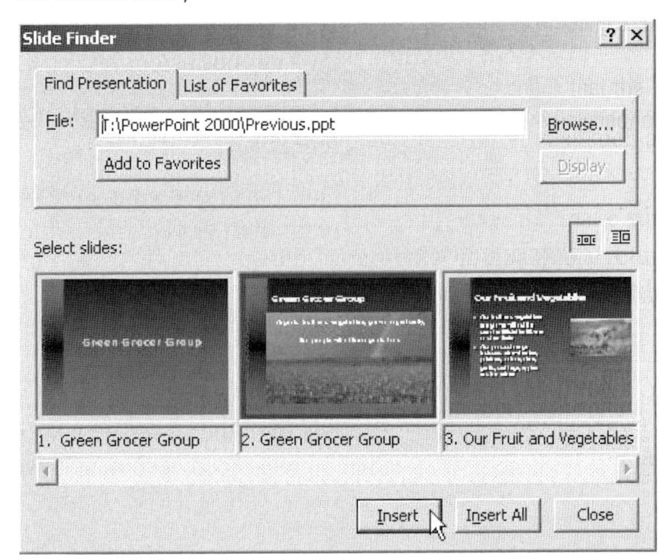

PowerPoint inserts the slide into your presentation after the cursor point. Note that while the content of the new slide comes from the old presentation, it loses its original formatting and needs to be adjusted.

6) Adjust Slide 2, 'Green Grocer Group', so that the graphic fits the slide properly:

   - Choose **Format | Slide Layout**.
   - Select the *Title Only* layout in the *Slide Layout* dialog box.
   - Click **Apply**.

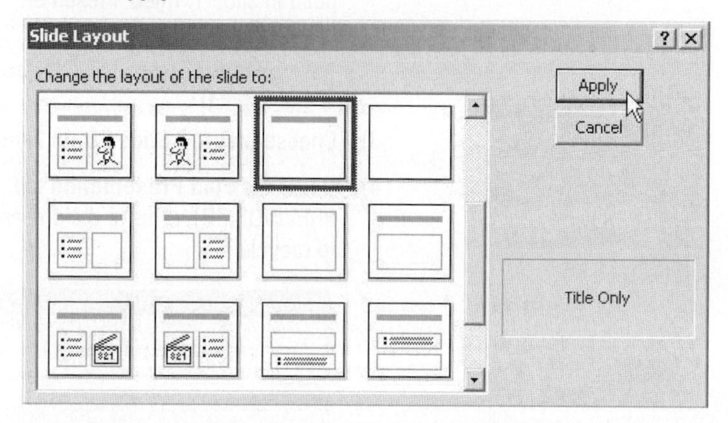

Well done! You've merged a slide from one presentation into another. It looks good doesn't it? And it didn't take too much time!

Making text presentable

Now that you've got your outline, you must make it 'presentable'. How do you do that? There are a few important points that you must keep in mind when preparing your text:

- Break up your information into 'bite-sized' pieces. Concise 'bites' of information are better suited to screen display.
- With text, less is more: if your audience are reading, then they are not listening!
- Use the slides to complement what you are saying, not to repeat it.
- Don't overload your slide. As a guide, restrict each slide to a maximum of five lines of text.

Less is definitely more in PowerPoint presentations. A slide with too much text looks ugly. Nothing puts an audience off more than looking at a 'wall of words' on a slide.

You want your audience to listen to you. Don't distract them by giving them the complete text of your speech on the slide. People will at least scan each new PowerPoint slide you show – by looking at the slide titles and then skimming through the content. Only show enough at a time to reinforce your spoken words.

Research shows that our short-term memory can hold a maximum of five to nine pieces of information. This is the limit of your audience's attention span. (If you want to find out more, read George A. Miller's article 'The Magical Number Seven, Plus or Minus Two: Some Limits on Our Capacity for Processing Information' (www.well.com/user/smalin/miller.html).) Never present more than nine pieces of information on a slide, and for safety, limit yourself to five.

So, how do you apply the 7±2 rule to a PowerPoint presentation? It's quite easy really. You:

- Limit the number of lines per slide to 7±2 (for safety, go for 5).
- Limit the number of words per line to 7±2.

Now let's apply the 7±2 rule to our PowerPoint presentation.

Exercise 2.3: Breaking up your information

1) Open EX2.2.PPT.
2) In Outline view, select slide number 7, titled 'What Makes Green Grocer Group?'. There are six pieces of information here that you can divide across two slides.

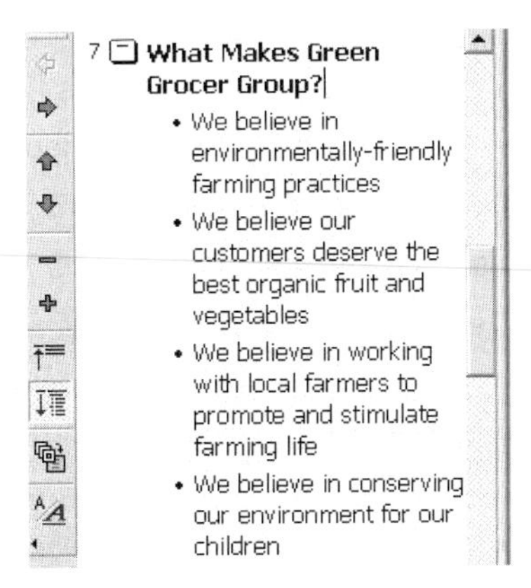

3) In the Outline pane, put the cursor at the beginning of the fifth bullet point. Select all of bullet point 5 and bullet point 6.

• Our fruit and vegetables are grown without the use of artificial fertilizers or chemicals
• Our product range includes: apples, strawberries, potatoes, onions, okra, garlic, cabbage, apples and tomatoes.

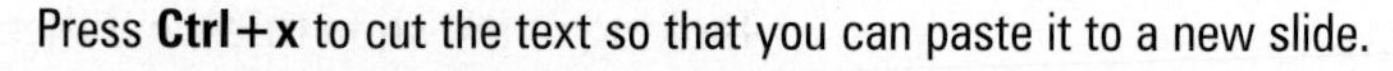

Press **Ctrl+x** to cut the text so that you can paste it to a new slide.

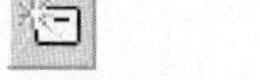

New Slide button

4) Click the **New Slide** button.

5) In the *Slide Layout* dialog box, select the *Text & Clip Art* layout and click **OK**.

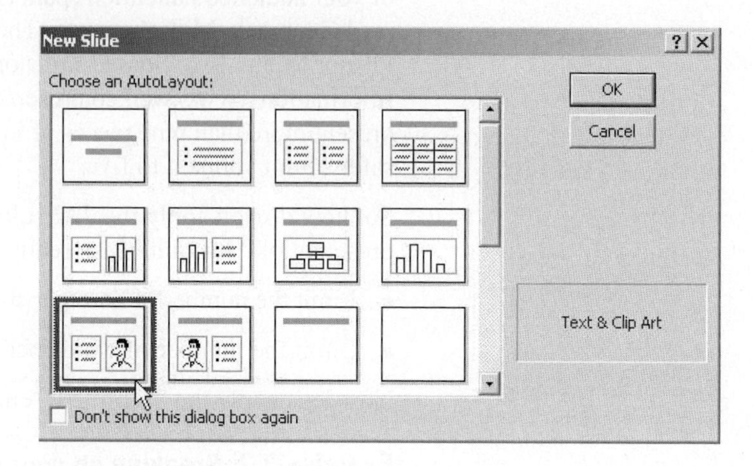

A new slide 8 appears.

6) In the *Click to add text* placeholder, press **Ctrl+v** to paste the selected text to the new slide 8.

- Our fruit and vegetables are grown without the use of artificial fertilizers or chemicals
- Our product range includes: apples, strawberries, potatoes, onions, okra, garlic, cabbage, apples and tomatoes

7) In slide number 8, type the title of the new slide and centre-align it:

`Our Fruit and Vegetables`

8) Double-click the **Clip Art** icon to add a graphic.

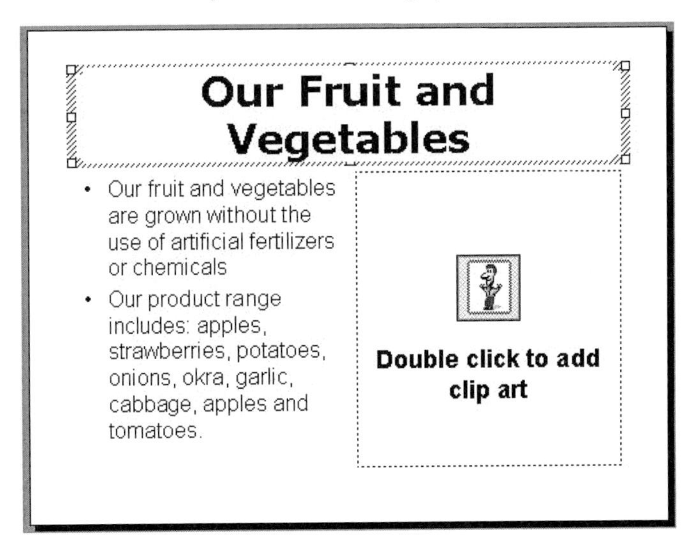

9) In the *Microsoft Clip Gallery* dialog box, type the following piece of text in the *Search for clips* box:

```
Vegetables
```

Scroll down to view the clips of vegetables.

10) Click the graphic of the potatoes and choose **Insert clip** from the menu displayed.

Your slide 8, 'Our Fruit and Vegetables' should look as shown.

Our Fruit and Vegetables

- Our fruit and vegetables are grown without the use of artificial fertilizers or chemicals
- Our product range includes: apples, strawberries, onions, okra, garlic, cabbage, apples and tomatoes

Chapter 2: summary

You must tailor your presentation to the needs of your audience. Choose language, tone, imagery, level of detail and examples that are appropriate.

A *logical sequence* of information will help your audience to understand your presentation better. *Break* your message into small units, each of which contains 7 ± 2 pieces of information. Our *short term memory* imposes limits on our attention span: we cannot handle more than this amount of information at any one time. You may use the *outline* feature in Word to plan your presentation. You can *export* this outline into PowerPoint.

You can also *merge information* on slides from another presentation into your current presentation.

Chapter 2: quick quiz

Circle the correct answer to each of the following questions about the information structure in PowerPoint.

Q1	What would be an appropriate number of slides to use in a 30-minute presentation?
A.	50 slides.
B.	20 slides.
C.	35 slides.
D.	5 slides.

Q2	True or False – our short-term memory can hold a maximum of five to nine pieces of information.
A.	True.
B.	False.

Q3	To merge slides from one presentation into another you choose ...
A.	**View | Files.**
B.	**Edit | Files.**
C.	**Insert | Files.**
D.	**Format | Files.**

Q4	What command do you use to export a Word Outline to PowerPoint?
A.	**Edit | Export to | Microsoft PowerPoint.**
B.	**File | Send to | Microsoft PowerPoint.**
C.	**Edit | Merge to | Microsoft PowerPoint.**
D.	**File | Export to | Microsoft PowerPoint.**

Answers

1: B, **2:** A, **3:** C, **4:** B.

3 Design structure

In this chapter

Your presentation might be full of the most interesting, compelling information, but if it is presented in a sloppy, haphazard or unattractive way, you simply won't get your message across. For this reason, you need to give as much attention to the design of your information as to the information itself. Design will either enhance your message or detract from it. Just as you structure the information in your presentation, you also structure its design.

This chapter will focus on the design structure of your presentation – how it can be created using certain PowerPoint features and how it impacts on your audience.

New skills

At the end of this chapter you should be able to:

- Discuss impact of design on the audience
- Choose appropriate font
- Choose appropriate line spacing
- Customize a template
- Create good colour contrast
- Customize a colour scheme
- Customize background fill
- Customize bullet points

New words

At the end of this chapter you should be able to explain the following terms:

- Design template
- Colour wheel
- Colour blindness

Syllabus reference

This chapter covers the following syllabus points:

- AM 6.1.2.1
- AM 6.1.2.2
- AM 6.2.1.1
- AM 6.2.1.4
- AM 6.3.1.3

Impact of design on the audience

Design can have a profound impact on how your audience perceives your message. There are many aspects to design, but here we will focus on just two: font choice and colour choice.

Choosing your font

Although PowerPoint offers you hundreds of fonts to choose from, it's best to limit yourself to one or two in any presentation. If you use more, you run the risk of distracting your audience. Just as consistency in terminology strengthens your presentation, so too does consistency in the use of fonts.

To serif or not serif?

What font should you use in a presentation? Should you use serif fonts such as Times New Roman or sans serif fonts such as Verdana?

Verdana
Times New Roman

Serif fonts were first developed in Roman times where they were painted on stone and then carved. They are particularly suited to printed text, as the serifs 'bind' the letters into recognizable word shapes, and thus aid legibility. However, in projected material, the serifs tend to blur the letters and result in text that is less readable. Therefore, it is advisable to use sans serif fonts in presentations, as they are easier to read.

Appropriate font size

Your choice of font size depends on two things:

- The size of the screen you will be projecting onto.
- The distance of the audience from this screen.

The minimum legibility standard is one inch (2.5 cm) of letter height on screen for a viewing distance of 30 feet (9 m). This means that in typical situations, 18 points on your computer screen is the absolute minimum. If you suspect that your room will be bigger than normal, or your screen particularly small, choose a larger font size. If in doubt, go large!

Your choice of font size for any piece of text should reflect its relative importance within the presentation: for example Verdana 36 point bold for title text and Arial 28 point for first-level bullets. Once you've chosen these fonts, keep them consistent throughout the presentation.

Adjusting line spacing

Line spacing is the space between one line of text and the next. In PowerPoint you can:

- Change the space between lines in a given paragraph.
- Change the space before a paragraph.
- Change the space after a paragraph.

By adjusting line spacing you can separate the different parts of the text on the slide, and bind together items that you want to bring together. The following exercise shows you how to adjust the line spacing on the Slide Master of your presentation. These changes will affect all line spacing within the presentation.

Exercise 3.1: Adjusting line spacing

1) Open EX3.1.PPT.
2) Choose **View | Master | Slide Master**.
3) Select all levels of the *Master text styles*.

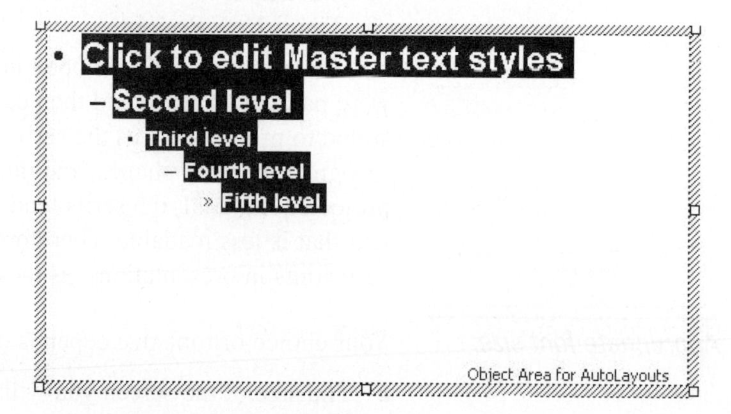

4) Choose **Format | Line Spacing**.
5) In the *Line Spacing* dialog box change:
   - *Line spacing* to 1 lines
   - *Before paragraph* to 0.5 lines
   - *After paragraph* to 0 lines

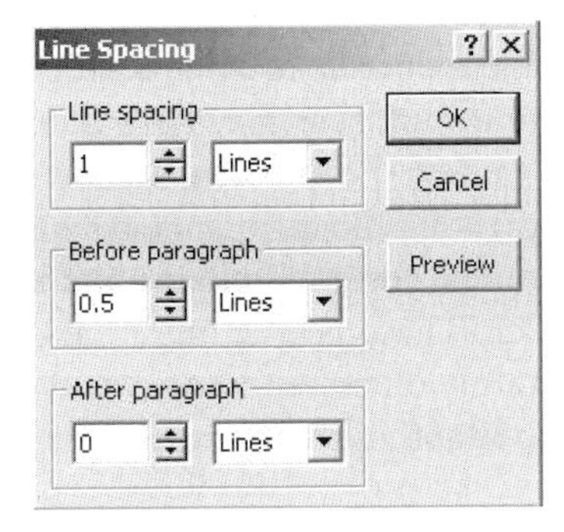

Click **OK**.

Your slide should look as shown.

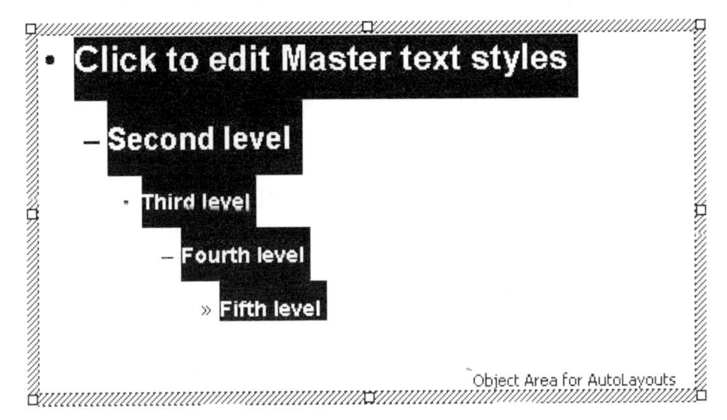

You can press the **Preview** button to view the changes and press **Cancel** if you are not happy with your choices.

Choosing colour

Audience perception can be 'coloured' by:

- Colour response
- Colour blindness
- Colour visibility

Colour response

Some colours and combinations of colours are pleasing to the eye whereas others are literally eyesores. Your choice of colour can provoke both a physical and an emotional response from your audience. For example, while yellow is the most visible colour in the spectrum, it needs to be used sparingly, as it can over-stimulate the eye and result in fatigue. The cultural significance of colour varies from country to country: for example, white is the colour of mourning in China and Japan, whereas in the West, we associate white with birth and new beginnings.

Colour blindness

Some members of your audience are likely to be affected by colour blindness. Colour blindness affects 8% of men, and 0.5% of women. People who are colour blind have difficulties perceiving the difference between certain colours. The most common form of colour blindness affects the ability to perceive green. These people might miss out on valuable information if you rely on colour to convey it. Steer clear of highlighting important issues in green, or making your hyperlinks green.

Colour visibility

It's important to use colours and colour combinations that the audience can see from a distance. After all, your information will appear, not on a printed page, but on a screen, and people will be sitting some distance away from it. The contrast between the colour of the text and the colour of the background of the slide will affect visibility too.

With all this information on colour in mind, let's look at a design template in PowerPoint. Remember, you want to use a template that will have a positive impact on the audience, that will not present problems for colour-blind audience members, and that will be highly visible when on screen.

Design templates

A template is something that serves as a model or example. You use a design template in PowerPoint to serve as a model for all the slides in your presentation.

Design template

A PowerPoint file that can be applied to a PowerPoint presentation to control its principal design elements. A template contains a colour scheme and one or more slide masters with font settings and possibly built-in graphics and text. PowerPoint templates have the file extension .pot.

The great thing about PowerPoint is that it comes with several built-in design templates. You can use them as they appear in PowerPoint, or you can customize them to suit your own needs. Let's open a design template and customize it to suit your presentation.

Exercise 3.2: Customizing a design template

1) Open EX3.2.POT.

2) Choose **Format | Apply Design Template**.

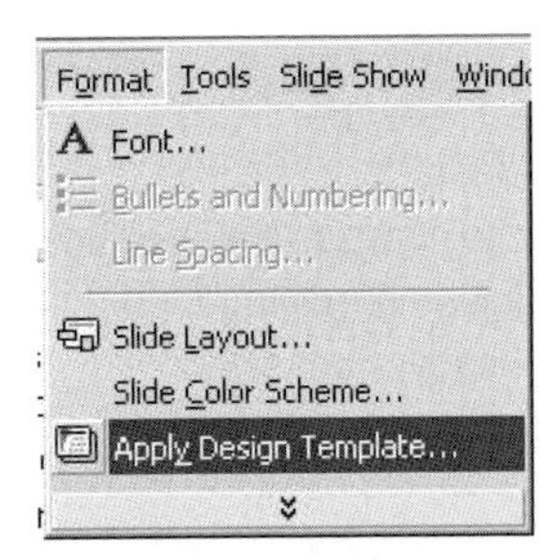

3) In the *Apply Design Template* dialog box, there is a list of available templates. Select the *Azure* template and click **Apply**.

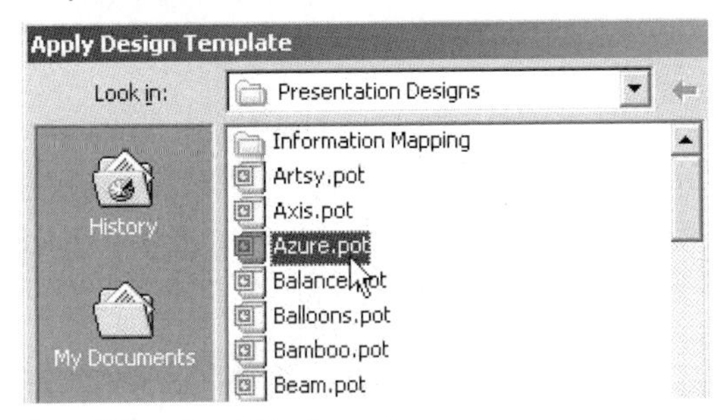

Your slides should look as shown.

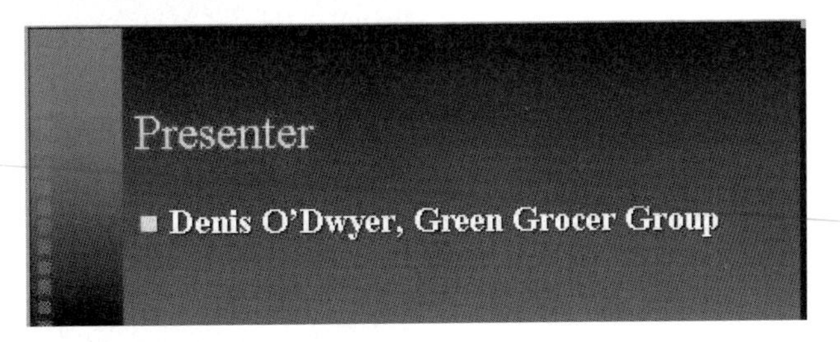

4) Choose **View | Master | Slide Master** and highlight the *Master title style*. Change the font, font size and weight to the following:

Verdana, 44 point, Bold.

(Remember, sans serif fonts work better in projected materials.)

5) Highlight the first level of the *Master text style* and change the font, font size and weight to the following:

Arial, 32 point, Bold.

6) Highlight the second level of the *Master text style* and change the font, font size and weight to the following:

   Arial, 28 point, Bold.

7) Move the *Master title style* box to the very top of the slide by clicking its outline and moving it up. (Notice how your cursor has changed to a four-headed cross?)

Line button

8) Click the **Line** button on the *Drawing* toolbar to add a line underneath the *Master title style* box.

   Keep the **Shift** button pressed down as you draw a line under the box as shown. (This ensures that the line is perfectly horizontal.)

9) Copy the line underneath the *Master text style* box by selecting it and pressing **Ctrl+c** and **Ctrl+v**.

   Drag and drop the new line below the *Object Area for AutoLayouts*.

Your slide master should now look as shown.

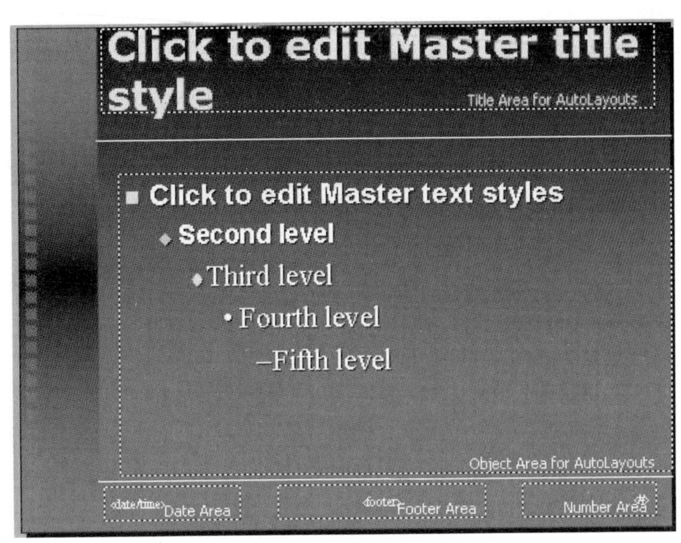

Well done! You've customized your first design template. You'll customize it further as you go through the rest of the chapter.

About colour schemes

Your colour scheme should help to communicate your message by making it easier to read, and by giving a consistent look and feel to your presentation.

Each design template in PowerPoint has its own colour scheme. These colour schemes have a range of coordinated colours for background, fill colour, hyperlinks and so on. You can customize these colour schemes to suit yourself. However, it's best to restrict your colour scheme to two or three colours. Too many colours compete for attention and can distract your audience. The following exercise shows you how to customize a colour scheme.

Exercise 3.3: Customizing colour schemes

1) Open EX3.3.POT.
2) Choose **Format | Slide Color Scheme**.
3) Under the **Standard** tab, select the colour scheme that is nearest the one that you want. For our purposes, let's choose the dark blue scheme.

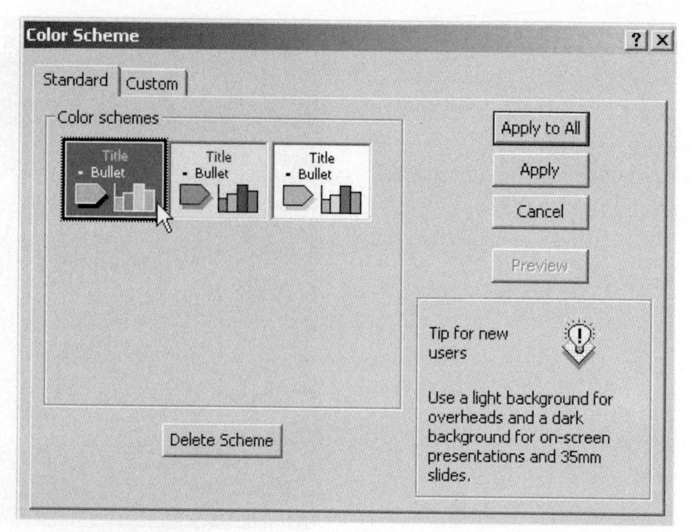

4) Click the **Custom** tab.

5) Under *Scheme colors* select the *Accent and hyperlink* option. You want to change it from mauve to yellow. Click the **Change Color** button.

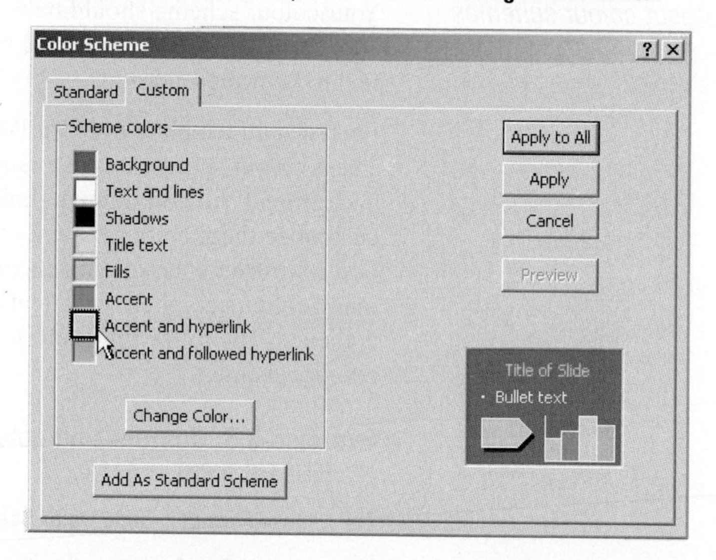

6) Under the **Standard** tab, select a bright yellow colour, and click **OK**.

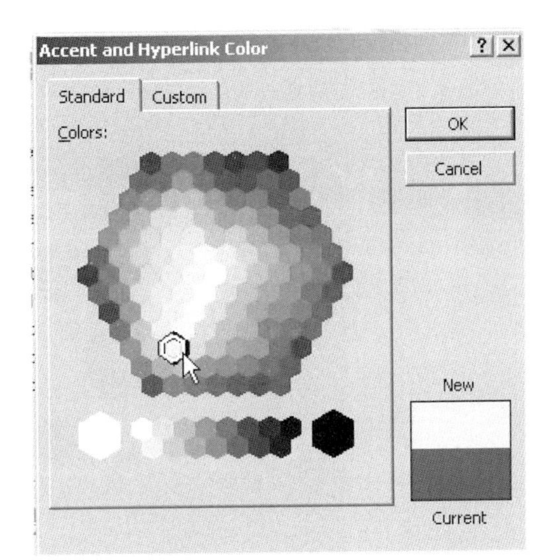

7) Select the *Fills* option. Click the **Change Color** button.

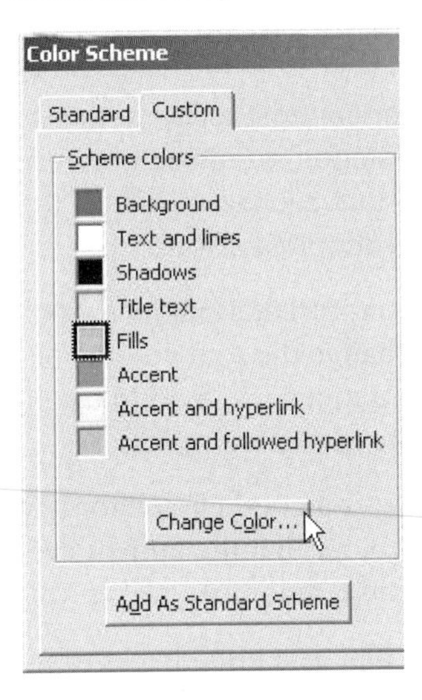

8) Under the **Standard** tab, select the grey colour at the bottom of the dialog box, and click **OK**.

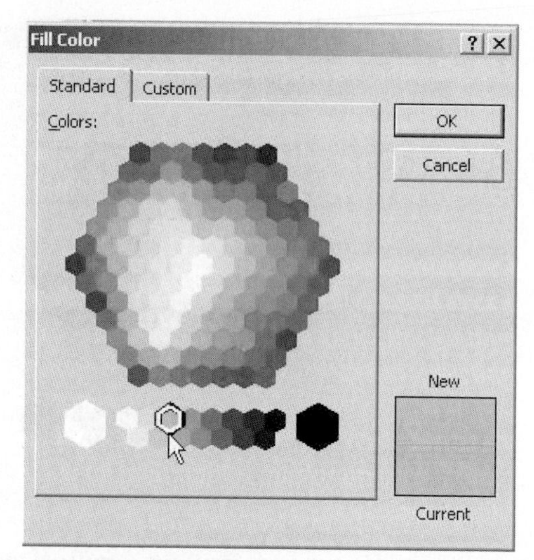

9) Click **Apply to All**. PowerPoint applies the new colours to all the slides in the presentation.

Colour contrast

Colour contrast refers to the degree to which elements in the presentation stand out from each other. Colour contrast is important because it affects the audience's ability to view and read your presentation.

For our presentation, let's work with the dark blue background and change the font colour for the title text to a soft yellow. In presentations it's good to use light text on a dark background (unlike in printed material).

Yellow is a good choice for a font colour as experts say it is the first colour that the human eye notices. It draws attention to the text and temporarily wakes your brain up!

Dark blue is a good background colour. Yellow and blue are also primary colours; they make a strong combination.

In the next exercise, modify the template to present the title text in yellow.

Exercise 3.4: Customizing font colour to create greater contrast

1) Open EX3.4.POT.
2) Choose **View | Master | Slide Master**.
3) Select the *Title Style* placeholder, then click the arrow to the right of the **Font Color** button on the *Drawing* toolbar.

Click to edit Master title style

A

4) Click the *More Font Colors* option and select the **Custom** tab. Use the cross hairs to select your colour and use the slider to adjust the luminosity. For the exercise, choose a bright yellow colour.

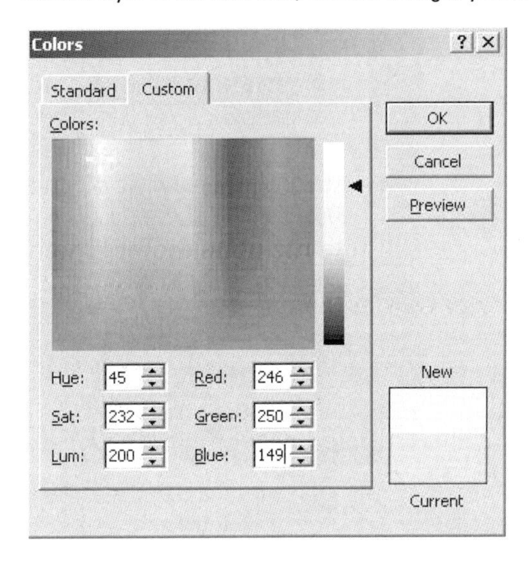

To ensure consistency in your colour scheme you can input the values directly into the *Colors* dialog box (as shown above). Click **OK**.

5) Click **Save**.

Customize bullet points

You can customize the bullet points in the slide master in two ways: by changing their shape and by changing their colour. If you want to change the type of bullet point, you choose **Format | Bullets and Numbering** and select the bullet style you want to use.

The following exercise will show you how to change the bullet point colour but you will keep the default bullet types.

Exercise 3.5: Customizing the colour of bullet points

1) Open EX3.5.POT.

2) Choose **View | Master | Slide Master**.

3) Highlight all the master text styles on the slide master.

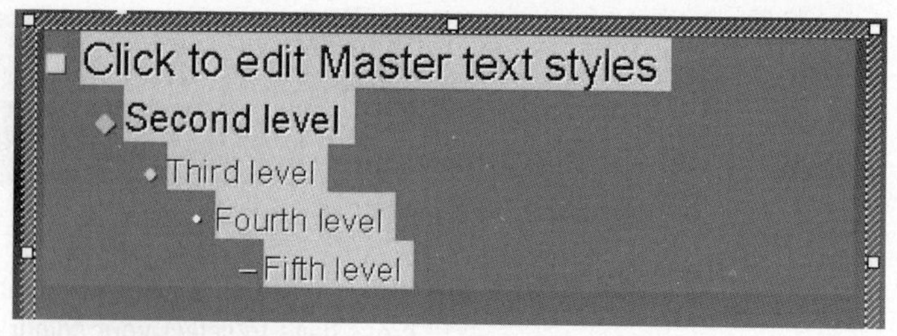

4) Choose **Format | Bullets and Numbering**.

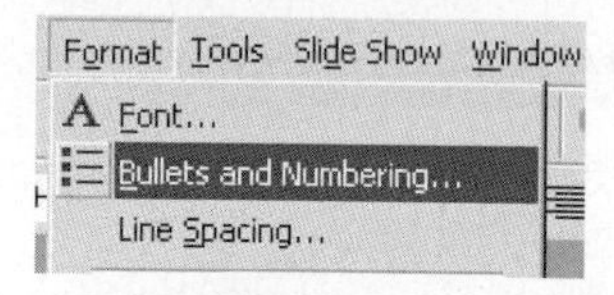

5) Under the **Bulleted** tab click the arrow to the right of the *Color* box. Our custom yellow colour is displayed in the **Color** menu. Place your cursor on the colour and click it. This changes the colour of the bullet points to light yellow.

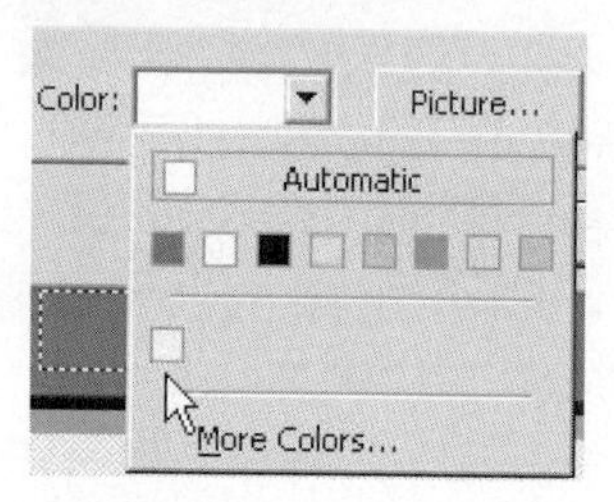

Click **OK**.

Your master slide should look as shown.

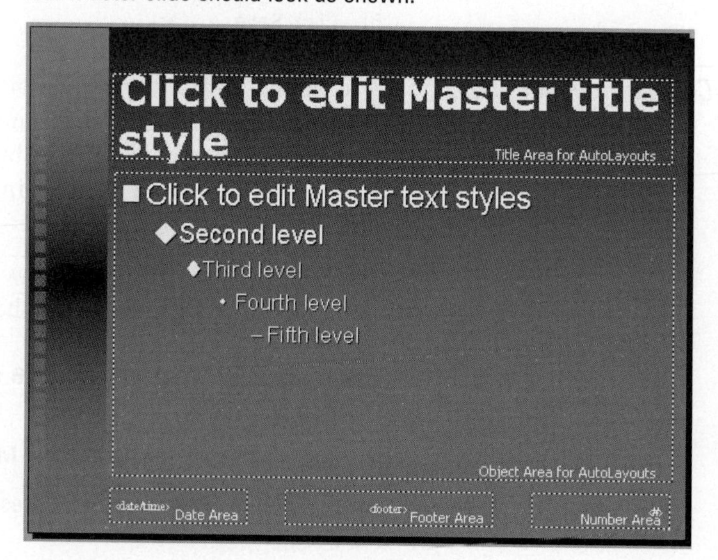

Custom fill effects

So far, the background of your slides is dark blue. You can change this background colour and you can apply special effects to the background, such as textures, colour gradients, patterns and pictures. To do this choose **Format | Background**. Then click the arrow to the right of the *Background fill* colour box and select the colour or fill effect of your choice. Click **Apply** to change just the current slide, or click **Apply to All** to change all slides in the presentation.

You can also apply a colour and fill effects to a placeholder or drawn object. In the next exercise, you will apply a colour gradient effect to a placeholder in the template's slide master.

Exercise 3.6: Customizing fill colour

1) Open EX3.6.POT.
2) Choose **View | Master | Slide Master**.
3) Click in the title placeholder. Click the arrow to the right of the **Fill Color** button. Select the *Fill Effects* option.

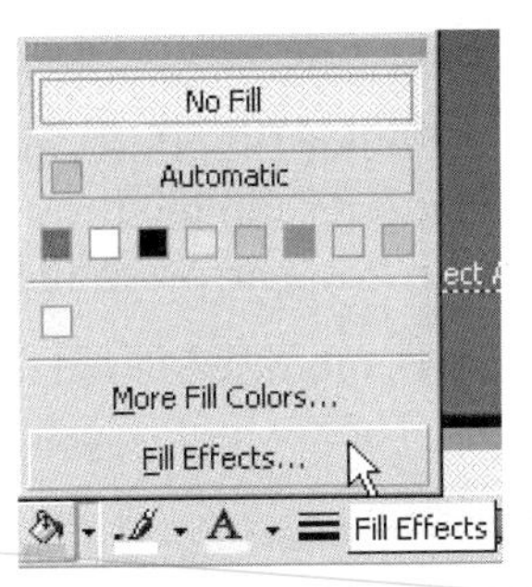

4) Under the **Gradient** tab, select the *Preset* option. Click the arrow to the right of the *Preset Colors* box and select the *Nightfall* option.

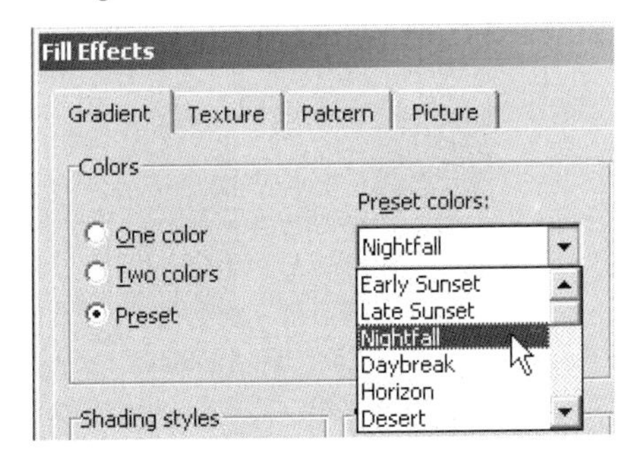

5) Under the *Shading Styles* section, select the *Diagonal up* option. Press OK.

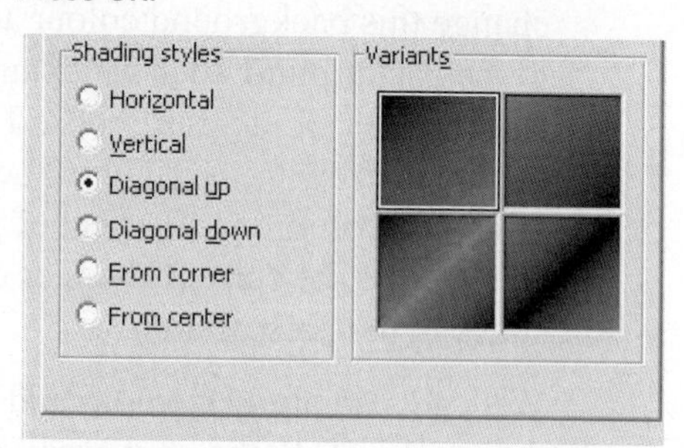

6) Switch to Normal view to look at the changes to your template – choose **View | Normal**.

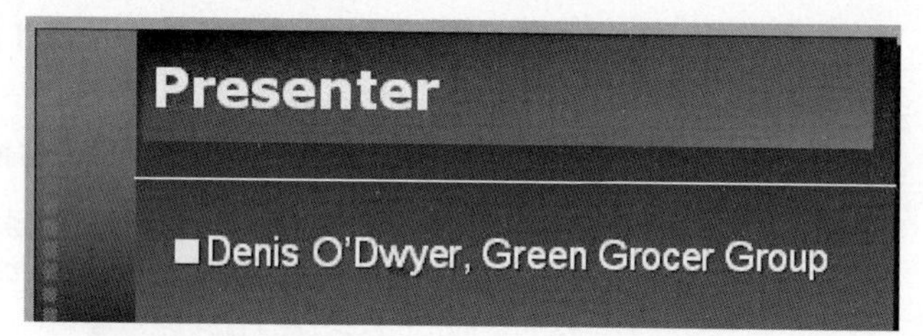

Other fill effects

Explore the other fill effects available in PowerPoint, such as textures, patterns and pictures. Remember, you can access these effects by clicking arrow to the right of the **Fill Color** button.

The **Textures** tab offers a range of textures you can apply to your slides. The texture selected below is of recycled paper.

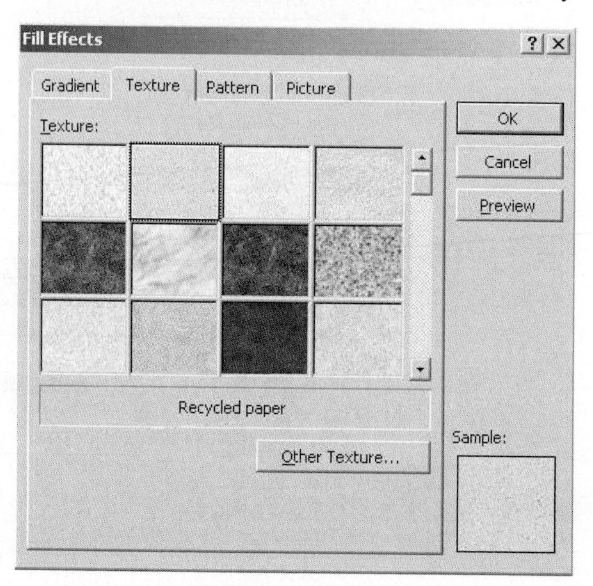

The **Pattern** tab offers a range of patterns as shown below.

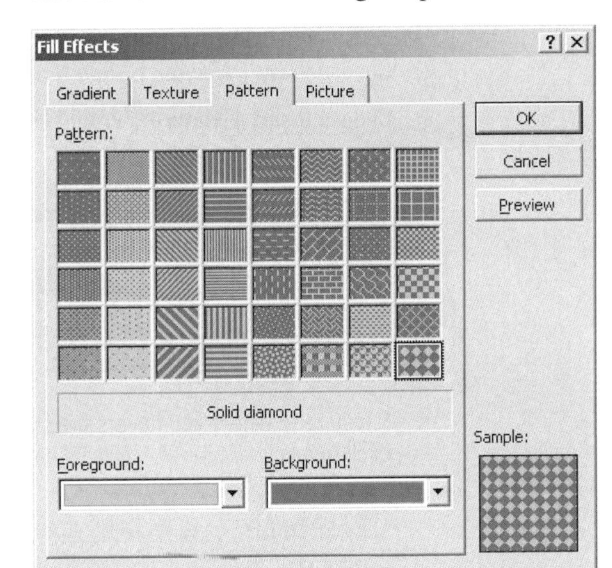

With the **Picture** tab, you can include a picture in your slides, either as a background image or as a unifying design element. You might use this, for example, to include a company logo or symbol in your presentation.

Inserting a logo

Inserting a logo is easy. The following exercise shows you how to insert a logo in the slide master, so that it subsequently appears on each slide in your presentation.

Exercise 3.7: Inserting a logo into your slide master

1) Open EX3.7.POT.

2) Choose **View | Master | Slide Master**.

3) Choose **Insert | Picture | From File**.

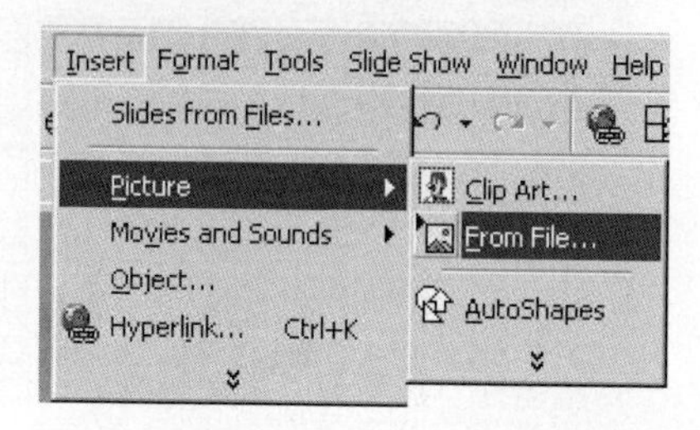

4) Navigate to where you have stored your company logo GGG.JPG. Click **Insert**.

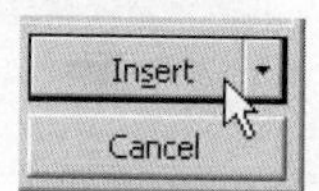

5) Drag and drop the logo to the *Date Area* box.

6) Save the template as CAPRI.POT.

- Choose **File | Save As** and type the following in the *File name* box:

  `Capri`

- In the *Save as type* box, select *Design Template*.
- In the *Save in* box, select the location where you want to save your template.
- Click **Save**.

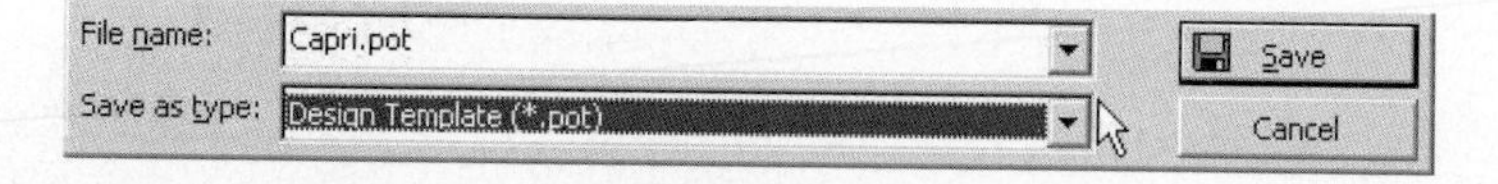

Applying the design template

So far you've created a new design template and customized it to suit your needs. Now, all that remains for you to do is to apply your new template to a presentation.

Exercise 3.8: Applying the design template

1) Open EX3.8.PPT.
2) Choose **Format | Apply Design Template**.
3) In the *Apply Design Template* box, navigate to where you have stored CAPRI.POT.

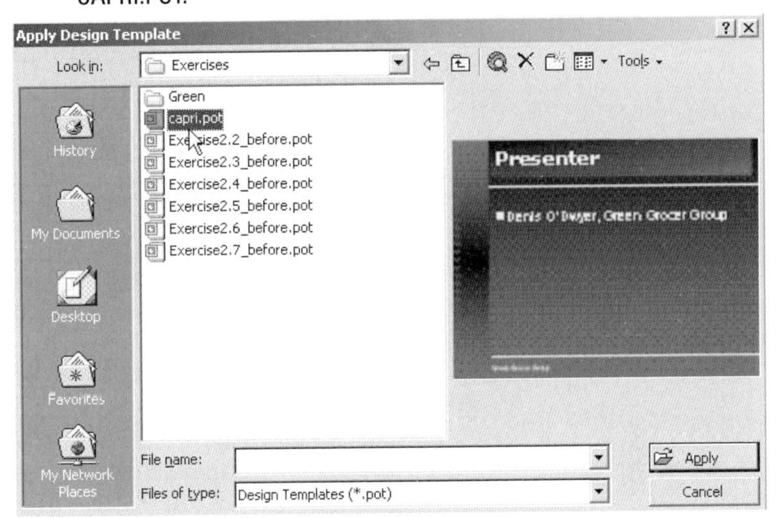

4) Select CAPRI.POT and click **Apply**.

   Congratulations! You've now applied a template to your presentation. Notice how each slide in the presentation has adopted the colour scheme and font characteristics that you specified in the template, and has the logo in the bottom-left corner.

Title slide

There's just one more thing to do. This presentation does not yet include a title slide: you will have to insert one yourself and adjust its design to make it consistent with the other slides.

A title slide is the first slide in your presentation, and it may also be used at other points to introduce a new topic or section. It is normally formatted differently from the rest of the slides in your presentation, while retaining the same basic design elements. In the following exercises, you will insert a title slide and change some of its design features.

Exercise 3.9: Inserting a title slide

1) Open EX3.9.PPT.
2) In the Outline pane, place your cursor before the text of slide 1, titled 'Presenter'.

   1 **Presenter**
   - Denis O'Dwyer, Green Grocer Group

3) Click the **New Slide** button, and select the *Title Slide* slide layout in the *New Slide* dialog box. Click **OK**.

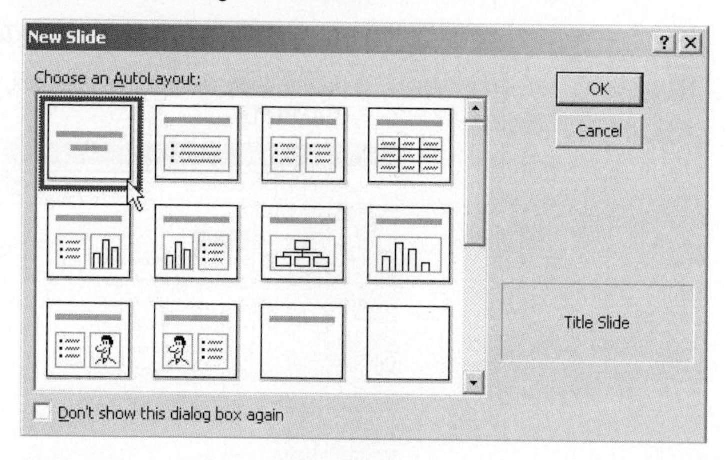

The title slide now appears as slide 1.

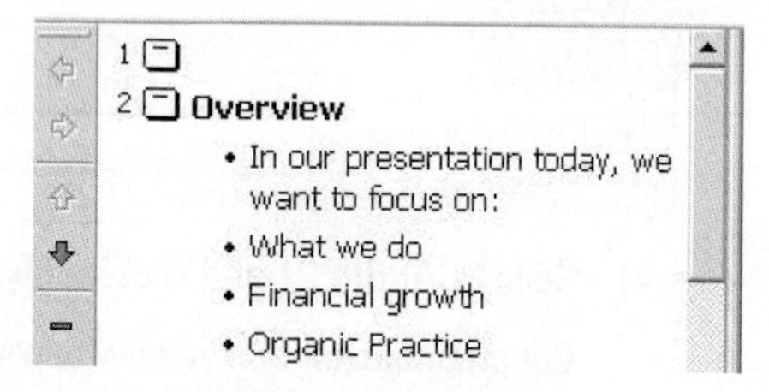

4) Type the following title in the *Master title style* placeholder:

`Green Grocer Group`

5) Choose the following font, size, style, positioning and colour:

Verdana, 48 point, Bold, Centred, White.

6) Select the *Click to add subtitle* box. Choose **Insert | Picture | From File.**

7) Navigate to where you have saved the logo of Organic Farming in Europe – ORGANICS.JPG, and click **OK**.

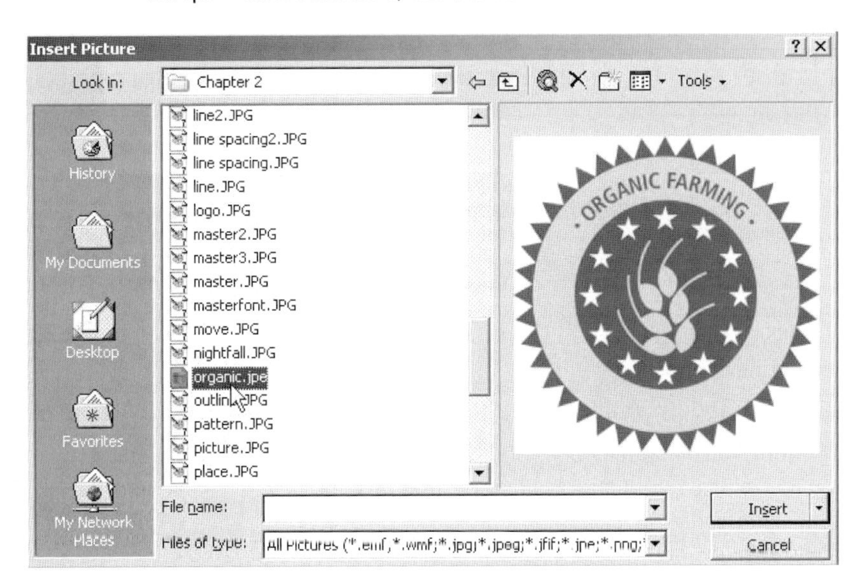

The graphic now appears on your slide.

8) Resize the *Subtitle* box so that it fits the logo as shown.

Well done! You've successfully created a title slide. To subsequently change any of the elements or characteristics of the title slide, choose **View | Master | Title Master**.

Stacking effect

Each element in your slide – text, drawn object, imported picture – is on a separate 'layer'. A slide might have several layers – a number of text boxes on an imported diagram, for example, or a background photograph behind your text, or a drawing consisting of a square, a triangle and a circle. The order in which these layers are drawn by PowerPoint can be changed to create different effects – you can make the elements overlap in different ways. You will need to do this particularly if you have complex graphics with explanatory text. When you select any object, PowerPoint offers you the following options:

- **Bring to Front** (bring the selected object to the front of the stack).
- **Send to Back** (send the selected object to the back of the stack).
- **Bring Forward** (bring the selected object one layer forward in the stack).
- **Send Backward** (send the selected object one layer backward in the stack).

These options are available from the **Draw** menu on the *Drawing* toolbar.

Exercise 3.10: Apply stacking effects to the title slide

1) Open EX3.10.PPT, and go to the first slide.
2) Click the **Rectangle** button on the *Drawing* toolbar and place a rectangle over the Green Grocer Group title.

Your title is now covered by the rectangle.

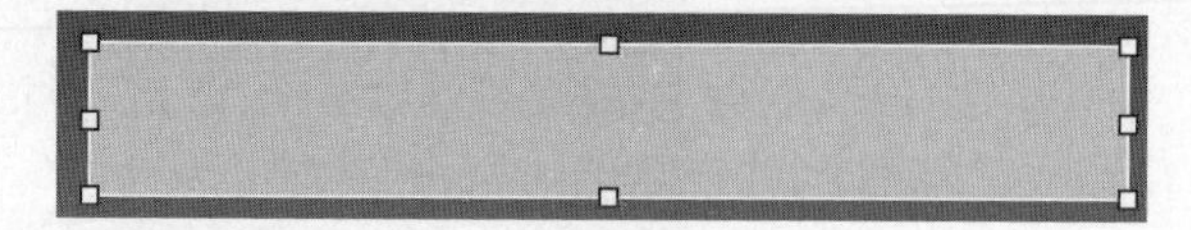

3) Choose **Draw | Order | Send to Back** from the *Drawing* toolbar.

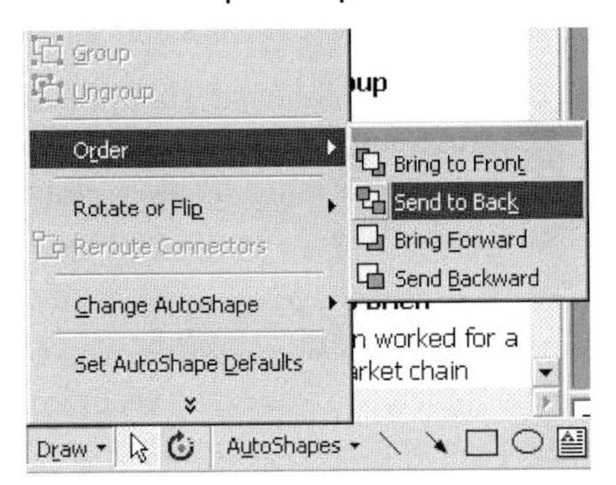

Notice that the rectangle has moved behind the text – the text can now be read, and the rectangle provides contrast.

Green Grocer Group

Exercise 3.11: Apply stacking effects to a picture or image

1) Open EX3.10.PPT, and go to the second slide, 'Presenter'.

2) Click at the start of the bulleted text 'Denis ...'. Press ENTER five times to move the text down the slide.

3) Click below the text or outside the text box. Notice that the picture obscures part of the text.

4) Select the picture and choose **Draw | Order | Send to Back** from the *Drawing* toolbar.

Notice that the picture is now behind the text, and the text is now readable.

Chapter 3: summary

Consider the *audience* and the presentation *environment* before you decide on your design: the various design elements – font size and style, colour scheme, use of graphics, and so on – must be chosen with these in mind. Design with the audience's needs in mind, because if you make it easy for them to see your slides, you have a better chance of getting your message across. Remember that colour has a profound physical and emotional impact on an audience – and that you cannot take everything for granted: cultural differences may affect how your message is perceived, and physical differences (poor eyesight, colour blindness) may impede the understanding of some of your audience.

Choose a point size that is suitable for the room in which you will be presenting. As a guide, never use type smaller than 18 point. For presentations, it is recommended to use a sans serif font, such as Arial or Verdana. And control *line spacing* so that each point appears both coherent and separate.

Your *colour scheme* should ensure a strong contrast between the foreground and the background. It is recommended to use a dark colour (such as navy blue) for the background and a light colour (such as bright yellow) for the text.

PowerPoint's *design templates* give you a basis on which to model your presentation. You can *customize* the design templates to your own requirements, by changing any of the elements in the Slide Master or Title Master, such as the fonts, the bullet characters, and the colour scheme. You can further customize the *background* by adding gradients, textures and pictures (such as logos).

When the template is customized to your satisfaction, you *apply* it to your presentation.

Stacking objects on your slides allows you to control how elements on your slide appear in relation to one another. You can move objects backwards or forwards on a slide so that they overlap in the way that you want.

Chapter 3: quick quiz

Circle the correct answer to each of the following questions about the design structure in PowerPoint 2000.

Q1	Which of the following statements about the Design Template are untrue?
A.	The Design Template has the file extension .pot.
B.	The Design Template cannot be customized.
C.	The Design Template comes with a title master and a slide master.
D.	The Design Template comes with a built-in colour scheme.

Q2	Which of the following is not an appropriate font size for a PowerPoint presentation?
A.	17 point.
B.	22 point.
C.	28 point.
D.	32 point.

Q3	To customize a colour scheme you …
A.	Choose **Format | Slide Color Scheme**. Under the **Custom** tab, select the components that you want to customize and click the Change Color button. Select the color you need and click **OK** and then press **Apply to All**.
B.	Choose **Format | Slide Color Scheme**. Under the **Standard** tab, select the components that you want to customize and click the **Change Color** button. Select the color you need and click **OK** and then press **Apply to All**.
C.	Choose **Format | Slide Color Scheme**. Under the **Custom** tab, select the components that you want to customize and click the **Add as Standard Scheme** button. Select the color you need and click **OK** and then press **Apply to All**.
D.	Choose **Format | Slide Color Scheme**. Under the **Custom** tab, select the components that you want to customize and click the **Change Color** button. Select the color you need and click **OK**.

Q4	Choose the sans serif font below.
A.	Times New Roman.
B.	Courier.
C.	Verdana.
D.	Garamond.

Answers

1: B, **2:** A, **3:** A, **4:** C.

Flowcharts

In this chapter

In this chapter you will create a flowchart to illustrate a series of actions and decisions. Flowcharts are useful tools for detailing the different steps needed in order to complete an action. In your presentation, you will use a flowchart to show the different steps in the organic certification process.

New skills

At the end of this chapter you should be able to:

- Insert the appropriate AutoShapes needed for a flowchart
- Position and resize a shape
- Insert text in an AutoShape
- Adjust text to fit an AutoShape
- Align AutoShapes
- Insert connector lines and arrows
- Insert text boxes

New words

At the end of this chapter you should be able to explain the following terms:

- Flowchart
- AutoShape
- Connectors

Syllabus reference

This chapter covers the following syllabus points:

- AM 6.3.1.2
- AM 6.3.1.4
- AM 6.3.1.5

- AM 6.3.2.4
- AM 6.4.2.1
- AM 6.4.2.2
- AM 6.4.2.3

The Drawing *toolbar*

The two main menus on PowerPoint's *Drawing* toolbar are:

- The **AutoShapes** menu
- The **Draw** menu

You use the **AutoShapes** menu to create the shapes you need for a flowchart, and you use the **Draw** menu to position these shapes.

There are other useful options available from the *Drawing* toolbar, such as:

- The **3-D** button
- The **Text box** button

These options can really add visual excitement to your flowchart and make it stand out. That said, remember that 'less is more' – be selective in your use of effects options. For example, don't add a 3-D effect to all the text and AutoShapes in a flowchart, as this may make the flowchart less legible.

Parts of a flowchart

The principal shapes used in a flowchart are:

Shape	Name	Purpose
▭	Rectangle (Process)	Indicates an action
◇	Diamond (Decision)	Indicates a question or decision
▢	Oval (Terminator)	Indicates where a process begins and ends

These parts are connected by lines or arrows to indicate the flow.

Now that you know what is involved, you can begin to create your own flowchart.

Exercise 4.1 Beginning a flowchart

1) Open EX4.1.PPT. Go to slide number 13, 'Organic Certification Process'.

2) Choose **AutoShapes | Flowchart** from the *Drawing* toolbar.

3) Click the shape labelled Terminator (third row, first on left).

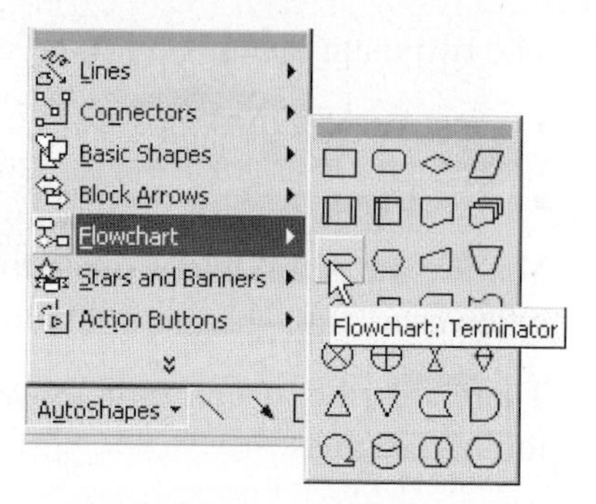

4) Click near the top left-hand corner of the slide and drag to create a terminator shape as shown.

If necessary, reposition the AutoShape by clicking in it and then dragging it.

Another way to reposition an AutoShape is to use specific co-ordinates. The following exercise shows you how apply co-ordinates to a terminator.

Exercise 4.2: Working on the terminators

1) Open EX4.2.PPT. Go to slide number 13, 'Organic Certification Process'.

2) Select the terminator and press **Ctrl+c** to copy it. Press **Ctrl+v** to paste it to the slide.

3) Reposition the new terminator, this time by specifying co-ordinates. Right-click the new terminator and choose *Format AutoShape*. Under the **Position** tab, input the *Position on slide* information as shown below. Click **OK**.

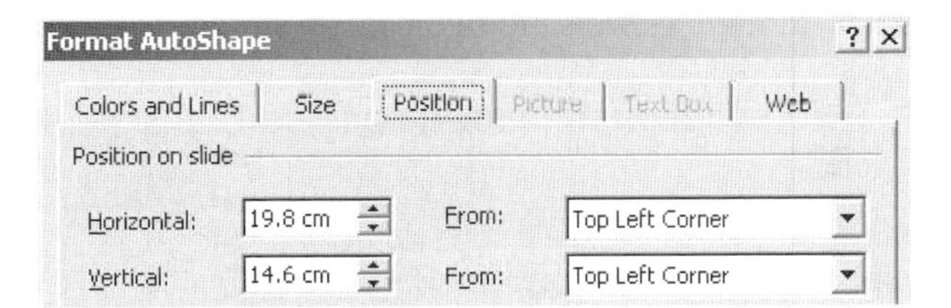

The new shape now appears at the bottom-right of the slide as shown below.

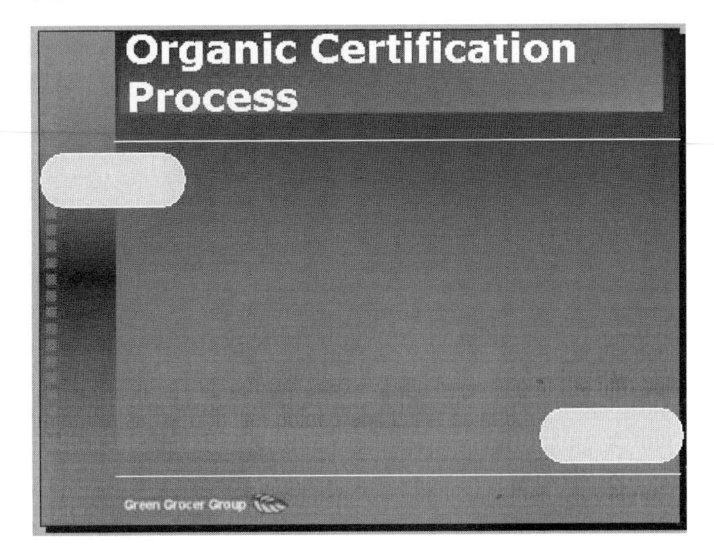

Now let's add more AutoShapes to the flowchart and then format their positioning and size.

Adding and aligning AutoShapes

You want to add more shapes to your flowchart. You need a rectangle for each step in the process, and a diamond shape for each decision. Make these shapes approximately the same size, and place them on the slide. (If you make a mistake, simply delete the AutoShape and start again, as in the exercise below.)

Exercise 4.3: Adding different AutoShapes

1) Open EX4.3.PPT. Go to slide number 13, 'Organic Certification Process'.

2) Select the first terminator and choose **Edit | Duplicate (Ctrl+d)**. A second oval appears. However, you want a diamond, as you will be illustrating a decision step.

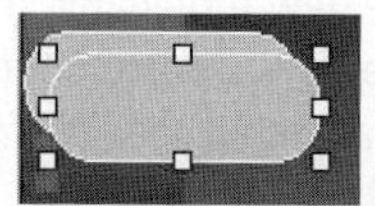

3) Choose **Draw | Change AutoShape | Flowchart** from the *Drawing* toolbar. Click the decision diamond shape at the top of the menu.

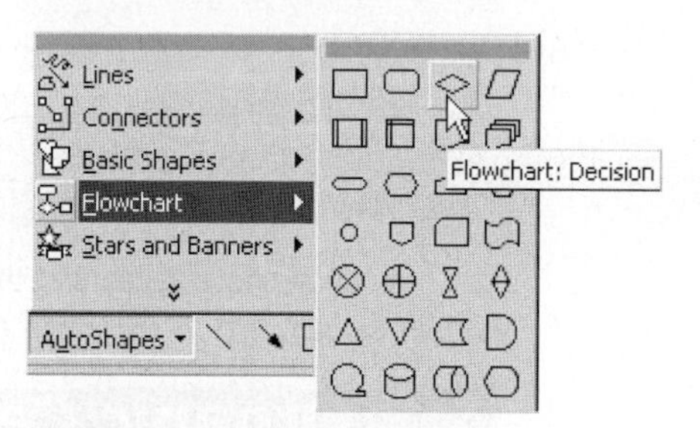

The new oval changes to a diamond.

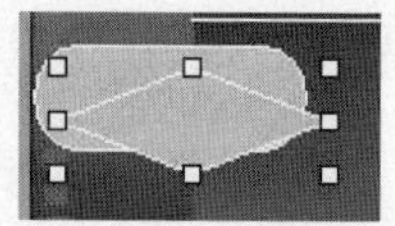

4) Drag the diamond to the middle of the slide. Your slide should look as shown.

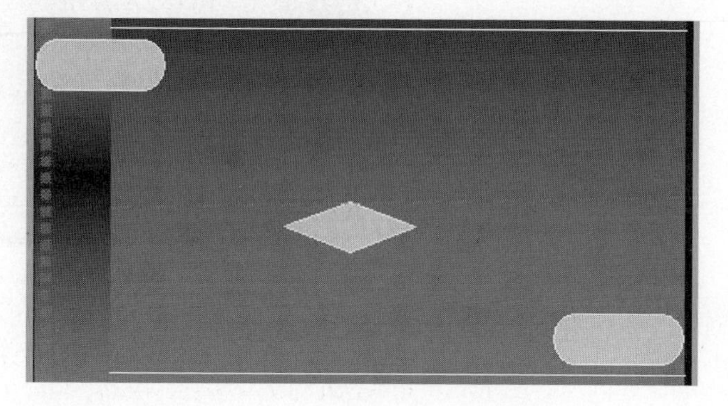

5) Duplicate the diamond by selecting it and pressing **Ctrl+d**.

6) Choose **Draw | Change AutoShape | Flowchart** and click the rectangle shape at the top of the menu.

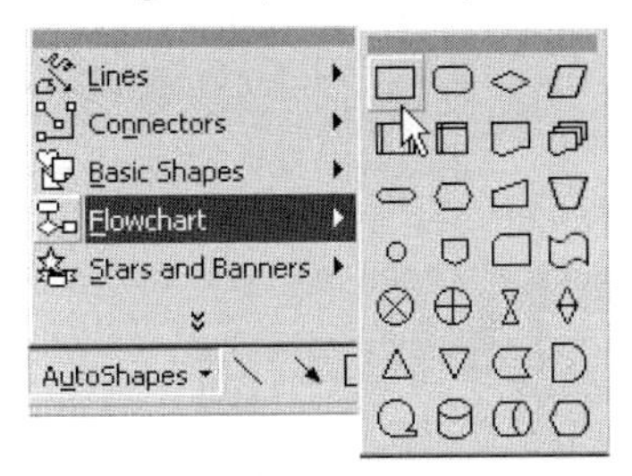

The duplicated diamond changes to a rectangle.

7) Duplicate this rectangle three more times so that there are now four rectangles on the slide.

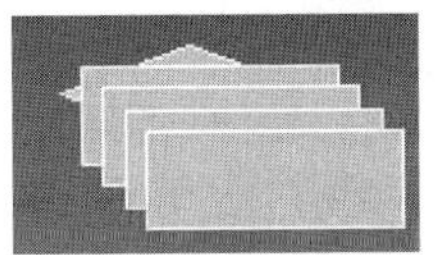

8) Drag the new shapes into position as shown below.

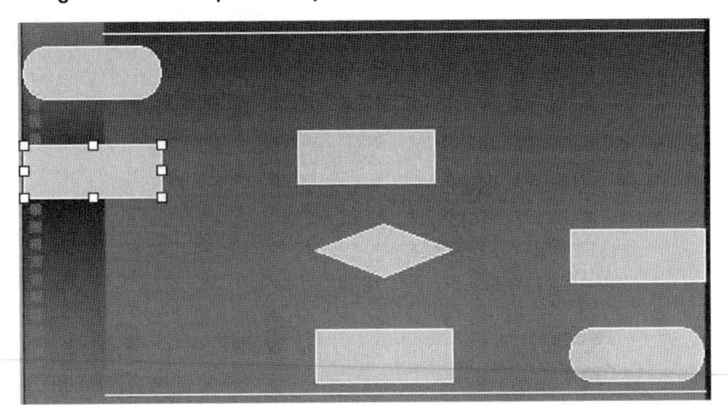

Fantastic! You've created all the AutoShapes that you need for your flowchart.

Deleting AutoShapes: to delete an object from a PowerPoint slide, select it and press **Delete**. Try this on one of the AutoShapes in the slide you have created, and then choose **Edit | Undo Clear** to restore it (or press **Ctrl + z**).

You now need to 'tidy up' the AutoShapes on the slide. You can do this by using the **Align or Distribute** feature on the *Drawing* toolbar. This enables you to align AutoShapes relative to each other. For example, if you want to align AutoShapes horizontally by their centres, click **Align Center**. You can also arrange AutoShapes at equal distances from each other, relative to the slide. You simply select the AutoShapes and choose **Draw | Align or Distribute| Relative to Slide** and select the distribute function that you need: **Distribute Horizontally** or **Distribute Vertically**.

The following exercise shows you how to align the different AutoShapes on a flowchart.

Exercise 4.4: Aligning AutoShapes

1) Open EX.4.4.PPT. Go to slide number 13, 'Organic Certification Process'.

2) Select the three AutoShapes in the middle of the slide: the two rectangles and the diamond. (Hold down the **Shift** key and click each of the shapes in turn.)

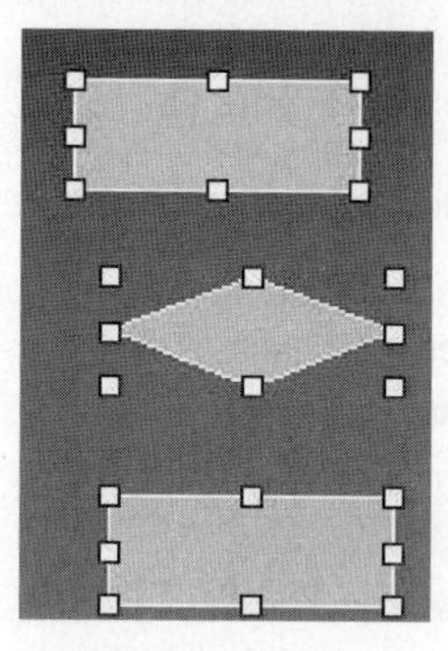

3) Choose **Draw | Align or Distribute | Align Center** from the *Drawing* toolbar. This aligns the AutoShapes by their centres, as shown.

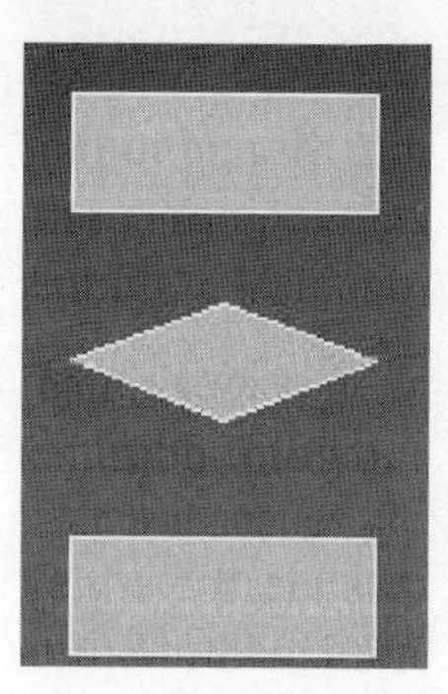

4) Select the top-left rectangle and the top-centre rectangle as shown.

5) Choose **Draw | Align or Distribute | Align Middle** from the *Drawing* toolbar. This aligns the AutoShapes by their middles, as shown.

6) Select the bottom oval and the right-hand rectangle as shown.

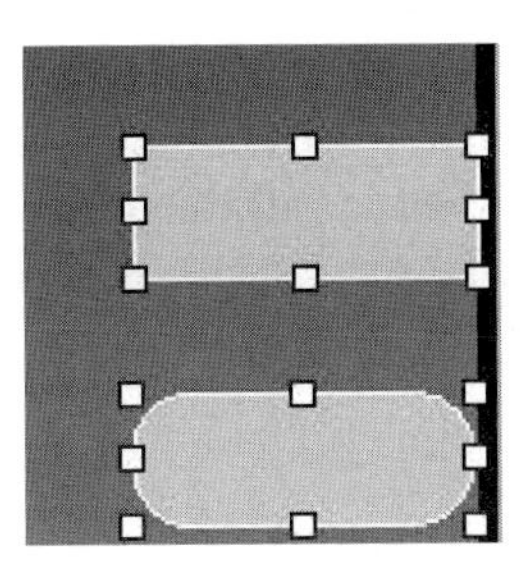

7) Choose **Draw | Align or Distribute | Align Centre** from the *Drawing* toolbar. This aligns the AutoShapes by their centres, as shown.

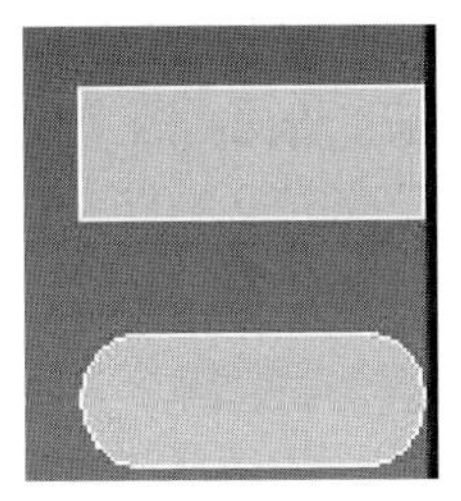

Well done! You've aligned the AutoShapes. Your slide should now look as shown.

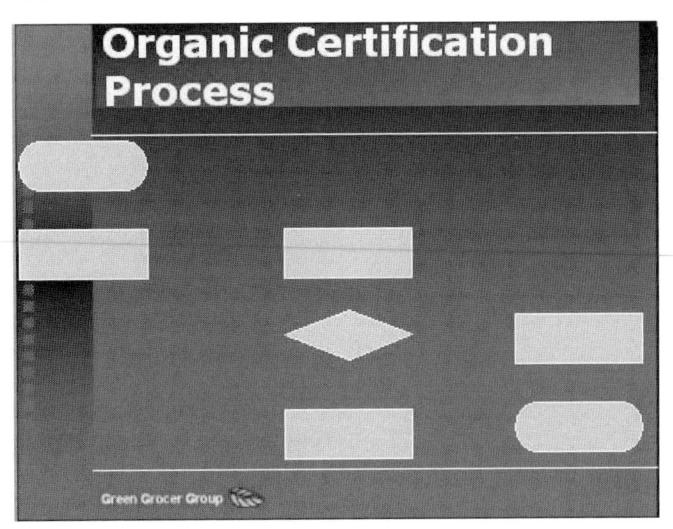

Now, your next step is to add some colour to the chart. Why don't you change the background colour of the AutoShapes? You can do this by using grouping techniques.

Grouping techniques

PowerPoint enables you to treat a group of objects as a single entity, and to apply effects to the group as a whole. This technique saves you time and effort, as you only need to apply one effect to cover all the shapes in the group. It also helps to ensure consistency throughout your flowchart.

The next exercise shows you how to group AutoShapes in order to apply colour effects.

Exercise 4.5: Grouping AutoShapes to apply colour effects

1) Open EX4.5.PPT. Go to slide number 13, 'Organic Certification Process'.

Shift key

2) Select all the AutoShapes except the ovals by holding down the **Shift** key and clicking each of the shapes in turn.

3) Choose **Draw | Group** from the *Drawing* toolbar. This groups the AutoShapes together, so that any action applied to one shape will automatically be applied to every shape.

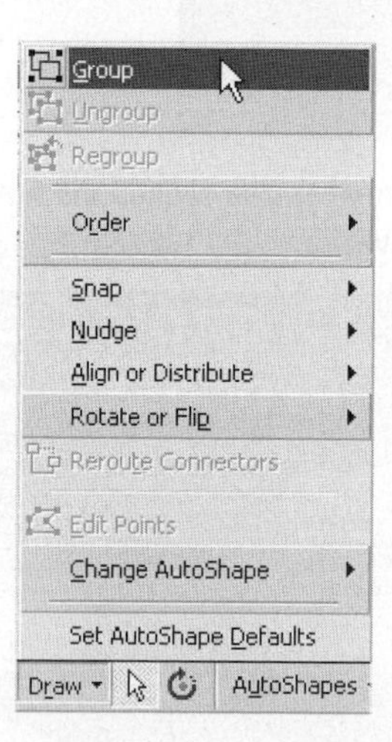

4) Click the arrow to the right of the **Fill Color** button. Select the *Fill Effects* option.

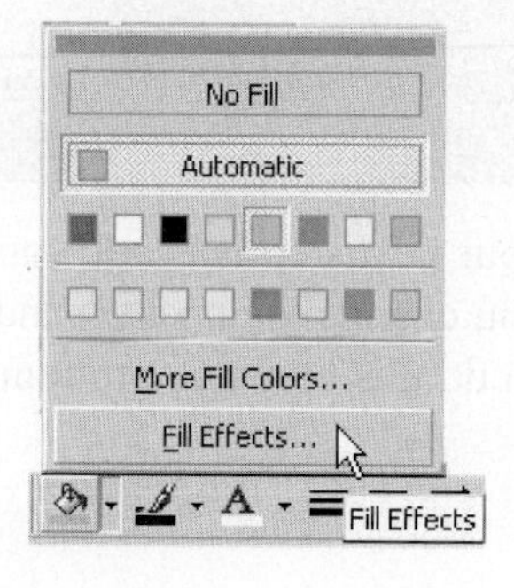

5) Under the **Gradient** tab, select the *Two colors* option. Select light grey as *Color 1* and white as *Color 2*.

6) Under *Shading styles* choose the *Diagonal up* option. Click **OK**.

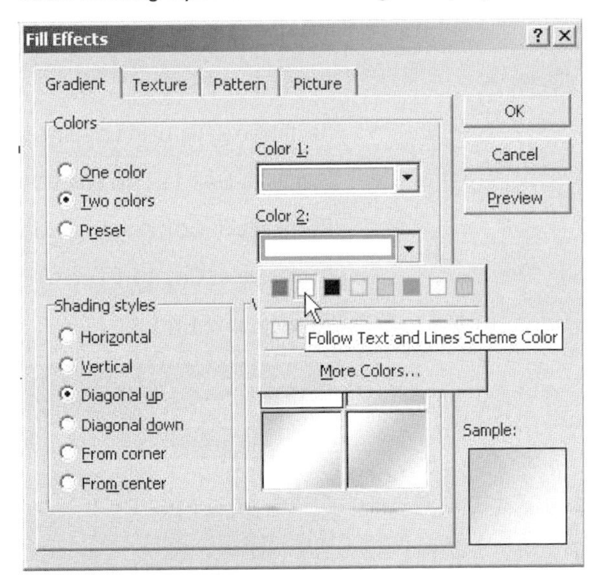

Your flowchart should look as shown.

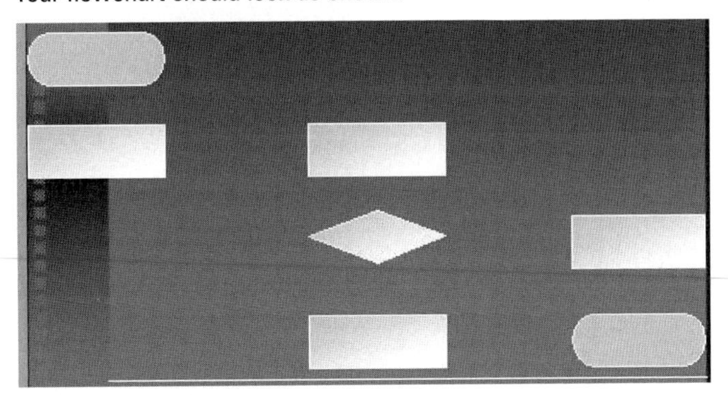

7) Choose **Draw | Ungroup** from the *Drawing* toolbar. Each shape is now independent.

What else do we need to put into the flowchart? Why, text of course, otherwise your audience won't be able to understand your flowchart!

Adding text to AutoShapes

Adding text to an AutoShape is easy. Make sure that your text is small enough to fit in the AutoShape but large enough to read. (Remember the 18 point minimum that we discussed in Chapter 3.)

Exercise 4.6: Adding text to AutoShapes

1) Open EX4.6.PPT. Go to slide number 13, 'Organic Certification Process'.

2) Type the following pieces of text into the AutoShapes:

   Terminator 1: `Start`

   Rectangle 1: `Submit application to agency`

   Rectangle 2: `Organic Inspection`

   Diamond: `Satisfactory?`

   Rectangle 3: `Correct and resubmit`

   Rectangle 4: `Certification`

   Terminator 2: `End`

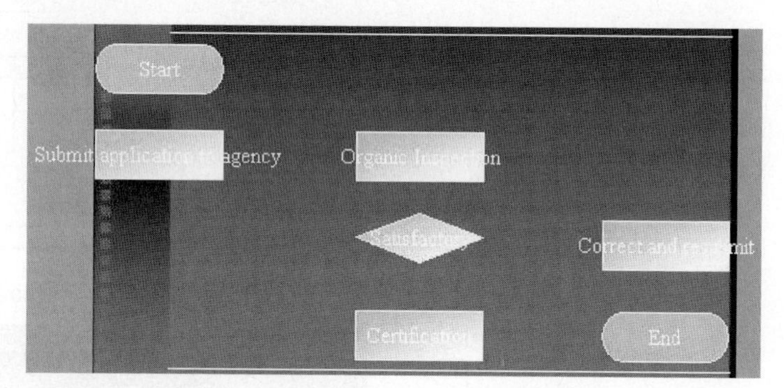

The font colour makes the flowchart hard to read doesn't it? Let's amend the text.

3) Group the AutoShapes again: select all the shapes and choose **Draw | Group**.

4) Change the font to Arial, 18 point, Bold, Black.

Note that the text in all the AutoShapes has changed font and colour.

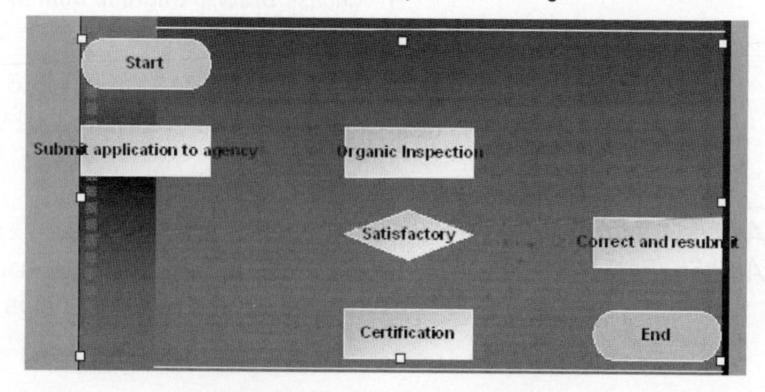

5) Choose **Draw | Ungroup** from the *Drawing* toolbar.

Note that the text in the shapes does not fit. Don't panic – you can adjust both the text and the size of the AutoShape.

Exercise 4.7: Adjusting text and AutoShapes

1) Open EX4.7.PPT. Go to slide number 13, 'Organic Certification Process'.
2) Select the top-left rectangle.
3) Place your cursor between the two words 'application' and 'to' and press **Enter**.

4) With the same rectangle selected, position the cursor on one of the corner handles.

Drag the double-headed arrow to enlarge the rectangle so that it accommodates the text.

5) Apply similar changes to the remaining shapes.

Your slide should look as shown.

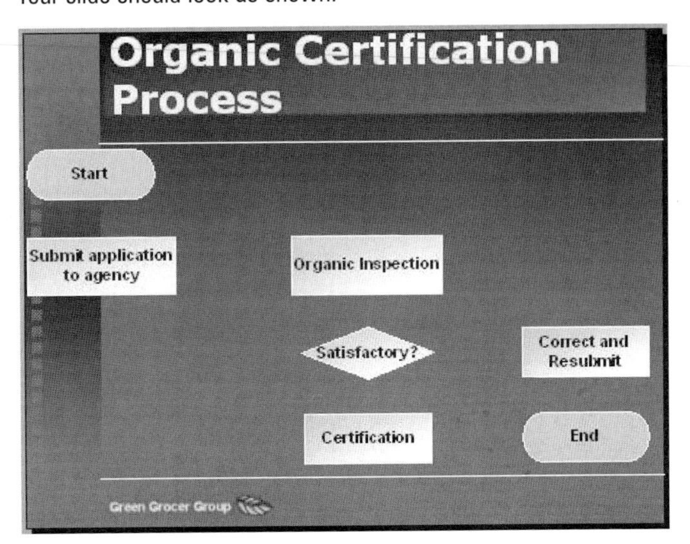

Arrows

In a flowchart, the flow is normally from top to bottom and left to right, in which case the shapes can be connected by a simple line. If the flow is in any other direction, the shapes must be connected by an arrow.

PowerPoint offers you two line options:

- The **Line** button on the *Drawing* toolbar.
- The **Connectors** option in the **AutoShapes** menu.

PowerPoint offers you three arrow options:

- The **Arrow** button on the *Drawing* toolbar.
- The **Block Arrows** option in the **AutoShapes** menu.
- The **Connectors** option in the **AutoShapes** menu.

You are probably already familiar with the **Line** button and the **Arrow** button on the *Drawing* toolbar but perhaps not so familiar with the **Connectors** option. In the following exercises you will add arrows and connectors to the flowchart.

Exercise 4.8: Adding arrows to a flowchart

1) Open EX4.8.PPT. Go to slide number 13, 'Organic Certification Process'.

Arrow button

2) Click the **Arrow** button on the *Drawing* toolbar.
3) Draw an arrow between the first terminator and the rectangle beneath it, as shown.

4) Duplicate the arrow (**Ctrl+d**).

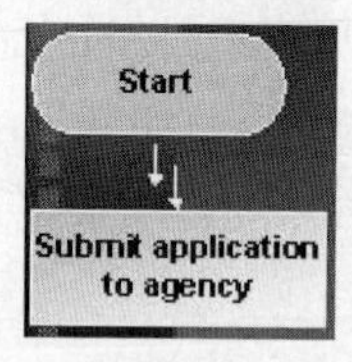

5) Drag the new arrow and position it between the centre rectangle and the diamond. Adjust its length to make it fit, as shown.

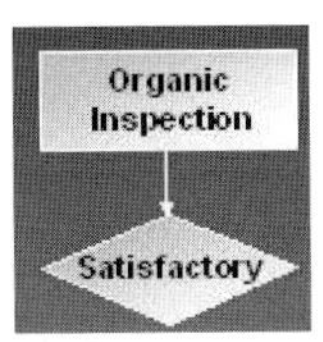

6) Add five more arrows to your flowchart:

- One arrow between the diamond and the rectangle below it.
- One arrow between the two top rectangles.
- One arrow between the diamond and the right-hand rectangle.
- One arrow between the bottom rectangle and the end terminator.
- One arrow between the right-hand rectangle and the second rectangle at the top.

Your flowchart should now look as shown.

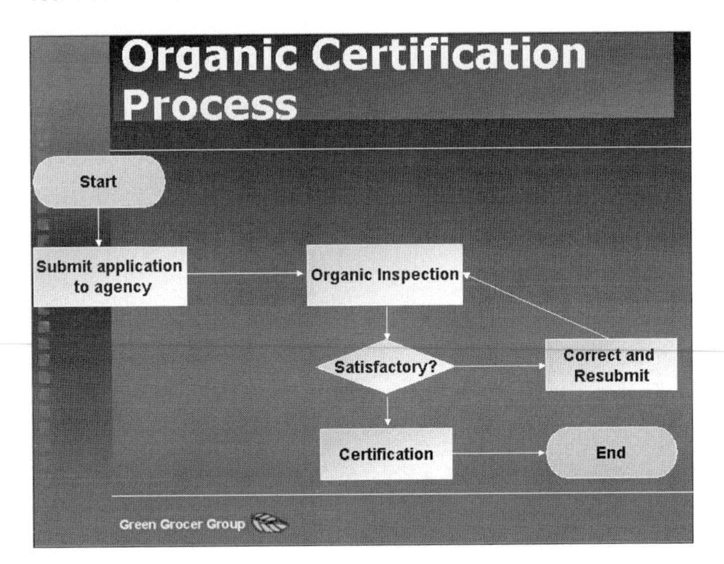

To complete your flowchart, you need to do two things:

- Add text to indicate the flow from the decision diamond.
- Use a connector line instead of the rather inelegant arrow joining the 'Correct and Resubmit' box to the 'Organic Inspection' box.

In the next exercise you will add two text boxes – one beside each of the arrows leading from the decision diamond.

Exercise 4.9: Adding text boxes to a flowchart

1) Open EX4.9.PPT. Go to slide number 13, 'Organic Certification Process'.

2) Click the **Text Box** button on the *Drawing* toolbar.

Text Box button

3) Draw a text box beside the diamond as shown.

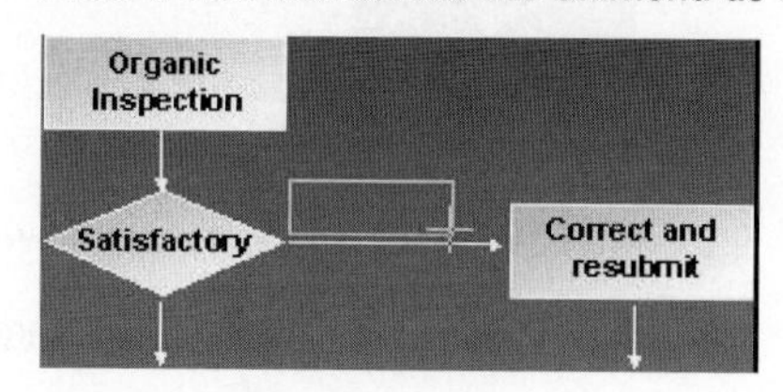

4) Type 'N' in the text box.

Change the font to Arial, 18 point, Bold.

Your text box should look as shown.

5) Similarly, draw a text box between the diamond and the bottom rectangle, with the letter 'Y' in it.

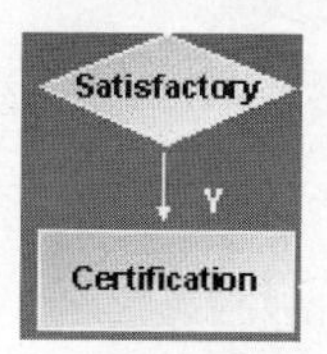

Your text boxes should now look as shown.

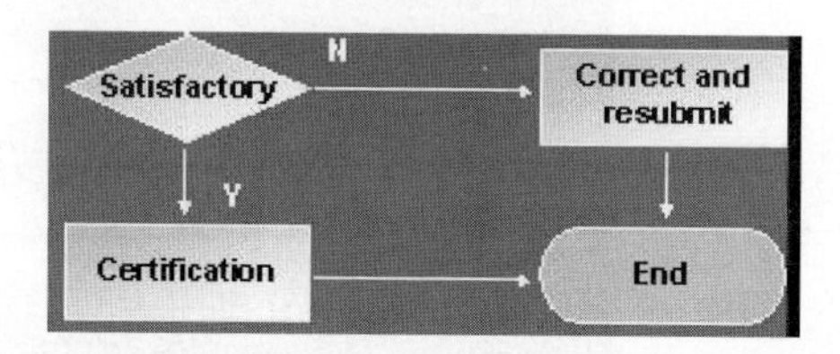

Connector lines

A connector is a special kind of line used to connect two flowchart shapes. The line 'sticks' to the shape even when the shape changes position and it's able to find the shortest route between the two shapes.

Connector lines can be straight, elbowed or curved, and they can have no arrow, an arrow at one end, or an arrow at each end. For flowcharting purposes, the best choice is:

- Elbowed
- One arrow

To draw a connector line, choose **AutoShapes | Connectors**, select the connector you want to use, click in the first shape you want to connect and then click in the second shape. Notice that four blue squares appear on the AutoShape itself; these are the possible attachment points for the connector.

When drawing a connector line, you will notice that the handles at the ends of the line change colour:

- Green: ending is not attached to a shape.
- Red: ending is attached to a shape.

If your connector has a yellow handle at its mid point, you can use this to change the shape of the connector without detaching it.

You can detach a connector line and 'reroute' it to another AutoShape: select it and then drag its handle (red or green) to the new shape.

Exercise 4.10: Working with connector lines

1) Open EX4.10.PPT. Go to slide number 13, 'Organic Certification Process'.

2) Delete the arrow joining the 'Correct and Resubmit' box to the 'Organic Inspection' box.

3) Select the rectangle with the text 'Correct and resubmit'.

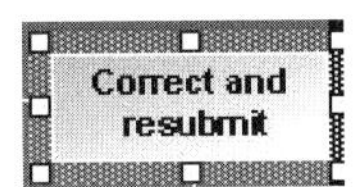

4) Choose **AutoShapes | Connectors** from the *Drawing* toolbar. Click the *Curved Arrow Connector* option.

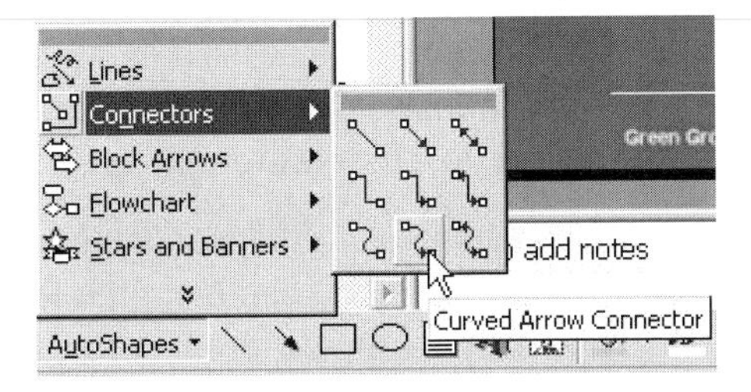

5) Draw a connector from the right-hand rectangle to the centre rectangle as shown.

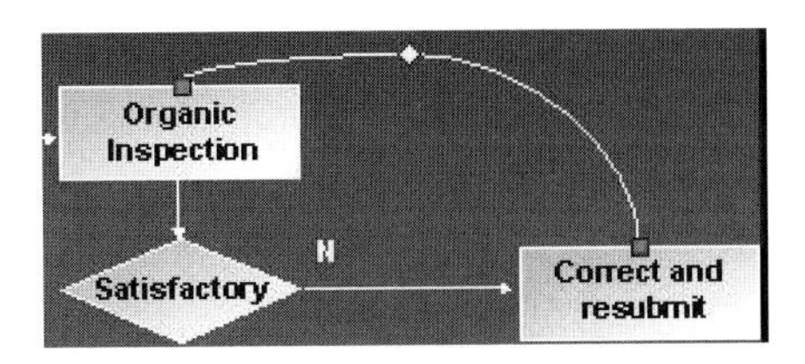

6) Curved connectors are not normally used in flowcharts, so let's change the connector type.

Right-click the connector and choose **Elbow Connector**.

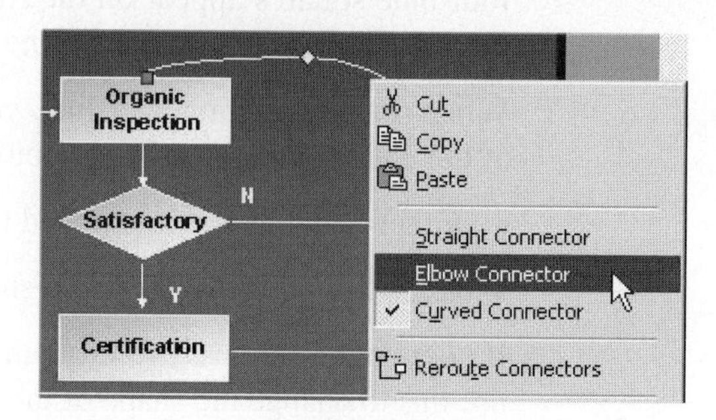

Your connector has now changed to an elbowed line.

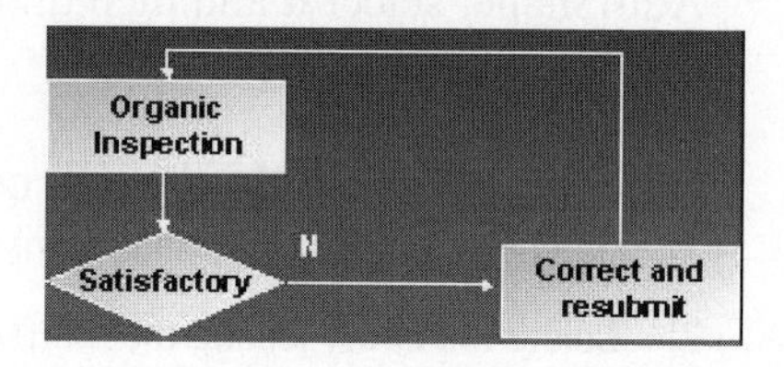

Chapter 4: summary

A *flowchart* is the graphical representation of a series of actions and decisions needed for a particular task or procedure. You use the following AutoShapes to create a flowchart: *diamonds*, *terminators* and *rectangles*.

Arrows or *connector lines* are used to link each shape in the flowchart. Position your shapes on a chart either by *dragging* the shape to the desired location or by using *specific coordinates*. Distribute the AutoShapes evenly by using the **Align or Distribute** option.

Group the AutoShapes together in order to apply effects to all of them. You can heighten the impact of your flowchart by introducing different colours, for example by adding a *graduated colour* to an AutoShape. You will need to *add text* to the AutoShapes and probably need to put *text boxes* into your flowchart to add extra information outside of the shapes. You can *adjust* the AutoShape to fit the text by stretching it.

Chapter 4: quick quiz

Circle the correct answer to each of the following questions on flowcharts.

Q1	What shape do you use for the start and end of a flowchart?
A.	◇
B.	⬭
C.	□
D.	○

Q2	What shape do you use for a decision step in a flowchart?
A.	◇
B.	⬭
C.	□
D.	○

Q3	Using specific coordinates, how do you position a shape in a flow chart?
A.	Right-click the shape and choose **Set AutoShapes Default** from the menu. Under the **Position** tab, input the *Position on Slide* information.
B.	Right-click the shape and choose **Format AutoShape** from the menu. Under the **Picture** tab, input the *Position on Slide* information.
C.	Right-click the shape and choose **Set AutoShapes Default** from the menu. Under the **Position** tab, input the *Scale* information.
D.	Right-click the shape and choose **Format AutoShape** from the menu. Under the **Position** tab, input the *Position on Slide* information.

Q4	True or false – a connector line 'sticks' to a shape even when the shape changes position.
A.	True.
B.	False.

Q5	What shortcut command do you use to duplicate a shape in a flowchart?
A.	**Ctrl+c**.
B.	**Ctrl+v**.
C.	**Ctrl+d**.
D.	**Ctrl+v**.

Answers

1: B, **2:** A, **3:** D, **4:** A, **5:** C.

5 Charts

In this chapter

Creating a good chart takes time and effort, but it's worth this investment. Charts help your audience to understand quantitative (number-based) information at a glance.

Keep your chart as simple as possible:

- Limit yourself to a few colours
- Use the chart as the main mechanism to convey your information – use as little text as possible
- Keep visibility issues in mind – remember the 18 point minimum guideline

New skills

At the end of this chapter you should be able to:

- Import a cell range from Excel
- Create a combination chart
- Change the scale of the value axis
- Change the display of the value axis
- Rotate a 3-D chart
- Elevate a 3-D chart
- Add and adjust labels

New words

At the end of this chapter you should be able to explain the following terms:

- Data series
- Combination chart
- Exploded pie chart

Syllabus reference

This chapter covers the following syllabus points:

- AM 6.4.1.1
- AM 6.4.1.2
- AM 6.4.1.3
- AM 6.4.1.4
- AM 6.4.1.5

Selecting chart types

The main chart types are:

- Column charts
- Bar charts
- Line charts
- Pie charts

So how do you know which type of chart to use?

Column charts

The default chart in PowerPoint is the column chart, in which numbers are represented by vertical bars. Column charts are useful when you want to compare quantities – for example, the sales of bananas in each month of the year, or the population of South American countries.

Bar charts

Bar charts are similar to column charts, except that the bars are horizontal. Bar charts are useful when the bars represent distances or speeds, such as the processing speed of different computers, or the personal best performances of different Olympic long-jump contestants. Bar charts are also useful if the label associated with each bar is lengthy, as the label can fit on a single line beside the bar.

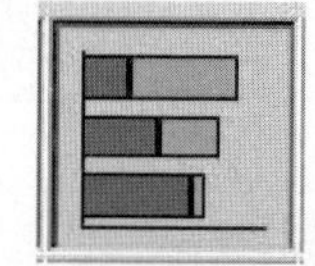

Line charts

Line charts are useful when you want to show trends, such as the changing pattern of cigarette consumption since 1956.

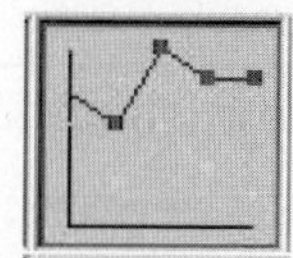

Pie charts

Pie charts represent the parts of a whole as segments of a circle. They are useful when you want to give a break-down of a figure, or show the percentages of a total – for example, the market share of different brands of DVD players.

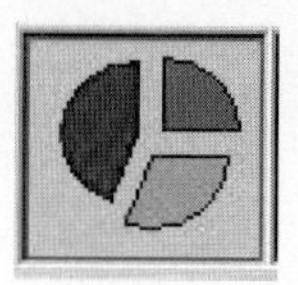

Using existing information for a chart

You want to show your audience some quantitative information. This information might originate in an Excel spreadsheet or an Access database. But no audience wants to look at a wall of figures. For their sake, you should create some visual interest by turning such information into a chart.

If your information comes from Excel, you can import a whole spreadsheet or a range of cells and use the information to build a chart. Let's work with the supplied spreadsheet END OF YEAR RESULTS.XLS. In the following exercise, you will import a cell range that will become the basis for your chart.

Exercise 5.1: Importing a cell range

1) Open EX5.1.PPT. Go to slide number 14, 'End of Year Results'.
2) Choose **Format | Slide Layout**. In the *Slide Layout* dialog box, select the *Chart* slide layout and click **Apply**.

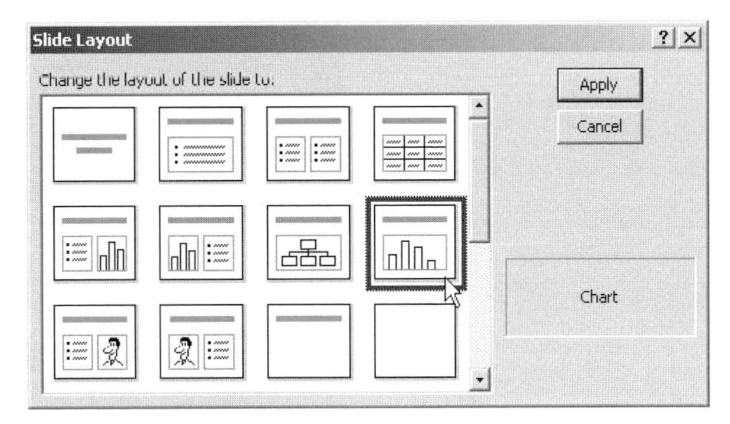

3) Double-click the chart icon. A default chart appears.
4) Choose **Edit | Import File**. Navigate to the Excel Spreadsheet END OF YEAR RESULTS.XLS and double-click it.
5) In the *Import Data Options* dialog box, select Sheet 1.

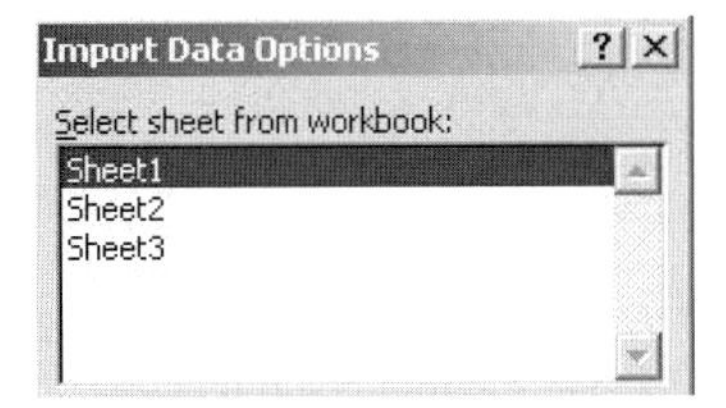

6) In the *Import* section, select the *Range* option.

   In the *Range* box, enter the following range of cells:

   A2:C5.

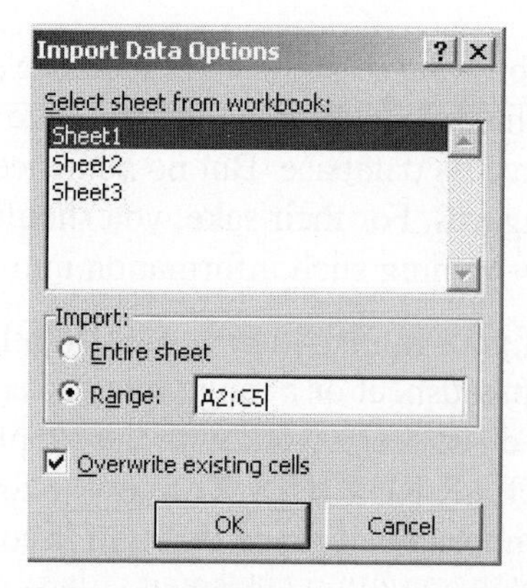

7) Select the *Overwrite existing cells* check box. Click **OK**.

The financial results from the spreadsheet are now represented in a column chart.

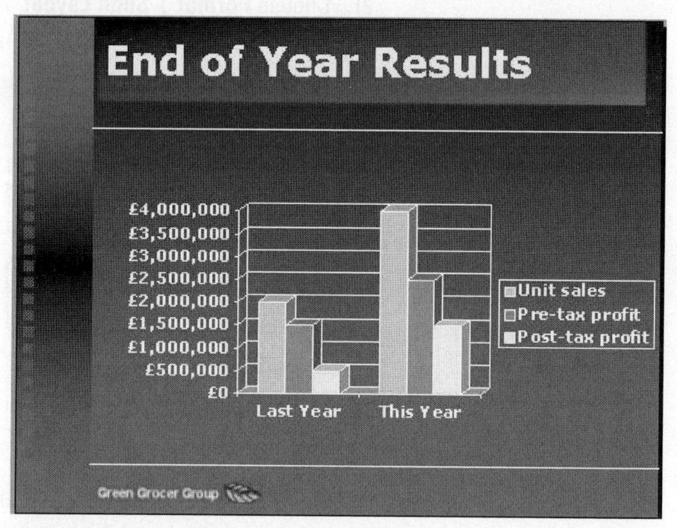

Notice that the datasheet has also changed.

		A	B	C
		Last Year	This Year	
1	Unit sales	2,000,000	4,000,000	
2	Pre-tax pro	£1,500,000	£2,500,000	
3	Post-tax pr	£500,000	£1,500,000	
4				

Well done! You've imported quantitative information (a cell range) and turned it into a column chart.

Combination charts

A combination chart is used to show the relationship between different *kinds* of information. You could use one, for example, to chart ice-cream sales against daily temperature. You can combine any of the different chart types within PowerPoint, but the most common choice is to combine a column chart with a line chart.

The only charts you can combine in PowerPoint are 2-D ones – PowerPoint does not allow you to create 3-D combination charts. (A 3-D combination chart would be potentially confusing.) In the next exercise you will convert your existing 3-D chart to a 2-D combination chart. This chart will contain both a column chart and a line chart.

Up to this point your chart has three data series, each of them shown as a vertical bar. When you convert it to a combination chart, one of the data series – the one relating to unit sales – will be shown as a line.

Exercise 5.2: Creating a combination chart

1) Open EX5.2.PTT. Go to slide number 14, 'End of Year Results'.
2) Double-click the chart so that the datasheet appears.
3) Right-click the chart area. Choose **Chart Type** from the menu that appears.

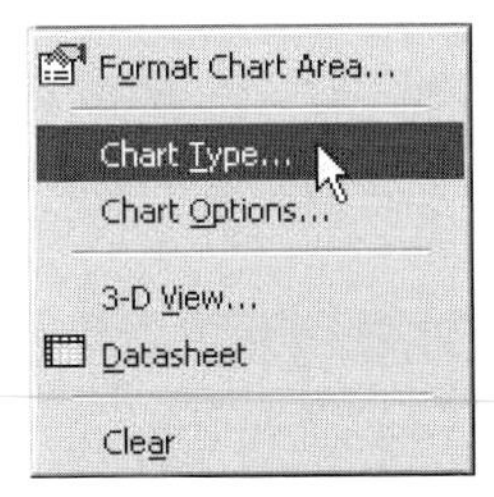

In the **Standard Types** tab, select the first chart sub-type, *Clustered Column*.

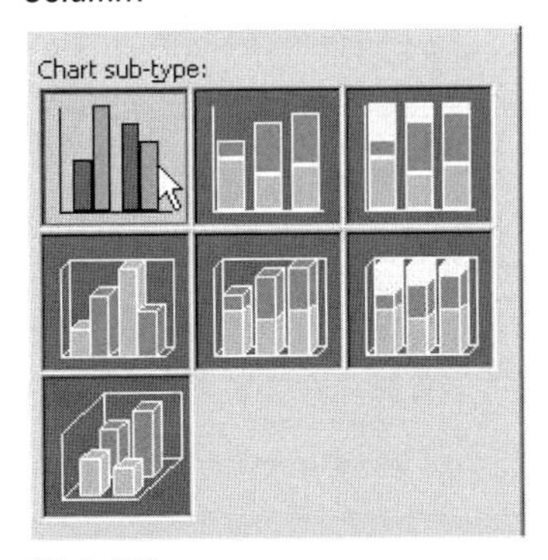

Click **OK**.

The chart is now 2-D.

4) Right-click either of the 'Unit sales' columns. (Unit Sales are represented by the first column in each group.)

Choose **Chart Type** from the menu that appears.

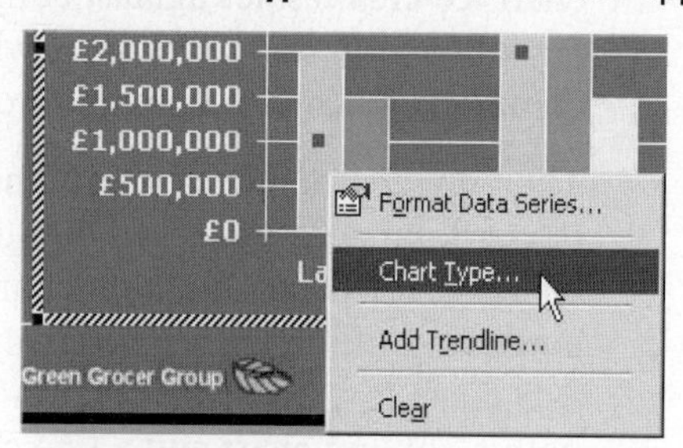

5) In the **Standard Types** tab, select the *Line* chart type.

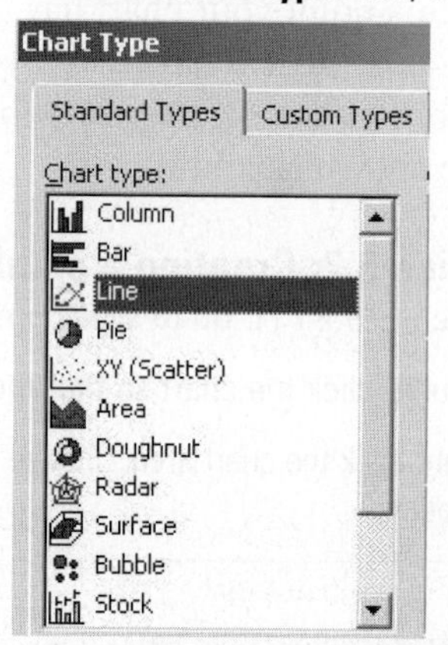

6) Select the first *Chart sub-type*. This is the chart type used to display trends.

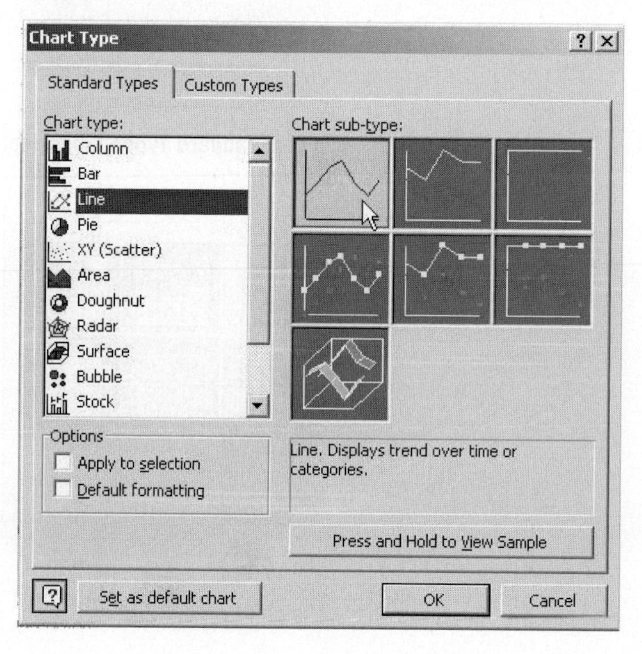

If you want a preview of the combination chart, use the **Press and Hold to View Sample** button. Click the **OK** button.

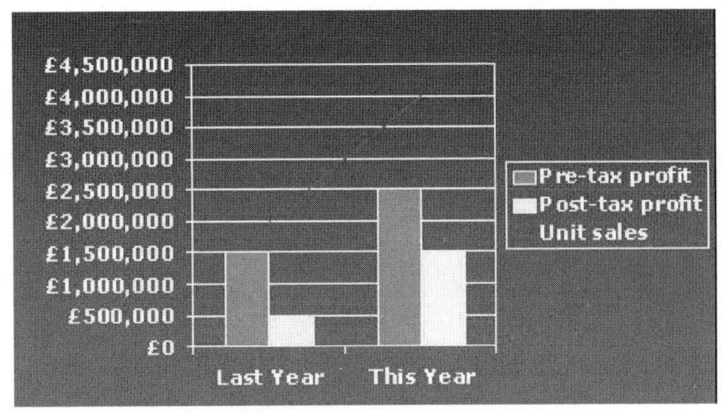

Well done! You have now created a chart that combines both a line chart and a column chart. However, the audience might find the line, in the line chart, hard to see. To make it more visible, change its colour and make it thicker in the following exercise.

Exercise 5.3: Formatting a chart

1) Open EX5.3.PPT. Go to slide number 14, 'End of Year Results'.
2) Double-click the combination chart so that the datasheet appears.
3) Right-click the line in the line chart. Choose **Format Data Series** from the menu.

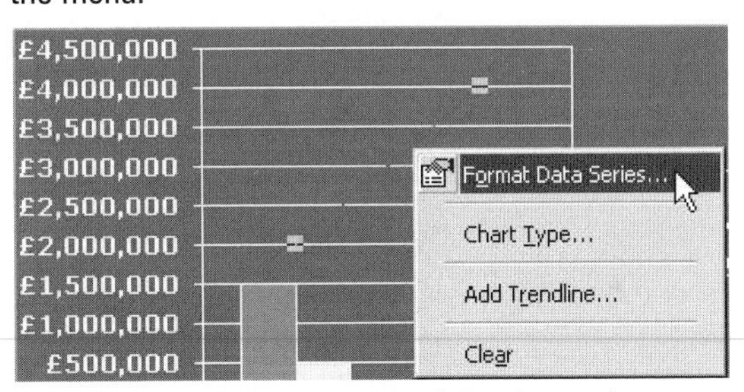

4) In the **Patterns** tab, select the following options:

   Under *Line*:

   - *Custom*
   - *Style*: first option (continuous line)
   - *Color*: orange
   - *Weight*: last option (thick line)
   - *Smoothed line*: select the check box

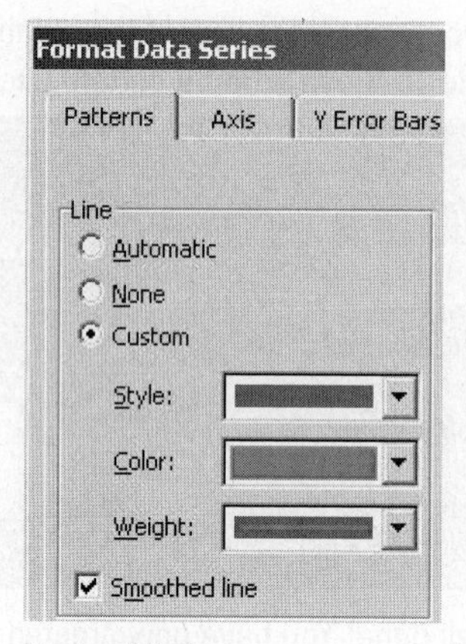

Under *Marker*:

- *Custom*
- *Foreground*: black
- *Background*: white
- *Style*: diamond (you will not see the diamond until you've changed the colours as above)
- *Size*: 12 point
- *Shadow*: select the check box

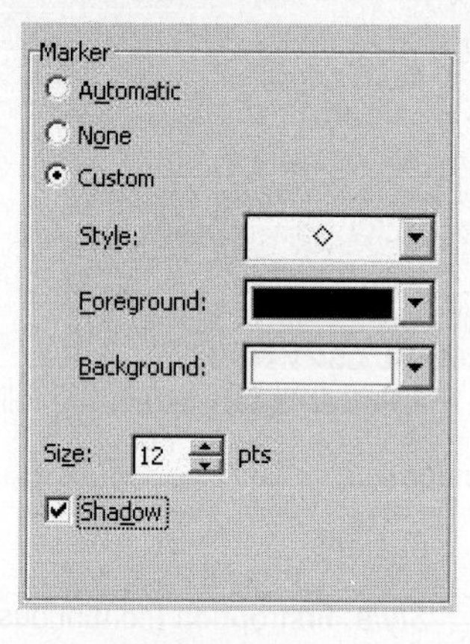

Click the **OK** button.

Your chart should look as shown.

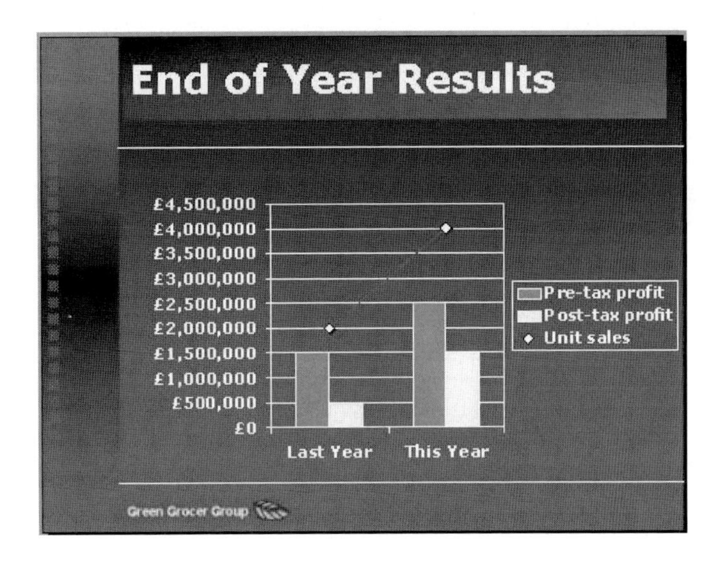

Occupational hazard!

It's an occupational hazard of working with PowerPoint that occasionally your right-clicks are misinterpreted. You might not have clicked on exactly the right place. Go back and try again.

Modifying scales

The Y-axis (vertical axis) in your chart shows the values of sales and profits (for this reason, the Y-axis is also known as the value axis). When the chart is created, PowerPoint allocates default settings to the Y-axis. You can modify these default settings in three ways:

- Change the scale of the Y-axis by specifying a minimum and a maximum value. This is useful if your data consists of high numbers within a narrow range (for example, sales figures, all of which lie between 10 million and 10.5 million). Changing the scale will enable you to highlight the differences.
- Change the units on the Y-axis – such as changing from hundreds to thousands.
- Change the interval between units on the Y-axis to simplify your chart.

Changing the scale of the Y-axis

To change the scale of the Y-axis:

- Right-click the Y-axis.
- Choose **Format Axis**.
- Under the **Scale** tab, input the minimum and maximum values that you want to use and deselect the corresponding *Auto* check boxes.
- Click **OK**.

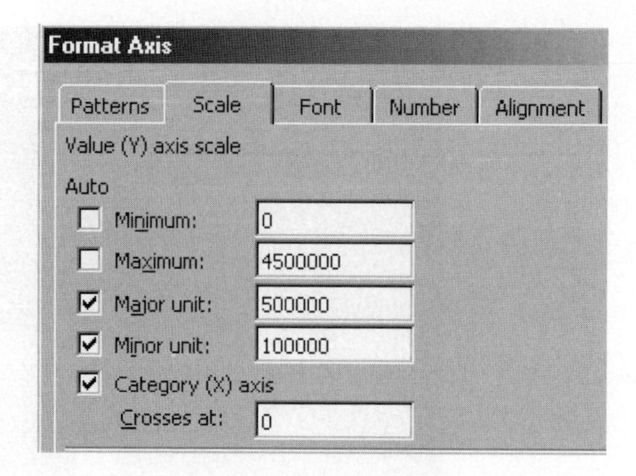

Changing the units used in the Y-axis

To change the units used in the Y-axis:

- Right-click the Y-axis.
- Choose **Format Axis**.
- Under the **Scale** tab, in the *Display units* section, click the arrow to the right of the *Display units* drop-down list.
- Select a value of your choice.
- Click **OK**.

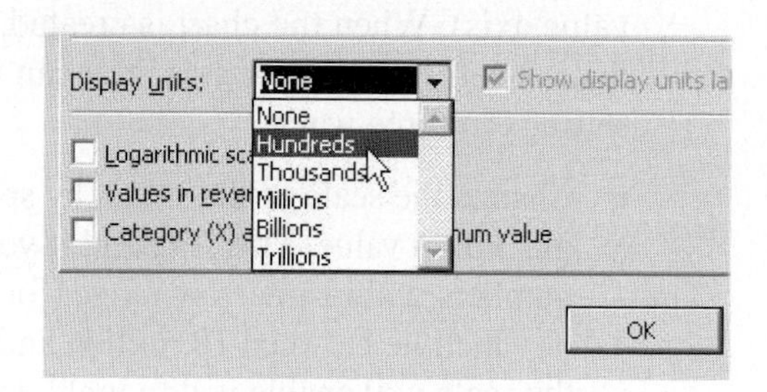

Changing the intervals used in the Y-axis

To change the intervals used in the Y-axis:

- Right-click the Y-axis.
- Choose **Format Axis**.
- Under the **Scale** tab, input the major unit and minor unit values that you want to use, and deselect the corresponding *Auto* check boxes.
- Click **OK**.

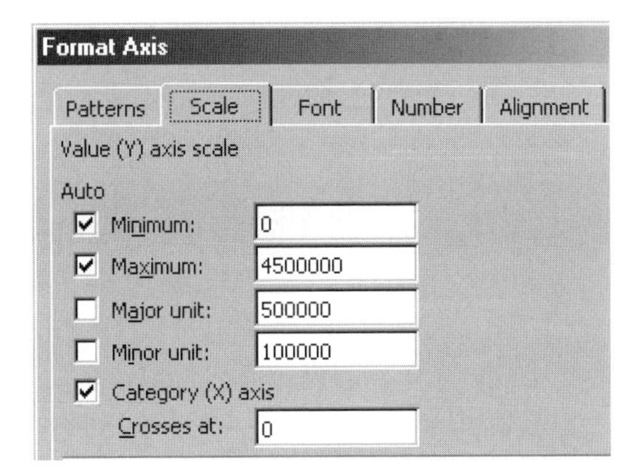

Pie charts

You will recall that pie charts represent the parts of a whole as segments of a circle. Note that if the numbers represented by the pie segments are percentages, then they *must* add up to 100. Otherwise, you will create a false impression.

In PowerPoint you can create different types of pie charts, from simple 2-D pie charts to exploded 3-D pie charts. An exploded pie chart is a chart in which one or more of the segments are separated from the others. You can rotate and change the elevation of these slices for greater emphasis, and you can label them to ensure that your audience can interpret the pie chart fully. For example, you can rotate the pie to bring a particular segment to the top. Take a look at the following exercise, where you rotate and change the elevation of an exploded pie chart.

Exercise 5.4: Adding 3-D effects to an exploded pie chart

1) Open EX5.4.PPT. Go to slide number 15, 'Best Sellers'.

2) Double-click the pie chart so that the datasheet appears.

3) Right-click the chart area and choose the **3-D View** option from the menu.

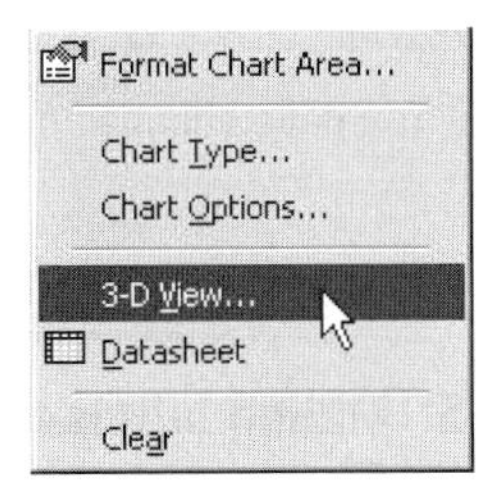

4) In the *3-D View* dialog box, change the elevation of the pie chart to 45 degrees. You can do this in one of two ways:

    - Click the **Up** and **Down** arrow buttons until the Elevation box reads 45.

    -or-

- Input the number 45 directly into the *Elevation* box.

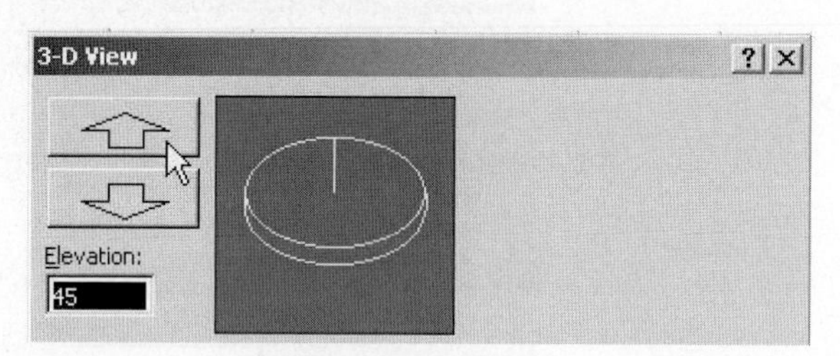

5) In the *3-D View* dialog box, change the rotation of the pie chart to 40°. You can do this in one of two ways:

- Click the **Left** and **Right** rotation arrow buttons until the *Rotation* box reads 40.

  -or-

- Input the number 40 directly into the *Rotation* box.

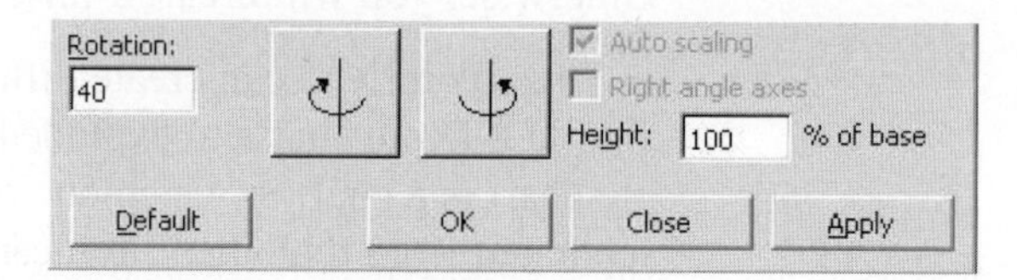

Click **Apply**, then click **OK**.

Your pie chart should look as shown.

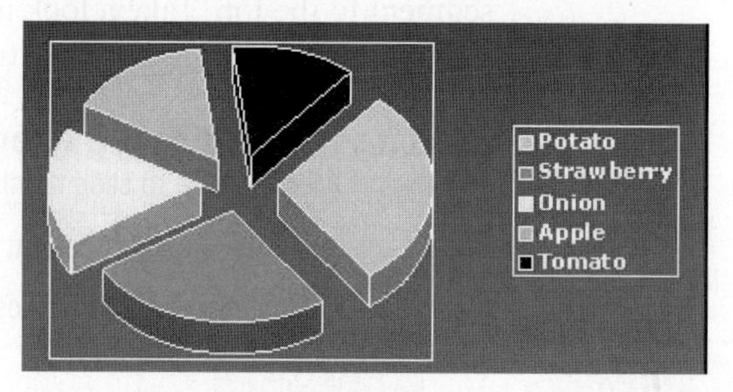

Well done! You have changed both the rotation and elevation of the pie chart.

Now add labels to the different pie segments.

Exercise 5.5: Adding labels to pie segments

1) Open EX5.5.PPT. Go to slide number 15, 'Best Sellers'.
2) Double-click the pie chart so that the datasheet appears.
3) Right-click the pie chart and choose **Format Data Series** from the menu that appears.

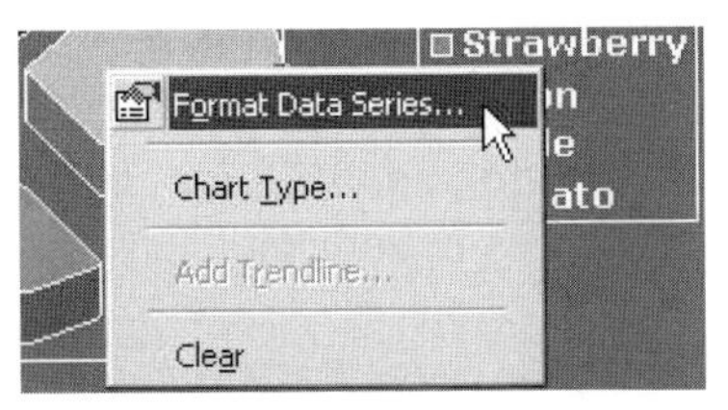

4) Under the **Data Labels** tab in the *Format Data Series* dialog box, select the *Show percent* option.

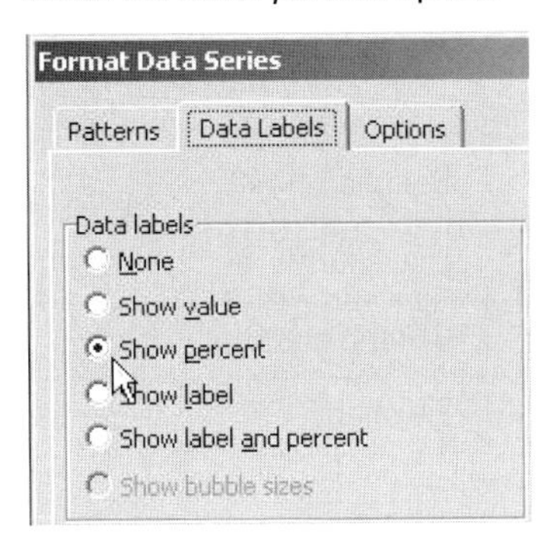

Click **OK**.

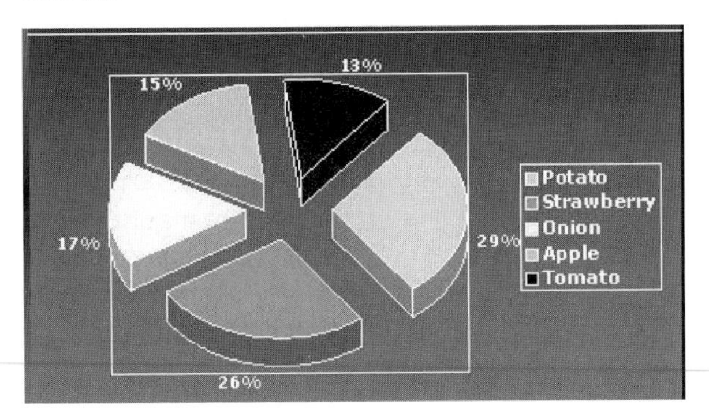

Your pie chart should look as shown.

Chapter 5: summary

You can import information such as a *cell range* from an Excel spreadsheet into PowerPoint. You can use this *quantitative information* to form the basis of a chart. There are several *chart types* to choose from: *bar charts*, *column charts*, *line charts* and *pie charts*. You can mix chart types together to form *combination charts*. A combination chart is used to show the relationship between different *kinds* of information. You can adjust your combination chart in various ways – you can change the *scale* of the *Y-axis* (value axis), change the types of units used on it, and change its intervals.

Pie charts represent the parts of a whole as segments of a circle. You can adjust a *3-D* pie chart by changing the degrees of *elevation* and *rotation* in the chart. And you can *label* the data slices in your pie chart.

Chapter 5: quick quiz

Circle the correct answer to each of the following questions about charts.

Q1	What's the best chart type to use for comparing quantities, such as sales figures?
A.	Bar chart.
B.	Line chart.
C.	Column chart.
D.	Pie chart.

Q2	To change the intervals used in the Y-axis you ...
A.	Right-click the Y-axis and choose **Format Axis**. Under the **Scale** tab click the arrow to the right of the *Display units* box. Select the values required and click **OK**.
B.	Right-click the Y-axis and choose **Format Axis**. Under the **Scale** tab input the major and minor unit values and deselect the corresponding *Auto* values. Click **OK**.
C.	Right-click the Y-axis and choose **Format Axis**. Under the **Scale** tab input the minimum and maximum values and deselect the corresponding *Auto* values. Click **OK**.
D.	Right-click the Y-axis and choose **Format Axis**. Under the **Number** tab click the arrow to the right of the *Display units* box. Select 1000s and click **OK**.

Q3	True or false – you can create 3-D combination charts.
A.	True.
B.	False.

Q4	To format a chart you …
A.	Right-click the chart and select **Clear**. Input the *Patterns* options and then input the *Marker* options.
B.	Right-click the chart and select **Add Treadline**. Input the *Patterns* options and then input the *Marker* options. Click **OK**.
C.	Right-click the chart and select **Chart Type**. Input the *Patterns* options and then input the *Marker* options. Click **OK**.
D.	Right-click the chart and select **Format Data Series**. Input the *Patterns* options and then input the *Marker* options. Click **OK**.

Answers

1: C, **2:** B, **3:** B, **4:** D.

6 Action buttons and hyperlinks

In this chapter

In this chapter you will learn how to create action buttons and hyperlinks in order to navigate through your presentation, and from it to other information resources. You route these hyperlinks and action buttons to specific locations such as individual slides, other presentations, websites, Word documents, and so on.

In this chapter you will also learn how to use the comment box, which is the PowerPoint equivalent of a 'sticky note'.

New skills

At the end of this chapter you should be able to:

- Place action buttons
- Format action buttons
- Place hyperlinks
- Reroute action buttons
- Reroute hyperlinks
- Insert comments
- Adjust comments
- Remove comments

New words

At the end of this chapter you should be able to explain the following terms:

- Action button
- Hyperlink
- Comment box

Syllabus reference

This chapter covers the following syllabus points:

- AM 6.6.1.1
- AM 6.6.1.2

Action buttons

A PowerPoint action button is an AutoShape that you place in a presentation to help you navigate through the slide show. Action buttons are especially useful when you want to go directly from one slide to another specific slide. If you want an action button to appear on every slide in a presentation you place it on the slide master. If you want an action button to appear on certain slides, then you place the button on those slides only. Look at the following exercise for an example of how to create and place an action button that will appear throughout a presentation.

Exercise 6.1: Creating and placing action buttons

1) Open EX6.1.PPT. Go to the Slide Master – **View | Master | Slide Master**.

2) Choose **AutoShapes | Action Buttons** from the *Drawing* toolbar and then select the **Home** action button.

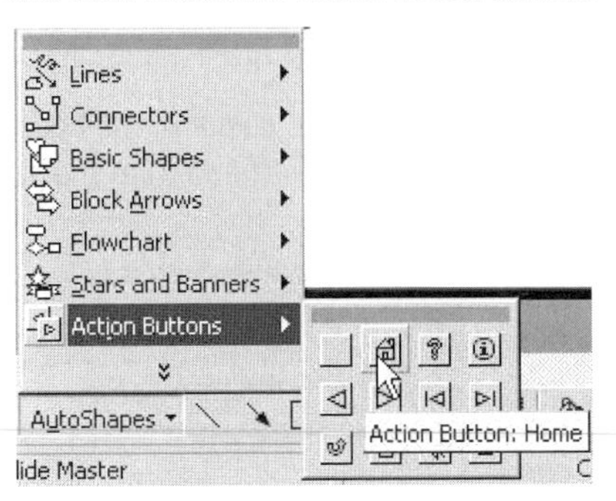

3) Place your cursor anywhere on the Master page; it turns into crosshairs. Drag the crosshairs to draw a **Home** button.

4) The *Action Settings* dialog box appears. Under the **Mouse Click** tab, select the *Hyperlink to* option. Choose *Next Slide* from the drop-down list.

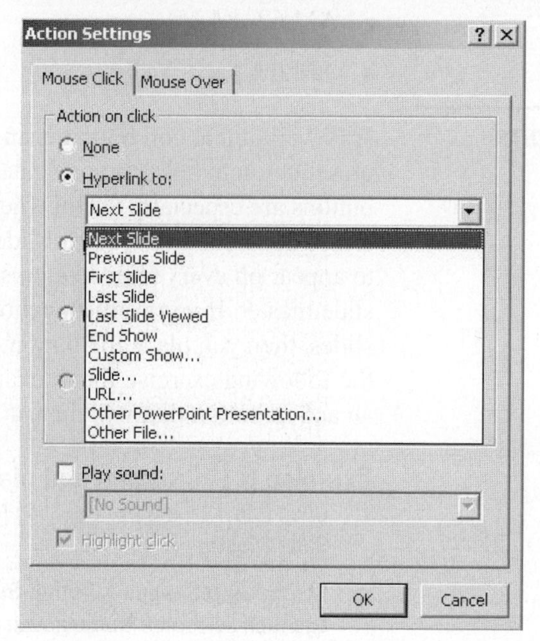

Click **OK**.

5) To adjust the colour of the action button, right-click it and choose **Format AutoShape** from the menu.

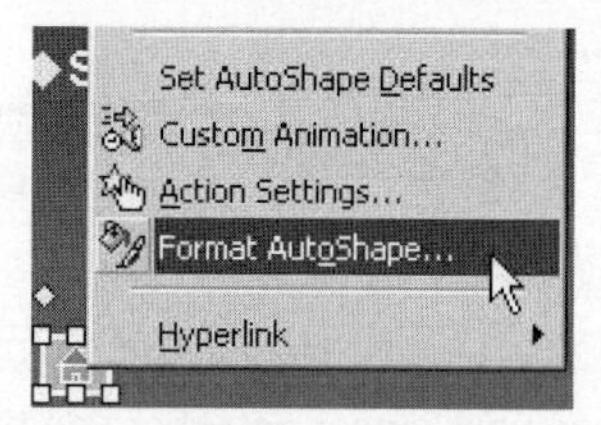

6) Under the **Colors and Lines** tab of the *Format AutoShape* dialog box, click the arrow to the right of the *Color* box. Select a light purple colour. (This colour is part of your colour scheme.)

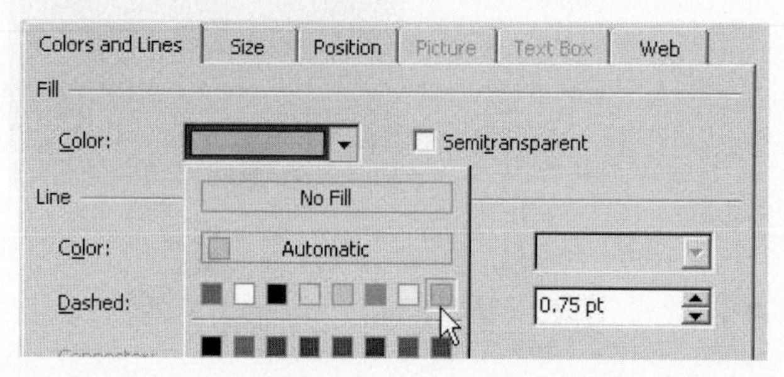

Click **OK**.

7) Use the arrow keys to move the action button to the bottom-right of the slide master (the number area). Resize the action button to fit the number area box.

Your slide master should look as shown.

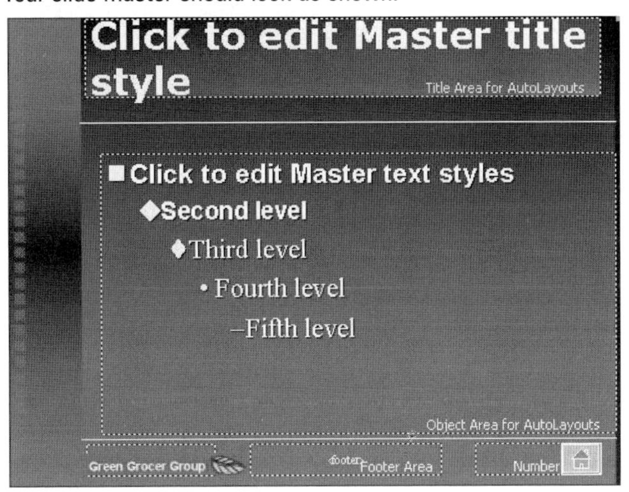

Assigning action buttons to other locations

You can assign action buttons to the following locations: websites, files, slides or other slide shows.

Assign an action button to a website

Start as in Exercise 6.1. In the **Mouse Click** tab of the *Action Settings* dialog box:

- Select the *Hyperlink to* option.
- Click the arrow to the right of the *Hyperlink to* box.
- Select *URL* from the list.

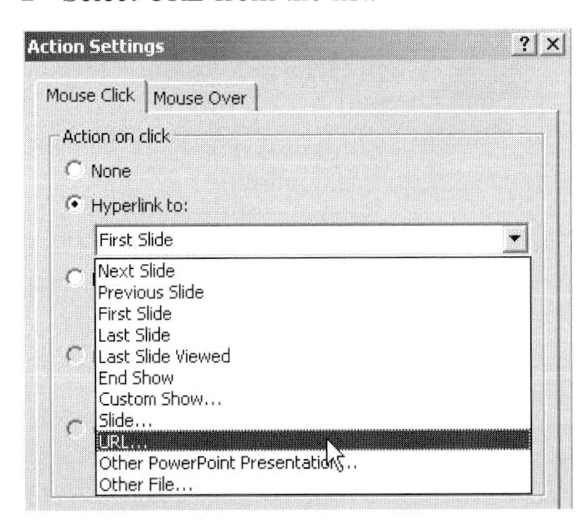

- Type the url you need in the *Hyperlink To URL* dialog box and click **OK**.

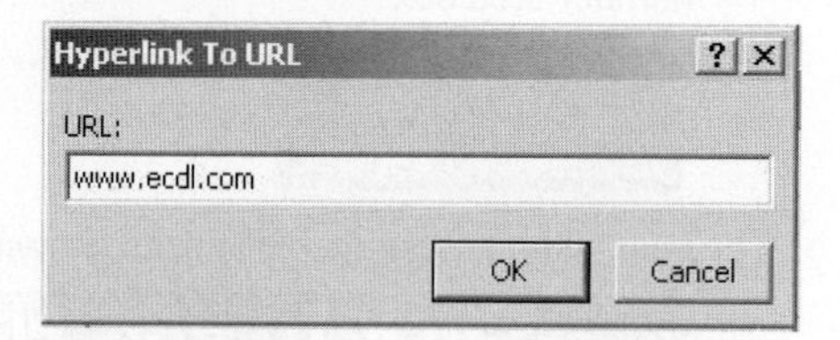

- Click **OK**.

Assign an action button to a file

Start as in Exercise 6.1. In the **Mouse Click** tab of the *Action Settings* dialog box:

- Select the *Hyperlink to* option.
- Click the arrow to the right of the *Hyperlink to* box.
- Select *Other File* from the list.

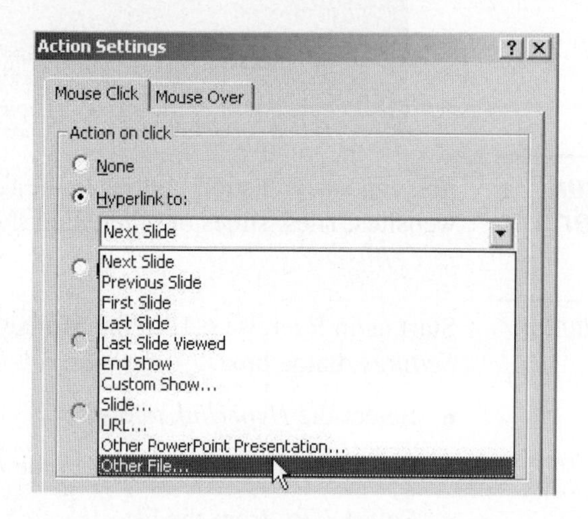

- Navigate to the file that you want and click **OK**.
- Click **OK**.

Assign an action button to a slide

Start as in Exercise 6.1. In the **Mouse Click** tab of the *Action Settings* dialog box:

- Select the *Hyperlink to* option.
- Click the arrow to the right of the *Hyperlink to* box.
- Select *Slide* from the list.

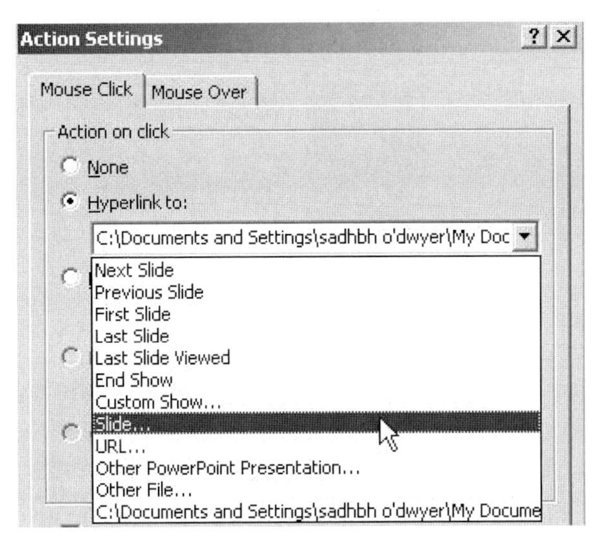

- Select the slide that you want from the *Hyperlink To Slide* dialog box and click **OK**.

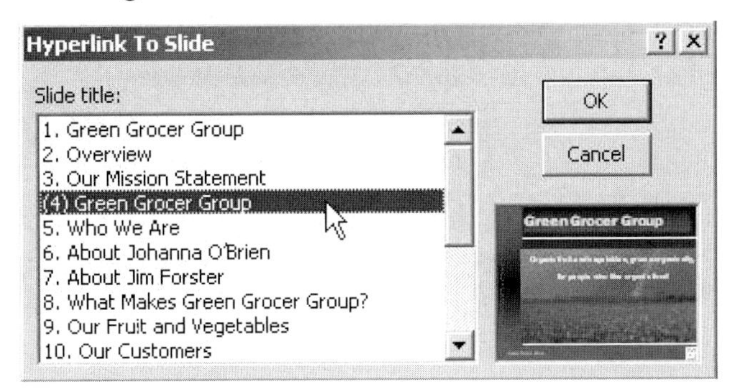

- Click **OK**.

Assign an action button to another slide show

Start as in Exercise 6.1. In the **Mouse Click** tab of the *Action Settings* dialog box:

- Click the arrow to the right of the *Hyperlink to* box.
- Select *Other PowerPoint Presentation* from the list.
- Navigate to the slide show that you want from the *Hyperlink to Other PowerPoint Presentation* dialog box and click **OK**.

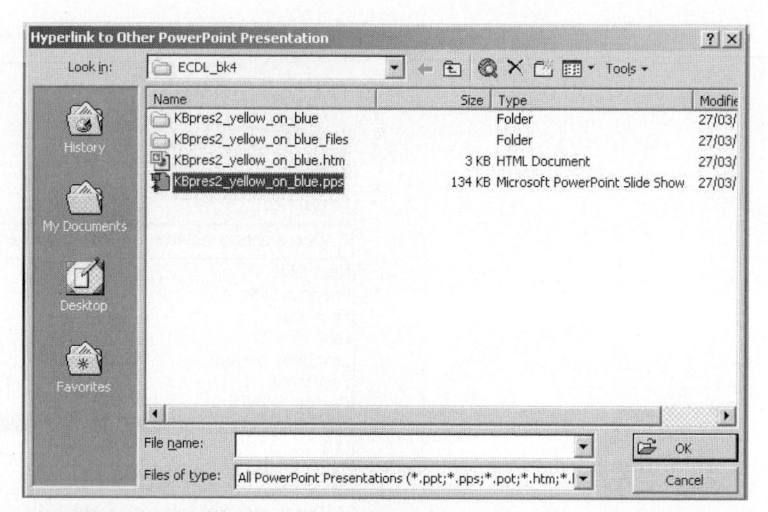

- In the *Hyperlink To Slide* dialog box select the slide that you want to display first, and click **OK**.

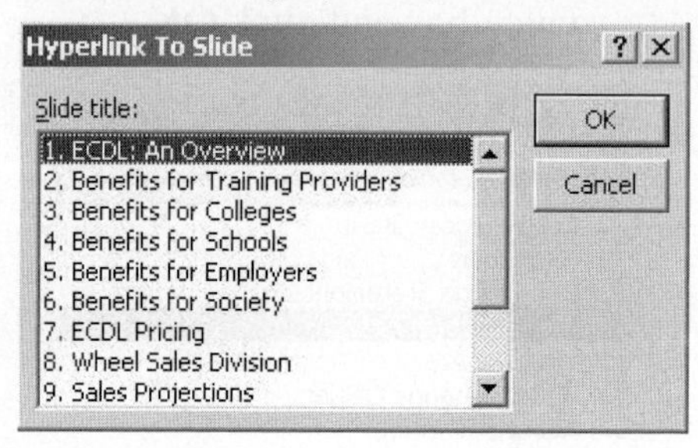

- Click **OK**.

Rerouting action buttons

If you create an action button but then decide to change its destination you can reroute it to an alternative location. When you set up the action button in Exercise 6.1, you assigned it to the *Next Slide* option. In the exercise below you will reroute this action button to the first slide of the presentation.

Exercise 6.2: Rerouting an action button

1) Open EX6.2.PPT. Choose **View | Master | Slide Master**.

2) Right-click the action button on the slide master. Choose **Action Settings** from the menu.

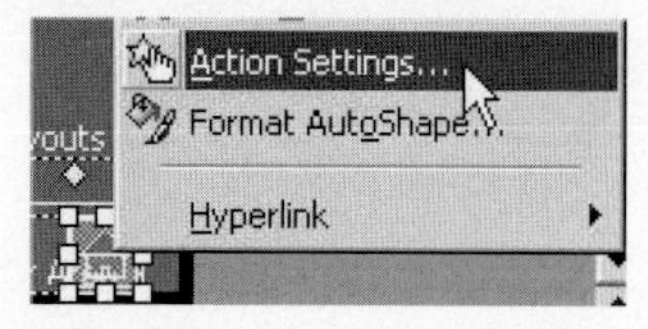

3) Under the **Mouse Click** tab, click the *Hyperlink to* option. Select *First Slide* from the drop-down list.

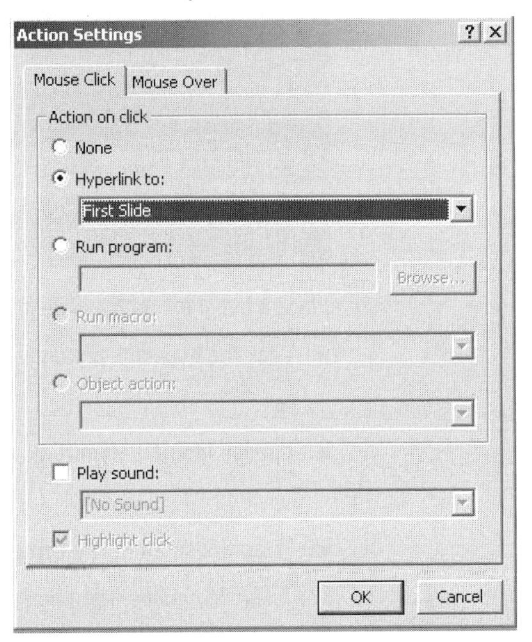

4) Click **OK**.

5) Go to Slide Show view and check that, from any slide, the action button brings you to the first slide.

Hyperlinks

Like action buttons, pieces of text, graphics or shapes can be hyperlinked to other locations: websites, slides, presentations or files. Note that hyperlinks are not active while you are creating your presentation – they are active only in Slide Show view.

In the next exercise you will create a hyperlink from a piece of text in your presentation to an organic farming website.

Exercise 6.3: Inserting a hyperlink in a presentation

1) Open EX6.3.PPT. Select slide number 12, 'Organic Farming Practices'.

2) Select the item that you want to hyperlink from – you can choose a graphic, a shape or a piece of text. Here you will link from a piece of text, as shown below:

Hyperlink button

3) Place a hyperlink on the slide in one of following ways:

   - Click the hyperlink button on the *Standard* toolbar.

   -or-

   - Choose **Insert | Hyperlink**.

   -or-

   - Press the shortcut key **Ctrl+k**.

   The *Insert Hyperlink* dialog box appears.

4) Click the **ScreenTip** button. In the *ScreenTip text* box type the following text:

   `European Organics`

   (This is the text that will appear when you place your cursor on the hyperlink.)

   Click **OK** to close the *Set Hyperlink ScreenTip* dialog box.

5) In the *Type the file or Web page name* box, type the url of the website you want to link to:

   http://www.organic-research.com

   (If you don't know the name of the website, you can browse the Internet for it. Click the **Web Page** button to navigate to your chosen site. Copy and paste the url to the *Type the file or Web page name* box.)

Click **OK** to close the *Insert Hyperlink* box.

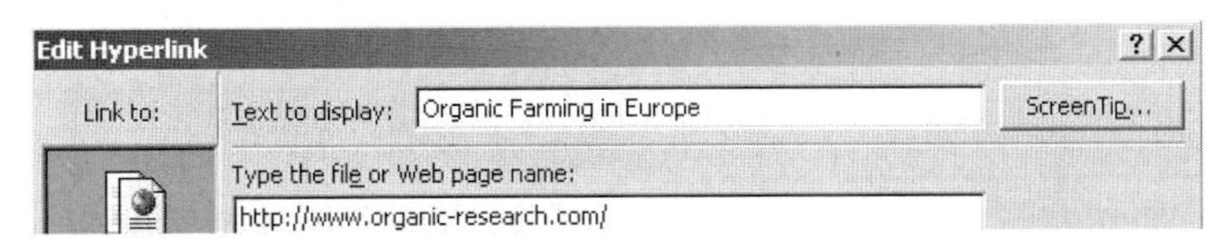

6) View your hyperlink in Slide Show view – press **F5**, or choose **View | Slide Show**, or click the **Slide Show** button.

7) Click the link to check that it works. Press **Esc** to return to the presentation.

Add a comment note

You can put the PowerPoint equivalent of a 'sticky note' on a slide. For example, if your presentation is being reviewed by other people, they might want to make a suggestion in a comment note. Or you might leave a comment note for yourself when you are working on a slide and you want to come back to it later.

Exercise 6.4: Adding a comment note to a slide

1) Open EX6.4.PPT. Go to slide number 12, 'Organic Farming Practices'.

2) Choose **Insert | Comment**. A yellow 'sticky note' appears in the left corner of the slide showing your name (or the name of the person who registered the application).

3) Type the following text in the comment box:

```
www.organic-europe.net – more up-to-date
information?
```

Denis O'Dwyer:
www.organic-europe.net --
more up-to-date information?

Assigning hyperlinks

In the previous exercise you created a hyperlink to a website. However, you can also assign hyperlinks to other locations: slides, files or other presentations.

Assigning a hyperlink to a slide

Place in This Document button

To assign a hyperlink to a slide you:

- Click the **Insert Hyperlink** button.
- In the *Insert Hyperlink* dialog box, click the **Place in This Document** button.
- In the *Select a place in this document* box, select the slide that you want to link to. (If necessary, click the + box, to see a full list of slide titles.)

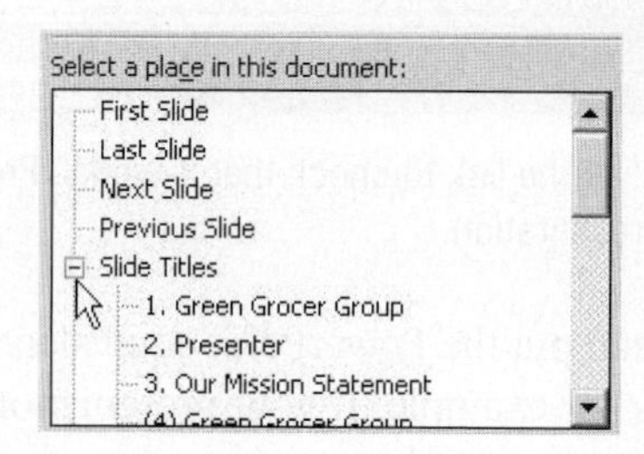

- Click **OK**.

Assigning a hyperlink to a file or another presentation

Existing File or Web Page button

To assign a hyperlink to a file or presentation you:

- Click the **Insert Hyperlink** button.
- In the *Insert Hyperlink* dialog box, click the **Existing File or Web Page** button.
- Click the **File** button in the *Browse for* section.
- In the *Link to File* dialog box, navigate to the file or presentation that you want and click **OK**.

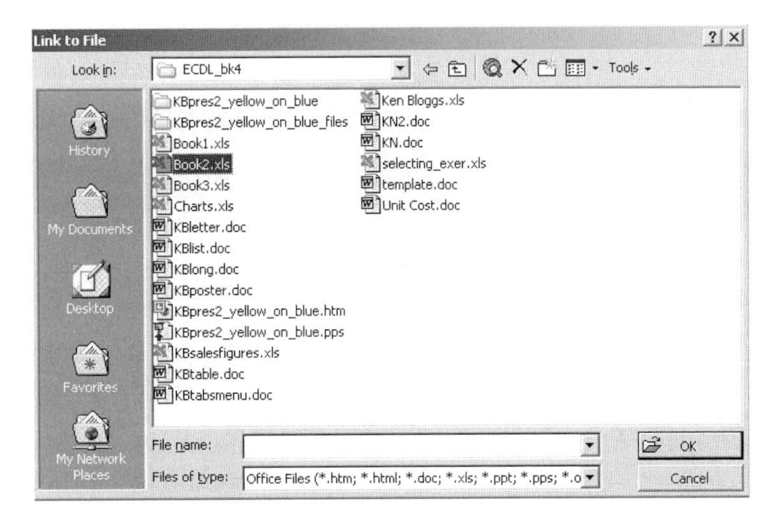

- Click **OK**.

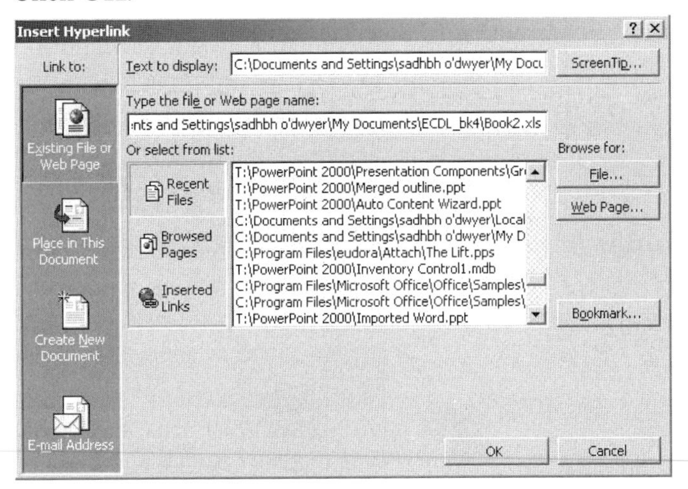

Rerouting hyperlinks

Just as you can reroute an action button, you can also reroute a hyperlink to another location.

Exercise 6.5: Rerouting a hyperlink

1) Open EX6.5.PPT. Go to slide number 12, 'Organic Farming Practices'. (This is the slide on which you put a comment note.)

2) Right-click the *Organic Farming in Europe* hyperlink. Choose **Hyperlink | Edit Hyperlink** from the menu.

   The *Edit Hyperlink* dialog box appears.

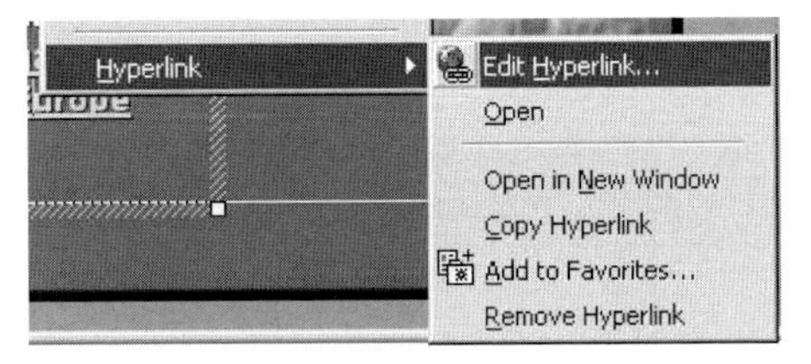

3) Copy the url of the website (www.organic-europe.net) from the comment note to the *Type the file or Web page name* box. Click **OK**.

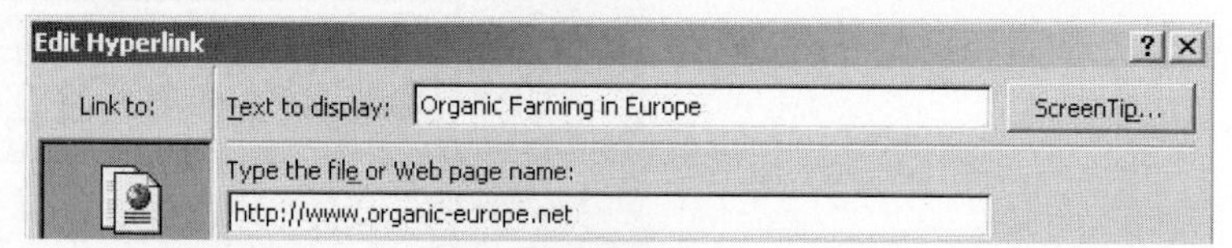

4) Remove the comment note – select the comment note and press **Delete**.

5) View your hyperlink in Slide Show view – press **F5**, or choose **View | Slide Show**, or click the **Slide Show** button. Check to see that the hyperlink works.

Chapter 6: summary

Action buttons are AutoShapes that help you to navigate within your slide show or from your slide show to another location. You can edit an action button or *reroute* it to another location. *Hyperlinks* link items such as text, graphics or shapes in your presentation to other locations. You can also *reroute* a hyperlink to other locations such as websites, presentations or files. The *comment note* works like a 'sticky note'. Insert a comment note to add suggestions or references to slides while you are still developing your presentation.

Chapter 6: quick quiz

Circle the correct answer to each of the following questions about action buttons and hyperlinks.

Q1	To reassign an action button to an alternative location you ...
A.	Right-click and choose **Format AutoShape**. Under the **Mouse Click** tab, click the *Hyperlink to* option. Select the alternative location from the drop-down list. Click **OK**.
B.	Right-click and choose **Action Settings**. Under the **Mouse Over** tab, click the *Hyperlink to* option. Select the alternative location from the drop-down list. Click **OK**.
C.	Right-click and choose **Format AutoShape**. Under the **Mouse Over** tab, click the *Hyperlink to* option. Select the alternative location from the drop-down list. Click **OK**.
D.	Right-click and choose **Action Settings**. Under the **Mouse Click** tab, click the *Hyperlink to* option. Select the alternative location from the drop-down list. Click **OK**.

Q2	To assign a hyperlink to a slide in your presentation, you click ...
A.	**Insert Hyperlink**. Insert the url of the hyperlink and then click the **Existing File or Web Page** button. Select the slide you want to use in the *Insert Hyperlink* dialog box. Click **OK**.
B.	**Insert Hyperlink**. Insert the url of the hyperlink and then click the **E-mail Address** button. Select the slide you want to use in the *Insert Hyperlink* dialog box. Click **OK**.
C.	**Insert Hyperlink**. Insert the url of the hyperlink and then click the **Place in This Document** button. Select the slide you want to use in the *Insert Hyperlink* dialog box. Click **OK**.
D.	**Insert Hyperlink**. Insert the url of the hyperlink and then click the **Create New Document** button. Select the slide you want to use in the *Insert Hyperlink* dialog box. Click **OK**.

Q3	The shortcut key to insert a hyperlink is ...
A.	**Ctrl+h**.
B.	**Ctrl+k**.
C.	**Ctrl+f**.
D.	**Ctrl+p**.

Q4	To reroute a hyperlink you ...
A.	Right-click the hyperlink and select **Remove Hyperlink**. Type the url in the *Type the file or Web page name* box. Click **OK**.
B.	Right-click the hyperlink and select **Edit Hyperlink**. Type the url in the *Type the file or Web page name* box. Click **OK**.
C.	Right-click the hyperlink and select **Copy Hyperlink**. Type the url in the *Type the file or Web page name* box. Click **OK**.
D.	Right-click the hyperlink and select **Edit Hyperlink**. Type the url in the *Type the file or Web page name* box.

Q5	True or false – a comment can be seen in Slide Show view.
A.	True.
B.	False.

Answers

1: D, **2:** C, **3:** B, **4:** B, **5:** A.

7

Custom shows and slide shows

In this chapter

Usually, a presentation will follow a linear path from the first slide to the last. However, details of financial performance might not be of relevance to farmers, for example, and details of crop performance might not be of interest to financiers. PowerPoint enables us to produce custom shows, where you specify different paths through the slides, each path containing a different subset of the slides. In this chapter you will specify two custom shows within your presentation.

Also in this chapter, when you save your presentation, you can save it as a slide show and you can adapt the slide show to suit the particular location and audience.

New skills

At the end of this chapter you should be able to:

- Create a custom show
- Run a custom show
- Edit a custom show
- Create a summary slide for custom shows
- Create a slide show
- Set up slide shows for different audience types

New words

At the end of this chapter you should be able to explain the following terms:

- Custom show
- Summary slide
- Slide show set ups

Syllabus reference

This chapter covers the following syllabus points:

- AM 6.6.1.4
- AM 6.6.2.1
- AM 6.6.2.2
- AM 6.6.2.3

Custom shows

If you are presenting at different times to different groups of people, your presentation is likely to contain some slides that are particularly relevant to a particular audience, and other slides that are of no relevance to them whatsoever. By creating custom shows, you can present a selected group of slides from your presentation, in a particular order, to each different audience.

Custom show

A custom show is a subset of slides from within a presentation, designed to appeal to a specific audience.

Creating a custom show

Before you create your custom show, you must decide what slides you wish to work with. There are two different audiences for the Green Grocer presentation:

- Suppliers to the Green Grocer Group.
- Investors in the Green Grocer Group.

Each group has a common interest in the Green Grocer Group, but each requires different levels of detail about different topics. Therefore, you will create a custom show with slides on organic practice and another custom show with slides on financial performance.

Here's how you do it.

Exercise 7.1: Creating custom shows

1) Open EX7.1.PPT.
2) Choose **Slide Show | Custom Shows**. The *Custom Shows* dialog box appears.

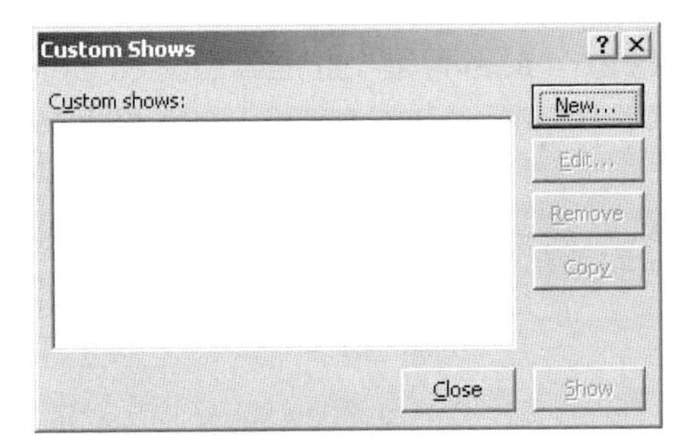

3) Click **New**. The *Define Custom Show* dialog box appears.

4) In the *Slide show name* box, give your custom show a name:

`Organic Practice`

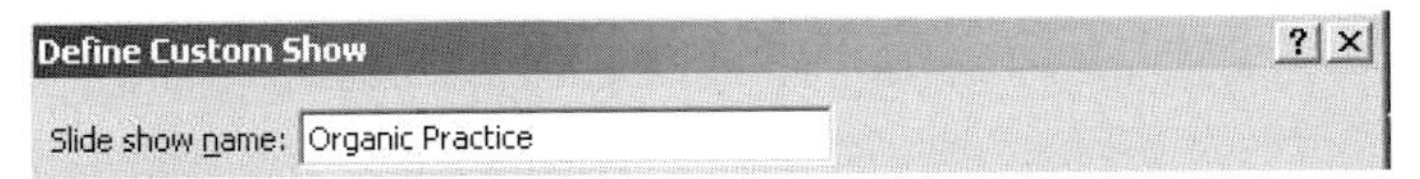

5) From the list of slides shown in the *Slides in presentation* box, select in turn each slide you want to include in the custom show and click the **Add>>** button. This moves them to the *Slides in custom show* box. Select slides 9, 10, 11, 12 and 13.

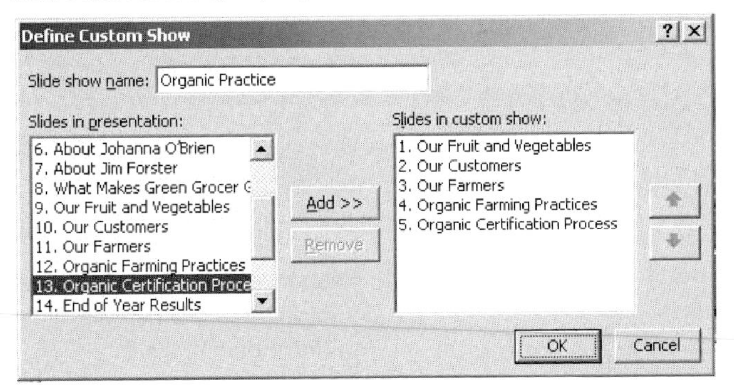

Click **OK**.

6) Create a second custom show in exactly the same way, called 'Financial Growth', and including slides 14 to 17.

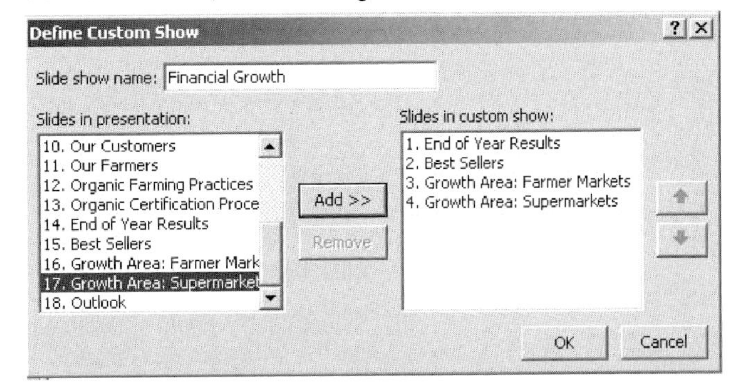

At any time, you can view a custom show by choosing **Slide Show | Custom Shows**, selecting the custom show and clicking **Show**.

Editing your custom shows

Now that you have created a custom show, you can return to it and edit it to suit you. You can reorder the slides, include more slides, or remove slides you previously used. The next exercise will show you how.

Exercise 7.2: Editing your custom shows

1) Open EX7.2.PPT.
2) Choose **Slide Show | Custom Shows** and select the Organic Practice custom show.

   Click the **Edit** button.
3) Rearrange the order of the custom show slides. Select slide 5, 'Organic Certification Process', and click the **Up** button to move it to the top of the list. Click **OK**.

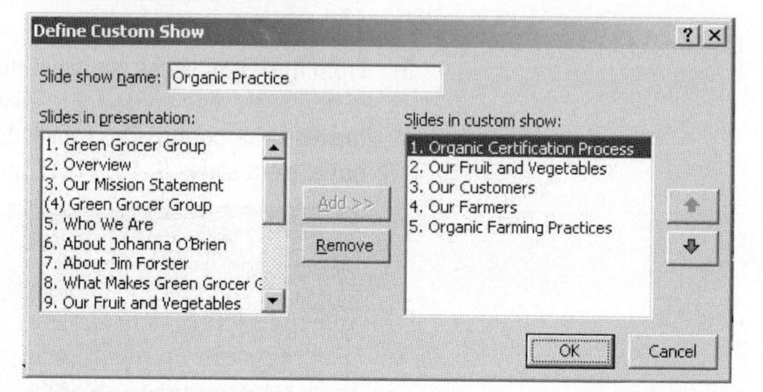

4) Select the 'Financial Growth' custom show and click the **Edit** button.
5) Rearrange the order of the custom show slides. Select slide 3, 'Growth Area: Farmer Markets', and click the **Down** button to move it to the bottom of the list.

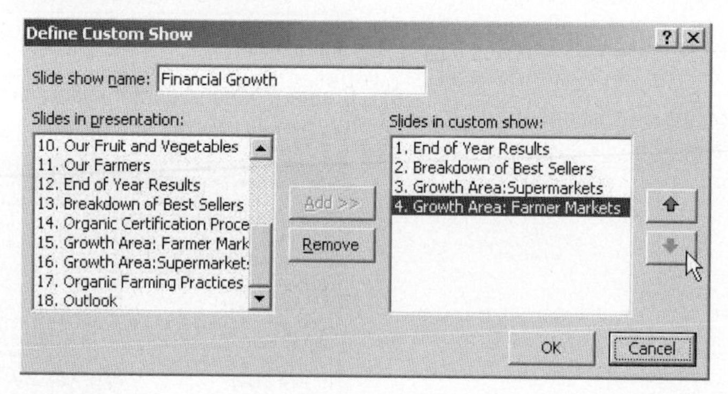

   Click **OK**.
6) Select each custom show in turn, and click **Show** to view them.

Summary slides

Summary slides are especially useful when you have custom shows in your presentation. A summary slide is like a table of contents, in that it contains slide titles. A summary slide is often used as a 'launchpad' for custom shows. You include the custom show slide titles on a summary slide, and then hyperlink from them to the custom shows.

> **Summary slide**
>
> *A summary slide gives the table of contents of a presentation. It usually contains hyperlinks to custom shows.*

The following exercise shows you how to create a summary slide.

Exercise 7.3: Creating a summary slide

1) Open EX7.3.PPT.
2) Choose **View | Slide Sorter**.
3) Select all the slides whose titles you want to appear on the summary slide. In this case, select the first slide of each of the two custom shows you've created: slides 13 and 14. (Click **Ctrl** and select them in turn.)

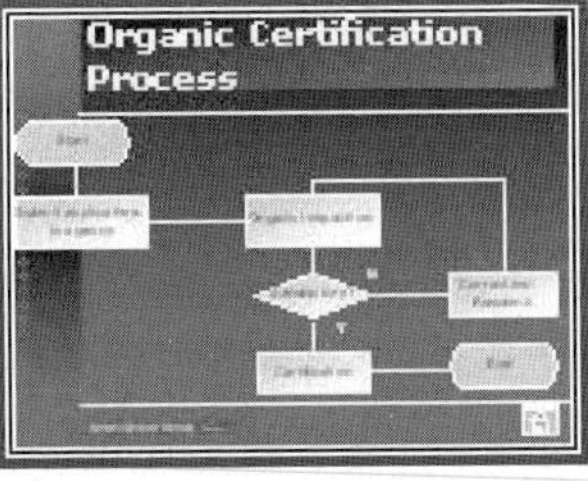

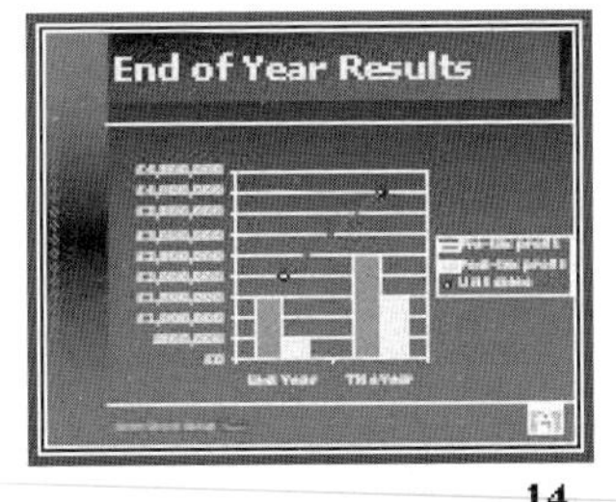

13 14

Summary Slide button

4) Click the **Summary Slide** button on the *Slide Sorter* toolbar.

   A new slide appears as number 13, 'Summary Slide'.

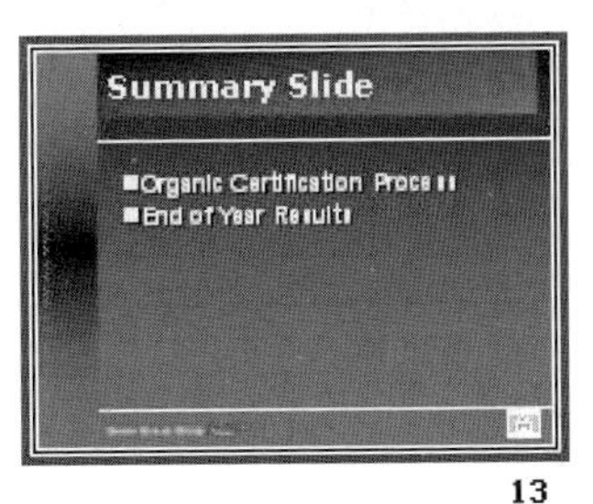

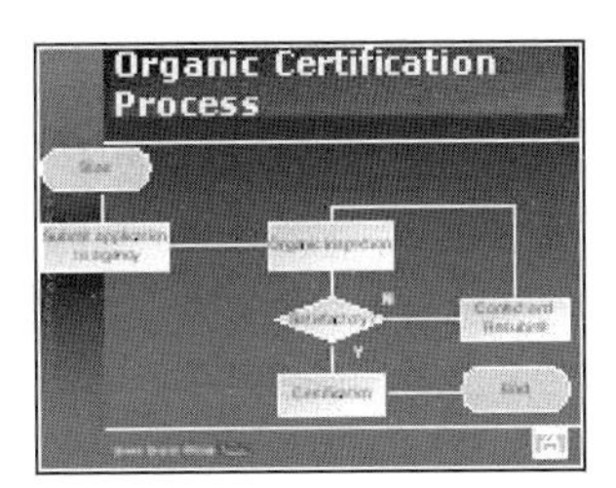

13 14

Notice that it contains the title of the first slide in each of your custom shows – 'Organic Certification Process' and 'End of Year Results'.

5) Let's change the position of the summary slide. Drag the summary slide from slide 13 to the position of slide 3.

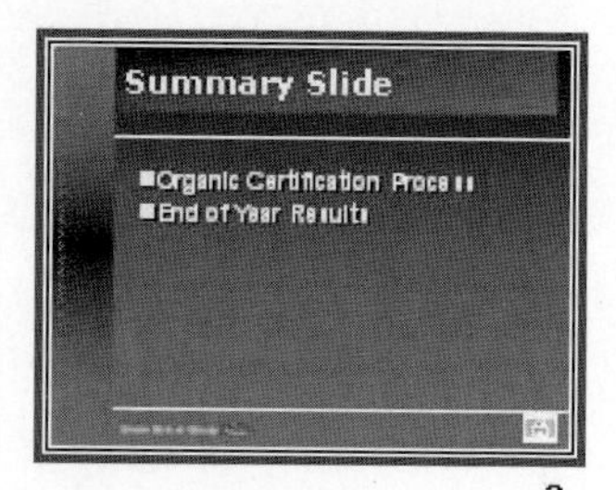

6) Edit your summary slide by double-clicking it:

- Change the title of the slide to the following:

  `Overview`

- Type the following text before the first bullet point:

  `In this presentation we will focus on:`

- Add the text `(of interest to growers)` to 'Organic Certification Process'

- Add the text `(of interest to financiers)` to 'End of Year Results'

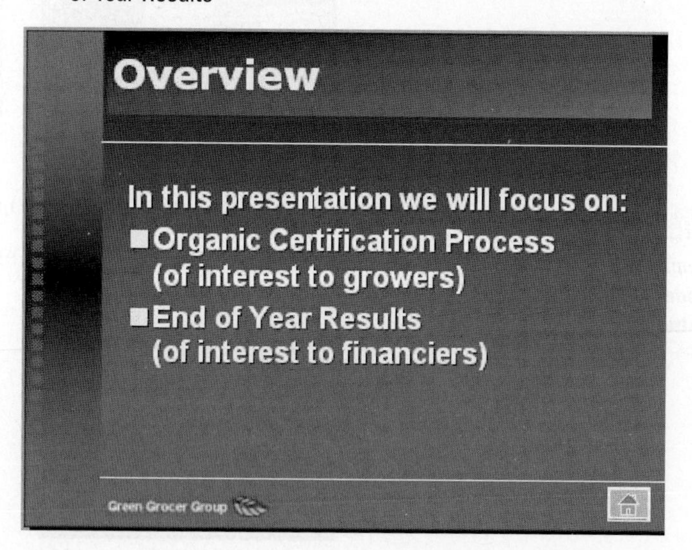

Activating your summary slide

Your summary slide contains your custom show names. Now you must activate them, so that you can navigate to the custom shows from the summary slide. You do this by assigning a hyperlink to each of the titles on the summary slide. The following exercise will show you how to do this.

Exercise 7.4: Accessing custom shows from the summary slide

1) Open EX7.4.PPT. Go to slide 3, 'Overview'.
2) Select the second bullet point 'End of Year Results'.

Insert Hyperlink button

3) Click the **Insert Hyperlink** button.
4) In the *Insert Hyperlink* dialog box, click the **Place in This Document** button.

5) In the *Select a place in this document* box, select the 'Financial Growth' custom show.
6) Select the *Show and return* check box. Click **OK**.

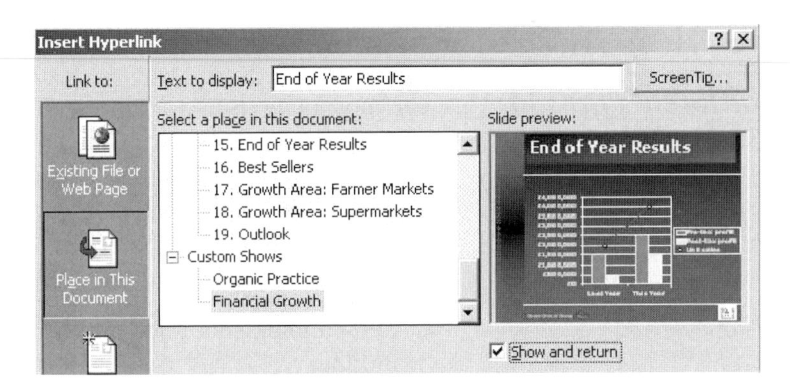

7) Repeat steps 2–6 to link the Organic Certification Process title to the Organic Practice custom show.

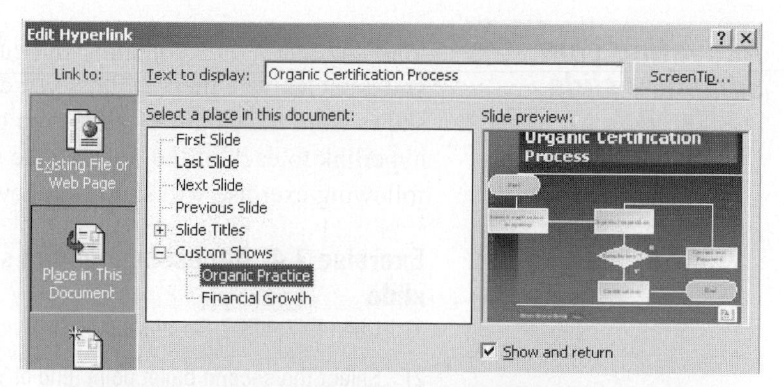

Your summary slide should now look as shown.

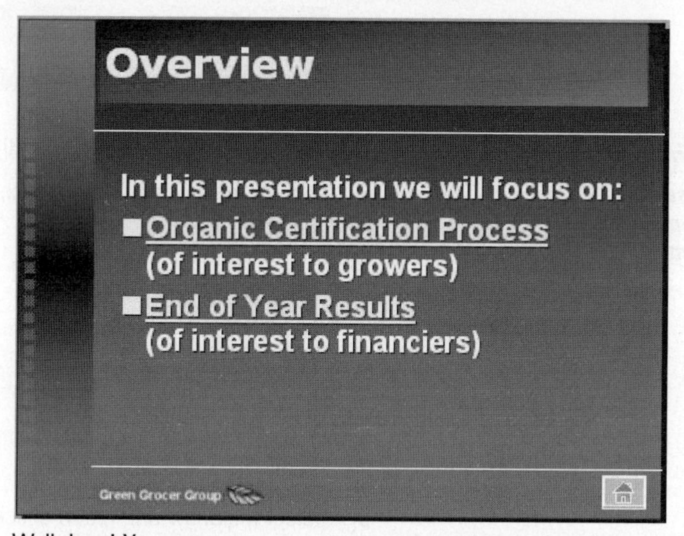

Well done! You can now access your custom shows directly from the summary slide.

Different types of slide shows

The most obvious use of a presentation is as a slide show supporting a presenter with an audience in a conference room. This requires that the audience be in the same place at the same time as the presenter, who controls the delivery of the presentation. However, there are other ways of using PowerPoint presentations. For example:

- Self-running slide show for website use – such as a company intranet.
- Self-running slide show for use in a kiosk – such as in a trade show.
- Slide show with limited viewer control – such as sharing on a computer network.

To choose one of these options, you first save your presentation as a slide show. (A slide show has the ending .PPS, but unlike a presentation PPT file, a PPS file will automatically open in Slide Show view.)

Exercise 7.5: Save a presentation as a slide show

1) Open EX7.5.PPT.
2) Choose **File | Save As**.
3) Ensure the following appears in the *File name* box:

   EX7.5
4) Click the arrow to the right of the *Save as type* box and select *PowerPoint Show (*.pps)*.

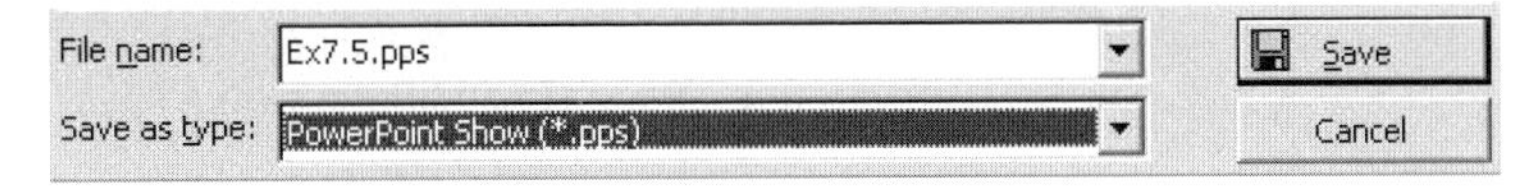

Click the **Save** button.

You now have a slide show called EX7.5.PPS.

Setting up slide shows

You can create different slide show setups by using the **Set Up Show** command. For example, in the following exercise you will set up a self-running slide show to run on the company network. You will not be present at the slide show, but the viewer will work through the slides by herself.

Exercise 7.6: Set up a self-running slide show

1) Open EX7.6.PPT.
2) Choose **Slide Show | Set Up Show**. The *Set Up Show* dialog box appears.
3) Under *Show type* select:
   - *Browsed by an individual (window).*
   - *Loop continuously until 'Esc'.*
   - *Show scrollbar.*
4) Under *Slides*, select *All*.
5) Under *Advance slides*, select *Manually*.
6) Click **OK**.

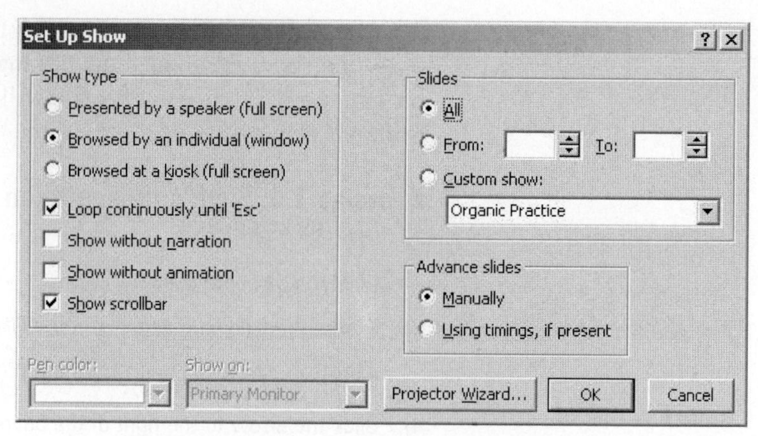

7) Press **F5** to see how your slide show will appear to the viewer. The viewer can navigate through the slides in different ways:

- **Page Up** and **Page Down** keys.
- **Forward** and **Back** buttons on the *Web* toolbar.
- Choosing **Browse | Advance** or **Reverse** on the menu bar.

Chapter 7: summary

PowerPoint enables us to produce *custom shows*. A *custom show* is like a presentation within a presentation; you specify different paths through the presentation slides and each path contains a different subset of the slides.

A summary slide is like the table of contents of your presentation, and you can use it to place hyperlinks to custom shows.

You can *set up* your slide show in different ways. For example, you can set up a self-running presentation that can be viewed at a kiosk in a trade show, or set up a slide show that can be viewed over your company network.

Chapter 7: quick quiz

Circle the correct answer to each of the following questions about shows.

Q1	To view a custom show you ...
A.	Choose **Slide Show | View Show**. Select the custom show that you want to view and click **Show**.
B.	Choose **Slide Show | Custom Shows**. Select the custom show that you want to view and click **Edit**.
C.	Choose **Slide Show | Custom Shows**. Select the custom show that you want to view and click **Show**.
D.	Choose **Slide Show | Set Up Show**. Select the custom show that you want to view and click **OK**.

Q2	A self-running slide show ends in ...
A.	.PPA.
B.	.POT.
C.	.PPT.
D.	.PPS.

Q3	In which view do you create a summary slide?
A.	Normal view
B.	Slide Sorter view.
C.	Outline view.
D.	Slides view.

Q4	To set up a slide show to run continuously you ...
A.	Choose **View | Slide Sorter**. Click the **Summary Slide** button and select the option *Loop Continuously until 'Esc'*. Click **OK**.
B.	Choose **Slide Show | Set Up Show**. Click **OK**.
C.	Choose **Slide Show | View Show**. Select the option *Loop Continuously until 'Esc'*. Click **OK**.
D.	Choose **Slide Show | Set Up Show**. Select the option *Loop Continuously until 'Esc'*. Click **OK**.

Answers

1: C, **2:** D, **3:** B, **4:** D.

Transitions

In this chapter

In this chapter you will learn about transitions, and about the different ways of timing and advancing the slides in your presentation. Transitions add visual interest to your slide. You can advance slides manually or automatically. If your presentation is well scripted and rehearsed, or it is running independently, in a kiosk for example, you are likely to choose automatic advance; if you expect interaction with your audience, you are likely to choose manual advance.

If you choose automatic advance, PowerPoint enables you to fine-tune your timings while rehearsing your presentation.

New skills

At the end of this chapter you should be able to:

- Apply transition effects
- Apply transition timings
- Apply manual advance to slides
- Apply automatic advance to slides
- Rehearse and adjust automatic advance timings
- Switch between automatic and manual advance

New words

At the end of this chapter you should be able to explain the following terms:

- Transitions
- Slide advancing
- Rehearse timings

Syllabus reference

This chapter covers the following syllabus points:

- AM 6.6.1.3
- AM 6.6.1.5

Transition effects

A transition is the way in which a slide first appears in a slide show. A slide can 'dissolve' into another slide, for example, or 'wipe' across the screen – PowerPoint offers 42 different transition effects. These special effects help to keep your audience interested.

In this chapter you will apply transition effects to your presentation and vary the speed of the transitions. One word of warning, however: transitions should not take away from the content of your presentation. If you use too many different transition effects, your audience will be distracted. Therefore, don't use more than two or three: consistently using a small number of transition effects will add strength to your presentation.

Transition

A transition is the way in which a slide first appears in a PowerPoint slide show.

Choosing transitions

Think about your choice of transitions carefully. A good way to familiarize yourself with the transitions available is to apply the *Random Transition* effect to your presentation. In Slide Show view you can then see the different transitions at work and you can pick the ones that you want. Note that *Random Transition* uses all the available transition effects and is not suitable for presenting to an audience.

Exercise 8.1: Applying the random transition effect

1) Open EX8.1.PPT.
2) Choose **Slide Show | Slide Transition**.
3) Click the arrow to the right of the *Effect* box, and select the *Random Transition* effect.
4) Select a transition speed of *Fast*.

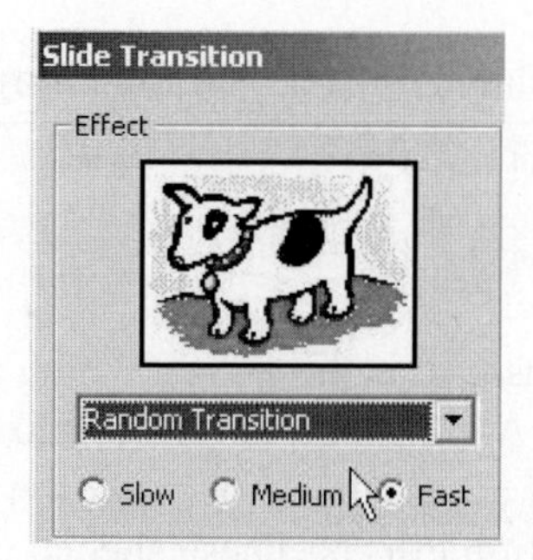

5) Select the *On mouse click* check box to advance the transitions manually.

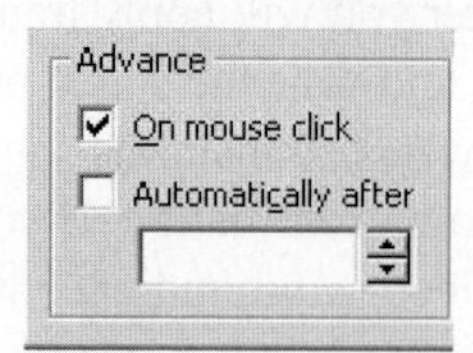

6) Click the **Apply to All** button to apply the *Random Transition* effect to all the slides in the presentation.

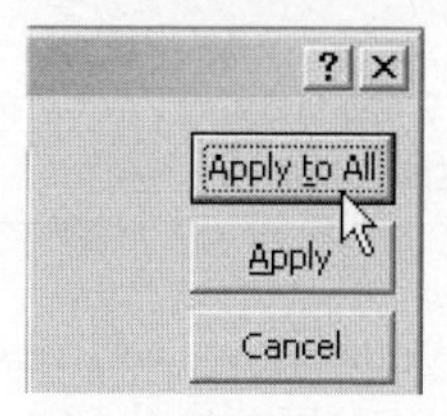

You've now applied the *Random Transition* effect to your presentation. Press **F5** to see how the various transition effects look during a presentation. When you've finished viewing, you can then choose the transition effects that are most suitable.

Applying transitions

In the previous exercise, you saw the range of available transition effects. The ones that you will use in these exercises are:

- *Box Out*
- *Dissolve*
- *Wipe Down*

Use the *Box Out* option for the majority of the slides in the slide show and keep the *Dissolve* and *Wipe Down* options for emphasizing special points.

Exercise 8.2: Applying selected transition effects

1) Open EX8.2.PPT.

2) Choose **Slide Show | Slide Transition**.

3) Click the arrow to the right of the *Effect* box and select the *Box Out* effect.

4) Select a transition speed of *Medium*.

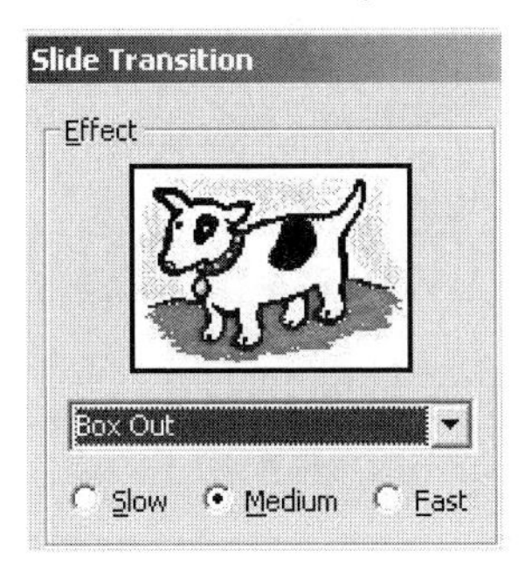

5) Select the *On mouse click* check box to advance the transitions manually.

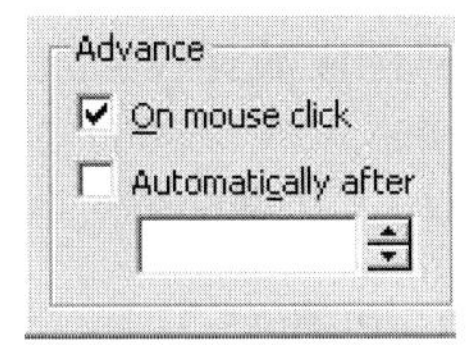

6) Click the **Apply to All** button to apply the *Box Out* effect to all the slides in the presentation.

7) In the Outline pane, select slide 15, 'End of Year Results', and slide 16, 'Best Sellers'.

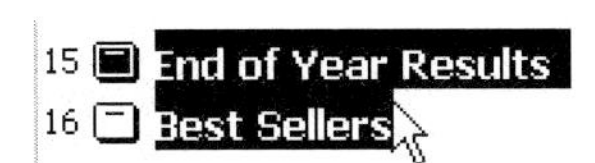

8) Choose **Slide Show | Slide Transition**. Click the arrow to the right of the *Effect* box and select the *Dissolve* effect.

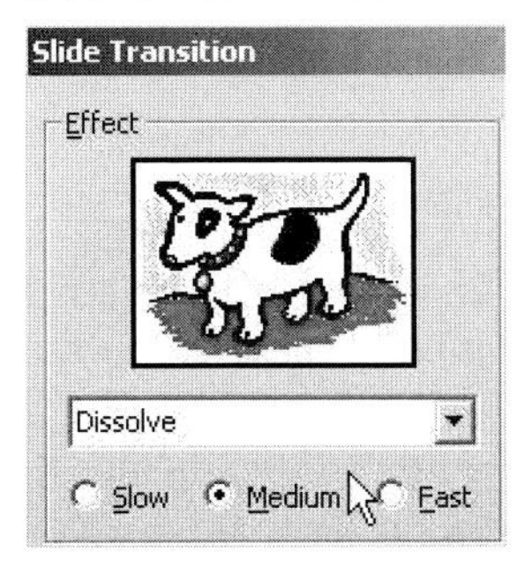

9) Click the **Apply** button.

10) In the Outline pane, select slide 1, 'Green Grocer Group'.

1 Green Grocer Group

11) Choose **Slide Show | Slide Transition**. Click the arrow to the right of the *Effect* box and select the *Wipe Down* option.

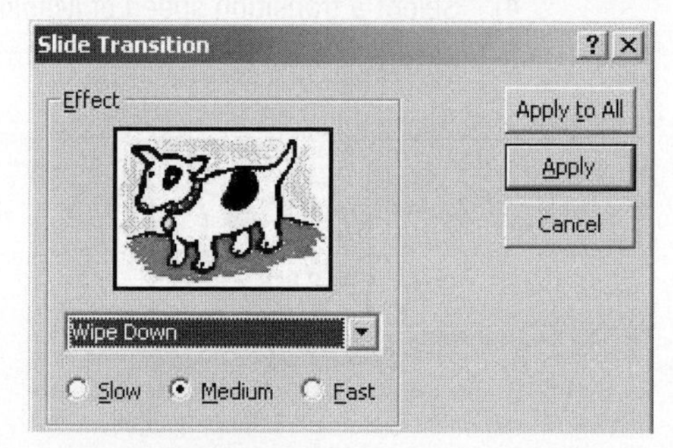

12) Click the **Apply** button.

Congratulations! You've applied the *Box Out* transition effect to the majority of the slides in the presentation. And, for greater emphasis, you've added the *Dissolve* effect to two slides in the presentation, and the *Wipe Down* effect to the title slide. Look at your presentation in Slide Show view and view your progress.

Transition timings

Transition effects can be run at three different speeds: fast, medium and slow.

In the next exercise you will edit the timings of your transitions.

Exercise 8.3: Editing transition timings

1) Open EX8.3.PPT.

2) Go to slide 2, 'Presenter'.

3) Choose **Slide Show | Slide Transition**.

4) In the *Slide Transition* dialog box, select a transition speed of *Slow*.

5) Click the **Apply** button.

6) View your presentation in Slide Show view. Note the difference between the transition to the second slide and the following transitions.

Advancing slides

How do you want to advance the slides in your slide show? Would you prefer to do this manually or automatically? Before you make a decision, let's see what's involved.

Manual advance

If your presentation entails a lot of audience participation, you must choose manual advance, as you can't predict the length of time you will spend on each slide.

You advance slides by clicking the mouse or by using any of the following short-cut keys:

■ Next slide	**Page Down** button
■ Previous slide	**Page Up** button
■ First slide	**Home** button
■ Last slide	**End** button

A disadvantage of using manual advance is that you might block the view of your audience when you lean over to click the mouse or use the short-cut keys. You could solve this problem by using a wireless mouse – this would enable you to walk around the room while advancing the slides.

Automatic advance

If you can predict the length of time you will spend on each slide or if the slide show will run unattended, you will choose automatic advance. However, some people are uncomfortable with automatic advance settings, as they feel restricted by them. If this is the case, you can remove the automatic advance settings and revert to manual advance.

Exercise 8.4: Setting up automatic advance

1) Open EX8.4.PPT.
2) Choose **Slide Show | Slide Transition**.
3) Under *Advance*, select the *Automatically after* check box.

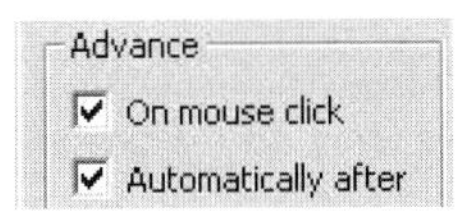

4) Input an advance time of 15 seconds.

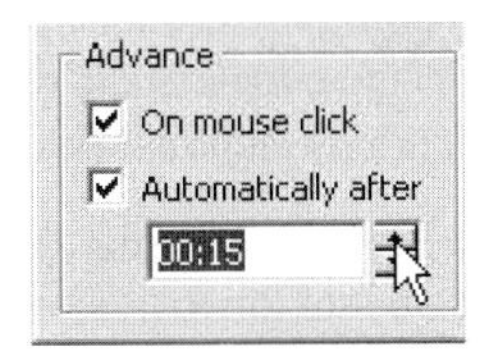

5) Click the **Apply to All** button to apply the changes to all the slides in the presentation.

Press **F5** to view the automatic advance timing.

Note: If both the *On mouse click* and *Automatically after* check boxes are selected, the next slide will appear *either* when the mouse is clicked *or* after the advance time specified, depending on which comes first.

Rehearse timings

Every presentation benefits from rehearsal. Rehearsal is especially necessary if you have set up automatic timings for your slides. You can rehearse timings with the *Rehearse Timings* feature, which enables you to test the automatic timings you have allotted to your slides. You might find that some slides require less or more time than you have allowed.

Let's explore the *Rehearse Timings* feature and see if some of the slides in the presentation could benefit from a timing change.

Rehearse Timings

If you choose automatic advance, Rehearse Timings enables you to run through your slide show in real time to check that the timings fit your presentation, and to fine-tune them, if necessary.

Exercise 8.5: Using the rehearse timings option

1) Open EX8.5.PPT.

2) Choose **View | Slide Sorter**.

Rehearse Timings button

3) Click the **Rehearse Timings** button on the *Slide Sorter* toolbar.

PowerPoint launches into Slide Show view with the *Rehearsal* dialog box in the top left corner of the slide.

4) Deliver your presentation as if you were in front of your audience, but advancing from slide to slide using one of the manual methods. (If this is a self-running presentation, check that the viewer will have enough time to absorb the information on each slide.)

5) When you have finished your delivery, click the **Close** button in the top-right corner of the *Rehearsal* dialog box.

6) While you were rehearsing, PowerPoint recorded the time that you spent on each slide. It now asks if you want to keep the new timing: press **Yes**. The timing allocated to each slide now matches your actual delivery speed precisely.

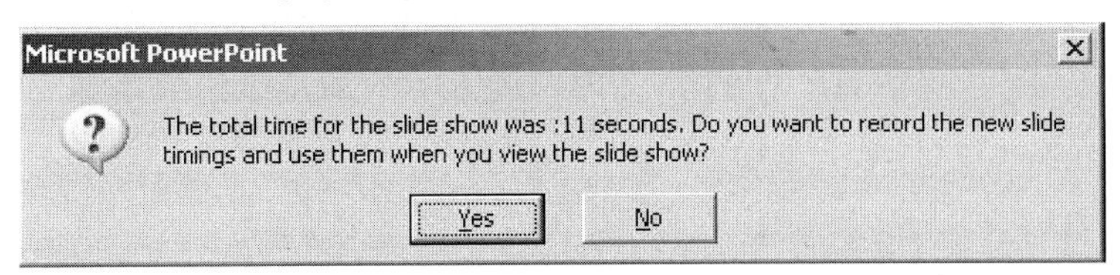

Removing the automatic advance timings

You can easily remove the automatic advance timings and revert to manual advance. You will see this in the following exercise.

Exercise 8.6: Remove automatic advance timing

1) Open EX8.6.PPT.
2) Go to slide 1, 'Green Grocer Group'.
3) Choose **Slide Show | Slide Transition.**
4) In the *Advance* section of the *Slide Transition* dialog box deselect the *Automatically after* check box.

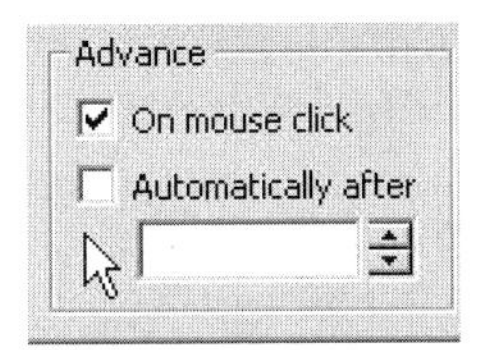

Leave the *On mouse click* check box selected.

5) Click the **Apply** button.
6) Press **F5** to view your presentation in Slide Show view.

Chapter 8: summary

A *transition* is the way in which a slide first appears in a slide show. Slide transitions are useful as they help to keep your audience interested. PowerPoint offers a wide range of transition effects, such as *Box Out* and *Dissolve.*

Advancing from one slide to the next can be done either *manually* or *automatically*. If you use automatic advance, you need to decide on the length of time each slide is displayed. PowerPoint refers to this as slide *timings*.

You can *rehearse* and *adjust* your slide timings with the *Rehearse Timings* option. If you want, you can remove the automatic timings and revert to manual advance.

Chapter 8: quick quiz

Circle the correct answer to each of the following questions about transitions.

Q1	Find the example of a transition effect from the list below.
A.	Disappear.
B.	Charcoal.
C.	Wipers.
D.	Box out.

Q2	For manual advance, which shortcut key do you use to go to the previous slide in a presentation?
A.	**Page Up**.
B.	**Page Down**.
C.	**Ctrl**.
D.	**Space bar**.

Q3	How do you rehearse the timings of your slide show?
A.	Choose **View | Normal**. Click the **Rehearse Timings** button and deliver your presentation as if you were in front of the audience. Advance the slides manually.
B.	Choose **Slide Show | Set Up Show**. Click the **Rehearse Timings** button and deliver your presentation as if you were in front of the audience. Advance the slides automatically.
C.	Choose **View | Slide Sorter**. Click the **Rehearse Timings** button and deliver your presentation as if you were in front of the audience. Advance the slides manually.
D.	Choose **Slide Show | Slide Transition**. Click the **Rehearse Timings** button and deliver your presentation as if you were in front of the audience. Advance the slides automatically.

Q4	How do you remove automatic advance timings for all slides?
A.	Choose **Slide Show | Slide Transition**. Deselect the *Automatically after* check box and select **Apply to All**.
B.	Choose **Slide Show | Slide Transition**. Deselect the *Automatically after* check box and select **Apply**.
C.	Choose **View | Slide Sorter**. Click the **Rehearse Timings** button and press **Close**.
D.	Choose **View | Master | Slide Master**. Click the **Slide Transition** button and deselect the *Automatically after* check box and select **Apply to All**.

Q5	True or false – a PowerPoint slide show will not work if you select both the manual advance and the automatic advance options.
A.	True.
B.	False.

Answers

1: D, **2:** B, **3:** C, **4:** A, **5:** B.

9 Animation effects

In this chapter

You can apply animation to each element in a slide (text, graphics, drawn objects). When you do, the elements will appear in a sequence and in a manner that you specify.

In this chapter you will explore animations in depth. You will edit existing animations and apply animation techniques to text and charts. You'll take your animation skills further by working with multimedia tools, such as audio effects and movies. Let your own creativity take over!

New skills

At the end of this chapter you should be able to:

- Change the order in which elements appear on a slide
- Edit animation timings
- Add animation to text
- Add animation to charts
- Insert audio effects
- Insert movies
- Identify audio and movie file types

New words

At the end of this chapter you should be able to explain the following terms:

- Animation order sequence
- Dimming

Syllabus reference

This chapter covers the following syllabus points:

- AM 6.5.1.1
- AM 6.5.1.2
- AM 6.5.2.1
- AM 6.5.2.2
- AM 6.5.2.3
- AM 6.5.2.4

Editing your animations

Animations are very flexible. You can change the following:

- The sequence in which the elements appear.
- The manner in which each element appears.
- The advance method used to reveal each element.

Exercise 9.1: Editing order and timings of an animation

1) Open EX9.1.PPT.
2) Go to slide number 10, 'Our Fruit and Vegetables'.
3) Choose **Slide Show | Custom Animation.**

   Note that the following check boxes have been selected in the *Check to animate slide objects* section:

   - Picture frame 4
   - Picture frame 5
   - Picture frame 6

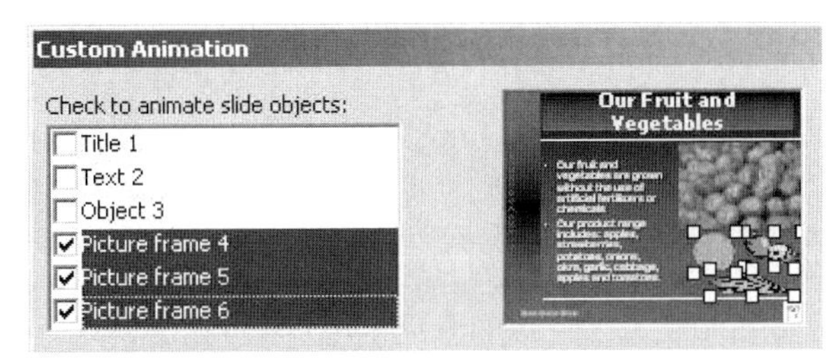

4) Click the **Preview** button to see the order in which the animated elements appear.
5) Select the **Order & Timing** tab of the *Custom Animation* dialog box.
6) Select *Picture frame 6* in the *Animation order* box, and click the **Move Up** button to send it to the middle of the animation sequence.

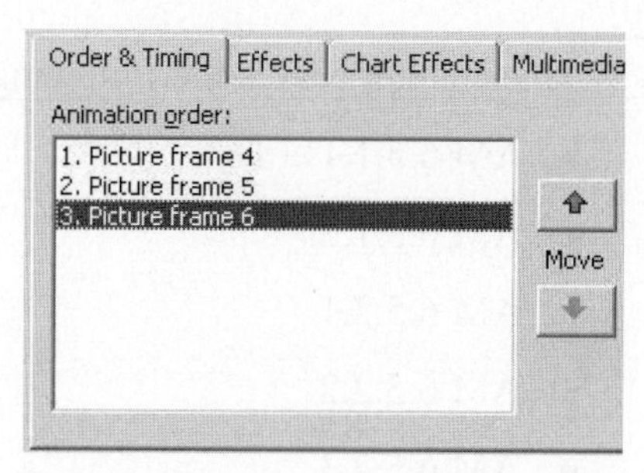

The animation sequence should now look as shown.

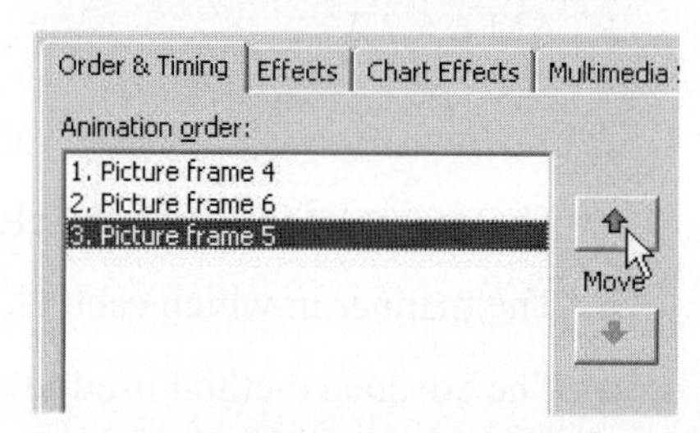

7) In the *Start animation* section, select *On mouse click*. Each element will now appear in sequence when you click the mouse. (If you want elements to appear with automatic timing, select *Automatically* and input a number of seconds in the *Automatically* box.)

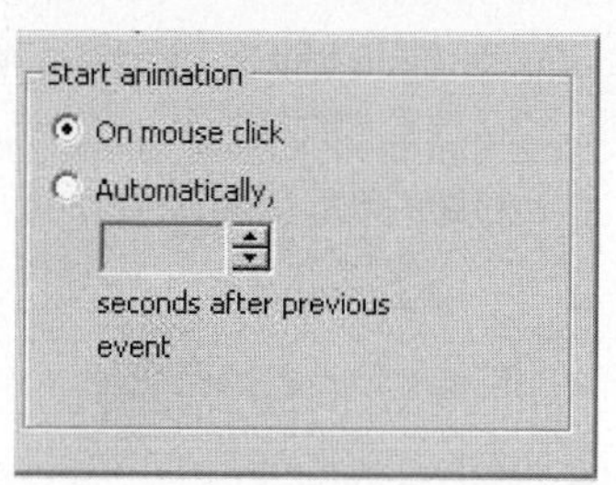

8) Click the **Preview** button to see the effect of your changes. If you are happy with your changes, press **OK**.

   In Slide Show view, you can verify that clicking the mouse causes each element to appear in the sequence you specified.

Animation effects

You might think that the word animation refers to moving graphics only. In fact, you can in addition animate other elements, such as text and drawn objects. In addition PowerPoint animations can be used to add sound effects and dynamic changes of colour to elements on a slide.

A particularly useful animation effect is dimming, in which a piece of text or another slide element changes colour, or even disappears from the slide once it has been seen, or the next element is displayed.

Dimming

Dimming is an animation effect that causes a slide element to change colour (typically to a lighter shade) or to disappear when the next element is introduced.

Try the following exercise to see how effective text animation really is.

Exercise 9.2: Animating text

1) Open EX9.2.PPT.
2) Go to slide 12, 'Our Farmers'.
3) Choose **Slide Show | Custom Animation**.
4) In the *Check to animate slide objects* section, select the *Text 2* check box.

5) Select the **Effects** tab in the *Custom Animation* dialog box. Here you will add audio, movement and colour to your text.
6) Select the following options to add animation and audio effects.

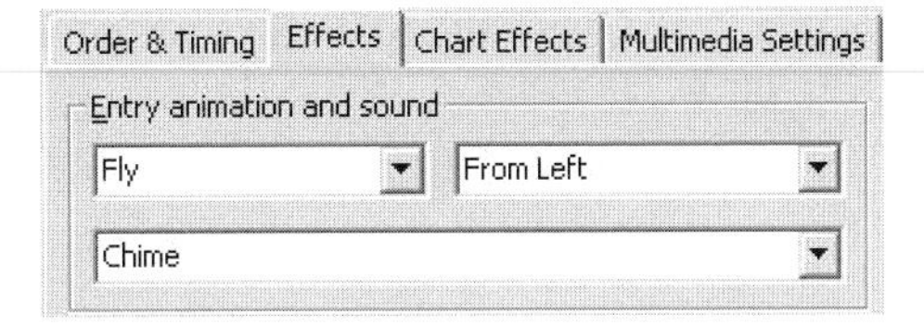

7) Select the following options to add motion.

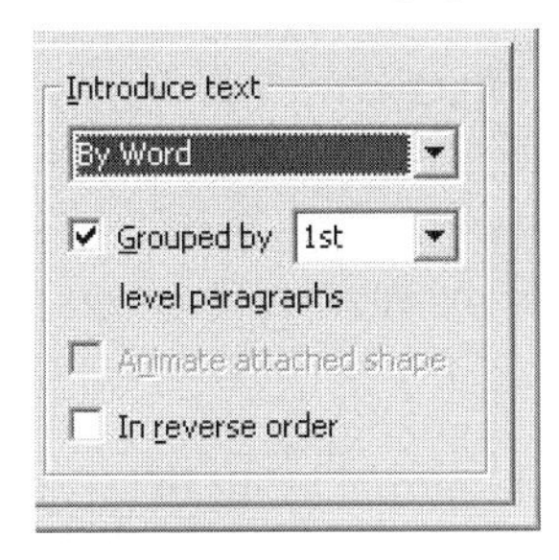

(If you want, try out each of the motion effects: *All at once*, *By Word* and *By Letter*. Press **Preview** to see which effect you prefer.)

8) Now apply the dimming effect. Click the arrow to the right of the *After animation* box and select *More Colors*. This is where you choose the colour that your text will change to when the next element appears in the slide.

9) Click the **Standard** tab of the *Colors* dialog box. Select the bright yellow colour shown in the diagram and click **OK**.

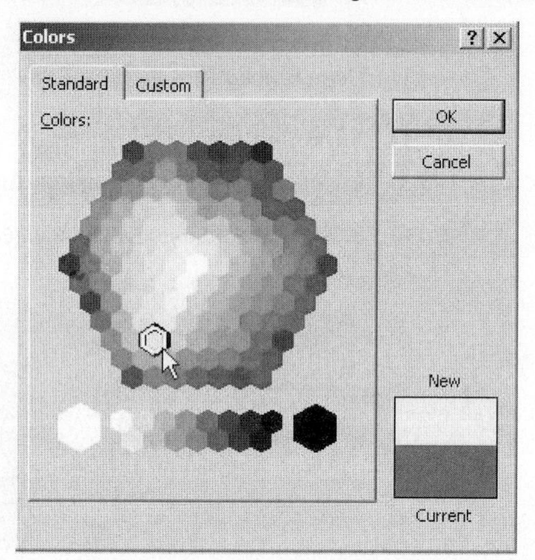

10) Click the **OK** button to close the *Custom Animation* dialog box.

11) View the slide in Slide Show view.

Exercise 9.3: Dimming drawn objects

1) Open EX9.2.PPT again, and go to slide 14, 'Organic Certification Process'.

2) View the slide in Slide Show view to see how animation has been applied to the groups of drawn objects in the slide.

3) Choose **Slide Show | Custom Animation**.

4) In the **Order and Timing** tab, select Group 8.

5) In the **Effects** tab, click the arrow to the right of the *After animation* box and select a light blue colour. Click **OK**.

6) View the slide again in Slide Show view. Notice that the group of objects you selected is dimmed when the next group is displayed.

Animating chart elements

PowerPoint enables you to animate charts, and thereby bring 'boring old numbers' to life. As with text and graphics, you can add motion, dynamic colour and audio effects to a chart. You can animate all the types of charts you saw in Chapter 5: pie charts, bar charts, line charts and so on.

Exercise 9.4: Animating chart elements

1) Open EX9.4.PPT. Go to slide 15, 'End of Year Results'.
2) Choose **Slide Show | Custom Animation**.
3) Select the *Chart 2* check box.

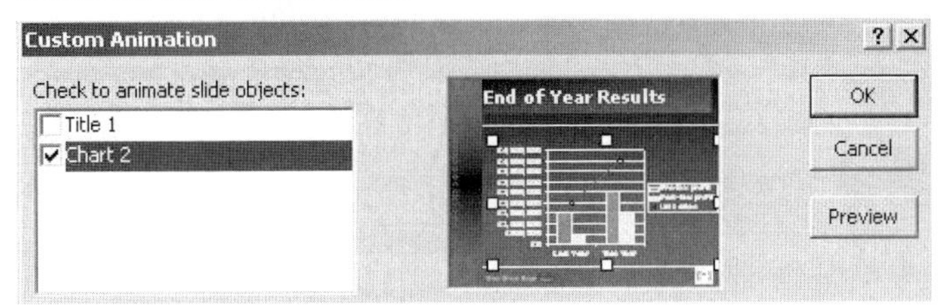

4) Select the **Chart Effects** tab.
5) Click the arrow to the right of the *Introduce chart elements* box. Select the *by Series* option and select the *Animate grid and legend* check box.

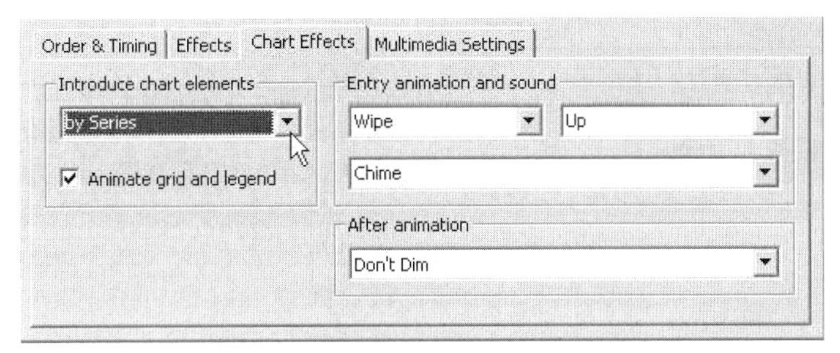

6) In the *Entry animation and sound* section, select the following:
   - *Wipe*
   - *Up*
   - *Chime*

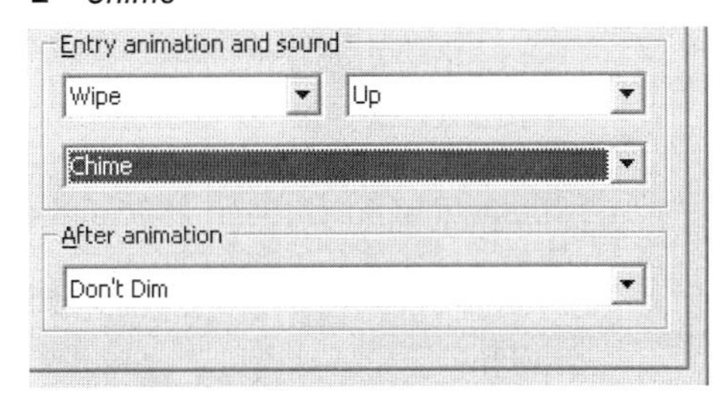

7) Click **OK**.
8) View your animated chart in Slide Show view. (Don't forget to turn on your speakers to hear the sound effects.)

In this exercise you animated the chart by series. However, depending on your chart type, you can choose other options in the *Introduce chart elements* box:

- *by Series* – this applies the animation effect in turn to each complete data series.
- *by Element in Series* – this applies the animation effect in turn to each data point in each data series.
- *by Category* – this applies the animation effect in turn to each complete grouping of data points on the Category axis.
- *by Element in Category* – this applies the animation effect in turn to each data point on the Category axis.

Try out the various options to see these animation effects at work. Note that some options are available only with certain chart types.

Audio effects

So far we have applied PowerPoint's pre-supplied audio effects, such as the *Chime* effect, to our animated slides. However, you can also use audio effects from other sources. You do this by:

- Inserting audio effects from PowerPoint's *Design Gallery Live.*

  -or-

- Recording your own audio effects.

  -or-

- Inserting audio effects from a CD.

Keep in mind that audio effects come in a range of file types, some of which are not compatible with PowerPoint 2000. The list below shows the type of audio files that are compatible with PowerPoint 2000.

Compatible PowerPoint 2000 audio file types	
AIFF, AIF, AIFC	Audio Interchange File Format
MPEG	Motion Pictures Expert Group
MP3	Layer 3 Motion Pictures
MIDI, MID, RMI	Musical Instrument Digital Interface
WAV	Microsoft Wave
ASF, ASX	Microsoft Streaming Format
CDA	CD Audio

Design Gallery Live contains a variety of items that you can include in your presentation to make it more interesting, including clip art (such as the vegetables used in Chapter 7), photographs, video clips and sound files. In the next exercise, you will use one of the sound files from the gallery. Note that you must have access to the Internet to do this!

Exercise 9.5: Inserting audio effects from *Design Gallery Live*

1) Open EX9.5.PPT.
2) Go to slide 1, 'Green Grocer Group'. Click anywhere in the slide.
3) Choose **Insert | Movies and Sounds | Sound from Gallery**.
4) In the *Insert Sound* dialog box, click the **Clips Online** button.

Clips Online button

Click **OK** to confirm that you have Web access and want to go to the *Design Gallery Live* website.

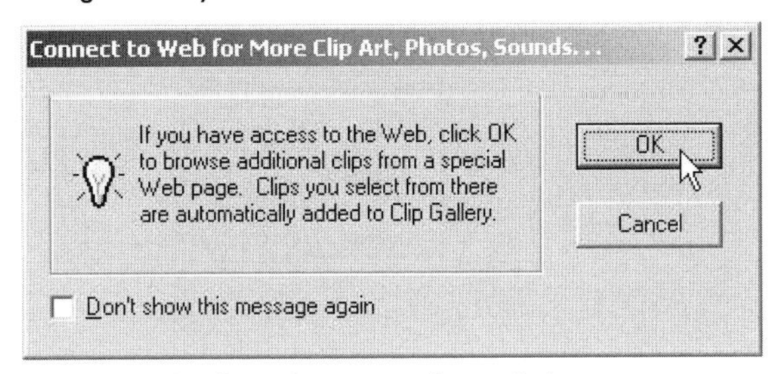

Connect to Web for More Clip Art, Photos, Sounds...
If you have access to the Web, click OK to browse additional clips from a special Web page. Clips you select from there are automatically added to Clip Gallery.
OK
Cancel
Don't show this message again

5) Complete the *Search* area as shown below.

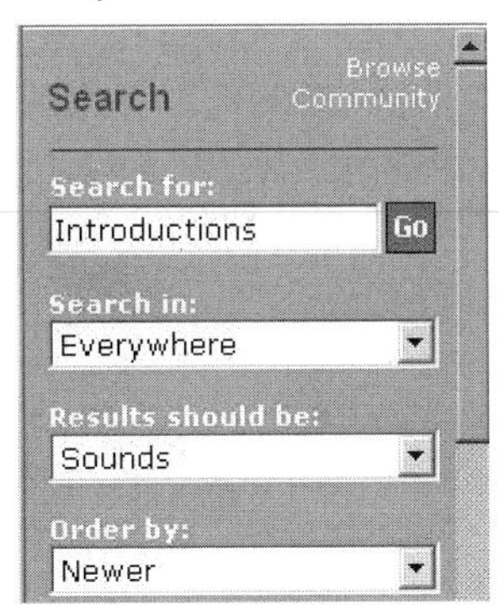

Click **Go**.

6) Download the *Pizzicato Open* audio clip by clicking the arrow box below its file name.

The *Pizzicato Open* audio clip is now in the *Microsoft Clip Gallery* on your own computer.

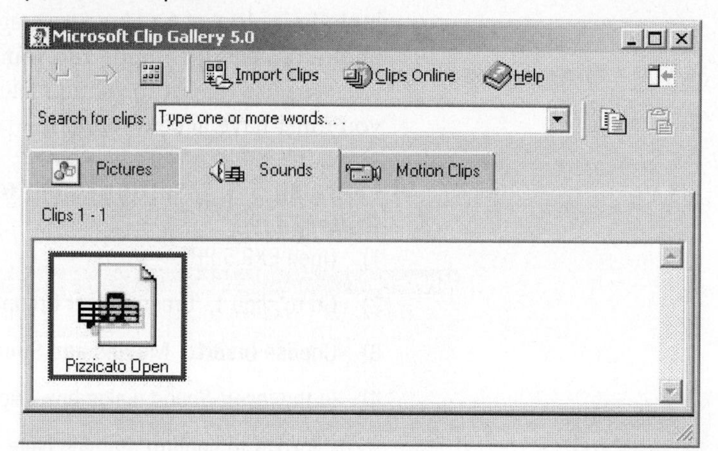

7) Select the audio clip in the *Microsoft Clip Gallery* and choose **Insert clip** from the menu list.

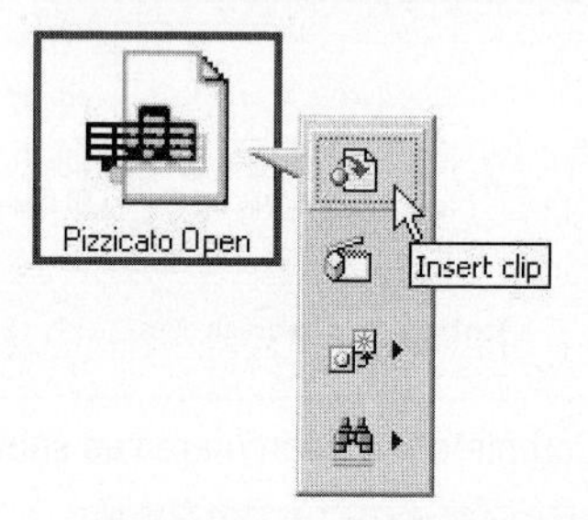

Close the *Insert Sound* dialog box.

PowerPoint asks you if you want the audio clip to play automatically. Click **Yes**.

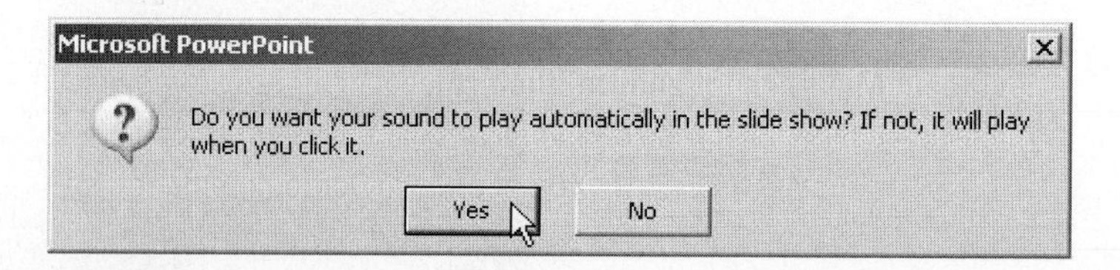

8) Drag the audio icon that appears on slide 1 down to the bottom-right of the screen.

Your audio effect will now play automatically whenever slide 1 is displayed in Slide Show view.

Other audio options

Apart from inserting audio effects from *Design Gallery Live*, you can insert audio effects from other sources, as follows:

- **Insert an audio effect from local sources**. Most programs, including Office, come with their own selection of audio effects. You usually save these programs to your local disk. To insert such audio effects, choose **Insert | Movies and Sounds | Sound from File**. Then navigate to the file you want to use in the *Insert Sound* dialog box.

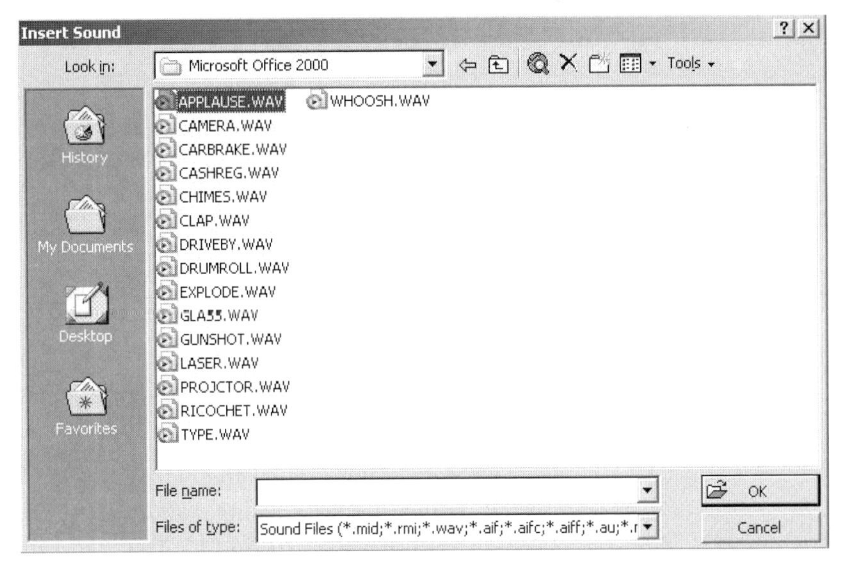

- **Insert an audio effect from a CD**. To insert a CD audio track, choose **Insert | Movies and Sounds | Play CD Audio Track**. Then follow the instructions in the *Movie and Sound Options* dialog box.

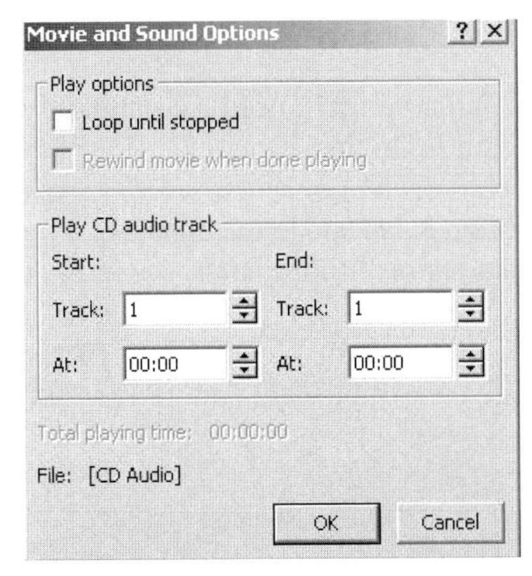

Inserting audio effects from a CD can be a good idea, particularly if you have a song that fits in with the message of your presentation. However, remember that, if the material is copyright, you should first ask permission.

- **Record a voice narration (for all slides)**. To record a voice narration, choose **Slide Show | Record Narration**. Then follow the instructions in the *Record Narration* dialog box.

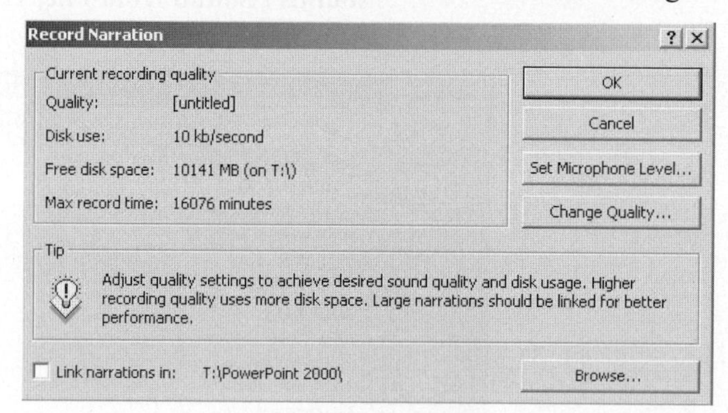

Recording your own audio is especially suitable for Web-based presentations or other self-running slide shows. You will need a computer with a microphone and sound card in order to record.

- **Recording audio effects (for single slides)**. To record an audio effect for a single slide, choose **Insert | Movies and Sounds | Record Sound**. You then follow the instructions in the *Record Sound* dialog box.

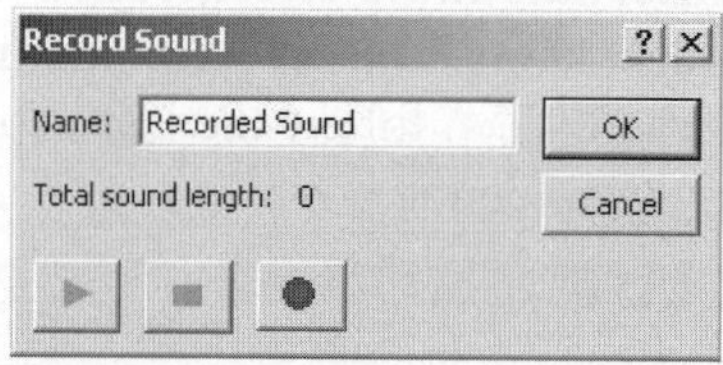

Again, you will need a computer with a microphone and sound card to do this.

Inserting movies

Movies can add to the impact of a presentation. But, as with any animation or illustration, you must ensure that your movie supports your information – a movie that distracts the audience is worse than no movie at all. As with audio files, only certain movie file types are compatible with PowerPoint 2000, as shown opposite.

PowerPoint 2000 compatible movie file types	
AVI	Audio Video Interleave
WMV	Windows Media Video
MPEG	Motion Picture Experts Group
QUICKTIME	Apple QuickTime
SWF	Macromedia Shock Wave Flash
ASF/ASX	Microsoft Streaming Format
GIF	Graphic Interchange Format

In the next exercise, we will insert a movie that is in .WMV format.

Exercise 9.6: Inserting movies

1) Open EX9.6.PPT.
2) Go to slide 9, 'What Makes Green Grocer Group'. There's a lot of information on this slide, so you'll need to add a new slide to share it.

   Select bullet points 1 and 2 and press **Ctrl+x** to cut them.

   9 What Makes Green Grocer Group?
   - We believe in environmentally-friendly farming practices
   - We believe our customers deserve the best organic fruit and vegetables

3) Click the **New Slide** button.
4) In the *New Slide* dialog box, select the *Text & Media Clip* slide layout and click **OK**.

   A blank slide 10 now appears.

5) Insert the following text in the title place holder:

   `Company Ethos`

6) Select the text place holder and press **Ctrl+v** to paste the text to the new slide. Your slide should look as shown.

7) Choose **Insert | Movies and Sounds | Movie from File**.

8) In the *Insert Movie* dialog box, navigate to where you have stored the movie file FIELD.WMV.

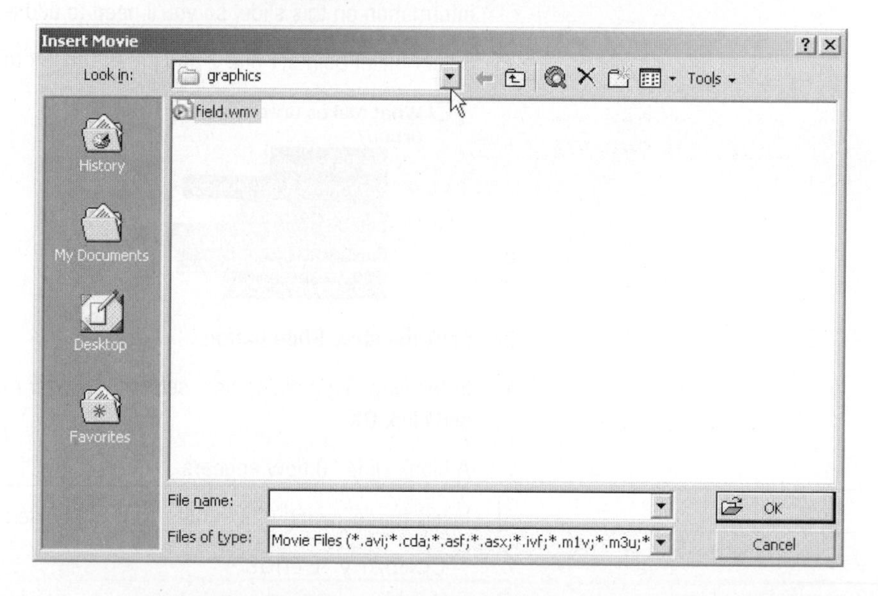

Select the WMV file and click **OK** to insert the movie in the presentation.

9) PowerPoint asks you if you want the movie to play automatically. Click **Yes**.

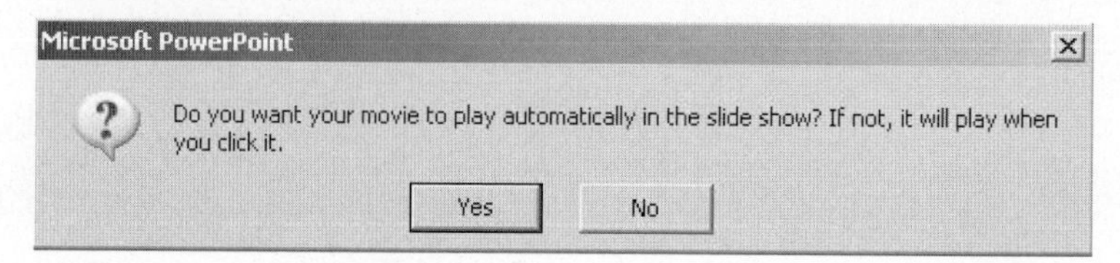

10) View the movie in Slide Show view. (In Normal view, it just appears as a static photograph.) Doesn't it look great!

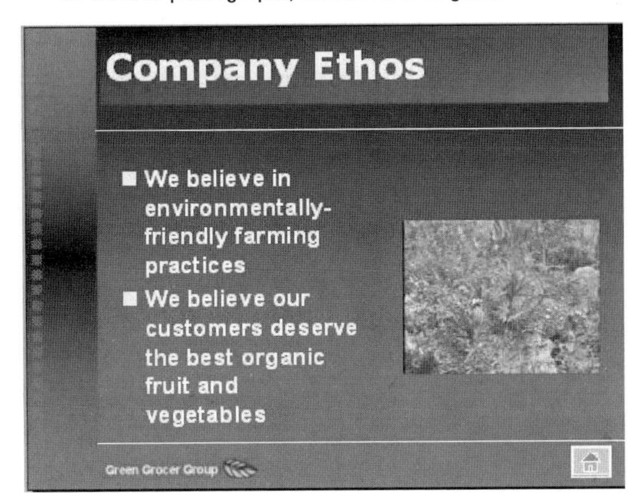

Note: In the *Custom Animation* dialog box, you can change the order in which the different slide elements appear. You can choose to play the movie before the text or play the movie after the text. The choice is yours!

Animated gif movies

Animated gifs work in the same way as cartoons: a series of graphic images are displayed in rapid succession in order to give the appearance of movement. They are commonly used in presentations and in websites. Animated gifs are sometimes referred to as 'movies'.

In the following exercise you will insert an animated gif from *Design Gallery Live*.

Exercise 9.7: Inserting animated gifs from *Design Gallery Live*

1) Open EX9.7.PPT. Go to the slide number 20, 'Outlook'.
2) Double-click the **Clip Art** icon.
3) In the *Microsoft Clip Gallery* dialog box, click the **Clips Online** button.

Clips Online button

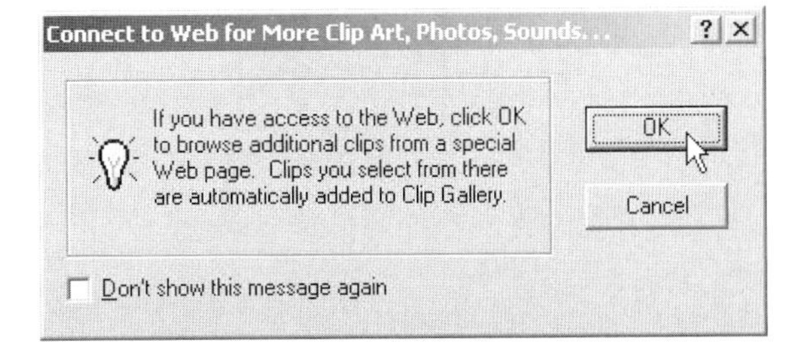

Click **OK** to confirm that you have Web access and want to go to the *Design Gallery Live* website.

4) Complete the *Search* area as shown below.

Click the **Go** button.

5) Download the animated gif shown below by clicking the arrow box underneath its file name.

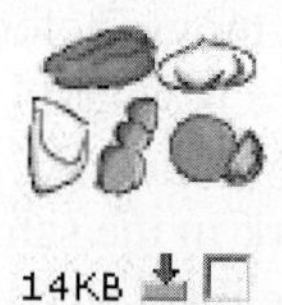

Select the **Click to Download** button.

The animated gif is now in the *Insert ClipArt* dialog box, contained within your own computer.

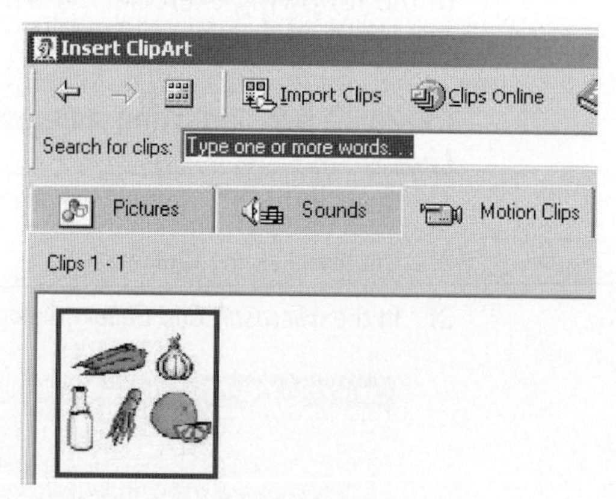

6) Select the animated gif and choose *Insert clip* from the menu list.

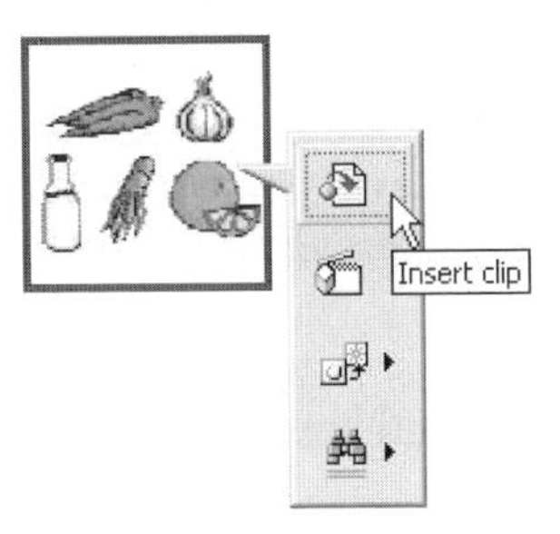

Close the *Insert ClipArt* dialog box. PowerPoint inserts the animated gif in slide number 20.

7) Move the gif to the Clip Art placeholder.

8) Your gif will not be animated in Normal view. Click the **Slide Show** button to see the animation at work.

Your slide should now look as shown.

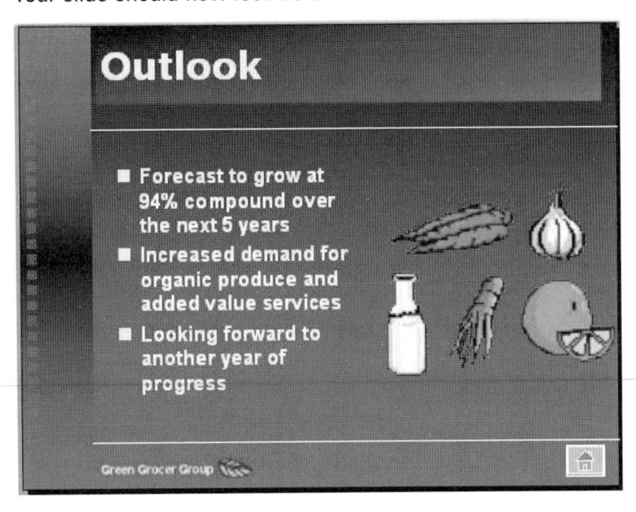

Chapter 9: summary

Animation effects specify how elements in a slide (text, graphics, drawn objects) behave, and the sequence in which they appear.

You can edit the *order* in which the animated elements appear and the *advance method* used, namely *mouse clicking* or *automatic timing*. PowerPoint's *dimming* effect can make your text (or drawn object) change colour, or even disappear from the slide when the next object appears.

You can also animate *charts* in PowerPoint so that series or groups of data points appear in different ways, and in different sequences.

Multimedia effects such as *audio* and *movies* add an extra dimension to your presentation. You can insert audio effects from *local* sources, from *Internet* sources such as the *Design Gallery Live*, from a *CD*, or from your *own recordings*. You can *make* your own movie for the presentation or download one (such as an *animated gif*) from *Design Gallery Live*.

Chapter 9: quick quiz

Circle the correct answer to each of the following questions about animation effects.

Q1	True or false – a WAV file is a movie file.
A.	True.
B.	False.

Q2	To dim bullet points to a specific colour you ...
A.	Choose **Slide Show | Custom Animation**. Select the text you want to animate. Under the **Order & Timings** tab, click the sound and motion animations you need. Click the arrow to the right of the *After animation* box and select *More Colors*. Select the colours you need and click **OK**.
B.	Choose **Slide Show | Custom Animation**. Select the text you want to animate. Under the **Multimedia Settings** tab, click the sound and motion animations you need. Click the arrow to the right of the *After animation* box and select *More Colors*. Select the colours you need and click **OK**.
C.	Choose **Slide Show | Custom Animation**. Select the text you want to animate. Under the **Effects** tab, click the sound and motion animations you need. Click the arrow to the right of the *After animation* box and select *More Colors*. Select the colours you need and click **OK**.
D.	Choose **Slide Show | Custom Animation**. Select the text you want to animate. Under the **Chart Effects** tab, click the sound and motion animations you need. Click the arrow to the right of the *After animation* box and select *More Colors*. Select the colours you need and click **OK**.

Q3	To insert an audio effect from *Design Gallery Live* you ...
A.	Choose **Insert | Movies and Sound | Sound from File**. Click the **Clips Online** button in the Insert Sound dialog box. Click **OK** to access the *Design Gallery Live* website.
B.	Choose **Insert | Movies and Sound | Sound from Gallery**. Click the **Import Clips** button in the *Insert Sound* dialog box. Click **OK** to access the *Design Gallery Live* website.
C.	Choose **Insert | Movies and Sound | Record Sound**. Click the **Clips Online** button in the *Insert Sound* dialog box. Click **OK** to access the *Design Gallery Live* website.
D.	Choose **Insert | Movies and Sound | Sound from Gallery**. Click the **Clips Online** button in the *Insert Sound* dialog box. Click **OK** to access the *Design Gallery Live* website.

Q4	To insert a movie from your local disk, you ...
A.	Choose **Insert | Movies and Sound | Clipart**.
B.	Choose **Insert | Movies and Sound | Movie from Gallery**.
C.	Choose **Insert | Movies and Sound | Record Movie**.
D.	Choose **Insert | Movies and Sound | Movie from File**.

Answers

1: B, **2:** C, **3:** D, **4:** D.

10 Graphic editing and graphic effects

In this chapter

A picture is worth a thousand words – and you will communicate your message much more effectively if you support your text with relevant graphics. You have already seen how to insert Clip Art images and charts into your presentation. In this chapter, we will look in more detail at graphic editing and graphic effects. Typically, editing a graphic involves changing its position or orientation on the slide, cropping it so that only a part of the original is seen, and making it bigger or smaller. Other effects are available: you can place a shadow behind an image; you can turn flat objects into 3-D; you can make an image semi-transparent, so that text can be read 'through' it. And, depending on the graphics software you have available to you, you can alter the image by blurring or sharpening it, bending or stretching it, and applying a wide range of special effects. You can also convert the image from colour to shades of grey or black-and-white, and change its colour depth and file format.

New skills

At the end of this chapter you should be able to:

- Edit a graphic
- Crop a graphic
- Flip, mirror and rotate a graphic
- Apply different effects to a graphic
- Convert graphics to different file formats

New words

At the end of this chapter you should be able to explain the following terms:

- Cropping
- Greyscaling

Syllabus reference

This chapter covers the following syllabus points:

- AM 6.3.1.1
- AM 6.3.2.1
- AM 6.3.2.2
- AM 6.3.2.3
- AM 6.3.2.5
- AM 6.3.3.1
- AM 6.3.3.2
- AM 6.3.3.3
- AM 6.3.3.4
- AM 6.3.3.5
- AM 6.3.3.6

Moving graphics

In Chapter 4, you repositioned graphics in two ways: by dragging the graphic with the mouse, and by using the *Format AutoShape* command to specify a precise position for the graphic, using co-ordinates.

Both methods can be applied to any PowerPoint object – placeholders, drawn objects, AutoShapes or pictures – on your slide. The most common method is the simpler one of dragging. You might want to use co-ordinates if you need to align objects precisely in a certain way, or if you wanted to use exactly the same placement of objects on different slides. To use the co-ordinate method, right-click on the object, choose **Format AutoShape** (or **Format Picture**, or **Format Placeholder**, or whatever), and click on the **Position** tab. You can then specify the distance that the object should be located from the edge or the centre of the slide.

Cropping graphics

If you want to eliminate parts of an imported picture from your slide, in order to focus your audience's attention on a specific part of it, you *crop* it. PowerPoint's cropping tool is on the *Picture* toolbar. If the *Picture* toolbar is not displayed, either choose **View | Toolbars | Picture**, or right-click on the picture and choose **Show Picture Toolbar** from the pop-up menu. (Note that you cannot crop AutoShapes or placeholders.)

Exercise 10.1: Cropping a picture

1) Open EX10.1.PPT, and go to slide number 14, 'Organic Farming Practices'.

Crop button

2) Select the graphic and then click the **Crop** button in the *Picture* toolbar. (If the *Picture* toolbar is not displayed, choose **View | Toolbars | Picture**.)

3) Move the mouse pointer over any of the eight sizing handles on the picture. Notice how the pointer changes shape.

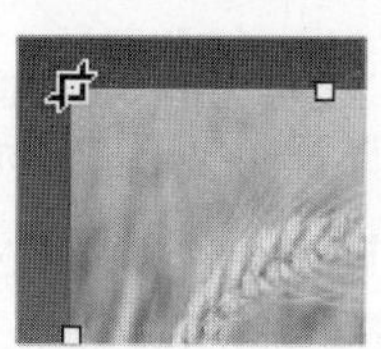

4) Drag the handle into the picture. As you drag, the cropped area is represented by a dotted line.

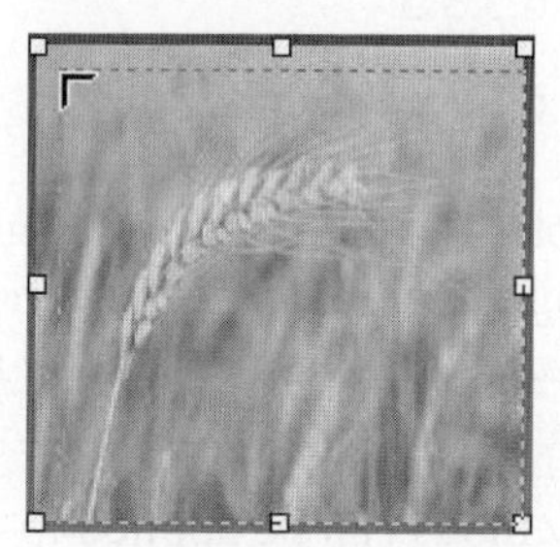

Release the mouse button when the part of the picture you want to eliminate is outside the dotted line.

5) Repeat this for each edge of the picture until you are left with a picture like that shown below.

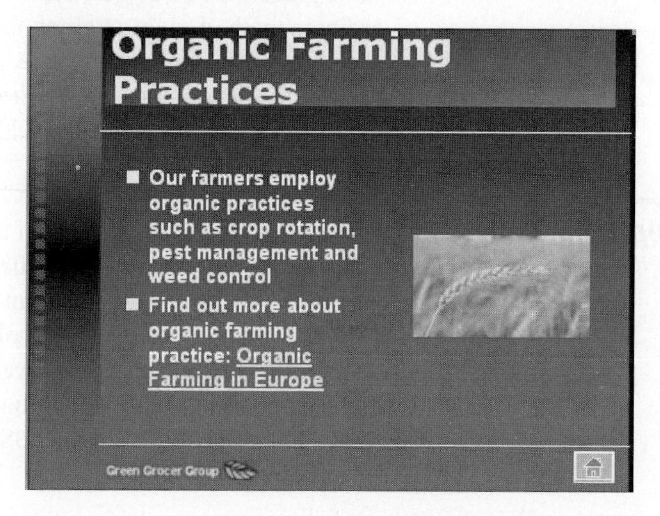

Resizing graphics

You can resize any graphic object (drawn object, AutoShape, imported Clip Art or picture) as described in Chapter 3, by clicking on it and dragging one of its sizing handles. Using the corner handles resizes the object proportionately (the object grows or shrinks without distorting). Using the handles in the middle of the sides grows or shrinks the object in one dimension only – the object is stretched or squashed.

Exercise 10.2: Enlarging a picture

1) Open EX10.2.PPT, and go to slide number 14, 'Organic Farming Practices'.
2) Select the picture that you cropped in Exercise 10.1.

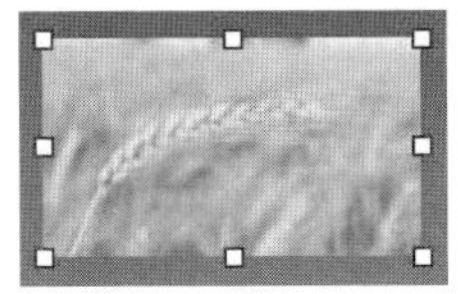

Notice how the sizing handles appear.

3) Drag one of the corner sizing handles to enlarge the picture so that it fills the space on the right of the slide, as shown below.

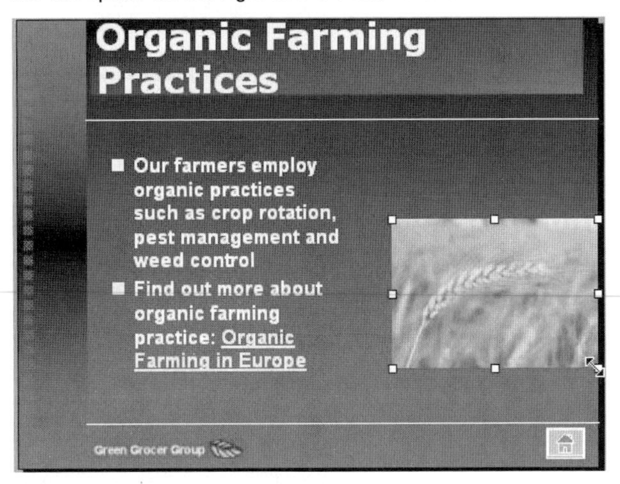

Well done! You've now successfully enlarged a graphic!

Flipping and rotating

The *Flip* and *Rotate* effects change the orientation of a graphic object on your slide.

- *Flip* (also known as *Mirror* in some graphics programs) creates a mirror image of the graphic. If you flip horizontally, you create a horizontal mirror image (in which the vertical axis remains constant): what was left is now right. If you flip vertically, you create a vertical mirror image: what was up is now down. Note that if you repeat the operation, you are back where you started.

- *Rotate* turns the graphic clockwise or anti-clockwise. PowerPoint offers you the option of rotating the graphic 90° either way, or of applying *Free Rotate*, in which you can rotate the object as much or as little as you like. Note that if you repeat the 90° rotation four times, you are back where you started.

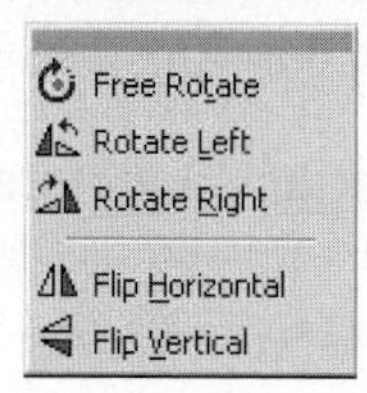

Try flipping and rotating in the following exercise.

Exercise 10.3: Flipping and rotating a graphic

1) Open EX10.3.PPT, and go to slide number 11, 'Traceability', and select the arrow AutoShape.

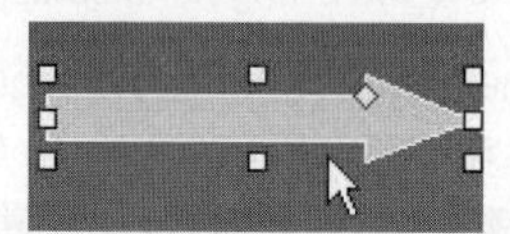

2) If the *Drawing* toolbar is not displayed at the bottom of the screen, choose **View | Toolbars | Drawing.** On the *Drawing* toolbar, choose **Draw | Rotate or Flip | Rotate Left**. Notice that the arrow now points upwards.

3) Repeat step 2. Notice that the arrow now points to the left.

4) With the arrow still selected, choose **Draw | Rotate or Flip | Flip Horizontal**. Notice that the arrow has turned around, and now points to the right again.

Because the shapes in the slide are symmetrical, the different effects of flipping and rotating may not be apparent. They will become more obvious in the next exercise.

Exercise 10.4: Free rotating a graphic

1) In EX10.4.PPT, go to slide number 11, 'Traceability'.

2) Click the arrow AutoShape. Choose **Draw | Rotate or Flip | Free Rotate**, or click the **Free Rotate** button on the *Drawing* toolbar. Notice that the sizing handles on the arrow AutoShape have changed into green circles – rotating handles.

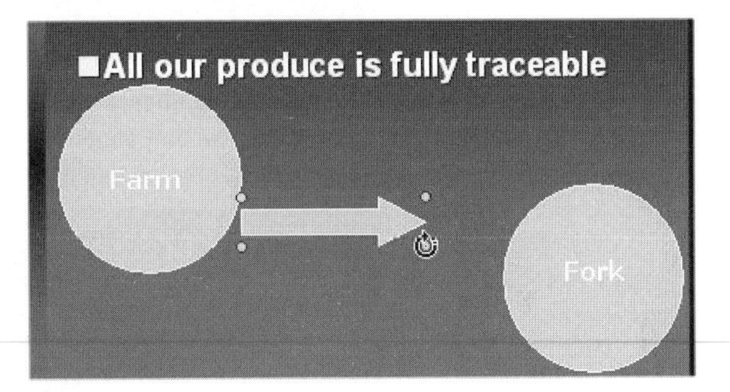

3) Click one of the rotating handles and drag it. Notice that, while you are dragging, the new position of the arrow is indicated by dotted lines.

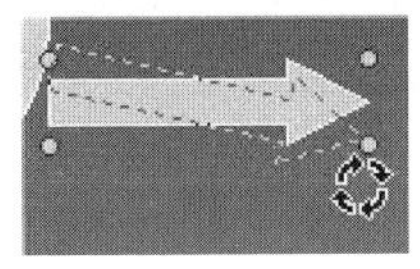

Position the arrow as shown below.

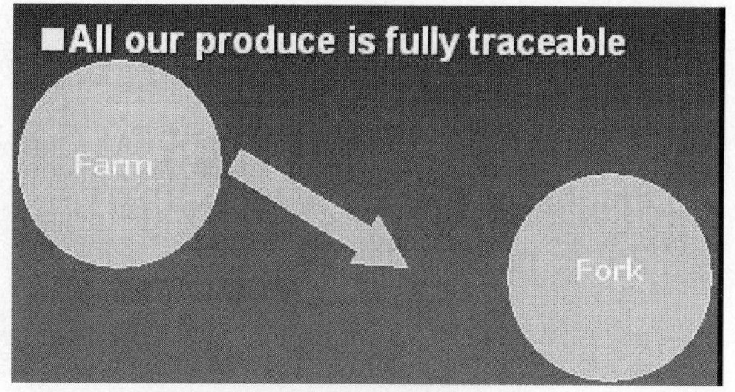

4) Now repeat the rotating and flipping exercises: choose **Draw | Rotate or Flip | Rotate Left**. Notice that the arrow now points up to the right, at 90° to the original.

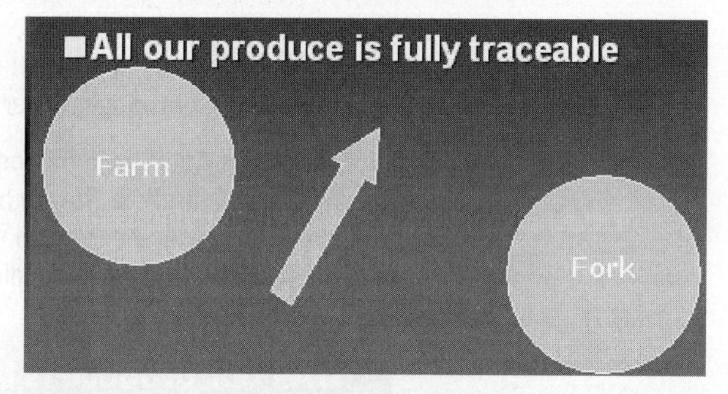

5) Repeat step 4. Rotating twice in the same direction turns the object through 180°, so that the arrow now points up and to the left (the opposite of its starting direction).

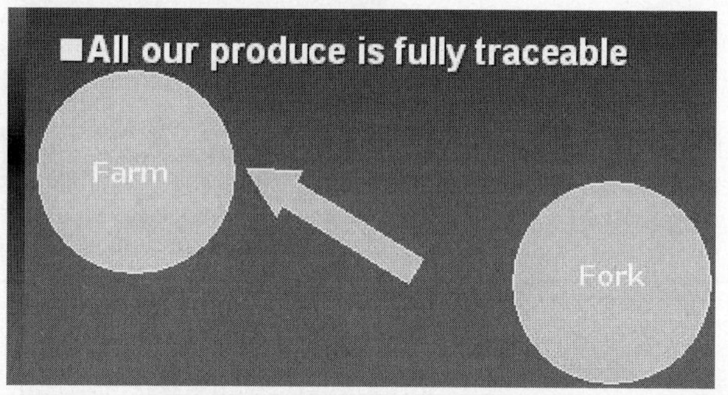

6) With the arrow still selected, choose **Draw | Rotate or Flip | Flip Horizontal**. Notice that the arrow has turned around, and now points to the right, but upwards, not downwards – it has been flipped around the vertical axis.

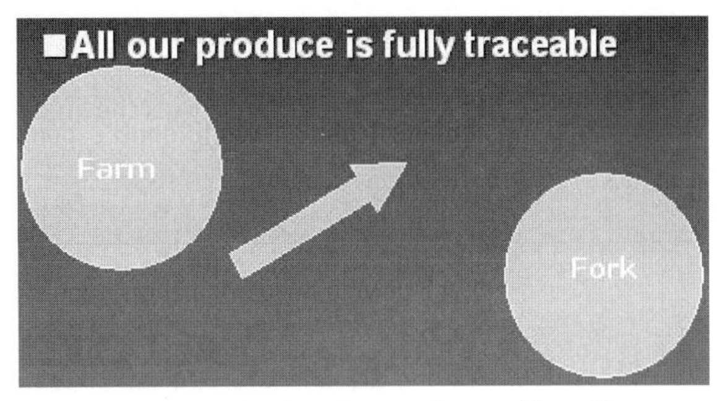

7) Change the arrow back to its starting position. Choose **Draw | Rotate or Flip | Flip Vertical**.

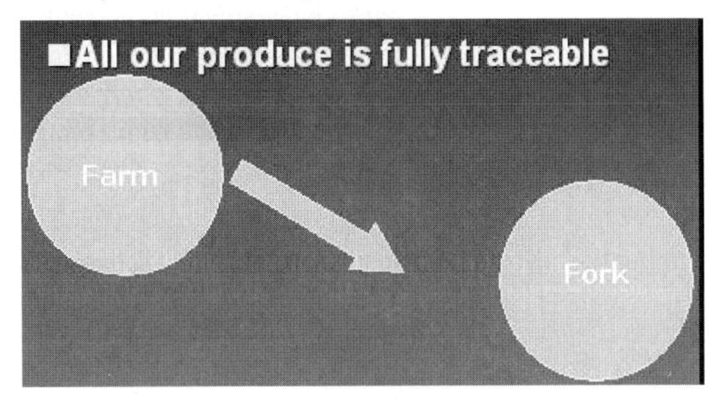

Converting pictures to drawn objects

Only certain kinds of graphic can be flipped and rotated: objects drawn in PowerPoint, using the drawing tools or AutoShapes, and imported objects that can be converted into a PowerPoint object or group.

If, when you select an object to rotate or flip, you find that all the options on the **Draw | Rotate or Flip** menu are greyed out, try to convert the object to a PowerPoint group, as in Exercise 9.5 below. Only certain kinds of graphic can be converted in this way – much Clip Art can be converted, but photos and other bitmaps, for example, cannot. If your graphic can't be converted, and you really want to flip or rotate it, your only option is to open the graphic in another graphics package, edit it there and then re-import it into your presentation.

Exercise 10.5: Converting a picture to a drawn object

1) Open EX10.5.PPT, and go to slide number 12, 'Our Fruit and Vegetables', and click the imported Clip Art image of the cabbage.

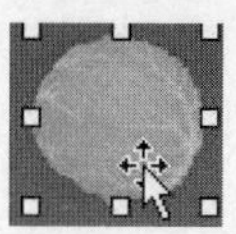

2) Choose **Draw | Rotate or Flip**, and notice that there are no options available to you.

3) Now choose **Draw | Ungroup**, and click **Yes** to confirm that you want to convert the picture to a Microsoft Office object. Notice that each tiny segment of the cabbage is converted into a separate object that can be manipulated in PowerPoint: you can move it around, enlarge or shrink it, stretch it – or rotate or flip it. For the moment, however, leave the entire group of objects selected.

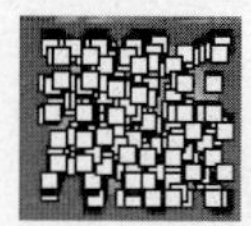

4) Choose **Draw | Group**.

   You can now treat the graphic as a PowerPoint object – all the options on the **Draw | Rotate or Flip** menu are available. Experiment with the cabbage, by rotating and flipping it.

Applying PowerPoint effects

You already know how to apply many PowerPoint effects. However, there are other effects that you can experiment with, such as:

- **Shadow**. This creates a background shadow behind the object, text or graphic.
- **3-D**. This adds a third dimension to a drawn object.
- **Semi-transparent**. This makes the drawn object or graphic semi-transparent, so that, for example, underlying text can be read through it.

Exercise 10.6: Create a shadow behind an object

1) Open EX10.6.PPT, and go to slide number 12, 'Our Fruit and Vegetables', and click the image of the apples.

Shadow button

2) Click the **Shadow** button on the *Drawing* toolbar.

3) Select the *Shadow Style 2* option from the **Shadow** menu.

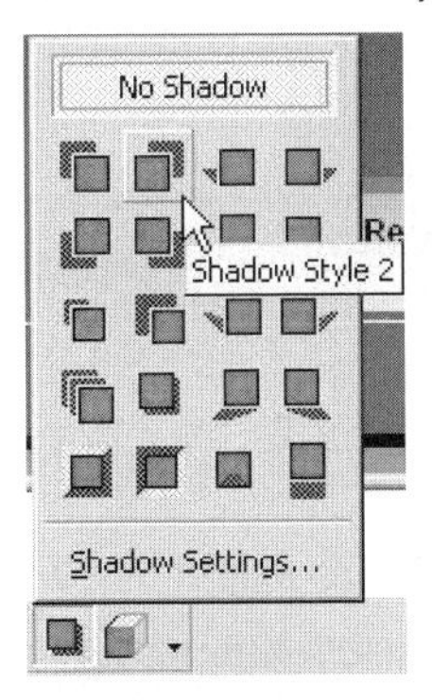

The apples should now look as shown.

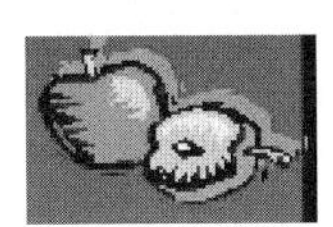

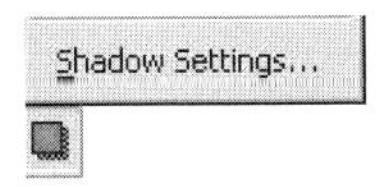

Shadow Settings

4) Click the **Shadow** button again, and select the *Shadow Settings* option.

The *Shadow Settings* toolbar now appears.

5) Use the buttons on the *Shadow Settings* toolbar to adjust the shadow effect – you can reveal more or less of the shadow by moving it up, down, left or right, and you can change its colour. Experiment with these options.

If you want to remove a shadow from an object, choose the *No Shadow* option on the **Shadow** menu, or click the **Shadow On/Off** button on the *Shadow Settings* toolbar.

Exercise 10.7: Make an object 3-D

1) Open EX10.7.PPT, and go to slide number 11, 'Traceability', and select the arrow between the two circles.

3-D Button

2) Click the **3-D** button on the *Drawing* toolbar.

3) Select the *3-D Style 1* option from the **3-D** menu.

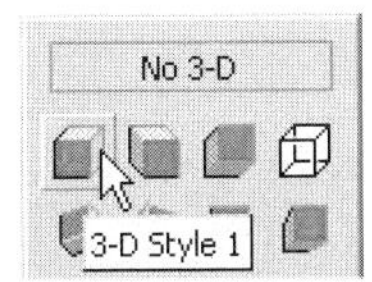

The arrow should now look as shown.

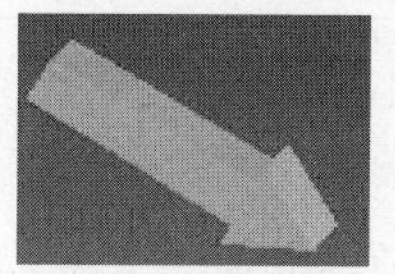

4) Click the **3-D** button and select the *3-D Settings* option.

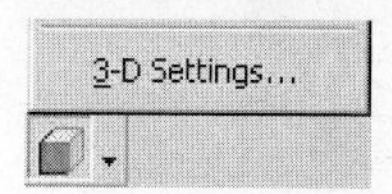

The *3-D Settings* toolbar now appears.

5) Use the buttons on the *3-D Settings* toolbar to adjust the 3-D effect, by tilting the arrow down, up, left or right, changing its depth and direction, and changing the angle of lighting, the surface texture and the colour. Experiment with these options.

To make it look like the one shown below:

- Leave the *Tilt* settings unchanged.
- Under *Depth*, choose 36 point.
- Under *Direction*, choose *Perspective*.
- Under *Lighting*, choose the top right.
- Under *Surface*, choose *Metal*.
- Under *3-D Color*, choose a light blue.

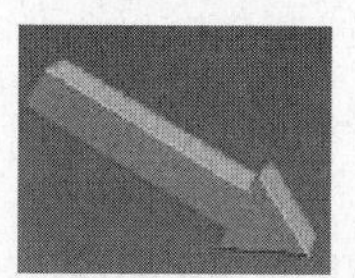

To remove a 3-D effect from an object, choose the *No 3-D* option on the **3-D** menu, or click the **3-D On/Off** button on the *3-D Settings* toolbar.

Note: You can apply the 3-D effect only to PowerPoint objects and imported objects that have been converted to PowerPoint objects.

Once you have manipulated the effects to your liking on one object, you can use the Format Painter to apply the same effects to other objects – as shown in the next exercise.

Exercise 10.8: Copy the style of one object and apply it to another

1) Open EX10.8.PPT, and go to slide number 11, 'Traceability', and click the arrow between the two circles.

2) With the arrow selected, click the **Format Painter** button on the *Formatting* toolbar. Notice that your cursor turns into a paint brush.

3) Click on the left-hand circle. Notice that it becomes a 3-D object with the same characteristics as the arrow.

4) Repeat steps 2 and 3 with the right-hand circle.

   Your slide should now look as shown.

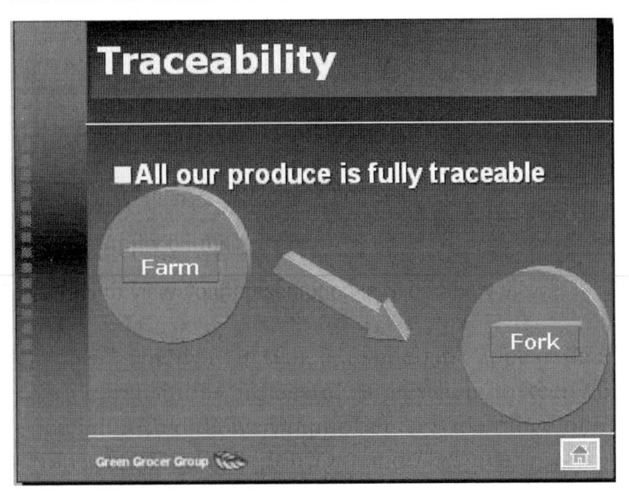

Exercise 10.9: Making an object semi-transparent

1) Open EX10.8.PPT, and go to slide number 11, 'Traceability'.

2) Right-click on the right-hand circle; choose **Grouping | Ungroup** from the pop-up menu; click anywhere outside the circle.

3) Right-click on the 'Fork' box; choose **Order | Send to Back** from the pop-up menu; click anywhere outside the circle.

4) Right-click on the circle; choose **Format | AutoShape** from the pop-up menu. The *Format AutoShape* dialog box is displayed.

5) On the *Colors and Lines* tab, select the *Semitransparent* check box and click **OK**.

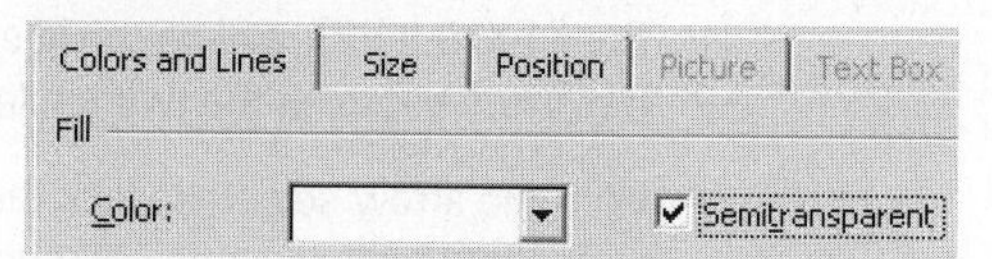

Notice the effect on the drawing.

6) Open EX10.9.PPT, and go to slide number 12, 'Our Fruit and Vegetables'; right-click the image of the cabbage. (Remember that you converted this image to a PowerPoint object in Exercise 9.5 – you can apply the semi-transparent effect only to objects created in PowerPoint or ones that have been converted.)

7) From the pop-up menu, choose *Format Object*.

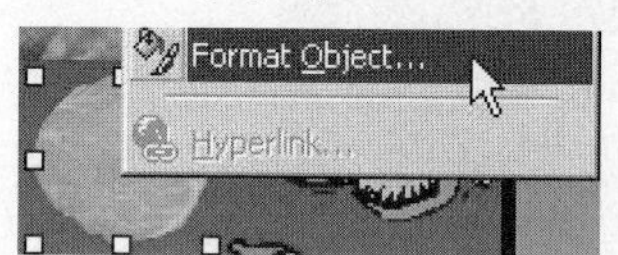

The *Format Object* dialog box is displayed. As above, select the *Semitransparent* check box on the *Colors and Lines* tab, and click **OK**.

Notice the effect on the image of the cabbage.

8) Click the image of the cabbage and drag it over the text on the left of the slide. Notice that you can now read the text through the cabbage!

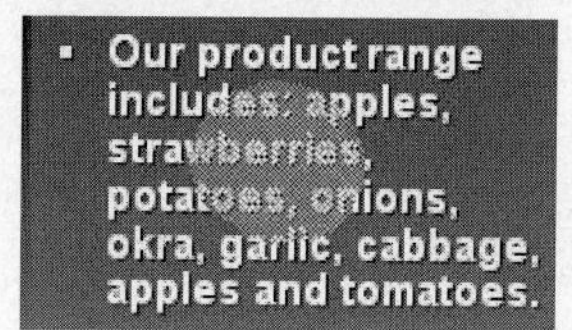

If the object you want to make semi-transparent is an unconverted Clip Art picture or a scanned photograph, click the **Image Control** button on the *Picture* toolbar and click *Watermark*.

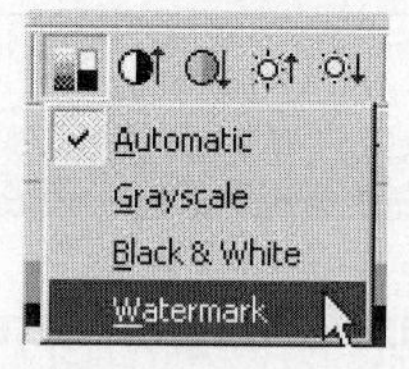

Exercise 10.10: Making parts of an object transparent

1) Open EX10.10.PPT, and go to slide number 1, the title slide, and right-click the logo. If the *Picture* toolbar is not displayed, choose **View | Toolbars | Picture**.

Set Transparent Color button

2) Click the **Set Transparent Color** button in the *Picture* toolbar. Notice that the mouse pointer changes shape.

3) Click the white area between the circular logo and the edges of the square. The white is eliminated, and the background colour or pattern shows through.

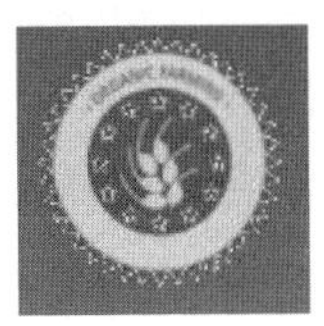

This feature is particularly useful for integrating graphics into your slides.

Note: The transparent effect is available only for certain kinds of graphics. Only one colour in a picture can be made transparent – this means that in a scanned photograph, for example, the transparent effect may not be noticeable, as what appears to be a single colour may in fact be composed of a range of colours, each slightly different from the next.

Adjusting the colour of images

There are three main reasons why you might want to alter the colours in your images:

- To enhance the picture and make the details in it easier to see.
- To make the picture harmonize with the colours in your presentation, or with other pictures.
- To reduce the file size of the picture, so that it takes up less disk space, loads more quickly, or can be e-mailed more easily.

Of course, you can also adjust the colours simply because it's fun, and can result in more interesting images. In the exercises below, you will adjust the contrast and brightness of an image, make colour substitutions in an image, and change the colour depth of an image.

Exercise 10.11: Adjusting brightness and contrast

1) Open EX10.11.PPT, and go to slide number 14, 'Our Farmers'.

2) Select the graphic and click several times on the **More Contrast** button in the *Picture* toolbar.

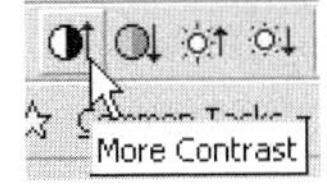

Notice how the picture changes as you click.

3) With the picture still selected, click several times on the **Less Brightness** button. You can continue to adjust the contrast and brightness of the picture, using the **More Contrast**, **Less Contrast**, **More Brightness** and **Less Brightness** buttons, until you are happy with the result.

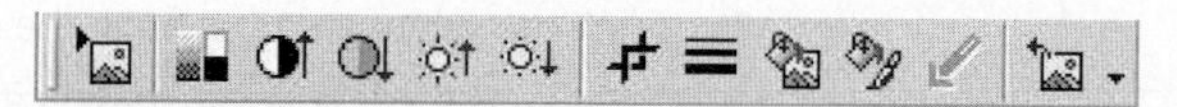

Reset Picture button

4) Click the **Reset Picture** button to get back to the original picture. (If you reset the picture, it will be restored to its original size – you will have to enlarge it again.)

In the previous exercise you worked on contrast and brightness; in the next exercise you will work on black-and-white shades.

Exercise 10.12: Converting a colour image to black-and-white

1) Open EX10.12.PPT, and go to slide number 12, 'Our Fruit and Vegetables'.
2) Select the potatoes graphic and click the **Image Control** button on the *Picture* toolbar.

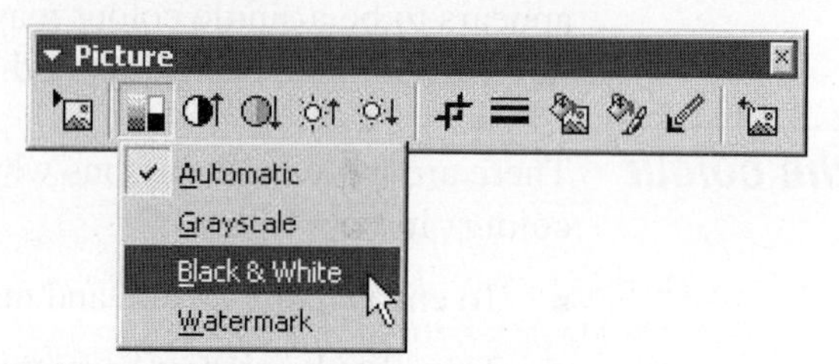

3) Select the *Black & White* option.

   The picture of the potatoes is now changed to black-and-white.

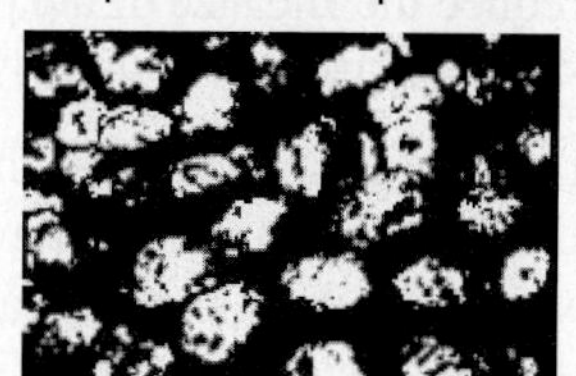

Clearly, this is not something you would do very often – black-and-white images (without any grey) are very stark, and it is difficult to interpret the picture. However, it is sometimes useful to convert a scanned document to black-and-white, as it maximizes the contrast, and can make the document more legible. Another way to make a graphic more legible is to convert it to greyscale.

Greyscaling and colour resolution

Graphics are made up of dots called pixels, or picture elements. Each pixel is represented in the computer by a number of bits. The greater the number of colours in the picture, the more bits are needed to represent each pixel. This means that graphics that use a wide colour palette are bigger files, and bigger files means that the files take longer to load, display and transmit.

There is a trade-off between colour depth and file size. One solution is to greyscale your graphics. When you greyscale a graphic, you convert all its pixels to shades of grey.

Whereas a full colour picture typically draws on a palette of 16 million colours (24-bit pixels), a greyscaled graphic typically contains pixels made up of 256 shades of grey, and each pixel is represented by eight bits.

Exercise 10.13: Converting a graphic to greyscale

1) Open EX10.13.PPT, and go to slide number 12, 'Our Fruit and Vegetables'.
2) Select the picture of the potatoes.
3) Click the **Image Control** button on the *Picture* toolbar, and select the *Grayscale* option.

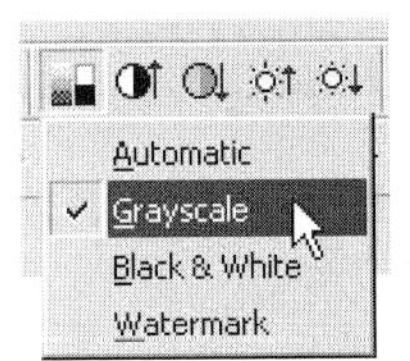

The picture of the potatoes is now changed to shades of grey.

This is a much better option – the potatoes are easy to see. You might use this option if you want to include a number of photos in your presentation, some of which are colour and some black-and-white (in the normal sense). Applying the greyscale effect to the colour photos will make them all consistent in style.

More sophisticated graphic effects

If you want to change a graphic more radically, PowerPoint may not be the tool for you. There is a very wide range of programs available with graphic editing capabilities.

Microsoft Paint

Microsoft Paint (which comes with Windows 2000) is a fairly simple program that enables you to skew an image, which is an interesting effect. To do this, open the graphic in Paint, and choose **Image | Stretch/Skew**. Experiment with *low* numbers for horizontal and vertical skew (try 5).

More usefully, Paint allows you to reduce the colour depth of an image by choosing **File | Save As**, and selecting from the *Save as Type* drop-down list. You can reduce the file size significantly, but you may lose detail in the picture. For example, the file size of a typical picture would vary as follows, depending on the format in which it was saved:

Format	File size
24-bit Bitmap (16 million colours)	119 KB
256 colour Bitmap (8-bit colour)	41 KB
Graphics Interchange Format (gif)	28 KB
16 colour Bitmap (4-bit colour)	21 KB
JPEG File Interchange Format (jpg)	10 KB
Monochrome Bitmap	6 KB

Adobe Photoshop

Adobe Photoshop is the favoured tool among graphic designers for editing and adding effects to graphics. (You can download a trial version of this graphics editing application from www.adobe.com.) It has many effects that you can apply to graphics – you can blur or sharpen the image, apply line-drawing or painting effects, shape your graphic with effects like *Twirl* and *Spherize*, or alter it further with effects like *Stained Glass* and *Embossing*. It's worth taking the time to explore the program to see its capabilities. For example, try the next exercise.

Exercise 10.14: Experimenting with Adobe Photoshop

1) Open Adobe Photoshop. Choose **File | Open** and navigate to BOWL1.JPG. Select the graphic and click **Open**.
2) Choose **Filter | Sketch | Charcoal**.
3) Click **OK** in the *Charcoal* dialog box.

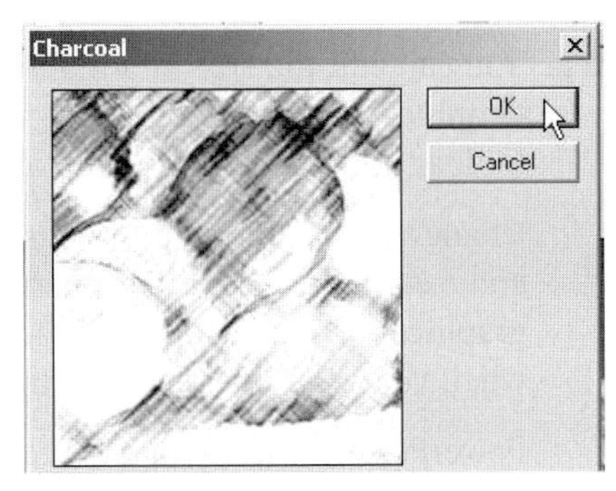

Your photograph now becomes a charcoal drawing. If this seems a little dark for your presentation, add the *Chalk & Charcoal* effect to lighten it up.

4) Choose **Filter | Sketch | Chalk & Charcoal**.
5) Click **OK** in the *Chalk & Charcoal* dialog box.

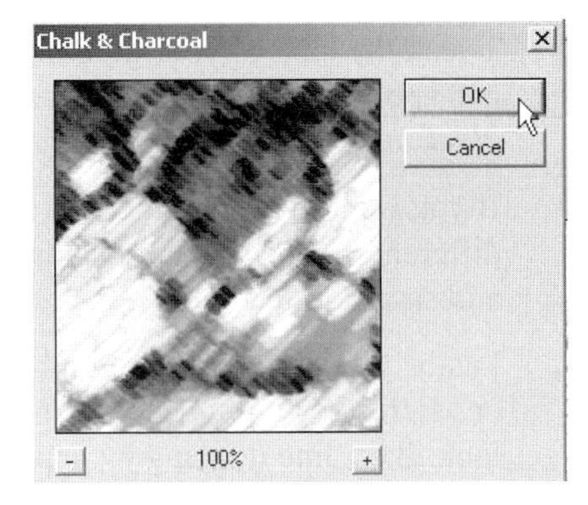

Your photograph now becomes a chalk and charcoal drawing.

6) Save the graphic as BOWL2.JPG.
7) Open EX10.14.PPT and insert the chalk and charcoal drawing into slide 5, 'Our Mission Statement'.

Your slide should now look as shown.

Chapter 10: summary

You can edit the size of a graphic by *cropping* it. You can use a Graphics Editor to do this but you can also use the *Picture* toolbar in PowerPoint to crop and *resize* a graphic.

Change the positioning of your graphic by *flipping*, *mirroring* and *rotating* it. As well as changing the physical size of a graphic, you can also *convert it to an object*. This is useful when you want to change a Clip Art picture into a drawn object.

PowerPoint comes with a range of graphic effects. For example, if you want to add more depth to a graphic you can apply a *shadow effect*. You can apply different shadow types and different shadow colours. Go even further by applying *3-D effects* to a graphic. Another useful effect is to make a graphic *semi-transparent* or parts of it transparent. (This is mostly used when integrating graphics into a slide.)

Tweak the look of your graphics by adjusting the colours. You can apply graphic *effects* such as *greyscaling*, *converting to black and white* and *changing contrast*.

If you want to change the size of a graphic file, you save it in a different *file format*. For example, you can open a .BMP image and save it as a .JPG.

Lastly, you can use other graphic editors like Adobe Photoshop or Microsoft Paint. A good experiment is to make a photograph look like a line drawing by applying Adobe Photoshop's *Chalk & Charcoal* effect.

Chapter 10: quick quiz

Circle the correct answer to each of the following questions about graphic editing and effects.

Q1	To make a right-facing arrow turn to the left you choose ...
A.	**Draw | Rotate or Flip | Flip Vertical.**
B.	**Draw | Rotate or Flip | Rotate Left.**
C.	**Draw | Rotate or Flip | Rotate Right.**
D.	**Draw | Rotate or Flip | Flip Horizontal.**

Q2	To convert a Clip Art graphic to a drawn object, you choose ...
A.	**Draw | Change AutoShape** and click **Yes** to confirm conversion.
B.	**Draw | Order | Bring to Front** and click **Yes** to confirm conversion.
C.	**Draw | Ungroup** and click **Yes** to confirm conversion.
D.	**Draw | Group** and click **Yes** to confirm conversion.

Q3	In PowerPoint, what *Picture* toolbar button is used to crop a graphic?
A.	
B.	
C.	
D.	

Q4	In PowerPoint, what *Picture* toolbar button is used to make parts of an object transparent?
A.	
B.	
C.	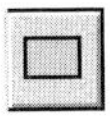
D.	

Answers

1: D, **2:** C, **3:** B, **4:** A.

11 Linking

In this chapter

Often, when you are creating a PowerPoint presentation, you want to use information that you have generated in another application – a Word document, an Excel worksheet or chart, or an Access database, for example. The most obvious way of doing this is to simply copy the information from the other application and paste it into your PowerPoint slide. In this chapter, you will learn about other ways of getting information from external sources into your PowerPoint presentation – by linking and by embedding.

New skills

At the end of this chapter you should be able to:

- Embed information from an external application into a presentation
- Link information from an external application into a presentation
- Display linked or embedded information as an icon
- Display linked or embedded information as an object
- Edit linked information
- Edit embedded information

New words

At the end of this chapter you should be able to explain the following terms:

- Embedded objects
- Linked objects
- Source files

Syllabus reference

This chapter covers the following syllabus points:

- AM 6.7.1.1
- AM 6.7.1.2
- AM 6.7.1.3
- AM 6.7.1.4

Multiple sources of information

When you are preparing your presentation, you might include information from a variety of sources, such as:

- An Excel spreadsheet.
- An Access database.
- A Word document.
- A graphic.
- Another PowerPoint presentation.

There might, for example, be relevant information about the Green Grocer Group in a financial spreadsheet.

Two situations arise:

- You want the presentation to reflect the financial position on the date you created it. In other words, you don't want to update the presentation when the spreadsheet subsequently changes.

  -or-

- You want the presentation to change when the numbers change in the spreadsheet, so that it always automatically reflects the latest financial situation.

With PowerPoint, you handle each of these situations differently.

Copying and pasting

If you simply copy the information from the spreadsheet and paste it into PowerPoint, the two copies are entirely independent – you can change one without affecting the other. However, the only tools you have at your disposal for changing the information that you have pasted into your presentation are PowerPoint tools – these might be fine for straightforward text, but if the information is in the form of a table, a worksheet or a chart, they are a bit limited.

Embedding

If you want to make the information in your presentation independent from the information in your worksheet, but you want to update it using the tools with which it was created, you need to embed the information in the presentation.

Linking

If you want to keep the information in the two applications synchronized, you need to link them. With linking, there is actually only one copy of the information. What appears in your PowerPoint presentation is a temporary graphic representation of the information. Changes can be made to the information only in the original application, and these changes are immediately reflected in the PowerPoint representation.

Embedded information

Information embedded in a PowerPoint slide is a copy of the original information. However, unlike copies made with the usual copy and paste functions, embedded information 'remembers' the application in which it was created. When you edit the embedded information, you are presented with the menus and toolbars of the original application. For example, when you edit an Excel worksheet embedded in a PowerPoint presentation, the PowerPoint menu bar and toolbars are temporarily replaced by the Excel menu bar and toolbars. However, the two copies are independent – if you change the copy that you have embedded in a slide, the original is unaffected, and if you change the original, the one embedded in your slide is unaffected.

You can present your embedded information either in full (as an object), or as an icon. You might choose to present it as an icon, for example, if your audience is going to view the presentation online and the embedded object is a large spreadsheet that would have to be very much reduced in size to fit on a slide.

In the exercise below, you will embed an Access database in your presentation, and show it as an icon. The same procedure can be used to embed a chart, a worksheet, a document, or a graphic in a slide.

Exercise 11.1: Embedding information

1) Open EX11.1.PPT.
2) Select slide 18, 'Best Sellers'.
3) Choose **Insert | Object**.
4) In the *Insert Object* dialog box, select the *Create from file* option.
5) Click the **Browse** button, and navigate to the Access database GREEN GROCER GROUP.MDB. Click **OK**.
6) Select the *Display as icon* check box.

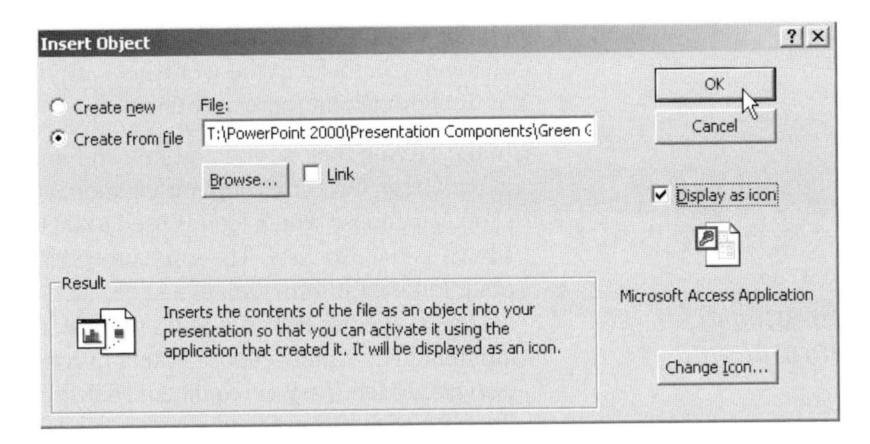

Click **OK**.

The **Access** icon now appears in the centre of the slide.

7) Move the icon to the bottom-left of the slide (use the arrow keys or drag-and-drop). If you wish, you can change the size of the icon by clicking on it and dragging one of its sizing handles.

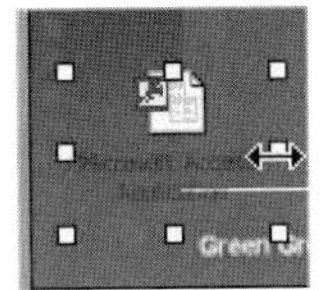

Your screen should now look as shown.

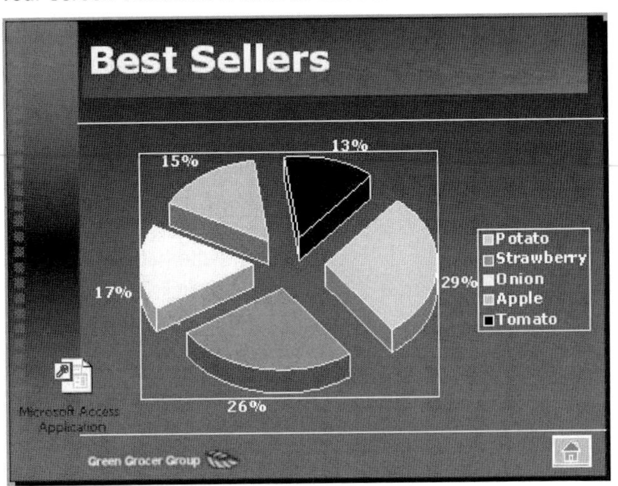

Linked information

Linked information in a PowerPoint slide is represented in the slide by a graphic object. The graphic may be an icon, or it may be a full-sized representation of the original document. In either case, the graphic provides a link to the original document in the original application. For example, in PowerPoint, to edit a linked Excel worksheet, you click on the graphic representation of it and the worksheet opens in Excel. Any changes you make to the worksheet are reflected immediately in the PowerPoint representation.

In the exercise below, you will link an Excel worksheet to a slide in the Green Grocer Group presentation, and show it as an icon. (You can choose which icon is used to represent the worksheet, as shown in the exercise.) The same procedure can be used to link other kinds of information to a slide, such as a Word document, a database, another PowerPoint presentation, or a graphic. To link to a graphic you simply choose **Insert | Picture | From File**. You navigate to the file you require and select it. Click the arrow to the right of the **Insert** button and select *Link to File*.

Exercise 11.2: Linking a worksheet to a slide

1) Open EX11.2.PPT.
2) Select slide 17, 'End of Year Results'.
3) Choose **Insert | Object**.
4) In the *Insert Object* dialog box, select the *Create from file* option.

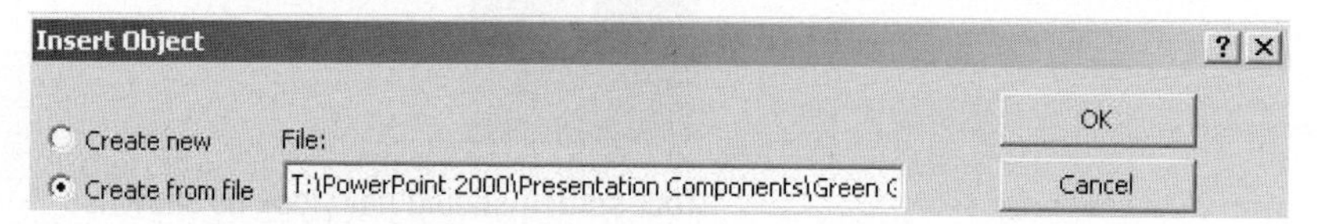

5) Click the **Browse** button and navigate to the Excel worksheet SUPPLIERS.XLS. Click **OK**.
6) In the *Insert Object* dialog box, select the *Link* check box.
7) Select the *Display as icon* check box.
8) Click the **Change Icon** button.

Change Icon button

Select the alternative Excel worksheet icon (as below) from the range shown and click **OK**.

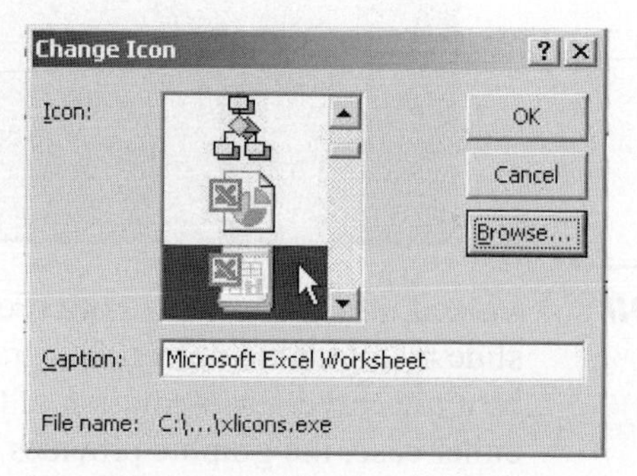

9) Click **OK** in the *Insert Object* dialog box.

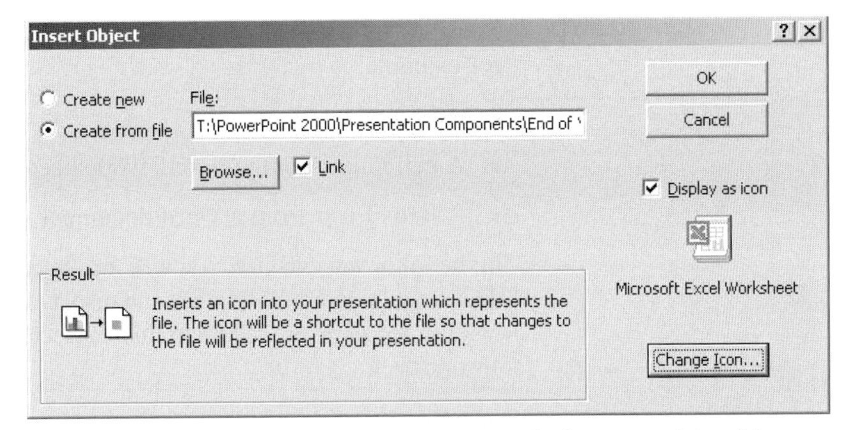

The Excel worksheet icon now appears in the centre of the slide.

10) Move the icon to the bottom-left of the slide. If you wish, you can change the size of the icon by clicking on it and dragging one of its sizing handles.

Your screen should now look as shown.

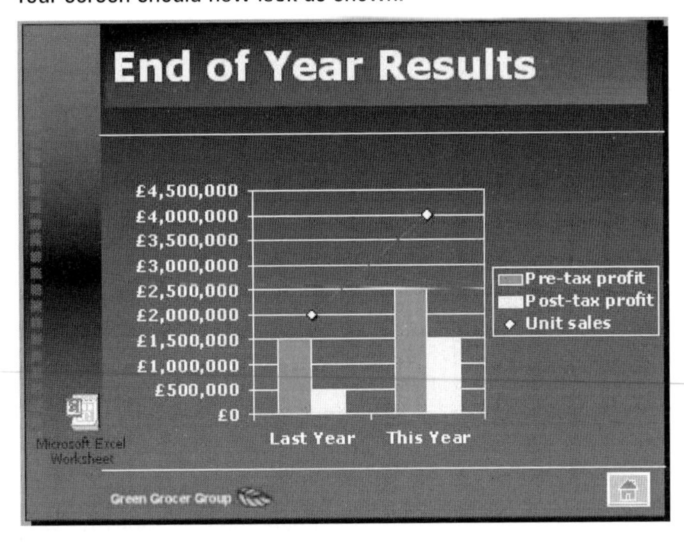

Linking part of a source file

In the previous two exercises, you represented the embedded and linked files as icons in your slides. That made sense: if the worksheet or the database table were shown in full as objects in the slides, they would have been too small to read. Most of the time, however, and particularly if you are projecting your slides, you will select a small part of the source document and show it as an object on the slide, instead of trying to show your audience the entire document.

You can embed or link a part of almost any document – for example:

- An Excel chart.
- A cell range from an Excel worksheet.
- A line of text from a Word document.

In the following exercise, you will link selected text in a Word document to your presentation and display it as an object. You will use the same procedure to link a selected range of cells in a worksheet.

Exercise 11.3: Linking part of a source file

1) Open EX11.3.PPT.
2) Select slide 17, 'End of Year Results'.
3) Click the **New Slide** button, and select the *Title Only* slide layout in the *New Slide* dialog box. Click **OK**.

4) Type the following in the title placeholder of the new slide 17:

```
What Our Customers Say
```

5) Open Word, and open WHAT OUR CUSTOMERS SAY.DOC.
6) Select the first two paragraphs below the heading (see below), and press **Ctrl+c** to copy them.

"I've never had such a range of organic fruit and vegetables available to me before."

"What I really like about Greeen Grocer Group is their dependability. When they say they deliver, they actually deliver, on time and to order."

"Our customers are still talking about the taste

7) In PowerPoint, in slide 17, choose **Edit | Paste Special**. The *Paste Special* dialog box appears.

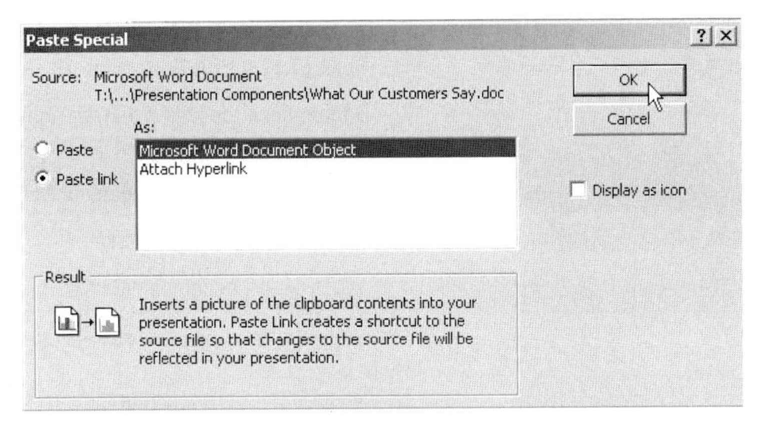

8) In the *Paste Special* dialog box, select *Paste link*. Ensure that Microsoft Word Document Object is selected in the *As* box. If necessary, deselect the *Display as icon* check box – you want to display the text in full, as an object, not as an icon. Click **OK**.

   Your slide should now look as shown.

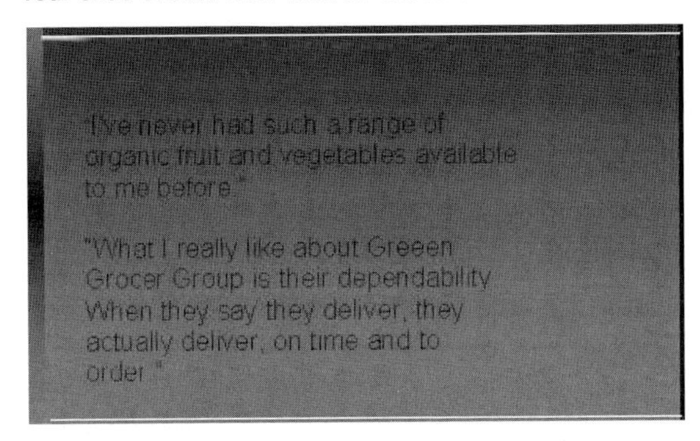

9) Click the **New Slide** button, select the *Title Only* slide layout, and click **OK**.
10) Give the new slide a title: Top Three Producers
11) Open Excel, and open the file SUPPLIERS.XLS.
12) Select the nine cells B2 to D4, and press **Ctrl + c** to copy them to the Clipboard.
13) In PowerPoint, choose **Edit | Paste Special**, and in the Paste Special dialog box, select *Paste Link*. This time, make sure that Microsoft Excel Worksheet Object is selected. Click **OK**.

Note that The text is displayed in PowerPoint exactly as it was created in Word or Excel. In the first slide you created, it is a reasonable point size (26 point), but the black font does not work well against the dark background. In the next exercise, you will edit some of the text, and change the font colour.

Exercise 11.4: Editing a linked file

1) Open EX11.4.PPT. Go to slide 18, 'What Our Customers Say'.

2) Double-click the linked text, or right-click it and choose **Linked Document Object | Edit**.

   The original document opens in Microsoft Word.

3) Change the spelling mistake:

   'Greeen' becomes 'Green'

   about Greeen Grocer Group

4) Select the first two paragraphs, as before, and choose **Format | Font**.

5) In the *Font* dialog box, click the arrow to the right of the *Font color* box and select the white colour. Click **OK**.

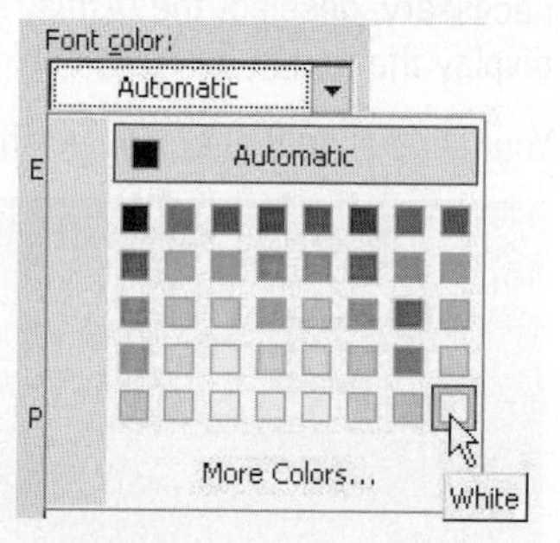

6) In PowerPoint, notice that the text in slide 18 has changed.

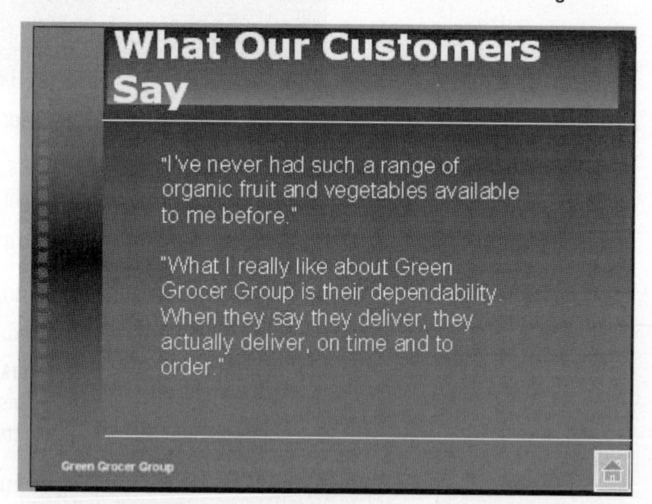

Congratulations! You've linked selected text from a Word document to your presentation, and seen how, when you change the text in Word, the changes are automatically reflected in PowerPoint.

Editing links

Not only can you change the linked information, you can also change the links themselves, in two ways:

- You can change the source file used for the information, as in Exercise 11.5.
- You can break the link, so that the information in your presentation is embedded, rather than linked, as in Exercise 11.6.

Exercise 11.5: Linking to a different source file

1) Open EX11.5.PPT.
2) Choose **Edit | Links**.
3) In the *Links* dialog box, select the Worksheet link.

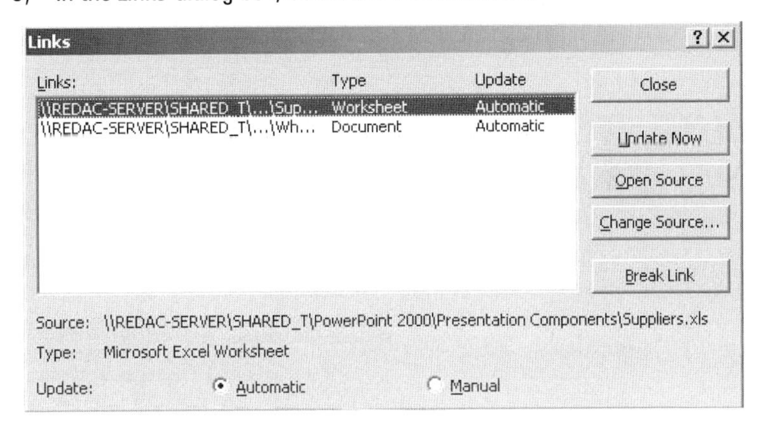

4) Click the **Change Source** button. Navigate to END OF YEAR RESULTS.XLS and click **Open**.

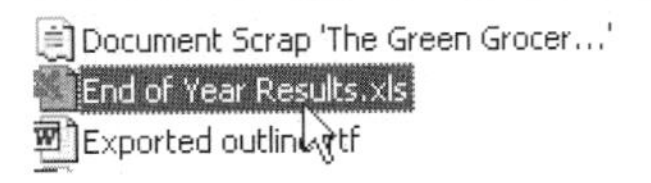

5) In the *Links* dialog box, click the **Close** button.
6) Check the effect of this change: go to slide 17, 'End of Year Results'; double-click the Excel icon, and note that the END OF YEAR RESULTS.XLS spreadsheet opens in Excel.

Converting linked objects into embedded objects

If you no longer want your presentation to be updated automatically when the source document changes, you need to break the link. Remember, however, that the linked document is represented in your slide either by an icon, or by a graphic representation of the source document. When you break the link between the representation on your slide and the source document, you are left with a graphic – either an icon or a 'picture' of the source document. This graphic representation can be edited only within PowerPoint – it does not 'remember' the application in which it was originally created.

Exercise 11.6: Converting a linked object to an embedded object

1) Open EX11.6.PPT.
2) Choose **Edit | Links**.
3) In the *Links* dialog box, select the Document link.

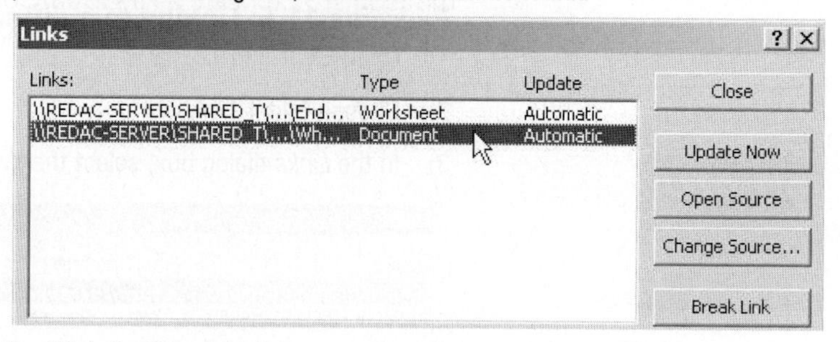

4) Click the **Break Link** button, then click the **Close** button.
5) Go to slide 18, 'What Our Customers Say'. Double-click on the text.
6) PowerPoint asks if you want to convert the linked object. Click the **Yes** button.

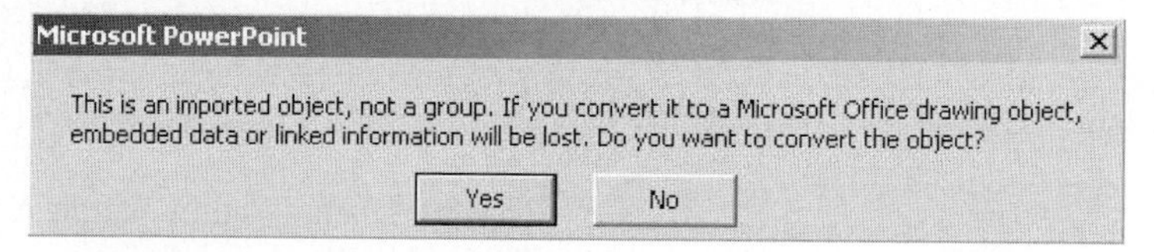

Note: The text is presented in a number of text boxes, each of which can be edited separately – for example, you can modify the text, or change the font size.

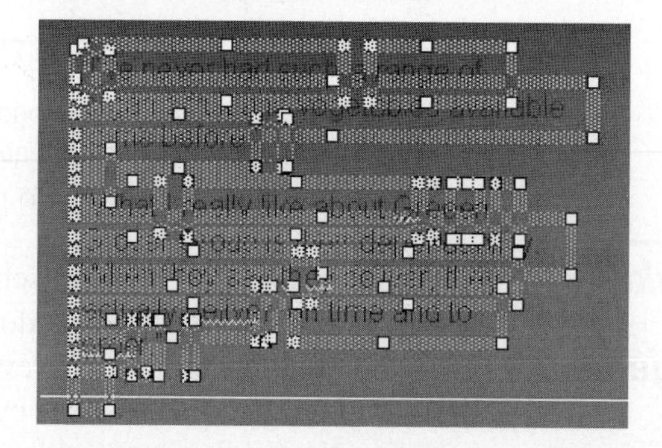

7) In the *Drawing* toolbar, click the arrow to the right of the **Font Color** button, and choose a yellow colour. The text in the slide changes colour (but the text in the original document is unchanged).

"I've never had such a range of organic fruit and vegetables available to me before."

"What I really like about Green Grocer Group is their dependability. When they say they deliver, they actually deliver, on time and to order."

Note: If you break the link from an icon to a source document, the icon still appears as a graphic object in the presentation – the data to which it referred does not appear.

Converting between an icon and an object

If you first chose to represent the source document as an icon, and subsequently wish to represent it in full as an object, right-click the icon, choose **Linked Worksheet Object | Convert** (or similar, depending on the source document type). In the *Convert* dialog box, deselect the *Display as icon* check box.

Similarly, if you first chose to represent the source document in full as an object, and subsequently wish to represent it as an icon, right-click the document representation in the slide, choose **Linked Worksheet Object | Convert**. In the *Convert* dialog box, select the *Display as icon* check box.

Where to keep your linked documents

PowerPoint needs to find a linked document in order to display it. For this reason, it's best to keep your linked documents in the same folder as your presentation. If you are copying your presentation to CD or to a floppy disk, make sure to copy any linked documents at the same time.

Chapter 11: summary

You can include information from many sources in a PowerPoint presentation. If you *embed* such information, the copy in your PowerPoint slide is independent of the original, but you can use the features of the original application to edit the information. If you *link* the information, PowerPoint shows a graphic representation of the original information, but all editing is done to the source document in the original application, and the graphic representation in PowerPoint is updated with any changes.

In either case, you can choose to show the information in full as an *object* or as an *icon* – double-clicking the icon opens the full embedded or linked document.

You can embed and link both *files* and selected *parts of files*, such as pieces of text, cells in a worksheet, or charts.

You can *change* the source file for a link, and you can *convert* a linked object to an embedded object.

Chapter 11: quick quiz

Circle the correct answer to each of the following multiple-choice questions about linking and embedding objects and icons.

Q1	To embed an information type as an icon you ...
A.	Choose **Insert | Object**, browse to your selected file, and click **OK**. Select the *Link* check box and select the *Display as icon* check box. Click **OK**.
B.	Choose **Insert | Object**, browse to your selected file, and click **OK**. Deselect the *Link* check box and select the *Display as icon* check box. Click **OK**.
C.	Choose **Insert | Object**, browse to your selected file, and click **OK**. Deselect the *Link* check box and deselect the *Display as icon* check box. Click **OK**.
D.	Choose **Insert | Object**, browse to your selected file. Deselect the *Link* check box and select the *Display as icon* check box. Click **OK**.

Q2	To insert part of a document as an icon you ...
A.	Copy the information that you need from the source file. Return to your PowerPoint presentation slide and choose **Insert | Paste Special**. In the *Paste Special* dialog box you select *Paste link* and Microsoft Word Document Object. Select the *Display as icon* check box and click **OK**.
B.	Copy the information that you need from the source file. Return to your PowerPoint presentation slide and choose **Edit | Paste Special**. In the *Paste Special* dialog box you select *Paste* and Microsoft Word Document Object. Select the *Display as icon* check box and click **OK**.
C.	Copy the information that you need from the source file. Return to your PowerPoint presentation slide and choose **Edit | Paste Special**. In the *Paste Special* dialog box you select *Paste link* and Microsoft Word Document Object. Select the *Display as icon* check box and click **OK**.
D.	Copy the information that you need from the source file. Return to your PowerPoint presentation slide and choose **Edit | Paste**. In the *Paste* dialog box you select *Paste* and Microsoft Word Document Object. Select the *Display as icon* check box and click **OK**.

Q2	True or false – if you update the source file an embedded database, the embedded information in the presentation doesn't change.
A.	True.
B.	False.

Q4	To change the source file you …
A.	Choose **Insert | Object**. In the *Links* dialog box you select the information type you want to change and click the **Open Source** button. Select the file you need and click the **Change Source** button. Click the **Close** button to return to your presentation.
B.	Choose **Edit | Links**. In the *Links* dialog box you select the information type you want to change and click the **Change Source** button. Select the file you need and click the **Open Source** button. Click the **Close** button to return to your presentation.
C.	Choose **Insert | Object**. In the *Links* dialog box you select the information type you want to change and click the **Change Source** button. Select the file you need and click the **Open Source** button. Click the **Close** button to return to your presentation.
D.	Choose **Edit | Links**. In the *Links* dialog box you select the information type you want to change and click the **Change Source** button. Select the file you need and click the **Update Now** button. Click the **Close** button to return to your presentation.

Answers

1: B, **2:** C, **3:** A, **4:** D.

12 Macros and set-ups

In this chapter

If you have a large number of slides, and you want to change certain details in some of them – use a different font for certain words, use a special animated effect, or add sound, for example – it can take quite a bit of effort and time to make the changes. Each change involves many steps, but the steps involved in each change are the same. Help is at hand, however! PowerPoint enables you to create macros that automate such repetitive tasks, and enable you to execute all the steps with a single mouse-click. You'll learn how to create and run macros in this chapter.

If you want to present one or other of your custom shows, or publish the presentation on the Internet or your company's intranet, or if the presentation is to run unattended in a kiosk or at a trade show, or if you need to pass the PowerPoint file to someone else, you need to set up your presentation to prepare it for final viewing. And if you want to use slides as graphics in word processed documents or web pages, you need to save the relevant slides as graphics. This chapter shows you how.

New skills

At the end of this chapter you should be able to:

- Record a macro
- Run a macro
- Create a custom button for a macro
- Check macro security levels
- Publish a slide show to the web
- Export slides as graphics
- Confirm slide show settings (custom shows and full shows)

New words

At the end of this chapter you should be able to explain the following terms:

- Macro
- Custom button
- Publishing to the web

Syllabus reference

This chapter covers the following syllabus points:

- AM 6.2.2.1
- AM 6.3.1.6
- AM 6.6.1.4
- AM 6.6.1.5
- AM 6.8.1.1
- AM 6.8.1.2
- AM 6.8.1.3

Recording macros

A macro is a recorded sequence of actions that can be played back with a single command. Typically, you go through the steps involved in executing a particular task, recording these as a macro. Then, any time you want to execute the same task, you can repeat the entire sequence of steps by choosing a single command or clicking a single button.

Recording a macro is just like taping a piece of music. You press **Record**, go through the sequence of actions you want to include in the macro, then press **Stop**. In the following exercise, you will record a macro that hides the selected text element when the mouse is next clicked.

Exercise 12.1: Recording a macro

Note: To do this exercise, the file EX12.1.PPT must be on your hard disk, as the macro is saved to the same location as the presentation. If you have not already done so, copy EX12.1.PPT from the supplied CD to your computer before starting.

1) Open EX12.1.PPT.
2) Go to slide 21, 'Growth Area: Supermarkets'.
3) Choose **Tools | Macro | Record New Macro**.
4) In the *Record Macro* dialog box, give your macro a name, say where it is to be stored, and give a short description, as below.

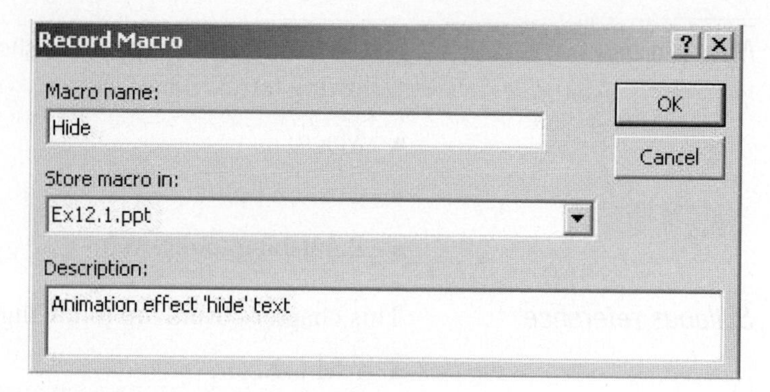

5) Press **OK**. The *Stop Recording* toolbar appears.

You are now in record mode – everything you do between now and pressing the **Stop Recording** button will be included in your macro.

6) Carry out the sequence of tasks that you want to record:

- Choose Slide Show | Custom Animation.
- In the *Custom Animation* dialog box, select the *Text 2* check box.
- In the Effects tab, select *Hide on Next Mouse Click* from the *After animation* drop-down list.

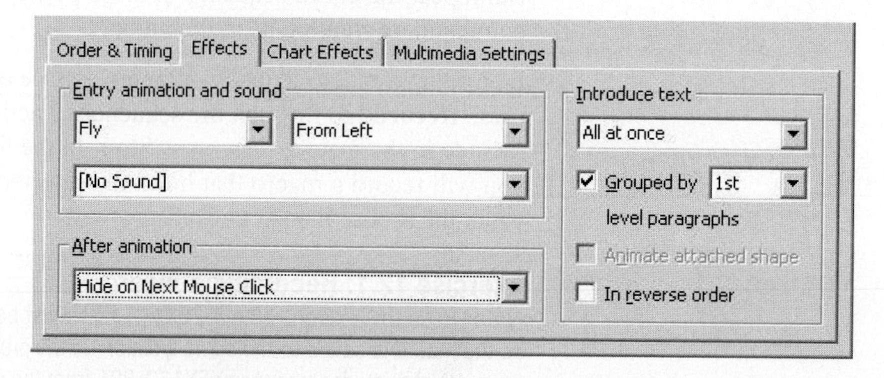

Click **OK**.

7) Press **Stop Recording** on the *Stop Recording* toolbar.

Well done! You've just recorded your first PowerPoint macro.

Macro names and locations

Macro names are best kept short and memorable: short, because you may want to use them on a toolbar button (see below); memorable, because if you have a number of macros, you will find it difficult to remember which is which if they are called names like 'macrol' and 'macro2'.

There are a few rules about naming macros:

- The first character must be a letter.
- The name may be made up of letters, numbers and the underscore character – no spaces or punctuation marks are allowed.
- Certain words are not allowed as macro names, such as Private, Public, Integer and Sub.

But don't worry! If you choose an invalid name, PowerPoint will tell you that it is invalid, and you can choose a different name.

Normally, macros are stored with the presentation for which they are created (as in the exercise above). Alternatively, you can store the macro with the template, so that it can be used with all presentations created from that template.

Running macros

Once you have recorded a macro, you can play it back any time you want to repeat the sequence of actions recorded in the macro. See how simple this is in the next exercise.

Exercise 12.2: Running a macro

1) Open EX12.2.PPT. (If necessary, confirm that you want to **Enable Macros**.)
2) Go to slide 20, 'Growth Area: Farmer Markets'. View it in Slide Show view; then return to Normal view.
3) Select the text that you want to apply the macro to, as below.

4) Choose **Tools | Macro | Macros**.

5) In the *Macro* dialog box, select the *Hide* macro and click the **Run** button.

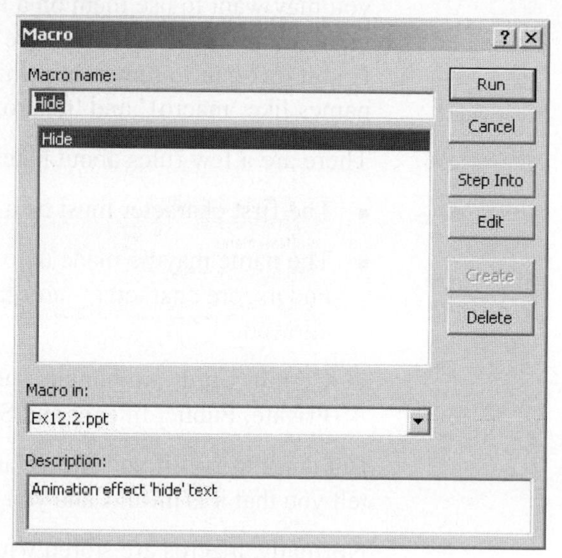

6) In Slide Show view, open slide 20, and note that the animation effect has been applied to the slide.

Note: If at any time you want to stop a macro, simply press **CTRL+Break**.

Creating custom buttons for macros

You can reduce the effort required to run a macro even further, by adding a custom button for the macro to a toolbar. In the next exercise you will create a custom button for the Hide macro and place it on a PowerPoint toolbar.

Exercise 12.3: Creating a custom button for a macro

1) Open EX12.3.PPT. (If necessary, confirm that you want to **Enable Macros.**)

2) Choose **Tools | Customize**.

3) In the *Customize* dialog box click the **Commands** tab and select the *Macro* option.

   Here you see the name of the macro you previously created: 'Hide'.

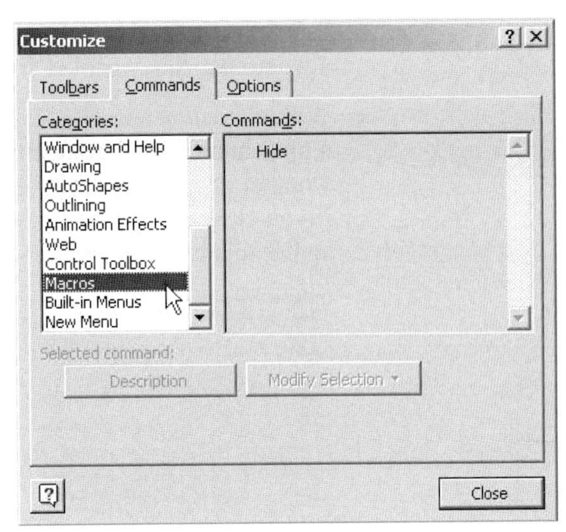

4) Select the 'Hide' macro and drag it to the *Formatting* toolbar.

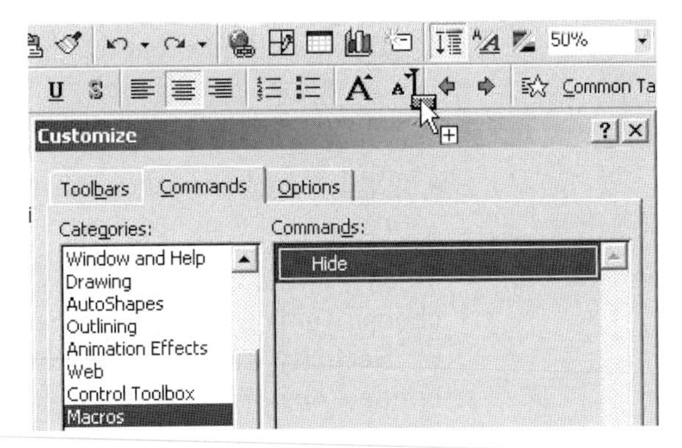

Well done! Your custom button should now look as shown.

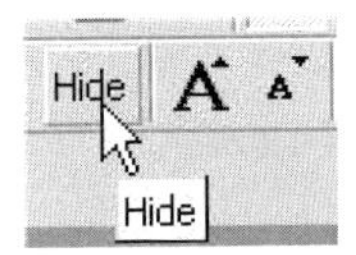

Clicking the button will have the same effect as choosing **Tools | Macro | Macros**, selecting the macro, and clicking **Run**.

Macro security

One of the most common ways of transmitting computer viruses is through macros. For this reason, you should be very cautious about opening any file that you receive from someone you don't know, and particularly careful if you know that the file in question contains a macro.

PowerPoint allows you to choose the level of security that applies to presentations that you open: low, medium and high.

- *Low* security level is not generally recommended – all macros are automatically enabled, irrespective of their origin.
- With a *medium* security level, PowerPoint will warn you that a presentation you are opening includes macros, and ask whether or not you want those macros enabled. For instance, if you close a presentation with macros and then open it again, this is what you see on your screen:

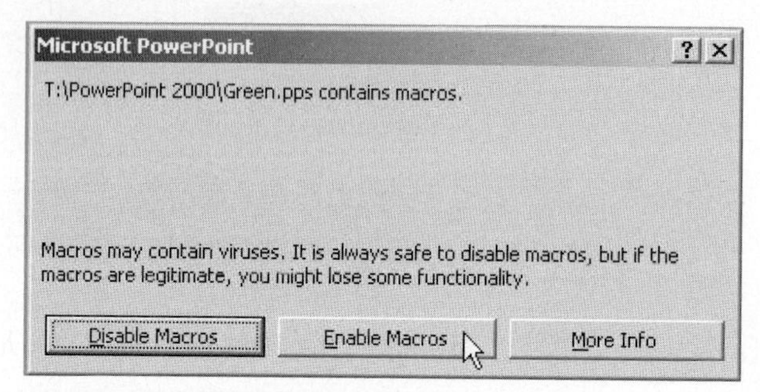

  Since you know that the macro in question is harmless, you are safe to click **Enable Macros**. However, if you are unsure, it is better to click **Disable Macros**.
- With a *high* security level, all macros are disabled, with the exception of signed macros coming from trusted sources.

To check your current macro security level, or to change it, choose **Tools | Macro | Security**. In the *Security* dialog box, in the **Security Level** tab, you can see the different security options, one of which is selected. You change the security level by selecting one of the other options. For this presentation, choose the *Medium* option.

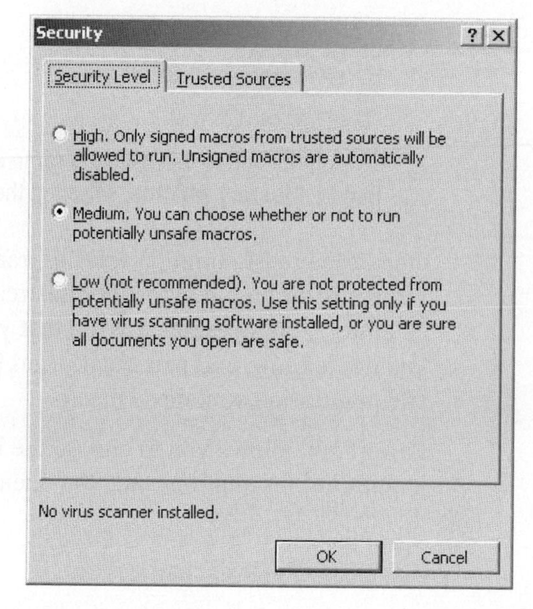

Deleting macros

You will very often use a macro when you are creating your presentation, but have no further use for it after that. It is good practice to delete such a macro, so that people to whom you give copies of the presentation do not have the macro on their PCs.

To delete a macro, follow the steps outlined in the following exercise.

Exercise 12.4: Deleting a macro

1) Open EX12.4.PPT. (If necessary, confirm that you want to **Enable Macros**.)
2) Choose **Tools | Macro | Macros**.
3) Select the macro that you want to delete in the *Macro* dialog box. In your case, it is the 'Hide' macro.
4) Click the **Delete** button.

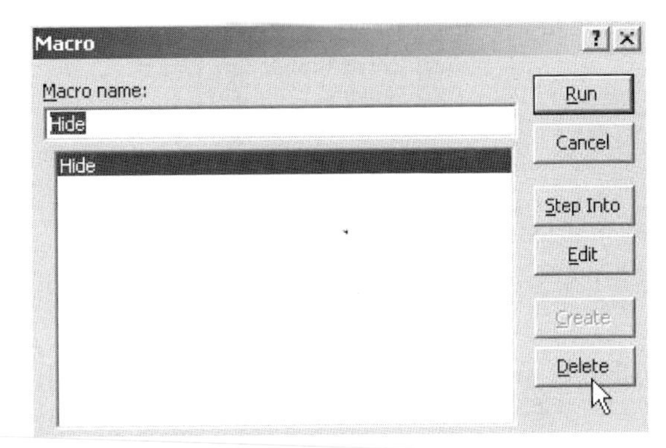

5) PowerPoint asks you to confirm that you want to delete the macro. Click the **Yes** button.

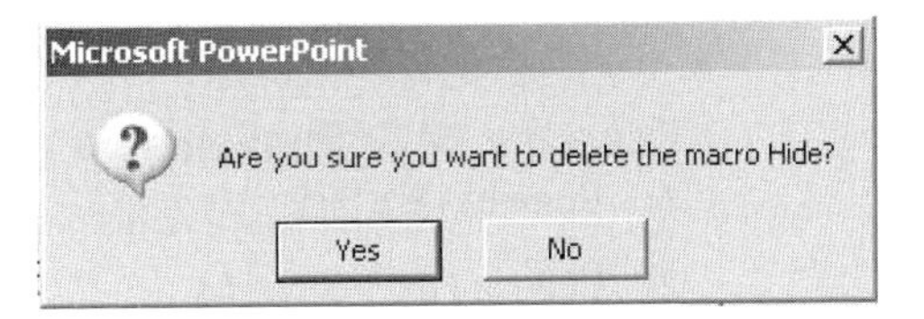

Setting up

You've designed and structured your presentation, set up all the slides, inserted graphics, applied animation and transition effects, rehearsed the timings and recorded your macros. Do you need to do anything else? Well, maybe, depending on how you are going to deliver your presentation.

If you are going to deliver your entire presentation yourself to a live audience, if nobody else is going to use it, either to prepare a similar slide show or to support their own presentation, and if you are sure that you won't have to send the file to someone who might or might not have PowerPoint on their computer, then you don't have to do anything else.

If, however, you want to present one or other of your custom shows, or publish the presentation on the Internet or your company's intranet, or if the presentation is to run unattended in a kiosk or at a trade show, or if you need to pass the PowerPoint file to someone else, you need to set up your presentation to prepare it for final viewing.

Publishing presentations to the web

You can set up your presentation in such a way that it can be viewed with a web browser, either on the Internet or on a corporate intranet. This is called publishing to the web. Your presentation will take on the attributes of a website, such as a navigation bar and an address bar.

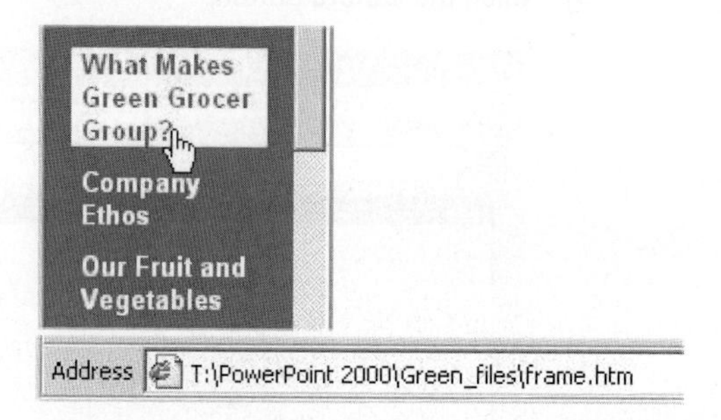

Slide titles will be displayed in a navigation bar, and viewers can simply click on a slide title to access that slide. You can choose to use your presentation animation or not.

The following exercise shows how to publish a presentation to the web.

Exercise 12.5: Publishing a presentation to the web

1) Open EX12.5.PPT.
2) Choose **File | Save As**.
3) In the Save As dialog box, click the arrow to the right of the *Save as type* box. Select the *Web Page (*htm; *.html)* option.

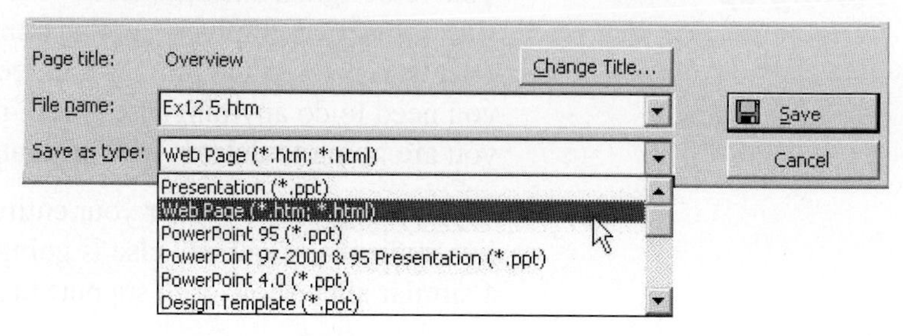

4) Select the location where you want the presentation saved and click the **Publish** button.

5) In the *Publish as Web Page* dialog box, select the *Complete presentation* option in the *Publish what?* section.

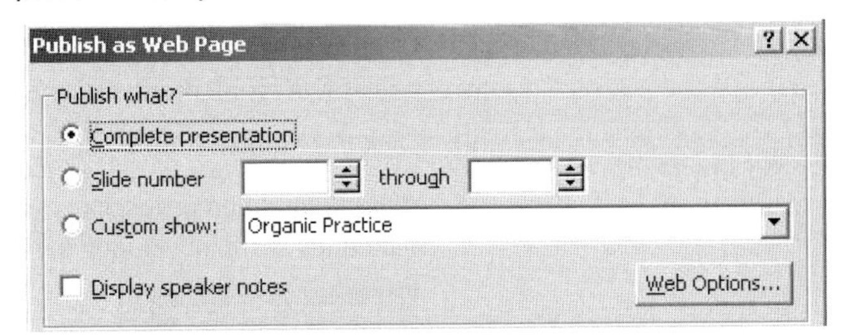

6) Click the **Web Options** button in the *Publish what?* section.

Under the **General** tab, select the options shown below.

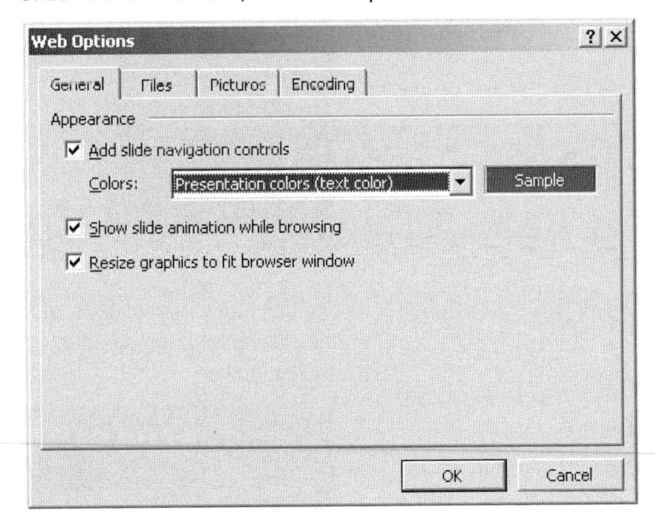

Click **OK**.

7) In the *Browser support* section, select the browser option of your choice. In this case select *Microsoft Internet Explorer 4.0 or later*.

8) In the *Publish a copy as* section, confirm or change the page title and file name. Select the *Open published Web page in browser* check box – this will enable you to see the result of the exercise immediately.

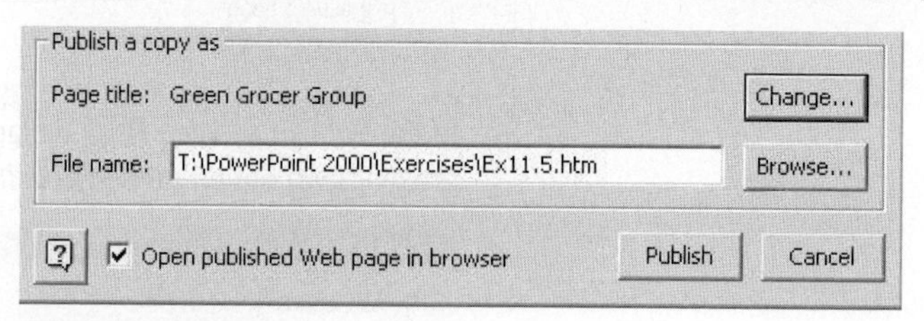

9) Click the **Publish** button.

Your presentation now appears in your Internet browser, with the slide titles in the navigation bar to the left.

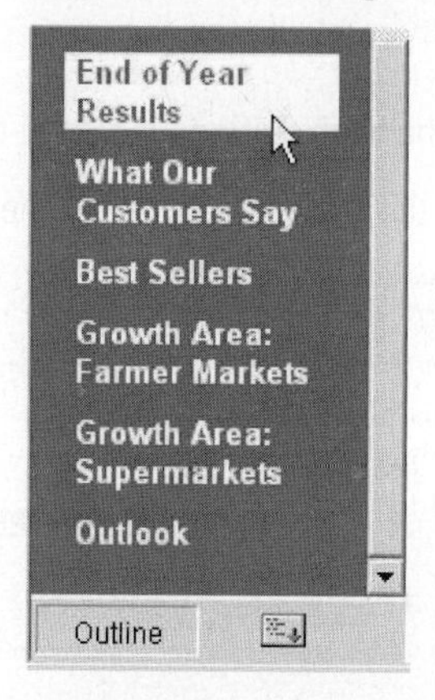

You can move from slide to slide sequentially by clicking anywhere in the slide area, or go directly to any slide by clicking on its title in the navigation bar.

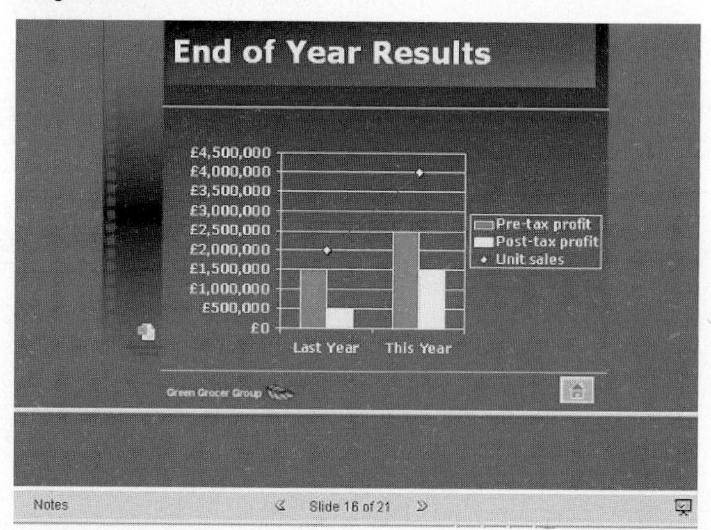

Saving slides as graphics

You can save an individual slide or your entire slide show as graphics that can subsequently be incorporated into a word processed document, for example, or a web page. You might do this if you don't want to publish your slide show on the web in the form of a presentation, but instead want to incorporate some or all of the slides into web pages, as graphic images. In this case, you save your slides in .JPG format. (The different types of graphic files were discussed in Chapter 10.) The following exercise shows you how to save slides as graphics.

Exercise 12.6: Saving slides in JPG format

1) Open EX12.6.PPT.
2) Choose **File | Save As**.
3) In the *Save As* dialog box, click the arrow to the right of the *Save as type* box. Choose the file type you want. You can choose from a range of graphic file formats, including .BMP, .GIF and .JPG. In this case, select the .jpg option (*JPEG File Interchange Format*).

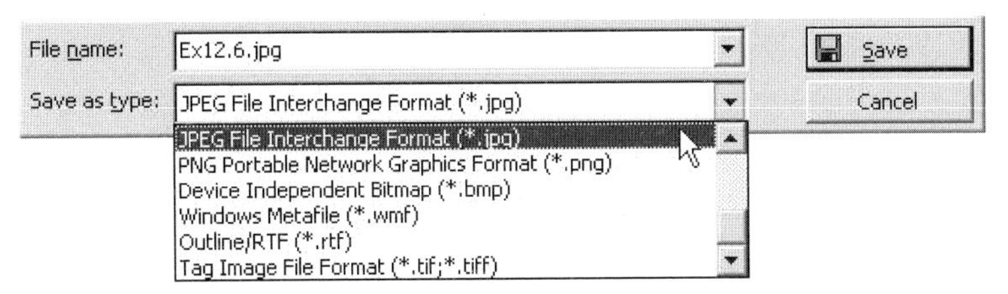

4) Select the location where you want the graphic files saved.
5) Press **Save**.
6) PowerPoint asks you if you want to export all the slides as graphics or just the current slide. Click **Yes**, as you want to create a graphic file for each slide in the presentation.

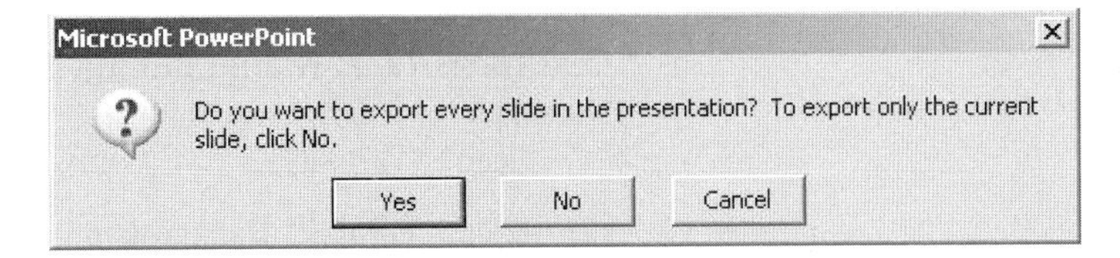

7) PowerPoint tells you that each slide has been saved in a sub-folder of the location you specified. (Here the sub-folder is called Ex12.6.) Click **OK**.

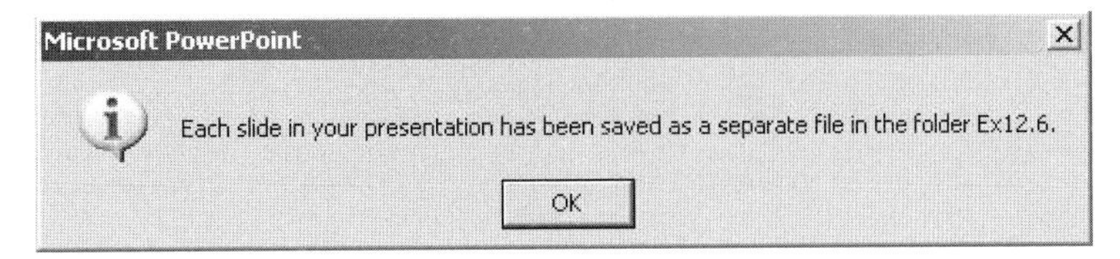

The graphic files are named SLIDE1.JPG, SLIDE2.JPG, etc. They can now be included in web pages, inserted into Word documents, or edited in a graphics application. Note that if you do make them available on a website, they will act as ordinary graphics – they will not have any of the navigation features of an interactive presentation.

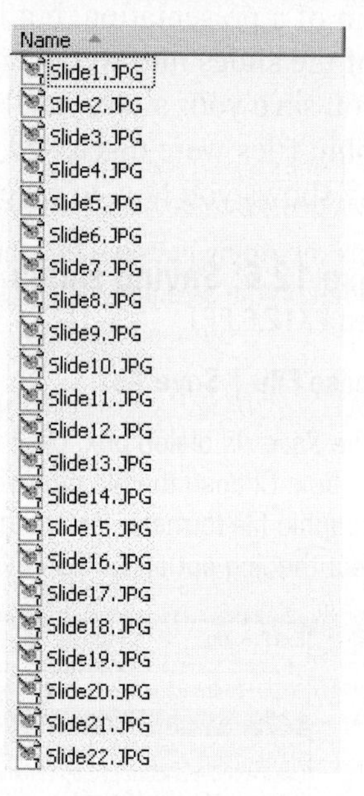

Setting up for a live audience

You can set up your presentation to show one or other of your custom shows, to use manual or automatic timings, to show or not show animations, and to show or not to show the background graphics from the Slide Master.

Hiding background graphics

If you do not want to show the background graphics included in the Slide Master, follow the steps in the exercise below.

Exercise 12.7: Hiding background graphics on one or all slides

1) Open EX12.7.PPT.
2) Choose **Format | Background.**
3) In the *Background* dialog box, select the *Omit background graphics from master* check box.

4) Click the **Apply** button – this means that background graphics will be hidden on the selected slide only. If you want to hide the background graphics for every slide in the presentation, you click **Apply to All**.

5) View the effect of your changes in Slide Show view.

Setting up custom shows

In the following exercise you will set up a custom show for slide show viewing. You will advance the slides manually, and turn off the animation effects.

Exercise 12.8: Setting up a custom show

1) Open EX12.8.PPT.

2) Choose **Slide Show | Set Up Show**.

3) In the *Set Up Show* dialog box, select *Custom show*. Click the arrow to the right of the *Custom show* box and select *Organic Practice* from the list displayed.

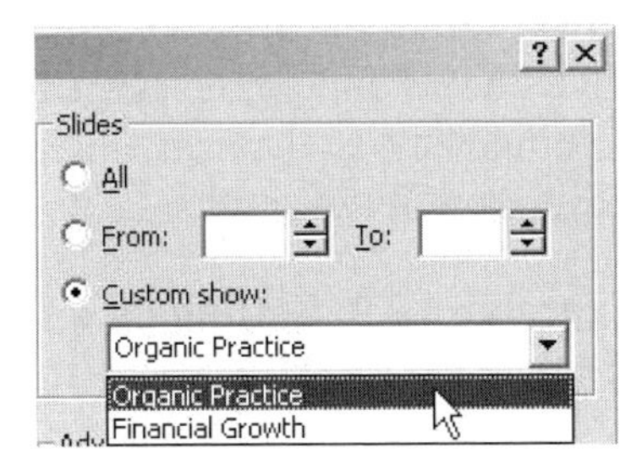

4) Select *Manually* from the *Advance slides* section.

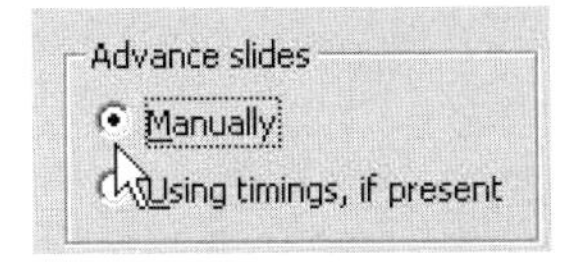

5) Select the following *Show type* options:

- *Presented by speaker (full screen).*
- *Loop continuously until 'Esc'.*
- *Show without animation.*

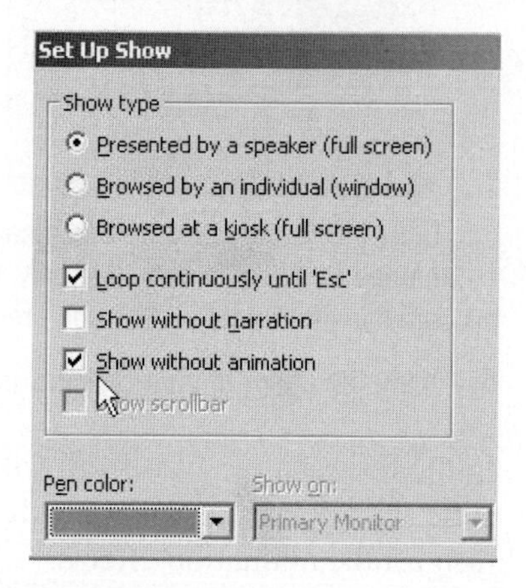

6) Click **OK**.

Well done! That's your slide show set up to show the Organic Practice custom show, to appear without animation, and to return to the first slide when the last has been seen.

Setting up full shows

The following exercise shows you how to set up a full show, complete with timings and animation, so that it can be opened directly from the desktop, and used by someone who does not have PowerPoint on their PC. This show will also loop continuously, so that it is suitable for unattended use at a trade exhibition, for example.

Exercise 12.9: Setting up a full show

1) Open EX12.9.PPT.
2) Choose **Slide Show | Set Up Show**.
3) In the *Set Up Show* dialog box, select the following *Show type* options:

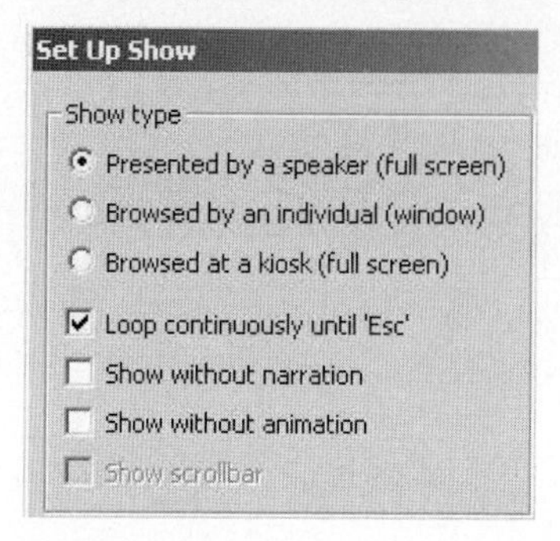

4) Select the following *Slides* options:

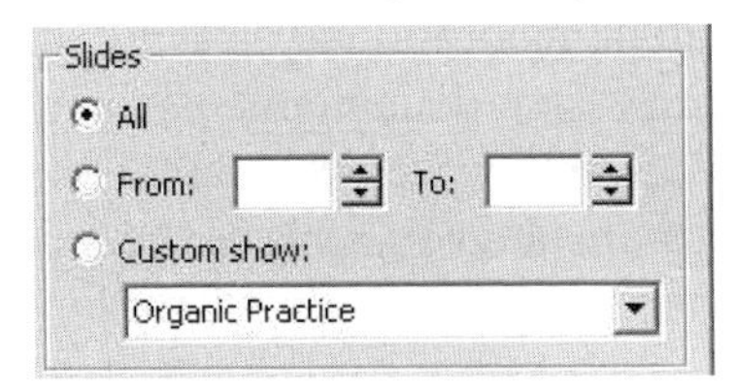

5) Select the following *Advance slides* option:

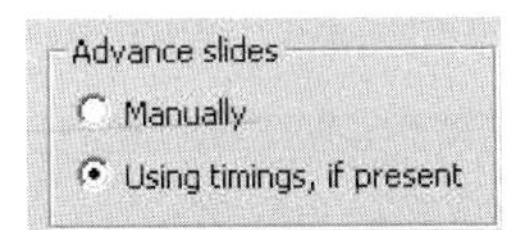

6) Click the **OK** button.

7) Choose **File | Save As**. Click the arrow to the right of the *Save as type* box and choose *PowerPoint Show (*.pps)*

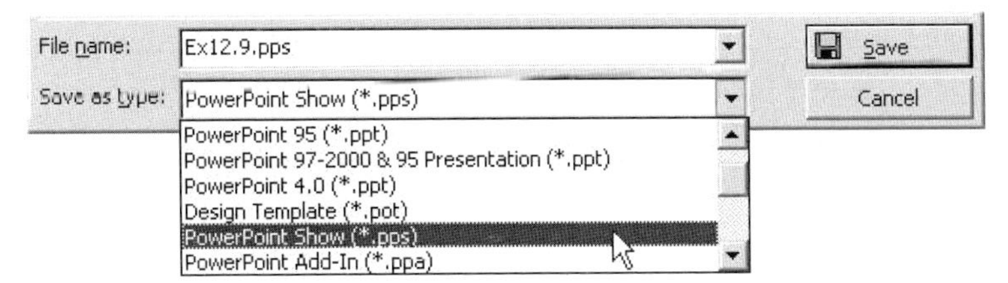

Click **OK**.

To deactivate continuous looping, choose **Slide Show | Set Up Show** and deselect the *Loop continuously until 'Esc'* check box.

You've now done *everything* you need for a successful PowerPoint presentation, and finished the ECDL Advanced Presentation course. Well done!

Chapter 12: summary

A *macro* is a recorded sequence of actions that can be played back with a single command. Recording and running macros is similar to recording and playing back a piece of music. You can create a *custom* button for a macro. If you decide that you no longer need the macro, you can *delete* it from your PowerPoint presentation.

When you are satisfied with the content of your presentation, you can set it up for final viewing. Your set-up will depend on the conditions under which the presentation will be used – live, in support of a speaker; viewed on a website; unattended at a trade show; or attached to an e-mail. You can *publish your presentation to the web*, in which case the presentation will be navigable in a web browser in the same way as in PowerPoint.

You can also export one or all *slides as graphics* (.JPGs) that can be incorporated as static images in web pages or word processing documents. You can exercise a variety of options when setting up your show: hide the background graphics, run a custom show or remove the animation. These options are available from the **Set Up Show** menu.

Chapter 12: quick quiz

Circle the correct answer to each of the following multiple-choice questions about macros and set-ups.

Q1	Which of the following is a valid macro name?
A.	2004macro.
B.	2004 macro.
C.	2004_macro.
D.	macro_2004.

Q2	How do you create a custom button for a macro?
A.	Choose **Tools | Customize**. Under the **Toolbars** tab select the *Macro* option. Select the macro you have created and drag it to the toolbar.
B.	Choose **Tools | Options**. Under the **Commands** tab select the *Macro* option. Select the macro you have created and drag it to the toolbar.
C.	Choose **Tools | Customize**. Under the **Commands** tab select the *Macro* option. Select the macro you have created and drag it to the toolbar.
D.	Choose **Tools | Customize**. Under the **Options** tab select the *Macro* option. Select the macro you have created and drag it to the toolbar.

Q3	True or false – slides saved as jpeg cannot be edited in the Internet browser.
A.	False.
B.	True.

Q4	How do you set up a show to run without animation?
A.	Choose **Slide Show | Set Up Show**, under the *Slides* section select the *Show without animation* check box and click **OK**.
B.	Choose **Slide Show | Custom Shows**, under the *Show type* section select the *Show without animation* check box and click **OK**.
C.	Choose **Slide Show | Set Up Show**, under the *Show type* section select the *Show without animation* check box and click **OK**.
D.	Choose **Slide Show | Set Up Show**, under the *Show type* section select the *Show without narration* check box and click **OK**.

Answers

1: D, **2**: C, **3:** B, **4:** C.

Index

Licensing Agreement

This book comes with a CD software package. By opening this package, you are agreeing to be bound by the following:

The software contained on this CD is, in many cases, copyrighted, and all rights are reserved by the individual licensing agreements associated with each piece of software contained on the CD. THIS SOFTWARE IS PROVIDED FREE OF CHARGE, AS IS, AND WITHOUT WARRANTY OF ANY KIND, EITHER EXPRESSED OR IMPLIED, INCLUDING, BUT NOT LIMITED TO, THE IMPLIED WARRANTIES OF MERCHANTABILITY AND FITNESS FOR A PARTICULAR PURPOSE. Neither the book publisher nor its dealers and its distributors assumes any liability for any alleged or actual damages arising for the use of this software.